"What a lovely writer Luanne Rice is."
—DOMINICK DUNNE

"[Luanne Rice's] characters break readers' hearts. . . . True-to-life characters dealing with real issues—people following journeys that will either break them or heal them." —*The Columbus Dispatch*

"A joy to read." —*The Atlanta Journal-Constitution*

"Addictive . . . irresistible." —*People*

"Rice writes as naturally as she breathes."
—BRENDAN GILL

"Luanne Rice has a talent for navigating the emotions that range through familial bonds, from love and respect to anger. . . . A beautiful blend of love and humor, with a little bit of magic thrown in." —*The Denver Post*

"Brilliant." —*Entertainment Weekly*

"Exciting, emotional, terrific. What more could you want?" —*The New York Times Book Review*

"Rice makes us believe that healing is possible."
—*Chicago Tribune*

"Good domestic drama is Rice's chosen field, and she knows every acre of it. . . . Rice's home fires burn brighter than most, and leave more than a few smoldering moments to remember." —*Kirkus Reviews*

"Rice masterfully weaves together a batch of sympathetic characters into a rich and vivid tapestry, all while exploring complex human emotions and the healing power of love." —*The Flint Journal*

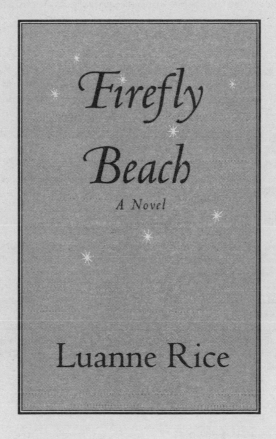

Firefly
Beach

A Novel

Luanne Rice

BANTAM BOOKS • NEW YORK

Firefly Beach is a work of fiction. Names, characters, places, and incidents either are the product of the author's imagination or are used fictitiously. Any resemblance to actual persons, living or dead, events, or locales is entirely coincidental.

2011 Bantam Books Mass Market Edition

Copyright © 2001 by Luanne Rice
Excerpt from *Secrets of Paris* by Luanne Rice copyright © 1991 by Luanne Rice

All rights reserved.

Published in the United States by Bantam Books, an imprint of The Random House Publishing Group, a division of Random House, Inc., New York.

BANTAM BOOKS and the rooster colophon are registered trademarks of Random House, Inc.

Originally published in paperback in the United States by Bantam Books, an imprint of The Random House Publishing Group, a division of Random House, Inc., in 2001.

This book contains an excerpt from the soon-to-be-published Bantam edition of *Secrets of Paris* by Luanne Rice.

ISBN 978-0-345-52686-1

Cover illustration by Robert Hunt

Printed in the United States of America

www.bantamdell.com

9 8 7 6 5 4 3 2 1

For Bill and Lois,
Bob and Anne

ACKNOWLEDGMENTS

With love and thanks to Carol Cammero, Rosemary McGinn, Jim Silvia, Jan Watson, Emily Andrews, Lisa Billingsley, Gerry Chylko C.Ss.R., William "Rip" Collins C.Ss.R., Ed Dunne C.Ss.R., Maureen Gattney R.S.M., Inge Hanson, Jayne Libby, April Fishgold, George Rose, and to all my friends from Westbrook, Old Saybrook, Old Lyme, and New York.

Firefly
Beach

$$*$$

PROLOGUE

DECEMBER 1969

THE HOUSE SMELLED LIKE CHRISTMAS COOKIES.

Butter, sugar, ginger, and spice. The aroma filled the warm kitchen; carols played on the radio. All their senses told Caroline and Clea that something wonderful was about to happen. The sisters were five and three, baking cookies on a snowy night with their mother. When the cookies cooled, they decorated them with white icing, silver balls, and red and green sprinkles.

Whenever the girls saw a crèche, they thought of their own family. Their mother was going to have another baby soon. The baby would be their new brother or sister, and the girls already loved him or her. The baby's crib was ready, just like the crib in the manger. The family had decided to name a boy Michael, a girl Skye. Caroline and Clea hoped for a Skye.

The doorbell rang.

Augusta Renwick, the girls' mother, wiped her hands on her dark green apron. The sight of floury handprints on their mother's big, pregnant belly made both girls laugh like crazy, and they ran with her to the door. On a night like this, anything could happen: Maybe Santa was there early, or maybe a small family in need of lodging had come to their house. Their father was away, painting the winter waterfront in Newport, but maybe he had come home early to surprise them.

It was a man with a gun.

He forced his way into the house. His gun was shaking in his hand. He closed the door behind him, as if he were a polite guest instead of a robber. Caroline and Clea huddled tight against their mother's legs. Her voice was calm but high, and she asked the man please to leave her children alone, to let them go, to not hurt them.

The man started to cry.

He pointed the gun at Caroline. Then at Clea. Then at Augusta. The black gun waved in the air as if it had ideas of its own. It kept coming back to point at Caroline. She stared at it, its small, mean-looking hole, and she knew that was where the bullet was. Even more awful than the gun was the man crying. Until that moment, Caroline had not known adults ever cried. She had never seen her mother or her father cry. The terrible sight choked her throat. She clutched her mother's thigh. The man's eyes kept darting to the photograph of their house, Firefly Hill, a study for a famous painting by her father.

"He's taken her," the man said. "Taken her away from me. Stolen her love, stolen everything I ever wanted, and now I've come to take what's his."

"What do you mean? Who are you talking about? You're wrong, it's a mistake—" Augusta began, her voice stronger than his.

"Your husband, Mrs. Renwick," he said. "I have the right man. He's with my wife at this moment. Do you doubt me? He's taken what I love from me, and I'm going to take what he loves from him."

"What he loves?" Augusta asked, and Caroline noticed her mother's hands shaking on her shoulder.

"His daughters."

Augusta gasped. Caroline heard that horrible high sound and couldn't believe it was coming from her mother. She pressed closer to her mother's legs, face-to-face with Clea. Clea looked scared and worried, her lower lip pushed out like when she was a baby, her thumb inching toward her mouth. Caroline gave Clea's thumb a small push, and in it went.

"Let them go," Augusta said softly. "They've done nothing to hurt you. They're innocent children. Let them be safe. You don't want to hurt them. I can see you're a good man. You're crying, you're a sensitive person. They're just little girls. . . ."

"We have a son," the man said. He pulled out his wallet, flipped it open to a picture. His hand fumbled, and the picture fluttered. At the sight of it, the man choked and sobbed. "My boy," he cried. "Oh, God."

Caroline saw the smiling face of a little boy about her age. He had blond hair and big blue eyes, and he looked like his father. "He's her pride and joy. We were so happy, all of us together. So happy. Oh, the day he was born . . ." The man hung his head and wept.

"What's his name, Mr. . . . ? What's your little boy's name?" Caroline asked suddenly.

"Joe. Joe Connor. That's his name. Come here," the man said, roughly grabbing Caroline's arm and pulling her away from her mother. He held her tight, and she heard a click come from the gun.

"No," Augusta wailed. "Please, Mr. Connor. Don't hurt her!"

"Shut up," the man said.

Caroline had never heard anyone tell her mother to shut up before, and she recoiled as if she'd been slapped. She looked up at the man and wondered if he was crazy. His eyes were terribly sad, sadder than any picture or real-life person Caroline had ever seen. Because of the excruciating sorrow in his blue eyes, she didn't feel afraid. She felt sorry for him instead.

"Don't say shut up to my mommy," Caroline said firmly.

"I want my sister," Clea cried, reaching her arms toward Caroline as their mother restrained her.

"Joe wouldn't want you to do this, Mr. Connor," Augusta said. "He wouldn't want you to scare my little girls, he wouldn't like to think of his father with a gun. . . . I'll do whatever you want. I'll make my husband stop seeing her. You have my word."

"What good is a person's word," the man asked, "when her husband doesn't love her anymore? When he loves someone else? You might as well promise me you'll stop the year from ending. It's over. It's all over now."

Caroline stood with the man's arm around her. She watched her mother's face. It melted like a warm candle. Her eyes drooped and her mouth frowned and tears poured down her cheeks. Caroline was watching her mother cry, now the second adult she had ever seen, and the sight of her mother's tears, more than the man's threat, suddenly filled Caroline with real panic.

"Take me," Augusta begged. "Let Caroline go. Take me and the baby instead. If you have to kill someone, kill us. But let her go!"

Her mother's voice rose on the word "go." It soared like a scream, like the wind howling through the trees on the hill.

"Let her go," the man repeated, blinking suddenly and swallowing his own tears. He looked at Caroline, then away, as if he didn't really want to see her.

"Please," Augusta said. "Take me. Take our baby."

"Don't say that," the man said, staring at Augusta's big belly.

The man gazed back at Caroline; he let himself linger on her eyes. They stared at each other, and Caroline felt herself getting less scared. A smile flickered on the man's lips. His hands trembling, he reached down to brush the hair out of her eyes.

"What's your name?"

"Caroline."

"You're Joe's age."

"I'm five now."

"Caroline," the man said, talking directly to her with tears running freely down his cheeks. "I came to take what your father loves, but I can't do it. I can't shoot a little girl like you."

"No," she agreed, and she had a sudden good feeling. As if everything would work out well.

"But he did this. Your father did this."

"Did what? My daddy did what?" Caroline asked, wanting to understand. Her mouth was dry. Reaching for the man's hand, her fingers ruffled the picture of Joe. "My daddy did what?" she asked again.

"Killed my family," the man said with a sob just as he raised the gun to his head and pulled the trigger.

The shot exploded in Caroline's ears. The burning smell of gunpowder made her gag, and the weight of the man crushed her to the floor. Blood poured out of his mouth and from the hole where he had shot out the side of his head. Her black hair was wet with it. She couldn't breathe because his body was on top of her. She screamed for her mother, crying with terror.

But her eyes were on the boy. Smiling up at Caroline was Joe Connor, six years old, his picture lying on the floor right under her face. The little boy whose father had just killed himself instead of Caroline or Clea or their mother and the new baby, whose mother didn't love him enough, who would never see his father again.

When Augusta Renwick, weeping, managed to pull the man's dead body off her daughter, she clutched Caroline to her breast and wiped some of the blood off her face and tried to hear what Caroline was saying to the picture of the little boy.

"I want my daddy," Caroline was crying. "I want my daddy now."

December 30, 1969

Dear Joe Connor,

I am your friend. Because your father came to our house and showed me your picture. I am sorry that he died, very very sorry.

Sincerely yours,
Caroline Renwick

January 14, 1970

Dear Caroline Renwick,

My father showed you my picture? He was nice and laughed a lot. We played baseball at Cardine Field. My father had a heart attack with you. I am glad you were with him.

Your friend,
Joe Connor

CHAPTER ONE

IT WAS THE LONGEST DAY OF THE YEAR. THE FULL MOON was rising out of the sea. The old dog lay on the grass beside Caroline, his chin resting on folded paws. Caroline, her mother, and her sisters sat in white wicker chairs. The gathering had an edge; family ghosts were circling around.

Caroline Renwick felt like a matriarch, but she was just the oldest sister. She loved her family. They were strong yet vulnerable, ordinary women who happened to be exceptional. Sometimes she felt she spent too much time with them, shepherding them along like a flock of eccentric sheep. Whenever that happened, she would jump on a plane, go on a business trip. It didn't matter where, as long as it was far enough away to give her mind a rest. But for right now, she was home.

As the moon rose, it grew smaller and colder, lost its pinkness and became silver. Stirred and panting, Homer raised his head from his paws . . . to watch. "Oh, girls," Augusta Renwick said, looking at her three daughters once it was entirely up.

"Isn't it incredible?" Augusta asked, staring out at Long Island Sound.

"A full moon on the longest day of the year," said Caroline. "That has to be a good omen."

"You're always looking for signs," Clea teased. "A full moon, shooting stars . . ."

"The North Star," Skye said. "Caroline taught me how to find it the last night I was ever really happy."

"The last *what?*" Augusta asked, smiling.

"Mom . . ." Caroline warned.

"My last happy night," Skye said sadly. She stumbled slightly on the words, making Caroline wonder how much she had already had to drink.

"You're happy *now,* darling," Augusta said. "Don't be ridiculous. How can you say something like that?"

"Easily," Skye said softly, staring at the old dog Homer.

"Mom . . ." Caroline started again, racking her brain for something light and conversational.

"Oh, Skye. Stop now," Augusta said, looking wounded. "We're celebrating the summer solstice! Let's get back to talking about stars. . . ."

"The North Star . . ." Clea said, laughing. "I don't need it anymore. If I want to go somewhere, I'll call my travel agent. No more hiking, no more hunting for this girl."

"Don't need *any* stars," Skye said.

"We all need stars," Augusta said. Then she said it again, as if it were very important: "We all need stars."

"We need cocktails," Skye said. "Isn't it time? The sun's down, the moon's up. There: I've got signs too. It's the cocktail hour. Right, Homer?" The ancient golden retriever thumped his tail.

"Well, it is," Augusta agreed, checking her small gold watch for added confirmation. She glanced at Caroline and Clea as if she expected them to interfere. Watching her mother, Caroline was reminded of a teenage girl on the brink of doing something her parents would disapprove of, daring them to stop her. Hearing no objections, Augusta walked into the house.

"Cocktails," Skye said to Homer.

"Drinking's not the answer," Caroline said. Instead of acting offended, Skye blew her a kiss. After all this time, their roles in life were clear: Skye misbehaved, and Caroline cleaned up.

Caroline shifted in her chair. She felt an unease deep down, worry mixed with fear. Lately she had been restless, cranky, dissatisfied with her bountiful life. She looked at Skye and saw a person she loved throwing herself away. She had to fight to keep from saying something sharp. For all these years, Caroline had been the glue holding her youngest sister together, and she felt as if Skye might finally be coming undone.

"Simon's not back, is he?" Clea asked, referring to Skye's scoundrel artist husband. "He's not coming tonight?"

"No, is Peter?" Skye asked, referring to Clea's husband, a hospital chaplain.

"No, he took the kids out for pizza," Clea replied.

"Peter's such a good guy," Caroline said, "wanting a night out with his kids."

"Caroline, how was your date the other night?" Clea asked.

"Fine," Caroline said, smiling as she shrugged.

"Who, that poor investment banker who drove all the way up from New York just to learn he doesn't have a snowball's chance in hell—" Skye began.

"Okay." Caroline laughed, getting up. "Enough." Thirty-six and never been married. The only Renwick girl never to tie the knot or even come close, she knew her sisters wished they could do something about her die-hard singleness.

"Seriously," Skye teased, tripping over the "s's." "Two

hundred miles in his 500SL to find out you don't kiss on the first—"

"I'll see what Mom's up to," Caroline said, walking away so she wouldn't have to hear how drunk Skye sounded.

* * *

She walked across the wide green lawn into her mother's house. Firefly Hill had been her childhood home. Hugh and Augusta Renwick had named their house on the Connecticut shoreline after Noël Coward's house in Jamaica, because on still June nights like these, when the moon rose out of the Sound, the dark fields around the old Victorian house and the thicket behind the beach below sparked with the green-gold glow of thousands of fireflies. The three sisters would run barefoot through the grass, catching the bugs in cupped hands.

And they had named it Firefly Hill because Noël Coward, to the Renwick family, meant martinis and conversation, wicked gossip and wit, wild parties and lots to drink—but never too much until way after dark. Caroline's father had been a famous artist; her mother had celebrated him with legendary parties here in Black Hall, the birthplace of American Impressionism.

The house smelled like home. Whenever she entered the place, the smell of her childhood was the first thing Caroline noticed. Salt air, wood smoke, oil paint, gin, her mother's perfume, and her father's gun oil all mingled together. She wandered through the cool rooms and couldn't find her mother.

There, sitting on the wide steps of the side porch, tucked back from her daughters' view, the sea breeze ruffling her mane of white hair, was Augusta Renwick.

Caroline hesitated in the darkened living room. Even alone, thinking herself unobserved, her mother had such poise, such theatricality. She gazed across the ocean with such intensity, she might have been awaiting her husband's return from a dangerous voyage. Her cheekbones were high and sculpted, her mouth wide and tragic.

She wore a faded blue shirt and khakis, tattered old sneakers. Around her neck were the black pearls Hugh Renwick had given her ten Christmases before he died. Augusta wore them always; to a party, to a ball, in the garden, to the A&P, it didn't matter. Her black hair had gone white when she was only thirty years old, but she had never dyed it. It was long and luxuriant, halfway down her back. Her eyebrows remained dark. She was still a dramatic beauty.

"Hi, Mom," Caroline said.

"Darling," Augusta said, emotional. "I just made the drinks and I was sneaking a quick one. Have one with me before we go back to your sisters."

"No, thanks."

Augusta patted the spot beside her. Caroline grabbed a seat cushion off the wicker rocker and placed it on the top step. The martini shaker, condensation clinging to the deep monogram in the sterling silver, rested between them.

"I was just sitting here, thinking of your father," Augusta said. Shielding her eyes, she looked across the waves, violet and silver in the moonlight. "He loved the June full moon. Didn't he? Couldn't he do a beautiful picture of that sky?"

"He could, Mom," Caroline said.

"Here's to Hugh," Augusta said, raising her glass at the moon, "and to the picture he could make of this moment. His wife and his oldest daughter and the longest day of the year. First one of the summer."

"First one of the summer," Caroline said, raising an imaginary glass.

"Oh, I miss him."

"I know you do."

There was a moment of silence, and Caroline could almost feel her mother waiting for Caroline to say "I do too." Augusta carried an air of sadness and longing around with her, and Caroline knew it had to do with the past, deep love, and missed chances. Hugh had died seven years before, of stomach cancer. As life unfolded, there seemed to be more things they all had to say to him, but he wasn't there to hear them. Her mother had loved him madly till the end.

Across the Sound, the lighthouses of Long Island had flashed on. To the west, the bright lights of some enormous fishing boat or work platform, moored over the Wickland Shoals, blazed like a small city.

"Come on," Caroline said, tugging her mother's hand. "Let's go back to the others and watch the moon."

Her mother left the drink things on the porch steps. Caroline felt relieved. As they crossed the yard, they felt the breeze in their hair. This was the time of day that reminded Caroline of her father more than any other. Her mother was right: She did hold things against him, but that couldn't stop the lump in her throat. Not all the memories were of bad things.

* * *

The fireflies had begun to come out. They twinkled in the rosebushes. They spread across the field, lighting the tall grass like a million candles. The fireflies made their beach magical. They danced down the gently sloping grassy hill, darting through the reeds and spartina above the sandy white strand. No other beaches along the shoreline glowed so intensely. Her father said his girls were special, that the fireflies lit their way and illuminated their beach so they could always find their way home.

Sometimes he would catch the fireflies and kill them, rubbing their lightning juice across Caroline's cheeks, anointing her with glowing war paint. Or he would pinch them between his big fingers and drop them into his glass, making his martini sparkle with stars, laughing with pleasure as he enchanted his daughters. For so long, Caroline had loved her father more than anything.

Clea and Skye were silent in their wicker chairs, watching the fireflies. Were they thinking of their father too? It seemed impossible that they weren't. Homer watched Caroline's progress across the yard, head on his paws. As she took her seat, he lifted his white face to kiss her hand. The night felt magical, as if the moon and the past and the ghost of Hugh had cast a spell upon them all. The Renwick women gazed at the moon and listened to the waves.

"What are you thinking?" Clea asked suddenly, leaning forward to tap Caroline's shoulder.

"About Dad," Caroline said.

Skye brooded in the moonlight, seeming to shiver. Their father was buried in the cemetery through the woods on the western edge of Firefly Hill, and Caroline watched Skye's gaze go there now.

"What are those boats?" Clea asked, pointing at the cluster of lights out by Wickland Shoals. "That's what I'm wondering."

"They anchored there today," Augusta said. "Two big white boats and a lot of little launches running in and out."

Leave it to Clea to be thinking something simple, uncomplicated, Caroline thought. She was the happiest Renwick sister, the least encumbered, the only one who had put the past behind her. Caroline gave her a smile. She turned to Skye.

"How about you?" she asked. "Why are you so quiet, Skye?"

"Just thinking," Skye said. But of course she would not say what about.

"We're all together, Caroline," Augusta said. "Let that be enough."

"I thought someone said something about cocktails," Skye said, rising unsteadily. "Can I get anyone anything?"

"I don't think so," Augusta said with a sidelong glance at Caroline.

But when Skye turned to walk precariously across the moonlit lawn, Augusta followed, linking arms with her youngest daughter. Homer rose, as if to follow. He seemed torn. Caroline scratched his ears, and he turned his eloquent eyes to hers. He had always sensed that Skye was the one who needed protection. But his great love was for Caroline, and both of them knew it.

Duty won. When Skye and Augusta headed up the gentle incline, Homer followed behind with his old head bent and his tail wagging. They disappeared inside the house. Caroline and Clea sat still, waiting. The music started: the tinkle of ice against silver, the complicit laughter, the clink of heavy crystal.

* * *

Unable to sleep that night Caroline turned her head and looked at the framed photo on her bedside table. It showed her, Clea, and Skye, all in summer dresses, at yet another party for their father, when Caroline was about sixteen.

Sisterhood is amazing. Caroline had known it almost forever, from when she was two, the moment she first realized her mother was growing large. It never ceased to amaze her: She and her sisters came out of the same womb.

Caroline knew it was the same for sisters everywhere. Whenever she met women who had sisters, she knew they *knew.* They understood the incredible connection. Staring at the picture, she tried to remember those girls from long ago. Her eyes focused on the image of herself: smiling but guarded, standing slightly behind Clea and Skye, as if to protect them.

"What were you thinking?" she whispered to her old self, to her younger sisters.

They grew up in the same house, with the same smells, the same sights, the same sounds. They had the same parents. They shared a room, fell asleep every night to the sound of one another's soft breathing. They shared the same images in dreams. They knew each other's nightmares. Some of their sweetest dreams were of one another.

"We walked each other to school," she said to herself, to her sisters.

When she looked at her sisters' bare legs, she knew every single scar. She knew the crescent-moon scar just under Clea's left knee, where she tripped in the night and fell on a piece of broken glass. She knew the inch-long scar on Skye's right ankle, from the time she snagged her foot on barbed wire, cutting through a pasture where none of them were supposed to be.

She knew the boys they liked. She had teased them about every single one. She helped them write love notes, she dialed boys' phone numbers for them so Clea or Skye could hear that boy answer and then hang up. Sometimes, and she would feel ashamed about this until she died, she flirted with them when her sisters weren't there. She wanted to see whether they liked her better.

Gazing at the picture, she knew they all had secrets. What about the different experiences, the things they'd never know about each other? They don't tell you everything, Caroline thought. The fights they heard their parents have when she was asleep. The only time in her life she ever cheated, on a math test in seventh grade, even though Caroline had helped her with her homework, she had pretended to "get it" just to please her.

The bad things that happened to her, the very bad things. The men she let touch her when she knew she shouldn't. The times she was scared. The times she didn't have a choice. The times she was in a place she didn't know, with no one to call, not even her sisters. The way it feels to kill another human being.

And even the miraculous times, the times when she was overtaken by the thrill of love, when the light of the moon on the water seemed to promise something Caroline could never understand, no matter that she was her sister, that they came out of the same womb.

Three sisters, three separate realities. Lots of combinations, lots of possibilities. Take one, get three. Two against one. Odd girl out. Secrets told to one but not the other. Then that one tells the first one, and everyone's mad at each other. Or secrets told to tell no one. Secrets she knows but would never tell. Secrets you imagine but don't know. Mistakes of life and death. The geometry of sisterhood.

CHAPTER TWO

A WEEK LATER, THE SISTERS WENT OUT FOR A MOVIE. Dropping Skye off at Firefly Hill, where she had been living since the departure of Simon, Caroline hitched a ride home with Clea. They all lived in Black Hall, within six miles of one another. Tonight they drove slowly, taking Clea's Volvo the long way around. Clea's husband and kids were out for the night, and she didn't have to rush home. Caroline loved driving around the shoreline with her sister. The car felt enclosed and warm, a sister-capsule orbiting the towns. They didn't speak for a few miles.

"What's with Skye?" Clea asked finally.

"I wish I knew," Caroline answered.

Caroline pictured Skye's handsome and ego-laden husband. Skye and Simon, both extraordinary artists, had lived a wild, bohemian lifestyle for as long as it had suited Simon. Running off with his model, he left Skye just before their fifth anniversary. Skye's dark moods had worried Caroline when they were kids, but they had gone dormant recently, until Simon met someone else.

"It's not because of Simon," Caroline said.

"What, then?"

"I think it's history catching up with her," Caroline said.

"What history?"

"She killed a man, Clea."

"But she didn't mean to," Clea said plaintively.

"That can't bring him back."

"She's drinking away her guilt," Clea said, "like Dad."

"Like Dad."

They drove on. Caroline lived in a small cottage of the Renwick Inn. Capitalizing on the family name, Caroline ran it as a hostelry that catered to artists. The inn itself was two hundred years old, a rambling white saltbox with seven chimneys and four secret closets. It had gardens and pine woods and outbuildings and a big red barn. It occupied one hundred acres on the Ibis River, a tributary of the Connecticut River, and it had once belonged to their grandparents.

Every year artists came to the Renwick Inn for the summer and parts of the other seasons to paint and escape the city and fall in love with each other. Every August at the end of the season Caroline held a renowned ball to celebrate love and creativity and new work and money in the bank. As Clea drove into the winding drive, Caroline saw that the parking lot was full.

"Good," she said. "Paying guests."

"Artists these days have to be pretty prosperous to afford the rates you charge." Clea laughed, counting the cars.

"Well, they're not all artists," Caroline said. "I just advertise as an artists' retreat because that seems to pull them in."

"It always did," Clea said, probably remembering their own childhood, all the would-be protégés and hangers-on who would congregate around their father, hoping for some of his talent or glamour or mystery to rub off.

Outside, the air was muggy, hot, and still. Heat rose from the lazy river, shimmering in the moonlight. The inn guests loved their ceiling fans, screened porches, mosquito nets, kerosene lamps. They paid extra for a certain rusticity. They wanted flickering candles, tangled gardens, dinners al fresco on weathered picnic tables, mismatched plates and glasses, a cozy bar with a fireplace, and plenty to drink. They disdained modern conveniences, so Caroline obliged by not providing air-conditioning, television, telephones, or electric alarm clocks.

"Will you come in?" she asked Clea, not wanting their night to end. "We have a great new chocolate cake I want you to try."

"Sure," Clea said.

Inside, they walked straight through the lobby. Guests were milling around, drinking and waiting for dinner. Michele, the manager, had everything under control. They walked straight past a row of their father's paintings to the back porch. Caroline settled her sister on a glider and ran to the kitchen. She set up a tray with chipped china coffee cups, a pot of coffee, and two big slices of cake.

"Hold me back," Clea said when she saw the cake.

"Wait till you taste it," Caroline said.

While conversation buzzed in the other room, the sisters hid out on the porch, eating the dense chocolate cake and watching a flock of geese land on the moonlit river twenty yards away.

"The river's pretty, but it's not the ocean," Clea said.

"We're saltwater girls," Caroline said. "Dad always said that."

They were facing the river, when suddenly an arc of headlights illuminated the trees. A line of cars pulled into the inn's circular drive. A truck rumbled up, and another. The sound of boisterous male voices carried across the property.

"Maybe they have us mixed up with the Catspaw Tavern," Caroline said, referring to the roadhouse five miles north.

"Let's go set them straight," Clea said, curious.

The two sisters walked into the lobby, where a pack of sunburned, unshaven men wearing frayed and grimy clothes were pouring through the front door. Michele, alarmed, stood at the reservations desk, ready with directions to the Catspaw. The Renwick Inn was refined, genteel. These men clearly had the wrong place.

"Got any vacancies?" asked one man. He had a mop of salt-damp black hair, a faded tee-shirt advertising a bar in Key West, and a chipped front tooth. His massive gut stretched the shirt to its limits; his tattooed biceps were as thick as Michele's waist.

"For rooms?" Michele asked, frowning.

"Yeah." The man laughed. "What'd you think I meant?"

"Well . . ." Michele said, gracefully ignoring the innuendo. She perused the reservations book. "How many rooms do you need?"

"Six," the man said. "We can double up. And some of us'll be staying on the boats."

"On the boats?" Michele asked, grabbing her chance. "You might be happier with a place nearer the marinas. I have a list of motels . . ."

"The boss wants this place," the man said, shaking his head. "He was definite about it."

"How long do you need the rooms?" Michele asked.

"Indefinitely. All summer, maybe. We're working offshore, got a big salvage operation going—"

"Loose lips sink ships," another man interrupted. He chuckled, but his eyes were serious. "Quit trying to impress the ladies."

"Offshore?" Caroline asked. "Just a little east of here?" She was thinking of the boats she had seen from Firefly Hill, their lights glowing like downtown.

"That's right," the first man said. He grinned proudly, revealing a broken tooth.

"We definitely don't have individual rooms available all summer," Caroline said. "But Michele might be able to find one or two for tonight, then move you around as things come available."

"Shit," the man said. "Boss'll be disappointed. Danny, you'd better run outside and tell him. Maybe he'll want to head back to the marina after all."

Some of the men had drifted into the dark, cozy bar. Candles flickered on every table, some of the old oak surfaces carved with artists' drawings and initials. Landscapes and nudes covered the walls. One by one, the houseguests looked up. They were either artists or people attracted by artists, and they regarded the seafarers with a mixture of alarm and curiosity.

Behind the bar was a particularly lush and decadent nude, depicting a large-breasted blond woman with tragedy in her eyes. The trick of the painting was that the background was money. At first glance it appeared to be foliage, but if you looked closely, it was coins and currency. To the artists, the picture was a sophisticated conversation piece, an excellent execution of trompe l'oeil done by one of Caroline's guests, who had gone on to become well known. But to the new visitors it was lewd and lascivious, and they stood around making loud toasts to the model's erect nipples.

Caroline stood quietly, listening to Clea and Michele ask each other what should be done. The language was growing raunchy. Some of the guests were squirming, staring with distaste at the men. Clea and Michele began to circulate among the tables, attempting damage control by offering drinks on the house.

"Are my guys behaving themselves?" came a deep voice from behind her.

"Not exactly," Caroline said, turning to see who had spoken.

The man was tall and fair. He had tousled blond hair,

streaked from the sun and salt. His blue eyes were wide and clear, and their serious expression was deep, in contrast with his smile. He wore a faded blue polo shirt, the tails untucked and the collar frayed. His arms were tan and strong.

"Hey, captain," called the man with the broken tooth and tattoos. "We want to buy you a drink."

"How about remembering you're not at sea anymore," the blond man said good-naturedly to his crew at large. "Be scientists and gentlemen." They listened with no apparent rancor, nodding and raising their glasses. One of them bought the man a drink, and it appeared to be a glass of cranberry juice. He held it, and Caroline could see how big his hands were.

"Danny says you're all booked up?" the man asked.

"I'm sorry," she said. "I can offer you two rooms for tonight, but that's just because we had unexpected cancellations. I think you'll have a hard time finding enough rooms for as long as you want them. Black Hall gets pretty busy in the summer."

"I'm disappointed," the captain said. "I've always wanted to stay at the Renwick Inn."

"Really?" she asked, skeptical but flattered.

"Really," he said.

"We get a lot of artists here," she said. "Not many sailors and . . . what did you say? Scientists?"

"Hard to believe, isn't it?" he asked, surveying his ragtag crew, desperately in need of razors and shampoo, drooling over the sad-eyed nude. "Half those guys are oceanographers and the other half are pirates."

"Which half are you?" she asked.

"I'm definitely a pirate," he replied.

"No kidding," she said. They stood there, smiling at each other. He had a sultry sexiness about him, but in spite of his easy way, there was something secretive behind his eyes.

"I run a salvage company in Florida," he said. "We dive on sunken ships, bring up what we can. Sometimes we contract out for government work, and sometimes we do our own thing."

"What do you salvage?" Caroline asked.

"Treasure." He grinned.

"Treasure?" she asked, still skeptical.

"Yeah," he said. "Sometimes it's just fishing gear and a water-logged outboard motor. A drunken captain who didn't know the water and went aground. Or a family sailboat the father didn't know how to navigate and hit a rock."

"I'm sure you didn't come all the way up from Florida to raise a family sailboat," Caroline said.

"That's right," he replied. "Earlier this year I went off Louisiana and brought up a chest of yellow topaz. A mound of silver pesos four inches high and eighty feet long. All from a Spanish brig that went down in 1784."

The romance of wrecks had always intrigued Caroline. Growing up at Firefly Hill, she and her sisters would look out to sea and imagine the ships that had gone down on the rocky shoals. There were legends about pirates and wreckers on this coast, and one memorable tale about an English ship lost in a terrible storm. "Do you expect to find something like that up here?" she asked, growing excited at the prospect. "Real treasure?"

"Maybe," he said, smiling enigmatically.

"The English ship. Is that what you've come for?" Caroline asked, suddenly understanding. She pictured the boats offshore, the secrecy in the men's expressions. The man had come north to excavate the old shipwreck.

Caroline had learned about it in third grade; all the Black Hall kids had. An English sea captain came to the colonies, his hold full of arms and the king's gold. He fell in love with the lighthouse keeper's wife, and she was going to run away to England with him. But their ship sank on the Wickland Shoals in a great gale. "Tell me her name, the ship that sank," Caroline said finally.

"The *Cambria*," the man said, watching her face.

"That's right!" she said, looking into his eyes. As she did, she had the feeling she knew him, had known him for a long time and knew him well. A strange sensation came over her: Her skin tingled, and the hair on the back of her neck stood on end.

"How did you find out about it?" she asked. "It's only a legend. People have looked before, and they've never found any trace. It happened nearly three hundred years ago, if it happened at all."

"It happened," he said softly.

"But how did you hear? It's a local story. I've never read anything about it."

"You told me about it," the man said.

"I told you?"

"In one of your letters you wrote about a ship that had sunk within sight of your house. The *Cambria*. You'd learned about it in school, and you could see the spot from your bedroom window. You're Caroline Renwick, aren't you?"

She felt the blush spread up her neck. Reaching out, she took his hand. It felt rough and callused, and his grip was tight and didn't let go. She recognized him now. He looked so much like his picture, that smile and the light in his eyes. She had carried his picture around for ten years, and she was surprised she hadn't recognized him the minute he walked in the door.

"Joe," she said. "Joe Connor."

"I should have called first," he said. "But we came north kind of suddenly."

"Joe," she said again.

"The Renwick Inn," he said. "I've always wondered whether it was you. Or your family, at least."

"It's hard to believe," she said. "That we've never met before. Of all the times for you to show up . . ."

"Life's strange," he said, still smiling. But something about the cast of his eyes made her see he was backing off. Whatever friendliness he had initially shown was tempered by their past, the secrecy of his business, or something else. He glanced around, nodded at his men in the bar.

"It is," Caroline said. "Strange that you wanted to stay at my inn, considering . . ."

"Considering what?"

"Everything. Considering everything."

"That's ancient history," Joe said. "You run an inn, and I need a place to put my crew."

"Your crew? Not you?" Caroline asked.

Joe shook his head. "I stay at the site, on board one of the ships. So do most of my guys, but we need a base on land. Showers, a bar, a restaurant."

"Looks like they're enjoying the bar," Caroline said, watching the bartender frown as he poured shots of Southern Comfort. "Can't say I remember the last time I saw someone drinking shots in there."

"My guys a little too rough for you?" Joe asked with an edge. He grinned. "Good thing you're booked. We wouldn't want to coarsen your place up. We'll finish our drinks and clear out."

Caroline brushed back her hair. She felt stiff, off balance. He'd be leaving soon, and she wanted to be glad. Meeting him brought back bad memories, a lot of hurt. She'd done plenty to block the pain out of her life, and she didn't need to open the door and invite it back in. So when she opened her mouth, her words surprised herself. "Like I said, we have two rooms free."

"Yeah?" he asked. "We'll take them."

Clea came forward, a worried look in her green eyes.

"Someone just made a pass at Leo Dumonde's wife," she said, "and Leo wants to fight him outside. I think he's trying to be Dad."

Caroline exhaled; she didn't have the patience just then.

Leo Dumonde was an abstract expressionist from New York, a man with a bigger reputation for investing than painting, and he was one of the artists who tried to live what he thought was the Hugh Renwick way: paint fast, fight hard. Exhibit timber, cheat on your wife, drink too much, hunt and fish enough to get noticed by the sports writers.

"Your father was the real thing," Joe said. "Leo Dumonde's a fake. He won't be stepping outside with anyone from my boat."

"You knew our father?" Clea asked, twinkling.

"Knew of him," Joe said. "The bastard."

Clea's smile evaporated.

"Clea, meet Joe Connor," Caroline said evenly, every one of her senses on guard.

"*The* Joe Connor?" Clea asked.

"I think so," he said, flashing her a wicked grin and shaking her hand.

"We've been wanting to meet you for a long time," Clea said.

"He's a treasure hunter," Caroline said. "He's here to raise the *Cambria,* and then he's going home to Florida."

"That's right," Joe said. "Renwick territory is a little too dangerous for me. Or at least it was when Hugh was around."

"We're our father's daughters," Caroline said sharply, the pain of Joe's rejection as sharp as it had been at fifteen. Amazed that it could still hurt, she felt her eyes fill with tears. He had been her friend, and he had cut her off without a second chance. Not even for her own sins, but for their fathers'. "You'd better not forget that."

"I never have," Joe Connor said softly.

* * *

Closing her office door behind her, Caroline went to her desk. Her hands were shaking, her heart pounding as if she'd just climbed a steep trail. Clea had driven away, and Caroline was glad to be alone. Pulling the curtains, she sat down.

The bar was noisy. She heard the loud voices, the excited laughter. It was a busy night at the Renwick Inn, and she knew she should feel pleased. Friends and acquaintances from the past often walked through her door. Sometimes they knew she owned the place, often they were surprised to find out. It never mattered: Caroline viewed those visits as serendipitous, lucky business.

Joe Connor was different.

Very slowly, she opened the top drawer of her desk. It was cluttered, filled with pens and receipts and mementos. Reaching back, rifling through the papers, she found what she was looking for. She pulled out the old picture and laid it on her desktop.

It was Joe's first-grade school picture, taken long ago. The little boy was smiling, his front tooth missing. He had blond hair, the back sticking up in a cowlick. The picture was stained brown, and dark flecks covered the boy's face. The flecks were his father's blood.

Caroline had held James Connor's hand while he shot himself. Crushed beneath his body, she had pulled his son's picture from the spreading pool of blood. Silent now, she sat at her desk and stared at Joe's face.

Her mother had given her permission to write to him. Against her better judgment, Augusta had let her find his address in Newport, even given her the stamp. Caroline, five years old, had written to Joe Connor, six years old, to tell him she was sorry his father was dead. She didn't mention the gun, she left out the blood. Her emotions were enough, her sorrow for another child who had lost his father. Her mother had helped her print the words, and the letter was short.

Joe wrote back. He thanked her for her letter. She could still remember his first-grade printing, his confusing words: "My father had a heart attack with you. I am glad you were with him."

Caroline responded. They became pen pals. On and off during the years, they wrote to each other. They sent Christmas cards, birthday cards, valentines. As the years went by, Joe began to ask about his father. From the questions, Caroline could tell that he had been lied to, that he had a totally wrong idea about his father's death.

Joe seemed to have the idea that their fathers had been friends. James Connor had met Hugh Renwick during one of his painting forays to Newport, guys from different walks of life who liked to drink together. Somehow James had ended up visiting the Renwicks and had a heart attack in their kitchen.

To Augusta's consternation, Joe's letters began to arrive more regularly. He and Caroline liked each other; when they became teenagers, they liked each other more. It drove Augusta crazy, seeing the name Connor in the return address. She'd grill Caroline about the letters, tell her to stop writing back. Reminded of her husband's infidelity, she couldn't stand Joe Connor.

The letters stopped. Caroline hadn't thought about that part in years, but the memory still carried power. She felt the color rising in her neck. Joe finally learned the truth, and not from Caroline.

Joe's mother had been too ashamed to tell him how his father had died, and one day someone in his family let it slip. An uncle or a cousin, Caroline couldn't remember. Joe finally learned that his father had committed suicide. The heart attack had been a lie, and so had the story about their fathers being friends.

James Connor had died among enemies. That was terrible, enough to break the heart of any teenage boy. But what was worse, the thing that brought tears to Caroline's eyes now, was the betrayal. She had been his friend. All along, reading his letters, she had known she should tell him the truth.

At the end, he couldn't forgive her. She had known and he didn't. He was seventeen and needed to know all he could about his father, and Caroline had held back a crucial fact: Her father had been having an affair with his mother, and James Connor had killed himself because of it. She had withheld the most important thing one friend could ever give another: the truth.

Truth was never big in the Renwick family, but that was no excuse. Sitting at her desk, staring at the bloody picture, she thought of Joe Connor out in her bar. If he were still a friend, she could buy him a drink, catch up on old times, get to know the man in person. But as it stood right now, he was just another customer.

September 20, 1972

Dear Joe Connor,

We have a shipwreck near our house! It happened long ago. The Cambria came from England loaded with treasure. My sisters and I look for coins on Firefly Beach. If we find some, I will send you one. Our beach is magical. Instead of lighthouses we have fireflies. Are you in fourth grade? I'm in third. The Cambria was a barquentine. It is buried in the mud.

> *Sincerely yours,*
> *Caroline Renwick*

October 16, 1972

Dear Caroline,

Why do you always write Dear Joe Connor? No other Joe lives here. Shipwrecks are cool, as long as you're not on them. Newport has plenty. Lots of barques. (The nickname for barquentine.) Yes I'm in fourth. How many sisters do you have? Keep looking for the treasure.

> Your friend,
> Joe

P.S. Of course it is buried in the mud. Otherwise, it would decompose. (That means "rot" to you third-graders.)

CHAPTER THREE

JOE CONNOR DROVE HIS TRUCK DOWN TO THE DOCK, feeling the air grow thick with sea mist. Behind him was a convoy of vehicles returning to the ship. Bill Shepard sat across the seat, but Joe wished he were alone. He hadn't been prepared for his reaction to meeting Caroline Renwick. He felt wired, as if he had either just landed or lost a black marlin. His hands were actually shaking on the steering wheel. He needed a drink, and he had quit drinking ten years ago.

For one thing, she was beautiful. Five-six and slender with incredible curves, the kind of body that sailors spend their lives dreaming about. Her face belonged on magazine covers, porcelain-pale with wide gray-blue eyes and high cheekbones, a tender mouth that wanted to smile but didn't right away. Her dark hair was long and wavy, and with her pallor it gave her a mysterious black-Irish look that made Joe think of whispers and passion and how her fingernails might feel digging into his back.

For another thing, the main thing, she was Caroline Renwick.

They had a past. All the letters and then, when he'd found out the truth, the rage. He had seen her father's

famous portrait of her, *Girl in a White Dress,* hanging at
the Metropolitan Museum of Art. But by then he was
deep into his hatred of the Renwicks. The lies had already come to light.

"Nice place, the Renwick Inn," Bill said, yawning as
he gazed out the open window.

"It is," Joe said.

"So, we'll be keeping a couple of rooms there, sort of
like a land base?" Bill asked. He was new to Joe's crew, a
diver they'd picked up at the tail end of the last excavation. He was young and eager, but he liked to talk too
much. Joe wasn't big on getting to know his team. They
did their work, he paid their salary.

"Yes," Joe said.

"Pretty girls," Bill said. "That owner chick and her sister. They friends of yours?"

"Not exactly," Joe said. "But close enough."

"I wouldn't mind getting to know her better,
that Caroline. Very hot, very hot. But she has that New
England—reserved look, real hard to get. You know?"

"That's because she is," Joe said harshly.

"Hey, you never know." Bill laughed in that drawn-
out southern way of his. He had a spooky cast to his
eyes, and his manner managed to make most things he
said sound snide. Joe felt a big knot of anger balling up in
his stomach, feeling like the right thing to do was defend
Caroline and not really knowing why.

"Listen," Joe said. "You want to drink, do it somewhere besides the Renwick Inn. When it's your turn to
bunk there, stay away from Caroline and her sisters."

"Sister," Bill corrected Joe. "There was only one."

There are two, Joe thought, remembering Caroline's
letters. He didn't bother to enlighten Bill.

"I'll tell everyone, not just you, but the Renwicks are
off limits. Let's just say they're friends of the family.
Okay?"

"Gotta respect that," Bill conceded. "But they're sexy as all hell. Too bad."

"Too bad," Joe agreed.

They were nearing the water. The saltier the air got, the easier Joe breathed. Going to sea, he always felt like a freed man. All the bonds of dry land, the problems and worries, slipped away. He loved the movement of waves under his feet, the sense of wind and tides having more power than he did. It had always been that way, since around the time he stopped writing to Caroline. He had escaped life by shipping out.

The road curved around, the coast grew rocky. In the back of his mind, Joe wondered where it was: Firefly Hill, the place where his father had shot himself. He could locate it on a chart—had done so a million times—but being so physically close sent chills down his neck.

On the USGS charts, the town was called Black Hall and the point of land, jutting like a crooked elbow into Long Island Sound, was called Hubbard's Point. Firefly Hill was a dot on the chart, the apostrophe in the name "Hubbard's Point," the highest point of land on the shoreline from Branford to Stonington. Firefly Beach was the family's name for their private beach; Joe recalled Caroline's story about having fireflies instead of a lighthouse.

Joe had dived for treasure in five of the seven seas, gotten rich doing it, found artifacts he still couldn't believe. But the *Cambria* was his Holy Grail. His Atlantis. Diving off Bosporus, his hold filled with Turkish gold and casks of Russian rubies, he had rocked the nights away in his cramped bunk, plotting his excavation of the *Cambria*. Finally, he laid legal claim to the wreck and brought his equipment and team and fleet north from Florida.

Was it just because the *Cambria* had sunk off the Black Hall shore? Within sight of Firefly Hill? Staring at the foggy road ahead of him, Joe thought to himself: Black Hall should be marked by a skull and crossbones on nautical charts. His reaction might have been less intense if the same name hadn't made him feel so happy for all those years, seeing it postmarked on Caroline's letters. He was bitter about the way she had held back the truth. But she had piqued his interest early with her letter about the *Cambria*, and here he was. In Renwick territory.

In too many ways, the Renwicks had shaped his life. Hugh had come to paint in Newport. Joe's mother worked for a lobster company, just a pretty fish lady with rough hands and sore feet, and when the artist with his easel on the dock had asked her to have a drink with him, it had been too exciting to turn down.

Although the affair didn't last long, from the very beginning Hugh owned Joe's mother's heart. When his father found out, it broke his. She spent her life loving a man she could never have, and the years and events made her bitter. She remarried, had another son, tried to live her life better the second time. But she could never stop loving Hugh Renwick and she had never been accessible to Joe.

After all these years, no one had ever told him the whole story of his father's death. Only the Renwicks knew what had happened in that house. Roman Catholic, his mother had kept even the fact of his suicide buried for as long as she could. That, plus the guilt she must have felt over the affair and what it drove his father to do, had turned the truth into a black secret that she had never talked about before her death. Joe felt the bitterness rising. He wanted to turn around and ask Caroline questions. But too many years had passed between them in silence.

He pulled into the sandy parking lot at Moonstone Point, parked his pickup truck next to the dockmaster's office. Half the trucks in the shabby old lot belonged to

Joe's crew, and more were pulling in. Most of them were already headed out to the *Meteor,* the research vessel his guys referred to as "the mother ship." He used the truck's CB radio to call the launch.

"Meteor, this is Patriot One, we're at the dock. Over," he said into the microphone.

"Roger, Patriot," came the crackling voice. "Coming to get you straightaway. Over."

"Make it fast," Joe said, his chest hurting with an old pressure. "I'm getting land legs, I've been here so long."

"Don't worry, skipper. We're on the way."

Joe clicked off, settling back to wait. He listened to Bill talk about the site, what they'd seen earlier that day. The project was exciting; in spite of himself, Joe breathed the salt air and began to relax.

Lives lost, hopes gone down. With the sunken ship came a hold of old dreams, the very specific lives of a ship captain and his mates. That's how Joe saw it: Raising a vessel's treasure was like meeting the dead. Their families, their habits, their fragile old bones.

He heard the high pitch of the launch's engine, the slap of its hull. Grabbing his chart case and duffel bag, he climbed out of the pickup truck. The sea was dark gray and choppy; clouds were thick on the horizon. The big mako bounded across the waves, sidled up to the dock.

Dan Forsythe, the launch driver, wore an orange foul-weather jacket over khaki shorts. "Hey, captain," he said.

"Hi, Dan," Joe said, climbing down the ladder. It was dead-low tide, a long drop from the dock to the water. In his mind, he was already back at work, calculating tomorrow's tides and currents, thinking of the operation.

"Water's rough. Hope that doesn't work against us," Dan said. "We going to try stabilizing the aft timbers tomorrow?"

"If the bottom hasn't shifted," Joe said.

They wheeled away from the dock, through the harbor crowded with pleasure boats, and out to sea. Lights were beginning to come on in the houses along the shore. Joe's eyes were drawn to them; he couldn't help it.

He tried to concentrate on work, but it was a lost cause. Black Hall stole his attention. Which one was Firefly Hill? He brushed the salt spray out of his eyes, gazing at the salt marshes and granite ledges. The houses slid by, and Joe thought of Caroline, of the darkness and trouble in her beautiful gray-blue eyes, her toughness and secrets. Now that he had met her, he couldn't get her out of his mind.

But then, he never could.

* * *

"What's he like?" Skye asked Clea.

"Can Mom hear you?" Clea asked, wanting to be sure they had privacy.

They were on the telephone. It was late, but Clea had called Firefly Hill the minute she got home from the Renwick Inn, after meeting Joe and leaving Caroline. The news of Joe Connor dropping into their midst was too crucial to keep from Skye.

"No," Skye said, "Mom's in the other room. Tell me."

"He's all grown up," Clea said. "Isn't it weird? All these years have passed, but I imagine Joe Connor still looking like that old picture Caroline always used to carry around."

"Six years old," Skye said, "with that cowlick and his front tooth missing."

"He's handsome," Clea said, "in a seaside kind of way. Very bright blue eyes, and he's tall. Strong, the way I guess men get when they go around lugging sea chests up from the bottom of the ocean." She spoke softly, not wanting to hurt Peter's feelings. As the hospital chaplain, he didn't do much heavy lifting. He visited the sick and soothed the bereaved, and Clea loved him more than she believed humanly possible. He was upstairs, reading one last story to Mark and Maripat.

"What is he, a fisherman?" Skye asked. "Like his father?"

"No, he has a marine salvage business. You know those boats we can see from Mom's? Those are his. He's a treasure hunter."

"How did Caroline seem, meeting him?"

"Well, she . . ." Clea began, but she was distracted by the sound of clinking ice cubes. "What's that? Skye, you're not still drinking, are you?"

"I'm having a nightcap," Skye said. "Here I am, in my old room at Mom's. Thirty-one years old, and I've moved back home. What a loser."

"That's not true," Clea said. Was Skye as bereft as she suddenly sounded? Or was it just booze talking? Clea had watched alcohol work its black magic before on their father.

"Tell me, Clea," Skye said calmly. "How did Caroline take meeting him?"

"She was shocked," Clea said.

"Because she loved him," Skye said in a low and dangerous voice.

"She didn't love him," Clea said. "She was only fifteen when they stopped writing to each other. It was just a crush."

"She loved him," Skye said. "She loved him more than anything."

Clea heard the tense edge in Skye's voice again, and she sat still, listening.

"Caroline used to talk about him," Skye said. "I remember. And she didn't stop carrying his picture. She kept it with her for ages afterward. She took it on every horrible trip, every time Dad left us alone."

"I know."

"Kept it in her backpack, one of those waterproof pockets."

"Don't, Skye," Clea said, feeling her heart start to pump.

"Joe would understand."

"Understand what?" Clea asked.

"Me," Skye said. "Caroline. Redhawk. The universe."

"He's a scruffy pirate with holes in his shoes," Clea said, her anxiety growing. "He's not an oracle."

"Where's he keep his pirate ship when it's not off Mom's?" Skye asked.

"*Meteor,* it's called. I saw the name painted on the side of his truck. At Moonstone Point, I guess. What do you want to say to him?" Clea pressed.

"That maybe it was an accident," Skye said. "Maybe his father didn't mean to shoot himself."

"Skye."

"It could have been," Skye said, her voice suddenly thick with tears, drunkenness making her sound maudlin. "You can see why I'd think that, can't you?"

"Skye, listen to me," Clea said. "You've had too much to drink. Go to bed, and you'll feel better in the morning."

"I think I could help him," Skye said. "I really think I could help him."

The sound of Skye's muffled sobs filled the phone.

Clea put her head down. She tried to gather her thoughts, to say something soothing that would defuse Skye's contorted grief, make her want to go to sleep. But before she could speak, Skye hung up the phone.

Clea sat still, wondering what to do. Was Skye going to do something crazy? Go to bed, she prayed. Go to sleep, Skye. Climbing the stairs, she decided to check on her children. For so long, she and her sisters had faced their past by not facing it. They busied themselves to avoid it. Clea had a family. If her family was happy, she could be too. Happiness was so cleansing.

She tiptoed into her children's rooms, kissed them each

as they slept. Whispering "sweet dreams" into Maripat's ear, she wished for her daughter's dreams to be free of all fear. She kissed Mark, wishing the same. Kissing her kids, Clea suddenly knew she had to call Skye back. She felt so frantic, she fumbled the buttons as she dialed the telephone.

Augusta answered. Clea heard the pleased warmth in her mother's voice that one of her daughters would call, even this late, even to talk to Skye instead of her. She called upstairs for Skye, and told Clea she must have gone out. Clea felt her heart banging. Her hands felt clammy. "Thanks, Mom," she said, blowing kisses into the phone as if nothing were wrong. Then she called Caroline.

"I think I just did something stupid," she said. "I just spoke to Skye. She's very upset, and I think she's gone down to the dock. She's drunk."

"You let her hang up?"

"What was I supposed to do?" Clea asked.

"I know," Caroline said. "I'm sorry, Clea. It's not your fault."

"It feels like it is," Clea said.

* * *

The town was small. Everyone knew Skye, and Caroline got the phone call. She immediately telephoned Clea to tell her, and sped to the Shoreline General Hospital. All three Renwick girls had been born there. Her heart racing, not knowing what she was going to find, Caroline tried to gain courage from that fact: Skye had come to life in this place.

"She's alive," the policeman said.

Caroline nodded, her knees going weak with relief.

"She's drunk out of her mind. No one's going to look the other way on this," he said. "She's going to get a DWI."

Caroline read his badge: Officer John Daugherty. She

knew him from around town; sometimes he brought his wife to the inn for dinner. "Did you find her?" she asked.

"Yes, I did."

"Thank you," Caroline said.

"She's a lucky person," he said. "She really cracked up good, and she could have gotten herself killed."

They stood outside the emergency entrance, the summer breeze soft and warm. Police cars had pulled in helter-skelter, their blue lights silently flashing, as if the hospital itself were the scene of a crime. Officer Daugherty had kind eyes and a calm voice, and he spoke with the soft regret Caroline remembered from the officers who had sometimes come to the inn to tell them they had picked up Hugh for drunk driving.

"Nature saved her," he said. "She left the pavement going eighty miles an hour, but her wheels hit a bog. There's a marsh along Moonstone Road, and her tires sank in deep. Even so, she had enough speed going to take down a fence and total her car."

"Moonstone Road?" Caroline asked.

"Yes. Heading for the docks. I can't help knowing she's married to Simon Whitford, but that's not the name she was saying when I got to her."

"What name was she saying?"

The officer lowered his voice, trying to be discreet. "Joe," he said. "She was calling for someone named Joe."

* * *

Caroline found Skye in a private cubicle in the emergency room.

Skye Renwick Whitford looked like an angel in white. White bandages, white sheets, pearlescent white skin. Except for the bruises' purple, black, wine-red. Her light lashes rested on high cheekbones. She was so thin, so small, she looked more like a child than a woman. The sight of her filled Caroline with such powerful love, she shook her head and had to take a step back.

Love expanded Caroline's chest and made her heart hurt. She stood at Skye's side, gazing down at her. She lay so still. Was she even breathing? Caroline watched for her chest to rise and fall. Skye's small mouth was open slightly under the cool green oxygen mask, her upper lip gashed and swollen. Her bruised eyelids twitched with dreams.

Caroline gently took Skye's hand. It was a sculptor's hand, rough as a workman's. Her fingernails were dirty with paint and clay. Bringing the tiny hand to her lips, Caroline smelled turpentine.

"Skye," she said. "Can you hear me?"

Skye didn't reply.

"You didn't mean this one, did you?" Caroline asked. "You didn't drive off the road on purpose. You were on your way somewhere."

"Skye?" Caroline tried again. "Why did you want to see Joe?"

The sight of Skye's face made Caroline stop. Her eyes were closed, but tears were sliding out of them, down her cheeks. Were her lips moving under the mask? The rushing oxygen sounded loud, a little unreal. Skye reached up and pulled the mask away.

"I didn't get to the dock," she said.

"No," Caroline said.

"It sounds stupid now," she said. "But it made sense at the time."

"Tell me anyway."

"I hate sobering up," Skye whispered. "My head hurts, and I feel like an idiot. Will you get me out of here?"

"I can't," Caroline said. "Not right now."

"Maybe his father made a mistake," Skye said, touching her bruised face. "Shot the wrong person."

"The wrong person?" Caroline asked, feeling sick. "Who would he have shot instead?"

"Me," Skye said.

"You weren't born yet," Caroline said. "You were still in Mom's womb."

"I wish he had," Skye said. "Then I wouldn't have been born."

"If you hadn't," Caroline said, putting her face right beside Skye's "I wouldn't have had you for a sister. Clea and I wouldn't have known you at all. Don't say those things."

"I wouldn't be a killer," Skye said.

"Oh, Skye," Caroline said, her eyes filling with tears. It always came back to this. How could she think it wouldn't?

Skye twitched, from pain or vodka or Demerol. Her voice was choked, her words hard to understand. Caroline wished her father were there. She wanted him to see Skye's agony, soothe her head with his rough, kind hands, tell her to forgive herself. His mistake had brought her here. Caroline squeezed Skye's hand. She searched her mind for something to say, something wise and comforting, but she felt too churned up herself.

"Joe," Skye said.

"Why are you calling for him?" Caroline asked. "What do you want him for?"

"We're connected. Don't you feel it?" Skye asked, her eyes wide open.

"I used to," Caroline said.

"More than ever now," Skye continued, almost unhearing.

Caroline held her hand and didn't answer.

Later, in the waiting room, she bowed her head so no one could see her face. How had they gotten here?

* * *

Six-feet-three, Hugh Renwick was a large man, and very strong; his ideas were huge to match.

He had been a great outdoorsman, as excessive in his sport as he was in his art and life, and he had wanted to teach his daughters the things other men taught sons. He gave them compasses and Swiss Army knives. He taught them to read the sky and mountain trails, to hunt for food.

His home had been violated by a stranger. The reason didn't count. Hugh, thinking that dangers lurked in every corner now, wanted his daughters to be able to defend themselves. Even if his affair with James Connor's wife was the cause of the attack.

They would drive away from the sea, north through pine woods and meadows of yellow flowers. The road followed a lazy brown river, and when Skye was young they would keep her occupied by telling her to count the red barns and black cows. Her father was so famous, the whole world wanted him, but on those trips he was theirs alone.

When they got to New Hampshire, to Redhawk Mountain, they would unload all the camping things. The trees were tall, and skinny green caterpillars dangled from branches by silken threads. Her father would help them pitch their tents; he would take the guns out of their cases. The .22-caliber rifles were heavy, especially when the girls were young, but their father taught them how to lift them slowly, to aim carefully.

Hugh's face by the campfire was shadowed with worry, for the fact that he had three daughters and the world was a cruel place.

Caroline had sat between Clea and Skye, listening to him, hearing the sounds made by wild things in the woods. He had told them that learning to shoot was necessary, to protect themselves against predators. His girls were sensitive and kind. Others were not, and bad men existed in a kill-or-be-killed world. They knew he was right, he had said, because of the man who had come to their house. Their father had spoken so gently, as if he were telling a bedtime story.

The fire crackled. Her sisters were warm beside her, and her father drew them close. He knew they loved wildlife, kept lists of the birds they'd seen. Each had her own garden at Firefly Hill. In some ways, hunting was like a nature walk. The softer you walked, the more creatures you saw. When it was time to kill, you became one with the animal. Mysteriously thrilling, the hunt stirred instincts most humans had long forgotten, a fantastic surging of life deep inside. He talked about hunting the way he talked about art: the ecstasy of life and death.

Caroline didn't believe it for a minute. She was thirteen, Clea was eleven, Skye was eight. Listening to their father, faces aglow in the firelight, the three girls were terrified. But they trusted him. He saw to their welfare with passion and kindliness, and if he said they should learn to shoot animals, they would.

Caroline's first kill was a squirrel. It sat on the branch of an oak tree, its tail curled over its back. She aimed the way her father had taught her, and squeezed the trigger. The squirrel toppled over. Just like a toy on a shelf, it fell off the branch. It lay on the ground, a black hole in its white fur. Caroline felt sick.

Her father wanted them to go their own ways, to explore the mountain and hunt on their own. If such independence was terrifying for Caroline, she could only imagine how it was for her younger sisters. She used to follow Skye. She would track her, fifty yards back, as if Skye were her quarry, just watching out for her.

Once Skye was crossing a narrow bridge across a fast stream. Halfway across she lost her footing, falling into the water. Caroline laid her gun down, kicked off her shoes, and went in after her. It was early spring, and the water came from melting river ice, farther north. The frigid water slashed around her, freezing her limbs, plastering them with the dead leaves of last winter. Her wool clothes weighed her down. Up ahead, Skye kept disappearing under the water.

By the time Caroline got her arms around Skye, they were in the rapids. The white water hissed in their ears. She spit out mouthfuls of cold water. Blinded by icy spray, she caught nightmare glimpses of snakes sunning themselves on the flat rocks they passed. Bumping into logs, tearing their clothes on sticks, Caroline clutched Skye with one arm and tried to grab branches and vines with the other.

Crashing down the river, Caroline felt the stones underwater. The force would drive the sisters into deep, swirling pockets, and they would be sucked under and spit out. Craggy boulders blocked their way, too slippery to grasp. The river pulled them forward. Caroline wondered how high the falls would be; she knew they were going over. She wondered if they would die.

But then the river evened out. The rapids gave way to a wide, peaceful stream. The roar faded away to silence and birds singing. Overwhelmed with her own life, the sense of safety, Caroline began to laugh with joy. She hugged Skye. But Skye didn't hug back. Her lips were blue. Weighed down by her jacket and boots, she felt like a sack of grain. Caroline pulled her to the riverbank. Skye was alive, and her eyes were open. But they wouldn't blink, wouldn't meet Caroline's.

"Skye, we're safe," Caroline said, rubbing her small hands.

"Did you see?" Skye asked, her voice small and frozen. "All those snakes on the rocks back there?"

"Yes, but—"

"I want to go home, Caroline," Skye said, the feelings breaking out. She began to cry hard. "Take me home. Please take me home."

But Caroline couldn't. She couldn't talk her father out

of what he thought was best. Falling in the icy river was part of learning how to be tough. Seeing snakes on the rocks was how you learned to keep from getting bitten. The lesson Caroline learned that day was slightly more disturbing: Just because she felt thrilled to be alive, overcome with rapture and gratitude, didn't necessarily mean her sister felt the same way. It didn't mean that at all.

Hugh had been so wrong. Caroline knew that now. Her father was dead, officially of cancer, but he had died years before, of a broken heart. Unable to bear what had finally happened to Skye, his baby, their beautiful girl, he had drunk himself to death, turning away from his family in the process. That more than the hunts themselves had filled Caroline with the bitterness she now felt. Because Skye was doing the same thing.

March 14, 1973

Dear the only Joe,

   I have two sisters. Clea and Skye. Clea is better than a best friend, and Skye is our beautiful baby sister. I wish we were all in the same grade together. Sometimes we want to talk so no one else can understand, and we do. It's hard to explain, but I know what they're thinking and they know what I'm thinking. It's like magic, only it's not. It's having sisters.

Your friend,
Caroline

June 19, 1973

Dear Caroline,

   Well, he's definitely not magic, but he's pretty cute. Sam. Good old Sam, my baby brother. Only he's a real baby—as in just born. Squawks like a seagull all night long. I took him out in my boat the other day, and my mother called the Coast Guard. She was really worried. Something about him not knowing how to swim (he's about the size of a flounder), but she missed the point. The kid loves water. Loves boats too. I swear, he wanted to row.

See you later,
Joe

CHAPTER FOUR

"MOM ADMITS SKYE MUST HAVE HAD A LITTLE TOO much to drink," Clea said, raising her eyebrow. The night before, while Caroline had maintained watch at the hospital, Clea had stayed home with her family, in touch only by telephone. She felt guilty, and it came through in the too-bright tone of her voice.

"Like a fifth of vodka?" Caroline asked.

The day was new, and they were on their way to Firefly Hill, to pick up Augusta and drive her to the hospital. Clea was at the wheel of her Volvo, and as they rounded the headland, Caroline caught sight of the big white ships on the horizon. They reminded her of Skye's last words the previous night.

"Did you tell Skye that Joe Connor was here?" Caroline asked.

"Oh, God," Clea said. "Why?"

Caroline was almost too angry to say. She felt tired and rumpled from spending the night at the hospital, and she hated these triangles of sisterhood, when two would know something the other wasn't supposed to. When she confided a worry to Clea and heard it come back from Skye. Or when she told some gossip to Skye and two hours later got a phone call from Clea, reporting the big news. Secrets among sisters were dangerous and nearly impossible to keep.

"Because she was on the way to see him," Caroline said flatly.

"She was?"

"She thinks if she hadn't been born, none of the rest would have happened."

"She was drunk. I thought she'd just go to bed," Clea said. "When she asked me about Joe's boat . . . I didn't think she'd drive. I can't stand thinking she crashed because of me," Clea said.

"Don't blame yourself, Clea," Caroline said.

"I can't help it. I should never have let her off the phone. Or I should have had her put Mom on the line."

"Blame has never gotten any of us very far," Caroline said. "So don't do it to yourself now."

They had arrived at Firefly Hill. The two sisters sat very still, staring at the door and wondering what kind of mood their mother was in. Would she be enthusiastic, ready to Visit the Sick with a big basket of freshly cut snapdragons? Or would she be frail, focused on her own arthritis or migraine headache to avoid noticing that her youngest child was going downhill fast?

The sun shone through a layer of high gossamer clouds. Not quite bright enough to throw dark shadows, it bathed the house and yard in an overall muted whiteness. A cold front was moving in, and the wind blew hard. Augusta appeared in the kitchen window. She was dressed, ready to go. At the sight of Caroline and Clea, she gave a hearty wave.

"Here we go," Caroline said, opening the car door.

"Have you seen Homer?" Augusta called, looking around.

The old dog sometimes disappeared. No one knew where he went. He could be gone for hours, or even overnight, but he always came back. Caroline didn't reply, knowing that Augusta's defense and denial were already locked in place. She just walked across the yard, to kiss her mother and drive her to the hospital.

* * *

At the hospital, all was quiet and blue. The lights at the psychiatric nurses' station had a shaded violet tone. Various monitors beeped and whirred melodically. The white-clad nurse pushing the medicine cart along the hall seemed to be swimming in contemplative slow motion.

From the far end of the hall, a patient let forth an eerie, ungodly howl, like someone in extreme agony. Standing with her mother and sister, Caroline had the impression of lurking in a strange undersea environment. For no reason at all, she wondered how it might feel to dive for treasure.

When signaled by the charge nurse, Caroline and Clea took their mother's hands and walked with her into Skye's room. The sight of Skye so still and pale, even more so than last night, made Caroline draw a deep breath. But her mother actually gasped. Caroline recognized this as a moment of truth: Her mother hadn't had time to polish, encode, or reinvent the situation. Unguarded, Augusta simply stared at Skye lying in her hospital bed. With frail fingers she touched her black pearls while tears ran down her cheeks.

The heart monitor glowed green in the otherwise dark room. Caroline and Clea stood back, letting their mother bend close to Skye, kiss her bandaged forehead. Augusta was silently crying, her shoulders shaking under her mink coat. A storm of emotion shivered through her thin body, but Caroline watched her force it down. She wiped her tears. She squared her shoulders.

"Skye. I'm here," Augusta said out loud.

"She can't hear you," Clea whispered.

"Skye. Wake up. Wake up, dear. It's your mother." Augusta spoke to Skye the way she talked to her daughters' answering machines, as if she knew someone was sitting there listening, unwilling to pick up the phone.

"Mom, she's sedated," Clea said.

"Caroline told me she spoke to her," Augusta said, sounding injured.

"Just a few words," Caroline said, wanting to cushion the fact that she had been there and her mother had not. That had always been the case, and Augusta was very sensitive about it. Caroline felt the all-too-familiar pressure in her chest. Skye was so injured and troubled, her mother was so infuriating and needy, and Clea was kowtowing to beat the band. Caroline wanted to rush out, slam the door behind her, head for the airport, and get on a plane to anywhere.

"If she needs her sleep, let's let her be," Augusta said, sounding frustrated. "She'll talk to me tomorrow. In the meantime, let's go find Peter. He's here, isn't he?" And she left Skye's bedside without another word.

Caroline and Clea drew together. With their mother gone, the old feelings came back: just the three of us, Caroline thought, holding Clea's hand and looking at Skye. The way it's always been. Three sisters on a lonely mountaintop, told to hunt by their father, holding hands when he turned his back. They had always taken care of each other.

Catching up with Augusta at the nurses' station, the women heard the charge nurse say that Peter was with Skye's doctor, who was just finishing up with another patient.

Augusta raised her dark eyebrows. No one could mistake her displeasure. She watched with silent disdain as the nurses moved methodically about their tasks. What did she want them to do? Caroline wondered. Make

Skye's doctor finish with his other patients faster? Serve cocktails?

"I'm going to go mad if that doctor doesn't hurry," Augusta said. She spoke in her normal voice instead of a whisper, and nurses up and down the corridor turned to look. "They'll have to admit me to this very floor if I have to stand here another minute."

"Mother, shhhh," Clea said.

"I have no respect for a doctor who makes the mothers of his patients wait like this," Augusta continued. "I think it's very rude."

Caroline and Clea exchanged a glance. Whenever their mother became this imperious, it meant she was very scared. She refused to accept the things she couldn't stand, the details of life she found too awful. Twisting reality was Augusta's way of marshaling her own sanity. Clea slid her arm around Augusta's slender shoulders, snuggling against the fur coat their mother had thrown on over her jeans and sneakers. Caroline felt her own rage start to abate.

"Doctors do it on purpose," Clea said. "They like to make the mothers really squirm, waiting to talk to them. Ministers do it too. Peter learned it in divinity school."

Augusta shook her head, her lips tightening. She was not about to laugh at anything. She was putting forth her best lofty grande-dame air, gazing appraisingly down the corridors as if she owned them. Like Caroline, Augusta Renwick had contributed to this hospital. Since Hugh's death, her sojourns here had been for opening ceremonies, board meetings, or events involving her chaplain son-in-law. Coming to the psychiatric floor to visit her youngest daughter was most assuredly not in her realm.

Finally Peter came along, wearing his clerical collar and dark trousers. He was talking to another man. He kissed Augusta and Caroline, then pulled Clea into a massive hug. Caroline watched the way they held each other, whispered a few words, looking deeply into each other's eyes until a slow smile came to Clea's troubled face. Then he introduced Dr. Jack Henderson, the head of their substance abuse unit.

"How do you do?" Dr. Henderson said.

"Pleased to meet you," Augusta said warily.

"Hi, Jack," Clea said, stepping forward.

Augusta shuddered, possibly at the idea of this doctor getting too close, at the prospect of him knowing anything too personal about the family. Caroline had met him before, seen him at a retrospective of her father's work.

"Hi," Caroline said, shaking his hand.

"Do you know each other?" Augusta asked.

"I collect your late husband's work," Dr. Henderson said.

"Really?" Augusta asked, lightening up slightly. "That's good to hear. Then you probably know that Skye takes after him. She's an artist herself."

The doctor nodded.

"She's a genius, doctor. Truly brilliant, and I am not saying that just because I am her mother." Augusta looked around the group for confirmation. Her eyes were glittering, as if tears were close by. "She's a sculptor. She was recognized by the art world years ago, when she was very young. Right, girls?"

"She was," Clea said. Caroline said nothing. She felt her mother lean against her slightly, and she held her hand for support.

"She's so talented . . ." Augusta choked up. Touching her throat, she pulled herself back together. "But she seems to be blocked."

"Blocked?" he repeated.

"I'm not an artist, so I don't know," Augusta said, "but

her father used to say he'd kill himself if he couldn't paint. An artist who can't make art . . . She's suffering so. Right, Caroline? We can see it, can't we?"

"Mom . . ."

"That's all it is," Augusta said, trying to convince herself and everyone else.

"Hmmm," Dr. Henderson said noncommittally.

"Mom, let's wait for Skye to wake up," Caroline said. "Let her talk to the doctor herself."

Augusta shook Caroline off.

"Artist's block," Augusta said, her voice trembling. "It explains everything, I think. She's so afraid she can't work anymore. And her husband left her. It's awful, it's just so terrible. . . ."

"Yes," Dr. Henderson said inscrutably.

"Who wouldn't drink a little under such trying circumstances? And I'm sure you know, alcohol fires the creative spirit. My God, could Hugh put it away! Skye takes after him even there, perhaps a little too much. If she could just moderate—"

"Excuse me?" Dr. Henderson asked.

"Perhaps you could suggest moderation!" Augusta said gingerly, offering the doctor his solution. "Half-measures don't come easily to any Renwick, that's for sure—"

"Mom," Caroline interrupted, stopping her.

"I believe moderation would help Skye. If she could just cut back a bit. You know, just stick to cocktails and wine with dinner. Don't you agree?" Augusta continued, unfazed, her hand cupping her chin as if she were a consulting physician.

"No, I'm afraid not," the real doctor said.

"Excuse me?" Augusta asked.

"Moderation rarely works with alcoholics. Total abstinence is the only way."

"Skye is not . . . an *alcoholic*," Augusta said, shocked and wounded.

Linking arms with Caroline and Clea, she glared at the doctor. Insulated by her family, she felt safe. She wanted him to see that the Renwicks were good people who loved one another. She wanted him to understand that although eccentric, they were not crazy, not the sort of people who became alcoholics. Bad things had happened to them, but adversity had built their characters. Caroline ached for her mother, recognizing that in her vulnerability she was terrified for Skye.

"Last night," the doctor said, "she told me about the hunting incident."

"Well," Clea said, holding Peter's hand. "Then you know."

Just then the doctor's beeper went off. He gave everyone an apologetic look, shook Augusta's hand, and hurried down the hallway. Everyone watched him go. Caroline had expected her mother to look relieved at his departure, but instead her pallor had increased. She had a thin film of sweat on her brow.

"Augusta, sit down," Peter said, leading her to a cluster of chairs at the end of the hall.

"It was an accident," Augusta said out loud. Her tone was quiet, almost humble. Tears spilled down her cheeks. Her hands trembling, she pulled at her pearls.

"It was," Caroline said quietly.

"Skye was just a child," Augusta said to Peter, her eyes wide. "She had no business shooting a gun in the first place. Haven't I always said that?"

"Yes, Augusta," he said. "You have."

"Skye wouldn't hurt a soul. She never meant to harm that man. A hunting accident, that's all it was. No one ever suggested otherwise, there were never charges brought."

"Skye isn't bad," Caroline said. "No one is saying that."

"He called her an alcoholic!" Augusta said.

"She drinks," Caroline said.

"Dad's drinking changed," Clea said, "after it happened."

"It was a tragedy," Augusta said, "a horrible thing that happened a long time ago. But there's no reason Skye should pay for it the rest of her life." Bewildered, she looked at Caroline. "Is there?"

Caroline shook her head. She was picturing the young man. She had heard the gunshot and Skye's scream, and she had been the first to find him. It had been fall, a bright blue day with yellow leaves covering the trail. He lay on the ground, the blood pouring from his chest. His eyes were bright and clear. His name was Andrew Lockwood, and he was twenty-five years old.

"Tell me why," Augusta said, staring straight into Caroline's eyes.

Caroline remembered taking her jacket off, pressing it into the hole in his chest. She could still feel the heat of his blood, see the question in his eyes. All the time, Skye, her voice as high as a baby bird's, asking what had she done, what had she done.

"Because she killed him, Mom," Caroline said quietly. "She didn't mean to, but she did."

January 7, 1977

Dear Joe,

I remember one of my letters to you, all about Clea and Skye and the magic of having sisters. Well, this one's not quite so nice. Did I mention my father? He's an artist. Okay, he's a famous artist. He tells us that he wants us to know How the World Works. (Boys have it easy, in case you're wondering) (according to him, anyway.) (I'm going parentheses-crazy.)

Girls have to be tough. Learn how to take care of ourselves. So he takes us hunting on Redhawk Mountain.

He loves us, you see.

He wants us to learn everything we can, really taste life. We camp out, go fishing and hunting. We go pretty far out in the country, and we have to fend for ourselves. I hate the hunting part. Killing is very hard—I know he'd be upset to know how much I hate hunting even squirrels.

At night, the woods are so dark, and we get scared. Sometimes very scared, especially Skye. I love her so much, Joe. Just writing this letter makes me cry, because if anything happened to Clea or Skye, I don't know what I'd do. They are the best, sweetest sisters in the world.

Write back soon. I'm starting to think you might be my best friend.

> *Love,*
> *Caroline*

Feb 2, 1977

Dear Caroline,

Hunting, cool! Your dad sounds great. Okay, I'll be your best friend. On one condition. Tell me the scariest thing that ever happened on the mountain.

> Love,
> Joe

March 4, 1977

Dear Joe,

The scariest thing. Okay, I'll tell you. It's how I feel. My father made Skye shoot a gun. She didn't want to, Joe. I'm so mad at him. He took something innocent and destroyed it. So I'm scared by how much I hate him right now. Hunting's not cool, not the way you said. It's horrible. Do you still want to be my best friend? Probably not. Even I don't.

Caroline

March 21, 1977

Dear Caroline,

I can tell you're upset by the way you didn't sign your letter "love." It's a little thing, but we best friends can be pretty sensitive. The gun thing sounds lousy. Poor Skye. I don't even know her, but since she's your sister, I figure she's okay. Your dad should forget about hunting and go back to painting. Or better yet, treasure hunting. He can teach you to dig for gold doubloons.

Love,

Joe

P.S. I'm only joking to make you smile. So smile!
P.S. again: Thought I forgot about the *Cambria*, didn't you?
P.S. double again: Smile, C.

CHAPTER FIVE

CAROLINE WAS PREOCCUPIED.

Michele Brady saw it right away, the way Caroline strode into the inn so purposefully, past the guests eating breakfast in the parlor, grabbing the phone messages off Michele's desk with barely more than a "good morning." Caroline looked gorgeous, as always: sleeveless black linen dress, black sandals, silver hoop earrings, silver necklace. She smiled, but it seemed forced.

Or pained, Michele thought, concerned. From certain phone messages, she had gathered that Skye was in the hospital again. That girl certainly gave Caroline plenty to worry about. Her whole family did. Even Clea, whom everyone in town considered to be the picture of respectability, was always calling Caroline for something. And Augusta didn't butter her toast without phoning Caroline for a consult.

Michele had been Caroline's assistant for ten years. At forty-two, she was just enough older than Caroline to feel rather protective of her. She was always telling her husband Tim about Caroline's crazy family, the things that went on. He was a professor of English at Connecticut College. Tim would listen with wry detachment, amusedly saying that Skye was New England's answer to Zelda Fitzgerald, or that the Renwick girls were like three divas in three different operas on the same stage.

Michele couldn't help laughing at Tim's take on the family, but she loved Caroline nonetheless. Caroline had hired her the year she opened the inn. They had spent the last ten years in separate offices, side by side, and although Caroline didn't specifically confide in her, Michele had been privy to the major moments in her life. She had watched Caroline transform from a . . . well, crazy Renwick girl into an astute and respected businesswoman. Caroline had always been loyal and kind, and those qualities had served her well.

Michele answered the phone, so she knew the general workings of Caroline's love life, business life, and family life. Over time she had watched Caroline build the Renwick Inn from a quirky little artists' retreat into an inn that attracted guests from all over the world. Some came for the location, others for the charm, still others because of the Renwick name.

Caroline's father was famous in a way usually reserved for actors or politicians, a man whose work hung in museums in New York, Paris, and London and whose wild nature had made him a favorite of magazine writers. One story in *Esquire* had called Hugh Renwick "the Hemingway of twentieth-century landscape painters." The author cited his bravery in World War II, his drinking and adultery, violence and self-destruction, the way his talent seemed to engulf everything—and everyone—in his life.

Doing the story, the author got drunk with Hugh. So did the photographer, who was famous in his own right. Their drunken escapades became part of the piece. They photographed him in a hunting jacket, with a rifle, somewhere in the woods at the edge of a bay in Maine. Hugh had told the story of an intruder that made it into the piece, a man who had entered his home and held his family hostage, finally blowing his own brains out.

Michele remembered Hugh's fury. It had saturated the magazine story: *his* home had been violated, *his* daughters threatened. He couldn't protect them twenty-four hours a day, but he could damn well teach them how to shoot a gun. He was sorry about the event on Redhawk Mountain, the hunting accident involving his daughter Skye. As Michele remembered it, the story didn't actually mention the name of the man she killed. All Hugh's sorrow and self-doubt had been edited out of the piece, leaving only rage and bluster.

Michele knew differently. Hugh Renwick was heartsick. As much as he had loved hunting, he celebrated life more. He loved nature. His adored his daughters. The world couldn't hold his passions; he had wanted excess and abundance for everyone, especially his family. But after the accident he turned inward. Michele had watched him mourn that young man every day, drinking alone in a dark corner of the Renwick Inn bar, his head bowed in silence.

Artists would approach him. He would be polite, sometimes let them buy him drinks. He could stare at the spot on the bar between his elbows for hours, watching the level of scotch in his glass rise and fall. Although he chose to drink at her inn, he couldn't stand to be with Caroline. It had killed Michele to watch her approach him, try to talk to him. He would turn surly, even belligerent. It was as if she reminded him of what was most precious in life, what he had failed to protect again and again. More than once, Michele heard him say that he had ruined Skye's life.

Three of his paintings hung in the bar. Hugh had done them when his daughters were young. Vivid and pure, they left no doubt about the love he had for the girls. Hunting scenes, set on Redhawk Mountain, each portrait depicted a different season, with each subject holding a different dead creature and weapon. Clea, in spring, held a rainbow trout in one hand and a fly rod in the other. Skye, in autumn, held a large knife and a writhing snake.

But it was Caroline in winter who took your breath away. Cradled in her arms was a small red fox. Blood dripped from its mouth. Snow covered the mountain and Caroline's cheeks were red. Her black hair blew across her eyes, but they showed through, clear blue and haunted. In her left hand she held the rifle that she had used to kill the fox. Her father had caught her compassion and regret; he had flooded the portrait with love for his oldest daughter. Michele shivered every time she looked at it.

Caroline walked out of her office. She had on her half-glasses, which gave her the look of a sexy librarian.

"What's this message?" she asked, ruffling a sheet of paper.

"Oh," Michele said, reading it. "He called first thing this morning. He left some rather complicated instructions about dialing ship-to-shore. I think he's one of those sailors who was here last night, drinking in the bar. They have Rooms Six and Nine, but I guess he's out on his boat."

"Did he say what he wanted?" Caroline asked.

"No. Just for you to call."

"Thanks," Caroline said. She walked into her office and closed the door.

* * *

Caroline dialed the marine operator and asked to be put through to the R/V Meteor. She held the line while the connection was made, staring out her window at the Ibis River, at egrets striding the shallows. She watched a kingfisher dive straight down, craning her neck to see what he came up with.

"This is Research Vessel *Meteor*," a man's voice said, the transmission crackling with static. "Over."

"This is the high seas operator. I have a call for a Mr. Joe Connor."

"Hold for Captain Connor," the man said.

A minute passed. Finally Joe's voice came over the line. The operator signed off, and Caroline said hello.

"It's Caroline," she said. "I got your message."

"Is your sister okay?" he asked.

"Why do you ask?" Caroline asked, surprised that he would know.

"She left a message at the dock office," Joe said. "Last night. Something about needing to see me, it was important."

"Did you talk to her?"

"Not in person. She said she was coming right over, but she never showed up. I wasn't sure where to reach her. So I called you."

"She's in the hospital," Caroline said tensely.

"Oh, no," Joe said, shocked. "What happened?"

"She had an accident," Caroline said.

"I'm sorry," Joe said. "Is she okay?"

"Not yet," Caroline said, her eyes welling up. His voice was kind. Speaking to him about Skye reminded her that they had once been close friends. She didn't feel friendship now, but the memory of their letters was powerful.

"Why did she want to see me? Do you know?"

"She was confused," Caroline said, not wanting to tell him more.

"I'm sorry," Joe said again.

"Thanks," Caroline said.

* * *

The dream had been so real, she had been back on the mountain.

She could smell the gunsmoke. The mountain air was

fresh and cold, the yellow leaves twinkling down like falling stars. Skye was holding her breath, standing just behind her. Caroline crept through the brush until she saw the deer Skye had shot. Big and brown, crumpled in a heap. She didn't want to look at it, but she made herself, for Skye's sake.

It was a man. He wore a brown corduroy jacket, the color of a buck. His hair was red, glinting in the sun. His eyes were wide, so amazed at it all. They held Caroline's as she crouched beside him. She knew she had to look into the man's eyes and never away, so she barely glanced at the wound in his chest, the blood pumping out of it like a natural spring.

She heard Skye start to whimper and then cry. She felt the man's dog, a young golden retriever, bumping against her with his wet nose, trying to kiss his owner and the stranger bending over him. She felt the cold air as she unzipped her red jacket, pulled it off. She felt his blood on her fingers, so incredibly hot as she pressed the jacket into the wound.

"Did I shoot him?" Skye asked. "Did I? Did I? What have I done?"

Caroline, who had never ignored her sister in her life, ignored her now.

"What's your name?" she asked, looking into the man's eyes.

"Andrew," he answered. He was not much older than Caroline, the age of some of the younger teachers at her college.

His eyes were so bright. They were calm and kind, reassuring Caroline that she was doing her best, that he understood she was trying to help. At first there was no fear in his eyes at all. Every second seemed longer than a heartbeat. Caroline felt the blood pumping out of his body, soaking her jacket, flowing through her fingers into the ground. Their campsite was only five miles down the dirt road, but that was too far. They would never make it for help. Time had paused for them, Caroline and Skye Renwick, Andrew and his dog.

"I thought he was a deer," Skye sobbed.

The sky was too blue. The day was too beautiful. The dog wanted to sniff the man's blood, kiss the man's face.

"Homer," Andrew said.

"He's just a puppy, isn't he?" Caroline asked, noticing the dog's puff-ball body, his eager yellow face. He was barely full grown.

"Yes," Andrew said.

"Call him, Skye. Call Homer," Caroline said, because the dog had blood on his muzzle from kissing Andrew, and she thought Andrew would look at him and see his blood and be afraid.

"Homer," Skye said, her voice thin and high, trying so hard. "Here, boy."

The dog ran to her. Only then did Andrew's eyes look away from Caroline. He watched his dog go, and then his gaze came back to Caroline.

"I'm going to die, aren't I?" he asked.

Caroline knew he was. She saw his lips turning white, felt his blood moving slower. She heard her sister crying behind her, felt the dog return to Andrew, wriggling between them as he snuggled closer to his master. Caroline thought of Joe Connor, of the lesson she had learned about how important it was to tell the truth about death, about how it was the least one person could do for another.

"I think you are," she said.

"Oh, God," Andrew said. His eyes turned afraid. It was so terrible to see. Caroline pressed harder on his chest, but she knew she wasn't doing any more good. His hands clenched and unclenched. Homer made a sound like a human crying, a mournful sob that came from deep inside. Skye stood right behind Caroline, her legs shaking against her sister's back.

"I didn't know," Skye wept. "I thought he was a deer."

"Homer," Andrew said.

The dog licked Andrew's face. There was comfort in that, Caroline knew. Even at that moment, with his life flowing through her fingers, she could see that he found peace in the presence of his dog. She could see it in the way he closed his eyes and let everything slip away. He didn't open his eyes again.

* * *

"A big bouquet," Joe Connor said to the woman at the roadside stand.

"Do you want just zinnias and sunflowers, or wild-flowers too?" the woman asked.

"Everything," Joe said.

He watched her work. She stood under the yellow-and-white-striped tent, pulling flowers from big buckets of water. She was heavy and very tan, dressed in a faded red housecoat, a scarf tied around her brown hair. She frowned. Watching an unhappy woman work hard reminded Joe of his mother.

"Did you pick the flowers?" Joe asked.

"Yes. And planted them too," she said, smiling proudly.

"They're pretty," Joe said, reaching into his pocket. The flowers cost five dollars, but he gave her a twenty. She started to make change, but Joe shook his head. The woman cast a quick glance at her husband, but he was sitting on a stack of milk cartons engrossed in the sports page. She nodded her thanks. But she put the money in the cash box instead of her pocket.

"Hey," Joe said, startling the man. "You should take your wife out for dinner."

The man grunted. His eyes were small and red. He looked mean, like a pig. Joe wanted to knock him off the milk crates.

"You should buy her a lobster," Joe said, "at her favorite restaurant."

"Yeah," the man said.

Joe drove away. He had problems in the area of unhappy women. He hated seeing women frown. He had watched his mother transform from a pretty, enthusiastic woman into a bitter, hurt, disappointed shadow. Working double shifts at the shellfish company, she had spent her free time waiting for Hugh Renwick to call. Drowning in guilt after her husband died. She had married again, but by then she had spent some miserable years.

Joe had wanted to bash heads. Everyone who had ever hurt his mother. The shellfish company owners, for making her work too hard. Hugh Renwick, for breaking both his parents' hearts. Joe's father had died in the Renwicks' kitchen, friendless and alone. And his gold watch: his father had died wearing his watch, the watch he had always let Joe play with, and Joe's mother had never bothered getting it back. The missing watch had been a symbol of everything Joe thought he had lost.

Staying friends with Caroline after learning the truth would have taken a miracle. For Joe's seventeenth birthday, his uncle had taken him out to the Spindrift to get him drunk. Joe was underage, but that was beside the point. They had sat on barstools, drinking boilermakers, while Uncle Marty told him the truth about his father's death. He was a jealous man, Uncle Marty said, out of his mind. Killed himself right in the Renwicks' kitchen. The kids had been there, Uncle Marty had said: Caroline and Clea. Caroline had watched his father die, heard his last words.

How could a friend know something like that, such a brutal part of his life, and not tell him? His friendship

with Caroline was over. Whiskey numbed the initial
shock, so Joe kept it flowing. He turned to the sea, stud-
ies, and drinking to forget. To block out how bad he felt,
how angry it made him. After a while he cut out drinking, but the first two still worked.

Trying to forget the flower stand lady, Joe did his er-
rands. He had supplies to pick up for the *Meteor,* letters
to mail, packages to send. His divers had collected some
timber fragments and rust scrapings, and he was sending
them to Woods Hole for analysis, in order to date the
vessel. Today he planned to enter the wreck, when the
tide was right, so he was in a hurry to get back. Nothing
like a dive to take his mind off his emotions.

Before returning to sea, he had one final stop to make.
He drove down Main Street, away from the small
business district, through the outskirts of town. He
pulled into the shady parking lot of Shoreline General
Hospital.

"I'd like to leave these flowers for a patient," he told
the blue-smocked lady at the information desk.

"What's the name, please?" she asked politely.

"Skye Renwick."

"Whitford's her married name," the lady said, smiling.
She didn't even bother typing Skye's name into the com-
puter, and Joe recognized the doings of a small town.
"I'm afraid she can't have visitors quite yet."

"All right," Joe said, relieved because he didn't want
to meet her anyway. He scribbled a note and handed
the lady his flowers. "Would you please see that she gets
these?"

"Aren't they beautiful?" the woman exclaimed. "I certainly will."

"Thanks," Joe said. He turned to walk out of the hospital. The air-conditioning stifled him. He couldn't
wait to breathe the sea air. In an hour or so he'd be in

the water, diving down to the wreck. He'd be away, he'd be free.

* * *

Caroline knew Skye wasn't supposed to see anyone, even family, but she stepped off the elevator with authority, a folder of papers under her arm, and she said a brisk hello to the nurses she passed instead of stopping to ask if it was okay for her to visit. No one questioned her. She had known they wouldn't, from all the times she had sneaked in when her father was sick.

Skye was awake. She was propped up in bed, staring at a card someone had sent her. It was a large, expensive greeting card with bluebirds, roses, a waterfall, and a rainbow on the front. It was supposed to be painterly and beautiful, but the artist had, perhaps unintentionally, given the bluebirds leering expressions in their large eyes. They looked like winged lechers.

"The word is out," Caroline said. "Fan mail is arriving."

Skye looked up and forced a smile. Her bruises had darkened and yellowed. The bandages around her head were disheveled from sleep; they hadn't been changed yet that morning. It was painful to look at her hands shaking from withdrawal, but Caroline couldn't take her eyes away.

"Who sent the card?" Caroline asked. Although, of course, she knew.

"Mom," Skye said, and with that she really did smile. She passed the card to Caroline, and her smile grew wider. It was a fact in the Renwick family that their mother bought and sent cards for all occasions, the more sentimental and glittery, the better. In turn, when Augusta herself received a card in the mail, she always checked the back to see how much the sender had spent on her.

Caroline turned the card over, to see the price.

"Wow," she said. "You really rate."

"A four-dollar card," Skye said, smiling harder. "You're not jealous, are you?"

"Don't rub it in," Caroline said, pretending to scowl. She read the handwritten message:

Darling,

When will you learn to ask when you need something? My car is yours whenever you need it. You had no business driving that old junker anywhere—never mind all the way to Moonstone Point. What ever possessed you to go there anyway? Come home soon! I am rattling around this big house without you!

Love,
Mom

"Vintage Mom," Caroline said, laying the card beside Skye's breakfast tray.

"She misses me," Skye said.

"She misses the point," Caroline said.

"Hmmm," Skye said.

"Not one word about vodka in that whole four-dollar card."

"Caroline, I feel bad enough," Skye said. "Don't rub it in, okay? I was an idiot, driving in the first place. I'm sure Joe Connor thinks I'm out of my mind. I know you don't understand, and I don't really feel like explaining it right now, but I had something I wanted to tell him."

"Tell *me*," Caroline said. She sat on the bed, waiting to hear Skye try to talk her way out of the situation. Skye's expression turned sullen.

"Don't torture me. I was hammered. I admit it."

"You don't remember, do you?"

"Blackout city," Skye confessed.

"It's not funny, Skye," Caroline said. "Last night your doctor told us you're an alcoholic."

"They say that about everyone," Skye said. "Look where I am: the rehab unit. It's how they make their money. They think everyone who has more than two beers is an alcoholic."

"Do you think you are?"

"No! Of course not! But I'm going on the wagon."

"You are?" Caroline asked, surprised. It wasn't something she had expected Skye to say.

"For now. I've been drinking too much. I admit it, okay? But things with Simon . . . and I can't get my work to go right . . . Does Homer miss me?"

"I'm sure he does. I stopped by to walk him this morning."

"Good, he was there?" Skye smiled, wanting to divert Caroline with speculation about Homer's secret life. He would take off, and they never knew when to expect him back. But Caroline wanted to stay focused on Skye. She sat still, not saying anything.

"I was worried," Skye went on. "What if he didn't come back? I mean, he's so old now. Doesn't it seem like he was just a puppy?"

"Something about Joe coming to town," Caroline said as if Skye hadn't spoken.

"What about it?"

"Stirring everyone up. Upsetting you."

"Not *me*," Skye said, smiling expectantly.

Trying her best to cajole Caroline, Skye hadn't noticed her bandage slipping over one eye. Reaching over, Caroline gently straightened it.

"When you were drunk," Caroline said carefully, "you said maybe Joe's father didn't mean to kill himself, and I know you had to be thinking about what happened with you. About shooting Andrew Lockwood."

"The beauty about it . . ." Skye said. She was sitting upright in bed, her knees drawn up. A white cotton blanket was spread over the sheets, and she had worked one of the threads loose, tugging the loop with her index finger. "Is that I don't really remember what I had in mind."

Both sisters seemed engrossed in the loop of thread. Skye wove it back into the blanket so seamlessly, Caroline couldn't detect where it had been. After a few minutes, Skye closed her eyes and faked being asleep. Caroline sat quietly at her side, wondering what to say. A candy striper walked in, wheeling a cart of flowers. She placed a large vase of beautiful flowers on Skye's table.

"Look," Caroline said, causing Skye to open her eyes. She handed her the small card.

"Oh," Skye said, frowning at the flowers. She read the card, then smiled up at Caroline. "They're from your boyfriend."

Caroline read the small card: " 'Get well soon. Call me when you want to talk again. Joe Connor.' My boyfriend? Not quite."

"He has nice handwriting," Skye said, grabbing the card. "Very masculine. Here, let me analyze it for you." She squinted, examining the words.

In spite of herself, Caroline was curious. Skye was no handwriting expert, she was just playing around. Even so, Caroline's interest was piqued. "What?" she asked.

"He is very lonely," Skye said, trying to sound mysterious. "He has no one to talk to. He searches for treasure to replace that vital thing missing in his life."

"Which is?"

"Hope? Love?" Skye asked. "His long-lost sweetheart. I don't know. You'll have to ask him. That will be three dollars."

"Sorry, I forgot my checkbook," Caroline said.

"It's okay," Skye said. "I owe you anyway."

* * *

When Caroline pulled up to Firefly Hill, her mother's car was gone. She walked up the porch steps and went in through the kitchen door. Homer was lying on his rug. At the sound of Caroline, he glanced over. Without actually moving, his eyes changed expression and he looked deeply happy to see her. Then his tail began to wag. It swished once, twice, across the tile floor. He clambered to his feet, wobbling on his legs. Then, with a little forward momentum, he came across the room to greet her.

"Hi, boy," she said, rubbing his head. "Good dog. You're a good dog, Homer."

He carried a faded blue hand towel in his mouth. The towel, or one like it, had been his toy ever since he came to live at Firefly Hill fourteen years ago. Her father had given him the first one. Caroline tugged the towel. Homer tossed his head, playfully pulling back.

"You win, Homer," Caroline said.

He stood at the door, waiting to be let out. Caroline walked across the yard, and he stayed close by: Today wasn't a day for one of his mystery sojourns. The ships were visible on the horizon, Joe Connor searching for treasure. Caroline stared at them for a minute, but Homer was eager to get to the beach.

He left his towel at the top of the tall stairway leading down the grassy bluff. It was painful to watch how slowly he moved, how every step seemed to tire his legs and hurt his back. His thick golden coat had turned thin and brittle, bald in patches. Watching him descend the steps, Caroline remembered him as a grief-stricken young puppy, his face dark with his owner's blood.

They walked down Firefly Beach, along the high-tide line. Bits of dry kelp and eelgrass stuck to his tufty fur, but he didn't care. He was happy to be outside with Caroline, the human he had loved most since Andrew Lockwood. When they turned back toward home, Caroline heard someone call her name.

It was Maripat. Her niece was nine, and she came running full tilt down the beach, holding a book in her hand. Homer barked, overcome with joy at the sight of another family member. His back leg faltered, and he went down. But he was up in time, panting happily, when Maripat got there.

She wore blue shorts and a tee-shirt Caroline had brought her from Nantucket. Her silky brown hair was long, pulled back in a French braid. She had the Renwick eyes, wide and clear, and she wore glasses with enameled green wire rims.

"Brought you something," Maripat said, kissing her aunt and patting the dog.

"For me or Homer?" Caroline asked.

"For you," Maripat said, smiling.

"What is it?" Caroline asked, accepting the book Maripat held out to her.

"Mom told me about your friend," Maripat said, "the pirate. Is he really a pirate?"

"He says so," Caroline said. "That's him, out there."

Maripat shielded her eyes, looking at the big white boats shining in the late sun.

"They look like yachts to me," she said doubtfully.

"Modern pirates," Caroline said. "They don't know what they're missing. Too much luxury and not enough creaky old planks. What's the book?"

"The ship that sank?" Maripat said, her eyes bright as she got to tell her aunt something she didn't know. "The *Cambria?* Well, she was an English barquentine, or brigantine, the one with more masts, I forget which."

"Barquentine, I think," Caroline said, thinking back to third grade.

"The captain was a rat," Maripat said. "Considering he went to the lighthouse and fell in love with the lady who lived there. And that she was married to the light-keeper."

"What a stinker," Caroline agreed.

"The lady had a little girl," Maripat said.

"That's right. I forgot," Caroline said, watching Homer dig a hole in the cool sand and lie down in it. "What were their names again?"

"The captain was Nathaniel Thorn, and the lady was Elisabeth Randall. The little girl was Clarissa." Maripat paused, her eyes shining, her excitement so palpable, there might have been an imaginary drumroll. "And that's her diary!" She thumped the book.

"Whose diary?"

"Clarissa's! Some old lady, her husband was in the Coast Guard and took over the light, found the diary, and had it printed. I'd kill my mother if she ever did that to me. But we had to read it in school, and when Mom told me about the treasure guy, I said oh-my-God. Read it!"

Together they opened the book, and Caroline read the first entry:

July 19, 1769

Today I found a finback whale which had run ashore. She was bigger than the lifeboat and the same color as the rocks of our island, and she was lying on the south shore with her eye wide open, just staring at the sky. Mama and I tried to free her for hours, until darkness fell. We kept her wet with sea water carried in the fire bucket, because Mama said if her skin dried out, she would die. And she bade me watch the whale's blowhole, because that was where she breathed, and if water got *in, she could drown. The tide took so long to rise! Tonight my arms ache from carrying water, from pulling on her tail to free her from the rocks. But it is worth it. Mama and I watched our whale swim away when the tide finally came to its full height, with a fat orange moon full on the water.*

"I like her," Maripat said. "Don't you? Doesn't she sound cool?"

"Very," Caroline said, touched that her niece had brought her Clarissa's diary. "This wasn't around when I was in third grade."

"Maybe they just didn't bother printing it back then," Maripat said helpfully. "Did you and Mom and Aunt Skye ever free a finback whale? Did there used to be many around here?"

"No, we never did," Caroline said, smiling. It cracked her up, the way Maripat thought her mother and aunts had lived "back then," in olden times, historical days like Clarissa Randall, when finback whales were as thick in the water as minnows.

"Are you going to show the diary to that guy?"

"Which guy?"

Maripat pointed out to sea. She seemed to be suppressing a smile, and Caroline wondered what Clea had told her about Joe. "Him," she said.

"I might, come to think of it," Caroline said.

"He's down in the shipwreck," Maripat said reasonably. "I think he should know about the people involved."

"That makes excellent sense. After I read it, I might let him borrow it. Is this from the library?"

"The school library. Only students can borrow there, but I signed it out till September. For you," Maripat said with shy pride.

"Thank you," Caroline said.

"He was like a brother to you, right?" Maripat asked, blushing slightly. "You were pen pals?"

"Sort of, when we were young," Caroline said. She sensed Maripat wanting to ask more. Her niece came from a totally stable home, with parents who had been married to each other forever, and she seemed fascinated with her two aunts and their troubled world of men. Ex-boyfriends, stormy love affairs, even broken friendships with boys intrigued her and got her curiosity working.

"Where's your mother?" Caroline asked.

"Up there," Maripat said, glancing up at the house.

"Let's go find her," Caroline said.

Together they waited for Homer to get to his feet. Caroline moved down to the hard sand, where it would be easier for him to walk. A fly buzzed around his nose, and it made her sad to see him ignore it. Not so long ago he would have chased that fly until he snapped it in his mouth.

"Poor Homer," Maripat said. "It's hard for him to walk."

"He's sixteen. That's old for a dog."

"You love him, don't you?" Maripat said. "He's like your baby."

"I've had him since he was a puppy," Caroline said.

"A brand-new puppy?"

"Well, not quite brand new," Caroline said.

"I wish Mom would let us get a dog," Maripat said. "And that she'd let her sleep on my bed. I'd get a girl dog. Not that Homer isn't nice—I know he's a boy and all—but one boy is enough in our house. Mark drives me crazy. . . ."

Caroline nodded, listening to Maripat chatter on, happily complaining about her brother, their lack of pets, her rival in swimming class, her father's thinning hair, her re-

cent discovery of lemon Popsicles shaped like great
white sharks. Caroline was grateful Maripat hadn't kept
asking about Homer. Questions came as easily to the
child as her next breath, and Caroline was pretty sure her
mother hadn't told her the story of Homer's first owner.
Caroline certainly didn't intend to tell her now.

Maripat led the steep parade up the stone steps.
Caroline and Homer brought up the rear. Petting the
dog, encouraging him along, Caroline took one last
glance at the ships at sea. Joe Connor. Telling the truth
about life and death could get you in trouble, no matter
which way you went.

When they got to the top, Homer paused for a moment. The western edge of the property was a nature sanctuary, a small forest of oaks and scrub pines. The woods
were cool and wild, and they sounded their mysterious
call. Homer cast Caroline an articulate look of love. Then
he swung around, walking quickly, disappearing into the
trees.

Never forgetting that she had first come upon him in
woods, Caroline watched him go.

April 2, 1978

Dear Joe,

I can't believe I've never asked you this, but do you have any pets? People always say it's possible to be a cat person or a dog person, but never both. I guess that makes me weird. I'm both. The problem is, I love saltwater so much, I want my animals to, too. I taught my first puppy how to swim. He sank first, and I dove down and found him walking through the seaweed. But then he floated up and swam like a champ. (Actually, I had to rescue him—but he ran right back in!) Cats are another story. They'd rather curl up on the window seat and listen to the waves.

Time for me to listen to my sisters. They want me to stop writing you and go outside with them. Until later!

Love,
Caroline

April 15, 1978

Dear Caroline,

This has to be short because I want to go sailing and the wind's perfect. Right now my only pet is my boat. She's fifteen feet, very fast, doesn't eat much. If I could live on the water for the rest of my life, I'd be happy. Maybe I will. You're a dog person and a cat person, and I'm a boat person.

Love,
Joe

CHAPTER SIX

"WHAT ARE YOU STARING AT?" AUGUSTA RENWICK asked, hating the silence. Her oldest daughter was standing at the big picture window facing seaward, looking across Long Island Sound with Hugh's shooting scope. When Augusta arrived home a few hours earlier, a troubled silence had billowed in, settling on the room like a great gray fog bank and encouraging Clea and Maripat to cut their visit short.

"Just a minute," Caroline said. Augusta felt hurt by her tone. She sat on the down love seat, curled up under a cashmere throw, needlepointing a pillow for Skye: swans and a castle, the motif from *Swan Lake*.

"I'm halfway finished," Augusta said just to make conversation. "*Swan Lake.* Wasn't that a happy memory for you and your sisters? The night your father took you to the ballet? Down to New York City in those black velvet dresses . . . You all came home wanting to be ballerinas. Maybe we should have encouraged Skye to study dance."

"Hmmm."

"She's always been so *critical* of herself. She thinks she can't paint, and now that she's having such a time, so blocked with her sculpting, it would be wonderful if she had something else to fall back on."

"You don't fall back on being a prima ballerina, Mom."

Augusta glanced over. Of course she had said the wrong thing. Speaking of Skye, she walked on eggshells with Caroline; she had no confidence in herself whatsoever.

But then, as if Caroline could suddenly read her mind, she smiled, trying to unhurt her mother's feelings, and said, "I just mean dancing's a life's work, like sculpting. I think it would be either or, not both. Obsessive professions."

"Like loving your father," Augusta said, trying to joke.

But Caroline wouldn't laugh. She shut down on that subject. She had always seemed so sternly competent, looking after her sisters like a mother hen when Augusta had abdicated her position, at times when things with Hugh had been the most precarious. Looking back, Augusta had a million regrets, but she knew one thing: She had never loved her daughters less than ferociously. That knowledge gave her courage to keep going.

"Any one of you could have danced the ballet," Augusta said. "Maybe not as your life's work, but you certainly had the grace and spirit for it. And your legs! Your father would look at your legs and say they were over the legal limit."

No comment. Augusta did her needlepoint, accepting Caroline's silence. All three girls were exquisite, temperamental beauties; right now, in Caroline's case, with an accent on the *temperamental*. Staring at her daughter, Augusta could only imagine the bad-parent accusations swirling around in her head.

Caroline had always been on edge, watching for something to happen, defending her little sisters against everything. Even their parents, Augusta thought, trying not to feel hurt. Watching Caroline now, staring off to sea, Augusta imagined her as a sentinel maintaining watch over the ones she loved. Her heart ached for her daughter, who didn't have enough love in her life. Always the one protecting other people.

She needed a man, Augusta thought. Beautiful but rather severe, with her dark hair all swept up, her clothing the colors of rocks or architecture: shades of granite and slate and brick and sandstone. Such a successful businesswoman, she intimidated all the men in town—scared them half to death. In her free time she traveled constantly, much too much. Or she hiked in the woods, alone.

"Caroline," Augusta said, rising. "What can be so interesting out there?"

"Come see," Caroline said. She handed the glass to Augusta, helped her steady it against her right eye. "There."

Augusta held the brass tube and tried to focus. The metal felt warm under her hands, from Caroline's grip. She blinked against the lens, twisted the eyepiece, trying to make sense of what she was looking at. A big circle of open ocean with a few boats in the middle.

"Fishermen," she said.

"No," Caroline said. "They're not."

Augusta laughed. Was Caroline joking? She lived here, looked out this window a hundred times a day. She knew fishing boats when she saw them. They'd surf the rip at Moonstone Reef, throw their lines overboard, hoping to catch bluefish and sharks. Hugh had fished there himself, although most of his sportfishing had been for big game in the Canyon beyond Block Island, or south, in the Bahamas or the Keys. Still, she stared at the boats. What was that plume shooting like a jet of water?

"What are they doing?" she asked.

"Diving for treasure," Caroline said.

Augusta lowered the lens. She gazed at Caroline's lovely gray-blue eyes and saw them so alive, so full of fire, she couldn't speak. Something was going on. It was like looking at a person having a religious vision.

"Darling, are you kidding?" Augusta asked.

"They're bringing up a shipwreck," Caroline said.

"Really?" Augusta asked. She adored things like shipwrecks. Why else would she live in a godforsaken mansion on the Sound if she didn't? Even more, it felt like a bond with Caroline. A shipwreck was something they could enjoy together. Curious, she raised the glass to her eye again. "How do you know?"

"A friend told me," Caroline said. "It's the *Cambria*."

"The *Cambria* . . ." Augusta said. The name sounded familiar.

"That fountain thing you're seeing is actually sand. They have a compressor on board their boat that blows sand away from the wreck so they can get to the gold."

"How exciting," Augusta said. She watched the spray of sand, tried to see the people on board the boats. At this distance, they were tiny and faceless, like toys. Even the big boats tossing on the waves looked miniature. Augusta smiled with pride. Leave it to Caroline to know everything going on in the area.

"How do you hear about these things?" Augusta asked, beaming. "It must be terribly top secret. I haven't seen a word about it in the papers. And no one's talking."

"I suppose it is a secret," Caroline said.

"You know I keep a secret better than anyone," Augusta said. But the awful look on Caroline's face made her heart sink.

"I know you do," Caroline said, making it sound like an indictment. She walked across the room, sat down in the Windsor rocker. In the time it took, she composed herself. When she directed her gaze at Augusta, her face was placid and neutral. Augusta swallowed. She was in for something she wasn't going to like.

"We have to talk about Skye," Caroline said.

Involuntarily Augusta touched the pearls around her neck. Why were they called "black" when they were actually the most amazing shade of dove gray? She glanced at Caroline.

"Have I ever told you your eyes are exactly the same color as my pearls?" she asked, smiling, still touching the pearls.

"Yes," Caroline said, patiently rocking.

"Eyes the color of black pearls. So rare . . . Some wonderful man will see that someday. He will. Ordinary men would look at you and say your eyes are blue, or blue-gray, but the right man will know immediately. He will tell you your eyes are the color of black pearls."

"Mom, you heard what Dr. Henderson said," Caroline said, leaning forward. "That she's an alcoholic."

Augusta shook her head. She had had time to process what the doctor had said. While she knew Skye was emotional, she refused to lend credence to the idea of her being an alcoholic. But Caroline was rocking away, determined to discuss it.

"He's crazy," Augusta said. "He doesn't know her. She's an artist, like your father. It's normal for artists to drink."

"Don't compare her to Dad."

"Such a terrible resentment," Augusta said sadly. "You and your sisters feel so angry at your father for those hunts, and all he wanted was to spend a little time alone with his girls."

"Turn us into boys," Caroline said, patting the dog.

"That is not true. He would attack anyone who suggested that he wished even one of you were a son instead of a daughter. He just wanted you to enjoy the outdoors, the way he did."

"It was a little more complicated than that," Caroline said kindly after the briefest of pauses.

"Well," Augusta began, but she trailed off. She didn't have the heart for an argument. Augusta was nonviolent. She didn't believe in guns or knives. She hadn't wanted her daughters exposed to danger, wild animals, or the thin night air. But she had adored her husband beyond all reason. When he had wanted to take the girls hunting overnight on the mountain, she hadn't spoken up, even though her heart had told her he was wrong.

"What do we do, then, Mom? Without blaming Dad or calling Skye an alcoholic, how do we help her?"

"We bring her home. We encourage her and love her."

"We will do all those things. We always have. But they're not enough anymore."

Augusta watched Caroline kneel next to Homer, who had started to scratch himself.

Working a seed pod free from where it had tangled in a clump of fur, Caroline pulled too hard. Yelping, he looked over his shoulder at Augusta, his big brown eyes liquid with injury.

"I didn't do it," Augusta said to the dog.

"Remember when we brought him home?" Caroline asked, stroking the old dog. His eyes were closed, his ribs visible through his rough yellow coat.

"He's a big pain in the neck," Augusta said, sounding less affectionate than she felt and ignoring Caroline's question. He had gotten Caroline and Skye through those first awful weeks after the hunting accident, although she knew that Caroline thought the opposite was true: that she had helped the dog in his grief.

"You love him, Mom," Caroline said. "You can't kid any of us."

"He'd be a stray if it weren't for me," Augusta said,

watching him slobber all over Caroline. "I wonder if anyone remembers that."

The young man had lived in New Hampshire, on a fellowship to Dartmouth, but his family was from San Francisco and wanted no part of shipping a dog across the country, to live in the middle of a city. The police had taken him to the pound in Hanover. Augusta had allowed Homer into her house because Caroline had been unable to bear thinking of him abandoned, because she had convinced Augusta that saving the dog would help Skye. And because Hugh had needed to do it as well.

"What about Skye, Mom?" Caroline asked now.

"I don't know what's set her off," Augusta said carefully. "What's making her so upset all of a sudden. I think we should let her come home, get some rest, and not go looking for trouble. The past is a minefield, and I for one am tired of it."

"Mom—"

"End of the story. Hear me, Caroline?" Augusta asked sharply. She pulled off her half-glasses and glared over Homer's head at Caroline.

"You're wrong, Mom," Caroline said, rising. "It won't be the end of the story."

"And what is? You and your sisters crying about your father to any stranger who'll listen? While I sit there and try to defend him? He loved you all. And I defy you to tell *anyone,* especially yourself, otherwise."

"Mom, the end of the story is Skye's funeral," Caroline said, her voice thick with anger and tears. Her black-pearl eyes were brimming, furious.

"Don't you dare say that," Augusta said.

"Maybe she'll fall and hit her head, or maybe she'll take too many pills. Maybe it won't be a car wreck next time. Or maybe it will. She killed a man, Mom, and I think it makes her want to die herself."

"Caroline," Augusta said dangerously, feeling her head starting to shake, the way it did when she got upset.

Caroline came across the room. She knelt before her mother's chair and held her hands. Seeing her elegant daughter kneel before her in such abject supplication was too much for Augusta to bear. She tried to push Caroline away, but Caroline wouldn't move. She stared straight into Augusta's eyes.

"Please, Mom," Caroline said, the tears just running down her cheeks. "It's you I'm thinking of almost as much as Skye. I know how you'll feel if something happens. You won't be able to stand it. You love Skye so much. Let's pull together now. Do whatever it takes to help her. Let's start by being honest, okay?"

Augusta took a deep breath. She leaned forward, touched the tip of her nose against Caroline's. Their eyes met, and, as always, Augusta was struck by the depth, the beauty, the compassion in Caroline's eyes. The emotion was enough to take your breath away. Hugh had caught it once, just once, in that portrait he had done of her, his famous *Girl in a White Dress*.

Backing away, Augusta brushed a stray wisp of raven hair off Caroline's forehead. She set her needlepoint aside. Arching her back, she stood tall. Looking down at Caroline, still on her knees, she thought of her own childhood, of going to church to pray for help. She wondered whether her children remembered their Catholic upbringing, whether they ever turned to prayer. Or whether they had stopped believing at the same time as Augusta and Hugh, right after the accident at Redhawk.

"Your father did love you," Augusta said, watching Caroline's face. It remained impassive. "Those hunts were his way. . . . He was larger than life, and he showed his love in extraordinary ways."

"I know," Caroline said.

"Would you like a cocktail?" Augusta asked. "I'm going to have one."

Caroline bowed her head. She didn't say yes, she didn't say no. She seemed to be thinking it over. She gave the appearance of devotion, of praying. Augusta would mix enough for two. She patted Caroline's head. Then she walked away, toward the flower room, where they kept the bar.

* * *

Extraordinary ways. Caroline sat at the top of the beach stairway with Homer, remembering her father. On the way to Redhawk, she was the navigator. She was supposed to say "head northeast" instead of "take a right," and when they came to an intersection and looked both ways, she would tell her father "clear," just like a copilot would say. She knew the things that made him happy, and she liked to do them.

One time she had a fever. Leaving for the mountain she had been healthy, enthusiastic. But that night, alone in her tent, she got sick. Her throat blazed, and her head ached. The hair on her head hurt. She had chills. She was fifteen, and when she got sick at home she knew how to take care of herself, but way out there she felt scared. Crying, she just wanted the sun to come up.

Her father heard her. He came into her tent, felt her head, held her in his arms while she shivered. In all the times they had camped out in their separate tents, she had thought she was all alone. Having her father come when she called was a surprise, and in her feverish state made her cry harder.

"You're sick, sweetheart," he said. "We have to go home right away."

He bundled her up, told her to sit still while he got her sisters. Caroline waited, unable to believe what was happening. She was fifteen, unused to being taken care of. The hunts were her chance to be with her father, but nothing had ever made her feel so loved as having him tell her they were going home. Knowing that she was sick, and giving her what she needed.

While her sisters took down her tent and their own, Caroline's father walked her to the car. He started it up, settled her in the front seat, frequently touching her head to see if the fever had gone down. He was so big and tough, with gray eyes that never showed his feelings, but Caroline remembered how worried he looked that night. It was after midnight; her sisters should have been sleepy, but they were excited. Leaning against her father, shivering in spite of the blasting heat, Caroline had felt so happy.

She had scarlet fever.

But then she thought of another time, years later, driving home from the same mountain after Skye had shot Andrew Lockwood.

They had spent the day at the police station. Skye was in one interrogation room, Caroline in another. So many questions: Did you know the man? Ever see him before? Was there any conversation before the shot was fired? A confrontation? Did your sister seem angry? What was her mood like?

Caroline was in shock. She understood that now, but at the time she had thought she was just tired. All she wanted to do was put her head on the desk and fall asleep. She kept seeing the man, hearing her own calm voice ask him his name. Hearing his voice say "Andrew." His eyes, his mouth, the feeling of his hand in hers. He was hers forever; no one would ever know him as well. Thinking of Andrew, she promised herself she would take care of his dog.

After the inquest, they drove home. They climbed into the station wagon, solemn but relieved. Everyone rallied around Skye. She had just been cleared of homicide. Augusta was at Firefly Hill, waiting to greet them. But Caroline was—as always—the surrogate mother. She wrapped Skye in a plaid blanket. She settled her in the backseat and Clea sat beside her. Caroline rode in front with their father.

The way-back was for Homer. They stopped by the pound to pick him up. Walking into the concrete building, they could hear the heartbroken howling. Handing Hugh papers to sign, the attendant went to get the dog. Caroline was sick with anticipation. She was afraid he would see his master's killers and bare his teeth. But at the sight of her, Homer stopped his noise.

Clea had the rear hatch up to let the dog into the way-back. She had made him a bed with an old beach blanket. But walking over to the car, Hugh shut the hatch door. He looked at Caroline.

"He likes you," he said.

"I don't know why," she said, looking away. "I was there when—"

"You're helping him, Caroline," Hugh said. "Let him ride in front with you. It'll make him feel safe." Her father's expression was unfamiliar, and looking back, Caroline realized she was seeing the first signs of agonized sorrow.

Homer traveled the whole way to Connecticut with his head on Caroline's thigh. He whimpered at first, but then he stopped. Clea had her earphones on, and she recited her French dialogue to herself. Skye, Caroline, and Hugh didn't speak at all. But every so often Hugh would reach across the seat to pat Homer's head. To look at Caroline and try to read her eyes. To pretend to smile.

Extraordinary ways.

* * *

Joe Connor stood in the *Meteor*'s cabin, watching the calm water. The wind had been steady all day, making waves that churned up the sea column. It had died at six, and now that it was too dark to dive, the surface was glass. He gazed forward as the line of the bow tilted up to meet the sky, then settled down. Overhead the sky was a jumble of stars. Joe looked back on his day, wishing he could have done more.

Strong currents had kept his crew away from the wreck. A weather system off Hatteras was making big waves offshore, creating a dangerous undertow. Joe had sent divers down every hour, had gone down himself in the morning, and again just before dark. But the water had been moving too fast to attempt much of anything.

Yet in the short time they had been on-site, they had moved forward. They had charted the wreck, cleared mud and sand. They had taken underwater photos, analyzed the timbers, examined the ship's construction. Their consensus was that the ship had been built in England before 1800, probably before 1750. Based on Caroline's letter written to Joe in 1971, he knew they had located the *Cambria*.

Caroline's letter and the gold.

They were beginning to uncover gold coins. The sea bottom was treacherous, a forest of broken spars: the vessel's splintered masts and yards. The jagged wood could snag a diver's air hose or slice through his wetsuit to the skin. Getting through the wreckage took care and concentration, like cutting a path through dense woods. But along the way they were finding treasure.

It cost a fortune to find a treasure. Joe was paying out of his own pocket, and he hated to see a day pass without real progress. He wanted to finish this project fast. A bunch of the guys had gone ashore to carouse at the Catspaw Tavern, and he was beginning to think he should have gone with them.

One of the launches was coming back. He heard the drone of the engine getting closer. He watched it circle the *Meteor* once, then tie up to the stern. Dan climbed aboard.

"Hey, skipper," Dan called, coming into the wheel-house.

"Forget something?"

"No, I just don't feel like going out. Tired of every-one, I guess."

"I know what you mean," Joe said. The crew got cranky on days when they couldn't dive much. Too much togetherness, hearing each other complain. Every-one began to miss their shore lives, their wives and chil-dren or girlfriends or whomever they cared about, and it began to show. Joe, who had never really made himself a shore life, missed having one at all.

"These came for you," Dan said, tossing some letters and a big brown envelope on the chart table. "The dock-master asked me to deliver them."

There was a letter from his brother Sam. He'd been feeling lonely, restless at sea, and the sight of the letter made him glad. At first glance the big envelope looked official. Probably lab work on the sail and timber frag-ments he'd sent to Woods Hole, or historical documenta-tion from his friend in the map department at Yale. But then he saw the familiar handwriting. He would have known it anywhere. He wondered why Caroline would be writing to him now. Only one way to find out. Lay-ing the other mail aside, he ripped open the package.

It contained a thick sheaf of photocopied papers. Joe glanced at them; they were dated 1769, written in small, neat penmanship. Caroline had sent a note on pale blue stationery. He could see by the telltale smudges that she had used a fountain pen, and he remembered that she had sometimes used one when they were kids.

Dear Joe,

My niece showed me this diary, and I thought it might interest you. It was written by Clarissa Randall, whose mother was the woman who ran away with the captain of the Cambria. I haven't read it all the way through, but it tells a little about what life was like living at a lighthouse in the 1700s, having one of your parents run away for the love of someone else and never come back home. Sounds too familiar . . .

It made me wonder if that's why you're diving on the Cambria. Not that it's any of my business, of course. I can't imagine how you're going to react to getting this from me, but I hope you'll take it in the spirit of scholarship. I do feel partly responsible for you being here, after all. Visiting my mother at Firefly Hill, I looked out the window and saw your boats. I felt kind of proud, actually.

The flowers you sent Skye were beautiful.

Yours,

Caroline

Joe glanced at the diary. Starting out, he had control of his feelings. He read the first few entries; it looked like the real thing, a faithfully reproduced handwritten account by a member of the woman's family. It contained descriptions of the area, a little about her family life. But as the meaning of Caroline's letter sank in, he felt the heat rising in his neck. Dan was right beside him, and Joe kept his face free of expression.

"She's a brave woman," he said.

"What?" Dan asked.

"Nothing," Joe said. Brave or crazy, he thought. What the hell kind of nerve did she have, making parallels between the *Cambria* and his family? Death and infidelity. Not exactly the kind of stuff he wanted to think about. Coming up here, he knew he'd have to face complicated emotions connected to his father. But he was a grown man, sober a long time, and he had put the past behind him, regardless of what Caroline Renwick might think.

Then, to make his night complete, he opened the letter from Sam. Knowing what it said, he read it anyway. He must have groaned, because Dan looked over.

"The kid still coming?" Dan asked.

"Yep," Joe said.

"He likes shipwrecks, huh? How's it feel to be a role model?"

"Fucking wonderful," Joe said, smiling ruefully.

"Kid's got balls, I'll give him that," Dan said, chuckling. "You send him packing every time, but he keeps coming back for more."

"He's tough," Joe said quietly.

The night was still. The *Meteor* rocked on the quiet sea. Joe stood at his chart table, staring at the letters. The green-shaded lamp threw soft light, easy on the eyes. Waves slapped the hull. Maybe he should ask Caroline out here so she could see that the excavation was about gold and scholarship, nothing messy and emotional. He wanted daylight, so he could work and dive. He didn't want to think about the people in his life, the people who could make him feel the way he did inside right now. Sad and angry, and as though he had lost something he couldn't quite name.

* * *

Caroline stood at the top of Serendipity Hill and stared out to sea. She was out of breath from climbing the steep and narrow trail. She gazed over the towns of Hawthorne and Black Hall, followed the Ibis River to where it met the Connecticut, then into Long Island Sound. Lights twinkled throughout the area. Caroline counted two lighthouses along the Connecticut coast and four across the Sound, on Long Island. She saw lights on a ship and wondered whether it was the Meteor.

A nightbird called up the hill. It sounded lonely and beautiful and reminded Caroline of nights on the mountain. She rested for a minute, sitting very still and trying to locate the bird in the trees. Its song was clear, coming from a grove of dark pines. The air smelled spicy. An owl swept through, its wings beating loudly.

As much as Caroline had hated the hunts, there had been parts of them she loved. The feeling of solitude, hiking up narrow paths that gave onto vistas of sweeping beauty, blue valleys heavy with summer haze. Sleeping outside, the feeling of air moving on her bare arms, had made her feel free. Caroline had always loved nature. She had loved the surprise of hiking, of coming across an animal or bird she hadn't expected to see. She just hadn't liked killing them.

Her father had tried to teach his daughters his sport, but you can't impose blood lust on those who don't have it. Caroline remembered killing the fox. She had felt like a murderer. It had been December, and that night she had seen the northern lights for the first time. She had held the fox in her arms. Its body had kept her warm.

Now, alone on her mountain perch, she looked for a star to wish on, in memory of Andrew Lockwood. She always did. Finding one, she shivered, even though the summer night was warm. Then she found one for her father. Thinking of her father wasn't always easy. But she made herself do it anyway.

Breathing the sea air, Caroline wondered whether Joe had received her package. She wondered whether her note would anger him, but it didn't matter. She hadn't written it for his reaction. Standing on the hilltop, watching the ship she imagined to be Joe's, Caroline felt a mystical communion with him. He had to love nature to spend so much time at sea.

Hating to hunt, Caroline was guilty of loving to catch fish. She loved the initial grab, the pull on the line, the tension between her and the fish. When she looked in its eye, she felt a strange kinship with the creature. Usually she let it go. She had spent time trolling Moonstone Reef. Stripers and blues were common in August; tautog and flounder lived on the bottom. She knew the wreck attracted fish, and she wondered whether Joe saw them or whether he had eyes only for the gold.

Maybe he wouldn't care about Clarissa's diary at all. Perhaps he only wanted the treasure, didn't care about the story behind it. He had run from his own story. By the time Caroline had been ready to tell him her part in it, he had been too angry to hear.

Or too afraid.

By the time Caroline walked down the trail, the half-moon had traversed the sky. She heard night creatures rustling in the trees, but she didn't feel afraid. Her feet were sure on the steep path; she held a walking stick in her hand. She followed the Ibis River to the inn's grounds, where the guests were having a party. She heard their music, their drunken cries. A group had taken off their clothes and were standing in the shallow water.

When she got to her cottage, she heard her phone ringing.

She almost didn't answer. At this hour it would be her mother. She would have been drinking, and she want to apologize for their unpleasant visit earlier. Caroline stared at the phone. She counted the rings: five, six . . .

But what if it were Skye? What if something had happened? Caroline picked up.

"Hello?" she said.

No one spoke. The line crackled with static. The call seemed to be coming from a long way away, from halfway around the world, or from another hemisphere, from an airplane over the ocean . . .

Or from a boat.

Caroline imagined she could hear the wind and waves. She listened hard. She could almost hear someone breathing. But no one was there. The call was nothing more than crossed wires. The static buzzed like a ferocious swarm of bees, and then it was gone.

The line was silent.

Caroline hung up.

Early the next morning, Michele teetered on a wooden ladder, starting to hang Japanese lanterns. The ball was days away, but it took time to get the inn ready. The trees were hung with a hundred candelabra, the dance floor was installed. Caroline called it the Firefly Ball, in honor of her parents, and she wanted candlelight to do the night justice. She had ordered beeswax candles from the Bridal Barn, and May Taylor had just brought them over.

May and her family—three generations of women—ran the Barn, planning weddings for women of the shoreline, making products from their herb garden. May and her five-year-old daughter, Kylie, seemed so excited about the ball, about the fact their wonderful, luminous candles would light every table.

Thirty round tables were stacked behind the barn, the long white damask tablecloths were expected back from the laundry that afternoon. The Japanese lanterns were bright and fragile; they danced on a wire strung around the perimeter of the inn's back lawn. She hoped the heat would return, as it always did, every year, for the night of the ball.

A tropical depression was chugging up from Savannah, bringing muggy air and temperatures in the nineties. Michele knew Caroline wished the night of the ball to be hot and steamy. Caroline loved the look of men without their jackets, their starched white shirts clinging to their sweaty backs; she wanted the women with bare shoulders and bare feet, dancing in the cool grass. The Firefly Ball was a night for artists to be wild and expressive, free of constraints and inhibitions.

Every year, Caroline chose a different theme—taking cues from various art forms. This year the theme was to be "My Favorite Painting." People really showed their different styles. Clea and Peter always attended in costume. Last year, for their favorite song, they had dressed as "Rhapsody in Blue," two lovers wrapped in blue chiffon. Skye and Simon had come straight from their studios in the barn, still in their paint-and-clay–stained work clothes, many of which were strewn, as the night progressed, in various bushes around the property. But Caroline the hostess always simply wore a gown.

Michele wondered what everyone would wear this year. She and Tim planned to dress as characters from Seurat's *Grande Jatte*. Michele had a long white dress and a parasol, and Tim would look adorable in his spats and bowler hat. Caroline always insisted that they attend as her guests—not to work, but to revel.

Standing halfway up the ladder, a crimson lantern in her hand, Michele spotted Simon Whitford. He was on the inn's porch, hands on his hips, squinting into the sun. He had that dark artist look to him, one of the brilliant ones who couldn't be held to the rules of ordinary men. But Simon was trompe l'oeil: a fake trying to be Hugh Renwick.

Poor Skye, Michele thought. Marrying a man with her father's fierce moods and none of his tender heart. Michele wondered why he was there. To see Skye, no doubt. Caroline certainly hadn't invited him to the Firefly Ball. The confrontation was coming: From her perch on the ladder Michele could see Caroline coming out of the inn, straight into Simon's path. She held on tight, leaning out for a better view.

* * *

Caroline had lain awake too long the previous night. The telephone call with no one there had unsettled her. She had tossed and turned, unable to get comfortable. After midnight, fog had closed in, swaddled the property, and given her a headache. The foghorns had wailed. Caroline had waited for the phone to ring again, but it never did.

But that morning at work, first thing, Michele had placed a message on her desk. It was from Joe Connor, an invitation to dinner aboard the *Meteor*. The telephone connection had been terrible, Michele said. So filled with static, it sounded like the ship might be riding out a thunderstorm. Afraid he would lose the transmission, Joe had talked fast, asked Michele to tell Caroline if she wanted to visit the excavation, she should be at the dock at eight on Thursday.

Bleary and frazzled, Caroline felt confused. He cut her out of his life, and now he wanted to have her over for dinner. Unsure of any of it, she walked down the back steps of the inn, straight into her brother-in-law.

"What the hell are you doing here?" Caroline asked, unable to believe her eyes.

"Hello to you too, Caroline," Simon said, grinding out his cigarette on the flagstone step.

"I don't want you here," she said.

"I'm here to see Skye," he said. "Where am I supposed to stay? We gave up our place. I'm hardly welcome at your mother's house."

"So you thought you'd stay at my inn? I think I'm safe in assuming you don't intend to be a paying guest. You lost your brother-in-law privileges when you walked out on my sister."

"Let me stay, please, Caroline? I'll sleep in the barn, in my old studio. I already checked—no one's using it right now. I need to see Skye. I want to help her."

Caroline chewed the end of her pen. She stared at Simon. He was tall and lean with wild black hair and gaunt cheekbones, sunken black eyes with that sexy fire that drove Skye crazy and made Caroline and Clea mistrust him to their bones. He was ingratiating and manipulative. He wore black jeans that rode low on his skinny hips and a clean white tee-shirt with laundry-faded paint stains. He looked malnourished, dissipated, and artistically tormented.

At her most cynical, Caroline wondered whether he had married Skye to complete the picture.

"Well. Speak of the faithless devil," came a voice from across the garden.

At the sound of Clea's voice, Caroline looked over her shoulder. Her beautiful sister came sauntering across the lawn, stunning in a salmon-pink sundress and big dark glasses. She circled Simon like a great white shark on a bleeding surfer.

"Hi, Clea," Simon said. Caroline didn't want to give him the benefit of the doubt, but he did sound miserable. Together, she and Clea were his worst nightmare. He had hurt their little sister—hurt her badly—and she wondered how he felt, standing in their midst, bearing the brunt of their scorn and derision.

"What brings you back to town? Is there a bank account you forgot to clean out?" Clea asked.

"Clea, I'll tell you what I just told Caroline. I want to help Skye. I made a mistake, okay? I love her, and I want her to take me back."

"Really?" Caroline asked, frowning. He hadn't told her that part.

"Yeah. Can I stay? In the barn?"

"I don't want you here," she said.

"Skye does."

"Why the hell would she want to see you?" Caroline asked, amazed at his arrogance, wondering how it could possibly help Skye to confront the man who had scorned her love.

"How do you think I found out about her accident?" Simon asked, palming another cigarette, wanting to light it so badly, his hand shook. "She called me. She needs me, just like I need her."

"She called him," Caroline said to Clea. The sisters gazed at each other for a few seconds, weighing this new information.

"That does make a difference," Clea said. "Although she's not in her right mind."

"She may have called you, but she doesn't need you," Caroline said to him, narrowing her eyes. "Let's get that straight."

"Think what you want."

"I'll let you stay," Caroline said. "I'll make sure something's free for you."

"I'll stay in the barn—"

Caroline shook her head. "In the inn, not the barn. You have one more chance to be good to Skye, and I'm not going to make you sleep in the hay."

"Thanks," he said. He moved forward, as if to embrace Caroline, but her look stopped him. Lowering his head, he backed away. Then he went toward the parking lot to get his things.

"Scum of the earth," Clea said, sighing, "but Skye loves him."

"For now," Caroline said.

The sisters walked across the brilliantly green lawn to the old red barn where Caroline had been headed before her encounter with Simon. Surrounded by stone walls and white fences, the soft red paint picturesquely peeling, the barn was a painting waiting to happen. Many artists, especially Hugh Renwick, had made it famous. Paintings of the Renwick barn hung in the Clark Institute, the Phillips Collection, the Guthrie, the Farnsworth, the Corcoran Gallery, and the Metropolitan Museum of Art.

Inside, the barn was cool and dark. It smelled of hay. Caroline's grandfather had kept horses and cows. Her father had taught his daughters to ride here; the box stalls were now individual artists' studios. The more expensive rooms at the inn came with barn rights. The stalls were occupied now, with guests painting, sculpting, and getting to know each other better. The unmistakable sounds of passion came from a stall/studio at the far end, making Caroline and Clea laugh softly.

"I lost my virginity in this barn," Clea whispered.

"At least twice." Caroline laughed.

"The Firefly Ball is upon us," Clea said, surveying the scene, feeling the excitement. Sunlight slanted down from the hayloft.

"Did I do the right thing, letting Simon stay?" Caroline asked.

"Skye is a grown-up," Clea said. "We forget sometimes. We can't protect her forever."

"Or at all," Caroline said. Then she heard herself say, "I sent Joe a copy of the diary Maripat gave me."

"You did?"

"And he invited me to his boat for dinner on Thursday night."

"Really!" Clea said, her eyes sparking as she smiled.

"Yes. But I don't know if I should go. Or if I want to."

"Why not?" Clea asked.

"Oh," Caroline said, shredding a piece of straw, "mainly because we don't like each other very much, I guess."

"Maybe you'll find out he's not so bad. I already know you're not. You'll both be in for a nice surprise."

"I was thinking about a quick trip to Scotland. Just for a few days, to check out a brand-new place that opened on one of the western islands. It's an old priory with great views of mountains and the sea, and there's a labyrinth. Doesn't a labyrinth sound fascinating? I read about it in the airplane magazine on my way back from Venice last time, and I need some new ideas for the inn. . . ."

"And you have to leave tomorrow? How convenient. I think you should stay, have dinner with Joe."

"I might." The pull to travel was strong. She had always done it to get her out of her own life. She went to beautiful country inns, visiting them with a vengeance, telling everyone it was for inspiration. Traveling like a fugitive—got to get there, got to check in, looking over her shoulder. If she kept moving, she wouldn't think too much. With Joe Connor in town, this might be one of those times.

Caroline yawned, shrugging.

"You look tired," Clea said.

"I am," Caroline admitted. "I hiked up Serendipity Hill last night—"

"Caroline, *Jesus*," Clea said.

"What?" Caroline asked, surprised by Clea's expression.

"I hate thinking of you on those cliffs at night . . . You could fall. Besides, you never know who else might be up there. You could get raped. I just read about two girls hiking the Appalachian Trail, they were raped and murdered—"

"Clea, it's okay. I didn't get into any danger on Serendipity Hill."

"No, but you'd fly to Scotland to avoid having dinner with a man on his boat."

Caroline opened her mouth to speak, paused, stopped.

"What?" Clea asked.

"You caught me," Caroline said, smiling. "I was just working out flight times in my head."

* * *

"I brought some old pictures," Augusta said to Skye.

"Mom, I'm tired," Skye said. She lay in her hospital bed. They had cut her pain medication down to Tylenol. But she felt so tired, so lethargic, all she wanted to do was sleep.

"These will cheer you up," Augusta said.

Skye stared at the picture album. Her parents had taken pictures of everything. Skye wasn't one of those youngest children who complained her parents had taken photos of the older siblings but lost interest when she came along. No. The Renwicks had four albums full of Skye alone. Each album was identical, Moroccan leather monogrammed *H & A*.

Augusta turned the pages. This selection of photos covered the early seventies, when Skye was very young. There were the girls on the beach, on the carousel, in a rowboat. Hugh at his easel, appearing young and intense.

"He looks like Simon," Augusta said, pointing. "You and I have the same taste in men."

"Mmm," Skye said.

A nurse came in. Shifts were changing, and she had to get Skye's vital signs. She slapped on the blood pressure cuff, gave the black bulb a few hard squeezes.

"What do we have here?" she asked, looking at the album.

"Family pictures," Augusta said, beaming.

"Beautiful," the nurse said. She wrote on her pad, stuck a thermometer in Skye's ear, glanced at the reading, and wrote it down.

"That's your patient, age two," Augusta said, tapping a photo of Skye holding a paintbrush.

"Quite the artist!" the nurse said.

"You have no idea," Augusta said proudly. She turned the page. "Those are Skye's sisters. They adored her, as you can see. That's her father . . . there he is again. Oh, don't look, that's me with short hair. God, what a mistake that was! That's my husband on his horse, that's the barn . . . there he is painting on the Quai de Tournelle . . ."

"Who are they?" the nurse asked, bending down for a closer look.

The black-and-white photo depicted a group of men wearing tuxedos. They appeared elegant and proud, some holding a paintbrush, a palette, or a small canvas. Others held rifles, bows, and arrows. They stood outside a massive stone building, reminiscent of a French château.

"Oh, they're members of a men's club," Augusta said with a concerned glance at Skye. Sensing Skye's discomfort, she seemed about to turn the page, but then her eyes lit on Hugh. Augusta sighed. Her fingers trailed across the plastic sleeve, caressing the photo.

"There's my husband, right there," she said softly.

The nurse peered at Hugh Renwick, standing in the center of the second row. His big shoulders filled his dinner jacket; his face was set, his eyes focused on the camera as if he wanted to attack it. He held a sable brush like a scepter. Glancing at the picture, Skye recognized where it had been taken and felt her heart start to race. She closed her eyes.

"They look so elegant," the nurse said. "So old-fashioned."

"Yes, courtly," Augusta said, furnishing what she considered the proper word. "They met twice a year, always wore black tie. They'd talk about their work, I suppose. They all had rather substantial careers. My husband was quite a well-known painter, you know."

"What's the place?" the nurse asked. "It's gorgeous. Is it in Europe?"

"No. New Hampshire, actually. Way up in the mountains, the Redhawk Club. It had marvelous gardens and secret places to paint. Places to hunt. Quite a few of the men enjoyed shooting."

"Only men?"

"Yes," Augusta said, and her voice took on a strange note of pride and self-defense. "Although my husband thought it was ridiculous. Our girls could shoot as well as any man."

Skye felt her heart pounding out of her chest. Her eyes were shut tight. She wanted a drink, she wanted a shot of morphine, she wanted to get out of where she was at that moment.

"Artists and hunters?" the nurse asked. "Seems like an interesting combination."

"They share an ecstasy for life," Augusta said. "My husband thought the two went hand in hand," Augusta said. As if she had just remembered Skye, the effect this conversation might be having on her, she quickly turned the page.

Skye breathed, and it came out a gulp.

The nurse, who had been taking her pulse, frowned and tightened her grip. As if she couldn't believe that her patient, lying down, could have such a quick heartbeat. Skye's eyes were shut tight. Her head was on the pillow, her face turned away. She tried to think of Caroline, to stop her heart from racing.

"Let me do this again," the nurse said, adjusting her grip on Skye's wrist. Skye felt the nurse's fingers on her vein, moving gently to find the right spot. "I got so side-tracked looking at those handsome men, I must have counted wrong."

Handsome men, Skye thought. The only face she could see belonged to Andrew Lockwood, with his brown eyes and straight nose and wide mouth, dying five miles down the trail from that beautiful château. She tried to push it from her mind, cover his eyes with darkness. The black peace of a moonless night, when the creatures of the hillside are safe from the hunter.

Safe, Skye thought, lying in her hospital bed, thinking of Andrew in his grave.

June 4, 1978

Dear Joe,

So many secret places in the world . . . Driving through the mountains, through forests and beneath cliffs, do you ever think about where the hidden roads lead? Some rich men with too much money built a palace that belongs in Europe. They say it's about sport and art, but it's just about showing off. It's so out of place, stuck right in the middle of the wilderness where there should be only pine trees and granite, not mahogany and marble. I think true artists would know better.

My sister Skye is a true artist. Not just her spirit, which is so beautiful and tender I can hardly write about it. No, not only that. You should see her work. One line from her pencil can become the beach or a cliff or a face. She is more talented than anyone I know. Even my father. How are you? As an artist, I mean.

Love,
Caroline

June 15, 1978

Dear Caroline,

Art, shmart. Secret places, though. Now, there's a subject. Newport has plenty. I can get into any mansion on Bellevue Avenue. I know a lot of the caretakers. Those places all have wine cellars, tunnels, secret staircases.

Sam drew a picture of my boat for you, but then he spilled orange juice on it. Oh well. Me, I'm no artist. Wind's blowing—got to go.

Love,
Joe

CHAPTER SEVEN

HER MOTHER HAD LEFT THE BOOK BEHIND, AND WHEN Skye was alone, she opened it again, to the picture of Redhawk. Seeing it had shocked her earlier; she had forgotten the picture existed. Now she stared at it, the cold stone and the men frozen on film, and her heart barely moved. The picture hardly stirred her at all.

The Redhawk Club. It had incensed her father to belong to a club that excluded his daughters. He had taken them everywhere. Taught them to shoot better than boys, talked with such pride about their accomplishments. People would tease him, saying maybe he should have had sons, and he'd start fights.

One day Hugh had driven his daughters through the club's wide gates, parked the car, and walked them over to the skeet range. Right in front of everyone, he had had the girls shoot clay pigeons, hitting every one. Turning away, just as the club manager walked over for a discreet reprimand, Hugh handed in his letter of resignation.

He had felt so victorious. If only they had loved his sport. Augusta had used the phrase "ecstasy of life"; Skye could hear her father saying it now. He felt wildly alive when he was painting, inspiration surging through his being, flowing onto his canvas, and the same thrill when he was on the hunt, tracking live things that fled before him under the fire of stars.

He had taught her to draw. They had studied anatomy, dissecting the creatures she had killed. She had drawn the muscle and bone and sinew while he told her that was *her;* she was an animal just like the ones they hunted. He wanted her to understand how primitive it was, that joyful surge she felt when she drew and sculpted, how closely connected to the deep and ancient need to hunt. That the burning passion of creation, when she forgot who she was, *that* she was, was no more or less beautiful or exultant than death.

Loving her father, Skye had tried to love hunting. Desiring the ecstasy and self-forgetting she knew in the studio, she fought so hard to fight her fear of the mountain. She felt shame and revulsion when she killed something, but she was afraid to tell him. Now, staring at the picture of Redhawk, she remembered how desperately she had tried to avoid those trips. Knowing how effective Caroline's fever had been, Skye always pretended to have a sore throat, hoping her mother would keep her home.

"Hey, baby," Simon said.

Surprised by the sound of a human voice, as if one of the men in the picture had spoken from the grave, she jumped.

"Hi," Skye said, her voice coming out in a slight croak.

They stared at each other, husband and wife. She swallowed hard at the sight of him: so dark and sexy and concerned. She could see he hadn't been eating right.

"What are you trying to do to me?" he asked, leaning against the doorjamb, his eyes full of worry. He moved slowly toward her hospital bed, gently moving the covers aside, bending down to give her a tentative kiss.

"*Do* to you?" Skye asked, confused.

"Cracking up the car," he whispered. "You'd kill me if you killed yourself."

"It wouldn't kill you," Skye said. "Don't say that it would."

"Want to bet?" Now that he was with her, he couldn't keep from touching her. Her bruised cheek, her hands, his lips against hers. She felt the heat of his body, the electricity in the air between them, and suddenly they pressed together, the skin between them an almost unbearable barrier.

"I love you, Skye," he whispered, "more than anything. I'm sorry, so sorry."

She didn't want to hear his apologies. She felt his arms around her, his hands stroking her back, and she felt she had been only half alive—an animal left to die on the trail—without him in her life.

"Say something," he said.

"Why?" she asked, because it was the only word she could imagine.

"Because I'm a jerk. Is that what you're asking? Why I left?"

Skye didn't know. She just wanted him to keep holding her. She felt their blood flowing together, just under their skin, and she felt the comfort of love, of affection, of human contact come over her. It soothed away her grief and despair. It pushed away her thoughts of Andrew. But because he wanted her to say something, he might pull back if she didn't, she said, "Yes."

"It was her fault, you know. Biba's." He said her name apologetically, as if the sound itself could hurt Skye. But Skye was numb. She closed her eyes and felt him rub her back. "She came at me full blast. You know artists' models, they take off their clothes for pay. What did I expect? For her to respect our marriage?"

"That's for us to do," Skye said quietly, before she could stop herself.

Simon stopped rubbing her back. He sat up straight, pushed his dark hair out of his eyes. Peering at Skye, he seemed to check her out.

"You okay? They planning to let you out of here soon, or what?"

"I hope so," she said. "I do."

Now that Simon had pulled back, her feelings changed. They went cold. It was as if his physical nearness had an anesthetic effect on her, as if the illusion of their love calmed her down, quelled the storms raging inside. She wanted him to hold her again, but she understood that a drink would work just as well. Or a painkiller.

"What's this?" Simon asked, glancing at the photo album.

"Just family pictures," Skye said, turning the page to a series of shots taken in St. Lucia, when she and her sisters were young. They stared at the images of palm trees, big white clouds in a bright blue sky, the black marlin their father had caught hanging above the dock beside their chartered boat.

"Hugh strikes again," Simon said with an admiring laugh. "Or did you kill that one?"

"He did," Skye said quietly.

"What you said before," she heard herself say to Simon, "that it would kill you, what I did. I'd never kill you. I'd never do anything to hurt you. You know that, don't you?"

"Yeah, baby," he said, rubbing her back again, sitting so close, their bodies were nearly one again. "I know that."

* * *

Augusta Renwick was curious about the treasure hunters. Ever since Caroline had been here—pointed out the ships at Moonstone Reef—Augusta had been glued to the window. Watching through Hugh's shooting scope, she kept hoping for a glimpse of some shining objects being raised from the depths.

Focusing on such glamorous activity, she was able to forget the fact that her youngest child was in the hospital. Not forget precisely, but set aside. She had seen Dr. Henderson in the hall outside Skye's room. They had circled each other warily. She mistrusted him. That eager voice with its phony warmth made her shiver.

Standing at the picture window, Augusta tried to see what the men on the boat were doing. Bending over something, raising it to the light. Must be something exciting, she thought. She adjusted the eyepiece for a clearer look.

That tiny act, the slight movement of her two hands as she twisted the spyglass, took her back twenty years: She had taken this very same shooting scope with her to spy on Hugh and one of his women in a glade north of Hawthorne, and she felt a rush of shame and fury. She had taken the girls with her. They had been young: nine, seven, and four. She hadn't told them what she was doing, but she suspected they knew.

Her girls were cursed with exceptional powers of perception.

She narrowed her eyes, focusing on the ship, but the thrill was gone. That flash of guilt from the past had destroyed it. What kind of woman took her daughters to spy on their father?

Maybe she should have a cup of tea. She walked into the kitchen. A cool breeze ruffled the white curtains at the windows. The air smelled fresh, of the sea and herbs from the garden. Augusta set a kettle on to boil, then walked out the screen door to the small, sunken herb garden. Homer followed her, panting.

Set in a circle, the garden had plants that dated back one hundred years. Augusta had taken snips and cuttings from her mother's garden in Jamestown and her grandmother's garden in Thornton. Whenever she came out to pick rosemary, sage, or thyme, she felt the endless love of those two wonderful women. Augusta had had no sisters of her own. She was an only child, and when she had borne three girls, she thought it was the most amazing blessing possible.

That she had daughters, and that they could be sisters to each other in a way that Augusta had never had sisters of her own, had made her feel so happy, as if she had provided something for them beyond measure. Sighing, she sat on a stone bench. She reached down, letting her fingers trail through a clump of mint. The stalks were dark red, the leaves fuzzy green. When she smelled her hand, she went back in time to her grandmother's garden, with all the love and comfort any child could ever want. The feelings she had wanted to give her daughters and their children.

She heard a car coming up the driveway. The sound broke the spell, but Augusta stayed where she was. She knew from the sound it was Caroline's old Jeep. Augusta might have walked around the house to meet her, or gone into the kitchen to set out an extra teacup, but she didn't. She knew that Caroline finding her in the herb garden would be a good thing. It would make Caroline sympathetic to her. The herbs themselves would be an unspoken connection to the good past, to Caroline's beloved grandmother and great-grandmother.

Homer bounded off on the trace of Caroline, and Augusta knew he would lead her back.

* * *

"Hi, Mom," Caroline said.

Augusta opened her eyes. She seemed startled, as if she had been sleeping. She sat on a bench in the garden, wearing her pearls and a straw sunhat, holding a handful of herbs. It touched Caroline to see her mother sitting there in the grandmothers' herb garden, enjoying the sun and the breeze.

"Caroline!" she exclaimed, smiling.

"I thought I'd take a swim," Caroline said. "Do you feel like putting on your suit and coming down to the beach?"

"That would be great," Augusta said. "Just let me turn off the teakettle."

Caroline went upstairs to change. She used the bedroom that had been hers as a girl. It faced the beach, and from her window she could see Joe's boat. Putting on her black tank suit, she walked barefoot through the back halls of Firefly Hill. It was bare and dark in this part of the house: The floors were dark oak, the wainscoting nearly black with age. The bedrooms and living rooms were bright and overflowing with pictures and furniture. But back here, this section intended for servants, had always been spooky; walking through it had always made Caroline and her sisters feel nervous of what lurked in the shadows.

She ran down the porch stairs and met her mother outside. They walked across the lawn, through the tall grass and wildflowers. Caroline preceded Augusta down the long flight of stone steps to Firefly Beach, one hundred feet below. A quarter of the way, she heard her mother stop. "You coming, Homer?" Augusta called.

The rangy old dog stood on the top step. His head was big and proud, the sun casting golden lights on his thinning coat. From this angle he looked young and magnificent. Caroline remembered how he had loved to run on the beach his first summer there. Born a mountain dog, he soon learned to love the beach.

"Homer?" Augusta asked again. She hesitated, looking up at the golden retriever. Her pose was tense, urgent.

She seemed to be willing him to move. "He's tired, Mom," Caroline said gently.

"I suppose he is," Augusta said. Without another word she followed Caroline down the stairs.

These swims were precious to both of them. Caroline made time at least two or three times a month in the summer to spend a late afternoon on the beach with her mother. They dove in together. The water was cold and salty, and Caroline swam out to the big rock and back. She felt the sea caress her body, giving her that feeling of rebirth she got when the tide was high and she was swimming with her mother. They'd been doing this for thirty-six summers, and every time she came to Firefly Beach for one of their swims, she prayed that they would have another: another swim and another summer.

Back on the sand, they lay in the sun on separate towels. It was nearly five o'clock, but the day was still warm, the light gilded. It glistened on the sea and made the tiny pebbles, wet from the waves, look like beads of amber. Caroline watched her mother open a book and start reading. Caroline looked out to sea. There was the *Meteor*, rocking on the waves. She'd be having dinner out there in just a few hours.

Caroline took Clarissa's diary out of her bookbag. It was the actual book Maripat had given her, so she held it carefully, away from the sand.

August 1, 1769

Today counted seven schooners and one brig and one barq. Found twenty-two red starfish. Ate two joe froggers after lunch. Saw three eagles, twenty osprey, and more than a hundred herring gulls. More than a thousand herring gulls. More than seven thousand herring gulls. But no friends! No little girls to play with. Only Mama and Pa, when he's not too tired. Tomorrow morning we're going for quahogs.

August 4, 1769

Pa got four geese. The bang from his gun scared me, and J was crying, but J couldn't find Mama. She wasn't there. J found her near to dark, by the south shore where we found the whale. The last place J looked, J came upon her. Mama as sad as when Grandmother died and we had to travel to Providence to bury her, but today no one is dead. She said she wasn't crying, but J know she was, and when J kissed her she tasted like tears. J told her about the geese, thinking she would be happy because we always cook one for Christmas, but it only made her cry more.

"What's that?" Augusta asked, curious.

"An old diary," Caroline said slowly. "A little girl writing about her life. This part is about her mother."

"Does she love her?"

"Very much."

"Good," Augusta said happily.

Caroline thought of how strange it was, Augusta asking whether the girl had loved her mother. What an odd thing for a mother to ask.

What made her so insecure? Had Augusta felt that way long ago, when the girls were young? Caroline took it as an explanation for the way things happened, the fact that their childhood had been so fragmented. The hunts, the fights, the separations and reconciliations between Augusta and Hugh. Caroline's heart ached for her mother, then and now.

"The diary was written by Clarissa Randall," Caroline said. "The daughter of the woman who died on that shipwreck."

"Right out there?" Augusta asked, shading her eyes as she stared at the ships on the horizon.

"Yes."

"Dear, how fascinating!" Augusta said. "I've been

keeping my eye on them. They seem to be making great progress. They work night and day. Oh, I have a great idea. . . ."

"What's that?"

"You should send the captain a copy of the diary! Wouldn't that be fun? And I'm sure he would find it extremely helpful. Maybe there's some secret code in the diary, some key to where the treasure is buried!"

"Mom," Caroline said.

"Darling, I'm serious. The captain would *love you* for it."

Caroline wanted to tell her mother the captain was Joe Connor. She felt it so strongly, the desire to explain that Joe was the ship's captain, that she had already sent the diary to him, that he was diving on the *Cambria* because of Caroline's letters from long ago. But Skye was in the hospital and her mother hated the Connors. In Augusta's mind the Connors were the enemy.

"Remember the treasure we found, honey? The gold chain?" Augusta asked, changing the subject herself.

"Yes, the one Dad gave you," Caroline said, trailing off.

"Are you going to Scotland?" Augusta asked after a long stretch of thinking about Hugh. "Didn't you say something about a quick trip?"

"Yes," Caroline said, suddenly wishing she were leaving tonight, "but I'm not going just yet."

"You pick up and go like no one I know," Augusta said, shaking her head. "Half the time I call Michele, she says you're on a plane to somewhere."

"Not half the time," Caroline said.

"I'm relieved, Caroline. That you're not going now. Skye needs you too much. I try to be there for her, but I know it's you she wants."

Caroline heard the pain in her mother's voice. She wanted to tell her it wasn't true, that she was a great mother, that Skye needed her more than anyone. But she knew Augusta wouldn't believe her, that the lie would only make her feel worse.

"She loves you, Mom," Caroline said, telling the truth.

"I know, dear. But I wish I'd done more earlier. That I hadn't missed my chance."

The words hung in the air, reminding Caroline of the failures of love. People tried so hard, but they often missed the most important connections. Slowly she looked out to sea, toward the white boat shining in the sun. She thought of Skye drunk, wanting to see Joe. Their tragedies were linked, there was no getting away from it.

Not even by taking the night flight to Scotland.

"This is lovely. Thank you for coming over to swim with me," Augusta said.

"It was my best swim of the summer," Caroline said, wishing she could give her mother something bigger, something more.

"I'm tired," Augusta said, gathering her things. "It's been so nice, sitting on the beach with you. Being together. That's all that counts, Caroline. When all is said and done, being together is the only thing that matters."

Augusta struggled to stand. Her feet slipped a little in the sand, but she caught her balance. As Caroline reached out her hand to help her to her feet, she was filled by a surge of love for her mother, for the way her mother lived, for the fears her mother tried so hard to bury, for the things her mother would never know. Caroline felt such tenderness for her mother, growing old, she bit her lip.

Homer must have seen the women approaching. He was on his feet, and he let out a joyful bark. Standing on the top step, atop the ledge, he was the sentry of Firefly Hill. He barked again and again, full of greeting and expectation.

"He must be hungry," Caroline said.

"No, dear," Augusta said, smiling as she checked to make sure her black pearls were still around her neck. "He's just happy we're on our way home."

Caroline didn't say anything, and the expression on her face didn't change. But walking along the beach, she felt strangely joyful. Soon the fireflies would come out, begin their nightly dance. There was the *Meteor*, across the sea to her right; she had no idea what tonight's meeting would be like. But the sand felt cool under her bare feet, walking just below the tide line, and she had to hold herself back from taking Augusta's hand. She was thirty-six years old, but it still made her feel so happy when her mother sounded like a mother.

July 7, 1978

Dear Joe,

I know we keep wishing for treasure from the Cambria to surface, but yesterday something great did happen. My mother and I went swimming, and I saw some gold glinting in the sand. Just as if a firefly had dropped down! I ran to pick it up, and it was a bracelet. Not from the Cambria, but from my very own family! My father had given it to my mother a long time ago, and she had lost it last summer. So it sat under the sand all winter, safe and sound, waiting for us to find it.

Don't give up hope, Joe: next time it'll be gold coins, and I'll send you one.

With love,
Caroline

July 15, 1978

Dear Caroline,

That sand is keeping more than your mother's bracelet safe. Those old ship spars are probably still in perfect condition. It's really great about the bracelet though. I wish I could go walking on a beach and find my father's gold watch. He always wore it, and sometimes I wish I had it.

Things are weird. If you're not careful, you can start missing things you barely remember.

Take care, C.

Joe

P.S. You really *do* have magic fireflies.

CHAPTER EIGHT

THAT NIGHT, JUST BEFORE EIGHT O'CLOCK, CAROLINE sat in her car at the dock waiting for Joe to pick her up. The evening had turned cold and crystal-clear, the sea flat calm without a whisper of wind. The sun had just gone down, and the horizon was deep red and purple, the sky darkening through shades of silver to violet to jet. The ocean was a sheet of onyx.

Caroline watched the launch approach fast, its running lights glowing against the sunset. She walked down to the dock, feeling nervous. The chill stirred her blood, heightened her awareness. Her father had taught them to pay attention to fear, to rely on their instincts. The back of her neck tingled, but it could have been the night air.

Wary, she raised a hand in greeting. Joe reached up to help her down from the dock to the skiff, and she handed him the bottle of wine she had brought. She wore jeans and a soft beige cashmere sweater over a silk tee-shirt; she slipped on the thick navy wool jacket she had carried from the car.

"Good idea," he said, nodding. "It's cold out on the water."

"Thought it might be," Caroline said.

"Clear and fine," he said, looking at the sky.

"Clear nights are sometimes the coldest," Caroline replied, wondering if they'd be talking about the weather all night. She tried a smile. "Thanks for inviting me."

"Thanks for sending me the diary," Joe said, smiling back.

He gunned the engine. The eighteen-foot skiff took off so fast, it nearly knocked Caroline off her feet. She hung on to the side rail, maintaining her balance. She was not going to let Joe see her hit the deck. She had a sailor's pride, and she made note of the fact he was driving like a jerk.

Spray flew back from the bow, tickling Caroline's face. The loud engine made conversation impossible. Joe stood at the console. All his concentration was on driving the boat. She found herself staring at his wrists. He was wearing a dark green chamois shirt with most of the nap worn off, and he had pushed back his sleeves. His wrists were bare, sturdy, covered with curly blond hair. They were safer to look at than his face. Glancing across the water, she spotted Firefly Beach, its grasses glowing with green-gold irridescence.

Several larger boats appeared in the distance. Bright lights illuminated the stem of one, and the plume of sand Caroline had seen from Firefly Hill was arcing out of the sea. People milled about on deck. Joe throttled back, said something she could not hear into the microphone. Someone replied, more static than human voice. Joe slowed down even more, so their approach was a quiet slap, slap over the small waves.

Red-and-white diving flags dotted the surface in two places. Joe steered the long way around to avoid them. He made the skiff fast to a ladder in the stern of the smaller boat. They climbed aboard.

The scene was exciting, the aftermath of chaos. A compressor thumped like a steam engine; the force of sand and seawater spitting twenty feet into the air rasped like a geyser. Divers in scuba gear lined the boat rail. Others swam between the boat and the flags, their sleek black heads glossy, like seals. Two people sat on deck, using soft brushes to clean sand off what looked like barnacle-encrusted baseballs.

"Hey, skipper," one of the men called. Motioning for Caroline to follow, Joe walked over. He bent down to hear what the guy was saying. He nodded, replied. Reaching down, he handed one of the balls to Caroline. Small enough to fit in the palm of Joe's hand, it appeared to have been underwater a very long time. Barnacles and mossy green seaweed covered its entire surface.

The ball weighed more than a barbell. It tugged Caroline down, she nearly lost her grip. Joe spoke, but she couldn't hear him over the compressor. She shrugged. Joe was grinning, possibly at how she had nearly dropped the weight on her toe.

"A cannonball. We found it today," Joe said, his lips against her ear.

"Wow," Caroline said, excited in spite of herself. She bent down for a closer look at the objects. There was a pile of coins, similarly covered by sea growth. Joe picked one up. He slid the coin into her hand. The barnacles were sharp and felt rough against her palm.

"From the *Cambria*," she said. It wasn't a question.

"Yes."

She turned it over, examining it. She tried to give it back, but Joe closed his hand around hers, giving it a rough push. His grip was so hard, it made the barnacle dig into her hand.

"Keep it," he said.

"Thanks," Caroline said, peering at her scraped palm.

The lights illuminating the sea were blinding, white-blue. The two large boats were rafted together; Joe helped Caroline climb over the rails, stepping from the smaller of the two boats to the larger. It was seventy feet long, sleek and magnificent, equipped for work. Everything was gleaming white fiberglass, stainless steel, aluminum. Caroline glanced into the wheelhouse, saw instruments and gauges blinking everywhere. It reminded her of the lair of some futuristic, mad oceanographer.

Everyone was busy, but they were noticing her and Joe. He led her from group to group, shouting introductions. Caroline nodded pleasantly, shook a lot of wet and cold hands. She was aware of the fact people were sizing her up. Did that mean they were comparing her to other women Joe brought out there? Or was she unusual, did he rarely bring women out at all? What difference did it make?

She stood in the wheelhouse while Joe called everyone together on deck. He gathered them in a huddle, said a few words, and the next thing she knew, the compressor was being shut down. The lights were turned out. En masse, like revelers leaving a party, the crew climbed aboard the smaller vessel. Someone started it up, and someone else moved the skiff, tying it off to a cleat at the stern of the big boat. Then everyone waved, and the boat chuffed away.

"That's better, don't you think?" Joe asked. "Now I can hear you. It was really pretty noisy." He was about six inches from Caroline. His hair was tousled and nearly as wet as if he'd been diving himself. He had a careless, rakish smile, a sharp expression in his dark blue eyes.

"What just happened?" she asked.

"I sent them to your inn," he said. "Gave them the night off."

"Really?" she asked, suspicious. "Alone at sea with Joe Connor. Are you planning to throw me overboard?" she asked.

"No," he said. "I just thought we had a few years to catch up on, and I didn't want the whole crew listening in."

"You didn't have to do that on my account," Caroline said, although she was secretly happy. To have a man cease and desist operations just so they could have a quiet conversation together was nice.

"Would you like a glass of wine?" Joe asked, and Caroline realized that he was holding the bottle she'd brought in his left hand. "Or something else?"

"Wine, please," Caroline said. "That would be fine."

He disappeared below for a moment, returned with a wineglass, a corkscrew, and a glass of what looked like juice for himself. They went up out on deck, into the cold night air. It felt brisk and sharp. The stars were just coming out, sparks of fire in the sky.

They leaned against the rail. With everyone gone, the ship was suddenly silent and very dark. Small waves splashed the hull. The generator hummed down below, but the sound was unobtrusive, even comforting. Green light from the loran screen glowed serenely in the wheelhouse, along with the warmth of a brass lamp. Caroline felt tension in her shoulders.

"This is beautiful," she said.

"You always loved the water," he said. "Saltwater."

"I still do."

"Me too."

"It's great that you're able to make your living out here. When did you first get the idea, hunting for treasure?"

"When I got your letter about the *Cambria*," he said.

She laughed, sipping her wine. "No, I'm serious."

"So am I. But the thought grew stronger when I was in graduate school. I did my first cruise in the Indian Ocean, on a small oceanographic ship researching sediment and salinity. But we snagged a wreck in our dredges, a ship dating back a thousand years or so, and it piqued my interest. A lot of gold came up that day."

"A thousand years?"

"Yeah. A Turkish ship in the silk trade, loaded with sapphires and rubies, gold medallions, statues, and ingots. Amber beads. Coins from the year 990."

"Amazing," Caroline said, imagining the thrill of Joe's first time on a ship that brought up treasure. "Did you ever actually work as an oceanographer?"

"For a few years. I worked at Scripps, in La Jolla, then at Woods Hole. But in my free time, all my reading seemed to be about wrecks. You know, local legends, failed dive attempts, anything I could find. On my vacations I'd travel to the most likely sites, size them up. I saved some money, did a real dive, and came up with enough stuff to sell and finance the next one."

"And you gave up oceanography altogether?"

Joe shook his head. "Never. I use it all the time. In some ways I practice it more now. I'm just not attached to an institution."

"And here you are, diving on the *Cambria,*" Caroline said, staring at the black water.

"I never forgot it," Joe said. "All this time, no matter which ocean I was in. I'd think of the *Cambria,* lying in New England water, and I knew I had to come here."

"Is it what you hoped for?"

"Yes," Joe said, staring at the black water as if he could see through it.

"I like that you're doing it," Caroline said, surprising herself, "instead of someone else. It seems right . . . You diving on the *Cambria.* I'm surprised no one's tried it before."

"They have," Joe said. "But the ship's in a tricky spot. It takes . . . well, a certain kind of operation to do it without getting hurt."

"You're saying you're pretty good?" Caroline asked, laughing as she sipped her wine.

"It's not that," Joe said uncomfortably. "But I have a great crew and a good ship. The money to do it right."

"And now you have Clarissa's diary."

"It's complicated," Joe said, "reading the diary, then diving down, getting involved with the lives connected with the wreck."

"Does it bother you?" Caroline asked.

Joe thought for a minute, watching the stars just above the horizon. "Yes," he said. "It's disturbing. But I still want to know."

"Why is it disturbing?"

"It's hard to be dispassionate, as I have in the past. I've come across human remains before, but . . ."

"But what?"

"They were just skeletons. The people never had names," Joe said. "Now I have the diary, and that makes everything more personal. And I'm not talking about the parallels you referred to in your note."

Caroline wanted to talk about their story, hers and Joe's, but she wasn't sure how. Words stumbled through her mind, linking their letter-writing days with this moment right now. How did they get from there to here? The wind was picking up. It made Caroline's fingers cold around the stem of her glass, her cheeks and forehead sting. She shivered, and Joe saw.

"Come on inside," he said.

"I like it out here," she said, looking around. The wind was strong in her face. It whipped her long, dark hair into her eyes, and she brushed it away. She had something she wanted to say to him.

"It's how I've always thought of you," he said quietly, interrupting her thoughts. "Outside. Totally alive, with nothing touching you but the elements. Like those trips to the mountain."

"Nature girl," she said, embarrassed.

With that he laughed and opened a door. They went through the wheelhouse. Caroline felt him close behind her. He didn't quite touch her arm to guide her through the narrow passage, but he almost did. She could feel the pressure of his hand in the air between them, and it made the skin on her wrist tingle.

She followed him down the companionway; it was like entering another ship entirely. All the high-tech sparkle and gloss up above gave way to old-world warmth and elegance down below. The entire main salon was teak. The burnished wood glowed in light cast from softly shaded brass lamps. Bookcases filled with texts and navigation tables lined one wall. Framed drawings of sailing ships hung over the settees.

All the furniture was built-in and gimballed for life at sea. The settees were covered with forest-green canvas, strewn with kilim pillows. There were brass barometers, wind indicators, fittings around the portholes, everything polished to a high shine. In one corner was a small ceramic fireplace surrounded by Delft tiles, with a fire already crackling inside.

"Here's how she looked," he said. He handed her a sketch. It depicted a beautiful barquentine, a three-masted vessel with the foremast square rigged and the main and mizzen masts rigged fore and aft.

"The *Cambria?*"

"One like her," he said, nodding. "The *Cambria* was English, carrying a load of arms, along with the gold. She went down in a gale in 1769. On Moonstone Reef."

"Right here," Caroline said, thinking of the ship lying in sand and mud however many fathoms directly under her feet. Seeing the sketch made the vessel seem more real. All shipwrecks were tragic, but as Joe had said, this one felt personal.

"It's sad," she said. "Kind of a love story."

Joe exhaled, shook his head. "What, the lady and the captain?"

"Yes."

"What about the lady's husband and kid?" Joe asked.

"Or maybe I've just been reading that diary a little too closely. I got your message about the similarities, loud and clear."

"Have you ever seen Wickland Rock Light?" she asked.

Joe shrugged.

"It's desolate. You can't get on or off without a boat. She must have been horribly unhappy," Caroline said. "I'm not excusing her, but she must have been desperate, doing what she did."

Caroline gazed at the drawing, imagining a young woman who lived in a lighthouse on a rock at sea, falling in love with the master of this ship. She heard herself defending Elisabeth Randall, but was that just so she could fight with Joe? She disliked Elisabeth for what she'd done. How bad could life have been that she would run off and leave her daughter? Caroline felt contrary, fired up, and she knew it had to do with old resentment at Joe, for the unfair blame he placed on her.

"Do parents think of their children first?" Joe asked. "When they're caught up in their own plans? I think you and I know the answer better than anyone."

"Joe," she began, raising her eyes. But he had disappeared. She heard him in the galley. Caroline tried to catch her breath, to get control of her emotions. She browsed through the library, calming herself down.

She watched Joe emerge with an orange-enameled casserole dish. He placed it on the gimbaled table, which was set for two. He refilled Caroline's glass, pouring himself more juice. Sliding a hidden panel, he pushed buttons that brought Mozart into the cabin from speakers in four corners of the salon. The sound was perfect, as sophisticated as she had ever heard. He stirred the fire.

"This is amazing," she said, pulling herself back together, trying to be nice. "I can't believe I'm on a boat. A fireplace!"

"It gets cold out here," he said. "Even now, in the summer. You should come out in November. Late fall in northern waters is not our idea of fun. But I know you're the Arctic type."

"Arctic?"

"Where was that mountain he used to take you hunting? Somewhere way up in Canada, wasn't it?"

"New Hampshire," she said, picturing Redhawk. "Not quite the Arctic Circle."

The table was square, set into a corner. Caroline slid into one side of the settee and Joe into the other. Caroline felt shaky from that earlier exchange. Their knees touching slightly, Joe served them both helpings of braised lamb shanks. With it came crusty French bread, salad greens tossed in vinaigrette, and baked chèvre.

"This is delicious," Caroline said awkwardly. "Did you make it?"

"I wish I could say so, but our steward did."

"I'd like to steal him for the Renwick Inn," Caroline said, joking.

Joe laughed. "He'd never go for it. He's from St. Croix, and he lives for the day we go back down south. To him, summer in New England is cruel and unusual."

"St. Croix," Caroline said. "I went down last winter to visit a few inns. There's a beautiful place way out on a headland, in an old sugar mill. Bougainvillea everywhere, and dark sand on the beach. I loved it."

"So you go south sometimes," Joe said without expression. "Not only north."

"No, there's life beyond the Arctic," Caroline said quietly. "I'm not as cold as you think."

Joe smiled. Noticing her glass was empty, he poured her more wine.

"Don't you like it?" Caroline asked, indicating the bottle of merlot.

"I don't drink," he said.

"Never?" she asked, thinking of Skye.

"Not anymore. I used to like it too much. I didn't get in trouble every time I drank. But every time I got in trouble, I'd been drinking. The pattern was pretty clear. And I got in some trouble."

"You did?" Caroline asked, fingering the stem of her glass, picturing the bottle beside Skye in the car wreck, knowing that many of the worst nights in their family had involved drinking.

"Yeah, I did," he said. "Drinking was fun for a while, but the fun stopped. I'd drink, and it took more every time. I felt empty, and the key word was always 'more.'"

"Oh," Caroline said. The emptiness: She knew it well. Sometimes she felt such bottomless sadness and grief and need and loneliness, she'd try to fill it with wine or travel or business success or helping her sisters.

"Anyway, it got to the point where one drink was too many and a hundred wasn't enough. So I stopped," Joe said.

"I have someone I'm worried about," Caroline said. "Who drinks too much."

"I'm sorry," Joe said.

Caroline wanted to tell him about Skye, but she held herself back. She felt cautious, on guard.

They finished dinner, telling each other safe stories about college escapades and travel fiascoes and the last movies they'd seen and where they'd each been last Christmas, Caroline at the inn and Firefly Hill with her family, Joe with his crew on Silver Bank in the West Indies.

Caroline took another sip of wine, but it didn't taste as good as it had before. She glanced up and saw Joe watching her. She tried to smile. But she felt the ghosts of both their pasts swirling around the table, waiting for an invitation.

They moved closer to the fireplace to have their

coffee. She took it black, strong, and hot. Topside, the wind was picking up, and she felt the boat begin to rock a little more. Joe stirred the fire and closed the glass door on it. He went up to check the anchor line. When he came back, he settled down again.

"Do you spend all your time at sea?" Caroline asked. "Or do you have a home somewhere?"

"Both," he said. "I have a place in Miami, but I'm at sea nine months a year."

"Miami is a long way from Newport, your old home, when I knew you," Caroline said, watching his dark blue eyes. Troubled, they darted to Caroline's face and away.

"Home wasn't . . ." He searched for the diplomatic explanation, but quickly gave up on it. "Well, I wanted to leave. In a way, I was surprised to find that you'd stayed so close to home. Put your father and those hunts behind you." He raised his eyebrows, acknowledging that he wouldn't drop the subject this time.

"You remember the hunts," Caroline said.

"How could I not? You wrote about them twice a year. He'd set you loose on a mountain with a canteen and a penknife and expect you to fend for yourself."

"He wanted us to be able to protect ourselves," Caroline said, surprised to find herself defending her father. She tried to remember her letters to Joe; at least one had been brutal with detail, filled with terrors of the hunt. But now, all these years later, she was revising the truth. She wished she had never told him. After all, her father had started them because of what his father had done. She drew herself up straighter.

"You were so mad," Joe said steadily. "The first time Skye went. She wasn't ready, you said. She was so scared, she didn't want to shoot a gun. Is she the one who drinks?"

"Why do you ask that?" Caroline asked, her heart racing.

"Because she crashed her car," Joe said.

Caroline sipped her coffee, but it was cold. She placed her cup on the table, looked Joe straight in the eye.

"Why am I here?" she asked coldly.

"I wanted to thank you," he said. "For the diary, for telling me in the first place. You're the reason I found the *Cambria,* after all. You told me about the wreck. . . ."

"But why did you ask me out here, to the *Meteor*?" Caroline persisted. Her heart pounded. Her mouth felt dry. She was sitting with Joe Connor after all the years of resentment, and she didn't know what to say.

"To talk to you," Joe said, his voice steady and low, "about that night."

"The night your father died," she said.

"When your sister called me—left me that message— I thought maybe she had something to tell me about what happened," he said. "Something new."

"She feels a connection," Caroline said quietly. "We all do."

"Because you were there when it happened," he said.

"I hardly remember," Caroline said. After all this time, she still didn't want to be the one to tell him.

"Tell me," Joe said again.

"I will," Caroline said, trying to keep her voice steady. "If you'll explain one thing."

"What?"

"Why did you start hating me?"

He didn't deny it. Staring at her, he spoke steadily. "Until I was seventeen, I thought my father died of a heart attack. I knew he died in your house, but I thought he was a friend of your father's from the docks, that he'd taken a break from fishing and gone off to visit him. I liked thinking he had died among friends. It made everything okay, thinking he had died with people who cared about him."

"I was a kid too, Joe. Just like you. It was too much responsibility to tell you what really happened."

"Tell me now," Joe said, looking directly into Caroline's eyes. "Please."

Caroline could summon her memory of that night in an instant. She closed her eyes, saw the kitchen at Firefly Hill. She could smell the cookies baking. She could see James Connor's eyes.

"He was sad," Caroline said. "That's what I remember most. So sad. He was acting crazy, but it was because he loved your mother so much."

"Did he say that?"

Caroline nodded. His questions were taking her back. She could see the gun in his shaking hand, the floury fingerprints on her mother's pregnant belly. The terror in Clea's eyes.

"He cried," Caroline said. "I'd never seen a grown-up cry before. He told my mother my father didn't love her anymore. Because he loved your mother instead. He was wild."

"Then he shot himself?"

"He was going to kill *us*," Caroline said, and she could see from Joe's expression that he hadn't known that part. He looked stunned.

"You and your mother?"

"Well, and Clea and Skye too. Even though Skye wasn't born yet. She came two days later, on Christmas, so I think of her as being there."

"But why?"

Caroline stared at him. His blue eyes were clouded with apprehension, his wide mouth twisted. He's afraid to hear, she thought. Suddenly she remembered seeing that six-year-old in the picture, all smiles, in his father's shaking hand.

"Because my father had stolen what your father loved," she said steadily. "I guess he thought that killing us would be taking what *my* father loved."

"His wife and daughters. My father was going to *kill you*."

"But he didn't, Joe," Caroline said. "Your father couldn't do it."

Joe closed his eyes.

"I've always thought of him as a good man," Caroline said, her throat aching. "A good man who was desperate. Crazed by love, you know?"

"Hmmm."

"He had this with him," Caroline said, reaching into her pocket. She had thought she might have this chance, and her fingers trembled as she handed Joe the photograph of himself, stained with his father's blood.

Joe accepted the picture. He held it, staring at it for a long time. When he looked up, his eyes were angry and glittering. He wiped them.

"What the hell," Joe said.

"He loved you," Caroline said. She could see that it cost Joe a lot to be near tears in front of her. He stared over her head, holding himself together. His eyes were closed, his dark lashes resting on weathered cheeks.

"He did," she said when he didn't speak.

In response, his mouth twitched. The seas were picking up. A line snapped free on deck, slapped against the planks like a live animal, startling his eyes open. A halyard clanked, metal against metal, in the wind. Joe's clear blue gaze went straight back to the old photo.

"I love that picture," she said. "I'll understand if you want to keep it. It belonged to your father, but I love it. It means so much to me."

"My picture?" Joe said, his voice harder than ever. "Why?"

"My old friend," Caroline said. "Joe Connor."

"I put an end to that, didn't I?" Joe asked.

"I couldn't believe it," she said, "when you told me not to write you anymore. I didn't know you thought our fathers were friends. I told myself you knew the truth. But I didn't think it was up to me to tell you the details."

"It wasn't," Joe said. "I used to think it was, but I was wrong. We were just young."

Caroline lowered her eyes, trying to stop her hands from shaking. Was he forgiving her? For harm she had never meant to cause in the first place? Why did she get the feeling that letting her off the hook, even to that extent, took a major effort? His lips were tight, his eyes hard and distant. She had the feeling he had gotten what he wanted out of her. Now he wished she would just disappear. When she looked up again, she caught him holding his picture, staring at it.

"It must have been awful," Caroline said, "for your family."

Some emotion flickered across Joe's face. He put the picture down, rested his chin in his hand. But he kept glancing at the photo. He touched the bloodstain with his finger.

"Was it?" Caroline asked. "What happened?"

"Nothing much," he said. "My mother remarried after a few years. They had a son, so she got the chance to do things right with him."

"Sam," she said.

To Caroline, sisters were a blessing. She couldn't imagine life without them. Maybe Joe felt the same way about his brother, because his eyes softened, and his mouth relaxed. He pushed the picture across the table to Caroline as if he were done with it forever. He may not have intended to send it flying, but it slid right off the gimbaled table onto the floor.

"Yeah," Joe said. "He's a pain in the ass, but he's a good kid. An oceanographer of all things, went to the same school I did. A twenty-seven-year-old know-it-all."

"Sounds like he looks up to you," Caroline said, smiling.

Joe shrugged. His smile faded as another memory took hold. He looked Caroline in the eye as if he had another bit of unfinished business. "I blamed your father for what happened," he said.

"I blamed your mother," she countered.

"He had no business putting guns in your hands. No matter what, but especially after what happened with my father. Right in front of you."

He exhaled, shook his head.

Caroline wondered how he'd feel if he knew the whole story. She wasn't about to tell him, and she doubted Skye would call him again. She closed her eyes, thinking about what had happened at Redhawk.

"I know how you feel," she began, her voice straining. She stopped when she saw Joe shaking his head.

"No, you don't," Joe said.

"What do you mean?"

"My father killed himself," Joe said. "It's pretty bad to find out your father was so miserable, he'd rather blow his head off than come home."

"I know," she said. Caroline's heart was pounding, her hands shaking. The waves had picked up, and the boat pitched beneath them.

"You don't, Caroline," Joe said, trying to keep his voice even. She could see that he thought he was alone, that his pain was exclusive, that Caroline was just a witness. "I'm sorry, but you just don't."

"I was there, Joe!" she cried, the words tearing out of her throat. If he didn't understand how that had been for her, if he wouldn't believe how much she had cared . . . "I was with him! It's one of my first memories, your father dying. I cared so much, Joe. About him *and you*." She had so much emotion inside her, she felt it bursting in her chest. "We were almost the same age, you and I— all I could think of was: That little boy's father died." She broke off to get control of herself.

Joe watched her, not saying anything or moving closer.

"Our parents were so angry at him, and they wanted us to be too. My father went crazy knowing he'd threatened us. That's *why* he gave us guns, because of what happened."

"That's why he took you hunting?"

Caroline went on as if she hadn't heard. "My parents *hated* your father, and they wanted me and Clea and Skye to feel it too. We didn't though. You can't believe how upset they'd get that I wanted to write to you. But I had to do it."

"Why?" he asked.

"To console you."

"You were only five," Joe said. "Why should it have been your job to console me?"

"It wasn't my job. But I couldn't get you out of my mind," she said.

She felt the boat pitching. She wondered how earthquakes felt, to have the ground shift underneath your feet. She felt Joe's arms come around her. His embrace was rough at first. He pulled her to her feet. She couldn't look at him, but his hand on the back of her neck was gentle. He traced the skin beneath her hair, and she heard herself moan through her tears.

His lips brushed her cheek, and she raised her face to meet his kiss. His face was coarse with two days of not shaving, and his grasp was tight. They kissed as if they were saving their own lives. It tasted like salt: the sea, tears, and blood. The kiss was harsh and violent, and it made Caroline feel as if she were standing on deck in a storm. His touch shivered down her skin, made her tingle and shudder as he whispered her name.

Scared by the emotions she was feeling, Caroline tried to push away. Joe's eyes were dark, even more angry than they had been at the beginning of their discussion. But he wouldn't let go. He looked bewildered, as if he couldn't believe he'd just kissed her. Gripping Caroline's arms, he held her still. His mouth brushed her cheek, and he whispered something she couldn't understand. When he pulled back, his eyes were almost tender. The expression lasted only an instant. He let go of her.

"I'd better get back," she said shakily.

Caroline felt a sharp mixture of pain and longing, tension and relief. But she could breathe easier than she had since coming to the boat. Without looking at Joe, she bent down to retrieve the picture on the floor. She brushed it off, slipped it into her pocket. If he saw, he didn't say anything.

They headed up on deck to feel the wind on their faces. Cold air had swept down from Canada, and it slashed across the open ocean. Caroline pulled her jacket around her. The boat rose and fell. The wind had whipped the waves into whitecaps; Caroline could see them in the starlight, crested with foam. Standing on deck, she felt like crying and didn't know why.

The old ship lay wrecked on the reef below. The seas were high and rugged. If they waited much longer, it wouldn't be safe to take the launch. Caroline climbed over the lurching rail, her nerves tingled with danger. The black ocean foamed and chopped. Her fear had such primal power. She was an expert swimmer, but she thought if she fell in, she would disappear. Sitting close to Joe as he took the wheel, their arms touched through their heavy jackets.

He drove less aggressively than he had on the way out, as if he had exorcised some demons. Or perhaps he was just being cautious in the building seas. Caroline's hand closed around the coin he had given her that day. Clutching it as the small boat flew across the sea, getting closer to shore, she felt it was a talisman to keep them safe. A creature slashed through the water, bright as neon, and she jumped. The fish left a trail in the water, phosphorescent fire.

When their feet were on dry land, Joe stood before her, not knowing what to say. She had the feeling he wanted to apologize for his kiss. Her voice trembled, but she spoke anyway, to take him off the hook.

"Thanks for dinner," she said.

"Thanks for coming."

"Are you sure you can make it back to the *Meteor*?" she asked, staring at the whitecaps, at the small boat tossing at the dock.

"Yes, I can make it back," he said.

Why did she feel disappointed? That kiss had started something. A feeling of heat filled her chest, and she realized that she wanted Joe to hold her again. Caroline shivered, the desire was so unexpected and strong and unfamiliar.

The waves hit the dock; she felt the spray in her face. It cooled and soothed her, and she let it push her feelings for Joe away. A poet once wrote that cathedrals were never built beside the sea because it was so beautiful it would distract the people from praying. Caroline agreed. Most of her travels took her to other oceans, and she felt the need for another one soon. She had to get away from this.

Glancing over at Joe, he seemed about to speak. He took a step toward her, but something stopped him.

A car was coming down the road. They could hear it over the wind, and they turned in time to see a yellow cab drive into the sandy parking lot. A single passenger sat in back. He paid the driver. When he got out, he grabbed a soft black bag and an enormous backpack from the trunk.

The man stood alone, silhouetted against the dockmaster's office light. The taxi drove away.

"Hey, a welcoming committee!" the man called. His voice was exuberant, full of humor.

"Holy shit," Joe said.

Joe stuck his hands in his jeans pockets. His posture was straight, his sturdy shoulders thrown back. A small smile crossed his lips, but he did his best to keep the pleasure out of his eyes.

The man was young. He looked like a college kid; he had a baseball cap on backward. He had a lanky build, wore wire-rimmed glasses, and was coming straight toward them with a ridiculous grin on his face. Pulling off his cap, he revealed short blond hair, darker than Joe's.

"How'd you know I was coming tonight?" he asked, dropping his bags to give Joe a bear hug. "I was trying to make it a surprise. Standing out here, waiting for me. Jeez!"

"I didn't know," Joe said. He let the young man hug him for so long without getting prickly or pushing him away, Caroline started to smile. She knew a sibling reunion when she saw one.

"Hi," the newcomer said, stepping back and catching sight of Caroline. He had a wonderful, wide-open smile, and it occurred to her: Joe would look like that if he ever looked really happy.

"Caroline, this is my brother, Sam Trevor. Sam, this is Caroline Renwick."

They shook hands. Was it Caroline's imagination, or did Sam react to her last name? If nothing else, she had learned tonight that the Renwick name was evil magic to Joe, and she didn't suppose it would be any different for his younger half brother.

"Nice to meet you," Caroline said.

"Same here," Sam said, his grin back full force. "You coming out to the boat?"

"Heading home, actually," Caroline said.

"Yeah, she was just leaving," Joe said, unintentionally abrupt. Or perhaps he had meant it to sound the way it did, rude and dismissive.

"Still an old grouch," Sam said, laughing. "He tries the

same thing with me, and I don't even hear him anymore."

"I didn't mean—" Joe said, looking at Caroline apologetically.

Caroline smiled. She didn't know which was the truth, Joe being mean or Joe being contrite. No matter which, Caroline took her cue. She said good night to the men, climbed into her car, and pulled out of the parking lot.

Only when she reached the main road did she see a flash of light in the eastern sky. It was bright and fast, close to the horizon. She saw another, higher in the sky. Shooting stars, she thought. It was the night of the Perseid meteor shower, and she had been too absorbed in Joe Connor, in their past and present—in their kiss—to gaze up at the sky and count the shooting stars.

Holding tight to the barnacle-encrusted coin Joe Connor had given her, Caroline Renwick drove slowly back to her inn.

August 5, 1978

Dear Joe,

I dreamed about you last night. It was the strangest thing. I was standing on a rock, in the middle of the Sound, with waves crashing all around. They were about to sweep me away, when all of a sudden I heard your boat. You were rowing out to get me. I heard your oars hitting the water, and my heart was beating so fast and hard, I thought I was going to drown. But I knew you were coming, Joe. You did too. In my dream, you looked just like you. But in real life, I don't even know if I'd recognize you. I think I would, just from your letters. Wow, I'm glad I survived that dream.

Gratefully yours,
C.

August 14, 1978

Dear C,

If I thought you were going to drown, do you think I'd row? I'd take the fastest motorboat I could get.

Love,

Joe

P.S. I've been thinking about that too. What it would be like to see you in real life.

CHAPTER NINE

AT THE HOSPITAL, SKYE WANTED TO HEAR EVERYTHING. If she ignored the antiseptic smell, the nurses walking by, and Skye wearing pajamas during the day, Caroline could almost imagine they were just two sisters having coffee. Only it was tea, lukewarm, in paper cups. And her sister's face was bruised, shades of yellow and fading purple.

"What's he like?" Skye asked.

"He has an amazing boat," Caroline said. "Like a floating laboratory, so high-tech, you can't believe it. They analyze the sediment and artifacts right there—"

"Not the boat," Skye said. "Him."

"He's guarded," Caroline said, flushing as she remembered his arms around her shoulders, his deep kiss. "Very guarded . . . never mind about that. How are you?"

"Why won't you let me care about you?"

"What are you talking about?" Caroline asked, shocked by the question.

"I want to know about you, and you always turn it back to me."

"I answered you—"

"In the most *perfunctory* way, just to get me off your back. You're like this all the time. Maybe you don't even know you're doing it." Skye exhaled. "Does he realize he's in love with you?"

"Skye," Caroline said, shaking her head.

"He is. Of course he is. Why else would he come to Black Hall? Don't tell me it's for that sunken ship. There are plenty of buried treasures around the world. He's here for you. You got under his skin all those years ago, and now he's come to sail away with you."

"That's not true," Caroline said.

"Love," Skye said, staring out the window.

"Love is not the answer to everything," Caroline said, shaken by Skye's accusation. "No matter how much you want to believe it."

"Is he what you expected? After all this time, does he match the picture you had of him in your mind?"

"I don't know," Caroline said, comparing her image of Joe as a cowlicked child with the serious blue-eyed man. Oddly enough, they weren't completely different, only the man had lost that boy's loving, open smile.

"It must be like a wish finally coming true," Skye said. "Seeing someone so important after all this time. It would be like . . ."

"Like what, Skye?" Caroline asked, alarmed by the change in her sister's tone.

Skye's head was down, but when she started to talk, Caroline could tell she was trying not to cry.

"Like Andrew Lockwood coming back to life," she said.

The sisters sat in silence. What if it were possible? Caroline could see him now, that other tragic boy from their past. His eyes were brown, not blue, and he had lived in the mountains, not by the sea. She put her arm around Skye.

"Did Homer come home? Mom was here this morning, and she said he was gone again all night."

"He's back."

"Where do you think he goes, Caroline?"

"I don't know," she said.

"Simon told me you're letting him stay at the inn. Thank you."

"Don't thank me," Caroline said, sipping her tea.

"Did Joe ask about me? The reason I called?"

"Yes, he did."

Skye shook her head. Her face was pale, and it seemed to be getting paler. Caroline knew her sister well, and she could see that she was uncomfortable, embarrassed about the drunken phone call. Caroline's first impulse was to comfort her, but she held back.

"Shitfaced to the max," Skye said. "What can I say?"

"What are you going to do about it?" Caroline asked.

Skye opened the drawer of the bedside table. She removed a gray pamphlet titled "Forty Questions." Glancing at the questions, Caroline could see that they were meant to help a person determine whether or not she was an alcoholic.

"It's rigged," Skye said.

"How?"

"It makes me seem like an alcoholic."

Caroline let Skye's statement hang in the air. In the hallway, a voice came over the public address system anouncing that Dr. Dixon was wanted in the emergency room. Someone on the floor had their television turned up high. Game-show bells and laugh tracks sounded noisy and festive.

"Dad wanted us to feel the ecstasy of life," Skye said. "Had you ever felt it, Caroline?"

"Yes," she said, thinking of the moonlit nights, the cries of nightbirds. She thought of dusty trails and thorny banks, wild animals screeching in the night, adrenaline flowing in her blood.

"It was incredible," Skye said. "I hated it, I was so scared, but I got used to it."

"To what?"

"To the surge. That feeling of really being alive. But we can't sustain it."

Caroline thought of kissing Joe last night. "Maybe we can," she said.

"I think I'm supposed to die young," Skye whispered.

"You can stop drinking instead," Caroline replied.

"It's complicated," Skye said. "You make it sound so easy."

"I don't think it's easy."

"I don't even know if I want to."

"That's for you to decide," Caroline said, sounding peaceful but feeling the opposite.

Skye didn't respond. She was staring at the pamphlet of forty questions, frowning at it as if she wished it would disappear.

* * *

Michele warned Clea: Watch out.

Caroline was in a horrible mood. She refused to accept the salmon from the fish man, she told Michele she hated daisies on the tables in the bar, and she asked a group of rowdy young artists from Montreal to keep it down even though they were making no more noise than any other rowdy young artists over the last hundred or so years.

Clea had pulled up with a trunkful of old clothes to ask what Caroline thought she and Peter should wear to the ball. She half considered leaving, to come back another day, but ignoring problems had never done anyone in the Renwick family any good. So she walked into Caroline's inner office.

"Since the theme this year is favorite paintings," Clea said, "I thought we should go as one of Dad's. I mean, don't you think?"

"If every one of Dad's paintings burned in hell, I'd be happy," Caroline said, furiously tapping numbers into her calculator.

"Dad was many things, but he did make beautiful pictures," Clea said, stepping back and lowering her voice to speak to Caroline the way SWAT negotiators speak to hothead terrorists.

"I saw Skye this morning," Caroline said.

"How was she?"

"Weighing the options. Whether she'd rather die young or give up drinking."

"Are you serious?"

"Yes. Dying young sounds so romantic, doesn't it? Artistically drinking oneself to death. Too bad it's so messy. And it makes people so mean."

"Like Dad."

"We're not supposed to notice he drank," Caroline said. "Or else we're supposed to excuse it because he was Hugh Renwick."

"What do you mean?"

"He got away with things no one else could. He had Large Concerns. Life was dark, and brutal, and harsh, and infested with evil. You know? And he saw so *deeply* because he was this great artist. He couldn't *not* see."

"Why are you in such a bad mood?" Clea asked, struck by Caroline's intensity, by the anger in her gray eyes.

"Lies were the truth in our family, have you ever noticed?"

"Like what?"

"Like Dad drank because Skye shot a man. He was so broken up with guilt over letting her hunt, he shut himself up in his studio or my bar with a bottle of scotch. Supposedly because he loved us so much, right? Because he had wanted to protect us, and instead he'd ruined us. But what a lie!"

"How?"

"Because if he really loved us, he would have stayed in our lives. He was here, but he was gone."

"He lost hope," Clea said quietly.

"But why?" Caroline asked. "We still loved him. I don't know about you, but I still needed him. More, if that's possible."

"I know."

Caroline squeezed her eyes shut. Slashing the tears away with her index fingers, her chest shook with repressed sobs. Clea watched; Caroline would never just let it out. This was the thing they couldn't understand, the way their father had just decided to depart. He was *right there,* sitting in plain sight, but he was a million miles away, in a haze of scotch.

"He'd brought daughters into such a barbaric world," Caroline said. "So much for 'the ecstasy of life.' Too bad his philosophies were in such dire conflict. He forced us to hunt our entire childhood, and suddenly he never took us to the mountains again. It was over."

"It wasn't over," Clea said. "He was sick. That's how I see it—sick with grief."

"You're more understanding than I am," Caroline said.

"Feeling bitter doesn't work," Clea said, covering Caroline's hand. Caroline allowed it; no one could say the things to her Clea did. Maybe because she hadn't seen Andrew die, Clea was softer, more trusting and un-guarded, than either of her sisters. She didn't suffer in the same way as Caroline and Skye.

"He wanted to be near you, Caroline," Clea said. "It's why he came to your inn."

"To drink!" Caroline said, holding back a sob.

"What's wrong?" Clea asked. "You sound awful."

"Am I aloof? Do I stop people from caring about me?"

"Not exactly," Clea said, alarmed by how frantic Caroline sounded.

" 'Not exactly?' What's that supposed to mean?"

"You're . . . competent. That's what it is. You handle everything so well, you give people the idea you don't need them."

"I need them plenty," Caroline said angrily, crumpling up her paper, starting over. "I need Skye to get a grip on herself."

"Uh-huh," Clea said, seeing the contradictions in her sister, the fact that even in a fury she could still not express her own needs—Caroline once again projecting her own feelings outward onto those she loved.

"I'm sorry," Caroline said. "But if you'd heard Skye, you'd understand. She is in bad shape. We have this whole family legend going about art and drinking. Skye and Dad. What a lie."

"Maybe that's why I married a minister," Clea said, smiling at Caroline. "Finally, a man I can trust." But even as she said the words, she knew they were true. She could never love an ordinary man, one who thought white lies were okay, who might believe a secret affair was acceptable if no one found out, who could lie to himself and his family about drinking himself to death.

Caroline turned her attention to her calculator and stack of receipts. Clea watched her flip through invoices, her fingers skipping over the keys. This was Caroline in action, Caroline being excellent. Clea had observed all her sister's escape attempts, and this was one of the most effective.

"Did you have fun last night?" Clea asked.

"What?" Caroline asked, her fingers stopping mid-click.

"Last night?" Clea asked, smiling. "Did you have fun?" When Caroline didn't reply, she went on. "You did go to the *Meteor*, didn't you?"

"Yes," Caroline said. She closed her eyes, gathering her thoughts. Her gray eyes flew open, and she exploded, "You should have heard him, he's just as crazy as Skye. Even more so! You'd think I'm to blame for every single person's crummy childhood from here to Boston."

"You're not to blame for mine," Clea said.

"He wanted an account of what happened the night his father died. It was horrible."

"It sounds it," Clea said soothingly.

"He basically grilled me. I told him what I could, and he started off being very high-and-mighty, saying I could not know how he felt. But he must have felt sorry. I think he did, because he pulled me over—so hard, it hurt my shoulder—and kissed me."

"Kissed you?" Clea asked.

Caroline nodded, miserable. She stared at her hands. Clea sat back, not wanting to say the wrong thing. Caroline never reacted to men this way. She was so guarded, she set herself so apart, she never let them get to her. Their father had schooled them in the ways of men and women, and Caroline had chosen her armor carefully and early. But it was off right now, Clea could see, plain as day.

"He shouldn't have done it," Caroline said. "He can't stand me."

"If he can't stand you, why did he kiss you?"

Caroline blinked. Her lashes were long and dark. They rested for a second on her pale cheek, then opened. Her eyes were clear, periwinkle blue, and full of distress.

"To shut me up," Caroline said. "Animal instinct, I don't know. I think he wanted to rip my throat out, but he kissed me instead."

"You've missed him," Clea said.

Caroline nodded, miserable.

"Don't be ashamed about that," Clea said softly.

"It's still there, the connection," Caroline said. "We

read each other. He knows about Skye, that she drinks. I didn't want to tell him too much, but he guessed. She's broken, Clea. I saw her in the hospital today, and I don't think she'll ever be okay again."

"She will be," Clea said.

"How do you know?"

"Because we love her," Clea said. "And love is all there is."

Caroline looked up. Clea smiled, filled with tenderness for Caroline. Clea watched Caroline's face change. "I told Skye the opposite today. That love can't fix everything."

"Then you were wrong," Clea said. She believed in love. She believed in it hard and strong, with everything she had. With all the grief in their life, the methods of violence, she knew that their love for each other had saved them so far. It had made them strong. And watching Caroline right now, Clea knew that her big sister had suffered as much as Skye.

Maybe even more than Skye. And Clea believed that the love Caroline needed, the one that was going to help her, was sitting offshore right then. In a boat, on the waves, over a murderous reef within sight of the house where it had all begun, Caroline Renwick's true love was waiting. Clea knew it. Gazing at her sister, she glowed with such tender affection, she thought her face would crack.

"He has a brother," Caroline said. "I met him."

"I'm happy for him," Clea said. "Sisters are better, but brothers are good."

Caroline was silent after that. She looked everywhere except at Clea.

"So," Clea said. "Joe Connor finally kissed you."

"Hmmm," Caroline said, wiping her eyes. "What are you smiling about?"

"Nothing," Clea said, smiling even wider. But even as

she said it, she knew she had just told a lie. She had used the wrong word; she should have said "everything."

* * *

On the porch that night with Peter, Clea sipped lemonade and watched her children chase fireflies. It was time for bed, but they were keyed up, and they ran though the side yard with wild abandon. They swooped and yelled, trying to stave off bedtime for a few more minutes. When they stopped, when she and Peter tucked them in, their eyelids would flutter and close within seconds.

"Why are you so quiet?" Peter asked, his rocker creaking on the wide floorboards.

"I'm worried about my sister."

"Skye? She's getting the help she needs—if she'll take it . . . you know it's up to her in the end."

"Not Skye. Caroline."

"Why?"

Clea's eyes filled with tears. "She's so armor-coated. Ever since we were little she's been that way. So busy looking out for us, making sure Skye and I were happy and taken care of."

"She's a good sister."

"The best," Clea said.

"So why are you worried about her?"

"I want her to fall in love," Clea said.

"She will when it's time."

A picture of Caroline, her eyes haunted, her arms around Skye, came back to Clea. They were at Redhawk, and Skye had just shot a person dead. "Caroline's always been there for us," Clea said. "Both times . . ."

"Both shootings?" Peter asked.

"Yes," Clea said. She had been only three when James Connor had come into their house, but she remembered

Caroline holding her, standing between Clea and the gun, shielding her with her own body.

"That's because she loves you," Peter said.

"Why did God put such violence in our lives?" Clea asked, taking his hand. "Such terrible things? Why did He put those deaths in our lives?"

"Maybe to show you how much you love each other," Peter said, using his handkerchief to dry Clea's eyes.

"We do," she whispered, thinking of Caroline, wishing and praying that she would let down her guard, let someone love her the way she loved them.

"Caroline has been afraid," Peter said. "I think we know that's what her traveling is all about."

"She acts so brave, but she's not."

"No, she's not," Peter agreed.

"How lucky we are," Clea said, sniffling. "You and I."

Peter didn't reply, but he held her a little tighter. Words weren't necessary just then. Clea looked up at the sky in time to see a shooting star. It made her suddenly feel so happy, she had to hold back tears.

August 30, 1978

Dear Caroline,

Had any good dreams lately? Maybe you don't like motorboats. I'm wondering if that's why I haven't heard from you lately.

I went spearfishing off Breton Point yesterday. The surf gets pretty crazy there, and I got really pounded. The America's Cup boats were sailing by, and I started wondering if you like sailing. Or if maybe you'd want to come to Newport to see the Cup boats. They're Twelve-Meters, really sleek and beautiful. My dad used to take me to see them. The next race is in 1980. I'm hoping I can find a way to crew on one.

Write soon. Hey, are you going out with anyone?

Still your friend,
Joe

November 24, 1978

Dear Joe,

Sorry I haven't written lately. Actually, I was embarrassed about telling you my dream. I'd never told anyone that before. No, I'm not going out with anybody.

I've never seen the Twelve-Meters in person. My father has painted them before, and he's hung out with some of the sailors. He talks about Ted Hood and Baron Bich, and this brash young guy named Ted Turner who reminds my dad of himself. He says art collectors love the Twelves.

That's a long way of saying yes. I'd really love to come to Newport. But how?

Love,
Caroline

CHAPTER TEN

"MAN, YOU ARE EQUIPPED," SAM SAID, DRINKING HIS morning coffee in the chart room with Joe. His eyes were big, his tone admiring as he carefully examined the *Meteor*'s electronics. He looked over the satellite equipment, from communications to engine room monitoring. He noted the airtime access routes via nautical programs like INMARSAT and AMSC and nodded approvingly.

Leaning over the computer station, he played with the navigation software. He clicked the keyboard, displaying a chart of Long Island Sound.

"You can read the charts either north up or course up, just like on radar," Joe explained. "The program interfaces with our depth sounder and autopilot, automatically figures in tides and currents. Under way, we can upload and download to the GPS receivers and exchange waypoint data."

"That's the difference between gold hunters and federal funding," Sam said. "I'm out there tracking humpback whales on an ancient rustbucket, where the idea of modern electronics is radar and the oldest GPS in existence. Shit, Joe," Sam said, downloading bathymetric charts, watching the graphic fly by. "Blindingly fast."

Joe smiled, then took a big gulp of coffee. He had not seen his brother in a few months, and the first thing Sam wanted to do was check out the new technology. It made Joe uncomfortable the way Sam looked up to him so blatantly. The kid had a short break from his own research, but he had flown down from Nova Scotia to interview for university jobs and spend his free time aboard Joe's boat. It bugged Joe, but he couldn't pretend it didn't please him too.

"So, what's happening down below?" Sam asked. "You making progress on the wreck?"

"It's slow, but yeah," Joe said. "I'd forgotten how murky New England water is. Cold and filled with particulate, makes it hard to work."

"Pretty funny, considering you're a New Englander born and bred," Sam said.

"Been a long time since I've lived up here," Joe said stonily.

Sam laughed. "Yeah, but you still sound like one. All crusty and cantankerous. You want to be one of those Florida guys who gets fat walking the beach and fishing the Keys, but forget it. You're too much of a codger."

"A codger. Hmmph," Joe said sternly. No one saw through him like Sam, and no one else could get away with saying the things Sam did. Joe did his best to keep the older-brother barrier up, and Sam did his best to rip it down.

"That what Caroline thinks of you?" Sam asked, laughing.

"Caroline?" Joe asked, startled by her name.

"Yeah. I was kind of surprised to see you with her. I mean, she's a Renwick, and I know how you feel about the old man. . . ."

"We had some unfinished business," Joe said, his mouth tightening. "It's finished now."

"She seemed nice," Sam said. "Growing up, the way

you and Mom'd talk about them, I got the idea all Renwicks were bad folks. Really wicked, you know?"

"She's not wicked," Joe said. "She's just the wrong guy's daughter."

"You gonna hold people's fathers against them, what does that say about me?" Sam asked. Joe leaned over the computer, pushing the zoom-in key for a closer look at the chart. He punched another key for the sea-surface temperature. His mouth was dry. Joe and his stepfather had never gotten along. Sam knew it, and he was driving home a point Joe didn't want to face.

"Drop it," Joe said quietly.

"It's just that I had the feeling I showed up at the wrong time last night," Sam said. "Seemed like you two were in the middle of something."

"I told you," Joe said. "We'd finished what we had to say to each other. Now, you gonna get dressed, or what?"

"I'm dressed," Sam said blankly, standing there in his shorts and WHOI tee-shirt. Behind his glasses, his eyes were wide and still sleepy.

"Get into your wetsuit. I'll take you down to the wreck, show you around," Joe said.

"Great!" Sam said, leaving his coffee mug on the chart table as he stumbled over a spare searchlight waiting to be installed. Shaking his head, Joe carried the cups down to the galley. Sam was like a big clumsy puppy waiting to grow into his paws. But he did see things. He saw through Joe like no one else.

Passing through the main salon, Joe thought of last night. He had kissed Caroline Renwick. Right here, he thought. Her perfume lingered in the air. The ship smelled like salt, diesel, coffee, and fish, but Joe was stopped dead by the scent of jasmine. He shook his head, walked on.

Caroline. He had had no business kissing her. The point was, he hadn't been thinking. He hadn't had much of a choice. His arms had slipped around her, his mouth had found her lips, his voice had whispered her name. It was as if Joe himself had had nothing to do with it.

Joe Connor would never kiss Caroline Renwick. Hate was a strong word, but it could honestly be said that Joe hated the Renwick family. He had drunk over it, guzzling scotch and feeling the ill will burn down with the liquor.

But facts were facts. Joe was a scientist, and he understood the irrefutable truth of certain data. He had stood in this room last night with his arms around a beautiful woman, their bodies pressed together and her tongue working hot magic, and he had wanted her more than he had ever wanted anyone. She had whispered shivers down his spine, mustered the hair on his arms to stand on end. He had held her with more tenderness than he knew he had; he hadn't wanted to let her off the ship.

That moment at the end, when she had told him how she had cared for his father and for Joe himself—how she hadn't been able to get Joe out of her mind—had pushed him over the edge. The compassion in her voice, all directed at him, was too much to handle. He could have walked away or kissed her; too bad anger still had him by the scruff of his neck. He wanted to be done with it; he really did. That familiar lifelong resentment.

"Ready?" Sam asked, flashed with excitement. He stood in the companionway, zipping up his wetsuit. Looking at his brother, Joe thought of the youngest Renwick sister. He had sensed Caroline's anguish, felt grateful he didn't have to worry about Sam that way.

"Wash these," Joe said, thrusting the coffee mugs at Sam. "What kind of sailor are you anyway, waiting for someone to clean up after you?"

"Sorry, captain," Sam said, grabbing the mugs so Joe could get changed. But he didn't sound sorry at all. He sounded affectionate, slightly condescending. As if he knew Joe's gruff manner was an act. As if he suspected that behind the cranky exterior was a good brother, a decent man, a lonely guy who would forgive if he could.

* * *

Skye and Simon went for a walk in the hospital garden. The paths were full of white-garbed nurses pushing people in wheelchairs. A few big maples provided shade, and the paved paths were lined with low boxwood hedges. Rows of lemon-drop marigolds and brilliant zinnias filled the geometrically positioned flower beds. Skye had rarely seen a garden she didn't want to paint, but this was one.

When they found an unoccupied stone bench, Skye sat down gingerly. She had been on her feet for less than ten minutes, but she felt exhausted. The effort made her so dizzy, she had to bend over. If there had been a patch of grass, she would have curled up on it.

Simon reached into his pocket and took out a cigarette. He lit it, blowing the smoke over Skye's head. She could hear the annoyance in his exhalation. She looked up.

"What's wrong?" she asked.

He shrugged.

She tried not to worry. She was the sick one, the person needing care. But she was so attuned to Simon's moods, to his needs and tempers. When he wanted something, she had trained herself to give it.

As a child, she had watched her father bang around his studio in a rage, or sulk in silent scorn for days on end. No matter how he acted, her mother would jump to attention. And so had Caroline, Clea, and Skye.

"How much longer are you going to let them keep you here?" Simon asked.

"I don't know. Now that my injuries are better, they're trying to talk me into signing into rehab."

Simon gave a slight laugh, an appreciative expression in his eyes. "With all the drunks and junkies?"

"Yes. The substance abuse unit."

"You're not seriously considering it, are you?"

"I haven't said yes yet."

"It'll fuck with your art, Skye. Turn you into another middle-of-the-road mediocre conformist. So you drink too much. You're not a little housewife with a carpool and a mortgage. You're a sculptor."

"Half the time I'm too hung over to sculpt," Skye said, staring at her hands, trying to remember the last time she had touched clay.

"Look at the artists who drank. The writers. You're emotional, and it shows in your work. If drinking pushes you over the top, I say let it." He moved closer to her on the bench, nudged her with his hips. "I don't want to lose my drinking buddy."

"I know," Skye said. It was one of the things she feared: If she was sober, how would she and Simon get along? So much of their relationship involved drinking. Wild nights with the ideas flowing faster than the scotch, decadent Tuscan lunches with wine and grappa when they pretended they were back in Badia on their honeymoon. Then again, there were the vicious, drink-induced fights, the nights when fine wine turned into booze. She wouldn't miss those.

"Lets you know you're alive—" Simon said, "—a great bottle of Calon-Ségur. Or a nice, fresh spring wine from Portugal. Remember that trip to the Algarve? We stayed naked for six days eating shrimp and drinking that cool white wine?"

"I remember," Skye said.

He pulled out pencil and paper and spread it out on

his knee. Then he glanced at Skye and started to sketch her.

Skye leaned back on her arms and tried to relax. He was a good artist. He felt high today, because a major collector had praised his work and agreed to visit his studio. Skye felt guilty though, because the art world considered her work superior to his. She knew it bothered him, and she suffered for it.

Her eyes closed, she heard his pencil flying across the paper. It seemed like such a loving gesture—a return to their early days—him drawing her outside on a sunlit day. She had boxes full of beautiful sketches he had done of her, just as her mother had so many pictures done by Hugh. It made Skye feel proud and lovely, to be loved by an artist. Her blond hair was tangled, and she knew her face was pale, but she decided to trust Simon.

"Here," he said finally.

The sketch was beautiful. Simon's style was spare, his lines simple; the body horizontal, the hair flowing down, the eyelids closed. He had drawn Skye in death, lying on a tomb.

"You're killing yourself, staying here," he whispered. "Closed off from the world, from your inspiration."

"I need help," Skye whispered.

"You need to make art," Simon said. "That's your gift. Don't waste your passion trying to fit in with the rest of the world. Express it in clay. Otherwise you're just choking yourself. Come with me now. Walk straight out of this place."

"I can't," Skye said.

"You can," Simon said, reaching out his hand. "Do it. We need each other. Haven't we always?" He had passion in his eyes.

Skye nodded. His words were true, the path was clear. His picture was a portent of things to come, and it terri-

fied her. Skye could not stay here alone. She would try to
stop drinking on her own.

He held out his arms, and as Skye walked into them,
somehow she knew she was letting her sisters down.
How did Caroline do it? Never compromise for love?
On the other hand, Caroline was alone. Their father had
warned them to protect themselves. Their mother had
taught them to sacrifice everything for men.

Skye took her husband's hand. Together they walked
out of the garden.

* * *

Clea was just throwing a load of laundry into the washer
when the telephone rang. She poured in the detergent
and ran to answer.

"Hello," she said with a don't-hang-up breathlessness.

"Clea, it's me," Caroline said.

"What's wrong?"

"Skye left the hospital. Just walked away without
telling anyone."

"Where is she?" Clea asked, feeling cold.

"I don't know. I stopped by, and she was gone. No one
saw her leave—"

"Oh, Caroline." Clea heard the panic in her sister's
voice. Their grip on Skye was so tenuous. Clea heard a tone
on the telephone line, indicating that she had a second call
waiting.

"Just a second," she said. "Maybe she's calling now."
Clicking off, Clea took the other call. "Hello?"

"Darling," said Augusta.

"Mother, can I call you back?" Clea asked, her heart
skittering. "Have you heard from Skye?"

"Heard from her? She's up in her room right now.
She's had enough of the hospital, and she came home,

where she belongs. With Simon. Now, listen. We have to talk about our costumes."

"Costumes? I've got Caroline on the other line. Let me tell her about Skye. She's frantic."

Clea returned to Caroline's line. "She's at Mom's. Safe and sound."

"What happened? Why'd she leave the hospital? If that idiot Simon's trying to svengali her into doing something crazy, I'll kill him. Is that her on the other line? Tell her I want to talk to her. Can you link us up?"

"It's Mom. I'll make it quick," Clea said. "Sit tight, and I'll get back to you with the whole story. Okay?"

"Goddamn it," Caroline said, signing off.

"That was Caroline on the other line—" Clea repeated to Augusta, adjusting her tone accordingly.

"Marvelous," Augusta said. "I need to tell her as well. I've worked out what I'm going to be for the Firefly Ball."

"The ball?" Clea asked, wiping her brow. "Mom, what about Skye? Caroline and I are so worried about her."

"I am so thrilled you girls are close," Augusta said with profound warmth. "I am so very grateful. Do you know how lucky you are to have sisters? Did I ever tell you how much I wanted sisters when I was a little girl, how I used to play with my dolls all alone and feel so sad?"

"Yes, Mom, but—"

"Now, darling. About the ball. I thought I'd go as something from Picasso's rose period. A harlequin, in fact. Everyone will expect me to dress as a painting of your father's—they'll all just take it for granted—and I'll shock them to death! It will be the most fantastic surprise!"

"A harlequin," Clea said, giving up.

"Is it too playful?" Augusta asked. "Too whimsical for a woman my age? I mean, who would expect Hugh Renwick's widow to dress as a Picasso? A harlequin, at that!"

"It sounds perfect," Clea said.

"I'm envisioning the little black mask, the bold checks, the curly-toed slippers. Really divine . . ."

Clea listened and talked for another few minutes, until her mother was done. Augusta was at her most brittle. Focusing on the ball was easier than thinking about Skye walking out of the hospital, and Clea was glad Caroline was not there to hear it.

"You'll look great," Clea said.

"Mmmm," Augusta said.

Silence filled the line. Clea took a deep breath. Just as she was about to bring Skye up again, Augusta headed her off.

"Would you and Peter and the children like to come over for cocktails?" Augusta asked. "I could call Caroline. We really need to do something to welcome Simon back into the fold. As much as I despise what he did to Skye, he is her husband."

"Not cocktails, Mom," Clea said.

"A barbecue, then. Something festive."

"Maybe she should rest," Clea said.

"She's *fine*," Augusta said. "You should see her. As bright as ever. God, I'm glad to have her home."

"I know, Mom," Clea said.

"Let's not mollycoddle her," Augusta said. "She needs our strength and support, not a lot of tiptoeing around. She needs to get back on her feet, back to life again."

"She's been ill," Clea began, realizing how painful it was for Augusta to accept that Skye needed to recover from something beyond her injuries.

"And she's well now. She's pulled through with flying colors. She's all better in time for the Firefly Ball. Won't Caroline be thrilled? She'd be so let down if Skye wasn't able to be there."

"I don't think Caroline would mind," Clea said, knowing how hard it might be for Skye, newly sober, to mill around a party where liquor was flowing freely, bottles of champagne chilling in tubs all over the lawn, trays of drinks being passed all night.

"Well, if you change your mind about tonight," Augusta said, "we'd love to have you all over. We could have a lovely time, planning our costumes for the ball."

"Don't drink in front of Skye, Mom," Clea said.

"Even her doctor didn't suggest anything as ridiculous as that," Augusta said shakily. "My God, Clea. Do you think the world stops just because your sister got drunk last week?"

"No, but I think it should," Clea said. She said good-bye and hung up. Then she called Caroline to tell her the details.

By the time Caroline called Augusta to throw in her warning, it was too late. Cocktail hour was under way. All was well. Augusta and Simon were having martinis, as usual, but Skye was drinking a diet Coke. Skye knew she could not drink. She didn't seem bothered at all. In fact, Augusta said, she had insisted that her mother and husband not forgo martinis on her account. That would have upset Skye more than anything.

* * *

Several nights later a bunch of guys from the *Meteor* converged on the inn for dinner. They had booked one table, but when they arrived, it was obvious they needed two pushed together. While they waited in the bar, Caroline helped Michele rearrange the dining room. They had to ask a party of four to switch tables, but they bought them a round of drinks to smooth the move.

Caroline headed into the bar, menus tucked under her arm. She tried to be cool, glancing through the group for Joe. He wasn't there. His crewmates were laughing, talking loudly about the artifacts they had found that day, excited about the progress. Spotting Sam, Caroline walked over.

"Hi, there," she said, smiling.

His grin was huge. Brushing dark blond hair out of his eyes, he knocked his glasses off his nose. Bending over to retrieve them, he spilled beer on the floor.

"Yikes," he said. "Sorry. You're Caroline, right?"

"Right. And you're Sam."

"I wasn't sure it was you," Sam said, bobbling his beer mug to shake her hand. "Last time I saw you, it was pretty dark." Still grinning, he seemed to be studying her. Caroline flinched, embarrassed.

"What?" she asked.

"You don't look evil and despicable," Sam said, peering down at the top of her head, ducking for a better look at her eyes.

"Is that what you've heard I am?"

"All my life," Sam said. "This is kind of momentous, me standing here talking to a Renwick. If I hadn't seen Joe doing it the other night, I'd feel disloyal. Fraternizing with the enemy, you know?"

"Think how it makes me feel, serving you dinner," Caroline said.

"I see your point," Sam agreed. "So, are you and Joe all made up now?"

"What does he say?" Caroline asked.

"Say? Joe doesn't say anything. Haven't you figured that out by now?" At Caroline's blank expression, Sam nodded. "Joe likes geophysics best, but he'll also talk about salinity in the water column and advancements in marine technology. He's pretty good on the subject of satellite navigation, and you can't shut him up once he gets going on new methods of carbon dating the stuff he finds in wrecks. But otherwise . . ."

"A man of few words," Caroline said.

"You got it."

Some of the scientists and pirates had made their way down the bar. They were talking to a group of pretty women watercolorists from Atlanta, up for their annual week at the Renwick Inn. Caroline stared at Sam Trevor and felt herself starting to smile. He had that effect on her, as she suspected he had on nearly everyone he met. He had a cute gap between his front teeth. His blue eyes crinkled at the corners. His glasses were crooked, as if he frequently sat on them.

"Why do you think he came here?" Caroline asked. "With all the wrecks in all the oceans, why did he decide to dive on the *Cambria*?"

"You've got to be kidding," Sam said, jabbing her with his elbow as if she'd just made a good joke.

"I'm not," she said. "I promise."

Sam turned serious. "She's a substantial wreck," he said, "historically and from a treasure-hunting point of view. Joe goes for the gold. No matter what the other factors, if he's not going to get rich on a dive, he doesn't do it."

"Really?"

"Really. The *Cambria* went down on a shoal, so you'd think the water would be shallow. But she slid into a trench, one of the deepest in Long Island Sound."

"Trench?"

"A geological feature of the sea bottom," Sam explained apologetically. He wasn't being a showoff, Caroline could see. He was a young nerd, pure and simple. He and Joe might have shared the same field, but their styles were completely different. Looking at this bespectacled scientist, she thought of Joe, his dark tan and sun-lightened hair, his pirate eyes and sexy arms, and she smiled at how different—yet the same— two people could be. Like herself and her sisters.

"So, the hole is deep, but Joe has the equipment. The tides and currents are fluky. The water's cold, and most of Joe's crew are southerners. The wreck is unstable—the bow lies on rock, and the stern's wedged in muck—he has to constantly analyze how the structure behaves under stress. . . ."

"Sounds impossible to me," Caroline said, laughing nervously.

"Does to other salvage teams too. That's why it's good for Joe. He's got the best boat going, and a crew to match. The site happens to be excellent for his area of geological interest. First and foremost, my brother's an oceanographer. He takes risks no one else would, and it always pays off for him."

"Were those the other factors you mentioned before? The risks?"

"No," Sam said, blinking his owl eyes. "The other factor is you."

Caroline felt her face redden. She looked down at her shoes, then back at Sam. His face was kind, as if he had just broken some hard news to her and was waiting for her to absorb it.

"Me?"

"Well, yeah. You must know that. Whatever happened between you guys wigged him out big-time. Coming anywhere near you had to carry a lot of weight in his decision to salvage the *Cambria*."

"Wigged him out," Caroline mused.

"Yeah. Frankly, I'm surprised we're having dinner here. At the Renwick Inn. No offense or anything. But the Renwick name . . ."

"Strikes fear into the hearts of pirates," Caroline said.

"Exactly," Sam said solemnly.

"Does that mean he won't be joining you tonight?" Caroline asked, hoping she sounded casual.

"No, he'll be here," Sam said.

* * *

Caroline wasn't sure how she felt when she saw Joe Connor park his truck and climb out. She watched him stretch. She saw his tan forearms flex, his shoulder muscles strain under his blue plaid shirt. He tucked the tails into his jeans, and she noticed his flat stomach, his broad chest. He was tall and handsome, and as she remembered kissing him on board the Meteor, she felt her face flush.

But fresh in her mind were Sam's words: "evil and despicable," that Caroline had "wigged Joe out" early, that he was surprised Joe would even want to eat at her inn. She felt her back stiffen.

He stood in the lobby with his feet planted wide, his rough hands in the pockets of his jeans. She felt the tingle in her neck.

"Hi, Joe," she said.

"Hi," he said, looking surprised to see her. "You work this late?"

"I own the place," she said. "I'm around here most of the time."

"Kind of like the captain," he said, trying a smile. "You're never quite off duty."

"Your table's ready," she said, leading him into the dining room.

Everyone ordered steaks and salad, though the Renwick Inn was obviously an oyster and fois gras kind of place. Joe watched his crew swilling beer, ripping into the rare beef, telling sea stories, and he sensed the artists recoiling. Twice he told his men to lower their voices and watch their language, but the volume kept creeping up. So did the expletives.

Joe had told himself Caroline wouldn't be there tonight, but now that he had seen her, he couldn't stop watching for her. All his attention was focused on the dining room door. She drifted by twice, looking sleek in her long black dress. Both times, she glanced over at the big table. But that was probably because they were causing such a ruckus. Sam was telling a long story about raising research money from the National Science

Foundation, and Dan kept interrupting with a tale about prostitutes in Fiji. Joe hardly heard. His eyes were on the door.

After dinner they took over the bar. Several artists from New York called them to their table. They compared tattoos. The artists had flowers, butterflies, and barbed wire. The sailors had women's names, ships' insignias, and serpents. More beer flowed. A few guys supplemented theirs with shots of Southern Comfort. Joe remembered the old drinking days, could practically feel the hot burn going down. He watched Sam drink a shot and realized he had never drunk with his brother.

Without telling anyone, Joe stepped outside. The fresh air felt good. Standing around bars didn't feel right anymore. The old desires came back strong. Being at sea, he didn't get to enough AA meetings. He knew it, and he tried to keep himself out of slippery places.

Joe stood in the herb garden. The heady smell of thyme and verbena reminded him of Greece. The summer night was warm, the breeze still. The inn was brightly lit. Music and loud voices came from the bar, and he had the familiar sense of being apart from the action. Watching through the old glass windows, he saw Caroline walk into the bar. She glanced around, and Joe wondered who she was searching for. He thought maybe she was looking for him. For just that second the scent of herbs grew stronger, made him dizzy.

An old Porsche pulled up. Two people got out. They clutched each other, wobbled against their car, kissed long and hard. Pulling apart, they laughed and hurried into the inn. They stumbled into the bar, and ordered drinks. The girl was beautiful. Small and slim, she looked like Caroline, only blond. She raised her glass to clink the man's, but Caroline stepped between them. Curious, Joe went inside.

"Don't, Skye," Caroline was saying, her hand on the girl's wrist. "Do you remember Dad standing in this exact spot? Do you remember how it made us feel to watch him disappearing?"

"Caroline, she's a big girl," the man said, too cool to register any expression in his eyes. He was skinny, dressed in black, with long, dark hair falling across his sickly, pale face. Some of the artists knew him; they had walked over, then faded back at the first sign of an altercation.

"Stay out of it, Simon," Caroline snapped.

The glass was full of champagne. Joe saw it catch the candlelight. The bubbles flowed in a thick stream to the surface. The girl wavered. She looked from Caroline to the skinny artist and back again.

"It's just one glass," she said.

"Think of Dad," Caroline said, her voice catching in her throat.

"This has nothing to do with him," Skye said, fixing her sister with a wild stare. "Leave me alone."

"We can leave," Simon said. "If that's what you want. We arranged to meet *friends* here—inn guests, as a matter of fact. Trent and Anya, you must know them. They live on St. Marks Place, take their two weeks here every summer. . . ."

"Simon, shut up," Caroline said dangerously.

"I hate when you fight," Skye said. "Don't fight." She took a sip, and another. With something that sounded like a sob, Caroline walked out of the bar.

Joe started to follow her. But Sam beat him to it. Joe watched his younger brother follow Caroline Renwick out the double glass doors. She hurried through the herb garden, down the path that led to the river, and Sam was right behind her.

* * *

"Caroline!"

Moving fast, Caroline heard the man's voice. She didn't want to stop, didn't want to face anyone. Ten minutes ago she had been looking for Joe Connor, but right now he was the last person she wanted to see. She didn't want anyone trying to help her. Her eyes brimming, she started walking faster.

"Caroline," she heard again.

"I'm fine," she said, trying to compose herself. She turned to look at him, forcing herself to stay calm, and was startled to find Sam bearing down on her instead of Joe.

"Are you okay?" he asked.

"I'm fine," she repeated. Being caught off guard by Sam undid her completely, and she welled up.

"You're not fine. You're a wreck," he said.

"No, I'm—"

"You can't stop her, you know," he said.

"I could have refused to serve her," Caroline said. "That's what I should have done. Told my bartender to shut her off, not even give her that one glass . . ."

"She would have gotten it somewhere else. Who is she, your sister?"

Caroline nodded. She wiped her tears with the backs of her hands. With Skye in the hospital, she had begun to feel safe. Like maybe Skye would get some help, maybe there was hope. But then Simon had come back, she had walked out of the hospital, and now she was back to drinking.

"I know how it feels," Sam said. "I watched my brother nearly kill himself for years."

"Joe?"

"Yeah. I probably shouldn't tell you, he used to have a drinking problem."

"He told me himself."

"He was so miserable," Sam said. "He drank to feel

better, but it only made everything worse. I didn't see him that often, but sometimes . . . He'd be home for Christmas, or one time he took me to Maine, sailing for summer vacation . . ." Sam's eyes clouded with the memory. "He was like Jekyll and Hyde. The best brother in the world one minute, a lunatic the next. That's when he talked about you most. When he was drunk."

"Oh," Caroline said, wondering what he said.

"He was crazy, those times. Out of his mind, not knowing what he wanted, what would help."

"You must have been very young," Caroline said, feeling sorry for the little boy watching his older brother self-destruct. But was it any easier for a grown woman? She felt the tears rolling down her cheeks.

"Yeah. It sucked."

"Well . . . Joe had some bad things happen," Caroline said slowly, thinking of their conversation on board the *Meteor*. "That I suppose didn't affect you. But . . ." She spoke very carefully. "Why Skye and not me? We had such similar childhoods. The same bad things happened to both of us. Or almost."

"Maybe it's the 'almost,' " Sam said.

Caroline had never known how to cry for help. When the bad things happened, she was always the one reaching out her hand. She wouldn't change that, wouldn't have it any other way, but right now she felt very off balance.

"Who knows?" Sam went on. "I know only one thing, and that's that they have to stop on their own. We can't do it for them."

"Everything okay?"

At the sound of Joe's voice, Sam handed Caroline his handkerchief. She blew her nose. The sound was so loud, it scared the ducks in the river. They took off, their webbed feet paddling the water.

"She's okay," Sam said. He sounded oddly proud, as if

he had been appointed Caroline's guardian, reporting back to Joe.

"Yeah? You sure?"

"I'm sure," Caroline said.

"Worried about your sister," Joe said. It was a statement, not a question.

"Yes."

Joe nodded. Dim light slanted through the trees. The ducks had circled around, were coming in for another landing. They were silhouetted against the moon. Across the river, a whippoorwill called.

"Would have been better if she'd decided to drink somewhere else," Sam said helpfully. "Instead of Caroline's inn."

"Wouldn't have made a difference," Joe said.

Caroline nodded, feeling miserable. She wanted to go back to the inn, but she was afraid to see Skye. She felt scared and angry and hopeless. Sam took a step toward the inn. Joe and Caroline faced each other. Tree branches blocked the moon, but his face looked pained in the half-light.

"What are those for?" Sam asked, pointing at the Japanese lanterns.

One entire string was illuminated, stretching from the inn's back porch to the barn. The lanterns hung still, as if caught in the trees, sparking the windless night with colors of persimmon, amber, turquoise, and scarlet.

"They're for the Firefly Ball," Caroline said.

"What's that?"

"Just a party," Caroline said, swallowing hard. Joe was staring at her, and she couldn't tear her eyes away from his. Thinking of Skye, tears welled in her eyes, then spilled down her cheeks. Sam was gazing at the lanterns, and he didn't see his brother reach for Caroline's hand and hold it. Caroline's fingers brushed Joe's scraped knuckles, and she wondered what it was costing him to make the gesture.

"Do you have it every year?" Sam asked.

"Yes."

"Can we come?"

"Sam," Joe said harshly, looking away from Caroline just long enough to miss seeing the smile pass across her eyes.

"Sure," she said. "I'd like that."

"Just me? Or Joe too?"

"All of you come, okay? The whole crew. It's a costume ball."

"What should we come as?" Sam asked.

"Pirates, of course," Caroline said, staring straight into the hooded blue eyes of his older brother, the toughest pirate of all.

January 6, 1979

Dear Caroline,

How to get you to Newport . . . that is the question. I was going to surprise you, drive down to Connecticut and pick you up, but I'm sort of grounded. A bad combination of beer, my mother's car, and my little brother.

The thing is, I really want you to come. I've got plenty of charts, and I've thought about sailing down to get you. Narragansett Bay, to Block Island Sound, to Fishers Island Sound, past the Thames River, to Black Hall.

And Firefly Hill.

Shit, who am I kidding? It would take so long to get to you, and it's the middle of winter. I was an idiot, doing what I did to get grounded. The thing is, idiots usually do the same thing again. Miss you, C.

Love,
Joe

February 4, 1979

Dear Joe,

If you got hurt or if you hurt Sam in that grounding incident, I'd never forgive you. You have to come get me! It's the only way I'll get to Newport to be with you. I miss you too, so much I can hardly stand it. How can I, when we don't even know each other? Or do we? Hurry, J.

Waiting impatiently,
C.

CHAPTER ELEVEN

*

IN THE SUNROOM, AUGUSTA WAS SEWING LONG CURLS OF black felt onto a pair of ballet slippers. She had an art book on the hassock in front of her, open to one of Picasso's harlequin paintings, copying it with studious diligence. She adored harlequins. So secretive, so playful: mysterious jesters! She congratulated herself again on her inspiration.

A character by Picasso would be recognizable. She didn't want to insult any of Caroline's less sophisticated guests by attending the soiree as anything too obscure. She could have chosen to be a character in a painting by Karsky or de Cubzac, artists no one had ever heard of, then spend the whole night explaining herself to people. Forget that.

And Augusta knew she had a good figure. The harlequin was long and slender, like Augusta herself, and she would look marvelous and sleek in the checked suit. It would be attractive, amusing, and witty.

The only problem was, Hugh had loathed Picasso.

As an artist, Hugh had admired his work. Who didn't? Who could look down on the man who had single-handedly revamped the twentieth century, who was the master of line, who had conjured cubism? Who could feel disdain for the artist who viewed a human face head-on and saw the profile instead?

No, Hugh had envied Picasso *for his life.* To Hugh Renwick, Pablo Picasso was "Pablo," an equal. And since the English translation of Pablo was Paul, Hugh had privately referred to Picasso as Paul. To call him Pablo, or, worse, Picasso, was to kowtow to an arrogant Spaniard.

Hugh was insanely jealous of Picasso. The women, the adoration, the adulation, the South of France, the bullfights, the legend. Hugh had had his own share of women, adoration, and adulation, but coastal New England was hardly the Riviera, and bullfighting had all other blood sports beat.

Fishing and hunting just weren't the same thing, especially since Hemingway, whom Hugh had actually known and referred to as Papa, had already made them his province. Hugh had taken the girls on his hunting trips, and Papa would have laughed. Daughters weren't sons when it came to hunting. Especially when they were so sensitive, and life had dealt them such a shocking blow.

Hugh was never as tough as he'd thought. He had affairs, he killed animals, he tried to live like Picasso. But once his daughters were affected, he had fallen apart. Destroying himself with drink, he had left this world. And left Augusta.

Dr. Henderson might say that Augusta's choice of a costume revealed a certain hostility for her dead husband. Her beloved—but resented—dead husband.

Quietly sewing her harlequin shoes, Augusta imagined what Hugh might think if he could see her costume. She had loved her husband with passionate intensity. She missed him more every day. In fact, she sometimes admitted to herself, it was easier to love him now than when he had been alive. Harsh realities didn't intrude quite so much. She had been a jealous woman.

Not only of the other women, but of her own daughters. God help her, she thought, remembering how she had felt watching him paint Caroline.

Hearing the kitchen door slam, she glanced up just as Skye walked in with Simon.

"Hi, dears," she said. As soon as she saw Skye, she knew: She'd been drinking. Her eyes were red, her hair disheveled. It was five o'clock, and she looked as if she had just gotten up: hung over and remorseful. Augusta's heart fell.

"Where were you last night?" Augusta asked.

"We stayed at the inn," Simon said. "Some of our old friends from the East Village are up for a few days, and we met them there."

"Skye, would you like something cold to drink?"

Skye nodded. Augusta walked to the flower room. She filled a crystal pitcher with ice water. Surprisingly, her hands were shaking. Tipping three aspirin into a tiny ceramic bowl, she placed everything on a tray and carried it back to the sunroom.

"I'm so thirsty," Skye said, drinking a tall glass. She filled another, took the three aspirin, drank the water down.

"What happened last night?" Augusta asked, shaken. "I thought you had decided to stop drinking for a while."

"I did. I stopped for a week. But it seems so pointless . . ." Skye tried to laugh.

"Pointless, ah . . . my beautiful little existentialist. Shall we discuss Camus?" Simon asked, coolly lighting a cigarette.

"Only if you make some martinis first," Skye said. "Mom, you're ready for one, right?"

"Well, yes," Augusta said cautiously. "But I'm not sure you should."

"Mom, do I really want to be one of those holierthan-thou abstainers? We hate them," Skye said, shaking her head.

"Personally, I think moderation is the best approach," Augusta said. "But your sisters have a very definite opinion on this. They think you should stop entirely."

"They're jealous," Simon said, exhaling a long stream of smoke from between his thin lips. "Of Skye's creativity."

Augusta's skin crawled at his audacity, although she considered the possibility that he was right.

"Will you quit talking about that and make the drinks instead?" Skye asked, a tremor in her voice. Alarmed, Augusta noticed that her lips were nearly white. Skye rarely snapped at Simon, just as Augusta had almost never spoken angrily to Hugh. Skye had to be under severe stress to talk to him that way, but already she was retreating.

"I'm sorry, Simon," she said, passing a hand across her face.

Simon glared at her. He looked sullen and skinny, his dark eyes sunken like some dissipated raccoon's. That he even considered himself in the same league as Hugh was pathetic, Augusta thought. She indulged him only because she understood Skye's love for him. It couldn't be explained, and it couldn't be quenched.

"I'll make the drinks," Simon said darkly.

"Simon's right," Augusta said, squeezing Skye's hand as a feeling of queasy panic rose in her chest. "You'll feel so much better when you're back in your studio."

"Oh, Mom," Skye whispered.

Nothing made Augusta feel so helpless as trying to get through to one of her girls and being unable to.

"I don't want to be an alcoholic," Skye said, tears sliding down her face.

"You're not one," Augusta said.

"I hate the word."

"So do I."

"I want to drink less, I know I have to. I can do that, right?"

"Of course, darling. I'll help you. We'll each have one, no more. Okay?"

Skye nodded. But her tears continued to fall.

Simon returned with a silver tray full of drink things. He had even remembered to bring a tiny dish of mixed nuts. The silver shaker, the vapors redolent of gin and vermouth, the three tiny olives. Skye's eyes were dull as she watched him pour the martinis into chilled glasses. It occurred to Augusta, clear as crystal: Skye should not be drinking. At all.

Augusta felt afraid. Filled with dread, she didn't know how to stop what she had started. Caroline would be devastated when she found out.

They raised their glasses, arms extended, to clink.

"Here's to Skye!" Augusta said. "Home again, where she belongs."

* * *

Caroline sat on her back porch alone. Wrapped in a shawl, she rocked gently in the glider, thinking of last night. She had walked along the riverbank with Joe and Sam while Skye got plastered in the bar. The men had told her: You can't do anything. It's up to Skye.

A small oil lamp burned on the table beside her. The night was dark and heavy, and the artists were quiet. A dog barked in the distance; nightbirds cried across the marsh, and their sound filled Caroline with uneasy memories of long, long ago.

She thought of Joe. Last night he had been here with her. Right here, by the river. He had held her hand. They hadn't acknowledged it, hadn't said anything. Sam didn't seem to notice, and when they returned to the inn, Joe had dropped it and stepped away. But for their walk through the reeds, he had offered her comfort. And Caroline almost never took that from anyone.

Amazing, she thought. She planted her feet firmly on the floor and pushed the glider back and forth, like a boat rocking on the waves. She was sitting there, on her own porch, not dashing out of town. Amazing. Totally unlike her. She opened the folder beside her. She took out Clarissa Randall's diary.

While Joe was miles at sea, excavating the ship that held Elisabeth Randall's bones, Caroline was safe at home, reading the writings of her daughter. It made Caroline feel strangely protective of the little girl, a keeper of painful memories. Little girls needed looking after; Caroline had realized that always.

Clarissa had such small handwriting. It traced across the page, delicate as spiderwebs. She had used a quill pen. Caroline recognized this, occasionally still using one herself. As a girl, she had found a seagull feather, used her father's X-acto knife to slice a sharp point, and dipped it in India ink to write in her journal.

> August 15, 1769
> A very bad storm today. The biggest waves I have seen since last winter, and a wind to shake the tower and make me feared it would blow the light out. Pa told us a ship ran aground on Wickland Shoals with no loss of life and all hands lucky to be alive. It makes me glad we live here to light the lamp.

> August 17
> Mama gone almost all day. I wanted to find her, so I looked all over. Imagined her blown into the sea by the gale, so I was very afraid.

Pa told us about pirates working the coast, bad men who take what isn't theirs and sometimes hurt others in their selfishness. Mama has such beautiful things, I thought, what if pirates took her? She wears Grandmother's cameo at her throat always. And she has the pearl and garnet pendant Pa gave her for their wedding. Pirates would surely find such treasures irresistible. I thought what if they hurt Mama taking her things! Or what if they steal her away to sail on their ship with them and cook their meals and be a wife to their captain.

But I was wrong. Mama came home. When I asked her where she had been, she gave me a funny look. She told me women have secrets just like girls, and sometimes she needs to be alone with her secrets for a while. Her secrets keep her well, she said. What a funny thing to say! But she does seem happy. So should I be.

August 18

Again, Mama disappeared! Now it seems exciting, a game. She has a secret place! Where could it be? Wouldn't it be perfect if it was one of mine? Let's see: I have Lightning Rock, the tallest granite boulder on the north end. Also the tidal pools on the south shore, where we found the finback whale at summer's start. I have the pine barrens, the green bowl, the beacon room atop the light. Should I let Mama keep her secret, or should I find her out?

August 20

Captain Thorn of the Cambria paid a visit. He brought whale oil and lavender. Don't like him.

August 22

Windy. Went to the boathouse to play, and saw Mama talking to Captain Thorn. Don't like him. He is from England, and he talks that way that makes Pa laugh. Mama bade me not tell Pa of their meeting. Walking home, we found a lobster shedding its shell in the rockweed. Mama cooked it for Pa, and he let me eat the little claws. Still haven't found Mama's secret place.

Reading the pages, Caroline found herself breathing hard. Clarissa had found her mother's secret place, and she didn't even know it. Captain Thorn was her mother's secret, but Clarissa's mind was too innocent to realize. Like all those times Hugh had been away from home with Joe's mother or some other woman, and Caroline had thought he was somewhere painting.

August 24

Today porpoises swam by the beach, just ahead of a whale. I wanted to swim with them, but Mama said no. She sat so quiet on the sand, sad like I haven't seen her for weeks. The tern babies begging their mamas for fish made her cry, and I said what's wrong, Mama? Usually the baby birds make us laugh. But she said to be a good girl, to take care of myself no matter what happens. That when mamas aren't there to take care of their babies, they have to know the babies will survive.

August 29

I can scarcely believe. Mama is gone! Captain Thorn took her aboard the Cambria, and she drowned on Moonstone Reef! Dear God, give me back Mama!

Caroline read the horrible words, biting her lip. The poor little girl. Abandoned by her own mother, and for what? So the woman could die with her lover at sea in a storm? Clarissa had been left to deal with everything by herself, with no help from the people who were supposed to protect her. Even worse, she had lost a parent she loved.

Across the marsh, the whippoorwill called. Seagulls cried, and other shorebirds, but the whippoorwill's song was unmistakable. It rang through the night, making Caroline think of Redhawk. That mountain trail, covered with yellow leaves, where she had begun to lose her father.

The cordless telephone beside her rang.

Caroline stared, thinking of Skye. She answered.

"Hello?"

"Hi. It's Joe."

"Hi," Caroline said. She shivered, although the night was hot. She held the phone with both hands and wondered what the sea looked like tonight.

"Are you all right?" he asked. "You were pretty upset last night."

"I'm fine," Caroline said.

"The thing is," Joe said, "you're probably not, but you can't change what she does."

"That's what you said. And Sam."

"He should know. He watched me drink for a long time."

"He's a nice kid."

Joe made a sound halfway between a snort and a laugh. "He's a character."

Caroline smiled. She had liked watching the brothers together, and she enjoyed hearing Joe soften every time Sam entered the picture. She heard Joe breathing against the receiver, and she closed her eyes. A warm breeze blew, lifting the hair on the back of her neck. All she had ever wanted was a friend, she thought. Why was that so hard?

"I called because I thought of something that might help," he said. "Maybe it won't help Skye, but it might help you."

"What?" Caroline asked.

"Just be honest," he said. "As honest as you can, about everything."

"I am—" she said, feeling hurt.

"I know. I believe you are. But . . ."

Caroline was silent, listening to his breath. Something inside her was changing, a profound shifting of ground that had to do with her isolation, the past. She knew it had started when Joe came to town, and it had to do with Skye slowly killing herself. She had always taken care of the ones she loved, but right now she knew she needed some help of her own. She held the receiver tighter.

"Sometimes you have to go deeper," Joe said. "I can't explain it, but it worked for me. Once I figured out what I was trying to hide from, I . . . was more ready to think of stopping."

"Stopping?"

"Drinking. There's a saying," Joe said. "The truth will set you free."

Caroline nodded. She closed her eyes again, thinking of what he had said. Her mind filled with an image of Skye, ten years old, alone on the mountain. She lay in her tent. It was August, the night was cool. Beneath her sleeping bag, under the thin tent floor, writhed snakes. Outside, coyotes howled. Skye lay with her eyes wide open, clutching her knife.

Andrew Lockwood would not cross their path for several years, but death was in the air. They were so young, and they were too alone. Caroline had learned never to complain.

"The truth feels too hard," she whispered.

"No," Joe said, realizing for the first time himself that the opposite is really true. "It might feel that way, but it's not. It's freedom."

Caroline listened to the phone echo. She heard static on the line, voices in the background. Jostling, as if Joe were fighting to hang on to the phone.

"Hang on," Joe said reluctantly. "Someone wants to speak with you."

"Caroline, hey!"

"Hi, Sam," she said, pulling herself together.

"What're you doing tomorrow afternoon?"

She could hear Joe in the background. They scuffled over the phone. The headset clattered, shuffled along a desktop. She heard laughter, a muffled shout, Joe speaking in a stern and insistent tone. Sam regained control of the phone.

"Well?" he asked, as if nothing had happened. "Are you busy?"

"I have a bank board meeting in the morning," she said. "But otherwise the day is clear."

"Joe's lecturing at Yale. It's open to the public."

"What time?" Caroline asked.

"Three o'clock. At Crawford Hall."

"Does Yale offer a degree in treasure hunting?"

Sam laughed. "No, but tomorrow the treasure hunter turns back into a scientist. If you come, you'll get to hear him speaking on the joys of sediment. I'm going to teach there, you know."

"At Yale? Really?"

"Well, they haven't offered me the job, but they will once—" Again Sam chuckled, losing control of the phone. Caroline heard Joe telling him to shut up, but his tone was joking, and there was laughter in his voice.

"I'll try to be there." Caroline waited for Joe to come back on the line, but Sam disconnected first. The line hummed.

* * *

After lunch the next day, Caroline swung by Clea's to pick her up. Together they headed west, down 95 toward New Haven. Clea didn't seem to find it strange that they would be going to Yale University to hear Joe Connor lecture on sediment. She simply smiled, told Caroline she looked beautiful in her navy blue dress, pearl earrings, and bracelet.

"Thank you," Caroline said. She cast a quick look across the seat. "Am I too dressed up?"

"You're perfect."

"I'm not really sure why we're going," Caroline said. "Except Sam sounded so excited, and I don't want to let him down. He's a cute kid."

"That's a good reason to drive all the way to New Haven in ninety-five-degree heat. To hear someone lecture about mud," Clea said, smiling inscrutably.

"If you didn't want to go . . ." Caroline muttered.

"I wouldn't miss it for anything," Clea said.

Route 95 was crowded. Traffic started building in Guilford, and by the time they reached the big bridge curving past the oil tanks at the head of New Haven harbor, they had just enough time to get there.

"See that big stone tower, looks like a cathedral?" Clea said, pointing across New Haven's concentrated skyline. "That's Harkness. Right in the middle of Yale, two blocks from Crawford Hall."

"Remember coming to Yale right after Dad died?" she continued.

"Yep. He had left that painting to the museum, and we all had to put on party dresses and drink tea with the trustees. Mom told the server to fill her teacup with sherry."

"And she was outrageous so they wouldn't see how sad she was."

"How much she hated doing things without Dad."

"Let's not talk about it," Clea said, shuddering. "Let's pull a Mom and put it right out of our heads."

Caroline turned off the expressway, took a right on York Street. She drove past the colleges of Yale, the granite buildings and big iron gates, and found a parking spot on the corner of Prospect and Grove. Without another word about the past, she and Clea walked up a tree-lined path to Crawford Hall.

Granite steps led into an arched and vaulted stone entrance hall. Graduate students and members of the public milled about the cool space. Joe's lecture was one in a popular series on maritime topics; it had been publicized in local papers and *The New York Times*. People were beginning to file into an auditorium.

Sam waved them over. He was sitting in the second row and had saved a seat for Caroline.

"This is my sister, Clea," she said, and they shook hands. Sam got everyone else in the row to shift down one, and they took their seats, with Caroline between Clea and Sam. Sam wore khaki pants, a denim shirt, and a tie. His hair was neatly combed, but it kept falling in his eyes anyway. He had a notebook open, as if he intended to take notes.

Dr. Joseph Connor walked onto the stage, taking his spot at the lectern. He wore a brown tweed jacket, a white shirt, and a striped tie. His manner was comfortable, like a sexy young college professor. He cleared his throat, gripping the lectern with tanned hands. Looking into the audience, he was relaxed, as if he had stood before many students, delivered many lectures.

He talked about roaming the seas in the R/V *Meteor,* diving on shipwrecks and exploring the ocean floor. He spoke of research as a by-product of his treasure hunts. He explained how climate and sea level responded to past changes, how sediments were packed in complicated patterns of layered wedges. Cylinders of gray mud were brought up and dated by the ship's paleontologist through microfossils contained therein.

"Drilling holes deep in the seabed to retrieve cores of mud and rock allows us to interpret the earth's distant past, going back thirty-five million years," he said. "Diving on a ship such as the *Cambria* is a way to interpret the last two hundred."

He spoke of how his work combined geology and archaeology, how he juxtaposed his interest in the sea bottom with curiosity about human behavior. At his signal, the lights were dimmed, and he began to project slides on a screen at the front of the auditorium.

"Our current site," he said, "is a perfect example. The *Cambria* was an English barquentine, her holds full of the king's gold. She went down in a storm in 1769, and all hands were lost, including the captain and a woman who had fallen in love with him." Joe paused, clearing his throat.

The screen showed a three-masted ship. It was the drawing Caroline had seen hanging in the *Meteor*'s chart room. Joe clicked a button, and pictures of gold coins and barnacle-encrusted cannons appeared. Another click, and a page of Clarissa's diary filled the screen.

"The woman was a wife and mother, and she left behind a little girl," Joe said. "The child kept a diary, and recently I came into possession of a copy."

"The one Maripat gave you!" Clea whispered to Caroline. Caroline nodded, eyes on Joe.

"It gives us a context," he said. His voice was deep and sonorous; it filled the auditorium. "The record of earth's history is probably written with more fidelity in the oceans than anywhere else on earth. Except, maybe, in the diary of a little girl who lost her mother. It's historically accurate, and purely true, words of grief written by someone who never expected them to be read. Clarissa has helped us piece together the story of the artifacts we bring up from the sea bottom.

"The diary was given to me by the same person who told me about the wreck in the first place, many years ago," Joe said, and Caroline felt herself blush in the darkness. "Our own histories intersected in a way that parallels the story of the wreck. At one time you might have said we were close friends. At another, someone might have called us enemies. Everything is changeable. Even the truth, or perceptions of it as time passes. On a dig like this, that can't help but seem significant.

"We bring up a lot of artifacts aboard the *Meteor*, a lot of sediment. It's not clear until later which will be helpful and which won't. We never know until we get to the lab whether the metal we find is gold or nickel. Whether our test bores hold a decipherable record of sea-level change or just mud. But then"—he took a deep breath—"nothing is just mud."

The audience laughed, and when they realized Joe was finished, they began to clap. Caroline sank lower in her chair. She stared at Joe, and she could swear that he had found her in the dark, was staring at her. His blue eyes were bright and clear, squinting past the beam of light. The auditorium lights were switched on, and he continued to stare at her while audience members milled around him.

"That was interesting," Clea said, leaning past Caroline to speak to Sam. "Your brother is an excellent speaker."

"They've asked him to come to Yale next year," Sam said, "as visiting professor. I'm not insanely jealous or anything."

"I thought you were the one interviewing," Caroline said.

"Are you a professor?" Clea asked.

"No, but I'd like to be. I interned at Dartmouth for a semester, but now I'm on a boat in the North Atlantic, sending out résumés from every town in Newfoundland and Labrador that has a post office. I interviewed here, they haven't given me any word yet. But my brother . . ."

"Really, here? Joe at Yale?" Caroline asked, still watching Joe, wondering whether he was thinking about accepting. Would he actually settle in the area, give up constantly traveling for a while? She tried not to care what his answer would be, even though he was coming toward her with his eyes focused on her like test bores.

"You made it," he said. "Thanks for coming."

"I enjoyed your talk," Caroline said, looking straight at him. "*Dr.* Connor."

"Hope you didn't mind me using you to illustrate a point," he said.

"I guess that depends," Caroline said slowly.

"On what?" Joe cocked his head. His eyes held a glimmer of a smile. He waited.

"It ought to be obvious, Joe," Sam said.

"Really? Tell me," Joe said.

"Whether she's your friend again," Clea said. "Or still your enemy."

"God, the whole family's in the act," Caroline said, making a joke to cover her discomfort.

"My friend," Joe said quietly. "She's my friend."

* * *

Driving home, Caroline played his words over in her mind: "She's my friend."

"It was good to hear him," Clea said. "He'd make a good professor."

"Yes," Caroline said.

"Wouldn't it be nice if he and his brother could teach together?"

"It would."

"At Yale. So close by. We'd probably see him once in a while," Clea said, her voice neutral, "now that you're friends again. . . ."

"Clea," Caroline said. Her voice was stern, but her face was smiling.

Once they got off the highway, they drove through the village of Black Hall. It contained large white ship-builders' houses with black shutters and window boxes full of red geraniums, white petunias, and blue lobelia; white picket fences; a yellow Georgian mansion with white columns, once a boardinghouse for the American Impressionists, now a museum; a gas station; stately beech and maple trees; American flags everywhere; two white churches: one, a famously painted Congregational, the other Catholic. Heading south, out of town, they passed the marshes and inlets of the Connecticut River; a third white church, this one Episcopalian; and the fish store with its blue fish weathervane.

"Want to stop by Mom's?" Caroline asked on the spur of the moment. "To see Skye?"

"Great idea," Clea said.

By keeping the steeples on the left and the water on the right, they eventually got to the sea road. The road tunneled through a dark forest of hemlocks and old oaks, the branches meeting overhead. The ledge rose on the right, and the road burst free of any tree cover. A vista of open water spread before them, rough water dancing under sunlight, Joe's ship riding on the waves.

A long drive wound upward through the forest. Wrought-iron lightposts, each topped with an evil-looking bat, lined the way. Her father had commissioned them from an artist he knew in Vermont. They had skeletal black wings, some spread and others drawn close about their spindly bodies; when lit, their eyes glowed red. Hugh had installed them to scare intruders away from Firefly Hill, so nothing bad would happen there again.

Caroline's stomach flipped. What would they find when they got there? She told herself not to care, that

Skye was a grown woman in charge of her own life. She tried to pretend they weren't stopping just to check up on her.

When they got there, Skye was drunk.

Augusta was needlepointing, looking upset. Simon and Skye were sitting together on the sofa, flipping through a design magazine. Skye could hardly hold her head up.

"Hi," Caroline said, her heart falling. Clea stood beside her, saying nothing.

"Skye spent the day in her studio," Augusta said dubiously. Her eyes were red-rimmed and haunted. She looked at Skye, then away. Skye had a bottle of beer tucked behind the sofa leg. She reached down, looked Caroline straight in the eye, and took a slug.

"All she needed all along," Simon said wearily.

"Needed you, baby," Skye whispered. "Needed your big . . ."

How drunk was she? Caroline wondered, listening to Skye whisper little pornographic promises into Simon's ear. It made her heart ache—literally—to watch her beautiful sister demean herself this way. Augusta pretended not to hear, an anguished expression in her eyes. Clea breathed heavily, as if she had just run up a hill. The whole family feels it, Caroline thought.

"Skye," Caroline said sharply.

Skye ignored her. She kept tickling Simon, murmuring her sexy words into his ear, just slightly too loud.

"Skye, stop it," Caroline said.

Skye's face reacted as if she'd been slapped. "He's my husband."

"Then respect him, and wait till you're in private to talk like that." The words were out so fast, they surprised even Caroline. Is this telling the truth? she thought. Is that what I'm doing now? Clea squeezed her hand.

Skye blushed. Simon scowled, said "Christ," and left the room. But Augusta looked relieved. Caroline watched her mother, noticed the way her mouth relaxed, her fingers stopped working her black pearls so incessantly.

"Get a man of your own," Skye said darkly.

"You turn ugly when you drink," Caroline said. "Do you know that?"

"What did you do in your studio today?" Clea asked, quickly trying to make peace.

The silence was heavy, the storm about to break. Caroline and Skye glared at each other. Homer stuck his wet nose in Skye's face. Surprised, she tossed her head. The interruption seemed to make her forget the fight. "What?" she asked.

"What'd you sculpt today?" Caroline asked. "Mom said you were in your studio."

"That," Skye said, pointing.

Caroline's gaze fell on a piece of clay. It sat on a table beside a cut glass vase overflowing with day lilies, beach roses, honeysuckle, larkspur, sweet peas, and mint. Six inches high, the clay looked like a three-peaked mountain range. Skye's work wasn't generally abstract. Her sculptures of the human figure were usually vivid and emotional; she filled her subjects with yearning. She usually sculpted women known for their fire and passion: Joan of Arc, Sappho, Lena Horne, Amelia Earhart.

"What is it?" Caroline asked, kneeling down.

Clea knelt beside her. She turned the piece around to see it better.

"Redhawk," Skye said bitterly. "Can't you see the mountaintops?"

"No," Clea said, looking into her eyes. "It's something else. Isn't it?"

Skye nodded, her eyes suddenly swimming in tears.

"Oh, the mountains," Augusta said, from across the room. "I used to feel so left out! But I wanted my girls to have their time with their father. . . ."

"It's not Redhawk?" Caroline asked, wondering if the degenerative state of Skye's art would become a permanent result of her drinking.

Skye shook her head. She was crying freely now. She reached for her beer. But she didn't drink. She gripped the bottle until her knuckles turned white.

"It's sisters," she whispered.

"Us?" Caroline whispered back, shocked, trying to shield the disappointment in her voice.

Skye nodded. "You, me, and Clea."

"I love it," Clea said fiercely.

Caroline stared at the piece. Primitive, unfinished-looking, a child might have done it. The three shapes were connected but separate. They touched at the bottom, leaned away from each other at the top. The sculpture showed none of the skill or technique that marked Skye as an artist, but staring at it, Caroline was suddenly filled with wild emotion.

"Can you see?" Skye asked through her tears. "The three sisters?"

"I see," Caroline said through tears of her own. "I love it too."

Caroline's affirmation set loose something in Skye, and her body was racked with sobs. She couldn't hold them back. She sat on the sofa, clutching the brown beer bottle, and both of her sisters climbed up beside her. The three Renwick sisters held one another as tight as they could.

We're like Skye's sculpture, Caroline thought. Three lumps of clay thrown together. Joe's sea mud. Thinking of Joe, remembering the truth, Caroline held on tighter.

Sisters. Three sisters. She thought of Skye's initial explanation, that her sculpture was of mountains, and she knew that was partly true also.

With three sisters, truth doesn't come in one piece, Caroline thought. Skye's drinking might be Caroline's travel. When one sister was ready to tell the truth, the others might still want to hide. Stop hiding, she thought, holding her sisters.

* * *

After the talk at Yale, Joe couldn't wait to get back to the wreck.

"You gonna teach there?" Sam asked, his left foot stuck in the right leg of his wetsuit.

"Doubt it," Joe said, watching Sam tangle himself up even more.

"Why not?" Sam asked, yanking his foot free and banging it on a cleat. Joe reached over, undid his brother's ankle zipper. He had a distant memory of stuffing the kid into a snowsuit.

"Why should I? I like what I do. Just because you want to teach at Yale doesn't mean everyone does."

At sea the sky was clear and the views were long. Joe took a deep breath and thought how that was exactly how he had liked his life to be: clear, with long views. Nothing crowding him. Just him, the wreck, the ocean, and the mud.

"You gotta grow up, man," Sam said. "You're out here being a pirate, and there's a university filled with students waiting to learn about muck. You know? Fossil-laden rocks and mud, telling the story of time. Just like you said in your lecture. Beautiful, man."

"Thanks," Joe said dryly. Sliding off his shirt and pants, he put on his own wetsuit. Sam handed him a single air tank, which he strapped on. They were ready to dive.

"I mean it, Joe," Sam said sternly. "Dry land's where it's at for you. Especially around here. Near Black Hall."

"Why near Black Hall?"

"Think about it, idiot. Just think about it."

Joe pushed Sam overboard. He watched him splash around, sputtering with surprise. Joe followed him into the cold water. The brothers spit in their masks, then slid them over their eyes. Sam blinked at Joe, tried to dunk him. His big brother pushed him away but he swam back good-naturedly. The water felt cold on Joe's hands and neck. He took a sharp breath, then another and another, trying to get used to the temperature. Years of warmer waters had taken the New Englander right out of him.

"Black Hall," he said to Sam, treading water. "Jesus."

"Think about it," Sam said.

They stuck the regulators in their mouths and dove.

Sunlight penetrates to a depth of two hundred feet, but to the human eye darkness takes over before that. Diving beside Sam, Joe sensed the wreck looming ahead. It hung on the reef, an outcropping of glacial moraine, a dead forest of black timbers. The three spars were broken in half, their yards and halyards trailing in the sand.

Divers, members of his crew, moved about their work like bees going in and out of a hive. There was an air of flight about them, the way they hovered and swerved, bubbles rising. They swam through a ragged hole in the ship's bow, a dark cave yawning at the sea bottom. And they swam out, holding bits and pieces of the ship and its loot.

Sam zipped ahead, eager to enter. Joe put out a warning hand to hold him back. The spotlight illuminated Sam's wide eyes behind his mask, and Joe was filled with a protective rush for his brother. The kid's enthusiasm got him into trouble every time, riding his bike into traffic, saying yes to the first job that came along.

Joe motioned for Sam to wait there. The wreck was too dangerous. Sam's eyes tried to argue, but Joe was firm. He made his face angry, his eyes threatening. Sam let out a big breath of air, backed off. Joe wished he could feel as if he had just won something, but instead he felt guilty for disappointing his younger brother.

Swimming through the silent deep, Joe felt somber—for leaving Sam behind, and because he felt as if he were about to enter a tomb. Which he was; swimming into the wreck of the *Cambria,* Joe felt a sense of duty. He wanted to honor Clarissa's mother. In his mind Clarissa was frozen as a little girl, that eleven-year-old child whose mother had sailed away and never come home. Reading her diary, he had gleaned information that made identification of her mother's skeleton possible. He tried to keep his emotions out of it.

Joe swam into the black hole. Down a long and treacherous path through the twisted and upside-down interior, he followed the dim light that marked the site. His heart skittered inside his chest, but he fought to remain steady. He was glad he hadn't let Sam come in here. It took great calm to keep breathing correctly underwater. He had watched divers suffer the bends, nearly explode from a surfeit of nitrogen built up from gulping for air, giving in to panic. So he thought of Clarissa and made himself breathe right.

Blue-bright lights glowed up ahead. They illuminated the *Cambria*'s crushed stern, the old mahogany splintered and covered with barnacles and mussels, now part of the reef itself. Fish darted in and out; the sand machine pulled debris away from the treasure site. Divers worked meticulously, uncovering coins.

He saw the two skeletons. They were clustered together, off to the side. Their mouths gaped, their bones protruded. They might have been screaming for help, for forgiveness.

Joe told himself not to feel.

He hovered about them like a fish himself, striving for dispassion. He felt his heart beating madly in his chest. Taking too much air, he looked away. Then back again. These people had died for love. They had sailed away with dreams of escape, their desire for each other pulling them away from everything else. This lady had had a daughter.

Was it worth it? Joe wanted to ask her. Dying on this reef, taken by surprise, by some sudden storm. They hadn't gotten more than twenty miles away from Elisabeth's lighthouse. Joe thought of his father, dying fifty miles from home. Of his mother and Hugh Renwick, of the mess and madness their affair had created.

Joe felt his heart hammering. All his life he had used women as a port in a storm, one after the other, avoiding anything messy or long-lasting, and this was why: Just look at the agony. He swam closer to the skeletons. Taking a light from Dan, he shined the beam down on the two gaping skulls, searching.

There it was: the object that identified Elisabeth Randall. Joe's hands were heavy, his throat ached. According to Clarissa's diary, she had worn it always. Shreds of weed clung to the vertebrae, with a solid object thickly coated with algae and old barnacles nestled in the clavical bones. Joe reached in, gently dislodged it. Over the years and through the wrecks he had trained himself to be unsentimental about death. He had done it a hundred times, reached into a pile of bones and removed a gold chain or diamond pendant or pocket watch. Clinical, scientific. He had taken the loot and never looked back.

But Elisabeth's cameo should have been Clarissa's.

Time should have passed the way it was supposed to between a mother and child, with the mother growing old and leaving her most precious things to her daughter. Joe thought of his father, his gold watch, how after he died Joe had never seen it again. Parents die far from home, and they take their things with them. The things that might give their kids comfort or solace or even an answer or two.

Not that things were enough, but they were something to hold on to. Objects to hold and examine, reminders of someone who had once loved you. And sometimes they were all you had.

Joe stared at the bones. He tried to pray for the woman, but somehow the prayer included Caroline and Sam. His throat burned. His weight belt dragged him down, his breath rasped in his ears. Restless, the cameo safely retrieved, he turned to leave the wreck.

As soon as he emerged, he looked around for Sam. Not seeing him right away, his heart started pumping. *Jesus,* he thought. Diving with someone you cared about was too fucking much work. He swam around the wreck, moving faster, looking through the groups of workers.

He found Sam at the reef. Away from the wreck, unimpressed by the gold, Sam was after his own treasure. Fish. A biologist, his interest lay in pelagic species, just as Joe's lay in sea mud. A thought went through Joe's mind: What if we did both end up at Yale? What if we found a way to live near each other instead of two oceans away? What if we both did what we were trained to do and taught at a good university?

Not forever, Joe thought, because that was too much to consider all at once. But for a while?

Sam was speaking. Two hundred feet beneath the surface, his brother was swimming among the fish of Moonstone Reef, forming words with his lips. He had taken the regulator from his mouth, and he was enunciating in an exaggerated way. His mouth moved, saying the same words over and over. Watching him form the syllables, Joe read his brother's lips.

"Black Hall," Sam was saying, the bubbles exploding toward the surface. "Black Hall."

March 14, 1979

Dear Joe,

Okay, so I got a little carried away in my last letter. I think it's bizarre, the way I can't wait to see you and I don't even know you yet. Ever since you mentioned sailing here, I keep watching the horizon for sails.

I think something's happening to me.

Love,
Caroline

April 20, 1979

Dear Caroline,

Something's happening to me too. Keep watching—I'll come as soon as I get my mainsail repaired. It blew out in a gale last week. I shouldn't have been on the water, but I thought I'd take advantage of the wind to sail to Connecticut (i.e., you).

Love,
Joe

CHAPTER TWELVE

SKYE SAT IN HER STUDIO, TRYING TO FEEL LIKE SCULPT-
ing. Facing north, the room was cool. Her clay was ready.
She sat in her regular place, on a tall metal stool pulled
close to a smooth stone table. Her roughened fingertips
trailed across the slippery surfaces. Her tongue felt thick.
Her head pounded. She felt a constant, dull pain in her
left temple; unconsciously, she kept touching it, prodding
it, seeing if it hurt more when she pressed it with her
finger.

She had fallen last night. Walking from the garden to the
house, she had stumbled and gone down. She had skinned
her knees and struck her head on a rock. The heels of both
her hands were scraped raw. She had been covered with
bits of grass; sand and tiny pebbles were pressed into her
skin. When she came to, Homer was licking her face.

It scared her. She didn't feel dizzy, and a look in the
mirror had revealed no new bruises. But the side of her
head felt different, almost as if she had cracked her skull.
It ached. Her mother and Simon had been in the house,
and she had gone off . . . for what? She hardly remembered now. She had been in some sort of huff, and she
had stormed out to stare at the sea. Homer had just happened along, returning from one of his journeys.

Looking at her clay, Skye felt unmoved, uninspired. The connections she needed to sculpt were missing today. They had been harder and harder to find lately. Skye needed her passions to come through, from her brain to her fingertips, to give shape and emotions to the clay she held in her hand. Drinking blocked them. Liquor dulled the pain, but it also numbed the love.

Every morning she would wake up with a hangover and promise herself she would not drink that day. Even before her fall, her head had hurt. Skye had thought of the liquor crushing her head from the inside out. But at some point every day, she would get the craving. The emptiness inside was bigger than the ache in her head, and she would know a drink would take the worst feelings away. At least for a while.

She wanted one now. She looked at the clock on her table: three P.M. She made a bargain with herself. Just two more hours. Work till five, and then reward yourself with a glass of wine. You can do that. It won't kill you.

Simon walked into the room. He smelled of cigarettes and turpentine, and his bleary eyes told their own drinking story. He stood over Skye's clay, staring at it without speaking. What was he thinking? Skye wondered. Did he know she was in trouble? The word surprised her, and she wondered where it came from. Trouble.

"How's it going?" Simon asked, pouring a tall glass of water and guzzling it down fast.

"Fine," Skye said.

"Your mother's downstairs, chirping about her costume." Skye smiled at the image, and Simon continued. "She wants to know what we're wearing to Caroline's ball. Are we even invited?"

"Of course we are," Skye said. "Why wouldn't we be?"

"Because she hates me. And she's jealous of you."

Skye shook her head. It made her unhappy when

Simon criticized her sisters, and today it made her feel particularly bad. What would Caroline have to be jealous of? A hung-over, bloated sculptor who couldn't sculpt? Skye reached past her clay for one of the objects she kept on her desk. There was a flat gray stone, a pure white feather, the skeleton of a snake, a shotgun shell, and a pale and faded blue grosgrain ribbon.

"Why do you keep these things?" Simon asked, taking the stone out of her hand. "We've been married five years, and I don't know half the story. These little mysterious things—your Renwick family fetishes—you never talk about them."

"They're just objects," Skye said. "Things to look at."

Simon regarded her with bloodshot eyes. He seemed so weary. Life—drinking, art, trying to love Skye—had taken a toll on him, and it showed. His dark hair was long and stringy. He seemed to be making up his mind about something. He was letting her see his thought process: Should I stay or should I go? Simon liked to play with her mind. The worst part was, Skye felt too weak to fight him.

"This, then," Simon said, putting down the stone and picking up the shotgun shell. "Why do you keep it?"

"To remind me of the deer it killed," Skye said, picturing the moonlit night on the mountain, the doe thrashing against the tall rocks, the black blood pouring out of her throat, the sound of the dying deer's hooves spasmodically clicking against the boulder. The first creature she had ever shot. For a long time, just looking at the shell could bring tears to her eyes.

"This," he said, touching the white feather.

"It came from a swan," Skye said. "My father gave one to each of us the night he took us to *Swan Lake*."

"He gave you swan feathers," Simon said, pursing his lips, fascinated by any story about Hugh Renwick, no matter how obscure.

"To remind us of nature. That nature was the great inspiration, love and nature—even for Tchaikovsky."

"Took you to the ballet and gave you swan feathers. Awesome," Simon said, shaking his head. "The snake."

"The snake reminds me of danger," Skye said. "To be careful."

She stared at the snake's skeleton. It was long and sinuous, the largest object on her table. Its skull was flat and triangular. From a different angle, if you could look into its mouth, you would see its fangs.

"Is that the one that bit you?"

"No," Skye said. "One like it."

Simon touched Skye's head. She felt his fingers running through her hair, pushing it behind her ears. She closed her eyes and tried to prevent the shiver that shook her entire body. She remembered sleeping in her tent, feeling the snakes writhing under the polythene sheet beneath her.

"When the poison took hold," he said, "did it feel warm and sleepy, like scotch? Like smoking a joint?"

"No," Skye said. "It felt black, and it hurt. I felt the air being squeezed out of me, and I thought I was going to die. But Caroline sucked it out."

Simon made his fingers feel soft and boneless against the back of her neck, as if he wanted her to think of snakes. Skye flinched uncontrollably.

"Your father left you all alone. With no one but Caroline to look after you. And Clea, only I'll bet she never even left her tent. He should have dropped her off in the suburbs. Talk about the blind leading the stupid."

"Stop, Simon."

She stared at the sculpture she had started days earlier. The three sisters. Caroline, Clea, and Skye. Huddled together, three lumps of clay, protecting each other on the mountain.

"Caroline was older. She should have known that you

were going to pitch your tent right over a fissure like that. Didn't she see it?" he asked.

"It was covered with grass," Skye said. "Soft mountain grass. She thought it would feel good under my tent, like a mattress. There wasn't much grass on the mountain."

"A rattlesnake den," Simon said, beginning to touch her neck again. "You must have freaked when they came up through the hole. After dark, all alone in your tent, your sisters in theirs. Poor Skye. You must have gone crazy, feeling those things wriggling around under your sleeping bag. Hey, maybe Caroline got a kick out of it. She might have known, told you to put your tent there on purpose. Sick of being your mother."

"She never would."

"That's right. Saint Caroline. What's the blue ribbon?"

"Oh, the ribbon," she said, not wanting to remember. "I wore it one day."

"With another man?" Simon asked. "One you liked more than me?"

Skye shook her head.

"Where'd you wear it?"

Skye paused. "To Redhawk," she said.

"The mountain," Simon said. "The weekend you shot the guy?"

"Yes."

"I'm married to a killer," he whispered in her ear.

Skye felt the tears in her eyes. She stared at the ribbon. She had worn her hair long then, tied back in a ponytail to keep it out of her eyes. So her aim would be better.

"Do you ever feel powerful?" Simon whispered. "Knowing that you took a life?"

"No, I feel horrible," she whispered back.

"I know you do. I know how much you've suffered for it. But deep inside, under all the conscience, isn't there a little part of you that feels like God? The part that craves experience . . . wants to feel everything intensely?"

"No, Simon," Skye said. She stared at the blue ribbon. The dark spot on one end, the patch of faded rust, was Andrew Lockwood's blood. While Caroline sat beside him, holding his hand as he died, Skye had bent down to catch Homer, and her ribbon had trailed through the blood.

"The hell you don't."

"You're my husband, you should know me by now," Skye said, her voice now shaking. She couldn't go on talking about this; she needed a drink. She wanted to feel the warm relief spreading through her head, taking the excruciating thoughts away.

"Show me you love me," he said, pressing down on her shoulders. "Come on, show me."

She climbed off her stool, falling to her knees.

Kneeling before Simon, she wrapped her arms around his waist. She placed her cheek against his thigh. She felt tired and sick. More than anything, she wanted to disappear, and she thought: How did I ever let this happen? How did I ever turn into a woman who feels this way, does these things?

"Do you want to?" he asked.

"Yes," she whispered, the lie easier than the truth.

He tangled his fingers in her hair and pulled her head back. She felt tears on her lashes. She tasted salt in her throat. He's my husband, she thought. Is this love? I'm just doing this so we won't have to talk anymore. She reached for his zipper. She tugged it down, reached inside.

Homer nuzzled her face, his big brown eyes so friendly, gazing at her with unconditional love.

"Hey, boy," she said.

"Jesus Christ," Simon snapped. "Get him out of here."

Skye tried to push Homer away, but he wouldn't go. Skye noticed that his ears were nearly bald, like a stuffed animal who had been loved so hard, his fur had worn off. Homer sidled between Skye and Simon. He pushed against Skye, edging her away from Simon.

"What the fuck," Simon said, giving Homer a swat.

The old dog just stood there, looking up at Simon with dignity in his cloudy brown eyes. Simon raised his hand again. Homer didn't flinch. He didn't bare his teeth, and he didn't wag his tail. He just stared at Simon as if he expected the worst from such a man.

"Don't hit him," Skye said.

"He ruined it," Simon snapped, zipping up his pants. "Her fucking dog ruined it. Jesus. Caroline couldn't have done better if she was here herself."

Skye felt like laughing. She kept her head down, feeling the laughter exploding in her chest, and she wondered if she was losing her mind. She was a hung-over drunk who wanted to get drunker, who'd rather do what her husband told her than face the fact she didn't like him, and she was under the protection of her sister's sweet golden retriever.

Simon stormed out of the studio. Skye heard the door slamming behind him, his footsteps on the stairs, heard him start the car and drive away. Homer lay on the floor beside her. He had long since forgiven her for the accident that had brought them together. Lying down beside him, her cheek on the cool stone floor and her hand on Homer's paw, Skye closed her eyes and wished she could forgive herself.

* * *

Caroline surveyed the inn grounds. The Firefly Ball would start at dusk, and she wanted to make sure everything was ready. A white film of heat clung to the trees, the lanterns, the inn itself. Long white linen tablecloths wafted desultorily in the slight breeze. The band had set up. The bass player stood alone onstage, shirtless in the hot sun, testing the sound system.

Bars were set up at either side of the dance floor. Champagne was chilling in the barn, waiting to be wheeled out after dark. Caroline approached Michele, who was running around with a clipboard.

"Tell the bartenders I don't want them to serve Skye," Caroline said.

"What?" Michele asked.

"She's been sick. She's not supposed to drink alcohol with her medication," Caroline said.

Michele saw through the lie. But she was loyal to Caroline, and she knew how worried she had been. "I'll tell them," she said. "Will your mother be here?"

"Of course," Caroline said, a smile breaking through the stress. "Augusta wouldn't miss it for anything."

"The guys from the boat said you invited them—" Michele said, "—the treasure hunters. They're all excited."

"Really?" Caroline asked.

"Yes, and, Caroline?"

Caroline turned to look at Michele. Michele held her clipboard to her breast. She was smiling like a proud parent.

"You look beautiful."

"Thank you," Caroline said, blushing. Knowing how much she had to do, she had dressed for the ball early. Her dark hair was swept up in a French twist. She wore a long white dress with a rustling sweep to the skirt, and no jewelry except pearl earrings.

"Are you supposed to be any painting in particular? Your father's *Girl in a White Dress?*"

"I hadn't planned it that way," Caroline said. But she knew it was true. She knew that she had dressed as herself in the famous picture painted by her father.

"That's the same dress you wore, isn't it?" Michele asked.

"No," Caroline said. The white dress she had worn

while her father painted that portrait had been given away long ago, donated to the Wadsworth Atheneum for an exhibition of garments worn in famous paintings. But looking down, she realized this dress was very similar.

"So many people will recognize the picture," Michele said. "I think it's your father's best-known."

"You're probably right," Caroline agreed, adjusting a bouquet of flowers on one of the tables. But she knew she hadn't chosen her father's painting because it was well known, because a great number of guests would recognize it. She had chosen to wear the white dress because one person would recognize it.

Caroline knew Joe Connor had seen her portrait at the Met. She knew because he had told her so. It was a small thing, but it was a connection. And connections were sometimes all that counted.

September 8, 1979

Dear Joe,

I have something to tell you. It has to be in person. Why is Newport so far from Black Hall? Hurry! But make sure you're safe.

Love,
Caroline

September 30, 1979

Dear C,

Actually, Newport isn't at all far from Black Hall. The problem is, you're there and I'm here. Until we're both here or both there; well, you get the idea. A new mainsail costs more than I have at the moment.

What do you have to tell me? I think I might know, because I want to tell you the same thing. Sometimes I feel as if I don't have anyone but you, C. My mother has her new family—Sam and his father. I live here, but I don't belong the same way as Sam.

It's different with you. You make me smile like no one else. Every time I see your handwriting, I know everything's going to be okay. There's one person in the world I trust, and it's you. I know this is a long letter, but it's late and I can't sleep. I'm thinking of you, Caroline. I wish you were here. I might as well say it.

I love you.
Joe

CHAPTER THIRTEEN

ALL DAY THE TEMPERATURE HAD HOVERED IN THE nineties, and at dusk the sky was pearl white, the sun a shimmering red ball. As the sun set, the moon rose. It climbed high and white in the hazy dark sky, and beneath it the paper lanterns illuminated the Firefly Ball as music filled the night.

The raw bar glistened with fresh clams and oysters on ice. Caroline and Michele had arranged some of the shellfish like a painting by Degas. The guests had created haystacks after Monet, erected beach umbrellas and white tents after Boudin. Candles twinkled, and the band played "Every Time We Say Good-bye."

Guests milled about, dressed as their favorite paintings. Many of the costumes were old-fashioned, *The Luncheon of the Boating Party* by Renoir and *Madame X* by Sargent, the graceful long dresses, providing the most inspiration for the women. May Taylor came as the Hugh Renwick portrait of her grandmother Emily Dunne, founder of the Bridal Barn. Her russet hair piled high, she looked sweet and elegant at once. Clea and Peter came dressed as an Irish couple from Hugh Renwick's *Galway Dance*, and Skye and Simon came in black, as themselves. Having made another of their unstable, uneasy truces, they came together, with Augusta, and they took a table between the river and the dance floor.

Caroline saw her family arrive. She hung back, watching. Caroline did not know what to say to Skye. She knew her so well and loved her so much. But somehow they had lost the ability to communicate. Their last few times together, they might as well have been speaking different languages.

"Caroline!" Augusta called, spotting her.

Smiling, Caroline went to join her family. Augusta looked mischievous, dressed in her harlequin costume and her black pearls. Everyone rose, and she kissed her mother, her sisters, and their husbands. They complimented one another on their costumes, and everyone remarked on the beautiful job Caroline had done with the ball.

"Your father would be so proud," Augusta said, squeezing her hand. Behind her harlequin mask, her eyes glistened. Augusta grew more sentimental every year. "You should give yourself a lot of credit, honey."

"Thanks, Mom," Caroline said, pleased. Her parents' approval had always mattered to her and it always would.

"That dress," Augusta said, gazing at Caroline. "It's remarkably like the one you wore . . . do you remember that sitting? On the porch at Firefly Hill?"

"Yes, I remember." How could she forget? It was late in the year, the last weekend before it snowed. Andrew Lockwood had been dead a month, and the family was in shock. It was the last real painting her father had ever done. When he completed *Girl in a White Dress,* he put away his paints for good.

"It finished him, Caroline," Augusta said.

"What did?"

"That painting. It took all he had. When he was done, he said he had nothing left inside. He was never really himself after that. But he caught something. . . ."

Caroline took a second look at her mother. She sounded bitter, as if Caroline's costume had reminded her of too much loss, misfortune, and injustice regarding her and Hugh.

"Caught what?"

"That quality you have inside. That reserve . . ."

"My coldness?" Caroline said with a touch of fear, remembering what Skye had said, wanting to be contradicted.

"No. You were young and emotional, and you were holding it all inside. The effect was very mysterious and alluring. I remember looking at the face your father painted and knowing the world would think he was in love with her. The girl in the picture."

"Mom!" Caroline said.

Augusta turned away to hide the harsh disappointment in her eyes. If Caroline hadn't known better, she would have said her mother's sour tone was jealousy. But it couldn't be.

"*Girl in a White Dress.* You look beautiful," Skye said quietly. She had a glass in her hand; it looked like mineral water.

"So do you," Caroline said.

They were shy with each other, two dogs circling. Clea leaned forward. "Listen," she said. The band was playing "Goodnight, My Someone." Skye had sung it in eighth grade, in her spring concert, and Caroline and Clea had skipped out of high school to sneak in and hear her. The song united the sisters in an old memory, and Caroline and Skye tried to smile at each other.

"Goodness," Augusta said. "Look!"

The crew from the *Meteor* had arrived. A band of pirates, dressed in torn shirts, eye patches, and salty trousers, they shouldered their way through the crowd to the bar. Polite clusters of guests parted quickly, as if the men were real pirates. The crewmates grouped at the bar, grabbing beers and surveying the party.

"Are they supposed to be here?" Augusta asked dubiously.

"They're friends of Caroline's," Clea said.

The skinniest pirate slapped his beer down on the bar and began making his way over. He moved with purpose, homing in on Caroline, as if he were swinging across the deck on a shredded topgallant. Dressed with a red kerchief tied over his short blond hair, a white shirt with comically billowing arms, Sam stood before Caroline with his hands on his hips.

"Ahoy!" he said. He had an eye patch over the left lens of his wire-rimmed glasses.

"Hi, Sam," Caroline said. "This is my family. Everyone, this is Sam Trevor." She sounded normal, and she smiled at Sam, but inside she felt something change. Sam was here, and so was Joe, and Joe's presence made everything different.

"I'm here to keep up the bad name of pirates everywhere," Sam said apologetically.

"By doing what?"

"Kidnapping you," Sam said, holding out his hand, "for a dance."

Caroline followed Sam onto the dance floor. The band was playing medium-slow, and they had plenty of room to move. Sam did his best; he really did. He knew where to put his hands and how to move his feet, but he lurched to a completely different rhythm than Caroline and the music. Caroline saw the embarrassment in his face. She adjusted her movement to his, overwhelmingly fond of him for trying.

"Sorry," he said, his face red.

"For what? I wanted to dance with you," Caroline said.

"It's dangerous, dancing with me," Sam said. "I trip."

"Do you like music?"

"I love it," he said.

"That's all that counts," Caroline said as if she were talking to a younger brother. "Just enjoy yourself."

"Thanks," Sam said. They danced silently for a minute. His muscles relaxed slightly, and he didn't seem as tense. But his rhythm was just as bad. As they moved around the dance floor, Caroline looked through the crowd. She saw the pirates drinking at the bar, but she didn't see Joe.

"How's the wreck?" Caroline asked.

"Cool. I dove on it twice this week. Joe took me down."

"Oh. Is he . . ."

There he was, the head pirate. Joe Connor stood off to the side, leaning against a tree. He wore a white shirt, ripped at the shoulders and chest. His black pants were tight, his feet were bare. He had on a black hat, low over one eye. The sight of him made Caroline shiver, as if the temperature had just dropped twenty degrees.

"We found skeletal remains," Sam was saying. "Partially buried in sediment and remarkably well preserved. We've retrieved quite a bit of the gold, in fact. . . ."

As Sam spoke, he became more excited and his dancing deteriorated. They wheeled around, and Caroline lost sight of Joe. When Sam twirled her back, she saw him again. He had started to move through the crowd. His blue eyes were dark, and they were on her. People stepped aside, watching him pass. He had an air of serious danger about him, as real as any pirate's.

The night smelled of honeysuckle and rosemary. Sam saw Joe coming, and he grinned. Caroline felt the heat spread through her chest.

"Would you like to dance?" Joe asked, looking straight at her.

"I have to let him, or he'll make me walk the plank," Sam said, stepping aside.

Caroline stood still, listening to the music play. People danced around them, jostling her. She was dimly aware of them and of Sam walking away. Joe watched her with dark eyes. He didn't appear to expect or want anything. He might have been a stranger, cutting in. Caroline nod-ded. Joe stepped forward, took her into his arms.

His body curved over hers, and she had to steady herself, catching her breath. They danced together, so close she could feel his breath warm against her ear. The music was slow and sweet. They did not speak, but Caroline loved the way they moved, like grass in a current, with grace and rhythm. Her throat ached, and she didn't know why.

"Thanks for dancing with Sam," he said after a minute.

"I wanted to," she said, surprised.

"The kid can't dance. He's got two left feet."

"He tries though. That's the important thing," Caroline said. Looking around Joe's shoulder, she could see her family. Simon and Skye had left the table. She hoped they would come dance, but Simon headed for the bar, and Skye stood off to the side, watching.

"Sam said you took him down to the wreck," Caroline said, wanting to put Skye out of her mind for now.

"Yeah."

"You showed him the bones?"

"Yes," Joe said, holding Caroline tighter.

She felt his arms around her bare shoulders, his mouth against her ear. He held her hand against his chest in his rough and scraped hand. Her fingers trailed through the hair on his chest and rested against his warm skin. She felt the tension in her own body and sensed it in his. They stopped talking. The music played, and Caroline rested her cheek against Joe's chest. She closed her eyes and wondered whether he could feel her heart pounding against his.

Augusta milled around. She drank martinis. As Hugh Renwick's widow she was a big hit. She found herself telling a group of young artists that the glass in her hand had actually once belonged to Hugh.

"Hugh Renwick drank from that glass?" a young man asked reverently. Like Augusta, he was dressed as a Picasso: the bull in *Guernica*. He wore a silly, lopsided mask of papier-mâché, but he looked adorable from the neck down in toreador clothes.

"Yes, he did," Augusta lied. "Would you care to sip from Hugh's hallowed goblet?"

"If it would make me paint like Hugh Renwick," the man said, eagerly taking the glass in both hands as if it were in some way holy, trying to make it meet his lips through the absurd bull mouth-hole.

"I can't guarantee that, dear," Augusta said wryly. "Hugh would be very displeased with both of us, dressed as Picassos instead of Renwicks. He loathed Paul, you know."

"Paul?" the bull asked.

"Picasso, dear," Augusta said, glancing around for her daughters. There were Clea and Peter, so sweetly social, just as adult children should be at fancy dress balls. Skye had wandered off somewhere, making Augusta distinctly nervous. She spied Simon, flirting with a young waitress, drawing her out with that passive-aggressive depression of his. Caroline was dancing with someone, blocked from Augusta's sight by the crowd.

"I would have come as a Renwick," the bull was saying, "but he did mainly landscapes and women. I didn't feel like coming as a red barn or a nude female."

"One understands," Augusta said, spotting Caroline.

She excused herself from the bull and paused to watch her oldest daughter. Caroline looked exquisite tonight. She radiated from within; her skin glowed like a peach, her wide eyes were clear and beautiful, her white dress fit her perfectly. Augusta felt stinging remorse for the old jealousy she had felt earlier. But it was true: *Girl in a White Dress,* coming so soon after the death of that young man, had finished Hugh. And Augusta had so desperately wished it had been she in the portrait, her husband's most famous picture.

When the crowd parted, Augusta got a good look at the man Caroline was dancing with.

He was the handsomest man Augusta Renwick had seen in years: over six feet tall with broad shoulders. He was one of the pirates. He looked physical enough to be a workman, but he carried it off with a sort of throw-away elegance. He had a sailor's tan and the clearest blue eyes Augusta had ever seen. But the thing that shocked her was the way he was looking at Caroline. His expression was fierce and wild, full of craving and longing.

"Mother?"

Augusta felt Clea's hand on her arm.

"Darling, who is that man with Caroline?"

"A pirate."

"I can see that. But who is he?"

"Just a friend, I think. Mom, have you seen Skye?"

"They're acting like lovers. Just look at the way he's staring at her."

"It's a slow dance. Mom . . ."

"I'm looking for Skye myself," Augusta said. She tore her gaze away from Caroline and her pirate to glance around. She sipped her martini, feeling disturbed. Was it more jealousy or just missing Hugh? She looked over again. The yearning in the man's eyes was matched by that in Caroline's and reminded Augusta of how passion ately she had desired her husband, how intensely she had feared losing him.

"She seemed quiet," Clea said. "Is she upset about something?"

Augusta sighed. Why couldn't they just have fun? Why did everything have to become so serious and moody? She hadn't raised her girls this way. She had given them free rein.

While other mothers watched every move, Augusta had let her daughters explore and grow. She had fought her protective instincts and allowed Hugh to take the girls hunting. He had wanted to teach them to fend for themselves, and she thought he had done it. All those nights alone on the mountain! Yet here they were, worried about Skye just because she had wandered out of sight.

"I'm sure she's fine," Augusta said.

"Look at Simon," Clea said.

He was leading the waitress onto the dance floor. She had left her drink tray on a table, kicked her shoes off, melted into his arms. Simon was smoking a cigarette. He talked with it in his mouth, the blue smoke curling into his eyes. Augusta thought he looked evil, dirty, and stupid.

"Why did Skye marry him?" Clea asked. "It's as if she deliberately picked the one man who would treat her the worst."

Augusta groaned, watching Simon's hands on the waitress's hips. "Your father would kill him," Augusta said.

"He'd kill Skye," Clea said. "He was so adamant about men, about us being strong and not being victims of anyone. That's all he wanted to teach us."

"He taught *you*," Augusta said. Hugh had cheated on Augusta, claimed he couldn't help himself, it was what men did. But more than anything, he had wanted to save his daughters from getting hurt.

"Taught me?" Clea asked.

"You married a good man. Dear Peter," Augusta said. "You're the only one. Skye married a bastard, and Caroline's all alone."

But even as Augusta spoke, she and Clea watched Caroline on the dance floor in the arms of the pirate. He looked like everything Hugh Renwick would warn her against. He was big and cool, with a wicked sexual intensity, and he had his arms wrapped around Caroline as if he had hunted her down and intended to own her. But the strange thing, the factor Augusta couldn't quite believe and had to check with a closer look, was the expression in his eyes.

The pirate dancing with Augusta's daughter looked for all the world as if he had fallen in love.

The song ended. Caroline stepped back. Joe stood still, not saying anything. He wanted to ask her to dance again. But this was her inn and her ball, and she probably had a million things to do. Guys were milling around, probably wanting to dance with her. But she didn't move. She just stood there. She was wearing that white dress Joe remembered from her father's painting, and all he wanted was to take her down to the river alone and dance with her there.

"Thank you," he said finally.

"Oh," she said. "It was fun."

Joe stared at her. It was strange; he didn't feel angry. Not at all. For the first time in a lot of years, he could think of Caroline Renwick and not feel the resentment rising. The opposite. He felt an unfamiliar tenderness, and it made him so uncomfortable he took a step backward.

"Well," she said.

The music was starting again. The paper lanterns swung in a light gust of breeze. Joe cleared his throat.

Caroline watched him, expectant. He reached into his pocket. He had brought something from the boat to show her, and his fingers closed around it now. He could ask her to dance again, hand it to her while they moved to the music. He could try to tell her what finding it had made him feel. . . .

Someone bumped him from behind.

Her brother-in-law, the creep Joe had seen drinking with Skye at the bar one week before, jostled into Joe, then Caroline. The guy had the smell of booze and drugs coming out of him. He was so busy feeling up the girl he was dancing with, he hardly noticed his own clumsiness.

"Oops," the girl said, eye to eye with Caroline.

"Where's Skye?" Caroline asked Simon, ignoring the waitress.

"She needed a walk," Simon said, the cigarette still in his mouth. Joe wanted to jam it down his throat and tell him to go find his wife.

"Dora, aren't you supposed to be working?" Caroline asked, barely controlling her fury.

"Sorry," Dora said, flying off the dance floor.

"I'm worried about Skye," Caroline said to Simon. "I want us to find her."

"I'm not her keeper," he said, watching the waitress from behind. "Neither are you."

"Doesn't mean you can't look for her," Joe said. "Especially if your sister-in-law asks you to."

"Who the fuck—" Simon asked, aggression making the cords in his neck stand out. He had the look of a beater in his eyes. He was small and mean, and Joe hardly had to use his imagination to see him hitting Skye. Quietly, Joe put himself between Simon and Caroline.

"Just look, Simon. Okay?" Caroline asked tensely.

"Fine," Simon said, throwing his cigarette on the floor. He walked away, leaving it burning. Caroline gave Joe an apologetic glance and followed him. Joe put out the cigarette in an ashtray on the bar. He stared after Caroline and then he went the other way. To look for Skye.

* * *

The log stretched across the stream. It had been there for some time. Sticks, feathers, and debris had caught on stray branches protruding from one end. The stream flowed beneath the log, lazy and blackish-green, just before it widened and joined the Connecticut River. Pine trees grew thick along one bank, while reeds whispered along the other.

Skye stood at one end of the log. The breeze ruffled her black dress. It tickled her bare legs. She watched the water move. A fish came to the surface, making rings in the dark water. Skye stared at the rings. She remembered a night on a different riverbank two hundred miles to the north. The stars had blazed low over the curving hills. Her father had dropped them off hungry, to make them hunt for their food. Sharpening a stick, she had waited in the rushes.

The frog was fat. She knew she was supposed to kill it. Stabbing down, she impaled its white moon body. Her father had shown her how to build a fire, and he had told her that cooking a frog was no different than cooking a fish. But somehow it was. The big frog had sleepy eyes and a smiling mouth. After she stabbed it, it twitched and gasped. As weak and hungry as she was, Skye had gone without eating. She had killed an animal for nothing.

"Not the last time," she said out loud now.

Haze hung over the stream, and Skye balanced on

the log. She held the silver flask in her hand. Music from the ball came through the trees; she could almost imagine she was at the ballet. Skye was *in* the ballet; standing on one foot, she twirled to the music and took a sip of vodka. Russian vodka, appropriate for *Swan Lake*.

Fireflies blinked in the trees. Skye took another drink. Knowing how worried Caroline was, how much she wanted to keep Skye from drinking, Skye had brought her own. She didn't want Caroline to feel compromised, serving Skye liquor she believed would harm her.

On the other hand, Skye did not want to be observed swigging from a flask. So here she was in the woods, dancing on a fallen log, remembering the first and only time their father had taken them to the ballet. *Swan Lake*. The dying swan. Wishing he'd taken them to more ballets, fewer hunts, Skye paradoxically hated *Swan Lake*. Tragically beautiful, it rang too many bells.

"The dance is over there."

The deep voice came from the shadows. Skye was so startled, she nearly fell off the log. Backing away from the sound, she felt the panic in her chest.

"Who's that?" she asked.

A man stepped forward, watching her with racy blue eyes. Tall, with a ripped shirt that revealed tan shoulders, he appeared menacing. He was dressed like a pirate; he didn't even seem to be wearing a costume.

"Don't fall," he said.

"Stay away," Skye said.

"I will."

Skye weaved on the log. The water was only six feet down. If he came toward her, she could jump. The black water would close over her head. She could hold her breath, swim for shore. The dying, stupid swan. She could play that role. The vodka she had already drunk made her dizzy.

"Sit down," the man said.

"Don't come any closer," she warned. Was he trying to help? Or would he grab her from behind, rip off her dress, hold his hand over her mouth to stifle her screams? The thought, blasting out of nowhere, made Skye turn and run. Her foot caught on a broken branch, and she started to fall.

The man caught her. He took two steps, and he was there. His arms around her, trying to steady her. Skye fought. She screamed, scratched him, tore at his eyes. They thrashed on the log, the man somehow keeping balance for both of them.

"Get away from me," she cried, grabbing his face.

"Skye—"

"I swear, I'll kill you, don't think I won't—" Skye said. Had he just said her name?

"Skye, sit down," he said. "It's okay, you're safe. Just sit down, for God's sake."

"Who the hell are you?"

The man gripped her upper arms. Skye's feet were barely touching the log. He held her steady. She had scratched his face; he was bleeding. Shaking uncontrollably, she looked into his face. It was familiar. Skye didn't know how she knew him, but she had seen him somewhere.

"Sit down, okay?" he asked cautiously. He touched his cheek, looked at the blood.

Skye's head throbbed. Her throat ached. Her stomach lurched, and she retched into the water. She didn't trust him for a second, but she didn't have a choice. Drunk, she felt wobbly and sick. She wanted a fast slug of vodka, but she had dropped her flask. The man helped her sit on the log.

Skye sobbed.

The man reached into his pocket, then handed her a handkerchief. "Here," he said.

Skye shook her head. She opened her eyes, looked around for the flask. Maybe it hadn't fallen into the stream.

"It's gone," the man said. "I saw it go in."

Skye gave him a desperate look. How did he know what she was looking for? Leaning forward, she saw the blood running down his cheek. She covered her eyes and moaned.

"Let's get off the log," he said. Offering her his hand, he waited for her.

"Why do you look so familiar?" Skye asked, trying to decide.

"I saw you at the inn the other night. You were at the bar with your husband."

Skye stared at him. That wasn't it. She knew his face, and she had known it for a long time. He was older now, but those blue eyes . . . the strong jaw, the straight nose. She blinked at him, trying to remember. She reached through the haze of vodka, past the fear of his unexpected presence.

"No," she said. She still felt afraid, but something about his blue eyes steadied her, reassured her that he wouldn't hurt her. She gave him her hand. He helped her off the log. The ground felt steady under her feet, but the sky moved overhead. She swayed,

"Skye, I know you can't hear me right now," he said roughly.

"I hear you," she said.

"No, you're drunk," he said. "But later, when you sober up, I want you to remember something."

"I'm not drunk—" Skye said.

"Yeah, you are. But tomorrow, when your head's

pounding and you're throwing up and you want to die, remember something, okay?"

"What?" she asked, her fingers trembling.

"You never have to feel this way again."

"Don't—"

"There's a way out," he said.

The man's eyes were deep and direct. He held Skye by her shoulders, and even though his voice was rough, it came out kind. He looked calm. Skye knew she knew him from somewhere, but the strangest part was, he sounded as if he knew her even better. She almost had it; she stared, trying so hard to remember.

They walked back to the party. The man held back branches so Skye could pass. They emerged from the woods, and almost immediately Caroline came walking over. She looked at Skye, then past her at the man. His eyes changed then. They had been hard, almost angry in their intensity, but they softened when Caroline came into view.

"Skye," she said, and Skye stepped into her arms.

Holding Caroline made her feel safe. Skye trembled from the vodka she had drunk and the shock of meeting a strange man in the woods, from dancing to *Swan Lake* and from remembering another time Caroline had held her close in other woods.

"You found her," Caroline was saying.

"Yes."

"Thank you," Caroline said. Skye's head was against her sister's chest, and she could feel Caroline shaking.

"Who are you?" Skye asked. "I know you . . ."

"Skye, this is Joe Connor," Caroline said.

The name sparked something deep inside. Skye tilted her head, looked at Caroline. She may have been holding Skye's hand, but Caroline's eyes were for the man. Overhead, the Japanese lanterns bobbed on the wire, bathing them in blue and red light.

"Oh, I do know you," Skye said, her eyes filling with tears.

Joe didn't smile or move. He stood very still, bleeding from where Skye had scratched him. She thought of that smiling boy in the picture, his wide-open face, his missing-tooth smile, the freckles across his cheeks.

There was nothing wide-open about the man who stood before her now. He's tough, Skye thought. That's what's so different, why I didn't recognize him at all. Life has made him wary. Skye knew, because it had made her that way too.

"Are you okay?" he asked guardedly.

Skye nodded.

"Try to remember what I said. Tomorrow."

Skye lowered her head, ashamed that he had seen her drinking from the flask.

"You were always one of us," Skye whispered.

"What?" Joe asked.

"One of us. You know . . . like a brother. I knew Caroline wrote to you, and I always imagined you knew what it was like."

"Only some of it," he said. "I was on the other side."

Skye shook her head. "No, you weren't. Our parents were, but not us. You were one of us."

It all made such perfect sense now. The summer night was hot, and fireflies were flickering through the trees, and she was standing in a tight circle with Caroline and Joe Connor. They were united by gunshots, other people's deaths.

Her mother was coming across the lawn. Simon was with her, a sullen expression on his face. Skye could feel his anger from there, and it made her stomach tighten. She would pay for his humiliation later. Clea and Peter were right behind them. Tagging along was a young man, bedecked in his pirate kerchief and black eye patch.

"Good God, where was she?" Augusta said. "I looked

up, saw her stumbling out of the woods with this pirate—"

Skye saw her mother glaring at Joe.

"First I see him dancing with Caroline, and the next thing I know, he's coming out of the woods with Skye!" Augusta said.

"Mom, he helped me," Skye said quickly to stop the innuendo. "I nearly fell in the water."

"What the fuck, Skye," Simon asked, yanking her arm. "A liaison in the woods?"

"Watch your mouth, tough guy," Joe said, calmly prying Simon's fingers off Skye's arm.

Simon was high. Skye could see it in his eyes. They glittered with violent rage, but he was too shocked by the rebuke to reply.

"Well, thank you," Augusta said properly, restoring decorum to the situation. "For helping my daughter. Mr.—?"

"Joe Connor," he said.

The name hung in the air.

"Connor?" Augusta asked.

"Yes," he said.

"Connor." Augusta repeated the word, the cold truth dawning in her eyes.

"That's right."

"Not James Connor's son?" Augusta asked with disbelief.

"Yes. He was my father." Joe sounded tougher than ever, as if he were ready for a fight. The anger was back in his eyes. Caroline stepped forward, trying to head off the confrontation, but Joe looked past her.

"Good God," Augusta said, her eyes filling with pain.

"Mrs. Renwick," Sam Trevor said, drawing himself up to his full height. He adopted the tone of peacemaker, firm but kind. "The past is the past. You have great daughters, we're just getting to know each other. Joe and I are friends of Caroline's. She invited us here."

"I did, Mom," Caroline said kindly. "Please, they're my friends . . ."

Augusta gave her a strange look, as if she had just betrayed the family and did not even realize it. She glanced at Sam, trying to make sense of what he had just said. Then she put her hand on Caroline's wrist.

"Do you remember what happened? I know you do . . . how terrible it was. His father hurt us all so badly. Please, walk away with me. Right now."

"Mom, listen," Caroline said, throwing a look at Joe, stepping forward to stop her mother from going on.

"To what?" Augusta asked desperately. "Words don't matter. They can't take away all the damage he did. I was a mother with young children, and he came into our house to kill us."

"But he didn't, Mom," Caroline pleaded.

"Murder in his heart," Augusta said.

"That's my father you're talking about," Joe said, holding her gaze.

"Your father . . ." Augusta said.

"Joe," Sam said calmly.

"I'm sorry he threatened your daughters. But I can't have you talking about him that way. Do you understand?"

"What I understand," Augusta said shakily, "is that I don't want you anywhere near my daughter."

"Come on, Sam," Joe said, turning.

"Joe, hang on, man," Sam said, still thinking there was a chance for peace.

Joe kept walking. He did not apologize to Augusta. He did not say good-bye to Clea and Peter, did not wait for his brother. He did not throw Simon a final look of disdain. He did not remind Skye of what he had said earlier. But mainly, even through Skye's drunken haze she could see he did not say good-bye to Caroline.

Caroline watched him go. Her hand on her breast, darkly elegant with her hair upswept and her white dress wrapping her long legs, she stood in the center of her family with an expression of total despair in her eyes, watching Joe Connor walk away.

November 1, 1979

Dear Joe,

I've never felt this way before. When I opened your last letter, I was ready to laugh because you're always so funny, or learn something new about you, or hear something about Sam.

But I didn't expect to read what I've been feeling. I love you too, Joe. I know we're young, we hardly know each other, we've never even met. Why don't any of those things matter to me?

Paintings are so strange. Sometimes I'll stand in a gallery, looking at a picture of a girl. She'll be sitting in a chair, or looking out a window, or walking on a beach, and I'll get a funny feeling in my throat. Somehow I'll know she's in love. I've always wondered how I knew that, because I'd never felt it before.

Now I do, and I know I was right all along. When I see those paintings, look at those girls, it's like looking in the mirror. It's like seeing myself, thinking of you. In love with you, Joe. I am.

C.

CHAPTER FOURTEEN

"HOW COULD YOU, CAROLINE?" AUGUSTA ASKED.

They were in the herb garden at Firefly Hill, the scent of verbena strong in the salt air. Waves broke on the shoal, rolled into the beach with a gentle rush. Offshore, the *Meteor* glistened and the blue water sparkled in the bright sun. Caroline couldn't bear to see it. She turned her back, facing her mother.

"I don't even know what you mean, Mom. Joe's my friend now. I wanted him there."

Augusta shook her head. She wore a long muslin dress and a straw sun hat. She huddled on the garden bench, fidgeting with her black pearls. Bending over, she pulled weeds from the bed of thyme and burnet. Then she stopped and rearranged a small cluster of scallop shells.

"Inviting him to the ball . . ." Augusta went on as if Caroline had not spoken. "Making him welcome when his family is responsible for so much unhappiness. So much unhappiness."

"His family?"

"You know what I mean," Augusta said, pulling off her dark glasses, gazing at Caroline with injured eyes. "His mother seduced your father. It's so ugly. It hurt me so much. Your father had an affair, honey. It broke my heart, and it drove her husband crazy. Literally crazy. He came here to our house," Augusta said, pointing at the kitchen door, "and killed himself in front of my babies."

"How long ago, Mom?" Caroline asked sharply. "How many years ago did that happen?"

"It doesn't matter how many years. We're still feeling the aftershocks. I came close to ending my marriage over it, Caroline. Your father took it into his head to teach you and your sisters to shoot, and your sister killed a man. Violence begets violence, and his father started the cycle."

"Dad did," Caroline said. "If you want to go back that far. By having the affair in the first place."

"This is getting us nowhere," Augusta said.

"Are Joe and I supposed to pay for *your* past?"

"I'm worried sick about Skye," Augusta said. "And now I'm worried about your judgment."

"Don't," Caroline snapped.

"You'll get hurt," Augusta said.

"I'm strong, Mom," Caroline said.

"I know. And we all rely on you," Augusta said. "Maybe too much." She reached across the garden bench to pat Caroline's knee, and Caroline took her hand.

How could people feel such powerful and conflicting emotions for each other? How often, when she was young, had Caroline hated her parents, her sisters? While knowing, with all her heart, that she would die for them? She sat beside her mother, smelling the soothing fragrance of sage and rosemary. Her mother softly stroked the back of her hand with her thumb.

"I saw you dancing with him," Augusta said. "Before I realized who he was."

"You did?"

"Mmm. I did. And I thought—" Augusta paused, considering.

"Thought what?"

"Caroline's done it."

Caroline closed her eyes. The breeze blew off the sea, and she lifted her face to feel it. Perhaps it had swept across the decks of the *Meteor,* perhaps it had passed across Joe's boat, his skin . . .

"What did you think I'd done?" Caroline asked.

"Fallen in love with a dangerous man," Augusta said.

Caroline shook her head.

"Like your father. Just as I'd done, as your sister Skye's done . . . I saw the man, the way you were looking at each other. His tallness, his rough body. And that love in his eyes."

Caroline could not move. She let her mother hold her hand, felt the soft pressure of her mother's thumb circling her hand. Augusta's voice broke.

"Maybe that bothers me more than the rest," she said. "You've kept yourself free for so long. Free and safe. Darling, I can't bear to think of you hurt."

"I'm strong, Mom," Caroline said again, her throat aching. It was true. She had learned all the lessons, and she had kept herself free and safe and strong—and alone. Her mother had nothing to worry about. She and Joe could never be together now.

"Thank God, Caroline," Augusta said, sniffling. "Do you forgive me?"

"For what?"

"For last night. Not for my emotions, but my behavior. For being so out of control . . ."

"You were shocked," Caroline said carefully, picturing Joe's face. Sam's. Forgiveness is not the only point, she thought, remembering something Joe had said. First we have to face the truth. It is about understanding. She squeezed her mother's hand, then let it go.

"I was," Augusta said.

"Where's Skye?"

"Inside. Asleep, I think."

"I have to talk to her."

Augusta nodded. She blinked at the sun. As if surprised to find herself sitting in the herb garden, she looked around. She brushed the tops of some lavender, smelled her hand.

"Your grandmother's herbs," she said. Her eyes filled with tears. "Sometimes I miss my mother and grandmother so much. They were wise women. Not like me. They were solid and old-fashioned, real mothers."

"You're a real mother," Caroline said, laughing with surprise.

"But I haven't been a very good one."

"Oh, Mom . . ." Caroline said, her eyes filling because sometimes she had felt the same way.

"I don't know what I'd do without my girls."

"We don't know what we'd do without you," Caroline said.

"Skye . . ." Augusta said, her voice trailing off, her eyes sweeping up the white house to a window where white curtains fluttered in the breeze.

"I know," Caroline said, following her mother's gaze to Skye's bedroom window.

"I've made so many mistakes," Augusta said, her voice thick. "And so much damage has been done."

"So much good too," Caroline said quietly, thinking of last night, of Joe helping Skye, of Sam running to the rescue, of Clea and Peter helplessly looking on. "There is so much in our families that's good."

* * *

Joe stared at the sea. The waves sparkled. The day was as sunny as a summer day got, but the old anger had closed in like fog in Maine. It hung thick and heavy, and it kept him locked in place. He handled his business, but his thoughts kept returning to the Renwicks.

Coming here was a mistake. Diving on the *Cambria*

was a success, but the rest left him muddled and fierce. He had wanted to put some things to rest by facing Black Hall. He had stirred them up instead. His hands in his pocket, he felt something unfamiliar. Frowning, he pulled out the cameo.

Pale and incandescent, the cameo showed the profile of a woman. Her face was noble and proud, with an unmistakable touch of sadness and strength around the mouth. Even on something so old and tiny, the emotion was apparent. Her hair was full, her forehead high. She reminded Joe of Caroline. He scowled.

"Boy, Mrs. Renwick was one mad old lady," Sam said, coming across the deck.

"Yeah," Joe said, slipping the cameo back into his pocket.

"She could go on, couldn't she?"

Joe nodded. He watched gulls gather on a school of feeding blues, the water choppy and silver with thrashing fish. He glanced at Sam. The kid seemed okay, well-adjusted, not too bothered by what had happened. In fact, he had a big grin on his face.

"Kinda spoiled a nice party," Sam said. "Chasing us away like that."

"She was right," Joe said.

"About what?"

"We had no business being there."

Sam raised one eyebrow. Behind his cockeyed glasses, it had the effect of making his frames look straight for once.

"Excuse me," Sam said, "but Caroline invited us."

Joe frowned, watching the gulls gulping down pieces of bait fish. He kept his eyes peeled for sharks. There weren't too many bad species in these waters, but every now and then a mako would come along.

"Well, she did," Sam said.

"I know that, knucklehead. But getting invited isn't

the point. I should have used common sense. We had no place at a Renwick party."

"Mrs. Renwick's just pissed because her husband had a thing for Mom. So what? They had their day, Mom married my dad, Mr. Renwick became the Hemingway of painters, and life went on. What's her big problem?"

"Sam . . ." Joe said warningly. He thought of the bloody details of his father's death, and stared angrily at the waves.

"It's not Caroline's fault, her mother being so jealous and neurotic."

"I know," Joe said. It was neither one of their faults, his nor Caroline's, that they had been born to the parents they had.

"Does this mean you won't be saying yes to Yale?"

Joe shot him a look. "I was never going to say yes to Yale."

"Shit," Sam said. "I had big hopes."

"Yeah? Of what?"

"You getting on the faculty. Putting in a good word for me."

"You don't need any good words from me, Sam," Joe said, a laugh escaping. "You've got plenty of your own."

"Still, it would have been nice. Both of us living in the area, teaching together. I wouldn't mind getting to know you a little better," Sam said, playing with a paper clip he had fished out of his shorts pocket.

"You know me fine," Joe said.

"Yeah, whatever. You left home when I was three. And then the drinking . . ."

The blues kept breaking the water's surface, flashing silver in the sun. The birds were feeding, diving. Joe touched the cameo in his pocket. It felt hot in his hand. He'd go below, look for the gold. *Yale. Jesus Christ.*

"You want to dive?" he asked Sam.

Sam shook his head. He was studying a hangnail that

had apparently been bothering him. "Nah, that's okay. I have work to do. My research . . . got to get back to Nova Scotia soon."

"Yeah, I remember those days." Joe tried a smile. "Got to get the data before your grant runs out."

"No shit," Sam said, trying to smile back. For Sam, it was a weak act. His mouth barely moved. His eyes were bitter with disappointment. He went back to the hangnail. Joe blinked, tried to get interested in watching the birds again, hating himself.

Black Hall.

He remembered his last dive with Sam, when he had found the cameo. The kid had been trying to talk him into Yale that day too. He had been swimming around, making Joe laugh, bubbles floating out of his mouth, silently forming the words with his lips: *Black Hall.*

What the hell was he pushing. That he and Joe should get a place in town, recreate the family life they never had? Teach together? Discuss their classes on the long commute? Become a team of Ivy League, treasure-hunting brothers? Live in Black Hall so Joe could fall in love with Caroline?

Joe exhaled, stood up, and arched his back. It was all a bunch of crap. Sam was a dreamer, and he always had been. He thought Joe didn't know him well, and maybe that was true. But Joe Connor loved his brother Sam as much as he had ever loved anyone—if he even knew what the word meant—and that was even truer.

Glancing across the sea, Joe faced toward Black Hall. He knew she was there. He had seen Caroline's face while her mother was carrying on. Those gray-blue eyes, the color of a safe harbor, so wild with love and worry for her mother and sister, things Joe could understand but had never had time to feel. How could he? Finishing grad school, finding treasure, giving lectures at places like Yale?

Joe had seen. He had looked in Caroline's face and read it all. But he had been powerless to do anything but the thing he did best: walk away.

And he did it again now.

Leaving his brother alone on deck, he turned his back. He touched the cameo in his pocket, and it scorched his hand. The salt wind stung his eyes. It burned the spot where Skye had scratched his face. Black Hall was far away, across the open water. Yale was for academics. Let Sam be the professor. Joe was a treasure hunter, plain and simple.

And treasure hunters worked alone.

* * *

Caroline waited for Clea to arrive.

Augusta had taken her needlepoint into the shade, as if she knew her daughters had something important to talk about that did not include her. Or perhaps she wanted it that way. Caroline and Clea climbed the back stairs. The stairway, dark and cool, smelled of ghosts and summer.

"What are we going to say to her?" Clea asked.

"I don't know."

Augusta had told Caroline that Simon had not come home last night. His car was still missing. Knowing Skye was alone, they walked into the room and stood at the end of her bed, watching her sleep. Caroline's heart was in her throat.

Skye was curled up, a white sheet pulled to her chin. She looked so young. Homer lay at the foot of her bed, curled up in a ball. At the sight of Caroline, he raised his head, eased off the bed, and stretched. His bones were stiff; he moved like a creaky old man. Trudging over to Caroline, he raised his white muzzle to be petted. They looked into each other's eyes, and Caroline saw his throat vibrating with unuttered sound. Her heart filled with love for the dog, and for the girl he had signed on to protect.

"Skye," Caroline said, her voice low.

"Wake up. It's morning," Clea said, in her best mother's voice.

Skye rolled over. She opened her eyes, saw her sisters then closed them again with a moan. Her eyes looked sunken, her mouth tight. She lay still, a rabbit trying to hide.

"Come on, Skye," Caroline said, opening the curtains. "We're going to the beach."

Skye took her time.

She showered. She fixed a cup of coffee, then felt too sick to drink it. She made some calls from the phone in the library—her sisters assumed she was looking for Simon. They did not ask. Simon was irrelevant.

Rocking on the front porch while Clea watered the garden, Caroline remembered going to Firefly Beach as children. She and her sisters had simply pulled on their bathing suits, run outside, flown down the worn cliff stairs. Now she sat with Homer, trying to be patient. He lay on his side with his eyes open, watching her rock back and forth.

But finally Skye was ready, and down the steps they went. Homer went through the garden, smelling all the rosebushes, giving the women a head start.

"I'm sorry about what happened with Joe," Skye began. "I feel like it was my fault that Mom—"

"Stop, Skye," Caroline said. "It wasn't your fault. It doesn't matter anyway. Okay?"

Waves broke just offshore and raced in white trickles over the sand flats of low tide. The sea air felt fresh and cool on their bare arms and legs as they walked through the shallow water. The *Meteor* rocked on her mooring, way offshore, and Caroline tried not to look. She felt uneasy enough.

When they reached a silvery log high above the tide line, deep in the spartina haunted by fireflies, driftwood from many winters ago, they sat down. Sandpipers skittered across the wet sand, and it glistened like a mirror. Skye held her head in her hands. Homer had been making his way slowly down the stairs. The minute his paws hit the sand, he took off in a run, flying down the tide line like a young dog.

Caroline nudged Skye.

Skye raised her head. Her dull eyes suddenly brightened. She smiled, watching Homer chase sea gulls away from a dead horseshoe crab. His shoulders were tired, but his face was proud. Tongue lolling out, he glanced at the sisters.

"Look," Caroline said. "He wants to make sure we see him."

"Good dog!" Clea called. "Scaring all the sea gulls."

He nuzzled the crab carapace. It was a large crab, the size of a dinner plate, its stiff tail a foot long. Turning the creature over, he made sure it wouldn't bite. Then he grabbed the shell in his teeth and carried it, tail swinging like a pendulum, to lay at Caroline's feet.

"He's your dog," Skye said. Caroline knew without looking that Skye was crying.

"He loves you," Caroline said. "He doesn't want you feeling bad all the time."

Skye didn't reply. She stared at the sand between her feet. She used her index finger to wipe her tears.

"What are we going to do, Skye?" Caroline asked.

"Do?" Skye asked, looking up. Her face was flushed, tear-streaked. It bore the brownish remnants of bruises from her car accident.

"Dad died drunk," Caroline said. "We never talk about

it. We say he had stomach cancer, that he died because the radiation didn't work, but that's not the whole truth."

"Stop, Caroline," Skye said.

"Let her, Skye," Clea said.

"You're in on this?" Skye asked, sounding betrayed. Clea nodded.

"Remember his last few months? How he spent all his time at my bar? How he wasn't supposed to have 'cocktails' with his medication, but he did anyway?" Caroline paused, but Skye wouldn't respond. "Drinking made him so mean, and Dad wasn't a mean man."

"He was dying, Caroline."

"But he didn't have to die drunk, Skye. He could have faced the truth, faced us. He could have let us help him. We would have told him it was okay, that we forgave him for whatever he thought we hated him for. Hated himself for."

"Don't say he hated himself," Skye said.

"He did. Last night Mom reminded me of something. He stopped painting. Just *stopped*."

"Remember how hard it used to be to get him out of his studio, to come down for dinner?" Clea asked.

"Even for Thanksgiving or Christmas," Caroline said. "Whenever he was home, he was painting in his studio. I'd want him to play catch, or to drive me somewhere, but if he had the door closed, all bets were off. Things changed right around the time he started drinking. All of a sudden, he never worked again. He just wouldn't let himself. And Dad loved to paint."

"So much," Clea said.

"Maybe he was blocked," Skye said. "You don't know how that feels."

"It felt like he stopped loving us," Caroline said. "I don't know about you, but that's how it felt to me. Blocked from painting, blocked from loving his family. Drinking all the time. We *loved* him, Skye."

"Maybe he couldn't help himself."

"I've never understood," Caroline said. "To be such a wonderful artist, to be able to express all that—important things—and to purposely lock it inside. That's what he did. Shut us out."

"He had Mom."

"He was mean to Mom too. She loved him so much, she'll protect him forever. But he shut her out too."

"Stop it," Skye said, putting her hands over her ears. Tears were streaming from her eyes. "It's because of me, I know that. I shot that boy. Dad couldn't bear it, he felt so guilty for putting the gun in my hand. So if I kill myself, do you think I care?"

"You have to care," Caroline said, grabbing Skye's hands.

"Why?"

"Because we need you. We love you so much—"

"You don't need anyone," Skye blurted out, jumping to her feet. "You're a bitter woman, Caroline. Listen to you! Attacking Dad like this!"

"I'm not attacking him. I—"

"You should feel sorry for him, being unable to paint. That must have felt like death. Worse than death, for Dad. You're so selfish, all you care about is your own agenda. Making *me* feel bad. I tried to apologize before for what happened with Joe, and do you even give a shit?"

"Skye!" Caroline said, stunned.

"You're so high and mighty. Miss Perfect. Simon always says it about you, and he's right. I agree with him."

"Cool down," Clea suggested, touching Skye's arm.

"I'm not perfect. I never said that—" Caroline said.

"You're more like Dad than I am. So what if I drink? At least I feel! You're so closed off, so steel-plated, you won't even accept an apology."

"You don't owe me—"

"*Owing* has nothing to do with it. I feel awful about what happened at the ball. Horrible! But what's it to you? What do you care if Joe walks out of your life? So what if he takes off? He'd find out soon enough how cold you are. You don't care. You're too busy living my life."

"I don't want to live your life," Caroline said.

"You act like you do. Trying to control me all the time . . ."

"Skye—"

"Why *wouldn't* you rather have my life?" Skye asked, weeping. "I'm the one who does things. I took the chance of falling in love with someone, marrying him. You just try to get me to leave him. You're like a frustrated saint. Martyring around all over the place. *I* killed Andrew Lockwood, not you, Caroline. You held his hand, you walked me out of the woods. But I killed him."

"Skye," Caroline said, struggling to keep her voice steady. "I never said—"

"Get mad, Caroline. *React!* Jesus Christ! Don't stay so calm, don't be so fucking afraid of upsetting me."

Paralyzed with shock, Caroline could neither speak nor move.

"And stop trying to take over my life," Skye said viciously. "You don't know how I feel about anything."

She ran down the beach.

January 2, 1980

Dear Joe,

It's been so long since I've heard from you. Please write back. I miss you. I still love you.

C.

April 30, 1980

Dear Caroline,

This is my last letter to you. You knew, didn't you? All that shit about trust, about best friends, about our families, about LOVE. And you knew.

You were there. My dad died in your kitchen. I know the whole stupid story now. Your family's not the only one with a gun. Did you hear the shot, C? Did you watch him die?

It sucks, you knowing all along. Did you just think I was a jerk? Were you and your sisters laughing at me? Or did you just think I wouldn't find out?

Well, I found out.

Don't write back. I hate you, your father, that house of hell you call Firefly Hill.

Joe Connor

May 12, 1980

Dear Joe,

Please don't hate me. I kept it secret because I didn't want to hurt you. Your father came here, it's true, you knew that already. I knew, but believe me, Joe: I never, never wanted to hurt you. The opposite.

I'm so sorry. If I could take it back—all of it, any of it—I would. Please, please don't hate me. You don't know what your friendship means to me. If you can't love me anymore, I understand. But don't hate me. I'm only sixteen, and you're only seventeen. I can't stand thinking of all that life waiting for me if you hate me.

Love,

Caroline

P.S. Please write back, Joe. Anything you want to know, I'll tell you. I'm here, and I always will be.

CHAPTER FIFTEEN

EVERY YEAR SKYE AND CLEA HELPED CAROLINE CLEAN up after the ball. It was a tradition, something neither of them ever missed. Skye was half dreading it; she didn't want to face Caroline after the scene on the beach the day before. But when Skye walked into the inn, Michele said Caroline had called in sick. She had asked not to be disturbed. Skye was on her way over, to knock on the door of her cottage, when Clea intercepted her.

"Hello, my little storm cloud," Clea said, kissing her.

"Is she really upset?" Skye asked.

"She's really tired."

"I want to talk to her—"

"She's sleeping late. Just let her rest," Clea said.

"Is it because of me—?"

"Even if it is, just leave her alone right now."

With guidance from Michele, Clea and Skye went straight to the task of cleaning up the ball. Every year it was the same thing. All the planning, the arranging, the antici- pation, the decoration, had lasted for months. All year, everyone at the Renwick Inn looked forward to the Firefly Ball. And when it was over, Caroline and her sisters pulled the whole thing apart. But this year Caroline wasn't around to help.

Taking down the paper lanterns reminded Skye of taking the lights off a Christmas tree. She stood on the ladder, looping the electrical cord over her arm. Swallows swooped in and out of the barn, brushing by her hair. She felt dizzy with a hangover and shame for what she had said to Caroline. Her mad twin had been in command.

When the telephone rang in the inn, she heard it jingle through the trees and almost fell off the ladder. She had left word with her mother that she was there, and she hoped it was Simon, looking for her. He hadn't surfaced since last night. But it was just someone calling for a dinner reservation.

"Hey, Michele," Skye asked when the manager walked by, taking another loop of wire. "Are the *Meteor* guys on the books?"

"No," Michele called.

Skye watched her walk across the wide porch, through the big door with its fanlight window. She knew better than to be surprised. But she felt an ache anyway, deep inside. She had worried all along that Joe's reentry into Caroline's life had been temporary.

"Hear that?" Skye asked Clea.

"Yes," Clea said.

"Shit," Skye said sadly.

"He'll be back," Clea replied with quiet confidence.

When they finally brushed the dirt off their hands and went inside the inn, Skye's back ached and her legs felt tired. She went into the bar for a beer but took a glass of ice water instead. There, pausing for a minute, her gaze fell upon one of her father's pictures. Very tiny, just four inches square, it showed a marsh.

Skye gazed at the watercolor, its greens and golds flowing into each other, just as they did in the salt flats themselves. She recognized the scene: It was the Black Hall marshes, with the Wickland Light shimmering in the background. When Skye looked at his pictures, she knew she was seeing one very specific moment in time. The cloud would pass, or the sun would move, and everything would change.

"He was a wonderful painter," Clea said.

"Amazing," Skye agreed.

"You inherited his talent."

"Thank you," Skye said.

"You heard what we were saying yesterday, didn't you?" Clea asked, gesturing at Skye's glass of water.

"Maybe a little," Skye said, sipping the water.

"You can't make beautiful sculptures if you're . . ."

Skye smiled, grateful that Clea had spared her the end of the sentence. Caroline would have said "dead" or "drunk."

"I know," Skye said.

On the other wall were the three portraits of Skye and her sisters Hugh had done after the hunts. Skye stared at the image of Caroline holding the dead fox. The winter light was cold and blue. The snow was deep, the stream black ice. The fox hanging limp with a line of blood drizzling from its mouth.

"Clea, look."

Staring at Caroline's portrait, Skye saw something she had never noticed before: Her father had painted a tear. It might have been a shadow, but from a certain perspective it was definitely a tear.

"Was that always there?" Skye asked.

"Yes," Clea said.

"Are you sure?"

"I'm positive. I used to wonder why Caroline had one and we didn't."

Looking at the picture, Skye had always felt sad, but she had never seen the tear before. Had Caroline actually cried the day she killed the fox? Had their father guessed that the hunts were laced with tragedy, that they would doom his family, not save it? Or had Caroline?

"Dad didn't usually make statements like that in his work. He'd leave everything to the imagination of the viewer. He must have felt pretty strongly about showing Caroline crying."

"She carries the weight of the world, Skye," Clea said gently, making Skye feel twice as guilty as she did already. "Dad just painted what he saw."

* * *

Joe Connor climbed out of the sea and let the dark water stream off his body. It ran down the deck into the scupper. He felt cold and clean. Night had fallen while he was down in the wreck. The fog had closed in; it wrapped the Meteor, heavy and gray, and sonorous tones of bell buoys and the foghorn at Moonstone Point carried across the water. He looked for Sam, but he wasn't on deck.

Operations were shutting down for the night. The compressor was off. Divers were slipping out of wetsuits, heading below for dinner. Joe was glad. Let them celebrate; today they had reached the mother lode.

The chests were buried under tons of mud and wreckage. Based on measurements taken of the keel, Joe estimated the vessel to be about two hundred and twenty tons, most of it corrugated aft, when the ship rammed the reef. The site was a nightmare of broken spars, splintered planks, mountains of ballast stones. But through careful tunneling, scientific estimation, and blind luck, that morning Dan had located the first chest.

Joe was the second man on the scene. They had swum down with lights, passing the bones of Elisabeth Randall. Joe's thoughts went straight to Clarissa, to the cameo he had found, to Caroline. Reminding himself that controlled emotions were key to breathing steadily underwater, he forced the thoughts from his mind.

Dan signaled from up ahead. Joe followed. Zigzagging through an obstacle course of jagged rocks and smashed wood, they shined their lamps into what looked like a devil's cave. Pitch-black, it was guarded by notched and pointed shards of wreckage. But just inside, nestled in the sandy sea bottom, was the chest.

Black wood encircled by bronze bands, it lay on its side. Two hasps had snapped free. Some of the gold had spilled out, creating a barnacle-encrusted trail of treasure. The divers followed it to the source, then hovered outside the possibly precarious "cave," trying to determine how many other chests were inside and how safe it would be to proceed.

"What do you think, captain?" asked Dan, coming up behind him on deck.

"It was an exciting day. You did good."

"Thanks," Dan said, grinning. He took a long drink of beer from a bottle. From down below came the sounds of the crew celebrating, retelling the triumphant moments.

"Seen Sam?" Joe asked.

"He's eating," Dan said.

Joe nodded. Sam had packed his bags. Walking past his cabin, Joe had noticed the knapsack and duffel bag full and stowed in the corner, ready to go. But since the other night, when they'd had their conversation about Yale, Sam hadn't said anything about leaving.

"We'll shore up those timbers tomorrow, just to be safe," Joe said.

"I say we go in with the hoist tonight, secure the chest right away. We can dive tonight, Joe. Let's—"

"We go tomorrow, Danny," Joe said. He spoke curtly, but with respect. He didn't like being second-guessed by his men. He was the captain, and he proceeded with a scientist's caution. Dan was a salvage man out of Miami, one of the professional pirates. He knew his stuff, but he was at odds with the oceanographers. Pirates were greedy by trade and by nature.

"Come on, Joe. The whole thing could shift—" Dan exploded.

"Tomorrow," Joe said, walking away.

He stood at the rail, trying to control his anger. He'd been on plenty of treasure operations where impatience had killed the whole enterprise. Wrecks had collapsed, the gold had been lost. Crewmates had died. So you had to move with care, one step at a time. On the other hand, he knew Dan was right: Just because you had found the gold today didn't mean it would be there tomorrow. The sea never stood still.

Joe was as impatient as the next man. He wanted to get out of there, finish his mission, get away from Black Hall as fast as he could; if the wreck weren't so unstable, he'd go down right then, yank the treasure chest up with the hydraulic winch, have his money counted by sunup, and be ready to go. The temptation was strong.

"Hey, aren't you gonna eat?" Sam asked, coming up with a plate of peach pie.

"Yeah, I was checking the charts."

Sam's brow was furrowed. He tried to straighten his cockeyed glasses, and the fork balanced on his plate clattered to the deck. "Here, this is for you," he said.

"Thanks," Joe said. He took the plate, watched Sam wipe the fork on his shirttail. The brothers' eyes met, and they grinned. On holidays, when Joe was home from school, they had always fought over washing dishes. They both hated the chore and they had both perfected ways of getting out of it.

"It's good pie," Sam said, handing him the fork.

"Hmmm," Joe said, taking a bite. "So. Were you gonna

tell me you're planning to leave? Or were you just going to go?"

"I was going to tell you," Sam said, trying to use his thumbnail to tighten the tiny screw holding the earpiece on his glasses.

Joe waited. Watching the awkward kid trying to get hold of that minuscule screw was putting his stomach in a knot. He had to hold himself back to keep from grabbing the glasses out of Sam's hand.

"I was planning to leave tomorrow," Sam said, fiddling with the screw.

"Hmmm," Joe said.

"Thinking about it anyway."

"Yeah?"

Sam looked up. He was waiting for Joe to talk him into staying. Joe could feel it in the pit of his stomach. He dug into the pie again, just for a diversion. He could barely eat the stuff. His appetite was gone, and he hadn't slept right in days, since the night of the ball. He was a mess of contradictions, and he knew it.

Joe wanted Sam to stay, but he couldn't wait for him to leave either. His few moments of sleep last night, he had dreamed of Caroline, of putting his arms around her and kissing her soft mouth, but when he was awake he thought of their parents, of all the history, of the scene her mother had caused.

"So," Joe said finally, putting down the pie plate. "You can't make up your mind."

"Not really."

"Well," Joe said slowly. "Tell me your reasons for both sides."

"Okay," Sam said, perching on the rail. He was so clumsy, so accident-prone, Joe had to fight the urge to grab him by the collar and haul him off to keep him from going overboard. It was an exercise in tolerance to let him stay there. "I should get back to work. The whales aren't in the passage, but I could be taking water samples, measuring salinity . . ."

"Stuff like that," Joe said, agreeing.

"Or I could stay here . . ."

"Yeah?"

"A little longer. The gold's pretty cool, and we found the mother lode today. I'd like to be here when we bring it up."

"Hmm," Joe said, smiling inwardly at the "we."

"So . . . you can see my dilemma," Sam said. "I don't want you to think I'm after anything. I mean, any of the gold."

"I don't," Joe said quickly.

"Because, frankly, I think gold sucks compared to other things. You know? Other things matter more."

"Yeah? Like what?" Joe asked, thinking of his own list.

"Well, family," Sam said. "Nature. The ocean. Love, I guess."

Joe nodded. He looked across the water, at the lighthouses blinking on the mainland. The night air sent a chill down his back. Love. Joe whistled.

"Oh, yeah," Sam said. "One more thing for the list. Good peach pie."

"That pie was great," Joe said, nodding. "Thanks for bringing it to me."

"No sweat. Great enough to matter more than gold?"

"Tough call," Joe said.

Sam was about to give up on his glasses. Sliding them back on, he glanced over and saw Joe holding out his hand.

"Give me your specs," Joe said, gesturing "come on," and Sam handed them over. Joe reached into his pocket, pulled out his knife. He had been away at school, absent from Sam's childhood and all the toys an older brother might have put together, bicycles he might have repaired, but standing on the deck of the *Meteor,* Joe tightened the screws on Sam's glasses.

"There," he said, handing them back.

"Hey," Sam said, putting them on. Although straighter, the frames were still crooked, and Sam was grinning.

"They look good," Joe said inanely.

"I think I need a new prescription," Sam said.

The *Meteor* rode higher on the rising waves, and the breeze was picking up. Here they were, standing on the deck of a treasure ship, talking about eyeglasses, when the feeling of good-bye was hanging in the air. *Good peach pie. Great.*

"So, how much longer you guys staying up here?" Sam asked.

The question took Joe by surprise. He hadn't thought in terms of the calendar. He had been thinking about the wreck, the gold, and some unfinished business on land. He wanted to visit Firefly Hill, see the spot where his father had died. He was his father's only son, and he wanted to pay his respects. But he knew none of it would take much more than a week.

"Ten days?" Joe asked. "At the most."

"Because," Sam said, "I was thinking I'd stick around for a few more days. Maybe help out, bringing up the gold or something. Recording sediment samples. Unless I'll be in the way."

Joe shifted his gaze from the horizon to his brother. He shook his head.

"No," he said. "You won't be in the way."

Sam nodded.

Joe wanted him there. But he wasn't good at saying what he wanted, getting the things Sam had mentioned earlier. If it was an object, if it lay on the sea bottom buried in silt, if centuries had left their mark in its metal,

Joe Connor was your man. But if it lived and breathed, if it had a name and knew the meaning of love, forget it. Joe was out of his element.

And yet, here was his brother, sticking around for a little while longer. Joe hadn't even had to ask. Imagine what might happen if he tried opening his mouth. If he tried leaving his ship, heading for solid land, driving to someone's door.

Tried to say what was on his mind, in his dreams.

Just imagine.

* * *

Skye sat on the window seat in the bedroom she still shared with Simon. She loved foggy nights. They made her feel safe and protected. She believed the fog hid sins, provided a place for people to hide. Skye had felt scared and sinful for so long, and the fog had always been a refuge.

She had clay under her fingernails. Today she had sculpted for hours in her studio. Somehow the tide had turned. She didn't understand how, but speaking up to Caroline had loosened something inside. Or maybe Caroline had finally hit home. Back at work she had tried again to do *Three Sisters*, a piece that would capture the way she felt about herself, Clea, and Caroline.

It had to show their closeness, but it had to show their separateness too. Skye had tried to sculpt it all different ways: abstract, very abstract, representational, surreal. She had formed one solid mass, meant to express her feelings about sometimes not knowing where she ended and her sisters began. One angry day, she had plunked down three separate balls of clay, unformed and unconnected, to show how immature she and her sisters really were and how little they really knew one another.

But ever since the other morning, on Firefly Beach with Caroline, something new was emerging. Skye was doing a piece of three women standing in a circle. They were holding hands, with one woman looking into the center of the circle, one looking out, the other looking in.

She found the combination intriguing. Because there were three, at all times two sisters holding hands would be facing the same direction. And one would be facing a different way. No matter how you looked at it, two would always be united. And one would be separate. But which two? And which one?

Doing the work, Skye felt a little safer than she had been feeling. She knew she was struggling. She needed that intense connection with her sisters, but at the same time she shrank from it.

For such a long time she had thought her main problem was the resentment she felt about Joe's father killing himself in the kitchen downstairs, her mother offering to trade her own life—and Skye's—for Caroline's. The beauty of a wild life, she thought. With so many traumatic events to choose from, how did you isolate the one that was making you would be relieved to die?

For all these years she had thought she was the only one to suffer. The others had found a way to beat the sorrow, to escape its spell. Out of three girls, why her? They had all survived the hunts, all carried guns. Why had she been the one to make an irrevocable mistake? To kill a man.

She never talked about it, had hardly ever told a soul. Her sisters knew some, and her father, but her husband didn't and neither did her mother. The details of that day were too private and terrible. If she told anyone, if she ever started talking about it, the facts might eat her alive.

Kill, she thought now. It sounded like what it was: sharp and hard and short and ugly like a bullet. She reached behind a book on the little window seat book-case and took out her vodka bottle. She refilled her small crystal glass and took a sip.

Drunk or just drinking, Skye had passed many hours trying not to think about the hunt, about the gun and Andrew Lockwood, about any of it. She had drunk to get loaded, to get wasted, to get happy, to get sad, because she loved the taste, because she was against killing ani-mals, because her husband liked rough sex, because she had nightmares about snakes under her tent, because her father had stopped loving her, because she hated *Swan Lake,* because she had gone to Redhawk, because she was mad at her mother for offering to trade her life for Caroline's, because Skye herself had killed a man dead.

Working on her small sculpture that day, her impres-sion of *Three Sisters*, Skye felt something shifting. A change in her breathing, a lessening of the pain deep in-side. Prey turning on the hunter. Thinking of the worst and knowing she wasn't alone. Nothing extreme, really. Unless you considered the desire to live extreme. Skye teetered on a suicidal seesaw: some days she wanted to live, many she would be relieved to die.

Just thinking that, huddled on her window seat clutching her secret bottle of vodka, Skye thought about living. She took a sip, tears rolling down her cheeks. The vodka dulled her feelings, made her fear more manage-able, but it killed so many other things too. When was the last time she had enjoyed a morning? Eaten and not felt like throwing up? Left the house and not wanted to hide from the first person she saw? Sculpted something she was halfway proud of?

"You never have to feel this way again."

She thought of the words Joe Connor had said to her, and she wondered what he had meant. She looked at her glass, took another sip. Skye no longer wanted to feel this way. She felt empty and desperate and sick and scared and ready to get better.

She wondered what she would have to do, and at the same time she wondered how a person could call a person on a ship at sea.

CHAPTER SIXTEEN

AUGUSTA'S GRANDCHILDREN WERE SPENDING THE DAY with her. They were outside, running in mad circles around the yard, loving the world of Firefly Hill as their mother and aunts had as children. Augusta sat on the porch with her tray of drink things and a few old scrapbooks, wishing the kids would tire themselves out and come sit with her. If only she had felt this way thirty years ago.

Augusta had not enjoyed her own children enough when they were young. The worst part was, she had realized it even at the time. She had had no choice in the matter. Like an illness she couldn't cure, she was consumed with their father. The best she could do for her daughters, as much as she loved them, was to *manage* them. Plunk them down with paints and paper; hand them seeds and dirt and a flowerpot; tell them to write poems about their school day. Being with their father had always taken top priority.

When they were tiny she had let them bake cookies and freeze Jell-O in ice cube trays, making a complete mess of the kitchen. She had let them eat their favorite foods, never forced them to have vegetables or fish. The year Caroline was twelve, she had made herself macaroni and cheese every night.

Anything to keep them occupied, so Augusta could be with Hugh. She had been so afraid of losing him. She seduced him every chance she got. Wore negligees in broad daylight just to get his attention. Read art history, studied the collections of great museums to help him further his career. Instead of helping her daughters with their homework.

Hugh had been her obsession. When he was away, she had assumed he was with other women. It drove her crazy, dominated her thoughts. She had tried to concentrate on her daughters, but her own insecurity was much too huge. When Skye would beg for a story or Clea would need help with her music lessons, Augusta would tell them to ask Caroline. So Augusta could be with Hugh.

Augusta's eyes filled, just thinking of him. She had loved him so much, and he had been so difficult. His work came first, then his fun, and somewhere down the list, Augusta and the girls. Or the girls and Augusta. She had never been quite sure of the order, and her jealousy and guilt over this fact grew even greater after the accident at Redhawk.

Hugh's love for the girls showed in their portraits. Especially the ones of Caroline. *Girl in a White Dress*, his most famous work, had caught her beauty, fragility, and solemnity. Augusta still remembered the day he sketched her, right there at Firefly Hill. Augusta had watched, feeling like the wicked stepmother in "Snow White," seething with the wish that Hugh was painting her instead.

Caroline had worn a straight white evening gown. She had stood on the porch, leaning against one of the columns, staring out to sea. Her eyes full of troubled passion, she had the air of a girl in a Greek tragedy. Augusta remembered staring at her oldest daughter, wondering what could make her feel such deep and helpless longing. The expression on her face was authentic sorrow, and it had wrenched Augusta's heart. Hugh had captured the emotion perfectly.

Flipping through the scrapbooks, Augusta sipped her martini and called up memory after memory. She found the articles she had clipped after *Girl in a White Dress* became such a sensation at the Venice Bienniale. Glancing through the piece in *ARTnews,* she ran her fingers over the photo of the painting. The colors were true: Caroline's glossy dark hair, the near-blue tinge of her columnar white dress, the dark blues and grays of the sea and sky.

But it was the look in Caroline's eyes that still took Augusta's breath away. Stunning and haunted. Augusta, and many of the most prominent art critics of the time, had never seen a portrait like it. Staring at Caroline's face as painted by her father, Augusta still wondered: What had caused such anguish? The deaths, she was sure. James Connor and Andrew Lockwood.

Tired of thinking about it, Augusta looked up. She did penance for the past every day, watching Skye dissolve. She couldn't mend that damage, but she could try to be a good grandmother.

"Children, aren't you tired?" she called, her hands cupped to her mouth. "Mark, Maripat! Come on the porch and have a snack."

"What kind of snack?" Mark asked, out of breath.

"Lemon squares," Augusta said, holding out the blue china plate. "I made them myself."

Each child took one. So polite, they said "thank you" and chewed slowly.

"Have another," Augusta said. "Go on. It won't spoil your dinner, and your parents never need to know. Would you like to see some old pictures?"

The children nodded. Augusta made room for them on either side of her. They were towheads, with Clea's beautiful skin and Peter's serious eyes. Mark rested his head on Augusta's shoulder; it made her smile from sheer joy.

Abruptly, she put away the *Girl in a White Dress* scrapbook. And she pulled out one from truly ancient times, her days as a schoolgirl in Providence and Narragansett. She had had a simple, happy childhood. The kind she had always intended to give her girls.

"There's my mother and father, our dog, Spunky . . ." she began.

"Are those your cats?" Maripat asked, pointing at Mew-Mew and Licorice.

"Oh, yes," Augusta said. "We adored our pets. They were just like members of the family!"

"Mommy used to go hunting," Mark said proudly. "She shot a wild pig once."

Augusta blinked. "Wild animals are different," she said stoically, thinking of her daughters hunting. "They can be very, very dangerous."

Eager to get back to happier thoughts, Augusta paged through pictures of her family on the Block Island ferry, in the Arcade between Westminster and Weybosset streets, on the beach at Newport, at her ballet recital in the church hall.

"Who's that?" Mark asked, pointing at a grainy photo of a small dog.

"Oh," Augusta said. "That's Tiny."

"Tiny's cute—a Chihuahua," Maripat asked, smiling at his skinny body and oversized head, his little tongue hanging out. He sat on a satin pillow on Augusta's bed.

The children were waiting, their big eyes looking up at her.

"Tiny," Augusta said, sighing. "Would you like to hear about him?"

"Yes!" Mark and Maripat said at once.

And so, because they had asked so politely, Augusta told them.

It had all started one morning in early June, when Augusta was nine. She had gone out in her dinghy to fish for blues. The sun was high, but the day was chilly. Anchored just beyond Pequot Island, she cast her line into the water. Fish were biting. The blues were running, and they fed upon one another in a cannibalistic frenzy. Augusta caught a six-incher in the process of being eaten by a larger fish.

"The sea roiled with blood and fish guts. Seagulls screamed overhead. You can just imagine. Blues in a feeding frenzy," she said. She told them about seeing something swimming on the surface. At first she had thought it was a shark fin, heading for the blues, on the scent of chum. But it had ears.

"Granny!" Maripat exclaimed.

"Yes, darling. It was Tiny."

"A dog? In the middle of the Sound?" Mark asked.

"Swimming straight for the blues. Now, you know, bluefish have needle-sharp teeth. They travel in gigantic schools, and when feeding, they have been known to massacre anything in their way."

"Granny, we know about bluefish," Maripat said patiently.

"Fine. Anyway, I scooped Tiny from the teeth of death. He was rail-thin, shivering like mad. Half dead. The poor little Chihuahua, I thought. He must have fallen off a yacht passing by."

"You took him home," Mark said.

"Sneaked him in. We already had a dog and two cats, and my parents said *no more*. So I took him up to my room. . . ." Augusta closed her eyes, remembering the cats. She felt a catch in her throat, sipped her drink to push it down. "Tried to feed him Spunky's food, but he wouldn't eat."

"He was probably so tired from falling overboard," Maripat said, touching Tiny's picture with her small finger. "Poor little fella."

"Yes." Augusta stared at the photo. She had taken it herself, posing Tiny on her pink satin pillow. He had sat there, so compliantly. She sighed. "Wouldn't eat. Wouldn't take water. He was shivering like mad, chilled to the bone from his time in the sea. I honestly thought he was going to die."

"Did he?" Maripat asked fearfully.

Augusta paused. "No. That night I took him into my bed. I brought the kitties in with us to keep him warm. We all huddled together, like a family of foxes in a den. Nice and warm, under my lovely down comforter."

"And you warmed him up?" Mark asked hopefully. "And he lived?"

"Oh, yes. He lived," Augusta said, cocking her eyebrow. She gave the children another lemon square. Maripat hesitated, but Mark gobbled his right up.

"And he got along with Spunky and Mew-Mew and Licorice?" Maripat asked, licking the powdered sugar off her fingers.

"Well, no."

"No?" Both children asked, looking disturbed. Augusta began to wonder whether she should have started this story at all. She tried to steer it back to something sweet and cozy.

"Finally, he felt like drinking. I gave him milk from one of my doll's bottles. Then I poured some more into a bowl. I had to go to school, but before I left, I let him have the rest of my cereal."

"Oh, he must have been so happy!"

"Mmm. I went off to school with Spunky—he always followed me. I got such good marks, children," Augusta said, going off on a tangent. "My teachers said I was a star pupil!"

"What about Tiny?" Maripat asked shyly.

"Well, I left him in my room so my mother wouldn't see him."

" 'Cause you hadn't convinced her to let you keep him yet," Mark said reasonably. "Did you leave the cats to keep him company?"

"Yes," Augusta said.

"And did they become best friends?" Maripat asked, happily sensing the end of the story.

"No," Augusta said, knowing she was in too deep. "He ate them."

Maripat's mouth fell open. Mark just stared at the picture album. Trying to comfort them, Augusta scattered some loose photos. Maripat tried to hold her tears inside, but they *spilled* out. "Why?" she asked.

"He wasn't a Chihuahua!" Augusta explained, wanting their sympathy. "It was horrible for me, returning home from school and finding cat fur and blood everywhere. Cat limbs all over the floor, chewed to the bone."

"Mew-Mew, Licorice!" Maripat cried.

Tearfully, Augusta told them about Tiny grinning at the end of Augusta's bed, covered with blood. His little tongue hanging out, a demoniacal mask on his face, his fangs dripping with blood as he sprang for her throat just before she slammed the door shut.

"He was a bandicoot, darlings," Augusta said, eyes shining. "A Vietnamese water rat, one of the most bloodthirsty species of mammal on earth. The veterinarian who came to remove what was left of the cats surmised that the bandicoot had come across the sea on a freighter, whose route had originated in Asia somewhere, and had fallen into our bay."

Just then, Clea walked in to pick up the kids.

They took one look at her and started to wail. Clea

dropped the bag of vegetables she was carrying. Opening her arms, she hugged them to her body. They sobbed against their mother's breast.

"Mom," Clea said, panicked. "What happened?"

"Mommy, Granny had a horrible pet that ate her cats," Mark sobbed. "An evil pet who looked like a Chihuahua but wasn't."

"You told them about *Tiny?*" Clea asked with disbelief.

"Well, yes," Augusta said defensively. "I did. They asked!"

"If they asked to play with matches, would you let them? If they wanted dessert before dinner, would you give it to them?"

Augusta tightened her lips, feeling awful. She didn't dare mention the lemon squares. All she had wanted was to spend a few hours with her grandchildren, have them love her a little more. She had thought the story of Tiny would be scary and thrilling.

"I thought children loved scary stories," she said.

Clea just shook her head. She eased Mark and Maripat off the porch, into the yard. Augusta watched her reach down, take first her daughter's hand, then her son's. She walked them toward the beach stairs, and they stood at the top, facing out toward the sea and listening to the waves. Their voices carried, and after a minute the tones of anxiety were gone and they were just a mother and two children talking.

Her chin wobbling, Augusta took another sip of her martini. It tasted warm, watered-down. She had never meant to make the children cry. Augusta had given them the lemon squares, shown them the old pictures only to make them love her. That's all Augusta had ever wanted from any of the children in her life; from any of the people, really.

She glanced around for Homer, the only creature who

seemed to take her for exactly who she was, faults and all. But he had wandered off on one of his mysterious outings. Even *he* was sick of her, and Augusta didn't really blame him. She felt like quite a failure. It always seemed to work out wrong.

* * *

"I am so mad at my mother," Clea told Peter.

"What did she do?" he asked.

Clea paused. She was sitting in the curve of his arm, watching their children swim back and forth in the pool. The night was clear. The Pleiades were bright, directly over the chimney, and all the other stars spread down the sky.

"She upset the kids. She told them a really awful story about a pet she had when she was little."

"How bad could a pet story be?"

"Well," Clea said, knowing this fell in the "only in our family" category, "it eviscerated her cats and could have killed my mother in her sleep. I'd say that's good for a few nightmares, wouldn't you?"

"Wow," Peter said. "I never heard about that one."

"Poor Mom," Clea said. "She doesn't get it. She's always been the same. It's as if she wants to do the right thing but can't. She never could."

"Lost in her own world."

"She's so anxious about being loved, she ends up driving people away."

"She should have a little faith."

"In other people? I don't know . . . my father wasn't the faithful type."

"In herself," Peter said. "She's a good woman, and she should trust her instincts. I've heard her say she wished she hadn't let your father take you hunting."

"That would have been a good one to trust," Clea said wryly. Her mother had tried to please him instead of listening to her own maternal instincts. How had that even been possible?

Peter and Clea sat quietly for a while. Clea felt drowsy, lulled by Peter's hand stroking her hair and the sounds of her children playing in the pool. She could get lost in feeling sorry for her mother. How awful it must be to go through life *shielded* from the truth. To be so afraid of your own feelings, you could fail to protect your children.

"Do you want to swim?" Peter asked.

"No, thanks. I'm so relaxed, I don't feel like putting on my suit."

"Just look at that," Peter said.

"What?" Clea asked.

"How confident Maripat seems in the water this summer. Remember how scared she used to be?"

"She would never go in the deep end," Clea said. Last year, when they had installed the pool, Maripat would sit for hours on the curved steps. She would hang on to the side, pulling herself around. Or she would swim the width of the pool and only with her father right beside her—gasping for air with terror in her eyes.

But this summer everything had changed. Clea had driven her to swimming lessons every morning. While Mark played soccer or went to the beach with his friends, Maripat spent hours in swim class, making friends and swimming alongside her teacher.

Peter and Clea now watched their daughter glide back and forth, stopping to splash her brother but neither afraid nor reliant on him. She swam on her own, lost in her thoughts, her strong strokes taking her where she wanted to go.

"She loves it," Peter said.

"She does," Clea agreed proudly. She had taken steps to help her daughter conquer her fear, to help Maripat feel strong and confident in something she had decided to do. It didn't take leaving her alone on a mountain, to pitch a tent and kill her food and lie awake listening to animals moving outside. Just driving her to swimming lessons.

* * *

Caroline was out of breath. She had spent the evening climbing Mount Serendipity, taking the north trail, the one that ran almost straight up the granite ravine. The night was black. It favored the hunted. The stars had come down to strike the crest. From the ridge she had looked southeast and seen the *Meteor*'s lights shining like stars in the Sound. Staring, she had wondered how much longer Joe would be there.

She had seen an owl flying low through the pines, starlight on its chestnut wings. Honeysuckle grew along the trail, and she now climbed down, breathing its sweet scent of summer. The trail forked halfway down. The wide path went straight to Black Hall Center. Melancholy without knowing exactly why, Caroline took the other, narrower one, that curved left toward the Ibis River.

Almost immediately Caroline saw the fox.

He was hunting along an old stone wall, skulking so close to the ground, she thought at first he was a shadow. His coat was glossy red, the tip of his tail pure white. Caroline stopped dead. She watched him stalk a chipmunk. He crept slowly, stone by stone. His ruff stood on end, his snout pointed straight at the prey. But then he heard Caroline.

They faced each other. Caroline's heart pounded. He looked so small, the size of a miniature collie. He bared his teeth. Lunging once toward Caroline, he flicked his tail and then sprang over the wall. Caroline wasn't afraid. She thought the fox was beautiful. Seeing wild animals up close was one of the best parts of hiking, and she tried to imagine how she had ever killed them. It was never a part of her personality. Yet she could recall perfectly the smell of gunsmoke, the feeling of her eyelashes against the sight.

At home, Caroline stood in her kitchen, breathing hard. She drank a glass of cool water, trying to calm down. Haunted by the memory, by the spirit of that fox, she stared out the window.

She wore khaki shorts and a long-sleeved blue shirt with the sleeves rolled up. Her hair hung loose around her shoulders. Kicking off her hiking shoes, she peeled off her clothes. She was thinking of how good the shower would feel, how she would make the water really hot, when the phone rang. Naked in her bedroom, she answered it.

"Hello?" she said.

"Caroline. It's Joe."

She hadn't expected to hear his voice. She held the phone in her hand but couldn't speak.

"Are you there?" he asked.

"Hi," she said.

"How's your sister?"

"I don't know," Caroline said. She hadn't seen Skye since the altercation on the beach.

"I hated to leave her the other night, and I'm sorry about what happened at your ball. I didn't mean to ruin it—"

"Don't be sorry," she said. "I should have told my mother you'd be there. Somehow I had thought I could keep you two apart."

The phone line crackled, and she imagined the static was normal for a call coming from out at sea.

"Our families. That's partly why I'm calling," he said. "I'd like to see Firefly Hill."

"Yes," Caroline said, understanding why that would be important to him.

"Do you think it would be possible? I know your mother doesn't want me there, and I don't blame her. But I want to visit—" he began, then stopped himself.

"I can arrange it," Caroline said. Did this mean he was getting ready to leave the area? "When would you like to go there?

"Soon," he said. "Tomorrow we're going to bring up the main chest. That should take all day. But once we get it, we'll be done. Anytime after that."

"How about Wednesday?" she asked quietly.

"Wednesday would be fine."

They arranged to meet at her place, and Caroline would drive him over to Firefly Hill. She would make sure her mother was out, so there wouldn't be any dramatic confrontations.

"Hey, Caroline—" he said all in a rush.

"Yes?"

The line was silent except for the static. It buzzed for a moment, neither one of them saying anything.

"Thanks," he said finally. Then he hung up.

* * *

Two nights later, Simon didn't even bother to sneak in. The old Porsche came up the driveway with the stereo playing so loud, it woke Skye out of a sound sleep. Entering the back way, he let the door slam behind him. He opened the refrigerator, poured himself a glass of something. When he was ready, he tromped upstairs.

When he entered their room, he had the good manners to move a little more quietly. Not suspecting Skye was wide awake, he stood at the window for a moment, drinking wine as he surveyed the moon on the water.

Probably he was thinking of the painting he would do. He would call it *Nocturne #62*—or whatever number he was up to—because he called all his paintings *Nocturne*-something. He was probably setting a price for it in his mind.

He unbuttoned his shirt, then ran his hand over his bare chest. Half turning from the window, he started unzipping his jeans. He was lost in thought. He sipped his wine. His face, illuminated by moonlight, was contemplative. Maybe he was thinking of how famous he would be. Or maybe he was thinking about the waitress he had just left.

"Did you have fun?" Skye asked from her spot in the bed, making him jump.

"Oh, you're awake?" Simon asked.

"Yes."

"Usually you're not."

That stung. Skye knew he meant that usually she was passed out from drinking too much. But she had not had anything to drink that night. She was shaking a little, her hands trembling under the covers. Her body was detoxing, and it wasn't easy. She had a dry mouth. A headache. But it was worth it. She wanted to pay attention. She wanted to see things—everything—even her husband coming home late from his tryst. Skye was tired of hiding.

"I'm awake now," she said quietly.

"Yeah. Well."

"Where were you?"

"What am I supposed to do? Give you an account of every move I make? If you wanted that sort of husband, you should have married Peter."

"I realize that now," Skye said, "but I want to know anyway. Where were you?"

"In my studio. Painting in the barn."

"Those aren't your painting clothes," Skye said.

"How would you know?" Simon asked, laughing. "They were right about the rehab, Skye. You do have a problem. You're too drunk most of the time to notice what the hell I wear to paint."

"I'm not drunk tonight," Skye said calmly.

"Whatever," Simon said.

"I want a divorce," Skye said.

That silenced him. He finished undressing. He drank a little more of his wine. She imagined that he might be wondering how he could continue to have it both ways: He wanted Skye and the comfort of her money and the prestige of her name, and he also wanted to go to bed with anyone else he desired.

Simon stood naked in the moonlight. He was tall and thin, and the blue light made his body look wet. Again he sipped his wine, stroked his chest. He started coming toward Skye. He sat on the edge of the bed, offered her a drink from his glass. She shook her head. Placing it on the table, he reached under the covers.

He slid his hands up under her nightgown. He brushed her skin, caressed her breasts. Skye hadn't been touched that way for so long. She bit her lip and arched her back. He kissed her neck, his tongue darting out to taste her skin. It felt so good, Skye thought she would moan. But she didn't.

"Um, Simon?" she said.

"Yeah?" He kept licking and sucking her neck, touching her hips and belly with his warm hands.

"Get out of my bed."

"You know you don't mean that," he growled.

"Get out of my bed," she said again. "Get your sleazy clothes off my floor, and get out of here now. Do you really think I want you to touch me after you've been with another woman? Didn't you hear me before? I want a divorce."

"You're fucking kidding me," he said. "You can't be serious." He sat up straight, staring down at her.

"I'm serious," Skye said, her throat aching.

He yanked himself off the bed. He tore into his clothes, slamming around the room. He was swearing, hate on his tongue. He wasn't getting his own way with her. He never would again. Somehow the courage Skye had found on the beach with Caroline and Clea was following her into the rest of her life. She was putting an end to anything that hurt her.

Simon left the room. Skye heard his boots on the stairs, and then she heard the door slam behind him as he walked out of the house. Trembling, Skye reached for the telephone by her bed.

It was five in the morning on Wednesday—nearly dawn—but she dialed Caroline's number anyway. That's the way it was between them: Anywhere, anytime Skye needed her, Caroline would be there. They hadn't spoken since their fight on the beach, but Skye didn't care. She had to reconnect with her sister. Trying to hold the receiver steady she heard Caroline's sleepy voice answer.

"It's me," Skye said.

"Are you okay?" Caroline asked, worry immediately in her voice.

"I'm fine," Skye said. "Caroline, I'm so sorry to call you so early."

"I'm glad you did," Caroline said.

"I just asked Simon to leave," Skye said. "It just happened, and I wanted to tell you. Can you believe it? I told him I want a divorce. I'm just so sick of it."

"Oh, Skye," Caroline said. "I'm glad."

"I just want to get better," Skye said. As she spoke, she felt her voice getting hoarser. She knew that what she was saying was so true, but so hard. Getting better: It should be the easiest thing in the world, but at five in the morning, trembling and desiring a drink to block it all out, to obliterate the pain, she had never imagined anything harder.

"I want you to get better," Caroline whispered.

"I haven't had a drink all day," Skye said.

"I'm so proud of you," Caroline said. And Skye remembered all the other times Caroline had been proud of her: At her spring concerts, her school plays, when she was six and did the best cartwheel in first grade, when she was twelve and made her first sculpture, when she went to college, when she moved to Rome, when she had her first one-woman show in New York.

Caroline had always been there, and Caroline had always been proud. Skye gripped the receiver harder to quell the trembling in her hands.

"I'm sorry," Skye said. "About the things I said on the beach."

"Don't be sorry," Caroline said. "It kills me to admit you have a point."

"You mean . . . you're sorry?"

"Did I say that?" Caroline asked, gentle laughter in her voice.

"I'm lucky to have you," Skye said.

"Took the words out of my mouth," Caroline said. "I'm lucky to have you too."

"I'm going to try to sleep now."

"Do you want me to come over?" Caroline asked. "Do you need me to sit with you?"

"No," Skye said, hanging on. She knew this would pass. She knew it would.

"Are you sure?" Caroline asked. "I'll just be with you if you like. We can walk down to the beach and maybe go for a swim." But even as the words came out sounding sure and positive, Skye heard her stop. She was doing it again, trying to make everything better when Skye had to do it herself.

Skye laughed, and this time Caroline really laughed back.

"That's okay," Skye said. "I'm fine by myself."

"I know."

"Anyway . . ." Skye trailed off, tired now. "Everything will be okay, just as long as you . . ."

"As long as I what?" Caroline asked.

"Love me," Skye whispered.

"That's the easy part," Caroline whispered back.

CHAPTER SEVENTEEN

CAROLINE STOOD INSIDE THE SCREEN DOOR, WHERE SHE had been watching for Joe's truck. She wore a buttermilk linen sundress and flat beige sandals, things she might wear to work. As Joe walked up the steps, she felt her pulse jump. Seeing him made her nervous, and as he approached the door, she wished she had not offered to do this.

Standing on the other side of the screen, he looked nervous himself, as if he weren't sure what he was doing there. He gave her a dazed smile. She noticed the lines around his eyes and mouth; he spent a lot of time smiling out in the sun. He wore chinos and a blue oxford shirt. Although the collar was frayed, the shirt was freshly pressed.

"Are you ready?" he asked.

Caroline had planned to ask him in, but she realized there really wasn't any reason for it. So she grabbed her bag. He held the door for her. Their hands brushed, and their eyes met. Caroline blushed, remembering their kiss. When they got to his truck, he put his hand on the passenger door handle.

"I'll take my car. You can follow me," she said, thinking it would be faster for him to return to the dock from Firefly Hill.

"That's okay," he said, pulling open the truck door. "You're doing this for me. The least I can do is drive."

He backed out of her driveway, circled past the inn, and headed east down Beach Road. They passed the Ibis marshes, where the river turned brackish and flowed toward the Sound. Stopping at Black Hall's only traffic light, they watched four teenagers fly by on their bikes. Sea gulls perched on the roof of the gas station.

Joe drove with his elbow sticking out the open window. His blond hair flew in his eyes, and he kept brushing it back. He turned on the radio, then turned it off. Caroline stared out the window, feeling so tense, she didn't know what to say.

"Did you get the chest of gold yesterday?" she asked finally.

"We didn't, actually," Joe said. "We tried, but the sea wouldn't cooperate. The wind kicked up yesterday morning, and then the currents shifted. My guys are thinking of mutiny, they're so ready to finish the job."

"What about today?" Caroline asked.

"Today I had plans," Joe said. "Besides, the currents are still fluky." He tried to smile, but his mouth was tight. His gaze slid over to Caroline. His face was drawn, and she noticed the bluish circles under his eyes.

They were on their way to Firefly Hill, the place where it had all started.

"Did you tell your mother I was coming?" he asked.

"I thought it was better not to." Caroline said. "But she won't be there. My sisters took her to Providence for tea."

"They know?"

Caroline nodded. "I told them. They're glad to help."

"No use upsetting your mother," Joe said.

"Are you okay?" she asked.

"Yeah," he nodded. He glanced over, then back at the

road. They were on the stretch where it hugged the rocky shore. The driving was treacherous, but Joe didn't seem to be able to keep from glancing over at Caroline.

"This is it," she said as they rounded the bend. She directed him to turn into the driveway, up the hill into a thicket of dark trees. At the top they emerged back into bright sunlight. Caroline wanted to point out the *Meteor,* which was visible on the horizon, but Joe was staring at the big white house standing between him and the sea. He must have been thinking of his father, his last hour. James Connor had driven up that hill, parked on the rough grass, walked across this very yard.

At the sight of Caroline, Homer trotted over with his towel. He dropped it to say hello, panting up at her with love in his eyes. Joe obviously knew dogs. He offered Homer his hand. The dog sniffed it, then turned quizzically back to Caroline. She took his big head between her hands, shaking it gently. Crouching down, she touched the top of her head to his.

"It's okay, Homer," she said.

"He wants to make sure I'm not going to hurt you," Joe said.

"He knows," Caroline said.

They walked across the back porch, into the mud room. The wainscoting needed paint. The linoleum was old and cracked. Framed fingerpaintings by all three girls hung on the walls. Caroline could have brought him in the front way, through the big hall with its sweeping stairway, but this was how the family always entered. It was the way his father had come in.

The kitchen was open and airy. Big windows gave onto the lawn, sloping to the ledge that dropped to Long Island Sound. Red clay tiles covered the floor. The big oak table had two coffee cups on it, left from Augusta's and Skye's breakfast. One wall was covered with pictures of the family in other places: Paris, Siena, St. Lucia, Colorado. Between two windows curved a silver fish, stuffed and mounted. It was a landlocked salmon, caught by Caroline at age thirteen.

Joe looked around the room. Caroline could see the pulse beating on the side of his neck. His blue eyes were steady, taking everything in. He stood in the middle of the room, a question on his face.

"Here," Caroline said, taking his hand. It felt big and rough, covered with scars and calluses. No matter what, she would have known the man it belonged to worked on the sea. Pulling gently, she led him to the spot where his father had died.

"Right here?" Joe asked. His tone was neutral. He might have been asking about some historical site that had nothing to do with him. But as Caroline nodded, his eyes began to betray him. They clouded over. His lashes lowered so she couldn't see.

"I don't remember everything," Caroline said, "but I remember thinking he loved you and your mother."

Joe made a sound deep in his throat. "At five years old?"

"Yes. Too young to understand what was happening—" Caroline paused, trying to say it right. Her throat felt dry. "But I understood the tears."

Joe wasn't looking at her. He leaned against the kitchen counter, examining some pebbles someone had left lying there.

"He was crying?"

"Yes," Caroline said, because she couldn't lie to him.

"And angry?"

"At first, yes," she said, trying to remember. She could see the man's red face, the gun wobbling in the air over her head. "But then he just seemed . . . sad. Very, very sad."

Joe moved to the kitchen window. He stood looking

at the sea, dark blue against the bright sky. His hands were jammed in his pockets. Beyond the breakers, across a long stretch of water, lay the *Meteor*. He stared at it intently, as if he wanted to fly away from Firefly Hill and be safely back on it. He shot a quick glance at Caroline.

"Where were you?" he asked with his usual wariness.

"That night?" she asked, surprised. She pointed at a spot eighteen inches from where his father had stood. "I was right there."

"A lot for a little girl," he said, still cradling the pebbles.

"Nothing compared to what it was like for you."

Again, a violent breath of air. "I wasn't even here."

"Do you think you should have been?" she asked softly. "Do you think you could have stopped him?"

A shrug. He turned back to the window. The sun was going down, and the cliff's shadow fell across the wide bay. Staring at him, Caroline could read his thoughts.

"He had your picture," Caroline said gently. "He was holding it, and for a minute we held it together, he and I. I've always thought—" She stopped herself.

"Go on."

"I've always thought your father had you with him. The last face he saw was yours. And he loved you so much."

Joe turned from the window. He shook his head, and for a moment he couldn't talk.

"No," he said simply. "The last face he saw was yours. You were with him, Caroline. With him when he died."

Caroline took two steps, and she was in Joe's arms. As he reached for her, she heard the pebbles he had been holding clatter to the floor. She understood his feeling because she wished she could have been with her own father at his death, but he had shut her out long before then. She felt her tears hot against Joe's neck. His strong arms gripped her body, his hands grasping each of her shoulders. He gulped hard, swallowing his own sobs. Behind him, the sea was silver and black, a crescent moon hung over the horizon.

"We loved them," Caroline said of their fathers. "We just thought we'd have them longer."

They stood locked in an embrace. Joe's hand stroking Caroline's hair. She had wanted to comfort him, but here he was, holding her close, whispering her name, telling her he'd never realized before, never pictured how it had been, how close she had stood to his father, how much it meant to him that she had been there.

The kitchen clock ticked loudly. Waves beat upon the beach, tumbling rocks in their wake. It was time to leave. Augusta would be home soon, and Caroline didn't want to face the explosion her arrival would bring.

Joe looked into Caroline's eyes. He wiped his own face with the back of his hand. Reaching into his pocket for a handkerchief, he offered it to her. She dried her eyes, folded it, and handed it back. She felt his reluctance at having to leave this place where his father had died, and she stood still, waiting.

Without another word, he just walked out the door.

He drove her home. As they got closer to her house, Caroline knew their time together was almost over. She glanced over at Joe. The lines in his brow and around his mouth were deep. There was something going on behind his eyes.

"Thank you for taking me there," Joe said when he caught her looking.

"Oh, Joe," she whispered, overcome.

"I'm glad I went."

Caroline nodded. Joe had recovered his tough reserve. A chilly breeze blew through the truck, blowing his hair into a windy mess.

When they reached the inn, he turned into the wide drive and continued left, down the private road that led to Caroline's house. Sharply trimmed privet hedges lined the road, and the branches of tall maples interlaced overhead. The approach felt safe and private, and at this time of day, just after sundown, it was already very dark.

Parking the car, Joe turned to her. His right arm was stretched out along the seat back. He had a strained smile on his face, as if this were good-bye. He stared at her for a long time, and she began to feel the color creeping into her face. They had come a long way, Caroline and Joe. She wished she could say what she felt, but she didn't believe he wanted to hear.

"Well . . ." she said.

"Yeah," he said, drumming his fingers on the steering wheel.

Gulls cried. Across the river, a whippoorwill began to call. Locusts hummed in the trees. The night sounds got louder.

"I have to get back to the boat, they're expecting me."

"I know," Caroline said, trying to smile.

Joe stared at her. He looked out the window. A minute passed.

"Say good-bye to Sam," she said, her hand on the door handle."

"I know I should leave," Joe said slowly. "But the thing is, I can't."

Caroline looked over, her pulse quick and light.

"We could have tea . . ." she began to say.

He opened his door even before she finished the sentence. They walked up her flagstone walk, and Caroline used her key to open the front door. Augusta always left Firefly Hill wide open, but Caroline had locks and alarms.

Joe entered, looking around. At Firefly Hill his attention had been on one spot, but here he seemed interested in everything. The rooms were spare and cool, done in the colors of dusk. Her floors were wood, stained deep brown and highly polished.

In the living room, she had a cream-colored sofa with a heathery dark blue throw folded across the back. A matching armchair sat by the gray stone fireplace. A single mahogany table held a blue glass vase containing wildflowers she had picked on her hike up Mount Serendipity. There were no rugs.

They walked into the kitchen, and Caroline turned on some lights. It was a cook's kitchen with a stainless steel stove and refrigerator, copper pans from Paris, plenty of counter space for chopping. The cabinets were made of warm, pale-gold natural wood. They seemed to glow from within. The kitchen table was round, lacquered black. In its center were tiny silver salt and pepper shakers, a silver sugar bowl, and a single framed picture of Caroline, Clea, and Skye.

Caroline filled a big copper kettle. She turned the heat on low, a ring of blue flame. Turning to Joe, she saw him studying the photo. It showed the three girls dressed in warm jackets, each holding a fish they had caught. Caroline was about eleven.

Replacing the frame on the kitchen table, Joe continued to look around the room.

"It's different from your mother's house," he said.

Caroline nodded, pouring milk into a silver pitcher.

"Hers is warm and cozy, all cluttered up with life," she said. "This place is . . ." She had been about to say "cool and spare, like me," but she didn't want him thinking she was feeling sorry for herself, looking for a contradiction. But the fact was, Caroline felt empty and alone, as if they had already had their tea and Joe was already gone.

"It's beautiful," he said. "I was thinking it's kind of mysterious."

"You were?"

"Yeah," he said. The woodwork in Caroline's kitchen was painted slate gray. One section of the wall was pumpkin. Joe went to the kitchen window, when he noticed six moonshells arranged there. Reaching into his pocket, he took something out. He examined it, then placed the object on the sill with the shells. He glanced over his shoulder at Caroline.

Slowly she approached. Her heart was beating fast. Caroline's desire for order was reflected in the shells, spaced at three-inch intervals in a straight line. Exactly three inches past the last shell, Joe had placed a cameo. Caroline stared at it.

"It's from the *Cambria*," Joe said in a low voice. "It belonged to Clarissa's mother."

Caroline, moving to touch the cameo, looked at Joe first. He took it off the sill and placed it in her hand. She stared at the fine rim of gold, worn to a thin line. The cameo itself was incandescent.

Held to the light, the carving was ivory, the background translucent pale green glass. The woman looked noble, with strong cheekbones and a straight nose, her hair drawn back, her chin tilted up.

"She looks like Clea," Caroline said.

"She looks like you," Joe said.

Caroline could barely see. For the second time that evening, she wiped away tears. She was incredibly moved, holding this jewel that had belonged to a family she had come to care about. She thought of Elisabeth Randall's bones lying in the eel grass, the tides sweeping in and out. The cameo felt light in her hand. It was so fragile and delicate, yet it had survived underwater for two hundred years.

"It's amazing," she said, handing it to him.

"I want you to keep it," he said, pressing it into her palm.

Caroline was stunned. She looked into Joe's eyes, and she saw the beginning of a smile. "I can't," she said, clearing her throat.

"Why?"

"Shouldn't it go to someone else? Clarissa's descendants? Or the town?"

"There aren't any Randalls we can find. And the town . . . it doesn't work that way." He laughed. "I'm a treasure hunter, remember? I filed my claim and got my permit, and this is treasure."

"Your daughter—"

"I don't have a daughter," Joe said.

"Well, if you ever do."

Joe was staring into Caroline's eyes, his blue eyes dark and unflinching. His wide lips wanted to smile; she could see it in the corners. He was amused with the awkwardness of her gift-taking, but she was always like this. At Christmas she felt uncomfortable when it was her turn to reach under the tree.

"I don't—" she began, looking at the cameo in her hand.

"You have to," he said a little roughly.

She was thinking of all the reasons she shouldn't accept anything from Joe Connor, all the anger and hurt that had passed between them, the way they had tried a friendship this summer, until the Firefly Ball came and his true feelings had come out.

"Sometimes it's more generous to take than give," he said.

"How?" Caroline asked.

"To let the other person give you what he has to offer. If you're always the one giving, you never have to feel disappointed, because you don't expect anything in return. But it's miserly in its own way. Because you never leave yourself open or give the other person a chance."

Caroline nodded, thinking of her father. And of herself: Skye was right.

"That's what my sister says."

"About you?"

"Yes."

"It's what my brother says about me," Joe said.

"Something we have in common," Caroline said. "Smart siblings—"

She never saw the kiss coming. He wrapped his strong arms around her, drew her body against his, and kissed her as if his life depended on it. Raising herself up on tiptoe, she reached up to hold him. She ran her fingers through his messy hair, felt the insides of her forearms around his face.

The teakettle began to whistle.

Joe stepped away, turned off the flame. He faced her again, breathing as if he had just run from Mount Serendipity.

Again, he took her in his arms. His body, which had felt strong and supple when they had embraced earlier, now felt rigid with an almost inhuman tension. *It feels like hugging steel,* Caroline thought. She trailed her fingers softly down his spine. His blue cotton shirt seemed thin beneath her fingertips. She could feel his bones and muscle. The sexual passion between them was enormous, but she sensed something different as well.

This was the love that had been building up between them since they were five and six. She could feel Joe Connor absorbing her warmth and love as she herself was consuming his. He wanted something from her that had nothing to do with sex; she knew that. She touched his face, softly stroking his cheek with her left hand.

Holding his hand, she led him down the hall. The

spareness apparent throughout Caroline's house did not extend to her bedroom. This was her private place, her sanctuary. She was most herself in this room, and allowing him inside made her feel vulnerable.

Everything was dark wood and white lace. The white lace curtains and eyelet coverlet had belonged to her grandmother. The dark mahogany four-poster was elaborately carved with roses and angels. The massive chifforobe and armoire came from Scotland. Bookcases were filled to overflowing, and the bedside tables were crowded with framed pictures of the people she loved.

He kissed her again. His mouth covered hers, and he wrapped her tighter in his arms. He let out a moan that sounded almost like grief as he slowly lowered her down to the bed. She could barely stand the tension that felt as if it had been building since she was sixteen years old. Caroline leaned into Joe, the full length and weight of his body pressing against hers. They kissed and kissed, undressing each other all the while.

"I'm sorry," he said when his hands touched the bare skin on her shoulders.

"Why?"

"My hands are too rough for such smooth skin."

Joe's hands were callused from hauling equipment, working underwater on the wreck, and the friction made Caroline's body tingle wherever they touched her. She felt the hair on his body, silky and fine, and she nearly lost her breath with the sexy maleness of him.

She lay back, letting him explore the soft curves and hollows of her body with his mouth and hands. He wanted her to stay still. He wanted her to lie back so he could love her, and he let her know this. "Shhh," he whispered, holding both of her hands just behind her head with one of his. "Please," she whispered, trying to get loose. "Please," he whispered back. She could neither touch him nor wrangle away. He made her lie there while he used his mouth all over her body.

He was steady and slow, and Caroline squirmed under the pressure of his tongue. Her nipples hardened. She arched her back, willing him to touch her breasts, finally reaching down to drag his hands up. His callused fingertips pinched and rubbed her nipples, sending a tense thrill straight between her legs. She clutched his head, encouraging him, bringing her hips up to meet his tongue. Everything exploded in red and blue stars behind her eyelids, and she gave out a shuddering breath.

He moved up the bed, his hands now gripping her shoulders, his flat, hard body pressing against her. She felt him enter so easily, water splashing against rock. She was so wet from her own excitement and from his mouth, and he was so hard. He moaned again. Caroline had not known a person could make such a sound of need and love and sex. She had never heard anything like it before.

They clung together, the blood pounding in Caroline's head making her feel in rhythm with Joe, their bodies hot and moist and full of fire, her legs wrapped around his waist, their love so intense, Caroline went deep inside, where she felt the connection they had always had and never really lost.

"Caroline," Joe said into her neck, his arms wrapped around her, "I love you."

"I love you," Caroline said back as Joe's eyes locked onto her gaze.

She touched his face. People weren't made to get this close to each other, she thought, scared by the depths of it. She was lying on the edge of the tallest and narrowest precipice she had ever known; if she moved left or right she would go over and never stop falling.

She had never felt this way before. She had let herself get physically close to men, but her emotions had never kept up, rarely even followed. But she and Joe had said "I love you" to each other and meant it.

"Joe," she said, again looking straight into his eyes, rocked at what was happening.

"I know," he said, smiling. His face glistened with sweat, his eyes sparkled in the cool light of night.

But what do you know? she wanted to ask. She wanted him to tell her. She wanted him to say the words, to name the moment, to tell her what *she* meant. But he couldn't do that. Only Caroline could. The feeling was there, just as it had been practically her whole life, ever since she had sent Joe that first letter. He was the boy who was everything to her, the one she had saved this feeling for her entire life.

"Look," she said, pointing.

Joe raised himself up on his elbow, looked toward the bedside table to where she was pointing. There, in the front row of framed photos, was the picture of him as a child.

"I knew I loved you all along," she said.

"I don't know why," he said, his voice rough with regret. "I made everything so hard."

"So did I," Caroline said, her throat aching, thinking of things Skye had said. "But here we are."

Lying next to Joe, she felt the truth: She had fallen in love. For the first time in her life, Caroline had given a man the power to hurt her. Her heart skipped. Joe could kiss her good-bye. He could sail away, go to sea in search of a different treasure, and there would be nothing she could do about it.

"What?" he asked, seeing her expression change.

Caroline couldn't speak. His eyes were so clear and blue, like the open ocean in October after a storm has blown through but a solid month before the first snow would fall. She felt so scared, she was frozen in place. Was *this* what her father had in mind? Teaching his daughters how to protect themselves against life, was it this feeling of absolute love and need?

"Whatever you're thinking," Joe said, still smiling into her eyes, "it's going to be okay. It is, Caroline."

"How do you know?"

"Because it's over," he said gently. "The bad stuff is over."

CHAPTER EIGHTEEN

WHILE THE COFFEE BREWED THE NEXT MORNING, Caroline walked barefoot to the inn to see what was for breakfast. A few of the guests were up early, but she breezed past them into the kitchen and filled a basket with peach muffins. Returning home, she covered the porch table with a damask cloth. The dawn light was turning from silver to rose to blue-gold, and she wanted Joe to see it. But when she went into the bedroom to get him, he grabbed her wrist and pulled her back into bed.

After a while they got dressed and walked down to the water. Fish were jumping and ospreys were hunting. A kingfisher, sturdy and blue, dive-bombed a school of minnows and came up with a beakful of silver. Joe held Caroline's hand. They stopped to kiss under the big willow tree. Walking a little farther, they stopped to kiss in a grove of pines.

"I have to get back," he said finally. "I didn't expect to be away this long."

"Will Sam be worried?" she asked.

"Sam, no. But some of the other guys will want to kill me. We're a few days behind, and they can taste the gold. I never do this."

"Do what?"

"Leave the boat overnight. Hold up the operation." He shook his head. "No one will be surprised though. They all saw it coming."

"What do you mean?"

"At the ball, the way you looked . . . I had to break a few heads—the comments they were making. They're nothing but a bunch of sea dogs, got the manners of hoodlums. Then they got on me for defending you, saying you'd hooked me good. But you did look beautiful. *Girl in a White Dress.*"

"What?"

"The portrait," he said. "It's the only painting by Hugh Renwick I can stand. I told you, I saw it once. I was walking through the gallery where it hangs, and it was there at the end of the room. I couldn't move. It was like being in the room with you. Only I wanted to know what you were thinking. There was something about your eyes. . . ."

"He painted that after we stopped writing, you and I."

"Did something happen?"

"Yes," Caroline said, thinking of Andrew Lockwood.

"Come out to the boat," he said. "Tell me there."

"I can't," she said, shaking her head. "I want to, but I have a ridiculously busy day."

"I want you there when we bring up the gold. I want you to see."

"What's it like?" Caroline asked, holding his arm, gazing at the river. "Finding the treasure?"

"I wish I could describe it," Joe said, bending down to pick up a stone. It was flat and smooth; he rubbed the surface with his thumb. "But you wouldn't believe me. You'd have to see for yourself."

"Is it more beautiful than this?" Caroline asked, taking the cameo out of her pocket, holding it to the light.

"When Marco Polo returned from China, he told about the wonders he'd seen," Joe said. "Because they were beyond the comprehension of the people of his own city, they accused him of lying. When he was dying, they asked him to confess his lies, because he was about to face God. And Marco Polo said, 'I never told the half of it.' "

Joe took Caroline's face in his hands, looked her deep in the eyes.

"That's how it is for you?" she asked, her heart pounding. He was telling her why he went to sea, the wonders he sought and found, the reasons he would always have to leave.

"Come out with me so you can see for yourself."

"I don't know," she said.

"Tonight? Tomorrow? I'll send the launch for you."

Caroline hesitated. She thought of the things Skye had said, about how she never let people close. About how she always lived her sisters' lives instead of her own. And of what Joe had told her: Generosity sometimes involved taking.

"I have things I have to do this morning," she said slowly, "but I can come out this afternoon."

"We'll pick you up at Moonstone Point," he said.

They walked back to her house. She held the cameo in her hand the entire way. Even when she kissed him good-bye, she didn't let it go.

*　*　*

Someone had been in Augusta's kitchen while she was out yesterday. She found beach stones scattered on the floor. Pictures shifted on the table. Two water glasses in the sink. Augusta had a suspicion, and she didn't like it. It was late morning, and she was waiting to ask Skye.

"Sit down," Augusta instructed, offering her cheek for Skye to kiss, hustling her into a place at the table. "I have breakfast all ready for you."

"Oh, Mom, I can't eat," Skye said. "I just want coffee."

Augusta just pretended she hadn't heard. When Skye smelled the muffins, when she realized Augusta had picked tiny wild blueberries from the bushes at the top of the beach stairs, she would change her mind. The muffins were small, their tops golden brown. Augusta took four from the oven, where they had been warming, and placed them in a lovely basket lined with a checkered napkin. She set the basket in front of Skye.

"Dear, I wish I could tell you this juice was fresh-squeezed," Augusta said, filling a glass, "but that is only partially true. I realized too late that I didn't have enough juice oranges. So I mixed it with canned."

"That's okay. I don't want—"

"I'll be desolate if you don't drink your juice. It's full of vitamins, you know."

"Mom, my stomach is a little—"

"We could make screwdrivers," Augusta suggested, assuming Skye was hung over. She knew that Skye should get her drinking under control, but maybe just this once it would actually help.

Yesterday's ride with Clea and Skye had left her anxious and tired. They had invited her along, but they spent the whole day acting nervous and distracted. Augusta had ridden in the backseat, doing her needle-point, knowing something was wrong. Arriving at home, she felt like Mama Bear: *Someone's been sitting in my kitchen.*

"Who was here?" she asked when Skye had taken some sips of coffee.

Skye didn't reply.

"Was it your sister?"

Holding her cup with two hands, Skye looked down.

"Tell me, Skye. I want to know."

"Shouldn't she feel welcome to come and go?"

"Not if she's with Joe Connor. Was he here? Answer me, Skye."

Skye couldn't speak because she didn't want to lie. Augusta felt the truth bowl her over, and she clutched her black pearls.

"I knew this would happen. Why else would he be in Black Hall, if he didn't want to come snooping around? I knew the instant I saw him at the ball."

"Maybe he wanted to visit the place where his father died," Skye said slowly. She took a bite of her muffin. Her tremor wasn't as bad as it had been the last few days. Still, Augusta couldn't bear to look.

"All this digging up the past," Augusta said. "It's horrible."

"The man was his father, Mom."

Augusta felt stung, and she wanted to strike out. She pictured Skye's studio, the new sculpture she was doing. She envisioned the talismans Skye had set out on her worktable, and she thought of the loathing she felt for them. To Augusta, they symbolized the wreckage of the painful past, everything wrong with Skye.

"I cleaned up your studio," Augusta said casually. "While you were sleeping."

"What do you mean?" Skye asked, looking up sharply.

"Those junky things. That dusty old blue ribbon, that horrible rattlesnake skeleton you had."

"Mom—"

"I threw them out."

"No."

Augusta nodded emphatically. "Surrounding yourself with negativity, no wonder you're depressed. How can you expect to do good work, lead a meaningful life, with snake bones lying right in front of you?"

"A snake bit me once," Skye said, her eyes piercing.

Augusta breathed steadily, poured more juice. "Don't be so dramatic. Not that snake—"

"It was poisonous," Skye said, her voice a little louder.

"It happened on the mountain, when you let me go hunting with Dad. Caroline sucked the poison out."

"It wasn't poisonous. If it was poisonous, I would have known. You would have been hospitalized, and if you think I'd let you go to the hospital without being right there at your side, you're crazy."

"Oh, God," Skye said, starting to laugh.

"What's so funny?"

"You weren't by my side, Mom," Skye said. "Caroline was."

"No, Skye. I think—"

"At the campsite, where it happened, and at the clinic later. And she was with me when I shot Andrew Lockwood, and she was with me when the police came, and she was with me when his parents walked into the inquest room and I had to look them in the eye."

"I was right here, waiting for you!" Augusta said.

"But Caroline was *with* me," Skye said quietly. "She always was. She was like a mother to me."

"I'm your mother," Augusta said, feeling panic rising inside her.

"But you weren't there, Mom. You never were. I was in trouble, and I needed you. Facing Andrew's parents was so hard."

"It was an accident, Skye. Even they knew that. . . ."

"You could have come. Didn't you think about how awful it was for me, seeing the people whose son I *killed?* I wanted to disappear, Mom. That's all I could think about."

"Darling, I was terrified for you. That you could be charged with murder. That was my only thought, that you couldn't go to jail."

"Mom, I killed someone! I wasn't thinking about *jail.* I was thinking they'd never see their son again. It was a beautiful sunny day, and he was *dead.*"

"Beautiful sunny day? Well, I was thinking about *you.* Going to jail, with God-knows-what for a cellmate, no freedom, no liberty, no beautiful sunny days. I was paralyzed."

"I know," Skye said. "But Caroline wasn't. She was there."

It hit home, hard and suddenly. Augusta had never been present for Skye. She had wanted to, planned to, imagined that she was, but she hadn't.

Trembling, Augusta pulled out her needlework. She had been hiding this from Skye, intending to keep it a secret until Christmas.

"Look what I'm making for you, Skye," she said, solemnly, showing Skye this symbol of her love, wanting it to obliterate the horrible past. She wanted to return to the comfort of *good* talismans instead of snake bones, to the old ways that had always let her pretend she had a happy family.

Spread out on the table was Augusta's nearly finished needlepoint pillow: *Swan Lake* with its mysterious forest, blue lake, graceful swans, enchanted castle. At the bottom were two dates—Christmas of two different years, thirty years apart.

"Do you see the significance?" she asked, her voice shaking. Her arms wrapped around Skye's shoulders, she traced the dates with her index finger, as if she were talking to a small child. "The Christmas my father took me to *Swan Lake,* and the year your father took you and your sisters."

"I'm falling apart, and you want to give me a pillow," Skye said.

"Darling, you'll be fine!" Augusta said, so afraid to hear the truth. She hugged Skye, practically shaking the needlework in her face, wanting her to see it and be happy, praying it wasn't too late.

"Mom, don't!" Skye said. "*Swan Lake* reminds me of Redhawk."

"But the ballet . . . your father took you. You loved it.

You'd listen to the music all night if you could, way past midnight, until I made you stop. . . ."

"You don't even know. You think what you want to think about everything," Skye said.

"Darling!"

"Mom, I hate *Swan Lake*. It reminds me of Dad. It reminds me of that fall day, of picking up the gun and shooting Andrew Lockwood. That's what I think of every time I hear that music."

Without speaking, Augusta reached for a pair of scissors. She found herself cutting the needlework in half, then in half again. She stared at the four pieces, two in each hand.

CHAPTER NINETEEN

JOE MET CAROLINE AS SHE STEPPED OFF THE LAUNCH. HE reached down to take her hand. Climbing aboard the *Meteor*, she let him pull her into his arms. He had on the bottom half of a black wetsuit. His bare chest felt warm in the sun, and salt crystals glistened in his blond hair. The crew stopped everything to watch.

"I don't bring girls out to the boat," Joe explained. "Twice."

"I don't take days off in the middle of the week," Caroline replied.

"Hey, Caroline," Sam said, bounding over in his diving suit. He shook his head, spraying water from his hair like a wet Lab. He kissed her on the cheek, apparently thrilled to see her. "You picked the best day to come out."

"I did?"

"Hell, yeah. You should see the treasure! It's like a real-life pirate's chest—ancient and covered with brass—and we've got the wires ready to hook up. Show her the winch, Joe."

Joe smiled at his brother's enthusiasm. "Right there," he said, pointing to a big stainless steel drum with quarter-inch wire spooled around. "We hit the engine and say the word, and we haul in the gold."

"We waited for you," Sam added. "We were all set to go the minute Joe got back from wherever the hell he was last night, but Joe said we had to hang tight."

"You did?" Caroline asked, blushing.

"Yeah," Joe said.

Caroline smiled.

"Got a wetsuit?" Sam asked.

"No," she said.

"Let her borrow one, Joe," he said. "You're gonna take her down, aren't you?"

Joe hesitated for a second. "Do you dive?" he asked.

"That's okay," Caroline said, laughing. She did dive; she had her scuba certification, and she had gone down on the local reefs before. But she was out of practice, and she wanted the operation to get under way. "I think I'll wait for you to bring it up."

"Okay," Joe said. "It won't be long." He zipped into the top half of his wetsuit while scanning the Sound. The blue surface was flat, painted with sunlight. It was one of those perfect summer days with no waves; the sea's only movement was its natural rhythm, low swells forming without peaks.

"Hey, skipper," one of the guys shouted. "We ready to go, or what?"

"Patience, Danny," Joe said, strapping on his tanks. "By dinner tonight you'll be packing for Athens."

"Athens?" Caroline asked.

"His next dive's in Greece," Sam said. "The brothers could've gone to Yale, but gold is gold."

"You're leaving tonight?" Caroline asked.

Joe's smile left his lips first, then his eyes. His eyes were clear, the color of deep water. "Not tonight," he said. But Caroline could see that it would be soon.

"Oh," Caroline said. Black Hall lay ten miles across the calm Sound, hills of dark pines rising sharply behind the town. Firefly Hill stood to the north. Caroline caught a glint of light and knew it was sun striking her family's picture window. She blinked, staring at it.

The pirates clustered on deck. They said a few words that Caroline couldn't hear, getting their strategy set. Then they split up and went over the side. Sam yelled good-bye, and Joe flashed her a grin. He went backward off the rail.

Caroline stared into the water. A few bubbles, a ring of ripples, were the only signs that anyone had been there. The men had disappeared completely. Last night, when Joe had seen the trouble in her eyes, he had said everything would be okay, the bad stuff was over. How could she have imagined that that meant he would stay?

Her father had armed them against danger, but he hadn't warned her about this part. Once you let yourself feel love, once you let it in, you take the risk. You lay yourself open to pure fear. The thought of Joe leaving was worse than any night alone on the mountain.

Something broke the surface. As Caroline stared, the sea began to dance with silver splashes. Two, three. A fish tail broke the surface. A sea gull circled overhead, letting out a jubilant cry. A common sight of summer: The bluefish were there. Trying to breathe, Caroline watched them feed.

Sunlight infused the top layer of water, and it twinkled above with plankton and particles of sand. The divers aimed down, flipping on lights to guide them into the murkier deep. Sam followed Joe. Diving always made him euphoric, and he'd start breathing too fast just when he was supposed to be cool and calm. *Think Tibet,* he told himself. *Meditate and focus on spiritual matters. Think anything but this.*

This. Who could believe Sam was diving with his big brother on a big-league wreck with major treasure? Sam had grown up idolizing Joe. He made no bones about it. Sam had never been good at hiding any feeling—not one—that he'd ever had. That Yale stuff, for example. Sam had been so disappointed when Joe had said he wasn't even considering the job. He had tried to act as if he didn't care, but Joe could see that he did. Sam had really blown it that time.

Just thinking about Yale made Sam's breathing go crazy. A year they could finally spend near each other, down the drain. Like all the other times Sam would show up and Joe would leave. *Don't take it personally,* he told himself. *That's just the way Joe is.* Sam's chest hurt. He pushed Yale away, straight out of his danger zone. Exhaling a long stream of bubbles, he narrowed his eyes. He peered through the dark water; ahead he could see the spars of the *Cambria*.

The wreck was a magic forest of broken timber. The divers swam in a line along the reef, circling around to swim the length of the old ship. She lay on her side, wide and austere as a great dead whale. The ribs of her black wooden belly curved out, the bow and stern tapered in. The masts had snapped off; they spiked out of the sand connected to the ship with evil loops of wire. Blackfish and cunners swam in and out.

Joe turned to face Sam. He gestured for Sam to stay put. Sam nodded assent even though he wanted to swim into the wreck behind Joe, watch the operation up close. But he wasn't in Joe's league as a diver. Sam's work off Canada's Maritimes didn't require much scuba action, and Sam knew he was present by his brother's grace alone.

In the precarious cave of the wreck, Sam would be in the way.

Joe was saying something. Sam squinted, looking through the celadon water. Air bubbles were flowing out of

Joe's mouth. Mask to mask with Joe, Sam read his lips: *Black Hall*.

No way. Joe couldn't be saying what Sam thought he was. Sam himself had mouthed the same words a few dives back, teasing Joe, wanting to tempt him to stay in the area, sign on at Yale, move into the town where Caroline Renwick lived. Sam had watched the way Joe changed when he was around her.

Black Hall. Sure as hell, that's what Joe seemed to be saying. But he couldn't be. Sam grinned, letting a whole passel of air out and shrugged to indicate he wasn't getting the message. Reading the word was wishful thinking on Sam's part. Sam's brother was a loner, a pirate, a treasure hunter. He'd never let anything like a woman or a brother hold him back.

Turning, Joe grabbed the cable. It ran from the winch on board the *Meteor* straight down to the wreck. Joe and Dan would attach it to the reinforced chest, bolstered by support and wrapped in straps, and they'd pull the gold out. Joe swam into the wreck. One by one the other divers followed. Engineers, geophysicists, archaeologists, professional salvage guys, they belonged in there, carrying out the delicate business of easing a chest of gold from the delicate labyrinth of old wood.

Sam had a different place in the sea. He was a biologist. He studied sea plants, ocean creatures. Once they got the gold, he'd hop a plane and return to his post up north. The cetaceans of Newfoundland needed to be counted. Seals needed to be observed. Herring stocks assessed. In the murky depths of Moonstone Reef, he tried to forget his dream of him and Joe at Yale.

Trying to remain patient, Sam Trevor saw a school of menhaden. The tiny fish flashed outward like an explosion of silver. Behind them came the bluefish, pewter torpedoes, eating machines. They pursued the bait fish, mouths open. The biologist hung back, observing the fish and tried to stop wondering whether his brother had actually been saying *Black Hall*.

* * *

In her studio at Firefly Hill, Skye worked on her sculpture of the three sisters. She wore a black ballet top and faded overalls, and she was covered from head to toe with a thin film of clay. Beside her was a bottle of Absolut and a crystal glass. The glass was full.

She couldn't stand her feelings.

She had just destroyed her mother. She pictured her mother's face, shadowed with despair. She could sculpt it, the bust of a woman who had just seen into the depths of her youngest daughter's empty soul. Old news, but it had shocked Augusta. Skye had seen it in her eyes. Vodka was the fastest way out. She sipped her drink and felt everything grow distant.

But her new piece was filled with love. Although the sisters did not have faces, Skye knew which one was Caroline, which was Clea, and which was Skye. All three had their heads tipped back just slightly, gazing at the sky with exuberance and gratitude. That's how Skye wanted to feel someday.

Exuberant and grateful. Skye raised the glass again and drained it.

The Renwicks had made secret-keeping and lie-telling an art form. What was the alternative? It they had told the truth, they would have fallen apart. Her parents would have gotten divorced, Skye was sure. She wished she could hold on to her picture of them as a couple in love, the way the stories made it sound. They had traveled the world together, always with their children, renting houses in beautiful places for Hugh to paint. They had made a fantasy world, and now it was finally disinte-grating.

Skye's name came from the place where she had been conceived, the storied Isle of Skye in the west of Scotland. When she was old enough, her parents would hold her tight and tell her about the tiny cottage, just big enough for a couple and their two little girls, with a peat fire burning all day and night. It had been a blissful time, a place where Augusta and the girls walked the sea path while Hugh fished for salmon and painted every day.

Christmas—nine months later—her father went off with another woman. That woman's husband came to Firefly Hill with the thought of killing the whole family, and that just about summed up the way of the Renwicks.

Hearing someone coming up the stairs, she turned to face the door. Simon stood just out of sight. She could see his lanky shadow thrown by the hall light, and she felt relieved it wasn't her mother. He paused out there for a long while, and she could almost feel him summoning up his courage. She heard him take a deep breath.

He entered her studio holding one red rose. Apology in his eyes. He wore black jeans, a green tee-shirt, and scuffed work boots. Very slowly, he walked across the big space, his footsteps echoing. When he got to Skye, he knelt before her and handed her the rose.

"This is for you," he said.

"Thank you," she said. She held the rose to her nose and breathed its sweet scent, trying to be unmoved.

"I picked it on my way in," he said with disarming truthfulness. "From the garden outside."

"Why?"

"I wanted to prove I belong here, that I'm part of the

family. I am, you know," he said, burying his head in her lap. Her hands were covered with clay, but she laid them gently on his hair.

"Your father made mistakes, Skye, and your mother took him back."

"Maybe she shouldn't have."

"Didn't you tell me he planted those roses outside as a symbol? He wanted to undo his mistakes, make things up to her. I'll be better to you."

Again, she smelled the rose. It was musky and sexy, like love and the end of summer. Skye thought of Caroline and Clea; for some reason, she felt tears hot behind her eyelids. She felt herself slipping away. She wanted to believe Simon. More than anything, she wanted to click into love and forget Redhawk and the blue ribbon and *Swan Lake* and the look in her mother's eyes.

"This is wrong," she said, pushing him away. "I have to be alone right now."

"Make love to me," he said.

"Simon, no."

"What's the matter?" he asked. "You were never like this before."

"I'm tired. I want to sculpt," she said, the two lies colliding head-on. She wanted to get rid of Simon as quickly as possible so she could get plastered on vodka and sleep the rest of the afternoon away.

"Which is it?" he asked, grinning as he caught her.

"The truth is, I need to be alone," she said, thinking fast. "I had an amazing dream last night, a major inspiration for a new piece, and I really feel like working." Her desire for isolation made the lie as easy as breathing.

"Sex," Simon said, sliding his tongue down her neck, his finger down her jeans. "You need to relax."

"Stop," she said, flinching. She pushed his hand away.

"I don't feel like stopping," he said, his breath hot on her neck.

The panic came over her. Feeling Simon's hand on her breasts, his mouth on her throat made her skin crawl.

"No, Simon. I said no!"

"You bitch," he said.

Skye took a deep breath. She closed her eyes, but only for an instant. She wanted to be completely present, right there for what was happening. She didn't want to escape into her imagination, into a momentary lapse of reality. Her husband had a vicious look on his face, and he had just called her a bitch. It was almost a relief.

"If you don't leave right now," she said, standing, "I'm going to call the police."

"What do you think the police will do?" Simon asked, smacking her so hard across the face that she saw stars. "You're my wife."

"Simon!"

"You don't want to make love? Fine. Then we'll fuck."

Shocked, Skye touched her eye, her mouth. The left side of her face stung; she could almost feel it throbbing in the shape of Simon's hand. He grabbed her by the collar, tearing her shirt. She felt her brain explode, as her eyes went wide with terror.

* * *

The fish were feeding. Caroline stood on deck, her hands on the starboard rail, watching the activity. Bluefish lunged into a school of menhaden, sending the baitfish flying like pellets into the sky. It was a full-blown feeding frenzy, with teeth snapping and half-eaten fish making a slick of oils and blood trailing the currents straight out to sea.

Caroline wondered what was happening below. A few crew members had stayed on deck to work the winch and stay in radio contact with Joe and the others below. Every so often they would pay out a little more cable. Take a turn on the winch. Crank up the engine. Check the *Meteor*'s position over the wreck, and back a few meters in reverse.

She watched the fish, trying to forget the pit in her stomach. The men on deck were talking about Greece, about diving for a treasure off Mykonos, about the warmth of the water and the beauty of the women there.

"They have it!" the winch operator yelled. "They've secured the chest!"

All the guys converged on deck. The big winch held a spool of wire like a giant's fishing line. The wire ran through a long, pivoted beam that swung out over the water down to the wreck below.

"Is this very dangerous?" Caroline asked one of the men.

"Shit, yeah," he said. "Once we start pulling, you know how much tension will be on that wire?"

"Picture the wreck as a house of cards," said an older man, a cigarette dangling out of his mouth and the tattoo of a battleship on his arm. "The gold is sitting smack inside. We gotta thread the wire through the structure, keep it from touching anything, then wrap it around the chest. We touch one card, the whole house goes down."

"It won't happen," the operator said. "Joe knows his stuff. We do this all the time."

"Gonna do it in Greece next month," someone else said.

The operator spoke into the mike. He pressed a finger against the earpiece, trying to hear better. He spoke again, and Caroline heard him say "Roger. Starting the winch." He punched buttons on the control panel.

Caroline watched the wire go taut. It was pulling the chest. Thinking of the house of cards, her stomach flipped. She gazed away, out toward the thrashing blue-fish. They had moved closer. Something dark was swimming toward them.

The thing was a shark.

Inside the wreck, darkness was total. No sun penetrated from the surface. Light shimmered from lanterns illuminating the chest, and Joe tried to see as he and Dan wrapped the case in cable. They had rigged up a series of metal arches, guiding the wire through the old ship. Designed to keep the cable from chafing and collapsing the wreck, the arches seemed to be holding.

Joe counted his men. He looked for Sam and felt relieved not to see him. The kid listened, Joe gave him that. Sam had always tagged along, followed Joe like a big puppy, but when Joe told him to back off, he did. *I do that too much,* Joe thought, yanking on the cable to test it. Tell Sam to back off. Tell *everyone* to back off. He thought of Caroline waiting on deck, and he moved faster. He gave the signal to start pulling.

The cable tightened. It scraped against the metal guides and supports. Joe's heart pounded, and he felt himself wanting to breathe too fast. He was glad Sam was outside the wreck, safe and free. This was the riskiest part of treasure hunting: getting the gold out of the unstable wreck. This was the part where people could get hurt.

The chest shifted. The wire stretched. The girded chest bumped along the sea bottom. Divers surrounded it, easing the encased old box over broken spars. Dan watched the cable, gauging its tension against the metal guides. He gave Joe a thumbs-up. Joe swam behind the chest, noticing a trail of coins spilling from a crack between the protective straps.

His main concern was getting the gold to the water's

surface. It was easier going now; the chest was off the sea bottom, being guided through the dark wreck. Bones lay strewn around, the remains of the *Cambria*'s crew. Clarissa's mother was among them, but Joe didn't let himself think of her. He was a pirate now, not a scientist, and he had to get the treasure.

As he swam out of the wreck, the water seemed bright. Joe felt relief. He searched for Sam, saw him waiting a safe distance away. The worst part was over. One by one his men were coming out, following the chest of gold. It hovered in the water, suspended in the hole in the *Cambria*'s hull. Half in and half out, it wasn't moving.

The cable was snagged.

Right away Joe saw the problem wasn't serious. The wire had eased between the metal arch and a ship's timber. Dan called for some slack, and the winch man let off some tension, unhooking the strap from a broken spar. The cable drooped. Joe swam over. He had just reached up to free the wire, when he saw the shark.

It was coming fast. Sleek as a jet, black on top with a white underbelly, the shark was headed straight for Sam. The creature twisted, opened its mouth to expose jagged teeth, slashed past Sam. Joe saw the startled look on Sam's face. Sam's eyes widened behind his mask. He opened his mouth, and a balloon of air bubbles escaped.

Joe grabbed a broken spar from the sea bottom. He didn't have a plan, he didn't even think. All he wanted was to protect his brother. He lunged toward the shark, trying to scare it away with his useless wooden club.

Joe's air hose caught on the metal guide. The cable had tightened up again, tugging the chest. Yanked back, Joe felt his air stop. All he had to do was slip out of his harness, leave his tank hanging where it was caught. But he was distracted by the shark and Sam. He saw Sam holding still, turning in place, watching the shark circle around. The shark flicked its tail and dodged away. Joe followed it with his eyes.

Fumbling with the harness, Joe smiled at Sam. The kid was a mess, freaked out over the shark and unaccustomed to seeing his older brother agitated. Sam swam forward, taking his regulator out of his mouth, ready to share his air with Joe.

Joe motioned him back. He had taken a big breath of air; he had plenty to take him to the water's surface. But Sam kept coming. He knew the buddy system, how you shared your air with a fellow diver in distress. Sam's eyes were focused on Joe, his mouthpiece held out like a gift.

Just then the chest swung free. It flew past Joe, on its way up. Snapping loose, the cable shook the wreck. The *Cambria* trembled, and the shock waves felt like an underwater earthquake. Joe steadied himself. He reached out, trying to push Sam away.

The wreck came down as if the ground had shifted. It tumbled in on itself, sending timbers everywhere. Divers scattered like baitfish. The school of blues exploded away, the shark had disappeared. Joe felt a timber strike his shoulder with a glancing blow. But Sam got hit hard. Joe saw the cable whip across the back of his head.

Sam's blood wafted into the murky water.

Joe darted toward his younger brother, but he couldn't swim. His arm wouldn't work.

No one had cared when Caroline pointed out the shark. They said they saw sharks all the time out here—it was no big deal, part of the job. Only gullible city people believed *Jaws.* Caroline had laughed, knowing she should believe them. She had lived by the sea her whole life, had never heard of one shark attack in Black Hall waters. *It's like the hunts,* she told herself: *We saw bears, we saw wolves, but nothing ever ate us.*

Caroline watched the chest shimmering beneath the surface. It was the size of a dinghy, blackened with time. Coated with green seaweed and raggedy barnacles, it came out of the sea, dangling on the cable, supported on all sides by strapping. The winch man maneuvered it onto the deck, water pouring from its seams.

Four black heads bobbed into sight. The divers were coming up. She looked for Joe and Sam, thrilled that they would all be able to see the gold together.

The divers were shouting. Climbing onto the swim platform, leaping onto the deck. Someone radioed for the Coast Guard, for a helicopter. Caroline ran to the rail. She stared at the surface, praying to see Joe and Sam.

"The shark?" she asked. She was thinking of hunters and prey, her worst fears.

"The wreck collapsed," someone told her, running by.

"Where's Joe?" she asked, her heart racing. "Where are they?"

Less than a minute passed, and they came up. Everyone was clustered around Sam. His face was pure white, streaked with blood. His eyes were half closed, rolled back in his head. Blood pumped out of a four-inch wound behind his ear.

Joe gasped air. He was trying to buoy up Sam, but his left arm was hanging limp at his side. His wetsuit was torn; Caroline saw the gash in his shoulder. Dan swam to his side, held him steady. Caroline held out her arms, tried to help as first Sam and then Joe were hauled onto the deck. People flew to the wheelhouse, then came back with blankets.

"He was trying to save me," Joe said, looking from Caroline to Sam. "He was just trying to pull me out of the way."

"He's hurt bad, man," Dan said, staring at Sam. "Losing blood fast."

"Coast Guard's on the way," Jeff called. "Sending a helicopter out right now."

"Sam," Joe said, his voice cracking. The sight of his exposed wound shocked Caroline. The jagged wood had plowed through his upper arm, slicing it clear to the bone. His own face was pale, his lips blue. Joe was losing a fair amount of blood himself, but he wouldn't leave Sam's side.

Someone found a towel, dabbed it against Sam's head. Sam's blood began pooling on the deck. The crew seemed paralyzed by their captain's distress.

"We need a fucking doctor," Dan said, spitting water. "Out the fuck here at sea, sharks swimming around, and not one of us is a doctor. All these eggheads and not one of them's a goddamn M.D."

"Where's the helicopter?" a young crewmember asked, scanning the sky.

Caroline pushed her way into the tight circle of divers. She knew first aid and she crouched down, touched Sam's face. It felt ice cold. Her throat tightened. She thought of Redhawk Mountain, of Andrew Lockwood. The memories broke her heart, and she knew she couldn't afford them right now.

Caroline pulled off her white shirt. She wore a bathing suit underneath, and the breeze chilled her skin. She pressed the shirt to Sam's head. She held it against the wound as hard as she could, feeling his hot blood soak into the fabric, forcing herself to look at his face so she wouldn't see Andrew's.

"Loosen his wetsuit," she instructed Dan and Jeff. "Cover him with the blanket and bring some more." She felt the side of his neck for his pulse and couldn't find it. She knew the cut was bad, that it might have scored an artery.

"Is he going to die?" Joe asked, his eyes red and brimming with tears.

Caroline looked over at him. The effort of will with

which Joe held himself up was enormous. His lips were a tight blue line. He had lost every trace of cool, of toughness. That emotional wariness she had observed ever since meeting him had vanished. It took a certain amount of courage to sit on deck surrounded by his men, tears rolling down his face, without wiping them away. He was hurt himself, close to passing out, but he hung on to Sam.

The helicopter was coming. Caroline heard the engine beating, far-off and faint like hundreds of birds.

"Is he going to die?" Joe asked again, never taking his eyes away from Caroline's face. She had to be careful with her expression. She knew how he felt about the truth. She knew that he wouldn't want her to lie, but she couldn't bring herself to say what she had seen once before, what she believed to be true. So she kept her eyes steady, her lips silent.

The tears in Caroline's periwinkle blue eyes were the only sign, the only giveaway to tell Joe that she had watched a boy losing blood before, that the answer to his question might very well be yes.

* * *

Breathing heavily, Augusta mounted the stairs to check on Skye. She would have admitted it to no one, not even to Caroline or Clea, but she felt finally and utterly defeated, a total failure as a mother.

The children had been such happy little girls. She could picture them now, running through the field at twilight, catching fireflies in their cupped hands. They were in constant motion. Augusta could see them perfectly in her mind's eye. She had sat on the porch steps, so full of love and delight, she thought she would rise like a balloon. Her daughters would dance and leap in arabesques of joy, and Augusta's eyes would fill with tears for what she had brought to life.

Whoever would have thought that twenty-five years later she would be checking her youngest, her darling Skye, to make sure she hadn't harmed herself? That she wasn't drinking straight from a bottle, that she hadn't taken an X-acto knife to the blue veins in her delicate arms? Over a death that had occurred so many years ago?

Skye, a killer.

Dear God, Augusta thought. The pain in her own family. She bowed her head, wiped her tears. How could she not have known how better to help? Her three girls, sisters looking after each other. Caroline, the surrogate mother. Thank God for her, that the others hadn't had to endure it all alone—their real mother too selfish and cowardly to protect them.

At the top of the back stairs, Augusta paused. She leaned against the banister, her arms full of white towels. She felt like a tired old washerwoman.

The door to Skye's studio was shut tight. Augusta stared at it. This was the moment she feared. When she would fling open her daughter's door, walk in, and discover Skye drunk.

Augusta straightened her spine. She took a deep breath and put an expression of put-upon ditziness on her face. She'd walk in complaining loudly that the world would never know about the mothers of sculptors, all the extra work they did to make sure their daughters could sculpt freely with clean hands.

She pushed the door open. She stepped inside. And her heart stopped just as Skye screamed.

"My God!" she said, dropping the towels.

There was Skye, blood streaming from her nose, while Simon stood over her, breathing like a bull. He held her from behind, and Augusta could see that he had hurt her. He had his pants undone, his belt trailing to the floor.

"Leave us, Augusta," Simon said. "This is between me and my wife."

"Skye?" Augusta asked again, ignoring him. She grabbed one of the clean towels and began walking toward her daughter. Was this a bad fight or something worse? Was he about to *rape* her?

Skye's nose was crooked. A lump was starting to swell under her left eye. Augusta crouched beside her, examining her eyes, stroking her hair. "Did he hit you?" Tears were leaking from Skye's eyes. Enraged, Augusta turned to Simon. "Did you hit her? So help me, Simon, if you . . ."

She glimpsed Simon's face. How ugly it looked, all contorted and red, the veins on his neck standing out like cords. His teeth were bared like a tiger's, and Augusta felt the rush of animal instinct herself. The hair on her neck stood up straight. She remembered feeling this way just once before: when James Connor had come into her kitchen and threatened her children.

Augusta put herself between Simon and Skye. She faced him head-on, their eyes met, and she saw the blow coming. She wasn't sure whether Simon was aiming for her or for Skye, but she held up her hands to protect them both. She heard Skye cry out, and the word "Nooooo!" lingered in the air, the whistle of a locomotive rounding a long curve before entering the tunnel.

It was Augusta he was aiming for, and he connected with a thud and a snarl. Augusta heard it as much as felt it, Simon's fist connecting with the side of her head, and her other senses were alive as well, she smelled and tasted her own fear, and she saw Skye, her baby daughter, her truest artist and purest spirit, pick up a pair of scissors.

"Skye," Augusta tried to say, but her brain couldn't push the name into her mouth. "Skye." *Don't, darling,* she wanted to say. *Don't. Don't.* Augusta felt herself slipping away, the words gargling in spit or blood. She might have been blacking out or she might have been dying, but for that moment, with all her heart, she didn't care. All she wanted to do was protect Skye. Protect her now, as she had been unable to protect her fourteen years before.

Unable to speak or act, Augusta Renwick lay crumpled on the floor of Skye's studio, powerless to protect her daughter from the forces that swirled around her family, and as she drifted into a place she had never been before, she saw Skye, a howl on her bloodied face, stab Simon Whitford through the heart.

CHAPTER TWENTY

THE LIFESTAR HELICOPTER FLEW JOE CONNOR AND SAM
Trevor down the Sound to Coastline General Hospital.
Dan drove Caroline by launch and truck, and she arrived
at the ICU frantic and terrified. A nurse told her they
were both going into surgery, that she had no details yet.
Uneasily, Caroline settled down to wait.

After an hour she asked for Peter, but they told her he
was busy with another family elsewhere in the hospital.
She tried to call Clea, then Skye, but no one was home.

The air was too cold. The orange vinyl chair stuck to
the backs of her legs. She rose every time a doctor came
through the door. The doctors wore loose green cotton
scrubs, their surgical masks pulled below their chins,
weary looks in their eyes. They spoke to the waiting
families, explaining the procedures and answering questions. Caroline watched the emotions in those families'
faces, feeling her own hands ice cold with worry.

Finally a young physician came looking for her.

"Are you Caroline?" she asked.

Caroline stepped forward. "Yes," she said, reading the
doctor's nametag.

"You're Joe's wife? Sister?" Dr. Nichols asked, looking
at her notes.

"Neither," she said. "But I was with them when it happened. I'm his friend."

"I see," Dr. Nichols said.

"Will they be okay?"

"Yes. Joe's out of surgery now. He'll need more work to repair the muscle damage, but he can take care of most of that when he goes home. He's from"—she checked her form—"Miami?"

"Yes," Caroline said, swallowing. "How's Sam?"

"Almost out of the woods, but not quite. He lost a great deal of blood. We're pumping more in right now. He's a lucky boy. Another twenty minutes and he wouldn't be here at all. He's a regular little bulldog."

"Bulldog?"

"Yes."

"Mmm," the doctor said, checking her notes. "He woke up from the worst head injury I've seen all summer and wouldn't let us give him anything until he'd asked about Joe. Had to know how his brother was." She smiled. "Joe's the same. He's in recovery right now, wanting to know when he can see Sam."

"Brothers," Caroline smiled, thinking of her sisters.

"Joe also wants to know when he can see you."

"Am I allowed in?" she asked. "I thought only family—"

"He has you down as next of kin," Dr. Nichols said, smiling. "Go on in."

Joe was asleep. He lay on the gurney, covered with a cotton blanket. The recovery room was kept cool, and Caroline saw him shivering. She asked the nurse for another blanket. The nurse smiled, checked Joe's shoulder, then covered him. The bandage was massive, pure white, stark against his tan skin. The slight pressure of the nurse's fingers was too much, and Joe flinched from the pain.

His eyelids fluttered open. Caroline leaned forward,

touched his cheek. His eyes were bloodshot, cloudy from the anesthesia. Seeing Caroline, he smiled. A shiver shook his body, and he clenched his teeth, waiting for it to pass.

"Sam," he said hoarsely.

"He's okay," Caroline said. "The doctor said they're giving him blood, he's asking for you."

"He's okay," Joe said, closing his eyes, latching on to the important part. "Alive and okay." The nurse returned with a shot. She sent the pain medication into Joe's already-inserted IV—speeding soothing relief quickly into his veins.

"Sleep," Caroline said, touching his cheek. She kissed him, feeling the two-day growth; waking up at her house that morning, he hadn't shaved. The memory pierced her heart, and she kissed him again.

"Don't go yet," Joe said sleepily. "Okay?"

Caroline stayed. She watched him fall asleep, sitting beside him until the nurse told her she had to leave. Standing in the hallway, Caroline closed her eyes and said a prayer. She heard someone call her name. When she opened her eyes to look, she saw Peter standing there. She didn't think there could be anything worse than seeing Joe so hurt, but there was.

"Come with me," he said, putting his arm around her. "Something happened; your mother is downstairs."

Clea met her outside the emergency room entrance. Red geraniums bloomed in tall stone pots. Two police cars were parked at the curb, and the officers stood beside their cars, talking. Three nurses were taking a break, leaning against the brick wall and smoking.

"See the police?" Clea asked. "They're here to talk to Skye."

"Skye?" Caroline asked, shocked. Seeing Joe upstairs already had her completely off balance. "Peter said Mom—"

"Simon beat her, Caroline. She told me he tried to rape her. When you see her—"

"Where is she?"

"Inside," Clea said, pointing toward the emergency room. "Mom got between them, and Simon hit Mom and knocked her out. Then Skye went after him with a pair of scissors. She hardly hurt him at all—it was self-defense—but it's awful," Clea said, her eyes wide. "The police—"

"They want to arrest *Skye?*" Caroline asked, her heart pounding.

Clea looked at Caroline and wiped her eyes. "They want to question everyone. To them it's just a domestic disturbance."

Suddenly the day became too much for Caroline. She had been holding up well, but now she pressed the heels of her hands against her eyes. She thought of Joe and Sam, her mother and Skye, and she leaned back against the brick wall with her eyes still covered.

"Being right there," Clea said, putting her arms around Caroline. "Seeing them right after the accident must have been terrible."

Caroline shook her head.

"I'm glad I was there," she said. "Joe asked for me, Clea. You're used to it, having Peter and the kids. Being the one someone asks for when they're hurt and scared, but, Clea . . ."

Clea gazed at Caroline, waiting for her to catch her breath.

"Joe looked for me on the boat. I saw him the minute they brought him up. He watched me while I was trying to help Sam."

"Of course he did," Clea said. "There's no one better, Caroline."

"He listed me as next of kin."

"He did?"

"Yes." Caroline looked at the sky. "Here at the hospital. They came to find me in the waiting room because Joe had put my name on the form. But he's leaving, Clea. As soon as he gets better, he's going to Greece." She tried to laugh.

"What?"

"Isn't it funny? That he's the one leaving? I finally want to stay put, and Joe's getting on a plane."

Clea knew there was nothing she could say. She just stood there, knowing that Caroline needed to feel all of the complex emotions roiling inside of her.

Caroline pushed off the wall. She linked arms with Clea. She swallowed her fear and walked with her sister straight into the emergency room. She asked the nurse on duty where to find Skye and Augusta; the nurse told her Augusta was having a CT scan and Skye was being questioned by the police. They were just about to head for the waiting room, when Caroline caught sight of Simon being led into one of the examining cubicles.

He wore a flimsy hospital gown. He stood at the far end of the emergency room, and to reach him, Caroline had to walk past many other patients, doctors, and nurses. He flinched at the sight of her. His skinny arms snaked out of the gown; his stick legs looked bony and pathetic. He had a pitiful expression in his beady eyes, and Caroline stood right in front of him, forcing him to look at her.

"Hello, Simon," she said in a normal voice.

"Hello, Caroline," he said warily.

"Why are you here?" she asked.

He pulled down the front of his hospital gown, revealing a square white bandage just below his collarbone. "Look what your sister did," he said. "She stabbed me."

"But you're walking. You're on your feet," Caroline said, trying to control the rage in her heart.

"They stitched me up," he said.

"Look at me, Simon," she said, tilting her head back to look up into his bloodshot eyes. "I'm taller than Skye."

"So? She stabbed me!"

"I'm taller than my mother."

"You're crazy, Caroline. You know that? Every frigging one of you is out of—"

"You hurt them," Caroline said, dropping her voice and reaching up to touch his chin. She wanted to choke the pathetic sneer off his ugly face.

"You hurt my sister and mother," she said again. "They're small women, Simon. They're wonderful, and they've both shown you more love than you ever deserved, and you put them both in this hospital."

"They attacked me," he said, trying to push her hand away.

"Attacked you?" Caroline asked.

"Crazy bitches."

With that, Caroline snapped. She jumped on Simon and began pounding him with her fists. She yanked his black hair, she clawed his evil eyes. She pictured him going after Skye, hitting her mother, and she saw blood. She heard her own cries, felt her blows connecting against his chest, the chest of a monster.

"Were you trying to rape my sister?" she screamed.

"Lady," a loud voice said. She felt herself being pulled back, and she looked into the broad face of a hospital security guard.

"Fuck you, Caroline," Simon said, scrambling back.

"Hey, are you all right?" a young nurse asked, a concerned look in her face. Caroline thought she was talking to Simon, until she saw the nurse looking at her.

"Call the fucking cops," Simon said. "I want her arrested."

"He hurt my mother and sister," Caroline said, staring at him.

"I need pain medication," Simon said. "My chest is on fire."

"Relax," the nurse said curtly. "Your doctor will see you soon."

Then, taking Caroline's arm, she led her toward the waiting area. "Leave it to the police," the nurse said. "If my mother and sister landed in here, I'd want to kill the guy too. But then you'd be in trouble, and who would that help?"

"No one," Caroline said. She was shaking. She hoped she had hurt Simon badly. She felt no remorse or regret for attacking him, only a desire to have hit him harder. Looking up, she saw Clea coming toward her.

"Can't I leave you alone for one minute?" Clea asked.

"No," Caroline said.

"You're going to get in trouble," Clea said. "I'd prefer not to visit you in jail."

"You're just mad you didn't hit him first."

"Did you connect?"

"I think so. My fist hurts."

"That's a good sign," Clea said, smiling.

Caroline shook her sister's hand, and they settled down to wait for news about all the people they loved.

* * *

Sam's head pounded. A thousand whales were slapping their flukes on the surface of his skull. Banging their tails pow. Whales' tails on the brain. He hadn't felt this bad since a sailing accident at age eight. He lay in his hospital bed, staring at a TV he couldn't see. He had his glasses, but when he put them on, his head hurt worse. When he took them off he saw three of everything, as murky as objects underwater.

Someone was coming into his room. A short, fat nun. A midget as wide as she was tall. Sam fumbled for his glasses, wanting to see her better. The nun had a very deep voice.

"What the hell are you doing, sitting up?" the voice asked. It was Joe.

"The nurse said I could."

"Bullshit. You're supposed to be flat on your back for another twenty-four hours."

"Look who's talking!" Sam said. He slid his glasses on, wedging the eyepieces under the bandage. There was his brother, sitting in a wheelchair. "You're supposed to be in surgery again today, getting your arm sewed on right."

"I already did, smart guy. First thing this morning. It's why they're making me sit in this thing. So I don't keel over." Standing up, he gave a macho stretch and pushed the chair away. "How do you feel?"

"Great. You?"

"Great."

The brothers smiled at their lies. Bowled over by the emotion, by how close they had come to death, they stared at each other.

They shook hands, and it turned into more of a clasp—the closest they would let themselves come to a hug. They were bandaged and bruised, broken open and stitched back. They had each nearly died trying to save the other. Gazing at each other now, they seemed to be taking inventory, making sure the other was in one piece.

Sam choked down a lump in his throat. Joe had his arm all bandaged, in a sling, pressed tight against his chest. Even in his hospital gown he had that tough-guy look that Sam in his wildest dreams would never have. A pretty blond nurse came in to check Sam's blood pressure, but at the sight of Joe, she lost interest. She ended up adjusting Joe's sling. Joe just stood there, curling his lip at her, looking mean to hide the fact he had nearly cried.

"Joe, you know you ought to be sitting in that chair," the nurse said, dimpling. She pulled Joe's hand, and he pulled back. "Just because they didn't use general anesthesia this morning doesn't mean your body isn't weakened. Now, sit!"

Joe just shook his head. He did it politely, but with a definite "get out of here" subtext in his baby-blues. The nurse blushed, patted his arm, forgot all about the task she was supposed to perform on Sam.

"So," Sam said, watching her leave the room. "What was that you were trying to say to me before the wreck collapsed?"

"Say to you? I was thanking you for trying to stick your air in my mouth."

"No, before that. Before you practically strangled yourself with your air hose, trying to bludgeon the shark. It was a blacktip, by the way. Rare for northern waters, but certainly not a danger to man. Actually, I enjoyed observing it."

"Bullshit. It was a mako. Worst shark in this region."

"Blacktip."

"Going straight for your jugular."

Sam shook his head. "Harmless species. But thanks anyway."

"Damn biologist," Joe said. "You're welcome. Thanks for the air."

"Anytime. So." Sam took a deep breath. He pictured Joe before he entered the wreck. Treading water, grinning widely, mouthing the words *Black Hall*. For those first bad hours, lying unconscious or close to it, Sam had basked in the salvation of thinking that his brother had made him a promise.

Sam's body was healing, but so was his spirit. Because he had convinced himself that Joe had been trying to tell him something. By saying *Black Hall* he was really saying *Yale*. He had made a decision to give up treasure hunting, stay in New England, be near Caroline and Sam. Sam felt himself grinning, and he couldn't stop.

"When were you going to tell me?" Sam asked.

"Tell you what?"

"Caroline."

Joe turned red. He tried to suppress the smile, but he couldn't. He nodded, a wry look on his face. "Yeah," he said.

"You're in love with her? That's what's going on?"

"It's true," Joe said, sighing as his grin got bigger.

"And you're gonna move in with her?"

"What?" Joe asked, the grin disappearing.

"*Black Hall*." Sam said, smiling so hard it made his temples burn, his skull throb, his ears ache.

"What are you talking about?"

"I saw you, underwater," Sam said, the smile dissipating a little. He wanted Joe to get it out, tell him that he'd changed his mind, decided to stay. That their little brush with death had hastened a conversion that was already under way, that he was finally figuring out what was important in life.

"Yeah?" Joe asked, waiting for a hint.

"You said *Black Hall*. As if you were trying to tell me something."

Joe frowned. "When we first went down? Before I entered the wreck?"

"Yes, then."

"I was saying 'Go over there,' 'Wait out here,' " Joe said. "Something like that. I didn't want you inside the wreck while we were bringing out the gold. I thought it'd be too dangerous."

"You mean you're not gonna go to Yale?"

"I told you, Sam—"

"But I thought . . ." Sam trailed off. He stared at the window. Somehow he had imagined that Caroline was going to change everything. He had seen the way Joe behaved around her, turning nicer and acting as if he were finally chucking off the old armor. Finally letting his guard down enough to fall in love. Sam had thought Caroline would keep him here.

"I told you, I'm not a teacher. You're the smart one. I'm not cut out for university life, doing research and lecturing students." Joe paused. "Not even at Yale."

Sam pulled his glasses off. His head was really starting to pound; the whales were at it again. Love and a headache, the combination made him think of his sailing accident. He had been in love for the first time, and he had lost the girl. True, he had only been eight. But now, losing Joe, he felt himself going into a tailspin.

"Sam?" Joe said, his voice too soft.

"What?"

"It has nothing to do with you. If I were going to teach, I'd want to do it with you."

"Yeah."

"I would, kid."

"Just forget it, Joe."

"We're going to see more of each other. I promise."

"You always say that," Sam said, sinking into his pillow. He was still weak and tired; he felt it now. He didn't even have the backbone to act his age, pretend he didn't care that Joe was going to leave again, go somewhere halfway around the world and see Sam only when Sam made the effort.

"I'm kinda tired," Sam tried to say. The words came out garbled.

"I mean it, Sam," Joe said. Sam's eyes were closed, but he felt his brother squeeze his hand. "This time it's going to be different."

* * *

Augusta lay in her hospital bed, drifting in and out of sleep. She had a concussion, and had suffered two seizures. An earthquake and two aftershocks, she thought of them. Her head ached terribly, but she refused to let anyone know. Caroline was sitting beside her bed, watching Augusta with that clear, steady gaze the whole family had come to rely on. The sight of her flooded Augusta with such gratitude she gave a big smile even though she had taken her bridge out.

"Caroline," she said, the word coming out as a croak.

"Are you thirsty, Mom?" Caroline asked.

"A little," Augusta said. She let Caroline push the button to raise her head, the little motor humming inside the bed. She opened her mouth as Caroline tilted the glass, poured a trickle of ice water into her parched throat. She swallowed, opened her mouth for more.

Caroline supported her head so carefully. She watched like an eagle, making sure Augusta didn't dribble on her chin. When Augusta had finished drinking, Caroline wiped her lips with a tissue. Augusta almost couldn't bear it, the love in her oldest daughter's eyes. When Augusta had given so little in return.

"Here we are," Augusta said.

"You and me," Caroline said, smiling.

"Toothless and bald," Augusta said. She was too tired to feel vain. They had shaved her head to stitch the cut, and she didn't have the energy to wear her bridge. All she wanted to do was sleep.

"You're still beautiful, Mom," Caroline said.

Augusta shook her head, but she felt better to hear it.

"How is Skye?" Augusta asked. "Have you seen her today?"

"She's fine," Caroline said.

Augusta nodded, looking away.

"What, Mom?"

"I almost feel . . . I don't have the right to ask," she said. "We turned you over to the universe a long time ago. Why should I think I can get you back now?"

" 'We'?"

"Your father and I."

"Oh, Mom," Caroline said. "You didn't pawn us."

Augusta waited for her to say more, but she didn't. Why should she? Caroline just didn't want to hurt her mother by agreeing with the truth: that Augusta had been a selfish

mother, unwilling and unable to go through the hard parts
of life with her three daughters. Wanting only the art and
the parties, the love and the fun and their father. Augusta
blinked, to focus her blurry vision.

"Mom, get well," Caroline said, such warmth in her
black-pearl eyes. "Don't think about bad things right
now. We need you at home."

"Have you ever needed me?" Augusta asked without
rancor. "I can't see why. I was a terrible mother."

"That's not true," Caroline said, her smile growing wider.
She meant it, Augusta could see. She felt tired, nearly exhausted from the effort of simply staying awake. Sleep was
coming, she could feel it deep inside herself.

"Do you know, I've been lying here, thinking about it
all. They're giving me medication that makes me so drowsy.
But I think about you girls, and your father and me, and I
keep trying to figure it all out. How it all turned out so
wrong. As if there's one little piece missing, and if I can just
get to it . . ."

"It didn't turn out all wrong," Caroline said.

"Our messy lives. We loved you girls so much. That
much I know. He wanted so desperately to protect you.
And when he couldn't, he turned away. There wasn't anything I could do to stop him."

Caroline touched her mother's forehead, soothing the
worry out of it.

"What good does it do?" Caroline asked. "Thinking
of that? It's over, Mom. Just get better."

"One little piece," Augusta said "I just want to put it
all together."

* * *

When the time came for Joe to leave the hospital, he
didn't really have anyplace to go. He had chartered the

Meteor out to a group of physical oceanographers from Woods Hole. They intended to record wave anomalies in the Atlantic Ocean—measure the heights and periods of standard waves, hoping for the occasional rogue. They were willing to pick up the *Meteor* in Black Hall and drop it off in Piraeus, doing their research as they crossed the Atlantic.

Fine with Joe. He felt relieved to have the *Meteor* on her way over. He had to be in Greece by the first of October, Mykonos by the seventh. The weather would be favorable then, the water clear. His operation was a joint venture with an archaeologist out of Marseilles. Their permit covered thirty days, and the Greek government was not known to be flexible with extensions.

Caroline had invited him to stay with her until he left.

Joe had hesitated. Not because he didn't love her or want to spend his last days in New England with her, but because he didn't want to hurt her. He knew he would leave Black Hall as soon as Sam was better, as soon as they let him out of the hospital. He had told that to Caroline. She had listened, taking it all in, then said she knew, she didn't care, she wanted him to stay anyway. Skye was staying at her house too. Not wanting her to return alone to Firefly Hill, Caroline had convinced her to stay in the guest room.

Joe and Caroline sat on her porch glider. The night was warm, and haze hung low in the marsh. Caroline wore a white cotton dress. Joe was slouched down at one end of the glider, and Caroline leaned against his chest, away from his sore arm. Homer lay at her feet, his head resting on folded paws, utterly content to be with Caroline.

"It's so quiet," Caroline said.

"It is," Joe said, playing with her hair.

"Sam looked good today. He liked the brownies Clea made him."

"Sam's in love with Clea," Joe said. "If Peter weren't such a good guy, I believe Sam would try to steal her."

"Everyone loves Sam," Caroline said.

"Even you?" Joe asked.

"He's my buddy," Caroline said. "I like that, the way our families go—"

"Go what?"

"I was going to say together," Caroline said quietly.

Joe nodded. His chest felt tight, the way it did when he stayed underwater for too long. That afternoon Peter had asked him about Greece, and Joe had felt the tendons in his shoulder start to throb as he thought about leaving.

"I like your family too. Skye and Clea." He grinned. "Your mother . . ."

"She's very polite about you staying here," Caroline said, smiling. "But I think it's because she knows it's not going to be for very long."

"It's not?" Joe asked, surprising himself by the way his voice lifted at the end.

"Is that a question?" Caroline asked.

"I guess not," he said. "Too bad you have your business to run. Otherwise I'd tempt you into coming to Greece with me. You keep telling me you love to travel."

Caroline lifted her eyes. Her expression was direct and sharp, not soft at all. She didn't smile. "Don't tease me," she said.

Easing out of Joe's arms, she lifted their empty water glasses. She walked barefoot into the house, and he heard her moving around the kitchen. He sat very still, wondering how it would feel to live there. To not be planning the next treasure hunt. His shoulder throbbing, he shifted on the glider.

The old dog looked up at him. Reaching down, Joe petted his head. Homer leaned into his hand, making friends. They had a lot in common, loving Caroline. Joe stroked the brittle fur, gentle and rhythmic.

"Should we go find her?" Joe asked. Homer struggled to his feet, limping into the kitchen.

Joe paused behind Caroline. She stood at the sink, rinsing the glasses. He could tell by the way she stood that she was upset, that he had hurt her.

"Caroline," he said, "I'm sorry."

She didn't move. She stood there, the water running over her hands. Joe put his hands on her shoulders and turned her around. Her cheeks were wet and there were tears in the corners of her mouth. Her eyes were stern.

"You have nothing to be sorry for," she said. "I'm just a little sad, okay? Aren't I allowed to feel sad?"

"You're allowed," Joe said. Because he felt sad too.

Homer stood beside Caroline. He gazed up at her, sensing her mood. As if he understood her need for comfort, he nudged her thigh with his head. She reached down to pet him, then lowered her head to his. Joe watched for a moment, realizing there was something eternal in the relationship between them. Homer was very old, past the age most dogs lived, and it hurt Joe to think he would soon die.

"Have you had him since he was a puppy?" Joe asked.

Caroline stayed where she was. Lovingly Homer bumped her head. When she stood, she wiped her tears.

"Not quite," she said. "I got him when he was about a year old."

"He must have been a beautiful young dog," Joe said. "Why did his first owner give him up?"

"He died," Caroline said.

"Oh, no," Joe said, petting Homer's back. His spine was visible through the reddish coat, and he arched into Joe's hand. Caroline reached for something on the table. It was Skye's hospital bracelet. She had cut it off her wrist earlier, leaving it on the kitchen table before going to her room for a rest.

"Skye killed him," Caroline said quietly.

"God," Joe said.

"We were hunting. She was only seventeen, and she thought she was shooting a deer, but it was a man." Caroline bowed her head.

"I'm so sorry," Joe said.

"She's never gotten over it," Caroline said. "It was just an accident, but that doesn't matter."

"No," Joe agreed, stunned.

"I was with her. She was beside herself—couldn't believe what she had done. I sat with him while she stood there. Poor Skye," Caroline said.

"He died there in the woods?" Joe asked.

"Yes," Caroline continued on. "I held his hand. He had such bright eyes. He was lying there, on the trail, and I remember thinking he looked so nice and *bright*. That's the word I kept thinking. So bright."

"Caroline," Joe said, moved beyond words. She had seen both his father and that young man die. He loved a woman who was so kind and sensitive, and all these years he had resented her for not telling him faster. Her father had sent them hunting because of something his father had started. "What was his name?"

"Andrew Lockwood."

"Homer was his dog?"

"Yes. It was a beautiful day, and they were just out for a walk. Homer was kissing him. Licking his face all the while, trying to make him better. When Andrew's eyes closed, Homer just licked his eyes. He never wanted to stop."

Joe looked at the dog's white face. He could see him

kissing his dying master, and knew why Caroline loved him so much. And why the dog loved Caroline.

"How's Skye?" Joe asked.

"I don't know," Caroline said. "It's with her all the time."

"Do you think she'd go to an AA meeting?"

Caroline paused. She glanced from Joe to Homer in that blank way of someone who had lost hope that a tragedy could be averted. She shrugged. "I don't know," she said. "I doubt it."

"It helps me," Joe said.

"I wish . . ."

"What?" he asked.

"That it could help her," Caroline whispered.

"Caroline," Joe said. Something was building inside him, and he had to get it out.

"What?" she asked.

"Come with me."

"To a meeting? But—"

"No, to Greece."

She looked shocked. Did she think he was teasing her like before? He pulled her into his arms. He said it again, looking straight into her gray eyes. "Come to Greece with me."

"Don't joke," she said.

"I'm not. Tell me one reason why it wouldn't work."

"My family," she said, "I can't leave them. And I have an inn to run."

"You love to travel, everyone knows it. Michele knows how to run the inn. And your family—"

She waited. She wanted him to finish the sentence: will be fine. But they both knew such predictions were impossible, that fate played tricks on people, that keeping watch was just an illusion. You could be standing right beside your sister, and she could kill a man. You could be ten feet away, and something terrible could still happen.

"Your family knows you love them. You'll be back."

"I will?"

"Yes. I'll talk to the guys at Yale. Not this fall, but maybe next year. I'm thinking of Sam too. Watching you with your family makes me want to do better with him. I've been on the run for a long time."

Caroline stepped away from Joe. Homer had retreated to an old blue blanket in the corner of her kitchen, and she leaned against the counter, watching him. He hadn't taken his eyes off her, and her sudden attention made him raise his head, bang his tail on the floor. Caroline leaned over to pet him, and to reach into a fold of the blanket. She pulled out a small towel, battle-scarred from many play sessions. Homer bit one end while Caroline held the other.

"My father started this," she said, tugging on the towel.

"With Homer?"

"Yes. When we first brought him home, he was so upset. He cried all the time, and he wouldn't play with any of the toys we gave him. Balls, bones. Then my father gave him an old towel. It was soft, and I guess it smelled like us."

"Homer liked the game?" Joe asked, wondering what this had to do with going to Greece.

"Yes. Homer loved it. He carried the towel everywhere, and when the first one got all chewed up, we gave him another. He'd always want my father to play with him." She paused, standing to face Joe. "My father liked it too. Till he got so sick. Then he stopped everything."

"His cancer, you mean?"

"No," Caroline said. "The kind of sickness that made

him drink and turn away. Like Skye now. I'm afraid to leave her."

Joe walked over to her. He felt his heart pounding. He had never wanted anything as much as this. He wanted her with him, but at the same time, he needed to help her. She was caught in a trap, trying to save someone who had to help herself. He took a deep breath, than held her face gently between his hands.

"Do you know what the opposite of love is?" he asked.

"Hate? Joe, I could never—"

"Fear."

"The opposite of love is fear," she said, frowning.

"We could be so fearful, we could let this go."

"I don't think I'm afraid—"

"You just said you're afraid to leave Skye."

Caroline nodded, seeing his point.

"And your father," Joe began. Talking about Hugh Renwick wasn't easy, especially when what he had to say was so filled with the understanding of one flawed man for another.

"What about him?" Caroline asked.

"Tell me something. How did Homer like your father?"

"He loved him," Caroline said. "It was so sad, ironic, really, that after my father died, Homer cried for him the way he'd once cried for Andrew. For days and days. He'd disappear from the house, go off on these long walks. He'd come home and howl on the porch."

"For your father."

"Yes," Caroline said, recognition dawning in her eyes.

"Even though your father had stopped playing with him. He might have turned away, but that didn't stop Homer from loving him."

Caroline nodded, her eyes briming. She bowed her

head for a minute. Joe waited, wanting to touch her but knowing she needed to decide for herself.

"I'm not afraid," she said suddenly, raising her eyes. They were full of tears, the most beautiful eyes he'd ever seen.

"You're not?"

"The opposite," she said.

Joe grinned, knowing she meant love, that they were picking up where their letters had left off so long ago.

"When do we leave for Greece?" she asked.

"As soon as Sam's out of the hospital," he said, taking her in his arms.

CHAPTER TWENTY-ONE

AUGUSTA WAS RELEASED FROM THE HOSPITAL RIGHT after Labor Day. She went straight to Clea's house, because Clea was the daughter best equipped to give their mother the care she needed. The bad blow Augusta had suffered had affected her motor skills and she needed physical therapy three times a week. This meant driving her to a rehabilitation facility and encouraging her to do her exercises at home.

Caroline gave her a fabulous black hawthorn walking stick with a sterling silver handle, which Augusta thought was marvelous. Antique and Irish, like something Oscar Wilde would have used had he ever needed a cane. Since they had shaved her head at the hospital, she was growing to enjoy being bald—or at least she was making the most of it. Her hair would grow back, but for now she wore the beautiful and dramatic silk scarves her daughters kept bringing her. She twisted them into turbans and thought she looked quite regal. Divine, considering.

But Clea felt overwhelmed. Her whole family considered her the rock. She kept house and cooked gourmet meals. She ran her children from day camp to flute and trumpet lessons to the movies all day long. She was the minister's wife, she stood by Peter's side at weddings and funerals, sickbeds and prayer services.

Having her mother under her roof was making her crazy. It wasn't Augusta's fault. For once, her mother was being meek. She seemed grateful for every saltine, every glass of seltzer water. Her doctors had told her she couldn't drink alcohol while she was taking anti-seizure medication, and Augusta hardly complained. Every day at five she would say, "Time for a martini!" But Clea wouldn't bring one, and Augusta wouldn't push it.

Mainly, Augusta stayed in her room and listened to music. It confused Clea to see her mother so quiet and contemplative. One day she called Clea to her bedside. Clea had thought she was going to ask for an extra blanket, or a glass of ice water, but instead, Augusta patted the quilt and asked Clea to sit by her side. Reaching for an English bone hairbrush, Augusta began to brush Clea's hair.

"Tell me something," Augusta said, slowly stroking Clea's hair.

"Like what?" Clea said, feeling goose bumps on the back of her neck from the unfamiliar pleasure of her mother's touch.

"Anything, honey. Just tell me a story. Anything at all."

"Well, Maripat and Mark both want to sign up for a new soccer league."

"About you, Clea," Augusta said. "I love the children, but I want to hear something about you."

"Oh, Mom," Clea said, her throat constricting, hardly knowing where to start.

"Something about Clea," Augusta said. "Tell me."

"But why?"

"I'm so sorry there has to be a 'why,' " Augusta said. "That you don't think it completely natural for me to wonder about you."

"You had Dad to worry about," Clea said.

"Yes, I did worry," Augusta said, brushing Clea's hair,

"that he'd find me boring, feel closed in, go off with someone else. You girls suffered for it."

"I'm fine, Mom," Clea said. "And Caroline is great." Caroline had announced her plans to go to Greece. While no one was totally surprised, the reality of her departure—for an entire year—felt daunting.

"But Skye's not."

"No," Clea said. Skye had moved out of Caroline's, back to Firefly Hill, where she could be alone. Clea had stopped by once with an extra pot of beef stew, and found her in bed at four in the afternoon, staring hopelessly out the window. Feeling her mother brush her hair, Clea closed her eyes. She tried to imagine how she would feel if she knew Maripat was suffering the way Skye was, and she knew her mother had a broken heart.

"What can I do, darling?" Augusta asked. "I know it's a case of too little too late, but I can't bear it. I can't bear to see her this way."

"I don't know, Mom," Clea said, reaching back for her mother's hand. It felt thin and frail, and when she turned around, she saw how old her mother looked. Augusta stopped brushing Clea's hair, letting her hands fall to her lap.

"With Caroline off to Greece, I don't know. . . ."

"She'll be back."

"I've let her handle so much for so long. She's taken care of Skye all her life, while I . . . wasted so much time."

They looked into each other's eyes, the two mothers of the family. They each understood how it felt to raise daughters, the special worries of letting their beloved girls out into this world full of dangers, and Clea tried to send her mother some of her own strength. Clea had gotten it from somewhere, and she liked to think some of it had come from Augusta herself.

"What happened?" Augusta said in the absent way of someone who has woken up from a bad dream. "That's what I asked Caroline. With all our gifts, all the love we have for one another, what went wrong? That's what I want to know. That one missing piece."

"Life, Mom," Clea said, holding her mother's hand. She thought "what if" all the time: What if Peter died, what if someone hurt one of the children, what if she fell through the ice in the pond? Terrible things happened when you least expected them. But so did wonderful things, so did joy. "That missing piece is life," she said.

"Life," Augusta said, tilting her head.

* * *

Skye was alone at Firefly Hill. She had agreed to have dinner with Caroline and Joe. What she wanted to do was pull the curtains, turn off the phone, and get the job done. She wanted to kill herself. She was so sick of living. Nothing touched the agony inside.

The house was a tomb. Memories everywhere. Homer's fur all over the furniture, but no Homer. He was at Caroline's, her mother was at Clea's walking with a cane and undergoing physical therapy because of the man Skye had brought into their home. Simon was in Boston. He had gone back to Biba, but he would have to face charges for assault and attempted rape in the coming months. Skye didn't care. She didn't love him anymore. She didn't need him—didn't need anyone. She loved only her father. She had recently imagined herself drinking with his ghost. Talking out loud to him, telling him how she felt, begging him to forgive her.

Someone knocked on the door. Expecting Caroline and Joe to just walk in, she felt surprised. She checked herself in the mirror: bloated face, circles under her eyes, her hair a rat's nest. She noticed a dark stain on the front of her sweater, but she didn't care. Slowly, every joint in her body aching, Skye went to the door.

It was Joe. He stood on the porch, all alone. Skye looked around.

"Hi," Joe said.

"Hi. Where's Caroline?"

"At home. Can I come in?"

Skye swung the door open. Without speaking, Joe walked past her. He waited until Skye remembered to ask if he'd like to come into the kitchen.

"What's wrong? Is she okay?" Skye asked.

"She's fine," Joe said, eyeing the bottle. Skye blushed. She hadn't drunk from it, but she had been staring at it for the last half hour.

"Would you like a drink?" Skye asked.

"Skye?"

His voice was so quiet, so calm and kind, it stopped Skye in her tracks.

"Would you like to go to an AA meeting instead?" he asked.

"AA?"

"Alcoholics Anonymous."

"You're one?"

"I'm one," he said, smiling.

"How did you know?" she asked, trembling. "What made you go?"

"It was over for me," he said. "I didn't want to do it anymore."

"I'm so tired," Skye said. She thought of the bottle, how she could drink it all night and not feel drunk, how nothing was chasing the pain away. She thought of her .22 out in a shed behind the house. She hadn't checked on it in a while, but for the last day and a half she had been imagining how it would feel to pick it up, do to herself what she had done to a man on a mountain trail.

"I was too," Joe said. "I was sick and tired of being sick and tired."

"That's it," Skye said, tears streaming down her face. "That's how I feel."

"You never have to feel this way again. Will you come with me?" Joe asked.

Skye took a look around the kitchen. There were the clay handprints she had made for her father in first grade. The bust of her mother she had done in high school. There were pictures of her and her sisters, dressed in their red-checked coats, ready to go hunting on Redhawk one Thanksgiving weekend. A picture of her father the year before she shot Andrew Lockwood; it was the last picture of him that showed him smiling. He had spent the rest of his life drunk.

"Dad," Skye said out loud.

"He'd want this for you," Joe said.

"I feel like I'm leaving him," Skye said. Then, giving Joe a defiant look, "I love him."

"Why shouldn't you? He's your father."

"Everyone blames him" she said.

"He's still your father."

Skye nodded. That's how she saw it: Before the hunts, before the shooting, there was a big man who taught her how to draw, carried her on his shoulders, took her swimming at the beach.

"You're not leaving him, Skye," Joe said, reaching out his hand.

The tears ran down Skye's face. She picked up her father's picture and held it to her breast. She felt so afraid of leaving the house. She and her father were so alike, artists who had made mistakes with the ones they loved, who drank because they couldn't bear the hurt in others' faces.

"Come, Skye," Joe said. "Please?"

She took a deep breath, put down her father's picture. If she looked too deeply into Joe's eyes, she would see more than she was prepared for right now. He was helping her out of love for Caroline, she was sure. Skye was sure Caroline knew what he was doing, that she was sitting home right now with Homer, wishing her heart out that Skye would go to the AA meeting with Joe. It would make leaving for Greece so much easier.

"You're taking her away," Skye said.

"Only to Greece," Joe said. "Not *away*. She could never go away from you."

"It's too far," Skye said.

"She hasn't left yet," he said. "She's five miles up the road right now."

Caroline leaving for Greece: another blow, another reason to take the dark path, hide out, turn away. It was so much easier to sleep than be awake, to drink than to stop.

"There's a saying in AA," Joe said. "Don't quit before the miracle."

"What's the miracle?"

"You'll know it when you see it," Joe said.

"What if I never see it?"

"If you quit, you'll never know what you might have missed."

Closing her eyes, Skye thought of the .22. She thought of her father and Joe's father; she thought of Andrew Lockwood. Their faces had been so clear, but now they were fading. She couldn't bring them into focus. Right now the face she was seeing was Caroline's.

Skye's eyes slowly opened, and she nodded.

"Okay," she heard herself saying. "I'll go with you."

* * *

Every morning Caroline found herself giving Michele a little more of the inn's business to handle. She took her to Coastal Bank & Trust, introduced her to the bankers, explained the workings of various accounts.

Michele was a quick study. She seemed eager. She learned fast, asked the right questions. Of course, she had been at the front desk for ten years, so she had a head start. Caroline noticed Tim hanging around some afternoons, taking a regular seat in the bar. Classes had started at the college, and he would sometimes drop by with colleagues or students to have a beer and talk about the artists of Black Hall. Seeing him there made Caroline happy. She knew he was at the inn to support Michele, that he would keep it up when Caroline was away.

Other days, Caroline wasn't sure she wanted to leave. How could she sail away with Joe and leave the inn behind? How could she leave her family? They needed her too much. Maybe she hadn't been the perfect sister to Clea and Skye, the perfect daughter to Augusta, but she had done her best, and so far hadn't they all survived? They wobbled along, the Renwick women, a troupe of off-balance acrobats trying to pedal bicycles across a high wire.

Sam was scheduled to be discharged from the hospital the following day, and she and Joe were supposed to leave a few days after that. Skye was now going to meetings. Caroline knew her sister's new sobriety came with no guarantees, but she had hope. She knew that she had no other option.

Caroline dropped in regularly at Clea's to visit her mother. Augusta was trying to be a good sport. She didn't like the idea of Caroline leaving, especially for

Greece—especially with Joe Connor. But she held her tongue. As if she had decided enough harm had been done in their lives, she seemed unwilling to do more. She didn't dislike Joe; she resented his father for the violence he had introduced to their family.

Three days before she was going to leave, Caroline drove Augusta to the hospital for a checkup. They were in the neurologist's office, waiting to see the doctor, when Joe and Sam walked in. Augusta froze. This was her first moment face-to-face with Joe Connor since the Firefly Ball.

"Hello, Mrs. Renwick," he said, holding out his hand.

"Hello, Joe," she said cautiously. She shook his hand, then his brother's. The boys kissed Caroline, and everyone seemed very chummy.

"Looks like we have the same doctor, Mrs. Renwick," Sam said.

"Call me Augusta," she said. "You too, Joe."

"Thanks, Augusta," Joe said.

Caroline and Joe had a million things to do before they left. They stood off to the side, by the receptionist's desk, going over a checklist. Augusta and Sam sat alone, not knowing quite what to say to each other. Augusta reached up to make sure her turban was in place.

"Hey, nice hat," Sam said, grinning. His skin was pale, the circles under his eyes dark and deep. Skinnier than ever, he must have lost ten pounds. He had a big white bandage on his head, exactly like the one Augusta had worn the previous week.

"Thank you," she said demurely. "Yours is quite nice too."

"Feeling better?" he asked.

"A little shaky these days. And you?"

"Wobbly as all hell. If you'll excuse my language."

"Think nothing of it," Augusta said, peering at him. She was looking for a resemblance to his brother, but saw practically none. Joe was strapping and sexy, while Sam was thin and gawky, handsome in an English-schoolboy way. Glasses, tufty hair sticking out of the bandage, a narrow face.

"Actually, my head hurts all the time," he said, leaning closer to her. "They're giving me anti-seizure medication, and it makes me feel like sleeping."

"Me too," Augusta said. "It's awful. I feel like I'm living in fog, and I'm not allowed to drink martinis. Do you have seizures?"

"I had one," Sam said, staring at his knees.

Augusta touched the back of his hand. The poor child. He was so young. "Did you hate it?" she asked.

"Yeah," he said. "I don't want to have another. My doctor said they're not uncommon with head injuries. Have you had any?"

"Two. Nightmare roller-coaster rides. Once they started, nothing on earth could stop them."

"Wow, it rots, huh? My brother would go crazy if he knew. He thinks the accident was his fault."

"Your brother," Augusta said, folding her arms and biting her lip as she watched Joe and Caroline laughing quietly.

"You don't like him?" Sam asked.

"Nothing to do with you, dear," she said. "But certain things from the past. And now he wants to take Caroline off to Greece."

"He's a good guy," Sam said.

"If you only knew the whole story. It started with his father, you see, coming into our home one Christmas Eve and threatening to kill us all. I hope I'm not shocking you—"

"I know the story," Sam said easily. "But you're missing the best part."

"Which is?" Augusta asked. She was changing in ways she couldn't comprehend, including allowing the possibility that this skinny child, his head addled, might have something to tell her about her family's tragedy.

"Your daughter's in love with him."

Augusta turned her head to stare.

Sam shrugged. "I don't want him going to Greece either. But do you honestly think you're going to stop them? You might as well decide to play ball."

"I've never played ball," Augusta said thoughtfully.

"You'd better start now, Augusta," Sam said. " 'Cause that's what life's about."

* * *

"I think I got Augusta to give you her blessing, dragging Caroline off to Greece with you," Sam said. This was his first walk outside, his first day out of the hospital. Warm in the September sunshine, he and Joe were heading down a road by the sea.

"You're a powerful man," Joe said.

"She's stubborn," Sam said. "But who can blame her? Not wanting to send her daughter off with a scoundrel like you?"

"Good point," Joe said, kicking a stone down the road. "But what about you? You gonna give me your blessing?"

Walking slowly, Sam caught up with the stone. He tried to kick it, missed, scutting his sneaker on the tar. His vision was off. He closed one eye, kicked again, connected with the pebble.

"It's not forever," Joe said. "My permit's only for thirty days."

"Thirty days in the Aegean, then on to—where?"

"Lamu," Joe said. They rounded the bend and came

upon a break in the trees. The Sound glittered in the sunlight, sparkling dark blue.

"Where's Lamu?" Sam asked, giving the stone an angry kick.

"The Indian Ocean. You know damn well."

"Is Caroline going with you?"

"Yes," Joe said.

Sam took a big breath of sea air, felt pain shoot down his neck. He was flying to Halifax the same day Joe and Caroline were leaving for Athens. His doctors told him his vision would improve, the pain would subside, and he'd probably never have another seizure again. But he had long ago lost the only girl who ever mattered, and he didn't look forward to missing Joe.

"You've got my blessing," he made himself say.

"Thanks," Joe said. He picked up the pebble they'd been kicking and handed it to Sam. Sam looked down at the small rock in his hand, then back up at Joe.

"What's this?" he asked.

"Objects are important," Joe said. "They remind us of things, you know? Like all that loot I brought up from the *Cambria*. Like my old man's watch—still don't know where it got to."

"What's a stupid stone supposed to remind me of?" Sam asked.

"Black Hall," Joe said.

"What about it?" Sam asked.

"A place to look forward to."

"We're here now. What's to look forward to?"

"Jobs," Joe said.

"I've got a job," Sam said. "On a research vessel out of Nova Scotia."

"I'll write to Yale from Greece, you do your part from Canada, we'll meet back here same time next year."

Sam stopped to stare at Joe. His mouth must have

been hanging open, because Joe reached over to close it for him.

"Didn't you hear me?" Joe asked, chucking Sam under the chin.

"I heard. You're full of shit." Sam stood his ground. He felt like charging his brother like a bull, knocking him over, pounding his face in the dirt. Joe had teased him unmercifully as a kid, and Sam felt he was doing it once again.

"Believe what you want," Joe said, shrugging.

"You take it too lightly," Sam said roughly. "Family ties. You're what I have left, with Mom gone. So don't play around—" Sam stopped, watching Joe's smile widen. For the first time, he began to believe that maybe Joe wasn't kidding.

"I'm not playing around," Joe said.

"Swear?"

"Swear."

"Yale? You really think I should pursue the position there?"

"If you want to hang out together, yeah."

"You think I'll get a job?" Sam asked, his throat aching right into his ears.

"Probably not," Joe said.

Sam laughed, blinking at the bright sun that was making his eyes water.

"Why would they want to give the job to a biologist who doesn't even know a mako when he sees one?"

"Blacktip," Sam corrected.

"Mako," Joe said.

* * *

Caroline and Clea visited Skye, and together they walked Firefly Beach. Homer explored the high-tide line for dead crabs and old lobster buoys. The sisters knew they were saying good-bye. It wasn't time to say the words yet, but the feeling was in the air. They strolled along, feeling the hot winds of summer give way to the cool breezes of autumn, full of gratitude that Skye seemed to be getting better. Secretly they were all trying not to worry that Skye would tumble without Caroline there to catch her.

With each AA meeting Skye attended, her desire for drinking lessened. But that first meeting remained sharp, so clear in her mind.

Quivering from alcohol withdrawal for the second time that summer, Skye had gone to that first meeting with Joe. The room was small and dingy, in the basement of a white church in Eastbrook. Signs covered the walls, those little sayings she and Simon had once made fun of: One Day at a Time; First Things First. Skye had felt so scared, so nervous. But the people were friendly and kind. They made her feel welcome right away. Joe had never been to that particular group, but he spoke to one woman, telling her Skye was new, and the next thing Skye knew, she was surrounded by women, all giving her their phone numbers, all telling her things would get better, that she never had to feel this way again.

One woman had said, "I wish you a slow recovery," and that was what was happening. Baby steps. She went to a meeting every day. Sometimes she went with Joe, sometimes she called one of the women she had met that first night, but mostly she went alone. One day at a time, Skye was not drinking.

That in itself was a miracle. She cried a lot. A *lot*. Some days all she could do was eat popcorn, lie on the sofa in the fetal position, and cry. She would talk to her sponsor, an older woman who had been sober for sixteen years, whom Skye already loved more than just about anyone but her sisters and mother, and who understood everything Skye was going through because she was an alcoholic too. Skye would cry as if it were the end of the world, and her sponsor would say, "Yes, but did you drink?" "No," Skye would say. "Then you're having a good day!" her sponsor would say, sounding jubilant, and Skye would know she was right.

"Are you all packed?" Skye asked Caroline.

"Almost."

"What do you need for Greece?" Clea asked. "A bathing suit?"

"Two, I think," Caroline said.

"None," Skye said. "Just you and Joe and the sea and sun. Naked."

Caroline smiled. She picked up a flat stone and skimmed it across the shallow water: seven quick jumps. Clea tried: three blooping ones. Skye found a perfect scaler and sent it surfing the sea: eight jumps. Her hand didn't shake at all.

The sisters turned toward the steep stairway and began the trek up. Homer went first. He moved stiffly, but then he got the rhythm. He took the steps one at a time; when he came to Firefly Hill, he had taken four at once.

"You leave tomorrow," Skye said.

"I know."

"Mom's coming home, and we'll be fine. We'll be together," Skye said to set Caroline's mind at ease.

"That's great, Skye."

"Are you excited?" Clea asked.

"Yes, very," Caroline said. But she didn't sound it. Her voice was hesitant. She was trying to smile, but her forehead looked worried. Homer brushed against her as if he knew they didn't have much time left together.

"What's the matter?" Skye asked.

"I feel like I'm forgetting something," Caroline said.

"Like what?"

"I don't know." Now she really smiled, as if she had been caught in her old pose: oldest sister, perfectionist, worrywart. She was leaving for Greece with the man of her dreams. She had to just let herself go.

"Well, you have till tomorrow to figure it out," Clea said.

"That's right," Skye said. "Mom's coming home, you're leaving home. We'll have a little party."

Having reached the top of the steps, they paused to catch their breath. Skye looked out to sea, feeling free. She didn't hate herself anymore. It was so new, life without drinking. The blue water sparkled, empty without Joe's white ships. Forgiveness was possible, even for herself. Her heart felt calm, she was taking everything as it came. For now anyway. For today.

"I can't believe it," Caroline said. Suddenly she smiled, as if it were sinking in. "I'm going away with Joe."

"It's about time," Clea said.

"The longest love story I've ever heard," Skye said, "because no one will ever tell me it didn't start when you were five."

"Good-bye," Caroline said, "will be very hard to say."

Homer had been lying on the grass, taking a rest. But suddenly his head lifted, and his sleepy eyes turned eager. He sprang to his feet, his sore legs buckling only slightly. Perhaps he had heard a bird, or an animal in the brush, because his scruffy mane bristled, and he let out a sharp yelp. Then, like the young dog he used to be, he ran across the wide field toward the pine forest and disappeared into the trees.

"Where does he go?" Caroline asked.

"The secret life of Homer," Skye said.

"He probably has a girlfriend in Hawthorne," Clea said.

"A pretty girl Lab who loves to swim and doesn't mind slobbery old towels," Skye said.

"Someone for Homer to love," Caroline said, sounding so unlike the Caroline from before, Skye had to turn away, to keep her sisters from seeing the tears in her eyes and getting worried all over again.

CHAPTER TWENTY-TWO

WHEN THE TIME CAME FOR CAROLINE TO LEAVE, HOMER wasn't back. Everyone else had gathered at Firefly Hill: Augusta; Clea, Peter, and the kids; Skye; Sam; Joe and Caroline. Augusta was on her best behavior, not trying to change Caroline's mind, getting along with Joe better than anyone had dared to expect. The family was together except for Homer. Mark and Maripat had been sent down to the beach to scout around for him. Perhaps it shouldn't have mattered so much that he be there—he was only a dog—but it did.

The men were loading the car. It was a bright September afternoon, cool and clear. The Renwick women had a few minutes alone in the kitchen, and they were making the most of it by sitting around the table for a cup of tea. Caroline wore her going-away clothes: a charcoal-gray suit, starched white shirt, the cameo at her throat. She had that overly composed, Carolinesque air to her. Augusta had come to recognize it as Caroline's matriarch look, and seeing it twisted her heart just slightly.

"You look great, dear," Augusta said.

"Thank you, Mom."

"As if you have absolutely everything under control,

every single detail in place. I wish I could be as collected and serene as you."

"Really? I'm a mess inside," Caroline said calmly. "For some reason, I feel as if I'm about to get seasick."

"Maybe you're pregnant!" Clea said happily.

Caroline gave her a long look, blowing on her tea. "I'm not," she said. "I just feel funny, like I'm missing something."

"Don't you want to go?" Augusta asked. "You can always change your mind. It's not that I don't like Joe. You know that, don't you?"

"You've been very nice to him, Mom."

"Well, if you're not in the mood to travel, you can wait here till he gets back. Although, frankly, I wouldn't let him out of my sight. I'm being very honest with you, Caroline. If you really love him, I wouldn't send him off to the Greek isles alone. He's a very charismatic man."

"Mom, he's not Dad," Skye said, smiling. "And Caroline's not you."

"I'm well aware of that," Augusta said. She smiled. She was being very brave about this. How could she say everything that was in her heart? Her oldest daughter was about to leave home just as Augusta felt she was on the verge of becoming a good mother.

"Mom," Caroline said, taking her hand.

"You don't have to worry about me," Augusta said, her voice strong. She knew what she had put her children through, knew how totally they had cared for themselves and each other over the years.

"We'll take care of her," Clea said.

"Or she'll take care of us," Skye said.

"Oh, Skye," Augusta said. She had been holding herself together, but hearing Skye's declaration, seeing her beautiful face nearly clear of bruises, made Augusta think she might break into pieces.

"Look what you did this summer," Skye went on.

"Got right between me and Simon. You protected me, Mom."

"I did, didn't I?" Augusta said with a certain amount of wonder. "I was never very good at it before though. Protecting you girls . . ."

"You're good at it now," Caroline said.

"I wish your father were here right now," Augusta said.

"I wish it too," Caroline said. Her throat was low, and she touched it as if it ached. "I think that's what's missing. Remember, Mom? We were talking about it a week or so ago? That one little piece?"

"Dad?" Clea asked.

"Dad," Caroline said.

"I miss him terribly," Augusta said.

"The summer's been about him, in a way," Caroline said. "With so much about James Connor and Andrew Lockwood, the hunts . . ."

"Homer getting old," Clea said.

"And me getting sober," Skye added.

"He was such an extraordinary man," Augusta said.

"And I never understood him at all," Caroline said. "So many things have become clearer this summer, but that part hasn't. If anything, he's farther away."

Her sisters looked quietly into their teacups, and Augusta sniffled loudly.

* * *

Caroline knew it was time to go.

Her mother patted her scarf, adjusting it carefully. She did look stunning, like an aging film star. Her scarf-turbans went perfectly with her black pearls, her New England–Hollywood looks. But seeing her mother, Caroline could tell that Simon's attack had taken something out of her. For the first time, Augusta looked old.

"Mom, are you okay?" Caroline asked.

"Just thinking of Hugh."

"We loved him, Mom," Clea said.

"It was never that we didn't," Skye said.

Augusta nodded. She looked tired and resigned, as if, like Caroline, she had spent too much time searching for the missing piece, the explanation that would weave it all together.

"Remember chasing fireflies?" Caroline asked. "Dad could do that with us for hours. It was always dark and hot, the middle of summer, and the stars were always out."

"Oh, sweetheart," Augusta sighed.

Caroline stared at her mother, trying to memorize her face. She would take it with her wherever she went, the image of her mother's eyes. She felt the pull of love, the eternal conflict of being a daughter.

"Remember when you were six," Clea said. "You caught a firefly, and you were so excited, you fell and squished it?"

"I started to cry," Caroline said steadily. "My firefly was dead, and Dad came off the porch. I remember him walking through the field, through the tall grass. He looked so gigantic."

"Hugh couldn't bear to hear you cry, Caroline," Augusta said. "Ever. When you were an infant, he'd pick you up at the least whimper. The nights he was home, he would walk you for hours, up and down the hall, just to keep you happy."

Caroline nodded, touching her lips. For some reason, she could almost remember that too. It was as if the family ghosts or angels had cast a spell on the table, made it possible to remember impossible things. Closing her eyes, she could feel herself in the palm of her father's hand, smell his scent of cigarettes and oil paint, hear him singing her a lullaby. Driving her home the time she had a fever. But none of those things was the missing piece.

"Chasing fireflies," Augusta said. "It wasn't just when

you were young. I vividly remember the summer Homer came to live with us, your father running through the salt hay with him, on the trail of anything that blinked."

"I loved Dad for that," Caroline said. It was true, she thought: With all the later hurt, during the years he spent drinking, she forgot the total love. "And I wish Homer would come back to say good-bye to me."

After a moment, Augusta reached for her cane. She motioned for the girls to stay where they were. She stood painfully, got used to her feet, and left the room. Caroline heard her thunking up the stairs, along the upstairs hall. She wondered how long her mother would keep the house. Firefly Hill was big and rambling, and maybe someday it would start to make sense for Augusta to live somewhere else. Somewhere smaller, more manageable.

Or maybe she would stay there until she died.

"I'm going to drive the mailman crazy," Skye said, "asking him for letters from you."

"You have to call from absolutely everywhere," Clea said.

"I've changed my mind," Caroline said. "I'm not going. Joe will have to find someone to take my place."

"Excellent thinking," Clea said. "Shall I tell him to move along?"

"Caroline?"

At the sound of her mother's voice, Caroline turned around. Augusta leaned on her silver-topped hawthorn stick, a gentle smile on her face. Clea and Skye stood still. Their mother seemed weakened by the exertion, but happy, content in a way Caroline had never seen her before.

"Go get them," Augusta said, nodding to Skye. "Please?"

"Who?" Skye asked.

"Joe and Sam," Augusta said.

Surprised, Skye stood still. Then she ran out the door

as fast as she could. They watched her run barefoot to the car, say something to Joe.

"What, Mom?" Caroline asked.

"I have something for your friend."

"Joe?"

Augusta nodded. She touched her black pearls, then she reached out her frail hand and touched Caroline's cameo. Caroline had found a length of black velvet ribbon and threaded it through the fragile gold clasps.

"Beautiful things," Augusta said, "from people we love. Objects matter."

"I know," Caroline said. She didn't know what was happening, but it began to dawn on her: Her mother was honestly making peace with Joe.

The screen door opened. The September evening was cool and a small burst of wind blew in. Skye stood there, smiling. Sam burst through the door, followed by Peter. Very cautiously, Joe followed. Caroline felt her heart quicken at the sight of him. He looked so handsome and tall, his white shirt tucked into his jeans. He smiled and said hello.

Augusta put out her hand. She stood tall and regal, her face stoic and dignified. Caroline watched Joe glancing around. His gaze lit upon the old kitchen table, the terra-cotta tile floor, old family photos, clay handprints of each of the girls. But Caroline knew he was thinking about his father. Caroline reached for Joe's hand, and he held tight.

"It was here, wasn't it?" Joe asked.

Augusta nodded.

"Right here," Joe said, staring at the place Caroline had shown him.

Augusta took four steps, stood in the exact spot where James Connor had fallen to the floor. "Here," she said.

Joe went to stand beside her. Caroline let go of his hand, and she leaned into her sisters, watching Joe and her mother. The moment seemed intense and private. Charged tension passed between them, the old woman and the son of the man who had died in her kitchen that Christmas so many years ago.

"He spoke of you that night," Augusta said in her low voice.

Joe nodded, frowning.

"I'm sorry, Joe," Augusta said, handing him something. "Please forgive me."

Joe examined the object in his hand. He held it up, and Caroline saw something heavy and gold.

"My father's watch," he said.

"I took it," Augusta said. "That night. If you had any idea . . ." She bowed her head, trying to control her voice. "When it was over, when your father was lying there . . ."

Caroline looked at Joe, saw him wiping away tears. She wanted to go to him, but the moment belonged to him and her mother.

"And Caroline was crying so hard, clutching your picture. Something made me take his watch. Forgive me, Joe. I don't know why I did it. I was rather crazed, you know? Your mother had my husband, so I thought I'd take something that belonged to her. I don't know."

Joe nodded. He gazed at the watch, turning it over and over in his hand. Caroline knew Augusta's explanation didn't matter. She knew what Joe's father's watch meant to him, and she had wondered: Searching his whole life for treasure, did any object compare to the sweet memory of his father's gold watch? And now Augusta had given it back to him.

* * *

"Thank you, Augusta," Joe Connor said. What he did next seemed so natural, it stole Caroline's breath away: He took her mother into his arms. Augusta dropped her cane in order to put both her arms around his neck. The stick clattered to the floor.

"You're welcome, Joe," Augusta said when she let him go.

But Joe held on. His hands still resting on Augusta's arms, he began to smile. His blue eyes widened.

"What, dear?" Augusta asked.

"Your pearls," Joe said.

"Oh," Augusta said, blushing with pride, brushing the pearls with her fingers. "Hugh gave them to me. They are rare black pearls, from one particular bay in the South Seas, near Tahiti or somewhere marvelous like that. But of course you probably know. Being a treasure hunter and all."

"Actually," Joe said, "I was thinking of how they remind me of Caroline's eyes."

Caroline caught her mother looking at her.

"Greece," Augusta said after a moment. "Hugh always said he'd take me there."

"I wish I were going," Sam said.

"They'll be back," Clea said reassuringly. "Yale, you know."

"Yale," Peter said. "Excellent school."

"Ah, Yale is just a four-letter word," Sam said. "Greece is where it's at."

"Take good care of her," Augusta said to Joe, looking him straight in the eye.

"I will," he said, gazing at her hard.

"Make sure," Clea said, standing beside Joe, her voice choked up. Skye didn't say anything, but she nodded.

"I promise," Joe said.

"He's getting better at promises," Sam said. "I swear."

"Enough out of you," Joe growled, but the look in his eyes was clear and full of love. "Why don't you get busy?"

"Get busy with what?"

"Finding that girl."

"What girl?" Sam asked, blushing.

Joe laughed. "See? You're such a damned academic, you've forgotten all about her."

"Sam's so adorable," Clea said. "There must have been hundreds of girls."

"Yeah, probably," Joe said, staying focused on his brother's eyes. "Only one who counted, though. But he's forgotten all about her."

"No, I haven't," Sam said, so quietly Caroline almost couldn't hear.

"A girlfriend for Sam?" Augusta asked. "How lovely! What's her name?"

"Hey, never mind," Sam said, now truly flustered. "We're saying good-bye to Caroline and Joe. That's all that matters right now."

Caroline smiled at him, her beloved's baby brother, and knew that some girl would be very, very lucky to have him. Then Joe took her by the arm, kissed her on the lips, and told her it was time to go. Her heart aching, she hugged them all: Clea, Skye, Sam, Peter, and the children. She told them that she loved them, she promised to write.

When she got to her mother, she stopped.

"Darling," Augusta said, "this is it."

"Thank you, Mom."

"For what?"

Caroline paused. For listening to the truth, for defending Skye, for letting Joe into their home, for having the courage to start to change, for the gift she had given her daughters that night: a way back to their father. If you start with love, can forgiveness ever be far behind? But she couldn't put those things into words.

"The missing piece?" she asked.

"Was that it?" Augusta asked, her eyes bright. "I want to feel like we found it, but I don't. Darling, I don't."

Caroline and her mother hugged, and neither wanted to let go. Clea and Skye had to step forward, to pry their mother away, whispering in her ears that it was time for Caroline to leave.

"Where's Homer?" she asked, looking around.

"We checked the beach, Aunt Caroline," Mark said. "He wasn't there."

"I want to say good-bye . . ." she said.

"He's so old, darling," Augusta said. "I don't like to say this, especially with you about to leave, but they're known to go off by themselves at the end."

"He's sixteen," Skye said.

"I want to see him," Caroline said. "We have to find him."

"There's only one thing to do," Sam said.

"There's no way we're leaving without you seeing him," Joe said.

"Let's look in the woods," Caroline said. She led the way.

* * *

They marched through the woods in swift silence. The scent of autumn was growing strong. The forest smelled of drying leaves and fallen pine needles, mushrooms clinging to the undersides of dead trees. It was the same time of year they had brought Homer here to live, and the old memories caused Caroline to feel a distant sadness, a longing for things long ago. She led her family, Joe, and Sam down the dry streambed, through the old cemetery where her father was buried, toward the curving path down the hill—the back way to Firefly Beach.

"Homer!" she called.

Her voice carried through the trees. Couldn't he hear it? Homer knew the sound of bags being thrown into cars, the excitement of travel. He had done it often with Caroline, and she believed that he realized what was happening now: that she was leaving. Old love was stirring in her, the feeling of his head under her hand, the memory of rescuing him from the concrete kennel when he was just a puppy.

A bark sounded. Was it Homer? Caroline felt the yearning. She wanted to see him for what might be the last time.

"Did you hear him?" Caroline asked, peering through the thick brambles. A bright opening led to the beach. "Homer!"

The old dog lumbered down the path from the sand, his eyes shining with love. Caroline crouched down, her arms open, watching him come. He had a big smile on his white face, his mouth drawn back and his brown eyes laughing.

"Where were you?" she asked as he crashed into her arms. He nudged his nose against her face, licked her eyes and cheeks and hands. She let him slobber all he wanted because she was so happy he was returning from his adventure to see her off. Running back the way he had come, he waited for her to chase him. He was leading her on a chase, though the thicket, over the silver green grass onto Firefly Beach.

"Where do you go, Homer?" Augusta called, following behind. "On your mysterious trips?"

"You're a traveler, aren't you?" Caroline asked when she caught him on the beach, looking deep into his eyes. "But you always come home."

Her heart ached with love for Homer, and for her entire family. How could she leave them at all? Why would anyone choose to walk away from all this, the comfort of their old home, this magical beach, the sure love of their sisters and mother and old dog? Homer sat on his haunches by a driftwood log, looking into her face with such keen emotion, she wished she could read his mind. Gentle waves broke on the sand, whispering secrets.

"Darling, you know I'm not one to shove you along, but don't you have a plane to catch?" Augusta asked.

"We do," Joe said, sinking down in the sand to pet Homer. The old dog looked long and hard into Joe's face. He seemed to be reading it: the blue eyes, the shape of his mouth, the strength of his chin. As if making up his mind, Homer sniffed his hair. He gave Joe a slight lick, then another. The gesture wasn't love, probably not even affection. But it was open and generous, a way of telling Joe to take good care of the girl they both loved.

"I'll bring her home soon," Joe said. Caroline nodded. She gave Homer a big hug, smelling the scents of drying grasses and sea air. Then, kissing him once on the nose, she stood up.

"Let's go," she said quietly to Joe, wanting to leave before she changed her mind.

"Okay," he said.

But Homer yelped. He lay down as if he were in pain. The fallen leaves were a reminder of another trail, from long ago, and Caroline felt her pulse quicken. She crouched beside him. Her hands traced his body, wanting to soothe him, but feeling for lumps or broken bones.

Rolling on his back, he wriggled in the white sand. His face was full of play. Caroline knew he was trying to keep her near. She was about to stand, to lead him back to the house, when Joe crouched down. Something under the huge drifthood log had caught his attention, and he twisted his neck for a better look.

"Look," he said.

"Oh, great," Sam said. "Our eminent geologist has just discovered some rare beach glass that requires his immediate examination. Stand back."

"No, look," Joe said softly, taking Caroline's hand.

"Whoa," Sam said. "This could be, like, the coolest way to give someone a diamond ring—like hiding it in the parfait, only better. What'd he do, get Homer in on the caper?"

"Sam, shut up," Joe said, gently directing Caroline's attention to the underside of the old tree. Silvered by weather, surrounded by sand and seaweed, was a message, deeply scored into the wood.

The second she saw it, Caroline knew. Her eyes filled with tears. She petted Homer, and she let Joe hold her hand. She stared at the words, letting the tears spill from her eyes. Blinking, she could almost see her father's old Buck knife: its handle worn, the blade carefully sharpened before every use. It wasn't that she recognized his carving, or that he had signed it with his initials. But she knew.

"Mom?" she said.

"Yes, darling?"

Everyone gathered around. Caroline felt them crowding beside her, crouching around her. Joe's arms held her tight, and Homer licked her hand.

"Dad was here," Caroline said.

Everyone bent down to read the words, but only Augusta read them out loud: " '*I love them all.*' "

"Dad carved that?" Clea asked.

"Certainly," Augusta said, eyes shining.

Skye put out her hand, touched each letter. Her shoulders shook with sobs, but she looked straight at Caroline, smiling.

Behind them, wind moved the reeds. A seagull began to cry, wheeling overhead. Slowly the beach became more alive. The birds were getting used to the humans' presence; very cautiously they began to come closer. Dusk settled on the sand, the last light evaporating into the violet sky. Caroline heard a twig crack and looked up in time to see a deer, approaching the creek. She thought of her father, of his love for nature. He had brought them somewhere beautiful after all.

"Why didn't he tell us?" Skye asked quietly, staring at the words. "Instead of just carving it?"

"It was right here, the whole time," Caroline said. How had Homer known? Had he followed her father?

Had he heard him cry, watched him drink his whiskey, tried to console him as he walked down Firefly Beach and knelt down to carve his message?

Augusta nodded. "This is just an outward sign, but—"

"Outward signs are good." Clea grinned.

"Especially when they're the missing piece," Caroline said.

* * *

It was time to go, that eternal moment between saying good-bye and actually leaving. Everyone had promised to write and call, everyone had kissed and hugged.

They were a close family. Was it possible to hold on too tight? All these years, living near Firefly Hill, Caroline had never wanted to go too far away for too long. As if in her absence shots would be fired. Someone would get hurt, the old dog would die. All her beloveds would disappear without her.

Now she knew that wasn't going to happen. Missing pieces do more than complete the puzzle, they fill an empty space. Caroline's heart was full of the knowledge that her family's love wasn't going anywhere.

Stepping away from the house, Caroline held Joe's hand. They stood still for a moment, breathing the salt air and the last herbs of summer. The waves rumbled over the tide flats. Gulls cried out at sea, and one lonely whippoorwill called from a distant marsh. Sam walked ahead.

Caroline looked toward the shoals, where the wreck of the *Cambria* still lay. She closed her eyes and thought of her father, whose ghost had been such an important part of this magical night. She wore Clarissa's cameo around her neck; Joe had his father's watch in his pocket. The stars were out, and she found one for Andrew Lockwood. Their dead were with them always, showing them the way.

"Caroline!" Clea called from inside the kitchen. "Look!"

"Look!" Skye said.

When she turned back to the house to see what her sisters were talking about, Caroline saw a firefly. It was September. The night was cool; fireflies should have been long gone for the summer. But there it was, undeniable, darting through the grass above the beach. Green-gold, it glowed like magic, like a whisper from the past. The firefly zigzagged through the night. Homer chased it just like when he was young, playing on the sand with Hugh.

"Good dog," Augusta called. "Good, wonderful dog."

Caroline gazed at her sisters and mother. They stood inside the kitchen, shadowed by the screen door. Homer walked slowly to the porch. He sat down, facing her. They watched each other for a long time. The sea broke on the shoal, and the waves rushed in. Joe squeezed her hand. Caroline squeezed back.

"We'll take care of him, darling," Augusta called.

"I know," Caroline called back.

Turning away, she walked with Joe Connor through the tall grass of Firefly Hill. He held the door of the car while she climbed in. Once inside, Sam gave Caroline several reassuring pats on the shoulder.

"Ready?" Joe asked, his clear blue eyes smiling.

"Ready," she said, waving to her mother and sisters.

"As ready as we'll ever be," Sam said. "We'll be back in a year."

"A year," Joe said. "Only a year."

"A year's not so long," Sam said.

"No, it's not," Joe said.

Joe started the engine. He pulled away slowly, so he, Caroline, and Sam could wave. Beach stones crunched under the tires. She had the missing piece in her heart; it would be there always. Homer followed the car down through the dark and graceful tree canopy to the ocean and roads that led away from, and back to, Firefly Hill.

"I love them all!" Caroline cried out the open window.

The night was silent as the car sped away, but she could swear she heard her mother's voice calling the same thing back.

November 6, 2000

Dear Everyone,
We made it!

    Greece is beautiful, just like the postcard: white churches, rocky cliffs, the bluest water in the world. But it's not home, and none of you are here. Homer would understand. We have the missing piece in our hearts, and it will bring us safely home to Firefly Beach.

                         WE LOVE YOU ALL,
                         C+J

DON'T MISS

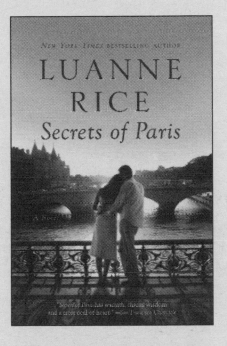

NOW AVAILABLE IN PAPERBACK
FOR THE FIRST TIME

Irresistible, long sought by readers, and at last available in paperback, *Secrets of Paris* is *New York Times* bestselling author Luanne Rice at her most incandescent—a deeply moving story of true love, abiding friendship, and a once-perfect marriage in jeopardy.

Turn the page for a special preview.

1

What I am about to communicate to you is the most astonishing thing, the most surprising, most triumphant, most baffling, most unheard of, most singular, most unbelievable, most unforeseen, biggest, tiniest, rarest, commonest, the most talked about, the most secret up to this day, the most enviable, in fact a thing of which only one example can be found in past ages, and, moreover, that example is a false one; a thing nobody can believe in Paris (how could anyone believe it in Lyons?).

—From Madame de Sévigné to Coulanges,
December 1672

LYDIE MCBRIDE OCCUPIED a café table in the Jardin du Palais Royal and thought how fine it was to be an American woman in Paris at the end of the twentieth century. The sun warmed her arms. People strolled along the dry paths, and the silvery dust mingled with the smell of strong coffee. It was one of the first hot spring days. Then something happened—cups clattered on the waiter's tray, or the breeze shifted, and Lydie thought of home. She felt a keen hankering for it: for her family, for her block in New York City, for the racetrack, for strangers speaking English.

"May I borrow your sugar?" someone asked in a low voice.

Lydie jumped. She had just been longing so hard to hear the English language, she wondered for an instant whether she had conjured the sound out of the May air. But then she regained her composure.

"Of course," she said, passing the china bowl to the woman at the next table. She watched her, a tall woman Lydie's age with dark hair twisted into a chignon, stir two sugar cubes into her coffee. This woman wore red lipstick perfectly; her eyes were hidden behind big sunglasses. Lydie, who never wore much makeup and had the sort of flyaway red hair that always looked uncombed, had the impression of much gold jewelry.

"I need some quick energy," the woman explained. "I just had a fitting at Chanel—an experience that never fails to take the heart out of me."

Lydie smiled at the way she made shopping at Chanel sound like torture—somehow Lydie knew that she lived here.

"What brings you to Paris?" the woman asked.

Lydie hesitated, trying to formulate the short version of a complicated answer. "Well, for work. Michael—my husband—is an architect. He's working on the Louvre, part of an exchange program. And I'm a stylist."

"A stylist? As in hair?"

Lydie laughed. "No, I work with photographers, doing pieces for magazines and catalogues. I set up the shots.

The editor tells me what he wants in a photo layout, and it's my job to get all the props."

"I think my husband uses stylists," the woman said. "He's in the jewelry business."

"Yes," Lydie said, nodding. "I work with jewelers a lot. He's French?"

"Yes, but we met in America. . . ." The woman trailed off, as if she thought the conversation was going on too long or growing too intimate. "I'll tell you something," she said. "I met my husband one day, he took me to Guadeloupe the next weekend, and then I enrolled in Berlitz, and then he asked me to marry him. You'll think I'm crazy, but it all took place in less than five weeks. The French understand, but Americans never do."

Lydie leaned forward, and she captured the moment, sure as a photograph: the way the sun struck the woman's hair, the blaze of primroses in a jardiniere behind her head, Richelieu's palace casting a shadow on the garden. "I don't think that's crazy," Lydie said. "I believe in love at first sight."

"Well," the woman said. She checked her watch, a tiny gold one with Chinese figures instead of numerals. Then she looked at the sky. "I should go. I'm running late."

Now Lydie checked her watch. She had planned to go to the Bibliothèque Nationale, to look up details of seventeenth-century weddings for a piece in *Vogue*. Then, like the woman, she gazed up. She felt unwilling to leave. The palace against the blue sky looked dark and ancient, as if it had stood there forever. She wanted to stall for time, to prolong this pleasant, casual conversation with another American. "Where are you off to?" she asked after a moment.

"Oh, home," the woman said. "I told my housekeeper she could go online."

"Your housekeeper?"

"Yes. I'm teaching her to use the computer. Didier bought it when personal computers hit Paris in a big way, but it just sits there."

Lydie regarded the woman more carefully. With her jewelry and clothes and slightly regal bearing, she gave the impression of someone who would want distance between herself and a domestic employee. "Are you training her to do your correspondence?" Lydie asked.

The woman smiled, but the smile seemed distant. "Kelly wants to improve her life. She's a Filipino, from the provinces outside Manila, and she's here in Paris illegally. She's just a little younger than I am—she's been to college. She shares a place with an amazing number of brothers and sisters. Her goal is to get to the United States."

"And you want to help her?" Lydie asked, sitting on the edge of her chair.

"Well, it's practically impossible."

"My parents immigrated to the United States from Ireland," Lydie said.

"It's especially hard for Filipinos," the woman said, again looking at her watch. She gathered her bags and stood. "Well. Hasn't this been fun?" she said.

"Maybe . . ." Lydie began.

"We should exchange phone numbers," the woman said, grinning.

And while Lydie wrote out her name and number on a piece of notepaper, the dark-haired woman held out a vellum calling card, simply engraved, with an address on the Place des Vosges and the name "Patrice d'Origny."

⌖

Walking down the rue des Petits Champs, Lydie felt in no hurry to get to the Bibliothèque Nationale. Even though she had hours of research to do for a photo series that was already a week overdue, she felt like playing hooky. The BBS wheels on a red BMW 750 parked by the curb caught her eye. Nice wheels, Lydie thought. She had spent many childhood Saturdays at her father's body shop in the Bronx—a cavernous place filled with smells of exhaust and paint, the flare of welding torches, the shrieks of machinery and metal tearing—without seeing many BBS wheels. Her father was the boss but wore blue overalls anyway. He would leave her in the office, separated from the shop by a glass window, coming back every fifteen minutes or so to visit her.

"What happened to that car?" Lydie had asked once, watching another wreck towed in.

"An accident, darling. He hit a tree off the Pelham Parkway, and he must have been drunk, because he knew how to drive."

"How do you know?" Lydie asked, when what she really wanted to know was what had happened to the man.

"See his wheels?" her father asked, pointing at the car, leaning his head so close to Lydie's that she caught a whiff of the exhaust that always seemed to cling to his hair and clothes. "They're BBS. A man doesn't buy wheels like that if he doesn't know how to drive."

To her father, "knowing how to drive" had covered more than mere competence. It was a high compliment and meant the driver was alert behind the wheel, unified with his car and the road, aware of the difference between excellent and ordinary machinery.

Walking away from the red BMW with its high-performance, nonproduction wheels, down the narrow Paris street, Lydie had the urge to drive fast. In America she raced cars for a hobby, but over here she hadn't had the desire. She had resisted this move to Paris. She had told Michael it was because she didn't want to leave her family, which now consisted of only Lydie and her mother. But Michael had said no, what Lydie did not want to leave was her family tragedy.

Eight months before Michael accepted the position at the Louvre, Lydie's father had killed his lover and himself. Margaret Downes. Lydie felt a jolt every time she remembered the name. After forty years of what everyone considered a great marriage, Cornelius Benedict Fallon had fallen in love with another woman. Lydie hadn't known and Julia claimed, even now, to have had no clue. Lydie knew there must have been clues, and she often felt furious with her mother for not seeing them. Because right up until the time the New York City detectives knocked on her door, Lydie had believed in her mother's myth of a happy family.

Lydie was her parents' only child; born relatively late in their marriage, she knew she was beloved. They had raised her to feel confident and live like a daredevil. A favorite story of her father's was of how Lydie at eight, watching the Olympics on television, had suddenly stood and done a perfect backflip off the back of the sofa. The second time she tried, she broke her collarbone. During high school she took up whitewater kayaking, tutoring children in a neighborhood few of her convent school classmates would even visit, and hitchhiking to Montauk on Saturdays. One day her father let her take an H-production Sprite for a spin. The intensity of concentration required to speed thrilled her, and from then on she thought of racing as a legitimate way to drive a car fast.

Cutting through the Galerie Vivienne, remembering that Bugeye Sprite and her old fearless self, Lydie felt her eyes fill with tears. The emotion was so strong she stopped in front of a wine shop, pretending to regard the window display while she cried. She thought of the car Michael had given her for Christmas, just before the shooting. They had shopped around together, and Lydie had fallen in love with a showroom stock Volvo 740 wagon. Michael had grinned at the idea of his wife racing a station wagon, the car favored by women living in the Litchfield Hills to ferry kids and groceries around Lime Rock. Secretly, he had bought it for her. Lydie closed her eyes, remembering that Christmas morning: in their apartment on West Tenth Street she had opened a small box containing brown leather driving gloves, a map of Connecticut with "Lime Rock" circled in red, and the keys. She hadn't even driven it since her father died. It sat in Sharon, Connecticut, in a garage behind her crew chief's house.

Michael had told her about the Louvre position as if he were giving her a gift even greater than the car: the gift of adventure, a year in Paris. But Lydie hadn't wanted to come. She had wanted to stay in New York; she couldn't imagine leaving her mother. She couldn't imagine leaving the scene. But in spite of lacking heart, she couldn't say no to Michael, who was incredibly excited about the move. And then, the day had come to pack their things into a crate that would cross the Atlantic on a Polish freighter.

Julia had sat on Lydie and Michael's bed, watching them pack. Lydie knew that although her mother felt abysmally sad at seeing Lydie go, she wouldn't dream of speaking up. Julia would think that by doing so she would spoil Michael's happiness. She was plump, especially in the bosom, with soft, curly gray hair and, even then, a perpetually happy expression in her blue eyes. Lydie could hardly bear to look at her that day; she rummaged through a dresser drawer. Coming upon her driving gloves, Lydie slipped them on, flexing the new leather.

"Can't wait to see you drive at Le Mans," Michael said. "It's only about two hours from Paris."

"I can't wait," Lydie said, doubting even then that she would drive in France.

"Oh, you two will have such a ball," Julia said, grinning. "All the museums and the restaurants. Your aunt Carrie and I spent a weekend in Paris one time. It was lovely."

"Flying to Paris from Ireland is like taking the Eastern Shuttle to Washington," Michael said. From his tone Lydie could tell he felt grateful to Julia for her enthusiasm.

"Well, we took the boat, but yes—distances are so different over there. It's a short trip from Paris to anywhere in Europe. You'll have a marvelous time."

"It'll be great," Michael said, speaking to Lydie.

She said nothing, but smiled at him. He was trying to assemble a cardboard carton. The sight of her tall husband—a whiz on any basketball court but a klutz when it came to anything remotely mechanical—trying to transform a sheet of corrugated cardboard into a vessel that would actually hold their belongings made Lydie laugh.

"Here, let me," she said, folding flaps, slapping on the plastic tape without even taking off her gloves.

"What a woman," Michael said, bending down to kiss her.

"She's one in a million," Julia said. "After she won her first race at Watkin's Glen, her father said she could do anything. Do you remember that nice dinner we all had afterward?"

"Sure," Lydie said, quivering with the memory. They had drunk champagne, and after dinner her father had bought her a cigar. She could picture her parents perfectly: their proud smiles, her mother's girlish smile, the absent way her father reached over to touch Julia's shoulder. It killed Lydie to think Margaret Downes had already brought her car in for its second paint job in six months, that Neil had already fallen in love with her. The happy expression on her father's face that night, so full of love, had been for Margaret.

Lydie crouched, assembling another carton. Michael sat beside her, pulling the tape out of her hands and holding them tight; he knew what the memory meant to her. Julia said nothing, looking on. She had started to cry but stopped herself. Lydie eased her hands from Michael's grasp, ripped off a piece of tape, closed a seam. Every crack she taped, every box she built, brought her closer to leaving. And, somehow, the idea of leaving the scene of her father's death and crime filled her with doom. She felt wild with an abundance of unfinished business.

"A year in Paris," Julia had said. "I can't imagine any couple who could enjoy it more than you."

But it wasn't working out that way, Lydie thought now, entering the Bibliothèque's vast courtyard. With their great luck, she had thought they would be the most frivolous pair in Paris. But Michael's exhilaration had turned to patience; he was waiting for Lydie to get back the spirit he had fallen in love with. So far it hadn't happened. Since coming to Paris, Lydie felt a gulf widening between herself and Michael, and she couldn't do a damned thing about it.

Just before a race, Lydie always experienced a vision. In a flash she saw the crash, the rollover, herself paralyzed in a hospital. And the vision always refined her concentration, made her take great care and drive more safely. Now, walking numb through the streets of Paris, she felt as if the crash had happened, and she hadn't even seen it coming.

❧

"Why didn't anyone tell us it stays light in Paris till midnight?" Michael McBride asked. He was watching Lydie cook dinner. They stood in the kitchen of their Belle Epoque apartment overlooking the Pont de l'Alma. A roasting chicken sizzled in the oven.

"It's nowhere near midnight," Lydie said, smiling. "It's ten-fifteen, and the sun's going down."

"Lydie!" Michael said, feeling impatient but vowing to stay calm. "I think you're missing my point. All I'm saying is that the sun would have set two hours ago in New York. It's something different, and I think it's neat."

"Paris is farther north than New York," Lydie said. "New York is actually on the same parallel as Rome."

Michael let it drop. If he opened his mouth again, he knew Lydie would come back with another rebuttal. They kept just missing each other these days. Sometimes they had full-scale fights. Like yesterday, when Michael had asked Lydie to meet him at Chez Francis for dinner and Lydie complained bitterly about how she missed Chinese takeout. Then Michael had accused her of deliberately trying not to enjoy their year in Paris and Lydie going on and on about eggrolls.

Still, watching her now, he felt a shock of love for Lydie. She moved around the kitchen with an unconscious grace, a small frown on her face when she concentrated on cooking the meal. He'd seen that same expression on her face when she raced cars. She looked delicate, with her pale skin and fine reddish-gold hair, but Michael had always thought of her as a tiger: strong, always moving, ready for anything.

"I met someone in a café today," Lydie said. "An American."

"Oh?" Michael said.

"We talked for a while, and it made me realize how much I've missed that. Someone to talk to."

"What do you call what goes on between us?" Michael asked. "A silent movie?"

Lydie smiled and laid down her wooden spoon. Taking her hand, Michael led her into the living room. He still felt a jolt when he came upon their furniture, which for seven years had sat in the same New York apartment, here, across the Atlantic, in Paris. There were the low mahogany table, the seascape by Lydie's mother, the sofa covered in a pattern Lydie called "flame-stitch," the ugly lounge chair his father had given him for his thirty-fifth birthday. Lydie, as a stylist specializing in interior design, had great taste, and it had pained Michael to inflict that

eyesore on her. But she had said it wouldn't do to hurt the old man's feelings.

"Her name is Patrice d'Origny," Lydie was saying. "She's married to a Frenchman and lives here permanently."

"Why don't you ask them for dinner?" Michael asked.

"Maybe," Lydie said. Although her voice still sounded subdued, her eyes looked happier than Michael had seen them in quite a while. After eight years of marriage, the sight of her smiling eyes, hazel framed with thick blond lashes, made the back of Michael's neck tingle. The feeling of excitement saddened him, because it was the only important thing between them that still felt true. He wanted to kiss Lydie, but she seemed to be concentrating on something.

"Why say 'maybe'?" he asked. "Why not just invite them?"

Lydie cocked her head slightly, as if she was trying to figure out her own hesitation. But the moment passed quickly. "Why not?" she said.

From her indolent tone, Michael doubted that a dinner with the d'Orignys would come to pass. He cursed himself for the disappointment he felt toward Lydie. But he'd been through it all with her: the sorrow, the mourning, the struggle to understand, and there didn't seem an end to it. Maybe he wouldn't feel so deprived if the contrast were not so great. Old Lydie versus new Lydie; he loved the old Lydie better.

He could see her now, one October day at Lime Rock,

the old Lydie speeding them around the track. She wore her racing overalls and sunglasses; she gripped the wheel with wicked intensity. "You scared?" she asked, possibly wanting him to be. But he wasn't. He was fascinated. He loved riding with her while she cranked the Volvo wagon up to 135 MPH. Seven miles down Route 112 Michael had pulled off the road and there, behind a red barn, Lydie dropped her overalls, laughing because she wore nothing under them, wanting Michael to be amused. Amusement was not what he remembered feeling. He remembered pulling her close, kissing her, feeling her shiver in the autumn air, making love to her on the cold ground.

And the words "cold ground" made Michael think of Neil Fallon. He and Neil had gotten along well, more like friends than father- and son-in-law. But Michael laid the blame for Lydie's transformation directly at Neil's feet. The man had lived his whole life as a good husband and father, an average businessman who had cared more about coming home for dinner every night than making a million dollars. He had devilish charm; on a bet he had truly, before witnesses, sold drunken Dennis Lavery his own car. With his elegant profile and wild black hair, Neil was so handsome that even Michael noticed. He was a Lion and a Knight of Columbus, a regular churchgoer who could be seen passing the basket at nine o'clock mass at St. Anthony's. By the time he started spending time with Margaret Downes, he had established himself as such a pillar that Julia and Lydie never questioned his absence or preoccupation. So how could Michael blame Lydie for falling apart when Neil, with his sharp-tongued, gentle-eyed Irish devil act, had turned out to be the Devil himself?

Michael knew that he was the only person Neil had told about Margaret Downes. Two nights before the shooting, Michael dropped his own car off at Neil's shop and hung around waiting for Neil to give him a ride home. Dented or mangled cars filled the six bays. Welding torches roared. An irate customer leaned across the office desk, haggling over the cost of replacing his Ford LTD quarter panel.

"I can't leave yet, but let's get out," Neil said, frowning, leaving his Danish office manager to placate the customer.

They road-tested a Ford pickup, down Zerega Avenue to the Hutchinson River Parkway. Neil drove easily, playing with the wheel and accelerating in a way that reminded Michael of Lydie. They headed north, toward Connecticut.

"What's up?" Michael asked after a long while; he had never known Neil to maintain a silence for more than a minute, and it alarmed him.

"I'm in love," Neil said, staring straight ahead.

"With someone . . ." Michael tried to hide his shock.

"With someone besides Julia," Neil said, finishing Michael's thought for him.

"What are you going to do?" Michael asked, with full Catholic knowledge that Neil could never divorce Julia, that Neil was talking about a mortal sin, that the situation was impossible.

"Not a damn thing. She won't leave her husband," Neil said, his voice bleak. "I want to see Margaret tonight; I'll have one of the fellows drive you home."

"That's okay," Michael said. "I'll take the subway."

"I want you to tell them you left me working at the shop."

"You want me to lie to Lydie and Julia for you?" Michael asked, making it as plain as possible that he thought Neil had sunk very low. Was Neil implying that if Margaret would leave her husband he would leave Julia?

"Yes," Neil said, sounding remote, without a trace of defiance. Then he shot Michael a dark look. "If you ever did this to Lydie, I'd kill you."

That was in Michael's mind now as he stared across his Paris apartment at Lydie: her father telling Michael he would kill him if he ever betrayed her. It had struck Michael odd at the time, for Neil to threaten, even if he hadn't meant it, to kill Michael. It proved that killing was on his mind; two days later he had shot himself and Margaret.

"I know what," Michael said to Lydie. "Get on the telephone, call your new friend, and ask her out to lunch tomorrow."

"Right now?" Lydie asked.

"Sure. Before you forget all about each other," he said, for he doubted she would call on her own.

Lydie went through her briefcase, found Patrice's card, dialed a number on the phone. Turning his back, Michael walked to the window. He heard Lydie speak French, then English. Horns blared on the Avenue Montaigne. The tour boats plied the river Seine beneath their window; their spotlights shimmered across the white walls, a twinkling of pale yellow, peach, and silvery grey.

"She invited me over," Lydie said, coming toward Michael. "Tomorrow, to her apartment on the Place des Vosges."

"That's great," Michael said. He felt a mixture of things: relief, as if this new friend of Lydie's could give to her some of the things Michael found himself increasingly unable to give, and hope. Hope that this could make her happy. He thought of her walking to the Place des Vosges tomorrow, of all the wonderful parks and monuments she would pass. The Grand Palais, the Champs-Elysées, the Place de la Concorde, the Tuileries, the Louvre. Let Paris make you happy, he thought.

"I'd better check the chicken," Lydie said. Michael had often heard her mother's theory that roast chicken was the truest test of a good cook. He went to her then, held the back of her neck. She tilted her head, and he looked into her eyes, golden in the half-light. He kissed her, thinking of the places they had kissed in spring: at the track, underwater, on a peak in the White Mountains, in Florence, on a hot subway platform at Fourteenth Street, now in Paris. The kiss felt right, and so did his arms around his wife. But the rest of it was unfamiliar. He thought the word "wife." It meant possession, love, sex: in that order. Then he thought "Lydie," which had once meant everything in nature and the world, and wished that it did not now only mean "wife."

Prologue

BRITTANY CALLAGHAN STARED IN THE MIRROR ABOVE her dresser, satisfied with the results. The blouse was sequined, fancy, but not too sexy. The jewelry was demure, nothing flashy. The long velvet skirt was elegant, slim, slit to the knee. It had taken her two hours to get ready, not that she needed that much time to look nice, but tonight was special, so she'd devoted more time than usual in her preparations.

Her makeup, applied just right, brought out the deep green of her eyes. Her roommate, Jan, had done her hair, managing to get the long mass of copper into a tight coiffure that would have earned Jan praise in her beautician's class. They made a great pair as roommates, swapping each other's skills as needed. Brittany could fix just about anything that went wrong in the apartment and kept Jan's car in top shape, while

Jan cooked most of the meals and did Brittany's hair for special events, since she never had time to get to a beauty shop herself.

They had been sharing an apartment in Seaview now for three years. It wasn't a big town by any means. Oddly, it wasn't by the sea either and the standard joke was that it was named in anticipation of "the big quake" that would show up one day, bringing the coast to them. A joke in poor taste, but if you lived in California, you either joked about earthquakes or you moved.

Seaview was one of the newer towns spread out inland away from the big cities, but within reasonable driving distance if you happened to work in the big city. The closest big one in their case was San Francisco. They were far enough away to not experience the chill weather and fogs off the Bay. They enjoyed such mild weather, in fact, that Sunnyview would have been a much more appropriate name for their town.

It was great having a roommate she got along so well with. Jan was petite, effervescent, always had a boyfriend on hand for anything she wanted to do, whether it was the same one or not, she didn't particularly care. She liked men, had a need to always have one around, even if she didn't take any of them seriously. Her only fault, if it could be termed one, was that she was a matchmaker at heart. She might not be able to settle on any one man in particular herself, but she saw no reason that her friends couldn't.

Brittany had proven to be a challenging subject for matchmaking though, and not for the usual reasons. She was beautiful, intelligent, responsible, had interesting careers, and admirable goals. She just happened to be six feet tall.

Height had always been a problem for Brittany, from childhood on. It put a serious restriction on the relationships she could develop, to the point where she had stopped putting any effort into developing one.

She had tried dating men shorter than her, but it never worked. The jokes would come out eventually about her height, or the man would get ribbed by his friends, or more often, their faces would accidently brush against her breasts—deliberately of course. She had decided, when she did marry, her husband would have to be at least as tall as she was. Taller would be nice, but she wouldn't hold her breath on getting that lucky, would settle for the same height.

Yet having such a problem did tend to make her notice tall men right off. Unfortunately, with a lot of really tall men, most of that height was naturally in their legs, and on some men, this tended to look a bit odd, particularly on the skinny ones. She'd take odd, though. She wasn't particular, just particular about not wanting to look down on her husband.

But a husband was a long way off for her, despite her age approaching thirty, or so she'd thought. Not that she hadn't wanted one eventually, but she was goal-oriented, and she had one major goal that all her efforts were put into these days, owning her own home that she built with her own hands.

To that end, she worked two jobs, part-time at the local health spa in the evenings and all day on Saturdays, where she kept herself in good shape while doing the same for others, regulating diets and exercise programs. Her full-time job through the week was with Arbor Construction.

Sunday was her only day off, and the only chance

she had to take care of the normal activities of life, like writing her family, balancing the checkbook, paying bills, house cleaning, laundry, shopping, repairing her car, etc. It was also the only day she had to simply relax, and she preferred to spend that free time catching up on sleep or working on designing her dream house, not working on a relationship. The two jobs gave her next to no time for socializing, which was why she had stopped trying—until she met Thomas Johnson.

She had tried seeing the same man more than once, every Sunday actually, tried it with more than a few men thanks to her roommate's persistence. But that never worked out well, because they soon resented that she wasn't available more often. She'd been waiting until after she had her house. She could quit the second job, then have the same free time that everyone else enjoyed. Then would be soon enough to start looking for a serious relationship.

Tom had changed her mind about that. She had begun to think she'd never find the right man for her, but Thomas Johnson filled the bill beyond her expectations. He was six foot six so he met her major criteria, but he was also exceptionally handsome and an established executive in advertising. She was blue-collar, he was white, but they still found common ground. He might make her feel self-conscious occasionally, but that was too minor a thing to counter her belief that he was the one for her. Stubborn certainty might better describe it, but then she *was* Irish.

Actually, her last name might give testament to that, but her family were Americans to the core. Her grandfather Callaghan had owned a farm in Kansas that he built from scratch and that her father inherited when

he died. This is where she and her three brothers grew up. None of the Irish part of their history had been preserved, if anything was known about it, because her grandfather had been orphaned too young to have learned any of it.

But their first names, well, it wasn't hard to guess that her parents had been a bit flaky when they'd started having children. They denied being part of the hippy generation, called themselves "free-spirited," whatever that meant, and in fact, they had met while hiking cross-country, and had gone off to see the world together. They were hitchhiking through England when the first child came along, and had been so impressed with that country, that their sons got named York, Kent, and Devon, in that order.

As the only girl who showed up last, Brittany got named after the entire country. Her parents took offense when it was pointed out that Brittany was actually a province in France, and not the shortened version of Great Britain.

Brittany had a no-nonsense attitude about life. You lived it, and eventually, you might even enjoy living it. That was actually a joke or meant to be, yet it wasn't that far off the mark on her own life. She actually liked her jobs, got a lot of satisfaction out of them, she just missed having the time to do all the little things in life that everyone else took for granted. But then she was no stranger to hard work and having little time for simple pleasures. Growing up on a farm, you went to school, then came home to endless chores. She hadn't had much free time then, and when she left home, even less.

She had made time for Tom, though. They'd been

dating for four months now, went out every Saturday night, spent every Sunday together. As a busy executive who often worked late into the evenings during the week, his time was also somewhat restricted, so he never complained that he couldn't see her more often, was probably relieved that she had no such complaints either. He hadn't mentioned marriage yet, but she didn't doubt that he would soon, and her answer was going to be yes. Which was why she had finally made the decision to give up her virginity to him.

It was an odd thing to still have at her age, odd enough that it caused a good deal of embarrassment if she was forced to own up to it. That usually only happened when whoever she'd been dating started putting the pressure on to have sex. But the result of her confession would always be the same, laughter on their part—or disbelief.

Tom didn't know. He merely thought she was being cautious. It was more than that. Heavy necking was fine, could be fun or incredibly frustrating, but going all the way required more than just liking, at least for her. She needed feelings first, strong feelings, and she had those now. . . .

"Tonight's the night then?" Jan said from the doorway of Brittany's bedroom with a knowing grin.

"Yes," Brittany replied and managed not to blush about it.

"Hot damn!"

Brittany rolled her eyes. "Let's not discuss it, or I'll get cold feet."

"Cold? It's a wonder your feet haven't moldered, you've waited so long—"

"Which part of 'not discuss it' did you misunderstand?" Brittany cut in.

"Okay, okay," Jan conceded with a chuckle. "Just trying to alleviate some of that nervousness you're drowning in. You've been tense about this all day, when there's no need. You *are* sure about him, aren't you?"

"Yes, I—" Brittany started, then groaned. "Oh, God, you're going to make me have second thoughts!"

"Don't do that! Okay, I'm shutting up. Zipped lips. You're going to have a great time tonight. Stop worrying. This guy's right for you. Hell, he'd be right for anyone! He's almost too perfect to be believed—no, scratch that. I didn't say that. Didn't I say I was shutting up?"

Brittany smiled, grateful for Jan's silliness. She *had* been tense, when she shouldn't be. She'd made the decision, had been agonizing over it for weeks, but was satisfied that it was the right step for her at this point. She *was* sure about Tom. That was all that really mattered—wasn't it?

Chapter 1

THE LY-SAN-TERS WERE FINALLY GOING HOME. THIS VISIT to his mother's homeworld of Kystran had been a much longer journey than Dalden Ly-San-Ter had counted on. Still he was glad he had elected to go along. Unlike his sister, Shanelle, who had gone there to study for a while, he had never been to Kystran before. He'd heard much about it from his mother, had seen computer-simulated pictures of life there, but it simply wasn't the same as seeing it firsthand. It was also something he hoped to never have to experience again.

But it was where his mother came from, and he felt he understood her a little better by seeing firsthand the things that made her so different from the Sha-Ka'ani people whom she now lived among. He had always been torn, nearly literally, in two by his parents. His

mother, Tedra, represented all that was modern and "civilized," while his father, Challen, represented old beliefs and what most worlds termed *barbaric*.

There was no compatibility between two social cultures of such complete and utter differences, and yet his parents had managed to become lifemates anyway. Not an easy thing for them, and not easy for their children, who grew up wanting to please them both.

Dalden had finally had to make a choice, and thankfully, his mother not only supported it, but had expected it. He was a Sha-Ka'ani warrior, after all. He could not *be* that warrior if he was going to slip every once in a while and talk as she did, or worry whether he would be displeasing her. So he had fully embraced his father's ways and never regretted it.

His sister, on the other hand, was comfortable with both cultures, could be a dutiful warrior's lifemate, as she now was, adhering to rules and laws that she knew were antiquated by most standards but worked well on Sha-Ka'an. Or she could go out and discover new worlds, as she had once planned to do.

Shanelle hadn't been the least surprised by her first visit to Kystran. Dalden had been nothing but surprised.

He had thought it would be fun. He had expected to be amazed. He even knew the language as well as his own, since, unlike learning it from a Sublim Tape, he already knew all the words that otherwise might not match up without explanations. But nothing could have prepared him for feeling so out of place, for being in a near-constant state of awe. His mother called it "culture shock."

Even after some of the awe died down, which it did

because they ended up staying longer than planned, he still couldn't be comfortable in a land where he wasn't just considered a giant, he *was* a giant by their standards.

Even during the short time they had stopped on the planet Sunder last year to collect Shanelle, his "runaway" sister, Dalden had felt he was dealing with children, those people had been so small.

The Kystrani weren't *that* small, but even their tallest was a good foot shorter than Dalden, and their average a lot shorter than that. It was distinctly uncomfortable to always be looking down on people, and to have those people always staring at you in fear or shock.

The fear was understandable. Some of the Kystrani still remembered all those years ago when warriors like Dalden had tried to take over their planet and had succeeded for a time, enslaving their women, taking away their rights, holding their leader hostage. It was Dalden's mother, with the help of his father, who had defeated those warriors and won Kystran its freedom again.

Tedra had become a national heroine in so doing, and that was the main reason their trip had been extended. They had gone because her longtime friend and old boss, Garr Ce Bernn, director of Kystran, was retiring and had requested their presence for the ceremony. Because it had been more than twenty years since she had been back to her homeworld, he had also arranged for her to be honored while she was there. This amounted to not one but many ceremonies, in many different cities.

Tedra De Arr Ly-San-Ter did not take honoring well. It embarrassed her. To her, she had just been doing her job as a Sec 1 back then, which was to rescue her boss and put him back in power—exactly what she'd done. She had then retired from her life of security enforcement to live with her lifemate on his planet of Sha-Ka'an and had never regretted it. All that honoring had put her in a testy mood that was still with her, even though it was over and they were nearing home.

The trouble was, as Dalden had heard Martha, his mother's Mock II computer, point out more than once, there had been no way to let his father know why they hadn't returned home two weeks ago when they were expected to. Long-distance communication did not include reaching across two star systems.

The distance had been shortened by the discovery of gaali stones on Sha-Ka'an as an energy source that far surpassed anything else known to either of their star systems, but communicating between those star systems was still only possible by the old-fashioned way of sending a ship within range. They would be home by then. So Tedra expected to be facing one very angry lifemate for the worry her longer absence would have caused him.

Dalden was merely amused, but his mother, who would hear no reassurances from him, was determined to fret and worry over the matter. He knew his father would be worried, extremely so. Challen didn't like it when he couldn't protect his lifemate himself, which was why he had "insisted" on Dalden's presence on this journey. But Challen would

understand, once informed of what had kept them. No difficulties would come from it, as Tedra seemed to be anticipating.

Brock, Challen's Mock II computer, who was in control of Dalden's ship, offered yet another reason for Tedra's short temper. She simply missed her lifemate. This was the longest she had ever spent away from Challen since she had met him.

Fortunately for the rest of them, since they spent most of their time on Tedra's ship with her, Martha was managing to channel most of the explosive feelings onto herself. It was one of her main functions and she did it extremely well, keeping Tedra from hurting innocent bystanders either with her deadly physical skills or with angry words, which might cause her later grief. Mock IIs were super-modern, super-expensive, free-thinking computers created for one individual only.

These unique computers couldn't be acquired without the buyer undergoing extensive testing first for the final programming that would bond them to their owner. They were more like a companion than an actual computer, their sole purpose being to assure the health, well-being, and happiness of the one they were created for.

Not surprisingly, there weren't too many Mock IIs in existence. Because they were so powerful—a single Mock II could run an entire computerized world by itself—their cost was prohibitive, so only highly advanced, rich worlds could afford one. Kystran, a very rich trade world, actually owned two. That Tedra had acquired a third when she lived on Kystran was due only to Garr losing a wager to her, and Martha had

been the payoff. That she had bought yet another for her lifemate was a minor point, due to Sha-Ka'an now being the richest planet in the two star systems because of the gaali stone mines there. Their family owned the largest of those mines.

Wealth meant very little to the Sha-Ka'ani, though. They were a simple people with simple needs. But when something specific was needed, it was nice to have the wherewithal to obtain it.

So, Challen had acquired a battleship to accompany his lifemate to Kystran. Her Transport Rover, while able to carry thousands, was a ship used for world discovery, not serious battle. Dalden and another fifty warriors had been sent to protect Tedra, but Challen had wanted her ship protected as well.

They had had no trouble from other ships, though; the trip had been completely uneventful in that regard. But they were all gathered in the Recreation Room six days from home when Martha announced she was picking up a distress call.

"From who?" was Tedra's first question.

"Sunder."

That answer caused major silence, for various reasons. They all knew the planet. All but Tedra had visited it last year, when Shanelle was trying to escape her father's choice of lifemate for her.

Tedra broke the silence first, wanting verification. "Isn't that the planet that Shanelle sought sanctuary on and didn't get it?"

"One and the same," Martha replied in one of her cheerful tones.

But Shanelle complained, "Mother, *must* you describe them like that?"

She had been sitting on an adjusticouch with her lifemate's arms wrapped around her. Falon Van'yer had been talked into letting his lifemate come on this trip, but not without him. And he hated space travel, really hated it. Yet Shanelle had wanted to come, and he would do anything to make her happy—within reason.

Shanelle now glanced back at him warily. He had good reason to despise the Sunderans and wouldn't like being reminded that they had tried to keep his lifemate from him, had even tried to make him completely forget about her. But Falon was looking absolutely inscrutable, though Ba-Har-ani warriors didn't usually hide their emotions. Kan-is-Tran warriors like Dalden and Challen didn't hide their emotions, either; they just had such unique control of their bodies that they seemed to lack any emotion of a strong nature, be it anger—or love.

But Tedra also had good reason to not like the Sunderans. Martha had given her a full account of all that had happened to her daughter while she was there, and if Tedra *had* been there, there would have been a lot of hurting Sunderans before she left.

She snorted now at Shanelle's complaint and turned her aquamarine eyes on Falon. "You know I love you to pieces and will, just as long as my daughter does," she told the *shodan* of Ka'al. "But she sought help from those people and they failed to supply it. It's a moot point that the help was needed against you in particular. And they want help from us now?"

Tedra's ending tone implied, *Fat chance they'll get it.* Falon merely nodded. Dalden knew better than to comment when his mother's dander was up. He left it

to Martha to point out the obvious, which she did now.

"They want help from anyone. We just happen to be close enough to hear it. And having heard it, there is no option of ignoring it—or did you suddenly become an uncaring, callous individual when I wasn't looking?"

That got a baleful glare out of Tedra, directed at the intercom on the wall that Martha's purring voice was coming out of. "I didn't say we wouldn't help, but I don't have to like it, do I?"

"Shanelle doesn't hold grudges against them," Martha pointed out.

"They did *try* to help me," Shanelle explained. "They just weren't very good at it. But they were dealing with Sha-Ka'ani warriors, so it's hard to hold them at fault for their failure."

"Not hard at all," Tedra insisted. "Incompetents have never been high on my list of want-to-know people. The Sunderans *did* have a weapon in their Altering Rods that could have worked without hurting anyone—physically," she quickly added for Falon's benefit, since he was the one who would have suffered if he had been made to forget about Shanelle. "And don't get me wrong. I'm pleased with the way that whole fiasco turned out in the end, and so are you. But that doesn't alter the fact that if you had really needed help of a life-threatening sort, you definitely picked the wrong people to get it from."

"Exactly," Falon put in.

Shanelle turned around to her lifemate. "You *agree* with her?"

"Absolutely."

Shanelle threw up her hands in exasperation. "I give up."

The distinct sound of chuckling was coming out of the intercom unit. "Now can we get around to helping the 'incompetents'?"

"By all means," Tedra said with a smile.

Chapter 2

IMPATIENCE WAS SETTING IN. FEW ANSWERS HAD BEEN supplied after they had arrived on Sunder and been escorted to General Ferrill's office. The little general had immediately gotten on Tedra's bad side with his belligerence and condescending attitude, particularly since the Sunderans were the ones asking for help this time around.

Normally she would have ignored it, but in her present fretting mood, it very quickly had them shouting at each other. Which was when Shanelle suggested tactfully that Donilla Vand be summoned to deal with them.

Ferrill had acceded to that request gladly, obviously uncomfortable arguing with a woman he had to look up at, and had left them there alone in his office. He had neglected to mention, however, that Donilla

would have to be fetched from prison. That information was volunteered by one of the military types standing guard at the door outside the office when asked what was taking so long.

When Shanelle had sought help from the Sunderans eight months earlier, Donilla Vand had been the general in command of Sunder's military forces. She was also the one who had explained how the women of Sunder had wrested control of the planet from their men, to keep them from going to war with their neighboring planet, Armoru.

It had been a global conspiracy made possible by the invention of what they called the Altering Rod. Sunder was, after all, quite advanced in the fields of science, having conquered all their known diseases. The rods had been created to control the minds of the mentally imbalanced, to make them useful citizens again. That they had been used by the women to take over all positions of power on the planet left many of them feeling quite guilty about it, Donilla included. So Shanelle wasn't really surprised that some of them had finally reversed the process to let their men take over again, though apparently the consequence was that those women had been sent to prison for what they'd done.

But there was no point in speculating about it until they knew for sure what had happened to put the men back in power. And they still didn't know what kind of help was needed or who had sent out a distress call, though that could be easily guessed at, now that the men were in power again. No doubt Sunder was in a state of war and possibly losing, now that their aggressive, war-minded men were ruling again.

Unfortunately for them, Tedra and her family were governed by the policies of the League of Confederated Planets, of which Kystran ranked twelfth, and by which the neighboring Niva star system also abided. Steps could be taken to prevent war, which had been done to keep more advanced planets from trying to take over Sha-Ka'an when it was discovered in the Niva system. But once war was declared, no help or hindrance could be offered, for the simple reason that some planets were too highly advanced for others to hope to compete with. For example, the battleship they had in their control could totally wipe out both Sunder and Armoru.

Nearly an hour had passed since the general had left them alone in his office. Tedra sat cross-legged in the center of his desk. The chairs in the room were too small to risk sitting in without breaking. Dalden, Falon, and Falon's brother, Jadell, were sitting on the floor, leaning against the walls. Shanelle was pacing the room, feeling the worst of their impatience, since she alone had any sympathies for the Sunderans, having gotten to know Donilla Vand during her short stay here and liking the women.

Not surprisingly, when Donilla finally arrived, Shanelle pounced on her with her first concern. "*Why* have you been imprisoned?"

Donilla smiled. She was a small woman, barely five feet in height, which was the norm on this planet. Their men only averaged half a foot more. To them, the Sha-Ka'ani really were giants, and Tedra and Shanelle, only a few inches short of six feet each, were close runners-up.

But Donilla showed none of the nervousness that

other Sunderans did in their presence. Her gray eyes
warm in greeting, Donilla held out a welcoming hand
to Shanelle.

"They didn't tell me it was you who answered our
call for help," the ex-general said. "I can't tell you how
often I worried about you, despite your assurance that
you would be fine. But since *he* is with you, dare I hope
that you are comfortable now with your father's
choice for you?"

The word *comfortable* didn't come close to describing life with a warrior, but it did bring a smile to
Shanelle as well. "Yes, I came here previously with
foolish fears, all of which have been put to rest. Happiness beyond measure is what my lifemate gives me."

"My woman is being modest," Falon said as he rose
from the floor to stand next to her.

The remark caused them all to laugh, even Tedra,
which momentarily relieved the tension of not knowing what was going on. Shanelle then took a moment to
introduce Donilla to her mother—she had met everyone else in the room the first time they were there.

Donilla, like most people who first met the Ly-San-
Ters, couldn't hide her amazement that Tedra could be
old enough to have children of twenty-one, when she
looked no older than thirty herself. Nor did either of
her twin children take after her in looks. Both Dalden
and Shanelle were blond and amber-eyed, while
Tedra's long hair was pitch black, her eyes a light
aquamarine. A woman of strict physical disciplines all
her life, she was aging very well.

Shanelle got back to the question that hadn't been
answered yet. "How did you end up in prison,
Donilla?"

Donilla replied, "Several months after you left us, I had an opportunity to meet with a large number of the women who, like me, had taken over key positions on Sunder with the use of Altering Rods. It wasn't hard to see that most of them weren't happy with the way things had turned out, any more than I was. Our original motive was sound, to keep Sunder from going to war. We just hadn't counted on the results leaving us with men who were barely recognizable from their former selves, or that we would feel so guilty about it. So, in effect, another conspiracy was begun. It wouldn't have worked unless enough of us were willing, because like the first instance, it had to be accomplished in a close time frame. One man back in power could do nothing if he had no support, after all. But we pulled it off again: we gave them back their identities and memories."

"And ended up in prison for it," Shanelle said indignantly. "I can't believe—"

"Yes, you can," Donilla cut in. "We took away their memories of who they were, took away their power, took away their aggression. They'll never trust us again."

"Sounds like you haven't stopped feeling guilty about it," Tedra remarked. "The way you went about it was underhanded, yes, but your motives were sound. And a few months' detention is long enough for trying to keep your planet from going to war, a noble effort in my book."

"Thank you—I think," Donilla replied, blushing slightly. "But if we didn't feel we deserved what we got, we would have made a fuss about it and been freed by now. Most of us see it as a vacation, one well

needed after the stress and worry of trying to keep our men under our control for so long. And it's not a real prison they've detained us in. We have all the luxuries we could ask for. It's more like a resort, just one with locks on the doors."

Shanelle would have discussed it more, but Tedra was more interested in the immediate problem and asked Donilla, "You know why we're here?"

"Yes. I may be locked away, but I'm still the only one Ferrill feels comfortable talking out his problems with, so he's kept me informed about everything that has happened since he took over again."

"If you're now at war with Armoru, we can't—"

"No, it's nothing like that," Donilla interrupted, smiling. "There was one benefit of what we did. We didn't make our men forget about what had happened during the years of our rule, and five years of seeing that we could get along just fine without conquering any more people made them not jump back into the race of who could wipe out their neighbors first. They have in fact continued our plans of defense rather than attack. We just might be ready and fully prepared when Armoru finally makes its move."

Tedra grinned. "Congratulations and welcome to the concept of Life Appreciation. But what, then, is the problem here?"

"A crate of Altering Rods has been stolen," Donilla admitted with a sigh.

"That's an internal problem. Why would you ask for off-world help for it?"

"Because the rods have been taken off Sunder, and we have no means to leave Sunder ourselves to retrieve them."

The Sunderans might be highly advanced in most fields of science, but space travel wasn't one of them. They hadn't even known that worlds other than Armoru existed until they had been discovered by the Antury six years earlier. They had, in fact, been trying to build their first spaceship at the time, not for space travel, but to get them over to the neighboring planet of Armoru with the intent of global war, with Armoru doing exactly the same. It had been a race about who could invade first, a race that Sunder dropped out of during the few years the women had been in power.

"Do you know who took them?"

"Yes, we don't get many visitors here, since we have so little to offer in trade. But these people came with the sole intent of buying the Altering Rods from us. This was strange in itself, since very few people know of the rods on our own world, let alone on other worlds."

"Did the Antury who discovered you know?"

"Possible, but doubtful—unless they have some means of reading our minds. The rods weren't something we were proud of by then. Shanelle was told about them because she needed reassurance on how we could help her against giant warriors like these here."

The rods had been used on those warriors and had even worked on most of them, making them forget that they had come there to find Shanelle. The process had failed on Falon, however, because he had refused to learn the Sunderan language before coming down to their planet, and for the rods to work, it was necessary for the targets to understand what was being said to them.

The other warriors who had come down didn't have Falon's deep distrust of all things unnatural to Sha-Ka'an, and since almost any ship computer could analyze a new language and create a Sublim so that the language could be learned in just a few hours, the old universal language that was so frustrating had long since become obsolete. Sublims made it possible to communicate with newly discovered worlds with ease. There were a few glitches, like some words not having an immediate association and so needing a visual or verbal explanation to make sense. But basically, Sublims worked amazingly well and were used by all world traders and discoverers.

"So what happened?"

"The visitors were honored, given the royal treatment, actually, being who they were. But the rods are naturally a sore subject with Ferrill. He refused to discuss selling them, and said only that the rods were locked away in our strongest vault and would never see use again."

"Why weren't they just destroyed after you stopped using them?"

"Because the men realized the day might come when *they* would find a good use for them."

"As in Armoru knocking on your doors with weapons in hand?" Tedra guessed.

"Exactly," Donilla replied. "Besides, quite a few women know how to make them now, and since they don't work on women, those women can't be made to forget how to make them. So the men felt that locking them away was sufficient. After all, our strongest vault is guarded by the military night and day, impossible for anyone on *our* world to break into."

"But not for someone from another world, obviously."

"No, indeed. They used some kind of gas that put everyone to sleep and an explosive unknown to us that easily opened our vault. They left the planet immediately thereafter, and were gone before the theft was even discovered."

"When was this?"

"Yesterday."

Tedra sighed and pushed the button on her computer-link unit. "Martha, I know you've been listening. What's the worst-case scenario on these stolen rods?"

"If they were stolen for profit, they could end up distributed throughout the galaxies and well-established policies could suddenly end up changing with no one the wiser as to why or how. Entire economies could be destroyed, wars would result, the League of Confederated Planets could topple."

That got a low growl and the demand, "How high is that on your list of probables?"

"Not very," Martha replied in one of her bored tones. "Considering who stole them, it's more likely that a single planet will be a target for takeover, pretty much in the same way it was done here. Quiet, efficient, without bloodshed, and without most of the populace even aware that they have been taken over."

"Considering who?" Tedra frowned. "And how do you know who our culprit is, when that hasn't been mentioned yet? Probables doesn't come close to dissecting a simple phrase like 'they were honored.'"

That resulted in a bit of computer chuckling, a sound Martha had created to perfection. "That's de-

batable, but the fact that there is only one ship within a day's travel of here does manage to narrow things down."

Tedra rolled her eyes. "A known race I hope, so we at least know what we're dealing with?"

"Better than that, you know them personally. It's Jorran of Century III, the very same High King who tried to make mincemeat of our Falon in the competitions last year."

"*Farden* hell."

Shanelle noticed Donilla's blush over her mother's swearing and whispered to her, "That's just the Kystrani word for bloody, pretty mild when you consider mother has seventy-eight languages to draw on for serious cussing."

Donilla grinned, but Martha, who had no trouble picking up whispers, said, "She's in shock. Give her a moment, she'll get around to some serious swearing."

Since everyone there could hear Martha, including her mother who was raising an annoyed brow at her, Shanelle was now the one blushing.

Chapter 3

TEDRA WALKED OUTSIDE THE MILITARY COMPOUND where General Ferrill's office was located. Dalden was deeply distracted and not paying much attention to anything other than walking. Shanelle was waiting to hear what Tedra would decide.

As far as Shanelle was concerned, having been apprised of the situation, they couldn't do anything but help. And that had nothing to do with Sunder or her liking for the Sunderan Donilla Vand, nor even her strong dislike of the High King Jorran, who had wanted to make her his queen by underhanded means. No, her concern was that an entire planet of unsuspecting people could become the victims of Jorran's tyranny. But Tedra might not see it that way and being more familiar with the policies of the Centura League, otherwise known as the League of Confeder-

ated Planets which strived to keep peace among all known planets, might be wrestling with good reasons why they shouldn't get involved.

Martha was being unusually quiet, even though her link was still open. But then, Martha only interfered when she knew that something might adversely affect Tedra. Otherwise, she let Tedra make her own decisions. That it often seemed otherwise was only because Martha covered all possibilities when she dissected a problem, from the most obvious to the least likely, and every variable in between.

Tedra finally stopped walking, and the frown she was now wearing said she wasn't happy with her own decision, but had made it nonetheless. "We need to get back to the ship and be on our way."

"You aren't going to help?"

"I retired from 'saving planets' twenty-one years ago," Tedra said matter-of-factly. "And the sooner we get home, the sooner we can notify the proper authorities to deal with this problem."

"Even though that might be too late? Once war is begun, the League won't get involved."

"I doubt Jorran's intention is to make war," Tedra replied. "Is it, Martha?"

"Highly improbable." Martha was using her bored tone again, which, unfortunately, usually precluded a bomb, which she dropped now. "Subjugation and utter domination are what he'll be looking for."

Tedra made a face. *Subjugation* was a word she seriously disliked; it was what the Sha-Ka'ari had tried to do to her own people. The Sha-Ka'ari were originally from Sha-Ka'an, but had been taken some three hundred years ago to a mining colony in the Centura star

system to be used as slave labor. But they were still incredibly huge warriors, and it didn't take them long to take over that colony and subjugate those people and any others they happened to conquer. They had lost touch with most of their old beliefs, didn't even know where they originally came from, and had developed much differently than the Sha-Ka'ani on the mother planet.

They were still considered barbarians, though, were still sword-wielding, slave-holding warriors, just a smaller variety, having interbred with their slaves for hundreds of years. But unlike Challen and his people, also considered barbarians, who pretty much snubbed their collective noses at the wonder that could be had from advanced planets, the Sha-Ka'ari weren't averse to using whatever was obtainable if they could put it to good use, nor averse to space travel.

Jorran's people from Century III were much like the Sha-Ka'ari. They were still medieval in development themselves, yet having been discovered and dealing for many years with off-world visitors, they didn't deny themselves the benefits of modern technology. They had trade ambassadors on almost all of the known planets, and their kings enjoyed space travel as well, but not much was really known about them, since they weren't members of the Centura League.

The League of Confederated Planets wasn't just one solar system, but half a dozen neighboring star systems now comprising seventy-eight planets that abided by one set of rules and regulations to the benefit of all. The Niva star system, newly discovered, had yet to be brought into the fold, though no one doubted it would be one day. Century III was another system

within traveling distance that, although it dealt well with the League, had yet to be invited to join.

And their own first dealings with the humanoids of Century III had been less than pleasant. The High King Jorran and his entourage had come to Sha-Ka'an the previous year, when the visitor restriction had been lifted for the competitions that Challen had opened to one and all in hopes of finding a lifemate for Shanelle among the winners. Shanelle hadn't known that was the purpose of the competitions, and the winner wasn't guaranteed to be chosen, but Jorran hadn't seen it that way.

He hadn't competed either, competition being much too undignified for his esteemed self. No, he had demanded to fight the winner who had gone through the process of elimination in the appropriate way, and Falon, being that winner, could have refused to fight him, should have refused, yet he didn't. No one suspected that Jorran's intention was to kill him, rather than just defeat him.

The competitions had been friendly matches of strength and skill, not the deadly fight Jorran tried to make of them. Falon didn't find that out until after he had accepted Jorran's challenge and Jorran used not a normal sword but a razor sword. This was a weapon so light and maneuverable that there was no way to avoid it by normal means, nor was Falon able to.

He would have died if a meditech unit hadn't been handy, he had been sliced up so badly. He would have lost the match as well if he hadn't given up using his own weapon and simply taken Jorran out with his fist instead, just before he passed out himself from loss of blood.

This was when Shanelle, fearful of having Falon for her lifemate, had run away. And Falon, determined to have her, overcame his own fears of space travel to follow her. Challen had already given her to him, and Falon wasn't going to let a mere thing like a universe keep him from her. Nor had the Sunderans been able to keep him away, despite their promises to the contrary.

"Shani, this is *not* our responsibility," Tedra said now. "Just because we know what those rods are capable of, and what a first-class jerk Jorran is, doesn't make this our problem. The League will be given all the information we have and will do what's appropriate with it. We are already late getting home, and I refuse to make Challen continue to worry."

"I will go after Jorran and see to the proper destruction of those rods."

Both women turned toward Dalden, his silence until now having made them forget he was with them. Shanelle was merely surprised that her brother would want to involve himself personally when matters outside of Sha-Ka'an had no interest for him. Tedra's own surprise was brief, her response less than diplomatic.

"No," she said.

Chapter 4

DALDEN SMILED AT TEDRA. SHE WAS HIS MOTHER, BUT HE was a Sha-Ka'an warrior full-grown, which made all decisions his own to make, and she knew that. She could make her objections known to him, but in the end the decision was still his.

"I have no choice in this matter," he told her. "You wondered how the High King could have had knowledge of the rods before he came here for them? That knowledge came directly from me."

"How?" she demanded, "and when? You weren't even home, had left with Falon to fetch Shani back. And Sha-Ka'an closed down to visitors again right after the competitions."

"All did return to their respective planets—except Jorran. He was still at the Visitors' Center when we returned. It was necessary that I go there as well, to ne-

gotiate with the Catrateri on Falon's behalf. They were still eager to trade for the gold from his country."

"But how did you end up having anything to do with Jorran, after what he tried to pull at the competitions? I would have thought you would have ignored him like the insect he proved to be."

"And I would have, but a man with such a high opinion of himself as Jorran has cannot comprehend that someone might dislike him or not want to be 'honored' by his attention. There was a dinner for a newly arrived ambassador. The Catrateri had been invited to it and insisted that we could continue our negotiations over fine food. Jorran invited himself, and of course the head of the Center would not think to insult him by asking him to leave."

"No, Mr. Rampon is the administrator there because he's about as diplomatic as they come. I doubt he even knows how to insult someone. It's just not in his genes."

"I could wish that it were not in mine."

This was said in such a tone that it brought an immediate blush to Tedra. Challen didn't insult people, after all, so Dalden certainly wasn't talking about the genes he had gotten from his father.

"Let's stick to specifics," she grumbled. "How did you happen to have words with Jorran? The dining hall at the Center is huge. You could have gone through the entire evening without getting within forty feet of that Centurian jerk."

"Except that he sought me out specifically, to question me about Falon. He did not pretend indifference, nor hide his underlying anger over the subject of his interest."

"Don't tell me his nose was bent out of shape figuratively, after Falon bent it out of shape literally? It's really too bad the meditech unit corrected that."

"I gathered the same, that he was still at the Center for no other reason than he had waited for Falon to return, with some sort of revenge in mind. Falon was unaware of this, or he might well have obliged him. But he had gone straight home to Ba-Har-an with Shanelle when we returned, and no visitors could get to his country, so the High King was forced to give up and go home, which he was scheduled to do the next rising."

"So mention of the rods occurred when he grilled you about Falon?"

Dalden shook his head, even sighed. "I would not speak of Falon with him, other than to give Jorran no doubt that Falon was beyond his reach. Speaking to him at all put a foul taste in my mouth that I tried to wash away with Mieda wine."

"You should have just left."

"I am aware of that."

"How did the rods get mentioned, then?"

"It was toward the end of the dinner. I spoke no more with Jorran, but I made sure I was close enough to hear anything he might say. He was talking with the people at his end of the table about the tedious process of mind control in Century III prisons, to rehabilitate their lawbreakers and make them useful members of their realm again. I mentioned that even a low-tech people like the Sunderans had mind control down to a fine art, and instantaneous, at that. It was a deliberate attempt at subtle insult of which I am ashamed."

That Dalden would have used phrases like *low-tech* and *fine art*, words he gained from having a "visitor"

for a mother, not words a warrior would use, showed just how drunk he had been that night. And he probably didn't even realize that whatever means Jorran's people would use for mind control was probably gained from offworlders; they weren't even low-tech, they were no-tech at all. Not that any of that mattered when the damage had already been done.

"Martha, did you know what Dalden had done that night?" Tedra asked.

"Sure did. You kept me on the Rover at the time, if you'll remember, so I could keep tabs on Shanelle. And after what Jorran tried to pull during the competitions, he was on my personal list of 'keep under surveillance' as well."

"*Why* didn't you mention this sooner?"

"Because Jorran's intention was to return to his world, which he did. Despite the fact that he left us furious, he had few options that might cause you trouble. His learning about the Altering Rods did set off alarms in my circuits, but when he gave absolutely no indication that it was something he felt he could take advantage of, I crossed him off my 'endangered species' list."

Tedra rolled her eyes. Martha's "endangered species" crack was her way of describing anyone she saw as a threat to Tedra's well-being. She was programmed against killing things herself, though she was rather good at threatening to do so, and she could defend and render harmless as needed. Tedra, on the other hand, wouldn't think twice about demolishing someone who threatened her life or that of any of her family.

"But there's no reason for Dalden to get involved, is

there, aside from guilt? This *can* be handled by the League, right?"

"In time to stop Jorran, no," Martha replied. "In time to prevent him from taking over more than one planet, you betcha. But that won't help the people who get forced to worship him as their new king."

Since that wasn't what Tedra was hoping to hear, it wasn't surprising that she slammed her palm down angrily on the link-unit so she wouldn't have to hear any more of Martha's less than supportive commentary.

"That isn't going to work," Shanelle pointed out.

"No, but after nearly two weeks on the ship where there is no shutting her up, since she has complete control of the farden thing, being able to do so now is a luxury I won't deny myself," Tedra replied.

"She can still hear you."

"Of course she can, but she can't reply."

"Wanna bet?" boomed out of the heavens.

Shanelle blinked, noticed the complete look of shock on Tedra's face, and then started laughing. "Droda help us, half the people on this planet are going to think their God just spoke to them." She fell to the grass and held her stomach as another round of laughter ensued.

Tedra wasn't amused, slammed the button on the unit again and growled into it, "You misbegotten metal nightmare, you know better than to cause global panic! You're in meltdown, right? You've totally lost it?"

"Relax, doll." Martha's voice came through the unit again in purring mode. "General Ferrill doesn't take chances with visitors anymore; he makes worldwide announcements warning his people to expect the bizarre and unusual for the duration. And since we've

been let inside their global shield this time, we're pretty hard to miss."

Tedra glared up at the two spaceships hovering in the sky above them. "Beside the point."

"Actually, that was the point," Martha said, using her tone that was laden with amusement. "Much as I might get a kick out of being mistaken for a god, that isn't going to happen here, when the Rover is in plain view for anyone who heard me on this side of the planet. And I have information that you require before you can make an informed decision, so shall we proceed?"

Tedra hated it when Martha dropped carrots like that. She would have preferred to tell her circuited friend to stuff it, but couldn't now.

"Proceed," she grumbled.

"I made a point of finding out all I could about Jorran when he became a contender for Shanelle. He's indeed a High King of Century III, but what isn't common knowledge is that he's a king without a kingdom. Probables tell me he had hoped to find a kingdom in Sha-Ka'an, through Shanelle. He's apparently been looking for one for quite a while now."

"Backtrack, old girl," Tedra said. "How'd he lose his kingdom?"

"He never had one."

"Then how does he hold the title?"

"That answer requires a bit of information about Century III."

"The brief version, if you don't mind."

"You got it. Century III isn't just the name of their main planet, but also of their star system. There are twelve planets in all, but only six are habitable, and

only the main planet had developed to the point of intelligence and world governance, ruled by one family that give themselves the titles of High Kings. The current family possesses seven High Kings. The planet used to be divided among the family, but that wasn't working out well with this last crop of seven, probably because they didn't have enough countries to go around. When they were discovered by the League and learned of space travel, they decided to divide up the planets in their system just as they had previously done with the countries."

"But they still came up one short?"

"Exactly. Now, the rest of the family are perfectly willing to share with Jorran, to give him anything he wants, but it's just not the same as having an entire people revere you as their only king. It seems to be a serious disgruntlement for him, and one he is finally taking steps to correct. His first option was to marry into a ruling family that would offer complete takeover eventually. He doesn't command a large army after all, nothing of the sort needed to go in and take what he wants by force. So this was his only option—until he learned about the Altering Rods."

"He learned about them eight months ago. Did it take them that long to find Sunder?"

"No, my guess is it took that long for Jorran to call in favors to get his own ship. He didn't have one when he came to Sha-Ka'an. They came with the Century III ambassador, which is how they returned home as well."

"Call in favors? Does he lack wealth as well as a kingdom?"

"Not at all, but keep in mind they don't produce

their own ships, nor are their people trained to fly them, nor are they likely to possess a Mock II capable of making crews obsolete. And they don't get ambassadors arriving from every known planet like Sha-Ka'an does, since they don't possess anything remotely as in demand as gaali stones are. They're on a few trade routes, but they're more a tourist attraction than a stopover for necessities. I'm frankly surprised it didn't take longer for Jorran to acquire his own ship and crew for this expedition."

"What type of ship did he get?"

"Your basic run-of-the-mill Trader, large cargo space, a few weapons to ward off pirates, good speed to outrun bigger ships, designed for long hauls."

"What kind of speed are we talking about?"

"A bit faster than the Rover, but about the same as that overpowered war machine that accompanied us."

"I take it you're not talking about Brock?" Shanelle couldn't resist saying, which got the expected snort out of Martha.

Brock and Martha got along much better than they used to, but there were still times when their objectives clashed, and this could well be one of them if Tedra decided to head out after Jorran herself. Brock would side with Tedra's original insistence of wanting to get her home with all speed, since getting her home and back into Challen's arms would be his main concern, ultimately insuring Challen's peace of mind. Martha, however, would know that Tedra was torn at the moment, wanting to help, but too worried about Challen's worry to be able to devote her full attention to helping.

Dalden was actually offering an alternative that

both Mock IIs would be able to support. Tedra hadn't reached that point of acceptance yet, though, and was still in questioning mode.

"From their current course, any idea which planet they have in mind for takeover?" she asked Martha.

"They are heading into uncharted space."

This surprised all of them. "You mean they're hoping to find a new, undiscovered planet out there?" Tedra concluded. "That seems like a rather stupid plan."

"No, actually, it's rather smart of them. That sector of space is uncharted, but there *are* solar systems in it, and there are rumors of at least one planet that's inhabited. But one planet in an entire solar system isn't worth putting them on a trade route when their system is so far off the beaten track, so no official World Discoverer has bothered to head over that way to verify or discount the rumors. But Jorran would want a target that is very far out of the way. This would pretty much assure him that no other off-worlders would be coming around to mess up his plans."

"Just how far off the beaten track are we talking about?" Tedra asked.

"Unknown data."

That was too abrupt, even for Martha, reminding Tedra that Martha based her probables on known facts, and rumors didn't fall even remotely close into that category. Martha hated being wrong about anything, after all, and rumors could be proven false.

So Tedra rephrased her question. "What's the general speculation, based on the rumor?"

"Three months for a Trader, five months for a World Discoverer."

"Three months even under gaali speed? *One* way? No one travels that far anymore without several stops along the way. Fuel isn't needed, but world communication is. Wars can be fought and won in three months, entire worlds can disappear in three months. No one likes being gone so long that when they come back, nothing is as they left it."

"World Discoverers are a spoiled lot, Tedra, and you know it. The Centura League would never have been formed if the old school thought like that, because the old school didn't have such high speed available to them. A year, two years was nothing to them, if it meant discovering a new world. Three months away would have been considered a short trip. Of course, today's three months is equivalent to more than a few years of travel back when space was first explored, but there's no need for a history lesson you're already familiar with."

"Three months—*six* months round trip." Tedra was looking at Dalden now and shaking her head. "You realize that's just travel time, doesn't count the time it will take to stop Jorran, reverse any damage he does if he can't be stopped before doing any, and find and destroy all the rods? This could conceivably take a year or more. You *aren't* going, and that's my final word on the subject."

Chapter 5

BRITTANY DIDN'T GET TO THE SHOPPING MALL OFTEN. Parking wasn't usually a problem, though, since Seaview wasn't a big town. It had only just gotten their first enclosed mall last year. Today, however, parking was a problem, and Brittany found out why when she got inside. The mayor was using the large community stage in the center of the mall to make a campaign speech. It was an election year. Mayor Sullivan was running for his second term.

The town was only four years old, so Sullivan was the only mayor it had known so far. He'd done a good job as far as Brittany was concerned, so he'd get her vote again. The town was growing at a steady pace thanks to him, which meant job security for her in her field of construction, so he could be forgiven for campaigning on a Sunday, her only day off.

Brittany even stopped to listen to him for a few minutes, though from the sidelines. Crowds like the one gathered around the center stage were things she tended to avoid, hating that penned-in feeling where you couldn't move without bumping into someone. Such crowds made her stand out like a sore thumb with her height, and getting rudely stared at was guaranteed to put her in a foul mood.

Actually, she hadn't been in the best of moods since her break-up with Thomas Johnson. She'd even given some thought to moving. But she was well settled in Seaview now, had a roommate she got along well with, even though Jan still tried to fix her up with dates that she didn't want. And she was meeting her goals here, was on schedule, would be able to quit her jobs and build her dream house in two more years.

She lived and breathed for that day, counted every penny, begrudged every worn-out purse and dented hard hat, not just because they cost her extra money but because, unlike some women, she actually hated to go shopping. And she had put off today's shopping excursion for two weeks now. But having to wash her work jeans every other night because three pairs had finally reached the irreparable stage with their worn-out seats was a pure waste of time, and she hated wasting time more than she hated shopping.

She had expected to be in and out of the mall in under an hour. She hadn't counted on the mayor and his campaign staff being there to draw her interest briefly. But she wasn't hearing anything she hadn't already heard on the six o'clock news, which she tried to catch each day while she ate dinner. She did have a few hours between jobs to eat, shower, take care of the

daily chores she shared with Jan, or whatever else couldn't wait until Sunday. Her spa job was from seven to ten at night, giving her no time for other than another quick shower and bed when she got home from it.

Brittany was just heading around the outer fringes of the crowd in the direction she needed to go for her favorite jeans shop when she saw *him* and did a double-take. Bumping into the person in front of her stopped her completely and she didn't even think to apologize, she was so amazed at the man's height. How had she missed seeing him work his way into the center of that crowd when her eyes were always drawn to tall men? You couldn't miss him. He stood more than a foot taller than everyone else there.

Had he been sitting down and only just stood up? There could be some chairs in the center of the crowd, she supposed. For that matter, he could be standing on one—no, she'd see a bit of waist if that were so, but all she was seeing was some incredibly wide shoulders and a golden mane of hair that reached them. And that wasn't nearly enough to satisfy her curiosity, which was why she quickly worked her way to the sidelines, to catch a glimpse of his face.

Brittany didn't realize that she'd been holding her breath, or was filled with anxiety, until she got that better look at the man and sighed long and loud in relief. The worry had been natural, because although her eyes were constantly drawn to tall men, they were usually disappointed as well. There had only been a few tall men over the years whom she had actually

been seriously attracted to, and only one whom she had come close to losing her heart to.

Thomas Johnson she would never forget, because he'd crushed her thoroughly in proving just how hard it was going to be for her to ever find the right man. She'd really thought he was it. Her instincts had said so. She'd even been willing to go all the way with him, though she could be grateful now that their relationship hadn't progressed that far before she found out that even he had a problem with her height. She was a good half a foot shorter than Tom, but that was *still* too tall for him. Damn jerk must have a thing for midgets had been her unkind thought before she'd shown him the door.

But this guy, surrounded by a sea of shorter heads, was absolutely gorgeous. And despite her immediate attraction, that sent off alarms in her head. Anyone who looked that good couldn't *be* that good. There had to be something wrong with him. Her instincts might be saying otherwise, but she could no longer trust them after Tom.

He was too young for her, that was it. Actually, it wasn't that he looked young—it was hard to look young when you were that big. It was more that he just didn't look old enough. Of course, age didn't matter much these days, when people were smart enough to have figured out that compatibility and common interests were much more important for holding a relationship together.

Brittany could apply that concept to her height problem as well, if it wasn't such a big bone of contention with her. And if she was going to hold his age

against him, then she ought to find somewhere to sit down and work on getting her pulse rate back to normal, because it was definitely leaping about in maximum attraction mode at the moment.

He wasn't listening to the mayor's speech, he was looking around as if he were lost, or didn't know what he was doing there. Brittany was still searching for something wrong about him when she realized that his expression had abruptly changed, was the very picture of a man about to panic. Claustrophobia big-time was about to happen.

She didn't doubt it, nor did she think twice before she barged her way in through the crowd, grabbed his arm, and dragged him a good distance away. Her good deed for the day. It had nothing to do with the fact that she *wanted* to meet him, and her rescue was a perfect excuse to. But she should have read the Girl Scout manual more thoroughly, because she must have missed the section that warned that good deeds just might change your life forever.

Chapter 6

RESCUES DIDN'T ALWAYS WORK OUT AS PLANNED. SOME of them that you thought were rescues might not even be so, might turn out to be intrusions instead.

This was Brittany's first thought when she turned to face the man whom she assumed she had pulled out of the jaws of his own personal hell. She had expected at the very least some gratitude, but she got merely a curious once-over from him. How deflating. Not that it mattered, when she was struck dumb by her own amazement.

Up close and personal put her system into overdrive. She never thought she'd see the day when a man might be too tall for her. But goodness, seven feet tall *and* properly proportioned for it!

The rest of him that she could see now, from the shoulders down, defied description. She was used to

bulging muscles after three years working in a spa, but the muscles on this guy seemed natural rather than a result of strenuous exercise. Everything about him was big, and yet a right kind of big. You couldn't create and mold that kind of physique, you had to be born with it.

He was also dressed in high fashion—heck, he was wearing what you might expect on a rock star, actually. A wraparound tunic with no buttons, belted at the waist, and a soft metallic blue in color. His black leather pants weren't the least baggy, nor did they have visible seams that she could find.

If she didn't know better, she'd think those pants had been poured on him, they were so skintight. Leather boots of the same color, with flat heels—no artificial height here—and just as soft-looking, went up to his knees. The fat medallion that was visible in the *very* deep V of his neckline, hanging from a thick gold chain, appeared mystic in design. It was plated to look like it was made of solid gold, which of course it wouldn't be, when it was the size of her fist in roundness and nearly as thick.

He had a fancy-looking little radio attached to his wide belt, with all kinds of buttons on it. At least she assumed it was a radio, since it had a thin cord plugged into it that ran up to one of his ears, one of those miniature earphones, she supposed.

Her thorough examination of him came to an abrupt end when he spoke to her. A deep rumble. Foreign. The accent was strong, distinctive; she just couldn't place what country it might be from.

"Do you require something of me?" he said.

She blushed, something she strived never to do, be-

cause pink cheeks just didn't go well with copper hair. "No," she answered, "and maybe I should apologize. You looked like you were having a claustrophobia attack." At his blank stare, she added, "You know, hemmed in by the crowd and panicking because you can't find your way out—never mind. I thought I was helping, but obviously not."

He seemed to pause to listen to the music coming out of his earphone for a moment before he replied, "Ah, you assisted me. Now I understand, and offer my gratitude."

He smiled at her. She wondered if fainting was allowed in the mall. *Good god in the morning, find something wrong with him, girl, before you fall instantly in love.*

Now that he had relaxed, with that incredible smile that almost doubled his appeal, his amber eyes said he liked what he was seeing, which thrilled her to the core. But then, as looks went, she had some nice ones—aside from her height. At least, constantly being hit on *despite* her height confirmed what her mirror said.

She had big breasts, dark green eyes that could turn murky or be crystal clear, and a thick mass of bright copper hair inherited from her grandfather that no beautician could quite match in color. Some nicely defined bones went with the package for a combination that was loosely termed a knockout. She wouldn't go that far in describing herself, but was glad she had a few nice features to make up for that last half a foot of height she could have done without.

They were staring at each other when they should be talking, or at least getting past all the standard first

meeting info, like name, profession, number of children they planned to have, and so on. And since he wasn't making the effort, that left it to her to get the ball rolling on getting acquainted, not something she had much experience at, since American men had that sort of thing down pat. But it was either that or let him walk away and never see him again, which at the moment was out of the question.

So she started from the top, telling him, "I'm Brittany Callaghan, and you are?"

"Sha-Ka'ani."

"Excuse me?"

The volume must have gotten turned up by accident on his radio, because even she could hear the tinny-sounding screeching coming out of his earphone that made him wince. He yanked it off his ear, held it a moment while he glared at it, then attached it again.

"I understand now it was my name you requested. I am Dalden Ly-San-Ter."

Brittany grinned at that point. "Let me take a wild guess. That's not a radio, but some kind of language translation recording you're listening to?"

"It does indeed assist me in understanding this language of yours that I have just learned."

"Just learned? You speak it amazingly well for only just learning it."

"Yet do I not have a translation for all of your words. Some require an explanation."

"Yes, I can see where brand names and slang might throw you off, as well as first names sounding like countries, like mine does." She took another guess on the next subject. "So, did you just get signed up for pro

basketball?" A blank look. "Uh-oh, if that didn't translate, then you can't be a professional player, though if you stay in this country long enough, the scouts will probably find you. Sorry for the assumption, but we don't see seven-footers every day, and those we do see tend to all be players—"

"I am not seven feet tall," he corrected her in a serious tone.

She chuckled. "So who's counting an inch or two when you're *that* tall? Not me."

"Is my height a problem?"

"Not a chance. Your height is absolutely perfect, just what the basketball scouts are always on the lookout for." Herself as well, though she didn't add that, and he didn't seem to be understanding anything she was saying again. "Never mind, I don't think I've got it straight yet in my head that you're not American. Heck, basketball might not even be a sport in your country. Where do you hail from, by the way?"

"Far from here."

She grinned. "That's obvious, but how far? Europe? The Middle East? I don't recognize your accent, and I'd thought television had done an admirable job of introducing us to the full range of foreign accents."

"My country would be unknown to you."

She sighed. "You're probably right. If Shaka-what-you-called-it is its name, I've never heard of it. But then, geography was never my strong point. Are you just visiting America, then, doing the tourist thing?"

"My time here will be brief, yes."

Another sigh. "Well, hell, so much for getting married." His blank stare this time brought on a chuckle

from her. "Don't panic, that was just a joke to loosen you up. You don't say much, do you?"

She blushed as soon as she said it, because she hadn't been giving him much chance to say anything with her nervous, nonstop chatter. A foreigner. Of all the rotten luck. But if they were growing them like this overseas, perhaps she ought to add a trip around the world to her goal list.

Her disappointment was almost a physical ache. Just a visitor. He'd have to leave the country when his visa expired. She'd never see him again . . . but that wasn't confirmed yet. His "brief" might only refer to Seaview. Foreigners did still move to America and apply for citizenship these days. Marriage worked wonders in cutting through that red tape, as well. She wouldn't ask, didn't want it confirmed, that he was just passing through.

"I will have much to say to you when my task is done here," he said.

She blinked, having forgotten her question. And those words sounded so promising, they managed to push her disappointment to the side.

"No time for socializing? Man, does that sound familiar," she remarked. "What task?"

"I seek a man. His name is Jorran, though he may call himself by a different name here."

"Are you a foreign cop, or a detective?"

"Is that what is required to find him?"

"Wouldn't hurt." She grinned. "Detectives have that find-what's-missing thing down pat. I don't think we have any in Seaview, though. Plenty of lawyers and even a pawnshop, if you can believe it. But there

wouldn't be much work for a professional detective in a nice quiet town like this. If this guy's a criminal, you can always ask the local police to help."

Screeching came from his earphone again, when his hand was nowhere near the unit to have adjusted the sound. What a strange translator—or was it? It seemed more like someone was actually talking to him through it, with the occasional yell thrown in, coaching him on what to say.

"Police would be more hindrance than assistance, when they would ask questions that would lead to many more questions, and have no understanding of the answers."

"That complicated, huh? Well, your best bet for finding a detective who won't ask too many questions is to head to San Francisco."

"There is no time for detours. Nor is the assistance I need of a complicated nature." His amber eyes seemed to glow for a moment before he added, "You could help me."

Brittany's pulse rate sped up rapidly. His tone *and* look implied something other than help. "I could?"

"An understanding of your people is needful, and help in determining if the one in power here begins to behave in an abnormal manner."

She frowned. The one in power here? Did he mean the mayor? She turned around to glance at the platform, to see that Sullivan was wrapping up his speech. Standard political jargon. Nothing unusual in that. Abnormal? What the heck did he mean by that?

Brittany turned back to ask him, and found herself alone. She turned in a full circle. He was nowhere to be

seen. People passed her. Shops were nearby. He wasn't. That gorgeous hunk of foreign masculinity had pulled a perfect disappearing act on her.

Crushed, she fell into the foulest mood imaginable. She didn't buy any jeans that day. She went home and broke a few things.

Chapter 7

"WHY DID YOU REMOVE ME FROM THE FEMALE'S presence?" Dalden demanded the second he materialized in the control room on board the battleship *Androvia*.

The question was asked of Martha. Though Shanelle was there as well and might know how to work the Molecular Transfer that could move people from place to place instantly, since she had learned how to fly spaceships during her time in Kystran, Martha was in control of every aspect of their ship and wouldn't relinquish any part of it to human error.

"Just listen to yourself, warrior, and you might figure that out on your own." Martha's placid tone drifted up from the huge computer console in the center of the room. "Or is so much emotion coming out of you a normal occurrence?"

"Are you blushing, Dalden?" Shanelle asked with some surprise.

Most blushes wouldn't be noticed with their identical golden skin tone; they had to be severe to show up at all. But Sha-Ka'ani warriors, who rarely blushed in the first place, had such natural control of their emotions that they wouldn't allow something so mundane as a blush to reveal emotions they maintained they didn't possess. They *could* feel embarrassment; you just had to know a warrior really well to guess when they might be experiencing it. Shanelle, as Dalden's twin, qualified for knowing him well.

But Martha had a whole list of complaints on her own agenda, and wasn't waiting for Dalden to answer insignificant questions from his sister. "You were supposed to be giving me a tour, not taking one yourself," Martha reminded him. "You were supposed to make contact with their leader. *She* isn't their leader."

"I did not initiate contact with her."

"You didn't try to end it, either."

"She wanted me."

"Sooooo . . . *what!*" was stretched out about five times longer than the words would take to say normally, just to stress how little that mattered in the scheme of things to Martha. "Women want you all the time, Dalden. Since when do you go haywire over it? And don't try to deny it when I am monitoring your vital stats."

"You're blushing again, Dalden," Shanelle pointed out, trying to keep from grinning.

She'd been there all along, and had been listening to Martha rant and rave about everything Dalden was

doing wrong on the planet before she lost patience completely and brought him back to the ship.

They had arrived yesterday. Since Dalden was determined to hold himself responsible for retrieving the Altering Rods, Tedra had finally given in and supported his decision. Her support meant that Martha had to go along, though, as well as all the warriors who had escorted them to Kystran. Brock could have handled it and was already in control of the *Androvia*, but with one of her "babies" going into deep space without her, Tedra would only trust Martha at the helm.

So the two Mock IIs had traded ships, with Brock taking Tedra home to Sha-Ka'an in the Rover, a short enough trip so Challen wouldn't complain too much that she'd made it alone. What hadn't been expected was that Falon would insist on going after Jorran as well, especially when he so disliked space travel.

Martha had expected it, though, pointing out that Falon hadn't gotten anywhere close to evening the score with Jorran after the High King tried to kill him. He had simply had more important things to deal with first, like chasing after his lifemate. But now he'd like to get his hands on Jorran to finish that long-ago fight more properly.

Of course, with Falon going along for the ride, Shanelle insisted on going, too, and although Tedra had objected most strenuously, Falon didn't, so that settled that. But understanding the Sha-Ka'ani way of life, as well as Martha's advanced and unique nature, Shanelle was the perfect buffer between Martha and the warriors aboard the ship. The warriors might get along well with Brock, who had been created for their

shodan Challen, so he was one of them. That couldn't be said for Martha, who had a tendency to provoke a warrior's placid nature without even trying.

It had taken two months and twenty-three days to reach their destination, the no longer rumored planet in that sector of the universe a verified fact now. But because the humanoids on the planet were advanced enough to have equipment that could see their ship when it neared them, even disguised as it was to look like a common piece of space debris, albeit a big piece, they couldn't remain hovering over the planet for more than a few seconds.

This was gotten around by Martha taking the ship down to the surface of the planet at incredible speed, halting it just before impact, and lowering it into a large body of water where it wouldn't be discovered. If it had been seen, it would be assumed a meteor had fallen and disintegrated before reaching the surface.

This was the planet that Jorran had come to, though his ship didn't remain near it for very long. His first impression was that this planet wasn't suitable for his purpose, and he left to find another. Martha didn't deal just with first impressions, however, and as it turned out, Jorran's ship had merely moved to a place of concealment behind the planet's single moon.

It had been easy to track and keep up with Jorran's ship, and the *Androvia* was designed to avoid being tracked, so Jorran wouldn't know that he had been followed. Concealing his ship in the area was a clear indication that he had gone down to the planet himself. Scanning his ship proved it had fewer bodies on it than it had arrived with. And having sneaked the android Corth II onto it to install a one-way data probe was

keeping Martha apprised of Jorran's men's positions on the planet, as well as giving her other pertinent information that Jorran was sending back to his ship.

Fortunately, the captain of Jorran's ship was proving to be a nosy sort who insisted on being kept apprised of the situation, and from a few choice words dropped during a communication, Martha was able to determine that the ship and crew were merely hired, and there was a time limit remaining on their employ, and most of that had been used up getting here. But Jorran wasn't going to dismiss them until the very end, in case things didn't go as he planned. It did, however, force him to make his move within a month, or give up and go home.

The rest of the time since their arrival yesterday had been spent gathering information about the planet and its people, and creating the Sublims necessary to speak the language. Corth II had come in handy for that as well, being sent to the planet's surface first to find an unused computer terminal that Martha could be connected to, and even Martha was impressed at the wealth of information she was finding.

"They might not be advanced to high-tech standards, but they are excellent recordkeepers and have at least mastered global computer connections, so that only one terminal is needed to access everything I require. But it's still in the primitive stages, which is why it's taking so long to access their vast stores of information."

That had been Martha's remark yesterday. By last night she had been complaining, "Did I say they were advanced? I have never encountered *anything* as slow as the machines those people call computers." She was still collecting data.

"Okay, we're going to take it from the top again," Martha said now. "And see if it sinks in this time. They are an aggressive, war-minded people up there on the surface. Their history is filled with violence from their very beginnings, and they think nothing of wholesale slaughter. And although the concept of life on other planets fascinates them, it also terrifies them, so Probables tell me that while there might be some of them who would greet off-worlders with open arms, most of them will go out of their way to destroy any visitors. They just aren't *ready* to be discovered yet. Have I made that clear enough yet?"

"The woman did not have war on her mind," Dalden pointed out stubbornly.

"We could hear perfectly well what she had on her mind, just as we know perfectly well what was on yours, all of which is redundant. I am stressing a point here, big guy, if you haven't figured that out yet, and if you don't get it by the time I finish, then you are *not* going back to the surface. Are you listening yet?"

"Is it possible not to, when in your presence?" Dalden replied stiffly.

A very good imitation of a sigh filled the control room, loud and prolonged. "We don't have time for bruised warrior egos, Dalden. My job is to get you back home in one piece and still breathing. If you can manage to recover the rods as well, then you're happy, Tedra's happy, and I'm happy. Which means I'll help you to do that. None of which means you have time for hanky-panky."

The third blush was immediate and quite vivid. Dalden had no trouble understanding the "ancients' language" that his mother and Martha both used, hav-

ing grown up hearing its use. Tedra had always been fascinated by the ancient history of her people, when most Kystrani couldn't care less, and only recent history was still taught in their learning systems. *Hankypanky*, one of those ancient words, equated to Sha-Ka'ani *fun*, or what was more universally known as sharing sex.

"Now, from the top once more, *no fraternizing with the local species*," Martha continued. "If even one of those humans figures out that you aren't one of them, you'd have billions of people trying to wipe you from their memories, and given their history, that means kill you on sight. They won't care that you're here to help them. They won't care about the wealth of advanced knowledge you could introduce them to. They would consider you a threat to their survival, not a benefit, and exterminate you accordingly."

Shanelle frowned at that point. "You said he'd have no trouble passing for one of them, Martha, as long as he left his sword on the ship."

"Nor will he, since they come in all sizes and shapes themselves, even Sha-Ka'ani warrior size. But that's *if* they aren't already looking for him."

"Why would they be?" Shanelle asked. "Didn't you say that they would have to conclude that we disintegrated, if they noticed us at all, because no disturbance of their water was caused by us?"

"Correct. They have viewing devices to see farther into space than the naked eye can, which means they could have seen us coming if battleships of this line weren't equipped with a wide selection of disguisers. It also means they probably *did* see Jorran's ship if it hovered long enough above them and if one of the op-

erators of those viewers was paying close attention, which fortunately isn't a guarantee, since they are operated by humans, rather than by computers."

"So if they are looking for anyone, it would be Jorran, not Dalden."

"Yes. But that means that Dalden can make no mistakes to draw attention to himself, or they'll think they've found what they're looking for in him. And these people are in a constant state of readiness for war. Though most of them have reached a point of wanting global peace, they are too diverse in cultures to attain it completely."

"I wish you could just get a fix on Jorran and zap him to us," Shanelle mumbled. "Problem solved."

"Already tried it, kiddo, without success," Martha replied in a matching mumble. "Without a homing link attached to him, I can't get a perfect lock on him, even if I can pick up his voice. I'd have to transfer the entire area he's in to guarantee getting him as well, which is out of the question unless we know for certain that he's alone. Besides, he's wearing one of those old-fashioned personal Air Shields that prevent contamination when visiting suspect areas."

"Never heard of it."

"Didn't think so. Personal Air Shields have long been considered inferior devices, since a simple pill these days can destroy any contamination in seconds, if there isn't a meditech unit handy to do the same. The shield around him isn't visible to the naked eye, doesn't prevent access to him other than of the germ type, but it definitely interferes with Molecular Transfer."

"As in, can't be used with?"

"Right. He'd have to turn it off for me to get at him,

and he's not likely to do that, if he's paranoid enough to wear an old-style shield in the first place rather than trust a meditech to cleanse and purify or a pill to prevent. But chances are his ship isn't equipped with an expensive meditech. Nor are the pills standard issue on Traders like his that usually have only contamination-free planets on their scheduled routes, so they have no need for such devices to begin with."

"Why was it discontinued for use if it still serves its purpose?"

"It became obsolete when Molecular Transfer first came into use. It worked fine when the only way you could get down to a planet was in a landing ship, but because Transfers can't be made while using one, if you transfer without the shield activated, you get contaminated before you can turn it on."

"That would be rather pointless," Shanelle agreed. "But wouldn't there be a time when Jorran might need to turn it off, like for cleaning up or sleeping?"

"Yes, but without a homing link on him, I can't keep him on track. I can zero in on him only when he communicates with his ship, but once he goes silent again, I lose him in the crowd. Besides, as long as he keeps the shield control within five feet of him, the shield will remain on him, even when he removes the control unit from his person, so I'm not counting on getting lucky there."

Shanelle sighed. "So we have to physically get our hands on him and the rods."

"Exactly, but Dalden should be able to manage that just fine once he finds him—as long as he stops being distracted by the locals."

No blush this time; in fact, Dalden's expression had

turned warriorish, as in no expression at all. Martha usually took such opportunities to try to provoke a reaction, one of her small forms of amusement, but with a specific task at hand, she restrained herself.

"I haven't determined if Jorran did his homework first, or just picked a country at random," Martha continued. "But there are many different forms of government here in the different countries, and a hierarchy of government in the one he did pick. Head of a town, then head of a state that has hundreds of towns, then head of the whole country. They don't have a head of the whole planet yet, haven't progressed to that. But there are a few countries that are considered world leaders: their opinion counts big-time and they have the power to back it up, if you know what I mean. He's picked one of the big leaders, but it looks like he's going to start small and work his way up. Didn't think he'd be that smart."

"Why is this smart, when it's not what he really wants?" Shanelle asked.

"Because what their leaders do here is quickly made known to all the populace, especially what the big leaders do. Whereas the actions of the little leaders, the ones who only govern a single town, tend to only be made known to that town. In other words, the fewer eyes on him, the better.

"He probably wasn't expecting this planet to be so hugely populated, since most planets grown to this size begin dispersing their people to other planet colonies before they deplete the mother planet's resources. Century III is still in the baby stages itself, with a gross population under five hundred thousand. This planet has people in the billions. They have mil-

lions jammed into little cities. They don't spread out, they spread up. There's just too many people here. It's no wonder any ship that has come close enough to check them out has run the other way instead of making contact."

"On the other hand, Jorran might be delighted by the overabundance of population," Shanelle remarked. "The more people falling at his feet in worship, the better."

"True, though I doubt it will matter when Probables tell me it's not going to work the way he's hoping, on a big scale—though he seems to think it will, and can cause a lot of grief in the trying."

"Why not? It worked perfectly on Sunder."

"Yes, because Sunder was a global unity that shared power between the military and science departments, and they didn't have world communication systems like this one does, where everyone can be apprised of what's going on in their world by just turning on a box in their homes and listening. On Sunder, the leaders could step down and appoint anyone they wanted to take their place, and most of the planet's people never knew the difference. On this planet the leaders are either elected by the people, born into the position, or take power by might. The general populace knows what's going on and if they don't like it, they most definitely aren't quiet about it. And he's picked the elected form of government, so he can't just use the rods to have one of the leaders resign and appoint him in his place."

"But won't that approach take much longer?"

"You betcha." Martha switched to a smirking tone. "It would take years for him to work his way up

through the hierarchy. And it's a good guess that Jorran won't figure that out before he runs out of time."

"Then couldn't we just sit back and wait for him to run out of time and go home? If he's back on Century III, we can file theft charges against him and get the rods back through normal diplomatic channels."

"We could," Martha replied. "But we won't, when he could decide to take the risk and strand himself here, the old do-or-die approach. And there is one other possibility we have to take into account."

"You mean you haven't told us everything yet?"

"It's those slow computers," Martha's new tone was thick with complaint. "I was concentrating on retrieving their history, military, science, and governmental records first, but I'm now getting information that introduces new options. Jorran doesn't have to get into a position of leadership to be in a position of power on this particular planet. Wealth is a highly motivating, highly powerful commodity here, so he could obtain his own empire in the field of finance instead. And in that case, those rods can do exactly what he needs."

"Have people shower him with their riches, without knowing why, and with nothing to prevent them from doing so?" Shanelle guessed.

"Exactly."

Chapter 8

"IS ALL THAT SILENCE BROODING, DALDEN, OR BECAUSE you've been paying attention?" Martha asked.

They were alone in the control room. Shanelle had been informed that Falon was showing signs of impatience in wanting to search for Jorran himself. Sending fifty seven-foot Sha-Ka'ani warriors to the surface for a mass search for Jorran would have hastened the search, but was out of the question. There might be humans of an equivalent size on the planet, but they were a rarity, not the norm.

Sending down even two warriors would be pushing it for drawing unwanted notice, which was why Martha was insisting the search begin with just Dalden. Shanelle, being in agreement, had rushed off to remind her lifemate of that.

"I understand what worries you, Martha," Dalden

replied. "I would not let the woman know that I am what she would call a barbarian."

Chuckling floated about the room. "She wouldn't think that. No, her word for you would be an alien. It would have no meaning to her that other worlds consider your world a bit barbaric in nature. She'd recognize only one thing, that you aren't from *her* world, and that would shock the hell out of her, taking precedence over anything she might have been feeling about you. I'd then have to bring her aboard the ship, erase her memories of you, and hope that it works on these humanoids. And you know I don't deal well with 'hope it works.' So why don't we just avoid all that—"

"I need someone who will immediately recognize another visitor like me," he interrupted. "I will not be able to know the difference, since they all sound strange to me. Jorran I will recognize."

"Not guaranteed, when he could change his looks. Did we say your task was going to be easy?"

Dalden ignored the commentary to continue to make his point. "The rest of his people I would not know. But she would know. She knew immediately that I was not from her town. She already thinks I am part of her world, a foreigner, she called me."

"I was there, remember? I heard every word."

"Then you can agree that to have her help would be a benefit to us."

"Of course I agree, but that doesn't mean it can be allowed. Other factors have to be taken into account, Dalden, the main one being that the longer you deal with one of those humans, the greater the risk of giving yourself away. The woman Brittany isn't even in a

position of authority, yet she asks the same questions you will run into from everyone. Those are a curious, bold people. Butting into others' business is a natural process for them. And she will continue to grill you with questions until you end up slipping and telling her something that you shouldn't."

"With most of those questions already dealt with, the risk has been lessened."

Martha chuckled. "I just love it when warriors prove they aren't all brawn."

"Does this mean—"

"Not so fast, kiddo." Martha did the interrupting this time. "I sent your sister out of here so I could speak plainly without embarrassing you. The woman Brittany does happen to be ideal for what you need, and you've passed with flying colors, making her think you're just someone from a different part of her world. I could wish you weren't attracted to her, so let me just stress: Jorran first, then rods, girl last on the agenda. If your reproductive instincts become a problem, get them out of the way. Too much trouble can be caused if that's all you're thinking about. So if it becomes a problem, take care of it, then get back to business. Can you do that?"

"Certainly."

"Why do I get the feeling that would have been your answer whether you believe it to be true or not? Never mind," was said with an accompanying sigh. "I know you wouldn't lie to me intentionally. I know you *think* you can do what needs doing. I've come to expect an abundance of confidence from any of you warriors, no matter the endeavor, and you and your father have proven time and again that your own confidence is rarely off the mark."

"Is the woman still in that place you sent me to?" Dalden questioned.

"No, but I have already accessed all pertinent information on her and have the location that she calls home. I've also launched a miniature viewer above her town so I can have visuals as needed and not have to depend solely on the viewers on the combo-unit."

A grid appeared on the computer monitor that enlarged and then enlarged several more times until it became more clear that it was an overhead view of a small section of the planet that included dwellings, foliage, and objects moving along the grids that looked similar to the flying vehicles of Kystran but without the capability of flying. A large red circle appeared on one section of the grid, another was drawn some distance away, then three more smaller circles.

Martha's voice was all business now as she explained, "Brittany Callaghan lives here." The first circle flashed brighter in color. "The leader called Mayor lives here." The second circle flashed. "The largest bank depositors live here." The three circles flashed together. "All three are corporations rather than individuals. I will monitor their accounts for any unusual withdrawals, but I am not overly concerned yet that Jorran might go the money route. His mentality is deeply set in being a titled ruler, rather than a wealthy despot, so he will at least make the attempt to become the mayor here."

"Can he succeed?"

"Sure, if he uses the rods on every male in town and waits to get elected by them through the normal process, but he doesn't have time for that. He'll more likely try something stupid instead like having the

mayor resign and appoint him as his replacement until the election. He'll be using those rods a lot to do it this way, and will have to have the support of the city council and every other man in a position of authority, as well as a full-blown history for himself to offer the public, because these people won't accept a stranger taking over, they will want to know *all* about him. But the rods will work to make people think they've known him forever and that he's a really great guy who'd make a perfect mayor for them."

Dalden frowned. "Then he *can* accomplish what he wants here."

Martha spared a moment to offer one of her more smirking-type chuckles. "He could if it were only men in the equation, but the women, at least in the country he's picked, aren't of the silent, do-as-they're-told variety. Many of them hold positions of authority themselves. The rods worked fine on Sunder because it was a conspiracy of women that took over there, so they only had the men to worry about. Here, it's the women who are going to throw a wrench in Jorran's plans."

"This is true on the whole planet?"

"No, he's just picked the wrong country to try to take over. It's up to you to get your hands on him before he changes tactics and picks another country, or goes after riches instead. The last thing we want is for him to lose himself in one of their big cities. It's hard enough trying to pinpoint his location in the small town he's in. It'd be impossible in one of their major cities."

"The amount of people in that place today cannot be called small by any standards."

Another chuckle. "That was not a normal place,

Dalden, it was a place the entire town goes to for shopping and other forms of entertainment, their version of a Sha-Ka-Ra market. You wouldn't find crowds like that in the rest of the town, though in a large city you just might. But the local news of the town had the mayor scheduled to be there today, which is why you were placed there."

"But was Jorran there?"

"Undetermined. The mayor was there, and we have to assume that Jorran will be following the mayor until he makes his move, which is why you will need to keep close to him as well. But keep in mind, you can't just grab Jorran when you do find him and expect no one to interfere, and we do *not* want those people yelling for their security forces. You can't give him a chance to use a rod on you, either. You need to stun him, turn off his shield, then I can get you both back to the ship and we will have the leverage to have the rest of the rods turned over to us. But you need to get him alone before you go assaulting him with a stun."

"The stunning and the turning off of his shield can be accomplished in a matter of moments, as is Transfer. Why must such precaution be taken?"

"Because I don't take chances with one of Tedra's babies. You know that. And there are too many unknown variables involved on this planet, things I am unaware of yet because their computers aren't up to my speed and aren't giving me all their information fast enough. I shocked a good many people today by putting you down in the center of them. I shocked many more taking you back out of their midst, since the Brittany female wasn't the only woman down there who couldn't take her eyes off you, kiddo. A

good many of them will now be visiting their eye doctors, which is okay, as long as we don't make a habit of shocking them. Had violence broken out in their midst, that whole crowd could have swarmed on you, and having you end up in what they call jail is *not* on the agenda."

"If I had my sword—" ·

"No, no, no, don't turn pure warrior on me, Dalden. I know what you're capable of, you know what you're capable of, but those people up there are not going to find that out for themselves. Swords are archaic here, used only by performers enacting their history. They are not worn in public without causing a great deal of curiosity. You have an excellent weapon in your phazor combo-unit: it covers all emergencies and gives me a six-sided view of the proceedings as well, and none of these humanoids will guess it is a weapon because they have nothing like it. It looks like what they call a portable radio, and Corth II even attached that wire to it so you can hear me without anyone near you hearing me."

"The woman could hear you."

"No, all she heard was noise, she didn't hear my words and wouldn't have understood them even if she did, which is beside the point. The communicator phazor unit has been made to look familiar to these people, so they won't question it. Now let's get back to the matter of the Brittany woman and using her to aid your task. The info I have gathered on her from all computer sources indicates that she has two places of employment that take up most of her time. You will need to tempt her away from these jobs to work for you. Just asking might do it, but let's not count on that. You will need to hire her."

"With what do I hire her? You can obtain their currency to do this?"

"Unnecessary," Martha replied. "Like the Catrateri, this is another planet that worships the metal gold, and that chunk you wear around your neck should be more than sufficient for the short-term employment you require. Now, are you ready to get back to business?"

"Indeed."

"Then hold on to your socks, kiddo, Transfer imminent."

Chapter 9

"IT CRACKS ME UP WHEN THIS JUNK MANAGES TO GET into the local paper. I mean, you expect it in the supermarket tabloids, but—"

"What junk?" Brittany asked as she closed the refrigerator, the cold soda she'd come for in hand.

Her roommate was sitting at their small kitchen table with a cup of coffee and a piece of coffee cake in front of her, even though it was midafternoon. Of course, Jan had only just gotten up an hour ago, having slept in later than usual today after a late night out with her current boyfriend. Several newspapers were there that she was catching up on reading, with one open in her hands.

"And on the second page, no less," Jan added as she glanced up at Brittany. "This is too funny."

Since Jan wasn't exactly laughing, Brittany took the funny part to be sarcasm. "What junk?" she asked again.

"Another UFO sighting."

Brittany rolled her eyes and headed out of the kitchen. Jan called after her, "No, really. Three people from Seaview swear they saw it. I wonder how long they stayed for happy hour."

Brittany came back and sat down across from Jan. "Some people actually take that stuff seriously, you know," she pointed out.

"We don't."

"No, but I can see why it would make the local paper, if three locals are claiming they saw something unusual. That's the first sighting in our area, which makes it newsworthy or at least of interest, even if it was just another weird-looking government plane being tested or a trick of the light. Besides, look at what those initials stand for, 'unidentified' being the word of note. I'm sure if the little green men ever do decide to pay us a visit, we'll have no trouble recognizing their transportation as a spaceship and calling it that."

Jan rolled her eyes now. "You are too kind, Britt. A flaky, delusional person is still a flake."

"No, actually, *those* sightings we probably never hear about, just as a known drunk isn't going to be taken seriously, either. The sightings that do make the news are usually from sober, respectable people who really do believe they saw what they claim to have seen."

"Or sensationalists who lie just to bask in the public spotlight," Jan countered as she continued to glance over the paper.

Brittany gave up with a chuckle. Her friend was one of those stubborn individuals who would adhere to an opinion to the bitter end, despite evidence that might suggest they have their facts wrong. She enjoyed such discussions, though, because she didn't let them frustrate her. She wasn't the type who had to be right all the time; she was perfectly happy to shrug and say we'll agree to disagree without getting hot under the collar about it, and go on to the next subject.

She'd still been in a rotten mood when she'd come into the kitchen, still furious that that gorgeous foreigner she'd met a few hours ago hadn't had the decency to at least say good-bye before disappearing on her. Trust Jan though to lighten her mood, however briefly.

They were three years apart in age, Jan the younger at twenty-five, but had hit it off immediately when Jan answered the roommate ad Brittany had run soon after she moved into the two-bedroom apartment. She could have afforded the place easily by herself, but her goals were already set, and having someone split the costs with her fit well into her plan. Besides, she wasn't a loner; she liked having people around, liked having someone there to talk to when she felt like it, or leave her alone when she felt like that, too.

But today she knew she wouldn't be good company. So she started to head back to her bedroom to lay on her bed and brood some more about all the things she should have said to that hunk to make him at least interested enough to ask for her phone number.

But again Jan arrested her attention, this time with a gasped, "Jeez!" and a moment later, "Oh, Jeez, I don't believe it!"

Brittany came back to stand in the doorway that separated the kitchen and tiny laundry room from the oversized living room. "What now?"

"We almost died yesterday and didn't even know it!" Jan exclaimed.

"Excuse me?"

Jan laid the paper down to stare up at Brittany wide-eyed. She was actually pale. "I thought meteors and comets got tracked coming toward us, like we had months' advance warning? Did *you* hear anything about this one?"

Brittany frowned. "A meteor passed by near us?"

"It didn't pass by, it was last tracked dropping into the Pacific, was already in the atmosphere when it was spotted, and then—gone."

"So there was no danger?"

"Are you kidding? It says here it was the size of a football field. If that thing had actually hit the water instead of disintegrating, the tidal wave would have been big enough to reach the next states over."

"But it obviously didn't hit."

"No, but that's beside the point. This one came in so fast that no one saw it coming."

"The size of a football field would be no more than a speck of dust in space, Jan. The observatories wouldn't pick up anything that small."

"I still don't like it that we hear about it *after* the fact," Jan grumbled.

Neither did Brittany, but she was pragmatic about things that she couldn't change. "If it came in as fast as you say, so it wasn't even noticed until it was already here, then nothing could have been done about it either way. Meteors flash through all the time, some hit,

most disintegrate. We can be glad they aren't the size of comets, and chalk this one up to it wasn't our time to go."

"Is that farm philosophy?"

Brittany grinned. "No, just old-fashioned acceptance of fate."

Jan snorted. "I'd rather make my own fate, thank you very much, which includes at least having the option of trying to run for the hills."

Brittany might have suggested Jan go back to school and figure out how to build better telescopes, but she preferred to get back to her brooding, so she shrugged instead and once again headed toward her bedroom. But she'd no sooner closed the door when another shriek of astonishment was heard from the kitchen. Brittany shook her head. She *did* wonder what could possibly top the story of the meteor to upset Jan this time, but decided she could wait to find out.

But less than a minute later she was heading back to the kitchen despite her resolve. Curiosity could be a major pain sometimes, and she did occasionally have an overactive imagination that could go haywire if her own curiosity started acting up. She began to think of other things that had nothing to do with news articles that might have made Jan cry out, and she was actually running those last few steps to the kitchen door to make sure her friend was all right.

She wasn't. Jan was slumped across the table, the coffee cup spilled, the cake just missed by her head, the newspaper scattered on the floor next to her chair. Behind her stood—him. Unbelievable. That gorgeous hunk of foreign masculinity in *her* kitchen? And he

looked annoyed and upset at the same time, if that was possible, as he stared down at Jan.

"What'd you do, scare the bejesus out of her?"

He hadn't seen Brittany yet in the doorway. He looked at her now and seemed to visibly relax, though he did sigh.

"She could not withstand the sight of me," he said by way of explanation.

"That's what I said—never mind. Help me get her to her bed."

There was no helping about it. He lifted Jan so easily that he could have been picking up the coffee cup, and simply waited for Brittany to lead him, which she did. A few moments later she stared down at Jan laying peacefully in her bed and had no idea what to do to bring her out of her faint. It wasn't as if she had any experience in the matter.

She sighed. "I really don't think we have anything in the medicine cabinet that covers fainting."

"I am told she will recover in due time."

"Told?" she said. "Or is that your way of stating your opinion? Oh, never mind," she added, realizing as she said it that she'd said it an awful lot to him in the brief span of their acquaintance.

She directed him out of Jan's room with a wave of her hand, followed him into the living room that adjoined both bedrooms, and pointed at the couch there. He took the hint, though he was very careful as he sat down on it, as if he were afraid he might break it. Come to think of it, some springs just might snap under his seven feet of solid man weight. He really was *big*. And although their living room was extra large in

comparison to the rest of the apartment, it looked cut down to half its size with him in it.

Brittany was still in a bit of shock herself that he was there, when she had been sure she'd never see him again. And the fact that Jan had still been sitting at the kitchen table meant she hadn't let him in, so it was no wonder his sudden presence had scared the heck out of her. Some overdue annoyance that he had just barged in on them rose now.

"Is it normal etiquette in your country to just walk into someone's home without knocking?" she asked. "There are laws against doing that here, if no one has bothered to mention that to you."

He didn't answer immediately. She had changed into shorts and a loose T-shirt when she got home, but he was still dressed as he'd been at the mall, and still had that radio, or translator, or whatever it was, attached to his belt, the miniature earphone still firmly in ear.

"I knocked," he told her. "Yet no one opened the door."

She found that hard to believe. As big as his hand was, any knocking he did could probably be heard over on the next block.

So she raised a brow at him. "You didn't figure, then, that maybe no one was home?"

Another pause before he said, "I knew that not to be the case."

Okay, so he could have heard them talking through the door, but then how the heck hadn't they heard his knocking? She might not have heard him after she'd closed her bedroom door, but Jan should have. And

why was she nitpicking when he was here? She still found that amazing. He'd actually tracked her down—but how had he?

She immediately asked, "How did you find me when my phone number is unlisted?"

Once again, a long pause before he answered, "I have excellent resources."

"No kidding," she agreed. "So much for thinking you needed a detective, when you've got the kind of access usually only law enforcement, government, or ambassadors—ahh, that's it, isn't it? Your embassy in this country is helping you cut through red tape?"

"For what reason would I cut tape of a certain color?" he replied.

Screeching out of the earphone. Well, he *had* answered immediately, without waiting for the coaching. Brittany almost laughed, but his wince restrained her. Poor baby. He was having a heck of a time coping with the new language he'd learned, and his translator was obviously of the impatient sort.

"How about we have a conversation without your hyperactive friend's help?" she suggested, staring pointedly at the radio on his hip.

He gave her a brilliant smile and removed the earphone, dropping the cord so it dangled over the couch by his feet, a good guess that was far enough for him not to hear anything else coming out of it. Brittany only vaguely noticed, though, that smile of his having dazzled her to the core.

"Be at ease," he said. "I will be fine."

"Was that for me or your friend there?" she managed to ask him.

"My friend. She worries overmuch about me."

The dazzling subsided completely, some unexpected bristling taking over. "She?"

"She is a computer."

Brittany blinked. "Was that a joke?"

"Why would you think so?"

She laughed. He was quite funny. "Probably because computers don't have emotions, so they can't worry. Now, what brings you here?"

"I need you."

Those words almost melted her on the spot. She had the greatest urge to hop across the coffee table between them, right into his lap. The butterflies in her belly had just gone absolutely wild. Never had she been so thoroughly turned on, and incredibly, just by words.

Chapter 10

I T TOOK BRITTANY NEARLY A MINUTE TO CONVINCE HERSELF that Dalden's definition of need was a far cry from hers. That he hadn't moved from his position on the couch sort of pushed her toward that conclusion sooner than her body was acknowledging. She *knew* she should have broken down and bought an air conditioner for the apartment; a blast of icy air would definitely be welcome at the moment.

She settled for sinking into the matching lounge chair next to the couch and inconspicuously fanning herself. Hearing his definition of need would probably help even more, so she asked, "What can I do for you that your embassy can't?"

"I must find the man Jorran in all haste," he told her. "Yet I am not assured of recognizing him if I see him,

because he may have changed his appearance from when I last saw him. You would know him, though, as you did me, for someone not from your country."

"Well, that's debatable," she replied, pointing out, "It was only your accent—"

"He will speak differently, as do I."

She chuckled. "I hope you're not talking about having a chat with everyone in town, just to hear their accents."

"If such is needful—"

"Time out," she cut in. "I was joking. We're a small town, but we still have a population now exceeding twenty thousand residents. If even half of those are men, you're talking a heck of a lot of time to track them all down for a little chat. And I was under the impression that you don't have a lot of time."

"Nor do I. Nor will it be needful. Jorran will wish to make contact with the one you call Mayor, so he will most likely be found in the vicinity of this leader."

"What's he want with Mayor Sullivan?"

"His position."

"His position on what?"

He looked confused. Brittany *was* confused. He tried to clarify. "He will try to become mayor here. I must stop him before he succeeds."

"He's here to run against Sullivan? But I thought he was a foreigner like you?"

"He is."

"Then I don't get it. You have to be an American citizen to run for political office in this country. How could he not know that?"

Dalden grinned, showing signs of relief. "Because he is as ignorant of your traditions as I am."

She grinned back. "Well, there you go, your problem is solved."

He sighed now. "Actually, it is not. I still must find him and remove him from your country before he causes problems here."

"Ah, international incident of the big sort, huh?" It was pretty obvious when he glanced down at the earphone at his feet that he was in need of an explanation. Brittany tried. "A big ruckus that would make the papers in both our countries, to everyone's embarrassment?" When he still looked blank, she added, "Oh, go ahead, pick it up. I'm sure *she* can make you understand."

He nodded, did so, and after a very long moment of having the earphone attached again, said to Brittany, "Your analysis is appropriate. Will you help me?"

"I'd love to, really I would, but I don't see how I can. You need someone with more time on their hands than I have. But with two jobs tying me up for most of the week, the only time I could help you would be on Sundays, and that doesn't seem nearly enough when you've made it clear you're in a hurry to get this wrapped up."

"You misunderstand, Brittany Callaghan. I wish to pay for your time, for you to work only for me until my task here is accomplished."

He lifted the large medallion off his chest and off his neck, leaning over to hand it to her. Her hand actually dropped before she put some effort into holding it up. The medallion was really heavy, with the added weight of the chain, which was more the size of a bicy-

cle chain than a piece of jewelry, probably weighing ten pounds itself.

She gave him a questioning look, to which he said, "That is a cheap metal where I come from, yet I am told it has high value here. Will it be sufficient to hire you?"

She glanced down at what was probably fifteen, maybe even twenty pounds of disk and chain. "How much gold plating are we talking about?"

"Plating?"

"The percentage of actual gold?"

"There is no percentage. It is only one metal. Are we misinformed, that you do not value pure gold?"

"You have *got* to be kidding."

She wasn't sure what gold was priced at by the ounce these days, but knew a chain not even a tenth the size of the one in her hand could cost upwards of six hundred dollars, and not even be pure gold at that. She did some quick calculations in her head and realized they were talking about a *lot* of money—if he wasn't pulling her leg about it being pure gold. And what was she even thinking about? It was way too much for what he was suggesting.

"Look, it probably wouldn't take more than a week to find your guy, even less if he really is going to be hanging out around the mayor. I can take a week off from my jobs, and you can pay me with the currency of your country the equivalent of a couple thousand American bucks. This," she added, handing him back the medallion, "is worth a small fortune, far too much for one week's work."

He pushed the medallion back at her. "It may require more than one week, and—it is all that I have to pay you with. I have not this currency that you speak of."

"No money, and here you are trying to dump a fortune in gold on me?" she rolled her eyes. "No offense, but you need a baby-sitter, big guy."

After a moment he grinned at her. "You have just endeared yourself to Martha."

"Who's Martha?"

"The voice in here." He tapped the earphone. "She suggests that 'baby-sitter' be added to the job you will do for me. What is baby-sitter?"

Brittany blushed. "You don't know? I mean, she didn't explain—? Never mind. I was just joking, really. But what happened to your money? Have you just run out, or were you robbed?"

"Neither. I had no requirement of currency until it became needful to hire assistance."

She stared at him long enough to draw her own conclusion and even thumped her head for not thinking of it sooner. "Credit cards, of course. And for some reason, you aren't equating them with money. Okay, no biggie. Your hotel might not advance you a couple grand, but the banks will tomorrow."

The look he was giving her said clearly that she was talking Greek to him again, but after the requisite pause while he attentively listened to Martha's explanations, he said simply, "I am reminded that I cannot return to my place of sleep until the new rising."

"Rising?"

He sighed after some brief coaching from the earphone and clarified, "Many call it a new day."

"Oh, tomorrow!" Brittany said, but then frowned. "Why not?"

He explained, "Because I was called back for an un-

needful consultation, I have exceeded my limit for returning there on this rising."

This was said with a degree of grouchiness. Not that
it mattered when she was completely baffled anyway.
She understood now how frustrating it must be for
him, needing translations for just about everything she
was saying. That must have been one heck of a lousy
language course he took, if such worldly things like
credit cards, hotels, and banks hadn't been included.
Talk about a simplistic definition for hotel—place of
sleep. She mentally rolled her eyes again.

The only other conclusion she could draw was that
he came from one of those countries that still got
around on camels, where most of their population had
never heard of such things. She hoped not.

And then it dawned on her and she asked, "Wait a
minute, are you saying you have nowhere to sleep
tonight, but tomorrow you will have?"

He nodded. She sighed, telling him, "I'm not even
going to try to figure out how that could be possible,
when it doesn't sound like you're referring to messed-
up hotel reservations. But you're welcome to sleep on
our couch, I suppose. My roommate Jan might object,
after the scare you gave her. Then again, after she gets
a good look at you, she might not. We eat around six.
The bathroom is through that middle door behind
you. In the meantime, how about telling me a little
more about yourself, so I can better understand what's
going on here and what's going to be expected of me
on this temporary job?

"And put this back on," she continued, tossing the
medallion at him so he couldn't push it back at her this

time. "Much as I could use what that thing will fetch, I'm not in the habit of taking advantage of foreigners. We'll find you a buyer for it tomorrow so you can pocket the bulk and just pay me the couple thousand I've asked for, to cover taking off from my regular jobs."

Brittany settled down into the chair to wait while the female on the other end of his earphone did her thing. Sooner than expected, though, Dalden smiled and said, "I am told you eat real food here. I look forward to sharing your meal."

Brittany burst out laughing. She couldn't help it, deciding it was probably his Martha who needed a translator, not him.

Chapter 11

THEY DIDN'T EXACTLY GET AROUND TO TALKING ABOUT him as Brittany had hoped they would. Somehow, the subject got turned in her direction instead, because Dalden's curiosity had been pricked earlier by one of her remarks that didn't get addressed immediately.

"What is the job you have here that ties you up?" he asked her.

Just by the way he said it, she knew immediately that he had taken the word literally and had envisioned ropes twined about her limbs. "Err, that was ties up as in restricts, as in, I don't have much time left in the day after I get home from work for anything other than sleep. Was that easier for you to understand?"

"Indeed," he acknowledged. "But I would still hear of your job."

She had no idea why she was suddenly embarrassed, had thought she had long since reached the immune stage where her job choice was concerned. And it had been a long haul getting there.

Because she worked in a field that most men considered exclusively theirs, she'd been called a libber and every other nasty name you could think of. She'd heard it all and learned to ignore it. She'd had whole crews refuse to work with her. She'd had architects turn down her contractor because she was on his crew.

It was a wonder she hadn't lost her quirky sense of humor, but she hadn't. It was, at times, the only thing that sustained her.

So why didn't she find a job where she didn't get so much grief?

She could have moved on to something else after she had learned all she needed to know about construction. But she was good at it, and she had yet to find anything she was as capable at that paid as well, and that was the bottom line for her when she had such an expensive goal. And one of the nice things about her profession was that she could quit for a few months, even years, and then get back into it and not feel that she'd missed anything, because it was what she would be doing when she quit to build her home. Not much changed in construction. Better tools were made, union reps came and went, dues were raised, benefits got better, but houses were still basically built the same.

Her delay in answering him brought the remark, "I am told you are defensive about your job. Why is that?"

Since that voice on the other end of the earphone couldn't possibly have guessed that just from her prolonged silence, she was beginning to think that his "I am told" was just his way of stating his own opinion, rather than something Martha was telling him. Besides, her hot cheeks had probably been a dead giveaway, and only he was seeing that. Martha might be able to hear them, but that was all she could do.

"I used to be," she admitted. "Hard not to be, when you get so much flak about an occupation from all sides. But I'm stubborn. I have a goal, to build my own home with my own hands. My grandfather did it, and the concept always fascinated me, which probably had a lot to do with finally making the decision myself. So everything I do now is done with that goal in mind, which includes my choice of work, so I could learn about all aspects of house construction from the ground up. Basically I'm a carpenter, though I can roof, lay drywall, and paint with the best of them."

"It is difficult here, the building of one's home?" he asked.

"Well, no, not if you have a well-paying job to afford it, or in my case, know how to build it yourself. I'm probably making it harder than necessary by wanting to have all the money up front first. I thought about taking out a home loan instead, but I really hate the idea of going that deep into debt. I know everyone does it, but that didn't mean I had to. And besides, I'm going to save tons of money by doing it myself, since it won't cost anywhere near what it would cost if I just went out and bought a house already built."

"You will build your home here in this town?"

"Yes, I've already bought the land. I could get started on it already, but that would be building it piecemeal in my spare time, which would take years. I prefer to have enough money to spare for all the materials and extra help I'll need when more than two hands are required, enough so I can quit both my jobs until it's done. And doing it myself, I'll make sure it's done right."

"I find it admirable that you know how to create a house from nothing."

She blushed profusely. That had to be the first time a man had ever complimented her about her job choice.

But then he spoiled it by adding, "And do not view it as a punishment."

"I think we need another time-out," she said. "Either things are done really weird in your country, or you've been given the wrong definition for punishment. The only work around here that can be considered punishment is forced labor in prisons. Now some folks might not like their jobs, some might even hate them, but doing them anyway isn't punishment, it's more a necessity until something better comes along. Punishment, on the other hand, is pretty much universally reserved for disciplinary measures. No one around here is going to punish someone by forcing them to build a house for them. Do you see the difference?"

He smiled at her in answer, but also added, "I see that you have a good understanding for what must be done when one breaks rules. And I am told 'chore' would have been a more appropriate word to express my thoughts in the matter of how you view your job."

She chuckled. "No, I don't see it as a chore; I actually like building things, whether it's cabinets, tables, or an entire house. I work mostly for Arbor Construction here. I like their foremen, get along really well with their crews due to long association, and they know I do good work, so I don't have to constantly prove myself like I did in San Francisco when I lived there."

"Prove yourself how? In challenge?"

She blinked, then grinned at him. "Another of those misdefined words? No, occasionally there'd be no work in the city, so I'd have to go to the union to get work, and those jobs were usually with small crews that I didn't know and I'd have to go through the whole proving process again each time, because not once did they ever accept me as one of them. So when Arbor relocated here and offered me a chance to move with them, I jumped at it. It meant steady work with the same crews, instead of being sent who-knew-where by the union. And I love it here. I come from a small town and prefer them small, where you actually get to know your neighbors and develop a real sense of community."

Something she had said surprised him, which he mentioned right off. "You have lived elsewhere than in this town? Marriage brought you here?"

"Good heavens, no, I've never been married," she replied, amused at how easily he'd gotten that information out of her without actually asking if she were married. His two questions combined, though, led her to guess, "I take it your countrymen tend to stay where they're born?"

"Indeed, only would marriage separate a woman

from the place of her protection." And then he sighed.
"I am reminded that our cultures are very much different, that women here even live alone."

She matched his sigh with the conclusions that remark drew. "Just how antiquated *is* your country?"

He grinned. "Barbaric, you would call it."

The grin suggested that he was joking. She hoped
he was joking. She decided to accept that conclusion
and forget about getting it clarified. Unfortunately, a
picture of men riding around on camels and locking
their women up in tents was hard to shake. She tried
shaking it by continuing the job discussion.

"I've tried other jobs, but haven't found any that
give me as much satisfaction."

"What other jobs?" he asked with interest.

She started to just tell him when she realized that
those other jobs were in that same "for men only" classification, or might as well be when so many people
still viewed them that way. So a little explanation was
required first, if she didn't want to start blushing again.

"I have three older brothers. With no sisters, I
tended to follow along in their footsteps, and did in
fact enjoy the same pursuits they did growing up, you
know, fishing, hunting, sports. You could say tomboy
was my middle name."

"Is it?"

She chuckled, because that had been a serious question, but rather than explain what a tomboy was, she
just said, "No," and continued. "We lived on a farm.
My oldest brother, York, was the tractor-fixer in the
family, so it wasn't surprising that he became a master
mechanic who now owns his own gas station back
home. Learning what I did helping him on weekends,

it wasn't surprising I became a mechanic's helper my-self for a few years. I could have gotten certified, but I knew that wasn't a job that I wanted to stay with when getting the grease out from under my nails became a never-ending source of annoyance."

That was said to amuse him, but his expression didn't change, remained merely attentive. Too attentive, actually. It was hard to tell if he were really interested in what she was saying, or just wanted to hear her talk. For all she knew, he could just be dissecting her words to better his grasp of her language, using her to teach him, so to speak. Or his interest could be purely on a base level, because he might be attracted to her, but that was wishful thinking on her part better left unexplored for the moment.

She got back to the résumé explanations. "My middle brother, Kent, moved to this state quite a few years ago. He'd always wanted to see more of the country and figured he might as well get paid for it, so he drives the big-load trucks cross-country. Visiting him one summer convinced me to move here as well, and after accompanying Kent a few times on his longer hauls, I decided to try my own hand at it. That job only lasted about a year, though; it was just too boring for my tastes, and boring on the road can be real dangerous."

"How do you equate danger with boring?"

"As in falling asleep at the wheel."

For some reason, his blank look said even that needed an explanation for him. Brittany decided to let Coach Martha deal with that one, and she must have, since he nodded understanding after a moment.

"You did not want to do something different from your brothers?"

She grinned at him. "Why waste valuable knowledge already learned?"

She had thought about joining the military, actually, but didn't volunteer that information. She was rather well-suited for it with her size, after all, but had nixed that idea, preferring to follow her own strict regimen rather than one forced on her. And she liked building things, liked leaving her mark in such a way.

"I did finally go my own way. My youngest brother, Devon, is what you might call a born farmer. He really loves growing things. I don't. In fact, I couldn't wait to spread my wings and get away from the farm. But Devon is still there helping our father, and will probably take over after our parents pass on."

"One grows, one builds, one fixes, one transports. You have a family well-suited for trade."

"Diverse, I think you mean."

He shrugged, allowing her her own interpretation. Annoyed for a moment that he wasn't going to make the effort that she had in explaining things, she almost wished she could borrow his "coach."

"And the other job that ties you up?" he asked next.

"That one's a piece of cake, at the local spa in the evenings and on Saturdays. Just one person could handle it, but there's two of us, so there isn't all that much to do, other than man the desk and offer guidance when someone wants to start up a strict exercise regimen. My coworker, Lenny, and I get along pretty well, too. We have an understanding: he doesn't try to hit on me, and I won't drop weights on his feet every chance I get."

Again, that was said just to amuse him, and again, it didn't. Actually, he sat forward and said in a concise,

somewhat ominous tone, "The man you share this job with hits you?"

Brittany rolled her eyes, explaining, " 'Hit on' has a completely different meaning from the 'hits you' that you're using. No, Lenny has never hit me. But he has tried a few times to get me to go out with him."

"Go out where?"

"Dating?" He wasn't the only one drawing a blank—his earphone was quiet, too. "Oh, come on, you have *got* to understand dating. You know, girl and guy getting together to get to know each other better."

"You speak of fun?" he said with a big grin.

It was that big grin that had her replying cautiously, "Well, sure, at least, it can be hoped a date will turn out to be fun, but that certainly isn't always the case, and some can turn out to be a real pain in the—"

She cut herself off. He was looking alarmed. And she heard the distinct sound of laughter coming out of his earphone. She gave up. She was either having her leg pulled halfway across the state, or whoever had taught him English didn't have a good grasp of it themselves.

She said, "We should probably stop at the library in the morning to get you a real English dictionary. It might take you a few weeks of studying it, but you definitely didn't learn all you should have the first time around."

"I am aware that we are having difficulty communicating, but I would not be able to read one of your books. I was taught in audio, not visual."

She sighed. "Was your teacher a complete idiot, or one of those rinky-dink language—?"

The screeching out of the earphone was seriously

loud this time, causing Dalden to yank it out of his ear before it did some real damage.

Brittany raised an eyebrow at him. "Let me guess. The gal on the other end of the line there was your teacher?"

He winced, but nodded. She chuckled, adding, "Okay, I'll assume, since you're still being taught by Miss Coach, that you haven't had a full language course yet, and you're actually doing pretty well, if we go with that assumption. It's not a major problem, just time-consuming, all this explaining stuff. No biggie."

The earphone had gone silent while she spoke, prompting him to risk putting it back on. It buzzed for a moment at a normal volume. The woman Martha was obviously temperamental, but able to recover swiftly and get back to business.

He said now, "I am told that your language is more familiar to us than was first realized. Taken from the computers, the language was basic. Hearing you speak it, the similarities are becoming noticeable."

"Similarities to what? Your own language?"

"No, to the ancient language of my mother's people, which I have full understanding of. If such continues apace, and other of your words have the same meanings, I will have the correct translations momentarily. Thus we will have no further difficulties in communicating."

"Huh?"

He held up a hand, silently asking her to wait on any further explanations. The noise coming out of his earphone now was a steady buzz, a nonstop low-volume

sound like a high-speed acceleration on a tape recorder, much too fast to be understood. It was probably broken. Good. She didn't really mind explaining things to him. But she did mind third-wheel Martha continuously butting in. How were they supposed to find any time alone to get to know each other better with that ever-present eavesdropper connected to his ear?

Chapter 12

"CAN THAT BE TURNED OFF?"

Brittany blushed as she asked it. She shouldn't have asked. It smacked of her obvious preference to be alone with Dalden.

Yet he didn't seem to notice any ulterior motive to the question and simply answered, "Only partially can Martha be disabled. The unit can be made so she cannot, or will not, speak, but there is no way to keep her from hearing when she is already hearing."

Brittany assumed that something got lost there in the translation, because it almost sounded as if Martha had some other means out of his control for listening in on him, which conjured up an image of her apartment being bugged with a spying device, which was absurd. And she was *not* going to start looking under tables.

The subject went no further, though, because noises were finally heard from behind Jan's bedroom door, a bit of swearing, then the door opened and Jan stumbled groggily out, rubbing her eyes. Seeing Brittany first, she said, "I had the weirdest dream," then noticing Dalden on the coach, "okay, so maybe I didn't. Who the—"

She didn't go any further, was absorbing Dalden's looks by slow degrees, to the point that her eyes got wider and wider. If someone could be said to be drooling without actually drooling, Jan was doing it. At least, she was until Dalden pushed off of the couch to turn to face her, so he didn't have to crane his neck to look behind him.

His neck-craning was nothing compared to hers. Jan was on the petite side and had to look up at Brittany if they were standing too close, but Dalden's seven feet were a bit intimidating. She'd been amazed at his handsomeness, but his size had her literally backing up until she was almost back in her bedroom.

She stopped at the door and said, "Holy cow!" And then as an explanation occurred to her, "One of your brothers, right? You could have warned me he was coming."

Jan had never met any of Brittany's brothers, but for some reason she assumed they were all a *lot* taller than Brittany was. Which wasn't the case at all. York was six-six, but both Kent and Devon were a bit shorter than that.

Brittany replied, "I'm happy to say he's no relation."

"Oh?" Jan's eyes swung to Brittany and, seeing the

blush, added, "Ohhhh," which made the blush even brighter.

Brittany made introductions and offered a bit of explanation about why Dalden was there. She then escaped to the kitchen with the excuse of getting dinner started, and stayed there until her cheeks cooled off. It was appalling that she'd blushed more in this one day than she had in the last several years.

She didn't have to worry about leaving Jan alone with Dalden. That longer "oh" had been clear understanding on her part. Jan even managed to disappear for most of the evening. She was a compulsive matchmaker, after all, had been trying to fix Brittany up with one guy after another in the three years they'd shared the apartment, and wasn't about to be a third wheel tonight when it was so obvious that Brittany was attracted to their guest.

Brittany cooked one of the most lavish meals she'd ever prepared. She even broke out the cookbook for it, not wanting to make a single mistake. Realizing afterward what she'd done, going to so much anxious effort to impress Dalden, she was disgusted with herself. If he couldn't like her the way she was, then there was no point in even thinking that they might be able to form a relationship, even if only a brief one. She wasn't going to change for anyone, was very comfortable with her life and her goals.

He was impressed with the meal, though—at least, he cleaned his plate thrice over. She knew men his size could eat a lot at one sitting, her brothers being testament to that, but even she was amazed at the amount of food Dalden consumed. Fortunately, she had pre-

pared enough side dishes that she didn't run short. Still, there were no leftovers, and thank goodness Jan had a sweet tooth, so there was half a chocolate cake available for dessert as well. With half of that and a full carton of milk, she was reasonably sure her guest was finally replete.

And then she got nervous.

It was natural, she supposed, with a few hours yet to kill before her usual bedtime, that she'd start thinking about sex. Not that it hadn't been in the back, or forefront, of her mind all day, when she'd never before met someone she was this powerfully attracted to. And since that attraction had seemed to be mutual, she was pretty much expecting Dalden to make a move on her at some point in the evening.

For an immediate distraction, she turned on the television. It wouldn't be the first time she had used it to ease awkward moments with new acquaintances. But Dalden didn't seem the least bit interested in it, was staring at her instead, which just increased her nervousness.

"What would you like to watch?" she asked him.

He chuckled. "Is that not apparent?"

Back came the pink cheeks. "I meant on the TV," she explained.

He finally glanced across the room toward where she nodded and, after a moment of visually examining the floor console sitting there, rather than what was on the screen, said, "It is a strange-looking computer."

"It's not a computer—" She paused with the incredulous thought. "Oh, come on, don't try to tell me you know about computers, but have never seen a televi-

sion set before, when television has been around *long* before computers."

"I am told it is a means of entertainment."

"But you didn't know that until Martha just told you, did you? How is that possible?" she asked, then answered her own question. "Okay, so maybe you live out in the boonies somewhere, and maybe your village doesn't even have electricity. But, newsflash, most computers require electricity, too. So how can you know of one and not the other, when most households have a TV or two or three, long before they even think about buying a home computer?"

He didn't reply. He got to his feet, moved to stand in front of her, and pulled her to her feet as well. One hand came to her cheek, and tilted her head so she would meet the eyes looking down at her. That easily all thoughts of questioning him were gone. She'd wonder later if it were deliberate on his part, to avoid answering her, but at the moment she was knee-deep in anticipation and simply didn't care.

"I like your concept of dating, now that I understand it," he told her. "But I think you will like the concept of my fun even better. We each of us know what the other wants, thus would dating best be seen to after we first have fun."

She could barely think to decipher what he'd just said, but managed to get out, "I get the feeling you have a really odd definition for fun."

"Not odd at all," he countered. "Though you may call it making love, you must agree no matter what it is called, it is fun."

"I—I agree it's reputed to be, yes, but—are you

suggesting we forget about the getting to know each other better part and get right down to the bottom line?"

He smiled beautifully. "If that means you will take me to where you sleep, yes."

Chapter 13

BRITTANY'S STOMACH WAS DOING THE BUTTERFLY THING. Her heart was slamming in her chest. Her instinct was to drag Dalden straight to her bedroom, and yet she had twenty-eight years of strict upbringing rooting her feet to the spot there in her living room.

He hadn't even kissed her yet. They'd only just met, not even six hours ago. How could she possibly give in to these primitive urges she was feeling? How could she not, when she'd been waiting so long for the right man to come along?

It wasn't as if she had to wait for marriage. Very few women did anymore in this day and age of self-gratification. And she'd been willing to sleep with Tom before he made that tactless remark that killed her feelings for him. But there was the rub. She'd had feelings for him after their many months of dating, had felt she

knew him really well. That might not have been the case in the end, but she'd *thought* it was. But she didn't know Dalden at all, and she was reacting to him in a purely physical way that had absolutely nothing to do with emotions.

She suspected she might be more old-fashioned than she'd thought when she heard herself saying, "I'm not sure I can relax my morals quite that much, Dalden, when I barely know you."

He didn't exactly look disappointed, but then he hadn't been told a flat-out no yet, either. "You require the dating first?"

"That's usually how it's done."

"Our finding each other cannot be considered usual, *kerima*. In all the universe, we have managed to meet. What is felt here, between us, is stronger than either of our cultures, stronger than any ideals."

Was it? She'd certainly never experienced anything like this herself before. Was he saying he hadn't, either? She was so thrilled with that thought, her knees actually got weak. But a small, rational part of her warned that some men would say just about anything they thought you wanted to hear if they sensed they were close to sexual victory.

She wished the rational part had kept quiet. She didn't want to think that Dalden might be one of those men. But she had to remind herself once again that she knew next to nothing about him. She'd told him practically her whole life history. He'd told her only that he was here to complete a pretty strange task and needed her help for it.

"Your uncertainty is felt," he remarked, his tone without inflection when there should have at least

been some disappointment in it. "Very well, tonight we see to dating, tomorrow we see to having fun."

She started to laugh. She couldn't help it. He still didn't get it, and she just didn't feel like explaining it any further. Nor was she given a chance to. He was suddenly kissing her. For him, that was apparently allowed, part of dating. Nor could she possibly have objected in that precious moment of tasting him for the first time.

His other hand came up to cup her left cheek. Her face was warmly cocooned between his large palms, his lips amazingly soft. He was touching her in no other way, just holding her face while he gently kissed her, and yet she felt as if he was touching her all over. To have felt all of him just then would probably have been too much for her senses, already on a thin thread of control.

She found out she was right when a few minutes later, he sat down in the chair she'd been in and drew her onto his lap. Wearing shorts, her legs were mostly bare, and all of that bareness was now exposed to the buttery-soft leather of his pants. It was one of the most sensual sensations she'd ever felt, not even remotely similar to leather upholstery. But that wasn't even half of what she was able to feel of him, sitting sideways on his lap.

Against her hip was the power and strength of his desire, impossible to ignore. One breast was pressed hard to his side; the other rubbed against his chest as he wrapped her arm about his neck. One of his hands was then placed high on the back of her thigh to keep her from sliding, not that bare skin had much chance of sliding on leather. His other arm fully supported her

back and drew her even closer to him as his mouth came down to hers again, this new kiss so different from before, deep, claiming, branding her his.

It was absolutely more than she could handle, the kiss along with touching him in so many places. The passion that overcame her was amazing. She had nothing to compare it with in her own experience. And it took her beyond thought, beyond anything except feeling and need.

She clung to him for all she was worth. She was kissing him back as if she meant to devour him. So she could hardly blame him for drawing the wrong conclusion.

"Have you changed your mind?" he asked. "You will show me where you sleep?"

She was gasping, while his tone was calmness itself. "No, no, I just . . . got a bit carried away."

"It was not my intention to punish you, yet does your dating seem to do that very thing."

"Huh?" Okay, so her thoughts weren't exactly coherent yet, but how could anyone equate punishment with kissing? "I thought you had the definition for 'punish' figured out. Need me to break out the dictionary?"

"Punishment may come in many forms."

Her thoughts were starting to clear, enough for her to realize he was probably talking about sexual punishment, the kind sometimes practiced when one half of a married partnership was annoyed with the other half.

"You mean like my telling you I've got a headache?" she said.

His frown was filled with sudden concern. "Your head hurts?"

She sighed. "No, that was just a comparison—never

mind. And you don't have to keep petting me. I've got it under control now."

From the moment he had mentioned punishment, he'd been caressing her in a very nonsexual way, soothing her to calmness like he might a child. Not that it did much good, when any touch from him at all was stimulating. But he didn't seem to need calming down himself. If she couldn't still feel that thick bulge against her hip, she'd swear he hadn't participated at all in the heavy kissing they'd just done. His composure was—unusual, to say the least, something else beyond her experience of men.

But then she noticed his eyes, and she was completely reassured that she wasn't the only one who'd gotten hot and bothered. He'd been affected, all right. His amber eyes were liquid gold, filled with enough passion for three men, the intensity unnerving in a man his size. And yet his control seemed almost superhuman. His breathing was normal. He hadn't broken a sweat. His tone was steady, his heartbeat probably the same.

But with that passion still there under the surface, just laying in wait, she figured it might be prudent to more fully distract them both. To that end, she asked, "What was that foreign name you called me?" His questioning frown added the prompt, "Cara something?"

"*Kerima*? It means little one."

She burst out laughing. "I know you're big, but I am, too. It's music to my ears, really, but it's kind of ridiculous to call me little."

"For your men, perhaps. For me, you are a perfect size. Any smaller, and I would fear to break you."

She grinned. "Let me guess. You've had the same

problem I have, of finding partners of an acceptable size."

He surprised her by shaking his head. "Size is of little matter. Frailty of body is of greater concern. But you are not frail, are you?"

"Wielding a hammer all day tends to build a sturdy frame, no pun intended."

"Pun—ah, you speak of house-building as well as body-building."

She blinked. "You got it without an explanation?"

"I have the proper translations now for all but what you call brand names."

"I don't get it. It just suddenly all clicked for you? A few hours ago you couldn't make head or tails out of some pretty common words, but now you can?"

"This is so."

"Then I think you'd better convince me that you haven't been pulling my leg all along, because what you're suggesting just isn't possible."

She had shot out of his lap, had her hands on her hips, was glaring down at him, so his remark wasn't really a question. "You are angry."

"Damn straight," she growled. "I don't like being made a fool of."

"Nor have you been," his calm tone continued. "The mistake was made because of the slowness of your computers. It has been corrected. I have been receiving the proper translations for several hours now."

"Language courses don't work that fast!"

"I am told you would understand 'new technology,'" he offered. "The means of teaching me is not known to all the universe yet."

"World," she mumbled, somewhat mollified, though

she was still incredulous that something had been invented that could speed along learning that fast. But apparently all the kinks hadn't been worked out of it yet, since he was still getting a few words wrong.

"Explain?"

"You keep using the word 'universe,' when you obviously mean *world*. Universe implies beyond this planet, but there's nothing out there in deep space, at least nothing alive, so 'world' is the better descriptive word for what you were talking about."

He smiled at her. "Are you certain?"

"That it's the better word?"

"That there is nothing out there?"

She made a soft snort, would have expounded on the concept that seeing is believing and so forth, but once again she got thoroughly distracted. She hadn't jumped very far away from the chair. He had sat forward, which narrowed the space between them even more, so he didn't have to even stretch his arms when his hands came to her hips to rein her back in.

"Ah . . . what are . . . you doing?" she asked a bit breathlessly.

He had circled her hips with one arm to put her in the position he wanted and keep her there. His other hand made a slow trip from the edge of her shorts down the back of her bare leg to nearly her ankle. His head was pressed squarely between her breasts.

He tilted his head up to answer her, a grin on his lips. "Dating you."

She would have laughed if her senses hadn't gone haywire again over what he was doing to her. Her breasts had seemed scalded by his breath. She had so much gooseflesh running down her legs, it was a won-

der she wasn't sprouting feathers. And yet he looked so boyish with that grin, so pleased with his answer, so delighted by what he was doing, that she didn't have the heart to correct him. But she had to, because she was afraid he still hadn't grasped where she was coming from, with her objections to their having his kind of fun right off the bat.

"No, this isn't really dating, this is the stage beyond that. Perhaps a better definition of dating would help. The kind of date we're talking about is a social appointment made by two people of the opposite sex to meet, usually for a specific purpose, like going to a movie, out to dinner, on a picnic, things like that. And typically while they are out together they do a lot of talking, which lets them get to know each other better. Now, I've been doing a lot of talking, but you haven't been doing much of any."

That finally got a frown out of him. "It will be a hindrance, my inability to talk?"

She brushed the hair back from his forehead. "You talk just fine, Dalden, just not enough about yourself. Can you understand my need to get inside your head, to feel like I know all there is to know about you, before we do anything so intimate as making love?"

He released her, slowly. "I am reminded I have a specific task here, and my need to join with you cannot interfere with it. When the task is done, then may I speak of myself. Until then, I am warned to keep my true self from becoming known to your people."

"So there's a specific reason you don't say much about yourself? Because you can't?"

He nodded. He sighed as well. He leaned back in the chair and stared up at her, and there was such

yearning in his eyes it made her catch her breath.

She couldn't imagine the reason behind his needing to be secretive, other than to not give that Jorran guy any warning that he was on his trail. The reason wasn't all that important, really. His hands were tied, so to speak. There was certainly nothing she could do about that, other than accept it. And he'd said he could talk freely when his task was done. There was hope in that.

Still, there was some definite disappointment in her own tone that she simply couldn't conceal when she said, "Then I guess we should concentrate on finishing your task. A good night's sleep and an early start in the morning will help for that."

"Will you sleep with me—here?"

It was amazing, what those simple words did to her. The urge to jump back in his lap and start kissing him again, and to hell with getting to know him better, was so strong that she had to take a step back to resist it. This kind of temptation was more than she'd ever experienced, more than she could reasonably be expected to handle. How could she say no when her body was thrumming with desire to say yes? But how could she throw caution to the winds and say yes?

Honestly, she told him, "I don't think I would be able to sleep, touching you."

"You will," he insisted with confidence as he held out a hand to her. "You will be soothed in my arms. The only thing that keeps you from me is these 'morals' you speak of. This is understood. But understand as well that having found you, I cannot bring myself now to let you go far from me. I will rest easier

with you in my arms. And you will know that you have nothing to fear of me."

There was no way she could say no now, not to a simple request for closeness. She knew she wouldn't sleep, she was wound up with too much sexual tension, and getting close to him again was just going to increase it. But she gave him her hand anyway and let him pull her back into his lap, where he positioned her for maximum comfort.

For a moment she felt like a child again, curled up in the lap of one of her parents. The lights were still on, and the TV droned on at low volume. It was silly to try to sleep in a chair when there was a perfectly good bed nearby. She almost mentioned it, but caution prevailed and she said nothing.

He said nothing more either. But his hand pressed her head to the bare part of his chest, where his tunic spread wide. And she didn't know how she did it, but she fell asleep listening to the steady beat of his heart.

Chapter 14

BRITTANY WOKE AT DAWN WHEN THE BIRDS ON THE two trees in front of her apartment building began their morning greetings. She didn't stir immediately, just opened her eyes and absorbed the fact that she was laying sprawled across a very big body and was utterly content to be there.

Dalden had moved down in the chair at some point in the night, to where he wasn't actually sitting in it anymore, was spread at a near prone angle, which was why she wasn't sitting either. She was actually laying on top of him, one leg bent across his hip, the other lost with his somewhere under the table in front of the chair.

She wondered what Jan had thought when she had come home and found them like that. The lights and

TV were off now, showing that Jan had quietly passed through the room without waking them. And Brittany and Dalden would probably be gone before Jan got up to go to work, since her job started much later in the morning than Brittany's—which reminded her she had to call Arbor and the spa to let them know she was taking a short vacation.

"Did you sleep well, *kerima*?"

She lifted her head to find those lovely amber eyes on her. "The birds wake you, too?"

"No, it was the sound of your purring."

She gasped, sputtered, and chuckled all at once. "I did . . . no such thing!"

He smiled at her. "Perhaps it was myself, then. I believe I could wish for no other thing than to wake with you in my arms every rising."

Brittany was a little shocked—actually, a lot. Those words spoke of permanence, of forever after, of never being parted. They were something a woman might say or think, but a man? When men tended to go through a heck of a lot of agonizing before they even came close to thinking about commitment? But then he'd used the word "wish," which could put the statement back into perspective. He wasn't really saying, Let's get hitched. He was just being fanciful.

That conclusion annoyed Brittany somewhat, enough to have her pushing off of him. "Careful, big guy, or you might get your wish."

She didn't get very far in the pushing. His arms around her tightened, and she quickly found it pointless to try to squirm out of that. So she gave him a look that said release me or . . . actually, she couldn't think

of an "or else" in his case, but she was sure he got the point. Not that it worked. He wasn't letting her move off of him yet, and that was all there was to that.

"What has annoyed you?" he asked.

"I'm not annoyed," she grouched.

"What has annoyed you?" he repeated, refusing to accept her evasion.

"Okay, you asked for it. I really dislike how men forever say things they don't mean."

"And women do not?"

"Not nearly as much, and besides—"

"Did you not *just* say something that you did not mean when you said you were not annoyed?"

"No. That was a flat-out lie. That isn't at all the same thing. I'm talking about things that get said between a man and a woman that can affect feelings, that can build hopes and dreams, that will finally shatter a relationship when it's realized that it's been nothing but BS."

"All this resentment over a wish I am inclined to grant?" There was suddenly a lot of screeching coming out of the earphone that was still attached to his ear, reminding Brittany that they weren't alone. "I am told you require asking, that I cannot decide the matter for you as I should."

"What are we talking about now?" she demanded.

"A difference in our cultures, one I find unacceptable. Asking can be done, but if the answer is not the right one, the question will be withdrawn and the matter seen to in the proper Sha-Ka'ani way."

She had the distinct feeling he wasn't talking to her just then, but to Martha. His own annoyance was sensed, rather than reflected in tone or expression, but

it was still crystal-clear to her. He hadn't liked the interruption from Martha any more than she had.

She had to wonder why he hadn't spoken to Miss Coach earlier. If the woman could hear every word they said, and was speaking to him through that earphone, wouldn't it have been much easier for him to have simply asked Martha for clarification of the things he'd been having trouble with last night, rather than making her guess what he needed to know?

Brittany knew to the second when his attention was fully back on her. His eyes absorbed her. His body seemed to as well, and, oh my, that bulge was back. He even shifted her and pressed her against it in that very spot that nature had intended it to go.

Swirls of desire took flight in her belly, so it was like a dash of ice water when she heard from him, "What is the meaning of bee-ess?"

She managed to get off him this time. Thrusting an elbow into his belly for leverage helped.

"I know you can hear me, Martha. So why don't you explain that one to him," Brittany growled as she stomped off to the kitchen to make coffee and call Arbor. The spa would have to wait a few more hours until it opened.

She had that flare of passion under control again by the time she turned back toward the living room with the coffee cups in hand. She didn't get far. Dalden was blocking the doorway, a normal-sized bath towel around his neck that seemed more like a hand towel around *that* neck, his tunic removed. Not enough time had passed for him to have showered, nor did he look damp, he just looked good, too good, good enough for her to want to meld with that body of his.

She'd already seen a good portion of his chest through the gap his tunic made, but it was nothing like seeing it all. The man was simply too huge. She'd never seen anything like his size before, not even in pictures. Without the height, he'd look really weird; with it, he simply looked gigantic. A fantasy giant came to mind, wielding a club as big as he was. She would have smiled at her own fancy if she wasn't so mesmerized by all that bare, golden skin.

No stressed muscles or overly taut skin to accommodate them, just natural bulges in his relaxed pose, the difference being that everything was oversized to begin with. And those arms, bigger than anything she could have imagined when they'd been concealed by his loose sleeves. The kind of strength represented by them had to be amazing. She wondered if they were registered as lethal weapons. And yet they'd held her with tenderness through the night. Her gentle giant.

She did smile this time, but had it and her fanciful thoughts wiped clear away when Dalden remarked, "Martha says that as long as you have spoken to her directly, you may be allowed to hear her voice."

"Wow, lucky me," Brittany said sarcastically as she shoved a cup of instant coffee in his hand.

"You can shelve that jealousy, doll" came out of the box clearly, which nearly made Brittany drop the other cup she was holding. "I'm not what you've been thinking. Try this one on for size: I was there for his birth, even assisted in it. That help? Yes, I can see that it does."

Brittany's face was going up in mortified flames. God, she had been jealous of a name, a voice, a faceless woman, without even once thinking the lady could be a little old grandmotherly type.

To cover some of her embarrassment, she asked Martha, "How can you see?"

"There are six viewers on the combo-unit attached to Dalden's belt, one on every edge, so no matter which way he's facing, I'm bound to get a good shot of what's going on around him."

"So it's a camera, too?"

"You could say that. Actually, why don't we call it a new advanced model of what's known to you as a cel-lular phone, under experimentation, and obviously failing. I should have whipped him up an old model instead, since I am now aware that your men of busi-ness walk around with them attached to their ears, so he wouldn't have drawn much notice using one."

"Not drawn notice?" Brittany replied. "Him? You're kidding, right?"

The distinct sound of chuckling came out of the box. "Aside from his looks. He needs to keep a low profile. We don't want Jorran alerted to his presence and hav-ing a chance to disappear on us."

"If he wants a low profile, we should probably stop by the mall on the way to City Hall and buy him some normal clothes. His rock star get-up might be fine for L.A., where people expect to see stars in fancy outfits, but we don't get many celebrities passing through Seaview."

None of those camera angles could have seen Dalden's blank expression, yet Martha still knew to share with him. "She's talking about their entertain-ment industry, Dalden, the gist of it being, she's going to buy you some local clothing this morning."

Brittany blinked. "I am? Okay, I suppose I am, but while you're on the phone, how about telling me why

he seems to be lacking any ready cash, or was he actually sent over to this country without any?"

"File that one under hard to explain, kiddo. There's a good reason for his lack, but not one that we can divulge at this time."

No other explanation came out of the box. Brittany wondered if Martha was waiting for her to fire off more questions, now that she could. But she didn't really have any more at the moment, at least none that she thought might get answered instead of being dumped into the "hard to explain" file. Well, there was one . . .

"I notice you don't have his accent. You don't come from his country?"

"No, my origins are very far from his. But the voice I use is irrelevant when I can simulate any tone, accent, or language imaginable. What you hear is only for your convenience."

Brittany was impressed. "A master linguist, then, or an impressionist?"

More chuckling. "You could say both, though just plain old master has a nice ring to it."

Whether Dalden was feeling neglected or not, he became Brittany's center of attention again when he asked, "Will you create a meal to sustain us for the day?"

Brittany grinned at him. "Why do I get the feeling that a bowl of cereal and milk won't do it for you? Never mind, I'll whip up some eggs and other breakfasty-type things while you take a shower."

"You will need first to show me how the water is acquired for it."

She raised a brow, though she shouldn't have been

surprised. A village without electricity was probably a village without proper sanitation.

Still, she'd rather not guess if she could get an answer, so she tried, "No showers where you come from?"

"We bathe in large pools."

She pictured big ponds with only a few trees and plants, an oasis, camels again—bah. She really was going to have to figure out just where his never-heard-of-before country was located. This imagining of primitive tents in a desert didn't say much for their ever being compatible. She and tents didn't get along well at all.

She headed to the tiny bathroom and leaned into the shower to adjust the single water control handle to get the water running at a comfortable temperature. The shower had been remodeled just last year by the landlord, and now had one of those newfangled spigots that concealed the shower turn-on valve under it. If you didn't know where it was, you'd never find it, so she could understand how Martha might not have been able to help him this time.

"My mother uses a different means, a solaray bath," he added while she was still leaning halfway into the shower, waiting for the hot water to show up.

"You mean a solar bath? Now that's a bit modern, and cost-effective, too. I plan to put up a few solar panels on the house I build, for the water heater at least. And I plan a really large bathroom, probably the same size as the bedroom attached to it. I've been dreaming of big ever since I first walked into this cubbyhole."

"I am accustomed to the bath being in the room of sleeping," he volunteered.

A pool in a bedroom? Now she was picturing a palace, or an incredibly large mansion.

She turned around to ask him once again just where the heck his country was, but found him towering over her, barely an inch separating them. Not surprising, since it was a really tiny bathroom. She couldn't turn around in it without banging elbows herself. With him in it, too, there was absolutely no space to maneuver without them bumping into each other.

It was hard to concentrate with him that close, but she managed to get out, "You can at least tell me the continent that your country sits in, can't you? So I can have something to relate to when you drop these little tidbits like pools instead of bathtubs and . . ."

That was as far as she got. Being lifted off her feet and deeply kissed worked pretty well to put an end to any kind of concentration. She was surrounded by his body, by his scent, by his taste. Her senses began rioting with her morals and were coming out ahead. And then she was set down and pushed toward the door.

"Be gone from my sight quickly, *kerima*, unless you wish to share the water and more with me now."

That was about as plain as could be, that he'd reached his limit of sexual forbearance. Caution prevailed and got her out of there real quick.

Chapter 15

"YOU CAN'T GO KISSING ME TO DISTRACTION EVERY
time I ask you something that you don't want
to answer. If it's secret, just say so. If I get fed up with
hearing that, *I'll* say so. Okay?"

They were in Brittany's car on the way to City Hall.
It was much later than they'd planned on getting
there. She'd fed Dalden before they left, and was definitely going to have to stop for some groceries on the
way home after that mammoth meal.

And there'd been an amusing moment when they
left the apartment and she told him not to mind the
rust-bucket look of her car, that she kept it in tiptop
shape so it purred. He, of course, misinterpreted that
and started looking around for buckets and *fembairs*,
the latter being what she figured he called cats.

It was now almost noon, since their brief stop at the
mall had turned into hitting every shop with men's
clothing, after it had been apparent from the first shop
that they were going to have trouble finding some
thing to fit Dalden. In fact, they never did. There had
been a few extra-extra-large T-shirts he could have
worn, but they just didn't look right on him, and be
sides, leaving those arms of his bare would draw as
much notice as his fancy tunic.

There was hope, though, at least for tomorrow. An
on-duty seamstress in one of the larger clothing stores
had felt challenged upon seeing Dalden, and after tak
ing some quick measurements, had promised to have
some jeans and a plain cotton shirt ready for him by
the end of the day.

Brittany had expected Dalden to draw some notice
but experiencing it firsthand in the mall that morning
went beyond even her own expectations. She hadn't
noticed yesterday because she'd been unable to take
her eyes off him herself. But he managed to affec
everyone that way. No matter where she looked, peo
ple were staring at him open-mouthed, boggle-eyed
he was causing traffic pile-ups of the pedestrian kind
One young kid even asked him for his autograph and
refused to believe he wasn't a celebrity. Keep a low
profile? Yeah, right.

There hadn't been much time between her apart
ment and the mall for talk, and besides, she'd been too
busy watching Dalden examining everything on the
dashboard, as if he'd never been in a car before. Yet
she'd wanted to wait until they were in the car, where
he wouldn't dare try to kiss her again, to bring up the
subject of his unique way of distracting her.

She wasn't expecting an argument. Her suggestion
had been so reasonable that it didn't leave room for arguing. But he put a new twist to it.

"Yet is it much more enjoyable, for both of us, to
kiss you to distraction," he said.

Undeniable, but beside the point. "Remember 'getting to know each other'? Part of that is answering
questions, not avoiding them."

"When I make you mine, Brittany Callaghan, you
may have all the answers you seek. I am told, however,
that you will not be happy with the answers."

Thank God the traffic light in front of them was red,
because Brittany temporarily forgot how to drive.
When he made her his? Again, that had such a ring of
permanence to it, coming from him. Not when they
made love. Not when her job was done. When he
made her his. The effect that had on her was swift and
primitive.

Driving down the boulevard was not the place for
this discussion after all. She tried zeroing in on his second remark to get her mind out of fantasyland. Unhappiness. Answers she wouldn't like. Okay, that
worked.

She gave him a quick glance, then glanced a bit
longer at the box on his hip, trusting that Martha's
camera views were working. "Are these 'I am tolds'
his opinion, or what you've been telling him, Martha?"

"You really don't want to hear his opinions, doll,"
Martha replied.

There was clear amusement in the older woman's
tone, which rubbed against Brittany's nerves. "Actually, I do," she said stubbornly.

"Really, you don't," Martha countered, then elabo-

rated. "From the information I've assimilated so far, your culture and his are so far on opposite ends of the spectrum, the distance could be described in light-years."

"Bah, I know an exaggeration when I hear it," Brittany replied.

Some chuckling drifted up from the box before Martha said, "If it means anything to you, and Probables is starting to lean toward it will, his mother's and father's cultures were also light-years apart, yet they've managed to adjust—or maybe I should say, she's managed to adjust. There's not much budging with a Sha-Ka'ani male."

"Was that supposed to be a warning?"

"You betcha."

Brittany snorted. She was beginning to think that Martha was toying with her, and getting a kick out of doing so. But it did worry her that Dalden wasn't trying to correct the impression Martha was trying to give her. In fact, he didn't look too happy. Actually, he looked a bit green.

"Are you all right?" she asked him.

"I am familiar with transportation that moves on other than legs, but I am not accustomed to the many stops and starts of your rust bucket."

She ignored the name he'd given her car and asked with a bit of amazement, "You're getting carsick? We *have* hit a bit more traffic than usual, the lunch-hour crowd, I suppose. But we're almost to our destination. Another minute or so. Can you last that long?"

"Last?"

"Without dumping your breakfast all over the car?" she clarified.

His expression turned a bit indignant over that remark, pretty hard to do when he'd been cringing with
nausea. "A warrior has more control over his body
than to reject an excellent meal."

"Delete that" came out of the box in an exasperated
voice. "What he means—"

"I got the idea, Martha, but let's not delete that warrior part just yet. He's in the military?"

"You could say that."

"I could, but you wouldn't? What's it called, then,
in his country?"

"The men of Sha-Ka'an merely keep themselves in a
constant state of readiness, sort of what you might
term the national guard, or the national militia, or—"

"I get it," Brittany cut in. "Not military, but available if needed."

"Exactly!"

"And where is this country?"

Not just a little chuckling, but nearly thirty seconds
of assorted humor sounds came out of the box before
Martha said, "Tenacious, aren't you? But you've heard
of classified info, haven't you? Yes, of course you
have."

"Oh, come on, you've told me the name of it. I can
go find an atlas and look it up myself."

"You can, but you'd be wasting your time. You
won't find it in any atlas."

"A country so newly formed it's not on the maps
yet?" Brittany said incredulously.

"Not new," Martha corrected. "But then, new is
subjective. What would be new to you wouldn't be to
him, and vice versa, of course."

Brittany could allow that there might be places in

the world still unexplored. But to have an entire country tucked away in one of them? OK, so it was possible. Actually, Dalden and his people were proof of that.

"*How* have they managed to remain undiscovered?" Brittany asked.

"You could say their—borders—are closed to visitors. No one gets in without permission, and permission is rarely if ever given."

"Are we even talking about a country? Maybe you've got town and country mixed up?"

"Actually, you're working on assumptions," Martha told her. "You're the one who called Sha-Ka'an a country. Dalden never confirmed or denied that. *Sometimes* he actually follows my directives."

The last was meant for Dalden, but it got no reaction out of him. He didn't look like he was paying attention to the conversation at all. His eyes were closed, his skin still off-color, his forehead damp. Brittany didn't doubt that his full concentration was still on keeping his breakfast where it resided.

But she knew she'd get no answers out of him, anyway. And as long as Martha was spilling some beans, even if dried-up useless ones, she'd rather keep trying to get at least one whole kernel out of her.

She tried a different tack. "I'm not asking for any great secrets. All I want to know is who I'm helping. There happen to be factions in this world that I'd be completely opposed to, and I don't want to find out later that I've helped one of them."

"Okay, listen up, because I'm going to break my own rules, but only this once. Sha-Ka'an isn't a country. Let's call it a place, and where his people as a whole get their name. His actual country is Kan-is-

Tra, and no, you won't find that on one of your maps either. His town is Sha-Ka-Ra. And none of the above have politics opposed to your people, so rest easy on that score. Now with no other information forthcoming about any of these locations, you'll agree what you've just heard has no meaning for you. Leave it at—"

"Damnit upside and down!" Brittany gave her exasperation free rein. "You can at least give me a region to relate to. Desert, arctic, tropics? Igloos, tents, *what*?"

"Ah, so it's the carpenter that's going nuts with curiosity? Very well, their architecture is pretty impressive, some of it ranking right up there with a sultan's palace, and no, you won't find any Sha-Ka'ani in that part of the world," was added with a chuckle. "Now give it up, doll. If he chooses to enlighten you when this is over, it would be info you can't be allowed to keep, so all of this is pointless. Whatever he tells you, I'll have to erase before we go home."

"Erase?" Brittany gasped. "Are you talking about making me forget somehow?"

"Necessary."

Brittany was outraged. "Is that how they've remained unknown? Anyone who finds out about them gets their memory tampered with?"

"Are we getting disturbed by the concept of self-preservation?"

Brittany hissed, "Messing around with someone's memories is a dangerous—"

"Not even close," Martha cut in this time. "Meticulous, exact, no guesswork involved. Only what needs to be removed gets removed. Everything else remains intact."

"Are you talking about hypnosis?" Brittany asked, her tone only slightly calmer.

"Something like that. That relieve your mind?"

It did—and it didn't. "You aren't planning on erasing my memories of him, are you?" was asked in a small voice.

"Lucky for me, I don't possess a single sentimental circuit. You'd be better off not remembering him, kiddo, believe me—"

"You need have no fear that you will be allowed to forget me, *kerima*" came from a new quarter.

"Not another word, warrior, until we go over the facts of Sha-Ka'ani life again," Martha warned in a seriously annoyed tone.

"What Martha has to say will be listened to, but it will make no difference when the decision has already been made," Dalden replied.

"You can't do that."

"It is too late for denials."

"I swear, you're getting more and more like your father every day."

The disgust in that remark was thick enough to cut, yet Dalden replied with some pride in his own tone, "I am pleased to hear you say so."

"Where is the common sense you inherited from your mother? Never mind," came out in a low growl. "We'll discuss this later. Her rust bucket has stopped moving. Finish the task at hand, and *then* we'll talk about decisions that don't have a chance in hell of working."

Chapter 16

"SLOUCH DOWN. SOME MORE." A SIGH. "I SUPPOSE that will have to do. Now stay there and let me do what you're paying me for."

Dalden watched Brittany walk away from him, a smile in his mind. He was aware that she had no doubt whatsoever that he would obey her and stay on the bench where she had told him to sit. She had no understanding yet that it was against a warrior's nature to take directives of any sort from a woman. But a woman could be humored. And special allowances had to be made when dealing with females from planets other than Sha-Ka'an. He understood that, for the most part. He didn't like it, but he understood.

But he continued to watch her as she moved about

the atrium in the place she called City Hall, stopping one person after another to speak a few words with each of them. It was, in fact, becoming increasingly difficult to do anything but watch her, when she was in the same area as him.

He wondered if it was the influence of his mother's Kystrani blood that was making him have unwarrior-like reactions around her, or simply because Brittany reminded him in many ways of his mother. Or it could be no other thing than the instinct he had been warned would take over when he found his true life-mate.

Whatever it was, it seemed to be beyond his control. Some *dhaya* juice could be wished for to eliminate the constant urge he had to carry her to some quiet place and make her his, but the abundant supply that had been brought along, which would have been more than sufficient for the original trip, hadn't lasted for this extended journey and had been exhausted the previous month. He had to wonder if even that would have been sufficient, when what he was feeling was beyond his experience.

She fascinated him in myriad ways. She spoke like a Kystrani Ancient. She was very much like his mother, taking matters in hand and issuing orders. She was bold, stubborn, creative. She took pride in a craft that a Sha-Ka'ani viewed as slave labor. She was independent. She felt she needed no other protection than what the laws of her country supplied her. She cooked and worked like a Darash servant and saw that as a normal thing to do. She was fulfilling the roles of both male and female and doing so happily. Her culture was so

different from his that indeed there seemed no point where the two could meet and coexist.

He suspected that Martha would point out all of this. He was prepared for it with a simple answer that even Martha couldn't dispute.

"Tedra's going to wish she had come along on this trip," came out of the combo-unit in Sha-Ka'ani, so anyone passing near wouldn't understand it.

"Why?" Dalden asked in kind.

"Because these people so resemble her Ancients, you might wonder if they didn't evolve from one of the original colony ships."

"Would they not be more advanced if that were so?" Dalden asked.

"Not if they lost all data and had to start over from scratch. Unlikely, though. And it's possible for two planets to evolve in exactly the same way, which would account for the similarities."

"You like Brittany," Dalden remarked. "This I have sensed."

A chuckle. "What you meant to say was that Tedra would like her. But let's not be tepid. Your mother would love the heck out of her. She'd be like a never-ending Ancients tape for her to listen to. Probables say they'd become great good friends."

"When your goals always center around my mother's ultimate happiness, how then can you object to bringing Brittany home with us?"

"Because unlike you, I can see down the road, and Tedra won't be happy if two people she loves are making themselves miserable."

"Such *would* not happen."

A sigh, prolonged, exaggerated; then in a no-nonsense tone, "Let's spend a moment to open your eyes beyond a squint, shall we? You and this female have the hots for each other. This is fine, even healthy. No one's objecting to you having a bit of pleasure while you're here, time permitting. But you have got to start looking at this thing realistically, Dalden."

"Why do you think I am not?"

"The fact that we're having this conversation was a good clue" came out sarcastically. Then, "A man can be and often is blinded by his sexual drive, and yes, that includes warriors. Take away that driving force, and a completely different perspective is open to them. If they still feel the same afterward, well, then, they're hooked. But half the time, and I do mean at least half, they find that it was no more than those primitive urges, and once satisfied, nothing is left, at least not enough to base permanent double occupancy on."

Double occupancy was the Kystrani term for two people wishing to share their lives together. They used to call it marriage, as they did here. The Sha-Ka'ani had no specific term for it, though even there it differed per country, what the partners called each other. In Kan-is-Tra, a warrior would choose the woman to be the mother of his children, and this was how she would be referred to. Generally, they called each other lifemates.

"In all your years on Sha-Ka'an, Martha, have you not learned that a warrior has a special instinct in the matter of his true lifemate? Many become impatient of experiencing this instinct and settle for a lifemate of indifference."

A snort came out of the box. "Careful, kiddo, or I might think you're talking about love—you know, that silly emotion that warriors insist they *don't* feel."

Dalden growled, "There is no similarity between instinct and that female emotion."

"I'm drawing a picture of rolling eyes. I've got eyes rolling on every monitor in the Control Room. You should see all these rolling eyes—"

"You cannot change the way a warrior is."

"Do I look stupid enough to try? But you've just hit it on the nose yourself, kiddo. It's because of that very thing that you and the carpenter will never see eye to eye on any subject. And without some common ground, of which you two don't have any, you simply can't coexist compatibly."

"We will."

"Stubbornness won't make it so. But I can see it's going to take more than just telling you it won't work. Okay, let's delve into a few of the specifics that my Probables are based on. The woman can accept being 'taken care of.' That isn't the problem, was the norm around here a few centuries ago, considered old-fashioned now, but not so long ago that she wouldn't know how it works. She'll be bored silly, just staying home and not working herself, but like Tedra, she could find other things to occupy her."

"I am pleased to hear you say so."

"You won't be after I've finished, because what she'll never get used to is the warrior's right to control all aspects of Sha-Ka'ani life, with the woman stuck in a role of subservient silence. They used to be like that, but the women here have crawled out of that hole, and having done so, they'll never crawl back in.

"Do you see what I'm getting at? It's against her nature to let a man make all decisions for her. It's against her nature to accept a situation she doesn't like without trying to change it. And she'd never accept that it can't be changed. The rules that warriors have made for the protection of their women are so contrary to the way she was raised, she'd laugh in your face if you try to enforce them on her. You'd have one fight after another on your hands, kiddo, never ending. That's how incompatible you and she are."

"Was I not to realize that you are describing life between my parents?"

A chuckle. "Must be the air up there."

Dalden didn't miss the jibe. "I do not lack intelligence, Martha."

"I know you don't, kiddo, but the warrior mentality gets in the way of it sometimes, which is why your people are still called barbarians. But we digress. I pointed out how it has worked for your parents, but you know me well enough to know there's a catch coming."

"Which is?"

"There's one big, and I mean really big, difference between your parents' case and yours. Tedra knows how to compromise. She also grew up with full knowledge of a universe filled with a diversity of races and cultures. Her schooling in World Discovery prepared her to deal with that diversity and taught her the basic premises of the Confederation, that each planet is unique, each culture to be respected, not changed. Discovered races aren't to be tampered with, aren't to be 'taught a better way,' are to be left alone to evolve at their own pace in the natural order of things. So as

much as she has wanted to change some of the things she really doesn't like about Sha-Ka'an, and you know exactly what I'm talking about, she wouldn't dream of seriously tampering with the way things are."

"She has assisted many of the women."

"Of course she has. But she hasn't tried to change the rules, she's merely helped some of the women to be removed from those rules."

"By sending them off-planet."

A shrug entered Martha's tone. "Whatever works, kiddo, is one of Tedra's mottoes. And besides, she usually gets anything she wants—in the long run. It might take a challenge loss or two first, but eventually, your father gives her what she wants. She just knows better than to go after the impossible, like trying to bring a planet classed as barbaric up a notch or two on the civilized scale, or trying to change the way a warrior views things. And now we get to why it would be a completely different scenario for your Brittany."

"But she is just like my mother."

"I hate to break it to you, warrior, but the way she talks is about all they really have in common. They were raised differently, with completely different cultures and beliefs. They probably have the same outlook on what rights a woman should have, because they both grew up in cultures of equality of the sexes. But it pretty much ends there. Yet this is only half the problem."

"I do not see what you have said so far to be a problem," Dalden insisted.

"And *that* is the other half. You *think* you'll manage to overcome her objections, but you're basing that as-

sumption on your father's success with Tedra. But you've overlooked a very simple fact. Because of your mother's blood, which is in many cases held against you, you've spent most of your life trying to be the ideal warrior. This included embracing and obeying to the letter the laws and rules of your people, even when you might have disagreed with them. You've strived not to be different. You are constantly trying to prove that Tedra's blood has had no influence on you. You *are* different, but you refuse to accept that. And we're talking years and years of struggle here, Dalden. Do you think you can set all that aside and finally *be* different?"

"There is no reason for me to change or be different from what I am."

"I rest my case. *That's* why it won't work. You won't compromise, and neither will she."

Chapter 17

BRITTANY HAD TO LAUGH AT HERSELF FOR THINKING that leaving Dalden on a bench under a slightly overhanging tree would keep him from notice, even slouched down to detract from his height. Her experience at the mall with him should have told her otherwise, and every time she glanced back his way, she noticed the stares, people stopped in groups of two or three to covertly look his way.

It wasn't just his size and handsomeness. There was a confidence about him that went beyond the norm, a unique presence that commanded attention and speculation. People who knew their own worth, or felt capable of accomplishing anything, carried that kind of confidence. Politicians, celebrities, billionaires came to mind—and perhaps specially trained military types,

too, which was the only thing she could think of to explain it in Dalden's case.

Of course, that was just her take on it. She felt his confidence, his utter lack of the common worries that plagued normal individuals. Other people just might be simply agog at his looks.

The end of lunch hour had not been the ideal time to start her job of finding Jorran, when most of the people passing through the hall just then were city workers on their way back to their offices. It meant there were too many people to talk to all at once, and that she was going to miss speaking to most of them.

The easiest and most common question to stop people with was to ask for directions. Usually she could move on to the next person within seconds, unless she ran into someone who simply liked to talk and could take five minutes to say three words, but that only happened once.

The mayor was on the premises. She'd ascertained that first, and briefly spoke with everyone in his waiting room, which was only three testy people who had missed their own lunches to try and get in to see the mayor instead, and apparently were wasting their time. She stayed out in the main hall after that, just kept her eye on the door to the mayor's inner offices for anyone new coming along.

After close to an hour, she finally had a reason to return to Dalden and, sitting down next to him, whispered to him, "Don't look immediately, but that guy over there to the left of us with the curly brown hair and the pasty white skin is pretty weird."

Dalden did look immediately, and frowned in the

direction where she had tilted her head. "Weird in what way?"

"He not only talks somewhat like you, but he also told me that I didn't see him, like he thinks he's invisible or something. And that silly stick he's carrying around like a wand—"

Brittany didn't get to finish. Dalden shot off the bench with such amazing speed that she was left with her mouth hanging open. She didn't think it was possible that someone his size could move that fast, yet within seconds, he was across the hall behind the weird fellow and putting an arm around his shoulder like they were friends. They weren't, of course, and there was a moment of grappling that seriously alarmed her, considering that the entire hall was probably watching them. But it didn't last long, and a few words were quietly said, then the weird fellow was following behind Dalden as docilely as you please, back to the bench.

Brittany's alarm was gone. It now seemed like it had merely been two friends doing the weird wrestling-type greeting thing. What was left was pure incredulity that had her simply staring at them as they reached her. What the hell had just happened?

"You did not predict this was a possibility?" Dalden was saying to Martha, still in Sha-Ka'ani. "That Jorran would not know to keep the rods off of women?"

"You didn't tell him," Martha replied. "And Ferrill wouldn't discuss the rods at all with him, so no, he didn't know they only work on males. I knew that, but I gave him more credit. I figured he'd be smart enough to test the rods before putting them to use.

He probably did, he just wasn't smart enough to include women in the testing, likely because he envisioned his new home to be like his old home, where women are only slightly up on the scale from slavery. Speaking of which, that was quick thinking on your part, kiddo, to use the rod on him and have him think he's your slave. They have them where he comes from, so this peon knows exactly how to imitate their behavior."

"Do you two know just how rude that is, to be talking that gibberish when someone is standing here who doesn't understand a word of it?" Brittany growled finally, her impatience turning to pure vexation.

"Didn't it occur to you that that was the point, doll?" Martha purred back at her. "Classified info, remember?"

That was hardly pacifying, and Brittany said as much. "If you think you're going to get away without telling me what just happened, you're crazy. And why is this man looking like he's about to bow down and kiss Dalden's feet?"

"Probably because he is," Martha replied dryly. Then, "Send him off to a safe distance, Dalden, so he doesn't get confused by what he hears."

Brittany watched as Dalden told the man to go stand in a corner and await him there, and he did just that. She guessed aloud, "He's not a stranger to you after all, is he? He's on your payroll or something like that?"

Martha shot that premise right down. "We've never seen him before."

"Then why is he doing what you tell him to do?" Brittany demanded.

Martha sighed, not once, but three times to stress the point that she felt her arm was being twisted. "All right, considering the matter is going to either be redundant or erased, I can divulge this much. A lot of amazing things have been invented where we come from, things that would defy belief. That rod Dalden just confiscated is one of those things. It was stolen, a whole crate of them, actually, and we have been tasked with retrieving them."

"What's it do?"

"You wondered how Jorran thought he could just waltz in here and become your mayor? Well, he thinks these rods will let him do just that."

"You haven't answered my question," Brittany pointed out, her impatience rising again.

"Oh, you wanted *de*tails?" Martha said with a big dose of innocence.

"What happens if I break your box?" Brittany snarled, glaring at it.

"Dalden gets another one" was answered in placid if somewhat smirking tones.

"Figures," Brittany mumbled.

Ten seconds of laughter followed before Martha continued, "Who would think a man's mind could be altered instantly with the power of suggestion and a mere touch of a rod? But someone figured out how to do just that. Call it hypnosis revolutionized, if you like. But someone who doesn't know the first thing about mind control can use one of these rods and completely alter a male subject's thoughts to anything

they want. Example being, Dalden used the rod on this fellow and told him he's his slave, and voilà, the man fully believes he's Dalden's slave. So until he's told otherwise, he will obey any directive Dalden gives him."

Brittany gritted her teeth, even counted to ten before she said, "Do you really expect me to believe that?"

"Did I not say inventions that defy belief? And weren't you subject to it yourself, when the fellow tried to convince you that you didn't see him?"

"Which just proves it doesn't do what you say it does. I still saw him perfectly."

"Lucky for you, doll, it doesn't work on women," Martha replied. "And lucky for us, Jorran and his people obviously don't know that yet."

"His people? You mean that wasn't Jorran that Dalden just took control of?"

"No, he can alter his looks, but not his height. Jorran's about as tall as you are. But we knew we'd have a lot of peons to deal with as well. Jorran travels with a full entourage, and the Altering Rods have likely been passed out to the lot of them. Getting our hands on Jorran will gather them all in, though."

"So that's what this is all about? Retrieving stolen property? Why haven't you just gone to the police about it?"

"Don't you realize the kind of mass paranoia that can be caused if word spreads about these rods and that there are people running around using them? Have you even realized yet what's possible with their use? A perfect stranger can be asked for all his worldly goods and he'll turn them over happily, then

go off and never know what happened to pauperize him. A man can be told to quit his job and do so, and never figure out why he did. People can be made to do things totally against their nature. Is it sinking in yet, why the fewer people who know about them, the better?"

"No. The police have the manpower to find them more quickly—"

"Brittany, Brittany," Martha cut in with a sigh. "You are missing the point. First you'd have to convince your law enforcement that the rods are real; then you'd have to swear them to secrecy. We now have one of the rods to do the first, but human nature will counter the second. Word *would* spread, and you'd have your whole town suspicious of everyone they see. Mass hysteria, paranoia, and panic. Is that what you're suggesting?"

"What *you're* suggesting is next to impossible, if there are a lot more people involved than you first led me to believe. How are we supposed to find them all?"

"We don't need to find them all, we only need to find Jorran. The rest will come voluntarily to us if we have him, and we'll take the lot of them back to where they belong. We happen to have a lot more manpower available to send in, but they would just alert Jorran to our presence, which we *don't* want to happen. If he suspects at all that we're here looking for him, he'll relocate and then we'll be reduced to zero chance of finding him."

"Won't he suspect something is wrong when the guy you entranced doesn't report in?"

"Not to worry, doll. You'll find I'm always one step ahead in any situation. Now, we really don't want to

send any more people rushing off to visit their eye
doctors, so point the big guy to a place where he can be
assured of some privacy to deal with our 'slave.'"

"Deal with him how?"

A chuckle came out of the box. "That's rich. You
don't really think we're here to kill anyone, do you?"

Brittany blushed profusely. She *had* sounded a bit
horrified there, and *had* been thinking the worst. But
what else did they suddenly need privacy for, if not to
dispose of this fellow they'd managed to capture?

"Interrogation," Martha continued, as if she'd been
able to read Brittany's mind. "And then he'll be sent
back to the enemy camp with no memory of us, but
minus his rod, of course, which he'll assume he lost.
But he'll be given a link to me, and once a day I'll get a
report in about Jorran's progress—an added bonus for
our side."

"You make it sound so easy."

"That *is* the easy part," Martha told her. "The hard
part is still in your court. We'd like to stop Jorran before he alters too many personalities or causes too
much irreparable grief."

"You don't think you'll find out from this fellow
where Jorran is now?"

"Highly improbable. Jorran will surround himself
with only a select few. The rest of his people will have
been turned loose to do his bidding without question.
They'll have means of communication in case directives get changed, but not with Jorran himself. It
would be beneath him to speak directly with mere
underlings."

"Like a crime boss?"

"Like an autocratic king."

"Not much difference there."

"An excellent observation, though the two might disagree—just on principle, of course. Now if we're done with the jokes, that place of privacy?"

Brittany sighed. She would have preferred to continue the discussion. The new piece of the puzzle was still missing some of its edges. But she supposed it was pointless to keep at it, once Martha was done with a subject.

"The bathroom around the corner over there would afford some brief privacy, but being public, that won't last long. My car would probably work," and she tossed the keys at Dalden. "Just turn on the air conditioner and keep the windows rolled up, and no one should be able to hear you."

"I was more concerned with sight," Martha said. "But I suppose that will do. And how about having a chat with your mayor while we're gone? We *do* need to make sure he hasn't been tampered with yet."

"You don't just get to have 'chats' with the mayor around here. I need an appointment first, then a good reason for it. He's a busy man. His secretary would object to taking up his time just shooting the breeze."

"His secretary a woman?"

"No, a man, actually."

"Dalden, get the little gal an immediate appointment before we adjourn to the parking lot with your slave."

Brittany's mouth dropped open when Dalden nodded, left to enter the mayor's inner realm with the Altering Rod, came back out moments later, collected the "slave," then left the building completely. She stared at the door leading to Mayor Sullivan's offices. Dalden

hadn't really managed to get her an appointment with him, just like that. She'd make a fool of herself, telling the secretary she had one. Yet wouldn't Dalden have come back to tell her it was a no go?

Chapter 18

BEFORE BRITTANY COULD TALK HERSELF OUT OF IT, SHE marched into the mayor's waiting room. She was expecting the worst, still not really believing what that Altering Rod was capable of. Yet the worst that might happen would be her getting laughed at and pointed to the door.

"Brittany Callaghan to see the mayor."

"Go right in, miss," the secretary said, barely even looking up at her. "He's expecting you."

He wasn't, of course. Dalden hadn't included in his suggestion to the secretary warning the mayor of his next visitor, which was probably standard procedure. A mayor would want to know who he would be dealing with, so he'd know which political face to wear. And Sullivan was quite upset that she just waltzed

unannounced into his office while he was eating a quick lunch there between appointments.

Security was about to be called. Brittany was about to panic. A double-talker she was not. And while there were a number of excuses she could have come up with for being there which she thought of later, nothing came to mind in that moment of staring at a very annoyed mayor.

And then Dalden was there, back much sooner than expected, and merely remarked as he passed her on the way to Sullivan, "It did not require a return to your rust bucket. The Centurian has been sent to Martha, who has pointed out that I may not have cleared a proper path for you here."

The mayor was so surprised by this new presence barging into his office that Dalden was able to reach him before he managed to get out, "Who—?"

The rod touched him, and Dalden's voice was calmness itself. "You were expecting the woman," he told the politician. "You will answer her questions truthfully and forget them when she leaves. You will ignore me."

He then dropped into a chair on the side, which broke. He growled, tried the one next to it more cautiously, and, settling there, grinned at her. The mayor didn't give him another glance, even when the chair broke, and Brittany had just enough time to pick her jaw up off the floor before Sullivan came around his desk, hand extended in greeting, all smiles now, and asked what he could do for her.

It was now alarmingly clear to her just how powerful those rods were and how much damage they could

cause in the wrong hands. Which was probably why she was a bit ruthless in her "interrogation" of the mayor. Backed with the assurance that he probably wouldn't remember her and certainly not what they talked about, there was no need for dancing around a subject or leading into it.

Directly, she asked Sullivan if he'd noticed an influx of foreigners in their town, if he had made any recent policy changes, if there were any differences in his routines that he'd found strange for any reason. She covered every subject she could think of, and a few others that Dalden thought to mention.

By the time they left him, it was pretty obvious that Jorran's people had started tampering with Sullivan, though not to any alarming extent yet. Yes, he knew Jorran. They were best friends. No, he couldn't recall where they'd met; no, he had no idea what Jorran looked like and didn't find that strange. He'd apparently been prepped for a meeting between them soon, but it hadn't actually happened yet.

But Dalden put a monkey wrench in Jorran's immediate plans by leaving Sullivan with some opposing facts, including that Jorran was his enemy and to be avoided at all costs. It was a temporary measure and could be got around with new suggestions. But it should buy them a little time, which hopefully was all they needed.

"Jorran will want the entire building neutralized before he involves himself, to minimize his own risk," Martha explained when they were out in the hall again. "But that could already have been done."

"Then where does that leave us?"

"Sticking around to make sure we spot him *before* he gets near the mayor. And continuing to pick up his men and send them to me."

Brittany assumed that the fellow they had found earlier had been put in a taxi, since Dalden had returned so quickly without him, and while under the influence of the rod he would go exactly where he was told. Which had to be to Martha. But that meant Martha had to be close by.

"How about having dinner with us tonight, Martha?" Laughter greeted that suggestion, which had Brittany demanding, "Now why is that amusing?"

Martha wasn't going to answer her, if the prolonged silence was any indication, so Dalden did. "She does not eat."

"What he *means* is, I don't socialize," Martha put in now, exasperation clear. "But you know how that is, don'tcha, doll. Never enough time to see to all that needs seeing to, et cetera, et cetera."

Brittany sighed. "Yes, indeed. Perhaps, then, when this is over?"

"No," Martha replied curtly.

"Yes," Dalden countered, and Brittany's face was lifted in his hand, his eyes consuming her. "When this is over, *kerima*, I will take you home with me. It will mean leaving all that is known to you behind. But in return, I give to you my life, yours to keep until the day I die."

"You call *that* asking?" came Martha's complaint in bitter tones.

Dalden's smile was brilliant, unrepentant. "It was decided when she slept in my arms without fear."

Chapter 19

IT WAS DECIDED? *"WHAT WAS DECIDED?"*

Brittany was asking Dalden to explain his cryptic remark, but it was Martha who answered in derisive tones, "The big guy just joined you at the hip. He was *supposed* to ask your permission first, said he understood that's how it's done around here, but he arbitrarily went ahead and did it his way rather than yours."

"Did what? I still don't get it."

"Does shackled ring a bell? Ball and chain? Hooked up? No? How about married?"

Brittany started chuckling. "Get real. It takes more than a few words to perform a marriage."

"Wanna bet?"

Brittany stared at Dalden, but he wasn't laughing. He was looking back at her as if he'd just bought her

and was quite pleased with the purchase price. She started to get annoyed.

She'd tried to go along with their joke and treat it as such, but it wasn't the least bit amusing when her feelings for this man were so new and fragile. She couldn't deny that the thought of being able to keep him was thrilling, but it was also unrealistic. For crying out loud, she'd just met him yesterday and still knew next to nothing about him. So for him to want to, or even think about, marrying her at this stage was so far-fetched, it was beyond imagining.

"Okay, chuckle-time is over," she said tersely, making no attempt to hide her annoyance. "Shall we get back to business, or do we go off on a honeymoon first?"

For an answer, Dalden took her hand and started to drag her out of the building. She heard Martha's alarmed voice from some distance away, since there was over six feet of stretched arms between them now.

"Stop right there, warrior. She was kidding! She didn't mean it. And you are *not* going to run off and have some fun now just because you gave yourself permission to do so—not when Jorran could walk in here at any moment."

Dalden stopped. He looked utterly chagrined until his gaze fell on Brittany, then he just looked inflamed. She caught her breath. Dalden in the throes of passion was an incredible turn-on. And he must have sensed that she felt so, because he closed the space between them, clasped her face in both hands, and kissed her right there in the center of City Hall.

Nothing like being taken out of mind and place. They could have been up on a cloud for all she knew, she was so consumed with him and nothing but him.

But it wasn't Martha's voice that brought her jarringly back to earth this time, it was one she could have wished to never hear again.

"Into exhibitionism these days, Britt?"

It was absolutely the worst interruption Brittany could think of. Thomas Johnson, ex-boyfriend, the one guy she'd actually thought about marrying—and having sex with—because she'd mistakenly thought there was more between them than there was.

They hadn't exactly parted amicably, after she'd kicked him out of her apartment that night and told him to drop dead on the way out. It was a small town and she'd known they would run into each other eventually, but she'd managed to avoid doing so up till now.

"Still breathing, Tom?" she said, hoping he'd take the hint and just leave. "What a shame."

"Aren't we bitchy these days."

She smiled tightly. "Only around you."

He chuckled, though it was forced. They both knew she wasn't kidding around, that her animosity was quite real. She'd invested three months of emotions in this guy. Then for him to admit he had a problem with her height after all that time, even though she was a good half a foot shorter than him. Not short enough for him to feel like a giant, apparently, which had to be what he was looking for.

Dressed in a well-tailored pinstriped business suit today, Thomas made her feel tacky in her blue jeans, white T-shirt, and sneakers, which she'd felt adequate for playing the tourist in City Hall. Come to think of it, though, he'd always made her feel inferior in one way or another. Blue eyes, wavy black hair, sexy, extremely

handsome—at least she'd thought so until she met Dalden.

"I tried to call you a number of times," Thomas informed her, like she might actually believe it when he knew her schedule, knew exactly when he could find her at home to receive any calls.

She let that pass, though, and attacked his motive instead. "Whatever for? Wasn't I clear enough that I didn't want to see you again?"

"Because you misunderstood that remark I made about your height. I wanted to explain."

"Oh, really? So you don't really think I'm too tall for you?"

"Well, for anything permanent, yes, but not for—"

"Get lost," she cut in, feeling some of the same acute embarrassment she'd felt that night. "I swear, you should get JERK tattooed to your forehead, just in case some poor fool doesn't figure it out right off."

"Britt—"

"My woman has suggested you leave her presence. Do so now before I assist you in the doing."

Thomas stared up at Dalden for a moment. He'd only glanced briefly at him before, then dismissed him as some dim-witted jock who got unevenly divided—lots of body, little mind. And even now, Dalden didn't seem all that threatening, standing behind Brittany with his hands on her shoulders, his expression calm despite what he'd just said.

Which prompted Thomas to remark snidely to Brittany, "Where'd you find this Neanderthal?"

"You can consider yourself really fortunate that he probably doesn't have a translation for that word," Brittany guessed aloud. "He's new to our country and

doesn't have a full grasp of the language yet. Should I translate for him? You think he might appreciate derision coming from a shrimp like you?"

Tom finally got the point that his physical well-being might be in danger. There was a smidgen of alarm, but it was quickly dismissed. They were in a public place, after all, and one that usually had a few policemen roaming around it. So he felt absolutely safe in the assumption that Dalden wouldn't start anything there.

Brittany was sure of that as well; she'd just hoped Tom wouldn't be and would back off. So they were both somewhat surprised when Dalden set Brittany to the side of him, then completely behind him, where she didn't have a chance of seeing what he was going to do.

What he did was pointless, though, when Martha was in interfering mode. Dalden had no sooner wrapped his large hand around the man's neck than his fingers were grasping thin air instead.

A low rumble of annoyance came out of him while Martha was saying in Sha-Ka'ani, "So the eye doctors around here are really going to make a killing this week, but better that than you splattering his blood all over this pretty white floor."

"Where did you put him?" Dalden demanded in the same language.

"Back outside. He'll think he was so scared of you, he ran *really* fast. And lucky for you. Starting a physical brawl in a building devoted to politicians is a sure trip to a local jail. Remember our discussion of their jails? Places to be avoided at all costs?"

Brittany had heard enough that she didn't understand. "You guys are doing it again," she complained

as she moved back around Dalden to find the space in front of him empty now. "And where did Tom go?"

"Who cares?" Martha countered. "We've had too many distractions as it is, when you're both *supposed* to be working toward our common goal of Jorran-hunting. Our friendly Centurian has volunteered that there are two more of his good buddies in there doing what he was doing, which was prepping everyone in the building for Jorran's arrival so that he's greeted by one and all with open arms. Find the other two and send them to me for new programming. *Then* we can get back to discussing Dalden's lack of warrior restraint in his dealings with foes and lifemates."

"Huh?"

Brittany didn't get any further explanation, which was becoming an annoying habit with these two. She almost preferred hearing the no-make-sense stuff that fell into the "classified info" realm than these cryptic remarks she thought she might understand if she could get past the disbelief stage. And this "warrior" label? Once mentioned—and Martha hadn't wanted it mentioned—it was now being mentioned much too often. Hardly indicative of a national guard type of part-time soldiers; more like a full-time career.

Well, he had the body for it, and he certainly had the reflexes. So he was a soldier, and they called themselves warriors where he came from. She could deal with that. Why did they try to fluff it off and downplay the fact that he was a military man?

Just more of the little oddities that didn't add up. And the main source of answers went off on Dalden's hip as he began covering all the offices in the building, getting to ask questions now without worry of caus-

ing alarm, because he took that rod with him. While Brittany was left with the foot-traffic crowd again and two hours remaining before City Hall closed shop for the day.

But she *would* get some answers, and pretty soon. She was working for them, helping them to round up this ring of thieves. Though *lunatics* might be a better word for people who thought they could just pop in and become an instant politician. She deserved better than double-talk, tasteless jokes, and when that failed, simply being ignored.

Chapter 20

BRITTANY HAD NEVER REALIZED HOW EROTIC A MAN could be in tight jeans until she saw Dalden in the pair that had been made especially for him. Or maybe it was just him. Actually, it probably *was* just him, because the sight of him when he came out of the dressing room, with the long-sleeved white cotton shirt tucked into those dark blue jeans was such a turn-on that she almost dragged him back into the dressing room.

Of course, helping him to look normal didn't help to keep eyes off of him. His amazing height and size couldn't be disguised. But at least he didn't look like a rock star now, though Brittany cracked up when the seamstress who'd supplied the new clothes hadn't wanted payment for them, but had blushingly asked for a picture of Dalden instead. She figured if he

wasn't a celebrity now, he would be one day, and she wanted proof that she'd sewn for him.

Night was approaching by the time they left the mall. Her first day working for Dalden had been pretty successful. Even though Jorran hadn't been found yet, three of his people had been rounded up and sent off to Martha for interrogation. With night just around the corner, her job was over for the day. And as much as she hated the thought of losing his company even for a little while, she supposed she ought to offer to get him back to his own lodgings.

So as she was driving out of the mall parking lot, she remarked, "I know you said you couldn't get to your hotel yesterday for some reason, but you implied you could today. Shall I drop you off?"

"My place is now with you."

She spared him a glance. "You want to sleep on my couch again?"

He smiled at her. "What we sleep on may be of your choosing."

The chair and laying there in his arms all night again flashed through her mind and brought on a blush, even though he was probably using the "we" in a singular sense, rather than meaning him and her together.

But if he was going to spend the night again, she'd have to feed him, and she really didn't feel like a trip to the grocery with him in tow. Besides, she could just picture shopping carts banging into each other in the aisles, cans and boxes spilling all over the place, if he walked into the local food store.

With quite a few hours before bedtime ahead of them, and since they didn't have to get up as early to-

morrow as she was accustomed to, she suggested, "Want to go out to dinner? Catch a movie? Go dancing maybe?" Then she grinned. "You know, a date?"

"Dancing?"

She rolled her eyes at him. "Why are you looking like that's another new word to you?"

Martha, quiet since they'd left City Hall, decided to explain, "There's no equivalent for it on Sha-Ka'an. It's a form of exercise that requires music, but music hasn't been embraced yet by the Sha-Ka'ani."

"No television, no music, but he's familiar with computers. Do you realize how bizarre that is?"

"Do you realize how diverse this world is in cultures?" Martha shot back.

Brittany sighed, allowing the point. "All right, dinner first, then we'll play it by ear. And since we're not exactly dressed for fine dining, how about a pizza? Or two." She chuckled, giving him another glance. "Or three."

"What is—?"

"Food! Just plain old Amer—well, it's an Italian dish, but I hear we've Americanized it so much, the original tastes nothing like what we serve up here. And there's a nice little parlor on the next block."

The pizza parlor was surprisingly crowded for that early in the evening, or for anytime, actually, considering it offered delivery service, which most people took advantage of. The crowd consisted of a children's soccer team celebrating a victory with a lot of the parents in tow. Which meant service was slow and they ended up being there for a couple of hours, rather than in and quickly out as was usually the case.

Dalden flipped out over the pizza, which made the

wait well worth it. But then Martha got interested in the ingredients for making it, which resulted in a long and detailed discussion, because she didn't just want to know the shopping list required, she wanted to know the process for making the ingredients from scratch. Raised on a farm, Brittany was able to answer most of her questions.

And then there were the interruptions, which she was getting used to by now. Dalden got asked for his autograph again, and two men stopped by wanting to know what team he played for. Brittany was amused that she wasn't the only one who immediately assumed he would be a basketball player. And she didn't know how it happened, but she came back from the bathroom at one point to find the entire soccer team piled up on his shoulders for a group picture with the "giant."

He seemed to be enjoying himself, and three large pizzas later, it was actually late enough to hit Seaview's one nightclub. Ordinarily she wouldn't have considered going dancing on a weeknight but since Dalden had no experience of dancing at all, she wanted to find out if it was something else he might enjoy.

The weekend would have been a better time for it, when the nightclub was hopping, but she had a feeling he'd be gone by the time the weekend rolled in again. They had made a lot of progress today, and Jorran's people had as well, supposedly, so the wanna-be mayor could well make his appearance tomorrow. Then Dalden would take control of him with that rod as easily as he had his lackeys, and he'd have no further reason to stick around. Task done, he'd be going

home—and Brittany refused to think of how much she was going to miss him.

She'd foolishly let herself get too attached too quickly. She still barely knew anything about him, yet even that didn't matter. It was going to be heartbreak, big-time.

She'd already been assured that she wouldn't be opposed to his factions, which left nothing else that she could think of that she might find objectionable about him. Martha seemed to think otherwise, that their cultural differences couldn't be bridged. But what did culture have to do with feelings, especially when her every instinct was telling her that he was the man of her dreams, her ideal mate? Even the fact that he might be younger than her had no relevance. Nothing mattered compared to the emotions he stirred in her.

So tonight was for fun, and for memories. But the thin crowd in the club was daunting. Only four other couples were there, and only one of them seemed inclined to dance. And contrary to Tom's snide remark today, Brittany wasn't an exhibitionist. So it took three and a half drinks before she was ready to get out on that nearly empty dance floor.

Dalden was fascinated with the place. The lighting was old-style disco, the music was typically blaring, and the one couple who pretty much stayed out on the floor were giving him a decent how-to demonstration. Martha continued to call it exercise, and an obsolete form of it banned in many places. Brittany would have asked for a definition of "banned" if she wouldn't have had to shout it, because their "banned" had to be something other than "not allowed."

"Are you ready to try it?" she finally asked him.

"I will try anything with you, *kerima*."

She was just tipsy enough to be really moved by how sweet that answer was. She gave him her hand, and led him out on the floor. A fast song was playing, not a hopping beat, but a steady tempo that could accommodate just about any style. She danced the way she'd learned to in high school, a bit on the sexy side, but the only way she was familiar with. He seemed to be swinging some kind of invisible weapon himself, his movements precise, and she almost laughed when she realized he wasn't dancing, he was doing exactly what Martha had called it, exercising. They were still having fun, and his eyes, which he never took off of her, said he was enjoying watching her dance more than anything else.

And then the music segued into a slow song, the first one played since they'd arrived. Dalden hadn't seen slow dancing yet; she had to show him how. He took the closeness a step further, though, and within moments, he was kissing her instead. And that quickly was she taken out of place and time, just like that afternoon, everything around her fading to nothing. All that was left was the man and his touch, consuming her.

"Martha, please!"

Brittany seemed to hear it from a distance, his voice. She didn't know what he was asking for, but it didn't stop what he was doing for more than a second. She was still being kissed, still being held so closely she could feel all of him. There was a tingling that had nothing to do with the drinks she'd consumed. And then there was softness under her, and a very big man above her, and it simply didn't dawn on her yet that she was in a bed with him, or to wonder how she got there.

Chapter 21

BRITTANY HAD BEGUN THE EVENING WANTING TO STORE up memories, because she was certain that was all she would have left of Dalden soon. She hadn't thought of lovemaking as an added possibility, but what better memory to retain of him than one of the most profound intimacy?

It was no longer a matter of her wanting some kind of commitment from him first, or needing to know him better. That previous reasoning seemed very old now, in the matter of importance. Her feelings had taken a big step forward even from just yesterday, yet despite that, there was the simple fact that she wanted him, and could no longer think of a logical reason to deny that need.

There was some small confusion left, that the matter was already at hand, that they were in her bed, in her

apartment, and already deeply involved in the mating ritual. She simply couldn't remember how they had gotten there, when her last memory of them was on the dance floor in that nightclub.

She was forced to assume that her drinks had gotten double shots without her knowing and the result had snuck up on her without warning. She'd heard of bartenders doing that, a male-helping-a-male-score type of thing they ought to be shot for. And although she was sobering up quickly now, she must have been quite bombed to have gotten them home without remembering it. Incredible as that was, there was simply no other explanation for it.

Her clothes were gone. She did recall them being stripped away with amazing speed. His were as well. And Dalden naked was a marvel to behold.

She didn't think it was possible for a man to fit her ideal specifications, yet Dalden did in every way imaginable. She hadn't thought it was possible for her to ever feel small, either, but laying next to him, she felt that, too. He was just so big, every part of him, so much power and strength on visual display. A normal-sized woman might have been scared senseless by it, but Brittany was delighted instead.

That urgent desperation she'd heard in his voice earlier was only slightly modified now. It was still there, the strength of his passion unleashed, but that didn't frighten her, either, because he seemed to have absolute control of it, now that he had her where he wanted her: naked, clasped to him, her body his to possess.

And explore. He did that. He molded her, moved her this way and that, positioned her exactly to his

preference, and explored every inch of her with his hands, his mouth, his golden eyes.

One of them had turned the light on in her room and left it on. She should have experienced some embarrassment because of it, but there was none at all, probably because she was too busy being fascinated by his body. She did feel almost dominated, but even that was all right, because she knew she could have control back if she chose to. She didn't. It wasn't as if she was confident yet in making love, having never done so before. So his guidance, or command of what they were doing, was welcome and left her more open to just feelings, and those were numerous and intense.

She was thrilled to a level hard to contain. What he was making her feel was exciting. That she was finally going to "do it" was exciting. That it was with *him* was exciting. It was a spiral upward, senses heightened, each new sensation a step closer to the pinnacle . . .

And then she remembered Martha, with her prying ears and six-sided viewers, and panicked, thinking they weren't alone. "Where is it? Martha's box?" There was no answer, at least not from Martha. "She's gone?"

"She would not intrude here."

That didn't mean she was gone, but it was good enough. At least the panic subsided, only to be replaced soon after with a different form. He had mounted her, was about to breach her. She scrunched her eyes closed, tensed to the max, but assured him, or rather herself, "I'm in good shape, I'm ready for this, go for it."

He stared at her tightly closed eyes. A bass rumble of laughter came out of him.

"You are in no way ready, *kerima*. You have not done this before?"

Brittany opened her eyes just a crack so she could squint up at him. "If I had, do you *really* think I would have put you off yesterday?"

He seemed so very pleased by her answer that she was immensely glad that she'd been able to say that. She'd waited a long time for the right man to come along, and he was the right man. Instinct told her that even if circumstances didn't, and even though Martha seemed to think there was no chance of their different cultures mixing. None of which mattered. This was something she had to do for herself. If she only had some hope that this wasn't going to be a onetime thing, it would be perfect.

That moment of sadness made her wrap her arms around his neck and squeeze. "Make me believe in happy endings, Dalden, even if we're not going to have one. Tell me this won't be the only time we love each other."

He leaned back so he could look into her eyes. "I cannot fathom your confusion. You are my lifemate. And until I have you in a place familiar to me, where I can be assured of not losing you, you will not be parted from me. Is this the assurance you need?"

Relief flowed out of her, made her glow with happiness. "Was it ever."

He smiled at her, kissed her cheek gently, nuzzled her neck. He was restraining himself now, for her, because she had interrupted her state of readiness with her worries. He was apparently willing to start over, which filled her with such a wealth of gratitude and warmth that her feelings for him escalated yet again.

His own state of need hadn't lessened. Hers was brought back to match his with amazing speed. Not that he rushed her; she just wanted this to happen so much, her body was cooperating perfectly with her mind. And it didn't even hurt that much. She probably had the liquor to thank for that—or Dalden's restraint and expertise. He entered her so slowly, so very carefully, distracting her with his kisses, that by the time she felt the uncomfortable pressure of him pushing against the virginal blockage, it popped open, causing no more than a minor gasp of surprise.

He went no further than that, though. He was practicing that amazing restraint of his again. Unbelievable, the control he had over his emotions and his body. It wasn't normal. It wasn't necessary, either, when her own heightened senses were clamoring for more of him.

Without words she tried to tell him, grasping his backside with both hands, trying to push him forward into her. That didn't work, of course. She couldn't budge him if he didn't want to be budged. She felt a moment of resentment, that he could so easily move her body exactly as he wanted, but she couldn't do the same with his. It didn't last, though, because he was smiling down at her, amused by her efforts, but obviously pleased, too.

He kissed her gently, then caught her gasp in his mouth as he slid the rest of the way into her. It was exquisite, more thrilling than she could ever have imagined, having him so deep inside her. And his restraint was still in full force—no swift pummeling, now that he could, but a slow, exacting ritual.

He was letting her experience every aspect of his

taking possession of her. She couldn't complain, not when the pleasure was immediately there and gradually increased, so that she could enjoy it longer—or would have, if her body didn't like what was happening too much!

There was no delaying her climax when it came; it washed over her in powerful waves, the pinnacle of sensations so intense she nearly fainted. He joined her in that, prolonging that unique pleasure, until it really was too much ecstasy all at once.

She awoke sometime in the middle of the night. She was wrapped around Dalden, covering him like a blanket. She tried to move, to turn off the light that was still on, but his arm tightened around her, refusing to let her leave his side even in sleep. She smiled and put her cheek to his chest again. He made a lumpy mattress, a hard pillow, but that was okay. Her contentment couldn't be measured in comfort.

Chapter 22

"**B**RITT, YOU AWAKE YET?" JAN CALLED FROM THE LIVING room. "You've got company."

Brittany knew she had company. She opened her eyes to see that her company was still sleeping, his feet hanging over the end of her bed quite a bit. It was an extra-length model and fit her just fine, but they really didn't make beds for seven-footers.

"Britt?" It was shouted this time.

Okay, so she wasn't quite awake yet, or she would have realized Jan wasn't talking about Dalden, that her friend likely didn't know yet that he'd spent the night.

"Coming!" she shouted back.

She leapt out of bed, yanked her bulky white terry robe out of the closet, wrapped it on, and stepped out

into the living room. She vaguely heard Dalden stirring behind her, but didn't dare look back at him, or she'd be really rude to whoever was there and simply tell them to get lost. She had a mind to anyway, up until she got a look at the man standing just inside their front door.

Jan was staring at him as if she were starving and he was six feet of chocolate cake. Brittany couldn't blame her. The man was unbelievably handsome; actually, way, way too handsome. She'd never seen anyone who looked that perfect, like he was created to someone's ideal specifications. He even fit her own specifications, was at least as tall as her if not taller. She wasn't sure she wanted to get close enough to see if he might top her by a few inches, when she was still doubting her eyes. He was even more handsome than Dalden, if that was possible, though in a different way, less masculine—*beautiful* was the word that came to mind.

He wore a one-piece jumpsuit that looked like some kind of uniform. His eyes were so green that the color was clear even from across the room. His hair was coal black, cut short, though not excessively short. And he carried some sort of large plastic container that Brittany did a double-take on when she realized it was filled with groceries.

She finally asked, "You sure you have the right apartment?"

He smiled at her. "Martha doesn't make mistakes. She sent me with some necessities for the big guy."

"Ohhhh, you're a friend of Dalden's."

That didn't get confirmed. Instead she heard behind her, "Corth II, Martha? Is that wise?"

"Just saving time, kiddo, since you depleted the little gal's cupboards yesterday," Martha's voice chimed in.

Poor Jan was staring wide-eyed now at Dalden's bare chest. He'd donned only the jeans before appearing in the doorway to the bedroom, and was hooking Martha's box over the denim. The female voice she'd just heard, with no body to go along with it, was probably confusing the hell out of her. She was also undoubtedly shocked to find Dalden coming out of Brittany's bedroom.

Tactfully, though, all Jan said was, "I think I need a cup of coffee," and disappeared into the kitchen.

Brittany wanted one as well, but decided some clothes might be a better idea first. "I'll just get dressed while you chat with your friend."

She'd still been staring at their visitor while she said it, which was possibly why there was some annoyance in Dalden's voice when he replied, "Corth II is not staying."

"It sounds like I'm not staying," Corth II said with a cheeky grin. "Nice to meet you, Brittany Callaghan, however briefly. Perhaps—"

"Be gone!" Dalden growled.

The man obeyed, though he seemed quite amused as he left. Martha was chuckling some as well.

"My, my, that was interesting," came purring out of the little box. "Losing some of that renowned Sha-Ka'ani control there, warrior? 'Course, I shouldn't be surprised, after you totally lost it last night."

Brittany frowned at the box on his hip. "Why are you picking on him, Martha?"

If a shrug could be heard in a voice, it was heard now in Martha's. "Just setting the stage for my expla-

nation, doll, before Dalden starts to fret over natural inclinations that he's convinced he doesn't possess. A fretting warrior is like a time bomb, which we don't need at this stage of the game."

"Martha has said too much already," Dalden said in grumbling tones.

"Martha hasn't said nearly enough yet," Martha countered. "But you can relax over some of those inclinations, warrior. Last night, you were provoked big-time. What you witnessed has been a form of sexual enticement for centuries. It's known to easily incite passions. Some cultures have managed to get rid of it, the thinking being that their people have enough stress to deal with, that sexual stress in that form only compounds the problem."

"Good grief," Brittany said incredulously. "You're talking about our dancing last night?"

"Watching you dance pushed him over the edge, doll, if you didn't notice at the time. You might want to make sure there is no more of that nonsense until after we've finished our task here."

"Some people consider dancing to be fun," Brittany pointed out.

"Some people are used to it," Martha shot back. "Dalden isn't one of them."

Brittany stared at Dalden and then blushed profusely. "I hope you don't think it was my intention to—to—"

He quickly closed the space between them, clasped her face in his hands, smiled at her. "I would change no part of last night, *kerima*."

She wouldn't, either—well, she wished she could recall getting back here. Black holes in the memory

were a bit frightening, in not knowing what you might have done during the missing time frame. But she supposed if she had done anything more stupid than driving under severe influence, he would have mentioned it by now.

Everything else she remembered clearly, including his assurance that she was his lifemate, that they wouldn't be parted until he had her in a place familiar to him. She would like to get "familiar" defined. Tacking "home" to it was unrealistic, when he could have just meant back to wherever his base of operations was for this assignment he was on. *Lifemate* was another word she needed his interpretation of. She knew the definition she'd like to put to it, but in some cultures, mate just meant friend, so she wasn't going to assume what it meant for him.

But she wasn't quite up to an interrogation yet, and what she suspected might be some considerable disappointment on her part as a result. She'd rather savor the contentment she'd felt last night awhile longer.

So she wrapped her arms around him, squeezed a bit, and said, "I'll endeavor to keep you out of any more disco-type establishments, but I'm sure we can manage to have fun without the dancing part."

Martha was chuckling. Dalden's smile widened considerably. And Brittany remembered too late that he referred to lovemaking as "fun."

She stepped back and snorted at the both of them. "That's not what I meant—bah, never mind. While I get dressed, why don't you unload the groceries your friend was nice enough to drop off."

"Corth II is not a friend."

"Fine. Enemy then."

"Nor that," he replied. "My mother considers him part of the family."

"She does? Which implies you don't?"

"Like my father, I have little tolerance for those of Corth II's ilk."

"Ohh—kay," she said, stretching out the word. "I suppose that made perfect sense—to you. And come to think of it, I'd just as soon *not* know what you mean by 'ilk.' I do find it odd, however, his having a number for a last name. Is that common in your country?"

"It is not a last name. He is the second in his line, an advanced model of Martha's creation, similar to the original Corth."

"Martha's son?" she said with surprise.

"Something like that."

"Something like—?" She frowned now. "Okay, I know I'm missing something here, and now I'd like that explanation. Martha, want to fill me in?"

"Not a chance, doll. I just love watching warriors dig holes they can't get out of."

Brittany made a face, but turned her questions back in Dalden's direction. "So why didn't this Corth get an original name?"

"Martha is a Mock II. It follows that anything that improves on the original, as she was, would get the same classification from her."

"I give up. You're talking like he's a machine, an android or something like that, when that's impossible."

"Why impossible?"

"Because we might be making strides with robotic gadgets, but nothing even remotely like what just walked in here. That was a man. I've got eyes. There was nothing mechanical about him."

He reminded her, "Inventions that defy belief, you were told."

She blinked at him, but then she chuckled. "I'm glad you've got a sense of humor, Dalden, I really am. It's an odd one, but none the less amusing."

"Woman—"

"This might be a really good time to drop the subject, children," Martha interjected dryly at that point. "You've overslept this morning. The big guy still needs to be fed. I was hoping we'd get to City Hall when it first opens, but now you'll have to backtrack again, to make sure no mischief gets caused before your arrival. Waste of time that could have been prevented if someone's alarm had been set."

Brittany blushed, mumbled something about grumpy old women, and went back to the bedroom to get dressed.

Chapter 23

"IT'S AS I SUSPECTED," MARTHA WAS SAYING AS THEY walked into the central lobby at City Hall. "Jorran's people were all turned loose on your fair town. The three that I have links to each abided the night in different locations, harmless for the most part. But *they* showed up here bright and early, unlike some—"

"There are times when you may ignore Martha," Dalden told Brittany, his arm around her waist. "Were it important for us to be here sooner, she would have woken us herself."

A snort first, then, "Actually, waking you myself, without any other distractions there to get you out of bed, would have guaranteed a *lot* more wasted time. Both blushing? I see you understand why I didn't do the waking, but sent Corth II over instead."

"Is there going to be a time when you can turn her off?" was Brittany's mumbled response.

"Indeed, but not for several more months."

Brittany frowned. "You don't really think it's going to take that long to find Jorran, do you?"

"No," he replied. "But Martha cannot be gotten rid of until I return home, and she is returned to being only my mother's nuisance."

"Tedra does *not* consider me a nuisance," Martha interjected in hurt tones.

"Can my father say the same?"

" 'Course not" came out with a chuckle that belied there'd been any real hurt in the last comment.

Brittany ignored the banter, was stuck on that "several months" remark. "Then you're not going straight home after you're done here?"

"Indeed we are."

Her eyes widened. "So it's going to take you a couple of months just to travel? Wow, I didn't think anything still took that long to cross the ocean. You must have a really old, slow ship lined up for the trip."

Martha wasn't the only one chuckling this time, and feeling herself the butt of yet another joke she couldn't possibly decipher, Brittany added, "Wrong guess? Maybe you plan to swim home?"

The sarcasm was clear to her ears, but Dalden didn't hear it, and said only, "Such would not be possible."

Martha was more perceptive, and replied, "No need to get bent out of shape, doll. You'll understand all too soon and probably wish you'd been left in the realm of 'unknowing' instead. In the meantime, how about you two getting to work? Same agenda as yesterday. Start with the mayor first and work your way out from

there, Brittany, while Dalden makes the rounds of the rest of the offices."

With a sigh, Brittany nodded and headed toward the mayor's reception room. With three rods confiscated yesterday, she now had one for her own use and Sullivan's secretary got to be her first test subject with it.

It still amazed her, the total hypnotic control those rods gave the user. She was sent right in to the mayor's office, had herself announced first this time so as not to startle the man again. And didn't once think that he might be in the middle of a meeting already, which happened to be the case.

Where was her mind today? Still savoring last night, of course, and not attending to current business. But that was no excuse to blunder like this. . . .

There were four other people gathered around the mayor's desk. They weren't talking, were merely relaxing in the plush chairs for the most part, looking bored. And Sullivan did stand up, all smiles, to greet her as if she weren't intruding on a meeting already in progress.

Was he still under the same influence from yesterday, ready to answer any questions she put forth and then forget about them? But she couldn't exactly grill him with these other people present. Nor could she use the rod on the lot of them without one or two realizing what she was doing before she reached them, and bolting to raise an alarm.

A hasty retreat was in order, and before she started blushing over this blunder, she jumped right in with, "Someone get their appointment times mixed up? If you'd like me to wait outside a few more minutes until you're done here, Mayor Sullivan, I—"

"Done with what?" he asked with a curious frown. "I was expecting you, wasn't I?"

"Yes, but—"

"Then sit, sit," he told her, wearing his public smile again. "What can I do for you today?"

The blush was coming up anyway. The four men must be members of his staff. And they still weren't saying anything, just watching the proceedings in a bored manner. Which really put her on the spot. Was she supposed to conduct her business with them present? Was that normal around here, for the mayor to be surrounded by his people during private appointments? She *had* caught him on his lunch break last time, after all. And if this was standard procedure, why hadn't they at least introduced themselves to put her at ease?

Annoyed that she wasn't going to accomplish her mission with them there, she pointed out their rudeness with some of her own by asking one of them directly, "Who are you?"

"An observer."

Fat lot that told her, so she held out her hand to shake his and even though he ignored it, she still said, "I'm Brittany Callaghan, and you are?"

"An observer" was repeated, but then, "Commence your meeting, woman, then begone."

She caught the accent this time. Like Dalden's but not quite the same, still very foreign-sounding. Alarms went off in her head. She needed to get the hell out of there and warn Dalden that they'd most likely hit the jackpot, and used that last comment to take offense over.

"Excuse me, I can tell when I'm not wanted," she

said tersely, and to Sullivan, "I'll reschedule, Mayor, when you're not being—observed."

She turned and started to march out of there on her high horse, only to be drawn up short because one of them had moved to block the exit. Nor was he little enough that she might have been able to push her way past him. He was her height, but with the physique of a nightclub bouncer, all brawn and happy to show it off. The price tag dangling from the lapel of his new suit was a bizarre touch, but not enough to detract from his seriously threatening demeanor.

And she heard behind her, "It is difficult to hide fear beneath other emotions. Most people cannot manage it. You fall into that group. Then the question becomes, What was said here to cause you fear?"

She swung back around. It was the same fellow she'd spoken to who had sensed her fear. The observer. He'd looked more important than the other three bored interlopers, which was why she'd addressed him. Jorran himself?

He was standing now, with that aura of command even more prominent, wrapped around him like a cloak. Tall, lean, with light blond hair and emerald green eyes, he held himself like royalty, was lacking only a crown to make the impression complete. But then the price tag hanging from his sleeve ruined the impression and threw her off again.

She noticed it as he crossed his arms. A brief, nervous glance at the other two men showed that their suits also sported them. Fashionable where they came from? Or was their country so backward that they simply didn't know that if you left the store wearing new clothes you just bought, you were supposed to remove

the evidence? And that they were all wearing brand-new suits for this appearance made her wonder why they had felt it was necessary. To replace desert robes, perhaps?

She was doing it again, making assumptions, when she should just deal with known facts. Trouble was, there were so few of those. And such blatant ignorance of the modern world was making it easy for her to put her fear aside. How was she supposed to take this plot seriously when these people knew absolutely nothing about the country and politics they were trying to gain control of?

He was waiting for her answer. She kept it simple. "I don't know what you're talking about."

A slight annoyance showed in his expression. "Of course you do. And you can own up to the truth, or I can have you arrested for attempting to assassinate Mr. Sullivan. He will, of course, swear that you did indeed try to kill him."

He was bluffing. He had to be bluffing. Send her to prison, and that's what that particular charge would do if the rods were used to support it, just because she wouldn't answer his question?

Panic mixed with indignation had her demanding, "Are you listening to this, Mayor?"

Sullivan was frowning at her. "All I hear is you talking nonsense to yourself."

That produced a sigh from Jorran, drawing her eyes back to him. "It is really too bad that he mentioned that. I was merely curious about what caused you to be suddenly afraid. Now we will have to detain you."

So it had been a bluff. Of course he wouldn't want to cause such a big to-do, which would only draw

more attention to himself. But detaining was just as bad in her book.

"And do not ask why he does not hear or see me, woman," he added disdainfully as he sat back down. "Your curiosity is unimportant."

That easily she was dismissed. And that was what made her angry. She was inconsequential, a nuisance to be brushed under the rug. She posed absolutely no threat to their carefully laid plans.

"Ask? I don't need to ask," she said with an equal amount of disdain. "I know exactly why he doesn't hear or see you."

Chapter 24

BRITTANY COULD CLAIM THE DEVIL MADE HER SAY THAT, but it was a known fact that anger was its own worst enemy, and she was no exception to that rule. She should have kept her mouth shut. She should have pretended that she was just what she seemed to be, just another appointment on the mayor's busy schedule. Now she had to admit that she knew more than they had counted on anyone knowing, and offer a reason for that without implicating Dalden.

He might be bigger than the lot of them, though the two bouncer types might cost him a bit more effort. He could still probably take them all down by normal means. But if all four of them were equipped with those rods, there'd be nothing normal about it. Dalden could be rendered harmless within seconds, and the

only end to that would be Jorran wins, Dalden and company lose. So it was imperative that they not know he was in the building looking for them.

Jorran was standing up again, and there was no "slight" to his annoyance this time. A short, rotund fellow had also moved behind the mayor and was whispering in his ear. It looked like she had just been made invisible as well, since the mayor proceeded to ignore her as he started browsing through some papers on his desk.

"Explain yourself, woman," brought her eyes back to the regal-looking Jorran.

She decided on the most plausible lie out of the few options she had. "I'm a news reporter assigned to City Hall. It's my job to ferret out anything of interest going on around here, and your crew and those sticks they've been waving around the last couple of days were most definitely interesting. I followed, I listened. A child could have put two and two together here, when your people haven't exactly been trying to hide what they were doing."

The last wasn't exactly true either, but he didn't address it, merely pointed out, "We have been following your town news. No mention of what you say has appeared in it, which means you lie."

"No, that just means I haven't finished writing the article yet."

"Then you have told no one else of your findings?"

Dilemma time. Cover her own butt and claim others knew, put the fear of imminent discovery into them, or keep them from panicking so Dalden could do his thing and round them up? Actually, there was no

dilemma, when Martha had mentioned that if they went into hiding, it would be impossible to find them again. No panic—well, aside from her own.

So she took an accusatory tack, complaining, "You're kidding, right? And get labeled as writing science fiction? I need more proof before I put my name to an article as unbelievable as this one is so far. I mean, what it seems those sticks of yours can do is just not possible. Maybe you'd care to explain what exactly it is they *do* do?"

"What is your conclusion?"

"I'm not paid to draw conclusions, merely to report what's newsworthy," she said. "But it's pretty obvious you want to be mayor."

"What is obvious is often proven irrelevant," he replied, then nodded toward the mayor as he added, "He does not do much that impresses me. He decides no matters of great import. I am not sure now that I want his title. I am taking a few days to observe and decide."

She almost laughed. The man wanted the mayor's job when he had absolutely no idea what it entailed. Or was he trying to throw her off the track?

"The position of mayor can't be encompassed in just a few days," she told him, "when the projects he undertakes can take months, even years to finish. A mayor's greatness or failure is seen at the end of his term, in what he has accomplished during that term. It's not a title, it's a job. He works for the people, for the betterment of the town, not for the betterment of himself."

A hand was waved to dismiss that reasoning. "The position will be what I make of it, not what the towns-

people have come to expect. Not that it matters. This is merely a stepping-stone to true rulership."

So much for the misleading theory. Sounded more like he was going into bragging mode now, which didn't hold much hope for her being released when they were done talking. She might as well hear it all, then . . .

"Rulership, huh? Don'tcha mean leadership? But just out of curiosity, how did you think you could manage to jump into an elected position of prominence in this country when you're not a citizen of it, or known to the populace?"

"I am known. The people in this building already think I am their mayor. He will make a speech today to the thing called media that he has been merely my puppet, that I have been making all decisions for him from the start."

It was on the tip of her tongue to tell him that such a speech would cause outrage—to say that the people had been duped—not have the desired effect he seemed to think it would give him. But just in case they couldn't stop him before then, why give him warning that he'd be digging his own grave with that course of action?

So she said instead, "Aren't you forgetting the other candidates running for the job?"

"If I decide to continue on this stepping path to the presidency, I will be the only candidate running for mayor during the thing you call election. The others will concede to the better man."

"You plan to use those rods to force them to drop out at the last minute, don't you?"

He smiled. It was such a confident, I-can't-lose sort

of smile. But that wasn't what had her belly rolling
with dread, it was the realization that the man could
do exactly what he planned to do, and what he
planned to do was much worse than she'd been told.

The presidency? He was out of his flipping mind,
and yet those rods could get him there. Men could be
told how to vote. The media could be given false information about him and make it nationally known.
Women who might suspect what was going on and try
to prevent it could be warned off by their bosses and
men in their families, or railroaded into jail as they had
threatened to do to her.

There were countless ways they could get around
any opposition, just with the touch of a hypnotic stick
and a few whispered words. Judges, other politicians,
top law enforcement positions, hell, even the high
brass in the military, all could be made puppets in Jorran's camp.

"Why bother with small potatoes, why not go
straight for the big seat?" she asked, trying to understand his reasoning. "Plastic surgery could make you
look like the current president." Hadn't Dalden been
worried that he had changed his appearance? "You
could just take over that way—"

"And assume his name?" was said indignantly.
"Never. I share no glory. It is my name that will be
revered, as it should be."

She forced herself to remember he'd said "if" earlier, that he wasn't fully committed on this path yet.
There was nothing standing in his way from his point
of view, since he didn't know about Dalden and
Martha yet. So what else was making him have second
thoughts?

"You've gone to a lot of trouble here, to be undecided in the matter. Perhaps you've realized that it's not going to work in the long run?"

The curious look he gave her wasn't doubt; it was laced with amusement. "Why would it not?"

"Because you're always going to have someone questioning who you are, where you came from. Everywhere you turn there will be reporters hounding you, demanding answers. You can fool a few people, but this country is comprised of millions, and every one of those millions is concerned with who leads them. And every time you open your mouth, you will generate even more questions."

"How so?"

"Because your accent points out that you're not one of us, so you have no business governing us. Now if you plan to have someone else do all the talking for you, you might get by for a while. But you strike me as a man who doesn't want to take second place to anyone."

He actually chuckled. "Your suppositions are based on what has been, not what will be. Do you understand that your governing foundation will be changed to *my* foundation? A king is not questioned. A king's word is law."

"And you would be king?" she said derisively.

"I am already king. I merely require a new country to rule. My indecision is in regard to your particular country. I have more information about your world now. I must weigh immediate power of a lesser degree against a greater, true power that requires much time and effort. I lean toward great power, but I abhor being made to wait for it."

Was he just hatched yesterday? How could he not know the different forms of government to be had, and that the one he'd picked was the least suited for what he had in mind?

She didn't get a chance to ask. The rotund fellow who'd put the mayor into complete ignore-mode said peevishly to Jorran, "You need waste no more time on this female, Eminence. I will see that she is disposed of."

Jorran gave that a moment's consideration before he replied, "No . . . no, I have enjoyed the discourse, Alrid, and wish to continue it later."

"She knows :oo much—"

"Get real," Brittany interrupted, afraid she knew where that line of reasoning was going to go. "I could have screamed my head off already, and had the cavalry arriving to bash down the mayor's door by now. But I'm a reporter, remember? I'd rather get an exclusive interview after the mayor makes his speech to the cameras. Everyone and their mother is going to want to know about the brains behind the puppet after that speech. Work with me, and I'll give you the best news coverage you could ask for."

"Why would you do this?" Jorran asked.

"Because it would be a *huge* boost to my career, which means more money for me. I've got a mortgage to pay, kids to feed." Bah, she was laying it on too thick. "Look, the fact is, I was getting nowhere with the article I'd planned to write, so I'd just as soon forget about that one for the real story. Fact two, you're going to need some good press coverage that you have some control over. The average reporter is going to write what they want to write about you, not what you want to be known."

"And you would write what I want known?"

"Exactly—for a price."

Jorran threw back his head and laughed. "Greed. This I understand perfectly. I was beginning to wonder if your species was capable of corruption. My faith is restored. You will remain with us to our mutual benefit."

He had bought it. She'd be put on the payroll. Amazing. She certainly wouldn't have believed that hogwash she'd tossed his way. It had to be the greed part, right up his alley, something he was comfortable dealing with. Not that it mattered, when it was probably going to be her shortest job ever—because she was fully expecting Dalden to take this guy out of commission before the mayor started spouting his rod-induced lies.

Chapter 25

"WE'VE GOT PROBLEMS." MARTHA'S VOICE CAME through the phazor combo-unit a bit erratically.

"Your impaired speech?" Dalden said as they returned to the main lobby.

"Not just that. Something has moved into the area that is causing major interference that makes Transfer too dangerous to consider. Do you notice anything unusual?"

A quick glance around the central hall had Dalden saying, "Other than Brittany is not here?"

"Yes, other than that. Strange equipment? Electrical storms?"

"Your viewers are not working, either?"

"Only sporadically, which is unacceptable. Corth II

is on his way with a few emergency essentials. He'll be a few minutes getting here, since I had to set him down out of the range frequency of that interference. It's imperative that it be located and disabled, whatever it is."

"It is more imperative that you tell me where Brittany is," Dalden countered.

A sigh. "She's still in the mayor's office."

"Why?"

"Probably because Jorran is in there, too. Hold it right there! If you go barging in, she's liable to get hurt. At the moment, she's fine."

"I will not leave her in there, Martha."

It was said so emphatically that only a fool would try to argue—or a computer. "She's fine, kiddo, *really* she is. I'm not getting full conversations with this interference, but from the bits and pieces I am getting, it sounds like she's got them believing that she's joined their camp and will be a benefit to them. Besides, he's not going to hurt her when he finds her interesting."

"I find these trees growing indoors interesting. That does not mean I would not cut them down."

"I meant interested as in bedtime fun—hold it right there! You don't chop someone up for what they are thinking, and that's as far as his interest has gone. She doesn't know he finds her attractive. He's the type who won't reveal emotions to anyone if they could be perceived as a weakness that could be used against him."

"You have had chains on me too long, Martha."

"Dalden, sweetie," she cajoled in syrupy tones. "We are almost done here. The end of this rising should see us on our way home. Don't blow it now because

you're impatient to get your hands around his neck. If it sounds like she's in the slightest trouble, you get the green light. But at the moment, we want him to think he's got the upper hand, so he'll leave here and you can then deal with him under less public scrutiny. Here, there are a good forty people or more who will jump to his defense."

"He has that many with him?"

"No, but you keep forgetting what I told you about the people in this country. They are an aggressive lot. They will interfere just because they can."

"Not if I stun them all."

Another sigh, much longer and riddled with static. "Tedra could pull that off, but you haven't had any practice with that phazor combo-unit. With calm, slow use and sightline up, you'd have no trouble with it, but Probables say that in your rush to stun them all before they can get to you, you'll end up missing one or two and risk the chance of the beam reflecting off something and coming right back at you. But in case you haven't realized it yet, Transfer isn't the only thing currently being affected by that local interference. Your weapon is out of order as well."

"Then what do you propose?"

"Let him get beyond the interference, or get rid of it first. And *please* keep in mind that you can't kill Jorran, much as you might be currently relishing the thought, or we lose the leverage for a recall on *all* of the rods. So the original plan still holds: disable his shield so I can Transfer him to the ship, but do it in the least crowded place so you won't be jumped by locals who think you're accosting an innocent party. The advantage is still ours, since he still doesn't suspect that we're here.

Ah, that's better." A sigh filled with relief, and minus any static.

"What?"

"Corth II has arrived and turned off the interference, though not very diplomatically," Martha complained. "I'll have to talk to him about threatening to break people who don't want to cooperate with him, and leaving stunned bodies all over the place. We're going to have to wrap this up, kiddo. We've got about an hour before those stuns wear off and all hell breaks loose around here."

Dalden grinned. "I will have to thank him for releasing me from your restraints."

"If I don't fry his circuits first," Martha mumbled. "But all systems are back in full operation—on our end. And those cameramen coming into the building haven't realized yet that they've been disconnected from making a live broadcast. So it was the media transmission equipment causing—Jorran is coming out. Show time."

"Show time?"

"Time for you to do your thing, warrior."

Quite a few people were coming out of the mayor's reception room. Dalden saw none of them until he saw Brittany and that she was all right. Jorran followed her. He looked harmless wearing local clothes, rather than his royal garb, but Dalden knew just how dangerous he could be, especially if he had a razor sword tucked into the pocket of his suit. Would he feel the need for a weapon here, or assume that the Altering Rod was all the weapon he needed?

At least a dozen people had come out, including the mayor. "How many are Jorran's people?" Dalden asked.

"Three of them," Martha replied. "The others with them are on the mayor's staff, though Probables say they've all been altered. *Your* main concern will be avoiding any rods pointed your way."

"I will have you to counter any suggestions that halt me, as Brock did for us on Sunder when we were told to forget my sister."

"That will work, but it requires time for the correcting speech to be said, time in which weapons can be used against you. *Avoid the damn rods!*"

"This might help," Corth II said as he sauntered up to join them. "The emergency essentials Martha called for, just in case the interference didn't get turned off. Not exactly needed now—except for the confidence gained in having the right equipment at hand."

The right equipment in this case was Dalden's own sword and his intricately carved arm shields. Martha was mumbling about creating spectacles, but Dalden had gone into ignore-Martha mode as he stripped off his shirt and strapped on the *Toreno* steel arm shields that wrapped about his forearms from elbow to wrist. They were his only protection, but then not much more was needed with a four-foot sword in hand. *Droda*, it felt good clasping his fingers around that hilt again.

"I owe you," Dalden told the android.

"Yes, you do, big-time." Corth II grinned at him. "Just keep that in mind the next time I flirt with your beautiful lifemate."

That got him a scowl, but Martha wasn't done, and suggested in reasonable tones, "You could at least make an effort to conceal that ridiculously long instru-

ment of death until you get close enough to Jorran to use it."

"Martha is too cautious where her owner's children are concerned," Corth II pointed out, more as a reminder for Martha, since Dalden already knew it from firsthand experience. "She cannot be faulted for that. It is against her basic programming to allow anything to cause Tedra distress if she can prevent it. But now that the target has been located, there is no reason not to capture him with no holds barred. I'll keep others from interfering."

"No more stunning unless absolutely necessary," Martha warned Corth II.

He just grinned cheekily and replied, "I have the third confiscated rod."

"Then why didn't you use it on those broadcast people outside?"

"Because we needed a guaranteed time frame, which the stunning has given us. Rod suggestions could have been countered, the machines fixed that I disabled, the interference turned on again—"

"All right already, I get the *farden* point. Let's wrap this up, children."

Chapter 26

BRITTANY WAS NERVOUS AS ALL HELL, AND BEING AFRAID
that it was obvious only increased it. She'd worn a
pullover sweater today with her jeans, so she could
conceal the Altering Rod up her sleeve for easy access.
Since City Hall was air-conditioned, she'd figured
she'd be okay in the thick winter sweater and had been
comfortable—until she came face-to-face with Jorran.
She was sweating now.

How did she get herself into this mess? This was no
longer just helping a man she'd flipped over locate a
wacko foreign thief. That had seemed easy, something
anyone could have done, adventurous even. These
people were dangerous. She had little doubt that the
fat man's "dispose of" was of the permanent sort. This
was a play for power, serious power. With that kind of

stake involved, they wouldn't care who got hurt—or died—in the process.

And where the hell was Dalden? One of the news-people had told the mayor they were having camera trouble, that someone had pulled the plug on their connection, so it would be a few more minutes before they were ready for his speech. That speech was going to turn this town upside down if Dalden didn't do something before Sullivan had a chance to speak.

Or if she didn't.

What would be the chance of her using the rod she had up her sleeve on Jorran before one of his two bruiser bodyguards put her out of commission? She wouldn't have to say much, just tell him to call this off, well, maybe also mention that he didn't want to be mayor—or president, maybe even suggest that he should go home.

She was standing close enough to him to do it. He'd moved in front of her, was so close that the few extra inches he had on her was blocking a good portion of the room from her view. But then the rotund fellow named Alrid was standing just as close to her at her back . . .

God, should she take the chance, or wait and see if Dalden was in the crowd gathering behind the camera-people? She peered over Jorran's shoulder to get a bet-ter view of the room, hoping to spot the big guy, and caught her breath when she did. He was there and marching purposely toward the gathering in front of the mayor's offices. But half naked and with a sword in his hand? A *sword*, for crying out loud?

Jorran had seen him, too. Jorran was smiling, not at

all confused by what he was seeing the way she was. They knew each other. That was apparent. Perhaps Jorran hadn't noticed the sword yet.

He turned to tell his men, "A Sha-Ka'ani warrior among us, how interesting. Do not interfere. This is going to be my pleasure."

"Jorran, if there is one, there will be more." There was distinct worry in Alrid's voice, in his expression as well. "We should—"

"Enjoy the diversion," Jorran cut in. "They are men, subject to the rods just like any other, and will make excellent bodyguards for me after my empire is established. But this one's family thwarted my plans. This one dies. The rest that we find, we will tame."

Such confidence went beyond mere bravery, it was certain knowledge of having a *huge* advantage. Brittany couldn't see what that advantage might be. Jorran lacked the muscle, the height, the brawn to compete with someone of Dalden's immense stature physically in close combat, which the sword Dalden held seemed to suggest he had in mind to do. How, then, did Jorran think to win without a gun or other long-distance-type weapon that could stop him before he was within arms' reach? And he had no weapon of that sort . . .

He had something. It was taken from the pocket of his coat before he shrugged out of it and tossed it at Alrid. A tube of some sort, it looked like, no more than six inches in length, grasped in his right hand. But it wasn't pointed at Dalden, it was squeezed, which caused an extension to shoot out of it, a little more than three feet of shining metal that was so thin, it could barely be seen if viewed from the side.

"What the hell is that?"

She said it aloud. Alrid heard her and answered, "A razor sword, capable of slicing a man in half with little effort. The Sha-Ka'ani is about to find that out."

Brittany blanched, and was rendered nearly immobile by the accompanying weakness that spread through her limbs. Jorran had said it. Alrid had just confirmed it. The plan was to kill Dalden, not just stop him or use the rod on him.

It was so utterly bizarre, that scene in the middle of City Hall. A bare-chested giant in tight jeans and knee-high boots with what looked like an old-fashioned transistor radio hooked to his belt, a mammoth sword in hand. And what appeared to be no more than a simple businessman in tailored slacks, silk shirt, and tie, with something hooked to his belt as well, a round disk flat on the side facing him, the size of an orange—and a sword so thin it couldn't really be called a sword, was more like an exaggerated razor blade.

It was no wonder everyone there was staring open-mouthed, disbelieving. People just didn't come into City Hall carrying swords and looking like they intended to use them. But then she noticed that one man was ignoring the two facing off in the center of the room. Corth II was there, and working his way around the side toward Jorran's bodyguards.

She came to life herself then, figured the tall though lean fellow was going to need help with the two bruisers, and she was the least likely to raise their suspicions. She started with Alrid, whom she needed to get past to reach the other two, touched his arm and told him he couldn't move or speak. She did the same with one of the bodyguards, but wasn't quick enough to reach the other before Corth II did.

The bodyguard might look the stupid sort, but apparently he wasn't. He recognized the threat to himself immediately and used his own rod on Corth II. Brittany was close enough to hear Martha's son say, "Sorry, big guy, but those don't work on me," before he grasped the offending hand touching him and, with absolutely no effort, broke it.

She didn't stop to wonder why Corth II was immune to the rods when no other man seemed to be. She was in active mode herself, and went ahead and used her rod on the bodyguard, telling him the same thing she had the other two, though she added for him, "You feel no pain."

Corth II chuckled at that, and told her, "You're too soft, beautiful."

"No, I'm just having a nervous breakdown," she answered in an agitated tone, "since nothing going on here right now makes any sense."

Others were beginning to be of the same opinion. The immobilizing initial shock had worn off, and now gasps, shouts, a general sense of panic were going on—and the loud clash of metal. Brittany turned to see that Dalden and Jorran had engaged in combat, and the audience, not having believed it could possibly have come to that, was reacting normally, some backing away intent on getting the hell out of there, some calling for the police, the newspeople avidly watching, those with cameras shooting the fight.

The people trying to leave the building were in for yet another surprise, no less equal to Brittany's, though, when she noticed the exits to the building were presently blocked. The several men standing there keeping anyone from entering or leaving were just as

tall as Dalden, just as brawny, just as bare-chested, golden-skinned, golden-haired—actually, identical to Dalden except for their facial features, and with sword belts strapped to their hips.

It was the identical part that gave her a clue. She didn't know how they'd done it, but it had to be an illusion, those extra bodies, to make Jorran and his people think the odds had just been upped in favor of the Sha-Ka'anis.

She did what she could to alleviate some of the panic, working her way quickly through the crowd, repeating over and over, "It's a local theater troupe, enjoy the performance, nothing to be alarmed about."

The spectators could now discount any blood they saw as fake. She wished she could as well. She had been deliberately avoiding looking out in the center of the room herself. She still heard the clash of metal on metal, knew they were still at it, but couldn't bear to watch.

She stopped by Corth to demand, "Why don't you help him disarm Jorran and get it over with?"

"He would dismantle me if I presumed to interfere in his personal fight," Corth II replied. "Warriors are touchy about such things."

"Dismantle?" she growled. "I'll dismantle you myself if he gets hurt."

A smile. "As long as there is life, he can be fully repaired."

What an odd way to say doctors could patch you up, if the wounds weren't mortal. His lack of worry should have reassured her. It didn't. And she finally looked toward the center of the room—and wished she hadn't. It was impossible to turn her eyes away now.

Blood *was* splattered on the white floor, though not too much of it, and apparently just Jorran's so far. There was a minor gash on his upper left arm that had cut the silk sleeve and left a red path in the material to his elbow. But most of the blood was coming from his nose and a cut on his cheek, which indicated that the flat of Dalden's sword might have smashed against his face.

Neither injury stopped the whirlwind motion of Jorran's other arm, which held his weapon. It was nonstop, his efforts to slice into Dalden, and with such speed, it was fairly obvious the razor sword weighed next to nothing. But he was having no success yet, because Dalden's arm shields, rather than his own sword, were constantly there to meet the razor blade and slide it off harmlessly to the side.

Dalden was also using his own weapon, just not as one might expect. When Jorran extended his reach too far in his impatience to inflict damage, Dalden grasped Jorran's right wrist to prevent another swing and slammed his own sword against a vulnerable spot, but with the flat of his blade, not the edge. He could have disarmed him. He could have killed him. He cracked ribs and broke noses instead.

"He's just playing with him," Brittany said aloud, some annoyance now mixed in with her worry.

"Yes," Corth II agreed.

"But Jorran isn't."

"No, indeed."

"Then why take the chance that Jorran will get lucky?" she demanded.

"Because he's a warrior."

"So instead of getting the job done by the easiest

and quickest means possible, he's got to do the macho thing instead? That's positively medieval."

"Actually, barbaric would better describe it" was Corth II's reply.

It was said with that cheeky grin of his, as if it were some kind of inside joke she should have grasped. She didn't, and it made Brittany want to hit him, a barbaric impulse of her own. Was she the only one who could see the difference, that macho grandstanding was misplaced when life hung in the balance?

Chapter 27

THEY CAUTIOUSLY CIRCLED EACH OTHER FOR A FEW MO-
ments. Dalden allowed the break, which was what
it was. Jorran was breathing heavily. Sweat beaded his
brow, soaked the silk shirt under his armpits, down
the center of his back and chest. It was hard work, trying to slice someone to bits. Dalden's exertion so far
had been minimal in comparison.

"Surrender is an option you may want to consider,"
Dalden remarked casually.

"Are you offering to do so?" Jorran replied.

"I am not the one losing."

"Nor am I."

"Are you not? Warriors learn from witnessing mistakes. Having seen the effectiveness of your razor
sword, Falon and I both have trained to deflect it."

"Practice does not equate to a razor intent on your life," Jorran smirked.

"True. But nor does your own experience prepare you for a Sha-Ka'ani warrior intent on yours."

Jorran wasn't expecting an aggressive move, when Dalden had shown him only defense thus far. Nor were his reflexes quick enough to avoid being lifted and tossed a dozen feet across the room.

Dalden added when he came to stand over Jorran, "Your fight with Falon was not to the death, from his perspective. Have you realized yet, there is a difference?"

This fight wasn't going to be to the death either, if Dalden could help it, but Jorran didn't need to know that—yet. And he was furious now. The toss had rattled him. It was not something one did to High Kings, tossing them about like so much refuse. The resulting anger was yet another point in Dalden's favor.

Jorran rolled away from him, went immediately on the offensive again. It was nearly a blur, the movement of that razor sword now.

It was finally an effort to keep up with the raging razor. Good. The fight had been too easy up till then. And he didn't want Falon, who was sure to be furious that it was not he facing Jorran here, to feel less able, because his previous fight with Jorran had not been as easy. Of course, Jorran's advantage then was that Falon had tried to use his heavy sword, while Jorran's weighed next to nothing. They knew now how to defeat a razor sword.

The anger was Jorran's downfall. The furious burst of energy it had produced brought him quickly to ex-

haustion. And the moment his swings slowed down, Dalden made his move to end it.

Instead of just deflecting the next swing, he thrust it away from him, throwing Jorran off balance. In quick succession, he then smashed Jorran's kneecap with the flat of his own sword, further unbalancing him, and while Jorran was absorbing the shock of that, Dalden disabled him completely by twisting his right arm behind his back until it broke.

It was overkill. At almost anytime during the fight, he could have snatched the contamination shield and let Martha take over. There would have been no punishment in that, though, merely defeat. Jorran deserved more than that. Dalden now ripped the shield from Jorran's belt and tossed it to Corth II, who smashed the metal in his hands as if it were a wad of paper. Only then did he let Jorran drop at his feet.

"He is yours, Martha."

"N—!" Jorran began to shout, but was gone before he could finish.

"And no meditech for him," Dalden instructed, ignoring the collective gasp that went up in the crowd when Jorran disappeared before their eyes.

"Wasn't planning on it," Martha agreed. "The slap on the wrist he'll get when we take him home isn't nearly enough for what he's done."

"Your silence was appreciated," Dalden felt the need to add, after spending several days with Martha's constant input, wanted or not.

"I know when not to distract, warrior," Martha said in unmistakably smirking tones. "And now you need to gather up all remaining evidence of our presence here, before we depart for our sector of the universe."

"What of the mayor? Is he still under Jorran's control?" Dalden asked.

"He was moved safely back into his office soon after the fight began, but Corth II got to him first with the forget-Jorran suggestions, as well as a few others. Amusing that some of the people present actually thought their mayor was pulling a publicity stunt, since they'd been rod-told that Jorran was the mayor already. Corth II will do a little more clean-up in that regard later today, while we're collecting the rest of the rods from Jorran's people."

"What other evidence, then, do you speak of?"

"Unfortunately, your entire fight was recorded by the news crews. We can't leave these people anything that's beyond their own technology to understand. Those here will discount what they've seen as illusion, like a disappearing act in a magic show, but any experts who could study those tapes would know better. So get rid of the tapes before I take you out of there. There are two of them, from the two shoulder-held cameras. The big television camera you don't need to worry about, it's still inoperative."

Dalden glanced toward the newspeople, but first saw Brittany, standing behind them. She was staring at him as if he weren't real.

"Is my lifemate all right?" Dalden asked Martha, his concern rising.

"She's fine, just a bit amazed over the violence she just watched you dish out. She'll get over it."

"Take her to the ship now, in case I need to get violent again in the recovery of evidence."

"I *really* don't think you're going to have any more trouble, kiddo. These locals are pretty much in awe of

you at the moment. But you're right, the rest of Jorran's crew is going to disappear in seconds, and with her standing among them, she won't be able to help but notice. Better just one nervous breakdown than a bunch of little ones."

"You *will* explain and calm her, yes?"

"Sure I will. Don't give it another thought. She'll be waiting for you in your quarters."

Martha's glib reply, for some reason, was not very reassuring. But the sooner he finished here, the sooner he could see to Brittany himself.

He watched her Transfer, along with Jorran's remaining people. Corth II and the half-dozen warriors at the exits remained, in case they were still needed. He then turned toward the newspeople.

Their cameras were still pointed at him. They tried to back up as he approached them, but there wasn't much room for that. And they were still recording, even when he stopped in front of them.

One of them, though obviously nervous, said, "Man, that's about the best special effects I've ever seen. Want to clean up some?"

A cloth was tossed at him. He looked down at his torso to find what might need cleaning up. He hadn't felt the cut that ran from his upper left side across his abdomen to his right hip until he saw it now. He patted the cloth along the line. It did no good. More blood immediately oozed out to flow down and soak into his jeans.

The cameraman, however, had expected the line and blood to be gone, was staring wide-eyed at the new flow. "That's—real, isn't it?"

Dalden looked back at him, and said only, "I require

the evidence you have recorded. If it can be removed from your camera and given to me, then I will not need to destroy the camera."

"Ah, sure, whatever you want, guy. No problem."

The man couldn't get the film out of his camera and into Dalden's hands fast enough. The other camera holder was still backing away, though not in nervousness. He was apparently looking for an exit. He had no intention of giving up his evidence.

Corth II became a solid, immovable wall at his back. "The big guy requires your film, bud. His option was to not destroy your camera to get it. My option is to not destroy you to get it. Which of us do you wish to deal with?"

"Okay, okay," the man tried, stalling until he could turn around to take a swing at Corth II. Big mistake, that. He ended up with broken knuckles that hadn't budged the face they struck, and wailed, "What the hell is that, a steel plate in your jaw?"

"*Toreno* steel to be exact, and not just the jaw, but the whole body. Welcome to your worst nightmare, friend," Corth II said as he prepared to flatten the guy.

"Enough with the showing off, children." Martha's voice rang out loudly with distinct displeasure. "Must I do *everything* myself?"

Not surprisingly, the heavy video camera disappeared from the man's hand, Corth II disappeared next, then Dalden and the remaining warriors followed. Martha was, after all, capable of doing almost everything herself.

A shocked silence remained in City Hall. It was finally broken by a chuckle from the fellow who still possessed his own camera, minus any film. "I'd sure

like to be there when you try to explain what just happened," he told his friend. "And why you shouldn't have to replace that camera yourself."

"I'm not the only one who saw things poof around here," the other man snarled.

"What you saw was one hell of a performance that you shouldn't have gotten involved in. But if you're lucky, those magic people will return your . . ." There was a pause due to the camera reappearing on the floor between them. "Wanna bet the film's not in it?"

Chapter 28

❦

HE FOUND BRITTANY WRAPPED IN A TIGHT LITTLE BALL on the floor of his quarters aboard the *Androvia*, her back against the padded wall, her face tucked against her raised knees, her long copper hair spread like a cape around her. She didn't look up when the door slid open and then closed behind him. She was rocking slightly, and making sounds of angst.

Dalden felt a constriction in his chest. Her pain was not physical, it was mental, and he wasn't sure how he could help that.

Martha had warned him that the shock from the Transfer had put Brittany into a refusing-to-believe-anything mode. Most people had warning beforehand, knew what Molecular Transfer was, knew it was going to happen prior to it happening. And even if they didn't know it was going to happen, at least they could

guess what had happened to them if they suddenly ended up in a place other than where they had been. That required knowledge of Transfer, which most of the known universe had, all except undiscovered planets like hers.

"Brittany."

She looked up instantly, her dark green eyes wide, full of fear and confusion. But then she shot to her feet, flew at him, clung to his chest. And in a small voice that steadily grew louder, said, "I was beginning to think you weren't real, that I'd dreamed you, too. You are real, aren't you? Tell me you're real!"

"Very real, *kerima*."

"You aren't going to disappear on me again?" she demanded sharply.

"You will never be far from me, not ever. I would not allow it."

She relaxed somewhat, leaned back to stare into his eyes, as if she might find all her answers there. She found none, but she did seem to find the reassurance she'd been in need of. She stepped away from him, agitation now taking the place of her fear, though the confusion was still rampant.

"You've got some explaining to do."

"I know," he agreed.

"You can start by telling me how I got here, and where *here* is."

"Martha has already told you—"

"Don't even think of feeding me that same line of bullshit that she did! It's all been a dream, and I've just woken up from it, right? I can buy that. But how did I get here to begin with, and when? Last night? So everything that happened in City Hall today didn't re-

ally happen, you didn't fight Jorran with swords, didn't get wounded—no, of course you didn't. There's no cut on your chest."

She was staring at his chest triumphantly, thinking she'd just managed to confirm everything she'd just said. "The cut was there, but is now gone," he was forced to tell her. "Such is the amazing ability of a meditech, which I was Transferred into upon arrival here."

"Dalden, are you okay—mentally? You don't really believe that nonsense, do you?"

He smiled at her concern for him. "You were told that all would be revealed to you after our task was completed. The time for answers is now."

"Then start telling me the truth, because this science fiction crap just doesn't wash. And you can start with where we are."

"In my quarters aboard the *Androvia*."

"Aboard as in—on a ship? Quarters without a bed or bathroom? Sure."

In this case, it was much easier to show her than convince her. He took her hand, pulled her over to the Sanitary wall, and pressed a button there. Walls immediately enclosed them in a small area, a toilet and sink slid out, the circular shower rose up from the floor to fill the corner, and a ledge dropped down with other amenities, including access to the dial-up closet. He took a moment to dial a light blue tunic. It was delivered in less time than it took to don it.

While she was staring incredulously at everything that had been revealed, he pressed the button to send it all back into concealment and dragged her over to the other corner of the room. Pressing the button there

slid out new walls, and a section of the floor flipped over, leaving a narrow bed in its place that would adjust in size once someone laid down on it.

These, too, he sent back before he said, "I feel confined here, which is why I do not leave these things out, but send them away until they are needed. I am told it is designed to make these rooms seem bigger than they are."

"I get it," she said, finally looking at him again. "This is a movie studio, right? Props, make-believe stuff that isn't really real."

He sighed. He had known this would not be easy, but he hadn't thought it would be impossible.

"You search for any answer but the truth," he told her.

"Show me *proof*!" She was getting agitated again. "If this isn't a studio made to look like a ship, show me what's outside of it."

"This room has no windows."

"Correction." Martha's voice came through on the audiovisual ship's intercom on the wall, proving she was in standby assistance mode. "Knowing how much you hate being reminded of what you're traveling in, Dalden, the windows were never revealed to you."

The walls began to move again, in Martha's control this time, opening up a long bank of windows made of something other than glass that revealed nothing but water and a lone fish swimming past.

"A submarine?" Brittany said in surprise, but then she frowned and added skeptically, "Or a large tank of water. You call this proof?"

Dalden growled in exasperation. Martha chuckled. "Give it up, kiddo. She doesn't require proof. She al-

ready knows what she's dealing with, she just refuses to accept it, and no amount of words will change that."

"Because aliens are a myth, perpetrated by the UFO craze!" Brittany shouted for Martha's benefit, but then she rounded on Dalden and slapped her palm against his chest. "Look at you, you're flesh and blood, you've got all the right parts in the right numbers, even if you are a bit big. There's nothing alien about you!"

"It pleases me to hear you say so," he replied. "This name you have for off-worlders is only slightly more tolerable than what I am usually called."

"He's referring to the name *barbarian*," Martha supplied. "It's how the rest of the civilized universe views his world, not because of the way his people look, dress, or even that they still fight with swords. It's their overall outlook, their primitive laws, their stubborn adherence to tradition that's outlived its time."

"You are *not* helping, Martha," Dalden said.

"Just telling it like it is, warrior. Why go through this stonewall disbelief twice? Besides, her idea of an alien is something bizarre-looking that isn't humanoid—another reason why she's having trouble grasping reality here. If you looked like the Morrilians with their oversized heads that accommodate their magnificent brains, she'd have no problem pointing at you and saying you're an alien."

Brittany wasn't listening. She was gripping the hair on both sides of her temples and saying to herself, "There has to be a logical explanation for this. There has to be."

Dalden moved to put his arms around her. "*Kerima*, your distress pains me. What must I do to ease it?"

She leaned into him, trying to accept the comfort he

offered. "Just tell me there's a really good reason for lying to me."

"Talk about a double-edged request," Martha said in one of her more distinct you've-annoyed-me tones.

Brittany swung around, searching for Martha's voice, since Dalden was no longer wearing his communicator. "The audiovisual monitor on the wall," he pointed out with a sigh. "She controls the ship, thus she has eyes and ears in every room."

Brittany marched to the monitor on the wall, which was presently blank. "Show yourself to me. I want to see the woman who has the gall to try to convince me I'm on an alien spaceship."

"I'll do better than that," Martha purred.

Dalden stiffened, but before he could warn Martha off, Brittany was Transferred out of the room. He swore, knowing where she'd been taken, and that he couldn't get there in time to prevent Brittany from further shock.

Chapter 29

BRITTANY *WAS* IN SHOCK. IT HAD HAPPENED AGAIN, THAT
moment of tingling, then waking in a completely
new location. Waking? No, she was standing up. Even
if they'd been able to put her to sleep somehow to
move her somewhere else, she wouldn't wake up on
her feet.

It had to be illusions, or perhaps rotating walls.
She'd seen enough moving walls since she got here to
know they had that process down pat and in high
speed, so she could be in the same room, just with new
walls and—and a really big computer console in the
center.

"This is the command center." Martha's voice
seemed to come at her from all sides. "If I weren't here,
this room would be filled with the specialists needed

to run a ship this size, all made obsolete with a Mock II on board. I'm the Mock II, by the way."

"What is a Mock II?" Brittany demanded. "And where are you hiding this time?"

"I'm currently housed in the console you're looking at. That's right, doll, I'm a computer, one of the most highly advanced computers ever created. Dalden let that slip the other day, but fortunately you decided he was just pulling your leg. Not an unrealistic conclusion on your part, since the computers you have on your planet are prehistoric dinosaurs compared to me, and those are all you've had for comparison—until now."

"More bullshit?"

"Your disbelief is wearing thin, child," Martha said with a sigh. "I'm going to make this brief before Dalden barges in here to retrieve you. He's not too pleased with me at the moment. You're causing yourself, and him, a lot of grief over nothing. He did good today. He should be celebrating his victory instead of having to deal with a hysterical woman who can't get past one simple little fact."

"A simple fact!?"

"Why don't you try using the logic you were crying for a few minutes ago? It's rather egotistical of your people to think that your insignificant planet, tucked away in this sector of the universe, is the only planet that supports life. Look at it this way: your solar system has moved into a well-established neighborhood, sorta like the new kid on the block. But there were other systems on the block first so much older than yours that the species in them were exploring far into space while you still had dinosaurs roaming."

"You don't get it. I'd have to be dreaming for this to

be real, but I'm not dreaming. I know I'm not, because I pinched myself and it damn well hurt. So stop trying to mess with my mind."

"We'd have to be pretty cold-blooded to try to pull what you're accusing us of trying to pull. Is that really how you see Dalden?"

Of course she didn't, which was why none of this made sense. There had to be a reason for these lies, but she couldn't hope to guess what it was and was driving herself crazy trying to find a plausible explanation.

"Just take me home already," she said wearily. "My job is done. You've captured your thief. You don't need me anymore. I want to go home."

"It's too late for that. It became too late when Dalden made you his lifemate."

"What the hell does that *mean*?"

"You were already told what it means. You chose to see that as a joke, too. It wasn't. And you're still not taking it seriously yet, but for him, it's about as serious as you can get. You're now his to protect, his to have and to hold, for life. There's no getting out of it, like you people do around here. There's no breaking it. It's a done deal, and it's permanent. So you go where he goes, doll, no ifs, ands, or buts. And where he's going is home to Sha-Ka'an, a planet in the Niva star system, light-years away from here."

"You just slipped up," Brittany said, pouncing on it, and pointing out triumphantly. "Light-years would take more than one lifetime to travel."

In response, chuckling filled the room. "With anything your planet can currently produce, yes, but the rest of the universe runs on different sources of power. This spaceship is powered by gaali stones, the newest

and most impressive known source, so it will only take us a couple of months to get home. But even crysillium, the last, now obsolete power source, was capable of similar speed, as well as the one before that. Your planet hasn't come close to knowing what real power is yet."

"You have an answer for everything, don't you?" Brittany said bitterly.

"'Course I do, I'm a Mock II. We don't stagnate, we grow with age."

"You mean upgrade," Brittany corrected.

"No, my parts can't be replaced, but nor will they ever need to be," Martha recorrected and made a brief attempt at explaining. "Imagine a simulated brain, superpowerful at birth, yet like any brain, capable of maturing. Yes, that means I'm capable of thoughts and decisions just like you, even though I am man-made."

"That's not possible."

"Doll, anything is possible for the Morrilians who created me. They are a *very* old species whose intelligence can be likened to godlike, if you need a comparison. I'm talking genius beyond anything you can imagine, beyond anything most worlds can imagine, even high-tech worlds far more advanced than yours. Ironically, they are a very simple people with few needs other than intellectual, and very nonaggressive, which is fortunate for the rest of the universe. That nonaggression is made part of all Mock IIs before they are sold."

"Sold? You're actually owned by someone?"

"It might help if you stop thinking of me as a person. While that's great for my ego, it's not very factual.

Mock IIs are designed to be compatible with one and only one owner, so all programming is geared to that one individual, and his or her happiness and well-being are our number-one priority.

"My individual is Tedra, Dalden's mother," Martha added. "And her happiness includes her family's, which is why I was sent along on this retrieval trip, not just to recover the Altering Rods but to make sure her son returns home in one piece. Remember her son, the Sha-Ka'ani who has decided that you're the only woman he wants to spend the rest of his life with? Do you *really* think that he would intentionally hurt you by messing with your mind?"

"I'm trying not to think. Thinking right now is going to lead to a nervous breakdown."

"I wouldn't allow that."

"You wouldn't be able to prevent it."

"Sure I would. Or have you forgotten the option I was going to use if Dalden had just had his fun with you and left you behind? You can be made to forget us and everything we've revealed to you. Is that what you want? To never see Dalden again, to have him leave you behind?"

"And the alternative is? To be taken off into deep space? To never return here, never see my family again? That *is* what the bottom line is here, right?"

Martha made a *tsk*ing sound. "One thing that hasn't been mentioned yet is that in the universal scope of things, Dalden's family is about as rich as rich can ever get, for the simple reason that they own the largest gaali stone mine in existence—power that the entire universe is in need of and is willing to pay just about

anything for. So with the right inducement, I'm sure you could convince your lifemate to bring you back occasionally to visit your family."

"I didn't get asked if I want to be his lifemate," Brittany said in a small, resentful voice.

"Warriors never ask. On Sha-Ka'an, it's a male decision that females have no say in. But just out of curiosity, what would your answer have been if you were asked?"

"Before all the rest of this was revealed to me, or right now?"

"Never mind. I'll ask that question again someday, but right now, you'll just say something emotional that has no bearing on your real feelings. Humans tend to do that a lot. Silly of them, and half the time those wrong answers cause even more hurt feelings, all of which could have been avoided with a little honesty up front."

"You have *no* idea what I'm feeling. You couldn't even begin to—"

"Now there's where you're wrong," Martha interrupted in a purring I'm-ready-to-impress-you tone. "You're not used to a computer of my caliber yet, but you'll find that it's pointless to argue or disagree with me, simply because my forte is probabilities. So even if I don't have all available facts to work with, I can still come up with the answers. Let's take yourself for an example."

"Let's not—"

"Too late. I'm proving a point, and I'm a bit hardnosed when points need to be proven. You flipped over the warrior when you first saw him. There was no getting around it, you were hooked. Even thinking

him 'foreign,' which was probably at the bottom of your list for acceptable mates, couldn't detract from the kind of attraction you were in the grips of. You threw up all the standard roadblocks your people favor for stalling the inevitable, but it took no more than a couple of intoxicants for you to break down all barriers and jump in with both feet to a full commitment. And you *did* commit yourself, by the way, which was all the 'yes' he needed to make his own decision to bind you to him for life."

"I'm not *agreeing* with you," Brittany said stiffly and with deliberate emphasis. "But what has any of that to do with now, with this ship, with your ridiculous assertion that you're aliens from outer space?"

"It's off-worlders, doll. That's what we're called. We're no different from your own people from Asia or India. You wouldn't understand their language until you learned it. You wouldn't take to their culture because it's not yours and you naturally prefer your own. But you can visit them and get along with them and might even like their countries and peoples well enough that you want to stay. The only difference between them and us is, instead of hopping over an ocean for a visit, it takes a spaceship for us to do so and vice versa. Besides, it's not that you don't believe any of this, it's that you don't want it to be true. And it's time for the final proof, so you can get around to relaxing and seeing this as an adventure rather than your worst nightmare."

"You want to rip my life to shreds and I'm supposed to find it adventurous?" Brittany snorted.

"You're going to be the first from your world to travel into deep space. You're going to see things that

will astound you. You should be excited by the
prospect, not crying that you want it to all go away.
The facts I have assimilated from your planet show
your species to be much more bold than what you're
showing me."

It was said in a derogatory tone. If the intention had
been to insult, it worked wonders. "What final proof?"
she bit out.

"You might want to have a seat," Martha said, and
one of the chairs in the room that were bound to the
floor turned in Brittany's direction. "And keep an eye
on that wall of observation screens that I'm going to
turn on with brief explanations for each. Biggest and
center is our frontal view. I've been raising us from the
ocean floor while we spoke. No point in hanging
around down there anymore when we have business
to complete on the other side of your moon. We'll be
on the surface in a moment, and then high-speeded
out of visual range of the planet's surface, so *sit*."

Brittany bolted toward the indicated chair and
dropped into it, gripped the arms for dear life.
"There's no seat belt!" she pointed out in a panic.

"What am I, an amateur?" Martha's tone turned aggrieved. "There isn't a pilot born who has a hope of
flying these things better than I. Don't worry about the
speed, doll, I adjust gravity within to accommodate for
it. You'll only feel a slight pull and shift in weight."

The screen had turned on to reveal mostly a torrent
of small bubbles in the water outside. Martha's voice
was heard vaguely echoing distantly in other parts of
the ship, warning anyone else on it that flight was imminent. Another screen lit up, but with a large dark
mass in it that looked like a misshapen rock.

"This ship is capable of disguise, and that's our current one. Nice rendition of a meteor, eh? I believe we even made some of your local newspapers when we arrived."

Brittany's eyes rounded on the computer as she recalled Jan telling her about the meteor that disintegrated just before it would have caused widespread disaster. "There were other UFO sightings last week. You didn't hide yourself in the ocean immediately?"

"That wasn't us. That was Jorran's captain being stupid. Watch the screens, I'm switching to a cloud disguise for the takeoff. Less conspicuous, since rocks are known to drop out of space to the surface of the planet, but not the reverse. And you'll be able to see through it, while anyone else will merely see a dense cloud— for a millisecond, just long enough for them to discount it."

The middle, larger screen revealed the break to the surface of the water, while the smaller screen showed a cloud hovering over the ocean. Another screen came on, showing a bottom view, and the ocean quickly became an entire view of the planet from the sky that steadily shrunk in size as it was surrounded by black space. The main screen now showed the moon steadily growing larger.

Brittany was beyond speech at that point. Had she just been taken off the planet with no hope of being returned to it? Or were these screens she was viewing mere computer-simulated special effects, made to look real?

Chapter 30

"DON'T BACKTRACK ON ME, GIRL," MARTHA SAID IN A sharply annoyed tone, somehow reading Brittany's mind just from her expression. "I've delayed Dalden getting here with the takeoff. He hates takeoffs, hates spaceships, hates space travel, and will be glued to a chair right now just as tightly as you are. His planet is not high-tech, if you haven't gathered that by now, but since they've been discovered, they've been forced to deal with the rest of the universe, which wants one of their resources. Now, you were accepting everything you've been told for a moment. Don't revert back to thinking we're trying to pull one over on you."

"I've seen space movies, Martha, *and* seen how they do the special effects to make them look real."

"And I thought Tedra wrote the book on being stubborn," Martha mumbled, then, in a more perky voice, asked, "How would you like to walk on the moon?"

"Are you out of your mind?"

A chuckle. "There you go mistaking me for a person again. The more apt comment would be 'out of your motherboard.'" Another chuckle. "No, it won't take but a moment to land—there, we've landed. And we just happen to have an emergency exit here in the Control Room that I'm opening—"

"Wait! Don't do that! Don't I need a spacesuit? The atmosphere isn't breathable—"

"Not to worry, kiddo. This battleship is capable of landing on any planet, no matter what it's made of, and creating its own air. I've released a domed shield around the ship and filled it with a breathable substance. Go ahead, the platform extending out from the door works like an elevator to lower you to the surface, currently in single-person length. It can be further extended to accommodate up to thirty people comfortably. The enclosing handrails will retract as soon as it touches ground, so you can get off."

Brittany stepped to the doorway. She didn't step on the short platform. Some twenty or thirty feet below was the surface—of the moon. She began to laugh, and only half hysterically. The moon, and she was within mere feet of it. A few rocky bumps, a few dents, but otherwise a flat gray surface lit almost white by the overhead lights on the dome. Beyond was infinite black space—the sun didn't reach this side of the moon. But inside, the dome was well-lit. It was a large dome, mammoth. It encompassed a really big ship.

"You're not going outside?"

"No, I'd rather our astronauts hold that distinction. They went through hell to get up here, while you make it seem like mere child's play."

"Sweetie, you're comparing apples and oranges. This battleship, which makes this seem like child's play to you, was designed by a people that have been in existence for more than twelve million years. How many years have your people been evolving? Look at your own age of inventions. In just a few hundred years, just about all the known improvements of your world came into being: electricity, flight, mass communication, convenient travel, and so forth. Look at your history and what you had available prior to these inventions. And imagine what you will create a thousand years from now. Your people are progressing normally; they are just still young compared to some of the worlds in other solar systems. If it's any consolation, there are other worlds out there younger than yours that haven't advanced nearly as far as yours has."

Brittany glanced back at the console. "Really?"

"Most definitely. Take Jorran's planet, Century III, for instance. Medieval in government, advancement, and mentality. They've been discovered, could buy modernization, but prefer their feudal way of life and a government that favors only a select few, the ruling house. And until those High Kings get toppled in revolution, nothing will change there. Another thousand years could pass and they'd still be medieval.

"Jorran is one of those High Kings of Century III, but the only one without his own kingdom," Martha continued. "It was his intention, with the rods he stole from the planet Sunder, to make your country his

kingdom first, then your entire world. He might have succeeded. The Sunderans haven't reached the space age yet, either, so they couldn't track Jorran down to retrieve their rods. We just happened to be passing by on our way home and picked up their distress call— and knew Jorran for the jerk he is, so we decided to put *canceled* to his plans. Our good deed for the century, you could call it."

"So you didn't have to come after him?"

"No, indeed. But by the time the proper authorities could have been notified to pursue him, he would have been long gone. And even if they could have found him eventually, the damage would have been done. We already had him on tracking, were able to follow him, were the only ones who had a chance of stopping him before he ruined too many lives."

"And Sha-Ka'an?" Brittany said. "How does it fit in the age of development?"

"Sha-Ka'an is unique. It's not really barbaric, that's just a convenient name the modern worlds give it. It's perfected some crafts beyond manufactured quality without the pollution of factories, has an ancient formula for making the strongest steel ever created that even a laser can't penetrate, has palatial-like architecture in some of its cities, regulates birth control as well as sexual aggression, treats gold like you would common metals—"

"How can they regulate sexual aggression?"

Martha chuckled. "With another thing unique to their planet, the *dhaya* plant. The juice made from it will put even the strongest sex drive on temporary hold, and no amount of stimulation can break through

its effect until it wears off naturally. In wine form it will prevent pregnancy."

Brittany frowned. "Why would they want to do away with sexual aggression?"

"Hold up, you've gotten the wrong impression. *Dhaya* juice is only taken in certain situations, when the warriors go off to hunt alone—and when they raid."

Brittany made a face. "Are we getting to the part that gives them their 'barbarian' label?"

"You betcha—at least, part of it. There's a difference, though, from what you're thinking. You hear the word *raid* and associate it with killing, pillage, mayhem. That's not what Sha-Ka'ani warriors are about. They don't go to war with each other. There are a lot of countries, each with their own leaders, but all in all, they consider themselves one. Raiding for them is sport, something fun to do. They'll go in, take something from their neighbor, try to keep it, but if the neighbor raids and retrieves it, they'll shrug and say well done."

"So it's just a game to them?"

"That's one way to put it. As for the other reasons for the label they wear, I've already mentioned it's a cultural thing, the way they view things and view themselves, the antiquated laws they uphold. These things differ slightly per country, yet one thing is universal on the planet. Warriors treat each other as equals, but treat their women like children."

"Excuse me?"

"You have enough to assimilate for now without getting into the things that still drive my Tedra nuts.

And Dalden will be here in about five seconds. He'll be glad to know you no longer think you're dreaming."

"Like children?" Brittany persisted. "You were joking, right?"

No answer, and the main door to the Control Room slid open to reveal seven feet of very annoyed male.

Chapter 31

DALDEN WAS REALLY ANGRY, THOUGH BRITTANY WAS A bit surprised that she could actually tell that, since it wasn't revealed in his expression. It was more that she sensed it, or maybe just that she was expecting it, after Martha had warned that he was annoyed.

He walked into the room, took her hand, and started walking out, dragging her with him. He didn't pause as he told the computer, "You have interfered with a warrior and his lifemate. You know that is unacceptable, Martha."

"Beneficial interference is acceptable," Martha disagreed. "Besides, since when do I ask permission when something needs doing? It's not as if there's a way to stop me, or that anyone using *common sense* would want to, when my actions calculate all Probables beforehand."

"Is there not?"

"Not what?"

"A way to stop you."

"Tedra would never agree to pull my plug," Martha replied in smirking tones.

"My mother is still answerable to my father. Would he hesitate?"

"Now just a minute . . . Dalden, come back here!"

He didn't, nor was it necessary for him to even stop, since Martha's voice followed them down a wide corridor and into an elevatorlike cubicle whose door closed, then immediately opened again to reveal a different corridor, this one with a slight curve to it. There had been no movement of the cubicle; at least, Brittany had felt no movement of the thing, yet it had apparently transported them elsewhere on the ship . . . oh, God, she really was starting to believe—everything.

"It's a good thing, actually, that it's going to take us nearly three months to get home." Martha's voice continued to follow them from each wall monitor they passed, every twelve feet or so along the corridor. "Plenty of time for you to settle into your commitment and possibly even get over some of the anticipated hurdles."

Mentioning expected problems didn't work to stir Dalden's curiosity, though it sure did Brittany's. He said merely, "Warriors have long memories."

"More's the pity," Martha mumbled, and then said, "It worked, by the way, which is the bottom line, if you haven't figured that out yet. *You* certainly weren't getting anywhere in the convincing department. And what's more important: that she accept what you are and where you come from, or that she continue to

think you were lying to her, which was going to put a big dent in the recent bonding you did?"

He stopped at that point to look down at Brittany, wanting confirmation. "Do you?"

She knew what he was asking her, and although she would have liked to relieve his mind, since he did seem to be worried about whether she believed them or not, she had to consider her own peace of mind first. And there *were* other explanations, albeit elaborate, incredibly expensive ones, yet ones much more palatable than that she was traveling into deep space. When she thought of what it must have cost to create a studio big enough to give her the impression that she was looking out at the surface of the moon when she'd looked through that door . . . it simply boggled the mind, the effort these people were going to in order to fool her.

Or maybe it wasn't just her; maybe there were other people being put through the same program. She'd hate to think all this trouble was being wasted on just one person, such subtle details, a new view behind every door, out every window. Was she a test subject? Had Dalden blown it by getting involved with her when he shouldn't have? Martha had certainly made enough complaints about that involvement, and enough predictions that it just wouldn't work, to stop it before it got started. But Dalden got involved anyway. . . .

"No," Brittany said, causing Martha to make a snorting sound of disgust, and Dalden to frown in confusion. She added tonelessly, "That's not to say I don't think that the reason for this elaborate deception isn't for my own good, which is why I'm going to ac-

cept it for now and trust that at least your emotions are real—"

"What emotions?" Martha cut in. "Don't tell me you haven't noticed yet that he doesn't have any."

"Excuse me? Everyone has emotions. You told me yourself that he was annoyed."

"Actually, that was an understatement on my part. He was furious, still is, but you'll never see a Sha-Ka'ani warrior stomping around mad to prove it. A Ba-Har-ani warrior, maybe. The ones from his country pride themselves on absolute calm under any circumstances, which means they've done away with the more common emotions that might interfere with that calm."

"Sure, if you say so," Brittany replied.

That got a chuckle out of Martha, but Dalden was more concerned with her "no." "I fail to understand. How can you not believe, yet be accepting?"

"It's called humoring, Dalden," Martha put in. "In other words, while she's not going to give any credit to what she sees or hears, she's going to smile and go along with it all. She's decided it doesn't matter. Actually, she *does* know better; she'd just prefer to decide it doesn't matter."

It was absolutely uncanny, the way Martha could analyze and dissect someone's thoughts and motives from just a few spoken words, like a psychiatrist guessing right the first time around. Brittany had to keep in mind that these people had probably done this before, knew just what to expect, and so had answers for everything already prepared. But given enough thought, she could come up with answers for everything as well, from a different, more believable slant.

She just couldn't come up with a good reason why she was being put through this program. Some not so good reasons, yes, but not a really good one. If she were a scientist or someone in a position of power, then yes, it might be for national security reasons or something similar, to see if she could be tricked into revealing secrets or joining their cause or whatever. But she was just an average person, so why would they need to mess with *her* mind? What, after all, could she do for them or tell them, if they did manage to get her to believe what they were trying to?

"You do not dispute what Martha said," Dalden finally remarked. "Is it true?"

"That I'm humoring you?" Brittany replied uncomfortably. "I prefer to think of it as keeping my sanity, so how 'bout we give it a rest for today, okay? I've been fed enough for one sitting, more than I can stomach. I'm here, I'll listen, I'll probably even ask questions. And I'll ooh and aah when I should. But—no more today. I'm mentally exhausted, and stressed beyond coping."

"She's only slightly exaggerating, Dalden, but she *could* use some form of relaxant—either a round or two of lovemaking, or a visit to the massager unit in the ship's gym. My Tedra swore by the latter, until she got introduced to the former. In our Brittany's case, though, I'd say the latter for the time being would be more appropriate. No point in testing her resolve at the moment on what she's going to believe or not. And since you are part and parcel of what gets believed or not, you'll avoid any hurt pride on your end by practicing hands-off for now."

The blush that had started with that "round or two

of lovemaking" was gone by the time Martha finished. Brittany groaned inwardly. She had already considered how Dalden would feel about her disbelief if *he* believed all this, but she hadn't given it any in-depth thought, really—until now. He'd see it as a lack of trust, obviously, which could cause a really big breach between them, and one that wouldn't be crossable unless one of them changed opinions.

She didn't want to lose him, but damn it all, had she even had him to begin with, or was that just part of the program, too? It was beyond comprehensible that she might have been seduced, her emotions deliberately tied up in knots, all as part of the program or whatever the hell it was these people were trying to accomplish.

"I'm reading higher levels of upset, Dalden. Take her to the massager unit *now*."

Chapter 32

BRITTANY HAD NEVER EXPERIENCED ANYTHING QUITE like it. She'd splurged and treated herself to a fifty-dollar massage once, after the completion of one of the more grueling jobs she'd worked on. She'd had the kinks worked out of her body in a most painful manner and had come away from that experience thinking that massages sucked, that causing more pain to forget about current pain just didn't work for her. Yet by the next day, all those kinks had been gone. This was nothing like that. This was total, 100 percent relaxation, an absolute pleasure, and she was sorry when the lid finally opened, asking her silently to get out.

She'd been afraid to get into it. It reminded her of a coffin, or more precisely, a sarcophagus, since it was shaped like a body. There were quite a few of them in the large gym, and dozens of other exercise machines

that she'd never seen the like of before either. She knew all the current best-of-the-best equipment available, yet nothing in this gym was familiar.

As for the massager, Dalden had assured her that she would enjoy the experience. He also complained that he couldn't demonstrate it for her, since they didn't make them in models long enough to fit him. Last, he assured her that if she wanted out of it before it was finished with her, she need only press up on the lid to have it open.

She'd had no trouble breathing after the top had closed on her, sealing her inside the box. That had really been her main hesitation about getting in. And then hundreds of little rollers and skin-pressers moved over her body from head to toe, above and below her, in a gentle, thorough massage. She had felt the tension leaving her body, the stress flowing out with it, felt so utterly loose and relaxed that she wasn't sure she'd be able to stand up.

When she got out she found that Dalden hadn't stuck around for a well-deserved "I told you so." But standing there apparently waiting on her was one of the loveliest women she'd ever encountered in person, the stuff models were made of, a face meant for the front page of magazines. Blonde, amber-eyed, golden-skinned and not quite as tall as Brittany, but taller than average. She was wearing a white one-piece jumpsuit that looked like a uniform and fit like a second skin, in a thin, stretchy material. She was also wearing a very friendly smile, even though her eyes were avidly curious.

Brittany was just as curious, and asked, "Who are you?"

The smile got wider. "My name is Shanelle Van'yer. Dalden didn't mention me?"

Brittany stiffened, ruining a good portion of the work that the massager had just done on her. "No, he didn't. Should he have?"

"I suppose not. I've been dying to meet you, though. I could not be*lieve* it when Martha told me that Dalden had chosen his lifemate. And after knowing you for only two days! Such impulsiveness just isn't in his genes."

"You know him well, then?"

"Shanelle, sweetie." Martha's voice interjected from one of the wall monitors across the room. "You might want to take a precautionary step or two back before she socks you one, because she's about as livid with jealousy as a humanoid can get at the moment."

Shanelle merely frowned. "Jealous? Why?"

Martha was quick to answer in one of her drier tones, "Possibly because you didn't make clear that you're a relation of Dalden's rather than a fun-sharing companion."

It was an utter exaggeration that she was livid with jealousy, but it still had Brittany blushing profusely, because she had just experienced some serious, but apparently unwarranted, negative emotion.

"A relation?" she asked.

"His sister, or to be more exact, his twin."

"Sister?" Brittany said hollowly, and her blush got ten times worse.

The beautiful Shanelle gave her a beautiful smile. "His only sibling, for that matter. Our father decided two of us were enough after our mother went through hell having us. Not that it was a really difficult deliv-

ery for her, just that they don't deliver babies where she comes from, so it was an experience she couldn't really relate to on any level."

Brittany stared at her. It was on the tip of her tongue to ask for a detailed explanation, but she decided there was no way an explanation was going to make sense.

Instead she said, "I think I'll have another round in this massager."

"The machine knows when you've had enough, can sense it by the looseness of your muscles, in the same way it senses the tightness, to know which areas need the most work. It won't operate on you again until you need it to work on you. It doesn't operate on 'want.' In that respect, it's like a meditech unit."

"What's that, a doctor in a box?"

"I know you were being sarcastic there, but that's pretty much exactly what a meditech unit is. It's one of the crowning achievements of Kystrani scientists. They're pretty expensive, so they haven't made the medical profession completely obsolete, since not all planets can afford them. Those that can tend to have one or more units in each town. Most ships also have a unit on them, except for the smaller traders. A battleship like this one would of course have quite a few."

"What exactly are we—you—talking about?" Brittany demanded.

Shanelle frowned. "Martha gave me a Sublim tape on your language. I thought I had it down pat. Wasn't I making sense to you?"

"I understood every word. I just don't know what you're talking about."

"The doctor in a box, that ring a bell?"

"That's ridiculous."

"No, it's called a meditech unit."

"Okay, I'll bite for the moment," Brittany said with a sigh. "What's it do?"

"Everything except bring life back—and deliver babies. It does everything a doctor can do, just a whole lot quicker. It accelerates the healing process to such an extent that it's almost instantaneous. It cures disease, mends bones and ripped skin and muscle, is so thorough in fixing anything that's abnormal that even old scar tissue gets erased."

"Do you realize what you're describing is nothing short of miraculous?"

Shanelle shrugged. "If it helps, a lot of worlds agree with you—or rather, disbelieve, just like you. Sha-Ka'an was the same, but it's kinda hard to dispute when you actually see someone injured beyond repair, about to die, and then after a Transfer to a meditech they are back to perfect health. It's so miraculous that the Sha-Ka'ani, who want absolutely nothing to do with off-world inventions and high technology, ordered at least one meditech unit for each of their towns. If something can save your life when nothing else can, that's worth having around, isn't it?"

"Sure," Brittany agreed. "If something like that really exists."

Shanelle grinned at her. "Let's hope you never need to find out."

"No, why don't we prove it to me instead."

Shanelle blinked. "You want to get injured just to experience something firsthand? I *really* don't think Dalden would allow that."

"You said it erases scars, didn't you? Well, I'm

loaded with them—no biggies, but lots of little ones, a hazard of my profession."

"She's got you there, kiddo," Martha's voice purred from across the room. "Take her to Medical. This ought to be interesting."

Brittany wasn't sure she wanted to go now. If Martha was all for it, then there must be some new trick awaiting her there. The massager had been nice, but she wouldn't be surprised if something like that had been invented already but just wasn't on the market yet for the general public. But this so-called meditech was about as believable as a spaceship was.

She followed Shanelle anyway. Curiosity was human nature, as well as walking eyes-open into traps because of it. So what would they tell her when she still had her scars afterward? That the machine was currently malfunctioning, or that the scars were too old to be erased?

There was a row of them in the pristine white room called Medical, but no technicians around to operate them. They were longer than the massager, wider, deeper, and really did resemble oversized coffins. Brittany almost balked at getting into one of them. This was ridiculous. The thing *couldn't* do what they said it could. Yet this was her idea; she couldn't back down from it now. Well, she could, but she preferred to not give a cowardly impression if she could help it.

The lid on the closest one opened automatically as soon as she got near it. The unit was low to the floor, the bottom about the height of a couch, easy to sit down and stretch out in. It was padded on all sides, and not as deep as its size seemed to indicate. Consid-

ering that there wasn't much depth to the lid either,
they would probably only accommodate lean people,
which was pretty silly when you considered people
came in all sizes and shapes.

"What happens when people with a weight problem need to use one of these?" she asked as she cautiously laid down on the one that had opened for her.

"I mentioned they aren't designed to deal with
pregnancies, didn't I?"

"I mean just your average person who likes to eat
too much."

"Ohhh, well, I suppose they would need to lose
some weight first."

"And die in the meantime?"

Shanelle smiled. "The world that created these is a
world that no longer uses its animal resources, the few
it has left anyway, for food purposes. They subsist on
food that has the texture, taste, and look of the real
stuff, but it's not real, and it's virtually impossible to
become overweight on such a regulated, nutritious
diet."

"But you also said these get sold to other worlds—
have they all conquered obesity?"

"No, indeed, but can you imagine a better incentive
to keep your body healthy? I'm sorry, that was a rather
tasteless bit of humor. Actually, most of the higher advanced worlds have 'conquered,' as you put it, such
health problems, if not through government regula-
tion then with simple intelligence and an appreciation
of a healthy environment. Then, too, you have mili-
taristic worlds that keep fit for other than health reasons. Either way, once a world has been discovered,
they can opt to advance their way of life, or continue to

progress normally. The League of Confederated Planets has a strict policy of noninterference if a planet opts for the latter."

"But why would anyone refuse such—miracles—if they were offered?"

"For any number of reasons, including ingrained culture, ignorance, natural distrust of off-worlders—" Laughter circled, echoed about the room from the many wall monitors, causing Shanelle to make a face before adding, "Okay, and warrior stubbornness."

"I think she was being amused by *my* distrust," Brittany said, making a face of her own.

Shanelle just grinned. "Don't kid yourself, kiddo. The Sha-Ka'ani have other worlds beat hands down when it comes to *not* liking off-worlders and off-world inventions."

Shanelle stepped back then, and the lid closed on Brittany. Panic flared, but didn't last long. Once again she was completely encased in one of their machines, but this one was simply like a soft heat that moved around her, passing over all her limbs, a tingle here and there, and then the lid popped open again.

Brittany frowned as she sat back up. No more than a few seconds had passed, barely enough time to hear the low hum on the machine as it came to life and to feel that gentle heat surrounding her. Just as she'd figured. They were going to claim the thing had malfunctioned.

She beat them to it. "Not working, huh?"

Shanelle frowned at her. "Why? You still have some scars left?"

Expecting excuses, Brittany hadn't even thought to look down for proof. She glanced at her left hand, the one that had suffered the most injuries during the

years she'd been learning her craft. She looked at both sides of it. Then she brought it up in front of her face for closer examination.

Her expression must have mirrored her incredulity, because Martha, viewing the room from the wall unit across from her, complained, "Oh, sure, I offer her a walk on the moon and she's still skeptical, but one little visit to a meditech and she enters 'have to believe it' mode."

Brittany snapped her jaw shut and gritted her teeth. "It's hypnosis, isn't it? The scars are still there, you've just convinced my mind not to see them."

"Hey, I'm impressed," Shanelle said with a chuckle. "That's a really good logical deduction if you're determined to doubt. But let's hope we don't need the meditech to prove any more points. Shall we adjourn to the Rec Room now? Dalden's probably done with Jorran by now and wondering why you're not where he left you."

Brittany had forgotten all about Jorran. "That egomaniac is behind lock and key, I hope?"

"Better than that, he's in a containing cell. It doesn't have doors, windows, or any other means to get out of it without Transfer. A very luxurious suite, actually, which in *my* opinion he doesn't deserve. But we don't mistreat prisoners, we just make sure those needing isolation get it. Though Martha has been Transferring his people aboard—they've all elected to travel with Jorran, rather than return home on their ship—they aren't going to be allowed to speak with him during the journey and are being delivered to an unused portion of the ship where they'll be kept happy but out of the way. Putting him with them would just be asking

for trouble. How's the collection going anyway, Martha?"

"Two rods left unaccounted for," Martha replied. "But two of Jorran's people haven't checked in yet to know he's been captured. Current estimate is another three hours before we can depart."

"The captain of Jorran's ship is being very cooperative," Shanelle explained as they headed out of Medical. "Once he got a look at the battleship hovering over him, he gave the exact coordinates for the remaining Centurians on his ship, wanting them all *off* it immediately, and he's making every effort to find the remaining two still down on the planet."

"Then he's not a Centurian himself?"

"No, it's just a simple trader with a full crew that Jorran hired to transport him to his new 'kingdom.'"

They had arrived at the Rec Room. It was a really big room, designed to entertain the ship's crew in their off-duty hours. This ship had Martha, rather than a crew, but the Rec Room was filled with men anyway—nearly fifty of them, and all huge like Dalden.

"You aren't going into shock again, are you?" Shanelle asked with concern. "Weren't you told that there were other Sha-Ka'ani here?"

"I don't—recall."

"These are my father's warriors, sent along to protect my mother on her trip to Kystran. We were on our way home from that planet when we got the distress call from Sunder. Mother insisted the warriors accompany us, and went home alone." Shanelle's voice rose to reach Martha amid the noise in the room, even though there was a wall monitor right behind them.

"Assure me again, Martha, that the Probables say she *didn't* get punished for that?"

"Stop fretting, doll," Martha replied. "You know your father is more understanding than that."

"Except when it comes to the protection of his lifemate," Shanelle said in rising agitation.

"Punished?" Brittany choked out.

"You don't want to know," Shanelle replied before she stomped off, really upset now.

"*Martha?*" Brittany demanded, her own upset getting out of hand.

But Martha just purred, "She was right, you don't want to know. Besides, Shanelle typically overreacts whenever she thinks her mother has earned her father's displeasure. In this case she's dead wrong, but there'll be no convincing her of that till she gets home and sees for herself." And then Martha added, "But why get into the oddities and peculiarities of a people you don't believe exist?"

Brittany opened her mouth to protest, then snapped it shut. She *did* want to know what they'd meant by punishment, but she'd be damned if she'd ask now. The Sha-Ka'ani didn't exist, she wasn't in a spaceship, none of this was the least bit real. But where the hell did they find *fifty* giants to participate in this bizarre scam?

Chapter 33

⊙

"TEDRA ISN'T FROM SHA-KA'AN?"

"No indeed, she was hatched on the planet Kystran in the Centura star system, which is fortunate for you, doll. I'm sure she'll set you up with all the modern conveniences from other worlds that she enjoys, which most Sha-Ka'ani refuse to introduce to their daily lives. Kystran is a major exporter of luxuries, a member of the Centura League of Confederated Planets."

Brittany had settled into a chair near the entrance to the Rec Room, with a monitor on the wall behind her. She wasn't about to proceed any farther into that room with all those giants lounging about, and Dalden not among them. She had felt the chair move under her when she sat on it, shrinking somewhat, but wasn't going to comment on it.

Martha was less reticent, had remarked nonchalantly, "The beds here adjust to size as well, just so you know. When you're ready to crawl into one usually isn't the time for such explanations."

Brittany hadn't thanked her for the warning. She'd been too busy trying to keep down her unease of being in a room with so many huge men. Those men were ignoring her for the most part, but that didn't reassure her one bit. Some were watching what looked like war movies on really big screens. Others were involved in wrestling matches. Still others were exercising on mats. Actually, most of them were doing things that should have been done in the gym instead. . . .

"They hate the gym," Martha said, back to reading minds. "It's filled with things that are foreign to them, and like Dalden, none of them really like things that are unnatural to their own world. They'll play the war games on the ship's entertainment system, because they understand they are just games, but when it comes to workouts, they'll do it their own way. They'd be practicing with swords like they do at home if I hadn't forbid it."

Swords—warriors. Brittany still found it incredulous that they'd found this many huge men for this convince-at-no-expense project. All of them were over six and a half feet; one looked even taller than seven!

She had mentioned Dalden's mother to get her mind off what she was viewing. And much as she didn't want to appear curious, she couldn't let that "hatched" comment pass.

"Are you going to try to convince me now that your Tedra isn't human?"

"Put the brakes on," Martha said, injecting surprise in her tone. "Where'd you get that from?"

"Your 'hatched' instead of born. Either you don't know that 'hatched' implies a hard-shelled egg, which I doubt, or you were being cute to confuse the issue."

A good bit of soft chuckling floated about Brittany. "Can't deny I do have my 'cute' moments." More chuckling. "But I was just calling it like it is in this case. Kystrani are a species so far advanced that they long ago did away with natural childbirth as you know it."

"They couldn't have. They'd be extinct, yet you don't talk of them in the past tense."

"They did almost come to extinction during the Great Water Shortage many years ago. They lost most of their plant and animal life, but didn't abandon the planet. They are one of many colony planets founded by the original Ancients more than two thousand years ago, so they got a lot of help from their sister planets. They adapted because of the shortage, created waterless baths, new food sources, oxygen, liquid, and with the bad comes the good. They now have the technology to populate barren, resource-deprived planets."

"You get an A-plus in distraction, Martha."

"Now who's being cute? And I wasn't avoiding the subject, merely supplying a little history. They've done away with natural childbirth for the simple reason that it's painful and dangerous. It also isn't selective breeding, and Kystrani prefer to cultivate intelligence that can better their way of life."

"But how?"

"Give it a little thought," Martha replied, "and your

best guess would probably be right, since your own planet is starting to experiment in the same area."

"Cloning?"

"Close. You call it artificial insemination. The Kystrani took that one step further by eliminating the female from being the holding tank, using man-made artificial wombs instead. Add to that worldwide birth control that's not left to individual choice, but administered in all food and drink on the planet, and donors from only the most intelligent. The whole process is monitored by Population Control. The children are then raised in Child Centers, where they are tested to determine their best match for life careers."

"It sounds very—cold."

"Tedra would agree with you. Child Centers teach everything a child needs, they just don't supply what only a child's parents could. Tedra had to go to Sha-Ka'an for that missing ingredient."

"You're talking about love, right?"

"You betcha."

"Then you're contradicting yourself," Brittany was quick to point out. "Or didn't you just try to convince me awhile ago that the Sha-Ka'ani have their emotions mastered to near nonexistence?"

"The males do, not the females," Martha clarified. "But I'm going to let you in on a little secret. Warriors truly are convinced that they can't love. Caring, yes, but not the deeper emotion of love. But my Tedra upset that notion all to hell with her lifemate, Challen. He loves her to pieces even though he tried to deny it to begin with. It was what she was missing in her life, so you don't think that *I* would have let her stay there with him if he wasn't going to supply it in big doses,

do you? But she had to almost die before he owned up to it. So expect a lot of frustration if you're going to try to make your warrior admit it."

"Thanks tons," Brittany said. "Just what I needed to hear."

"Now, don't get discouraged, doll. I like you. I'm not going to steer you wrong. And I've just given you a major advantage where your warrior is concerned: he might try to convince you that it's impossible for warriors to love, but you now know that isn't so. Just don't push it, would be my advice. He's Tedra's son, after all, which makes him quite a bit different from other Sha-Ka'ani, so he's likely to figure it out on his own, whereas most pure Sha-Ka'ani never do. Their own women don't buck the way things are. It takes off-worlders to stir things up and show them that ingrained beliefs aren't always what's real."

"So my role is to be teacher?"

Martha laughed. "That's a good one, and not even close. These men don't take to learning new ways, they think their way is the best way. I said show, not teach, and I meant *your* lifemate, not the whole planet. Tedra has tried to change things there, with little luck. Believe me, she hates their rules and laws just as much as you will. But you're stuck with them because *their* women don't mind them—yet. Your own people have followed the same path, subject to a male-dominated society up until they finally got tired of being treated like children and did something to change it. Sha-Ka'ani women just haven't reached that point yet."

"Talking to you, Martha, can be really depressing. God, I'm glad none of this is really real."

Martha sighed. "If it's any consolation, Tedra has been *very* happy with her warrior all these years. She wouldn't want to live anywhere but with him."

"In other words, she got converted to their ways rather than them learning from hers."

"No way. She just knows when to ignore things she can't change—and help where she can. She's gotten quite a few of their women off-planet and living where they can feel useful and needed."

"Which is the wrong thing to do. It takes dissatisfaction to want change. If she's shipping off the ones who aren't happy there, nothing will ever get changed."

Martha was back to chuckling. "I know that, and obviously you know that, but my Tedra needs to feel that she's doing something for those people, so *we* aren't going to point that out to her."

"To coin a phrase of yours, wanna bet?"

"So you're going to stir the pot?"

"You could always return me to my home instead," Brittany suggested.

Martha chuckled. "Blackmail?"

"Bargaining."

"You keep forgetting that you're dealing with a computer who can tell you exactly the end of that scenario. I send you home, I even take Dalden back to Sha-Ka'an without you, since there's no choice in the matter of who flies this ship. But then we have one very angry warrior, and one very angry Challen who will agree I overstepped my bounds. So I probably get unplugged, and Dalden gets another ship and comes to collect you, because there *is* no getting away from your lifemate. So at the most you've saved your-

self from this horrid new life you're imagining for six months, then get taken to Sha-Ka'an anyway, but with an angry lifemate rather than one who is presently going to go out of his way to please you. Now I ask you, which option is going to be more to your benefit?"

"Oh, shut up and go away."

"I can't go away. The best I can do is offer silence. But then you'll just sit there and brood about everything you *don't* believe, and since arguing with me is more healthy than brooding, guess which you get?"

"I'm not Tedra," Brittany nearly snarled. "I'm *not* your responsibility."

" 'Course you are. When Dalden made you his lifemate you became part of Tedra's family, and I think we've already covered this ground. Her family, every member of it, falls into my sphere of responsibility. She's a very caring woman. She gets upset when her personal people aren't happy. She feels their pain."

"So who gets priority when two of her 'people' are unhappy with each other?"

"Priority is given to the best-choice conclusion with all variables involved," Martha replied. "That may mean someone will have to bend a little, but compromise is necessary in many disagreements."

"Why do I get the feeling that I'll be the someone who has to bend?"

"Not even close, doll. I've known Dalden all his life and you not even a week, but keep in mind I said best-choice conclusion. Dalden has been due for some bending. He strives to follow only the one path, ignor-

ing half of his nature. This has caused him a lot of unnecessary grief that I'd like to see end. He'll be happier with himself, with who he is, once he accepts that he's not just a Sha-Ka'ani warrior."

Chapter 34

BRITTANY DID GET TO BROOD SOME, FOR ALL OF TEN MIN-utes. That was about all she could stomach of try-ing to assimilate all the fantastical information Martha had thrown at her. There was simply too much of it, too many bizarre inventions, too many advanced con-cepts mixed in with the barbaric. And even that didn't make sense. If there were such advanced, godlike worlds such as Morrilia, why weren't they educating the primitive worlds? Why leave them to struggle in ignorance?

But none of it was true. Whoever had designed this program she'd been unlucky enough to get picked for had a really strange imagination. Or maybe it was just Martha, instructed to improvise as needed, who had the overactive imagination. And where did that leave her? Imprisoned on this so-called ship for nearly three

months? Then what? Taken to some remote area that they had set up to convince her she was on another planet?

Somehow she doubted they planned to invest three full months on just one test subject. There was probably a time limit, a couple of weeks, a month at the most, to either convince her or admit it was all a farce and send her home—without Dalden.

Her heart constricted. He was one of them, part of the program. Work on the heart as well as the mind? God, she hoped not. She'd rather think their involvement hadn't been counted on, that at least *that* part of it was real.

But she still wasn't going to get to keep him when this was over. And she had to decide whether to cut that string to her heart now, before it got any stronger—or enjoy him while she had him. But hadn't she already decided to savor their time left, to stockpile the memories, anticipating that their time together *would* end? Of course, that was a decision made before their program went into full gear.

"Where is Dalden?"

"Done brooding already?" was Martha's reply.

Brittany sighed. "Tired of the headache already. Where's Dalden?"

"He's calmly assumed the role of ambassador and is presently explaining to Jorran why his demands aren't going to be met. I'm amazed he hasn't lost patience yet. Jorran's overwhelming arrogance is hard to stomach by any species."

"I suppose you've been listening in on them?" Brittany remarked.

"I'm capable of following *and* participating in every

conversation going on in this ship at any given moment," Martha boasted. "Computers aren't single-tasked like you humans, you know."

Brittany allowed herself a satisfying snort before suggesting, "How about directing me to him? I'd prefer not to stay—here."

"These warriors aren't going to bother you, doll." Martha went back to reading minds. "You're off-limits to them because they know who you belong to."

"I don't belong to anyone. Must you make it sound like slavery?" And then the thought struck her. "*Is* there slavery there?"

"Yes, in a few of the more distant countries. But before you go getting bent out of shape over that, kindly remember that there's still slavery in some of the far corners of your own world, and it was widely accepted just a couple of hundred years ago in your own country."

Brittany thumped her head mentally for even asking. Barbaric in the eyes of "most of the universe" would of course include things like slavery. A logical deduction. And much easier to convince the nonbeliever if the tall tale followed a logical path.

But Brittany proved just how single-minded humans were by repeating, "Directions? Or is there some reason I must stay here?"

"Out the door and right to the lift at the end of the hall. It's voice activated—or controlled by me." And then a chuckle. "Dalden doesn't even know that. He just assumes it's always going to take him exactly where he wants to go in the ship, because I always know where he wants to go and control it for him."

"Why not just tell him?"

"Weren't you listening when I mentioned that he doesn't like spaceships? The less he has to personally deal with the ship, the better."

"Will I get to explore this ship?"

"Sure, why not?"

Brittany could have thought of one major reason why not. If their ship was as big as it was being represented by them, then the size of the studio that had created this illusion would have to be mammoth to show her all of it. It would be much easier to restrict her to just a few rooms. Of course, when she got around to asking for that tour, they would probably come up with excuses to not allow it.

"Alone?"

Martha chuckled at that addition. "Doll, there's no such thing as being alone on a ship controlled by me. There are visual monitors in every single room that can't be turned off if I don't want them turned off."

"What about broken? Smashed? Demolished?"

"Are we getting hot under the collar? You could try, but they're made of unbreakable material. And why does that upset you?"

"Maybe I'm used to the concept of privacy?" Brittany growled. "Maybe I don't like the fact that there will *always be eyes on me.*"

"I'm not intrusive, Brittany. I view when I need to view, I don't view just for the hell of it."

"I'm not impressed by that hurt-feelings tone. If you're a computer, you don't have feelings."

Another chuckle. " 'Course not, but *you* don't think I'm a computer, remember?"

Before Brittany's blush got really bright, the door to the lift slid silently open. Dalden turned toward her

immediately. So did Jorran. It was a circular room in the middle of which was another circular room enclosed by see-through walls. Those curved, seamless walls extended from floor to ceiling. As Martha had mentioned, there were no doors, no openings of any kind. There had to be a trapdoor in the floor, though, that she just couldn't see, because their only way in or out, called Transfer, was stretching the limits of even their imagination, much less hers.

"Why is she here?" Dalden wanted to know.

"Shanelle took her to the Rec Room, where she thought you'd be, then abandoned her there when she got emotional again over what she assumed happened to Tedra on her return home. Nothing we haven't seen her do a dozen times since parting from Tedra, but you know how your sister is, and how poorly she deals with *that* subject."

"Why is she here?" Dalden repeated, showing that barbarians could be single-minded, too.

"Didn't care for my subtle warning about what *you* can expect to be grilled about later? Forgetting that the Rec Room is where your good buddies prefer to hang out? Brittany got intimidated."

The blush that Brittany had gotten under control immediately returned. And Dalden's expression softened now as he put an arm around her and said, "You need have no fear of Kan-is-tran warriors."

"I wasn't afraid," she insisted. "Martha embellishes. I was merely uncomfortable. And she said you were playing the ambassador here. I wanted to see how one plays at being an ambassador."

He made a face now. "As you say, she embellishes. I have not the diplomacy needed for such a role. But I

am capable of turning down Jorran's demands and making sure he understands why."

"Satisfaction in saying no?"

"Indeed."

"I suppose he's demanding that you let him go?" Brittany guessed.

Dalden shook his head. "He understands we are returning him to Century III and that he will be contained here for the journey. He has no difficulty accepting that as the consequence of losing the fight with me. But he remembers that a meditech fully healed him after his fight with my sister's lifemate, Falon. He demands that we heal him."

She was surprised. "You aren't going to?"

"We have decided that he is to have no more treatment than his own world would be capable of giving him, which is next to none. They have not yet progressed to the age of science or medicine."

She wasn't sure she understood that reasoning — and then it occurred to her that she didn't need to. She realized they hadn't just been telling her things. Telling was easy. They'd also been enacting their story, following their own scripts, and Jorran had been a major acting part.

He was one of them, of course. They'd actually had her believing what those rods could do, when in fact they did nothing, had been used on other members of the project who had merely pretended they'd been hypnotized. The mayor? His secretary? Either tricked into going along with the pretense or really hypnotized ahead of time. Jorran had just been their "reason" for coming here. So he had to be a continuing part of the script.

The damage done to him? Faked, of course, but damn, they sure did a good job of faking. His nose really did look crooked above the cloth he was holding below it to stem the fake blood. His broken arm was hanging rather limp at his side. He stood lopsided, to keep the weight off his supposedly broken kneecap.

Impressed, Brittany remarked casually, "You know, if I really thought Jorran was injured, rather than pretending to be, I'd tell you it's cruel to make him suffer like that when he could be mended."

Dalden frowned, but Martha chose to answer this time. "The man deserves some suffering. He's a member of the ruling family of his world. All they're going to do when we take him home is slap his wrist and tell him to not get caught next time. But even if he hadn't tried to take over your world, he's still on our endangered species list because he deliberately tried to kill Tedra's son-in-law so he could hook up with her daughter, for the sole purpose of taking over their world. He's *never* suffered any consequences for his merciless actions. Someone needs to show him that the way he does things just isn't acceptable to the rest of the universe."

"Why isn't he reacting to what you just said?" Brittany asked curiously.

"He didn't hear it. I turned off the communication speaker when you entered."

"Turn it back on. I'd like to hear what he has to say."

"You're too emotional to stomach it, doll. Make up your mind. You're either going to believe he's for real, in which case you have to believe everything else, or you're not. And if you're not, then what's it matter what he has to say?"

Touché. "Is he in pain?"

"No. Even medieval worlds have figured out painkillers of one kind or another, and he'll be given regulated doses in the air he's breathing for as long as needed. We're not out to torture him, merely to teach him a lesson, and even that will only be temporary."

"Why only temporary?"

"His bones will mend by the time he gets home, they just won't mend perfectly, so he'll probably leave us with a slight limp and not liking his pretty new nose job. But I have little doubt that he will find himself a meditech eventually that will put him back together perfectly. Even if he never leaves home again, his planet gets a lot of off-world tourists fascinated with their old-world culture, and most modern ships come equipped with a meditech or two."

Brittany stared at Jorran through the see-through wall. He was staring back at her, an abject appeal in his eyes. He wanted her to help him, was willing it, trying to play on her sympathies. He was a good actor, really good, was well-suited for the role of villain. He'd get no help from her, though, either way. Real or not, her only concern was whether Dalden could be cruel. He wasn't, though; he was just trying to administer some justice that he felt wouldn't be forthcoming from any other quarter. The logical path, something the good guys might do.

She tipped an imaginary hat to Jorran, turned to Dalden with a smile. "I can't wait to see the finale. When do we leave for Sha-Ka'an?"

Chapter 35

THEY DID LEAVE FOR SHA-KA'AN. AT LEAST, THEY wanted her to believe that. The announcement had been made. Everyone had heard it.

Brittany had been in Dalden's quarters when she heard it, staring out the long bank of windows. Those windows had shown her water before. When she had returned to Dalden's quarters, they were filled with black space and stars. After the announcement, some of those stars began to move. An amazing depiction of a ship moving swiftly through space—or an elongated computer screen giving that illusion.

So much to think about, way too much. She didn't want to deal with it anymore. It was depressing her. Even though she didn't really believe she was leaving Earth, she was somehow experiencing the same feel-

ings as if it were so. And it wasn't the same as leaving home for the first time. She might not get back to Kansas to see the folks very often since she moved out, but she *could* just hop in her car and go anytime she felt like it. There was security in having that choice. No such choice here.

The door slid quietly open behind her. She heard it, just didn't turn to see if it was Dalden or not. The depression that had settled in as soon as she was alone, was weighing her down. Too many emotions, doubts, fears, and so much of it centered on *him*.

He stood in front of her. He looked concerned, probably because she was on the verge of tears and looked it. Was he for real? How could he be? A barbarian from another world just wasn't acceptable. But did he believe it? As they could make her forget, could they make him have memories that weren't real, a whole lifetime of memories inserted in his mind to make him think he was other than what he was? She really wanted to believe that, rather than he was just another actor in this "play."

"So you are not as accepting as you claimed you would be?" he said.

"I know this isn't real," she replied tonelessly. "You say it is. One of us doesn't have our facts straight."

His hands came to her shoulders, pulled her close enough so they were just touching. She had to tilt her head back now to still meet his gaze. Those lovely amber eyes were filled with sadness.

"I cannot make it all go away for you," he told her. "I would not want to. That would mean giving you up, and I will never do that."

"You mean Martha's means of making people forget what has passed?"

"Yes."

"No, I wouldn't want that either." She laid her head on his chest, wrapped her arms tight around him. "But it's occurred to me that to accept this is to accept that I'll never see my family again. Can you understand why that thought is abhorrent to me?"

"Certainly, yet is it in error? Your star system is farther than most from mine, yet is it still reachable. You will see your family again if that is your wish."

She looked up at him again. "You mean that?"

"I am not breaking your ties with all that you know, merely loosening them for now," he replied. "You have a new family. You have me."

He was doing it again, amazing her at how easily he could adjust her emotions. He was reputed to have none, but he sure knew how to mold hers. A few words and half the burden had been lifted from her shoulders.

It wasn't the first time. Actually, it seemed to be a constant with him. The way he looked at her, touched her as if he cherished her above all things, said just what she needed to hear . . . it was no wonder she fell for him so hard and so fast. He might not love her, might not even be capable of it, but he sure knew how to make her feel loved. And every time he did, he bound her heart more firmly to his.

Was it by design? Deliberate? Part of the plan? Brittany shoved those doubts away, savoring the relief he just gave her. She hugged him tighter, thanking him without words. He might be too good to be true, but

he was one fantasy she could live with for the rest of her days.

"You're amazing."

"It pleases me that you think so."

"Don't get conceited," she said as she leaned back to grin at him. "I didn't say you were perfect. Close, but no cigar."

His hands continued to caress her in a gentle, soothing manner, rather than sexual. Was he still worried that she was falling apart at the seams? Or was he keeping Martha's "practice hands-off" warning in mind? She really hoped it wasn't the latter.

"What else—pleases you?" she tested, trying not to sound sexy, merely curious.

But that easily, his golden eyes filled with heat, and that quickly, he was kissing her. Martha wasn't always right. As a stress reliever, Dalden's lovemaking beat a massager, even their unique one, hands down. Just his kisses alone could do that, and for the simple reason that as usual, all thoughts, worries, fears, flew right out of her mind the moment his lips touched hers.

He lifted her, carried her to the bed, positioned her carefully on top of him as he laid back on it, so she wouldn't be distracted by any adjusting it did. As if anything could distract her just then. He took her into that realm of ecstasy again, so new to her, yet already addicting. His heat surrounded her, the strength of his passion thrilled her.

His lovemaking was all the answer she'd needed, yet he still said awhile later, "It pleases me when you want me. It pleases me to hold you close to my heart.

Everything about you, woman, pleases me. And it pleases me most to know that you are mine."

Tears came to her eyes. "Did I say you weren't perfect? You can have that cigar now."

He laughed, gathered her close. If she was dreaming, she really didn't want to wake up.

Chapter 36

IF BRITTANY DIDN'T HAVE SPECIFIC MEMORIES OF EACH and every day, she could almost think she'd slept through most of that trip, time flew by so quickly. She'd marked the days to begin with, but after two weeks and then a month passed, she had to give up the notion that they had a short time limit for convincing her. She was forced to conclude that the time involved was part of the project, to determine just how long it would take for her to crack. She was obviously just a test subject, after all. When they got around to doing this to their real objectives, they'd want to have a good idea of a time frame for it.

So much time spent on just her? Maybe not. The "ship" was certainly big enough that there could be dozens of others just like her there at the same time, and they just managed to keep her from running into them.

She *had* gotten that tour of the "ship" she'd asked for. And she had ended the day being even more impressed by the immense scope of this project, and the immense expense involved. Even if that lift wasn't really taking her to different levels of the ship, was just taking her back to the same floor where walls had been changed to make her think she was seeing different rooms, it was still a mind-boggling expense, the creation of all this. And she wondered if she was the only test subject who had yet to be convinced even partially, let alone fully.

They never lost patience with her disbelief, never tried to double their efforts to change her thinking. She was grateful for that, because it let her enjoy her time with them. It was almost like reading a book. Once she looked at it in that light, she found it an amusing pastime, to make them flesh out their story, to ask all kinds of questions about their part of the universe.

She learned that Dalden's mother was a heroine on her own planet, that she was also the one to first discover Sha-Ka'an and bring it to the attention of the rest of the universe. She knew that his planet was closed down to off-world visitors, that anyone arriving there had to stay in the Visitors' Center and conduct their business from there, that few exceptions were made to this rule. That wasn't always the case, but "tourists" had caused too much trouble in the early days of discovery, apparently, enough to make themselves unwelcome.

She spent a lot of time with Shanelle and learned that it was Falon's family that was ultimately responsible for ousting the visitors from their world. After his sister had been raped by one of them, they'd been ready to go

to war if the planet wasn't made off-limits to off-worlders. Brittany figured this was a very good excuse to not show her very much of Sha-Ka'an, but Shanelle had assured her that exceptions got made for lifemates, that she was a Ly-San-Ter now and so one of them.

From Shanelle she also learned that like her own world, each country in Sha-Ka'an was somewhat different from the next, some with different rules and regulations, some with different philosophies, and in some the people looked different as well, though the amazing height and brawn were apparently a planet-wide thing.

Shanelle's lifemate and his brother were examples of that. From a far distant town, they were black-haired and blue-eyed, while everyone from Dalden's town fell into the golden to light-brown hair and eyes category. The women from Falon's town apparently weren't quite as restricted, either, as they were in Sha-Ka-Ra, but that was one aspect of Sha-Ka'ani life that Brittany did *not* want to learn about yet.

She became friends with Shanelle. At least, the feeling was there that they were friends, even if it was all pretense on the younger girl's part. She even became friends with Martha, amazing as that was, when she had yet to meet the real Martha, and had to wonder if she ever would. But Martha had a dry sense of humor that Brittany took to—after she stopped allowing it to annoy her. And Martha was still her main source of information. Because she was faceless, Brittany could ask her things that she wouldn't ask the others.

One of those things was their differences in speech, which had confused her from the beginning. Several weeks into the journey she finally got around to asking

Martha, "Why do you and Shanelle talk—I guess normally is the word I'm looking for? While Dalden, and Jorran's people as well, for that matter, sound foreign? If Shanelle is his sister, why doesn't she talk like him?"

"Dalden speaks pure Sha-Ka'ani. What you hear is his translation of your language. The same with Jorran, who speaks pure Centurian. Shanelle and I, however, speak Kystrani, and not pure Kystrani, but their Ancient dialect, which includes slang. We speak it because Tedra has a fascination with her Ancients, to include using their slang, and my main dialect is set to be identical to her preference."

"But why would that be different, if you're using a translation as well?"

"Because of the similarities that we've found between the Kystrani Ancients and your people. Your history has closely followed theirs, so closely that even your slang is mostly the same. So in effect my language, the one Tedra prefers, is already the same as yours in basic content, as in same meanings, same slang, even same phrases. If I tell you that you got your socks knocked off when you met Dalden, you know exactly what I mean, don't you? A normal Sha-Ka'ani wouldn't have a clue, however, since they don't have a similar phrase in their language."

"Why didn't you say Dalden wouldn't have a clue?" Brittany had asked.

"Because he would. I told you Dalden is unique, a product of two cultures, though he'd prefer it were only one. Both of Tedra's children received a major part of their education from me, but only up to a point. Shanelle wanted to know everything and continued to learn, Dalden didn't. After he made the decision to fol-

low his father's path exclusively, he wanted no more teaching from me, and he's tried to forget everything he'd already learned about the rest of the universe. He *can* talk just like Tedra, he just won't."

"So he took after his father, and she took after her mother?"

"In speech, yes, but women tend to be better at adapting, and Shani is a shining example of that. She can be the absolute perfect Sha-Ka'ani daughter, obedient in every way but one, or she could move to Kystran and take up the life career of flying ships for trade or world discovery—she spent a year there learning those careers."

"Back up. Every way but one?"

"Come on, kiddo, common sense would tell you that since she's been educated on how things are elsewhere, she's not going to like every aspect of how they are at home. Ignorance is bliss, as the saying goes, and she's not ignorant, which is why she learned to fly. She had every intention of leaving home to find a lifemate on some other world—until she met Falon and got her socks knocked off just like you did."

"And she's happy to stay at home with him now?"

"Oh, yes." Martha spared a condescending chuckle. "There's something about that love emotion you people have that makes you perfectly willing to be where your mate is, whether you like where that is or not."

"Is this finally my preparation for not liking Sha-Ka'an?" Brittany said suspiciously.

"Not at all. You may love the heck out of it, once you get used to it. No crime as you know it, no fear as you know it, no worries about war, disease, sickness, jobs, or anything else you're used to worrying about."

"Utopia with a catch?"

More chuckling. "If everything was absolutely perfect, doll, you'd get bored real quick. Now back to Shani. She'd make an ideal ambassador for Sha-Ka'an, actually, because like Tedra, she's well versed in every known language in the universe, and respects each species for its own uniqueness. They both fully support the League's hands-off policy on underdeveloped planets, even though they might wish it were otherwise for Sha-Ka'an. They agree that a species must be left to develop at its own pace, for good or bad, that its full potential won't be reached otherwise. It's been proven by low-tech worlds that once they start trading with more advanced cultures, their own development stagnates, setting them back centuries in the way of personal growth."

"Why?"

"Because their creative people will naturally feel that anything that they could envision has already been created, so why bother."

"How is that avoided?"

"It's not, it's happened time and again. So now when the League discovers a new high-tech world, they rejoice, but when they discover a primitive world, they step very carefully. Trade gets restricted to the mundane, space travel isn't offered, educating the primitives on what's out there is minimal. A few non-League planets and rogue traders might break this policy, but for the most part, it's abided by."

"That doesn't sound like what happened with Sha-Ka'an," Brittany pointed out.

"They were an exception, because one of their natural resources is so greatly needed by the rest of the uni-

verse. But that's worked out well because they finally restricted off-world involvement themselves, so they get to progress at their own pace, while the League protects them from invasion by advanced worlds. And the League has a good representative there in Tedra. She's the perfect go-between, because she wants what's good for both sides."

In a contained environment like the *Androvia*, Brittany had expected to get bored pretty quickly, but she never did. She learned to play some of the games in the Rec Room, which really amazed her. She wasn't up to date by any means on computer-type games, never having owned a computer herself, but being able to control what seemed like real people in simulated wars and watch the action on movie-size screens was impressive. It was like watching a movie, but you were the director of it, or the master puppeteer in control of the actors.

And she had discovered a crafts room and ended up spending a lot of time there. It was for the crew, which the *Androvia* currently didn't have, or for people who might have personal hobbies they didn't want to give up just because they had elected space travel careers. Most of the stuff in the room made no sense to her, but the small section with stored wood and tools certainly did.

She cluttered up Dalden's quarters with her creations: a new table and chairs, and a nightstand—and she insisted the bed remain out at all times for it. She made a double-seated rocker that he'd never seen the like of and was sturdy enough for him to sit in with her. They used it each evening, sitting in front of the bank of windows, staring at the stars and the occa-

sional streaking comet, and once, another ship that
freaked her out until Martha's soothing tones assured
her it was just a passing trader.

No, she was never bored. Corth II amused her a lot,
too. He had a keen sense of humor and often used it
to try and annoy Dalden, successfully. Martha explained that while Dalden had never experienced jealousy before and would discount it as being an
emotion he wasn't capable of, he wouldn't experience
it where other warriors were involved because he
fully trusted them, while Corth II was a different matter, and unpredictable.

Which was why Dalden didn't mind her making
friends with one of the young warriors who had an interest in woodworking. Kodos had always had a desire to make things with his hands, but had never
come across anyone who could teach him how—until
her. That was his story, anyway, and one she chose to
accept, because teaching him was something else to
keep her busy and her mind occupied on other than
the end of the project.

No, Dalden didn't mind at all her counting Kodos
as a friend, but he did mind any time she spent with
Corth II, who was an outrageous flirt. His flirting she
didn't take seriously. And Martha's insistence that he
wasn't a real man but an android that she and her
good buddy Brock, another Mock II, had mutually created, Brittany filed away with another mental "yeah,
right." If Dalden knew he wasn't a real man, why
would he be jealous?

Martha, of course, had an answer for that, too: because an entertainment unit had been used for the android's body, he was fully capable of sex-sharing like a

normal entertainment unit, and Dalden knew that. But Corth II was anything but normal, was apparently a free-thinking computer that wasn't restricted to stationary housing, and answerable only to Martha and Brock.

Brittany had wanted to know why Martha hadn't given herself legs, since that was possible. Martha's reply was that you didn't tamper with perfection. Brittany had a good laugh over that.

She had made a point of not asking about things that she figured were going to upset her. Why rock an unsteady boat, after all? The rules and laws she'd been warned she would hate fell into that category. But the journey was coming to an end, so she was forced to finally put the matter to Martha.

"Isn't it time for me to learn their laws?"

"Not really." Martha used a bored tone, which was actually reassuring in this case. "As long as you're with Dalden, he's not going to let anything go wrong. When you're left to your own devices, *then* you'll need to know what you can and can't do alone."

"I am going to be told before I break any, right?" Brittany persisted.

"Tedra wasn't, but then Challen was just like you, convinced that she had to be from his planet and so already knew everything about his planet, including all laws. He refused to believe in off-worlders—actually, he knew she was telling the truth about who she was, he just didn't *want* to believe it. Sound familiar?"

That had annoyed her. They'd shown her some pretty fantastic things, or they would be fantastic if they were real. She just didn't believe anything was real.

So she wasn't the least bit apprehensive about arriv-

ing on Sha-Ka'an. If she thought she would be meeting Dalden's real parents instead of actors representing them, she'd probably be a nervous wreck, worried about all the normal things one worried about when meeting the family of the man she had committed to.

And she *was* fully committed. After spending nearly three months with Dalden, there was no doubt that her heart wouldn't be whole now without him. The thought of losing him when this was over and she was rejected as unconvinced, was so painful that she couldn't face it. Nor had she been able to seek reassurance or ask what was going to become of them when this was over, because he would just insist there was never going to be an "over" for them.

She sometimes thought that Dalden was actually as brainwashed as they were trying to make her, that he really did believe everything that had been told to her. She preferred to think that was the case, rather than that he was deliberately lying to her for whatever "good" reason. Lying would mean an end when the truth was finally admitted. And what would that end be? Go home, we're done with you? Or stay with me and be part of the program? Could she agree to put other people through what she was undergoing? She didn't think so, because bottom line, it was cruel to tamper with emotions to this extent.

But the journey was over; the announcement had already been broadcast that they'd be home in a few hours. And now she'd find out how they could possibly depict an entire planet—that was, if they were going to try. No studio could be that big. She'd have to be contained in a small part of it. But how would that be convincing? And they'd made the mistake of telling

her that there was plant and animal life unique to Sha-Ka'an, that even the air was different, edenlike, it was so pure and pollutant-free. Hard things to fake.

So was this going to be the end, then? When she stepped off the "ship," would they tell her, "You failed, you can go home now"?

Chapter 37

"IT IS TIME."

Brittany was staring out the bank of windows in Dalden's quarters at a very large planet that didn't come close to resembling hers. Hers was two-thirds ocean. This one had a lot of green, but very little blue. A nice computer simulation, like everything else she'd seen out those windows. And yet it looked so real it gave her chills.

"We aren't close enough to land yet," she pointed out.

"We are. For a ship of this speed, it is a matter of moments."

Dalden's massive arms came around her from behind to draw her back against his chest. It was comforting and frightening at the same time, because he

could be preparing her for their last moments together. The thought brought tears to her eyes, and she swung around to hug him tightly.

"Tell me this isn't going to be the end of us," she said in a voice that was as close as she could get to pleading.

Dalden lifted her face in his hands. His thumbs gently smoothed away the wetness on her cheeks. His own expression was intense.

"I feel your pain. What causes it cannot be allowed to continue. After today, there will be nothing else for you to fear."

"I hate to break it to you, warrior." Martha's voice suddenly floated about the room. "But you are *not* reassuring her."

He turned a chagrined look at the wall monitor. "What must I do to ease her distress?"

"Take her home, to her *new* home. Get her settled in. Introduce her to the family pets." Some positively wicked-sounding chuckling was inserted over that last suggestion before Martha continued. "It's really too bad this ship didn't come equipped with solaray baths. Three months of squeaky-clean without a speck of water might have done some convincing. But she's only had inanimate *things* to go by here, which she has discounted as being 'tricks' or things her own people could have invented. Fifty giant-sized warriors didn't impress her, when men *can* reach that height on her world. She thinks she's been on a simulated ship, thinks she's going to step off it and still be on *her* world. But you have things to show her now, live things. Living, breathing, unique, can't-be-shoved-into-the-'trick'-category things."

Brittany stepped back, bristling a bit with indigna-

tion. She really hated it when she got talked about while she was standing right there listening.

"I hate to break it to *you*, Martha, but you aren't re-assuring me, either," she said testily.

"Wasn't trying to, kiddo. I'm just telling the warrior what it's going to take to end your delusional state. But then I did toss you a bone; you just didn't catch it."

"Excuse me?"

"'New home.' 'Settled.' Sounds like a beginning rather than an end, don't it?"

It did, but words could be deceiving, or outright lies. She glanced at Dalden again, her skepticism plain. His own look turned determined, and she figured out why when he took her hand and marched her out of the room.

"You're taking me off the ship?"

"Indeed."

"Why not take me off the same way I was brought on?" Brittany asked.

Martha chose to answer, from the comm-link Brittany had been given a few days ago. She'd been warned to keep it with her at all times until she ran out of questions.

"Transfer can't be done here until we've actually landed," Martha said. "Sha-Ka'an is surrounded by a global shield that prevents access by ships without permission. A hole in the shield is opened above the Visitors' Center if permission is given, but even that opening contains a contamination shield. There is at least one meditech in each town, but that isn't nearly enough to help if disease gets introduced to the planet by visitors. The second shield the ship passes through

scans for contamination and, in the process, interferes with Molecular Transfer."

"But aren't we about to pass through it?"

"Yes, and I could send you straight to the palace once below the shield, but do you really want to miss out on seeing the sights on the way home? Your first ride on an airobus and then an *hataar*? The architecture in the countryside? Your first view of Sha-Ka-Ra from afar?"

"Things you think are going to make me a believer?" Brittany guessed.

"You betcha," Martha said in smirking tones.

Brittany snorted for Martha's benefit, but she was starting to feel some excitement. A beginning—that implied a life shared with Dalden. And she had reached a point of not caring where they shared it, as long as they shared it. She simply couldn't bear the thought of losing him now. But on another world? How could she accept that as being real?

Martha seemed to think she'd have no choice but to believe it by the end of the day. Dalden had pretty much said the same thing, that she'd have nothing else to fear after today. But where did that leave her? With Dalden, surely, but also with the fantastical concept of living on another world—and meeting his *real* parents. Oh, jeez.

Chapter 38

SHE COULDN'T HAVE IMAGINED IT IF SHE'D TRIED.
Brittany had been expecting a lot of spaceships laying around, nice, easy visual illusions. It was supposed to be a spaceport, after all. But none, zip, *nada*. Even the one she had just left wasn't visible by the time she was on the ground. They'd stepped out of it into some kind of tramlike thing that whisked them along for about a minute, then stepped out of that into a long tubelike tunnel that ended inside a large round building. Looking back, all she saw was the tunnel opening and a lot of wall surrounding it.

The building was immense, she'd give them that. It wasn't often that you saw a ceiling about ten stories high. There weren't very many people in it, though, for its size, and the few that were there were dressed strangely.

"It's just the disembarking terminal." Martha's voice started explaining from the comm-link on Brittany's hip. "For all arrivals. Ships don't land unless they need repairs. It's not good for them to shut down."

"So they just hover up in space depleting their fuel? Sure."

Martha didn't remark on her skeptical tone, said merely, "Fuel as you know it is obsolete. A ship can run forever on one inexhaustible gaali stone. And no, once inside the shield, they aren't let out of it until they're ready to leave. They connect to this hub to drop off passengers, then to the supply hub to restock, then return to this hub and float in standby above the center. It'd be a pretty impressive sight if seen from afar, but it was built to not be an eyesore to a people who don't want reminding that it's here, so it's a *very* long way away from any towns, even Sha-Ka-Ra."

A really good excuse to not show her the Visitors' Center from a distance. Their illusions must only be short-range.

She noticed the other tunnels then, like the one they'd come out of, ten in all, enough to accommodate a lot of passengers arriving at once, but no others were arriving except the people from their ship at the moment. There was a large open exit that they were heading toward, just a wide corridor that connected to yet another big building. No windows anywhere, to see what was outside. Now why didn't that surprise her?

"This Center is like a small city, at least what you would consider a small city—Sha-Ka'ani towns don't come this big," Martha said, continuing the role of tour guide. "It covers two square miles, the port taking up

half of that, the trade goods warehouses taking up another big chunk. The rest is devoted to housing for the Trade Ambassadors, security, personnel, and visitors who don't get to stay long. Then you have the areas for maintenance, supplies, repair, and anything else needed to make it a self-contained area."

"The planet doesn't sustain it?"

"No indeed, most of the planet refuses to acknowledge that it's here. It's run by the League for the benefit of League planets. Dalden's father is the only *shodan* who has to deal with it on a regular basis; all the other *shodani* go through him if needed."

She'd already learned that a *shodan* was like a mayor of his town, or to be more exact, a medieval lord ruling over his small kingdom. But even that didn't describe it perfectly. Problems got brought to him, decisions affecting the town were made by him, widows and orphans got full protection from him, yet any warrior could challenge him for the position and take it over if he won. It wasn't a hereditary position in Kan-is-Tra, though it was in some countries like Ba-Har-an where Falon came from. Even then, the son wanting to take over still had to take on all challengers for the privilege.

"Heads up, doll, you're about to meet the new in-laws," Martha said next.

"Huh?"

Brittany stopped short, forcing Dalden, who'd been leading her along by the hand, to turn to see what was wrong. He smiled reassuringly. He'd seen the couple up ahead also, standing at the end of the wide corridor.

The man was huge, as big as Dalden and just as golden, just as handsome, too, for that matter. And af-

ter spending three months with fifty warriors, she'd already figured out that they all preferred those leather pants they called *bracs* and the wraparound tunics. The woman was nearly as tall as Brittany, with long black hair pulled up into a high ponytail, and wearing a strange outfit that seemed to be made of sheer green scarves, a lot of them not actually see-through, the points reaching her sandaled feet, with a white cloak attached at the shoulders. She was beautiful, no doubt about it. And young, too young to be a grown man's mother.

Dalden did some explaining now. "Be at ease, *kerima*. Martha has been in contact with Brock since the last rising. So my parents expected us and due to our long absence, could not wait until we reached home. She would have told them all about you, is that not right, Martha?"

"You betcha."

Shanelle had already run forward, was embracing the couple. The warriors with them were filing past and continuing on, leaving the family to their reunion.

"Go ahead. Give me a moment to compose myself," Brittany told Dalden.

She smiled for his benefit, though it was an effort. He seemed somewhat nervous, too, a normal reaction, to worry if his parents would like her—if this was for real. Damn, he was good, sneaking in those little subtleties that she might have missed if she weren't already so attuned to him.

But the moment he was out of hearing she hissed at Martha, "You could have at least gotten someone old enough to play the part of his mother. If you're going to try to convince me that *she* is Dalden's mother, don't

bother. She's not much older than I am. Neither is he, for that matter."

A short round of chuckles. "Tedra has aged very well in comparison to average humanoids. The Sha-Ka'ani do also, due to their healthy environment, but Tedra has the added benefit of her Sec 1 training that she keeps up, grueling exercises that have honed her body into a lethal weapon—well, considered lethal on other worlds. But she's forty-four. I should know, she belongs to me."

"I thought that was the other way around and you belong to her?"

"Matter of opinion," Martha muttered.

Brittany didn't believe the handsome couple up ahead were Dalden's real parents, so what was she suddenly nervous about? Because the second phase of "convince at no expense" had begun, apparently. A spaceship hadn't done it. So now new actors and a make-believe whole planet were supposed to. She should be relieved. Her greatest fear before leaving the ship had been that she'd be back in her own bed by tonight, with the space next to her empty. But that wasn't on the agenda yet.

"Showtime," Martha said as the group up ahead stopped waiting for her to join them and approached her instead.

Martha was being cute, but that was too close to how Brittany viewed all of this. A show for her exclusive benefit, just actors following a basic script and improvising where needed.

"Welcome to Sha-Ka'an, Brittany Callaghan, and welcome to my family."

Oh, God, that sounded really nice. Her own family

had grown apart and rarely saw each other anymore. They kept in touch, but she missed that closeness of when they'd all lived together. One of her lessons on the journey had included that Sha-Ka'ani families usually stayed together, that when children reached adulthood they stayed in the same town, some in the same house. A few females might end up with a lifemate in another town or country, but that was a rare exception, since warriors tended to pick their mates from women known to them in their own town.

Following Tedra's welcome, she got a tight hug and a whisper by her ear. "Relax, kiddo, we don't judge here. When a warrior makes his choice there's no reversing it, so he gets wished happy. Some take a long time to decide, some know instantly. Either way, it's something they *know*. Too bad women never gain that kind of certainty."

Was that a joke? Tedra was grinning when she stepped back. Yet what she'd just said was kind of the reverse of the way Brittany knew things to be. Women knew right off when they were in love. It usually took the recipient of that love a heck of a long time to figure the same thing out. There were exceptions, surely, but on the average, women won hands-down in the instant-decision-making category.

Seeing her close up, Brittany still couldn't believe that Tedra was forty-four years old. "Aged well" was a definite understatement. She'd probably make a really cool mother-in-law, though. Brittany wasn't so sure about Challen, who was very intimidating with his size and his look that seemed to be analyzing, but was otherwise inscrutable.

Tedra now turned a stern expression on Dalden.

"Six months' absence, never again, Dalden. Contrary to the Ancients' adage, absence does *not* make the heart grow fonder, it's *farden* well painful. Never again. And your father agrees with me—for once."

"Do not give the impression that I never agree with you, woman," Challen rumbled curtly. "That would be an untruth of the size you call whopper."

Tedra snorted. "You only agree when it suits you, never when it suits me."

That caused a grin from the big guy. A yank to him that had to have hurt when Tedra collided with that big body. A slap on the backside that had to hurt even more.

"We will agree to discuss the matter of disagreeing later," Challen warned.

"Wanna bet?" Tedra shot back.

She then pushed away from him, grabbed Shanelle's arm, and marched off toward the front of the building. Challen and Falon followed more slowly. Dalden took Brittany's hand again to bring up the rear.

At her hip, Martha suggested in a cheerful tone, "Don't mind them, kiddo. Their way of joking around takes getting used to."

"Joking, huh? Sure."

Dalden gave her a glance. "Martha is correct, but it is my mother who will take getting used to. She does not behave as a Sha-Ka'ani woman should."

Brittany stopped, demanded, "And just how would a Sha-Ka'ani woman have acted? Smiled and thanked her lifemate for banging her around?"

Dalden looked confused, but Martha wasn't, and said instantly, "Put the brakes on, girl. Tedra's body is conditioned to take damage and not feel it. She wasn't hurt; if she even felt that love tap, I'd be surprised.

Challen would cut off his hand before he'd actually hurt her. Most warriors feel the same way about their women."

"Do you?" Brittany asked Dalden.

"Certainly," he replied, somewhat indignant that she'd needed that reassurance.

Certainly, she repeated dryly in her mind. But he was talking about physical pain, not the mental kind that could sometimes be just as excruciating. What would a warrior's philosophy be about that? As long as it didn't leave a bruise, it couldn't hurt?

She got the sneaky suspicion that phase two was going to be more emotional than visual. Bog her down with anxieties and uncertainties so she didn't notice when she started believing it all?

Chapter 39

⊂♡⊃

BRITTANY BEGAN TO RELAX ON THE SHORT RIDE TO Sha-Ka-Ra, Dalden's hometown. They weren't showing her things anymore, had perhaps finally concluded that it was a waste of their time and effort. She got flimsy excuses for this new tack, but she didn't really care.

There had been nothing outside the building to see except the front of the building they just left, and a hill on the other side was close enough to kill any views. It could have been an illusion; she wasn't allowed close enough to it to check it out. There were three vehicles there to transport the lot of them, and they all piled in.

Airobuses, they called them. They could have been remodeled normal buses. Remove the wheels, make

the front streamlined instead of flat, extend the length to twice normal size, and voilà, a space-age weird-looking vehicle.

There were cushy chairs in the first section behind the pilot's pit, but most of the vehicle was just a cargo bay. They were supposedly used to collect and deliver trade goods to the outer reaches of the planet, but they had to remain more or less invisible, so they had preset routes that took them high enough above the clouds to not be visible from the ground. They required pilots, even though there was nothing for the pilot to see other than a large monitor. No windows, even up front, the excuse being that if a warrior had to be brought to the Center on one for some reason, they made it as painless as possible for him by giving him no visible reminder that he was flying while he was in the air. There was no sound, either, no feeling of lift-off, no feeling of any movement at all, for that matter, just a low, steady hum barely heard.

The landing points for these buses were called stations, all of them located far enough from the major towns, again, to keep the people from being reminded of their existence. It didn't dawn on Brittany until they arrived at their station just what that was going to mean.

Views. Incredible, far-reaching views of the majestic sort. The station sat at the base of a mountain they called Mount Raik, a mass so tall its point was capped with ice even though the climate was tropical. Mostly flat land spread before it, some cultivated with grains and vegetables. Forests were in the distance, with multi-colored trees, reds, greens, yellows, blues—blue?—and every shade in between. She saw long purple shadows on the horizon that could have been other mountain

ranges, too far distant to define. She saw what might be a small lake in a field of wildflowers.

No telephone poles, no roads other than dirt paths, no buildings yet, no airplanes flying overhead to blow it for this look of Eden. And the air *was* clean, no smoke or pollutants floating on any of the horizons. Where on earth had they found such a place?

And then she saw the three airobuses, sitting on a paved landing pad, and what looked like a winding road leading up the mountain. They were too close to the mountain to see the town of Sha-Ka-Ra, which sat halfway up it, or so she was told.

"Are we going to walk up it?" she asked.

"My father has arranged transportation."

"Where?"

He took her hand and led her around the airobus that had been blocking a bit of the view. A small herd of *hataari* were now visible, about forty of them standing placidly off to the side of the pad. Some of the warriors were already mounting them; others standing there showed her just how big the beasts were, when their heads were barely a foot above the animals' backs, which meant those backs had to be as high off the ground as Brittany was tall. They were shaggy-haired, most of them black, a few brown, one tan, but all with white manes and tails that nearly reached the ground. Thin legs, extra-wide bodies, too wide to be horses—perhaps what prehistoric horses might have looked like? But even that was pushing it. They were like horses, but nothing like horses.

They were so funny-looking with their long shaggy coats, she started to laugh. They had to be made-up, Clydesdale horses probably—didn't they get that tall?

But someone's imagination had really gone wild in the creation of their costumes. The padding for the extra-wide trunks was a weird touch; it just made them look silly.

"What amuses you?" Dalden asked as he led her to one of the *hataar* and tossed her up on its back.

The suddenness of being on top of one of those things ended her amusement. There was no saddle, just a blanket covering its back and a harness contraption with reins and a post for gripping, which she did now while Dalden mounted behind her.

"Sure," she said, disgruntled. "Don't give me a chance to find the zipper on this costume."

His arms came around her, pulled her back against him. That easily did she relax and put aside her brief annoyance. He didn't ask her to explain, though if he were for real, he wouldn't have understood her remark. Martha did.

"I'm disappointed in you, doll," came the voice at her hip. "You know you're reaching now, grabbing at crumbs to explain away the obvious."

"Your obvious is so far-fetched, it's gone beyond silly now. If anyone's disappointed, I am. I expected better after such meticulous details on your spaceship."

"Hasn't it occurred to you that there's no choice in the matter of what's real? Yes, they are visually silly-looking. I've seen the animals you have in comparison that are sleek and beautiful. Not every world is so lucky in their beasts of burden. Believe it or not, some worlds have *hataar*-like creatures even more silly-looking than these."

"Sure, and I own a fantastic bridge I'll be glad to sell you."

"This habit you have of saying things you do not mean must end, *kerima*."

Brittany stiffened at Dalden's serious tone, but she caught her breath when Martha said, "Heads up, girl. He's home now and starting to sound like a warrior."

Brittany swung around to give Dalden a hard look. "What'd she mean by that?" No answer from him. "Martha, why'd you make warrior sound like a bad name?" No answer from that quarter, either, which caused her temper to erupt. "Damnit upside and down, don't you people *dare* spring any surprises on me at this late date! Have I fallen in love with a man who's only shown me half of himself? Is the other half some monster I'm going to hate?"

Dalden's expression softened, probably because she'd just admitted she loved him for the first time. She hadn't meant to own up to that yet. She didn't want it laid on the table if the end of the "project" wasn't going to be to her liking. But it was too late to take it back. She did love him—at least, she loved the man she'd come to know. But who was that? A man pretending to be an alien? A man so brainwashed he really believed he was an alien? Or a real alien who'd restrained his alien tendencies up until now, but now that he was home was going to release them? Just why *were* these people called barbarians?

Her barbarian put his hand to her cheek to draw her mouth to his. His kiss was soft, so tender. One of the things she loved so much about him was that despite his incredible size and strength, he was always so gentle with her. He wasn't a barbarian. No way in hell.

Chapter 40

IT HAD BEEN A LONG TIME SINCE BRITTANY HAD BEEN SO embarrassed that all she wanted to do was hide her face. Dalden was almost purring with satisfaction. He'd managed to distract her so thoroughly she forgot what they'd been arguing about, forgot that she should be watching things around her, forgot she was on the back of an animal and other people were riding along beside them.

He was proud that he could do that to her. He'd turned that sweet kiss into a raging inferno of passion—at least on her part. She'd turned all the way around to face him, her legs spread and laying over his, clinging to him, devouring him, lost in the moment. . . .

Until Martha's voice intruded dryly, "I could have sworn you were interested in architecture."

Kodos, riding next to them, was chuckling at Brit-

tany. Shanelle, on the other side riding double with Falon, rolled her eyes at her. Thank heavens their parents were sharing an *hataar* up ahead and hadn't noticed, or her mortification would have been absolute.

She hissed at Dalden, "If I thought that was deliberate, you'd be in big trouble."

He was seriously amused, if his grin was an indication. "Define big trouble."

"For starters," she said, stabbing a finger against his wide chest, "never speaking to you again."

"That would not be allowed," he said simply.

"Would not—!" she choked, unable to finish. "To paraphrase Martha, wanna bet? And don't think you can tease your way around it. They don't come much more stubborn than an Irish American, which I happen to be. Stubborn is often our middle name."

"I thought your middle name was Tomboy."

"Oh, cute, real cute. Pretend you don't know what the hell I'm talking about."

He disagreed. "You are telling me it is your nature to be stubborn. This is the nature of most women, so warriors expect it and find it amusing."

"Why amusing?"

"Because it is not a thing women succeed at very well—here."

"You might want to readjust that statement a little bit to include, until now."

He chuckled, then hugged her, then explained why he was suddenly so pleased with her responses. "You—and Martha—insist that you are different because you were not born here, but truly, *kerima*, your reaction to an unwanted lesson is no different from that of a Sha-Ka'ani woman."

She pushed out of his arms, narrowed her eyes on him. "Lesson? Just what were you trying to teach me there? That if I do or say something you don't like, you'll embarrass the hell out of me?"

"It was not meant to embarrass you."

"Then what was I meant to feel?"

"Exactly what you did feel."

What she'd felt was raw passion and a desire to make love with him right then and there. "I don't get it."

He didn't respond, which managed to infuriate her enough to say, "Martha, you and I are going to have a long talk before the end of the day, and you're coming clean this time."

But Dalden objected to Martha enlightening her, insisting, "Lessons are better learned by example than in the telling."

Brittany bristled, but before she could reply, Martha lit into the warrior. "Dalden, did that Sha-Ka'ani pure air muddle your brain all of a sudden? You've done fine until now, keeping it in mind that she's not Sha-Ka'ani. Don't blow it just because you're home, and don't make some assumptions based on one reaction when she's capable of reactions you've never seen before. Some of the things that you see as natural and right and your responsibility, she just isn't going to tolerate. That cultural difference I warned you about better be ringing a big bell, because it's real, it's huge, and it will cause problems of the like no warrior, even your father in dealing with Tedra, has ever faced before."

Brittany stiffened, feeling an ominous dread that frightened her. Dalden stiffened as well, though for different reasons. She didn't like hearing that she, specifically, was going to be the cause of trouble be-

tween them. He didn't like hearing that Martha was so certain he wouldn't be equipped to deal with it.

Brittany clutched him suddenly, the fear getting to her. "Whatever happens, we can work it out. Whatever it is she thinks I'm going to hate, I'll—I'll try to understand, I'll try not to hate it. We *will* work it out, Dalden."

He hugged her back, squeezing a bit harder than usual. "I am grateful, yet do you not need to make promises based on the unknown. We will indeed 'work it out.' I will allow no other thing to be."

His indomitable will managed to truly amaze her sometimes. They'd be fine because he said so. No matter what, no matter the obstacles, no matter anything. He'd have it no other way, wouldn't *allow* it. She wished she could grab hold of that certainty and take it to heart. But it was reassuring and took the edge off her fear.

"Did I mention architecture?" Martha's voice intruded in another really dry tone.

Brittany burst out laughing, the rest of her tension fading away.

Chapter 41

BRITTANY HADN'T MISSED TOO MUCH OF THE TOWN, just the approach. And Sha-Ka-Ra was bigger than she'd expected after Martha's remark that their towns didn't come in sizes she was used to—not so much in head count, but in the buildings being spread out with plenty of breathing space between each one. It was perched on a flat plateau, so nothing was built on the slopes of the mountain.

The main street was very wide, lined at regular intervals with trees of different colors—none that she actually recognized, though a horticulturist she was not—and lampposts. The posts were similar to what was used in the nineteenth century, when someone came by each night and lit the candles in them, but these used gaali stones that supposedly didn't need lighting, just uncovering, to reveal their soft glow.

She was looking forward to seeing one of these gaali stones she'd been told about up close and personal, a small one, though, since she'd been warned that large chunks were so bright they could blind. Yeah, right, something they couldn't prove to her, but she'd like to see how they were going to hide the seams of a battery compartment on the smaller stones.

Just now, though, she was experiencing some disappointment in finding that none of the buildings in the town were built of wood. Everything was light tan in color, either plaster or stone, she wasn't close enough yet to tell which. Mostly one-story houses, a few two-story, many with lovely arches, windows in all kinds of different shapes, each with its own yard and stable, its own garden. There were even some with balconies on their flat roofs, like sun decks. And clean. There wasn't a single piece of rubbish on the ground anywhere.

It was an even mix of old and new. The buildings were modern-looking, but the people weren't, and plenty had turned out to view the homecoming. Fifty men from this town had been absent for a long time, so their families were on hand to welcome them home. The procession started breaking up as each warrior was met by two or more members of his family. Oddly, never just one member, or more specifically, a lifemate. Even more oddly, now that it was noticed, there wasn't a single woman on the street standing alone.

Each woman there had a man with her. Each one was wearing one of those scarfy outfits they called *chauri*, each with a cloak draped behind them. They

came in a wide range of colors, but all solid colors. There wasn't a single garment on anyone that was a mix of colors.

She found out later that the only reason she hadn't been given a cloak the color of the house she now belonged to was because her white T-shirt and blue jeans were already the two colors representing Dalden's house. That he'd let her wear her jeans, when the women of his town weren't allowed to wear pants of any kind, had been an exception made just for her because she wasn't Sha-Ka'ani and he'd wanted his people to see that plainly. It wasn't such a strict rule anymore though, now that his country knew that other countries like Falon's didn't even follow that rule, so exceptions for visitors did get made now, when that didn't used to be the case. It *was* still their rule though, which was why she was going to be supplied with a full new wardrobe and was expected to wear it.

She didn't mind. She was definitely tired of jeans after wearing hers for three months, even though they'd been cleaned and returned to her each day by that thing Dalden called dial-a-closet. She'd been offered ship's uniforms but had declined. She had never felt that her height looked good in one-piece jumpsuits of the clingy sort.

Old-style again were the marketplaces—they looked like something out of a medieval fair, with small tents with tables in front of them, or goods laid out on rugs. Then a beautiful park with a pond in it and children playing, that could have been in any American hometown.

The streets were laid out in even, straight lines.

Turning one brought the biggest building in the town into view, a towering white stone castle. Brittany's jaw dropped. It wasn't a castle as she knew them; it looked more like something that could be found in a fantasy picture book. It wasn't one big building, either, but built in sections, some round, some square or rectangular. All of the sections were in different heights and shapes so that none of them were the same, yet they grew in height pyramid fashion, the shorter towers on the outside, the tallest at the center. There were conical roofs on some, spiral roofs, normal roofs, and flat roofs on others, even crenellated walkways on top of some of the towers.

Tall white walls surrounded the castle, with a wide-open archway spanning the street to enter the inner castle yard. And they were heading to it. This was where Dalden and his family lived.

It was too much. They couldn't have built something like that just for this project; it had to be something they'd found and were going to make use of. The whole town, for that matter. Maybe somewhere in Russia or that part of the world. Didn't they have strange-looking buildings like this? And beautiful untouched countrysides? And towns so different-looking from anything she was used to?

She felt better with that conclusion, on firm ground again, and ready to be impressed as they rode through the archway into the castle yard. There was a long rectangular building right in front, with steps spanning the length of it, and at the center, a tall pair of steel-looking doors flanked by two warriors guarding it.

There was a stable for the *hataari* out front, and she got her first sight of small men that worked in it. They weren't really small, just not giant-sized like the warriors, and they dressed differently, too, in thin white pants and shirts. *Darash* males of the servant class apparently, whom she'd been told about. They were descended from a people conquered so long ago that no one had the date of it anymore.

They weren't slaves, but were more like a mix between a medieval serf and someone from the servant class of eighteenth-century England. They were the working class, the ones who did all the menial labor warriors snubbed their noses at, though they didn't get paid for it. There were laws to govern them, they had some rights, but they couldn't just pick up and move like normal working-class people. For the most part, she'd been told, they were a happy lot who knew their worth in as much as the warrior society would probably collapse without them.

Dalden's parents led the way inside. Shanelle would be staying a few more days, but then would be leaving for Ba-Har-an, a country that used to take a good three months to reach by *hataar*, but now was just a few minutes away by airobus. The distance, or prior travel time, was why not much had been known about Ba-Har-an before Challen had been asked to contact them for trade with the League, plentiful deposits of gold having been scanned in that region that other planets were interested in.

But it wasn't really the distance that had kept the two countries virtual strangers for so long, but that the Sha-Ka'ani were a sedentary warrior species. They

might differ here and there in each separate country, but they pretty much universally weren't explorers. By nature, they preferred to stay, grow, and prosper in familiar surroundings.

Chapter 42

BRITTANY MIGHT HAVE BEEN PICKING HER JAW UP OFF the floor again after walking through the mammoth steel doors of the castle if she hadn't had prior warning—pools in bedrooms had been a clue—that inside wasn't going to look like a castle, but more like a palace. Even so, the bright, open airiness of the place made it unique: high ceilings, huge rooms, everything predominantly white, even the floors, which were marblelike granite.

Potted plants and flowering trees added greenery and other colors, and a blue carpet runner about twelve feet wide extended down the center of the hall where they entered. Two big rooms on each side of it were divided by arches, but arches so wide they were barely divisions, so that standing at the end of one room you could see clearly across to the end of the

other. Tall open windows at the ends of these rooms let in soft breezes that kept the place cool, as well as so much daylight they might as well have been still outside. More trees in great urns were in the two rooms, along with backless couches, tables. . . .

Brittany's interest perked yet again. Tables meant carpentry, but her kind or—bah, there was only one kind. Yet Kodos had said there was no one around here who could teach him how to work with wood, that most of the buildings in town had been built by the Darash so long ago that the knowledge of how to do so had been lost. A challenge loser could be made to build a building in punishment, but it tended to be of such poor quality that it would never be used.

"You expect to lose some challenges?" she'd teased her young friend.

He'd replied a bit indignantly, "I want to show a challenge loser how to build something properly so it can be useful, rather than task the next challenge loser with tearing it down, as is usually the case."

She hadn't asked much about these challenges, figured they were just another warrior sport. But that conversation had illuminated the early one she'd had with Dalden when he equated her job with punishment. Warriors apparently could be merchants, could direct Darash in farming, but the only thing they did with their own hands was sword-wielding. Amazing how these people managed to connect and combine their stories into a whole tale without loose ends.

The party divided then, with plans to gather again for dinner: Challen off to attend to *shodan* business, Tedra off for a catch-up session with Martha, Shanelle and Falon off to her old room, and Dalden pulling Brit-

tany along to his: down one hallway, then another, through a tower, then a garden outside with a covered walk that passed down the middle of it, into the next building, a few more hallways, some stairs, some more stairs. She was absolutely lost by the time they reached his room, which was so far away from the main sections of the castle that it might as well not be considered part of it.

The room covered the whole upper floor of the building it was in, so the balcony that surrounded it surrounded all of it. And yes, there really was a sunken pool in it, about eight feet round, like a miniature oasis with potted trees around it and a stone bench next to it. An extra-big bed was against the only wall that didn't have those open, arched windows. Not a normal bed as she knew it, it seemed to be a thick, stuffed mattress that fit into a full boxlike frame with no springs. Although it was very old-fashioned looking, the bedding appeared soft and comfortable.

There were a few more of those backless couches around a long, low table. Did they eat lying down? Carved chests sat between arches—detailed woodworking! The floors were again white marblelike stones but lightly veined with blue. Sheer light-blue curtains stirred at the windows, their only covering. There were no windowpanes or shutters.

"Tell me something, how do you keep out the flies and mosquitoes?" she asked Dalden.

"The what?"

"Insects, bugs, you know, tiny things that fly around in the air and make a habit of biting people."

"You will find such things in the lowlands, not up on a mountain."

"Ah."

"What think you of your new home?"

She knew he'd been eagerly awaiting that answer, though his expression was guarded. It was truly beautiful, his room, uncluttered yet lavish. But the whole place made her think of a sultan's harem. It brought home clearly that she was nowhere near her own home.

"It's big," she allowed.

"Indeed, a warrior has need of space to not feel confined," he agreed.

"I suppose."

"You do not like it," he remarked, clear disappointment in his tone now.

"I didn't say that," she said quickly. "It will just take getting used to."

"What do you not like about it?"

"Dalden, stop it. It's beautiful, really."

"You are mine, thus do I know you well, *kerima*, and you are not pleased with where you will live."

She held out her hand to him. When he clasped it, she brought his fingers to her mouth and bit one of his knuckles, hard. He raised a golden brow at her, though he barely felt any pain. He then grinned at her and pulled her to him. She pushed away.

"Bah, that wasn't an invitation. I was just proving you'll never know me as well as you think you do, which is a good thing. Surprises add spice to life, after all. As for these quarters, I *will* get used to them. But you saw where I lived. The house I had planned to build for myself would have been four times as big, but it still wouldn't be a castle. This place is like a—a fairy tale to me. Fairy tales are nice, but they are to be

enjoyed temporarily, not permanently. I can't see staying here forever."

"You wish to live elsewhere?"

Instead of answering that, she asked him, "Did you plan to always live here, even after you took a lifemate and started your own family?"

"There is ample room here for more than one family," he stated.

"Yes, but you're missing my point. You have no desire to spread your wings? To have a place that's exclusively yours, rather than your parents'? Where I come from, people tend to leave home as soon as they're done with their schooling, to get out and start their own lives. Parents nurture up to a point, then turn their creations loose and hope they become productive adults. You *are* an adult, right?"

That got her a scowl that she couldn't help chuckling over. It was so rare of him to display frowns of any sort, other than in confusion.

"Sorry," she said. "But I had to ask, when nothing else around here is what I'm accustomed to. Do women even work on your planet, you know, make things, build, create? Do they have occupations?"

"Not in the way you mean."

"Take me home."

"Yet they do have hobbies."

"Doesn't suffice for a working woman," she mumbled. "And yet you *do* have industry here, craftsmen, woodmills. Evidence is all over your town. Where do you hide it?"

"Kan-is-Tra has not these things. We do not tamper with nature above the surface of the ground, other than to add to it in the growing of food."

"And below the surface?"

"The gold metal is extracted in many areas of the world, including here in Kan-is-Tra. Usually Darash who live near each mine have the knowledge of crafting and shaping the metal into useful objects."

"And the furniture I've seen?"

"It is made in countries to the south. Twice a year we get huge caravans of merchants who bring these things to us. There are potters in the north. Most all Darash are skilled in weaving, sewing, and dyeing. Glassmaking is known in the east, but is generally not transported by caravan because it rarely survives the trip."

"I guess that's something," she said with some relief. "How hard is it going to be for me to commute to one of these craft countries to get a job?"

No answer and a really blank look. Brittany sighed, but recalled that there was a better information source attached to her hip.

"Martha, what wasn't to understand about that question?" she asked.

"He understood it, doll, he just didn't *understand* it, if you get my drift. Sha-Ka'ani women have simply never had a need to work. They go from one protector to another all their lives, so they never lack for support—which doesn't mean they don't have responsibilities. If you need an example, think of them as the medieval lady of the keep who keeps everything running smoothly, supervises the servants, and makes sure things get done and done right."

"That isn't work, that's home chores."

Martha chuckled. "The culture you came from had evolved in leaps and bounds in just the last hundred

years, and took giant leaps where women are concerned in just the last fifty years. So I know your
women didn't always have this 'gotta work' attitude.
You have it because you were born when it was already starting, and by the time you reached adulthood
it was already fully in place. You expected to support
yourself, expected to continue doing so even after you
married, because your people have let their economy
go bonkers, forcing them to hook up to combine in-
comes in order to get anywhere."

"And your point?"

"Look back just fifty years ago, when your culture
expected women to stay home and be housewives as
soon as they married, and work in only menial, unimportant jobs until then, and your women were *happy* in
this role. Like the medieval women before them, they
didn't bring home the bacon, but they worked: they
ran the home front, which was often harder work than
their mates were doing elsewhere. Now look what you
have here: a lot of 'housewives' comfortable with that
position just as your women were a few decades ago,
something you *can* adapt to because it's not so far off
the mark from your own history."

"Inactivity is going to drive me up a wall," Brittany
insisted.

"That's a distinct possibility, and one that Dalden
will have to think hard to rectify," Martha said. "Paying attention, big guy?"

He was, and replied stubbornly, "Hobbies will occupy her as they have my mother."

Martha all but snorted, "Don't kid yourself. Tedra's
job had been in security. There was strenuous exercise
to keep fit, and the occasional head-bashing to do, but

for the most part it was a boring job because Kystran was a peaceful planet. So she's happy to putter about with a few crafts here, but she doesn't spend much time at it. She spends more time involving herself with people, and to a degree, security at the Visitors' Center. In other words, Dalden, she's active in things she enjoys. Everyone needs *that* kind of activity."

"My lifemate will have it."

"But not enough, if I know you, and I do," Martha warned. "She needs to build things, *useful* things. It's what she enjoys doing and she does it damn well. Her craft could also be a benefit to your people, since she can create things unknown here. Like this, for instance."

Brittany had been really impressed with Martha's speech, so it was a bit of a shock to have the double rocker that she had built on the ship suddenly appear before them. No one had carried it in. It was just—there.

"By the way, Brittany, my girl," Martha said now in smirking tones, "if that's an illusion, then you probably won't want to try sitting on it or moving it out to the balcony where it would be ideal for enjoying the view. On the other hand, if you would like to sit on it, you'll probably have to accept that I just Transferred it to you, huh? Just like I did with all your belongings, now piled into Dalden's closet."

"What belongings?" Brittany said resentfully. "You people didn't exactly give me time to pack."

"Your things weren't needed aboard the ship. But Corth II collected all of what was yours, with your roommate's help—all except your rust bucket. There was no point in bringing that here when its fuel source is unique to your world."

"All of my things?"

"Yes, not that you'll get much use out of your own clothing, though you can probably convince the big guy to let you wear some of it in private."

Brittany didn't remark on that demeaning "convince." She noted the two doors on the wall without windows. The larger one led to the stairs they had mounted to get to the bedroom. The other she moved to now, and saw that it was a room a bit bigger than her bedroom at home, filled with standing racks that had local clothing draped over them, so just about everything was seen at a glance. And there piled on the other side was her own suitcase stuffed to the brim, and some boxes she and Jan had been storing in case they were needed come Christmastime, filled with what hadn't fit in the suitcase. Even her tools!

The room had no windows in it, yet it was well lit. She had to visually search for a moment to find the source of the light, a small wooden box high up on one of the shelves where Dalden's boots and belts were laid out. For that matter, there had been short ledges in his room between the windows with identical boxes on them. This one was open on top, light pouring out of it.

She was able to reach it and lowered it until she could see inside. A small blue rock was in it, about the size of a silver dollar, a single stone, the rough edges smoothed, but not perfectly round. She brought her other hand close to it, but there was no heat coming off of it as there should have been, considering this was what the light was coming from. Closer still and still no heat.

It took a moment for her to gather the nerve to actually touch it, then clasp it in her hand. Cool it was, and almost weightless.

She was fascinated, wanted to examine it closer in daylight to find the seams she couldn't manage to see just by turning it around. There had to be some. There had to be a battery inside it, making it a light.

She brought it with her back into the bedroom. The rocker was gone, but a glance around showed that the sheer curtains had been opened on one wall, revealing an archway out onto the balcony where Dalden had moved the rocker. He was out there, too, sitting in the rocker. She gritted her teeth. Obviously, the real thing had been there before they got there, transported ahead of them along with her belongings. *Transfer my ass*, she thought to herself.

She'd figure out later where they had the cameras hidden that could project illusions. Just now she was too interested in the gaali stone in her hand.

She started toward the balcony to join Dalden where it was brightest. She was maybe ten feet away from the large arch when a cat landed on the balcony from somewhere but couldn't stop from the momentum of its jump. It slid into the bedroom, coming to rest at her feet, whereby she promptly fainted. Understandable, considering that it was as big as she was.

Chapter 43

DALDEN'S SIGH WAS NOT A STRENUOUS ONE AS HE LAID
Brittany down on his bed. He sat down beside her
and carefully smoothed her hair back from her face.
Such a glorious color her hair was, unknown on his
world.

"Did she hurt herself in the fall, Martha?" he asked,
concern thick in his voice.

"Like intoxication that deadens natural reflexes,
fainters drop without trying to break their fall, so they
tend to suffer less bruising and breaking in the falling
than someone who was fully alert."

"You did not answer my question."

"Oh, you wanted specifics?" Martha's voice turned
dry. "She's fine, really."

He could be grateful for that, if nothing else. It was

everything else that was frustrating him to barely tolerable levels.

Martha had asked him to not follow his warrior instincts with his lifemate until she finally accepted him for who he was. But when would she? She was to have opened her eyes and accepted the truth when they arrived home, but still she wouldn't. Even the *hataar* she had discounted, claiming it an animal from her world in disguise. And the *fembair* had frightened her so badly she fainted, yet which animal would she claim *it* was from her world?

He was beginning to think his sister had truly cursed him all those months ago, when he'd helped to put her in Falon's control where she didn't want to be. She had been too furious to fully consider her words when she had shouted at him, *Stars, I hope the female you finally want for yourself isn't Sha-Ka'ani, and that she never gives you any peace!* It had been the worst thing she could wish for him, and it had already come half-true.

His woman wasn't Sha-Ka'ani. And her own stubbornness was going to keep an insurmountable wall between them. She loved him, yes, but not completely, nor would she as long as she continued to doubt who he was. This was already disturbing his peace. He had bided his time, though, had taken Martha at her word that Brittany would accept the truth once he got her home. That hadn't happened.

"Martha, have Shanelle come and collect her pet," he ordered.

"Not a chance," Martha declined. "The arrival of that furball was a good thing. I couldn't have planned it better myself."

"I will not allow her to be frightened again," Dalden said adamantly.

"She wasn't frightened, she just got a dose of shock too big for her to handle, no pun intended," Martha added, though she chuckled a bit. "But if you take Shank out of there before she wakes up, she'll just chock him up to another illusion. Let her get to know him, and there's no way she can deny him. Done deal."

"Our arrival here was to have been the 'done deal,'" he reminded her with clear annoyance.

Martha injected a sigh. "So I was a bit off on my estimate on the extent of her stubbornness. But she's borderline. She's clutching at straws now, and far-fetched ones at that, to maintain her disbelief. As soon as she realizes that the excuses she's coming up with to keep the wool over her eyes are more ridiculous than the truth, she'll open her eyes."

"How long?" he demanded.

"Practice some of that warrior patience that you men are renowned for. Give her one more week. Her 'project' scenario is like a security blanket to her. She clings to it because the truth frightens her."

"There is no *reason* for it to frighten her," he replied in frustration.

"Yes, we know that," Martha agreed. "But she can't see that far ahead."

"I happen to have perfect vision," Brittany mumbled in a groggy, testy voice as she came awake. "Which is a good thing, since this culture probably doesn't have eye doctors or glasses, does it?"

"Welcome back," Martha said cheerfully.

"I'm not sure I want to be back."

"Do you even think before you say things designed to inflict pain on the warrior?"

Brittany's eyes flew open in horror as that question sank in. She located Dalden next to her. She sat up immediately, and wrapped her arms around him.

"Martha is way off base," she assured him. "That wasn't said for you, but for her."

"Yet is it obvious that you do not like being here," he pointed out.

"No, if we're going to stay here, then I'll get used to it. I don't *have* to like it—really. What is important is that I *do* like being with you. Where doesn't matter. I'll be happy as long as we don't get parted when this is over."

He set her back from him, said sternly, "I have told you there can be no 'over' for us. You are mine for life, as I am yours. Such is the meaning of a lifemate. When will you accept this?"

"I—I think I do. It's just that everything else keeps getting in the way."

"Everything, as in your persistent belief that I am not a Kan-is-Tran warrior from Sha-Ka'an as I have told you I am? What, then, am I?"

"You're confusing me."

"You confuse yourself, woman."

Martha interjected, "I warned you the warrior was asserting himself, now that he's home."

"Be quiet, Martha!" they both said almost at once.

He had stood up in his agitation. Brittany's eyes flared as she finally noticed the *fembair* still in the room, spread out on the floor near the bed. Dalden had been blocking it from her view until he stood up. She didn't faint again, but the fear was back.

"Martha, get rid of that one!" she said in a high, squeaky voice, "that one" being yet another illusion, to her way of thinking.

"Contrary to *your* popular belief, I don't have any control over the local population, animal or humanoid. You can pet Shank, by the way. He won't bite."

That didn't reassure her. In this case, however, Dalden could not fault her disbelief. A *fembair* was a predator, the most vicious flesh-eater on the planet, something he would refrain from mentioning. Those that lived in the castle were tame, yet anyone who visited there and didn't know that would have the same reaction as Brittany.

It wasn't easy to tell these creatures apart. They were a non-interbreeding animal, so there was very little deviation in their looks. They all sported short white coats of an exceptional softness, long sleek bodies, and large round heads with great blue eyes. And fangs. He'd never taken one for a pet himself because they liked to sleep in beds and he didn't like sharing his—until now.

Explanations usually sufficed—for a Sha-Ka'ani who would not discount the existence of a *fembair*, merely that one could be found in a town, inside someone's house. They could make their home in any region of the planet, since the climates didn't vary greatly, they just preferred the wilds, far from people and cities.

The people of Sha-Ka-Ra were used to them wandering in and out of their town, and found it amusing that their *shodan* had managed to domesticate such a wild breed. All of which wouldn't matter to his life-

mate, whose disbelief stemmed from a different reason. He still had to try.

"Shank belongs to my sister," he told Brittany. "She raised him from a baby when she was but a child herself, so he is completely tame."

"If he's hers, what's he doing here?"

"It was a game from when we were young. I would lure him here with treats so she could not find him. It became a habit with him. He still comes here expecting treats."

"I—I hope you had some on hand to give him," she said, her voice still apprehensive.

"He is content with petting instead."

He sat down cross-legged on the floor next to the *fembair*. It immediately curled its large, supple body around him. He scratched behind its ears, under its chin. Purring began immediately.

"Come here," he told Brittany. A glance at her showed that she was adamantly shaking her head. "Come *here*," he repeated in a tone that would have made any Sha-Ka'ani woman jump to obey, but not his lifemate. "We are going to remove your fear of this feline," he explained more calmly.

"Just remove the cat instead," she suggested.

Martha scoffed at her. "You think it's an illusion. Since when can illusions hurt?"

That caused Brittany to frown. Dalden took advantage of her confusion to point out, "Can you not hear the sound of his contentment?"

She couldn't help but hear it purring so loudly it rumbled about the room. She abruptly left the bed, marched determinedly toward him, and squatted down next to Dalden, though still several feet from

Shanelle's pet. He unbalanced her, and tugged her into his lap to bring her closer to Shank. She still didn't take her eyes from the *fembair*, not once, and her body was stiff with fear despite her determination. Courage his woman had, to charge ahead, fear or not.

He took her hand, guided it to the top of Shank's head, and left it there. She didn't pull it away. And having touched the animal, she now wanted to examine it fully. She lifted the heavy head, stared into the big blue eyes, measured the length of the two four-inch fangs.

"Sabertooths are extinct," she finally said in an awe-filled voice.

He knew not what she was talking about. Martha did and merely replied, "On your planet they are."

"Nor did they ever grow this big," Brittany said.

"Careful, doll, or you might convince yourself you're in a new world."

Brittany made a low growl and shot to her feet. "I know what you've done. You found this place and have somehow kept the rest of the world from hearing about it. What is it, something in the water here that makes the people and animals grow exceptionally large? Or genetic engineering? Have you actually tampered with nature here?"

Whether he could have answered her or not, Dalden knew those questions weren't for him. Whenever she came up with a new nonreality, it was Martha she accused with it. Never him. To accuse him would mean she would have to discuss *with* him her disbelief.

They had both been reluctant to do that, to "rock the boat," as Martha would put it. But perhaps it was time for that boat to sink. It was becoming painful,

knowing that although she wanted to be with him, she wanted to be with who *she* insisted he was, not who he really was.

He needed advice from someone who had long dealt with an off-worlder.

He went to find his father.

Chapter 44

"WHERE'S HE GOING?" BRITTANY ASKED MARTHA when Dalden abruptly left the room.

"Probably off to kill something. Warriors tend to do that when they get frustrated."

"Something?"

"Don't sound so horrified, I was joking. But you, my girl, are going to have to start looking at this from his point of view. Every time you scoff at something we show you, you are scoffing at him. Every time you come up with one of your excuses, you're saying he isn't real. How do you think that makes him feel?"

"If he's brainwashed into believing all this, then it probably upsets him, but that's your fault, not mine. If he's just a really good actor playing his part, then I'll allow he might be frustrated that he's not convincing enough. But if you people would just figure out al-

ready that I'm never going to be convinced that you've brought me to another world in another star system, then he and I can both stop suffering with feelings we don't need to be feeling."

A big sigh. "Do you really want to be taken home and never see him again? Not that he'd allow it, but is that how you see this ending?"

"Why does that have to separate us? You admit the truth, I hopefully agree it's a necessary project for some greater good, and he and I can still be together— can't we?"

"The females in this society live with the males, not the other way around. For you to have him, you have to live here, in his world."

"Oh, I get it. Nothing else has worked, so now you're going to try using him specifically? The emotional angle? If I don't fall in line I lose him?"

"Your blood pressure is rising, kiddo."

"I have normal blood pressure!"

"Amazing how you humanoids can work your-selves into a snit without even half trying, and all on your lonesome. It makes my heart bleed, watching the way you struggle with so many conflicting emotions."

"According to you, you don't have a heart to bleed."

"Sector burn then, same thing."

Brittany made a sound of disgust and turned away from the door Dalden had left through. She didn't know why she continued to talk, or rather argue, with Martha, a faceless voice. The woman put new meaning into single-mindedness. Either that, or she was the head honcho in charge of the whole project, and every-one else was just window dressing.

Come to think of it, Dalden had never really tried

to convince her. He was just there, to comfort and soothe, to distract, to keep her mind off chaotic thoughts, to give her some peace. And if that was going to change now, she imagined she would go nuts within a month.

She finally noticed that the "prehistoric monster" was still in the room. God, it was *too* huge, as big as a horse. But she knew that genetic engineering could double the size of a creature. Could it be done again? And again? Until the result was something monstrous like this? Yet it was beautiful, sleek, well-proportioned, and probably graceful if it didn't have slippery floors to deal with.

Ironically, she really liked cats. She'd had several as pets when she was a child, and had one in the apartment when she first moved in, until it escaped out the door one day and never returned. That Jan turned out to be allergic to them was the only reason she hadn't gotten another yet. But she had planned to get a whole menagerie of them when she built her own home and had more room. But this one wasn't natural: it was a freak of experiments—or nature. And those fangs . . .

"Now you're being silly," Martha said, monitoring Brittany's edging backward away from the cat. "If that animal was the least bit dangerous to you, Dalden wouldn't have left you alone with it."

That was likely very true. He did seem to put great importance in protecting her. She decided she could safely ignore the beast. However it was created, it probably *was* a pet like they claimed.

But then Martha added, "There are more than just this one roaming the castle. Tedra and Challen both keep them as pets as well, so you'll come across more

of them. Try not to run the other way when you see one coming."

"Why?" Brittany asked in new alarm. "Will that make it attack?"

Martha chuckled. "No, you just strike me as someone who doesn't want it to become common knowledge what a coward you are."

Brittany became very still. "Are we resorting to insults now?"

"Well, aren't you?" Martha persisted. "You're terrified to face the truth, which is pretty silly in my book. This is a nice world. Barbaric, yes, but it's got its upside to compensate for that."

Brittany relaxed. It was typical of Martha to toss out an eye-opener like an insult just to lead into what she wanted to discuss. She should be used to it by now.

"Name one—and don't mention the air again, when clean air can be found in most mountainous regions like this."

"How about a temperate climate planetwide? There are no seasons like you have. The climate remains the same year-round in each country, a bit hotter up north, a bit cooler down south, but nothing extreme."

"Like there aren't temperate zones at home," Brittany snorted.

"Disease is unknown here. Must be that clean air you didn't want me to mention," Martha said dryly.

She would be amazed—if it were actually true. "Is it the air?"

"I don't know," Martha admitted. "It's never been analyzed. It could just as easily be the Sha-Ka'ani constitution. But there's no need for you to worry. There's

a meditech in the castle in case you catch something you shouldn't."

"I know damn well that thing isn't real. It's too bad I haven't caught a cold or the flu, to disprove your so-called meditech once and for all."

"I could probably order a virus for you. It might take a few weeks to get here, though."

"Cute, real cute. So far you're wasting your breath, Martha."

"What breath? Computers don't breathe."

"You know what I meant."

"Okay, let's try on faithfulness."

"Excuse me?"

"You'll find this interesting: a warrior who takes a lifemate will remain faithful to that lifemate for the rest of his life. I find that rather unique myself, since most cultures can't say the same, yours included."

"They love that deeply?"

A round of laughter. "You're forgetting they claim they don't experience love."

"You said some do."

"Some, yet all warriors with lifemates are faithful to them. It's more part and parcel with the protecting thing. It's a duty they take beyond serious, so it includes not only protecting from harm but also from emotional stress. And from fear. How many times now have you heard Dalden say he won't *allow* you to be afraid?"

"As if it's something he can control," Brittany scoffed.

"Don't kid yourself. He can and will assist you in conquering your fears, in one way or another. His methods might not be considered normal, but they'll

be effective. Warriors are firm believers in teaching by example. Lasting impressions are gained in that way that mere words can't hope to duplicate. Which is why the old crime and punishment philosophy goes over so well here."

"Are we *finally* getting around to discussing the laws around here?"

"No, I've concluded that the extra information I've been feeding you isn't helping and could be part of the problem. You haven't been given time to assimilate what you're learning. Besides, you know the basics, enough to stay out of trouble. No more pants for you; they offend warriors. Never leave home without an escort at your side, or without wearing a cloak of this house, so anyone who doesn't know you will see that you're protected. Be respectful of other warriors, obey your own. See? Very simple."

"Bah, you call those laws?"

"Well, actually." Martha began another round of laughing. "I don't, but they do. Rules might be a more appropriate term. They don't have the kind of laws you're used to, because they don't have the kind of crimes that require strict laws. Theft here is more a sport, a back-and-forth kind of thing. If something or someone gets stolen, they merely buy it back, steal it back—or be glad it's gone."

"Then nothing gets stolen with the expectation to keep it? Why does anyone bother?"

"Like I said, it's more a sport, something done for fun. There's also no such thing as murder; the warrior ethic simply doesn't allow it. Challenge can cause death, but rarely; it's more desirable to humiliate an enemy with challenge loss service. They have their

own rules that govern their behavior. Any disputes are brought to the *shodan* to decide. But you've let me get sidetracked."

"Is that even possible? For you?"

"My, aren't we feeling sarcastic today."

"I have a good teacher."

"I don't have an ego to bolster, doll, though I appreciate the effort. Now back to the subject, which was women. Women are the sole responsibility of their protector, be he father, lifemate, or *shodan*. Without a protector, they become claimable by any warrior who wants them, and a claimed woman isn't quite as desirable a position as a free one—for the women, that is."

Brittany stiffened, hearing that addition. "Why? And why haven't I heard about *this* before now?"

Martha injected a shrug into her tone. "It wasn't mentioned because it's never something you're going to need to worry about, as long as you obey those few simple rules we just discussed. As for why it's not a 'wanna-be' status, probably because it draws many parallels to slavery. A claimed woman can't be sold or mistreated, but they have so few rights, they might as well be considered slaves. Most women around here would rather enjoy the luxury of freedom."

"Free? When they can't go out without being led by the hand like a child?"

"Are we feeling aggrieved?"

"Damned right we are. You know I'm not going to be able to accept that when I come from total freedom of choice."

"So did Tedra, and she adjusted just fine. So will you. It just takes rearranging certain thinking and seeing the logic behind the protection that's offered. And I

could swear I said I was done feeding you information. Start asking Dalden your questions. The answers he gives you will give you a better understanding of him. Signing off, doll."

"Wait! Martha?" No answer, but the *fembair* was still there, watching her with those big blue eyes. "Go away, cat. Go on, shoo."

It didn't, but then it perked up and glanced behind him, as if it heard someone calling. She heard nothing, but animals had better hearing than humans. It then rose so fast it lost its footing on the shiny floor, regained it, ran toward the balcony, and leapt off it the same way it had arrived.

Brittany sighed in relief. Martha signed back on long enough to laugh.

Chapter 45

BRITTANY DID START STORING UP SOME QUESTIONS FOR Dalden, but he didn't return to his room. A Darash female servant showed up instead, to help her dress for dinner. And she did need help in figuring out how to get into a *chauri*.

The outfit really was just a bunch of scarves, thin, almost transparent squares of material. A bunch of them were sewn together at the tips. These were placed at the shoulders, sections then draped just so to cover what should be covered, the lot then belted about the waist to hold it all in place. The skirt was separate but put together just about the same way, a bunch of scarves sewn to a waistband and just left to fall as they would about the legs, the tips floating halfway down her calves.

Other than walking fast or encountering a brisk wind, the outfits probably remained quite decent. They were soft, feminine, cool, sleeveless, V-necked, shapely with the belt, and actually very pretty in the way they draped. Sandals that tied on her feet were provided as well, kind of weird-looking, but serviceable.

The only thing that looked out of place now was the link attached to her belt. She almost considered leaving it behind, but didn't quite dare yet, even though Martha was being conspicuously silent.

The girl, Talana, who brought the white *chauri*, said more were being made for her and would be delivered on the new rising. Her much smaller height and dark hair and eyes marked her clearly as a Darash, if her simple sleeveless tunic and long skirt didn't. Brittany wasn't used to servants, but Talana didn't seem at all servile. She was perky, full of smiles, and seemed to have a sweet nature. Other than calling her "mistress," she was merely being helpful.

Talana was also tasked with leading her to dinner. They were passing through that little outdoor garden when Brittany stopped abruptly, it finally dawning on her that she'd had no trouble understanding Talana, nor Tedra and Challen earlier, nor anyone else she'd heard speak since their arrival that morning.

She couldn't believe something that simple would have been overlooked, and her tone reflected her incredulity when she said, "You people finally blew it, didn't you?"

"Mistress?"

"How are you going to explain the fact that the peo-

ple here can understand me, if they are supposed to be a different race and language than mine?"

Talana was staring at her blankly, too confused to answer, but Martha proved she'd been eavesdropping all along when she said, "Took you long enough to notice, girl. But you got it a little backward. They aren't speaking your language; you're speaking theirs."

"Huh?"

"It really only takes one night of sleeping on a Sublim tape of a new language to have the basics of that language planted in the subconscious. Your world has started using a similar process, just not one as advanced as we have. And instead of just one session for you, I overdosed you a full week before arrival, to make the transition as painless as possible for you. Which is why it's taken you so long to notice that you have two completely different languages in your head now."

"Martha, why do you bother?" Brittany said with a sigh. "You *know* I'm not gonna buy this."

Martha's laughter had the distinct sound of triumph in it this time. "For once, kiddo, I don't have to convince you. You'll do that yourself with just a little thought. Take the word *chemar*. You know what it means, don'tcha?"

"Of course, it's—"

Brittany didn't finish. Martha had switched back to her own language with that last question, and she had answered in kind, naturally, without thought—just as she had been speaking the new language from the moment she first heard it spoken to her. Because she knew it so well, it had been automatic to respond with what she was hearing.

"It's too bad we gave you a simple communicator to

keep in touch with me, rather than a combo unit with viewers," Martha remarked. "I'd get a kick out of seeing just how white your face is about now."

Hot color suffused immediately. "Bright pink, if you must know."

"Finally amazed you, did we? With something you can't shrug off as being faked?"

Brittany ground her teeth. "Bull. Subliminal tapes are reputed to be a great learning tool, and you had three months to run one without my knowing about it while I slept. One day, my ass."

"If computers had patience to lose, I'd be losing mine about now."

That managed to surprise her. "You're giving up? It's over, then?"

"If you're never going to believe anything else, you should believe this. There isn't going to be an 'over.' There is never going to be a 'done.' The here and now is it. So get used to it. Start making the transition. You have a new life to live here; make the best of it."

"Just like that? 'Gee, how could I have been so wrong?' Is that what you expect me to say now?"

"Is it hereditary, this stubbornness of yours? Did your parents get along?"

"My parents got along fine. When they weren't fighting, they were kissing and making up."

"You said they were free-spirited."

"They grew up."

"Ah, finally the equation I've been missing. Okay, listen up, doll, because Probables did tell me what your problem is, and lucky for you, I'm still in a sharing mood. Your first fears were of the unknown. You equated aliens with weird-looking creatures. Those

fears should have been alleviated by now. The Sha-Ka'ani aren't exactly what you're used to in humanoids, but they're close enough. Your next fear is more personal and still with you."

Brittany did not want to hear this. "This isn't going to—"

But Martha couldn't be interrupted. "You're afraid to accept the happiness that Dalden offers because deep down, you see him as too good to be true. He's everything you want in a mate, everything, so you figure something must be wrong. In your mind, no one gets that lucky. Your emotions are revving up. Did I hit a nerve?"

"Go to hell."

"I'll decline that, thank you," Martha said with a chuckle. "But your warrior is about to arrive and collect you. He's had a nice little talk with his father, and has concluded that you and he need some time off to yourselves where you won't be disturbed. Which means I'll be left behind. Good luck, doll. You're going to need it."

That last didn't sound promising, so she was rather apprehensive when Dalden appeared. He was wearing one of those determined looks again. And when he took her hand and started leading her off without a word about where they were going, her apprehension escalated.

Chapter 46

"YOU KNOW, DALDEN, WHEN TWO PEOPLE DECIDE TO go on an excursion together, they usually discuss it fully beforehand, to make sure they both agree that it sounds like a good plan. That way, one or the other doesn't bring along any disgruntlement, and they both can enjoy the outing."

He didn't reply. In fact, she'd made a number of remarks since they'd left Sha-Ka-Ra, and he hadn't replied to them, either. He'd yet to say one word to her since he dragged her out of the castle.

Two *hataari* had been waiting out front for them. She had been alarmed, thinking she was to ride one of them by herself, but she wasn't. The extra mount was loaded down with stuff Dalden was taking with them, and it merely followed along behind them.

It was full night by the time they reached the bottom of the mountain. Very dark, no moon yet, but normal-looking stars. She wasn't disturbed that there were no constellations that she might recognize. She'd already figured that they'd had to take her to some far-off country she wasn't familiar with for their project to have any hope of working, and the stars she was used to obviously didn't show up on this side of the world.

She was sitting in front of him on the *hataar*. He had one arm locked firmly around her waist, so she had no fear of slipping. The other controlled the animal. They were traveling slowly, which was probably a good thing. Everything was in shadow, without much distinction. She could barely see the dirt road they followed, if it was even a road. But he obviously could.

She was still wearing the thin *chauri*, which felt rather odd—riding sitting forward with one leg dangling on each side of the animal, the scarf pieces of the skirt split, exposing her limbs halfway up her thighs. She wasn't cold, though. The weather didn't seem to change much come nighttime, was just as balmy warm as the day had been. And Martha's link *had* been left behind as she'd predicted, taken from her waist and tossed into the foliage back in that garden.

Dalden was wearing a little less than usual. He was bare-chested, except for his medallion. A sword belt had been added, along with the weapon it was designed to carry. Long, wicked-looking daggers were also strapped to each of his boots. He was wearing those arm shields again, too, that had been donned for his fight with Jorran that day in City Hall. He looked positively primitive in that getup, which probably

should have given her a clue that he wasn't the same Dalden she'd become used to.

When they passed into some woods that were so dark she gave up trying to see anything in front of her, she tried once again to get some answers. "How come you won't tell me where we're going?"

"When you say something that needs a reply, I will reply. Until then, my attention remains on the path, to assure it is safe."

Something that *needs* a reply? In other words, where they were going was none of her business?

"I don't know if I like the sound of that," she said with distinct unease.

"Your opinion was not requested, *kerima*."

She began to bristle indignantly. She couldn't help it. He was suddenly acting way too...too barbaric for her taste. It must be the clothes he was now wearing. Look primitive, become primitive?

"Martha was right. You—"

"Martha has been a hindrance," he cut in. "You may forget everything she has told you."

"Are we finally getting to the truth?"

"What truth would that be?"

"About where I am."

"Where you are is with me," he said simply.

"O—kay, then where are you?"

"With you." His chin came to rest on her shoulder. "I will always be with you."

That had a nice, secure ring to it, enough to mollify her somewhat for the moment. She supposed that if she tried, she could read between the lines of what little he'd just said. Martha had only been interested in

convincing her to believe the whole fantasy. Dalden apparently had a different agenda. He *was* the fantasy, or at least, a very big part of it. And for him, it wasn't important that she accept where she was, only that she accept who she was with.

Martha had said she'd convinced him to be patient, which pretty much meant that he'd held back up until now from showing her what he was really like. Was that what this was about, then? They were going off to be alone somewhere so she could meet the real Dalden— the barbarian she'd only seen little glimpses of so far?

She suddenly felt a very real fear. What if she didn't like the barbarian side of him? What if, as the word *barbarian* implied, he was so insufferable that she simply couldn't tolerate living with him?

They continued to ride through the wooded region, seemingly without direction. If there was a path, she no longer saw it. Miles passed with nothing to see because of the intense dark. As they got close to a clearing, it actually appeared brightly lit by the starlight.

"We will make camp here," Dalden said, dismounting and then lifting her down to the ground next to him.

Brittany had been falling asleep, and hadn't noticed the small clearing they finally entered and stopped in. A stream was nearby. She could hear it, just didn't see it yet. And a moon had risen when she wasn't looking, a great yellow ball seen through the trees.

"Is this our final destination, or do we move on in the morning?" she asked.

"We will stay here."

"And the purpose?"

"We are here to learn."

"Let me guess. I'll be doing all the learning, you all the teaching."

He had moved to unload the other animal. He glanced her way now with a raised brow.

"Your tone suggests you have brought some of that mentioned disgruntlement along with you. Have you not stressed, more than once, that you would be happy as long as you are with me? Was that not the truth? Does the place then make a difference to you?"

She sighed. "You're right. I don't know why I'm on edge—actually, I do know, but I'll get over it now that we're communicating again. We *are* communicating again, right? No more of that ridiculous silent treatment?"

"There is always a reason for what I do," he told her. "Wild animals make their home in these woods. Hunters come here to hunt them. Travelers pass through them between towns, as do raiding parties. My full concentration was needed to keep our journey safe. It was also my intention to be assured that Martha could not follow us with her short-range scanning, which she could have done from our speech. You do not need her protection any longer. You are *mine* to protect. Lastly, you have learned that there will be decisions that I will make that are not open to discussion."

"Wow, that was a great explanation—up to the end," she said drily.

He went back to the unpacking, but remarked in a tone without inflection, "You are determined to find fault with me. Why is that?"

"Martha warned—"

"Martha again?" he cut in. "Did I not say you should forget what she has told you?"

"You know that isn't possible."

"When most of what she has told you, you do not believe anyway?"

She blushed clear to the roots of her hair. Fortunately, Dalden wasn't looking and probably wouldn't have noticed those hot cheeks in the dark if he was. She *had* been expecting the worst after Martha's warning, had been expecting all kinds of unacceptable traits from him now. He said they were there to learn, and that *did* go both ways. What was wrong with that? She wanted to know him better, to know every single thing there was to know about him, didn't she?

"I'm sorry," she offered. "I did bring along some preconceived notions, but I'm putting them to rest now. Would you like some help with that? I was a Girl Scout as a kid, so I know how to erect tents, get fires started, gather food, and otherwise survive in the wild."

That gained his complete attention for a moment. "Truly? Such things are taught the females in your world?"

"Well, not the whole world," she was forced to admit. "It's a program offered in my particular country, with similar programs in a few others. It's not mandatory, and actually, very few girls join it these days with so many other activities to interest them instead. That's a shame, since it teaches some really good qualities, as well as useful things to learn. Enjoying camping with my brothers, I personally found it very beneficial."

He nodded, even grinned at her. "I am pleased you enjoy camping. Most of our women would complain

mightily at being taken away from the comfort of their homes. They fear the 'wild' as you call this."

She hoped their fear was without good reason, and at least he didn't say *Your wilds are different from our wilds.* As to her suggestion, he seemed to be ignoring it, probably because the tent turned out to be too big and heavy for her to handle, no thin nylon or army canvas, but a seriously thick material designed to keep out whatever might come snooping around. There were a lot of things to carry inside, though, after it was erected, and he let her help with that.

When they were done, a large fur rug had been un-rolled in the middle of the tent as their bed. Numerous sacks were brought in, as well as a gaali stone box that provided tons of light, making a campfire obsolete except for cooking. That wasn't needed tonight, since he'd brought along their dinner, already cooked.

They shared the meal. Dalden insisted on feeding it to her, which she didn't mind. Actually, he made it an erotic experience, whether intentional or not, that she thoroughly enjoyed. So she couldn't be faulted in thinking they were going to be making love soon after the meal.

"Come here."

Replete and mellow now, and having decided this camping trip just might turn out to be a lot of fun, Brittany didn't hesitate. She settled down on his lap, felt his strong arms come around her, and expected him to kiss her. He didn't.

He tilted her head in the right position for kissing, but there were other things on his mind. "Was that difficult, to obey me?"

It was the word *obey* that set off alarm signals really

loudly this time. Brittany stiffened and tried to move off him to a distance more appropriate for a discussion she didn't think she was going to like. But she was held firmly in place. A subtle reminder that if someone refused to obey, she could be forced to?

Chapter 47

BRITTANY TRIED TO GIVE DALDEN THE BENEFIT OF THE doubt, she really did. She allowed that she was overreacting to one simple word. Granted, it was a word that went against the grain for an independent woman who'd been making all her own decisions since she left home. But all she had to do, really, was give the word a less offensive meaning. After all, she hadn't been "obeying," and said so to answer his question.

"I didn't see it as an order, but a suggestion."

"Had it been an order?"

"Then it would have required thought on my part," she replied.

"Why?"

"Because I don't like orders. They are demeaning, suggesting I lack intelligence. That's why I didn't join

the military. I wouldn't have been able to handle hearing nothing but orders. And don't look so surprised; women can be soldiers where I come from. Wasn't it the same where your mother comes from?"

"I will allow that the technology of these other worlds make such possible, if you will allow that in a society where the weapons are only swords and strength, a woman cannot hope to compete."

That caused an image in her mind of her trying to wield a four-foot sword that she could barely lift against one of these barbarian giants. It was an absurd image that caused her to grin, then chuckle.

"Good point," she said.

Again he looked surprised, probably because he'd expected an argument. "You agree?"

"Sure, but that still doesn't mean I'm going to jump when you say jump."

"Even if an order is given for your own good?" Dalden persisted.

She gave that some thought, then allowed, "Some orders are acceptable, certainly, but you aren't my boss with power over my job, or my government, or the law. You're the man I live with in a mutual relationship. Why would you even want to order me around?"

"It is not a matter of want, but of necessity," he told her. "It is my right to protect you. No one else has this right more than I—even you. This is not something that normally needs explaining. Our women are taught from birth what they can and cannot do, and who they must obey in all things—and why. A warrior needs the assurance that if he finds his woman in danger, and must instruct her to remove her from that danger, she will not stop to argue about it. If he cannot

have this assurance, then he would restrict her more than is needful, and neither would be pleased."

"Okay, I see where you're coming from. If your women have been trained from birth to literally jump when you say jump, then you men probably take it for granted that they'll do just that. But you have to take into account that I wasn't trained that way, so instead of getting an old horse to follow new tricks, how about just keeping in mind that I'm not one of your women and so need to be treated differently?"

"Do you tell me you did not follow the rules of your father?" he said.

She frowned. "Not just my father, my parents. Both. Rules mutually decided on. Yes, when I lived with them I obeyed their rules, but it was with full knowledge that when I left home I'd be living by my own rules. Do you see the difference? Those were temporary rules, the rules for a child. Our children grow up knowing that eventually they'll be on their own, with no one but government and laws telling them what they can and can't do. You, on the other hand, are telling me that your people continue to treat your women like children even after they're adults. I'm twenty-eight years old, Dalden, in case that hasn't been mentioned yet. I am *not* a child."

His hands suddenly cupped her breasts fully, heat searing through the thin material of the *chauri*. "I do not see you as a child."

She blushed. He couldn't miss it this time with the gaali stone lighting the inside of the tent with daylight brightness. He smiled. She scowled.

"Don't sidestep the issue," she said. "I wasn't talking about sex, but general overall treatment. I've heard

the ridiculous rules you place on your women, that they have to dress a certain way, that they can't walk out their front door without having their hand held by some man. Has it even occurred to you how demeaning I would find such rules?"

Now he frowned. "You were told the rules but not why there are such rules?"

"Martha didn't want to discuss them at all, probably because she finds them as offensive as I do."

"They are not meant to offend, but to protect."

"If your town was a civilized town, then I could walk its streets without fear of being bothered. Are you going to tell me it's not civilized?"

"How many times were you told that Sha-Ka'an is viewed by modern worlds as a barbaric world? Did you truly think you would find equality between men and women here?"

The blush was back. She *had* been forgetting that. Not that it meant much when this was all make-believe anyway, but if she was going to go along with the program—or at least accept the possibility that Dalden really did believe all this—then she needed to keep in mind that nothing here was going to be what she would call normal. Why was she even fighting it? What she needed to figure out was if she could live with it—at least until the "program" was over.

"All right, so you're barbarians—I'm sorry, I know you don't like that word, but you brought it up. And you say these rules that I object to are for my own protection. Why? What happens if I don't follow them?"

"You will be punished."

"You have jails for this?"

"No."

"Whipping posts?"

"Do not be silly, woman," he said sternly. "Your punishment would be mine to give, and you know I would not cause you physical pain."

She did know that. He was always mindful of his greater strength, always so careful in touching her. She sighed, leaned forward to lay her head on his chest.

"I'm beginning not to like this discussion," she said in a tired voice.

He immediately began to soothe her with his hands. "We need not finish it now, yet it is my wish that you have no more questions when we leave here."

She was all for that. She'd avoided those answers, or had had them avoided for her, too long now.

"That must have been quite a talk you had with your father," she remarked.

"How did you—?"

"Martha."

"Ah, Martha. Indeed, she was thorough in her report. My parents were together to hear it."

"I take it you're ignoring her advice to continue patience with me?"

"My patience has not assisted you to full acceptance," he said.

"Dalden, I'm *never* going to accept this fantasy. If you can't accept that—"

"Answer me this, *kerima*," he cut in. "If you did believe everything that has been told you, would it change your feelings for me?"

"No," she said without hesitation.

"This is what my father pointed out to me. Martha's predictions of doomed failure did not take into ac-

count a woman's heart, which Martha can never fully understand."

"Then why bring me out here?"

"To assist you to a full acceptance of me."

"But I—"

He put a finger to her lips. "I will endeavor to explain what I mean. The culture differences that so worried Martha are indeed real. Already you have shown an unwillingness to embrace my culture. What you have yet to realize is there is no choice in the matter, for you or for me. If this were a different country in your world that you were visiting, would you refuse to obey its laws while you were there? Would you expect immunity from those laws simply because you were not born there?"

"No, but—"

Once again he didn't let her finish. "Then why do you resist doing so here? Because here is not real to you? Is your denial, then, the true problem after all?"

"But what's that got to do with a full acceptance of you?" she demanded.

"Everything, *kerima*," he said gently. "You *will* have to obey our rules. You *will* be punished if you do not. Can you accept this, and understand that it is not something I will enjoy doing? A warrior often suffers as much, if not more, in the punishment of his woman."

She didn't snort, though the urge was there. They treated their women like children—the punishments were no doubt of the same nature. His worry, and what was beginning to worry her as well, was, could she accept *him* enforcing one of those childish punish-

ments on her? Probably not. But she could compromise. She could follow their silly rules so that the matter would never be put to the test.

She said as much. "How 'bout I just obey the rules, so you can stop worrying about punishments you're never going to have to dish out? Will that ease your mind?"

"It pleases me greatly that you will make this effort," he said gravely.

Her brow knitted in a frown. "Then why don't you look pleased? That wasn't what you wanted to hear, was it? Do you *really* want my permission—and forgiveness—before the fact?"

"These things are not needful," he replied. "It is your understanding that I wish to assure. I have explained what can happen. I need to know that you understand why such things are necessary here."

She counted to ten before she lost it over what *wasn't* needed. She finally sighed.

"I think I'll take you up on that offer to drop the subject for now. You've given me a lot to think about. I need some time to digest it."

Having said that, she tried once again to move off his lap and out of his reach. Again, she couldn't. She narrowed her eyes on him.

"That's major advantage taking, using your strength against me like this."

"A benefit of a warrior," he said, grinning at her to show that he might be teasing, but she'd place her wager on not. "For what reason do you wish to move?"

"So I can sulk, of course," she retorted.

He shook his head at her, still grinning. "If we are done with discussing matters of importance, then it is time for—other things."

"Such as?"

"A benefit of being a woman."

It turned out to be quite a benefit that night.

Chapter 48

IT NEVER SEEMED TO CHANGE, THE COMPLETE AND utter distraction of Dalden's kisses. From the moment his mouth claimed hers, everything else was forgotten. Where they were, what they'd been discussing, her annoyance—all gone with the touch of his lips.

That was quite a power he had over her. If she didn't trust him, it might worry her, that power.

He stripped her in his lap, a task made too easy by the *chauri*. He merely placed his hands by her neck, moved them over her shoulders and down her arms in a slow caress, and the *chauri* went with them, baring her to the waist. She barely noticed because he was still kissing her, a deep "you're mine" kind of kiss that instantly ignited her passions—which was a good thing. His hands might be slowly caressing her, but the rest of him was on a much faster time schedule. A

slight change in her position and she was impaled and exploding with pleasure. All within a matter of minutes. And still sitting on his lap!

Dazed, breathless, still throbbing, she barely had a chance to notice his grin before he began anew. And thus it went for most of the night. She lost count of the many different pleasures she received. Her barbarian was inexhaustible. She wasn't, but sleep wasn't on the agenda. He had only to touch her again, to start the kissing again, and she was fully awake and in need.

Overdosed on pleasure. Absolutely amazing. This was his way, she knew, of making up for all the harsh "realities" of his world that she didn't like, by reminding her of the benefits—the benefits of being a woman. What he should have said was the benefits of being *his* woman.

She was hard pressed when she finally awoke the next day to get rid of the silly grin she was wearing. It was late. They'd slept the morning away, or at least she had. He was already awake and simply holding her next to him when her eyes opened. And he seemed no more inclined than she was to start up that depressing "this is how it is" conversation again.

He fed her leftovers from the night before. He wanted to know about fishing, which she'd mentioned more than once. They apparently had fish in their lakes and streams, but no one had ever bothered to think of adding them to their list for daily consumption. She didn't buy that, but had fun whittling a fishing pole with one of his daggers, borrowing some *hataar* tail hair to braid for a line, and showing him how to use the finished product in the stream nearby.

He was impressed, but he concluded there was no challenge in hunting fish, as he put it. He preferred larger game that would provide more than just one meal. She'd already figured out that he would be doing some of that kind of hunting on this trip, and he left around midafternoon to take care of finding their dinner.

She wasn't sure why she'd thought she'd be allowed to go with him. Actually, it was probably because when she'd hunted with her brothers, they'd all done it together. But women here weren't allowed to hunt whether they knew how to or not. Nor was it open to discussion. She was ordered to stay in the tent while he was gone, to not leave it under any circumstances, and that was that.

He did pause long enough to explain that the tent was her only protection while he wasn't with her. It would be considered her home, and as long as she was in it, any warriors who might come by wouldn't intrude without permission. It was also built sturdily enough to keep out any animals, so she'd be safe as long as she stayed *in* it.

She'd had to agree to do that before he would leave. She felt he was making too much out of nothing. She'd been outside while he was there, down to the stream, around the edges of the clearing. It was a peaceful setting. She wasn't worried about being left alone there, was more annoyed at being restricted to the tent than anything else.

But he assured her he wouldn't be gone long, gave her a parting kiss to give her something else to think about, and rode off. She paced about the tent for a

bit—prowled was more like it—until she finally shrugged off her annoyance and decided to grab a short nap to pass the time.

She'd no sooner laid down on the soft fur rug than she heard the *hataar* that had been grazing in the clearing run off. She didn't think much of it. If it was anything at all like a horse, even a bird flying past could spook it. The animal should have been staked. Dalden would just have to go chase it down when he got back. But then she heard other noises closer by, the sound of clicking, of something dragging on the grass, a couple of thumps.

She got slowly to her feet. She'd heard Dalden's *hataar* leave. She would have heard it return. It wasn't Dalden out there making noises around the tent edges. The sounds were too strange to be coming from a human anyway, so it was some animal investigating the tent. She still wasn't that alarmed. If it was a predator, it would have chased after the *hataar*—unless it counted the *hataar* as too big to handle.

She had no weapon other than her fishing pole, which wouldn't do her a bit of good against the two-legged kind of predator, but might scare off the four-legged kind. But she was more curious than anything else. This was an unplanned visit, so no illusions or costumes would be involved. She had a chance to see a perfectly normal-looking animal from her world, a deer maybe, or a bear, something to reinforce her version of where they were.

She just wanted a quick look. Dalden wasn't there to see her disobey his order, and she'd be back in the tent before he was. She unlatched the tent flap. The animal was on the left side of the tent. She stepped out-

side, moved slowly to that corner, and peeked around it—and stared wide-eyed at yet another oddity that defied belief.

It was a long, spiked tail that had been dragging on the ground. Her gasp drew slanted yellow eyes to her. She ducked back and dove back into the tent, but it used powerful legs to leap over the corner to try to stop her. It was so swift it had turned and landed in time to see where she went, and pushed its way in behind her. She didn't know that until she turned to secure the flap and saw it squatting there just inside the tent, staring at her.

She had absolutely no idea what it was. The animals she'd seen so far, though weird, still bore some resemblance to animals she knew. Not this thing. It was big, about four and a half feet tall, and fat, at least on the bottom half of it. The top half tapered to thin shoulders and a round head with pointy ears, no visible nose, those slanted yellow eyes, and a jutting jaw with lots of teeth. Its arms were misshapen and seemed too short compared to the rest of it to do anything. It maneuvered and balanced itself with the long tail and powerful, squat legs, each with three clawed toes. It was gray and hairless, its skin wrinkly. If not for all those exposed teeth, it would simply look funny.

She was nervous, but she didn't think anything that looked that weird could be dangerous. It could have just followed her out of curiosity. A lot of animals were more afraid of humans than vice versa, and this one might just need reminding of that. With that in mind, she picked up the fishing pole at her feet and thrust it forward like a sword, at the same time screeching really loudly. Nothing. It just stared at her.

Annoyed now, she poked her whittled stick at it a few more times, growling, "Get the hell out of my house. Go on. Scat! Shoo!"

One thrust actually touched it. It didn't like that, started some growling of its own, and that clicking sound again. Its teeth? The claws on its stubby arms? She couldn't tell, but decided one of them had to leave. And if *it* wouldn't . . .

She moved slowly to the front of the tent, forcing it to turn to keep its eyes on her. She hit her stick on the floor a few times, trying to get the thing to move back away from the opening that it was blocking. It did, but its growling increased. It was getting angry. It lowered its head nearly to the ground, raised it again.

She was afraid it was getting ready to rush her. She would have liked to back it farther into the corner before she exited, her hope being that if she made enough noise on that side of the tent from the outside, it would turn in that direction rather than follow her, and trap itself in the tent long enough for her to get away.

She ducked outside, screamed Dalden's name, ran her stick along the side of the tent as she raced toward the back, then ran straight for the stream. Water. A scent masker. And she'd noticed a few pockets deep enough where she could submerge if necessary. She just had to reach it while that thing was still trying to find its way out of the tent.

It landed in front of her. It had leapt an incredible distance to land right in front of her! And there was no stopping, as fast as she'd been running. She collided with it, tumbled over it, and rolled down the rest of the bank, coming to rest half in, half out of the stream.

She was dazed, but too frightened now for that to

stop her. She sat up. It was foremost in her mind that she had to get to the other side of the water. It might be afraid of the water, or at least wary enough not to cross it. That could be her only salvation.

It landed on top of her, breaking half of her rib cage, crushing one lung. There was no breath left for screaming, no breath at all. She fainted for a moment, and woke up to excruciating pain . . . wet, warm, bloody. She wasn't dead yet, but wished she was. Its hands really were useless. It was dragging her out of the water with its teeth, feeling like it was ripping off half her leg in the process.

Her last thought before the pain sent her back into blessed nothing was that Dalden had brought her across the universe to be eaten by a stupid beast. He wouldn't be pleased.

Chapter 49

"ARE THEY REALLY THAT STUPID?" TEDRA DEMANDED of the computer link in her hand. "To declare war on a League-protected planet is to declare war on the entire Confederation."

"Not stupid," was Martha's placid reply. "Just too primitive to think that far ahead."

Tedra was furious, not over the audacity of the inhabitants of Century III who had arrived en masse, but because Challen was taking this seriously *and* looking forward to a good old-fashioned war. But there'd be nothing old-fashioned about it. The Centurians weren't planning on landing for any hands-on fighting. They'd be bombarding from space.

Jorran had apparently done a lot of crying and complaining when he got home. That he hadn't been in the

best condition, left somewhat deformed by his mended injuries, had obviously enraged his relatives enough to want revenge on his behalf. You simply didn't treat a High King that way and expect to live to tell about it.

The highest High King of the lot, Cayden, head of their royal family, had confiscated every visiting ship in their star system, for a total of twenty-three ships, from common traders and swift privateers to battleships. An impressive flotilla, which was probably why Cayden had sounded so confident. He thought he had the upper hand.

Martha disagreed. "Rust buckets," she called his entire fleet, every one of them so ancient, they hadn't been converted to crysillium, much less gaali power. Which was why she wasn't the least bit concerned about this invasion. Still aboard the *Androvia*, she was just waiting for permission to blast the Centurians back to where they came from.

Challen was refusing to give that permission, which was probably a good thing. The Centura League strived to avoid war, to exercise any and all peaceful options first, resorting to war only as an absolute last measure. They expected planets under their protection to follow suit. Tedra knew that and would have been pointing it out, if she weren't taking this personally. Challen was also taking it personally, but for different reasons.

Demands had been made. If not met, war would be declared. So far they had stalled the Centurians, who were asking for Dalden's head, and his woman. Dalden wasn't around to offer it, had taken his lifemate off for some prime time alone. Even if they knew

where he'd gone, it would take time to reach him. Not that Tedra had any intention of letting him know that his head was on the table for negotiation, when Dalden was known to make sacrifices in the name of honor.

It wasn't that Dalden's death and his lifemate delivered into Jorran's hands was the restitution the Centurians wanted for the insult dealt to Jorran. This wasn't even considered by Challen. No, he was seeing this from a warrior's viewpoint, not a father's.

The Centurians dared to make war on Sha-Ka'an. And there wasn't a warrior on the planet who wouldn't be insulted by this and rise up joyfully to the occasion. The planet as a whole didn't know about it yet, however. The demands had come through the Visitors' Center and were relayed directly to Challen through his link to the director of the Center. One of the Centurian ships had managed to fool the Center into gaining entry before the rest arrived. The director was in their hands, the global shield already turned off.

A lot of damage—and deaths—could result if the Centurians started laser-blasting the planet. Which was why Challen was stalling. He wanted time to get his warriors to the Center.

Tedra just wanted a little extra time to think of all the ramifications before she mentioned that it wasn't necessary to go to the Centurians, that those who had taken control of the Center could be brought to them instead, instantly Transferred, just as Cayden could be. But when Challen became warriorish, he seemed to overlook what Mock IIs in super-high-tech warships were capable of. Or perhaps he didn't overlook it, he'd just rather do it his way.

And he was about to do just that, to leave with his warriors, who had been summoned to the castle. Tedra moved quickly to block his way.

He had only to look at her stubborn expression to warn, "Do not interfere, woman."

Which meant that if she did now, she'd be in trouble. He hadn't told her to be quiet, though, and she wasn't.

"Which would be more satisfying, to have Cayden laying in a pool of blood or to have him eat crow and beg your forgiveness for coming here?"

"The man is a leader of his people," Challen replied. "I would not belittle him with humiliation, but offer him honorable death."

"But which would be more *satisfying*?" Tedra persisted.

He gave her a chagrined look. She took advantage of his moment of indecision to add, "And he's not at the Center. Only Jorran and his crew are. High King Cayden is up on the biggest of their ships, calling the shots in what he thinks is complete safety."

"Jorran isn't at the Center, either," Martha suddenly put in to Challen. "You might want to hold off doing anything, big guy. I've just been contacted by Jorran to perform an emergency Transfer to a meditech."

"For him?" Tedra asked in surprise.

"No, for your daughter-in-law."

Tedra paled. "Was it in time?"

"Undetermined yet," Martha was forced to reply. "She's lost a *lot* of blood, is barely hanging on by a thread." It was eight suspenseful seconds before Martha was able to add, "Okay, Transfer was in time; she's out of immediate danger. I hate to say it, but Jor-

ran saved her life by contacting me. You are now officially indebted to the jerk."

Tedra swore a blue streak. Challen came to put his arms around her.

"It is doubtful his act was without self-interest," he said. "Was it, Martha?"

"No indeed. He wanted Brittany saved so he could take her home with him. Those idiots lucked out getting Transfer this time on one of their ships, but there's still not a meditech among them. He managed to find Brittany by scanning for her language. He Transferred to her location, killed the *sa'abo* that was ripping her to shreds, and knew that the only thing that could save her at that point was a meditech. And the only way for him to get her to one was through me."

"Where the hell is Dalden?"

"Scanning the surrounding area for him now," Martha answered. "But with him not talking, I'm not likely to get a fix on him. And he's guaranteed to go berserk if he shows up and finds all that blood at his camp but no Brittany. I had visual and it wasn't pretty. So I've sent Corth II there to await his return with explanations."

"Are you sure Jorran didn't Transfer him somewhere?" Tedra asked.

"He swears Dalden wasn't there when he arrived. I'm inclined to believe him. He's pretty shaken up."

"*He* is?"

"And Brittany wouldn't have tangled with a *sa'abo* herself if Dalden had been there," Martha pointed out.

That being true, the edge was taken off Tedra's fear for her son. Which left only the annoyance that they

couldn't deal as harshly with Jorran now, with their gratitude getting in the way.

"What was he doing searching for them?" Tedra asked next. "Are their demands just a ploy?"

"Probables tell me Jorran neglected to tell his relatives about me and the *Androvia*. The highest king is legit. He *is* here for revenge, his house offended by our treatment of one of theirs. But Jorran knows firsthand what they're up against, and that the only way he'd get what he wants would be to sneak in and accomplish it himself while we were otherwise distracted by Cayden."

"So he brought his relatives here knowing they'd get egg on their faces? Why?"

"When I mentioned that he liked our Brittany, I didn't think it was necessary to stress just how much he liked her. All things considered, we shouldn't have crossed paths with him again, so it wasn't an issue."

Tedra frowned. "How much are we talking about?"

"He wants her for his queen, and since she'll bring him no land, status, subjects, wealth, or other queenly gains, it's a safe guess his 'want' is strictly personal."

"*Farden* hell," Tedra mumbled.

"He's given up his advantage by rescuing her and giving her back to us for mending. Had he found them alone, it's a guarantee he would have Transferred them both to his ship and would be racing for home already, using Dalden as leverage to keep us from following. And Dalden wouldn't have found the journey pleasant. That Jorran found Brittany about to die put an end to those plans. Her dire condition has probably saved Dalden from endless torture. I hope the boy

takes that into account before he starts thinking about punishing her for tangling with a *sa'abo*."

"Did she have a choice?"

"That critter is too stupid to find its way inside a secured tent. Need I say more?"

"No, but near death—I'd say she's already suffered enough."

"Since when do warriors take previous suffering into account when lessons need to be taught? That only reinforces their need to assure the situation will never happen again, and we know the name of that tune."

That got Challen a glare from Tedra just on general principle. That he chuckled at his lifemate confirmed that Martha had called it right.

Chapter 50

IT WAS FORTUNATE THAT THE LID OF THE MEDITECH opened before Brittany's eyes did, or she would have thought she'd been sealed in a coffin. Not a thought far off the mark, since she had known that she was going to die. But she wasn't dead, or if she was, at least the pain that had surrounded her was now gone. Yet with Tedra standing there offering her a hand to help her up, she had to conclude she wasn't in Heaven, either.

She sat up, carefully at first, in case she was only imagining that the pain was gone. But it was. She could breathe normally now, too. And looking down at herself, she saw the evidence that she hadn't dreamed it all, her *chauri* in bloody shreds barely hanging onto her limbs. But no wounds on those limbs.

"It works from the inside out, which is why it doesn't require naked patients," Tedra remarked.

Brittany recognized *it*, the meditech that had put her back together. It sat in a small room by itself, she assumed in the castle. No one else was there, just Tedra—and Martha, if that was a computer link hooked to Tedra's belt.

"Would you like a list of the injuries that have been fixed?"

"No, I felt most of them as they occurred," Brittany said. "I don't need reminding, thank you."

Tedra winced. "You're taking this pretty calmly."

"I'm not calm," Britanny replied. "The shock hasn't worn off yet."

"Understandable. That was one of the nastier predators around here that you tangled with. *Sa'abo* bring down their prey by ripping out its neck, usually resulting in instant death. I'm glad it didn't reach yours."

"That wasn't the shock I meant. You really are his mother, aren't you?"

It must not be a computer link that was attached to Tedra's belt, or Martha would be gloating by now. Tedra merely smiled in understanding.

"It is a bit difficult to ignore being brought back from the brink by a machine, I suppose," Tedra said. "But don't try to assimilate everything you've discounted yet. You'll have plenty of time for that."

Assimilate everything? Things were rolling through Brittany's mind at high speed: the *Androvia*, all the different planets that had been mentioned, the different degrees of evolution, Sha-Ka'an on the bottom of the ladder in development, barbaric, yet amazing for all that . . .

Embarrassment began to override the shock. These people had been so patient with her, Dalden unbelievably so. She'd as much as called him a liar countless times with her continued disbelief, but he hadn't given up on her. He wasn't brainwashed, hadn't been playing a role. He was a real alien from a warrior caste of people who were barbaric in their customs and beliefs. And she was married to him, or bound to him by their equivalent of marriage—his lifemate.

"You'll want to go to your room and change clothes before Dalden is found and Transferred here," Tedra was saying, taking no pity on a mind gone haywire with the unbelievable suddenly turned real. "The less he sees of the trauma you went through, the better."

"Why? It wasn't his fault. He warned me to stay in the tent. There's no reason for him to blame himself."

That caused Dalden's mother to frown, and as if Martha had a visual of it, she proved she was present and accounted for by saying to her owner, "No need for confusion, doll. Our Brittany sees this from an Earthling's perspective, where their men have been conditioned to shoulder blame whether blame is theirs or not. She hasn't grasped yet that when a warrior's rules are obeyed, protection is guaranteed. So the only way for harm to occur is if the rules are broken. All blame is then on the rule-breaker, and the rule-giver is required to reinforce those rules with lessons guaranteed to leave lasting impressions, so the rules don't get broken a second time."

"Did you have to remind her of that, Martha?" Tedra said with a sigh.

"'Course I did," Martha replied in distinctly smirk-

ing tones. "Nothing like a big dose of reality to shake off the cobwebs that shock leaves behind."

It did take a few moments for those cobwebs to clear enough for Brittany to grasp what Martha had actually said in her long-winded way. She went very still.

"Let me get this straight. I just went through hell. If it weren't for mind-boggling inventions like Transfer and meditechs, I'd be dead right now. And you think Dalden's going to punish me on *top* of that?" No answer from either of them, which was answer enough and had Brittany shaking her head. "No way. He wouldn't."

"Let's look at the facts." Martha switched to her teacher tone. "The beast that nearly had you for dinner is about as dumb as they come. It could smell you in your secure tent. It could be certain you were in there. But it's too stupid to even think of looking for a way to get in at you. It would instead wait for you to come out. It might wait a long time, because it does smell food. But eventually it would get hungry enough to go look for food that it can actually see instead of just smell. Of course, Dalden would have returned before then and killed it with little difficulty. Warriors are good at that. So if you *had* stayed in that tent as you admitted you were told to, would you have gone through hell?"

"You're missing the point that I've already suffered enough."

"No, you're missing the point that you wouldn't have suffered at all if you had simply obeyed your warrior. And he's going to be furious that you came to harm because you didn't obey him—and make damn

sure you never put yourself in that kind of danger again. Are you understanding their logic yet?"

"I understand it," Brittany mumbled. "That doesn't mean I agree with it."

A chuckle from Martha. "Warriors don't require agreement. Tedra can assure you of that."

"Leave me out of this, old girl," Tedra replied. "I happen to be getting along just fine with my warrior this week. Don't remind me why I shouldn't."

"She's exaggerating, kiddo. My Tedra gets along with her warrior all the time. She might step out of line occasionally and suffer the consequences, but she makes sure Challen makes up for it big-time."

Brittany stared at her mother-in-law. "You come from a society much more advanced than mine. I would have thought that you, more than anyone, would find these rules and laws as barbaric as I do. Ordered to stay in that tent, I fully understand now. I didn't and found out painfully why I should have. But everything else? Unneeded escorts, clothes to mark your status—why don't the rules get put on the men instead? Why aren't they told that women are to be left alone? How can you accept being treated like a child?"

"Hot damn, I'm looking forward to this answer myself," Martha said.

Tedra ignored her instigating computer to hook her arm through Brittany's. She began to escort her to her room while she explained, "I don't accept being treated like a child, but I do accept the laws of the land. No one expects you to be a model of Kan-is-Tran womanhood overnight, not even Dalden. I had an easier time adjusting because my first month here was spent in a challenge loss, which was about as close as you

can get to slavery. Since I had agreed to the challenge, I had to honor the results of losing it, so I couldn't really complain about how belittling the position was. My point being, I was introduced to the way things are around here while I was on the bottom of the social scale. Which made it much easier to accept the things allowed higher up on the scale, even if most of those things grossly favor the male of the species."

"Grossly?" Brittany snorted. "How 'bout one hundred percent?"

Tedra grinned. "Face it, it's a male-dominated society, and because these males happen to come in giant-like proportions, they've had to make up a few little rules to keep themselves from hurting their women. The women raised here don't mind the rules because they've never known anything better. Are you getting that particular point yet? To them it's *not* barbaric, it's normal."

"And exceptions don't get made for visitors?" Brittany asked.

"Why should they? It's not as if a visitor from another world can be differentiated from a visitor from another country here. They don't have schools as you know them. They aren't taught about other people on their own world, much less about other worlds. They exist in black and white, and don't recognize much gray. They keep things simple, uncomplicated. If a woman doesn't have a protector, then she's up for grabs. You can't get much simpler than that. But once she has a protector, then she has to obey him to keep herself protected. You really can't get much simpler than that."

"You do realize that you've just defined childish?" Brittany said.

Tedra didn't try to deny it, at least not completely. "From an advanced perspective, certainly. But from their perspective, it's actually pretty civilized. They aren't killing each other to take what they want. They've set up laws that they all abide by, self-governed by their warrior code of honor. They are light-years beyond our own prehistoric people. They are unique, without comparison—actually, that's probably half your problem, kiddo. You need to stop comparing them to your own species."

"It's kind of hard to ignore twenty-eight years of my own upbringing."

"Because you're looking at things here while wearing modern glasses. Take off those glasses and you'll get a completely different view, one much easier to tolerate. I know that's asking a lot. It was also easier for me because I spent three years training for a career in World Discovery before I was allowed to switch to my preferred career in Security. And one little gem I learned in Discovery was that if you want to live on a world other than your own, you do so not with the intention of changing that world, but of adapting to it. These medieval worlds *must* be allowed to evolve at their own pace. It's not for us to tamper with them just because we know better ways of doing things."

"I hate to break up such an excellent lesson in how to deal with your local barbarian," Martha interjected sarcastically. "But Corth II just informed me that Dalden is now approaching his camp."

Brittany frowned. "If Dalden didn't find me and get me back here, who did?"

"Martha did."

"I thought her link got left behind."

"It was," Tedra said. "It was actually Jorran who found you, and only because he was specifically looking. He had his ship computer contact Martha for a Transfer directly to a meditech. You didn't have enough blood left for any other option."

"Specifically looking?"

"He has returned with an army for revenge—and you. Not that he'll be getting either, but because he more or less saved your life, we're having to deal with him diplomatically again. He's requested permission to speak with you and has agreed to leave afterward. Because it's a peaceful way of avoiding an outright war with Century III, we were inclined to agree. He's catching a ride here on an airobus as we speak."

"No Transfer?"

"He's used up his quota for the day—which reminds me. Corth II will be filling Dalden in on what happened, but you might want to point out to him that your meeting up with that *sa'abo* caused Jorran to change his original plan, which was to capture you both and cart you off to Century III, and Dalden probably wouldn't have survived the trip."

"Delete that," Martha said. "Jorran wouldn't have found them without her reverting to using her own language. It was what he was hoping for, the only way he could have located her. And she wouldn't have done that if she weren't alone with a *sa'abo* breathing down her throat."

"*Farden* hell, must you always get technical, Martha?" Tedra complained.

"Never mind that. Dalden wants Transfer now, and

I mean *now*. I warned you he'd go berserk when he saw all that blood."

"For stars' sake, you know how to stall someone better than anyone else. Let her at least change clothes first," Tedra said, then suggested, "Transfer him to Challen. *He* can calm him down some, if you can't."

Which made Brittany start to panic. If Dalden's mother was this worried that she was in big trouble, she was likely in some seriously big trouble.

Chapter 51

CHANGING CLOTHES WASN'T ENOUGH. BRITTANY WAS still smeared with dried blood, even though there were no wounds left to account for it. She had just enough time to drop into the sunken bath, scrub thoroughly, then drain the water—leaving a pink pool wasn't a good idea—and get into a fresh blue *chauri*. Not enough time to dry her hair completely, but that was a minor point. She wasn't trying to hide the fact that she'd been hurt, which Dalden already knew, just the visible reminder of how bad the injuries had been.

Tedra left Martha's link behind and told her to use her discretion if someone needed Transferring out of there until emotions settled down. At that point, Brittany had no idea who that someone might be,

since her own emotions were getting out of hand as well.

By the time Dalden finally walked into their room she had worked herself into a fine state of nervousness. And what kept repeating in her mind was he was for real, *really* for real. He wasn't someone playing at being a barbarian, he *was* a barbarian, and how the hell did you deal with an archaic mentality that, instead of offering comfort over an injury, was going to add punishment to it as well?

He didn't look angry. But she knew him well enough by now to know that he wouldn't look it. Wrapped in his warrior's calm, you had to search for more subtle signs than the obvious, and they were there: a certain stiffness, compressed lips—no warmth in his golden eyes.

Her problem, and the reason she couldn't shake the dread building in her, was that she didn't know what to expect from him at this point. He'd said he would never cause her physical pain and she believed that, but what about mental? Just what was a barbarian's idea of punishment if it wasn't whips and chains? Dumped in some dark, dank hole for a week? A month? Solitary confinement? Her only defense was anger, and she wrapped herself securely in it.

"Remove your clothes."

She blinked, stiffened, narrowed her eyes at him. "No way."

"Remove them," he repeated as he started to cross the room to her. "I need to see that you are whole."

That should have reassured her. He just wanted to see for himself that she was okay. She would have

wanted the same visual proof if he'd been the one injured. But this wasn't a normal situation.

"Forget it," she said and started backing away from him. "I'm not putting myself in a vulnerable position like that when you've got punishment on the brain. Do I look like I'm flipping out of my mind?"

She'd just given him a chance to deny it. He didn't take it. The anger wrapped more firmly around her.

"You can stop right there," she told him. "I'm fine, good as new. You *will* take my word for it. And I've already learned the lesson you think needs reinforcing, so there's no need for reinforcing it. I'll obey all future orders."

"Then obey this one. Remove your clothes!"

That was about as close as Dalden had ever come to actual shouting. Incredibly, it made her *want* to obey him, which was insane!

She shook her head at him, but dread was swiftly replacing her anger. She continued to back away. "That order has nothing to do with safety, just the opposite. And I'm warning you up front, I won't accept punishment from you. I absolutely refuse to accept it. So don't even *think* of—"

She'd run out of room for escaping, had come up against the wall behind her. Not that it mattered when his longer legs had already brought him within inches of her. And it didn't even take him two seconds to pull her away from the wall and peel that stupid *chauri* to the floor. He then turned her around, once, twice, held her arms out to the sides, and felt her limbs in a clinical manner.

Brittany bristled under the close examination, was

too indignant to be embarrassed over it. He should have taken her word for it.

She slammed her palms against his chest. A normal man would have at least been shoved back a little by it, since she put every bit of strength she had into it. Dalden wasn't budged. Her hands now hurt.

"Satisfied?" she growled. "I *told* you I was fine! Why couldn't you just believe me?"

He dropped to his knees in front of her, wrapping his arms around her. His head rested between her breasts. She was completely confounded by this, too surprised to think for a moment.

"I am sorry for my compulsion to see for myself," he told her with a great deal of feeling. "I am sorry for the pain you suffered," he added with even more feeling. "I am sorry I was not there to prevent it."

"Dalden, stop," she said, wrapping her arms around his head.

He didn't. "I am sorry you could not trust me enough to know that I would not give you an order without there being a good reason."

"Dalden, please, you're killing me with guilt here," she told him. "You have nothing to be sorry for. Look, if you must know, when I heard that animal outside the tent, I was hoping it was a normal animal. Our visit to the clearing was unplanned, and I wanted ammunition to discredit the Sha-Ka'an fantasy. And I was only going to satisfy my curiosity with a quick peek. But it saw me, and ended up proving me wrong instead."

His grip tightened on her. "I am sorry you had to nearly die before you could accept the truth."

She smiled. He didn't see it. "You and me both."

"And I am sorry that I must now make sure that you never let your curiosity interfere with an order given for your protection again."

She had begun to relax somewhat. Now all her muscles tensed again. He rose to his feet and picked her up to cradle in his arms.

"No!" she cried.

But he was set on his own path, was going to ignore anything she had to say. He didn't want to punish her, he *had* to, for her own "good." She knew that was where he was coming from, that he really did see this as being for her ultimate benefit, so nothing she said or did was going to stop it from happening.

She should just buck up and take it like a man. How bad could it be, anyway, if it wasn't going to cause her physical pain? But it was the principle of thing, damnit. She was too old to have lessons taught by way of punishment, as if she were a child.

It wasn't a law she broke, for crying out loud. That she could abide—break it and pay the fine or do the time. But a rule for her own safety should be at her discretion to decide whether to follow it or not. And the one she broke shouldn't even fall into that category. All he'd had to do was tell her that there were man-eating beasts in that woods and she would have damn well stayed in the tent.

He carried her to his bed, laid her on it, joined her there, and simply held her to him. He had to force it, she wasn't exactly laying still—until she realized that was all he was doing. He was trying to calm her first. He couldn't have missed her rigid stiffness. But there

was no way she could get calm under the circumstances.

He must have finally realized that, because he began to kiss her. New alarm bells went off. She didn't think this was to calm her. How could it when his kissing had just the opposite effect? No, she was afraid he was trying to make amends beforehand, to cushion the blow for the punishment that was coming—as if anything could.

She fought what he was making her feel, desperately fought it. She couldn't let him get away with this. She had a stand to make here. But it was impossible. She'd never once been able to resist his kisses before. What made her think now would be any different?

Within moments she was kissing him back. Despite the grievance she should be feeling, and would soon be feeling, here, now, there was only him, a man she absolutely adored—when he wasn't being obnoxiously barbaric. And he certainly wasn't at the moment.

Meticulously, he brought every one of her senses to full awareness, set her pulses racing, frazzled her nerves in anticipation. So quickly, the coiled tension spread through her body. She was trembling, on fire, brought so close to the ultimate pleasure, only to have him soothe it away and start over again.

She told him in countless ways that she was ready, but he was determined to prolong the anticipation, to bring her to such a height of need that she'd probably explode the second he entered her. And then his hands were gone, the heat of his body next to her gone, too. It

still took several moments for her to realize he'd actually left the bed.

Coming out of the daze, she sat up, growled, "What the hell was that all about?" But he hadn't just left the bed, he'd already left the room.

Martha was still there, however, and answered cheerfully, "You were just punished."

"How?"

"If you don't know—"

"I'm not kidding, how?"

"Sha-Ka'ani women are highly sexual. Warriors, at least those in this country, figured out long ago that the most harmless way to punish one's lifemate, if needed, was to bring her to an extreme state of desire, then leave her that way to reflect on the error of her ways. Being highly sexual themselves, they can't accomplish this without the help of *dhuya* juice, which temporarily kills their own sex drive."

Brittany began to laugh. So Dalden had been obnoxiously barbaric after all.

"You find sexual frustration funny?" Martha asked curiously.

"No, but it's not exactly something my people are unfamiliar with. In fact, we self-inflict it on ourselves all the time in the form of dating."

Martha made a snorting sound. "I have your definition of dating and it doesn't include—"

"Hold on, I meant what goes on when two people are getting to know each other. A few dates can lead to heavy petting, with the guy expecting to score, but the girl still undecided, so they both end the date frustrated. They could avoid the heavy petting, but since

that's a learning-about-each-other process, too, they typically don't avoid it."

"Trust a low-tech human species to do things the hard way."

"I suppose advanced worlds have figured out easier ways?" Brittany retorted.

"Certainly. Computer-matched compatibility, works like a charm."

"We happen to have computer dating, and I promise you, it doesn't work like a charm."

"Antiquated stuff," Martha scoffed, adding, "and irrelevant to our subject. So the proven effective Kan-is-Tran punishment didn't bother you at all, eh? If that's the case, I'd say you've got such an advantage over that boy it isn't funny."

"How do you figure?"

"The fact that their idea of punishment doesn't faze you. The fact that he'll be drowning in guilt and the need to make amends every time he has to punish you. I'd say that puts you in the driver's seat."

Seeing it that way, Brittany couldn't help grinning. "You gonna tell him?"

"Me? Now, why would I do that? I happen to like pulling the wool over on these guys. It's just so priceless when their culture conflicts with logic they can't dispute. Makes my day, I tell you."

Brittany snorted this time, to which Martha just chuckled. But after a moment, Martha added, "By the way, Dalden didn't take anything to help him get through that. It's standard for a warrior to at least drink the *dhaya* juice first. He didn't. He was determined that if you had to suffer, he was going to suffer

with you. And *your* body might be conditioned to shrug that kinda stuff off, but his isn't. At the moment, he's in a good deal of discomfort. He continues to impress me, that boy, with the depth of his caring. Has he told you he loves you yet?"

"No."

"He may never say the actual words, but you needn't doubt it now."

Brittany smiled to herself. No, she didn't doubt it at all.

Chapter 52

BRITTANY WASN'T SURE HOW TO DEAL WITH JORRAN, High King of Century III. She'd been briefed more thoroughly on the way to the room where he was waiting, about why he was there and what he had hoped to accomplish. He'd had every intention of more or less kidnapping her and forcing her to become his queen. He'd had every intention of killing Dalden, too, if he could have found him with her.

He'd brought a modern weapon with him this time to do it, since his razor sword hadn't been effective the last time they fought. It was what he'd killed the *sa'abo* with, without having to get close to it, and it horrified her that he could have killed Dalden just as easily with it.

He hadn't been let inside the castle with that

weapon, but he'd agreed to come unarmed into the enemy's camp, so he could speak with Brittany.

She'd been warned that he would probably try to talk her into leaving with him. She'd been warned not to trust anything he had to say, that duplicity was second nature to someone like him, who would say or do anything to accomplish his goals.

Jorran's relatives had already gone home. Martha had done no more than park the *Androvia* in the middle of their fleet of ships to make them rethink their demands. Considering that all twenty-three ships could fit inside the *Androvia*'s cargo bay, there hadn't been much to think about. The Centurians were a medieval people, and they recognized when they were outclassed and outgunned.

Challen hadn't been all that thrilled with the peaceful outcome of the "invasion." But when the Ly-San-Ters had become indebted to Jorran, that had pretty much ended any retaliatory sword practicing.

Dalden also couldn't do as he would have liked, which was to make sure Jorran never bothered them again in a more final way this time. Brittany was learning that warriors here weren't called warriors just because it sounded good. They could defend, exact retribution, and conquer just like anyone else, only they could do it in a *big* way if provoked.

She was left alone with him. Well, not really alone, since she had Martha's link with her. It had been Jorran's request, that privacy, and Martha wasn't going to reveal herself unless she had to. Dalden had refused to allow Brittany to get anywhere near Jorran *without* Martha's presence. He wasn't the least bit happy that she was being allowed to see him at all. It had taken

his father to get him to agree to it. And all because of the debt they owed Jorran.

It was Brittany's debt, actually. She was well aware of that. He'd saved her life. There was no getting around the fact that she'd be dead if he hadn't found her. So in an odd way, she could be grateful that he'd tried to kidnap her. How weird.

She waited for him to speak first. He looked nothing like the Jorran she'd met at home. He was wearing clothes from his own country, which included a fur-trimmed royal cloak, a long fancy tunic, and high boots. He looked now exactly like what he was, a medieval king, and his own clothing suited him much better than a business suit.

He must have been thinking something along the same lines because his first remark to her was, "Their barbaric clothing does not suit you. I would dress you in fine silks befitting a queen."

"I'm old enough to dress myself, thank you."

"I did not mean to insult."

She sighed. "I'm sorry, I didn't mean to give offense, either. I owe my life to you. I am deeply grateful."

He nodded, expecting no less. "Grateful enough to give that life into my keeping?"

"I've already given my life to another for keeping. You know him well. He *is* my lifemate."

He waved that aside. "Their barbaric means of joining in marriage are not recognized on my world."

"Nor on mine, but in my heart I recognize it. So it's binding for me."

He seemed surprised to hear that. "You *want* to stay with him?"

She couldn't imagine why he might have thought

otherwise, but perhaps a little explaining was in order. "Jorran, when I said I would help you in my world I lied. I was wholeheartedly against what you were trying to accomplish. I was assisting the Sha-Ka'ani in stopping you. If you've been thinking otherwise all this time, I'm sorry."

He shrugged indifferently. "None of that matters. I saw in your eyes, on their ship, your real feelings for me."

She frowned in confusion, trying to remember that day of major shocks. "Sympathy? You mistook my compassion for something more. I didn't like it that they were denying you medical treatment, even though they assured me you weren't in pain. I wouldn't have liked seeing anyone left like that—but I see you're whole again. You must have come across a meditech between then and now."

"Only today," he replied with some bitterness. "In their Visitors' Center. We have not such things on my world."

"Then I'd say you have reason to be grateful as well, that you have no lasting scars from what happened. My people would have put you in prison for the rest of your life for what you attempted, if they'd been the ones to stop you. The Sha-Ka'ani only returned you to your own home with a few deformities they knew you could eventually fix."

"So in your mind that exonerates them?"

It was on the tip of her tongue to say that in her mind, he was the villain, but she diplomatically bit her tongue. "I'm just glad that no lasting damage was done—to anyone."

They'd been standing a good ten feet apart. He ap-

proached her now. It was all she could do not to try to keep that original distance, he made her that nervous. And as she'd feared, he touched her, though harmlessly, a mere brush of his fingers against her cheek.

"You have a strange way of looking at things," he remarked softly.

"Not strange, just different from how you view things. It doesn't mean I'm right and you're wrong, or vice versa. We just come from vastly different cultures."

Jeez, was she telling him what she should be telling herself? What Martha had tried to make her see all along? The Sha-Ka'ani weren't really barbarians, they were just different. Their way of doing things was normal for them, worked for them, so it was the right way. To compare them with other cultures, her own in particular, was ludicrous. They were unique. They'd evolve in their own way.

"You would like my culture," he said wistfully. "I would make you a queen. What can your barbarian offer you to equal that?"

There was no hesitation in her answer. "Himself, which is all I need to make me happy—because I love him deeply, with all my heart."

Chapter 53

MARTHA APOLOGIZED FOR NOT WARNING HER THAT Dalden had listened in on her conversation with Jorran, that it was the only way he would allow her to be left alone with the man. Brittany wasn't too happy about that. They hadn't spoken since he'd punished her. She had wanted to enjoy some of his amends-making before she officially forgave him, not have him hear secondhand that she still loved the heck out of him.

Not that it mattered. When she did finally see him again that day, he wasn't interested in talking. He marched her straight back to their room, where they spent the rest of the day and half of the next making sure neither of them were still suffering over that silly punishment.

She was beginning to wonder, though, if his drag-

ging her off to places without a word of explanation was going to be a standard practice, because he did it again the next afternoon. He tossed a white cloak over her shoulders, took her hand, and pulled her behind him out of the castle, across most of the town, and through some of the park that fronted the edge of the mountain.

He stood behind her, wrapped his arms around her, and said nothing while she absorbed the incredible view before them. All of the verdant green valley that spread at the base of Mount Raik could be seen, woods and lakes beyond, and in the far distance, even a long range of other mountains which were a mere purple haze.

It took her breath away, all that beauty. And then Dalden said, "You will build our house here."

She swung around to stare at him incredulously. "*I* will?" she gasped.

"The design will be of your choice," he replied matter-of-factly, as if he weren't astounding the hell out of her. "You will keep in mind, however, that a warrior requires a good deal of space to keep from feeling confined."

She grinned at that point. "You're talking a big house, I take it?"

"Yes."

"A *really* big house?"

"Yes."

She beamed ecstatically—until she recalled that his country didn't have lumber mills. "I'm not sure I can work with the materials you have available here."

"Martha has assured me that she can obtain anything you require."

"It will take me a long time to build something of the size you're talking about," she pointed out next.

"You will have help. Kodos and his lifemate, Ruriko, would like to assist you. Corth II will be available, also. And I will rarely be far from your side, *kerima*. You are likely to have other volunteers as well, once the town sees what you are doing. Sha-Ka-Ra has stood here for centuries without change. Change is not required, but it is not discouraged, either, and there are many who regret that we have no knowledge of creating things. Kodos has shown that clearly in his desire to learn your craft."

"He actually agreed to let his lifemate work beside him, when your women have never known real jobs?"

Dalden gave her an aggrieved look. "To keep peace in his household, he was—persuaded—to agree. He made the mistake of telling her too much about your culture. She was greatly intrigued."

Brittany winced. "I'm not heading for trouble here, am I? I *really* don't want to go down in history as the instigator of the women's movement in Sha-Ka'an. Not that you don't need a women's movement, but it's been pointed out to me that you need to figure these things out for yourselves, not have them forced down your throat by other species."

He cupped her face in his hands. "Do you intend to make trouble?"

"Well—no."

"Then no trouble will occur."

"Yeah, sure," she mumbled.

He chuckled at her. "I am teasing you, *chemar*. I should tell you that I have come to a realization that

has taken a burden from me. Long ago I made the decision to follow my father's ways completely, to ignore my mother's. It was a good decision at the time. It was not easy when I was young, to be so divided by such vastly different beliefs. But this left a hollowness in me, as if I were not whole. Finding you, knowing you, loving you, has shown me that—"

She squealed and threw her arms around his neck. "You said it! You said you love me!"

He set her back from him, gave her a stern look. "Do not try my patience, woman. You know very well the depth of my feelings for you."

"Well, yes." She grinned, not the least bit intimidated by that look. "But it's still nice to *hear* it occasionally."

He rolled his eyes, but drew her back against him. "What I wanted to share with you was that I am no longer divided. Half of me is Kystrani, and I can embrace that half, which comes with full knowledge of other worlds, other beliefs, other ways—including yours. Such things will no longer be ignored simply because they are unknown here."

"You're trying to tell me you've got me figured out?" she asked.

"I am telling you that you do not have to change completely just because you will live here now. I am telling you that your ways are understood, that such understanding will temper how you are dealt with. This does not mean you can ignore what you have thus far been taught of *our* ways. Until a warrior will not take for himself any woman he wants who is not obviously already claimed, you will obey our laws for your *own* protection."

"Yes, I will."

"Until our world is rid of beasts that can cause you harm, you will obey *my* orders."

"Yes, I will."

He frowned at her. "Why do you not argue with me?"

"Because this is Sha-Ka'an. These rules work here. They wouldn't work anywhere else, but here they work just fine. Besides," she added with a grin, "after the gift you've given me today, you're in my good graces big-time."

He kissed her deeply, then gently—they were a long way from any privacy. "You may build hundreds of houses, whole towns, if it will make you happy."

"I was talking about your love," she replied in a softly purring tone.

That did it: he took her hand again and started dragging her off to find some of that missing privacy.

Brittany laughed to herself. He wasn't really barbaric, her lifemate. A warrior, yes. Adamant when it came to protecting her, yes. A bit domineering, but understanding, too. And gentle. And caring.

And how the hell did she get so lucky?

THE PURSUIT

KIMBERLY MACGREGOR WAVED THE LETTER IN HER hand to gain her husband's attention as he entered her sitting room. "Megan has written again," she told him. "She has invitations piling up, too many as usual, but in this case that's ideal. Let her pick and choose the best ones. She's sounding really excited about this. Want to read the letter?"

"Nay."

That answer was too abrupt and a bit disgruntled-sounding for a man of Lachlan MacGregor's easy temperament.

"You aren't having second thoughts about letting Melissa go to London, are you?"

"Aye."

"Lachlan!"

His disgruntled tone was now accompanied by

a matching look. "I dinna like asking the Duke and Duchess o' Wrothston for favors."

Kimberly relaxed. She should have known. Lachlan might get along famously with Devlin St. James when he and his wife Megan came to visit them at Kregora Castle, or vice versa, but it wasn't always that way. They had in fact met under bizarre circumstances which didn't account for Lachlan's remark about favors.

"This was Megan's idea, so there's no favor involved," she reminded him. "As soon as she heard that all of Melissa's beaux were being frightened off by my over-protective brothers, she suggested Meli come to England where the MacFearsons are unknown. You agreed it was a good idea. I agreed it was an excellent idea. And Meli is looking forward to it. So don't be having second thoughts now."

"I assumed she'd be staying at Wrothston, as we do when we visit them in England, no' in London town," he grumbled. "The lass has been tae Wrothston enough tae be comfortable and feel right at home. London's no' the same, and she'll be nervous enough—"

"Nervous?" Kimberly interrupted. "Our daughter is excited about this trip, she's not the least bit nervous. If anyone's nervous it's you, and you and I aren't even going until later in the summer.

Is that it, then? You're letting your worry for her override your better judgment?"

"Nay, I just dinna want her feeling she has tae find a husband afore she comes home. That's tae much pressure tae be putting on her at her young age. You have assured her—?"

"Yes, yes, I've assured her she can be an old maid if she'd like."

"Och, this isna funny, Kimber."

She tsked at him. "You're the one making too much out of it. Most young girls her age go through this; I did myself. Now I might have been nervous about it, but Meli really isn't. She plans to have fun, to make some new friends, to be awed by such a big town as London is, and she even figures she'll probably find a husband while she's at it. But that's not at the top of her to-do list by any means. She thought we wanted her to make a concerted effort to get affianced, but I've assured her if she does, that's fine, and if she doesn't, that's fine, too. Maybe you should tell her the same before she leaves, so she can just relax and let what happens happen. Now have we covered all your last-minute doubts?"

"Nay, 'tis still a huge undertaking tae be putting on the duchess on our behalf."

"Would you like us to go as well for the whole

summer instead of just a few weeks as we planned?"

He looked appalled. Just as she expected. "You said that wouldna be necessary."

"Nor is it. We covered Megan's willingness already. And furthermore, she isn't planning any events herself; she merely has invitations lined up that she was no doubt going to accept anyway. Besides, she adores Meli and is an old hand at this sort of thing. She sponsored me, didn't she? And had a hand in matching you and I to wedded bliss."

That made him grin. "Is that what we've been having, darlin'? Wedded bliss?"

She quirked a golden brow at him and asked, "You don't think so?"

He pulled her to her feet, then meshed her hips to his. "I'd be calling it heaven m'self."

"Would you now?" She grinned back at him, then made a face. "Bah, you're not going to get out of this subject that easily. Why are you really having doubts? And no more of these lame reasons that don't wash."

He sighed. "I had the hope remaining that our lass would end up wi' a fine Scot brave enough tae ignore the legend and trounce any o' your sixteen brothers that think tae bully him."

"What an unkind thought," she said, and smacked his shoulder before she moved away from him. "I love my brothers—"

"I know you do, Kimber, and I even tolerate them m'self, but you canna deny they deserve a trouncing or two for scaring off all o' Meli's suitors. If we didna have friends in England willing tae sponsor her for a season there, the poor lass could end up permanently unwed, and I want m' daughter tae be as happy in wedlock as I've made you."

She chuckled. "Listen to that bragging."

"True nonetheless," he said with complete confidence.

"Perhaps," she allowed with a teasing grin, but then grew serious again. "As for Meli and her future happiness, is the nationality of the man she loses her heart to really of importance to you? And before you answer, keep in mind that if you say yes, your English wife will be insulted."

He laughed. "Half English wife, though one could wish yer Scottish half didna come from the MacFearson himself."

She ignored the reference to her father this time. "Answer me."

"Nay, darlin', the hope was no' that her husband be Scottish exactly, was more that he just hail from closer tae home than England is. I'm no' looking forward tae our lass moving far away is all," he ended with another sigh.

She moved closer again to cup his cheeks in her hands. "You knew that would be possible."

"Aye."

"You also knew that her prospects in our neighborhood were very slim. We don't exactly live close to any towns up here, and the other clans nearby don't have any sons of an age appropriate for our lass. And being the MacGregor's daughter limits her choices even further."

"Aye, I ken that as well."

"So this is all just a father bemoaning the loss of his only daughter in marriage, even before she's married?" she asked in exasperation.

He nodded with a sheepish look. She decided not to scold him for such silliness but said instead, "Lach, I'll be just as unhappy to see her go, but we knew from the day she was born that she would be leaving us one day to start her own family, and even then we didn't expect her to start that family near Kregora Castle. Granted, we weren't thinking as far as England, but still—"

Kimberly amazed even herself when she suddenly burst into tears. Lachlan gathered her close and made all the soothing sounds appropriate to providing comfort. She finally pushed away from him, annoyed with herself.

"Don't ask why that happened," she mumbled.

He grinned at her. "I'm sorry, Kimber. I didna mean tae refresh all your own misgivings."

"You didn't. Unlike you, I'm delighted Meli

has this opportunity for a season in London. I just"— she paused for a sigh of her own—"just had the same hope as you still lurking, though I thought I had given up on that long ago. And it is pointless. Even those few young lads who did come to call on her live miles away, which is probably why you weren't all that displeased when my brothers ran them off."

"Miles away is no distance a' tall up here; they just didna impress me too much is all, and rightly so as it turned out. Look how quickly they turned tail when your brothers started in on them. That last one made his excuses after one wee warning from Ian Two that he'd be displeased if his niece was e'er made unhappy."

"I think it was because he had a fistful of the poor boy's shirt when he said it."

They both laughed for a moment, remembering how quickly the suitor had fled. He'd practically run for the door the moment after he'd made his excuses. The laughter eased their misgivings.

"Och, well, this trip canna be avoided I suppose," Lachlan conceded.

"No, it can't."

"Speaking o' which, is Meli done wi' her packing?"

"She's not leaving for three more days, plenty of time to finish that up. She's gone to see my fa-

ther and probably will be spending the night. Actually, I think her intent was to assure my brothers that she forgave them for ruining her prospects here at home—a few of them have been quite gloomy over that if you didn't know. She was also going to assure them that when the right man for her comes along, she'll know it herself, so they needn't worry on that account."

"She actually thinks saying so will assure them of anything?"

"Well, she's hoping." Kimberly grinned. "My brothers can be reasoned with—some of the time."

For Dylan, a warrior at heart

AVON BOOKS
An Imprint of HarperCollins*Publishers*
10 East 53rd Street
New York, New York 10022-5299

Copyright © 2001 by Johanna Lindsey
Excerpt from *The Pursuit* copyright © 2002 by Johanna Lindsey
ISBN: 978-0-06-137932-1
ISBN-10: 0-06-137932-8
www.avonromance.com

First Avon Books special printing: June 2007
First Avon Books paperback printing: March 2002
First William Morrow hardcover printing: May 2001

Avon Trademark Reg. U.S. Pat. Off. and in Other Countries, Marca Registrada, Hecho en U.S.A.
HarperCollins® is a registered trademark of HarperCollins Publishers.

Printed in the U.S.A.

10 9 8 7 6 5 4 3 2 1

JOHANNA LINDSEY

HEART of a WARRIOR

AVON BOOKS

An Imprint of HarperCollins*Publishers*

Johanna Lindsey

"First rate romance."
New York Daily News

"One of the most reliable authors around.
Her books are well-paced and well-written,
filled with strong characters, humor,
interesting plots—and, of course, romance."
Cincinnati Enquirer

"Johanna Lindsey has a sure touch
where historical romance is concerned."
Newport News Daily Press

"She manages to etch memorable characters
in every novel she writes."
Chicago Sun-Times

"The charm and appeal of her characters
are infectious."
Publishers Weekly

"Long may she continue to write."
CompuServe Romance Reviews

Chapitre premier

Accueil et présentations

Objectif à court terme: être la meilleure animatrice de formation que la ville ait jamais connue.
Obstacles: aucun, en fait. Le coin manque cruellement de bonnes formatrices. Ce n'est même pas un vrai défi.
Objectif à long terme: trouver l'amour et le bonheur avec Richard, l'élu de mon cœur, le seul, le vrai.
Obstacles: Richard est à l'étranger.

N'est-ce pas que vous adorez le changement? Nous en avons tous besoin pour progresser, pas vrai? Sans cela, on n'aurait jamais inventé la roue, la pénicilline, ou le fer à lisser. Nous devrions l'accueillir à bras ouverts, nous y plonger, le soutenir, parce qu'il nous offre à tous une possibilité de nouveau départ, comme le printemps après l'hiver. Les saisons passent: la vie recommence. Pas de mort, pas de fin, juste du changement.

Quel ramassis de conneries.

Dans la vraie vie, qui aime que les choses changent? Qui se réjouit sincèrement quand tout ce qu'il a appris à connaître, ce en quoi il a investi de l'énergie et de la confiance, s'écroule soudain avec fracas comme une table suédoise bon marché ? Qui penserait en rentrant de trois semaines de vacances : *Oh, des squatters se sont installés pendant notre absence ; comme c'est merveilleux, ça va me donner l'occasion de développer mon sens de la négociation ?* Personne.

Mais je dois présenter cette théorie comme si j'y croyais, que j'étais capable de joindre les mains et de sourire d'une joie sincère au commencement de chaque nouvelle magnifique journée que Dieu fait, sans être pour autant une idiote pathétique qui s'enthousiasme pour un rien. Je dois vendre ça parce que c'est mon travail. Non, je ne suis pas agent immobilier. Ce que je fais a bien plus de sens que de vendre une maison à Monsieur Tout-le-Monde. Je travaille pour Love Learning, le meilleur prestataire de formation de la ville, et je suis Beth Sheridan, la meilleure formatrice de Love Learning. Aujourd'hui, je fais « Gérer le Changement », et dans à peu près trois minutes je dois entrer dans une pièce pleine de caissiers, de guichetiers et de conseillers financiers de la banque de la grand-rue et leur présenter la « Journée 1 : préparation ». Autrement dit, je dois tous les convaincre que le changement, c'est merveilleux et fantastique, que ça entraîne évolution et révolution, que nous faisons tous de nouvelles expériences qui nous enrichissent.

C'est de la connerie pure et dure.

Si le directeur de l'établissement a inscrit son personnel à ce stage, c'est probablement parce que la succursale va fermer dans trois mois et qu'il veut qu'ils le prennent non comme un « licenciement » mais comme une « opportunité ».

Non, non, je ne dois pas penser comme ça, sinon ils le liront sur ma figure. Je dois être positive, optimiste et passionnée, pour qu'après cinq jours passés à m'écouter ils puissent retourner sur leur lieu de travail enthousiastes et pleins d'allant, impatients de rencontrer l'horrible changement qui les attend et d'avoir l'occasion de le « gérer »… avant de faire une visite surprise à l'agence pour l'emploi. Il va falloir que je croise les doigts dans mon dos.

Il y a trois mois, je ne ressentais pas ça du tout. À l'époque, j'y croyais encore, et j'étais chez moi, en nuisette, la peau dûment hydratée, dans l'attente, l'expectative, non, l'impatience dévorante, d'un changement. Mon patron, Richard Love, propriétaire et fondateur de Love Learning, devait venir à 20 heures ce soir-là pour m'annoncer quelque chose : une nouvelle importante qu'il ne pouvait me communiquer par téléphone. Il voulait me le dire de vive voix. Je savais ce que c'était.

Richard et moi étions ensemble depuis huit ans. Pas à proprement parler en couple, mais nous avions une relation, c'est sûr. Tout avait commencé lors de mon embauche à Horizon Holidays, la grosse société de voyages qui se trouve sur un rond-point du centre-ville. Apparemment, Rupert de Witter, le patron, ne voulait pas prendre trop de place en ville – pour des raisons écologiques. Du coup, il avait fait construire ses locaux sur le terre-plein d'un carrefour giratoire, ce qui ne me semblait pas franchement malin. De quelque côté qu'on sorte du bâtiment, il fallait toujours traverser une route. C'était vraiment agaçant, surtout si on faisait juste un saut à la pharmacie ou autre. Après, il ne fallait pas se plaindre que ça prenne du temps de faire l'aller et retour.

Quoi qu'il en soit, j'étais recrutée comme assistante du directeur des formations, et, à cette époque-là, c'était Richard Love. J'avais vingt ans, j'étais sortie de l'école deux ans plus tôt, et c'était mon premier vrai boulot. Il avait vingt-sept ans, c'était mon patron, et il avait passé cinq années dans l'entreprise. Il était directeur ; il donnait des ordres, et les gens obéissaient. Moi aussi.

La première chose que j'ai remarquée quand on me l'a présenté, c'est sa taille. Il se tenait de l'autre côté du bureau, de dos, les bras croisés, à contre-jour devant la fenêtre, si bien que tout ce qu'on voyait, c'était une grande ombre. Le type des ressources humaines devait lever le nez rien que pour s'adresser en bredouillant à la nuque de Richard.

— Euh, monsieur Love, je vous ai amené votre nouvelle assistante.

À ce moment-là, Richard s'est retourné et m'a regardée. Et c'est arrivé. Ses yeux noisette ont rencontré les miens, et un lien à toute épreuve s'est formé entre nous. Un frisson électrique a parcouru mes veines, et, inexplicablement, j'ai senti une force incroyable m'attirer vers lui comme le rayon tracteur d'une soucoupe volante. Nos regards ne sont restés rivés l'un à l'autre qu'un très bref instant, mais ces quelques secondes ont suffi pour que nos âmes se dévoilent et se reconnaissent. Je ne respirais plus, les horloges avaient cessé d'égrener les secondes, le bruit des voitures s'était tu. Tous les occupants de la pièce étaient fascinés par la magie de l'instant.

— Alors, elle a un nom ? aboya Richard tout à coup.

De toute évidence, il tentait de masquer sa confusion.

— Oh, euh, oui, désolé, voici Beth Sheridan.

Deux ans plus tard, nous quittions cet endroit, main dans la main. C'est une métaphore, bien sûr. Mais je lui aurais tenu la main s'il n'avait pas marché si vite. Et s'il n'avait pas eu les bras chargés de fournitures chipées dans la réserve. Il partait pour protester contre la nullité de M. Rupert de Witter et sa politique de formation débile ; je me suis précipitée à sa suite pour lui témoigner mon soutien.

Horizon obligeait chaque membre du personnel à suivre tous les stages, sans tenir compte du domaine de chacun ou des bénéfices qu'il pouvait ou non en tirer. La « tactique de la désinfection préventive », c'est comme ça que Richard avait surnommé cette organisation. Ainsi, tout le monde recevait une formation Excel ou PowerPoint, y compris les filles de la vente par téléphone, même s'il était peu vraisemblable qu'elles en aient besoin pour discuter de Séjours Peinture avec des vieilles dames de Llandudno.

— C'est un gaspillage de ressources, c'est stupide ! hurlait souvent Richard au bout du fil avec Rupert de Witter en roulant des yeux dans ma direction et en jetant des perforeuses à la volée.

Parfois, dans un temps mort, nous passions une éternité – cinq ou six minutes, pas moins – à rêver de stages sur mesure pour nos salariés.

— Ne serait-ce pas merveilleux, Bethy, me disait-il, de ne dispenser aux gens que la formation dont ils ont réellement besoin ?

Le menton dans la main, il me regardait d'un air rêveur. Captivée, je hochais la tête. Je ne me sentais jamais plus proche de lui que dans ces moments.

13

Finalement, Richard lui-même fut convoqué à un stage intitulé : « Souris, Mode d'Emploi », malgré son diplôme d'informatique. Il était un peu dépité. Je crois qu'il a lâché une phrase comme : « C'est quoi, ce bordel ?! » Et c'est là qu'il a fait comme dans *Jerry Maguire* et qu'il est parti, ne gardant que sa moralité et son assistante éblouie – moi. C'était exactement comme dans le film, à part la scène des poissons – il n'y a pas d'aquarium chez Horizon Holidays. Richard était décidé à donner le meilleur à ses clients, à l'image de Tom Cruise ; et, à l'image de Renée Zellweger, je l'ai suivi avec des étoiles dans les yeux. J'ai craqué quand il m'a dit :

— Alors, tu viens ou quoi ?

J'y suis allée.

Depuis, c'est devenu incontestablement mon film préféré.

La morale triomphe de l'argent, et l'amour triomphe de tout. Jerry prend sa revanche sur ceux qui l'ont abandonné, tout simplement en étant meilleur qu'eux, avec personne d'autre que Renée pour l'aider, et il tombe amoureux d'elle à la fin. Exactement comme pour nous. Sauf que Richard ne s'est pas fait virer. Oh, et puis il met un peu plus longtemps à craquer pour moi que Tom pour Renée. Mais la différence, c'est que je suis prête à attendre.

Il y a six ans que nous avons quitté Horizon ensemble, et dans cet intervalle nous avons monté Love Learning et travaillé comme des malades pour en faire le meilleur prestataire de formation de la ville. Notre engagement, c'est de dispenser des cours tellement efficaces que nos clients voient une amélioration dès que leurs employés en reviennent. Nous faisons du sur-mesure ; le rêve de

Richard est devenu réalité. Je me suis tuée à la tâche pendant six ans pour ce résultat.

Richard est brillant pour tout ce qui touche à l'argent, l'immobilier, les impôts et autres, alors il s'est concentré là-dessus et m'a laissé le champ libre pour ramener des contrats. Je me suis donnée à fond : j'arrivais tôt, restais tard, travaillais les week-ends, parcourais la ville en quête d'inspiration, infiltrais les entreprises pour cerner leurs besoins en formation, écumais Internet, les bibliothèques, conférences, réunions et ateliers, le plus souvent sur mon temps personnel. Après quatre mois à accumuler les semaines de soixante-dix heures, le manque de sommeil et l'excès de caféine, le temps passé à chercher, à espionner, à épier et à explorer a vraiment commencé à payer. J'ai eu la chance d'être la première de toute la ville à repérer dans un très court article d'un magazine pour industriels une petite citation insignifiante du patron d'une chaîne de restaurants qui voulait faire entrer ses établissements dans le XXIe siècle.

« Bien sûr, avait-il déclaré, probablement avec un hochement de tête sentencieux, tous mes collaborateurs vont devoir être à nouveau formés. »

Je suis restée à contempler cette phrase. J'entendais sonner les cloches, j'avais des papillons devant les yeux, un vrai feu d'artifice. Sans doute le manque de sommeil.

Je suis passée à l'action. Bon, comme il était minuit, je suis d'abord allée me coucher. Mais j'ai démarré dès le lendemain matin. Je me suis rendue dans le premier restaurant de cette enseigne que j'ai trouvé et j'ai persuadé le responsable que s'il cherchait des cours pour l'ensemble de son personnel, Love Learning pouvait répondre à tous ses besoins. Il l'a cru.

Ce fut le point de départ. À partir de là, plus rien ne pouvait m'arrêter. Je me suis aperçue que plus un contrat était juteux, plus il intéressait Richard ; il fallait pour cela que les autres prestataires de formation n'aient pas encore fait d'offre. Cela signifiait que je devais contacter les entreprises avec nos brochures avant qu'elles aient publiquement annoncé leurs recherches de services. À moi donc de découvrir ce dont elles avaient besoin avant qu'elles l'aient révélé.

J'avais un don pour ça. Sans doute grâce aux quatre mois entiers que j'avais passés plongée dans les lectures sur l'éducation, j'étais capable de sentir le potentiel d'une remarque faite en l'air dans un article sans aucun rapport. Par exemple, une fois, en regardant les infos régionales, j'ai vu le directeur local de l'hôtel *Hippocampe* qui était interviewé parce qu'une star de seconde zone avait séjourné dans son établissement et s'était plainte du room service. Du coup, je suis allée le rencontrer pour lui demander si une formation en Service à la Clientèle pourrait lui être utile. Et lorsqu'un restaurant de la zone d'activité a été menacé de fermeture pour raisons d'hygiène, je n'ai pas pu m'empêcher de faire remarquer, alors que je m'y trouvais justement, que si les employés avaient un peu plus de temps disponible, ils pourraient en consacrer davantage à la propreté. Le directeur s'est montré très intéressé par notre nouveau programme d'Organisation des Tâches.

Love Learning s'est agrandi, et Richard a dû embaucher huit personnes : sept autres animateurs et Ali, notre assistant administratif. Pour conquérir Richard, je me suis arrangée pour coiffer nos concurrents au poteau, signant sans cesse des contrats alléchants. Richard a gagné beaucoup d'argent, très vite.

— Bethy, Bethy, Bethy, m'a-t-il déclaré un jour, les mains sur mes épaules – ce qui me récompensait largement pour l'épuisement, la malnutrition et la dépendance au café –, où serais-je sans toi ?

Il me regardait droit dans les yeux, et la chaleur de ses mains me brûlait à travers mon chemisier, laissant certainement dix petites traces de grillé sur ma peau pendant que je le contemplais. Je me mis à trembler, et ce n'était pas un symptôme du manque de caféine. J'entrouvris les lèvres, le souffle coupé, le cœur battant la chamade, et j'attendis qu'il me dise qu'il ne pouvait vivre sans moi, qu'il m'aimait passionnément, d'un amour profond, qu'il ne supporterait pas de passer un jour de plus sans…

— Je serais fauché, tout bonnement. Non, ne me regarde pas comme ça, Bethy, c'est la pure vérité. Je suis riche grâce à ton travail acharné. Comment pourrions-nous fêter ça ?

— Eh bien, ai-je croassé, la bouche sèche, on pourrait…

— Je sais ! Allons manger !

Il avait les yeux brillants, l'air extatique, et il était parfaitement clair que ce qui le rendait si heureux, c'était mon dur labeur, mon dévouement à l'entreprise, nés de ma loyauté et de mon admiration pour lui.

— Bon sang, quand je pense à tout cet argent, je suis fou de joie ! s'est-il exclamé en enfilant sa veste. J'adore être riche !

Bref, peu importe. J'aimais passer du temps en tête à tête avec lui. Ces petites fêtes impromptues autour d'une pizza ou d'un chinois étaient les meilleurs moments de ma vie.

La reconnaissance, ce n'est pas l'amour, comme se plaît à le répéter Vini, ma colocataire, avec un hochement de tête entendu. Eh bien, elle se trompe, et, même si elle a raison, ça se ressemble beaucoup. Et même si ça ne se ressemble pas, c'est toujours mieux que rien. On a des sourires, de la nourriture, et parfois même un contact physique. À mes yeux, c'est exactement comme de l'amour.

Et donc, à 19 heures ce soir-là, il y a trois mois, j'étais épilée, gommée, parfumée et hydratée, et je m'étais installée sur mon canapé, essayant de me mettre à l'aise. Un changement allait se produire, je le savais. Je sentais dans mon cœur fébrile, ma peau qui picotait après le rasage, mon estomac noué, qu'après huit ans à me côtoyer Richard allait enfin se rendre compte qu'il était tombé amoureux de moi au premier regard. Certes, je n'avais pas pensé que ça lui prendrait huit ans, mais ce n'était pas grave. Le moment tant attendu était venu.

En réalité, ce que j'avais en tête, sur mon canapé, il y a trois mois, ce n'était pas vraiment le confort. C'était la séduction. Il fallait que j'arrive à m'affaler – non, à prendre place – sur le siège d'un air naturel, tout en plaçant mes jambes de la façon la plus séduisante possible. J'avais apporté le grand miroir de ma chambre et l'avais appuyé contre la télé pour pouvoir observer le résultat. Je devais dévoiler une bonne étendue de peau nue, sans pour autant jouer les Britney Spears et montrer ma culotte, et c'était loin d'être évident dans cette minuscule nuisette. Les trois premières tentatives se sont soldées par un échec – pour des raisons que je préfère passer sous silence – et juste quand j'adressais des sourires coquins au miroir pour la quatrième fois en murmurant : « Voyons Richard, que veux-tu dire ? » la sonnette a retenti.

Il a une heure d'avance. Une heure entière, putain ! Je suis pétrifiée, les yeux rivés sur mon visage horrifié dans la glace absolument ÉNORME qui n'a rien à faire dans le salon. Il faut que je la déplace. Richard va se demander pourquoi j'ai un miroir en pied au beau milieu du séjour. J'avance d'un pas vers l'objet, mais je sais que je n'ai pas le temps. Il est incroyablement lourd, et pour l'apporter ici cet après-midi j'ai dû le traîner dans le couloir, en le faisant passer d'un côté sur l'autre. Ça m'a coûté une demi-heure d'efforts et la peau de mon gros orteil. La sonnette retentit à nouveau. Tant pis, la glace va devoir rester là. Par chance, j'ai surestimé le temps qu'il me faudrait pour allumer toutes les bougies et j'ai commencé à 17 h 30. J'avais l'intention d'en éteindre quelques-unes parce que vingt-huit – une pour chaque année de mon existence avant cette minute – ne me semble plus une si bonne idée, mais il est trop tard maintenant. Je me dirige vers l'entrée d'un pas langoureux, tel un léopard qui traque sa proie, racé et séduisant, consciente d'être magnifique : le moment où ma vie va changer est arrivé.

« Tu as une panne de courant ? » sont ses premiers mots, alors qu'il entre à grands pas dans le salon, vêtu d'un jean et du manteau caramel que je connais si bien. Je referme la porte avant de le suivre dans la pièce. Quand j'entre, il me regarde pour de bon, et je sens mon estomac se nouer. Je lui lance un regard séducteur et m'assieds sur le canapé. J'arrive à me positionner à merveille. Puisque le miroir est toujours en place, j'y jette un rapide coup d'œil : Oui ! Je suis superbe ! Des jambes et du décolleté en veux-tu en voilà, mais pas de faux pas à la Britney. Parfait. Je lui décoche une œillade par en dessous – il est encore debout – et je constate qu'il semble désorienté. Il parcourt la pièce du regard, agite ses mains dans ses poches, faisant tinter ses clefs et de la monnaie, il est un peu rouge et il se mordille la lèvre inférieure de cet air gêné qui me fait fondre. De toute évidence, il est complètement transi et ne trouve pas ses mots. C'est fantastique. Je ne fais pas un geste, profitant de l'instant, gardant ma pose parfaite – malgré l'engourdissement qui gagne mon pied gauche – et le dévore des yeux, les lèvres entrouvertes, le cœur battant à tout rompre.

Alors il s'exclame :

—Oh, merde ! Bethy, il y a quelqu'un avec toi ?

Il se couvre la bouche avec sa main, et ses yeux s'arrondissent alors qu'il remarque ma tenue, les bougies, le miroir…

—Non, personne. Bien sûr que non.

Il sourit :

—Allons, Bethy, ne fais pas l'idiote. Tu n'as pas besoin de me faire des cachotteries.

Avec un regard en direction de la glace, il hausse les sourcils, me gratifie d'un sourire entendu :

—Petite cochonne…

J'entreprends de me relever, mais je ne me suis pas entraînée et j'ai du mal à garder ma dignité. Pour finir, je dois tenir ma nuisette d'une main pendant que je glisse vers l'extrémité du canapé avant de m'appuyer sur l'autre pour me remettre sur mes pieds. Du coin de l'œil, j'aperçois mon reflet dans l'immense glace, pauvre fille en train de se redresser laborieusement comme une créature du passé réveillée d'un sommeil de mille ans par une explosion nucléaire. En nuisette.

—Non, Richard, c'est vrai. Il n'y a que toi et moi.

Il pose sur moi un regard intense, de mes pieds nus au reste de mon corps pas très habillé non plus. Puis, après ce qui semble une éternité, il ajoute :

—OK. Bon, écoute, Beth, j'ai quelque chose à te dire. Il s'est passé un truc. C'est tellement fabuleux, inattendu…

Il ne me quitte pas du regard, les yeux brillants, un sourire aux lèvres. Une excitation à peine contenue se lit sur ses traits.

Ma voix n'est plus qu'un murmure :

—Oui ?

—Beth, je suis amoureux.

—Oui.

—Profondément, à la folie, passionnément amoureux.

—Oui.

—Elle s'appelle Sabrina.

—Non.

—Quoi ?

—Rien.

—Ah. OK. Bon, écoute, Sabrina est portugaise, alors devine quoi ? Je pars au Portugal ! Demain. Je commence une nouvelle vie ! (Il s'approche et me dévisage.) Je vois bien que tu t'inquiètes pour Love Learning. C'est typique de toi, toujours consciencieuse. Mais ne t'en fais pas ; j'ai tout arrangé. Chas, mon beau-frère, fera tourner la boîte pour moi. Je te donne les clefs du bureau. Chas devrait arriver vers 10 heures, tu pourras les lui passer?

Bref. Pas la peine de s'étendre. Il suffit de dire que Richard a quitté le salon, mon appartement et le pays à la vitesse de l'éclair, et que je ne l'ai pas revu depuis. C'était bien un changement, juste pas celui que j'avais en tête.

Alors maintenant, je vais dans cette salle de formation pour expliquer aux employés de la banque que le changement est positif, super, que c'est une idée fabuleuse, désirable, séduisante, et, dans mon dos, je ne croise pas les doigts, je fais le V de la victoire. Un petit salut aux enfoirés absents.

Chapitre 2

Besoin de changement

Objectif à court terme : convaincre les employés de la banque qu'ils devraient aimer, chérir et embrasser le changement.

Obstacles : Dieu va sans doute me foudroyer en plein milieu de « Préparer l'Action ».

Objectif à long terme : inchangé – épouser Richard, ou quelqu'un d'autre.

Obstacles : il est toujours au Portugal. Et il n'y a personne à l'horizon qui vaille la peine qu'on s'y intéresse.

Je suis professionnelle, donc je ne montre pas mes sentiments. Je ne les dévoile pas, même par accident, en ricanant sans le vouloir. J'ai le contrôle absolu de mes expressions faciales et autres signes non verbaux, à chaque instant, et je m'assure de toujours présenter au monde une agréable contenance. Et ce, pour deux raisons principales. Premièrement, tout le monde le sait, rien n'est moins attirant qu'une femme délaissée. Je refuse de jouer le rôle de la pauvre fille aigrie, dévastée. Être toute ma vie malheureuse et cassée parce qu'on m'a laissée tomber un jour serait un gâchis pur et simple.

23

Sans compter que ça pourrait miner sérieusement mes chances d'attirer quelqu'un d'autre. Même si ça n'a aucune importance pour le moment : alors que la première partie de « Journée 1 : préparation » s'achève après quatre-vingt-dix minutes, j'ai compris qu'une fois de plus aucun mec potable ne participait au stage. C'est trop déprimant : avec qui les employées de la banque peuvent-elles flirter ?

J'éteins les lumières et la cafetière avant de retourner au bureau, laissant les stagiaires apprendre à se connaître autour d'un café et d'une carte heuristique. Autrefois, ils auraient aussi eu droit à des biscuits, mais nous avons dû cesser d'en acheter. Les petits ruisseaux font les grandes rivières, d'après Chas. Le budget semble beaucoup plus serré depuis le départ de Richard.

De retour au travail, je me dirige de ma démarche la plus séduisante vers mon bureau et m'assieds, les jambes repliées sous ma chaise, comme la reine, conservant sérénité et élégance en toute circonstance. En m'observant, on ne devinerait jamais à quel point j'en ai plein le dos. Alors que j'ouvre une session sur mon ordinateur, je m'efforce de paraître préoccupée, pour donner l'impression que je suis plongée dans mes pensées. Personne ne me regarde, donc vous pourriez croire (et je vous pardonne) que je suis vraiment dans une profonde méditation. Je continue à garder un tout petit sourire, comme si l'objet de ma rêverie me faisait plaisir ; j'ai les jambes sagement pliées en diagonale sous ma chaise, les pieds croisés au niveau des chevilles (les varices frappent à tout âge) ; j'ai coincé gracieusement derrière une oreille mes cheveux châtains, coupés aux épaules ; je porte un peu de gloss, mais pas trop, un maquillage naturel. Je suis certaine que, dans cette posture, j'ai l'air absolument adorable, toute simple, et c'est exactement ce que je recherche.

Un jour, alors que nous étions allés manger une pizza, Richard m'a dit : « Ça, c'est ce que j'appelle une jolie femme. Regarde sa peau... pas une imperfection. Et pas peinturlurée comme un camion volé. C'est ça, la beauté naturelle. » Je me suis retournée pour voir de qui il parlait. Une fille d'une vingtaine d'années était installée derrière moi, ses cheveux châtains tombant sur les épaules, à peine maquillée, les pieds croisés sous sa chaise comme la reine.

Il lui adressait des sourires par-dessus mon épaule, apparemment incapable d'en détacher les yeux. Jusqu'à ce que je m'étrangle avec un bout de pizza au point de frôler la mort.

Du coup, je sais ce qui plaît à Richard, et c'est cette image que j'ai adoptée. Tout ce dont j'ai besoin, c'est qu'il revienne et qu'il me voie. Quand ça arrivera, je serai prête. C'est la deuxième raison pour laquelle je prends toujours un air enjoué et adorable.

Vous avez déjà remarqué que quand le héros observe la fille en secret, par la fenêtre ou dans une pièce bondée, elle n'est jamais en train de se curer l'oreille, de se gratter l'aisselle, ou même de regarder dans le vide d'un air d'ennui profond ? Il la surprend toujours à rire avec une amie, à venir en aide à une personne handicapée, ou à distribuer de la nourriture. Lorsque Superman scrute à travers les murs pour voir Loïs dans l'ascenseur qui monte vers le toit, elle se tient juste debout avec grâce, bien coiffée, les pieds élégamment posés, immobile. Enfin quoi, elle est toute seule dans cette cabine, merde, pourquoi ne remonte-t-elle pas sa bretelle de soutien-gorge ou ses bas, ou ne s'extirpe-t-elle pas un bout de céleri coincé entre ses dents du fond, comme tout le monde ? Elle s'arrange pour être séduisante, même si c'est absolument inutile. Heureusement, d'ailleurs, parce que son mec peut la voir où qu'elle soit, quoi qu'elle fasse.

Je n'ai pas l'espoir secret que Superman me reluque à travers les murs en permanence ni qu'il me sauve un jour d'une mort certaine quand l'ascenseur en panne fera un piqué du troisième étage, puis me porte avec amour en survolant la ville dans les rayons de lune jusque devant chez moi, où il me quittera à regret pour aller sauver une autre vie. Bien sûr que non. C'est complètement ridicule. Mais ce dont je suis sûre, c'est qu'un jour Richard reviendra. Un jour. Dans dix minutes, six semaines ou un an, je ne sais pas, mais ça arrivera et, à ce moment-là, j'ai l'intention d'être jolie. Même s'il a pu être provisoirement détourné par la couleur locale – à mon avis assez bas de gamme – d'une bimbo exotique plutôt que de craquer pour moi, ça ne veut pas dire que je ne suis pas la femme de sa vie.

Dès qu'il aura compris qu'il m'aime depuis des années, il va revenir dans ce bureau comme Richard Gere à la recherche de Debra Winger dans *Officier et gentleman*. Il fera le tour de la pièce pour me trouver et m'apercevra avant que je l'aie reconnu. Il ne me lâchera pas du regard, son visage s'adoucira, un sourire s'y dessinera pendant qu'il observera ce que je fais, et il saura, au fond de son cœur, qu'il est enfin à sa place. Ou alors, il va m'envoyer un texto. Dans tous les cas, l'idée c'est que je dois être prête, à chaque instant, dans une jolie posture ou une occupation valorisante, parce qu'il n'y aura pas de signe avant-coureur et que je n'aurai pas le temps de me fabriquer une expression séduisante ou de mettre du gloss.

Je n'exclus pas de rencontrer en attendant un mec superbe lors d'un stage, au supermarché, dans une file d'attente à la banque, dans la rue, dans un parking, un pub, un magasin de chaussures, une bibliothèque, une station-service, peu importe. Ce genre de Rencontres Fortuites arrive tous les jours. Et alors, quand Richard reviendra, je pourrai lui dire : « Tu as loupé le coche, chéri. » J'adorerais ça.

C'est pour ça que je suis assise à mon bureau, donnant à qui me regarderait l'illusion d'être plongée dans mes pensées. J'appuie doucement mon menton sur ma main. Bon, en fait, je ne fais pas reposer tout le poids de ma tête sur ma main, ça me ferait un double menton, mais cette posture me confère un air intéressant, pensif.

Actuellement, nous sommes huit formateurs à Love Learning, plus Ali, notre assistant. Je suis assise à côté de Fatima, dos à dos avec Grace et face à Derek. Ma table, c'est celle dont la séparation est recouverte de coupures de journaux, d'articles de magazines, de documents imprimés, d'interviews, de critiques, de rapports et de graphiques. Sous l'une des feuilles est cachée une petite photo de Richard que j'ai prise à son insu avec mon téléphone. Elle est un peu floue et pas très grande, mais c'est la seule que j'aie. Il est debout à côté de son bureau, les yeux baissés, une main dans la poche. Personne ne sait qu'elle est ici, alors ne le répétez pas.

Près de moi, Fatima se lève. Elle porte un tee-shirt où est écrit en grand :

Qu'est-ce qu'on fait là ?

Et en dessous, en tout petit : « On pourrait être au bar. » De toute évidence, elle n'anime pas de formation aujourd'hui.

—Coucou, Beth, tu as de très jolis cheveux, ce matin. Comment ça se passe, avec le stage « Changement Machin » ? Tu es excellente pour celui-là, à te voir on croirait que c'est trop facile. Moi, je suis si nerveuse que je m'embrouille à tous les coups, avec tout le monde qui me regarde et qui m'écoute en s'attendant à ce que je me trompe. Fais-nous baver, dis-nous s'il y a des beaux mecs ?

Fatima n'est pas faite pour ce boulot.

—Fatima, réponds-je avec un sourire serein, un groupe, c'est tellement plus enrichissant que le physique des mecs. Franchement, tu n'as pas autre chose à penser ?

Son sourire s'efface un peu alors qu'elle se rassied.

—Non, non, ce n'est pas ce que je voulais dire, bien sûr que je sais que… je veux dire, je ne suis pas… c'est juste que… tu crois que tu vas bien t'entendre avec eux, à part ça ?

—C'est trop tôt pour le dire. Mais ils ont l'air de s'intéresser. Pour l'instant.

—Ah, ben tant mieux, ça sera plus sympa pour toi, pas vrai ? Il n'y a rien de pire que d'animer une séance avec des gens qui ne sont pas passionnés, on n'arrive pas à les captiver, quoi qu'on fasse. Une vraie perte de temps. Tu veux du thé ?

Je soupçonne Fatima d'être incapable de réveiller les stagiaires quand bien même elle leur expliquerait comment changer la paille en or ; mais je garde cette pensée pour moi.

— Oui, s'il te plaît, Fati. Merci beaucoup.

Elle se dirige vers la cuisine, et je me tourne à nouveau vers mon ordinateur. J'ai une pause d'un quart d'heure devant moi, qui sera consacrée à considérer mon écran d'un air intéressé, tout en sirotant une boisson chaude. Je risque un discret coup d'œil vers la porte, au cas où. Non, toujours au Portugal.

Fatima met des heures à préparer ce thé. Ça m'arrive parfois d'y passer du temps parce que je suis toujours soit distraite par une pensée qui me fait sourire, soit occupée à contempler un arc-en-ciel avec sérénité ou à nourrir les oiseaux ; mais Fatima se contente de verser de l'eau chaude dans les mugs, sans chichis. Je consulte ma montre et essaie de calculer combien de temps prend chaque étape. Disposer les sachets dans les mugs : quatre secondes ; ajouter l'eau : huit secondes ; attendre que ça infuse : deux minutes…

Un hurlement retentit dans la cuisine.

La réaction dans le bureau est immédiate. Toutes les têtes se tournent de concert vers la porte, puis à nouveau vers la pièce pour voir si quelqu'un d'autre y va. En face de moi, Derek se prend aussitôt à tousser et à se racler la gorge sans relever la tête, l'idée étant, j'imagine, de faire croire qu'il n'a pas entendu parce qu'il s'est éclairci la voix juste à ce moment-là. Hum, hum.

Heureusement que ces gars-là ne sont pas à Skull Island. Quand cette malheureuse jeune femme pousserait un hurlement de terreur en voyant King Kong pour la première fois, ils se mettraient tous à examiner une intéressante formation rocheuse ou à feuilleter un magazine.

—C'est bon, dis-je en me levant rapidement, j'y vais.

J'arbore un air inquiet et surpris en me dirigeant vers la porte. Et ils devraient tous être reconnaissants, franchement. Fatima se blesse au travail environ une fois tous les quinze jours, et personne ne lui vient en aide aussi souvent que moi. Si elle s'y prend au bon moment, avec de la chance je lui prodiguerai de tendres soins au moment où Richard débarquera au bureau en demandant où je suis. Soigner une amie fait partie du top 5 de ce que je voudrais que Richard me voie faire en arrivant.

Ne vous méprenez pas. Je ne me réjouis pas que Fatima se soit fait mal. Bien sûr que non ; enfin, je ne suis pas sadique ! En entrant dans la cuisine, je vois tout de suite qu'elle a une vilaine brûlure sur le dos de la main gauche et l'avant-bras. Mais le malheur des uns fait le bonheur des autres, comme dit Chas. Je suis sûre que Fatima serait ravie de savoir que sa douleur a un bon côté. Elle n'aura pas souffert pour rien, dans ce cas. Et quand je parle de mon attitude inquiète n'allez pas penser que c'est un masque hypocrite, parce qu'au contraire je me fais réellement du souci. J'ai juste besoin d'être certaine que ça se voie, donc j'accentue mon expression. À peine.

Fatima renifle un peu en regardant tantôt son bras blessé, tantôt la diabolique bouilloire, comme si elle espérait la faire culpabiliser. Ou, soyons honnêtes, plus probablement pour comprendre ce qui a bien pu se passer.

— Hé, Fati, ça va ? lui dis-je en baissant les yeux vers la serviette humide qu'elle tient sur sa main gauche.

— Oui, ça va, répond-elle d'une voix larmoyante. Je me suis ébouillantée, c'est tout. Quelle idiote !

Je penche la tête de côté et lui adresse un sourire compatissant. Non seulement c'est très joli à voir, mais en plus ça m'évite d'acquiescer.

— Oh, ça peut arriver à tout le monde. Écoute, est-ce que tu veux que ce soit moi qui te fasse une tasse de thé, finalement ? Puisque tu n'es plus vraiment en état de le faire.

Elle hoche la tête et me sourit avec gratitude. Je me retourne donc pour laver ostensiblement des tasses sous le robinet d'eau chaude, mais elle est déjà repartie d'une démarche mal assurée.

Je lui apporte son thé. Je marche à pas lents, le visage toujours solennel et anxieux, les cheveux coincés derrière les oreilles parce que ça me donne l'air plus sérieux. Quand j'arrive près du bureau de Fatima, je lui mets la main sur l'épaule et lui adresse un sourire rassurant. Le sourire rassurant fait partie de mes plus réussis, alors j'essaie de l'employer à la moindre occasion.

— Oh, merci, Beth, c'est gentil, dit-elle. Tu n'aurais pas dû, tu sais, vraiment, j'aurais pu le faire moi-même, je ne suis pas si gênée que ça. Remarque, me connaissant, je me serais sans doute à nouveau renversé de l'eau sur la main, ou bien j'aurais trébuché sur la table basse, ou fait tomber les tasses ou la télé…

Elle n'exagère pas ; elle a déjà fait tout ça.

Mike, qui a le poste de travail en face du sien, a tiré son fauteuil pour s'asseoir à côté d'elle. Le bureau de Fatima est couvert de morceaux de papiers et de formulaires.

— Décrivez les conditions et l'environnement le jour de l'accident, lit Mike. (Il lève les yeux de l'imprimé.) Qu'est-ce que tu en dis, pour aujourd'hui, Fati ? On met « Gris et ennuyeux » ?

J'ouvre la bouche pour faire une blague sur la déco de la cuisine, mais je me ravise. Je vais garder ce bon mot de côté pour le sortir au moment propice.

Le seul autre événement marquant de la journée est l'arrivée de Chas par la porte à panneaux, déboulant sans s'annoncer dans la partie principale du bureau lors de ma pause de l'après-midi. Il entre dans notre champ de vision à peu près aussi souvent que la comète de Halley, du coup nous abandonnons tous nos activités pour contempler le spectacle.

Le jour où il a débuté chez nous, quand Richard m'a demandé de lui remettre les clefs, je l'attendais sur le seuil et je l'ai vu arriver en deux-roues. Je veux dire en vélo, pas en moto. Vous vous rendez compte ? À bicyclette en costume trois pièces, avec une serviette en cuir dans le panier du guidon et des pinces en bas de son pantalon.

« Ah, je vois que vous avez remarqué mon mode de transport écolo et économique, qui sauve des vies ? s'est-il écrié en passant lestement une jambe par-dessus le cadre avant de s'avancer vers moi, debout sur une pédale, se poussant de l'autre pied par terre. » Il s'est donné une grande tape dans la poitrine. « Excellent pour le cœur, vous savez. Cette petite merveille va me maintenir en bonne santé. »

Pas s'il se fait écraser par un camion à ciment.

Dans le bureau, il commence par cligner des paupières pendant quelques instants, désorienté, puis s'éclaircit la voix pour attirer notre attention, sans s'apercevoir que nous le regardons déjà tous avec des yeux de merlan frit. Finalement, il se lance en déclarant que nous avons besoin de changement. Pour une fois, je suis d'accord avec lui et fais mine de me lever, souriante, pour lui souhaiter de la réussite dans sa nouvelle carrière. Mais il continue. Il nous dit que nous ne disposons plus que de trois semaines avant la fermeture saisonnière de Noël, le 22, et qu'il attend au minimum un contrat signé par chacun d'entre nous, car, depuis le départ de Richard, le succès et le roulement auxquels nous sommes habitués se sont mis à décroître. Il présente ça comme si c'était notre faute parce que nous nous serions « reposés sur nos lauriers » et que maintenant nous devons « donner un coup de collier » et « prendre le taureau par les cornes ». Il conclut en essayant de nous motiver par l'évocation d'un phénix et de flammes, ajoute très vite que si nous ne le faisons pas, au moins quatre postes seront supprimés et que la boîte coulera peut-être, puis disparaît à nouveau. À peine avons-nous eu le temps de nous tourner, bouche bée, les uns vers les autres, qu'il réapparaît.

— Et tant que j'ai votre attention, dit-il en nous montrant tous du doigt, merci de vous souvenir de ce que je vous ai dit la semaine dernière. Je continue à trouver des lampes et des appareils électriques allumés alors que vous avez fini de vous en servir. Vous devez éteindre chaque appareil quand vous n'en avez plus besoin. Je ne plaisante pas : c'est crucial, mesdames et messieurs. Ça économise de l'argent et c'est ça qui sauve des emplois. Faites-y attention.

Et, sur ces paroles, il disparaît une fois de plus. Comme pour la comète, nous savons qu'il est quelque part dans le coin, mais nous avons également la certitude qu'il ne reviendra pas avant un certain temps.

J'ai l'impression qu'il fait tout ce qu'il peut pour ne pas voir que nous avons déjà subi l'un de ces changements bénis des dieux, profondément épanouissants, qui transcendent la vie – fabuleux en un mot – dont je vous ai parlé. Richard est parti, Chas est arrivé. Vous voyez ce que je veux dire ?

Fatima me tire de ma rêverie en m'attrapant brusquement le bras.

— Oh, Beth, tu as entendu ce qu'il a dit ? Quatre postes supprimés. À ton avis, ce sera qui ? Tu crois que je vais perdre mon boulot ?

Je lui souris :

— Fatima, tu ne devrais pas te faire de souci.

Pas la peine, parce qu'en fait c'est une certitude absolue. Elle pourrait aussi bien commencer à vider son bureau tout de suite.

Son visage s'éclaircit un peu, et un rayon d'espoir l'anime. Juste comme ça.

— Vraiment ? Tu crois que ça va aller pour moi ? Parce que je ne sais pas ce que je ferais. Je ne peux pas me permettre de perdre mon job. J'ai un chat, des cours de guitare et un abonnement au satellite. Je ne peux pas me retrouver sans emploi.

Aujourd'hui, on est lundi 4 décembre, alors après le travail j'ai rendez-vous avec Vini pour les courses de Noël. J'ai vraiment hâte. Je tremble déjà d'enthousiasme à l'idée d'une Rencontre Fortuite avec celui qui se révélerait être mon âme sœur. Et aussi, bien sûr, il se pourrait que Richard vienne juste d'atterrir à l'aéroport et fasse un rapide saut en ville pour m'acheter un cadeau – ou une bague! – avant de se précipiter au bureau par le plus court chemin. Tenir des articles à paillettes ou à plumes dans mes mains me rendrait particulièrement adorable quand il me verrait, je pense, surtout si l'une des plumes vient se loger dans mes cheveux. Alors Richard, ou qui que ce soit, pourra l'enlever délicatement, ou souffler pour la chasser, lisser mes cheveux doucement du bout des doigts et dire : «Vous prendrez bien un café?»

Et aussi, il faut que j'achète une robe de chambre pour mon oncle Colin.

— Tu sors?

Tout va bien, pas de panique. C'est une voix de femme. Ce qui est logique, puisque je suis dans les toilettes des dames à me brosser les cheveux et à remettre du gloss avant de me rendre au centre-ville. C'est l'un des rares endroits où je suis certaine de ne pas être observée par Richard. Bien que je n'exclue rien. Quand il reviendra enfin, il sera peut-être tellement impatient de me voir qu'il fera irruption ici. Dans le miroir, cela dit, ce n'est pas lui. C'est Grace.

Grace est mon ennemie numéro un. Elle est tout le contraire de moi. Elle se fiche totalement de faire des bonnes présentations ou des recherches exhaustives, et elle a l'air du genre à coucher avec le fiancé de sa sœur la veille du mariage. Elle est complètement fausse. Exactement comme la couleur de ses cheveux. Une chevelure aussi blonde et soyeuse, ça n'existe tout simplement pas dans la nature. Et quel que soit le temps passé sur une plage personne n'arrive à un bronzage si parfait. C'est de l'autobronzant, pas de doute, mais elle ne l'avouera jamais.

Non que j'aie le moindre reproche à faire à l'auto-bronzant. J'en tamponne un peu sur mes bras et mon visage durant l'hiver, juste pour neutraliser mon teint blafard. C'est plus par gentillesse pour ceux qui me regardent, en réalité. Les stagiaires n'ont pas besoin de contempler Blanche-Neige pendant leurs sessions. La différence entre Grace et moi, c'est qu'elle s'en recouvre entièrement de la tête aux pieds, été comme hiver, et ensuite se balade en disant qu'elle a passé deux semaines à Dubai.

Je lui adresse un doux sourire dans le miroir :

— Non, je vais juste faire les magasins.

Elle s'approche de la glace :

— Ah, c'est sympa. Plus amusant que d'aller chasser des pauvres contrats, en tout cas. (Elle claque la langue et roule des yeux de façon théâtrale.) Quelle bande de demeurés…

Je fronce les sourcils. C'est trop puéril ! Je veux dire, je sais que je ne pars pas à la chasse aux contrats ce soir, mais c'est juste parce que j'ai autre chose de prévu. De toute façon, je ne doute pas un instant que mon immersion imminente dans les magasins d'usine du coin ne me souffle une idée de génie sur les prochaines personnes à démarcher. Mais Grace, apparemment, ne voit pas plus loin que le bout de son nez.

— Qu'est-ce que tu veux dire ?

J'évite de regarder son reflet en face parce que, quand je reporte ensuite les yeux sur moi, c'est toujours un peu décevant.

Non pas qu'elle soit plus jolie que moi. Pas du tout. C'est juste que, à côté de son bronzage permanent et de sa blondeur peroxydée, j'ai l'air d'avoir le teint tout pâle et les cheveux ternes. Alors que par rapport à Cath Parson, qui occupe le bureau en face de Grace, je suis Miss Univers. La beauté est dans l'œil de celui qui est à côté de vous. Si seulement Cath était dans la pièce en ce moment !

Grace se penche vers le miroir pour mettre du khôl, la bouche béante de concentration.

—Oh, tu sais bien, tous les autres vont se précipiter après le boulot pour essayer de décrocher des contrats. Comme si c'était une question de vie ou de mort. Tu vois ? (Elle me lance un coup d'œil dans la glace et secoue la tête avec tristesse.) C'est consternant…

—J'en déduis que tu penses que ce n'est pas important ?

—Bien sûr. Ça n'a aucune importance. En tout cas, pour le moment.

Elle s'arrête, brandissant son crayon khôl comme une baguette magique, prête à jeter un sort, et se tourne vers moi.

—Et toi, tu en penses quoi ?

Elle est maligne, n'est-ce pas ? Si je la contredis et lui assène qu'elle est incapable de vision à long terme, immature, pathétique, sans oublier vaniteuse, et qu'elle ferait mieux de se remuer pour sauver l'entreprise et nos emplois, ça me met dans le même panier que tous les collègues qui, selon elle, sont des demeurés. Mais si je l'approuve je… euh… l'approuve, ce que je déteste, par principe.

Pour finir, je me contente de hausser les épaules, en toute neutralité.

—Chacun pour soi, dis-je, très satisfaite de ma formule.

Je gagne sur les deux tableaux : je me montre adulte et sereine, sans pour autant reconnaître que c'est une bonne idée de ne pas aller courir après les contrats ce soir. Tout simplement brillant. Je réprime un sourire et reporte mon attention sur mon reflet.

—Tout à fait, répond-elle en retournant à son khôl. J'ai des choses beaucoup plus amusantes à faire. À demain.

Elle remet son sac sur son épaule d'un grand geste et disparaît.

Évidemment, elle n'est pas restée pour me demander à quoi je vais passer la soirée. Je suis tentée de la suivre pour pouvoir lui raconter mes projets dans l'ascenseur, mais le bon sens l'emporte, et je choisis de finir de retoucher mon maquillage. Je ne le sais pas encore, mais plus tard je serai drôlement contente de ce choix.

Chapitre 3

Conscience

Objectif à court terme: m'éclater en faisant les courses de Noël avec Vini.
Obstacles: aucun. Ce sera facile parce qu'on s'éclate toujours comme des folles quand on sort toutes les deux.
Objectif à long terme: inchangé. Plus, m'éclater tout le temps.
Obstacles: trop occupée à m'éclater pour y penser.

Aah, les courses de Noël. C'est tellement rigolo! Il fait un froid polaire, la nuit tombe tôt, mais ce n'est pas grave, car toute la ville est décorée de jolies guirlandes lumineuses de toutes les couleurs. Partout on ne rencontre que des familles aux joues rosies, emmitouflées dans des écharpes de laine et des moufles, chargées de brassées de paquets joliment emballés; ces troupes glissent sans effort d'un magasin à l'autre et dénichent le cadeau idéal dans l'immense variété des babioles du meilleur goût. Dans un stand de la zone piétonne, des vendeurs joyeux proposent des cacahouètes pimentées et du vin chaud; au coin de la rue, le père Noël agite une cloche pour une bonne cause; au milieu, autour de l'énorme sapin, un groupe d'enfants entonne des chants de Noël.

Oh non, attendez! Ça, c'était une carte de vœux. En réalité, ça ressemble plus à une scène de *L'Armée des morts*, quand un groupe de survivants se barricade dans un centre commercial pour échapper à l'invasion des zombies.

Pour rejoindre Vini devant la poste, j'ai un sacré bout à marcher. Enfin, quand je dis « marcher », je devrais plutôt parler de me frayer un chemin, en me faufilant à tout petits pas, à travers une foule en mouvement apparemment constituée de zombies pressés de se nourrir de ma chair. Bon, j'exagère un peu, mais ils ne sont pas très plaisants.

—Oh, désolée, est-ce que mes côtes ont cogné votre coude? dis-je à une dame qui me bouscule.

Mais elle est déjà partie, avant d'avoir eu le temps de se repentir. Quelqu'un m'écrase les orteils avec ses bottes.

—J'espère que je ne vous ai pas éclaboussé avec mon sang?

Un objet long et pointu, peut-être un cerf-volant Teletubbies ou un fusil à canon scié, me heurte la figure, me faisant hurler: « Argh, bordel de merde! », mais dans une zone piétonne, personne ne vous entend crier; le type au glockenspiel fait trop de bruit pour ça.

Vini m'attend devant l'unique cabine téléphonique qui subsiste dans notre centre-ville. Les magasins ouvrent en nocturne ce soir, nous avons donc beaucoup de temps devant nous, et elle aime traîner dans les lieux surpeuplés, de toute façon.

Je la trouve en conversation avec une femme blonde très mince, qui prend sa carte de visite avant de s'éloigner.

—Salut, Vini. Tu ne m'as pas attendue trop longtemps?

— Ne t'inquiète pas, j'étais un peu en retard aussi. Et ça m'a donné l'occasion d'observer ces gens exceptionnels qui peuplent notre délicieuse petite bourgade.

— Et?

— Eh bien, tu as vu la nana avec laquelle je discutais? (Je hoche la tête.) Elle pourrait faire Keira Knightley sans problème.

— Merde alors! C'est super.

— Tu m'étonnes! Ça fait des mois que je cherche une Keira.

Vini dirige sa propre agence de sosies, Fake Face. Son affaire tourne maintenant depuis plus de cinq ans et rencontre un énorme succès. Vous seriez surpris du nombre de losers qui pensent que leurs soirées, anniversaires, réunions, et même leur vie, seront miraculeusement embellis par la présence d'un ou d'une inconnu(e) portant une perruque de Catherine Zeta-Jones ou une moustache de Tom Selleck. Je ne critique pas : Vini a gagné beaucoup d'argent grâce à ces demeurés. Elle est vraiment douée pour ça, en fait. Elle est capable de repérer un Paul McCartney dans la queue de la station-service ou une Grace Kelly sortie fumer une clope devant la banque à l'heure du déjeuner. Elle a une bonne quarantaine de clients.

— Bon, dit-elle en me prenant par le bras, allons faire ces courses ; je suis dans les starting-blocks.

Et c'est ainsi que nous plongeons dans la foule. Nous entrons tout d'abord à *Whytelys*, le grand magasin, mais nous sommes aussitôt séparées par une femme avec une poussette double, qui, vu son air, pourrait avoir *Les Armes de destruction massive pour les Nuls* caché dans son sac à langer. Vini danse cette gigue spéciale qu'on mène, sur la pointe des pieds, pour éviter de se faire défoncer les chevilles par une poussette, et je l'aperçois, le regard affolé, en train de disparaître derrière le stand des huiles essentielles.

Après un moment d'hésitation, je décide de continuer sans elle. Bon, elle s'en sortira. Je suis sûre qu'elle sait se défendre dans un grand magasin bondé. Et on se retrouvera plus tard chez *Pizza Hut*.

Je poursuis ma progression dans la boutique et m'arrête pour regarder autour de moi, émerveillée. Les sapins scintillants, les pères Noël en feutrine et les rennes pétrifiés aux yeux vitreux sont si nombreux qu'il ne reste pratiquement plus de place pour les produits exposés. Les clients se promènent sur la pointe des pieds comme s'ils étaient perdus dans une forêt enchantée. Je garde un air de joie enfantine, parce que c'est l'une des dix expressions que j'aimerais avoir quand Richard reviendra. Je suis certaine que c'est adorable. En plus, ça me permet de cacher le fait qu'en réalité je me suis arrêtée ici pour passer mes compagnons de shopping en revue. Les manteaux caramel comme celui de Richard retiennent particulièrement mon attention, mais tout ce qui porte un pantalon est bon à prendre.

Vous devez me trouver horrible, non? Tout ce que je voulais dire, c'est que je ne m'intéresse pas aux femmes. Ni aux messieurs en robe. Vraiment pas.

— Ça va? s'enquiert une voix dans mon dos.

Elle appartient à un homme, et je sens une bouffée d'excitation monter en moi. C'est Richard. Il me demande comment je vais après trois mois de séparation! En tout cas, je n'ai pas entendu sa voix depuis si longtemps que je ne suis pas sûre que ce ne soit pas lui. Oh là là, c'est peut-être enfin le moment ! De quoi ai-je l'air ? Aussitôt, je passe mon apparence en revue dans ma tête : je sais que ma posture est bonne, car je joue toujours la joie enfantine, et c'est bien ; cheveux : sans doute un peu ébouriffés, mais de façon charmante ; maquillage : parfait, je l'ai retouché au travail, cela ne fait que quarante minutes ; vêtements : bien, puisque rien d'autre que mes magnifiques bottes marron ne dépasse de mon manteau blanc cassé. Je suis belle. Mon cœur s'accélère d'une mesure, alors qu'à l'extérieur il apparaît clairement que ça m'importe peu qu'il soit parti au Portugal depuis trois mois et que je continue à mener ma vie, avec plaisir et enthousiasme, sans penser à son absence.

— C'est juste que vous êtes là, sans bouger, depuis un bout de temps, ajoute la voix. Je me demandais si vous alliez bien.

Crotte. Ce n'est pas Richard. La déception me donne un bref pincement au cœur, mais je reprends aussitôt du poil de la bête : il y a un homme qui me parle ! C'est une Rencontre Fortuite, juste comme je l'avais imaginé. Quel dommage que Vini ne soit pas là pour voir à quel point elle s'est trompée !

Sauf que, maintenant qu'il m'a adressé la parole pour la deuxième fois, j'ai l'impression qu'il faudrait vraiment que je réagisse d'une manière ou d'une autre. Au minimum, je dois lui montrer que je l'ai entendu, ce qui me semble soudain très difficile. J'aurais dû me retourner dès qu'il a parlé, mais j'étais trop occupée à me demander si c'était ou non Richard. Maintenant, ça paraît bizarre que je ne l'aie pas fait. Merde alors, dois-je me retourner en souriant ? Avec un air curieux ? Perplexe ? Effarouché ? Ou pas du tout ?

—En fait, reprend la voix, j'ai hésité à vous aborder : j'ai d'abord cru que vous étiez un mannequin.

Il fait des blagues. C'est très bon signe. Ça signifie qu'il veut me faire rire, ce qui montre qu'il… euh… a envie de me voir rire. Je devrais simplement rire, et me retourner. Ou peut-être juste sourire, et me tourner.

Oh, et s'il était en train de se payer ma tête ? J'esquisse un petit sourire et tourne légèrement la tête, si bien que je me retrouve à regarder ses chaussures. Elles sont noires.

—Puis je me suis dit que les mannequins, en général, n'ont pas « robe de chambre » écrit au feutre sur le dos de la main.

Oh, merde, merde, merde. Le pense-bête. Je ne m'en souvenais plus, et il l'a remarqué. Mais comment a-t-il fait pour le voir ? Alors ça, c'est parfait pour me donner un air élégant et sophistiqué, n'est-ce pas ?

—À moins que quelqu'un n'ait noté ça pour indiquer aux magasiniers à quel endroit de la boutique ils devaient vous poser. Ça veut peut-être seulement dire que vous devriez en porter une, et je suis en train de me ridiculiser en tenant une conversation à sens unique avec une Barbie géante.

Je pouffe discrètement à travers mes lèvres fermées.

—Et maintenant que j'ai commencé, je n'ai plus d'autre choix que de continuer à vous parler jusqu'à ce que vous me répondiez. Ce qui fait que si vous êtes un mannequin, évidemment, je suis parti pour une très longue nuit. (Il se tait un instant.) Bon, ne nous voilons pas la face, pour une très longue année.

Cette fois, je ris pour de bon et tourne enfin la tête pour croiser son regard. Ce que je découvre avec un choc, ce sont les yeux chaleureux et souriants d'un homme que je pourrais bien trouver extrêmement séduisant.

—Ah, Dieu merci, vous êtes vivante. Et ma réputation est sauvée.

—Ça n'a jamais fait l'ombre d'un doute.

—Bah, c'est facile à dire pour vous. Vous allez bien, donc, je vois?

Je me retourne à présent pour lui faire entièrement face. Oh, ces yeux! Je pourrais sans problème me réveiller à côté d'eux même quand il aura atteint la quarantaine. Pendant un court moment, j'imagine la scène : c'est mon anniversaire ; penché vers moi, appuyé sur un coude, il attend que je m'éveille ; sur la table de nuit, dans un écrin de velours repose un magnifique anneau serti de rubis et de diamants. Je suis ravissante, allongée, vêtue de soie, les cils longs et fournis, les lèvres rose pâle étirées en un petit sourire qui témoigne de mes rêves. J'ouvre les paupières, les fais battre un instant, découvre qu'il me regarde, sourit davantage…

—Finalement, je ne suis plus très sûr : vous allez vraiment bien?

Je reviens à *Whytelys*. L'homme est toujours là, mais il commence à avoir l'air un peu inquiet. Vite, je hoche la tête et réponds d'une voix sourde :

—Oui, je vais très bien, merci.

—Eh bien, tant mieux. Je suis content de l'entendre. Bien que ça me laisse quelque peu perplexe. Je veux dire, je vous ai trouvée complètement immobile et silencieuse au milieu d'un grand magasin à trois semaines de Noël. Si ce n'est pas causé par une maladie, alors je suis forcé de penser que vous le faisiez simplement pour jouer un tour cruel aux gens pleins de bonnes intentions qui vaquent à leurs affaires.

Je viens de m'apercevoir qu'il a les cheveux châtains. Et un long pardessus noir. Et une serviette en cuir.

— Pas du tout, dis-je avec douceur. J'étais seulement éblouie par les merveilles qui s'offraient à ma vue.

— En effet. (Il se retourne pour suivre mon regard.) Spectaculaire, n'est-ce pas ? C'est un tribut tellement approprié au jour que les chrétiens reconnaissent comme la naissance officielle de leur religion tout entière.

— Winnie l'Ourson en costume de père Noël. Quoi de plus approprié ?

Il rit :

— Rien, en effet ! Sauf de la lingerie bordée de fourrure rouge.

Nous nous tournons tous les deux et posons les yeux en même temps sur un négligé vaporeux accroché non loin de mon coude gauche, puis nous détournons immédiatement pour regarder quelque chose – n'importe quoi – d'autre.

— Hum… oui. Vous avez raison. Donner et recevoir des sous-vêtements vulgaires et des peluches à cette période de l'année a un sens profond et représente… euh…

— L'amour du prochain, propose-t-il avec un grand sourire, et de toutes les merveilleuses créatures de Dieu.

— Oui ! Même celles qui n'existent pas en vrai.

— Absolument. Et l'orgie de nourriture et d'alcool à laquelle nous allons tous nous livrer est le symbole de…

— La nourriture spirituelle que nous pouvons nous procurer en accueillant la parole de Jésus.

Il hoche la tête d'un air sage :

—Ah, bravo ! Dieu merci, il reste au moins une personne qui n'a pas oublié la vraie signification de Noël.

Nous partons tous deux d'un petit rire. Il remonte légèrement sa manche *(Il porte des boutons de manchette ! Ça existe encore ?)* pour consulter sa montre. Merde !

—Bon, commence-t-il.

Je ne veux pas qu'il finisse. Pourtant je ne peux pas non plus lui montrer que je ne veux pas qu'il termine sa phrase.

—Moi aussi, interviens-je. Des courses à faire, une robe de chambre importante et symbolique à dénicher.

Je fais un geste vers les mots écrits sur ma main.

—Bien sûr. Bien. D'accord. Bon, dans ce cas… (Il se tait, passe la main dans ses cheveux, puis reprend.) Oh, et puis zut. C'est Noël, quel moment plus parfait ? Je ne pense pas, si vous n'êtes pas trop occupée, que vous pourriez… avoir envie de…

—Putain, j'ai cru que je ne te reverrai jamais !

Nous sursautons tous les deux, et soudain je me souviens que je suis au milieu d'un magasin. Qui grouille de monde. Très bruyant. Nous levons les yeux pour découvrir une femme avec des mèches roses qui se dirige vers nous, l'air décidé, en faisant des signes de la main. C'est Vini, bien sûr, mais je me demande si je peux faire semblant de ne pas la connaître pour finir d'entendre ce que cet homme était sur le point de dire.

—Où tu étais fourrée, bordel ? s'écrie-t-elle en me rejoignant.

OK, plus moyen de la snober, maintenant. Je me détourne de Vini pour regarder mon interlocuteur qui sourit toujours, bien que son expression ait à présent un je-ne-sais-quoi de définitif.

—Bon, dit-il.

Au même moment je m'exclame :

—Vini.

—Tu ne devineras jamais qui j'ai vu, affirme-t-elle en me prenant par le bras. Par ici, grouille-toi.

—J'ai été ravi de vous rencontrer, assure-t-il en penchant la tête vers moi.

Il commence à se dégager de notre échange.

—Moi de même.

—Quoi ? demande Vini, qui vient seulement de remarquer qu'en fait j'étais en pleine discussion. (Ses yeux font l'aller et retour entre l'inconnu et moi.) Oh, merde, désolée.

—Au revoir, dit-il en reculant d'un pas.

Il se détourne. J'ai envie de l'attraper par le bras pour l'empêcher de partir. Je remue les doigts tandis que le film se déroule dans ma tête :

Moi : « Attendez, ne partez pas. » (J'ai la main posée sur son bras.)

Le Séduisant Inconnu : (Il se retourne vers moi.) « Je n'ai pas le choix, vous ne comprenez pas ? Il doit en être ainsi. »

Moi : « Non, ce n'est pas une fatalité ! Vous n'avez pas besoin de partir. J'ai ressenti… quelque chose. Ne me dites pas que vous l'avez ressenti aussi ! »

LSI : (Il fait quelques pas vers moi et entre dans mon espace d'intimité. Il parle d'une voix basse et précipitée.) « Un… lien. Entre nous ? »

Moi : (D'une voix sourde.) « Oui. »

LSI : (Il hoche la tête.) « Oui. Je l'ai senti également. Mais vous avez de la compagnie. Je ne peux pas… »

Moi : « Oh, laissez tomber, ce n'est que Vini, ça lui est égal. Alors, qu'alliez-vous me dire ? »

J'ai le bras qui me fait mal, et qui est même en train de bouger tout seul vers le manteau de l'inconnu, mais celui-ci s'éloigne hors de ma portée, et Vini tire mon autre bras.

— Mais viens !

Il n'est plus là, de toute façon. Je finis par me tourner pour suivre Vini. Elle part précipitamment à travers la foule, et c'est difficile de ne pas la perdre. Surtout que mes pieds semblent avoir décidé de rester où ils sont, et que le reste de ma personne est d'accord avec eux. Tant pis. Le film se serait probablement éloigné du scénario original si je l'avais réalisé :

Moi : « Attendez, ne partez pas. » (J'ai la main posée sur son bras.)

LSI : « Enlevez votre main de mon bras ! »

Je fais de mon mieux pour suivre Vini tout en regardant constamment autour de moi pour essayer de le revoir. Bien que nous nous soyons éloignées de l'endroit où il a été vu pour la dernière fois et que la logique veuille qu'il soit quelque part derrière nous. Mais bon, la logique importe peu dans ces histoires, bien sûr. Dans une situation comme celle-là, il pourrait très bien me croiser sur le trottoir dans une demi-heure ou se trouver devant moi dans la queue à la caisse.

Nous finissons par ralentir et nous arrêter au rayon Homme, où flotte comme toujours une légère odeur de cuir. Vini revient vers moi et me reprend par le bras pour me conduire vers les caleçons rayés. Je continue à regarder autour de moi, guettant encore LSI, tout en cherchant déjà la personne que Vini veut me montrer. À tous les coups, c'est quelqu'un qui ferait un sosie potable. Ce doit être une star intéressante, sinon elle ne prendrait pas la peine de m'amener jusqu'ici. Je ne vois pas qui ça peut être. Qui rêve-t-elle de trouver depuis longtemps ? Le gamin qui joue Spiderman ? Peter Parker ? Ah non, je suis bête, ça c'est le nom du personnage. Je suis un cancre. Ah, comment s'appelle-t-il ? Tony quelque chose, je crois. Non, pas…

— Là-bas. Vise un peu. Près des cravates.

Je regarde. C'est un homme en manteau caramel. Richard.

— Écroule-toi, dis-je.

— Quoi ?

Je ne parviens pas à détacher mes yeux de lui, mais Vini n'est pas très coopérative. Je la supplie d'une voix plus pressante :

— Écroule-toi. Fais comme si tu avais un malaise.

— Non.

À regret, je me tourne vers elle :

— Pourquoi pas ?

— Beth. Bordel de merde, je ne veux pas. Je me suis déjà ramassée avant de sortir.

— Allez, Vini, s'il te plaît… Moi, je le ferais pour toi, tu le sais bien.

— Non.

Donc, Richard, après s'être précipité en avion du Portugal, avoir fait des excès de vitesse sur le chemin depuis l'aéroport dans sa course folle pour me retrouver et me dire quel idiot aveugle il a été, qu'il m'aime et ne veut plus jamais être séparé de moi, s'arrête à *Whytelys* pour regarder les slips kangourou blancs en promotion.

Nous nous cachons aussitôt, accroupies, derrière les shorts de cyclisme en lycra. Après un coup d'œil à Vini, je me concentre sur Richard. Je ne veux pas qu'il me voie comme ça. Cette position est tout en haut de ma liste des tabous, avec se gratter, vomir, se moucher et acheter des tampons. Et je ne veux pas que nos retrouvailles larmoyantes se déroulent de part et d'autre d'un présentoir de sous-vêtements soldés. Le scénario idéal – j'aide Vini après un malaise quelconque – n'est pas parti pour se réaliser, il ne me reste donc plus qu'une seule solution.

Je me tourne vers Vini :

— Il faut qu'il me voie ailleurs dans le magasin, dans un endroit plus favorable. Je ne peux pas le laisser me repérer ici.

Il s'éloigne vers les caisses, et je me relève.

— Si ça t'ennuie tant que ça, pourquoi tu ne vas pas lui parler ? Enfin quoi, c'est l'homme de tes rêves, bordel de merde !

— Ça ne se passe pas comme ça, lui dis-je.

Je m'approche des sous-vêtements. Ses mains ont touché ces slips kangourou ; ses doigts ont caressé ces coutures, se sont glissés à travers cette ouverture, ont tiré cet élastique. Quelle chance il a, ce slip !

Le manteau caramel s'éloigne de plus en plus, et disparaît dans la foule. Si je ne me dépêche pas, je vais le perdre. Cela fait des mois que je planifie la façon dont je lui apparaîtrai lors de son retour, et je veux que tout soit parfait. Je veux qu'il m'observe à mon insu, comme ça je suis certaine de me présenter à mon avantage. Je file entre les portants vers l'endroit où je l'ai aperçu pour la dernière fois, et plusieurs personnes lèvent la tête pour me voir passer, comme un troupeau d'herbivores qui cesse de brouter en se demandant si le tyrannosaure arrive.

Je débouche d'un tournant et m'arrête net. Il est là, dans la queue de la caisse, plusieurs articles en tissu blanc dans la main. Les slips kangourou.

La file d'attente est longue : il va rester immobile, tourné dans la même direction, pendant une éternité, ce qui me donne largement le temps d'entrer dans sa ligne de mire. Et juste devant lui – Alléluia ! – se trouvent des décorations de Noël ! Des tas de jolis objets scintillants que je vais pouvoir tenir en souriant avec une joie enfantine. Je ne pouvais rêver mieux. Je passe rapidement mon apparence en revue : cheveux… *Oh, et puis merde, dépêche-toi d'aller là-bas.*

Je ne me précipite pas, parce que, évidemment, quand on flâne dans un magasin on n'est pas pressés. De toute façon, même si je voulais, je ne pourrais pas : il y a neuf millions de personnes dans le passage. Mais j'ai l'air sereine et heureuse lorsque j'arrive aux décorations de Noël. Je choisis une boule en verre qui miroite tout particulièrement et la tiens dans la lumière. Des petits éclats lumineux dansent de façon charmante sur mon visage et mes cheveux, et j'esquisse un léger sourire plein de douceur, qui ne déforme pas mes traits mais les embellit simplement. Et je sais qu'à l'instant où il lèvera les yeux et me verra son cœur s'arrêtera, il aura le souffle coupé, il sera mien. Je lance un regard furtif dans sa direction.

Ce n'est pas Richard.

Chapitre 4

Préparer l'action

Objectif à court terme : Vini pense que je devrais oublier Richard, mais je crois au contraire que c'est à moi de fixer mes propres objectifs. Je l'oublierai quand je serai prête.

Obstacles : ça n'a aucun intérêt d'oublier quelqu'un qui va revenir.

Objectif à long terme : peut-être que je pourrais retrouver le Séduisant Inconnu et faire ma vie avec lui.

Obstacles : je ne sais pas qui il est, ni où il est.

Pendant une seconde, le vernis s'est craquelé. Pendant un bref moment, ma rayonnante, bienheureuse joie enfantine s'est transformée en amère, écrasante déception. Je ne m'en suis pas aperçue sur le moment, bien sûr ; j'étais trop submergée par mon amère, écrasante déception. Mais après coup, maintenant que nous sommes rentrées à la maison, blotties dans le salon avec les lumières du sapin allumées et une bougie parfumée à la cannelle, je peux regarder en arrière et me dire, en toute honnêteté, que je n'étais pas à mon avantage à cet instant. En fait, heureusement que ce n'était pas Richard qui achetait ces sous-vêtements parce qu'il m'aurait vue le visage déformé, hideux. Sauf que, bien évidemment, si cela avait été lui, mon expression aurait été tout à fait différente. J'espère que j'aurais été capable de lui servir mon air de bienvenue, digne et les yeux brillants, mais vu ma totale perte de contrôle, je n'en suis plus si sûre.

Vini garde un silence plutôt puéril sur la question. Je lui jette un regard, mais elle est ostensiblement plongée dans un article sur les pêcheurs de la mer du Nord dans le programme télé. C'est évident qu'elle veut me punir. Je sais qu'elle pense que je perds mon temps avec Richard. Je ne comprends pas pourquoi : il représente exactement ce dont nous avons passé nos nuits à discuter et à rêver, toutes les deux – beau, intelligent, drôle et, disons-le, riche. L'argent, c'est un critère pour Vini. Pour ma part, ça ne m'intéresse pas du tout. L'homme de mes rêves pourrait vivre dans une petite cabane ou quelque chose similaire, ça ne me dérangerait pas. Ça n'aurait pas d'importance du moment qu'on s'aime, n'est-ce pas ? Et, quand on vieillirait, je pourrais l'aider à monter sa propre entreprise, et on pourrait s'installer dans un logement un peu mieux.

Mais Vini est très différente de moi. Vous n'avez peut-être pas remarqué, mais premièrement elle a des mèches roses qui ont l'air, vous savez, fabuleusement punk et déjantées sur elle, mais ne conviendraient pas à quelqu'un comme moi. Et elle s'habille toujours de couleurs pétantes, par exemple des bottes mandarine avec une jupe en daim violette et un chemisier de cachemire orange et marron, ou une veste en vinyle rouge. Elle dit qu'elle exprime sa personnalité, et je hoche la tête chaque fois en prétendant qu'elle est magnifique, tellement originale et patati et patata ; mais au fond de moi je crois qu'elle cherche juste à se faire remarquer. Et ça marche, à tous les coups. Personnellement, je pense que c'est humiliant que les passants vous dévisagent comme ça, ou pouffent et se donnent des coups de coude, et qu'il y a de bien meilleures façons d'attirer les regards que de porter des tenues excentriques. Rien de mal à susciter l'attention par un beau manteau de marque, par exemple, ou un pantalon stylé et bien coupé.

— Mais tu ressembles à tout le monde, affirme Vini qui n'a rien compris, quand j'essaie de le lui suggérer. Des fois, on n'est vraiment pas sur la même longueur d'ondes.

— Ooooh ! s'exclame-t-elle brusquement depuis le canapé.

Je relève la tête d'un coup pour la regarder :

— Quoi ? Quelque chose que tu voudrais me dire ? À propos de Richard que je devrais oublier, et la vie qui continue ? Encore ! Mais tu ne le connais même pas, Vini. Tu ne sais pas comment on est ensemble. Tu fondes ton opinion sur cette unique soirée où il s'est saoulé et t'a accidentellement frôlé la poitrine, et ce n'est pas du tout représentatif. J'ai travaillé avec lui pendant huit ans, et il s'est toujours montré parfaitement correct avec moi. Il est charmant, drôle, attentionné, et, bon, je suis amoureuse de lui. Ça devrait te suffire. Le fait que, techniquement, il soit à l'étranger en ce moment n'a pas d'importance.

Un court silence s'installe, puis elle redresse la tête et me considère d'un air sérieux :

— Putain, tu savais que ces pêcheurs passent des jours et des jours par un temps affreux et glacial, avec des vagues énormes, risquant leur vie à chaque minute ? (Je la dévisage.) Tout ça pour quelques cabillauds minables. Quoi ?

— Tu n'as pas entendu un mot de ce que j'ai dit ?

Elle fait la moue :

— Tu as parlé ? Désolée, j'étais plongée dans cet article. Redis-le-moi.

— C'est plus la peine. Laisse tomber.

— Oh, d'accord…

— De toute façon, tu ne comprendrais pas…

— Vraiment ? Pourquoi ça ?

— Ça ne fait rien, manifestement tu as beaucoup de choses à lire, je ne veux pas te déranger.

Elle jette le magazine et se retourne sur le canapé pour me faire face :

— OK, mademoiselle, vous avez mon entière attention maintenant. Et, au passage, Richard n'est pas « techniquement » à l'étranger ; il est à l'é-tran-ger, bordel. Et il ne m'a pas frôlé le nichon par accident, l'autre fois, il me l'a franchement empoigné. Et, tant qu'on parle de ça, il t'a manifestement échappé que Richard est parti avec sa copine, Beth, bordel. Co-pine. Ce qui me conduit à subodorer qu'il ne s'imagine pas rentrer en courant pour t'épouser dans un avenir proche.

Je reste silencieuse un moment avant de répondre :

— Tu as écouté, alors.

— Oui, je t'ai écoutée. Je t'écoute toujours, merde ! C'est pour ça que je fais semblant de ne pas t'entendre, parfois. Bordel, Beth ! C'est tellement ridicule, tu ne t'en rends pas compte ? Putain, tu m'as carrément demandé de me rouler par terre comme un poisson à *Whytelys* aujourd'hui, juste pour que Richard te voie faire semblant de me venir en aide. Soit il t'aime pour ce que tu es – une très jolie formatrice qui n'a pas l'ombre d'un brevet de secourisme –, soit non. Et aucun scénario d'urgence bidon n'y changera rien.

—Oh, tu es juste…

—Non, Beth, je ne suis rien du tout. Il y a des indices, tu sais, si seulement tu voulais bien ouvrir les yeux. (Elle se tire l'index en avant avec l'autre main.) Indice numéro un : jamais, en huit ans, il n'a fait le premier pas. Et, euh, numéro deux : il a une copine. Ah, et n'oublions pas le numéro trois, crucial : il est au Portugal avec elle. (Elle tourne à nouveau son regard vers moi et hoche la tête d'un air sage.) Ça, pour moi, c'est l'argument décisif.

Je préférerais qu'elle n'affirme pas ce genre de choses. Ça me fait douter de mon bon sens.

Après un long silence, je réponds :

—OK, tu as gagné. Je vais oublier Richard et essayer de me trouver quelqu'un d'autre.

Elle laisse un blanc démesuré et se met en quatre pour avoir l'air absolument abasourdie :

—Vraiment ? Tu penses ce que tu dis ? Je veux dire, tu vas chercher activement quelqu'un d'autre ?

Je hoche la tête :

—Oui, je suis sérieuse. Je vais chercher activement un nouvel homme à aimer. Tu es contente ?

Elle arbore un large sourire :

—Putain, tu sais quoi, Beth ? Je suis carrément sur un nuage. Si tu es sérieuse, je suis en extase.

—Bien.

—Excellent.

Elle ramasse le magazine télé et se met à le feuilleter sans entrain. Nous discutons sans conviction pendant quelques minutes des programmes de ce soir, puis une idée me frappe. Pourquoi se croit-elle autorisée à critiquer ma vie amoureuse presque parfaite, alors que sa nouvelle manie a été de sortir avec toute une série de sosies de sa propre agence ? Juste parce qu'ils ressemblent vaguement à quelqu'un de connu. Je la regarde, les paupières plissées, et ajoute d'un air ultradétaché :

— Alors, comment ça va, avec Johnny Depp ?

Elle claque la langue :

— Beurk. Ce n'est pas Johnny Depp, Beth, c'est le capitaine Jack Sparrow. Il y a une grosse différence, tu sais.

— Vraiment ?

— Ben, évidemment. Tu voudrais coucher avec Edward aux mains d'argent, toi ?

Nous restons toutes les deux les yeux dans le vague un moment.

— Non. Non, tu as raison. Alors, comment ça va ?

Elle soupire :

— C'est la même histoire qu'avec Yan Solo.

— Oh non, tu rigoles ?

— Nan. Enlève-lui le costume, et il se met à ressembler à Martin Hunt, du magasin de bricolage.

— Ce qui est sans doute sa vraie identité.

Elle hoche tristement la tête.

— Ah, pauvre de toi.

— Tu m'étonnes. Bordel, ce chapeau, avec le khôl et la perruque… (Elle ferme les yeux quelques secondes.) Il était très convaincant. Mais une fois que je l'ai déshabillé…

— Martin Hunt.

— Martin Hunt. (Elle soupire.) On a été photographiés par des paparazzis, un jour, tu sais.

— Vraiment ?

—Ouais. Bon, en fait c'était Adam Beresford, du *Herald*, mais quand même.

—Hum.

Franchement. Et avec ça elle pense que c'est moi qui me fais des films ! Au moins, l'homme dont je suis amoureuse est réellement celui qu'il prétend être, il ne fait pas semblant d'être un acteur qui fait semblant d'être un pirate imaginaire mal dégrossi, avec du khôl.

Vini et moi, on n'est pas meilleures amies depuis toujours. Quand on était à l'école, on ne se fréquentait pas du tout. Elle, c'était l'excentrique avec les yeux maquillés en noir et des Dr Martens, une mère morte et un père poivrot, qui vivait dans une caravane et travaillait chaque soir et chaque week-end au restau du coin juste pour payer les factures. Elle était du genre qui participe au club de maths, tandis que j'étais pom-pom girl. En fait, il n'y avait ni club de maths ni pom-pom girls, mais, s'il y en avait eu, c'est ce qu'on aurait fait. Et je ne pense pas que sa mère soit vraiment morte, elle habite juste à Southampton. Mais elle vivait pour de vrai avec son père.

Il est chauffeur de taxi, donc évidemment il ne peut pas passer son temps à boire, sinon il perdrait son permis. Et c'est vrai qu'elle travaillait le samedi dans un grand magasin. On a commencé à louer cet appartement ensemble grâce à un site de retrouvailles entre copains, comme quoi il faut toujours garder son abonnement à jour. J'ai aussi trouvé mon plombier de la même façon, ainsi que la personne qui s'occupe du jardin. C'est mieux que les pages jaunes.

—Vini, je crois qu'il serait temps de changer.

—De quoi tu parles ?

Elle parcourt la pièce des yeux, feignant de penser que je fais allusion au papier peint.

Je soupire :

— Chaque homme que tu as eu depuis, disons, un an et demi, est un de tes clients.

— Bordel de merde, Beth, ce n'est pas parce que je touche douze pour cent sur leurs contrats que je me suis jetée tête baissée dans un truc véreux. Je ne vais pas me retrouver avec des gros plans de ma main dans les journaux nationaux, ni me faire radier de l'ordre des agences de sosies.

— Non, je sais. Ça existe ?

— Non.

— Ah, OK. Écoute, j'essaie juste de t'amener à comprendre que tu vis toujours dans tes rêves. Comme quand on avait quinze ans et qu'on était toutes persuadées que Richard Gere allait passer dans une voiture rutilante et nous demander le chemin, et qu'on lui répondrait que ce serait plus simple si on lui montrait directement, donc on monterait à bord et on partirait pour une longue balade romantique avec lui, à l'issue de laquelle il contemplerait, fasciné, la fille magnifique à ses côtés en se demandant comment il pourrait un jour parvenir à…

— Ouais, c'est bon, je n'ai pas besoin d'un résumé de *Pretty Woman* maintenant, merci. Va à l'essentiel, histoire que je puisse avoir des gosses avant de mourir.

— C'est exactement ce que je veux dire. Tu voudrais des enfants, mais tu n'essaies même pas d'avoir une relation sérieuse.

— C'est toi qui dis ça ! Des deux hommes de ta vie, il y en a un qui est sur un autre continent, et l'autre, ah non, attends, il n'y en a pas d'autre.

—Techniquement, c'est encore l'Europe, donc c'est…

—Ta gueule.

Je me tais. On se regarde en chiens de faïence. Au bout de quarante-cinq secondes, elle détourne les yeux et dit « Pfff ». Ce qui signifie qu'elle reconnaît que j'ai raison.

—Vini, le temps passe, tu sais. On a toutes les deux vingt-huit ans. Je n'accepte pas – je refuse absolument – d'être célibataire à trente ans.

—Et d'être une trentenaire célibataire avec de multiples partenaires ?

—Non. Pas question. Jamais de la vie. Je refuse. Donc si Richard ne rentre pas…

—Et il ne rentrera pas.

—Alors je dois m'y mettre maintenant. Il me faut au moins une année pour préparer le mariage, ce qui me laisse un peu moins d'un an pour trouver l'homme avec qui je veux passer le reste de ma vie, le pousser à comprendre qu'il ne peut pas vivre sans moi, à débouler sur mon lieu de travail pour me soulever de terre et me porter jusqu'à sa voiture. Trop facile !

—Super plan. Sûr de marcher.

—Ben, ça vaut le coup d'essayer. Et je crois que tu devrais faire pareil. Parce que quand j'aurai rencontré ce mec, je n'aurai plus besoin de colocataire. Tu vois ce que je veux dire ?

—Bon, on dirait que je n'ai plus trop le choix…

—Super ! On va s'y mettre ensemble. Puisque nous savons que ce que nous avons fait jusqu'ici ne marche pas, nous avons toutes les deux besoin d'un changement drastique. Ne me regarde pas comme ça, c'est nécessaire, et, si on le fait comme il faut, on aura de la stabilité et de la sécurité avec un seul homme pour toute la vie.

—Ooh. Je suis impatiente.

Je sens qu'elle n'est pas très emballée par cette perspective. Je la connais depuis longtemps et, comme je suis de nature sensible, j'arrive parfois à déceler des choses qu'elle ne dit pas.

—Vini, si tu n'es pas convaincue à cent pour cent, dis-le-moi maintenant. Je n'ai vraiment pas envie de devoir te traîner, de t'entendre râler sur tout et de te voir essayer de te carapater avec le premier mec qui aura les cheveux de John Travolta.

Elle secoue la tête :

—Non, non, tu as raison. Tout n'a pas été rose : il est temps de tenter une nouvelle approche.

—Bien. Donc tu es prête à tout changer, y compris et surtout le type de personnes qui t'a attirée jusqu'à maintenant ?

—Oui, d'accord.

—Tant mieux, parce que la première chose que je veux que tu fasses, c'est d'enlever ces habits.

Non, tout va bien, je ne cache pas un amour secret et interdit pour ma colocataire. Bien sûr que non. Je suis amoureuse de Richard, vous vous souvenez ? Oh, et au cas où vous supposeriez que j'ai renoncé à lui, eh bien ce n'est pas vrai. Franchement, vous imaginez que je vais dire : « OK, tu as gagné, je laisse tomber », après huit ans ensemble ? Vous y avez cru ? Allons ! Je pensais que vous commenciez à me connaître. Quand j'ai parlé de besoin de changement, c'était Vini que j'avais en tête, pas moi.

Donc voici mon plan d'action : d'abord, Vini la ferme au sujet de Richard. Super. Deuxième point : elle arrête de porter ces tenues horribles et mal assorties, et devient élégante. Super aussi. Troisième point, et il s'agit plus d'un à-côté que d'un facteur de réussite à part entière, nous nous mettons toutes deux activement à la recherche de quelqu'un dont nous pourrions tomber amoureuses, je pourrais vraiment trouver. Et alors je n'aurais plus besoin d'attendre Richard. Parce que, en dépit du fait que tout ce que j'ai dit à Vini soit un mensonge, c'est vrai que je suis inquiète à l'idée d'être célibataire à trente ans. Je veux dire, bien sûr que Richard sera rentré d'ici là, donc ce n'est pas vraiment un problème, mais quand même. Une toute petite, minuscule, microscopique partie de mon cerveau chuchote aux autres : « Et s'il ne revenait pas ? » Et c'est à cette petite partie que les autres sont de plus en plus nombreuses à prêter attention.

Chapitre 5

Saisir sa chance

Objectif à court terme : Ce soir, je me fais teindre les cheveux.

Obstacles : Une profonde réticence, ça compte ?

Objectif à long terme : (le faux) rencontrer un homme, commencer une nouvelle vie avec lui, vivre heureux et avoir beaucoup d'enfants.

(Le vrai) Attendre Richard et l'épouser quand il reviendra.

Obstacles : Vini.

C'est le lendemain, mardi 5 décembre, que ça se produit. J'arrive tôt pour préparer la prochaine séance de mon stage « Gérer le Changement ». Je suis là juste avant 8 heures, ce qui me permet de voir mes collègues débarquer. Fatima est la première d'entre eux, l'air inquiète, légèrement penchée en avant comme pour protéger le haut de son corps d'une agression. Elle garde sa main brûlée contre sa poitrine ; de l'autre, elle porte un petit sapin de Noël. Elle me jette un coup d'œil et m'adresse un sourire nerveux.

— Salut, Beth. Ça va ? Tu as un joli chemisier. Ooh, j'adore tes chaussures, elles sont nouvelles ?

—Merci, Fati. Non, ça fait des siècles que je les ai. Et ta main ? Comment te sens-tu, aujourd'hui ?

Elle hausse les épaules et essaie, sans succès, de sourire avec désinvolture :

—Oh, tu sais, ça peut aller. J'ai quelques élancements, mais ça reste supportable. C'est bien fait pour moi, de toute façon. Peut-être que je ferai plus attention la prochaine fois. Regarde, j'ai apporté un sapin.

Elle le soulève, au cas où je ne l'aurais pas vu.

—Super. Tu vas l'installer où ?

Elle parcourt la pièce des yeux.

—Je ne sais pas. T'en penses quoi ? Près de la porte ?

—Hum, ce serait sans doute mieux dans le coin à côté de la photocopieuse. Les gens risquent de se prendre les pieds dedans si tu le mets dans le passage.

—Ah oui, bonne idée. Je vais faire ça.

Je la regarde porter le sapin, qui n'est pas décoré, à l'endroit désigné.

—Tu as essayé de trouver des nouveaux contrats, hier soir ?

Elle hoche la tête d'un air anxieux en revenant vers son bureau :

—Oui. Dès que je suis sortie du travail, j'ai fait tout le tour de la ville, tous les magasins auxquels j'ai pu penser. Je ne suis pas rentrée avant… (Elle regarde sa montre.) 23 h 30. Ou minuit. Je sais plus.

—Fati, tu n'as pas marché dans les rues jusqu'à minuit, quand même ?

—Ben, j'ai un peu perdu la notion du temps. Et après quelques heures, j'étais complètement prise dedans. Je n'arrêtais pas de me dire « ça va marcher dans celui-là, ou celui-là, ou celui-là… »

Sa voix s'éteint et elle se laisse tomber sur sa chaise.

— Mais c'étaient lesquels, les magasins ouverts à cette heure-là ?

Elle hausse les sourcils :

— Oh, tu serais étonnée. Dans la vieille ville, tu sais, de l'autre côté de la rocade, il y avait plein d'endroits qui n'étaient pas fermés.

Je connais ces boutiques, et ce n'est pas exactement le style qui recherche des formations, si vous voyez ce que je veux dire. Les talents qu'ils emploient sont du genre qu'on apprend sur le tas.

— Tu as réussi à en caser un ?

— Non, ça n'a pas marché hier. En fait, c'était un peu… (Elle se tait de nouveau et reste un moment le regard dans le vague.) Mais ce soir je vais y arriver. Je suis motivée.

Et elle lève les yeux vers moi avec un sourire confiant. Je lui rends son sourire et hoche la tête, mais je la vois se rembrunir un peu alors qu'elle se tourne vers son écran d'ordinateur.

Putain de merde, je me sens presque coupable de n'avoir encore rien fait pour décrocher des nouveaux contrats. J'espérais trouver l'inspiration pendant ma virée shopping d'hier avec Vini, mais j'ai été tellement distraite par le Séduisant Inconnu, puis par la présence de Richard, puis par son absence, que je n'y ai plus du tout pensé. Ça ne fait rien, il me reste presque trois semaines. Depuis que celui qui me donnait envie d'accumuler les nouveaux clients s'est barré à Faro, je suis un peu apathique et déboussolée, mais quand je regarde le visage anxieux de Fatima, je sens la vieille flamme se rallumer. Je dois pouvoir me motiver suffisamment pour

66

rapporter un gros contrat et sauver le poste de Fatima ; elle n'a pas vraiment de raisons de s'en faire. Je l'observe à nouveau et remarque que son collant a filé et que des aiguilles de sapin se sont prises aux deux extrémités de la déchirure. Heureusement qu'elle n'anime pas de groupe aujourd'hui : les stagiaires auraient du mal à se concentrer.

Dans la demi-heure qui suit, personne n'engage la conversation avec moi en arrivant, et je n'adresse la parole à personne non plus. En les regardant, je devine que Fatima est la seule à avoir essayé de trouver des contrats hier soir, et elle a tenté sa chance au mauvais endroit, comme les nazis lorsqu'ils cherchent l'arche perdue dans *Indiana Jones*. Cath Parson, si léthargique que boutonner un cardigan semble le sommet de ses efforts, se sera probablement installée à proximité d'un cendrier, pour ne plus en bouger de la soirée ; Ali, notre assistant administratif, et Skye, la plus jeune formatrice, auront perdu leur temps et tout leur argent de poche dans une salle de jeux vidéo ; Mike aura allumé son ordinateur pour voir s'il avait remporté son enchère sur des graines de courge géante. Pour Derek, je ne sais pas : je ne le connais vraiment pas. Je l'imagine lisant un recueil de récits historiques relié plein cuir, au coin du feu. Mais je suis certaine que Sean, qui occupe le quatrième bureau de l'autre îlot de travail avec Grace, Skye et Cath, aura passé toute la nuit dehors à boire, à parier, ou encore à regarder les filles dans un club de striptease. J'ai toujours pensé que c'était le genre à doubler ses deux meilleurs amis en remplaçant la statue d'or par une imitation avant de s'enfuir avec l'unique cheval dont la bande dispose. À supposer qu'il se trouve dans cette situation. Je ne crois même pas qu'il connaisse mon nom.

Bon. Il me reste une demi-heure avant le début de ma séance. Je recommence à m'exercer à lire mes notes d'un air sérieux.

— Bonjour, Beth.

Oh non, c'est Grace. Je me compose un doux sourire et relève la tête :

— Salut, Grace. Ça va ?

Merde, elle est magnifique : blazer en daim écarlate, jupe noire étroite, bottes rouges. Je déplie ma jambe, sur laquelle j'étais assise, pour remettre mon pied dans ma chaussure à talon compensé rose, qui traînait par terre.

— Oui, merci, répond-elle en s'installant à sa table derrière moi.

Elle enlève sa veste d'un haussement d'épaules puis se relève pour la suspendre à un cintre qu'elle garde dans le tiroir de son bureau. Ensuite il faut encore qu'elle aille l'accrocher tout en haut du portemanteau, ce qui lui donne l'occasion de s'étirer dans son polo noir moulant. Quelle pimbêche ! Pourquoi ne s'est-elle pas contentée d'enlever ce blazer avant de s'asseoir ?

— Ça a marché, hier soir ? dis-je.

Je parle de la recherche de contrats, bien entendu, mais la connaissant elle va sans doute me raconter qu'elle a tiré le gros lot et s'est tapé un inconnu sous le porche d'un magasin de pièces automobiles.

— Non, pas trop. En fait, je n'ai même pas essayé. Et toi ?

J'aime sa réponse ambiguë, qui ne révèle rien.

— Non, rien du tout. Comment ça se fait que tu n'aies pas cherché, alors ?

Je savais bien qu'elle n'en avait pas l'intention : elle l'avait sous-entendu quand nous avons discuté dans les toilettes avant de partir. Tout en allumant son ordinateur, elle tourne son siège vers moi :

— Ben tu sais, j'avais autre chose à faire, hier soir. De plus amusant. Et bien plus important qu'un stupide contrat.

— Plus important ? Plus important que de sauver cette boîte et nos emplois ?

Elle acquiesce, les yeux écarquillés :

— Oh là là, oui. Un million de fois !

Elle fait pivoter son fauteuil pour regarder son moniteur et repousse ses cheveux d'un grand geste. Ils sont si longs qu'ils manquent de me cingler le visage. Je détourne rapidement la tête.

— De toute façon, j'aurais tort de m'en faire, pas vrai ? Tu vas évidemment signer un énorme contrat quelque part et nous sauver tous. N'est-ce pas ?

Elle se tourne pour me décocher un coup d'œil sur ces derniers mots, puis reporte son attention sur son écran.

J'éprouve une bouffée de ressentiment teinté d'incrédulité et m'agrippe au rebord de mon siège. Est-ce qu'elle vient vraiment de sous-entendre (ou de confirmer, en réalité, parce que je m'en doutais depuis quelque temps) qu'elle va se contenter de rester là à balancer ses cheveux à droite et à gauche pendant que j'écume toutes les entreprises de la ville pour, après trois semaines d'efforts infatigables, finir par décrocher le genre de prestation dont Chas a besoin pour sortir la société de l'ornière ? Je sens mes doigts se tendre vers cette chevelure incroyablement artificielle. Elle est juste hors de ma portée.

— Je plaisante, Beth, dit Grace tout à coup, en se tournant à nouveau vers moi. J'avais des choses prévues hier soir, mais je vais essayer aujourd'hui. Il faut bien le faire, n'est-ce pas ?

J'acquiesce en silence et me retourne vers mon propre ordinateur. Alors là, je me sens dévastée. C'est quoi son problème, à elle ?

— Tu ne trouves pas que Grace est magnifique, aujourd'hui ? me chuchote Fatima en se penchant vers moi. J'adore sa veste. Elle est trop classe, cette fille !

À l'heure du déjeuner, Vini m'appelle pour me dire qu'elle l'a.

— Mais tu l'as, quoi ?

— La teinture.

Comme je ne crie pas de joie, elle ajoute :

— Pour tes cheveux.

— OK. C'est bien.

— Rentre à la maison le plus tôt possible. On s'occupera de ta coloration, et après on sort.

— On sort ? (Hélas, c'est parti !) Où ça ?

— Pas la peine d'être aussi négative. Tu voulais découvrir de nouveaux horizons, tu te souviens ? Ça commence à 19 h 30, alors rentre avant 18 heures.

Avec une patience d'ange, je réplique :

— Je suis toujours là avant 18 heures, Vini. Tous les jours de la semaine, depuis qu'on habite ensemble, je suis toujours rentrée avant 18 heures. Et maintenant tu m'appelles pour me dire de rentrer avant 18 heures ? C'est un peu comme si tu me téléphonais pour me dire de décrocher le combiné. Je serai là vers 17 h 30, comme d'habitude. D'accord ?

— OK, te décoiffe pas la touffe. Je voulais juste être sûre. À tout à l'heure.

Ça ne me plaît pas. De toute évidence, nous n'allons pas simplement dans un pub ou une boîte, il s'agit plutôt d'un événement puisqu'il y a un horaire. Un spectacle où elle imagine qu'on peut rencontrer de beaux célibataires. Ah là là, j'espère que ce n'est pas une pantomime. Il n'y aura que des pères divorcés en pull à col rond…

Attendez un peu. Les paroles de Vini remuent une pépite de souvenir qui brille juste sous la surface. Elle a parlé de « nouveaux horizons ». Ça me rappelle un article que j'ai lu la semaine dernière dans un magazine nautique. Sur le moment, j'ai pensé qu'il y avait du potentiel, mais je n'en ai rien tiré. Je l'ai quand même arraché. Je n'y crois pas ! Je me penche et commence à décrocher tous les papiers punaisés sur la séparation devant moi ; je les parcours puis les rejette jusqu'à ce que finalement les mots que je cherchais me sautent à la figure. « Horizon prend l'eau ? » Je balaie la pièce des yeux pour m'assurer que personne ne regarde dans ma direction et n'a aperçu le titre, mais tout va bien. Puis je me penche et déplie l'article entre mes mains. Il traite des résultats d'Horizon, en baisse pour la troisième année consécutive, et de la situation épineuse que traverse son P.-D.G., Rupert de Witter. « Quelles mesures prendra de Witter pour faire entrer sa compagnie dans le XXIe siècle ? » s'interroge le journaliste. « Quelles qu'elles soient, il doit agir vite. »

Je garde les yeux rivés sur ces mots, le cœur battant la chamade alors que les sous-entendus de l'article et les difficultés de Rupert de Witter m'apparaissent clairement. De Witter doit agir, maintenant, pour redresser la barre. Et je suis aussi certaine qu'on peut l'être que sa politique de formation dépassée sera l'une des premières choses dont il se débarrassera.

Je n'y crois pas. Je dois démarcher Horizon Holidays.

Je ferme les paupières. Un contrat avec Horizon serait pharaonique : assez pour sauver Love Learning sans problème. Mais ça va être beaucoup plus difficile que ce que vous pourriez croire. Quand Richard a claqué la porte, je voulais qu'il sache que je le soutenais et du coup je ne l'ai pas caché à Rupert de Witter. C'est-à-dire que, pendant que Richard hurlait dans le téléphone, j'ai dit « Exactement » et « Tu as complètement raison » une ou deux fois, en fond sonore.

En réalité, peut-être que Rupert de Witter ne m'a pas entendue. C'est possible. Mais il aura été conscient que je suis partie avec Richard. Il est certain qu'on lui a parlé de notre mutinerie dans les heures, voire les minutes, qui ont suivi notre départ. À l'évocation du nom de Richard, il a sans doute hoché la tête, peu surpris. Il s'y attendait. En revanche, en apprenant que l'une des assistantes de Richard avait également démissionné, il a probablement passé quelques minutes les yeux rivés sur son élégant centre de table, les sourcils froncés.

— Qui peut bien être Beth Sheridan ? se sera-t-il enquis. Est-ce que je la connais ? Pourquoi est-elle partie ? Quel est son problème ?

— Oh, elle n'est restée chez nous que deux ans, lui aura-t-on répondu. Elle doit avoir dans les vingt et un ans, pas plus. Elle est folle amoureuse de Richard, apparemment. Elle le suit partout comme un petit chien malade. Ça fait un peu pitié, en fait.

— Ah oui ! (Et il aura ri d'un air cruel.) Quelle petite dinde. Elle ne sait donc pas que dans six ans il fichera le camp au Portugal et que tout son dévouement et son travail acharné n'auront servi à rien ?

Ils ont dû bien rigoler, j'en mettrais ma main à couper. Et maintenant je me retrouve à devoir démarcher Rupert de Witter. Merde! Va-t-il se souvenir de moi et me chasser de son bureau dans un grand éclat de rire? Non, non, bien sûr que non, ça ne va pas se produire, parce que quand il se rappellera ma défection il n'acceptera même pas de me recevoir.

Un autre élément vient s'ajouter à cette situation déjà embarrassante.

Rupert de Witter est à tomber par terre.

Je veux dire complètement sublime, du genre qui provoque battements de cœur accélérés, incapacité à trouver ses mots, mouvements de crinière, crise de gloussements inexplicables… Ses épais cheveux blonds couvrent son front et lui cachent parfois les yeux; ses dents sont si blanches et parfaites qu'on se demande si ce sont bien ses dents de naissance (bon, évidemment, il ne les avait pas à la naissance; ça aurait été effrayant, même si elles avaient été brillantes et bien alignées); ses yeux sont bleus, je pense, mais c'est difficile à dire, à cause de la mèche et de ses cils fournis, qui ne sont pas blonds, au passage. Et le corps qui va avec suffirait à lui tout seul à semer l'émoi dans les régions les plus secrètes de votre personne.

En fait, je ne l'ai jamais rencontré. Une simple assistante de formation n'avait rien à faire avec le Grand Patron. Mais on peut voir son portrait sur la dernière page de chaque brochure d'Horizon. Il y a quelques mots, censés être une lettre de lui à tous ses clients, dans ce goût-là: « Horizon Holidays met tout en œuvre pour créer de parfaites blablabla, et moi-même, en tant que directeur général, je vous garantis que blabla. » Tout en bas figure une reproduction de sa signature, puis vient la photo. Elle est prise en plein air, et il y a manifestement une légère brise, car ses cheveux sont un peu décoiffés, sans être hirsutes non plus. Juste assez pour vous donner envie d'y passer les doigts. Avant de lécher de la crème fouettée sur son visage. Il sourit, bien sûr, découvrant ces dents magnifiques, et il se tient sur le pont d'un bateau, en polo bleu pâle, un pull blanc cassé noué négligemment sur les épaules, une main gracieusement posée sur le bastingage.

Honnêtement, c'est ridicule. Je n'ai plus vu quelqu'un d'aussi artificiel depuis que j'ai quitté le collège. Et il est là, à dire à tous ses clients qu'il va s'assurer personnellement que leurs vacances soient aussi merveilleuses qu'ils le désirent, alors qu'il arbore un bronzage d'institut, des mèches décolorées et des dents refaites. Qui pourrait y croire ? On dirait un acteur !

Mais il est sexy à en pleurer. Et j'ai travaillé pour lui. Sauf que j'ai quitté l'entreprise à grand fracas, en signe de désapprobation. Et chipé quelques chemises à rabat. Mais il ne s'en est peut-être pas rendu compte. Et à présent il faut que j'aille le trouver pour le convaincre qu'il devrait abandonner sa vieille politique de formation mal fichue au profit d'un prestataire qui s'est créé par mépris de lui et de sa société.

OK.

Ce dont j'ai besoin, c'est d'une entrée en matière, une idée de génie qui puisse me faire pénétrer dans son bureau sans qu'il s'aperçoive que c'est moi, Beth Sheridan, le petit chien malade de Richard Love. Ou des lunettes noires. Ça marcherait aussi.

74

Je n'ai pas le temps d'y penser maintenant. Je dois aller animer la prochaine session de « Gérer le Changement » dans cinq minutes. J'aurai peut-être une illumination pendant la séance. Bien sûr, le fait est que les bénéfices d'Horizon sont en baisse pour la troisième année consécutive et que le conseil d'administration s'inquiète. Gagner un ou deux millions de moins que l'année dernière doit être terriblement stressant pour Rupert, et il est certainement aux abois, à l'affût d'une solution.

Il est sans doute, en ce moment même, assis dans un confortable fauteuil en cuir de veau, dans un vaste cabinet de travail aux murs de verre, les yeux rivés sur le paysage urbain, le menton posé sur son poing, devant un café qui refroidit sur son imposant bureau en chêne, les cheveux brillant dans la lumière des spots, à se demander quelle peut bien être la raison de ces mauvais résultats. Et si j'ai de la chance, ses pensées vont se tourner encore une fois vers sa politique de formation, et vers les mots que Richard Love lui a jetés à la figure il y a six ans :

— Tu n'es qu'un sale maquereau !

Non, non, pas ça. L'autre phrase. Sur sa politique de formation, dépassée et inefficace. Est-il en train de se demander si Richard Love avait raison, il y a si longtemps ? Sa vision des connaissances est-elle obsolète ? S'est-il, lui, Rupert, montré borné ?

— Tu es vraiment un patron très arrangeant, Rupert.

À l'instant précis où je me dirige vers la salle de cours pour la prochaine séance, tout en l'imaginant en train de se maudire pour son manque d'ouverture d'esprit d'il y a six ans, Rupert de Witter, comme dans mes pensées, regarde par une fenêtre et observe le panorama. En revanche, il n'est pas dans un bureau. Il déjeune avec un ami et associé, à l'une des meilleures tables d'un restaurant très sélect, le *Madeleine's*, qui surplombe le lac et les cygnes de Fieldwood Park.

C'est là que toutes les stars de cinéma de la ville viendraient se restaurer, s'il y en avait. Malheureusement, le reste de l'agglomération avec sa zone piétonne et ses échoppes de restauration rapide n'est pas à la hauteur du *Madeleine's*, qui ne suffit pas à les attirer.

— On peut avoir l'addition, Julian, s'il vous plaît ?

— Bien sûr, monsieur de Witter. Je vous l'apporte.

— Merci.

Rupert se tourne vers son compagnon de table et hausse les épaules.

— Tu crois ? Peut-être. Mais ça me semble une demande raisonnable, et je peux me le permettre, alors pourquoi pas ? Au-delà d'un certain seuil, on ne sait plus comment dépenser son argent, de toute façon.

Son vis-à-vis sirote son verre d'un air pensif.

— Je ne pense pas qu'il y ait beaucoup d'hommes d'affaires qui voient les choses comme toi !

Rupert acquiesce :

— Je sais. Tu as raison. C'est le signe qu'on vit dans un triste monde, gouverné par l'argent, si la plupart des employeurs refusent d'ouvrir une crèche d'entreprise simplement parce que ça amputerait trop leurs bénéfices. Mais pourquoi les gens devraient-ils être pénalisés quand ils deviennent parents ? (Il secoue la tête.) J'espère que le jour où je sauterai le pas – si ça se produit – je n'aurai pas l'idée de demander à ma femme d'arrêter de travailler pour s'occuper des enfants. Pourquoi devrait-elle le faire ?

Elle a une carrière, aussi importante pour elle que la mienne pour moi.

— Ta femme ? Bon sang, pourquoi tu ne m'as pas invité au mariage ?

Rupert sourit.

— C'est juste une hypothèse, mon vieux. Je suis sûr qu'il y a plein de parents à Horizon qui pensent comme ça. Et ce sont eux qui sont le plus intéressants pour moi en tant que chef d'entreprise, parce qu'ils sont prêts à tout pour garder leur emploi. Je serais idiot de ne pas les aider.

— Je suis bien d'accord. C'est exactement mon avis.

— C'est vrai ?

— Ouais. À cent pour cent. Il y a tellement de mamans qui devraient être incitées à reprendre le travail. Tu sais, des femmes intelligentes et jolies qu'on ne devrait pas laisser bêtement à la maison à changer des couches.

— Tout à fait.

— Et si tu es malin je crois vraiment que tu devrais les faire travailler. Tu sais, c'est criminel, le nombre de filles vraiment sexy qui ne reviennent pas au boulot parce qu'elles ne peuvent pas se payer de bon mode de garde et qu'elles n'ont pas...

— Tu veux dire « intelligentes ».

— Hein ?

— Tu as dit « le nombre de filles vraiment sexy qui ne reviennent pas... »

— Je n'ai pas dit ça !

— Si, Hector, mon ami, ce sont tes propres mots.

Hector reste un moment silencieux avant de s'avouer vaincu :

— Bon sang, vraiment ? Hum.

Il pouffe de rire.

Rupert se carre dans le dossier de sa chaise :

— Tu sais, je vois à différents petits indices que tu n'as peut-être pas la tête entièrement à cette réunion. Je me trompe ?

Hector regarde Rupert avec franchise et baisse le chef d'un air piteux :

— Désolé, Rupe. Tu as raison, je suis un peu distrait aujourd'hui.

— Tout va bien ?

Hector répond avec un grand sourire :

— Très bien, en fait. Et même mieux que ça. C'est une distraction positive.

Rupert, qui portait son verre à ses lèvres, s'arrête à mi-chemin :

— Sans blague ! Hector s'est trouvé une copine.

— Pas la peine de…

— Eh ben, ce n'est pas trop tôt ! Je croyais que tu avais définitivement renoncé, après Miranda.

— Mais c'était le cas, en fait. En tout cas, je ne cherchais plus. Tu sais, maman était malade, et je ne sortais pas tellement, j'avais décidé de ne pas y penser pendant quelque temps. Mais cette personne m'est tombée dessus. Elle est juste… apparue dans ma vie, comme ça. Tu te souviens de notre rendez-vous ici, il y a six semaines ? Le jour où maman est morte ?

— Bien sûr. Tu as interrompu notre discussion pour répondre au téléphone, alors que ce n'était même pas au sujet de ta mère.

— Eh bien, c'était elle. Rachel. Il fallait que je décroche… Je ne pouvais pas ne pas le faire.

—À ce point? Ça devient intéressant. Alors, elle est comment?

—Ah, par où commencer? Elle est super marrante, Rupe. La première fois que je lui ai parlé, elle avait trouvé mon portable et elle s'est mise à me faire une petite blague à propos d'une demande de rançon. Et elle a continué, sans dévier. Ça m'a fait rire.

—Pour une fois que c'est dans ce sens-là.

—Exactement.

—Alors, le mariage, c'est pour quand?

—Bon sang, Rupert, attends un peu! On n'est même pas encore vraiment ensemble.

—Ah bon? Mais pourquoi? Je veux dire, si elle est tellement fantastique, qu'est-ce qui te retient?

Hector hausse les épaules:

—C'est compliqué. Mais j'y travaille.

—Vraiment? Laisse-moi deviner, son ex est toujours dans les parages? Il ressemble à Brad Pitt et n'accepte pas leur séparation? Il l'appelle jour et nuit, l'attend sur le paillasson avec des fleurs pour la supplier de changer d'avis? Dans ce cas, tu ferais mieux de l'oublier, mon vieux.

—Merci pour le vote de confiance, Rupe.

—Ce n'est pas contre toi, Hec. C'est juste que, tu sais, Brad Pitt: personne n'a ses chances contre lui. Je crois même que je virerais ma cuti si c'était Brad qui me le demandait.

—Hum. Bon, même si l'image que j'ai à présent dans la tête est très séduisante, si on passait à autre chose? Je te tiendrai au courant. En attendant, qu'as-tu pensé de ma proposition?

Rupert prend un dossier en papier bleu posé sur la table, puis le repose:

— Ouais, ça m'a plu. Démarre tout de suite. Et pour revenir à notre précédent sujet de conversation, quand tu as dit qu'elle était apparue, qu'est-ce que tu voulais dire exactement ?

— Donc le système que j'ai créé correspond bien à ce que tu veux pour Horizon ? Il fait bien tout ce dont tu as besoin ?

— Oui, mec, je te l'ai dit. On fait des pertes, donc on doit travailler autrement. J'envisage également de changer notre politique de formation.

— Vraiment ? C'est intéressant. Tu penses externaliser ou continuer avec…

— Oublie le boulot, Hector, et réponds-moi. Comment est-elle apparue ?

— Ah ah ! Je vois. Je comprends. Tu fais le cynique, avec tes histoires de Brad Pitt, mais en fait tu voudrais bien savoir comment je m'y suis pris, n'est-ce pas ? L'idée te plaît, et tu voudrais faire pareil. J'ai raison ?

— Pas forcément. Peut-être que je m'y intéresse seulement parce que tu es l'un de mes plus vieux amis.

— Oui, bien sûr. C'est ça, je te crois.

— Tant mieux. Alors, c'est quoi, la réponse ? Comment quelqu'un comme moi rencontre-t-il quelqu'un comme elle, sans qu'elle sache qui je suis et qu'elle me coure après seulement pour l'argent ?

Hector hausse les sourcils et pince les lèvres :

— Désolé, je n'ai pas la solution, vieux. Aucune idée.

— Super.

Hector se penche en avant avec un regard de conspirateur :

— Il y a bien une chose que tu pourrais essayer…

Chapitre 6

Premiers pas

Objectif à court terme : me faire verser des produits chimiques sur la tête et feindre d'en être heureuse.

Obstacles : les cheveux teints, c'est tout le contraire de ce qu'aime Richard.

Objectif à long terme : tout ce que je veux, c'est me marier à quelqu'un qui m'adore. Ce sera peut-être Richard, peut-être pas (probablement pas, une fois que ma chevelure sera artificiellement embellie).

Obstacles : je n'arrive pas à trouver de salle correcte pour la réception. Ah ah.

Quand je termine la session de l'après-midi, après avoir été retardée par quelqu'un qui croyait intelligent de me poser des questions pertinentes et intéressantes, je n'ai plus le temps de faire des recherches sur Horizon ni sur Rupert : j'ai pour instructions d'être rentrée avant 18 heures, et il est déjà 17 h 15. Il ne reste plus que Chas, qui attend à la porte, jouant avec ses clefs. Je n'aperçois que le sommet luisant de son crâne par-dessus les séparations des bureaux alors qu'il jette son trousseau en l'air et le rattrape. Ou, du moins, les tripote, les laisse tomber, essaie de les rattraper tandis qu'elles roulent sur son ventre en tintinnabulant, et finit par se pencher pour les récupérer par terre. Trop cool, le mec.

—Allons, Elizabeth, dit-il. (Il a découvert mon prénom en consultant la liste du personnel et non en parlant avec quelqu'un en chair et en os.) Le monde appartient à ceux qui se couchent tôt.

Il est ridicule, mais aujourd'hui ça m'est égal. J'ai la tête pleine de Rupert de Witter. Oh non, comprenez-moi bien. Je ne rêve pas de lui torse nu, avec un regard passionné rivé sur le mien, en train de m'embrasser et de m'embarquer sur son yacht pour un week-end en Méditerranée, où ses yeux magnifiques suivraient, comme aimantés, mes moindres mouvements, et où il finirait par me dire qu'il veut passer le reste de sa vie avec moi. Rien de tout cela. Il est beau, c'est vrai, mais c'est un crétin. Je sais bien que je ne l'ai jamais rencontré, mais j'ai une connaissance directe de lui par les hurlements que j'ai entendu Richard pousser sur lui au téléphone. Il est inflexible, puéril, arrogant et incapable. S'il occupe toutes mes pensées, c'est simplement parce que j'ai besoin de trouver une façon d'arriver à lui. Je ne pense pas plus loin que le moment où l'on m'introduira dans son bureau. Pour l'instant, tout ce que j'ai réussi à imaginer pour la suite, c'est de m'écrouler par terre en gloussant de rire, et je ne crois pas que ce soit très fructueux.

—Allez, sors, on n'a pas toute la vie !

Je lève les yeux et découvre Vini debout à côté de la portière conducteur de ma voiture. Le véhicule est à l'arrêt, garé devant notre appartement, et je m'aperçois avec horreur que je ne me souviens pas d'avoir conduit jusqu'ici. Je me retourne pour regarder derrière moi, m'attendant presque à voir un charnier dans mon sillage, la route jonchée de corps sanguinolents et gémissants, et de voitures fumantes au capot enfoncé, mais il n'y a qu'un petit chien gris qui traverse la rue en trottinant. Je suis effondrée. C'est la première fois en huit ans que je ne me suis concentrée ni sur ma conduite ni sur mon apparence au volant. Normalement, je conserve un sourire un peu rêveur, au cas où l'on m'apercevrait à travers le pare-brise, mais ce soir j'ai passé tout le trajet à penser à ce satané Rupert de Witter. C'est mal. Je prêterai davantage attention à la route la prochaine fois, surtout que ça implique de manœuvrer une tonne d'acier, d'étincelles électriques et de liquide explosif dans les rues d'une calme banlieue résidentielle.

À peine ai-je posé un pied dans l'appartement que Vini me traîne jusqu'à la salle de bains et m'ordonne de me déshabiller. Elle est très créative. Enfin, pour les cheveux et les ongles. Elle n'est pas du genre à fabriquer des cadres photo avec des vieux sachets de thé, ou des tables basses en bouchons de stylo. Dieu merci! Mais elle est douée pour les soins de beauté, ce qui est parfait, vu la carrière qu'elle s'est choisie. Un jour, elle a transformé une jeune personne étique à la chevelure fine et sans tenue, qu'elle avait dénichée sur le parking de l'hypermarché, en Marilyn Monroe. C'était incroyable.

Ah non, en fait c'était Marilyn Manson. Mais ça reste impressionnant.

Donc, bien que je n'aie pas tellement envie de changer de couleur de cheveux, je me remets entre les mains gantées de Vini. Elle me recouvre la tête de sa mixture, protège ma peau tout autour avec du coton, puis m'ordonne de demeurer assise sans bouger sur les toilettes pendant vingt-cinq minutes. Excellent. Ça me donne le temps de penser à une technique pour approcher Rupert de Witter.

Je sais ! Je vais lui envoyer des fleurs, avec une carte : « De la part de Beth, de Love Learning. Pour vos formations, sans hésitation. »

Non. Peut-être pas. Les gens qui envoient des fleurs ont généralement un autre message à faire passer. Non que j'en aie reçu très souvent. Deux fois dans toute ma vie, en fait. La première, c'était à l'école quand j'avais quinze ans, en lot de consolation pour le concours d'arts plastiques. J'avais fabriqué une belle sculpture en paille et papier mâché de Jésus sur la Croix, la peau grise, des caillots de sang tout autour de la tête, la chair en lambeaux au niveau des mains et des pieds. Il avait même les côtes saillantes après être resté là-haut un jour ou deux. Le gagnant, qui a remporté le lecteur CD portable, avait présenté quelque chose avec un œuf peint, ce qui m'a semblé sacrément cliché pour une décoration de Pâques. La deuxième fois, c'était des années après, mais le message était à peu près le même. John Wilson, de l'agence immobilière dans la zone piétonne, m'a envoyé un bouquet pour m'annoncer qu'il me larguait. « Chère Beth, je t'ai essayée, et j'ai conclu que tu n'étais pas au niveau sur certains points, donc je ne te garde pas. Je t'envoie ces œillets pour que tu aies moins l'impression d'être une ratée. John. » Bon, ce n'est pas exactement ce qui était écrit. Mais c'était l'idée.

Pas de fleurs, alors. Des ballons. Oui ! Pas de sens caché : des baudruches, c'est juste de la joie gonflable, avec un message poignant et sincère bien visible. Je pourrais faire imprimer un texte du genre «Love Learning, centre d'éducation et de développement», et j'ajouterais une carte avec mon nom et mon numéro de téléphone.

C'est vraiment merdique comme idée. Où ai-je la tête? Comment puis-je avoir des pensées pareilles? Les ballons ne sont pas un support publicitaire sérieux. Il va penser qu'on est une bande de clowns, pas des professionnels. Il aura raison.

— Bon, allez, c'est l'heure du rinçage, dit Vini en rentrant dans la salle de bains.

Pendant les dix minutes suivantes, je suis penchée au-dessus de la baignoire; le sang me monte au cerveau et m'empêche de réfléchir.

Après un rapide coup de sèche-cheveux, qui me fait l'effet de recevoir des gifles sur les oreilles, Vini m'emmène vers un miroir et me dévoile mon image, comme dans une de ces émissions de relooking. Sauf qu'elle le fait en arrachant une serviette mouillée, avec les mots:

— Alors, je suis la meilleure?

Je suis blonde. Je m'attendais, je ne sais pas, à un acajou ou peut-être à un châtain un peu plus clair que ma teinte naturelle. Voire à du noir. Rien de vulgaire, en tout cas.

Mais la différence est saisissante. La couleur qui encadre mon visage m'a transformée. Mon teint paraît plus éclatant, mes yeux plus bleus, même mes lèvres semblent plus pleines. Je suis vivante, vibrante, et même, eh bien, oui, sexy. Je tourne la tête de droite à gauche, et ma chevelure suit le mouvement, comme dans une pub pour un shampoing.

— Je suis blonde, dis-je bêtement.

— Merci, j'avais vu. Alors, qu'est-ce que tu en penses ?

Je me tourne vers elle, avec l'impression que je pourrais désormais porter un haut transparent qui laisse voir mon soutien-gorge. Il faut que je m'en achète un comme ça.

— C'est vulgaire.

Je reporte mon attention sur mon reflet. Je ne veux pas en détourner les yeux.

— Noon, non, ce n'est pas vrai. C'est sexy et magnifique. Et ça te va vraiment bien, j'ajouterai. Ça éclaircit ton teint. Je le savais.

— J'ai l'air d'une traînée. Que vont penser les stagiaires, quand ils me verront ?

Elle hoche la tête de façon suggestive :

— Ils vont penser : « Putain de bordel de merde, je ne m'étais pas rendu compte que la formatrice était si SEXY ! »

Je lui jette un regard sans perdre mon reflet de vue :

— Mais c'est tellement artificiel. Tout le monde va le voir.

— Ben oui, c'est clair. C'est l'idée. C'est quoi, le problème ?

Le problème, c'est que j'ai passé les huit dernières années de ma vie à cultiver un style frais et naturel parce que je sais que c'est ce que Richard préfère. Vini vient de mettre tout ça par terre en un seul soin. Mais je ne vais pas le lui dire. Elle croit que je l'ai oublié, souvenez-vous.

— Vini, j'ai consacré beaucoup de temps à me préparer… pour cette formation, et un changement aussi soudain et spectaculaire que celui-ci (Je porte la main à mes cheveux.) pourrait avoir des conséquences désastreuses sur… l'efficacité du stage.

Elle reste bouche bée. Je la vois du coin de l'œil.

— Tu n'es pas heureuse d'être magnifique ?

— Ce n'est pas ça qui compte. Ou peut-être que si, justement. Si je suis trop belle, personne ne me prendra au sérieux. Tu me trouves vraiment magnifique ?

— Ah oui, bordel. Et toi aussi. C'est juste que tu ne veux pas l'admettre. Allez, regarde-toi : tu es superbe.

Je considère mon reflet, les sourcils froncés. Que va dire Richard en me voyant ? J'ai l'air complètement artificielle. Certes, mon visage est rajeuni, l'éclat de mes yeux ravivé, et mon allure tout entière est celle d'une femme incroyablement glamour et sexy, mais et alors ? Rien de tout cela n'a d'importance si… J'observe le miroir avec une attention accrue… Non, non, ça ne m'apporte rien, si… J'adresse un rapide sourire à l'image dans la glace avant que Vini le voie. En réalité…

— OK, Beth, dit-elle, tu peux arrêter de faire cette tête. C'est magnifique, tu es éblouissante, et c'est l'un de tes premiers pas vers une nouvelle vie, mais tu penses que ça fait pute.

J'acquiesce, le visage sévère, et je remarque dans le miroir que mon hochement de tête fait danser mes cheveux, qui scintillent dans la lumière.

— Tu penses que j'aurais dû te prévenir, pour te laisser le choix ?

Même mouvement de tête : on croirait voir une pluie de diamants.

— Et que peut-être j'aurais dû m'en tenir à quelque chose de moins connoté, comme de l'acajou ou un brun profond ?

— Oui.

Nouveau hochement : des éclairs étincellent sur ma couronne.

— Alors, teignons-les en noir. Numéro 001, c'est ça ? « Brun Boue Nature » ?

— Non !

— Ha ha !

— Merde.

— Je t'ai eue !

Finalement, ce n'est pas à une pantomime qu'elle me traîne. Pourtant, en cet instant, alors que je traverse le parking de l'hôtel *Hippocampe*, je préférerais. Je regarde avec nervosité l'affiche qui annonce en grandes lettres effrayantes : « Fast Love : Speed Dating… Ce soir ! » et je sens mon estomac se serrer encore davantage.

— On est vraiment obligées de faire ça ? dis-je à Vini pour la huit centième fois.

Ça fait une demi-heure qu'elle a cessé de me répondre.

Quand on s'est mises d'accord pour que chacune change sa conception des relations amoureuses, je ne pensais pas à ça. J'imaginais plutôt quelque chose comme, je ne sais pas, rencontrer quelqu'un dans un train et finir au lit ensemble dans l'après-midi. Pas, je cite : « Trois minutes de relations sociales, toute une vie de relations sexuelles. » Mais je suis sûre d'une chose : ma nouvelle couleur me va comme un gant.

Cette coloration a été un véritable atout dans la négociation, cela dit. Avant de quitter la maison, Vini a accepté de changer de style vestimentaire, en échange de ma blondeur. Je lui ai fait mettre un jean, des bottes marron et une veste en daim fauve ; je la regarde franchir d'un pas vif la double porte de l'hôtel. Elle est superbe.

À l'intérieur, c'est exactement comme je m'y attendais. Le hall est plein de gens tristes mais bien habillés, qui font les cent pas, l'air pataud avec leur fleur à la boutonnière, essayant désespérément de paraître à l'aise dans leurs sous-vêtements neufs. Évidemment, je ne peux pas affirmer qu'ils ont des sous-vêtements neufs, mais je le devine à leur façon de bouger. Une femme dotée d'un énorme postérieur passe à côté de moi en roulant des fesses. Sa démarche est si chaloupée qu'elle rivalise avec le *Titanic*, et elle porte manifestement un string en dentelle qui lui donne l'impression – erronée – d'être sexy. Au bar, des dames d'une cinquantaine d'années, les yeux maquillés en bleu pâle et les lèvres rose vif, tiennent leur verre de vin du bout des doigts en gloussant pour laisser croire qu'elles sont si jeunes que c'est la première fois qu'elles boivent de l'alcool. Je capte des odeurs variées, tantôt whisky, tantôt eau de Cologne, parfois poisson, selon l'impression que les hommes veulent donner d'eux-mêmes : Indiana Jones, James Bond ou Forrest Gump.

— Jamais de la vie.

Vini, qui se rue avec enthousiasme vers le comptoir, se retourne pour me faire face :

— Quoi ?

— J'ai dit, jamais de la vie. Nan. Plutôt mourir. Pas la peine d'insister. Non. Jamais. Non non.

— Quoi ? Tu plaisantes ! Enfin, on était d'accord.

— Ah, pardon. Je n'ai peut-être pas été claire. J'ai dit…

Je lui tourne le dos et me dirige vers la porte. Cela aurait pu être une sortie réussie, si je n'avais pas eu la route barrée par une chicane de losers chauves. Le plus proche de moi croise mon regard et hausse les sourcils d'un air coquin avec un sourire grivois :

— Eh bien, bonjour, dit-il avant de rejeter brutalement la tête en arrière pour aspirer à grand bruit tout l'air de la pièce par les narines.

— Tu n'as pas intérêt à filer, me dit Vini qui arrive par-derrière. (Je me tourne vers elle, soulagée de trouver un prétexte pour m'éloigner de Moby Dick.) De toute façon, ce n'est pas aussi pourri que tu pourrais le croire.

Nous sursautons de concert quand une marionnette de ventriloque, coiffée d'un chapeau de père Noël, surgit devant moi et s'exclame :

— Bonzour, zolie madame, ze m'appelle Doddy. Vous voulez bien être ma copine ?

Je lance un regard éperdu à Vini qui contemple, bouche bée, la marionnette. J'écarquille les yeux et m'exclame, avec un grand geste des mains :

— Tu crois ?

— Ce n'est pas représentatif, affirme-t-elle en m'attrapant le bras pour m'écarter en toute hâte de ce coin de la pièce. Essaie, d'accord ? Si ça se trouve, ça va te plaire.

— Tu as peut-être raison. De toute façon, la seule chose que j'avais prévue pour ce soir, c'était de m'arracher les ongles avec une pince.

— Super. Je vais nous chercher un verre.

Restée seule, je parcours à nouveau la salle des yeux, et le regrette aussitôt. À côté de la porte est installé une sorte de guichet d'accueil, où des gens surexcités font la queue pour recevoir un papier. Il n'y aura personne qui puisse m'intéresser dans cette file d'attente digne de la soupe populaire. Je tire cette conclusion du premier de ces messieurs, qui porte un déguisement d'autruche complet, avec de fausses jambes qui pendent sur les côtés pour donner l'impression qu'il se tient en selle sur l'animal. Je le dévisage, bouche bée. Manifestement, cet homme est resté longtemps assis à un endroit que je vous laisse deviner, et, au terme d'une réflexion longue et intense sur tout ce qu'il a bien pu rater avec les femmes jusqu'alors, il a décidé qu'un costume d'oiseau géant était la solution. Merde, je donnerais cher pour voir les techniques qu'il a rejetées au profit de celle-ci !

J'examine quelques-unes des dames en me demandant quelle est la chanceuse qui repartira avec l'homme-oiseau ce soir. L'une d'elles porte une jupe à carreaux avec un chemisier rayé. Parfait. Si l'on en croit les choix qu'elle a faits jusqu'à présent, il se peut qu'elle trouve que le déguisement d'autruche soit une bonne idée. Derrière elle, j'aperçois une petite brunette qui se tient toute seule près du mur. Enfin quelqu'un qui a l'air normal et qui s'est regardé dans le miroir avant de venir. Elle porte un jean classique, des bottes noires, un cardigan marron, une marionnette de Mordicus sur la main gauche. Non, mais je rêve ! Et Mordicus adresse de grands gestes au ventriloque de tout à l'heure. Je cligne des yeux. Où suis-je tombée ?

Paniquée, je jette un regard derrière moi et aperçois Vini qui traverse la pièce vers moi, tête baissée.

— On s'est trompées de salle, dit-elle d'une voix pressante.

Elle me prend par le bras et me tire dans la direction d'où elle vient d'arriver.

— Quoi ?

Elle secoue la tête et se dépêche de m'entraîner vers une double porte en verre, à l'opposé de celle par laquelle nous sommes entrées. Une fois dans le couloir, nous nous retournons vers les battants que nous venons de franchir : au-dessus se trouve une gigantesque bannière qui explique tout :

—Congrès des marionnettistes ? dis-je avec surprise. Toute une salle pleine de marionnettistes ? Réunis en congrès ?

Elle acquiesce :

—Apparemment.

—Ça alors… De quoi peuvent-ils bien parler ? Avantages comparés des ficelles et des mains ? Comment faire dire « maman » correctement à votre poupée ? La bonne méthode pour faire pleurnicher Peggy la Cochonne ?

—C'est peut-être les marionnettes qui discutent, répond Vini, sibylline, avant de s'éloigner d'un pas vif.

Restée près de la porte, j'hésite un moment en observant les conversations. Vous savez quoi, je crois que Vini a raison. La poupée de ventriloque entretient une discussion animée avec Mordicus, pendant que son propriétaire boit un verre d'eau ; et le type à l'autruche consulte sa montre sans se préoccuper du fait que son oiseau est en train d'agresser une dame qui tient un petit âne qui parle. Alors là, c'est La Quatrième Dimension.

Je suis Vini dans le couloir, dans une direction que j'aimerais être celle de la sortie, mais je me doute que ce n'est pas le cas, hélas. Au sortir d'un tournant, je la retrouve devant une porte en verre ornée d'une affiche collée à la Patafix : « Ici, Soirée Speed Dating ». Je soupire. J'espérais qu'elle s'était trompée de date et que nous allions pouvoir abandonner ce projet. Le battant est doublé d'un rideau qui empêche de voir les ratés qui vous attendent avant que vous vous soyez décidés à entrer. D'ailleurs la vitre a un grillage intégré, sans doute pour éviter qu'elle ne vole en éclats en cas de bagarre.

—Vini, vraiment, je ne suis pas sûre que ce soit une bonne idée…

Elle est en train de tendre le bras vers la porte et arrête son geste en m'entendant.

—Moi non plus, Beth. Quoi ? Tu penses que c'est comme ça que je rêve de rencontrer l'âme sœur ?

—Euh… non, je voulais dire… je ne…

—On est XXIe siècle, tu sais. C'est comme ça qu'on fait, aujourd'hui. On est beaucoup trop vieilles pour les soirées étudiantes. C'est ça, ou… les marionnettistes.

—Je crois que je préférerais y retourner plutôt que d'entrer ici, dis-je en désignant la tenture d'un mouvement de tête.

—Ah non, je ne pense pas, Beth. Arrête tes salades. Ces gens avaient des marionnettes. (Elle imite une bouche avec ses doigts.) Des marionnettes, Beth.

—À ton avis, pourquoi y a-t-il un rideau sur cette porte ?

—Je ne sais pas. Parce qu'elle est hideuse. Allez, viens.

—Tu n'as rien compris. C'est pour empêcher les clients potentiels de regarder à travers la vitre avant d'entrer. Et tu sais ce que ça montre ?

—Je sens que tu vas me le dire.

—Ça signifie que les gens qui sont à l'intérieur sont de tels losers que, si on les voyait, ça nous dissuaderait de franchir le seuil. Franchement, du speed dating, Vini ! Tu as vraiment envie de sortir avec quelqu'un qui fait ça ?

On ne va rencontrer que des serial killers psychopathes ultraviolents et des fans de Star Wars.

— Beth, tu es tellement…

À cet instant, la porte s'ouvre, un homme en surgit et se cogne directement dans Vini.

— Oh, pardon, s'excuse-t-il en se retournant pour la regarder. (Il esquisse un sourire.) Ça va ?

— Oui, répond-elle, les yeux levés vers son visage, quelque part près du plafond. Tout va bien, merci.

— Oui, dit-il sans s'éloigner, tout va bien.

— Je me présente : Lavinia, ajoute-t-elle en lui tendant la main, ce qui me donne le sentiment désagréable que je vais me retrouver toute seule pour le speed dating.

— Bonjour, Lavinia, répond-il en lui prenant la main. Moi, c'est Adam.

— Bonjour, Adam. Est-ce que vous allez…, demande-t-elle en indiquant la porte, restée à moitié ouverte comme pour nous inviter à entrer.

— Quoi, au speed dating ? Oh là là, non ! Je me suis juste trompé de salle. Je cherche le congrès des marionnettistes. Vous ne savez pas où c'est ?

Vini, qui avait toujours la main de l'homme dans la sienne, la laisse tomber comme s'il s'agissait d'un lombric et lui désigne le couloir du menton :

— C'est par là.

C'est intéressant de voir le visage de l'inconnu changer, manifestement surpris qu'elle puisse être choquée qu'un adulte participe à un congrès de marionnettistes. Je regarde ses mains, à la recherche d'un signe qui trahirait sa passion, comme des morceaux de feutrine jaune.

— OK, merci.

Il reste là, balançant les bras en attendant que quelque chose se produise. Puis il comprend que ce ne sera pas le cas.

— Bon, eh bien, c'était très agréable de vous rencontrer, Lavinia. Et vous, se hâte-t-il d'ajouter en se souvenant tout à coup que je suis juste à côté d'elle. Au revoir.

— Au revoir, répond-elle.

Comme il ne donne pas le moindre signe de vouloir partir rejoindre les marionnettes, elle me met la main sur l'épaule et me pousse vers la porte.

Et c'est ainsi que je me retrouve à l'intérieur, sans avoir vraiment eu l'intention d'entrer. Derrière moi, Vini ferme la porte très doucement, le visage appuyé contre l'ouverture. Le marionnettiste est sans doute encore là, en train de regarder le battant se refermer. Il va rater tout le spectacle s'il ne se remue pas un peu.

Vini me rejoint, et nous avançons dans la pièce. Plus petite que celle où nous sommes entrées par erreur, elle contient une quinzaine de tables disposées en cercle, chacune assortie de deux chaises. Chaque guéridon, décoré d'une guirlande, est placé sous un bouquet de gui. En fond sonore, on entend George Michael chanter son cœur brisé dans *Last Christmas* : ce n'est peut-être pas le meilleur choix pour accompagner des gens qui essaient de démarrer une nouvelle relation amoureuse.

Une ou deux tables sont déjà occupées par des femmes un peu nerveuses qui passent la main dans leurs cheveux, jettent un coup d'œil dans le miroir de leur poudrier, pincent les lèvres. À l'autre bout de la pièce, près d'un petit bar, les hommes font la même chose, à leur manière : les mains enfoncées dans les poches, ils cherchent leur pénis pour lui donner une tape rassurante :

— Alors Popaul, prêt pour un peu d'exercice, après tout ce temps ?

J'ai envie d'aller leur dire de ne pas s'en faire : ce n'est pas pour ce soir.

Chacune de nous reçoit un grand triangle de plastique avec un chiffre – Vini a le cinq et moi le six – et une feuille qui comporte des numéros et des cases, puis on nous explique les règles. Nous allons rester assises à nos tables, et les hommes se déplaceront dans la pièce. Ils passeront trois minutes avec chacune d'entre nous, pendant lesquelles il est recommandé que les temps de parole et d'écoute de l'un et de l'autre soient équivalents. J'espère que les messieurs se sont également préparés à ça. Pourtant, j'en doute : s'ils en étaient capables, que feraient-ils ici ? À la fin des trois minutes, une cloche retentira, et nos compagnons se décaleront vers la table suivante, tandis qu'un autre homme s'installera en face de nous.

Vini se tourne vers moi :

— Ça a l'air super, non ? s'exclame-t-elle en se dirigeant vers nos places.

— Oh oui, réponds-je à voix basse, vraiment super.

Nos tables sont côte à côte. Quelques secondes plus tard, la sonnerie se fait entendre, et la chaise en face de la mienne est soudain envahie par un grand type en pull à col polo. Je sens mon cou qui me gratte, rien qu'à le regarder.

— Je m'appelle Gordon. Numéro huit.

Il me montre, au cas où je n'aurais pas compris, le chiffre « huit » épinglé sur sa poitrine.

—Moi, c'est Libby, dis-je en décidant sur le moment que je ferais mieux d'utiliser un pseudonyme, au cas où il se mettrait en tête de me harceler.

Il a, sans l'ombre d'un doute, des sourcils de serial killer. Ou plutôt un monosourcil de serial killer.

—Salut, Libby. Bon sang, il fait chaud ici, pas vrai ? Mon Dieu ! Je transpire comme un crapaud-buffle.

Quelle belle image de lui-même il vient de me donner dans les deux premières secondes de notre relation. C'est difficile de trouver une réponse après une telle déclaration.

—Est-ce que les crapauds-buffles transpirent vraiment ?

—Hein ?

—Je veux dire, c'est des amphibiens, n'est-ce pas ? Quand ils ont chaud, ils n'ont qu'à aller s'installer au fond de l'étang pendant une petite demi-heure, non ?

Il me dévisage. Je peux facilement l'imaginer en train de ne pas cocher ma case sur sa feuille.

—Vous êtes quoi ? Zoologue ? reprend-il.

—Oui.

—Ah ! Bon alors, est-ce que les chevaux transpirent ?

—Oh oui. Abondamment.

—Super. Parce que je transpire comme ça.

—Ah bon.

Le suivant est aussi catastrophique :

—Mais quand j'arrive au niveau neuf, un énorme rocher déboule de nulle part et m'écrase. Ça m'a pris une éternité de m'en sortir. Vous savez ce qu'il fallait faire ? Le faire exploser, mais avant de grimper à l'échelle de corde. Trop débile.

Au bout de trois quarts d'heure, il y a une pause de trente minutes, et Vini et moi nous retrouvons au bar pour comparer nos notes.

— Est-ce que tu as coché quelqu'un ? demande-t-elle immédiatement. Moi oui.

— Au secours, ce n'est pas vrai, j'espère ? Je n'en ai pas coché un seul.

— Pas un seul ? Vraiment ?!

— Aucun.

— Mais qu'as-tu pensé du numéro dix, avec ses beaux yeux ?

— Il n'y en a aucun qui m'ait plu.

— Pas même le numéro onze, avec sa voix sexy ?

— Tu ne captes pas, Vini. Il n'y en a aucun qui m'ait plu.

— Bah, tu es juste trop difficile, conclut-elle.

Elle n'a pas tort. Mais quand on a passé huit ans de sa vie avec Richard Love, comment les autres pourraient-ils être à la hauteur ? Vini se penche pour me donner une petite bourrade d'encouragement sur le bras :

— Allez, ne fais pas cette tête, tout n'est pas si catastrophique. Essaie de les imaginer au pub ou ailleurs, détendus et avec plus de trois petites minutes pour faire bonne impression.

En toute honnêteté, ce qui me plaît le plus à leur sujet, c'est bien qu'ils n'aient que trois minutes.

Nous retournons à nos places, et l'infatigable cloche retentit de nouveau, annonçant l'arrivée d'une nouvelle bête de foire.

— Salut, moi c'est Brad, dit-il en se penchant par-dessus la table pour me serrer la main.

Ses doigts enserrent les miens, et lorsque je lève les yeux vers lui, j'éprouve un choc : c'est le Séduisant Inconnu, du grand magasin. Il a laissé sa serviette en cuir à la maison et porte une tenue plus décontractée – chino noir, pull fauve –, mais c'est bien lui. Ma respiration s'affole un peu, et je perds toute contenance pendant un moment. Oh là là, j'ai peine à en croire mes yeux. Alors que je le regarde s'asseoir, il plisse un peu les paupières et tourne légèrement la tête comme s'il m'observait à travers le viseur d'un appareil photo.

— On se connaît, dit-il. On s'est déjà vus ?

J'opine du chef. Il tient toujours ma main, apparemment décidé à me garder captive tant qu'il n'aura pas éclairci la situation. Il se penche vers moi et hausse les sourcils.

— Oui, désolée, salut, Brad, moi c'est Libby. On s'est rencontrés hier à *Whytelys*. Je suis – j'étais – le mannequin.

Il sourit avec délices :

— Ah oui, c'est ça ! Bon sang, vous êtes…

Je commence à avoir chaud, et je me sens rougir. Il va me déclarer que je suis magnifique, et je dois bien avouer que lui aussi. Des yeux d'un brun profond, avec de légères pattes-d'oie, les cheveux châtains, quelques rides d'expression – on dirait même des fossettes – sur les joues… J'ai des sensations bizarres dans le ventre.

— complètement différente. Vous avez changé de coloration, n'est-ce pas ? C'est très joli.

Bon, OK, pas magnifique. Mais il m'a quand même complimentée sur ma chevelure. Et déjà il a remarqué. Je suis sortie une fois avec un type qui a passé deux jours sans s'apercevoir que j'avais le bras dans le plâtre.

— Merci.

C'est tout ce que je parviens à marmonner. Allons, Beth, temps de parole et d'écoute équilibré !

— Vous…, commence-t-il, avant de s'interrompre. Non, rien. Oubliez ça.

— Quoi ?

Il soupire en riant :

— J'allais dire : « vous venez souvent ici ? » mais vu ce qu'on vient chercher ici ce serait un peu insultant.

— Speed dating en série, vous voulez dire ? Personne n'a craqué pour moi les dix-sept premières fois, alors me revoilà.

Il pince les lèvres en souriant :

— Ce n'est pas exactement ce que je pensais.

— Ah.

— Mais maintenant que vous le mentionnez, je n'aurais pas imaginé que vous puissiez avoir besoin de venir plus d'une fois.

— Vraiment ? Dans ce cas, comment expliquez-vous que ce soit ma quatrième fois ?

Il a l'air sincèrement surpris, et ça me fait très plaisir.

— Quatre fois ? Vraiment. Hum.

Il se détourne un peu, les sourcils froncés, le regard lointain. Après un moment, il se tourne à nouveau vers moi :

— Eh bien, après mûre réflexion, je suis forcé de conclure que si personne n'a coché votre case c'est parce que vous les intimidez.

— Vous croyez ?

— Oui, forcément. À titre d'information, il faudrait que vous soyez moins… séduisante.

— Vraiment ?

— Oh oui.

Il baisse les yeux vers la table. Je me sens rougir quand il me regarde à nouveau. Il sourit, un peu gêné.

—Ce que vous devez faire, c'est de ne pas vous laver les cheveux pendant quelques semaines avant de venir la prochaine fois. Essayez de les faire paraître ternes et mous, si possible. Et peut-être porter un vieux survêtement, ce genre de choses. Ce sera moins impressionnant.

Je lui rends son sourire :

—Merci pour le conseil.

—Tout le plaisir est pour moi.

Après un court silence, je reprends :

—En réalité, c'est ma première fois.

Il hoche la tête :

—Je l'aurais parié. (Il détourne à nouveau les yeux et toussote.) Hum. C'est horrible, en fait, non ? En arriver à ce marché de l'amour, je veux dire. C'est presque comme de retourner à l'école, pour qu'on nous explique comment faire.

—Je suis bien d'accord. Ce que je ne supporte pas, ce n'est pas tant d'avoir la peau flétrie par l'humiliation, c'est plutôt le sentiment de ne pas être à la hauteur dans le monde des adultes, comme si je n'avais jamais vraiment dépassé mes seize ans.

—Mais au moins, avec cette méthode, il n'y a pas de mystère ni d'incertitude. Pas besoin de lire les signes, de se poser des questions. Est-ce que je lui plais vraiment ? Peut-être qu'elle n'est pas très intéressée. Est-ce que j'ai mal interprété ? Est-ce que je suis en train de tout rater ?

Je souris :

—En effet, rien n'est plus romantique que de cocher la bonne case.

Il lève les mains en riant :

—Bon, OK, là vous m'avez eu. Ce n'est pas romantique du tout. Mais ça peut venir après, non ? Vous savez, on n'est pas censés s'en tenir à ça. Ici, on voit juste s'il y a une petite étincelle, si ça peut coller. Une fois que la rencontre est faite, les soirées au clair de lune et les balades en bateau peuvent arriver n'importe quand.

Sa voix s'est faite toute douce, ses yeux sont rivés sur les miens. Dans ma tête se dessine une image de ce à quoi un rendez-vous avec Brad pourrait ressembler :

—Waouh, pique-nique à la belle étoile et feu d'artifice au-dessus de l'eau… Est-ce qu'on a droit à tout ça, en sortant avec vous ?

Il fronce les sourcils d'un air interrogateur tout en me souriant :

—Voyons, Libby, je n'ai pas parlé de pique-nique ou de feu d'artifice.

—Ah bon ?

—Non. Je pensais à un film et à un kebab après.

—Ah, et quel film ce serait ?

—*Nine Dead Gay Guys*, répond-il sans s'emmêler les pinceaux.

—Hum. C'est une histoire d'amour ?

—Oh oui.

Je pouffe :

—Eh bien, ça promet d'être romantique. C'est très tentant. Maintenant, parlez-moi du kebab. On le prendrait où ?

—À *Kev's Kebabs*, juste à l'angle de la bibliothèque.

J'acquiesce :

—OK. Il y a souvent la queue ?

—Pas trop. Une ou deux personnes.

—Parfait. Donc pas trop d'attente. Et il sera comment?

Il se penche vers moi avec un air de conspirateur :

—Il sera chaud, fumant même, très juteux, vos papilles vont exploser, et vous aurez la bouche pleine de sauce qui vous dégoulinera jusqu'au menton… (Il se tait soudain et baisse encore une fois les yeux.) Euh…

J'ai les joues en feu et l'estomac qui se tortille. Je me racle la gorge :

—Eh bien, apparemment, Kev sait y faire.

Je le vois se détendre, souriant, et son regard cherche à nouveau le mien :

—Sans l'ombre d'un doute. C'est le meilleur.

—Naturellement. C'est d'un rendez-vous romantique que nous parlons : bien sûr, il ne faut aller que dans les meilleurs endroits.

Il sourit :

—Libby, je suis vraiment content que cette soirée ne soit pas un ratage complet. Je commençais à penser qu'il n'y avait personne ici qui ne soit pas dans un coma profond. (Il sort un papier de sa poche et baisse d'un ton.) C'est quoi, votre numéro?

Je mets un moment à répondre. Faut-il lui donner mon numéro de portable, juste comme ça, sans passer par l'étape des cases à cocher? Qu'est-ce que cette société propose comme assurance si la personne à laquelle ils transmettent vos coordonnées se révèle être un assassin sanguinaire? Est-ce que je peux me faire rembourser, si je lui ai donné mon numéro moi-même au lieu de passer par eux, et qu'ensuite il me fend la tête d'un coup de hache pendant le dessert?

La cloche retentit, et on entend les chaises poussées à la va-vite. Brad se lève lentement, les mains toujours posées sur la table.

—C'est quoi, votre numéro, répète-t-il d'une voix pressante. On doit être raccords.

Je comprends alors qu'il ne me demande pas mon téléphone, mais mon numéro Fast Love, celui de ma table, pour cocher ma case. Mon triangle en plastique est tombé, et je me penche pour le ramasser. Il se dirige à présent vers la table suivante et se retourne à plusieurs reprises pour me regarder. Il ouvre trois fois la main : cinq, cinq et cinq. Quinze. Waouh.

Oh là là, où ai-je pu fourrer cette feuille ? Elle n'est pas devant moi, et je dois me tortiller pour regarder sous la table, puis sous mon siège. Ouf, elle est là, coincée sous un pied. Je penche la chaise dangereusement et réussis à extirper le papier du bout du pied puis à le pousser sur la moquette jusqu'à mes doigts.

Le formulaire dans une main, je ramasse le triangle de plastique qui porte mon numéro et le lève, car, pour que ça fonctionne, chacun doit avoir coché la case de l'autre. Si l'un d'entre nous est seul à le faire, nos coordonnées ne seront pas communiquées. Je regarde dans sa direction, juste quand il est sur le point de s'asseoir à la prochaine table, et le supplie mentalement de tourner les yeux vers moi. S'il vous plaît, s'il vous plaît, juste un petit coup d'œil pour que je puisse lui montrer mon numéro. Et là, par miracle, il me regarde. Je me dépêche d'agiter mon triangle dans sa direction avec un sourire. Avec un haussement de sourcils, il lève six doigts d'un air interrogateur : il veut vérifier qu'il a bien vu, pour être certain. Par acquit de conscience, je retourne le jeton pour vérifier, et le chiffre est bien là, profondément gravé en noir, numéro six, donc je hoche lentement la tête en levant six doigts à mon tour. Brad saisit son stylo et trace une grosse croix, en prenant tout son temps pour être sûr que je le voie, dans une case en haut de la feuille. Il tourne le papier vers moi pour me montrer que sa marque, noire et gigantesque, se trouve bien en face du six, et du même coup d'œil je constate qu'il n'a coché aucune autre case. Je l'imite en traçant un grand trait en face du numéro quinze, avant de l'entourer de plusieurs cercles et de grosses flèches qui traversent la feuille dans toutes les directions pour venir pointer le quinze ; puis je tourne le papier vers lui, pour qu'il voie la case cochée, les flèches et les ronds. Il rit et opine du chef, puis je le vois s'asseoir et saluer poliment son hôtesse d'un signe de tête.

Chapitre 7

Évaluer les résultats

Objectif à court terme : avoir des nouvelles de Brad. Tout de suite. Ah oui, et contacter Rupert de Witter.

Obstacles : aucun, puisque chacun d'entre nous a coché la case de l'autre. Mais il se pourrait que j'oublie de contacter Rupert de Witter.

Objectif à long terme : je vais peut-être me débarrasser de Richard et, à la place, concentrer tous mes efforts sur Brad. Dans ce cas, mon objectif serait de dire à Richard, quand il reviendra : « Tu as loupé le coche, chéri ! »

Obstacles : il n'est toujours pas là, donc impossible de le lui assener. En plus, il faut d'abord que j'aie une vraie relation avec Brad. Au cas où.

En ce moment, je lis un roman dont l'héroïne est hideuse. J'en suis à la page 34. Je n'avance pas vite, parce qu'elle n'arrête pas de répéter qu'elle évite les miroirs, marche la tête baissée et redoute les rencontres, car les gens reculent avec horreur devant sa laideur chaque fois qu'ils la croisent. Pas très passionnant.

Ce n'est pas très crédible, en plus, n'est-ce pas ? Vous savez, les filles qui gardent les yeux rivés sur le trottoir, n'ouvrent jamais la bouche, ne sortent pas de chez elles et n'essaient pas de se faire belles ne deviennent pas des héroïnes. Leur vie de piétonnes terre à terre n'est pas sujette à faire un roman. Ce sont elles qui finissent par travailler dans une jardinerie, une bibliothèque, un théâtre ou n'importe quel endroit peu fréquenté par les hommes.

Le héros n'a pas l'occasion d'être pétrifié, enivré ou enchanté à leur vue si elles ne lèvent jamais les yeux. Il faudrait qu'elles sourient un peu, qu'elles essaient de donner l'impression de passer un bon moment. Peut-être qu'elles se teignent les cheveux.

Avec ma nouvelle couleur, je me sens davantage comme une héroïne. Ça ne veut pas dire que ce n'était pas le cas avant. Vous savez, c'est évident : une relation avec le patron, qui m'a brisé le cœur et dont j'attends désormais le retour. Classique. Mais ce sentiment s'est atténué depuis qu'il est parti. Je m'efforce tout de même chaque jour de conserver mon prestige en étant toujours prête pour son arrivée impromptue, mais ça n'est pas facile, contrairement aux apparences.

Mais maintenant que je suis blonde, c'est un nouveau départ. Je me sens légère, comme une bulle, et j'ai l'impression de flotter comme un bouchon, de rebondir contre les meubles alors que je conduis ma séance de la matinée bille en tête.

Bien sûr, ça pourrait aussi être Brad, et non ma blondeur, qui me pousse à cabrioler.

Nous sommes le lendemain du speed dating, c'est mon premier jour au travail avec cette coloration, et quand je suis arrivée ce matin, j'ai fait sensation.

— J'aime bien tes cheveux, Beth, m'a dit Derek avec un signe de tête.

— Mince, tu es magnifique, Beth ! Pas vrai, Mike ? Regarde-la, elle est splendide. Waouh, Beth, c'est absolument superbe. Comment elle s'appelle, cette couleur ?

Ça, c'était Grace.

Mais non, je rigole. Ça, c'était Fatima, évidemment. Grace a dit :

— Beth, tu es aussi blonde que moi. Ça alors, les teintures d'aujourd'hui sont vraiment excellentes, n'est-ce pas ? Ça aurait presque l'air naturel.

Et là, elle a rejeté ses cheveux par-dessus son épaule comme pour montrer… quelque chose. Quoi au juste, je ne sais pas : arrivée à ce point de la conversation, je m'étais détournée.

La réaction la plus étonnante a été celle de Sean : il est entré dans la pièce, est passé à côté de moi, et au dernier moment il s'est retourné d'un coup pour me regarder à nouveau. C'était vraiment surjoué, mais ça m'a plu. Il m'a dévisagée un certain temps avant de dire « Waouh ». C'est tout. Ah, et il a aussi sifflé, comme Fred Astaire ou je ne sais plus qui.

De toute façon, ça m'est égal parce que je vais recevoir un message de Brad aujourd'hui. La nuit dernière, j'ai rêvé que c'était Brad Pitt que j'avais rencontré au speed dating, et quand je me suis réveillée je ne savais plus si c'était vrai, ou si c'était seulement dans mon imagination que j'avais fait la connaissance d'un certain Brad. Puis je me suis dit que Brad Pitt était trop occupé pour venir faire des rencontres à l'hôtel *Hippocampe*. Et Angelina ne serait pas très contente, en plus. Quelle dinde, qu'est-ce qu'elle imaginait, qu'il allait arrêter de se montrer en public ? Il faut qu'elle ouvre les yeux et qu'elle se fasse à l'idée que son mec est un sex-symbol international, et qu'il a besoin de liberté.

Mais ce n'était pas Brad Pitt, évidemment. Et ce n'était pas non plus un Brad imaginaire. Celui que j'ai rencontré hier soir était un homme bien réel, en chair et en os, et totalement sublime. J'en suis sûre parce que quand j'ai demandé à Vini ce qu'elle pensait du numéro quinze, elle m'a répondu, chaleureuse et enthousiaste :

— Il est potable, si tu aimes ce genre-là.

Et je sais qu'elle préfère les barbus, donc c'était un sacré compliment.

Depuis que Richard est parti, il n'y a pas beaucoup d'hommes qui me regardent. Aucun, en réalité. Les deux seuls endroits où je me rends sont le bureau et le supermarché, et la probabilité de rencontrer dans l'un de ces endroits un mec qui soit attirant, disponible, et qui ne sorte pas de prison est proche de zéro. Après trois mois de célibat forcé, ça m'arrive peut-être un rien trop facilement de trouver un homme à mon goût. En tout cas, c'est ce que pense Vini. Je ne m'en étais pas aperçue.

— J'ai rêvé ou tu le draguais ? m'a-t-elle demandé alors que nous quittions un magasin de chaussures, il y a quelques semaines.

— N'importe quoi ! Bien sûr que non.

— Ah bon, alors c'était quoi, tous ces «Oh là là, je suis vraiment désolée de vous obliger à retourner dans l'arrière-boutique encore une fois, vous êtes en nage, je vais devoir vous frotter avec une serviette mouillée, hi hi hi» ?

— Je n'ai jamais dit ça !

— Ah bon, ben ça y ressemblait. Tu lui as quand même proposé d'aller lui acheter une glace, bordel ! Tu le draguais.

— Non. Et quand bien même ?

— Quand bien même ? Putain, Beth, il devait avoir seize ans ! Est-ce que tu as regardé au-dessus de sa ceinture ?

— Évidemment.

— Il avait quelle tête, alors ?

— Arrête tes conneries, Vini.

— Non, non, tu ne vas pas t'en sortir comme ça. À quoi il ressemblait ? Allez ! Commence par les cheveux : ils étaient comment ?

Je ne pense pas qu'il soit utile de rapporter toute la conversation. Je vous laisse imaginer la suite. J'étais simplement préoccupée par les chaussures que je voulais acheter, ce qui est parfaitement compréhensible, surtout qu'il s'agissait d'une magnifique paire d'escarpins noirs avec des sequins brodés. Ou peut-être des bottes. Ce n'est pas surprenant que je ne me sois pas souvenue de lui. En plus, quand on essaie des chaussures, et que quelqu'un se tient devant vous pour voir comment vous vous en sortez, ce n'est pas sa chevelure qui est à hauteur de vos yeux.

Donc, après avoir expédié ma séance du matin (« De qui s'inspirer ? ») et avoir été retardée par un type agaçant qui s'ingéniait à couper les cheveux en quatre, je me précipite vers mon bureau – mais sans courir – et ouvre une session sur mon ordinateur. J'aurai forcément un mail de Brad, maintenant. Quand nous avons rempli nos formulaires en arrivant, nous avons dû fournir nos coordonnées. J'ai donné mon adresse Hotmail et mon numéro de portable, donc je devrais avoir un message dans l'une des deux boîtes, soit de lui, soit de Fast Love qui me communique son mail. Je suis tellement surexcitée que j'ai du mal à taper correctement mon mot de passe, et je passe à deux doigts de bloquer mon accès. Oh non, si j'en arrive là, je vais devoir donner un interminable coup de fil à l'un des tâcherons de la société d'informatique à laquelle Richard a acheté les ordinateurs, pour changer mon mot de passe, et j'ai mal à la tête rien que d'y penser. Je suis légère et aérienne comme une bulle aujourd'hui, donc je suis certaine qu'en réponse à sa demande monocorde de mon numéro de contrôle à seize chiffres je serai capable de le lui communiquer facilement et avec bonne humeur. Ou de me taper la tête sur le bureau en hurlant.

C'est ainsi qu'après deux tentatives infructueuses pour entrer mon mot de passe je préfère par prudence éloigner mes doigts du clavier et jeter d'abord un coup d'œil à mon téléphone. Non, ni texto ni appels manqués. La connexion est bonne en ce moment, mais il est possible qu'elle ait été coupée juste à l'instant où un message essayait de passer. Ça arrive parfois, il paraît. Je l'éteins et le rallume, mais il ne se passe toujours rien, alors je m'écris rapidement à moi-même – «Coucou Beth, ça va? Moa oui, à +» – et l'envoie. Parfois, un texto qui passe dans le tuyau en pousse beaucoup d'autres qui étaient coincés. Mais ça ne marche pas. Même mon propre message n'arrive pas. C'est ridicule, le téléphone est juste là, il n'y a même pas de chemin à parcourir.

OK, je vais appeler Vini à la maison et lui demander s'il y a eu des coups de fil.

—Non, m'informe-t-elle. Sauf si tu comptes Philip de Northern Finance, qui a gaspillé les deux secondes que j'étais décidée à lui consacrer : il m'a demandé comment j'allais. Abruti. Je lui ai répondu que j'étais triste parce que tout est fragile et voué à disparaître, et que notre existence n'a pas de sens puisque quoi qu'on fasse on finira tous par mourir, alors à quoi bon essayer ?

—OK, donc pas d'appels ?

Silence lourd de sens.

—Tu… attends un appel ?

J'hésite avant de répondre. Je ne lui ai pas parlé de l'échange de numéros avec Brad. Mes pires cauchemars concernant la soirée ne se sont pas réalisés, et c'est entièrement grâce à Brad, mais je ne veux pas qu'elle le sache. Ah non, elle va devenir complètement insupportable si elle apprend que le speed dating marche vraiment. Dans la voiture, au retour, je mourais d'envie de sourire aux anges, de sautiller sur mon siège et de crier : « La vie est belle ! » par la fenêtre, mais pour bien lui faire comprendre que cette sortie avait été une pure perte de temps, comme je l'avais prédit, je suis restée grincheuse et n'ai prononcé que des monosyllabes. C'est une chance que je sois si consciente des messages et des signaux que ma contenance laisse paraître, parce qu'elle ne s'est pas doutée une seconde de mon état d'esprit réel. Mais, évidemment, ça ne fait que repousser le moment où elle découvrira qu'elle avait raison ; je ne peux pas l'éviter indéfiniment.

Attendez. Peut-être que si. Et si je lui disais que Brad et moi, c'était une Rencontre Fortuite à *Whytelys*, point final ? Il n'est jamais allé à l'hôtel *Hippocampe*, n'a jamais coché la moindre case. Oui ! Ça va marcher, et elle ne saura jamais où nous nous sommes réellement connus. Et le meilleur, c'est que c'est presque vrai. Tout le monde sait que quand on ment il faut rester aussi près que possible de la vérité ; mon plan est parfait, magnifique, parce qu'il est si proche de la vérité qu'il n'y a presque aucune chance que je sois démasquée.

— Toi, tu as coché quelqu'un hier soir, pas vrai ? s'exclame Vini juste à ce moment-là.

Merde.

Je reste silencieuse quelques instants avant de répondre, d'un ton sans doute assez peu convaincant :

— Non.

— Tu mens !

— Ce n'est pas vrai : cet homme est celui que…

— Je le savais ! Ça se voyait, dans la voiture tu n'arrêtais pas de gigoter et de te tortiller, ça sautait aux yeux. Merde, Beth, pourquoi tu ne m'as rien dit ? Ah non, attends, laisse-moi deviner. Tu ne voulais pas reconnaître que mon plan avait marché, et qu'il était meilleur que le tien ! C'est ça, pas vrai ?

— Vini, ne sois pas aussi bête. Tout ne tourne pas toujours autour de ton nombril, tu sais. De toute façon, j'ai du travail. Je te raconterai plus tard. Ciao !

Bordel de merde.

OK. J'ouvre une session sur mon ordinateur maintenant, et, cette fois, je ne me trompe pas de mot de passe. Pour ne rien vous cacher, j'ai dû l'écrire sur un bout de papier, parce que j'ai toujours la tête embrouillée, mais ne vous inquiétez pas, je l'ai avalé aussitôt après. Richard insiste beaucoup pour qu'on fasse très attention à la confidentialité, et ce n'est pas parce qu'il est absent en ce moment qu'il faut se relâcher. Même si, franchement, j'ai du mal à imaginer que quelqu'un force l'accès à mon compte pour vendre ma présentation PowerPoint «L'Importance d'Être Honnête» sur eBay. Mais Richard dit toujours qu'on ne peut faire confiance à personne.

—Ça va, Beth? demande tout à coup Sean, dans mon dos.

Je sursaute et fais pivoter ma chaise un peu trop violemment. Je dois freiner avec les pieds pour éviter de tourner à trois cent soixante degrés devant ses yeux. Je parviens de justesse à m'immobiliser en face de l'endroit où il s'est arrêté pour me saluer en passant.

—Euh… salut, Sean. Merci, ça va. Je te remercie.

Puis, pour faire bonne mesure, j'ajoute:

—Désolée.

Il sourit et fait un pas dans ma direction, en se penchant légèrement comme si nous partagions une blague secrète:

—Laisse-moi te dire que tu n'as… rien… à te reprocher. D'accord?

Je hoche la tête, mais me force à garder la bouche fermée. Ses petits silences avant et après le mot «rien» sont pleins de sous-entendus, et j'essaie désespérément de comprendre. Pour ne rien arranger, je suis abasourdie qu'il ait décidé de s'arrêter pour me parler. Je pense que c'est seulement la deuxième fois qu'il s'adresse à moi personnellement depuis que je le connais. La première fois, il m'a dit: «Salut, je m'appelle Sean Cousins. C'est où, ma place?»

Il s'attarde encore une seconde ou deux pendant lesquelles j'essaie de le repousser par télékinésie. Ça a peut-être même marché, car finalement il se détourne pour s'éloigner, avec un petit clin d'œil au dernier moment.

Pour un peu, j'en resterais bouche bée – ne vous inquiétez pas, je n'en fais rien. Mais, sincèrement, Sean Cousins qui me fait un clin d'œil? Sean, c'est le gars qui donnerait probablement sa fiancée aux indigènes en échange d'un bateau pour quitter l'île. Que se passe-t-il? Pendant un instant, je parcours bêtement la pièce des yeux pour m'assurer que je suis dans le bon bureau.

C'est le cas, évidemment. Je n'ai pas vraiment cru que j'étais ailleurs. Mais vous ne pouvez pas me reprocher d'être un peu perplexe. C'était aussi inattendu que d'imaginer Vini avec des boucles d'oreilles en perle. Elle est plutôt du genre à porter un piercing en tête de mort sur le nez.

OK. Ne pensons plus à Sean. C'est peut-être la crise de la quarantaine. Ça ne fait rien. J'ai finalement réussi à ouvrir une session sur mon ordinateur, et je me dépêche de consulter ma boîte Hotmail pour voir quel message drôle et romantique Brad m'a envoyé ce matin, après avoir sans l'ombre d'un doute passé la nuit à songer à moi et au tournant merveilleux que sa vie est en train de prendre. Il sera poétique, affectueux, chargé d'espoir, peut-être un peu anxieux, se demandant si j'éprouve le même sentiment, s'il peut oser espérer que ce sera le début de quelque chose, le premier jour d'une belle relation pleine de passion, qui nous liera à jamais.

Merde. Il n'y a rien.

OK, bon, je ne suis pas déçue. En fait, c'est certainement une bonne chose qu'il ne m'ait pas encore contactée, parce que ça risquerait de me déconcentrer de l'autre tâche vraiment importante que je dois accomplir aujourd'hui, dont les détails vont me revenir dans une minute.

Un homme comme Brad a forcément un travail et ne peut probablement pas envoyer de mails ni téléphoner pendant la journée, de toute façon. Il m'appellera sans doute ce soir, ce n'est pas la peine de paniquer. Je peux attendre jusque-là sans problème. Ou je peux vérifier de nouveau dans quelques minutes. Pour le moment, je suis concentrée à cent pour cent sur…

Je pense que je vais poser mon téléphone sur le bureau. Je ne l'entends jamais sonner quand il est dans mon sac.

Où en étais-je ? Ah oui, concentrée à cent pour cent. Mais sur quoi, déjà ? Ah oui : trouver une façon d'attirer l'attention de Rupert de Twitter, alors qu'il est très certainement entouré de personnes qui essaient toutes d'attirer son attention en même temps.

Je ferme ma boîte Hotmail, ouvre celle de ma messagerie Love Learning. Malheureusement, mes idées n'allaient pas plus loin que ça. Merde. OK, ne t'inquiète pas, concentre-toi. Qu'est-ce que je sais de lui ? Rien d'autre que les informations qui me viennent de Richard, et qui ne me donnent pas envie d'être aimable avec lui. Maintenant que j'y pense, je l'ai bien rencontré moi-même une fois, de façon informelle, au supermarché, il y a des années, quand je travaillais encore à Horizon. Je l'ai reconnu d'après les brochures, même s'il présentait nettement moins bien dans les rayons que sur le papier glacé de la photo. Il ressemblait moins à un adonis aux traits ciselés, aux mâchoires carrées, et plus à un ivrogne aveugle. Il a embouti mon Caddie avec le sien.

—Oups, désolé, m'a-t-il lancé distraitement, sans poser les yeux sur moi.

—Ce n'est rien, ai-je répondu, en décidant à la dernière seconde de ne pas ajouter « monsieur » ou « monsieur de Witter » en m'écartant sur le côté.

—Oh, et à propos vous ne sauriez pas où sont les anchois, par hasard ? m'a-t-il demandé subitement en levant la tête du morceau de papier en lambeaux qu'il tenait dans la main et en me regardant presque pour de bon, cette fois.

—Ah non, je n'en sais rien. Désolée.

—Vous savez quoi, vous avez raison. Les anchois, c'est dégueulasse. Merci du conseil.

Et il s'est éloigné lentement en traînant les pieds.

Donc tout ce que je sais de lui, c'est que c'est un connard qui aime les anchois. Ou les trouve dégueulasses. Oh, et qu'il est multimillionnaire. Ce qui signifie qu'il est doué pour les affaires, donc absolument sans pitié. Merde ! Je dois choisir les mots de mon mail pour qu'ils le surprennent, qu'ils soient si brillants qu'il se redresse sur sa chaise, se donne une tape sur le front et s'écrie :

—C'est donc là qu'on s'est trompés ! Passez-moi Love Learning !

Mais je n'ai pas l'ombre d'une idée. Je regarde l'aiguille de l'horloge glisser lentement de 12 h 52 à 13 h 13, avec la même panique grandissante qu'on éprouve quand on passe un examen et qu'on n'a pas le moindre élément de réponse pour aucune des questions. Finalement, alors qu'il ne me reste plus que dix minutes avant la fin de la pause-déjeuner, je trouve enfin. Ce n'est pas exactement le message renversant, passionnant, que j'espérais inventer, mais c'est un début.

Cher monsieur de Witter,
Vous arrive-t-il de porter des chaussures ? Si oui,
pouvez-vous m'en envoyer la description, dès
que possible ?

Bien à vous,
Beth Sheridan,
Love Learning.

Je sais, ce n'est pas vraiment une rhétorique explosive,
accrocheuse, qui suscite la réflexion. J'imagine Rupert
de Witter assis dans son bureau vitré, lisant ce mail
pathétique puis rejetant sa frange décolorée en arrière,
dans un éclat de rire moqueur, et tapant une réponse
acerbe comme une remarque du jury de *X Factor* :

C'est vraiment moyen. Vous devriez vous cantonner
aux pubs et aux boîtes de nuit où votre style de mails
aura sans doute du succès. En tout cas, ça ne peut pas
marcher avec les grandes entreprises, mon petit.

J'essaie d'évacuer cette image de ma tête et de me
consoler avec la pensée qu'un homme qui passe trois
heures toutes les six semaines dans un salon de coiffure
où on lui tartine des mèches de teinture blonde avant de
les enrouler dans du papier d'aluminium a des chances
de ne pas être concentré à cent pour cent sur ce qui est
important, comme la dette des pays du tiers-monde ou
une grammaire correcte. Je suppose que ses assistants ne
doivent employer que des mots d'une syllabe. Bon, c'est

trop tard pour s'en inquiéter maintenant, je l'ai envoyé. Seigneur, s'il vous plaît, faites qu'il réponde. Amen.

Pendant le reste de la journée, je crée l'étonnement parmi les stagiaires en leur donnant une série de petits exercices… qui me permettent de quitter la pièce toutes les demi-heures pour vérifier mes mails et mon téléphone. Ils doivent imaginer que j'ai un problème digestif, ou que j'ai développé durant la nuit un trouble obsessionnel-compulsif qui me pousse à courir surveiller régulièrement si le parking ne grouille pas d'aliens. À moins que ce ne soit de la schizophrénie ? En tout cas, c'était en pure perte, car personne ne m'a laissé de message.

À la maison, Vini fait le ménage à tour de bras. Elle aime garder ses distances par rapport aux tâches domestiques et à la saleté en général.

— Salut, dis-je sans enthousiasme en m'affalant sur le canapé.

— Salut ! répond-elle avec un grand sourire. Tu veux un thé ? J'ai acheté des gâteaux.

Elle arrache ses gants en caoutchouc et file dans la cuisine.

Oh là là, que se passe-t-il ? Me suis-je trompée d'appartement ?

Je ne l'ai encore jamais vue comme ça, pendant toutes nos années de colocation. En général, je la trouve plutôt assise par terre avec un verre de jus de grenade, penchée sur ses pieds pour se vernir les ongles en noir.

— Tu vas bien ? lui dis-je en la suivant dans la cuisine.

Je rêve, elle porte un tee-shirt rouge sur lequel est écrit « Happy Kissmas » en lettres pailletées. Et un jean. Je m'accroche au comptoir pour ne pas tomber : j'ai la tête qui tourne.

Elle acquiesce, enthousiaste :

—Ouaip ! Pourquoi ça n'irait pas ?

—Vini… est-ce que tu as mis… du gloss rose ? dis-je en la dévisageant.

Elle se tripote les cheveux et pince les lèvres, gênée.

—C'est juste un essai. Y a pas de mal à ça, pas vrai ?

—Non, non, bien sûr que non. Je suis juste un peu… surprise, c'est tout.

—OK, bon, peu importe. Écoute, je dois sortir. J'ai une réunion très importante. Mon avenir tout entier pourrait en dépendre. J'ai fait un ragoût, il est dans le four, laisse-le cuire une heure et demie, d'accord ? Et ne m'attends pas.

Je chancelle encore de la nouvelle du ragoût qu'elle m'en assène une autre :

—Ah, et j'ai acheté un programme télé en ville, il est sur la table.

Et, sur ces mots, elle disparaît. Avec ma veste en daim fauve et mes bottes, encore une fois. Elle se rend tout le temps aux cérémonies pour lesquelles elle a fourni des sosies : ce n'est pas une surprise. Cette réunion importante, qui pourrait changer sa vie, consiste sans doute à regarder Nicole Kidman inaugurer une station de lavage auto dans la zone industrielle…, mais elle est tellement différente. Elle portait plus de rose que je n'en pouvais voir, et ça ne lui ressemble pas du tout. Peut-être qu'elle a vraiment décidé de prendre un nouveau départ.

Je me retrouve donc seule ce soir. Parfait. Je vais enfin pouvoir faire quelques recherches sur Horizon et Rupert de Witter. Je sors mon téléphone de mon sac et le pose sur le bureau à côté de moi, juste au cas où il sonnerait sans que je l'entende. Il n'y a rien de plus agaçant que d'appeler sur un portable et que la personne ne décroche pas. Je veux dire, à quoi ça sert d'en avoir un, dans ce cas-là ? Enfin, je me connecte à Internet.

Le site d'Horizon Holidays est magnifique. Leurs informaticiens ont manifestement fait d'immenses progrès depuis l'époque de « Souris, Mode d'Emploi ». Je clique sur divers icones pour naviguer sur le site – une plage pour les séjours à la mer, un avion pour les vols, des béquilles pour l'assurance – sans trouver l'inspiration.

Ce qui me surprend, en visitant chaque page du site, y compris « à propos de nous », c'est de ne voir aucune autre photo de Rupert que celle qui figure sur la dernière page des brochures. C'est la même photo depuis mes débuts chez eux, il y a huit ans. Pourquoi ne l'a-t-il pas mise à jour ? Et pourquoi n'y a-t-il aucun cliché promotionnel – lui sur un paquebot, ou lors d'une remise de prix, ou quelque chose comme ça ?

Bon, le site Web ne m'apprend rien d'utile, à part peut-être que Love Learning devrait en avoir un aussi. Sauf que nous n'avons plus notre directeur diplômé en informatique pour nous aider.

J'éteins l'ordinateur et saisis mon portable. Pas la peine de me voiler la face : je ne peux pas me concentrer sur ce satané Rupert de Witter. J'ai toujours une bonne connexion, donc ce n'est pas ça le problème. Le téléphone fixe fonctionne également : la tonalité me prouve que la ligne est en service et que Brad n'est pas en train d'essayer de me contacter.

Je ne comprends pas. Je suis certaine qu'il était intéressé, hier soir. Je veux dire, je n'ai pas inventé ce badinage et ce langage non verbal éloquent. Récapitulation rapide de

Brad assis en face de moi à Fast Love : les yeux (d'un beau brun brillant, avec des pattes-d'oie et de longs cils fournis) rivés sur moi ; la bouche (lèvre supérieure légèrement plus pleine, sensuelle et sexy) souriante ; le corps tout entier (hummmmm…) penché vers moi, bras ouverts, mains doucement posées sur la table… Un tiraillement dans mon ventre me fait glisser dans mon siège et respirer plus vite. Ooh, ça fait longtemps. Je me redresse et toussote. *Allons, Beth, reprends-toi.* Je jette un coup d'œil en direction de la porte, mais bien sûr personne n'est là, et surtout pas Richard.

OK, donc il est évident pour quiconque m'observerait que j'ai le béguin pour lui. Et je crois pouvoir dire sans me tromper que c'est réciproque. Alors pourquoi ne m'a-t-il pas encore appelée ? Pourquoi sa main ne s'est-elle pas dirigée vers le clavier de son téléphone à l'instant où il a ouvert les yeux ce matin ?

C'est manifestement un signe de la duplicité masculine. Ils vous sourient, rient avec vous, se montrent si délicieux qu'on a envie de les caresser du bout de la langue, vous font perdre tous vos moyens, avant de vous planter là comme une déco de Noël jusqu'à ce que vous preniez racine. Ces salauds… on est vraiment mieux sans eux. Sauf s'ils appellent.

Une image saisissante me vient subitement : Brad gisant face contre terre au bord de la route, la chemise tachée de traînées de sang, parmi les éclats de verre, son bras fracturé étendu, son téléphone toujours serré dans la main, mon numéro affiché sur l'écran, incapable de presser le bouton pour m'appeler à cause d'une collision inattendue avec une bétonnière. Oh là là… s'il ne m'a pas téléphoné, c'est parce qu'il a eu un horrible accident.

C'est fantastique! Je me lève d'un bond et me mets à danser autour de la pièce en chantant *Brad s'est fait écraser, wouoh ho* sur l'air de *Walking on Sunshine*, souriant d'une oreille à l'autre en me berçant de cette merveilleuse idée.

Je ne suis pas sérieuse, évidemment. Ce n'est qu'un fantasme, et je le sais très bien. Je remplace rapidement la bétonnière par une petite camionnette blanche d'électricien : je voudrais qu'il soit sur un lit d'hôpital, pas dans un cercueil.

Une heure plus tard, je suis couchée, les yeux rivés au plafond. J'ai beau essayer de me convaincre qu'il a subi d'atroces blessures et ne peut composer mon numéro de ses doigts écrabouillés, je sais que c'est peu probable. En réalité, s'il ne m'a pas contactée, c'est qu'il a choisi de ne pas le faire. J'aurais dû m'en douter dès le départ : à présent je me rends compte que le speed dating n'est que l'un de ces merveilleux petits changements dont je vous ai parlé ; et, comme nous le savons tous, le changement est horrible et cruel parce qu'il vous promet tant, vous montre qu'autre chose est possible, qu'une vie meilleure existe, vous attend, juste à votre portée, et que tout ce que vous avez à faire, c'est de tendre la main.

Mais je sais que c'est un faux espoir, une farce tragique, parce qu'on ne peut l'évaluer, comme le speed dating, que par son succès ; et alors que je suis étendue dans l'obscurité, seule une fois de plus, mon jugement personnel ne peut être autre que : le speed dating, ça craint.

Chapitre 8

Persuader et influencer

Objectif à court terme : être trop occupée pour penser à… j'ai oublié son nom.
Obstacles : penser à Brad.
Objectif à long terme : attendre que Richard s'aperçoive qu'il ne peut vivre sans moi, j'imagine.
Obstacles : on peut dire qu'il prend son temps.

Mes rêves sont peuplés d'images floues : quelqu'un, derrière un mur en verre dépoli, les mains posées contre la vitre dans un geste suppliant, la bouche formant un trou d'ombre dont s'échappe une plainte indistincte et assourdie. Je regarde, les yeux plissés, mais malgré mes efforts je ne parviens pas à voir qui c'est. C'est forcément Brad, ou alors Fozzie, l'ours du *Muppet Show*.

Mais aujourd'hui je ne vais pas me laisser aller à penser à lui. Ni à Brad. Ah ah. Non, je vais me concentrer sur de Twitter et ce satané contrat. Brad est soit en train de subir une traction transosseuse, soit c'est un salaud de menteur hypocrite, donc s'il doit appeler un jour, ce sera quand il aura retrouvé l'usage de ses muscles, et ça peut prendre des semaines. Ça ne sert à rien de continuer à perdre du temps à consulter mon téléphone et ma messagerie électronique tous les quarts d'heure.

Bien sûr, ça ne prend que deux minutes de jeter un coup d'œil à mes mails en arrivant au bureau, donc ça ne compte pas. De toute façon, il n'y a pas de message de lui. Quel branleur !

Ou bien, quel pauvre homme, réduit en bouillie !

Fatima vient d'entrer, et elle porte un chapeau qui ressemble à un énorme gâteau en feutrine orné de bougies, et qui joue *Elle est vraiment phénoménale* quand on appuie sur le bord. Et il y a même des petites ampoules qui s'allument pour faire les flammes.

—C'est pourquoi, le chapeau, Fati ? demande Mike, dont le manque d'imagination me sidère.

—C'est mon anniversaire, couine-t-elle, illuminant les ténèbres de Mike. Souhaitez-moi un joyeux anniversaire !

Tout le monde s'exécute :

—Joyeux anniversaire.

—Qu'est-ce que tu as reçu ? lui dis-je alors qu'elle s'assied.

—Ooh, regarde, mes parents m'ont offert un téléphone, répond-elle en le sortant de sa poche. Il fait appareil photo, vidéo, Bluetooth, WAP et lecteur MP3.

—Ooooh…

Je prends le nouveau portable, le tourne et le retourne dans ma main :

—Tu sais ce que c'est, un fichier MP3 ?

Elle secoue la tête avec enthousiasme :

—Pas vraiment.

—Et le Bluetooth ? Et le WAP ?

—Non, non, mais c'est justement pour ça que j'ai demandé ce cadeau, pour apprendre.

—D'accord. Bonne idée, Fati.

—C'est aussi mon avis. Écoute, tu viens prendre un verre au *Bell Pull* à la pause-déjeuner ? C'est ma tournée.

J'hésite. Je sais que pour décrocher ce contrat avec Horizon il va falloir que je m'investisse et que je travaille dur, et je dois vraiment faire des recherches. Si Rupert de Witter me répond, ce serait mieux que j'en sache un peu plus sur lui et sa société avant qu'on se rencontre. D'un autre côté, fêter l'anniversaire d'une amie serait une jolie occupation si quelqu'un m'apercevait après avoir passé environ trois mois sans me voir, décidé à me trouver et à me faire sienne. Cela lui montrerait bien qu'il ne me manque pas du tout.

—Ma foi…

—Allez, Blondie, dit une voix traînante dans mon dos. (Je pivote dans mon siège pour découvrir Sean tout près de moi, la tête penchée de côté, le regard rivé sur ma personne.) S'il te plaaaaaît, viens boire un verre à la pause-déjeuner. Ce n'est pas tous les jours l'anniversaire de Fatima, n'est-ce pas ? En plus, elle a dit que c'était sa tournée, alors elle serait… très déçue… si tu ne nous accompagnais pas.

Il laisse de nouveau des silences dans ses phrases, et je suis cette fois encore obligée de me creuser la cervelle pour en comprendre le sens.

—Euh…

—Allez, Beth, steuplaît, s'écrie Fatima. J'aimerais vraiment que tu viennes, même si c'est que pour une demi-heure. Ça ne sera pas pareil sans toi. S'il te plaît !

—Elle a raison, ce ne sera pas pareil, ajoute Sean.

Il hausse les sourcils, avec un sourire coquin à la Mel Gibson, avant de tourner les talons et de regagner son bureau.

C'est extraordinaire. Sean avait toujours fait comme si je n'existais pas, et maintenant il m'a carrément donné un surnom. Cette coloration devait être vraiment haut de gamme. Je reporte mes yeux sur Fatima qui a tiré sa chaise près de la mienne et se penche le plus possible vers moi, les mains jointes. Le chapeau a un peu glissé et s'incline dangereusement d'un côté en tremblotant. Je recule légèrement mon siège : je ne voudrais pas qu'il me tombe dessus.

— OK, je viens. Mais je ne peux pas rester longtemps, Fati. J'ai quelque chose de vraiment pressé à faire.

— Hourra ! hurle-t-elle. Youpi ! Joyeux anniversaire, moi !

Après une matinée vraiment stressante à discuter de la gestion des conflits, je décide de jeter un petit coup d'œil à ma messagerie Hotmail, juste au cas où quelqu'un m'aurait envoyé quelque chose de très urgent et important, par exemple, vous savez, des informations sur une carte de crédit à zéro pour cent, ou autre. Ce n'est pas le cas, et je ne peux m'empêcher de remarquer que Brad non plus ne m'a pas écrit. Mais, et c'est très intéressant, ma boîte professionnelle contient une réponse de Rupert de Witter. Ça me surprend : je n'attendais pas de nouvelles de lui avant quelques jours, au moins. D'un autre côté, il ne doit pas être si occupé, s'il trouve le temps d'aller bronzer en institut toutes les six semaines, n'est-ce pas ? Je suppose que ce sont ses assistants qui font tout le travail et lui apportent juste un parapheur à signer de temps en temps, comme le capitaine de l'*USS Enterprise* dans *Star Trek*.

—Je vous laisse les commandes, Numéro Un. Je me téléporte sur cette nouvelle planète pour rafraîchir mon bronzage.

—Bien reçu, mon capitaine.

En tout cas, il m'a répondu :

De : Rupert de Witter
À : Bethsheridan@lovelearning.co.uk
Objet : Chaussures

Chère mademoiselle Sheridan,

Merci pour votre question. J'ai la joie de vous informer que j'ai en effet un penchant pour l'habillement des extrémités basses de ma personne, et on m'a vu exhiber des chaussures en de nombreuses occasions.

Aujourd'hui, mon équipement à ce niveau-là est assez terne : noires, à lacets, pointure 44.

J'attends de vos nouvelles avec impatience.

M. R. de Witter,
Horizon Holidays.

Je le relis, le sourire aux lèvres. Est-ce bien vrai ? Est-ce bien là le crétin arrogant dont Richard ne cessait de se plaindre ? Il me semble au contraire charmant et bien élevé. Ce sera moins difficile que ce que je craignais de le persuader de me rencontrer puis de signer un contrat, s'il n'est pas « ignorant comme un cochon, un vrai trou du cul qui a du yaourt à la place du cerveau », comme Richard me l'a dit. Mon idée des chaussures, pourtant assez minable, a l'air de prendre, et bien mieux que je ne l'avais espéré. J'ai essayé une approche humoristique, déroutante, pour susciter son intérêt, mais, en vérité, comme je pensais qu'il n'était qu'un crétin arrogant sans esprit ni intelligence, je n'imaginais pas qu'il comprendrait.

Et si la réponse avait été écrite par l'un de ses assistants ? Il est sans doute très occupé, le crétin en question, donc ce ne serait pas étonnant qu'il charge quelqu'un de répondre en son nom. Mais c'est signé de son patronyme, pas un truc du genre « Tarquin van Hoople, assistant de M. de Witter ». Peut-être que Rupert a dicté le message, et que Tarquin l'a tapé. D'après Richard, c'est un abruti sans éducation, donc je pensais que sa réponse, si j'en recevais une, serait dans ce style : « Oui, bien surre que j'est des chossure, pourquoi vous me demandais sa ? »

C'est au contraire très encourageant de voir qu'il est assez intrigué par mon message pour s'assurer que sa réponse soit dans un français correct.

Je meurs d'envie de répondre, mais bien sûr nous allons tous au pub dans une minute. Et c'est le moment que choisit Chas pour faire irruption. Je détache à regret mes yeux de l'écran pour le regarder.

— OK, tout le monde, écoutez-moi bien, commence-t-il en claquant des mains. (On dirait qu'il vient de voir une pièce de théâtre ringarde.) On a un petit problème, là, continue-t-il, en balayant la salle d'un regard sévère.

Près de la porte, Fati, toujours coiffée de son chapeau, met son manteau. Elle s'arrête et se retourne vers Chas.

— Je crois que vous savez tous ce dont je veux parler. Je pense que vous êtes tous parfaitement au courant de ce qui se passe. Love Learning a des ennuis, et ce n'est pas nouveau. Pourtant, certains d'entre vous ne font pas les efforts qu'ils devraient.

Ses yeux qui parcouraient la pièce s'arrêtent à présent sur Fatima. Son visage s'allonge alors qu'elle jette des regards nerveux autour d'elle, le chapeau géant tremblotant sur sa tête.

— Je ne tolérerai pas que certains ne mettent pas la main à la pâte, reprend-il d'une voix basse et menaçante. Je n'accepterai pas quelqu'un qui pense qu'il suffit de traîner à ne rien faire pendant que tous les autres travaillent. Je ne veux personne qui ne prenne pas ce boulot au sérieux.

Maintenant, tout le monde a le regard rivé sur Fatima qui se tortille sous son chapeau. Les yeux de Chas semblent la transpercer. Elle finit par lever un bras pour retirer son couvre-chef, qu'elle garde à la main. Ce geste simple paraît libérer Chas de sa fixation, et il se détourne enfin d'elle et recommence à s'adresser à l'ensemble de l'assistance :

— Et maintenant je veux que chacun d'entre vous me fasse un rapport sur ses recherches de contrat. Derek ?

Pendant que Derek bredouille des explications sur ses démarches, je reporte mon attention sur Fatima. Accroupie à côté de sa place, elle essaie d'enfoncer l'objet du délit sous la table le plus loin possible, en se parlant à elle-même :

— Connerie de chapeau… Qu'est-ce qui m'a pris de le porter ?… J'aurais dû m'en douter…

Elle a un pauvre sourire tremblant, mais je peux voir d'ici qu'elle a les yeux très brillants. Elle renifle discrètement une fois, bat des cils rapidement, se passe la main sur les yeux, puis repousse sa chaise sous son bureau et se relève.

— Beth ? interroge Chas tout à coup.

Merde. Je ne veux pas lui parler de mon projet, sinon tout le monde sera au courant des difficultés d'Horizon alors que j'aimerais garder l'avantage. Mais je ne veux pas non plus qu'il pense que je me suis tourné les pouces :

— Oh, euh, j'ai quelque chose sur le feu.

— Pas suffisant, aboie-t-il. Sean ?

Pas suffisant ? Putain de bordel de merde ! Comment peut-il oser ? Il ne sait donc pas que je suis responsable à moi toute seule de pratiquement tous les progrès de Love Learning et que sans moi il n'aurait probablement même pas ce poste ? Eh bien, il faut croire que non, puisqu'il n'est là que depuis trois mois. Mais j'ai travaillé ici pendant six ans avant qu'il arrive : de quel droit se permet-il de dire que mon travail n'est pas suffisant ? Je serre les poings et les mâchoires, et parviens de justesse à me retenir de grogner comme un animal. J'ai envie de lui sauter sur le dos pour lui arracher la tête avec mes dents et la recracher dans la cage d'escalier, mais je me contente de prendre un air profondément offensé.

— Et finalement Fatima, dit-il d'un ton doucereux. Quelque chose à nous proposer, mon poussin ?

— Je… ou… hum… la ch… c'est…

— Oh, écoute, ce n'est pas grave, ma puce, ne t'embête pas avec ces idioties de contrats. Ils sont vilains. Continue donc à faire… ce que tu fais, quoi que ce soit, et laisse-nous nous occuper des choses difficiles. D'accord, poussin ?

Fatima a les lèvres qui tremblent et les larmes qu'elle avait réussi à contenir finissent par rouler sur ses joues, mais Chas ne s'en aperçoit pas, car il a reporté son attention sur nous tous, avec un froncement de sourcils lourd de sens :

— On éteint les lumières, tout le monde. OK ? On ne remplit pas la bouilloire jusqu'en haut. On imprime en recto-verso. Les boissons chaudes pour les stagiaires sont désormais à 30 pence. Compris ? Les petites économies ici ou là feront la différence. Je ne veux pas avoir à le répéter. D'accord ? (Il garde les sourcils froncés pendant quelques secondes, avant de changer délibérément d'expression pour afficher un sourire béat.) Et maintenant, on a un anniversaire à fêter, pas vrai ? C'est moi qui paie la première tournée.

Un peu plus tard, au pub, Fatima paraît plutôt éteinte. Apparemment, elle avait prévu des petits jeux – un quiz musique, quelques tours de magie, la patate chaude – et elle met son programme à exécution, mais mon petit doigt me dit que son sens de la fête est un peu en berne :

— Bordel de merde, Cath, tu la fais passer, cette patate !

— Elle me fait de la peine, me murmure Sean à l'oreille sur le chemin du retour.

— Pardon, tu disais ?

Sean déballe la boîte de chocolats qu'il a gagnée et me la tend pour que je me serve. Il porte des mitaines.

— Fatima. J'ai de la peine pour elle. Elle travaille dur, elle fait de son mieux. Ce n'est pas sa faute si elle n'a pas la bosse du commerce.

Je le dévisage, abasourdie. Je veux dire, je sais que je ne le connais pas bien, mais j'ai toujours pensé qu'il était du genre à tuer et à dévorer son propre chien. La compassion pour une collègue écervelée ne fait pas partie des qualités que je lui aurais attribuées. Je l'ai sans doute mal jugé.

Maintenant que je le regarde pour de bon, son air un peu négligé, voire miteux, qui a toujours évoqué pour moi un joueur professionnel en déveine, est en réalité plutôt sexy, dans un style dangereux, pas comme il faut. Il a quelque chose en lui qui, tout d'un coup, me donne envie de m'approcher pour lui couper les cheveux.

— Non, tu as raison. Elle ne mérite pas d'être traitée comme ça.

— Carrément. Chas est un vrai connard. (Il se tient si près de moi que son bras ne cesse de frôler le mien.) Alors, dit-il avec un hochement de tête tandis que nous marchons d'un même pas, de la buée sortant de sa bouche.

— Alors ?

— Alors, mademoiselle Sheridan, répond-il avec un grand sourire. Vous êtes très jolie.

Aussi bizarre que ça puisse paraître, je commence à m'y habituer et je ne rougis même pas. Peut-être parce que je suis déjà rouge, après deux verres de vin chaud.

— Merci.

J'essaie quand même d'avoir l'air étonnée, parce que c'est bien plus séduisant que de répondre tout simplement : « Oui. »

— Comment ça va, pour toi ?

— Bien, merci. Et toi ?

Il me regarde de la tête aux pieds de façon éhontée, et j'aurais raison de protester, puis il répond :

— Vraiment bien, Beth. Vraiment… bien.

— Tant mieux.

Je lui souris, mais je ne vois pas trop sur quoi peut déboucher cette brillante conversation.

— Comment ça se passe, le travail ? Ton truc sur « Gérer le Changement » ?

— Bien, je crois. Ça touche à sa fin. Plus que deux jours.

— Je suis sûr qu'ils te dévorent des yeux, pas vrai ?

— Oh, euh, eh bien…

— Je parie que tu les hypnotises carrément.

— Hummm.

Je ne peux pas lui donner raison : ça aurait l'air prétentieux. Mais je ne veux pas non plus le contredire et affirmer que je suis parfaitement quelconque. Par chance, juste à ce moment, je repère sur le toit d'une maison des décorations lumineuses qui doivent avoir une empreinte carbone de la taille de la cathédrale Saint-Paul à Londres, et ça me permet de changer de sujet :

— Regarde ! Oooh, c'est impressionnant ! Je crois que je vais faire le tour pour voir s'ils ont un père Noël. Je te retrouve au bureau, d'accord ?

— Je t'accompagne, répond-il vivement. J'adore les décos de Noël.

— D'accord. Ce sera chouette.

Merde, merde, merde.

Nous marchons en silence quelques minutes avant de prendre la première à gauche.

— Oh, regarde, s'exclame-t-il, tu avais raison, il y a un père Noël.

Nous nous arrêtons pour contempler l'étalage clinquant qui comprend, allez savoir pourquoi, une Blanche-Neige et sept nains en guirlande électrique.

— Tu as un vrai don pour prédire les choses avant qu'elles arrivent, non ?

Je le dévisage. Manifestement, il a remarqué mes excellents résultats en matière de prospection, mais n'a pas vu les heures que j'ai passées en douloureuses tractations. Il préfère croire que je suis douée, au lieu de reconnaître que je travaille plus.

— Pas vraiment. Je veux dire, c'était plutôt évident. Une maison qui a autant de décorations lumineuses sur le toit a neuf chances sur dix d'avoir toute une scène animée avec rennes, chalet du père Noël, lutins et crèche.

Il a vraiment les yeux très, très bleus, vus d'ici. Il me regarde avec tant d'intensité, sans ciller, que j'en ai la chair de poule. Je me creuse désespérément la cervelle pour trouver une réponse, mais rien ne vient. C'est vraiment difficile de me concentrer alors qu'il me dévisage comme ça. Allons, Beth, réfléchis.

— Tu as raison, dit-il sans me lâcher du regard. Tu es très futée.

— Merci.

— Bien sûr, tu as déjà un contrat géant dans ta manche ?

Je détourne les yeux pour contempler à nouveau la vue merveilleuse qui s'offre à moi. Dans l'herbe, près de la remise, brillent trois champignons lumineux.

— Non, pas vraiment. J'ai quelque chose en tête…

— Je le savais ! Beth, tu es impressionnante. C'est quoi ? C'est un gros truc ?

Je pose une nouvelle fois les yeux sur lui. Il n'est que 13 heures à peine passées, mais le ciel est couvert et menaçant, et certains lampadaires s'allument déjà. Dans cette lumière, c'est vraiment difficile de déchiffrer son expression.

—D'accord, Sean, je vais te le dire, mais tu dois me jurer de ne le répéter à personne, OK?

Il hoche la tête, brûlant de curiosité:

—Promis.

—OK. Bon, alors, je peux te dire que… (Il se penche vers moi, et pour un peu je verrais une étincelle dans ses yeux.) Oui, c'est un gros truc.

Il bat des paupières.

—C'est… Oh, OK, bon, c'est super. Fantastique, Beth. Je suis vraiment content pour toi.

—Merci, Sean.

Il se détourne pour regarder la rue. Puis reporte son attention sur moi:

—Oh là là, tu frissonnes. Allez, rentrons. Il est bientôt 13 h 30.

Vous n'avez pas cru que j'allais lui dire, quand même? Allons! Il suffirait que ce type me fasse un tout petit peu la cour du jour au lendemain, et vous pensez que je vais rendre les armes comme un laideron en peine de se débarrasser de sa virginité? Vous devriez pourtant commencer à me connaître, maintenant.

Mais je vais devoir faire très attention à lui, dorénavant. De toute l'équipe, il est celui que j'imagine le plus facilement essayer de m'extorquer des informations par les moyens les plus odieux, vraisemblablement en me ligotant et en me séquestrant jusqu'à ce que je craque. Dans un endroit sombre et secret, où personne ne nous entendrait, il se collerait à moi de façon menaçante, et je sentirais son haleine brûlante sur mon visage. Tout à coup, je m'aperçois que j'ai le cœur qui bat à se rompre, et lorsque je le vois marcher à mes côtés, j'ai la chair de poule.

Avant de retourner dans la salle de formation, je prends le temps de me connecter à ma messagerie et de répondre à Rupert de Witter. « Pas suffisant », me dis-je avec haine en vrillant la porte en bois des yeux. Ce n'est pas mon avis. Je suis seulement en train de préparer un contrat avec l'une des plus importantes sociétés de toute la ville. Je relis le message de Rupert et je me surprends à sourire en cliquant sur « Répondre ». C'est vraiment fantastique qu'il soit entré dans le jeu. J'irai trouver Chas pour lui mettre le nez dedans quand j'aurai les documents signés. Je veux dire, au sens propre, je lui écraserai la figure dans les papiers.

En même temps, le fait que Rupert relance la plaisanterie pourrait signifier qu'il me prend pour une petite rigolote. Je lève mes doigts du clavier. Merde.

Bon, il est trop tard pour y penser, maintenant. « Quand le vin est tiré, il faut le boire. » Je termine mon message et clique sur « Envoyer ». Au moins, il semble apprécier mon approche et être intéressé. Mais, comme Fast Love me l'a si bien montré, ça ne veut rien dire.

De : Bethsheridan@lovelearning.co.uk
À : Rupert de Witter
Objet : Chaussures noires à lacets, pointure 44

Cher monsieur de Witter,
Merci beaucoup pour votre prompte réponse.
Si vos chaussures sont de pointure 44, puis-je en déduire que vos pieds font également du 44 ? Je suis certaine que vous ne serez pas surpris d'apprendre que de récentes études ont montré que quatre-vingt-neuf pour cent de la population

choisit ses souliers de la même taille que ses pieds, ce qui me permet de tirer la précédente conclusion. Corrigez-moi si je me trompe.

Bien à vous,
Beth Sheridan,
Love Learning.

C'est seulement après avoir envoyé le mail et éteint l'ordinateur pour me rendre dans la salle de formation que je m'aperçois que je n'ai pas vérifié s'il y avait un message de Brad. Zut! Toute cette émotion à propos de Sean l'a chassé de mon esprit.

La session de l'après-midi se termine avant l'heure. Elle est prévue pour durer trois heures, avec une pause d'une demi-heure au milieu, et un exercice d'une quinzaine de minutes, mais je fais la présentation en quatrième vitesse et donne le travail à faire à la maison. Ça ne me ressemble pas, mais, pour la première fois de ma carrière, j'ai la tête ailleurs pendant la séance. Cela ne m'est jamais arrivé auparavant. Même pas quand l'équipe olympique de natation d'Australie est venue en ville. Je reconnais qu'après le boulot je me suis précipitée au centre sportif, mais ça n'a eu aucun retentissement sur mes performances professionnelles. Non que les stagiaires s'en plaignent: ils se réjouissent simplement de sortir quarante minutes en avance.

Si je n'ai pas la tête à ce que je fais, c'est en partie à cause de Sean, et en partie à cause de Brad, mais surtout à cause de Rupert de Witter. Je suis très impatiente de voir s'il m'a répondu, mais, pour cela, je dois d'abord me rendre à mon bureau. Quand je passe à côté de Sean, il me suit des yeux, du coup je marche très lentement, feignant d'être absorbée dans les dossiers que je porte. Puis je dois atteindre la partie supérieure de l'armoire à classeurs pour les ranger. Ils ne viennent pas de là, mais c'est à cet endroit que j'ai envie de les mettre. Comme je m'étire, mon chemisier s'échappe de l'arrière de ma jupe et remonte même un peu, dévoilant quelques centimètres de peau. Finalement, je le sens arriver derrière moi, la chaleur de son corps m'enveloppe, et son souffle fait frissonner les petits cheveux sur ma nuque. De toute évidence, il est venu me prendre doucement les classeurs des mains et, les yeux rivés sur les miens, les poser sans effort à leur place, au-dessus de ma tête.

— Espèce d'endormie, qu'est-ce que tu fais ? dit une voix qui n'est pas celle de Sean. (Je me retourne et me retrouve nez à nez avec Mike, les poings sur les hanches.) Ces dossiers ne vont pas là. Il faut les mettre ici, dans le deuxième tiroir en partant du bas.

— Oh, quelle idiote ! Merci, Mike.

Je m'assieds. Bon, ben ça, c'est fait. Je jette un coup d'œil furtif à Sean, mais il ne me regarde pas. Il devait avoir les yeux sur moi à l'instant, cela dit, et c'est parfait. Maintenant, je dois aller voir si j'ai une réponse de Rupert.

Incroyable : il a répondu.

De : Rupert de Witter
À : Bethsheridan@lovelearning.co.uk
Objet : Ampoules

Chère mademoiselle Sheridan,
Merci pour votre mail, que j'ai reçu aujourd'hui.

Vous avez raison de supposer que mes pieds font également du 44. Je trouve intéressant que vous mentionniez le fait que la plupart des gens aient les pieds de la même taille que leurs chaussures. Est-ce un phénomène national, ou seulement régional?

Bien à vous en pensée,
Rupert de Witter.

Ce qui me frappe tout d'abord c'est qu'il a signé avec son prénom cette fois-ci, et pas seulement l'initiale. Puis je remarque qu'il n'a pas écrit Horizon Holidays sous sa signature. Ensuite, je vois le titre qu'il a donné au message et j'éclate de rire. Il a de l'humour! Je ne m'attendais certainement pas à ça, d'après ce que Richard m'avait dit de lui. Il n'était pas rare qu'on – c'est-à-dire moi – l'entende déclarer: «Cet emmerdeur est aussi drôle et futé qu'un cul de babouin.» Ou autres variations sur le même thème. Au fond de moi, j'ai toujours pensé qu'en réalité les babouins ont un postérieur vraiment rigolo, si c'est bien ceux qui ont l'air de s'être brûlé les poils du derrière.

Bien que tout se passe mieux que je ne l'espérais – ce qui n'est pas bien difficile, puisque je m'attendais à n'importe quoi entre un refus abrupt et un franc «Allez vous faire foutre!» –, la rapidité des réponses de Rupert pose un problème inattendu. Je croyais que ça lui prendrait plusieurs jours de s'arracher à son institut de beauté et de répondre à mon message, ce qui me laisserait le temps d'apprendre des tas de choses intéressantes sur Horizon. Et, bien sûr, de préparer mon prochain mail fantastiquement intelligent. Mais il riposte du tac au tac, et je commence à être à court d'idées. Mon plan de départ – comparer les formations aux chaussures parce qu'elles doivent être parfaitement ajustées – est en train de s'épuiser, et au rythme où ça va, il est vraisemblable que je le rencontre assez rapidement pour en discuter.

Je me dépêche de me connecter à nouveau au site d'Horizon, dans l'espoir que quelque chose me frappe. Et aussitôt c'est le cas : son visage me saute aux yeux. Le voilà, les cheveux dorés et brillants, la peau bronzée, les dents très très blanches. Oh là là, il est magnifique. Et mille fois plus drôle et charmant qu'un cul de babouin. Non, un million de fois, voyons, c'est quand même d'un derrière que l'on parle. Et ne l'oublions pas, il est très riche. Je me penche vers la photo pour la contempler. Je suis tellement fascinée que j'appuie tout le poids de ma tête sur ma main. Bon Dieu, qu'est-ce que je donnerais pour te rencontrer… Merde, je vais te rencontrer ! Et re-merde, comment vais-je m'habiller ? Je ferme les yeux alors qu'une image délicieuse se forme dans mon esprit : Rupert se lève pour m'accueillir quand j'entre dans son bureau d'une démarche aérienne, vêtue d'une robe bustier noire, très *Pretty Woman*.

De surprise, il ouvre sa bouche magnifique en s'avançant à ma rencontre.

— Vous êtes en retard, dis-je.

— Vous êtes belle.

— Vous êtes pardonné, réponds-je avec un grand sourire.

Je me redresse. *Allons, Beth, reprends-toi.* Une tenue de soirée, ça ne va pas, la tête ? Tu seras en tailleur, parce que tu iras pour le travail, pour essayer de le convaincre de te confier l'ensemble de la formation de son personnel, pas pour une partie de jambes en l'air et la promesse d'une longue vie heureuse. Bien que, si je n'arrive pas à obtenir l'un, je me contenterai de l'autre.

Oh non, je perds la tête. Son visage tellement sexy me déconcerte à tel point que je ne sais pas comment je vais faire pour parler en sa présence. Ou rester à la verticale. Et habillée. Je parcours rapidement le reste du site à la recherche d'une autre source d'inspiration, jusqu'à ce que je trouve : sur l'une des pages, on peut voir une petite photo du plateau de vente par téléphone, avec quelques télévendeuses souriantes et Joan, la superviseuse, debout derrière elles, la mine sévère, les bras croisés. Le cliché a l'air récent, ce qui signifie qu'un photographe s'y est rendu au moins une fois, pour prendre des vues. Ça ne me donne pas l'idée de me mettre un appareil photo autour du cou et de coincer une fausse carte de presse dans la bordure de mon chapeau ; mais peut-être que je pourrais me faufiler subrepticement et faire un peu d'espionnage. Éventuellement, engager la conversation avec quelqu'un dans l'ascenseur sur la satisfaction qu'on a dans le travail. Horizon Holidays est tellement immense que personne ne peut connaître tout le monde, pas même Rupert de Witter lui-même. En fait, c'est sans doute lui qui connaît le moins les gens, vu qu'il passe la moitié de son temps enfermé dans son bureau au septième étage, l'autre moitié à se faire retoucher les racines. Je pourrais peut-être même le rencontrer et me faire passer pour l'une de ses employées. Je me plaindrais de la formation !

Et alors, quand on se verra finalement pour de bon, il hochera la tête en disant : « Bien joué. » Ça lui donnera sans nul doute envie de coucher avec moi. Je veux dire, de signer un contrat avec moi.

Pour tuer le temps dans la voiture en rentrant chez moi, j'imagine plein de scénarios dans lesquels je m'illustre par des actions héroïques ou hilarantes devant une foule d'admirateurs, sous les yeux de Rupert. Je sais, ça vous étonne que Richard ne figure plus dans mes pensées. Eh bien, ne vous inquiétez pas, je suis toujours amoureuse de lui, tout ceci n'est qu'une distraction en attendant qu'il vienne réclamer mon cœur. Et si ça devait prendre de l'ampleur, j'ai encore en tête l'option : « Tu as loupé le coche, chéri. »

J'aurais mieux fait de passer le temps en me concentrant sur la route : ce n'est qu'en entrant dans l'appartement que je me rends compte que je n'ai aucun souvenir du trajet, encore une fois. Je ne sais même pas si c'est bien avec ma voiture que j'ai roulé jusqu'ici. J'aurais aussi bien pu monter dans celle de quelqu'un d'autre pour rentrer à la maison. Ou ailleurs. Je pourrais avoir commis un crime en chemin. Pointé une carabine à canon scié sur la figure d'un vendeur ; embouti un distributeur de billets avec une voiture-bélier ; ou pris une rue en sens interdit. Je regarde mes mains, comme si je m'attendais à y trouver un flingue fumant, ou du sang. Mais tout ce que j'ai, ce sont mes clefs de voiture, et ça me rassure.

Qu'est-ce qu'il a donc pour me faire oublier ainsi ce que je fais, ce Rupert de Witter ? Ah oui, bien sûr, il est tellement sexy qu'on en fondrait de plaisir. C'est pourtant simple !

Vini m'attend dans l'entrée, serrant dans ses mains un paquet de vêtements qu'elle me tend à la minute où je franchis la porte :

— Enfile ça, je t'emmène.

Je scrute le ballot. Pour commencer, il est noir et semble constitué d'un vieux pantalon de survêtement.

— Qu'est-ce que c'est ?

— Mon vieux survêt'. Allez, dépêche-toi.

— Non merci, Vini. Si on sort, je vais essayer de faire un petit effort. Ce qui veut dire que je vais mettre une jupe ou un jean.

— Non, pas là où on va. Allez, Beth, ça va être marrant.

Ça ne me dit rien qui vaille. La dernière fois qu'elle m'a demandé d'endosser des habits confortables, c'était pour un cours d'expression corporelle à la maison de quartier. On devait s'identifier à un arbre. Je ne suis pas près de recommencer.

— Pas question. Laisse tomber. Jamais, *nada*, *niet*, *no*, *nein*.

— Écoute, ce n'est pas « Danse avec la Terre », ou je sais plus comment ça s'appelait. Je veux juste aller à la salle de sport. C'est sympa, ça fait du bien, et c'est plein de beaux gars musclés et athlétiques qu'on pourra draguer.

— Donne-moi deux minutes.

Chapitre 9

Apte au service (I)

Objectif à court terme : remarcher.
Obstacles : je ne peux pas. Je ne veux pas.
Personne ne peut me forcer.
Objectif à long terme : mourir. Vite.
Obstacles : je n'arrive pas à attraper de quoi
mettre fin à mes jours.

Donc, je ne suis pas apte au sport. Je pense que je le
savais déjà.

Chapitre 9

Apte au service (II) – Adaptation

Objectif à court terme : me traîner jusqu'à Horizon Holidays. Essayer d'y faire quelques pas. Me tenir, toute raide, à côté de Rupert et découvrir des éléments intéressants. Ensuite, rentrer à la maison.
Obstacles : il n'y a pas un seul de mes muscles qui ne soit en train de saigner.
Objectif à long terme : que la douleur s'arrête. S'il vous plaît, Seigneur, qu'elle s'arrête.
Obstacles : je ne peux pas bouger les bras pour prier.

OK. Laissez-moi vous dire une chose à propos des salles de sport. Premièrement, les gens y portent des lunettes de soleil. Pour quoi faire ? Je veux dire, on est au milieu de l'hiver, il est 19 heures, il fait très froid et sombre, on n'en a pas besoin. En fait, je pense qu'au fond d'eux-mêmes ils savent très bien qu'ils n'en ont pas besoin et que c'est pour ça qu'ils se les calent sur le haut du crâne.

Évidemment, cela rend le jogging ou tout autre exercice énergique assez délicat, parce que les lunettes aiment bien glisser sur le nez ou carrément par terre.

Par conséquent, la première chose que j'aperçois en entrant, ce sont de nombreuses femmes à la silhouette irréprochable, en tenue de Lycra, bougeant avec précaution sur les tapis de course, essayant de ne pas se mettre à transpirer pour éviter d'abîmer leur fond de teint.

—Allez, me dit Vini, enthousiaste, en me traînant vers les vélos d'appartement. Le vélo, c'est facile.

OK, bon, c'est vrai. La dernière fois que je suis montée sur une bicyclette, j'avais quatorze ans, mais aussitôt que je suis en selle, ça me revient. *OK*, me dis-je, *tout va bien, je peux le faire.* Je règle le chronomètre pour un entraînement de vingt minutes, puis je commence à regarder autour de moi.

Très vite, je comprends deux choses. Premièrement, le plan de Vini a un gros défaut : on ne peut pas draguer les beaux types musclés ici. La salle est presque entièrement remplie de femmes de différents formats. Il y en a pour tous les goûts, si vous aimez les dames : c'est incompréhensible qu'il n'y ait pas plus d'hommes. J'en découvre un ou deux tout au bout de la pièce, mais ils sont totalement absorbés par les poids qu'ils soulèvent, et, pour être honnête, ils ont fort à faire : il y en a une quantité à ramasser et à remettre en place. Ils doivent le faire devant un miroir, qui plus est, afin de pouvoir imaginer à quel point ils auraient l'air fantastiques s'ils levaient une voiture pour dégager un enfant.

Pour ne rien arranger, tout le monde a des écouteurs et se déplace donc comme s'il était parfaitement seul. Personne ne semble même conscient de la présence des autres ; ils font juste en sorte d'éviter de se cogner, comme des chauves-souris, utilisant, je suppose, un sonar particulier aux salles de sport.

Deuxièmement, vingt minutes sur une bicyclette, c'est beaucoup trop long.

— On essaie les vélos elliptiques ? propose alors Vini.

Nous traversons la pièce.

Je ne vais pas entrer dans les détails. Je suis très bonne dans mon boulot. Je suis intelligente et raisonnablement marrante, plutôt séduisante, je sais faire des super tiramisus, je suis douée pour le Scrabble, je suis élégante, propre, et je me défends en calcul mental.

Mais je ne sais pas tenir en équilibre sur un vélo elliptique. Pas la peine d'en faire un plat.

Le lendemain, vendredi, je me trouve assise dans la plus grande immobilité à mon bureau, occupée à suivre l'aiguille des yeux en redoutant qu'elle n'arrive sur l'heure où je devrai quitter ma chaise. Je me concentre pour me lever sans faire de crise d'hyperventilation.

Je projette pour cet après-midi une visite d'espionnage chez Horizon, mais après que Vini m'a montré tous les merveilleux bénéfices d'une bonne séance d'entraînement à la salle de sport, par exemple le renforcement du cœur et des poumons, l'amélioration de la circulation sanguine, la perte de poids et l'allongement de l'espérance de vie, j'ai passé la journée à attendre la mort. Ce matin, elle est partie avant que je me lève. Je pense qu'elle m'évite, ce qui est inutile, car elle a moins à craindre de moi aujourd'hui que jamais auparavant.

Aujourd'hui, c'est le dernier jour de l'atelier « Gérer le Changement », et je vais le rater. Et vous savez quoi ? Je m'en fiche. J'ai dit à Derek que je m'étais coincé le dos, ce qui explique mes mouvements raides comme ceux d'un robot. (Je ne vais pas avouer que je suis courbaturée à cause du sport. À mon âge, c'est pathétique.) Du coup, je lui ai demandé si ça l'ennuierait de faire la séance de bilan à ma place. Je savais qu'il serait d'accord : c'est le genre de personne qui croit que, sans lui, c'est à peine si les autres arrivent à s'en sortir.

— Je suis heureux de te rendre service, Beth, dit-il, les yeux mi-clos. C'est la moindre des choses.

Ce qui signifie vraisemblablement qu'il pense sauver de justesse mon atelier de l'échec. Sans doute le groupe sera-t-il déçu, et quelque peu déconcerté, de se retrouver face à face avec un crétin en costard-cravate au lieu de moi, mais j'ai d'autres chats à espionner.

J'ai décidé d'y aller après le déjeuner, ce qui me laisse la matinée pour traîner une fois de plus devant ma messagerie. Bien qu'il soit presque 10 heures, Fatima n'est pas encore arrivée, et cela ne lui ressemble pas ; mais ça signifie que je peux être tranquille pour écrire des mails spirituels, intéressants, et terriblement séduisants à une certaine personne, sans être interrompue.

Je relis le dernier message de Rupert, qui date d'hier, où il me demande si la concordance des pointures des chaussures et de la taille des pieds est un phénomène national. Je souris en le parcourant, et je me dis qu'il est très attirant, dans le style homme d'affaires au cœur de pierre. Mais je ne dois pas laisser ma célibatairite aiguë troubler mon jugement. Je clique sur « Répondre ».

De : Bethsheridan@lovelearning.co.uk
À : Rupert de Witter
Objet : Confort

Cher monsieur de Witter,

Merci beaucoup pour votre récent courrier. J'ai consacré du temps à des recherches approfondies pour répondre à votre question, et les résultats sont très surprenants. Il apparaît que les pieds des porteurs de chaussures sont contenus dans des souliers très exactement de la même pointure, et ce aux quatre coins du pays. Pour tout dire, parmi la totalité de mon échantillon, je n'ai trouvé qu'une seule personne qui montre une différence significative entre taille du pied et pointure de la chaussure. Ses pieds étaient de pointure 24, et ses chaussures du 38; elles semblaient appartenir à un autre membre de sa famille proche. Je l'ai interrogée sur cet écart par rapport à la norme et les motivations de ce choix, mais sa réponse n'a pas été concluante: «Je suis une princesse» n'a pas été considéré comme une explication satisfaisante de ce comportement peu ordinaire. Malgré un questionnement répété, le sujet n'a fourni aucune information, et s'est finalement endormi.

J'ai une hypothèse concernant le phénomène de la concordance de la taille des pieds et des chaussures, et serai heureuse de vous l'exposer, si vous le souhaitez. J'attends vos instructions.

Bien à vous,
Beth Sheridan,
Love Learning.

OK. Maintenant, il ne me reste plus qu'à patienter jusqu'à ce qu'il réponde. Sans bouger. Je me tournerais bien les pouces, mais la douleur lancinante et horrible dans mes muscles transforme le moindre mouvement en torture médiévale. Bon, ça devrait aller, du moment que personne ne…

— Salut, Beth, dit une voix dans mon dos.

Je pivote vers la personne qui vient de me parler. Avant de crier «Aaaaargh, putain de bordel de meeeeeerde!» Silencieusement, dans ma tête, bien sûr. En apparence, je suis calme comme la Petite Sirène, et je fais des jolis sourires alors que des millions de poignards transpercent chaque centimètre carré de mon corps. Elle croyait souffrir, avec seulement quelques couteaux dans les pieds. Elle n'était vraiment pas en droit de se plaindre. Enfin, techniquement, elle ne s'est pas plainte du tout, n'est-ce pas, puisqu'elle était muette.

— Tout va bien? reprend la voix.

Je me rends compte que j'ai certainement l'air un peu bizarre, raide comme un piquet, osant à peine respirer, les yeux rivés droit devant moi et souriant comme une demeurée.

— Oui, très bien, merci.

Je réussis à lever juste un peu les yeux sans bouger le cou et découvre Sean qui se penche un peu pour essayer de croiser mon regard.

— Je ne te trouve pas bien. Enfin, je ne veux pas dire ça. Tu es très bien. Vraiment très bien. Ce que je veux dire, c'est que tu n'as pas l'air en forme. Tu es sûre que ça va?

— Oh oui, je me suis juste coincé le dos hier. Tout sera rentré dans l'ordre dans un jour ou deux. Promis.

Il tire la chaise de Fatima et s'assied à côté de moi, à mon grand soulagement. Je commençais à avoir mal aux sourcils.

— Tu veux un massage ? (Il entrelace ses doigts pour les étirer.) Il paraît que je suis très doué pour ça…

— Non, merci, ce n'est pas la peine.

Il repose les mains dans son giron :

— C'était juste une blague, Beth. Il ne faut pas avoir peur.

Crotte, j'ai l'air terrifiée ? Ce n'est pas le genre de message que j'ai intérêt à envoyer quand un bel homme me propose de me masser. Je me concentre aussitôt sur mon front et mes paupières pour leur donner une expression plus détendue :

— Oh non, non, désolée, j'ai juste peur de la douleur, c'est tout. Mon dos me tue.

— OK. Tu es pressée de te remettre à ce que tu faisais ?

Je m'aperçois en l'entendant que j'ai reporté mon attention sur mon ordinateur, qui vient de me signaler par un bip l'arrivée d'un mail. Je détourne à regret les yeux de l'écran pour regarder Sean :

— Euh, oui, un peu. Désolée, j'ai l'esprit occupé.

— Est-ce que je peux faire quelque chose pour t'aider ?

Je me tourne complètement vers lui. Pendant toutes ces années, je lui ai prêté des intentions cachées, juste parce qu'il a des petits yeux et une voix traînante. Après tout, peut-être que c'est un type bien, parfaitement honnête, et que j'ai eu tort de me fier aux apparences.

— Euh, dis-je, un œil sur l'écran d'ordinateur, en me demandant si je peux le mettre au parfum.

Ça ne pourrait pas faire de mal, finalement ? C'est un collègue, nous avons certainement les mêmes objectifs ?

Et, comme on dit, l'union fait la force. Il pourrait peut-être même m'aider.

Tout à coup, je reprends mes esprits.

—Non merci, Sean. C'est très gentil de ta part, mais je m'en sors très bien. Je vais bientôt m'absenter, donc il n'y a pas grand-chose que tu puisses faire de toute façon.

Bon Dieu, j'ai eu chaud !

—Vraiment ? Et tu vas où, comme ça ?

Je penche légèrement la tête *(Aïïïe !)* et souris :

—Tu ne lâches pas facilement, n'est-ce pas ? Pourquoi est-ce que tu as tellement envie de savoir ce que je fais ? Tu veux me voler mon idée ?

Il fronce les sourcils et s'écarte de moi en se redressant et en reculant un peu la chaise :

—C'est ce que tu penses ? Tu crois vraiment que je suis comme ça, Beth ? Que j'essaie de te parler, de me rapprocher de toi, juste pour m'immiscer dans ta vie et découvrir quel pauvre contrat tu cherches à décrocher ? Si c'est ça… (Sa voix s'éteint, et il secoue la tête.) C'est…

Il hausse les mains en signe de défaite, secoue à nouveau le chef, sourit et fait mine de se lever.

—Non, écoute, je suis désolée, je plaisantais. Je ne voulais pas dire ça. Bien sûr que je ne pense pas comme ça.

Il s'arrête dans son geste :

—C'est vrai ?

—Oui.

—D'accord. (Il se rassied.) Parce que la vérité, c'est que j'ai vraiment envie de passer du temps avec toi. De te parler. De te regarder. Sans aucune arrière-pensée, juste parce que… bon, ça doit être évident, non ?

— Tu sais, on pourrait sans doute le croire, mais en fait non.

Il rit :

— Voyons, Beth ! Tu me plais. Grave. Sors avec moi. Ce soir.

Je le dévisage. Ce n'est pas du tout ce à quoi je m'attendais. En fait, peut-être que si, puisque je n'avais pas la moindre idée de ce qui pouvait bien se tramer. Mais Sean et moi, on se connaît depuis plusieurs années : pourquoi est-ce qu'il passe à l'attaque aujourd'hui ? Est-ce que ça pourrait être ma nouvelle coloration ? Après toutes ces années, il a finalement le béguin pour moi à cause de mes cheveux ? Ah, j'aimerais vraiment savoir combien cette teinture a coûté. Il faudra que je demande à Vini où elle l'a achetée. J'imagine sa réponse :

« Oh, j'ai fait un troc un peu risqué avec un vieux Chinois tout ratatiné, quelque part, dans une boutique. Il a parlé de trois règles importantes… »

Je reporte mon attention sur Sean. Il a un regard suppliant, hanté, qui le rend extrêmement séduisant. Rien n'est plus sexy qu'un mec torturé par la possibilité qu'on l'envoie balader.

— OK, finis-je par répondre. Je le vois se détendre, soulagé.

— Ah, super. Écoute, tu veux que je passe te prendre, ou tu préfères qu'on se retrouve quelque part ?

Hum. C'est loin d'être parfait : en tant qu'homme, il aurait dû savoir planifier une soirée de séduction, et devrait donc venir me chercher et m'entraîner dans la première activité de notre rendez-vous. Patinage sous la lune ou pique-nique au champagne sur les rives d'un lac. Mais manifestement, il n'a rien prévu.

—Je préfère te rejoindre, dis-je.

Je ne veux pas qu'il croie qu'il doit arranger quelque chose. Je veux dire, il ne devrait pas avoir besoin que j'essaie de lui donner l'impression qu'il faut qu'il le fasse : il aurait dû y penser tout seul. C'est comme de demander à quelqu'un de vous offrir des fleurs.

—OK, parfait. Où ça ?

De mieux en mieux. La moindre des choses serait qu'il suggère un endroit magnifique ; comme ça, même si je dois m'y rendre par mes propres moyens, au moins je saurais que ce sera magique à l'arrivée.

—Que dirais-tu du *Perroquet du Pirate* ? Sur Willoughby Road ?

Il opine :

—Je vois où c'est. On dit 20 heures ?

Même l'heure est un peu vague, et le fait que ce soit une question montre bien qu'il veut que je confirme. Pour l'amour du ciel !

—Vingt heures, c'est très bien, dis-je.

Il hoche la tête, l'air heureux :

—Super. Je te retrouve là-bas, alors. (Il sourit, puis se lève, les mains appuyées sur les cuisses.) J'ai hâte d'y être.

J'opine du chef :

—Moi aussi.

Bien que je n'aie pas la moindre idée de ce qu'il espère. Il doit savoir que je suis prise. Et je ne pense pas que ce sera lui qui me fera parler du coche à Richard. Celui qu'il a loupé, vous vous souvenez ?

Il finit par rejoindre son bureau, après avoir rangé la chaise de Fatima à sa place. L'image de ma collègue en train de fourrer son chapeau au même endroit hier me revient en tête, et je me demande vaguement où elle est en ce moment. Elle est peut-être en larmes au fond de son lit. Je vais l'appeler dans une minute. Quand j'aurai regardé le message qui vient d'arriver.

Oui ! C'est encore un mail de Rupert. Je sens des bulles d'excitation pétiller en moi alors que je rapproche mon siège du bureau, comme si j'étais plus près de lui par ce geste. Je clique sur le titre, impatiente de lire sa réponse.

De : Rupert de Witter
À : Beth Sheridan
Objet : Soulagement

Chère Beth,
Je suis très heureux que vous m'ayez enfin répondu. Je commençais à croire que je n'aurais plus jamais de vos nouvelles, et cela aurait été bien dommage. Nos petites conversations sur le port national de souliers sont pour moi comme un rayon de soleil. Bien que je n'aie nul désir d'abréger notre correspondance, j'ai le sentiment qu'il faut que je hâte la conclusion de cet échange, afin que nous puissions nous divertir en évoquant d'autres sujets.
Je suppose que vous finirez par arriver au constat que chacun est plus à l'aise et mieux armé pour être efficace s'il est équipé de chaussures de la bonne pointure et de la bonne forme ? Et que cette remarque vous conduira à l'idée que toute chose dans la vie devrait nous convenir aussi bien que nos souliers, et que c'est le cas, par exemple, des enseignements que nous recevons ? Me trompé-je ?

Puis, oserai-je le suggérer, vous m'informerez probablement que toutes les formations de Love Learning sont faites sur mesure pour répondre aux demandes des stagiaires, afin que les ressources – c'est-à-dire le temps et l'argent – ne soient pas gaspillées par des stages dont les gens n'ont ni le besoin ni l'usage. Puis, vous conclurez en me demandant si j'aimerais vous rencontrer pour que vous puissiez me montrer comment Love Learning peut améliorer les performances de mon entreprise, avec des résultats visibles en moins d'un an?

La réponse est oui. Avec grand plaisir, et aussi vite que possible. Je suis impatient de faire votre connaissance. Faites-moi savoir par retour de mail quel jour dans les deux prochaines semaines ne vous convient pas pour un déjeuner. Les jours où vous avez rendez-vous avec votre petit ami, par exemple. Ou ceux où vous vous rendez au spectacle de Noël de vos enfants.

J'attends votre réponse avec impatience.

Bien à vous,
Rupert.

Oh, mon Dieu. Seigneur. Doux Jésus. Il est prêt à tout pour me rencontrer. Humm. Je sens une agréable chaleur se répandre dans mon ventre – tout en bas – à la seule évocation de son visage. Pour cette figure-là, je pourrais parler du coche à Richard.

Mais allons, Beth. Il est intéressé par la formation, pas par ce que tu as dans la culotte. À moins que ça ne soit une brochure sur la communication non verbale, ou quelque chose du même style.

Je rougis. Mon Dieu, qu'est-ce qui me prend?

Le fait est qu'il a répondu à mon message quelques minutes seulement après l'avoir reçu. Ce qui signifie, soit qu'il n'a rien à faire de ses journées – et nous savons que ce n'est pas vrai, puisqu'il doit aller se faire blanchir les dents – ou qu'il était devant son ordinateur, à attendre mon mail avec impatience. Et, de toute évidence, il me demande si je suis célibataire. Pourquoi me poserait-il cette question s'il n'était intéressé par rien d'autre que par ma documentation?

Mais, à ce moment-là, je me mets à penser au message lui-même. Il a vu clair dans mon jeu sur les chaussures, ce qui me fait me sentir un peu bête. Manifestement, il m'a vue venir gros comme une maison, et avait probablement tout compris à la minute où il a lu mon premier mail, dans lequel je lui demandais s'il portait des souliers. Et depuis il n'a fait que jouer avec moi. Crotte!

Dans le feu de l'action, je riposte aussitôt par un autre message.

De: Beth Sheridan
À: Rupert de Witter
Objet: Re: Soulagement

Est-ce que vous vous moquez de moi?

Et avant que j'aie eu le temps de regretter mon geste, Ali crie qu'il y a un appel pour moi. Ooh là là… déjà?! Je ferme la messagerie et verrouille l'ordinateur afin que nul ne puisse espionner mes tableurs Excel, puis je pose la main sur le combiné.

C'est de toute évidence Rupert de Witter qui m'appelle, sans nul doute, pour parler de couchers de soleil rouge sang qui embrasent le ciel au-dessus d'une eau noire aux profondeurs insondables ; ou de formation. En attendant qu'Ali me le passe, je rejette mes cheveux en arrière sans y penser, mon pouls s'accélère, et j'arbore un tout petit sourire clandestin.

Quand ça sonne, je décroche, avec un coup d'œil en direction d'Ali, installé dans le coin.

— Je ne sais pas ce qui te fait sourire comme ça d'une oreille à l'autre, dit la voix d'Ali dans le téléphone. C'est Fatima.

Fatima était dans un état épouvantable. Elle tremblait, reniflait et hoquetait à tel point que j'avais du mal à la comprendre. Pour finir, un homme à l'intonation de professeur d'anglais a pris le combiné pour m'annoncer qu'elle avait été arrêtée lors d'une descente dans certains établissements très fréquentés de l'autre côté de la rocade et avait besoin qu'on vienne la chercher au poste de police.

— Quoi ? fut tout ce que je réussis à articuler dans un premier temps.

L'idée que Fatima s'était fait ramasser en ville, coiffée d'un gâteau d'anniversaire géant en feutrine, avec une palanquée de maquereaux, de dealers et de prostituées toxicomanes évoque pour moi l'image d'un enclos de velociraptors qu'on ouvrirait pour y pousser Tinky Winky. C'est l'heure de dire « au revoir », les Teletubbies…

— El…, fut ma deuxième tentative, parce que je voulais m'assurer d'avoir bien entendu.

— Qu…, fut ma question suivante.

Mais bien sûr, je connaissais déjà la réponse, donc je finis par bredouiller :

— J'arrive, avant de raccrocher.

Donc, nous sommes dans la voiture, en route vers l'appartement de Fatima. Elle est effondrée sur le siège passager, à renifler et à se frotter les yeux.

— Tu essayais de trouver des contrats ? dis-je, parce qu'elle vient juste de m'expliquer que c'était ce qu'elle faisait ce matin. (Elle opine du chef, épuisée.) Mais pourquoi dans cette partie de la ville ? Je croyais que tu y étais déjà allée et que tu avais vu que ces boutiques ne correspondaient pas à ce que nous recherchons.

— Ben, je n'avais pas pris la décision définitive de ne pas réessayer là-bas. Pas vraiment. Je veux dire, quelle que soit la boîte qui signe dans la case, ça nous va. Ce n'est pas notre problème, quel boulot ils font.

— Non, Fati, tu as raison, ça ne nous regarde pas. Sauf s'ils exercent une activité illégale. Cela les exclut plus ou moins complètement de notre programme.

— Ben, comment j'étais censée savoir que ce qu'ils faisaient est illégal ? Je suis de Taunton.

Elle a les yeux braqués droit devant elle, les bras croisés, comme si elle venait de me donner une explication crédible, qui exclurait toute sottise de sa part.

Puis elle ajoute :

— Je ne peux vraiment pas me permettre de perdre mon boulot, Beth.

— Non, je sais bien, Fati, mais tu ne peux pas passer tout ton temps à te faufiler dans les quartiers malfamés de la ville pour inciter les drogués, les prostituées et les psychopathes ultraviolents à s'inscrire à un stage « Traiter les Réclamations ». Je ne pense pas qu'ils se préoccupent beaucoup de l'après-vente quand ils viennent de te refourguer un sac plein de substances illicites. À mon avis, leur façon de régler les problèmes, c'est simplement de te planter un couteau entre les côtes.

Je m'aperçois que quand elle a prononcé la dernière phrase ses lèvres tremblaient tellement que sa voix chevrotait. Vous savez, quand on se rend compte d'un coup que quelque chose vient de se produire, quarante secondes après, et qu'il est déjà trop tard pour empêcher la situation d'empirer. Comme quand le Héros dit :

— Oh, ouais, je sais ce qui s'est passé, et ça ne me dérange pas du tout.

Alors, le Meilleur Ami répond :

— Ah, Mec, tu ne peux pas savoir à quel point je suis content de t'entendre dire ça. Je n'avais vraiment pas l'intention de coucher avec ta fiancée, surtout pas huit fois, mais c'est arrivé, et je suis vraiment soulagé que tu sois enfin au courant, parce que ça m'a pourri la vie ces derniers mois. Je suis toujours ton Meilleur Ami, et je sais que Sarah veut toujours se marier avec toi.

Puis il se rend compte, quarante secondes trop tard, que le Héros faisait en réalité allusion à la montre que son père lui avait léguée et qui vient d'être réduite en bouillie, mais au moment où il s'arrête de parler tout est fichu, et le Héros lui colle une beigne. Eh bien, je me suis sentie comme ça.

Sauf que, quand je regarde Fatima, c'est à moi que j'ai envie de coller un marron.

Je me gare et me tourne vers elle :

— Fatima, je suis désolée, je ne voulais pas dire ça. Bien sûr que non, tu ne vas pas recevoir de coup de poignard entre les côtes, c'était juste une plaisanterie. Mais qu'est-ce qui se passe ? Pourquoi est-ce que tu veux tellement décrocher un contrat au point de te jeter au milieu de dangereux psychopathes armés, drogués à l'héroïne ?

Elle lève les yeux vers moi et les frotte vigoureusement. Puis elle me répond :

— J'ai des dettes.

Ah, ah ! Bien sûr. C'est une histoire de sous. Je hausse les sourcils, attendant la suite. Je sais d'avance que ce seront des usuriers véreux qui menacent sa famille. Ou une société fantôme qui exige des fonds sous peine de saccager l'entreprise de son frère. Ou encore peut-être un amant secret qui a fait un coup et n'a pas remis tout le butin au commanditaire, qui maintenant demande le reste. Mais elle ne dit rien de plus. Je vais devoir lui tirer les vers du nez.

— Alors, c'est des sous que tu dois ? (Elle acquiesce.) Ils te réclament de l'argent qui ne leur appartient pas, ou bien c'est toi qui l'as emprunté ?

— Je l'ai emprunté, dit-elle d'une toute petite voix.

Bon, c'est déjà mieux que si elle l'avait subtilisé sur leurs extorsions de fonds.

— OK. Qui te l'a prêté ? Une petite annonce dans une cabine de téléphone ? Quelqu'un que tu as rencontré en boîte ? Le petit copain de la cousine du voisin d'un ami ?

— Non. (Elle renifle et me regarde dans les yeux.) La Barclays.

Je cligne des yeux :

— La Barclays ?

Elle hoche à nouveau la tête :

— Oui, le taux d'intérêt était vraiment compétitif.

— Tu veux dire, la banque Barclays ?

— C'est ça. Tout s'est bien passé jusqu'ici. Mais maintenant je m'inquiète.

Subitement, une image me traverse l'esprit : une fille aux longs cheveux blonds, souriant de ses dents blanches et bien alignées, vêtue d'un tailleur-pantalon turquoise et d'une cravate, se tient devant la porte de Fatima avec une batte de baseball. Je secoue légèrement la tête :

— Bon, OK. Alors, qu'est-ce qui t'inquiète ?

Elle détourne les yeux. À cet instant, je me souviens de l'amour de Fatima pour l'exagération, et l'envie de me coller une beigne me reprend. Pourquoi n'y ai-je pas pensé avant ? Elle a probablement emprunté 2 000 livres pour acheter une voiture, une télé, ou quelque chose comme ça, et maintenant elle panique.

— Si je perds mon travail, dit-elle doucement en s'adressant au lampadaire à côté duquel nous sommes garées, je ne vais pas pouvoir rembourser.

Là, elle n'a pas tort, mais est-ce que les banques n'ont pas une sorte de garantie qui couvre le chômage ?

— Tu n'as pas pris l'assurance ?

Elle fait « non » de la tête :

— Je ne pouvais pas, c'était trop cher.

Je la dévisage, bouche bée. C'est peut-être un peu plus que 2 000 livres.

—Fati, tu dois combien?

Elle se retourne et me saisit le bras:

—Beth, je ne peux pas me permettre de perdre mon boulot, vraiment pas. Que dirait ma mère? Déjà qu'elle pense que je suis idiote d'avoir emprunté 15 000 livres…

—Quinze mille livres!

Ça m'échappe avant que j'aie le temps de tourner ma langue dans ma bouche.

—Ben, ma Mini coûtait 9 500 livres, Beth. Je n'aurais pas pu acheter la télé plasma, les meubles de ma chambre et ma guitare électrique, si j'avais pris moins, pas vrai? Et je n'en ai plus que pour six ans.

Je déglutis plusieurs fois avant de demander:

—De combien sont les mensualités?

Je préférerais presque ne pas entendre la réponse au cas où elle m'abîmerait les tympans ou me foudroierait sur place. Je sens un tambour qui roule quelque part, en fond sonore. Ne pas réagir, ne pas réagir. Et le gagnant est…

—295 livres par mois.

—Deux cent…

Je bredouille, les sourcils levés, la main collée sur la bouche, les yeux écarquillés rivés sur la pauvre Fatima qui tremble sur le siège passager. Oups, j'ai oublié de ne pas réagir. Avec peine, je baisse la main et reprends une expression neutre:

—OK. Donc tu dois trouver ces 300 livres par mois.

—Non, Beth, quand même pas. C'est juste deux cent…

—Quatre-vingt-quinze, oui, je sais.

—Mais si je ne signe pas de contrat, Chas va me virer et je ne pourrai plus rembourser. Qu'est-ce que je vais faire? Je vais finir en prison pour dettes, j'en suis sûre.

—Fatima, personne ne... (J'hésite.) En prison pour dettes?

—Ma mère m'en a parlé.

—Ah, je vois. OK. Bon, écoute, je suis aussi certaine qu'on peut l'être que tu ne devrais pas te faire de souci à ce sujet.

—Mais maman dit...

—Non, je sais, mais je pense que tu ne dois pas suffisamment. Ce doit être plus de... euh, 16 000 livres pour... ça.

Son visage s'éclaire un peu:

—Tu crois vraiment...?

—De toute façon, tu n'as qu'à revendre la Mini et tu pourras rembourser la plus grosse partie, non?

—Ça fait un mois que j'essaie de la vendre, mais personne n'en veut. Je voudrais seulement récupérer le prix que j'ai payé, mais tous ceux qui viennent la voir ont l'air de penser que parce que je l'ai eue pendant cinq mois je devrais demander moins.

—Comment ils peuvent savoir combien tu l'as achetée? Ou que tu l'as depuis cinq mois?

Elle ouvre la bouche pour s'expliquer, mais je l'arrête d'un geste:

—Réflexion faite, ne réponds pas. Je crois que je peux deviner toute seule.

—Bref, dans tous les cas, et si je n'arrive pas à la vendre? Et que je perds mon boulot?

—Personne ne va perdre son boulot. Je te le promets.

—Ah, tu ne peux pas promettre ça. Tu n'en sais rien. C'est facile de faire des promesses, mais celle-ci tu ne peux pas la tenir, puisque ce n'est pas toi qui décides. C'est Chas. Et il me déteste.

—Mais non. (En fait, elle a raison, il la hait.) C'est un vieil emmerdeur bougon, il est odieux avec tout le monde, c'est tout.

—Non, Beth, il en a après moi. Je l'ai vu dans ses yeux. Il meurt d'envie de se débarrasser de moi.

—Bref, peu importe. Ça n'a aucune importance, qu'il te déteste ou non, parce que tu ne vas pas perdre ton poste. Je te le garantis.

—Mais comment peux-tu m'assurer ça ? Comment est-ce possible ?

J'hésite. Non, je ne vais pas parler à Fatima du projet avec Horizon. Non que je la soupçonne de vouloir me voler l'idée, mais parce qu'elle pourrait la révéler à tout le monde par inadvertance. Mais je peux quand même lui donner un peu d'information :

—Je te le promets, lui dis-je en lui mettant la main sur le bras, parce que j'ai déjà un énorme contrat, assez gros pour qu'on n'en ait pas besoin d'autres, et que ça va sauver la boîte, et notre job à tous.

Et je suis récompensée par la vision de la bouche de Fatima qui s'ouvre, et un couinement qui s'en échappe alors qu'elle se jette à mon cou et me serre très fort.

Chapitre 10

Désir de changement

Objectif à court terme : mais qu'est-ce qui m'a pris de dire ça, bordel de merde ? Je pourrais aussi bien grimper dans un arbre pour miauler à la lune, des brindilles plein les cheveux.
Obstacles : j'ai apparemment perdu la raison.
Objectif à long terme : me faire interner et passer mes journées à suçoter des couverts.
Obstacles : je ne peux pas me faire confiance. Me connaissant, je vais aller m'inscrire dans une pension pour chiens.

Ironie du sort, j'étais tellement occupée à réconforter Fatima que je ne me suis même pas demandé à quoi je ressemblerais aux yeux d'un observateur caché, et justement il y avait quelqu'un qui me regardait discrètement. Mais je n'ai pas remarqué. De toute évidence. C'est pour ça qu'il était caché.

Le temps de déposer Fatima chez elle et de me traîner jusqu'au bureau, il est 14 heures. Je meurs d'impatience de vérifier si Rupert a répondu à mon dernier message, mais c'est seulement parce que je suis désormais motivée à mort pour décrocher le contrat. OK, oui, d'accord, peut-être également en partie à cause de son charme et de son esprit. Et de son corps superbe. Mais pas de son yacht. Je me précipite dans la pièce aussi vite qu'il est possible en n'ayant plus de muscles, et je rouvre ma boîte mail, sans même essayer d'avoir l'air mystérieusement plongée dans mes pensées. Je veux dire, j'ai sans doute l'air mystérieusement plongée dans mes pensées, comme quelqu'un qui court vérifier sa messagerie, mais je ne m'en préoccupe même pas.

En plus de Rupert, du contrat et du visage de Fatima ruisselant de larmes, je pense au temps qui commence à me manquer. Je ne sais pas si vous vous en souvenez, mais j'ai une grosse journée, aujourd'hui. Je dois tout d'abord séduire Rupert – au sens professionnel, bien entendu – par mail, maintenant ; cet après-midi, j'infiltre Horizon Holidays ; et je finis par un rendez-vous de rêve avec Sean plus tard dans la soirée. Je m'accorde au maximum deux heures pour réussir cet échange de mails, afin d'arriver chez Horizon vers 16 h 30, à temps pour me faufiler discrètement et rencontrer quelques employés dans les escaliers alors qu'ils prennent le chemin de la maison.

Bien que, en y repensant, je ne sois plus aussi certaine de pouvoir me faufiler discrètement. Rupert a, de toute évidence, un esprit tellement futé et alerte qu'il devine mes moindres intentions. Il sera probablement en train de m'attendre dans le hall, avec du champagne, des ballons, et des bombes à confettis. Ou des chiens de garde.

Et je ne pense pas qu'on puisse considérer le fait de marcher à pas lents et raides en se tenant le bas du dos comme « se faufiler discrètement ».

Ma boîte de réception finit par s'ouvrir, et deux messages de Rupert me sautent aux yeux. Si j'en crois l'ordinateur, qui ne se trompe jamais, le premier est arrivé une minute après l'envoi de mon dernier mail dans lequel je lui demandais s'il se moquait de moi. Je clique, tout excitée, et me penche en avant.

De: Rupert de Witter
À: Beth Sheridan
Objet: Plates excuses

Ma chère Beth,
Je suis sincèrement désolé. Parfois, je suis un vrai guignol, et je n'ai même pas pensé que vous pourriez trouver mon dernier message blessant ou insultant. Je vous supplie de croire que je ne voulais pas vous offenser. C'était juste une lamentable tentative d'humour, je le crains, mais j'aurais dû comprendre depuis longtemps que je ferais mieux de laisser l'humour aux gens qui en ont. S'il vous plaît, répondez-moi et accordez-moi votre pardon.

Bien à vous et la tête basse,
Rupert.

La lecture de ces lignes semble allumer un petit feu sous ma chaise. Je me tortille un peu, puis m'appuie contre le dossier de mon siège quelques instants, pour m'éloigner de l'écran, comme si je risquais la combustion spontanée en restant trop près.

Mais je dois garder la tête froide et me souvenir que ce type est un homme d'affaires sans pitié qui serait sans doute prêt à dire n'importe quoi pour tourner la situation à son avantage.

Le message suivant a été envoyé trois minutes plus tard.

De: Rupert de Witter
À: Beth Sheridan
Objet: Au revoir à jamais

Beth,
Cela fait maintenant un temps considérable que je n'ai pas eu de vos nouvelles, et j'en déduis qu'il vous est impossible de me pardonner. Cette situation est pour moi intolérable, et je vais quitter cette terre de misères pour aller vivre au Népal. Je vous prie de garder un tendre souvenir de moi.

Votre ami,
Rupert.

Je pouffe à voix haute avant de mettre précipitamment la main sur ma bouche et de regarder si personne ne m'a entendue. On dirait que non.

OK. Il faut que je réfléchisse et que je trouve la façon et le moment opportuns pour répondre et donner au contrat la meilleure chance d'être…

Merde, je dois écrire une réponse, et maintenant.

De: Beth Sheridan
À: Rupert de Witter
Objet: Yétis

Très cher Rupert,
Vous allez me manquer. Pensez-vous avoir le temps d'observer les animaux? J'aimerais avoir une photo

de yéti si jamais vous en voyez un. Il paraît qu'ils pullulent dans cette région du monde.

Bien à vous comme toujours,
Beth.

Oooh… Je laisse mon curseur pendant une éternité sur le bouton «Envoyer» avant de me décider à cliquer. Si j'expédie ce message, je reconnais clairement que notre échange concerne désormais plus que la simple formation. Je veux dire, j'ai beau le tourner et le retourner, je ne vois pas comment il pourrait penser que mon allusion aux yétis est une tentative à peine voilée de l'amener à signer un contrat, comme l'histoire des chaussures.

Les yétis = les mythes ; Les faits = la formation ?

Nan. Il va savoir que j'ai décidé de changer de niveau avec lui.

Je clique. C'est envoyé. Les dés sont jetés.

Le reste de l'après-midi se traîne comme dans *Lost in Translation*. J'ai hâte que ça se termine, mais l'heure n'arrive jamais. Mon ordinateur bipe de temps à autre, mais ce sont le plus souvent des blagues de Vini ou des instructions de Chas. Chaque fois, je sursaute et me tourne avec impatience vers l'écran, les yeux écarquillés, tout le corps tendu ; puis je m'avachis à nouveau en lisant le nom de l'expéditeur. Il y a aussi un message de Sean, qui est parti pour l'après-midi conduire un atelier «Écrire un Rapport» dans la salle de séminaire d'un hôtel et qui doit utiliser leur wifi. Apparemment, il a hâte de me retrouver, mais j'ai beau savoir que je devrais être enthousiaste et faire de mon mieux pour être contente, je m'affale quand même sur ma chaise en voyant que ce n'est pas Rupert.

Je n'ai pas de nouvelles de lui de tout l'après-midi, et, à 16 h 45, je range mes affaires et me prépare à partir. Il est plus tard que ce que je voulais, parce que je suis sortie me promener pour faire passer le temps plus vite, mais j'ai marché beaucoup plus loin que prévu. Puis j'ai dû me mettre en mode Puissance Décuplée par la Panique pour revenir sur mes pas. Et maintenant, alors que je me gare non loin du rond-point d'Horizon, j'ai l'estomac noué et je me sens à la fois excitée et anxieuse. Je vois sans cesse le beau visage de Rupert qui me tient des propos comme « Je suis désolé, je t'en prie, pardonne-moi », et dans mes moments d'égarement « Tu es la personne la plus fabuleuse et la plus jolie que j'aie jamais rencontrée. Je ne survivrai pas si je ne t'embrasse pas tout de suite et si je ne passe pas le reste de ma vie avec toi », ou ce genre de choses.

Je me faufile par la porte tournante en verre et m'aperçois que le hall est désert. Ce qui me convient parfaitement, parce qu'il est impossible d'entrer sans être repéré par une porte tournante. Je pénètre plus avant, et ma première impression se trouve confirmée : le réceptionniste est absent. Quand je travaillais ici, c'était un type adorable du nom de Ron. Son absence me déconcerte. Se pourrait-il qu'il soit mort ?

Allons, allons, Beth, reprends-toi. Le fait qu'il ne soit pas là ne signifie pas automatiquement qu'il ait passé l'arme à gauche. S'il était décédé, ils n'auraient pas laissé le guichet vacant pour toujours, avec ses stylos, ses bonbons et son journal restés exactement comme il les a quittés en ce fatal dernier matin, comme s'il était juste allé aux toilettes. Un charmant hommage rendu à cet homme doux et serviable, mais ce serait complètement idiot.

À moins qu'il ne soit mort qu'aujourd'hui. Ils n'auraient pas encore eu le temps de le remplacer, n'est-ce pas ? J'essaie d'imaginer Rupert de Witter, horrifié, en compagnie des collègues de Ron désespérés, regardant les secouristes lui administrer un massage cardiaque frénétique, puis se penchant vers Carol de la comptabilité pour lui demander à voix basse de bien vouloir prendre le relais à la réception.

Non, non, Rupert de Witter n'est pas sans cœur à ce point, j'en suis certaine.

Je me glisse un peu plus près du comptoir, tel Bruce Willis dans l'un des *Die Hard*, redoutant ce que je vais trouver de l'autre côté. Est-ce que le corps froid et sans vie de Ron repose face contre terre dans une mare de sang, derrière le guichet, fauché là où il se tenait, défendant bravement l'entreprise qu'il avait appris à aimer ?

Non.

En fait, un rapide regard circulaire dans le hall montre qu'il n'y a de cadavre nulle part : ni sur le sol, ni sous la table, ni derrière l'énorme sapin de Noël qui clignote en silence près des ascenseurs, pas même debout, les yeux ouverts, dans l'armoire des fournitures de bureau, prêts à tomber dès que j'ouvrirai la porte. Je me dirige vers les ascenseurs ; tout ce calme me met les nerfs en pelote.

Les bureaux des dirigeants se trouvent aux septième et huitième étages, et je décide de descendre au sixième. Peut-être que je pourrai en attraper un dans la cage d'escalier. Je me souviens que certains de ces crétins descendaient les sept étages en courant à la fin de la journée, au lieu de prendre l'ascenseur, pour rétablir leur circulation après être restés assis sur leur chaise pendant huit heures à manger des croissants. Ça aurait peut-être été plus efficace de monter les sept étages en courant chaque matin, mais ça aurait pris beaucoup trop de temps. Sans compter que ça aurait été bien plus dur.

En débouchant d'un tournant après être sortie de l'ascenseur au sixième, j'ai des frissons et la chair de poule : il n'y a personne ici non plus. L'épaisse moquette étouffe le bruit de mes pas, mais je marche quand même sur la pointe des pieds. Je me dirige à pas furtifs vers le luxueux coin-cuisine que je n'ai vu qu'une fois, quand je me suis « perdue » et que je suis arrivée là « par erreur », et me colle contre le mur à côté de la porte. Par mesure de sûreté, je sors mon portable de mon sac, compose le 112 et laisse mon doigt sur le bouton d'appel, prête à appuyer au premier signe de présence d'un commando terroriste : « J'ai un téléphone je suis bien décidée à l'utiliser si vous faites un pas dans ma direction. » J'inspire un grand coup, hésite une seconde, puis me jette dans la cuisine.

Je vois tout de suite trois tasses sales et une assiette pleine de miettes à côté de l'évier, mais pas de sbires masqués cachés derrière le distributeur de boissons chaudes. Sur la touche d'appel, mon pouce est tellement crispé que je manque d'appuyer par erreur, alors je l'éloigne doucement, puis je fais passer mon téléphone dans l'autre main pour détendre mes muscles quelques secondes.

De retour dans le couloir, j'entends, ou plutôt je sens, les basses d'une sono poussée à fond, mais ça ne vient pas de cet étage. Je le ressens dans mes pieds, donc ça doit venir de quelque part en dessous.

Je retourne dans l'ascenseur et appuie sur le 5. Quand les portes s'ouvrent à nouveau, je rencontre la même atmosphère déserte, sinistre et silencieuse. La scène se reproduit au quatrième étage, mais ici les vibrations sont plus nettes. Je descends encore.

Cette fois, quand les portes de l'ascenseur s'ouvrent, j'entends une assourdissante cacophonie de musique à plein volume et de cris : c'est la fête. Une décoration de Noël un peu fatiguée pend au plafond en compagnie des vestiges d'une autre, dont il ne reste plus que les extrémités collées à la Patafix. Bien sûr ! Ce n'est pas une odieuse bande de terroristes sadiques devenus fous et cherchant la vengeance : c'est la fête de Noël. Soulagée, je reprends mon souffle, et j'efface le 112 de mon téléphone, verrouille le clavier et le range en sécurité dans mon sac.

C'est super ! Je peux me mêler discrètement à la foule, bavarder avec les gens au sujet de leur travail sans éveiller les soupçons. Ils penseront simplement que je suis l'une des dactylos ou des employées de l'ombre.

Je sors de l'ascenseur et tourne à droite, vers les salles de conférences. La première, qui ressemble plus à un auditorium en réalité, sert pour les grands événements de la vie de l'entreprise, et, bien entendu, c'est là que se déroule la fête. Je me glisse incognito dans la pièce et me dirige vers le bar.

En fait de comptoir, c'est une longue table de réunion, avec des quantités de bouteilles dessus et derrière, mais c'est bien suffisant. Une nappe blanche aurait atténué l'ambiance de foyer d'ouvriers, mais je devine que les employés ont préféré dépenser l'argent en alcool qu'en fanfreluches. Je me sers du vin blanc – il n'y a pas tellement de choix – et me retourne vers le reste de la pièce. À qui vais-je m'adresser en premier ?

Perchée sur un tabouret à ma droite se trouve une jeune femme en guêpière moulante et jupe de satin brillant, aux cheveux bruns et courts. Je lui souris en haussant les sourcils d'un air de dire : « Tu as envie de bavarder ? » mais elle secoue la tête pour signifier : « Tu veux ma photo ? » OK, pas elle, donc. À côté d'elle, une fille avec des bottes et une jupe noire trop serrée sue à grosses gouttes et fixe son gobelet en plastique d'un air angoissé. Elle semble tellement mal à l'aise qu'on n'a même pas envie de se tenir près d'elle.

Quelqu'un sur la piste de danse, alors. Je les observe tous de mon siège. Un type déboutonne sa chemise d'un air enjôleur, faisant glisser ses manches sur ses bras tandis que la femme devant laquelle il danse lance des regards nerveux à la ronde. Tout à coup, il rejette la tête en arrière et arrache son vêtement, révélant un ventre blanc et imberbe, qui commence à bedonner. Il fait tourner la liquette au-dessus de sa tête et la jette à travers la pièce à une horde imaginaire de fans hurlantes. Je parie que sa moitié ne va pas être contente…

Je ne suis pas sûre qu'un des danseurs soit en état de discuter des avantages et inconvénients de travailler pour Rupert de Witter. La fille en minijupe qui était assise à côté de moi est entraînée par un très jeune et très beau garçon, ce qui l'élimine. Ainsi que lui. Il ne reste plus à sa copine qu'à faire des efforts désespérés pour avoir l'air d'être très contente d'avoir été abandonnée toute seule au bar, parce qu'elle mourait d'impatience de pouvoir reprendre son souffle. Je me tourne vers elle pour engager la conversation, mais mes yeux se posent sur un visage à trois mètres derrière, et je me pétrifie.

C'est Rupert de Witter. Il est là, à la fête, assez près pour me voir, si jamais il se retourne. Je le reconnais tout de suite grâce à ses mèches platine et à sa barbe de trois jours soigneusement négligée. J'ai la gorge sèche, et tous mes organes semblent vouloir changer de place dans mon abdomen. Je ne peux détacher les yeux de ses larges épaules. Enfin, si, je peux, mais seulement pour regarder d'autres parties de sa personne. Il parle, avec de vigoureux hochements de tête, manifestement en grande conversation avec quelqu'un, donc je ne vais pas me présenter. Bon, de toute façon, ce n'est pas le moment, puisque je suis entrée sans y être invitée, et que j'ai volé un verre de liebfraumilch tiède. J'aurais du mal à lui demander un rendez-vous plus formel pendant que ses agents de sécurité me chasseront de l'immeuble :

— J'ai une possibilité, lundi à 10 heures ?

— Et qu'on ne vous revoie pas !

Je choisis donc de m'avachir un peu plus dans mon siège et de me détourner légèrement de lui, afin de pouvoir le dévorer des yeux sans en avoir l'air.

Je bois une goutte, et m'étouffe en essayant de réprimer la quinte de toux provoquée par la douceur écœurante du vin qui descend dans ma gorge. Je ne veux surtout pas attirer l'attention et les faire se tourner vers moi. La conversation semble toucher à sa fin, car Rupert tend la main à son interlocuteur, qui la retient dans les deux siennes. Hum. Il serait sans doute intéressant de bavarder avec ce type, quand Rupert sera parti. Je pivote à nouveau de façon à me trouver quasiment dos à dos avec eux, puis lance un regard discret par-dessus mon épaule alors qu'ils se séparent et que je peux enfin apercevoir le visage de l'autre homme. Et me voilà de nouveau pétrifiée.

C'est Brad.

Pas Brad Pitt. Pas un Brad imaginaire inventé en rêve. Je veux dire le vrai Brad en chair et en os que j'ai affronté en trois minutes à la soirée Fast Love, qui ne m'a pas recontactée, et dont j'attends l'appel ou le message avec langueur depuis des jours. Oh, enfin! Alors que je le dévisage, bouche bée, je sens qu'un changement s'annonce, et, cette fois, je suis certaine que c'est une bonne chose. Cette fois-ci, le changement est grand, beau, charmant et drôle, et ma bouche esquisse un sourire involontaire tandis que je me lève de mon tabouret pour aller lui parler.

Attendez une minute. Je me rassieds. Ce salaud n'est pas dans le plâtre de la tête aux pieds. Il n'a pas de béquilles, pas même le bras en écharpe. En fait, je ne vois pas le moindre petit pansement. Ce qui signifie clairement que s'il ne m'a pas appelée ces cinq derniers jours, c'est parce qu'il a choisi de ne pas le faire, et non parce qu'il ne pouvait appuyer sur les boutons à cause de ses doigts cassés.

Putain de merde, heureusement que je ne suis pas allée le voir, je me serais couverte de ridicule. Évidemment, je ne me serais pas jetée sur lui pour lui lécher la figure, mais j'aurais eu l'air heureuse de le rencontrer, et ça aurait été humiliant.

Je jette un nouveau regard, l'air détaché. Il sourit à présent à Rupert, et je sens une agréable agitation dans mon ventre. Il est tellement incroyablement sexy. En fait, à côté de Rupert avec ses mèches, son teint doré et ses dents phosphorescentes, Brad a l'air grand, massif et viril naturellement, sans l'aide d'aucun adjuvant chimique injecté dans une quelconque partie de son corps. Il représente le changement le plus séduisant que j'aie jamais vu.

OK. C'est ça. Je vais aller lui parler. Je veux dire, qui suis-je pour le juger, après tout ? Je crois que par pur esprit de justice je devrais donner à cet homme une occasion de se justifier, parce qu'il y a certainement une explication toute simple au fait qu'il ne m'ait pas contactée, et, avouons-le, ce serait idiot de ne pas le faire.

Mais que lui dire ? « Salut, Brad, tu te souviens de moi ? La fille que tu n'as jamais rappelée ? » Ça semble un peu pathétique. En fait, ça fait penser à Glenn Close, dans sa grande époque *Liaison fatale*. Ou même à Cruella. Dans un cas comme dans l'autre, il y a plus de chances que ça le pousse à fuir vers la sortie qu'à m'entraîner vers une chambre à coucher.

Bon Dieu, Beth, allons, reprends-toi. Il n'y a pas de chambres pour consommer une union, ici.

Il y a des salles de ré-union, cela dit.

Oh là là. OK. Je vais juste aller le trouver avec un petit sourire nonchalant et lui dire : « Eh bien, bonjour, c'est marrant de te voir ici. » Et alors il me répondra : « Ah, Libby, c'est vraiment super de te revoir, j'ai essayé de t'appeler, mais mon chien a mangé le fil du téléphone. » Non, non, il va m'expliquer : « Je suis désolé de ne pas t'avoir appelée, j'ai dû partir le lendemain pour une réunion urgente. À Pretoria. » Non, pas Pretoria. Je ne suis pas une spécialiste de la géographie, mais ils ont sans doute le téléphone, là-bas. Ce sera une réunion urgente à… merde, quel est l'endroit où il n'y a pas de réseau aujourd'hui ?

Ça ne fait rien, ça ne fait rien. Je vais aller lui parler. C'est une fête, on peut être détendus – et se contenter de bavarder et de flirter, et, quand tout aura été clarifié et expliqué, on peut fixer une date pour un prochain rendez-vous. Et ce qui est beau, c'est que je peux l'entretenir en toute authenticité de son boulot ici, de ce qu'il pense de Rupert, de la formation, et j'aurai juste l'air de m'intéresser à lui, ce qui est le cas, mais en même temps, je collecterai des données pour mon enquête et ma future proposition. On ne pourrait rêver mieux !

Non. Attendez.

Je me pétrifie encore une fois, une fesse déjà levée du tabouret. Si j'y vais maintenant, tout de suite après l'avoir vu discuter avec Rupert, et que j'engage la conversation sur son travail et tout, et que plus tard il s'aperçoit que je fais des recherches sur Horizon pour mon offre de formation, il va croire que tout ce que j'avais en tête en venant lui parler, c'était d'en apprendre davantage sur Rupert. Ça fera trois ou quatre mois que nous sommes ensemble, dans un bonheur sans nuages, et il commencera à songer à passer aux choses sérieuses, et tout à coup il découvrira que Love Learning est désormais l'unique prestataire de formation d'Horizon Holidays. « Quelle coïncidence », se dira-t-il, en tripotant un écrin de velours rouge qui renferme un magnifique solitaire monté en bague, « ma Libby travaille chez Love Learning. » Oh non, attendez, il va penser : « Ma Beth travaille chez Love Learning », parce que d'ici là nous aurons été complètement honnêtes l'un avec l'autre et je lui aurai révélé mon vrai nom. Bien qu'il puisse choisir de continuer à m'appeler Libby : ça deviendrait mon petit surnom d'amour.

De toute façon, on parlera vraisemblablement de LL, et de moi, comment il s'est trouvé que j'ai réussi à convaincre Rupert de Witter de changer, après des années à prendre les choses à l'envers. Et à ce moment-là, en train de m'attendre dans la salle à manger, alors qu'un superbe saumon rôtit dans le four, que le champagne est au frais dans le frigo, que la lumière des bougies scintille sur les verres de cristal et les couverts en or, il comprendra soudain que je me suis servie de lui. Il aura froid partout et il laissera tomber l'écrin de velours rouge, puis moi, dans cet ordre-là, juste là où il se trouve, et il attrapera sa veste et sortira de ma vie. Même si, techniquement parlant, je suis innocente. Mais je n'aurai pas l'occasion de le lui expliquer, parce que le lendemain il déménagera à Hong Kong.

Oh non ! C'est tellement typique de ma vie. Mon bonheur, si longtemps attendu, va m'être arraché comme ça, juste à cause d'un petit malentendu idiot. Je ne peux pas permettre que cela se produise. Je me rassieds convenablement sur mon tabouret et me détourne entièrement de lui. Il ne m'a vue que trois minutes, il ne pourrait pas me reconnaître de dos, n'est-ce pas ? Je me tasse sur moi-même, au cas où.

Une minute plus tard, je jette un rapide coup d'œil derrière moi et constate que Rupert et lui sont partis. Pffiou… Je crois que finalement je ne vais pas m'embêter à engager la conversation avec quiconque, maintenant, et que je vais juste m'en aller. L'espionnage, c'est carrément épuisant. Je regarde une dernière fois les couples qui dansent, se tenant par le cou, les hanches aussi serrées qu'une presse à fleurs, tourbillonnant sur *Lonely This Christmas*, et je suis frappée par l'idée que la fête de Noël n'est peut-être pas la meilleure occasion pour des entretiens de fond sur la satisfaction professionnelle.

Plus loin dans le couloir sombre, devant la porte de l'une des petites salles de réunion, Rupert de Witter fronce les sourcils. Il scrute le corridor obscur, plissant les yeux comme si cela pouvait l'aider à voir mieux. Il secoue la tête.

— Tu as dû l'imaginer, lui dit son associé.

— Je ne crois pas, Harris. Même si je peux me tromper. Après tout, je ne l'ai rencontrée qu'une fois.

— Qu'est-ce qui se passe ? demande un troisième homme, qui sort de la pièce.

Harris se tourne vers lui :

— Rupert pense avoir vu une mystérieuse inconnue.

— Ah bon ? Qui ça ?

— Eh bien, Hector, si je le savais, répond Rupert sèchement, ce ne serait pas une mystérieuse inconnue, qu'en dis-tu ? Ce serait, Carol, de la compta, ou Val, de la télévente.

— Qu'est-ce que tu entends exactement par « mystérieuse inconnue », alors ? Je veux dire, tu l'as déjà vue quelque part… Elle travaille ici ?

Rupert secoue la tête lentement, sans cesser de scruter l'obscurité :

— Je ne sais pas. C'est possible. J'ai l'impression de l'avoir déjà vue. C'est probable.

— Bon, alors… le mystère est résolu. Tu l'as déjà vue ici, mais tu ne lui as jamais parlé.

— Non, non. Je suis certain de l'avoir déjà rencontrée, mais pas ici. On a bavardé. Pas longtemps, je le reconnais, mais j'ai fait sa connaissance. (Il sourit.) Elle m'a vraiment plu. C'est juste qu'à l'époque je ne savais pas qu'elle travaillait pour moi. Si c'est le cas. (Il fronce les sourcils.) Mais si elle bosse ici comment ça se fait que je ne lui aie pas plus parlé, qu'on ne se soit pas croisés davantage ? Et si ce n'est pas le cas, qu'est-ce qu'elle fiche là ?

— Pourquoi tu ne lui poses pas la question ?

Rupert se tourne vers Hector et lui adresse un regard acéré :

— Je ne pense pas, non.

— Pourquoi pas ?

— Parce que. (Il se retourne vers la porte ouverte.) Allez, finissons ce que nous avons à faire.

— Ne sois pas idiot. Va lui parler.

— Non.

— Vas-y, intervient Harris en poussant doucement Rupert dans le dos. Ce n'est pas difficile. Tu dis juste : « Salut, moi c'est Rupert de Witter, je suis fabuleusement riche, charmant et absolument canon, puis-je vous offrir un verre ? » et là elle te répond : « Ah, bonjour Rupert, je suis la princesse héritière Incognita du Danemark, j'accepte avec plaisir. » Après ça, tu vas chercher une boisson, tu lui demandes si elle aimerait s'asseoir, tu prends place et tu engages la conversation. Facile.

Rupert réfléchit et se racle la gorge :

— OK. Attendez-moi une minute. (Il s'élance à sa rencontre, puis s'arrête.) Qu'est-ce que je fiche ? Elle est déjà partie.

Il fait demi-tour et revient vers les autres.

— Tu peux la rattraper, si tu te dépêches, le pousse Harris. Allez ! Tu vas lui plaire. Ou alors c'est qu'elle est bête.

— Peut-être. Mais elle avait l'air pressée de s'en aller. Elle rentre sans doute chez elle, ou bien elle va à une autre soirée. Je vais juste la mettre en retard.

Hector roule des yeux :

— Bon sang, Rupert, pourquoi tu n'essaies pas ? Au moins tu serais fixé. Je veux dire, qu'est-ce qui peut arriver ? Au pire, elle t'envoie balader. Point barre.

Rupert opine :

— Je sais, tu as raison. (Il se détourne, le regard rivé sur le couloir désert.) C'est juste que je n'ai pas envie de lui courir après dans le corridor pour l'attraper par le bras. Ça serait un peu extrême, non ?

— Alors, que vas-tu faire ?

Rupert secoue lentement la tête :

— J'sais pas, mon vieux. Elle me plaît vraiment, mais je n'ai aucun moyen de la contacter. Et je ne sais même pas si je lui plais aussi. Si j'en étais sûr, je serais en train de dévaler le couloir à l'heure qu'il est. Elle est tellement chouette, Hec. Enchanteresse, radieuse, et moi je suis juste…

— Rupert de Witter, millionnaire.

— Ouais, bon, ça ne veut rien dire, pas vrai ? On sait tous les deux par expérience que ça ne signifie pas que tu vas plaire à une femme. Ou, en tout cas, pas à celle à qui tu voudrais.

— Alors, à cause du risque de ne pas plaire à la fille qui t'a tapé dans l'œil, tu ne vas rien tenter ? Ce qui fait que tu es certain de finir tout seul, alors que, dans l'autre hypothèse, il y avait seulement une probabilité que tu finisses célibataire.

— Ouais.

— Sans blague ? Alors même qu'il y a plus de cinquante pour cent de chances qu'elle craque pour toi ?

— Oui. Quand on se reverra, je ne veux pas être essoufflé, paniqué, et vêtu d'une chemise que je porte depuis le matin. J'aimerais lui faire bonne impression.

— Tu es bête.

— Merci. Tu as raison. (Il se tait un instant.) Non, tu as tort. Complètement tort. Je viens juste d'avoir une idée pour la retrouver.

— De quoi tu parles ?

— Je ne te dis rien, mon vieux. Ça pourrait me porter malheur. C'est un plan. Pense à Clark Kent et tu devineras peut-être.

— Tu vas mettre un collant bleu et te balader avec ton slip par-dessus, en sauvant les gens des immeubles en feu et en empêchant les barrages de céder ?

— Non, ça, c'est Superman, idiot. Allons, vieux, reprends-toi !

Chapitre 11

Un panel de possibilités

Objectif à court terme : Waouh ! Richard, Sean et Rupert. Et peut-être Brad. Trois hommes et un point d'interrogation. Je dois faire de l'un d'eux une certitude.

Obstacles : je crois que je suis peut-être un tout petit peu cinglée.

Objectif à long terme : sans doute commencer à porter un entonnoir en aluminium sur la tête pour me protéger des rayons extraterrestres.

Obstacles : les entonnoirs, c'est vraiment ridicule.

— Bon Dieu, les hommes, c'est vraiment comme les bus, pas vrai ? remarque Vini le lendemain matin.

— Tu veux dire, aucun pendant une éternité, et ensuite trois d'un coup ?

— Non, je veux dire qu'ils sont toujours en retard, jamais fiables, couverts de pisse et qu'ils suivent perpétuellement la même voie.

Elle est dégoûtée parce que les frères Bogdanov sont arrivés bourrés à l'inauguration des lumières de Noël dans la zone piétonne. Igor tenait à peine debout, semble-t-il. Ce n'était pas un bon jour pour Fake Face.

Assise à la table de la cuisine, je couve Vini d'un regard suspicieux. Je suis sûre à presque soixante-quinze pour cent de l'avoir vue hier soir au *Perroquet du Pirate*, avec un homme. J'ai entraperçu des mèches roses en arrivant, et j'ai eu l'impression qu'elle se trouvait à côté de quelqu'un de très grand, puis ils ont disparu, et mon attention a été attirée ailleurs. J'attends qu'elle m'en parle, mais plus le temps passe, plus je suis certaine qu'elle n'en fera rien. Ce qui est contraire aux règles. J'ai mentionné mon rendez-vous avec Sean hier soir, en application de l'article 3 – je ne me souviens pas de la formule exacte, mais il s'agit de tenir l'autre au courant –, alors que, de son côté, elle enfreint clairement le règlement. Je ne suis pas contente.

Je ne lui ai pas raconté les événements d'hier après-midi. Je n'arrive pas à croire que j'aie pu penser que c'était une bonne idée de m'infiltrer chez Horizon. Ou que j'y parviendrais. J'ai dû finir par m'exfiltrer, parce que j'ai cru voir Brad sur le trottoir en sortant. J'ai aussi cru voir Elvis Presley bavarder avec E.T., donc j'ai pu me tromper. En rentrant à la maison, j'étais d'humeur à prendre un agréable dîner diététique – saumon poché, fleurettes de brocoli à la vapeur, salade verte, puis sorbet allégé au citron, le tout accompagné d'une eau minérale pétillante ; ou d'une demi-bouteille de pinot grigio et d'une boîte de chocolats au lait – suivi d'un bain avec des bougies parfumées, avant de me coucher tôt avec un Dan Brown. Mais, bien sûr, j'avais toujours mon rendez-vous de rêve au programme, donc j'ai dû me contenter d'une douche rapide, de vêtements propres et d'un bol de soupe de poulet. Et en route pour le *Perroquet du Pirate*.

Après avoir presque vu Vini, j'ai repéré Sean, qui, Dieu merci, était arrivé avant moi. Entrer seule dans un pub, c'est déjà affreux, mais devoir s'asseoir seule pour attendre quelqu'un équivaut à montrer ses seins à un car de supporters de foot avinés en criant : « À donner en échange de beaucoup de câlins ! »

De toute façon, je n'ai pas eu à le faire, puisqu'il était là. Il m'a offert un verre, et nous avons commencé à parler de films, je crois, mais je n'arrivais pas à oublier Rupert de Witter et Brad. Je veux dire, le fait qu'ils se connaissent est presque inexplicable. C'est comme si, je ne sais pas, il y avait un gigantesque plan dessiné par quelqu'un et que nous n'étions rien de plus que des pions, suivant à notre insu une voie que nous ne choisissons pas, parce que tout a été écrit il y a des millénaires. C'est complètement hallucinant ! Cela prouve sans l'ombre d'un doute l'existence de Dieu, et à partir de là toutes les religions du monde peuvent enfin se réunir et mettre fin aux conflits et à la misère, sans distinction de race ni de croyance.

Non, attendez. Cela vient probablement plutôt du fait qu'Horizon est l'un des principaux employeurs de la ville. Ce n'est pas vraiment surprenant que Brad y travaille, en fait. La plupart des habitants du coin y ont bossé à un moment ou à un autre.

De toute évidence, Brad occupe un poste haut placé, d'après la façon dont il parlait à Rupert de Witter. Ils avaient l'air de vraiment bien s'entendre, comme de vieux amis. À cet instant se forme dans ma tête une image de Rupert et de Brad en train de lutter, vêtus de chemises de bûcheron et de grosses bottes, sur un sol très sec, soulevant d'énormes nuages de poussière alors qu'ils roulent alentour en grognant et que je me tiens non loin, dans une magnifique robe jaune, me tordant les mains, morte d'inquiétude.

—Beth ? Hou hou !… Tu es là ?

C'est à ce moment-là que Sean s'est aperçu que je ne l'écoutais pas le moins du monde, ce qui était très gênant. J'ai dû inventer une excuse :

—Oh, je suis vraiment désolée, Sean, j'étais ailleurs. Je suis un peu préoccupée par cette histoire de contrats.

Il a hoché la tête :

—Oui, moi c'est pareil. Comment ça avance, de ton côté ?

—Pas aussi bien que je l'aurais voulu, en fait. Et toi ?

Et ce qu'il m'a dit alors m'a clouée au sol, complètement pétrifiée :

—Eh bien, il se trouve que j'ai eu une sorte d'illumination. J'ai pris conscience tout à coup que *Whytelys* ne nous a jamais demandé d'intervenir, depuis tout le temps qu'on existe, et qu'il est possible que leur formation ait besoin d'être dépoussiérée. Je les ai appelés, en me disant qu'il y avait une chance sur mille, j'ai un peu baratiné, et j'ai décroché un rendez-vous avec le directeur régional mardi après-midi.

—*Whytelys* ? Le directeur régional ? Mardi après-midi ?

Remarquez comme je suis allée droit au but en éliminant tous les détails sans importance.

—Ouais. Je suis plutôt fier de moi. Ça pourrait être suffisant pour sortir la boîte de l'ornière, pas vrai ?

Eh bien, c'était la fin de l'histoire : si Sean a eu du mal à capter mon attention avant, qu'est-ce que ça a été ensuite ! J'aurais aussi bien pu ne pas être là. D'ailleurs, dix minutes après, je n'y étais plus.

—J'ai passé un super moment, a-t-il conclu sur le parking en essayant d'opérer un rapprochement prudent.

—Oui, moi de même. À lundi.

Et j'ai filé.

Merde alors! *Whytelys*. Quelle idée de génie, bordel! Comment ai-je pu être assez bête pour ne pas y penser? Bon, parce que j'ai fait une vraie fixette sur Horizon et Rupert de Witter. Mais *Whytelys* serait incontestablement une meilleure idée. Bon Dieu, c'est une chaîne qui a des magasins dans tout le pays, qui suffirait à faire tourner Love Learning, quand bien même on perdrait tous nos autres clients. À côté, ma possible conquête d'Horizon ressemble à une deuxième place à la course en sac d'enfants de six ans, comparée à une médaille d'or olympique.

À peine arrivée au bureau le lundi matin, j'aperçois Sean qui vient à ma rencontre. J'ai tout juste le temps d'avoir l'air présentable. Je suis encore partagée au sujet de son affaire avec *Whytelys*, ce qui ne me donne pas une belle expression, et je ne sais pas comment me comporter. Devrais-je être enthousiaste et heureuse qu'il soit sur le point de résoudre à lui tout seul l'ensemble des problèmes d'argent de Love Learning, nous évitant ainsi à tous perte d'emploi ou baisse de salaire, et nous assurant bonheur et sécurité? Ou devrais-je être complètement vexée? Vous voyez ce que je veux dire. Je finis par opter pour une expression neutre, qui conviendra en toute circonstance sans me trahir aux yeux des observateurs.

—Tu as l'air chiffonnée, me dit-il en s'asseyant à la place de Fatima. Tout va bien?

—Oui, très bien. Non, je vais parfaitement bien. Pas du tout chiffonnée. Pourquoi ça? Non, je suis juste très contente que tu fasses ce truc avec *Whytelys*. Je veux dire, ça nous enlève à tous une épine du pied, pas vrai?

Il tressaille en entendant le nom de *Whytelys* et lance autour de lui un de ces coups d'œil furtifs vraiment appuyés qu'on voit tout le temps dans les mauvaises séries britanniques :

—Oui, j'imagine. Écoute, Beth, c'est justement ce dont je voulais qu'on discute. (Il rapproche la chaise de Fatima de la mienne et me regarde fixement.) C'est parce que j'ai confiance en toi que je t'ai parlé de… ce qui commence par W. (Il hausse les sourcils d'un air interrogateur pour s'assurer que j'ai compris, et j'opine, puisque c'est le cas.) Mais tu es la seule, OK ? Alors, s'il te plaît, ne le répète à personne. Je sais bien que c'est une bonne chose, quelle que soit la personne qui rapporte le contrat, mais je suis vraiment enthousiaste et j'aimerais vraiment faire le suivi moi-même. Tu vois ce que je veux dire ?

J'acquiesce à nouveau, plus vigoureusement :

—Oh oui, complètement. Je vois exactement ce que tu veux dire. Ne t'en fais pas, je serai muette comme une tombe. Promis.

Il se penche davantage vers moi :

—Je savais que je pouvais te faire confiance. Merci.

Il se lève, m'adresse un clin d'œil et un sourire, et retourne à son bureau.

Je sais ce que vous pensez. Pourquoi ne lui ai-je pas rendu la politesse hier soir en lui parlant du contrat avec Horizon ? Parce qu'il n'a aucune raison de s'intéresser à un petit voyagiste miteux installé sur un rond-point, maintenant qu'il a *Whytelys* dans son escarcelle. Non, en réalité, Horizon n'est ni miteux ni petit, mais il est vrai qu'il se trouve sur un rond-point et que c'est une seule société. Alors que *Whytelys* est présent dans tout le pays. Alors, pourquoi ne pas me confier à Sean ? Pourquoi ne pas lui faire confiance et lui témoigner le même respect dont il a fait preuve à mon égard ?

Parce que je ne lui fais pas confiance, vous vous souvenez ? Vous avez oublié son chien, sa fiancée, l'unique cheval ?

OK. Je me connecte à ma messagerie Hotmail pour voir s'il n'y a rien de Brad. Ça reste possible qu'il ait été malade la semaine dernière, coincé au lit, dans un délire fébrile, au bord de la mort, même, et qu'il n'ait pas pu se lever et sortir avant vendredi. Et maintenant il est au travail et il peut enfin taper le mail qu'il a écrit et réécrit dans sa tête depuis le premier instant où…

Non. Il n'a rien envoyé. Mais, dans ma boîte professionnelle, il y a un message du magnifique Rupert, qui me met le ventre en émoi alors que je me penche pour le lire.

De : Rupert de Witter
À : Beth Sheridan
Objet : OK, pas à jamais.

Très chère Beth,
Eh bien, me voilà de retour du Népal après un voyage catastrophique. Je ne me doutais pas que la colonie de yétis serait aussi importante. Pourquoi ne m'avez-vous pas mis en garde ? Une nuit, une famille complète a attaqué notre camp et s'est enfuie avec tous nos flacons de shampoing et d'après-shampoing, nous contraignant à précipiter notre retour.
Malheureusement, je n'ai pas pu les prendre en photo, parce que mes camarades m'ont interdit d'utiliser mon appareil après la perte de notre

après-shampoing. Mais je vous ai quand même rapporté un cadeau, cela dit. C'est un moulage en plâtre d'une empreinte de pied. Les petites échoppes touristiques qui fleurissent partout dans l'Himalaya les vendent treize à la douzaine, de même que des cendriers artisanaux en terre cuite en forme de pied, des pierres précieuses locales taillées en d'amusantes formes de pied, et des ceintures en cuir assez jolies. J'espère que vous me pardonnerez.

Votre ami,
Rupert.

Qu'est-ce qu'il est drôle ! Je lis le message une deuxième fois, puis une troisième, souriant d'une oreille à l'autre pendant toute la lecture. Bon, ce n'est pas exactement un sourire d'une oreille à l'autre : c'est l'expression inconsciente de l'amusement que je ressens, mais un peu atténuée pour que je n'aie pas l'air d'une folle. On ne sait jamais qui vous observe. Je jette un rapide coup d'œil autour de moi : personne, mais on ne sait jamais quand quelqu'un va s'y mettre.

Mais regardez-moi ce mail ! Rupert de Witter est tout simplement en train de flirter avec moi. C'est tellement évident, avec ce ton pince-sans-rire au sujet des yétis qui s'enfuient avec l'après-shampoing ! Je réprime mon hilarité en posant une main sur ma bouche.

Il me drague, n'est-ce pas ? Hein, c'est vrai ? Je veux dire, pour autant qu'il le sache, je pourrais aussi bien avoir soixante-huit ans, être grand-mère de quatre petits-enfants, avoir les cheveux bleutés et les jambes bandées, alors il se montre peut-être seulement amical.

Mais s'il pensait vraiment que j'ai les jambes bandées m'écrirait-il sur ce ton ? N'essaierait-il pas au contraire de donner à notre échange une tournure professionnelle et raisonnable ?

Une pensée vient de me traverser l'esprit. Et s'il s'était souvenu de mon nom, à cause de mon passage dans son entreprise ? Cela aurait deux conséquences géniales et merveilleuses : la première, c'est qu'il sait que je n'ai pas soixante-huit ans, que je ne suis pas grand-mère et que je n'ai pas d'œdème, et donc qu'il est bien en train de me draguer ; la deuxième, s'il garde un souvenir d'il y a six ans, ça veut dire que je l'ai marqué, bien que je ne l'aie jamais rencontré !

Non, non, attendez. Si je ne l'ai jamais rencontré, comment pourrait-il savoir que je n'ai ni soixante-huit ans, ni des œdèmes ?

Pfff, à cause de la conversation qu'il a eue avec l'un de ses assistants quand Richard a claqué la porte, et que je l'ai suivi discrètement, pour monter Love Learning :

— Beth Sheridan est partie aussi ? a demandé Rupert, un peu surpris. C'est qui ?

— L'assistante de Richard, lui a-t-on sans doute répondu. Elle n'a que vingt-deux ans, ou quelque chose comme ça, elle est folle amoureuse de lui. Elle le suit partout.

— Vraiment ? Elle semble incroyablement sexy et intéressante, il faut que je retienne son nom, comme ça je pourrai un jour l'épouser.

OK, cette dernière réplique est un peu ridicule, mais c'est certainement possible qu'on lui ait donné mon nom à cette époque et qu'il s'en souvienne à présent. Oh, mon Dieu, donc il connaît mon âge !

Eh bien, il n'y a qu'une façon de le savoir. Je souris béatement en cliquant sur « Répondre ».

De : Beth Sheridan
À : Rupert de Witter
Objet : Bon retour parmi nous !

Mon cher Rupert,

Je m'arrête. Est-ce trop direct ? Je retire brusquement mes mains du clavier et les pose aussitôt sur mes genoux, comme si elles risquaient d'agir sans ma permission et de me mettre dans l'embarras. Je relis ces trois mots, une fois, puis deux, puis je parcours toute notre correspondance, dans l'ordre, avant de terminer à nouveau par ce morceau de phrase. Non, ça passe. Il a signé « Votre ami », et commencé par « Très chère Beth », donc « Mon cher Rupert » est sans doute exactement dans le ton.

Mon cher Rupert,

Mais que peut-il bien vouloir dire quand il me demande de le pardonner ? Est-ce qu'il parle toujours du message dans lequel je croyais qu'il se moquait de moi ? Ou s'agit-il d'une facétie sur le fait qu'il n'ait pas pu prendre de yétis en photo ? Alors, dois-je poursuivre la blague en lui disant que ça ne fait rien ? Ou faut-il répliquer avec sérieux en lui disant que je le pardonne, que ce n'est pas grave, que j'avais compris dès le départ que c'était une plaisanterie, blablabla ?

Je vais reprendre la boutade. Il peut déduire du fait que je lui réponde que je l'ai excusé.

Mon cher Rupert,

Mais de quoi je parle ? *Allons, Beth, ressaisis-toi.* Je suis en contact avec Rupert de Witter pour une seule et bonne raison : lui faire signer un contrat. Je dois absolument rester concentrée là-dessus. Pour me motiver, je jette un coup d'œil à Fatima qui vient d'arriver. Aujourd'hui, elle porte un tee-shirt qui proclame en grosses lettres roses :

Gagnante du Maillon faible

Je cligne des yeux et relis. C'est sans doute un parent cruel qui le lui a donné pour rire à ses dépens. Certainement un cousin. C'est là que je repère une phrase écrite en tout petit, en-dessous :

Sonnez en face.

— Ah ! dis-je d'une voix forte.

Fatima se tourne vers moi :

— Ça va, Beth ? demande-t-elle, vraiment inquiète. (Elle remarque alors que je souris et en fait de même.) Quoi ?

— Je viens juste de voir ton tee-shirt. Il est extra.

Tout heureuse, elle esquisse un sourire et regarde vers le bas, comme pour se rappeler ce qu'elle porte :

— Merci. J'ai craqué dès que je l'ai vu et j'ai pensé qu'il m'irait vraiment bien, tu sais, parce qu'il n'y a pas moyen que quelqu'un croie que j'ai gagné au *Maillon faible*, pas vrai ?

Mike est assis avec elle, occupé à regarder des formulaires posés sur son bureau, et, en l'entendant dire ça, il lève le nez de ses documents et secoue doucement la tête :

— Tu as des tas de qualités merveilleuses, tu sais, réplique-t-il, d'un ton qui me semble paternaliste.

Mais Fatima rougit un peu et se tourne vers lui :

— Tu le penses vraiment ?

— Qui veut faire une pause-thé ? dis-je précipitamment, afin d'empêcher Fatima de se couvrir de ridicule. Je vais en préparer. Allez, vous avez vraiment travaillé dur.

— Pendant quarante minutes ! pouffe Fatima.

— Oui, mais…, dis-je d'une voix hésitante.

C'est un peu délicat de justifier une coupure après seulement quarante minutes, mais j'ai vraiment envie de parler à Fatima pour me remémorer ce que je cherche à obtenir de Rupert de Witter. En dehors de… bref, je n'en dis pas plus. Mais j'ai vraiment l'impression de m'être un peu écartée du sujet. Commencer par des contrats de formation pour terminer par des yétis, on peut difficilement dériver davantage.

— Allez, prenons un chocolat chaud. Il pleut, c'est l'hiver, qu'est-ce qu'il faut de plus pour vous convaincre ?

J'ai beaucoup de mal à éteindre mon ordinateur et à m'en éloigner, en sachant qu'à l'autre bout de la ligne Rupert espère que je réponde. Je me sens comme Ralph Fiennes dans *Le Patient anglais,* quand il laisse Kristin Scott Thomas l'attendre au fond d'une grotte dans le désert. Bon, OK, Rupert ne va pas mourir paralysé de souffrance, gribouillant ses dernières pensées désespérées avec son sang sur un morceau de papier avant de périr lentement de déshydratation et de froid, et se faire dévorer par les rats en m'attendant. Mais il se peut qu'il s'ennuie un peu.

— Alors, comment ça se passe pour vous, la chasse aux contrats ? dis-je à Fati et à Mike en leur tendant les tasses fumantes. Il y a huit chaises dans la cuisine, disposées en U, toutes libres, et Mike a choisi de s'asseoir juste à côté de Fatima. Leurs coudes se touchent presque : ça n'a pas l'air confortable.

— Oh, affreux, répond Fati du tac au tac. Je n'arrive à rien. Je ne sais pas ce que je vais faire, si je ne trouve pas quelque chose.

Mike se tourne vers elle avec un sourire :

— Ne t'en fais pas pour ça, dit-il d'un ton horriblement condescendant. (Je sens ma lèvre supérieure se retrousser de dégoût, mais je parviens à lui rendre sa position initiale.) Ça va marcher, j'en mettrais ma main à couper.

Elle se retourne à nouveau vers lui et baisse le menton, très Lady Diana, en le regardant. Le grand numéro de la fausse timide qui essaie d'avoir l'air de le draguer.

Non, je me trompe. Elle le drague franchement :

— C'est tellement adorable, Mike, dit-elle.

Je la dévisage en clignant des yeux. Pardon, mais qu'est-ce qui est adorable, exactement ? Elle le remercie de lui dire de ne pas s'en faire ? Super ! Ça ne serait pas mieux de lui venir réellement en aide, espèce de connard prétentieux ?

— Et je te remercie vraiment pour ton aide.

Ah. OK.

— Ça me fait plaisir, Fatima, tu le sais bien. On y arrivera, n'aie pas peur.

— Oh oui, j'espère. C'est juste que je m'inquiète à cause de Chas, tu sais ? Tu vois, parfois je me dis que même si je parviens à dégotter un énorme contrat qui rapporte plein d'argent, il me sacquera malgré tout parce qu'il me hait.

—Il ne te hait…, dis-je.

Mais au même moment Mike déclare :

—C'est son problème.

Je me tourne vers lui, les yeux écarquillés :

—Mike ! Tu ne vas pas être d'accord avec elle, quand même ?

J'arrondis encore plus les yeux et les roule un peu, pour dire : « Ne la conforte pas dans sa crainte que le patron la déteste, ou bien elle perdra confiance en elle au point d'être incapable de réfléchir. Et alors elle risque de faire quelque chose de complètement idiot, comme de frayer avec d'effroyables repris de justice, dans une tentative désespérée de sauver son job. » Mais il n'a pas l'air de comprendre. Il ne me reste qu'à m'exprimer un peu plus ouvertement :

—Enfin, tu ne vas pas lui donner raison quand elle affirme que Chas la déteste, n'est-ce pas ? Ce serait ridi…

—Bien sûr, qu'elle a raison ! rétorque-t-il, sûr de lui. Ça saute aux yeux de tous ceux qui travaillent ici, et le nier reviendrait à prendre Fatima de haut.

Moi, je la prends de haut ? Quel hypocrite ! Et maintenant c'est moi qu'il prend de haut ! Bordel de merde, il vient de toute évidence de s'autoproclamer Roi de la Prise de Haut et s'est donné comme but sacré de parcourir le pays d'un bout à l'autre en prenant de haut et en traitant avec condescendance tous ceux qu'il croisera sur son chemin.

—Ce n'est pas grave, Beth, me dit Fatima avec un sourire tremblotant. J'ai toujours su qu'il me détestait. Et si Mike est d'accord, alors c'est que j'ai raison.

Je tente de protester, sans trop y croire :

—Mais Fati…

Elle secoue la tête :

—Pas la peine d'essayer de me remonter le moral. Ça va. Je voudrais juste le pousser à bien m'aimer. En fait, ajoute-t-elle d'un ton enjoué qui m'inquiète, j'ai une idée. Si je lui fabriquais un chapeau rigolo ? Tu penses qu'il… Pourquoi tu me regardes comme ça ? Qu'est-ce que j'ai dit ?

Oh non… Comment lui expliquer ?

—Non, pas de chapeau, Fati, dis-je, en espérant qu'elle ne me demande pas…

—Pourquoi pas ?

—Eh bien, euh…

—Parce que tu ne devrais pas gaspiller une seule seconde de ta vie pour quelqu'un qui t'apprécie pas à ta juste valeur, décrète Mike.

Je me tourne pour le regarder. Il est plutôt doué : Fatima n'a même pas l'air gênée.

—OK, bon, dans ce cas, je vais juste m'en remettre au réchauffement climatique, soupire-t-elle, sibylline.

—Hein ?

Elle me sourit :

—Le réchauffement climatique. Tu en as entendu parler ? Tout d'un coup, tous les habitants de la planète commencent à prendre conscience que les autres ne sont pas aussi nuls qu'ils le croyaient, et, assez vite, tout le monde est copain. S'il est touché par ce phénomène, il va se mettre à aimer tout le monde, n'est-ce pas ? Même moi. Je n'ai plus qu'à espérer que ça se produise.

Je la dévisage, mais elle se contente de siroter son chocolat chaud en poussant des petits soupirs de satisfaction.

— Fati, c'est ta mère qui t'a parlé du réchauffement ?

Elle acquiesce :

— Ouais. Pourquoi ?

— Comme ça.

Bon. Me voilà revenue à mon bureau, après cette pause pour le moins surréaliste. Je garde les yeux rivés sur mon écran vide pendant quelque temps, histoire de remettre de l'ordre dans mes idées.

OK. Fatima. Fatima est très endettée, et elle est prête à tout pour rembourser, donc je dois décrocher ce contrat pour la sauver. Je sais que Sean a de bonnes chances de signer avec *Whytelys*, mais aujourd'hui Horizon apparaît comme la meilleure piste, donc je dois me concentrer là-dessus. Je reporte mon attention sur les trois derniers mots que j'ai écrits sur mon écran :

Mon cher Rupert,

Et soudain je me rends compte que tous ces mails absurdes avec Rupert ne sont rien d'autre que cela : des absurdités. Il est sans aucun doute l'homme le plus sexy et le plus merveilleux que j'aie jamais (presque) rencontré, et, en toute honnêteté, je ne pensais pas seulement au contrat lors de cet échange de messages. Au fond, j'espérais un peu avoir l'occasion de boire de la liqueur de whisky directement dans son nombril.

Mais ce n'est qu'un fantasme. Un rêve irréalisable que je dois chasser de mon esprit afin de ramener la conversation sur l'offre de service.

Oh, mais…

Non. J'ouvre les yeux, surprise de m'apercevoir que je les avais fermés. *Allons, Beth.* Je dois écrire un mail raisonnable au sujet de Love Learning, et laisser les yétis en dehors de tout ça. Je peux, sans être désagréable, me référer à nos précédents messages à propos des chaussures qui doivent être bien ajustées et essayer d'arranger une entrevue.

Mon cher Rupert,

Mais alors, si je veux paraître sérieuse et tenter de fixer un rendez-vous, je dois m'adresser à lui de façon professionnelle. Je ne peux pas lui donner du « mon cher Rupert », puis lui demander de consulter son planning pour la semaine prochaine. Je vais bientôt devoir le rencontrer dans son bureau et lui serrer la main, et ce sera un peu embarrassant si je l'appelle « mon cher Rupert ».

Oh, mon Dieu, entrer dans son bureau et lui serrer la main ! Cette pensée transforme mes entrailles en *jelly*. Que quelqu'un aurait arrosée de whisky, puis flambée.

Alors, que faut-il faire ? Mon objectif, mon unique objectif à présent, c'est le contrat, mais c'est un peu difficile de ramener à nouveau la conversation aux chaussures. Comment faire pour ne pas le vexer, ni lui donner à penser que je ne suis qu'une froide professionnelle ?

Mais j'ai besoin qu'il considère que je suis professionnelle, et que j'ai la tête froide, n'est-ce pas ? Je veux qu'il signe dans la case, donc je dois l'impressionner par mon professionnalisme. Bon. Alors qu'est-ce qui m'a pris de faire l'idiote avec des histoires de yétis ? Jouer les évaporées, c'est bien mignon, mais ça ne suffit pas à convaincre les hommes d'affaires aguerris de valider des contrats.

Cher M. de Witter,

Non, trop froid. Je le vois d'ici, ouvrant le message et clignant des yeux, effaré. Il va s'écarter de l'écran d'un bond, comme s'il venait de recevoir une gifle. Puis il lira la suite, dans laquelle je radoterai sur la politique de formation et sur ce que Love Learning peut offrir, et sur le moment où il serait disponible pour un premier rendez-vous afin de passer en revue les différentes possibilités. Il secouera la tête, poussera un soupir, et s'exclamera à haute voix : « Alors, c'est de ça qu'il s'agissait depuis le départ ? » Non, il ne va pas dire ça, puisqu'il sait bien que je ne l'ai contacté que pour conclure un accord. Il l'avait deviné dès le début. Ce qu'il laissera échapper à voix haute sera plutôt quelque chose comme : « Et dire que j'ai cru que nous étions amis… » Non, il ne dira pas ça, parce que nous ne sommes pas amis. Il va soupirer et fermer les yeux, en s'appuyant sur le dossier de sa chaise, et il va s'écrier : « Quelle salope ! » Oui, c'est ça.

Ce qui ne me laisse pas d'autre solution que de poursuivre la plaisanterie. C'est vrai. J'ai les mains liées. J'ai envisagé sérieusement d'y mettre fin, mais il est parfaitement clair pour moi que si je le faisais je mettrais en péril tout espoir d'obtenir sa signature. Et s'il y a une chose dont je suis certaine, c'est que de continuer la blague ne peut pas nuire à mes chances avec lui. À mes chances de signer un contrat, je veux dire.

Mon cher Rupert,

J'étais ravie de recevoir votre message, même si j'ai bien entendu été horrifiée par la nouvelle de votre terrible rencontre avec les yétis. Ça a dû être affreux. Je suis sûre que vous trouvez un peu de réconfort dans l'idée qu'au moins ils seront présentables pour leur prochaine soirée.

Ce que vous me dites sur ces babioles en forme de pieds vendues dans les boutiques de souvenirs de l'Himalaya est très intéressant. Avez-vous eu l'occasion de découvrir quelle était la pointure des yétis? Je me demande si leurs chaussures sont à la bonne taille, car, comme nous le savons tous, des chaussures mal adaptées mettent tout le monde de mauvaise humeur, ce qui expliquerait leur mauvaise conduite.

Votre amie,
Beth.

Quel trait de génie! Je me félicite intérieurement: m'être débrouillée pour ramener la conversation sur les pieds et les chaussures me permettra de trouver une ouverture parfaite.

Attendez, je reçois un nouveau message. Waouh, c'était rapide!

De: Rupert de Witter
À: Beth Sheridan
Objet: Enfin!

Coucou Beth, c'est moi, Rupert. Vous êtes là?

Chapitre 12

Problèmes particuliers

Objectif à court terme : Il faut que je garde la tête froide. Ce n'est qu'un être humain, comme moi. Avec environ un million de fois plus de sex-appeal et de pièces de 1 livre, que les autres personnes que je connais.

Obstacles : c'est un beau millionnaire ! Oh, comment, mais comment, vais-je faire pour garder la tête froide ?

Objectif à long terme : retrouver la parole et m'installer dans une maison de retraite pour collectionner des pots de yaourt.

Obstacles : il faut d'abord que je décroche ce contrat avec Horizon.

Je suis pétrifiée dans mon fauteuil, les yeux rivés sur ce dernier message. Soudain, il ne s'agit plus seulement d'écrire un mail et de le laisser quelque part où il le trouvera. Ça se passe maintenant, tout de suite, c'est une vraie conversation. Je le vois tellement clairement dans ma tête, son visage, ses cheveux, et le reste de son corps, posté devant son écran attendant ma réponse. Je dois avoir le regard vitreux. Humm, il a dû renverser du café sur sa chemise, parce qu'en ce moment il est assis là, torse nu. Sa poitrine et ses bras sont fermes et bronzés, doux et galbés. J'ai du mal à en détacher les yeux. Il arbore un sourire plein d'expectative, mais on devine une pointe d'anxiété, alors qu'il attend mon message, qui s'affiche brusquement sur son écran avec un petit bip.

Oui, je suis là.

Comment diable ce mail est-il arrivé là ? Je jure devant Dieu que je n'ai rien écrit.

Mon ordinateur émet un nouveau son, et j'ai la main qui tremble un peu en ouvrant le message. Pas seulement la main, soit dit en passant.

Eh bien, coucou! C'est vraiment super de se parler pour de vrai, au lieu de simplement se laisser des petits mots. Plutôt absurdes, d'ailleurs, devrais-je dire. Comment en est-on arrivés à évoquer les yétis? J'ai failli m'étrangler avec mon bagel en lisant ça!

Oublie qu'il est millionnaire, concentre-toi sur le sexe. Oh non, ce n'est pas une bonne idée. *Oublie le sexe, concentre-toi sur les millions.* Non, ça ne va toujours pas, je ne parviens pas à oublier le sexe. J'ai pris une brochure d'Horizon quand j'y étais vendredi, et je l'ai ouverte à la dernière page, où se trouve la photo de Rupert. En vérité, elle est ouverte à cette page-là depuis que je l'ai. J'ai toujours pensé qu'il était beau à en mourir sur cette photo, mais maintenant, en la regardant, je vois aussi qu'il est gentil, attentionné, sensible.

OK, en avant. Je dois répondre. Garder son intérêt en éveil.

Les bagels sont bien connus pour ça. C'est terriblement sec. Savez-vous qu'on déplore quatre morts par ingestion de bagel chaque année dans le monde ? Si seulement les gens s'en tenaient aux croissants, ça sauverait des vies.

Quarante-six secondes plus tard, je reçois un nouveau message.

Je suis abasourdi, et ferai certainement plus attention à l'avenir. Merci de m'avoir prévenu.
Pour parler d'autre chose (sans rapport avec les bagels), j'aimerais vraiment m'entretenir avec vous de vive voix. À quel numéro puis-je vous joindre ?

Oh, mon Dieu. Il veut m'appeler. Mais je ne peux pas ! Ça va être un désastre ! Son sex-appeal et ses millions vont me distraire, et je serai aussi drôle et futée qu'un cul de babouin. Qui, comme vous le savez, est rigolo, mais dans le mauvais sens du terme. C'est-à-dire marrant comme d'avoir la jupe remontée dans la culotte, une moustache de chocolat, ou la fourrure du derrière brûlée. Je vais me transformer en drôlesse hystérique et bavarde comme une pie. Il se peut que je me mette carrément à baver.

Le truc, avec les échanges de mails, c'est qu'on a le temps de réfléchir avant de répondre. Ensuite, on peut se relire plusieurs fois, corriger un mot ici, en remplacer un là, jusqu'à être certaine de présenter au monde la version la plus exacte, la plus « vraie », de vous-même : celle qui est d'une éloquence infaillible, drôle, futée, et – ce n'est pas le moins important – incroyablement sexy. Je suis sûre que si les hommes politiques et les rock-stars droguées jusqu'aux yeux ne s'exprimaient que par mail ou par texto, les tabloïds feraient faillite. Imaginez comme l'histoire aurait été différente si Bill Clinton avait tapé « je n ai pas eu de reltns sxl ac cette femme » du bout du pouce sur son téléphone portable, puis s'était relu, s'était dit : « Oh non, attendez une minute, qu'est-ce que je raconte ? » et avait effacé les négations avant de l'envoyer. Humm. Ou pas.

Bref, c'est la panique. Intérieurement, je suis blême, je me ronge les ongles, je fronce les sourcils, je jette des regards anxieux autour de moi, et je me balance dans mon fauteuil. Mais ne vous en faites pas : en réalité, je ne fais rien de tout ça. Extérieurement, je suis calme et maîtresse de moi, avec juste l'ombre d'un petit sourire, l'image même de la sérénité ; alors qu'en secret je remue frénétiquement chaque compartiment de mon cerveau à la recherche : a) d'une bonne excuse pour ne pas lui donner mon numéro ; ou b) d'une bonne excuse pour faire des pauses de cinq minutes dans une conversation téléphonique. En ce qui concerne le a), je n'en vois aucune. Les coordonnées de Love Learning sont dans les Pages Jaunes, donc s'il voulait vraiment me parler, il pourrait les trouver facilement. Hum. Je me demande pourquoi il ne le fait pas. Je veux dire, je ne sais absolument rien de lui, à part qu'il adore, ou déteste, les anchois. Peut-être qu'il voudrait mon numéro personnel pour pouvoir me pister jusque chez moi et traîner devant mon appartement avec des jumelles et un hachoir à viande.

Non, non, c'est ridicule, c'est de toute évidence mon téléphone professionnel qu'il me demande, c'est pour ça qu'il a écrit « À quel numéro puis-je vous joindre ? », et non « Quel est votre numéro de téléphone à la maison, votre adresse, votre code postal, et vous arrive-t-il de vous habiller près de la fenêtre ? »

J'ai du mal à me le représenter, pas vous ? Je veux dire, Rupert de Witter, millionnaire sexy (respirer à fond, faire le petit chien, et ça ira), traînant dans les buissons devant chez quelqu'un ? Maintenant que j'y pense, si ça me met dans une telle panique d'imaginer Rupert en possession du numéro de Love Learning, je ferais mieux de m'inquiéter de tous les psychopathes boutonneux et de tous les pervers sexuels qui peuvent également se le procurer. Bien que j'aie du mal à concevoir des tas de monstres violents et assoiffés de sang, vautrés sur leurs bureaux, plongés dans des recherches Google frénétiques sur les prestataires de formation et les agences de développement personnel. Fermant le portable d'un geste sec quand leur mère entre dans la pièce.

— Qu'est-ce que tu fais, Herman ?

— Rien, maman.

— Est-ce que tu étais encore en train de regarder des sites de formation et de développement personnel ?

— Non, maman, bien sûr que non.

— Eh bien, j'espère pour toi. Tu sais ce que le juge a dit.

Ce qui signifie, je pense, qu'il n'y a aucune bonne excuse pour ne pas lui donner le numéro, ce qui ne me laisse que le b) : trouver une excuse valable pour de longues pauses dans les conversations téléphoniques. Et la seule qui me vienne à l'esprit, c'est la mauvaise transmission satellite, ce qui est ridicule parce que pour ça il faudrait que je sois à Bornéo ou autre.

Encore que, je pourrais m'y être rendue en voyage d'études, pour observer les techniques que les habitants de Bornéo mettent en œuvre lors de leurs stages, afin d'améliorer les résultats.

Heureusement, à cet instant, mon ordinateur émet un nouveau son, et ça me rappelle que je dois me reprendre, arrêter de perdre la tête, et lire ce nouveau message. Avant de l'ouvrir, je me fais la remarque que cela fait maintenant plusieurs minutes que Rupert m'a demandé mon numéro de téléphone, et comme il sait que je suis assise devant mon écran il doit se poser des questions face à mon silence. Et Dieu m'en est témoin, moi aussi. Je me penche, espérant qu'il ne soit pas fâché. Qu'il veuille encore me parler. Qu'il ne veuille plus.

Le mail vient de Sean.

De : Sean Cousins
À : Beth Sheridan
Objet : Réitération ?

Salut, toi. Je n'ai pas encore eu l'occasion de te parler aujourd'hui. Tu as l'air très occupée, donc je ne vais pas venir te déranger à ton bureau. Je voulais juste te demander si tu aimerais qu'on remette ça, un autre jour ?

S.

Hum. Une réitération. Voilà un mot propre à faire rêver une jeune fille. Je suis très surprise qu'il ait envie de sortir à nouveau avec moi, car je sais que je n'ai pas été d'une très agréable compagnie vendredi soir. En fait, j'ai

210

passé toute la soirée à penser à deux autres types, bien qu'il ne s'en soit pas douté. Je ne lui ai jamais dit : « Tais-toi une minute, s'il te plaît, j'essaie de fantasmer ! » Du moins, je crois. Mais ça n'a pas pu lui échapper que j'étais ailleurs pendant tout ce temps... surtout lorsque je me suis ruée vers ma voiture juste quand il s'approchait pour m'embrasser. Et pourtant il réitère sa demande. Comme c'est curieux... Une pensée étrange me vient. Serait-il possible qu'il ne s'intéresse pas à moi pour mon esprit brillant et ma conversation passionnante, qu'il se fiche de savoir quels sont mes films préférés ou ce que j'étais en train de faire lorsque j'ai appris que Lady Di était morte, et qu'il veuille juste aller voir ce que j'ai sous la jupe ? Est-ce qu'un homme peut être superficiel à ce point ? Ça alors, je crois que je viens de faire une grande découverte.

Je clique sur « Répondre » et commence à taper : « Sean, je ne crois vraiment pas... », mais, à ce moment-là, l'alerte sonore de ma boîte de réception retentit une fois de plus, et ma main me ramène par un geste automatique vers mes mails. La vue du nom de Rupert dans la colonne des expéditeurs efface tous les autres correspondants, comme dans l'une de ces illusions d'optique avec des points roses. Je double-clique pour ouvrir et m'installe confortablement, un sourire aux lèvres, pour lire le long message qui s'affiche.

De : Rupert de Witter
À : Beth Sheridan
Objet : Mauvaise transmission satellite

Ma chère Beth,

Mes yeux se brouillent à ce moment et je suis incapable d'aller plus loin que le titre. J'ai subitement l'impression que quelqu'un joue à pierre-feuille-ciseaux sur ma colonne vertébrale avec des doigts glacés, et j'en ai la chair de poule. Je jette un coup d'œil autour de moi, comme si je m'attendais à le voir, accroupi derrière la photocopieuse dans son costume et ses chaussures à lacets pointure 44, muni de ces fameuses jumelles, en train de m'espionner. Aussitôt, je secoue la tête pour chasser cette pensée. C'est sans doute l'idée la plus idiote qui me soit jamais venue, et ce n'est pas peu dire. Il ne peut pas se cacher dans le bureau, parce que c'est un open-space, il n'y a aucun endroit où échapper aux regards. Et de toute façon, en me regardant avec des jumelles, il ne verrait pas dans mon esprit. Bien sûr qu'il n'y a rien d'aussi sinistre. En fait, il y a sans aucun doute une explication très simple. C'est soit une preuve irréfutable de l'existence de Dieu, soit une coïncidence. Deux esprits qui se rencontrent.

Je lis la suite.

Ma chère Beth,

J'ai trois théories pour expliquer votre absence de réponse immédiate à mon dernier message :
1) Vous avez dû quitter votre bureau – vraisemblablement pour dresser en urgence une carte heuristique ou dessiner un organigramme sur un papier gigantesque, ce qui n'est pas très confortable ;
2) Vous êtes à l'étranger pour un voyage d'études et vous m'écrivez sur un PC professionnel depuis votre chambre d'hôtel à Nairobi, et la transmission

satellite est mauvaise (Je ne sais pas s'il y a réellement une transmission satellite pour Internet ? Je pensais que tout l'intérêt, c'était d'être plus ou moins instantané. Mais je peux très bien me tromper sur ce point.);

3) Ma troisième hypothèse, qui me dérange vraiment, est que vous avez été gênée que je sollicite votre numéro de téléphone et que vous êtes en train de vous demander pourquoi je souhaite l'obtenir, et si vous devriez ou non me le communiquer.

En réponse au 1), je veux que vous sachiez que j'attendrai toute la journée devant mon écran, donc quand vous aurez fini ce que vous faites, je serai là.

Si c'est le 2), j'attendrai une réponse dans la demi-heure qui vient, bien que si vous êtes à Nairobi, vous avez des choses beaucoup plus intéressantes à faire que d'envoyer des mails à un homme d'affaires qui s'ennuie devant son ordinateur en Angleterre.

Et si jamais c'était le 3) – c'est peu probable, je sais, mais j'ai besoin de prévoir chaque possibilité –, j'ai pensé qu'il serait bon que je vous informe que je viens de trouver le numéro dans les Pages Jaunes, donc si je voulais le connaître pour de sinistres raisons, rien de ce que vous ou quelqu'un d'autre pourriez faire ne m'arrêterait plus désormais. Ha ha ha, le monde tremblera devant moi, etc.

Rupert.

Au moment où j'achève la lecture, deux événements s'enchaînent rapidement. D'abord, j'entends le téléphone sonner sur le bureau d'Ali. Et ensuite Ali me crie à travers la pièce qu'il y a un appel pour moi.

J'attrape ma brochure d'Horizon sur mon bureau et me concentre sur la photo de la dernière page pendant quelques secondes, le temps qu'Ali me passe la ligne. Humm, le voici, beau comme un dieu. Mon ventre gargouille et se tortille quand la communication arrive, et je tends la main pour décrocher le combiné qui me révélera la voix qui va avec ce visage magnifique.

— Tout va bien, Beth ?

La voix d'Ali me parvient dans le téléphone, et je lui réponds par un hochement de tête rêveur.

— Hum, oui. C'est juste… (que je suis sans voix alors que je suis sur le point de m'adresser à l'homme le plus sexy de la planète, qui est aussi très drôle et charmant à vous en donner des frissons dans le ventre, voudrais-je dire.)

Mais comme j'ai perdu la parole, je me contente d'un grognement. Puis, je tousse un peu et me tape la poitrine, utilisant la paume de ma main comme défibrillateur maison. Comme attendu, mon cœur redémarre.

— OK, bon, le voilà.

Et il raccroche. Après quelques secondes passées à me demander que dire en premier, je croasse :

— Beth Sheridan. Que puis-je faire pour vous ?

— Vous savez, j'étais en train de me poser la même question.

Oh, hummm… Quelle voix ! Je chancelle un peu dans mon fauteuil, alors que mon sang reflue de ma tête.

C'est l'équivalent auditif de la première gorgée de Baileys qu'on boit lors d'une fête alors qu'on n'y a plus touché depuis Noël : chaude, riche, et, de façon déroutante, agréablement familière. Un léger vertige me prend.

— Pardon, qui est à l'appareil ? dis-je, tentant de paraître occupée à balayer mes notes d'un dernier regard avant une brillante intervention que je serais sur le point de présenter.

— C'est Rupert, annonce-t-il d'une voix qui me fait fondre, de Witter. D'Horizon Holidays.

— Ah, bonjour, réponds-je comme si je le découvrais à l'instant. Vous avez trouvé mon numéro, alors ?

— J'ai été obligé, pour deux excellentes raisons. Et sans doute davantage.

— Oh, très bien. De quoi s'agit-il ?

— OK. Premièrement, pour vous prouver que je n'avais aucun motif sinistre pour vous demander vos coordonnées, et qu'en fait je pouvais les obtenir facilement sur Internet, au service des renseignements ou dans les Pages Jaunes. Comme n'importe qui pourrait le faire, et comme je l'ai fait. Ou plutôt mon assistante.

— Ah !

Je ne fais pas exprès de paraître cool : je suis seulement incapable de prononcer des consonnes.

— Et deuxièmement j'avais très envie de vous parler.

Impossible également de proférer une voyelle, à présent. Silence prolongé, alors que nous attendons tous deux que je réponde. Comme je n'en fais rien, il ajoute :

— Pour fixer un rendez-vous.

Je hoche la tête, tout en parcourant du regard le reste du bureau. Il n'est pas là, bien entendu, caché sous la table, mais je veux avoir l'air de dominer la situation aux yeux d'un potentiel observateur. Donc je prends un air pensif, avec une petite moue, et opine à nouveau du chef. Ma figure exprime l'idée que : « Cette proposition me plaît beaucoup et que j'en vois clairement les avantages réciproques », même si ce n'est pas le cas.

— En fait, reprend-il, avant de signer un contrat, je dois toujours rencontrer la personne avec laquelle je négocie, surtout quand elle évoque les yétis dans sa correspondance préliminaire. C'est une formalité à laquelle je suis très attaché dans de semblables circonstances.

Je pouffe de rire, et retrouve partiellement la parole :

— C'est fréquent ? réussis-je à croasser.

— Quoi, qu'on me parle de yétis ? Non, pas vraiment. C'est assez rare, en réalité. Pour tout vous dire, c'est la première fois. Ça m'a pris par surprise, comme vous le savez.

— Ah oui, le bagel. J'espère que vous êtes parfaitement remis ?

— Eh bien, j'ai frôlé la mort, mais il a fini par descendre. Êtes-vous libre demain ?

Tout l'air contenu dans mes poumons s'échappe d'un coup, mais heureusement j'arrive à étouffer le bruit. Demain. Oh. Mon. Dieu. Je le rencontre demain. Je prends quelques inspirations profondes pour me donner une voix digne et calme. Et ne pas couiner de joie, surexcitée.

— Miss Sheridan ? dit-il dans mon oreille. Vous êtes toujours là ? Oh, pardon, c'est bien Miss, n'est-ce pas ? Non, euh, ce que je veux dire…

Il se tait soudain, comme si quelqu'un venait de poser la main sur l'émetteur de son côté. J'entends le son étouffé d'un raclement de gorge, puis la ligne revient à la normale.

—Désolé. Donc, vous êtes libre demain?

—Demain, c'est parfait, dis-je dans un souffle, et ma voix paraît merveilleusement calme et sexy, même à mes propres oreilles. Et c'est en effet Miss.

—Excellent, répond-il.

Je ne sais pas s'il parle du rendez-vous ou du fait que je ne sois pas mariée. J'entends à sa voix qu'il sourit, sans l'ombre d'un doute, et je ferme les yeux un instant. Puis les rouvre aussitôt en m'apercevant que je ne peux pas regarder sa photo avec les yeux fermés:

—Où cela? Voulez-vous que je vienne dans vos locaux?

—Non, je préférerais faire ça en terrain neutre. Hum, non, je ne voulais pas dire… vous savez, «faire ça»… Ce n'est pas…

—Un endroit neutre sera parfait, réponds-je avec naturel.

Je me sens posée et séduisante. Je ferme à demi les yeux, mais pas complètement, pour laisser passer la lumière qui rebondit sur la photo de Rupert.

—Quel est le lieu qui vous conviendrait?

Je n'entends rien d'autre qu'une respiration laborieuse pendant quelques instants. Peut-être qu'il est asthmatique. Peut-être qu'il est excité. Tout à coup, je me mets à frissonner.

—Tout va bien? dis-je doucement, à moitié par inquiétude, à moitié par désir d'écouter encore cette voix douce comme un lait pour le corps.

Surtout par inquiétude, bien sûr. S'il est en pleine crise d'asthme, ça explique pourquoi il trébuche sur les mots comme ça. Mais s'il est excité, aussi.

— Humm, répond-il avant de se râcler la gorge. Désolé.

Je ferme à nouveau brièvement les yeux au son de cette voix. Elle est tellement magnifique, que j'ai l'impression de l'avoir écoutée toute ma vie. C'est soit ça, soit il a la même voix que Daniel Craig.

— J'essaie juste de trouver un endroit neutre.

— Peut-être la Suisse ?

Il éclate de rire :

— Oui, pourquoi pas ? Mais c'est un peu loin, vous ne pensez pas ?

— Humm. Oui, un peu. Je dois être rentrée à 17 h 30 pour faire la fermeture.

— Dans ce cas, que diriez-vous de Paris ?

— Oh oui, bien sûr, c'est plus faisable. Avec l'Eurostar, ça ne me prendrait que quelques heures. Je pourrais vous rejoindre là-bas pendant ma pause-déjeuner et être de retour pour mes séances de l'après-midi.

L'idée me vient soudain qu'il est peut-être absolument sérieux et qu'en le prenant ainsi à la rigolade je passe à côté d'un merveilleux voyage en jet privé, en hélicoptère, ou autre. Il a forcément accès à ce genre de choses. Pourtant, je n'y serais pas allée, bien sûr. C'est mon devoir, en tant que professionnelle, de refuser. Si jamais ça se savait, on risquerait un scandale dans l'édition locale du *Herald* : « Dessous de table pour des tarifs de formation avantageux ».

—Oh, je ne sais pas trop, répond-il. Je crois que nous en avons pour la journée. Je pensais prendre ma montgolfière.

Des images et des sons déferlent dans mon esprit, l'une après l'autre : la montée, douce et silencieuse ; les bouffées de vent et d'air chaud ; un panier à pique-nique ; le tintement de deux flûtes à champagne ; de magnifiques collines moutonnantes ; un premier baiser dans les nuages.

Je secoue la tête comme un chien de dessin animé, et les visions éclatent telles des bulles de savon. Il faut vraiment que je me reprenne. Je n'ai même pas encore rencontré cet homme. Je crois que mon besoin désespéré de m'assurer cette signature commence à perturber ma rationalité. C'est certainement ça. Oui, ce n'est que mon angoisse professionnelle, ainsi que le fort sentiment de responsabilité que j'éprouve à l'égard de Fatima en ce moment.

Ou alors c'est ce visage.

Non, allons, maintenant, Beth, concentre-toi. Décroche ce contrat avec Horizon, comme ça tu pourras retrouver un comportement normal.

Ouais, c'est ça. J'arrive presque à me convaincre, jusqu'à ce que mes yeux rencontrent à nouveau la photo de Rupert et que je sente une chaleur torride m'enflammer une fois de plus.

—Je suppose que votre épouse a l'habitude que vous rentriez tard, n'est-ce pas ? m'entends-je demander, bien que je puisse jurer que je n'ai pas ordonné à mes lèvres de remuer.

Je les attrape et les serre l'une contre l'autre avec mes doigts, pour les empêcher de prendre d'autres initiatives.

Oh non, il n'a pas répondu. Qu'est-ce qui m'a pris de mentionner sa femme ? Qu'est-ce que cela – ou plutôt elle – vient faire dans la conversation ? Ça ne concerne en rien mon rendez-vous professionnel avec lui. Et maintenant son long silence montre que ma question a soulevé des problèmes particuliers auxquels il doit réfléchir quelques instants. De toute évidence, il vient juste de comprendre que je suis comme la cliente folle de la table 4 – la femme mûre, rondouillette, qui bat des cils avec coquetterie en demandant à tous les jeunes serveurs horrifiés qui n'ont pas plus de dix-sept ans, ce que leur petite amie pense du fait qu'ils fassent la conversation à une bande de *desperate housewives* – et il va me donner une réponse dans ce goût-là : « Je ne vois pas en quoi... »

— Je ne suis pas marié.

— Pardon, vous dites ? Oh, vous n'avez pas de femme ? Ah.

Et, malgré moi, je sens un énorme soupir de soulagement m'échapper. Mais je le réprime aussitôt, et ôte du même coup mon sourire béat, en me pinçant les lèvres.

— Non. (Il se tait.) Je cherche toujours.

— Ah.

Je suis de nouveau incapable de prononcer une consonne.

— Donc personne ne s'impatiente, quelle que soit l'heure à laquelle je rentre.

— Humm.

— Même si ce n'est qu'au matin.

— ...

— Oh, Beth, écoutez, je suis désolé, ce n'est pas le sujet. Qu'est-ce qui me prend ? Vous savez, c'est difficile de rester concentré, avec vous.

—Non. Hum hum. Non, n'essayez pas de me faire porter le chapeau. Nous étions en train de parler de votre montgolfière.

—Et vous m'avez demandé si j'étais marié.

—Non, je vous ai demandé si votre femme avait quelque chose contre le fait que vous rentriez tard.

—Et, quelle que soit la réponse, cela vous donnait l'information que vous n'aviez pas sollicitée directement. Donc, non, je ne suis pas marié.

Il est vraiment rusé. Il voit clair dans mon jeu, exactement comme pour mon entrée en matière avec les pointures de chaussures. Zut.

—OK, Einstein. Moi, au moins, je ne me suis pas emmêlé les pinceaux dans le genre « Oh, c'est bien Miss, n'est-ce pas ? Non, oups, désolé, euh, n'importe quoi, qu'est-ce que je raconte, désolé, je ne voulais pas dire ça. »

Il rit à présent.

—OK, vous m'avez eu. Disons que nous sommes quittes.

—Et célibataires tous les deux.

Bordel de merde ! Quel est le problème de ma bouche aujourd'hui ?! Je crois qu'elle est comme moi, préoccupée de savoir ce que ça ferait de se poser sur ce beau visage.

—En effet, il semble bien.

Cela sonne comme s'il opinait avec intérêt. Avec plaisir, même. Ou bien avec horreur, comme quand on s'aperçoit que la personne à laquelle on s'adresse est folle à lier ?

—Alors, Beth, où allons-nous nous retrouver demain ? Il fait sans doute trop froid pour la montgolfière, et puis ça prend une éternité de la monter, et je ne me souviens jamais où j'ai rangé le gonfleur.

— Vous ne pouvez pas souffler ?

— Je pourrais, mais ça me fait toujours tourner la tête.

— Vous n'avez pas assez de souffle ?

— Je le crains. Alors, que diriez-vous d'aller déjeuner quelque part ? Au *Madeleine's* ?

Au *Madeleine's* ! J'ai vécu dans cette ville toute ma vie, et je dois reconnaître que je n'y suis jamais entrée. C'est très chic, huppé même, et je ne suis jamais sortie avec quelqu'un qui soit chic et huppé à ce point. Et ce n'est pas le genre d'endroit où l'on va tout seul.

— Au *Madeleine's*, c'est parfait, réponds-je simplement, comme si j'y mangeais tous les quatre matins. On dit 13 heures ?

Je prie Dieu que ce soit dans mes moyens. Je me contenterai peut-être de la soupe. Seigneur, faites qu'il y ait de la soupe.

— Treize heures, c'est noté. Je vais réserver une table. Je vous retrouve là-bas.

— Merveilleux. Je suis impatiente.

— Moi de même.

Nous raccrochons tous deux, et je garde les yeux dans le vide pendant quelques secondes, tout en essayant de ne pas me laisser aller à un éclat de joie, et de me limiter à un petit sourire énigmatique. J'ai rendez-vous demain avec Rupert de Witter ! D'Horizon Holidays ! Le multimillionnaire !

Jésus Marie Joseph dans une montgolfière.

Dans son bureau, Rupert remet le combiné en place et laisse sa main posée dessus pendant un moment, un sourire distrait sur les lèvres.

—Alors, demande une voix à sa gauche. (Il lève les yeux vers Harris qui le regarde avec intérêt depuis son fauteuil.) Comment ça s'est passé ?

—J'en ai eu une, pas de problème. Demain, 13 heures.

—Au *Madeleine's* ? Vingt dieux, comment tu as fait, si près de Noël ?

—Trop facile, Harris. Ils me connaissent, là-bas, tu sais bien.

—Mais si toutes les tables sont réservées, ils ne peuvent pas en sortir une de leur chapeau, pas vrai ?

—Eh bien si, ils en ont sorti une, mais pas de leur chapeau. Ils étaient complets, mais quand ils ont su que c'était moi, ils ont dit qu'ils allaient en installer une dans le kiosque.

—Non ! Ils ne vont pas ouvrir le kiosque en hiver. Il y ferait un froid de canard.

—C'est là que tu te trompes, mon vieux. Ils vont le bourrer de radiateurs et l'éclairer avec des bougies. Ce sera enchanteur.

—Ah, OK. Enchanteur. Hum.

Il se frotte le menton, pensif.

Rupert le contemple quelques instants :

—OK, allez, qu'est-ce que tu en penses ? Non, ne me dis pas « rien », tu as manifestement quelque chose à dire. Crache le morceau.

—OK, bon, je me demandais simplement s'il s'agissait d'un déjeuner de travail ou d'un rendez-vous romantique ? Tu sais, au *Madeleine's*, dans le kiosque, avec des dizaines de bougies, de la musique douce, du bon vin, des plats raffinés, le clair de lune…

—À 13 heures, Harris ?

—… et vous deux.

—Et cinq radiateurs électriques.

—Ah oui, et les radiateurs.

Rupert réfléchit un moment :

—En vérité, je ne sais pas trop. Au début, elle m'a impressionné par son originalité et son humour, et ça ne pouvait qu'être bien pour Horizon : un regard neuf sur notre politique de formation. Mais ensuite, après quelques mails, elle a commencé à me plaire pour toutes sortes d'autres raisons, sans rapport avec le travail. Elle a une façon d'écrire… charmante, intelligente, captivante. Quand j'attends ses messages, c'est comme, je ne sais pas… d'attendre les résultats d'un examen. Ouais. Lorsqu'on se demande si on a fait suffisamment bien pour convaincre, si on a bien compris, si on a réussi.

—Ce n'est pas très sexy comme comparaison, tu sais.

Rupert se passe la main dans les cheveux :

—C'est vrai ? Je me suis peut-être mal exprimé. (Il se tait.) Non, non, peut-être que tu as raison, en fait. Ce n'est sans doute pas sexy. Je veux dire, nous échangeons juste des mails, pour le moment, rien de plus. Mais ça m'intéresse. J'aimerais que ça débouche sur autre chose. Et ça commence par le déjeuner de demain.

—OK, je comprends. Mais tu ne m'as pas répondu : ce déjeuner, c'est pour le travail ou pour le plaisir ?

Rupert reste silencieux, une main posée sur l'arrière de la tête, puis sourit et hausse les épaules :

—Je ne sais pas. De toute évidence, il faut que je la rencontre pour régler les questions professionnelles. Et ça me permettra de la voir en chair et en os, et de décider si j'ai envie de poursuivre ou non. (Il lève les sourcils.) Enfin, je crois que mon opinion est arrêtée sur ce point, en fait.

Harris le dévisage un moment :

— Attends une minute. Ce ne serait pas la fille que tu as aperçue à la fête, vendredi ? Celle que tu avais déjà rencontrée ?

— Non, c'est quelqu'un d'autre.

— Mais bon sang, Rupert. Qu'est-ce qui t'arrive ? Je croyais que l'autre te plaisait vraiment ?

— Mais elle me plaisait. Elle me plaît toujours. Mais ça ne sert à rien d'y penser, puisque je ne connais ni son nom, ni son lieu de travail, ni rien du tout. Je ne parviendrai jamais à la retrouver, alors autant tourner la page.

— Bon, OK, dans ce cas mettons les choses au clair. Celle que tu vois demain, c'est… qui, exactement ?

— Elle travaille chez Love Learning, le prestataire de formation que Ricky Love a monté quand il est parti d'ici.

— Et tu ne l'as jamais rencontrée ?

Rupert secoue la tête :

— Pas que je sache. Mais Rhonda pense que son nom lui dit quelque chose.

— C'est vrai ? D'où ?

Rupert hausse à nouveau les épaules.

— Elle a peut-être bossé ici à une époque. Rhonda a une excellente mémoire des noms. Elle va vérifier ça pour moi.

Harris hausse les sourcils :

— Tu parles d'une coïncidence ! Mais tu ne la connaissais pas à l'époque ?

— Non, comme je te l'ai dit, pour autant que je sache, nous ne nous sommes jamais vus.

— Pourtant tu as des sentiments pour elle ?

Rupert baisse les yeux, puis regarde encore une fois Harris et opine du chef.

— Donc, elle pourrait avoir cinquante-neuf ans, huit petits-enfants, et être aussi large que haute ?

Rupert secoue la tête avec dédain :

— Oui. Ça n'a pas d'importance.

— C'est vrai ?

— Oui. Ne me dévisage pas comme ça : je suis parfaitement sérieux. Évidemment, je préférerais qu'elle ne soit pas beaucoup plus âgée que moi, mais même ça, ce n'est pas important. Elle me fait rire, elle est de bonne compagnie. Ça suffit à me séduire. Bon sang, combien de gens très beaux à regarder ai-je rencontrés, qui ne savent pas faire une phrase ? Ils te font mourir d'ennui en te parlant de leurs cheveux, de leurs chaussures ou de leur téléphone portable. Les gens comme ça pensent qu'ils n'ont pas besoin de faire le moindre effort, parce que leur plastique leur ouvre toutes les portes. Et le pire, Harris, c'est que, la plupart du temps, ils ont raison. Tout le monde est tellement superficiel de nos jours, comme si la beauté était le principal pour tous. Ne vous en faites pas pour l'esprit, les bonnes manières ou la conversation. Si vous avez une belle peau et une taille de guêpe, vous êtes sûr de réussir. Ça me fait chier.

Harris lève les mains avec un grand sourire :

— Hé, vieux, je rigolais. Il se trouve que je suis d'accord avec toi ; je te faisais marcher. De toute façon, ça n'a pas d'importance, dans le cas présent, pas vrai ?

Rupert le dévisage :

— Qu'est-ce que tu veux dire ?

— Eh bien, tu ne te rappelles pas comment est Ricky Love ? Tous ceux qui travaillent pour lui doivent répondre à certains… critères.

Le silence s'installe pendant que Rupert considère Harris, puis se lève et se dirige vers la fenêtre, en se frottant le visage de la main. Il regarde la rue pendant quelques secondes avant de se tourner vers son compagnon :

— Donc, tu dis que… tu crois… qu'elle pourrait être… belle, en plus du reste ?

Harris opine :

— Sans l'ombre d'un doute. À moins que ce triste pervers n'ait changé ses habitudes. Mais ça m'étonnerait fort.

Rupert se laisse tomber sur son siège et contemple un point de son bureau :

— Eh ben…

Dans son fauteuil, Harris se penche vers l'avant :

— Rupe, écoute, je viens juste de penser à un truc.

Rupert lève les yeux :

— Quoi ?

— Tu as dit qu'elle avait pris l'initiative de te contacter. OK. Donc elle t'a écrit, à toi, Rupert de Witter, probablement en recopiant l'adresse de la brochure d'Horizon ?

— Sans doute.

— J'en déduis qu'il existe une forte probabilité pour qu'elle ait vu la photo de la dernière page. Tu ne crois pas ?

Le silence s'éternise tandis que les deux hommes se dévisagent, chacun attendant la réaction de l'autre.

— Merde, dit finalement Rupert. Ça m'était complètement sorti de l'esprit.

Harris pince les lèvres :

— Ça fait des années que j'essaie de te faire mettre ce portrait à jour…

— Oui, oui, je sais. J'aurais dû le faire, mais ça n'a aucune importance, n'est-ce pas ? Je veux dire, tout le monde ici est au courant, alors qu'est-ce que ça peut faire ?

— Eh bien, rien. Avant. Mais ça commence à avoir de l'importance maintenant, tu ne crois pas ?

Rupert garde les yeux rivés sur lui pendant un moment avant de répondre :

— Je ne peux pas y aller. (Il secoue la tête.) C'est impossible.

— Bien sûr que si. Il suffit que tu t'approches d'elle et que tu te présentes.

— Bon sang, non ! Qu'est-ce qu'elle va bien pouvoir penser, après avoir vu cette photo ? Non, non, je ne peux pas y aller.

Il laisse tomber sa tête dans ses mains.

— Oh, allons…, dit doucement Harris. Que fais-tu de tout ce que tu as dit sur l'apparence, qui n'est pas importante ? Sur la superficialité des gens ? Je suis certain qu'elle ne te trouvera pas moins à son goût, et il faudra bien que tu sortes d'ici tôt ou tard. Il faudra bien qu'elle voie ton visage.

— Non. Jamais. Je ne le ferai pas. Laisse tomber. Bordel. Putain de bordel de merde !

Soudain, il lève les yeux vers Harris, et son expression passe du désespoir sans fond à un espoir infinitésimal.

— Harris, vieux frère. Tu es mon comptable. Va au rendez-vous.

— QUOI ?

— Non, non, je ne te demande pas de te faire passer pour moi. Tout ce que je veux, c'est que tu ailles déjeuner avec elle, que tu règles les affaires professionnelles, que tu lui parles un peu de moi, tu sais, que tu lui dises à quel point je suis formidable, et ensuite tu rentres ici et tu me racontes tout sur elle.

— Non.

— Harris, s'il te plaît. En tant qu'ami ? (Harris fait « non » de la tête.) En tant qu'associé ? (Il secoue la tête plus fort.) Très bien. Je ne voulais pas en arriver là, mais tu ne me laisses pas le choix : tu es viré.

— Ah, c'est bas, Rupert. C'est vraiment bas.

— Oui, je sais. Et je suis désolé. Mais j'ai vraiment besoin de ton aide. Je veux dire, je ne te demande pas de marcher sur des braises ni de manger à *Eggz & Beanz*. Ça va être un délicieux repas aux chandelles, dans le kiosque du *Madeleine's*, en tête à tête avec une jeune femme drôle, charmante, et probablement jolie. Je paie.

— Encore heureux !

— Tu y vas, alors ?

Harris ferme les yeux, puis regarde Rupert d'un air las :

— OK. Mais tu as une dette envers moi.

— Bien sûr, vieux, bien sûr. Et n'oublie pas de lui dire quel type formidable je suis, OK ? Et, à part ça, je peux faire une note de frais pour le repas, n'est-ce pas ?

Chapitre 13

Respect des engagements

Objectif à court terme : trouver une activité passionnante qui me tienne occupée pendant environ vingt-sept heures, afin que je puisse consulter ma montre et constater avec surprise qu'il est l'heure que je parte pour mon rendez-vous à déjeuner.

Obstacles : qu'est-ce que je pourrais bien faire qui prenne aussi longtemps ?

Objectif à long terme : une séance de sexe de vingt-sept heures avec Rupert de Witter. Hummm…

Obstacles : je ne suis pas sûre que ce soit réellement possible.

J'aimerais pouvoir faire avancer le temps jusqu'à 12 h 59 et entrer au *Madeleine's* maintenant, chaussée de mes chaussures les plus sexy, une brochure en papier glacé sous un bras et un sac Gucci sous l'autre. Mais j'ai d'autres choses à faire avant.

Premièrement, on est toujours lundi, donc si j'entre au *Madeleine's* avec ces fameux escarpins aux pieds à 12 h 59 aujourd'hui, personne ne m'attendra, et quelqu'un sera gêné de constater qu'il n'y a pas de réservation à mon nom : ce sera moi.

Du coup, j'ai programmé diverses activités pour me tenir occupée d'ici là. À 12 h 59 aujourd'hui, j'ai prévu d'être dans la cuisine, en train de retirer la cellophane de mon sandwich diététique dinde farcie-airelles. Je dégusterai aussi, sans doute, un gâteau à presque zéro pour cent de matière grasse, et une barre chocolatée, que je tremperai dans une tasse de thé. Puis, je ne pourrai échapper à un gros après-midi de travail, suivi d'une soirée avec Vini, et d'une nuit passée à me tourner et à me retourner dans mon lit. Mais tout ça ne m'amène qu'à 7 heures, et il me restera donc l'horrible perspective de six heures de néant à traverser pour atteindre 13 heures et mon rendez-vous.

La première heure s'écoule comme un spectacle de Noël. Vous savez que si vous serrez les dents et continuez à sourire courageusement ils finiront par entrer dans le vif du sujet. Je lance un coup d'œil à l'horloge, certaine que cinq heures viennent de passer et qu'il doit être bientôt l'heure de rentrer à la maison, mais il n'est que 11 h 45. Crotte.

L'heure suivante s'écoule comme l'ère mésozoïque. Des espèces entières y sont nées, ont évolué au-delà de leurs limites, et se sont éteintes. Je sirote mon thé, mais il a refroidi. Ça ne fait rien, ça passe le temps.

L'alerte de ma boîte de réception retentit ! Youpi ! Dans ma hâte à me distraire de l'horloge, je me jette pratiquement tête la première dans mes mails, mais, à ma grande déception, ça ne me prend pas longtemps, et c'est un message de Sean. Vous vous rendez compte qu'il ne faut que huit secondes pour recevoir et ouvrir un nouveau courrier?

> Coucou! Ça va? Je voulais savoir si tu avais eu l'occasion de lire mon précédent petit mot, où je te demandais si tu aimerais qu'on sorte ensemble à nouveau? Qu'en dis-tu? S'il te plaît, réponds-moi vite, pour abréger mes souffrances!

> Sean.

Hum. Drôle d'idée de mettre un point d'exclamation après un mot comme «souffrances». Je veux dire, ce n'est pas comme s'il avait écrit quelque chose comme «Surprise!» ou «Réveille-toi!» Ça donne l'impression qu'il dit «abréger mes souffrances» avec un sourire ironique. Ou plutôt, comme c'est un mail, un e-sourire ironique. E-ronique. Dans tous les cas, à quoi sert de sous-entendre que ça le fait souffrir de se demander si oui ou non j'ai envie de sortir à nouveau avec lui, s'il efface toute la souffrance par un point d'exclamation? Ça n'a aucun sens. Je m'aperçois qu'en essayant de démêler cette question je me suis mise à froncer les sourcils, et je m'applique donc à détendre mon front. Est-il ou non plongé dans la souffrance? Cela semble peu probable. En fait, la seule explication crédible, c'est que ce type soit un parfait dé…

— Tu as vu mon mail, Beth?

— Merde! Tu m'as fait sursauter!

En fait, l'unique raison pour laquelle j'ai tressailli comme ça, c'est que j'ai été surprise dans une activité répréhensible. Il se tient juste derrière moi, les mains appuyées sur le dossier de mon siège, mais ce n'est pas comme s'il pouvait lire dans mes pensées. Je ferme les yeux et pose la main sur ma poitrine, à moitié pour lui montrer qu'il m'a vraiment causé un choc, à moitié pour masquer mon air coupable. Il plisse un peu les paupières et s'accroupit à côté de moi.

— Bon sang, désolé, ma puce, je ne voulais pas te faire peur. Ça va ?

— Oui, oui, ça va. *(Mais si tu m'appelles encore une fois « ma puce », je t'arracherai les amygdales avec les ongles et je te mettrai les testicules à la place.)* Et toi ?

Il me gratifie de ce geste si masculin qui consiste à opiner d'un coup de menton vers le haut, et m'adresse un large sourire :

— Ça va au poil. Tu as vu mon mail, alors ?

— Oh oui, merci. Euh, je n'ai pas encore eu le temps de répondre, désolée. Je suis très occupée.

Il écarquille les yeux comme Macaulay Culkin quand il voit le père Noël dans *Maman, j'ai raté l'avion*, et affiche un air pressant, affamé. Il se penche plus près de moi :

— Occupée ? Par quoi ?

— Oh, tu sais, le boulot. Préparations, recherches, toujours la même chose.

— Et chasse aux contrats ?

Il respire comme s'il osait à peine y croire.

— Eh bien, oui, un peu de ça aussi. Pourquoi ?

— Ça marche ?

J'ouvre la bouche pour lui annoncer que j'ai organisé une réunion demain midi, mais je me rends compte qu'il s'attendra à ce que je lui disc avec qui, puisqu'il ne m'a rien caché de son rendez-vous avec *Whytelys*. Donc je la referme sans rien révéler. Puis la rouvre :

—Non, pas vraiment. Je n'arrive pas à passer le barrage des standardistes, jusqu'ici.

—Tu as essayé où ?

J'hésite avant de répondre. Je me torture les méninges à la recherche d'une histoire à lui raconter, mais, de toute évidence, il interprète mon silence de travers et reprend la parole avant que j'aie eu le temps de m'expliquer :

—Oh non, écoute, ne parlons pas de ça ici. Je suis juste venu te demander si tu aimerais aller prendre un verre demain soir ? On pourra discuter librement à ce moment-là, d'accord ?

Bon, c'est non, évidemment. Je veux dire, vous imaginez dans quel état je serai après avoir déjeuné avec Rupert ? Je suis certaine que je serai incapable de m'exprimer ou de marcher, et que je ne voudrai donc pas faire autre chose que de passer la soirée avec lui, ou même simplement avec son souvenir. Et des parties secrètes de ma personne me pressent de rester disponible, au cas où le déjeuner se déroulerait vraiment, vraiment bien.

—En fait, Sean, demain ce n'est pas…

—S'il te plaît, Beth.

Il pose sa main sur mon bras, et je la regarde. Je sens sa chaleur à travers mon chemisier. Il n'est pas loin de s'embraser.

—Je ne veux pas me retrouver tout seul chez moi, demain soir. Je ne le supporterai pas.

Et, à ma grande surprise, ses yeux commencent à s'embuer.

—Ah. Tout va bien ? Qu'est-ce qui se passe ?

Il secoue la tête, jouant l'homme fort et muet, et se frotte les paupières :

—Rien. Désolé. Écoute, s'il te plaît, viens prendre un verre avec moi demain. Je te devrai une fière chandelle. S'il te plaît…

Un mec qui pleure. Qu'est-ce qui pourrait être plus séduisant ? Ah oui, je sais, juste une chose : un type debout sur son yacht. La brochure d'Horizon est toujours sur mon bureau, ouverte à la dernière page, et la photo qui s'y trouve irradie quasiment de lumière et de magnétisme. Mes yeux sont involontairement attirés vers elle. Oh, merde, j'avais vraiment envie de garder la soirée libre…

—OK, alors. Un verre, pour te rendre service.

—C'est fantastique ! (Il arbore un grand sourire et se relève d'un coup, toute trace de larmes effacée.) On se retrouve au *Perroquet du Pirate*, comme l'autre fois ? À 20 heures ? J'ai hâte d'y être !

Il conclut par un clin d'œil au ralenti, qui me met mal à l'aise, et il retourne à son bureau.

Crotte de crotte. Bref, il y a un bon côté. Vini dit toujours qu'il faut se faire désirer, donc être prise demain soir, c'est plutôt cool. Je prie juste le Seigneur que Rupert m'invite à dîner pour pouvoir répondre : « Désolée, je ne suis pas libre ce soir. » Sans ça, passer la soirée avec Sean n'a aucun intérêt. Bien entendu, je pourrais prétendre être déjà engagée, même si je n'avais pas rendez-vous avec Sean, mais, pour être honnête, je ne le ferais sans doute pas. En plus, cela me donnera l'air sincère. C'est nécessaire quand on se montre distante et inaccessible, surtout si au fond de soi on préférerait boire de la liqueur dans son nombril.

L'après-midi traîne en longueur. Heureusement que je n'avais pas de tâche à accomplir aujourd'hui, parce que j'ai été bien trop occupée à passer le temps. J'ai fait ma liste de Noël sur un tableur Excel. J'ai dressé une liste complète de choses à faire, y compris écrire ma liste de Noël, histoire de pouvoir tout de suite barrer l'un des points. C'est très agréable. J'ai fait le tri dans mon sac à main, et établi une liste de tout ce que je dois racheter pour remplacer ce que j'ai jeté. J'ai pris trois tasses de thé et suis allée quatre fois aux toilettes ; et franchement je suis à court d'idées. Finalement, à 15 h 30, un événement intéressant se produit. J'ai décidé d'ouvrir ma messagerie personnelle, au cas où j'aurais reçu un mail de Brad, et juste pendant que je fouille dans ma besace à la recherche de ma lime à ongles, que je ne trouve pas à cause de toutes les listes, mon ordinateur émet un son.

Je laisse aussitôt tomber mon sac – la lime atterrit par terre – et me précipite sur la boîte de réception. S'il vous plaît, s'il vous plaît, s'il vous plaît, que ce ne soit pas une pub pour accroître la taille de son pénis.

Ce n'est pas ça. Je regarde de plus près le nom d'expéditeur, que je ne connais pas.

De : VPickford@FastLove.co.uk
À : esp79@hotmail.co.uk
Objet : Coordonnées

Chère Elizabeth,
Suite à votre participation à la réunion Fast Love la semaine dernière, l'un de mes autres clients a très envie d'entrer en contact avec vous, mais malheureusement il semble que le numéro de téléphone que vous nous avez confié soit erroné. Vous avez également sélectionné le participant

en question sur votre coupon-réponse. Il ne dispose pas d'ordinateur et ne peut donc vous envoyer de mail. Pourriez-vous par conséquent me communiquer dès que possible un numéro que je puisse lui transmettre, afin qu'une solution satisfaisante pour tout le monde soit mise en place prochainement?

Bien à vous,
Val Pickford.

En lisant ce message, je me décroche tellement la mâchoire qu'elle en tombe presque par terre. Est-ce que c'est vrai? Est-ce que Brad essaie de me joindre depuis tout ce temps? Est-ce qu'il a tenté frénétiquement de remplir l'engagement qu'il avait pris en cochant ma case, alors que j'ai sans le vouloir donné un faux numéro? Putain de bordel de merde, quelle nouille! J'en rirais presque, tant c'est idiot et merveilleux.

C'est bizarre qu'elle me dise qu'il n'a pas d'ordinateur. Je veux dire, je sais qu'il travaille chez Horizon, je l'y ai vu. Et je sais avec certitude qu'il y a des tas d'ordinateurs là-bas. Est-ce un mensonge? Ment-il à Val Pickford, ou à moi?

Aucune importance! Je lui demanderai quand je le verrai. C'est-à-dire aujourd'hui ou demain, si je règle ça maintenant. J'envoie mon numéro de portable à Val par mail sur-le-champ, avant de composer celui de Vini. Elle sera sur le cul.

Attendez une minute. J'appuie aussitôt sur «Raccrocher» et remets le téléphone dans mon sac. Vini n'est pas au courant officiellement pour Brad: elle a seulement deviné que j'avais craqué pour quelqu'un, mais je n'ai pas confirmé. Et elle ne m'a toujours pas expliqué son utilisation si peu conventionnelle d'un gloss rose, ni sa présence au *Perroquet du Pirate* l'autre soir, donc je ne vais certainement pas lui faire le plaisir de lui parler de cette histoire. Ouais, et en plus je sais qu'elle va essayer de me dire que j'ai fait exprès de mal noter mon numéro de portable pour saboter toute chance de rencontrer quelqu'un de nouveau parce que je suis encore amoureuse de Richard.

Richard. Ça fait longtemps que je n'ai plus pensé à lui.

De toute façon, elle se trompe complètement. Je veux dire, quel serait l'intérêt de donner un faux numéro ? Tout ce que j'avais à faire pour annihiler la possibilité d'avoir un coup de cœur pour quelqu'un d'autre et d'être heureuse jusqu'à la fin des temps, c'était de ne cocher aucune case. Tout bête. Aucune nécessité de faire l'idiote avec des faux noms et des faux numéros.

Sauf que, comme Vini me le fera remarquer, j'ai utilisé un pseudonyme.

Et alors ? De toute façon, ça ne compte pas. Il fait partie de mon identité. Mes parents m'appellent toujours Libby, ou Elizabeth, ou Beth. Mais ce n'est pas la question. Le fait est que je n'avais pas besoin de mentir sur mon prénom ou mon numéro parce que, si deux participants ne se choisissent pas mutuellement, personne ne reçoit ni coordonnées ni adresse, dans tous les cas. Je reprends le téléphone.

Oui, mais Vini va prétendre que je l'ai fait inconsciemment. Je repose brutalement l'appareil. Elle prétendra que je n'étais pas consciente de ce geste, mais que ça lui en dit plus long que tout ce que je peux essayer de lui raconter sur le fait que j'ai oublié Richard et que je suis prête à tourner la page. Je l'ai fait exprès pour contrecarrer mon désir d'être heureuse, même si je ne m'en suis pas rendu compte sur le moment.

Merde, elle a vraiment réponse à tout. Ce qui me ramène à l'idée que je ne peux pas lui parler du numéro de téléphone. Il faudra juste que je lui dise plus tard que Brad a mis une semaine à me contacter parce que… parce que… ah oui, parce qu'il s'est fait écraser en sortant du speed dating! Fabuleux!

Mon portable sonne dans mon sac, et je me retrouve pétrifiée. Waouh, c'était rapide. Je reste quelques secondes les yeux rivés sur la besace, comme si elle allait se transformer par magie en prince charmant, puis je la ramasse, l'ouvre d'un coup et me mets à farfouiller frénétiquement à la recherche de mon téléphone.

Il m'annonce un message non lu et me demande très poliment: «Lire maintenant?» Non, vraiment, je pense que je vais attendre jusqu'à demain. Bien sûr que je veux le lire maintenant! J'appuie un grand coup sur la touche verte.

Kikou, toi, beautée! Sa fais des jours et des jours ke j essait de t apelé, mais pas moillen. G T impassien de te revoire des que tu veut. Apele moi ou par texto, biz, Nigel n° 15 gros bizous

Quoi? Mais qui c'est, ce Nigel? Je contemple le message, les sourcils froncés, sans même me soucier des rides de mon front. Qu'est-ce qui peut bien se passer? Je ne sais pas qui est ce type, mais je devine à son orthographe que je ne l'ai pas coché. Même si la

239

survie de l'espèce en dépendait. Le monde se porterait mieux sans ces gênes-là. Je sais – oui, je sais – que je n'ai coché qu'une seule case, et c'était celle de Brad, qui avait le numéro quinze. Donc comment est-ce que ce débile a pu avoir mes coordonnées ?

Je me retrouve à observer toute la pièce, comme si je m'attendais à trouver une explication sur le poster de gestion des ressources humaines, mais, bien entendu, il n'y a pas plus de réponse sur celui-ci que d'habitude. Je reporte mon attention sur le téléphone et relis le message. Il est évident que finalement ça ne vient pas du délicieux Brad. Je m'affale quelques instants dans mon fauteuil, la déception et la tristesse me tirant vers le bas comme la gravitation universelle. Puis la colère me regonfle à bloc. La seule personne qui soit au courant que je suis allée au speed dating la semaine dernière, c'est Vini. Ce qui signifie que soit Nigel existe et s'est réellement procuré mes coordonnées d'une manière ou d'une autre, ce qui est impossible puisque je sais que je n'ai coché personne de ce style, soit Vini me fait une blague.

Oh non… La chienne ! Sans aucun doute, elle se souvient que je lui ai demandé ce qu'elle pensait du numéro quinze, et elle s'en sert à présent contre moi.

J'appuie aussitôt sur la touche « Répondre » et tape un message :

C'est coule d'avoire de tes nouvel. Rejoint moi demain soir au Péroquet du Pirrate, 20h30. L.

Parfait. Comme ça, elle va se sentir coupable de m'avoir donné de faux espoirs et elle devra s'expliquer avant demain soir pour m'éviter d'y aller. Non, attendez, je sors avec Sean au même moment, et c'est évident que je vais me trahir. Elle saurait que c'est une fausse réponse. Aussitôt, je change pour « mercredi », et j'appuie sur « Envoyer ».

La journée s'achève enfin, et je rentre à la maison, où je reste assise à attendre le lendemain. Vini est dans la cuisine, en train d'enlever une à une les airelles lyophilisées d'un bol de céréales.

— Coucou, dit-elle. Tu as passé une bonne journée ?

Je plisse les yeux. Elle veut m'amener à mentionner le message de Nigel pour pouvoir me faire une sorte de « Je t'ai eue ! » complètement infantile, mais je ne vais pas lui faire ce plaisir :

— Oui, merci. J'ai rendez-vous pour déjeuner demain avec Rupert de Witter.

— Putain, c'est pas vrai !

— Bah, si. Pourquoi pas ?

Elle ramasse toutes les airelles dans sa main et les jette dans la poubelle.

— Tu parles du Rupert de Witter d'Horizon Holidays, l'homme le plus riche de ce trou paumé ? Celui qui est par conséquent totalement impossible à rencontrer quelque part ?

— Hum, ouais, je pense.

— Bordel, Beth, comment tu fais pour avoir autant de chance ? Ce type a forcément un planning complètement dingue, sans doute bouclé jusqu'au mois de mai, et toi tu as réussi à obtenir un rendez-vous aussi vite ? C'est incroyable.

— Vini…, dis-je.

Puis, je me tais.

Elle a raison. Les hommes d'affaires comme Rupert ont des vies si remplies que leur agenda doit être tenu

241

par quelqu'un d'autre. Parfois par deux personnes. Alors comment a-t-il pu arranger un déjeuner avec moi demain, en un coup de cuillère à pot ? Il avait justement une possibilité à cette heure-là ? C'est peu probable. Il a annulé quelque chose pour me voir ? Une brûlante sensation de plongeon m'envahit de la poitrine jusqu'aux cuisses. Est-ce que ce serait possible ? Non, non, c'est aussi invraisemblable que le fait qu'il soit libre si vite. À moins…

Non, je ne veux pas y penser. C'est un déjeuner d'affaires, point final. Ce n'est pas plus important à ses yeux que d'innombrables autres déjeuners d'affaires qu'il a eus par le passé, qu'il aura aujourd'hui, demain, et toute la semaine, sans l'ombre d'un doute. Il a dû avoir une annulation de dernière minute, comme le coiffeur. Les gens obtiennent toujours des rendez-vous invraisemblables à cause d'annulations de dernière minute. Les autres gens, je veux dire. Ça ne m'arrive jamais, à moi.

— De toute façon, je sors dans une minute.

Elle engloutit les céréales, debout près de l'évier.

— Tu vas où ?

Elle hausse les épaules d'un air dédaigneux. Un peu trop dédaigneux, en fait :

— Oh, nulle part, rien du tout, juste un repas d'affaires. À plus !

Et elle laisse tomber son bol dans l'évier avant de filer dans sa chambre.

Je la suis des yeux. Je connais Vini. Elle mange des céréales avant de sortir dîner pour ne pas être affamée en arrivant au restaurant, comme ça elle pourra picorer délicatement dans son assiette. Ce n'est pas à un repas d'affaires qu'elle se rend.

Pour me venger, après son départ, je farfouille dans la penderie de Fake Face. Elle garde certains costumes à la maison pour les prêter à ses clients quand des tenues ordinaires ne conviennent pas. Il y a là Indiana Jones, Jack Sparrow, Neo de *Matrix*. Elle m'a formellement interdit de toucher à ce placard, et encore plus d'en sortir quoi que ce soit, et, Dieu m'en garde, de l'enfiler. Ouais, bon, je n'ai jamais eu besoin de passer l'un de ces déguisements auparavant — même si j'ai tout essayé, bien entendu, même Forrest Gump, pour le principe — mais maintenant j'aimerais quelque chose de monstrueusement sexy pour demain midi. Mes vêtements ne sont pas trop mal, mais je pense que je ferai plus femme d'affaires si je porte une jupe plus courte et des talons plus hauts. Et peut-être du vernis à ongles.

Je m'attarde un moment devant le survêtement de *Charlie et ses drôles de dames*. Bon Dieu, ce serait fantastique, non? Je pourrais entrer à grands pas, me montrer puissante et autoritaire, comme quelqu'un qui sait se servir d'un flingue. Je pourrais même arriver avec un casque et secouer ma chevelure en l'enlevant. Oh, c'est une image séduisante… Rupert me dévorant des yeux alors que je franchis le seuil. Je sais que je suis plutôt pas mal dans ce costume, et maintenant avec les cheveux blonds en plus… Non, voyons, Beth, tu vends des formations, tu ne poursuis pas des dealers sur ta moto. Je finis par trouver une panoplie qui pourrait avoir été portée par Michelle Pfeiffer — jupe au-dessus du genou, chemisier en soie ivoire, chaussures sexy — et le cache dans ma chambre pour demain.

Je passe le reste de la soirée à me préparer. Je ne vais pas entrer dans les détails, mais il est question de cire.

En fait, cela fait un bon moment que je n'avais rien fait de tout ça, donc, quand j'arrive au bureau le lendemain matin, j'ai la peau plus douce qu'elle n'a été depuis des mois, et la tenue soyeuse à la Michelle Pfeiffer ondule sensuellement sur mon corps.

À peine ai-je enlevé mon manteau que Sean me siffle comme le loup de Tex Avery, et je me sens tout à coup vulnérable.

— Dis donc, tu déchires aujourd'hui, Blondie, souffle-t-il à voix basse. Ce look de secrétaire sexy te va vraiment bien. Vivement ce soir.

Et il me gratifie une fois de plus de son clin d'œil au ralenti qui me donne la chair de poule.

Qu'est-ce qu'il peut bien sous-entendre? Il ne croit quand même pas que je me suis habillée comme ça pour lui? Bon Dieu... Faudra que je pense à me vêtir le plus mal possible pour notre rendez-vous, pour lui faire comprendre. Vini aura bien quelque chose à me prêter.

OK, le déjeuner est à 13 heures, donc il me reste à peine plus de trois heures à tuer, si je compte trente minutes pour aller en ville et trouver une place de stationnement. Je sors subrepticement la brochure Horizon du tiroir de mon bureau et laisse traîner mes yeux sur la photo de la dernière page. Humm... Je la range à la hâte, attrape mon sac et mon manteau, et me dirige vers le centre-ville.

À ma grande surprise, je me gare très facilement, sans doute parce qu'il est encore tôt, et je me retrouve à 10 h 15 en train de flâner sans but dans la ville, essayant d'avoir l'air de quelqu'un qui a fort à faire. De fait, j'ai fort à faire – je dois dénicher un cadeau pour ma petite cousine Charlotte et pour ses parents –, mais je ne peux rien entreprendre avant le déjeuner avec Rupert. Je ne peux pas paraître maîtresse de moi et séduisante si je débarque au *Madeleine's* avec sous le bras une paire de pantoufles lapin, un tournevis électrique et un bain de pieds bouillonnant.

En fait, la question est plus de me sentir maîtresse de moi et séduisante en arrivant. Je pourrais très bien laisser les lapins dans le coffre, mais je saurais quand même qu'ils sont là.

Alors, comment tuer le temps jusqu'à midi trente ? Je traîne dans la zone piétonne, les mains dans les poches, regardant autour de moi, et soudain mes yeux tombent sur *Whytelys*. Bon, c'est un énorme bâtiment de cinq étages au milieu de la ville, avec toute une série de boules de Noël dorées de la taille d'une citrouille et des ampoules de toutes les couleurs qui clignotent et qui scintillent dans toutes les vitrines. Je ne pouvais pas le louper. Mais, à cet instant, une idée me traverse l'esprit.

Sean a ce rendez-vous avec le directeur régional cet après-midi, sans doute plus ou moins à la même heure que mon déjeuner avec Rupert. Et si je me promenais un peu dans le magasin pour voir si je peux trouver des infos utiles pour lui ? Ensuite je l'appellerai au bureau, lui communiquerai ce que j'ai appris, et il pourra s'en servir dans son topo de tout à l'heure.

C'est fantastique ! Non seulement ça me donnera une bonne occupation qui m'évitera d'avoir l'air de m'être fait poser un lapin, mais en plus ça signifie que si Love Learning est sauvé par le contrat avec *Whytelys*, je pourrai dire que j'y ai participé.

Ça a l'air affreux, et ce n'est pas ce que je pensais. Je voulais simplement dire que je n'aurai pas à me sentir cent pour cent redevable à Sean. Ni moi ni personne.

J'entre donc et me fonds discrètement parmi les cardigans brodés et pantalons bleu marine qui font face aux coffrets de produits à la gelée royale. Ma tenue de Michelle Pfeiffer paraît un peu voyante dans cet environnement, et je me dis que je ferais mieux de prétendre être là pour affaires. Je ressors aussitôt pour faire un saut au *Virgin*, où j'achète un classeur et des feuilles, puis, à la dernière minute, des intercalaires. Je mets les feuilles dans le classeur, y fourre les intercalaires et le serre contre ma poitrine. Enfin, je retourne à *Whytelys* et me rends d'un pas décidé au Service Clients, où je demande à parler à la gérante.

Il apparaît qu'elle ne sait rien de la politique de formation :

— Je gère le magasin, moi, c'est tout, me dit-elle. Dans les chemisiers, je m'y connais. Les cravates, ça passe. Pour les sels de bain, oreillers parfumés, cintres molletonnés, je suis celle qu'il vous faut. Mais la formation ? Aucune idée. C'est les gars du siège social qui s'en occupent. Des mecs qui restent assis sur leur cul toute la journée à décider ce qu'on va faire dans les prochains mois ! Comme s'ils s'y connaissaient pour faire tourner une grosse boîte comme ça, hein ?

— En effet. (J'ouvre ostensiblement mon classeur et tiens mon stylo pointé sur la première page.) Mais vous devez savoir quelle formation reçoivent les membres du personnel quand ils sont recrutés ? Par exemple, est-ce qu'ils font un stage préparatoire ? Est-ce obligatoire de passer un brevet de secourisme… ?

— C'est comme je vous disais : s'il faut arranger les chemises de nuit à fleurs, je sais faire. Si vous cherchez des pantoufles en daim, venez me trouver. Mais si vous souhaitez discuter formation allez au siège social. Vous voyez ce que je veux dire ?

—Oui, je vois. Vous n'auriez pas leurs coordonnées, par hasard ?

—Je dois pouvoir vous trouver ça. Deux petites minutes. Nerys ! hurle-t-elle, et au rayon des *Christmas puddings* une femme replète avec une guirlande dans les cheveux sursaute, puis arrive en courant :

—Oui ?

—Le numéro du siège social pour cette dame, s'il te plaît Nerys.

—Ah, d'accord. OK.

Nous suivons toutes deux du regard le petit corps grassouillet de Nerys qui part, comme un bouchon au fil de l'eau, en direction de la porte « Accès Réservé au Personnel » au fond du magasin, puis la directrice se tourne à nouveau vers moi :

—Il vous fallait autre chose ?

—Non, c'est parfait, merci beaucoup.

—Vous savez qu'il y a un pain d'épice offert si vous prenez un Latte Pain d'épice dans notre salon de thé ?

—Non, vraiment, je n'ai besoin de rien, merci beaucoup.

—Comme vous voulez. Bonne journée, dans ce cas.

Et elle joint les mains derrière son dos et s'éloigne d'un pas raide, arrangeant un caraco ici, un cardigan là.

Lorsque Nerys revient, j'envisage de lui demander quelle a été sa formation quand elle a débuté, mais après m'avoir tendu le numéro de téléphone sur un bout de papier, elle disparaît en toute hâte avant que j'aie pu ouvrir la bouche. Zut !

Eh bien, c'était une pure perte de temps. Excellent : objectif atteint, donc. Même s'il me reste encore une heure à tuer avant de me mettre en route pour le *Madeleine's*. Que vais-je faire maintenant ?

— Il t'a plantée là, ma jolie ? me souffle un homme en passant.

— Non ! dis-je avec indignation.

Comment ça se fait qu'on ne puisse pas être tranquille quelque part sans que quelqu'un se sente obligé de vous faire une remarque ? Bordel de merde !

— Je t'invite, si tu veux, me lance-t-il par-dessus son épaule, et à cet instant je remarque qu'il a de belles épaules, bien larges.

— N'y comptez pas.

J'ai répondu avec un sourire et, sans le faire exprès, je laisse mon manteau s'ouvrir.

Il fait mine de s'arrêter, et je vérifie aussitôt que je ne suis pas sortie toute nue sous mon manteau par inadvertance. Non, tout va bien, les habits sont là. Je lève les yeux vers le type qui trébuche un peu, secoue la tête avec un grand sourire, avant de s'éloigner en me saluant d'un geste de la main.

Attendez ! Je manque de le retenir. Mais je ne le fais pas. Mon cerveau est déjà en train de donner l'ordre à mon bras de se lever pour lui rendre son geste, mais je réussis à l'en empêcher. Dieu merci. Le rendez-vous imminent avec le délicieux Rupert me met dans un tel état que je me transforme en danger pour la société. Il vaudrait peut-être mieux que je m'enferme dans la voiture pendant l'heure qui vient, avant de me faire arrêter. Je prends le chemin du retour.

En passant devant l'animalerie, je décide d'aller voir si je ne pourrais pas trouver un cadeau de Noël pour le chat de ma mère. Je sais, c'est grotesque. Je parie que c'est même contraire à la religion. Mais maman vit seule, et Sybil est son unique compagnie. Et nombreux sont les gens qui ne considèrent pas Noël comme une fête religieuse, de toute façon.

Alors que je flâne dans les rayons de friandises pour félins et de cadeaux pour chiens, j'entends tout à coup une conversation à la caisse. Un mot en particulier fait tilt. Quelqu'un dit : « formation ».

— Tu crois qu'ils auront envie de le faire ? demande une autre voix.

— Peu importe qu'ils aient envie ou pas. Je les envoie, et ils ont intérêt à apprendre quelque chose.

C'est fabuleux ! Je me tourne dans cette direction et accélère un peu le pas, préparant déjà mon entrée en matière. En plus, j'ai la panoplie de circonstance, y compris le classeur et le stylo ! Fantastique !

Mais alors que je suis sur le point d'entamer ma manœuvre d'approche, je suis prise d'une hésitation. Et même je m'arrête complètement et reste immobile quelques secondes. Puis je repars vers la porte, quitte le magasin, et attrape mon portable dans mon sac. J'ai du mal à croire que je suis en train de faire ça, et je secoue lentement la tête en composant le numéro du bureau :

— Coucou, Ali, tu peux me passer Fatima, s'il te plaît ?

Quand Fatima décroche le téléphone, paniquée et essoufflée, je lui annonce qu'elle ferait peut-être bien de donner un coup de fil à *Instinct Animal*, puisque j'en sors et que je les ai entendus parler de « Relations Clients ».

— Tu… qu…, répond-elle en guise de remerciements.

— Ce n'est rien, Fati, dis-je d'une voix rassurante. Bonne chance.

Puis je lui lis le numéro indiqué sur l'enseigne et raccroche.

Pfff. C'était bizarre. J'ai juste offert ce coup-là à quelqu'un. C'est la première fois que je fais un geste pareil, depuis le temps que je travaille à LL. Incroyable. C'est sans doute parce que j'ai totalement confiance dans ma démarche auprès d'Horizon. Et je suis tellement surexcitée en ce moment que je perds un peu la tête. Ce qui me fait penser… Quelle heure est-il ? En consultant ma montre, je m'aperçois que j'ai toujours mon téléphone dans la main, et le morceau de papier que Nerys m'a donné dans l'autre. C'est encore le destin. Pas la peine de lutter. Quelque part, un être supérieur me pousse à appeler ce numéro, et il a organisé cet instant pour que ça se produise. Ce n'est pas moi qui décide, je ne peux rien y changer. Et, de toute façon, ça ne peut pas faire de mal, n'est-ce pas ? Je prétendrai tout simplement que je suis l'assistante de Sean Cousins et que je fais quelques recherches pour préparer son entretien de cet après-midi. Ce qui est vrai, si l'on n'y regarde pas de trop près.

— *Whytelys*, bonjour, dit une voix féminine dans mon oreille, à ma grande surprise.

Je me croyais encore en train de débattre avec moi-même, mais il semble que j'aie déjà pris une décision et composé le numéro.

— Oui, bonjour, j'appelle de la part de Love Learning. Serait-il possible de parler à quelqu'un au sujet de la politique de formation de votre magasin, s'il vous plaît ?

Elle me met en attente, et j'écoute *Jingle Bells* à la flûte de Pan pendant quelques secondes.

Je finis par entrer en communication avec une certaine Annette, mais elle n'est pas au courant de la réunion de Sean.

— Vous êtes sûre ? Il a rendez-vous avec le directeur régional.

— Vous savez de quel directeur il s'agit ?

— Euh, en fait, non. Ça a été arrangé avec le directeur régional, donc je pensais que…

— Eh bien, nous avons quatre directeurs régionaux, mais Love Learning n'apparaît dans aucun des agendas, donc si vous ne pouvez pas me donner le nom de la personne que vous venez voir…

— Oh non, non, ça ne fait rien. Ne vous embêtez pas.

— Vous voulez prendre un autre rendez-vous ?

Écoutez, je ne lui ai pas demandé de dire ça, pas vrai ? Je veux dire, je ne suis pas en train d'essayer de voler son contrat à Sean. Non, non, ça n'est pas en train de se produire, parce que je vais y mettre un frein. Je vais tout simplement dire à Annette que « merci beaucoup, mais ce n'est vraiment pas la… »

— Oui, s'il vous plaît, ce serait parfait.

Oh, bordel de merde ! Ma bouche a repris le contrôle.

À la fin de la conversation, j'ai un rendez-vous avec l'un des directeurs régionaux à 15 heures, mardi prochain, le 19, dans leurs locaux. Que je pourrai décommander sans problème après en avoir parlé à Sean ce soir. Je veux dire, c'est vraiment juste au cas où il y aurait eu un malentendu et où son rendez-vous de cet après-midi serait passé à la trappe. Je promets que je le laisserai aller à cet entretien la semaine prochaine, si sa rencontre de tout à l'heure n'a pas lieu. Bouche, tu peux te taire.

Chapitre 14

Recueil d'informations

Objectif à court terme : déjeuner sans baver.
Obstacles : le visage de Rupert.
Objectif à long terme : le visage de Rupert.
Obstacles : déjeuner sans baver.

Je retourne rapidement à la voiture et roule pendant huit minutes vers le *Madeleine's*, où je me gare sous un sapin de Noël géant. Et maintenant je me retrouve avec une vingtaine de minutes à tuer avant de pouvoir entrer. Bordel de merde. Qui aurait cru qu'une adresse aussi chic puisse se trouver si près de la voie rapide ? Ce n'est pas grave, je vais juste attendre dans la voiture jusqu'à 13 h 04, comme ça j'aurai l'air de ne pas avoir regardé ma montre toutes les deux minutes depuis ce matin. Quoi qu'il advienne, je ne dois pas arriver la première.

Très exactement six minutes plus tard, je me laisse nerveusement guider par le maître d'hôtel. Attendre dans la voiture était une idée stupide, comme je m'en suis rapidement rendu compte, pour des raisons obscures et subtiles auxquelles on ne pouvait pas espérer que je pense dans mon présent état d'esprit.

Je veux dire, qui aurait deviné que le temps serait si glacial ? De toute façon, Rupert aurait peut-être repéré une harpie pâle, à la figure transie, assise congelée sur le siège conducteur, et il aurait roulé des yeux devant ce comportement loufoque, avant de s'apercevoir que c'était moi.

Et me voici donc en train de passer à côté de tous les convives vêtus de ces horribles cardigans brodés que je regardais un peu plus tôt chez *Whytelys*, en direction d'une place au fond. Non, pas d'une place au fond. Mince alors, où allons-nous ? Nous avons dépassé toutes les tables et franchissons à présent les portes vers une terrasse en bois. Oui, c'est charmant, mais il fait hyperfroid, bordel ! Je suis entrée pour avoir chaud, merde ! Il me conduit vers une sorte de structure au bout de la terrasse. Oh non, c'est là que je vais ? J'ai une bouffée de panique irrationnelle, et je me demande si cet homme fait seulement semblant d'être le maître d'hôtel dans le but d'attirer des jeunes femmes innocentes dans un appentis dérobé, caché aux regards, où il les garde pendant des semaines enchaînées à un radiateur avec pour unique compagnie une vieille scie rouillée. Mais à cet instant il ouvre la porte pour me faire entrer, et j'en ai le souffle coupé.

On se croirait dans le chalet du père Noël. Il ne manque que le père Noël lui-même. Il y a la place pour cinq tables, mais une seule est mise. J'ai un bref aperçu de la table magnifiquement dressée, avec des couverts en or scintillants, des verres en cristal étincelants, des fleurs, des papillotes de Noël, des chandelles, dans une harmonie de blanc cassé soyeux et d'or. Puis je me rends compte que si tout miroite et brille ainsi, c'est parce que la pièce est remplie de bougies. Elle flamboie presque littéralement. Il n'y en a que deux sur la table, mais, tout autour de la salle, chaque mur porte au moins vingt chandeliers, peut-être même trente, et chacun présente une magnifique bougie dorée dont la lueur vacille. Je ne sais pas s'il y a ou non des radiateurs, mais il fait bien chaud. Délicieusement chaud. Et la pièce est animée du mouvement des flammes. Je franchis le seuil, captivée par la vue qui s'offre à moi, tandis que le maître d'hôtel se tient juste à l'extérieur.

Je me tourne vers lui :

— Est-ce que vous… ? Je veux dire, est-ce… ? Est-ce toujours… ?

Il sourit d'un air sagace :

— Ah, M. de Witter a demandé cet arrangement tout particulièrement, madame.

Je reste bouche bée. Je m'en rends compte, mais je ne peux pas m'en empêcher. Il y a sans doute une goutte de salive sur ma lèvre inférieure, mais je m'en fiche. Il a demandé cet arrangement tout particulièrement. Rupert. Rupert de Witter, l'homme avec qui j'ai rendez-vous. Il a fait ça, spécialement. Pour moi. Il l'a fait pour moi.

— Je suis certain que M. de Witter ne tardera pas, madame, ajoute le maître d'hôtel avec un sourire.

À ce stade de la conversation, je tiens à peine sur mes pieds. Dans ma tête se bousculent de brûlantes pensées charnelles, et le feu intérieur qui couve en moi à l'idée de rencontrer Rupert entre brutalement en éruption ; le brasier se propage à toutes les autres parties de mon corps, comme si quelqu'un avait laissé une traînée de paraffine de mon ventre vers l'extérieur. Je me retourne pour le remercier et remarque que ma première impression, celle d'un petit moustachu de quarante-cinq ans, est fausse : je me rends compte à présent qu'il est en fait très attirant dans le genre *latin lover* et qu'il a un timbre très sexy. Pour un peu, je sentirais mes pupilles se dilater en le regardant. Je me mouille les lèvres :

— Merci beaucoup, dis-je d'une voix rauque. C'est… incroyable.

Il s'incline légèrement :

— Tout le plaisir est pour nous, madame. J'espère que vous témoignerez votre satisfaction à M. de Witter… ?

J'écarquille les yeux, que je gardais mi-clos dans mon humeur torride. Quoi ? Qu'est-ce qu'il vient de sous-entendre ? Que je couche avec Rupert ici même, en guise de remerciement pour le déjeuner ? Tout ça pour quelques bougies ? C'est un véritable outra…

Je commence à fermer les yeux alors que je sens ma tête retomber et mes genoux flageoler.

Non. Où ai-je l'esprit ? Quelle idée ridicule ! Comment peut-il oser ? Quoi qu'il pense de moi, debout et bouche bée comme Simplet, je ne suis pas une pauvre traînée qui…

Oh, attendez ! Non. Il sous-entend certainement qu'il aimerait que je dise à Rupert à quel point j'ai été ravie, comme ça ils auront tous un bon pourboire. Et la visite de Rupert encore de nombreuses fois à l'avenir.

Oh non, je devrais m'asseoir et m'enchaîner à la chaise, pour le bien de l'humanité.

Donc je n'ai qu'un quart d'heure à tuer. Je commande une boisson, et lorsqu'elle arrive je la sirote d'un air décontracté, comme s'il m'était indifférent de me trouver ici ou ailleurs. Puis j'en demande une deuxième. Encore neuf minutes à attendre. Je me sens incroyablement sexy, installée ici, la lueur des chandelles dansant partout sur mon corps, la chaleur des flammes rosissant mes joues (à moins que ce ne soient les deux verres de sauvignon à jeun) et ma jupe de Michelle Pfeiffer remontée sur mes cuisses (c'est prévu pour faire ça quand on s'assied). Pendant un moment, j'imagine que je suis Rupert de Witter qui arrive, et j'essaie de me voir à travers ses yeux. OK, j'ai l'air bien. Même si c'est un peu difficile à dire, car le vin m'est monté à la tête. Mes cheveux sont comme il faut : à la lumière des bougies, le blond tourne au doré. J'ai les paupières qui tombent légèrement, alors j'écarquille un peu les yeux, pour finalement les laisser revenir à leur forme normale. Je ne voudrais pas qu'il croie que je viens de voir quelque chose d'effrayant derrière lui. Je trouve mon sourire un peu benêt, donc je le modère aussi. Oui, c'est bien : yeux charmeurs, cuisses satinées et doux sourire secret. Parfait.

La porte s'ouvre soudain à la volée, et je sursaute dans mon siège avant de me retourner vers le nouvel arrivant, qui se met à parler :

— Oh, Miss Sheridan, Beth, je suis désolé de vous avoir fait attendre.

J'ai le cœur qui bat la chamade, le souffle court, mais j'offre une apparence calme et alanguie alors que je lève les sourcils vers l'homme qui s'avance dans le chambranle. Et qui n'est pas Rupert de Witter.

— Qui êtes-vous ? Où est Rupert ?

C'est sorti avant que je puisse me reprendre. Ça sonne affreusement mal, je m'en rends compte, comme si je n'étais qu'un second rôle, une blonde idiote qui va se faire larguer par l'intermédiaire du comptable du héros.

— Je suis le comptable de Rupert.

Merde.

—Je me présente : Harris O'Neill. Rupert a été appelé à la dernière minute, malheureusement, et il m'a demandé de venir vous adresser ses excuses.

—Oh.

Il fait quelques pas dans la pièce.

—Vous permettez ? s'enquiert-il en désignant la chaise opposée à la mienne, avant d'attendre poliment mon accord.

J'essaie de répondre : « Mais bien sûr, je vous en prie » avec grâce, mais ce qui menace de sortir est : « Pourquoi n'êtes-vous pas Rupert ? », et je me contente donc d'un hochement de tête.

—J'espère que vous resterez quand même pour déjeuner ? dit-il en rapprochant son siège de la table. (Il est plutôt pas mal, dans le genre comptable en costume gris et cravate.) Ils servent de très bonnes choses. (Il se penche vers moi par-dessus les assiettes, m'enveloppant dans le parfum de son after-shave, et baisse la voix.) C'est Rupert qui paie, alors autant en profiter. Et la facture passera en note de frais, du moment que nous faisons notre affaire en même temps.

Quoi ? Qu'est-ce qu'il sous-entend ? Maintenant il faut aussi que je couche avec le comptable de Rupert, ici, par terre, dans cette pièce magnifique, la lueur des bougies vacillant sur nos corps nus qui s'étreignent, à deux pas d'un restaurant plein de gens qui pourraient nous voir s'ils quittaient leur table et venaient jusqu'à la porte, et le serveur qui va entrer et nous prendre sur le fait d'un instant à l'autre, tout ça dans le but de pouvoir faire passer l'addition en note de frais ? Je sens ma respiration s'alourdir, mon cœur battre à se rompre. Il a quelque chose de Matt Damon…

Non, non, mais qu'est-ce que je vais m'imaginer là ? Mais enfin, qu'est-ce qui m'arrive ? Il faut vraiment que je m'attache quelque part. Et pas au comptable de Rupert.

Concentre-toi, Beth, allons. Pourquoi es-tu venue ? Pourquoi as-tu envie à ce point de rencontrer Rupert de Witter ? Un indice : ce n'est pas pour coucher avec n'importe qui sur cette terrasse.

— Eh bien, c'est pour ça que nous sommes ici, n'est-ce pas ? finis-je par répliquer, en suant légèrement et en me tortillant sur ma chaise, tout en donnant l'impression de n'être ni terrassée par la déception ni frustrée sexuellement au point d'en devenir perverse.

— Parfait. Avec un peu de chance, la partie affaires ne nous demandera que quelques minutes, et ensuite nous pourrons prendre du bon temps. Bon sang, je meurs de faim. Les croquettes de saumon sont sacrément délicieuses, au passage. (Il attrape la carte.) Vous êtes déjà venue ?

J'hésite avant de répondre. Mon instinct me pousse à mentir et à faire comme si je mangeais ici tous les quatre matins, pour qu'il revienne aux oreilles de Rupert que je n'étais pas totalement submergée par l'expérience, mais après avoir vu *Madame Doubtfire* je sais que quand on prétend être autre chose que ce que l'on est, le résultat est une catastrophe.

— En fait, non, jamais.

— Eh bien, je ne suis venu qu'à deux reprises, et j'ai pris les croquettes les deux fois, donc je pense que je vais essayer quelque chose d'autre aujourd'hui. (Il examine le menu.) Hum. Venaison, peut-être. (Il lève les yeux vers moi et m'adresse un grand sourire.) Et du coup ce sera la dernière fois que Rupert me paie un déjeuner !

— Bah, vous le remplacez, n'est-ce pas ?

Il baisse la carte pour me regarder :

— Vous savez quoi ? Vous avez raison. Et il me doit une fière chandelle, avec ça.

Il continue à me scruter, puis sourit avant d'ajouter :

— Mais je dois reconnaître que je suis très content qu'il me l'ait demandé.

Ah. Que dois-je répondre ? Je ne peux pas lui dire que j'en suis moi aussi très heureuse, parce que ce n'est pas vrai. Même s'il a de très beaux yeux, je préférerais plonger mon regard dans celui de Rupert. Je finis par opter pour un sourire énigmatique et un hochement de tête qui n'engage à rien, et cela semble le satisfaire.

Une fois que nous avons commandé nos plats et notre bouteille de vin, Harris lève son verre dans ma direction :

— À Rupert et vous, dit-il d'un ton joyeux.

Et je suis aussitôt transportée au jour de notre mariage.

Je suis magnifique avec ma robe en soie crème et mes perles sauvages… Oh, ne pensons pas à ma tenue, regardez seulement Rupert ! Il porte une chemise à haut col avec une cravate rouge sombre, un gilet et un costume queue-de-pie gris foncé. Nous sommes côte à côte sous la tente, et il a les yeux rivés sur moi, admiratif, son regard balayant chaque parcelle de mon corps, dévorant tout ce qu'il voit, comme s'il ne pouvait se rassasier de cette vue.

— … relation d'affaires, conclut Harris, qui prend une lampée de vin.

Je cligne des yeux. Ah, d'accord. Merde, j'ai raté quelque chose ?

— Tout à fait, dis-je en sirotant mon verre.

— Rupert est un employeur sacrément chouette, en fait, continue Harris. Ça fait presque neuf ans que je travaille pour lui, et on ne s'est jamais disputés. Bien sûr, c'est un vrai cauchemar, avec ses reçus et ses livres de comptes ; il n'écrit jamais ses dépenses précisément, il loupe les échéances, il est toujours en retard aux réunions, ne fait pas ses paperasses correctement et imagine que je peux lire dans ses pensées, mais, à part ça, c'est un type formidable.

En l'écoutant parler, je me dis que ce repas sans Rupert n'est peut-être pas une telle perte de temps, après tout. De toute évidence, ce Harris connaît très bien Rupert, et c'est une chance unique pour moi de collecter quelques informations sur Horizon et son patron. Mentalement, j'ouvre un calepin et mâchouille le bout de mon crayon.

Je ne suis pas trop sûre d'aimer ce que j'ai entendu jusque-là, cela dit. Il semble un peu irresponsable. Vous voyez, il possède cette société de voyages monumentale, et il ne prend même pas la peine de se rendre aux réunions ? Il ne sait pas ce que c'est, de diriger une entreprise ? Est-ce qu'il a idée du nombre de personnes qui dépendent entièrement de lui ? Est-ce qu'il paie ses factures en temps et en heure ?

Harris tente de déchiffrer mon expression, qui doit être pleine de désapprobation, parce qu'il commence à avoir l'air paniqué et lève les mains :

— Oh là là, non, écoutez, je ne voulais pas dire… en fait, c'est un type bien sous tous rapports… Ce que j'essayais d'expliquer, c'est juste qu'il est comme ça avec moi. Je ne suis que son comptable, souvenez-vous. Je ne m'occupe que de sa fortune, qui ne l'intéresse pas. Il me rend dingue avec sa négligence envers l'argent, parce qu'il se retrouve à payer plus d'impôts que nécessaire. Je le vois chaque année, quand les échéanciers arrivent, mais il s'en fiche. J'ai l'impression de ne pas faire mon travail correctement, vous savez, de ne pas faire le maximum pour lui, mais il me garde. (Il sourit, mais malgré cela il a l'air triste.) Il me donne même une prime à Noël. Alors que, comparé à ce que je pourrais, je ne lui ai presque rien fait économiser. Je crois juste que le pognon est tout en bas de sa liste de priorités.

Oh là là… qu'est-ce qu'il pouvait dire de plus sexy ? Un millionnaire qui ne s'intéresse pas à l'argent ? Est-ce seulement possible ? J'imagine qu'avec de telles sommes, même en étant complètement écervelé, on ne peut pas se retrouver dans le rouge, n'est-ce pas ?

Par association d'idées, je pense à Fatima. L'opposé exact de Rupert. Pas millionnaire, se préoccupe des sous, horriblement endettée. Une pensée me traverse subitement l'esprit. Oh, ça alors ! Je déjeune avec un comptable : peut-être que ce gars pourrait me donner des conseils pour elle ?

— Hum, donc Harris, vous êtes comptable ?

Il sourit :

— Ouais. Pourquoi ?

— Eh bien, une de mes copines de bureau, Fatima, a des problèmes d'argent. Enfin, elle a des problèmes d'absence d'argent. Elle est dans un état pas croyable, vraiment anxieuse et malheureuse, elle pleure au travail, elle a peur de se faire licencier. Elle a un peu perdu la boule, pour être franche, elle fait des choses qui ne lui ressemblent pas, elle fréquente des types douteux, se fait arrêter…

Je me tais. La situation de Fatima paraît vraiment horrible, maintenant que je viens de tout mettre bout à bout. Comment a-t-elle pu en arriver là ? Et que se passera-t-il si Chas décide en effet de se séparer d'elle ? Et il n'est pas exclu qu'elle finisse par fomenter un braquage de banque pour essayer de rembourser ses dettes.

— Beth, n'ayez pas l'air si inquiète. Honnêtement. Votre amie – Fatima, c'est ça ? – elle va s'en sortir. Il y a toujours un moyen, du moment qu'elle est rationnelle.

— Vous croyez ?

— Oui, bien sûr. Qu'est-ce qu'elle a acheté ? Des choses qu'elle peut revendre ?

Je hoche la tête. Ah, c'est super ! Il va avoir une idée comme seuls les comptables en ont, grâce à toutes leurs années de formation spéciale, et une fois que Fatima aura fait ce qu'il propose, ses ennuis seront résolus. Je sens déjà le soulagement gonfler ma poitrine.

— Oui, elle a une Mini. Qui lui a coûté 9 500 livres. Qu'est-ce qu'elle doit faire ?

Je le dévisage, les yeux écarquillés, retenant mon souffle, attendant qu'il se mette à cracher des diamants et règle tous les problèmes d'un coup.

— Il faut qu'elle la vende, qu'elle rembourse ce qu'elle doit et qu'elle s'achète une voiture moins chère.

Pétrifiée, je garde les yeux rivés sur lui. J'arbore toujours mon expression pleine d'espoir de réponses, les sourcils levés, les lèvres entrouvertes, mais Harris s'est remis à siffler du vin et ne le remarque pas. Crotte et crotte, toutes ces années de formation intense et compliquée pour ça ? « Vendre la Mini et acheter une voiture moins chère ? » Eh bien, merci mon Dieu de m'avoir suggéré de lui poser la question, quel soulagement de pouvoir transmettre à Fatima les conseils éclairants d'un vrai comptable.

—Oui, après mûre réflexion, et ayant examiné toutes les possibilités, Fatima et moi avions déjà plus ou moins compris que c'était la meilleure solution. Seulement, elle a du mal à la revendre. Personne ne veut payer 9 500 livres pour une Mini de troisième main.

—Ah, je vois. Quel dommage…

Il porte à nouveau son verre à ses lèvres, prend une gorgée et le repose. Mais il n'ajoute rien, et aussitôt nos plats arrivent, alors il m'adresse un grand sourire, s'empare de ses couverts et attaque son assiette de bon cœur, et j'en déduis que c'est tout, qu'il ne va rien résoudre, qu'il n'a rien à me proposer.

Les croquettes de saumon sont délicieuses, cela dit. C'est bien la seule chose positive dans tout ce fiasco. Maintenant que Harris est complètement bourré, il est assez peu probable qu'il me révèle une mine d'informations sur Rupert. Alors que je mange, je commence à sentir poindre un minuscule sentiment de rancœur envers Rupert qui n'est pas venu. Je veux dire, Harris est très sympa, mais ce n'est manifestement pas le meilleur comptable que la terre ait connu. Et mon rendez-vous galant – pardon, ma réunion de travail – était prévu avec Rupert, pas son comptable. Pourquoi l'avoir envoyé à sa place pour l'amour du ciel ? Pourquoi ne pas avoir tout simplement annulé et trouvé une autre date ? Vini avait raison, c'est absolument impossible de le rencontrer, ou que ce soit et quel que soit le moment.

—Tout va bien ? demande soudain Harris en levant les yeux vers moi.

Je sens ce qu'on peut lire sur mon visage : c'est « emmerdée », et ce n'est pas bien. Je me force à sourire, et Harris se détend à vue d'œil.

263

—Oui, très bien, désolée. Je songeais juste au travail. Il va bientôt falloir que j'y aille, en fait. Est-ce qu'on peut régler nos affaires maintenant ?

—Oh oui, bien sûr. J'aurais dû y penser. (Il plie sa serviette et la laisse tomber dans son assiette vide.) Écoutez, Beth, Rupert aurait vraiment voulu être là, vous savez. Je lui ai parlé encore hier : il était impatient.

—Oh non, écoutez, ça ne fait vraiment rien. Je peux vous expliquer Love Learning aussi bien qu'à lui, alors je vous en prie, vous savez, ce n'est pas un… c'est tout à fait… ne vous en faites pas.

—Le truc, continue-t-il comme si je n'avais rien dit, c'est qu'il n'aime pas déléguer. Vous voyez ce que je veux dire ? Il aime s'impliquer dans les moindres détails, quand c'est possible. Cette boîte lui prend tout son temps.

—Eh bien, oui, c'est exactement ce que j'aurais…

—Le problème, ajoute-t-il, c'est qu'il ne se garde pas de temps pour sa vie privée, vraiment. C'est bien rare qu'il passe la soirée ailleurs qu'au bureau, alors il n'a quasiment aucune occasion d'avoir une vie sociale.

Quoi ? Qu'est-ce qu'il essaie de me dire ? Est-ce une mise en garde ? Je hausse les épaules et tente de donner l'impression de ne pas me sentir concernée :

—Ah, vraiment ? C'est bien dommage, n'est-ce pas ? Alors, quelle sorte de…

—Oui, oui, c'est dommage, reprend-il d'un ton pressant, en se penchant à nouveau par-dessus la table. Il fait passer son travail avant tout le reste, et ce n'est pas bon pour lui. Il finira tout seul et plein de regrets, et ce n'est pas ce que je lui souhaite.

Il prend encore une goulée de vin, d'une main assez tremblante, et c'est tout juste s'il arrive à reposer son verre correctement.

—Non, évidemment, vous êtes son ami, donc vous ne voulez que…

—Ce dont il a besoin, Beth, c'est d'une raison de travailler moins. Parce qu'en ce moment il n'a rien d'autre que le boulot, donc il bosse encore plus, ce qui l'empêche de trouver autre chose. Vous voyez ce que je veux dire?

Il me dévisage avec une telle intensité que je dois détourner les yeux :

—Hum, eh bien, je ne suis pas sûre…

—C'est un cercle vicieux, Beth, et il faut le casser. Il a besoin de quelque chose qui donne du sens à sa vie, parce que, ces temps-ci, il ne travaille que pour l'argent, alors que ça ne l'intéresse même pas.

—Aaaah, d'accoooord…

À ce moment, le serveur entre pour débarrasser la table, et Harris lui demande de mettre l'addition sur la note de Rupert.

—Tout s'est passé comme vous le souhaitiez, monsieur O'Neill? s'enquiert le garçon.

Quelque chose me fait soupçonner que Harris est déjà venu plus que deux fois avant aujourd'hui.

—Oh oui, merci, Dan. Parfait. Ne vous en faites pas, je le lui dirai.

—Merci, monsieur, répond Dan en sortant presque à reculons.

Harris se retourne vers moi :

—Allez, Beth, craquez cette papillote avec moi. Ensuite nous discuterons de ce que l'adorable Love Learning peut faire pour les hommes d'Horizon Holidays.

Chapitre 15

Petites révélations

Objectif à court terme : obtenir un autre rendez-vous avec Rupert. Il me doit un tête-à-tête.
Obstacles : l'expression « tête-à-tête » fait constamment apparaître dans mon esprit une image troublante, qui m'empêche de faire quoi que ce soit. Ne serait-ce que respirer.
Objectif à long terme : coller ma tête contre celle de Rupert. Alors, peut-être que nous la perdrons ensemble.
Obstacles : le rencontrer pour de bon serait déjà un début.

Il est à peu près 15 h 20 quand je retourne à mon bureau, et j'y trouve un énorme bouquet de fleurs. Mon visage se fend d'un grand sourire idiot, et je n'essaie même pas de le contenir. Sourire avec délices en recevant des fleurs de la part d'un millionnaire invraisemblablement sexy est tout en haut de ma liste de ce que je veux être en train de faire lorsque Richard viendra me chercher. J'imagine Rupert au téléphone avec le fleuriste, lui dictant le texte pour la carte, les pensées tournées vers moi tandis qu'il pèse chaque mot, chaque variété de fleurs, et je sens mon cœur se gonfler, battre et appuyer sur mes poumons, accélérant ma respiration. Je m'assieds, enchantée, et commence à fouiller le bouquet à la recherche du bristol.

Chercher le message me donne l'occasion d'apercevoir le type de fleurs qu'il a choisi pour moi. Je vois beaucoup de petits pétales roses, dans un nuage de verdure, et encore beaucoup d'autres sortes de pétales roses. Elles sont vraiment jolies. Très belles. Pas très originales, mais ça ne fait rien. Je suis tellement ravie de recevoir des fleurs pour une raison agréable, pour une fois. Ce n'est que mon troisième bouquet, et les deux précédents m'avaient apporté des mauvaises nouvelles.

Mais envoyer un bouquet c'est un peu un truc de vieux, en fait, non ? Et si j'arrête de me mentir, je sais très bien que ce n'est pas Rupert en personne qui a appelé le fleuriste. C'est sans doute son assistant qui l'a fait, pendant qu'il était plongé dans cette activité si importante qu'il n'a pas pu venir au rendez-vous qu'il avait lui-même proposé et arrangé. Donc, il me laisse tomber et ensuite il pense que tout va bien sous prétexte qu'une Lucy ou un Howard quelconques a passé un coup de fil à *Interflora* et inventé quelques phrases basées sur le compte-rendu que Rupert lui aura fait des événements d'aujourd'hui. Je sens une moue se dessiner sur mes lèvres, et je décide aussitôt de la réprimer. Ricaner devant les fleurs qu'un millionnaire lambda m'a bêtement fait livrer en guise d'excuses après m'avoir posé un lapin n'est pas en haut de la liste de ce que je voudrais être en train de faire quand Richard reviendra. Même pas dans le top 10.

Peut-être qu'il vaudrait mieux que j'oublie Rupert. On ne s'est jamais rencontrés, dès le premier rendez-vous il m'a fait faux bond et, maintenant, il m'envoie un bouquet de clichés pour se faire pardonner. J'ai pu me tromper sur lui en lisant les mails qu'il m'a écrits.

—Elles te plaisent ? demande Sean en venant me voir.

Je ne veux pas lui révéler qui me les a expédiées, ni pour quelle raison, ni que ça m'agace, ni pourquoi, donc je lui adresse un large sourire.

—Oh oui, je les adore. N'est-ce pas qu'elles sont magnifiques ? Ce sont mes couleurs préférées. Et ce parfum…

J'enfouis mon visage dans les pétales et inspire longuement, mais je ne sens rien d'autre qu'une désagréable odeur de cellophane.

—Absolument enivrant, dis-je en émergeant du bouquet.

—Super. Je pensais que tu aimerais toutes ces nuances de rose, donc c'est ce que j'ai choisi. Juste pour te dire, tu sais : j'ai vraiment hâte d'être à ce soir. Je pars pour ma… réunion… maintenant.

Et il me gratifie une fois de plus de son clin d'œil au ralenti. Aaargh !

Je le suis des yeux pendant qu'il s'éloigne, et tout à coup je prends conscience que le rendez-vous auquel il se rend est celui avec *Whytelys*. Ça tient toujours, donc. Eh bien, tant mieux : ça signifie que je peux annuler l'entrevue que j'ai organisée avec eux par inadvertance. Je le ferai demain, pour laisser à Sean une chance de me dire, ce soir, comment ça s'est passé.

Le bon côté de l'absence de Rupert ce midi, c'est que ma soirée avec Sean ne vient pas interférer avec d'autres invitations que j'aurais éventuellement pu recevoir. Même si j'avais l'intention de prétendre que j'étais déjà prise, n'est-ce pas ? Ce qui signifie que mon rendez-vous avec Sean n'a aucun intérêt. Mais je pense que je lui dois bien ça, après avoir accidentellement peut-être contacté *Whytelys* derrière son dos. En regardant les fleurs, je me rends compte à quel point ce bouquet rose inodore va bien avec Sean. Comment ai-je pu croire une seule seconde qu'une malheureuse petite botte rose comme celle-ci pouvait provenir de quelqu'un comme Rupert de Witter ? Il ne fait sans doute jamais livrer de fleurs. Plutôt des bracelets de diamant ou des premières éditions rares. Et, si jamais il en envoie, ce doit être des orchidées ou autre végétal vraiment exotique. Pas de pauvres bégonias fuchsia, ou Dieu sait ce que c'est. Quand j'y ai plongé mon visage, j'ai bien vu qu'elles ne venaient pas d'*Interflora* mais du seau en plastique noir placé à côté du minuscule sapin de Noël à la station-service du coin de la rue. C'est pour ça qu'il n'y a pas de carte. Pour un peu, je me sentirais submergée d'émotions.

Allez, on se remet au travail. J'ai un atelier « Motivation » la semaine prochaine et j'ai vraiment besoin de le préparer, mais je n'ai pas la tête à ça. Je me connecte à ma messagerie, et pendant que j'attends qu'elle s'ouvre une image me traverse l'esprit : Harris se dirigeant vers le bureau de Rupert.

Rupert se dépêche de le faire entrer, impatient et anxieux à la fois, le fait asseoir et se penche sur la table devant lui, en demandant : « Alors ? »

Mais Harris a une légère migraine. Il a abusé du vin. Il fait signe à Rupert de s'écarter et se lève :

— Donne-moi une minute, Rupe. J'ai besoin d'un peu d'eau.

—J'y vais, répond Rupert en se hâtant vers son bureau pour servir Harris avec la carafe qui s'y trouve.

Il la renverse sur la table, mais ça lui est égal. Il revient à grands pas vers Harris et lui tend le verre avec autorité. Harris ferme les yeux et boit à longs traits sous le regard de Rupert, bras croisés.

—Tu n'étais pas censé te saouler, dit-il d'un air de reproche. Je voulais que tu sois vif, que tu prennes des notes dans ta tête.

Harris secoue la tête. Avec précaution.

—Je ne suis pas saoul. Je suis seulement dans l'esprit de Noël.

—Ouais, OK, alors, Harry. Peu importe. Parle-moi juste d'elle, s'il te plaît, et ensuite tu pourras rentrer te coucher.

—Qu'est-ce que tu veux savoir ?

Rupert hausse les épaules, lève les mains :

—Je ne sais pas. Elle était drôle ?

Harris hoche la tête. Avec précaution.

—Un peu.

Rupert opine également du chef :

—OK. Bon. D'accord. En fait, ça, j'étais déjà au courant. Tu as réussi à te débrouiller pour m'amener dans la conversation ?

Harris le dévisage :

—Tu n'as pas envie de savoir à quoi elle ressemble ?

Rupert lui rend son regard, le visage de marbre :

—Je ne sais pas. Je ne me suis pas posé la question.

—Sans blague ? Tu es sûr ?

—OK, si, j'y ai pensé. Mais, au fond, je ne sais pas si je veux vraiment avoir la réponse. Est-ce que je veux savoir… ? Non, ne me réponds pas. Laisse-moi réfléchir une minute.

Harris attend en silence pendant que Rupert fait les cent pas. Finalement, il reprend la parole :

— OK, écoute. Que dirais-tu que je te raconte maintenant comment ça s'est passé, et si tu décides plus tard que tu veux savoir à quoi elle ressemble tu m'appelles ?

Rupert s'arrête et se retourne :

— Je ne sais pas. Est-ce que ce serait… ? OK. Oui, d'accord. Non. Oui. Oui. C'est une bonne idée. Comment c'était ?

J'espère que les exigences d'Harris sont beaucoup moins élevées que celles de Rupert et qu'il est en train de lui dire en ce moment même que je me situe quelque part entre Victoria Wood et Halle Berry. Je veux dire, l'humour de l'une, le corps de l'autre. Et n'oublions pas qu'il était bourré. Ça aide.

Bon, j'ai besoin de me concentrer sur ce que je fais. J'ai ouvert ma messagerie, bien que je n'attende rien de particulier. Rupert n'aura pas écrit, puisqu'il a passé la journée à une quelconque réunion urgente. Même si je me demande bien quel genre de situation est suffisamment pressante chez un voyagiste pour prier quelqu'un d'annuler un rendez-vous à déjeuner. Un accident obscur avec une banane gonflable ? La nouvelle renversante que la bière locale bon marché provoque maux de tête et nausées ? Un bateau de croisière en panne de cocktails ? Je me tourne vers mon écran, et, à ma grande surprise, il y a bien un message de lui. Je suis parfaitement consciente qu'il m'a froidement posé un lapin aujourd'hui, mais j'ai du mal à me retenir d'afficher malgré tout un immense sourire. Finalement, je lis le message.

De : Rupert de Witter
À : Beth Sheridan
Objet : Déjeuner aujourd'hui

Chère Beth,

Me pardonnerez-vous ? Dites oui, s'il vous plaît. Je m'en veux terriblement de vous avoir laissée tomber ce midi, et je ne peux qu'imaginer à quel point vous devez me haïr à présent. J'aimerais que vous sachiez que seule la plus grave, la plus sérieuse des urgences liées aux vacances pouvait me retenir loin de vous. Et c'était le cas.

Apparemment, plus j'attends un événement avec impatience, plus il a de risque d'être empêché, donc il était pratiquement inévitable que notre déjeuner d'aujourd'hui n'ait pas lieu. Si nous parvenons malgré tout à trouver une autre date, je ferai de mon mieux pour être moins impatient. Ainsi nous aurons peut-être une chance. Même si je ne suis pas certain d'être capable de me dominer à ce point.

De toute manière, j'ai eu une idée qui était presque aussi bonne que de venir moi-même : j'ai envoyé mon comptable jouer les espions. C'est une technique bien connue chez les voyagistes. De cette façon, je saurai tout de vous grâce à Harris, si bien que lorsque nous nous rencontrerons à l'avenir je serai mieux préparé.

S'il vous plaît, répondez-moi et accordez-moi votre pardon.

Bien à vous,
Rupert.

Mon pardon ? Il n'y a rien à pardonner. De toute évidence, il n'y pouvait rien si quelque chose de vraiment sérieux s'est produit. Où avais-je la tête ? Une panne de cocktails, pour l'amour du ciel ! J'imagine qu'il a passé une journée harassante à essayer de résoudre une horrible catastrophe à propos d'un séjour, qu'il a passé des coups de fil délicats, fait des déclarations à la presse, et je suis là, à évoquer une banane gonflable géante.

Alors que je relis le message pour la quatrième fois, je comprends réellement ce qu'il veut dire dans le deuxième paragraphe. Pour être juste avec moi-même, il faut expliquer qu'il aurait pu écrire : « Mon âne n'avait plus de cacahouètes, bien à vous, Rupert », sans que je cherche à comprendre. Je me contente d'afficher un sourire mièvre, complètement enchantée qu'il m'ait envoyé un mail après avoir passé la journée à se débattre contre une catastrophe. Mais quand je saisis enfin le sens de son propos la brûlante sensation de plongeon m'étreint à nouveau le ventre. Il dit que plus il attend un événement avec impatience, plus il a de chance d'avoir un empêchement. Et ensuite il dit que ça signifie qu'il était inévitable que notre rendez-vous n'ait pas lieu. Ça veut forcément dire qu'il était impatient de me rencontrer. Qu'il était vraiment impatient de me rencontrer. À tel point que c'est lui qui nous a empêchés de nous retrouver. Indirectement, je veux dire.

Ça ne paraît pas très probable, en fait. Par exemple, il devait être enthousiaste quand il montait Horizon. Il a dû être impatient d'acheter des choses. Je sais avec certitude qu'il s'est tenu au moins une fois sur le pont d'un yacht d'apparence très coûteuse, sous un soleil éblouissant et un ciel d'un bleu profond. Il devait attendre ce moment avec impatience, et pourtant il existe une preuve photographique qu'il a bien eu lieu. Je clique aussitôt sur « Répondre ».

Vous essayez de me faire croire que vous n'avez jamais été impatient de partir en vacances, d'aller à l'opéra, ou d'acheter une voiture ? Juste parce que si vous étiez impatient ça n'allait pas se produire ?

J'ai cliqué sur « Envoyer » avant même d'avoir réfléchi. Merde, j'espère que je n'ai pas l'air querelleuse, sarcastique ou cynique. Parce qu'il y a peu de choses moins séduisantes que…

Oh mince, déjà une réponse !

Bonjour ! Vous êtes là ! Comment s'est passé le déjeuner ? Non, ne me répondez pas. En tout cas, pas maintenant.

Il se trouve que je n'aime pas l'opéra – je ne suis pas Richard Gere (malheureusement) –, donc j'étais plus impatient de me couper les ongles des pieds ce matin que je ne le serais de m'y rendre. Et quand vous avez déjà acquis chaque voiture qui vous faisait envie, ça n'est plus très attirant non plus.

En général, quand j'ai besoin d'un nouveau véhicule, j'envoie quelqu'un me l'acheter.

Je plaisante. Je ne possède pas toutes les voitures que j'aie jamais désirées, bien entendu. Et ça me fait toujours plaisir de m'en procurer une nouvelle. Je ne suis pas gâté à ce point. Mais je n'aime pas l'opéra, et j'étais vraiment impatient de vous rencontrer. Je n'ai pas pris beaucoup de plaisir à me couper les ongles des pieds, cela dit.

Votre Rupert.

PS : Vous pensez que j'ai eu tort d'évoquer les ongles des pieds ?

OK, tout va bien, calme-toi, il n'y a pas de sens caché dans ce message, ce n'est pas une déclaration d'amour éternel ni d'adoration, avec la promesse tacite qu'il m'appartiendra corps et âme pour toujours. C'est une coquille. Il voulait de toute évidence écrire « Amicalement vôtre, Rupert », et il a simplement oublié un mot. Et une virgule. Par erreur.

Aussitôt, je me connecte sur Internet et entre « Freud » dans le moteur de recherche. Je ferme illico la fenêtre. *Jésus Marie Joseph sur le divan, Beth, reprends-toi !*

Je saisis la brochure d'Horizon et l'ouvre à la dernière page. Bon, allez, j'avoue. Elle était déjà ouverte à la dernière page, pliée, avec la photo de Rupert sur le dessus. En la regardant, je sens une fois encore mon ventre chauffer et se tortiller, et je songe à ce « Votre Rupert ». C'est absurde, je sais. Il est tellement beau et riche, il n'y a pas moyen qu'il s'intéresse à une petite personne sans intérêt comme moi. Il ne peut sans doute pas faire un pas sans se cogner à une *playmate*. En fait, il avait probablement une fille magnifique avec lui sur ce yacht fabuleux le jour où le cliché a été pris. Je me penche vers la photo, les yeux plissés, le nez presque collé au papier. Est-ce une ombre pulpeuse mais étrangement superficielle et égocentrique que je devine sur le pont derrière lui ?

— Tu fais des recherches, c'est ça ? dit une voix traînante derrière moi, ce qui me pousse à me redresser d'un coup.

Sean est tout près, avec son manteau, ses clefs de voiture à la main. Il ajoute :

— Ne travaille pas trop.

— Oh non, ce n'est pas ça.

Je referme la brochure d'un geste sec et la laisse tomber négligemment sur le bureau, où elle se rouvre immédiatement à la dernière page :

— Je rêve juste à mes prochaines vacances.

Il hausse les sourcils :

— Vraiment ? Tu pensais recevoir des informations par télépathie avec le boss, alors ?

Du menton, il désigne la photo souriante de Rupert caressé par le soleil.

— Quoi ? Ah, tu veux dire… ça ? Non, non, c'est juste… c'est… bah c'est… c'est mon ancien patron. Tu te souviens ? Je bossais chez Horizon, alors ça me fait bizarre de revoir cette image, après toutes ces années. Tu vois.

— Ah, OK. Bon, ne te laisse pas embarquer au point d'oublier notre rendez-vous de tout à l'heure au *Perroquet du Pirate*, d'accord ?

Il me fait un clin d'œil et quitte la pièce. Dieu merci, parce que pendant qu'il parlait je me suis aperçue que le dernier message de Rupert était là, en évidence sur mon écran, et je suis passée en mode panique parano. Est-ce que Sean l'a vu ? A-t-il eu le temps de le parcourir ? Qu'en aurait-il pensé s'il l'avait lu ? En déduirait-il que j'ai une liaison avec Rupert de Witter ? Devinerait-il que je travaille sur un contrat avec Horizon ? J'espère voir juste en supposant que la réponse est « non » à chacune de ces questions.

Le départ de Sean a attiré mon attention sur le fait que non seulement ce cher collègue est déjà revenu de sa réunion chez *Whytelys*, mais qu'en plus il est 17 heures passées et que tout le monde est parti. Ali et Skye sont en grande conversation à l'autre bout de la pièce, et, sans l'ombre d'un doute, Chas est toujours dans son bureau, mais, à part ça, je suis toute seule. Bien. Je vais écrire encore un message à Rupert, et ensuite j'y vais. Je dois me préparer pour mon rendez-vous de rêve numéro deux. La réflexion sur l'atelier « Motivation » attendra demain.

De: Beth Sheridan
À: Rupert de Witter
Objet: Parties du corps

Cher Rupert,
Je suis pour la discussion franche et ouverte sur les parties du corps à la première occasion. De cette façon, personne ne craint qu'elles n'apparaissent plus tard dans la conversation. Je peux vous dire dès à présent, en toute franchise, que je vais quitter le travail dans peu de temps et que je me rendrai à la salle de sport pour me muscler l'intérieur des cuisses, qui est très décevant, comparé à l'extérieur. Vous pourriez à votre tour

mentionner vos biceps, et je vous répondrai par des détails concernant mon abdomen. Nous pourrions échanger des informations ainsi en toute liberté, en sachant que cela nous évitera toute gêne à l'avenir.

Cependant, je voudrais émettre une restriction pour les ongles des pieds. J'oppose également mon veto aux poils de nez.

Bien à vous,
Beth.

Oui, je sais, c'est très coquin. Je suis clairement en train de faire monter notre marivaudage d'un cran. Je suis sur le point de ne pas l'envoyer. Je garde mon curseur sur le bouton « Envoyer » plus de dix secondes avant de finir par cliquer semble-t-il par pur agacement.

Encore plus frustrant, alors que je meurs d'envie d'avoir la réponse, je n'ai pas le temps de l'attendre, puisque je dois me préparer pour ce rendez-vous avec Sean. J'ai prévu d'apporter le plus grand soin à mes préparatifs, car je veux que tout soit parfait. Je vais devoir m'entraîner un peu pour le maquillage, avant de l'appliquer pour de bon. Ce sera difficile d'atteindre la perfection pour les cheveux. Et il y a la tenue. Je vais devoir la choisir très attentivement, si je veux trouver quelque chose qui accentue tout ce que je souhaite mettre en valeur, et qui masque tout le reste. Ça ne sera pas facile, mais quand je ferai mon entrée dans le bar, je veux qu'il se retourne et qu'il me voie, répugnante à en vomir.

Chapitre 16

Grandes révélations

Objectif à court terme : me rendre absolument repoussante.

Obstacles : mon estime de moi, ma fierté personnelle, ma décence profonde et ma chevelure magnifique.

Objectif à long terme : me faire ~~Rupert~~ le contrat avec Horizon.

Obstacles : le rendez-vous avec Sean. Je n'ai pas le temps.

Il se révèle que sortir de l'appartement déguisée en héroïne de Ken Loach n'est pas aussi facile qu'on pourrait le croire. Je n'ai pas pu le faire. Je ne sais vraiment pas comment toutes ces bonnes femmes vêtues de pantalons de survêt blanc en éponge et de débardeurs arrivent à franchir le seuil de chez elles. « Chapeau bas », comme dirait Chas. La prochaine fois que j'en vois une – ou une bande – dans ce genre-là en train de traîner devant la poste, je hocherai la tête pour rendre un silencieux hommage à quelqu'un qui a des couilles. Enfin, je ne vais pas vraiment leur parler. Ni, vous savez, établir de contact visuel. Pourtant je peux – je ne vais pas dire les « admirer » – leur lancer un coup d'œil furtif, et détourner aussitôt les yeux avec un regard nouveau.

Mais cela va à l'encontre de chacun de mes instincts et de chacune de mes croyances, de tenter de paraître la plus hideuse possible pour sortir. En plus de l'estime de soi, il y a la possibilité que je sois aperçue, comme vous le savez, ce qui serait catastrophique si j'avais l'air d'avoir accouché à l'instant. D'un enfant nommé Destiny.

J'ai essayé, je vous assure. Je me suis frotté la figure jusqu'à ce qu'elle soit rouge et luisante, tiré les cheveux en une petite queue-de-cheval, et même étalé de l'ombre à paupières grise sous les yeux. Puis, après avoir enfilé le survêt de Vini et la polaire grisâtre informe qu'elle porte toujours quand elle ne se sent pas bien, je me suis approchée, joyeuse, du miroir, pour voir l'impression générale, et j'ai éclaté en sanglots.

Je me suis donc démaquillée et tonifiée, frisé les cheveux au fer, et remaquillée pour ne pas avoir l'air de ne m'être nourrie que de chips depuis huit ans, puis j'ai passé un jean et un long gilet marron. Après une heure quarante de préparatifs, j'avais réussi à avoir l'allure de quelqu'un qui n'a consacré que peu de temps et d'efforts à son apparence, parce qu'aller plus loin avec celui qui l'attend ne l'intéresse pas. Parfait.

Ah, que je déteste le *Perroquet du Pirate* ! Il offre un décor d'île déserte, avec de faux palmiers, des oiseaux tropicaux et des bananes en plastique partout. Tous les serveurs doivent être déguisés en corsaires, et quand j'arrive l'hôtesse me dit d'une voix monotone :

—Bienvenue au *Perroquet du Pirate*, ma belle, oh oh, où les morts ne mentent jamais.

Je lui jette un regard et remarque qu'elle a relevé son bandeau sur son front. De toute évidence, soit elle en a eu assez de ne pas voir en relief, soit ça la faisait transpirer. Au milieu de ce paysage des Caraïbes trône un sapin de Noël incongru, l'air gêné d'être là, essayant de se fondre dans le décor près de la cheminée, et des flocons de neige en plastique pendent du plafond. Je me dirige vers Sean.

—Salut, désolée pour le retard, dis-je en m'asseyant en face de lui sans lui laisser le temps de se pencher vers moi pour une raison ou une autre. C'est pour moi ? (Il y a un ballon de vin blanc sur la table devant moi.) Merci.

Je prends une gorgée. La soirée s'illumine.

—Ouais. Alors, comment ça va ? On n'a pas tellement eu l'occasion de bavarder au boulot. Tu as bien bossé, aujourd'hui ?

—Oh oui, vraiment. J'ai été très productive.

Je hoche la tête d'un air entendu, avant de serrer aussitôt les lèvres sur le bord de mon verre pour clore la conversation.

—Vraiment ? (De toute évidence, Sean n'a pas saisi l'allusion.) Qu'est-ce que tu faisais, de la recherche de contrats ? Par « productive », tu veux dire que tu en as décroché un ?

Je pose mon ballon de vin et le regarde. Il est penché vers moi, les bras étendus sur la table, les sourcils joints et levés à la fois, la bouche ouverte. Soit il est fasciné par ma recherche de contrats pour une raison qui m'échappe, soit il vient d'avoir une petite attaque. Et là, ça me revient.

—Ne parlons pas de moi. Et toi ? Comment s'est passée ta réunion avec *Whytelys* ?

Mais avant que j'aie fini ma question il secoue la tête :

— Putain, c'était horrible. (Il ramène ses bras vers lui sur la table et s'appuie sur son dossier avec un soupir.) Ils n'étaient absolument pas intéressés. Ils n'avaient même pas envie de m'écouter. Il semblerait qu'ils aient eu des échos merdiques d'Eastern Star Bank, mais je n'en sais pas plus. Pour autant que je sache, chez Eastern ils étaient satisfaits de notre boulot. Tu te souviens de quelque chose ? Non, moi non plus. Je ne sais pas. En tout cas, ils m'ont pratiquement jeté en bas de l'immeuble en se moquant de moi. C'était une vraie humiliation.

— Tu plaisantes ? Merde, Sean, ça a dû être affreux.

— Oh oui, crois-moi.

— Je ne comprends pas. Pourquoi ont-ils accepté de te recevoir, si c'est ce qu'ils pensaient ?

Il hausse les épaules avec amertume :

— Pour rire un bon coup, apparemment.

— Oh non, ça m'étonnerait. Ils n'iraient pas perdre leur temps à... (Je me tais. Une pensée vient de me traverser l'esprit.) « Ils » ? C'était qui, que tu as vu ? Ils étaient plusieurs ?

— Ah non, non, juste une personne. Je voulais dire, tu vois, *Whytelys* collectivement.

— Ah, OK. Alors, tu as rencontré qui ?

— Le directeur régional. Je te l'ai dit.

— Bah oui, mais... je pense... que j'ai lu quelque part... (Je hausse les épaules avec une désinvolture parfaite.) Il n'y a pas plusieurs directeurs régionaux ? Disons, peut-être, je ne sais pas, quatre ?

Il me dévisage :

— Bah merde, Betty, peut-être bien, mais le gars que j'ai vu n'a pas pris la peine de m'informer, alors qu'il me jetait de son bureau, qu'il y en avait trois autres comme lui qui me trouveraient sans aucun doute tout aussi divertissant.

Il fait l'un de ses roulements d'yeux qui veulent dire « mais ce n'est pas vrai ! » et prend une gorgée de bière.

Ce qui me dissuade aussitôt de lui parler du rendez-vous que j'ai pris. Je veux dire, ce type est de toute évidence humilié et brisé après cette réunion calamiteuse : comment pourrais-je lui dire que j'ai fixé une autre date par précaution ? Il va croire que je m'attendais à ce qu'il échoue, parce qu'il est arrogant, condescendant, paresseux, incapable de s'exprimer, sexiste, un vrai mer...

— Bon sang, j'avais vraiment besoin de ce contrat, soupire-t-il tout à coup en se frottant les sourcils.

— Oui, je vois de quoi tu parles.

Il se redresse, ses yeux rencontrent les miens, et je m'aperçois qu'ils sont subitement chargés d'une ferveur et d'une intensité qui me vrillent.

— Non, Beth, tu ne sais pas, bordel ! Tu n'en as pas la moindre idée, parce que tu mènes ta petite existence où rien ne va jamais de travers et où ton seul souci, c'est de choisir chaque matin ce que tu vas mettre pour aller travailler. Quand la boîte fermera et qu'on sera tous au chômage, garde une pensée pour ceux d'entre nous qui seront dehors dans la vraie vie, si tu veux bien, pendant que tu emballeras tes mules roses en plume de cygne pour retourner chez papa-maman.

C'est incroyable et insupportable, mais j'ai les yeux qui commencent à picoter, et l'émotion m'envahit. *Pour l'amour du ciel, c'est ce connard de Sean, à quoi est-ce que tu t'attendais ?* J'essaie de chasser mes larmes par quelques battements de cils et de me calmer par l'idée apaisante qu'il est de toute évidence sujet à de violentes sautes d'humeur et pulsions meurtrières en raison d'une toxicomanie sévère. Ça me remonte le moral. Manifestement, il s'inquiète maintenant de savoir comment il pourra continuer à se payer sa came. *Eh bien, pas de chance*, me dis-je en moi-même. *Tu aurais dû penser à ça avant de devenir dépendant d'une substance illicite.*

À cette pensée, je me sens beaucoup mieux ; je renifle et fais mine de me lever :

— Eh bien, c'était une charmante soirée…

Il tend brusquement la main pour m'attraper le bras :

— Non, Beth, dit-il d'une voix pressante. S'il te plaît, ne pars pas.

Je baisse les yeux vers lui :

— Pourquoi pas ?

Il ne me quitte pas du regard, mais après une ou deux secondes il retire sa main de mon bras pour la mettre dans la poche arrière de son jean. Il en sort son portefeuille. Ah, s'il s'imagine que je vais rester pour un autre verre… Mais ce n'est pas de l'argent qu'il en tire. C'est trop épais et rigide. C'est un petit rectangle blanc, et je me rassieds lentement quand il me le tend.

— C'est mon fils, explique-t-il simplement.

En contemplant la photo, je plonge mon regard dans les yeux d'un enfant de sept ou huit ans. Il essaie de sourire, parce que c'est ce qu'on attend de lui quand on le photographie, mais ce n'est pas naturel. Il est dehors, on dirait un parc ou quelque chose qui y ressemble, avec des balançoires dans le fond, et il tient un cornet de glace. La crème a coulé sur sa main et son avant-bras en épais sillons collants qui descendent jusqu'à son coude.

Il porte un tee-shirt Bob l'Éponge et un short orange qui découvre des genoux potelés.

Sean est papa. Il a un petit garçon. J'ai du mal à le croire. Tout ce temps-là, je pensais que c'était un flambeur superficiel, secret, indigne de confiance, doublé d'un homme à femmes, et il s'avère qu'il est père. Comment ai-je pu confondre ces deux états ? Comment ai-je pu me tromper à ce point ? Je lève la tête pour porter sur lui un regard neuf après cette grande révélation, et je suis surprise par ce que je découvre. Sean le papa est bien plus séduisant que Sean le mauvais garçon. Soudain, je devine comme ses yeux doivent être chauds quand ils se posent avec amour sur son précieux enfant, et cela me réchauffe moi aussi. Ça m'embrase, en fait. Je me sens comme Kirsten Dunst, quand elle comprend que lorsqu'elle regarde son geek de petit ami à lunettes, elle contemple en réalité l'immense, l'athlétique super-héros Spiderman. Je considère Sean d'un œil neuf, et subitement tous les regards secrets et sournois, tous les actes qui inspirent la méfiance, les gestes suspects trouvent une raison, une explication, et c'est celle-ci, dans ma main, ce magnifique garçonnet blond qui plisse les yeux et essaie de faire plaisir à la personne qui le photographie.

Mais maintenant que j'y pense, qu'a fait Sean pour me rendre méfiante et suspicieuse à son endroit ? À peine plus que de s'exprimer d'une voix traînante, sourire d'une certaine façon, et ne jamais raconter ce qu'il fait de ses week-ends. C'est pour cela que j'avais choisi de croire que ses loisirs étaient illégaux, de mauvais goût ou honteux. Je ne peux en réalité me souvenir d'aucune action concrète à mon égard qui puisse justifier ma méfiance. En fait, il s'est montré très ouvert et honnête avec moi, il m'a parlé de son idée de *Whytelys*, m'a tenue au courant de la date et de l'heure du rendez-vous, m'a avoué à quel point ça s'était mal passé, alors même que ça doit le mortifier de l'évoquer devant moi. Et maintenant, les yeux posés sur lui, je ressens l'amère morsure de la honte en repensant à la façon dont je me suis conduite face à sa confiance et à son respect. Je lui ai donné un coup de poignard dans le dos, ai retourné le couteau dans la plaie, puis cassé le manche pour qu'il ne puisse l'enlever et sauver sa peau. Je suis une vraie chienne. Je suis pire que ce que je pensais de Sean, et qui était faux.

—Elle date d'il y a trois ans, dit soudain Sean en tendant la main pour reprendre la photo. C'est son anniversaire, aujourd'hui. Il a neuf ans. (Il se perd dans la contemplation du cliché et semble oublier un instant que je suis là.) Joyeux anniversaire, Alfie, mon grand. J'espère que le singe te plaît. (Il lève les yeux vers moi, l'air à nouveau anxieux.) Je lui ai acheté un gros singe en peluche. Tu penses que c'est trop bébé pour lui? Je veux dire, il n'a que neuf ans, c'est encore un tout petit…

Je tends le bras pour poser ma main sur la sienne:

—Je suis sûre qu'il va l'adorer. Ça vient de son papa, n'est-ce pas?

Il hoche la tête:

—Oui, tu as raison. Bon sang, j'espère que tu as raison. C'est juste que je ne sais pas ce qui intéresse un enfant de cet âge-là. Il vit avec sa maman et son beau-père, alors je ne le vois qu'une fois par semaine. Ils lui ont acheté une PSP.

—C'est quoi?

— Une console de jeux portable. C'est vraiment chouette. Plutôt cher, aussi. J'aurais aimé la lui offrir, mais je n'ai vraiment pas les moyens. Et si…

Il ne finit pas sa phrase, mais je sais ce qu'il veut dire. Si Love Learning coule, que pourra-t-il encore faire pour son petit garçon ? Je le dévisage, et je comprends parfaitement son anxiété face à la recherche de contrats, ses questions répétées sur mes résultats de ce côté, le stress qu'il doit éprouver, l'inquiétude de vouloir faire plus pour son fils et la possibilité de devoir peut-être commencer à faire moins. C'est exactement comme dans *The Full Monty*.

— Écoute, Beth, je suis désolé d'avoir été désagréable tout à l'heure. C'est juste… je voudrais en faire tellement pour lui. Je veux l'emmener en vacances, juste lui et moi, et lui faire vivre une expérience fantastique, quelque part. Je veux lui offrir exactement ce qu'il souhaite pour son anniversaire. Je veux qu'il m'adore, qu'il m'admire, qu'il souhaite me ressembler. Je veux être son héros.

Il se frotte les yeux avec le pouce et l'index, et je détourne le regard vers un coffre à trésor en plastique sur le bar, qui déborde de fausses pièces d'or et de pierreries. Il y a un petit bonhomme de neige en coton posé à côté.

Je me tourne à nouveau vers Sean et remarque qu'il arbore à présent un sourire triste :

— Quoi qu'il en soit, reprend-il, merci beaucoup d'avoir accepté de passer la soirée avec moi. Je déteste être tout seul à la maison quand c'est l'anniversaire d'Alfie. Et aujourd'hui avec le fiasco chez *Whytelys*… je suis vraiment content d'avoir de la compagnie. Et je le dis parce que je le pense. Laisse-moi t'offrir encore un verre.

Ne nous voilons pas la face, c'est peut-être la dernière tournée que je peux me permettre de te payer !

Alors qu'il se lève, je pose ma main sur son bras, comme il l'a fait voilà quelques minutes :

— Attends une seconde, Sean.

Il regarde ma main, puis se rassied :

— Quoi ?

Il me dévisage avec intérêt, ses yeux bleus et francs rivés sur les miens, sans faiblir ni se détourner, sans ciller, soutenant mon regard avec calme.

— Sean tu n'as pas besoin de t'en faire pour l'avenir de Love Learning.

Il hausse les sourcils d'un millimètre :

— Pourquoi tu dis ça ?

Je déglutis.

— Parce que j'ai découvert qu'une des plus grosses sociétés de notre ville va très bientôt se mettre à la recherche de formateurs, et je suis la seule à le savoir.

Il sursaute un peu et se redresse dans son siège :

— Tu es sérieuse ? Comment tu le sais ? Que tu es la seule, je veux dire ?

Je souris. C'est agréable.

— Parce qu'ils n'ont pas encore rendu publiques leurs intentions. Je l'ai appris par hasard et j'ai contacté le P.-D.G. Il a confirmé.

Il me dévisage, bouche bée.

— Vraiment ? Donc la boîte ne va pas couler ? Je ne vais pas perdre mon boulot ? Bordel de merde, Beth ! C'est fantastique ! C'est avec qui ?

— Horizon Holidays.

— Horizon ? C'est cet immeuble sur le rond-point, au centre-ville ? Ils recherchent des formations, vraiment ?

Bon sang, cet endroit est énorme, ça suffirait certainement à sauver Love Learning, n'est-ce pas ? Tu es certaine d'être seule dans la course ? Je veux dire, tu as rencontré quelqu'un ? Tu as signé ?

— Euh, non, pas exactement. Pas encore. Mais je suis confiante.

Il a l'air tellement sérieux, tellement troublé, que j'ai soudain un violent désir de lui offrir du réconfort et de le consoler, de le protéger. De bercer sa tête contre ma poitrine. Quoique… cette dernière pensée vienne peut-être d'autre part.

— Vraiment, répète-t-il, comme s'il avait du mal à se faire à l'idée. Tu es la seule à le savoir ? Putain, c'est génial ! (Son angoisse cède enfin la place à un grand sourire, et il finit par s'autoriser à me croire.) La journée avait commencé de façon plutôt merdique, a empiré, s'est transformée en catastrophe ; et maintenant c'est l'un des plus beaux jours de ma vie, tout ça grâce à toi. Allez, prenons un autre verre pour fêter ça.

Ce n'est plus le même homme, n'est-ce pas ? Et il est changé, pas seulement par rapport à ce qu'il était avant que je lui parle d'Horizon. Je veux dire, il est complètement différent du Sean avec lequel j'ai travaillé ces dernières années. Il est enthousiaste, surexcité, pour un peu il sauterait sur sa chaise. Et comme Kirsten Dunst j'arrive soudain à l'imaginer se balançant à travers les rues de la ville, à quinze mètres de hauteur, sauvant les gens d'immeubles en flammes et d'épaves de voitures. En Lycra très moulant.

— Tu ne lui as quand même pas dit ? me demande Vini incrédule, un peu plus tard.

—Eh bien, il n'y avait pas de raison…, dis-je.

Mais elle secoue la tête :

—Est-ce que ce n'est pas l'homme qui abattrait et dévorerait son propre chien ?

—Je ne suis pas certaine qu'il mangerait vraiment…

—L'homme qui vendrait sa petite copine pour s'échapper ?

—Tu sais, ce n'est pas vraiment le genre de…

—L'homme qui mettrait le feu au bâtiment pour cacher ses détournements de fonds, même si sa femme, son meilleur ami et son père se trouvaient à l'intérieur ?

—J'ai peut-être exagéré…

—Tu veux dire que tu as peut-être perdu la boule, conclut-elle calmement.

Et ça vient d'une fille qui porte du mascara orange.

Le lendemain, il est déjà à son bureau quand j'arrive, et c'est sans doute la première fois que ça se produit. Il lève les yeux quand j'entre dans la pièce et m'adresse un grand sourire. C'est fini, les clins d'œil au ralenti qui me donnaient la chair de poule. Mais, en fait, qu'est-ce qu'il y avait de si effrayant là-dedans ? Je lui rends son sourire, sans montrer mes dents – cette nouvelle phase de notre relation ne signifie pas que je puisse me permettre d'avoir l'air d'une folle – et marche lentement vers mon poste. Je sens son regard qui me suit, alors j'essaie de faire en sorte d'être sexy, vue de profil. Puis je lève le bras par-dessus la tête pour me passer doucement la main dans les cheveux, avant de m'asseoir et de replier un pied sous moi, en gardant un tout petit sourire d'un bout à l'autre de l'opération, pour conserver un air de…

—Poste 457, s'il vous plaît, demande Sean d'une voix forte.

Je me retourne pour le regarder et je m'aperçois qu'il me tourne le dos, voûté au-dessus de son téléphone portable. Bon. Bah, peu importe. Je reviens à mon ordinateur et ouvre une session.

Un frisson brûlant me parcourt subitement, quand je me rappelle, pleine d'attente, que j'ai envoyé un mail très coquin à Rupert hier et que je suis partie avant d'avoir reçu sa réponse. Qu'est-ce qui m'a pris de faire ça ? Je devais être complètement bourrée, en perte totale de contrôle, après les deux verres de vin que j'avais bus au *Madeleine's* trois heures plus tôt.

La question est : a-t-il répondu ? J'ai presque peur de regarder. Je vais sans doute me faire rabrouer sèchement et poliment, avec un message du genre : « Chère Beth, merci pour votre mail. Je le trouve très informatif, bien que peut-être pas tout à fait en adéquation avec la politique actuelle d'Horizon. Je vous souhaite de réussir dans vos prochaines démarches. Veuillez agréer, etc., R. de Witter. »

Quel salaud d'hypocrite, alors que c'est lui qui a poussé Harris à me saouler, pour commencer ! Sans doute uniquement dans le but de voir si j'allais me déshonorer en me faisant culbuter sur cette terrasse en bois si glamour. Il me prend vraiment pour une traînée, pour s'imaginer des choses pareilles ? Eh bien, s'il a l'intention de changer son fusil d'épaule et de faire le vertueux, je ne suis même pas sûre d'avoir envie de travailler avec lui, et encore moins de passer le reste de ma vie avec lui, à élever nos trois enfants. S'il me recontacte après un message comme celui-là, en me suppliant de signer un contrat, ou un registre – l'un ou l'autre –, je crois que je vais devoir dire : « Tu as loupé le coche, chéri. »

Mes yeux tombent sur la photo de la brochure d'Horizon. C'est peut-être une réaction un peu hâtive, finalement. Je veux dire, avec tout le travail que j'ai consacré à ce contrat, ce serait absurde de tout mettre par terre maintenant pour une raison aussi triviale et stupide. Je pense que je peux prendre sur moi et lui pardonner. Comme ça on pourra se réconcilier en bonne et due forme.

Il n'y a pas de message. J'ai parcouru ma messagerie si vite, en ne laissant pas mes yeux sur les noms plus d'une demi-seconde, qu'il est possible que je l'aie raté, du coup je regarde à nouveau. Puis encore une fois. J'ai envie de retourner la boîte mail pour regarder derrière, d'y plonger la main et de fouiller dans le fond, en finissant par la renverser et la secouer. Ça ne sert à rien : il n'a pas répondu.

Bordel, c'est bien pire.

Ce n'est pas grave, ce n'est pas grave. Je dois préparer cet atelier « Motivation » – ou au moins commencer – aujourd'hui, sinon ça va foirer complètement. On est mercredi 13, et le séminaire a lieu lundi, donc j'ai maintenant trois jours de travail pour être prête. C'est large, du moment que je ne suis pas dérangée. Des mails de Rupert, voilà qui me déconcentrerait fortement, donc, en fait, c'est mieux qu'il ne m'ait pas répondu. Je suis contente.

Le problème, c'est que l'absence de message me déconcentre presque autant que d'en recevoir. Je passe le reste de la journée très occupée à regarder dans le vide, à contempler la pièce, à tapoter des doigts sur le clavier, sans but, et à ranger mon tiroir de bureau, mais toujours pas de mail. Je jette un coup d'œil à Sean et l'entends au téléphone.

— Oui, oui. Ça semble idéal. Il y a combien de places ?

De toute évidence, il règle des détails pour son prochain stage, qui est demain, je crois, sur « Comment Mener un Entretien », quelque part. Fatima parle avec Mike à voix basse :

— Des cochons d'Inde, s'étonne-t-elle, vraiment ?

Même Cath Parson, la femme-paresseux, qui se déplace plus lentement que le courrier interne, semble presque animée. Elle tape quelque chose, et je pense qu'elle atteint la vitesse de dix mots par minute. Donc il n'y a que moi qui n'aurai rien à présenter à Chas la prochaine fois qu'il entrera dans notre orbite. Super.

— Beth ! Téléphone ! crie soudain Ali, me faisant sursauter, de même que Fatima et Mike.

— Oh, Ali, tu m'as vraiment fait peur à hurler comme ça, pour l'amour du ciel. Tu aurais pu empêcher mes cheveux de pousser, dit-elle.

— Quoi ? répond Ali.

Pendant ce temps, Fatima commence à expliquer :

— Bah, ma mère m'a dit…

— Oh, OK, je vais la chercher. (Il couvre l'émetteur de sa main et reprend en criant.) Désolé, ce n'est pas pour Beth, c'est pour Fatima. Fatima, c'est pour toi.

C'est bizarre. Comment a-t-il pu croire que l'appel était pour moi, alors qu'il était pour Fatima ?

Je veux dire, quelle que soit la façon dont vous le prononcez, Beth et Fatima ne sonnent pas pareil. Fa-ti-ma. Be-th. Rien à voir.

Bordel, il faut vraiment que je me mette à ce truc sur la « Motivation ».

—Devine quoi ? s'exclame Fatima, le souffle court, en apparaissant à mes côtés cinq minutes plus tard.

Aujourd'hui, son tee-shirt proclame :

Je connais la réponse.
C'est juste que je l'ai oubliée.

—Quoi ?

Elle s'assied et fait rouler sa chaise à côté de moi.

—Quelqu'un vient voir la Mini. Ce soir ! T'imagines ? Je suis trop contente ! Je vais finalement pouvoir rembourser tout ce que je dois, et ça n'aura plus d'importance que je garde mon job ici. Enfin, non, évidemment que ça en aura, je ne veux pas perdre mon boulot, j'adore bosser ici, c'est génial, mais au moins je n'irai pas en prison, et c'est la meilleure nouvelle de tous les temps !

Et, de fait, elle joint les mains dans sa joie sincère devant le changement béni des dieux qui va s'instaurer.

Je m'apprête à la détromper gentiment mais, à cet instant, Ali crie qu'il y a un appel pour moi, et cette fois c'est vrai, alors Fatima s'éloigne.

—Beth Sheridan à l'appareil, dis-je, consciente que je vais devoir passer la plus grande partie de la journée de demain à consoler Fatima de sa déception, parce que la seule et unique personne qui l'aura appelée au sujet de la voiture, depuis qu'elle a accepté de baisser un peu son prix, ne l'aura pas immédiatement achetée, résolvant ainsi instantanément tous ses problèmes et mettant fin à la pauvreté dans le monde par la même occasion.

Puis j'entends la voix à l'autre bout du fil :

—Beth ? C'est Rupert.

Chapitre 17

Apporter un soutien

Objectif à court terme : traverser les prochaines minutes sans évoquer la pensée de lui passer les doigts dans les cheveux.
Obstacles : je n'arrive pas à m'enlever cette idée de la tête.
Objectif à long terme : est-ce que la vie va continuer, après ce moment ?
Obstacles : …

Je déteste être prise au dépourvu. Ce coup de fil arrive tellement comme un cheveu sur la soupe, après une journée sans mail de lui, que j'ai le souffle un peu coupé. J'essaie de prendre quelques inspirations profondes mais silencieuses pour me calmer.

— Beth ? Vous êtes là ?

— Ouais, oui, je suis là. Bonjour. Comment allez-vous ? J'allais juste rentrer chez moi.

— Eh bien, je suis content de vous avoir attrapée au vol. Vous avez passé une bonne journée ?

— Incroyablement banale. Et vous ?

— Pareil. Des réunions intenses, des décisions budgétaires, problèmes de personnel, approbations, désapprobations, acceptations. Vous voyez.

— Oui, c'est exactement ce que j'ai fait aussi.

Ah, c'est affreux ! C'est tellement évident que nous évitons tous deux de parler du message vraiment coquin et déplacé que j'ai envoyé hier. Cette minute se place donc officiellement parmi les moments les plus gênants de mon existence, juste derrière la fois où mon professeur d'art dramatique a écrit : « Merci, Elizabeth », à côté d'une déclaration d'amour éternel que je lui avais adressée dans la marge de ma copie et que j'avais oublié d'effacer.

Avec un peu de chance, Rupert sera trop gêné – voire mortifié – pour évoquer mes propos d'hier, et nous allons simplement continuer comme ça, à faire comme si rien ne s'était passé, jusqu'à ce que nous finissions tous deux par l'oublier. Ou par mourir de vieillesse, c'est selon.

— Quelle coïncidence ! dit-il. C'était bien, le sport ?

OK, peut-être pas alors.

— Le… euh… le quoi ?

— La salle de sport. Vous avez dit hier que vous alliez vous y rendre pour tonifier vos cuisses. « L'intérieur » de vos cuisses, si je me souviens bien.

Oh, merde. Merde, merde, merde. Pourquoi n'ai-je rien préparé à l'avance pour ce moment ? Tout le monde sait que quand on envoie un message suggestif, coquin et déplacé au millionnaire follement sexy avec lequel on essaie de signer un contrat, on devrait toujours prévoir une réponse drôle et intelligente en prévision des questions qu'il posera plus tard.

— Non, non, vous vous trompez, réponds-je sur une inspiration subite. J'ai dit que j'allais rendre visite à mon cousin Nestor. Vous n'avez manifestement pas fait attention.

Il s'ensuit un silence perplexe. Je l'imagine en train de rejeter la tête de côté comme si ma phrase l'avait heurté physiquement comme une gifle. Mais non, il sourit :

— Oh, désolé. J'ai dû faire erreur.

— Je ne me suis rendue qu'une seule fois à la salle de sport, et à la minute même où je me suis écrasé le visage sur le sol j'ai juré de ne plus jamais y mettre les pieds. Donc je n'ai pas pu dire ça hier.

J'ai la satisfaction de l'entendre réprimer un reniflement amusé, et cela me fait sourire moi-même.

— Vous avez bien raison. Alors, comment va Nestor, ces temps-ci ?

— Oh, beaucoup mieux. Il vous envoie ses pensées. Il vous dit merci pour le panier de muffins.

— Le pa… (Et il pouffe de rire.) Vous n'êtes vraiment pas banale, Miss Sheridan.

— Je suis flattée que vous l'ayez remarqué. La banalité est tellement dépourvue d'intérêt, n'est-ce pas ?

Il rit à nouveau, mais doucement, d'un air perplexe, et je me prends à regretter de ne pas lui avoir répondu plus sérieusement cette fois-ci. Pourquoi ne me suis-je pas contentée de soupirer : « Oh, merci, Rupert », d'une voix douce, sexy, pleine de promesses, qui aurait fait germer bien des idées intéressantes dans sa tête ?

— En fait, j'avais une raison de vous téléphoner, finit-il par dire.

— Je n'en attendais pas moins.

— Eh bien, vous ne vous trompiez pas. J'ai une bonne raison. Je vous ai appelée pour fixer un autre rendez-vous. Pour régler cette histoire de Love Learning. Et je vous promets que cette fois je viendrai. Promis juré. Quand êtes-vous disponible ?

Toute ma vie, qu'en pensez-vous ? Non, non, je ne vais pas dire ça. En plus d'être triste et gênant, c'est aussi complètement ringard.

Et déplacé, en plus.

— Eh bien, il faut que je consulte mon agenda. Je sais que je suis très prise jusqu'à lundi prochain, mais je devrais pouvoir me libérer ensuite. Et pour toute ma... hum... le... euh... la semaine. (Putain, je vous jure que j'ai failli dire « pour toute ma vie ».) Je ne veux pas dire que je peux me libérer pour toute la semaine. Je veux dire, vous voyez, je pourrais me rendre disponible pour une réunion à n'importe quel moment de la semaine.

Qu'est-ce qui me prend ? Je suis certaine que l'idée que je pense vraiment à un voyage d'une semaine ne l'a pas effleuré.

— Quel dommage ! J'allais justement envoyer un texto au gérant de l'hôtel *La Belle Étoile* à Paris.

Je me tiens coite.

— Bref, la date. Que diriez-vous de mardi prochain, pour déjeuner, dans ce cas ? Le 19. Au *Madeleine's* ? À moins que vous ne préfériez un autre endroit ?

Je sais que je me suis engagée vis-à-vis du directeur régional de *Whytelys* pour le 19, mais je vais sans doute annuler. Ou bien envoyer Sean. Ce qui me libère.

— Oui, le 19, c'est parfait. Et je n'ai rien contre déjeuner à nouveau au *Madeleine's*. Ça m'a vraiment plu.

Oups. Cette phrase suspecte laisse vraiment entendre que je n'y avais jamais mangé avant le repas d'hier. Avec un peu de chance, il ne va pas remarquer.

— Vous y étiez déjà allée ?

Crotte. Je m'apprête à répondre « Oh oui, bien sûr, j'y suis tout le temps fourrée », mais je me souviens d'un coup que la seule chose qui peut sortir d'un pipeau, c'est la catastrophe. Je pense à toutes les répercussions affreuses qui ont découlé de mensonges : tant de guerres inutiles, de vies innocentes sacrifiées, de dictateurs élevés et de rois tombés. Et, bien sûr, il y a aussi *Madame Doubtfire*.

—Non, en fait, dis-je rapidement. C'était la première fois. Merci beaucoup pour le déjeuner… C'était merveilleux.

—Super. (J'entends à sa voix qu'il sourit de toutes ses dents.) Donc vous êtes désormais une habituée du *Madeleine's*. Magnifique. Est-ce que j'envoie une voiture pour vous chercher, ou vous préférez qu'on se retrouve là-bas ?

J'hésite. La perspective de pouvoir regarder la tête de Grace alors que je m'enfuis à bord d'une limousine, vers un rendez-vous à déjeuner avec un millionnaire sexy, est très tentante. Mais si le déjeuner se déroule exceptionnellement bien, mon véhicule va rester sans surveillance sur le parking de Love Learning toute la nuit.

—Je vous retrouve.

—Je vais réserver la table alors. (Il se tait un instant.) Est-ce que vous avez aimé… l'arrangement ?

—Vous voulez dire les bougies ? Oh oui ! C'était éblouissant. Magique. Je n'avais encore jamais rien vu de tel. Ils font toujours les choses comme ça, dans ce kiosque ?

—Pas toujours. (Sa voix se fait basse.) Je pourrais redemander le même numéro.

J'ai un frisson, comme s'il parlait d'un numéro de chambre et non de table :

—Ce serait merveilleux.

—Alors d'accord. Je m'en occupe. Et, en plus, comme ça, nous risquerons moins d'être dérangés.

—Hum.

J'ai du mal à évacuer l'image de la chambre d'hôtel de ma tête. Maintenant je vois un panneau « Ne pas déranger » suspendu à la poignée de porte. Et l'écriteau se balance doucement au rythme de ce qui peut bien se passer à l'intérieur.

—Ça va ? me souffle soudain la voix dans le téléphone, me faisant prendre conscience que je n'ai rien dit depuis un moment.

—Oh oui, tout va bien, merci. Désolée.

Il émerge de notre salle d'eau, ruisselant au sortir de la douche, et s'approche du lit où je suis allongée.

—Je pensais seulement à des draps de bain.

—Des « draps de bain » ?

Merde !

—Non, non, pas des draps de bain. Des lapins. Je me souvenais juste que j'ai cru en voir un quand j'étais au *Madeleine's* hier.

Il y a un silence perplexe, et je l'imagine en train de sourire et de froncer les sourcils en même temps :

—Vraiment ? C'est curieux.

—Je sais. C'est ce que j'ai pensé. J'ai pu me tromper, cela dit.

Merde, est-ce que je pourrais avoir l'air encore plus cinglée ?

—Écoutez, il faut que j'y aille, dit-il après une pause.

—Oh, oui, moi aussi. J'allais…

—Rentrer à la maison, finit-il à ma place, me donnant la chair de poule.

—Oui, c'est ça. C'est ce que j'allais faire.

—Je sais. À la semaine prochaine, Beth. Treize heures, mardi. *Au Madeleine's.*

—Je voudrais déjà y être. (Merde.) Non, je veux dire, j'y serai. Je ne voulais pas dire…

—À mardi.

Il a raccroché.

Ce qui signifie que je dois tenir presque toute une semaine avant de pouvoir le rencontrer. Bordel, qu'est-ce que je vais bien pouvoir faire de moi jusqu'à mardi ? De mercredi à aujourd'hui, c'était assez facile ; pourquoi est-ce soudain devenu tellement difficile à présent ?

Je lance un regard plein d'espoir en direction du bureau de Sean, mais il n'y a personne. Il vient de partir pour toute la journée et il sera absent demain pour son truc : « Comment Mener un Entretien ». Il a passé tout son temps à s'en occuper et m'a à peine parlé depuis notre dernier rendez-vous. De toute façon, même s'il appartient à la catégorie papa sexy, il n'entre pas dans celle des millionnaires sexy, et c'est avec un membre de ce club très fermé que je déjeune la semaine prochaine.

Oh, ne vous méprenez pas ; je ne craque pas pour Rupert à cause de ses sous. J'aurais flashé sur lui dans tous les cas. Ça ne fait qu'accroître son pouvoir de séduction. Je veux dire, ça fait partie de lui, n'est-ce pas ? S'il n'avait pas cette personnalité et ce caractère, il n'aurait jamais fait fortune, donc, sans son argent, il serait une tout autre personne. Aimer Rupert, c'est aimer sa richesse.

Je me demande si j'ai le temps de faire de la chirurgie esthétique avant mardi.

—Nan, nan, me dit Vini d'un air docte dans la soirée, en secouant la tête. Pendant quatre à dix jours, tu seras bleue et bouffie. Ce n'est pas avant quatorze à trente jours, selon l'opération, que tu pourras mettre le nez dehors sans pansement.

—Vini…

—Bordel, non. Pas moi. C'était Joan Collins. Elle s'est fait refaire les paupières il y a quelques années. Tu la connais : elle travaille à la poste. C'est elle qui s'est occupée de ta vignette auto l'année dernière.

C'est ainsi que jeudi soir, poussée par le désespoir, j'accepte de sortir avec Vini. Je lui apporte mon soutien, c'est tout.

—J'ai vu ça dans le journal aujourd'hui et j'ai trouvé que ça avait l'air super, me dit-elle pendant que je me lisse les cheveux. Je ne voulais pas t'en parler, parce que je pensais que tu ne voudrais pas venir. Et que tu me rôtirais les pieds.

—Pourquoi je ferais ça ?

En fait, elle n'a pas encore reconnu m'avoir envoyé ce faux texto signé « Nigel ». Elle va peut-être enfin le faire.

—À cause du ratage total de la dernière fois. Tu sais. Aucune chaussure à ton pied.

J'ai une impression bizarre. De toute évidence, elle ne crachera pas le morceau. Bon, je ne vais pas la forcer à s'excuser.

—Ça ne fait rien. Disons que c'était un coup d'essai.

Elle scrute mon reflet dans le miroir :

— Tu n'es pas en train de te monter la tête à propos de ce Rupert, si ? Parce que ça va être exactement comme avec Richard, tu sais.

Je la dévisage à mon tour :

— Mais j'espère bien.

Je croise les doigts dans mon dos.

Une heure plus tard, nous nous présentons à l'hôtel *Oast House*.

— Ce n'est pas du speed dating, me dit Vini sur le parking. C'est du *pick n' mix*. Ou du *mix n' match*. Ou quelque chose du genre.

— Et en quoi c'est censé être différent du speed dating, exactement ?

Elle se tourne vers moi d'un air agacé :

— De plein de façons, Beth. Il n'y a pas de règles, cette fois. On est juste dans une pièce, avec plein d'autres célibataires. C'est comme n'importe quelle soirée, sauf que là, on sait tous que chaque personne présente : 1) est célibataire ; et 2) ne veut pas le rester. Si tu veux plus que trois minutes, tu peux prendre plus. Si tu as envie de moins, pareil. Si tu veux te faufiler dans une salle de réunion déserte et faire des cochonneries derrière le projecteur, fonce. Tu es magnifique, au fait.

— Merci.

Je baisse les yeux pour me regarder. Sous mon manteau, je n'ai qu'un jean noir et un tee-shirt rose : rien de spécial.

— Ce n'est pas les habits, idiote. C'est les cheveux. Un jean et un tee-shirt, ce n'est pas magnifique.

— Merci. Encore.

— Faut pas le prendre comme ça. Je te fais un compliment. Tu as l'air d'être quelqu'un.

Le plaisir m'envahit en entendant cette phrase. Je sais qu'elle ne veut pas dire que j'ai l'air d'être importante, qu'il faut compter avec moi, que j'ai le bras long. Elle sous-entend que je ressemble à une célébrité. Elle est toujours en quête de gens qui pourraient passer pour quelqu'un et n'hésite pas à aborder de parfaits inconnus pour leur donner sa carte. Je me suis souvent dit à quel point j'étais heureuse qu'elle ne m'ait jamais fait le coup, parce que je veux n'être semblable qu'à moi-même, et à personne d'autre. Je me suis répété ça mille fois depuis qu'elle a monté Fake Face.

Quand nous entrons dans la salle du *mix n' match*, je remarque immédiatement avec un pincement au cœur qu'il y a cette fois aussi de petits bouquets de gui accrochés avec espoir un peu partout au plafond. De toute évidence, les gens qui organisent ce genre de soirées ne se sont jamais retrouvés célibataires à Noël et s'imaginent que des bisous forcés vont nous donner le sentiment d'être aimés.

Il n'y a que deux autres personnes dans la pièce, et ce sont deux femmes. Nous échangeons un sourire, mais ce n'est pas un de ces sourires pleins de solidarité féminine qui disent : « Salut, ça va, n'est-ce pas que c'est gênant, j'aimerais qu'on n'ait pas besoin de faire ça. » C'est plutôt du genre : « Est-ce que vous êtes plus jeune, plus mince, plus jolie que moi ? » Nous nous approchons juste assez pour nous assurer qu'elles sont plus vieilles que nous – et pas qu'un peu. Je ne sais pas si je dois m'en réjouir ou si ça doit me démoraliser complètement. Je vais chercher des boissons et nous nous installons près du mur.

— Pourquoi est-ce qu'il n'y a pas de chaises? Ou de tables?

— Parce que, comme ça, c'est plus comme une soirée, et les gens se mélangent plus facilement. On n'est pas là pour boire un verre ensemble, garde ça en tête. On est là pour rencontrer quelqu'un.

— Est-ce que ça veut dire que je renonce définitivement au gars avec qui j'ai bien accroché au speed dating, alors? lui dis-je avec un regard oblique.

Elle se tourne vers moi, la bouche vissée sur le goulot d'une boisson alcoolisée à la pastèque :

— Bah, s'il ne t'a pas donné signe de vie…, répond-elle d'un ton innocent.

— Non, pas un mot, réponds-je, avant de hausser les sourcils, pleine d'attente.

Ça y est, c'est sûr. C'est l'occasion rêvée pour avouer, dans un torrent de remords, le tour horrible qu'elle m'a joué l'autre jour. Qu'elle a compris à quel point c'était cruel, presque aussitôt après avoir envoyé les messages, et qu'elle aurait voulu pouvoir revenir en arrière. Et qu'elle n'a pas pu se résoudre à m'annoncer qu'elle avait fait quelque chose d'aussi méchant, parce qu'elle ne supportait pas l'idée que j'aie moins d'estime pour elle. Et elle ne voulait pas admettre devant moi, ni devant elle-même, qu'elle était capable de faire du mal à quelqu'un, encore moins à sa propre colocataire et meilleure amie.

— Ah, c'est dommage, soupire-t-elle avant de reprendre une lampée de sa bouteille.

Bon Dieu, elle est douée!

Ou bien. Elle n'a en réalité pas envoyé ce texto. Ce qui signifie qu'hier soir un dénommé Nigel à l'orthographe incertaine a passé la soirée assis à attendre…

Une idée me traverse soudain l'esprit :

— Tu as toujours le numéro de l'organisatrice ?

— Du speed dating ? Oui, pourquoi ?

Je prends mon téléphone portable dans mon sac. Vini n'essaie même pas de déguiser sa consternation.

— Ne fais pas cette tête. Je veux juste en avoir le cœur net. Juste au cas où il y aurait eu un malentendu, ou autre chose.

— Bordel, c'est exactement comme avec Richard, une fois de plus !

— Ce n'est absolument pas pareil. Ce que j'ai partagé avec Richard, c'était tellement plus que d'être assise à une table pendant trois minutes.

— Certes. Voilà le numéro.

Quand la dame décroche enfin son téléphone, le fond sonore m'indique clairement qu'une autre séance de speed dating est en cours. Je me demande pourquoi ces soirées sont si nombreuses. Sûrement que si ça marchait il n'y aurait pas besoin de continuer à en organiser ?

— Eh bien, j'ai vérifié mes papiers, dit-elle en reprenant le combiné après une attente d'une minute. D'après ma liste, il n'y a rien de positif pour toi, ma puce.

— Mais c'est faux ! Je suis certaine à cent pour cent que nous avons chacun coché la case de l'autre.

— Je sais que ça paraît dur, ma chérie. Mais parfois les gens qui semblent vraiment sympas ne le sont pas.

— Mais il a dit qu'il…

—Écoute, je vais être franche avec toi, ma belle. Il essayait sans doute tout simplement de t'embarquer chez lui.

J'écarquille les yeux, et Vini m'adresse un grand « Quoi ? » Je secoue la tête et murmure :

—C'est possible ?

—Oh, ma pauvre, ça arrive tout le temps ! Les mecs font tout un foin en cochant ta case, et ensuite ils ne s'embêtent même pas à rendre leur feuille en partant. Tout ce qui leur reste à faire, c'est de s'arranger pour te croiser par hasard sur le parking, ou quelque chose dans ce goût-là, et l'affaire est dans le sac. Tu l'amènes chez toi, puisque tu l'as vu cocher ta case, donc tu sais que ce ne sera pas un coup d'un soir. Sauf que tu ne reçois jamais ses coordonnées, parce qu'il n'a pas rendu son formulaire.

J'en ai la mâchoire qui se décroche. Et je ne fais même pas l'effort d'y remédier.

—Le salaud…

—Je suis d'accord, ma chérie. Les mecs, ça se passe seulement en dessous de la ceinture. Je suis désolée que ça n'ait pas marché pour toi. Mais nous organisons une autre soirée dans deux semaines. Si ça t'intéresse ?

Elle se fout de moi ?

Pendant que je raconte à Vini ce que la dame m'a expliqué, les participants du *mix n'match* commencent à affluer. Vini les examine avec attention, presque comme si elle cherchait quelqu'un, mais pour ma part j'ai une boule d'angoisse dans le ventre : cette foule ne m'évoque rien de plus qu'un congrès de marionnettistes. Sans les marionnettes. Donc encore moins attirante, si c'est possible.

— C'est parti, murmure Vini, en se lançant joyeusement dans la cohue.

Je reste immobile quelques instants, à essayer de trouver du courage.

— Ça va, ma belle ? dit une voix à ma gauche.

Je tourne la tête et me prends aussitôt à regretter de ne pas avoir plongé dans la bousculade à la suite de Vini. De toute évidence, ne pas bouger est une grave erreur : ça vous laisse vulnérable, sans défense.

— Moi, c'est Éric.

— Salut, Éric, réponds-je.

Il porte un chapeau de père Noël en feutrine, tiré sur le côté, en ce qu'il doit imaginer être un angle coquin. J'évite délibérément de croiser son regard, de lui sourire, de lui donner mon nom, ou d'avoir l'air le moins du monde intéressée. Je ne veux surtout pas envoyer les mauvais signaux.

— Tu es déjà venue, alors ? me demande-t-il en m'aspergeant d'une fine pluie de postillons. Nan, ça m'étonnerait, une bombe comme toi.

Je cligne des yeux plusieurs fois.

— Pas vraiment.

Je me suis à présent entièrement détournée de lui et regarde dans la salle d'un air intéressé.

— Comment tu t'appelles, alors ? reprend-il, sans percevoir, semble-t-il, mon message implicite « barre-toi, tu ne m'intéresses pas. »

— Euh, Paula.

— Salut, Paula. Enchanté de faire ta connaissance.

Il me tend la main bien que je ne le regarde pas. Je lui tourne presque entièrement le dos, mais j'ai encore son visage rougeaud et souriant dans mon champ de vision, sa main tendue, pleine d'espoir que je la serre.

— Désolée, euh…

— Éric. Tu te souviens ?

— Éric. Désolée, faut que j'aille faire pipi.

— Dacodac. Je vais te chercher une boisson en attendant. C'est quoi, ta drogue préférée ?

Mais je ne réponds pas. Je traverse la salle bondée en courant, avec mes talons aiguilles, passant entre les gens engagés dans des conversations timides ou les contournant, en décrivant des zigzags parce que j'ai un jour reçu un mail qui expliquait que c'était la meilleure façon d'échapper à un poursuivant. Je sens dans mon dos émaner la chaleur des vaisseaux sanguins enflammés d'Éric, mais je ne vais pas me retourner pour regarder, même si je suis certaine qu'il ne peut plus me voir, parce que, connaissant ma chance, il sera encore en train de me suivre des yeux, et dès que nos regards se croiseront il va…

— Aaaah !

J'ai enfoncé mon épaule gauche dans quelqu'un. J'étais tellement occupée à ne pas regarder derrière moi que j'ai oublié de regarder devant.

— Oh, je suis désolée, je vous ai fait mal ?

Alors que je me tourne, je me tais, et mon regard s'arrête sur la grande silhouette aux épaules larges, puis sur le visage sexy et mal rasé, et enfin, avec un battement de cœur, sur les magnifiques yeux marron de Brad.

Chapitre 18

Communication efficace

Objectif à court terme : ne pas tuer Brad ni coucher avec lui. Pour le moment.
Obstacles : c'est sans doute l'homme le plus sexy que j'aie jamais eu envie de tuer.
Objectif à long terme : Tuer Brad ou coucher avec lui.
Obstacles : si je le tue, je ne pourrai pas coucher avec lui.

Brad qui m'a échappé après le speed dating, Brad avec lequel j'ai ressenti une connexion intense, un énorme béguin, puis connu des jours sans signe de vie. Je le dévore du regard. De la gloutonnerie visuelle. C'est affreux, mais je ne peux pas m'en empêcher, je le contemple sans fin, les yeux écarquillés, les lèvres entrouvertes, souriant malgré moi ; tout à coup je m'aperçois qu'il fait la même chose, les yeux rivés sur moi.

—Vous êtes… ? Est-ce que c'est… ? Libby ? C'est toi, n'est-ce pas ? Bon sang, tu es là ! J'espérais tellement que tu sois là ! Comment ça va ? Tu étais passée où ?

J'ai la bouche qui frémit et les bras qui font un sursaut d'un millimètre dans sa direction alors que je parviens de justesse à me retenir de lui sauter au cou avec un sourire crétin. Mais, juste à temps, je me souviens de ce qui s'est produit la dernière fois qu'on s'est vus, des paroles exactes de l'organisatrice du speed dating, et du but précis que cet homme attirant, beau à s'en lécher les babines, essayait d'atteindre. Mon sourire se fige et se détache de mes lèvres comme dans un dessin animé ; on pourrait presque l'entendre tomber. Brad cherche à se faufiler dans la culotte de quelqu'un d'autre, ce soir. De toute évidence, il se sert de ces soirées de célibataires pour… eh bien, rencontrer des gens. C'est terriblement triste et pathétique.

— J'étais exactement là où je suis d'habitude, dis-je, avec de gros efforts pour paraître distante et hautaine alors que je ressens une intense, presque irrésistible, attraction pour lui.

Je ne suis pas certaine du résultat, cela dit, surtout qu'il a l'air incroyablement content de me voir. Et – même si ça n'a aucune sorte d'importance puisque ce n'est qu'un prédateur froid et sans cœur – sexy à en avoir une boule dans la gorge. Je croise les bras et détourne légèrement la tête, autant pour éviter qu'il ne s'aperçoive que mes pupilles ont pris d'elles-mêmes la décision de se dilater que pour jouer l'indifférence.

— Mais c'est où, ça ? (Il fait un pas dans ma direction, me coupant efficacement du reste de la pièce.) Ça fait huit jours que je te cherche partout : je n'ai rien trouvé, pas même une trace d'ADN.

Mes pieds tentent de se rapprocher de lui, et je les force à faire un pas en arrière. Puis c'est mon corps qui se met à essayer de se pencher vers lui, sans l'aide de mes pieds. Je manque de tomber.

— À la maison, dans la voiture, parfois au super-marché. Au travail. Tu sais bien. Ou du moins tu saurais si tu avais vraiment eu l'intention de découvrir le moindre indice à mon sujet.

Il recule un peu, et ses sourcils tressaillent sous l'effet de la surprise. C'est ça, c'est un bon comédien.

— Qu'est-ce que tu racontes ? Bien sûr que je voulais te retrouver ! C'est même l'unique raison de ma présence ici ce soir, parce que je ne voyais pas d'autre moyen de te croiser. Et tu m'as vu cocher ta case. Numéro six. Je me le rappelle encore. C'était la seule case que j'aie cochée.

Oh, bon, dans ce cas, cherchons un endroit calme pour faire plus ample connaissance. Je me retiens difficilement de le dire. Mes lèvres forment les mots, et je dois remuer la mâchoire pour les empêcher de sortir. Ce qui doit me faire ressembler à l'une de ces vieilles femmes qu'on voit dans le bus qui mâchent du vide en permanence. Très sexy. Pour occuper ma bouche, je finis par marmonner :

— Vraiment ? Mais tu n'as fait ça que pour me convaincre que tu voulais me connaître mieux, tout ça pour que je sois davantage tentée de te suivre, plus tard, sur le parking, quand tu…

En réalité, nous ne nous sommes pas croisés par hasard parmi les voitures, n'est-ce pas ? En fait, je ne l'ai plus vu du tout par la suite.

— Quand je… ?

Un tout petit sourire apparaît sur ses lèvres incroya-blement charnues, brillantes, bordées d'un soupçon de barbe naissante en dessous. Pendant que je les contemple, le sourire s'élargit. Merde, j'ai les yeux rivés sur sa bouche ! Je détourne le regard à grand-peine.

— Tu sais bien, quand tu m'aurais tendu un piège sournois et sinistre, dans lequel je serais tombée parce que je t'avais vu cocher ma case, mais évidemment tu n'as même pas rendu ton papier à la fin de la soirée, donc ça n'était…

Mon débit s'est ralenti au fur et à mesure que je parlais, et je finis par m'arrêter complètement.

Il a maintenant les yeux écarquillés, les sourcils levés, et toujours un grand sourire :

— Donc tout ça n'était qu'un complot sophistiqué pour te pousser à coucher avec moi sans te communiquer mon numéro de téléphone, mon adresse, ni aucune autre information ? C'est ça ? C'est vraiment ce que tu as imaginé ?

— En fait, je ne pensais pas ça jusqu'à il y a dix minutes. Ensuite j'ai cru cette histoire pendant un moment. Et puis après j'ai de nouveau cessé d'y accorder foi.

— J'aurais pu aller en boîte, pour trouver un coup d'un soir, tu sais.

Et, à cet instant, il se fait l'une de ces pauses inexplicables dans les conversations, qui ne semble se produire que quand quelqu'un soit parle à voix haute de coup d'un soir, soit dit du mal de la personne qui se tient juste derrière lui. Les mots de Brad paraissent suspendus en l'air en lettres capitales.

— Tu es vraiment un connard, lui crache à la figure une femme qui passe à côté de nous.

Nous reculons sous le coup et la suivons des yeux pendant plusieurs secondes, mais elle ne s'arrête pas, ne se retourne même pas vers nous. Finalement, nous nous tournons à nouveau l'un vers l'autre.

—C'était qui?

Il hausse les épaules avec nonchalance:

—Ma mère.

Je fais entendre un petit rire délicat. C'est ce que j'espère, en tout cas: au point où j'en suis, je pourrais aussi bien m'esclaffer en montrant tous mes plombages, et je ne serais même pas capable de me retenir si je m'en rendais compte.

—De toute façon, écoute, pourquoi est-ce que j'aurais besoin d'en passer par tout ce mensonge compliqué, alors que, comme je le disais, il existe d'autres solutions? dit-il en baissant la voix et en lançant des regards furtifs autour de lui.

—Ah, bordel, te voilà enfin, Libby, s'écrie Vini en se précipitant vers moi.

Je lui ai demandé, dans la voiture, de m'appeler comme ça. Je ne croyais pas qu'elle y penserait.

—Ah, coucou, Vini.

Je lui adresse un sourire reconnaissant. Elle a dû me repérer quand ses yeux, comme ceux de toutes les personnes de la salle, se sont posés sur Brad pendant ce silence subit.

—Qu'est-ce qui se passe?

—J'ai rencontré quelqu'un, explique-t-elle d'un ton surexcité. Tu te souviens de ce type au congrès des marionnettistes?

—Lequel? Bon Dieu, pas celui qui se tenait à califourchon sur la fausse autruche?

—Non, non, pas lui.

—Celui avec le berger et toutes les petites chèvres?

—Non, pas lui. Écoute…

—Celui avec le cheval au bout de l'avant-bras?

—Non. Putain, tu vas me laisser parler ? C'était le gars qui sortait de la pièce de Fast Love quand on entrait. Tu te souviens de lui ? Adam.

—Ah oui, je me rappelle très bien. Il n'avait pas de marionnette, n'est-ce pas ? Mais il les cherchait, et c'est mauvais signe. Tu ne vas pas sortir avec quelqu'un qui est atteint de fièvre marionnettiste, Vini !

Brad essaie sans grand succès de réprimer un éclat de rire. Vini le foudroie du regard avant de se retourner vers moi :

—Je suis sortie avec pas mal de branleurs dans ma jeunesse, Lib, donc je ne pense pas que je vais l'éliminer juste pour ça. Pas encore.

—OK, mais il n'apporte pas de marionnettes à la maison. Je suis sérieuse, Vini. Je refuse de trouver Kermit à plat ventre dans la salle de bains quand je me lève, ou de me cogner dans une marionnette de cheval sur le palier. Je me fiche de savoir à quel point c'est sexy.

—Oh, ta gueule ! répond-elle, soudain grincheuse. (À présent, Brad glousse franchement, et il se cache la bouche de la main pour faire semblant de tousser.) Ouais, ouais, ah ah, très drôle. Je suis contente d'avoir pu te faire rire. Je suis juste venue te dire que je partais, OK ? Adam et moi, on va ailleurs. J'ai l'impression d'être une cible ambulante, ici, alors on va chercher un endroit plus calme.

—Il y a une jolie petite tente rayée sur la plage, dis-je obligeamment, en essayant de ne pas rigoler. Très cosy.

Brad s'étrangle à grand bruit derrière sa main et se détourne carrément, les épaules secouées de rire.

—Ouais, super, merci. À plus.

Et elle s'éloigne, la tête haute.

— Mais qui c'était ? explose-t-il, dans un dernier effort pour réprimer son hilarité.

— Ma coloc, Lavinia. Vini. Elle portait le numéro cinq, la semaine dernière, tu te souviens ?

Il reprend aussitôt son sérieux.

— Non, désolé, je ne me souviens pas. Une fois que je suis arrivé au six, j'ai oublié tous les autres numéros.

Il me sourit avec douceur, et je sens fondre certaines parties de mon corps. De nombreuses parties.

— Et tout ce que je me rappelle, c'est le numéro… (Je me tais.) Attends une minute. Tu avais quel numéro, exactement ? Parce que je sais que j'ai coché le quinze, mais après j'ai reçu un message bizarre de quelqu'un qui prétendait être… quoi ?

Il secoue la tête :

— Je n'avais pas le quinze. J'avais le seize.

— Mais non, tu avais le quinze, j'en suis sûre.

— Le seize.

— Non, je m'en souviens, parce que tu m'as montré ta main trois fois : cinq, cinq, cinq. La dernière fois que j'ai vérifié, trois fois cinq faisaient quinze. Ne me dis pas que ça a changé ?

— Non, c'est toujours vrai. Tu as raison, trois fois cinq, quinze. Et je t'ai montré trois fois cinq, mais ensuite j'ai ajouté un. Cinq et cinq et cinq. Plus un. Total : seize.

Je le dévisage, les yeux écarquillés.

— Oh non. Ce n'est pas vrai, je n'ai pas fait ça ? Mais comment est-ce que j'ai pu louper… ?

Et là, ça me revient. Mon papier était tombé par terre, et je paniquais à l'idée de ne pas réussir à le rattraper et à noter son numéro avant que la personne suivante arrive, et j'ai dû rater son «un» final pendant que je regardais frénétiquement autour de moi…

Du coup, je me couvre la bouche de la main.

—Oh… merde! Tout est ma faute. Oh non. Tout ce temps, et c'était… Je suis vraiment désolée. Quelle idiote! Je dois avoir des raviolis grillés à la place du cerveau.

—L'image est évocatrice, mais ne sois pas trop dure avec toi-même. Tout est bien qui finit bien, n'est-ce pas?

Il fait un pas imperceptible dans ma direction. Cette fois-ci, je ne recule pas.

—Je ne sais pas. Repose-moi la question dans une heure.

Il sourit et me boit des yeux :

—Je n'y manquerai pas. (Il se tait, puis m'attrape vivement les bras.) Ça va?

Oups. J'ai les jambes qui flageolent un peu. J'espérais qu'il ne s'en était pas aperçu.

—Oh oui, tout va bien. Je suis juste un peu…

Un peu quoi? Fatiguée, j'allais dire, mais ça me donne l'air… je ne sais pas, un peu pathétique. Je pourrais prétendre être saoule, mais c'est sans doute un gros tabou quand on apprend à se connaître. Donc quelle explication puis-je donner?

—Tu veux t'asseoir? demande-t-il doucement, l'air inquiet, mettant ainsi terme à mon dilemme.

Il penche la tête pour être à hauteur de mes yeux. J'opine du chef :

—Oui, je crois que j'aimerais bien.

Avant que mon désir hors de contrôle me pousse à m'allonger, nue.

Il me conduit à une table flanquée de deux sofas, dans le coin, puis part nous chercher des boissons. Quand il revient, je projette un puissant rayon tracteur avec mon corps, comme dans *Star Trek*, pour attirer vers moi le divan, où Brad pourra s'asseoir à mes côtés et où nos cuisses pourront se rencontrer. Mais ça ne marche pas. Il hésite une seconde, puis fait le tour de la table pour s'installer en face de moi. Je le dévisage avec désespoir – non, pas désespoir, déception – et je remarque qu'il semble un peu perplexe. Ou bien troublé. Je ne suis pas certaine d'aimer ça. Peut-être que mon langage corporel est un peu trop expressif : je suis étalée sur les coussins, penchée en arrière, les trois premiers boutons du chemisier défaits, les genoux légèrement écartés, les yeux à demi fermés, les lèvres humides et entrouvertes, alors je me redresse comme une bibliothécaire et m'apprête à me coincer les cheveux derrière les oreilles. (Je ne le fais pas en vrai : je ne suis pas stupide.)

— Je crois que je t'ai vue, dit-il avec un sourire soudain.

— Vraiment ? Quand ?

« Et pourquoi n'es-tu pas venu me voir et me demander de t'épouser ? » me retiens-je d'ajouter.

— Hum, laisse-moi réfléchir.

Il pince les lèvres et lève les yeux, dans un effort pour se souvenir. Mais franchement, allons, ça ne peut pas faire si longtemps que ça, on se connaît depuis neuf jours.

— Vendredi dernier. Le 8. À 13 h 17.

Je bats des cils.

— Oh, sans blague ? Bah, tu prétendais que tu n'avais même pas trouvé d'ADN, et maintenant tu m'annonces que tu m'as vue. Pourquoi tu n'es pas venu me dire bonjour ?

— Eh bien, je l'aurais fait, mais tu étais dans ta voiture.

Oh non ! À tous les coups, c'était l'une de ces fois où je rentrais à la maison en rêvant à Rupert, sans penser à l'expression idiote qu'on pouvait lire sur mon visage. Je ressemblais sans doute à une folle. « De quoi j'avais l'air ? » parviens-je de justesse à m'empêcher de m'exclamer. Au lieu de quoi, je dis :

— Ainsi c'était bien toi qui m'as servi ce hamburger au drive-in, l'autre jour. Tu as un deuxième travail ?

Il sourit :

— Tu as deviné. Je fais du bénévolat chez eux, deux fois par semaine.

Je hoche la tête avec sérieux.

— Admirable. C'est bien de savoir partager.

— C'est pour ça que je le fais. Alors, comment va cette fille, avec qui tu étais ? Celle qui était dans ta voiture ? Quand je t'ai vue, elle avait l'air au trente-sixième dessous. En fait, c'est pour ça que je ne suis pas venu te parler.

Oh, merci, Seigneur ! Je n'étais pas en train de conduire.

— Ce n'était pas faute d'en avoir envie, pourtant, ajoute-t-il.

Je prends conscience de nouvelles informations. Tout d'abord, la douceur de sa voix dans ces derniers mots. Ensuite, le fait qu'il voulait venir me parler quand il m'a vue. Et la troisième chose, la plus importante, dont je me rends tardivement compte, c'est que non seulement je n'étais pas au volant, l'air grincheuse, mais il m'a surprise occupée à consoler Fatima après être allée la chercher au poste de police, la semaine dernière. J'ai été vue en train d'aider une amie ! Et je n'ai même pas remarqué qu'on m'observait, ce qui signifie que tout ce que j'ai fait était parfaitement naturel, et pourtant j'étais séduisante.

Je m'aperçois soudain qu'il attend toujours une réponse à propos de Fatima.

—Euh, elle va bien, vraiment. Enfin, non, pas complètement. Elle a quelques problèmes. C'est pour ça qu'elle pleurait. Je suis vraiment inquiète à son sujet.

—Ça se voyait. (Il me regarde droit dans les yeux pendant une seconde, avec un sourire chaleureux.) J'aurais aimé pouvoir te parler ce jour-là.

—Moi aussi.

Nous sirotons nos verres en silence pendant un moment. Il pose son regard sur moi, puis le détourne, et le ramène vers moi. Je m'en rends compte, parce que je ne peux pas détacher mes yeux de lui. Il finit par se racler la gorge.

—Donc nous savons tous deux pourquoi je suis là ce soir, dit-il avec un sourire jusqu'aux oreilles, mais qu'en est-il de toi ?

Je secoue la tête :

—Non, non, attends un peu. Nous ne savons pas tous deux pourquoi tu es là, pas du tout. Toi, tu le sais, mais dans mon esprit, tu es ici pour un coup d'un soir. (J'ai baissé un peu la voix sur ces derniers mots, au cas où.) OK, tu m'as convaincue que ce n'était pas le cas, donc tu dois être ici pour des raisons valables. Ce qui est un peu… eh bien, superficiel, étant donné que tu as coché ma case la semaine dernière et que tu t'es démené pour me faire comprendre que tu n'avais donc plus besoin de chercher. Et pourtant, te voilà : en train de chercher. Pourquoi ?

Il me contemple d'un air sérieux pendant quelques instants, et je sens la chaleur envahir mes joues. Et mon cou. Et d'autres endroits. Et alors il déclare :

—Toi.

—Humm ?

—Libby, je suis ici parce que je voulais te trouver. Je pensais que tu avais compris ?…

—Euh… tu… tu es… ?

Il sourit et penche un peu la tête en avant.

—Contrairement à toi, quand je n'ai pas reçu tes coordonnées de la part des organisateurs de Fast Love, je n'en ai pas déduit que tu étais une nymphomane avec une seule chose à l'esprit.

—Mais moi non plus, je n'ai pas cru ça de toi.

Il pousse un soupir amusé.

—Eh bien, quelle que soit l'intention que tu m'aies prêtée, la réciproque n'est pas vraie. J'ai pensé qu'il y avait eu un imbroglio avec les formulaires, ou quelque chose comme ça, et que tout ce que j'avais à faire, c'était de te trouver. À ce moment-là, la seule information que j'avais sur toi, c'était que tu t'étais rendue une fois à une soirée pour célibataires, donc c'était mon unique piste. Par conséquent, me voici.

—Oh.

Vous savez, en y repensant, ça me semble grotesque d'avoir pu le prendre pour un Don Juan dans ce genre-là. Je veux dire, il aurait vraiment fallu qu'il soit bon acteur pour réussir cette mise en scène.

—Pour ne rien te cacher, je ne pensais pas vraiment te trouver là. Ni dans aucune autre soirée pour célibataires. Tu détonnais complètement, la dernière fois. En plus, je sais que tu pensais que c'était un ratage total, fréquenté uniquement par des obsédés sexuels. (Il m'adresse un sourire espiègle.) Ce qui m'amène à me demander ce que tu fais ici exactement ?

—Vini, réponds-je simplement.

Il hoche la tête d'un air de comprendre :

— Bien sûr. C'est quoi, son vrai nom ?

— C'est son vrai nom.

— Non, sérieusement ?

— Mais je suis sérieuse. Ses parents l'ont appelée Lavinia parce que c'était original et que ça compensait son patronyme tellement banal.

— C'est quoi, son nom de famille ?

— Jones.

— Jones ? Tu plaisantes ? Vini Jones, comme l'acteur ? Pas possible !

— Mais si. En fait, je pense que choisir Vini comme diminutif de Lavinia était un véritable coup de génie de sa part, tu ne crois pas ?

— Eh bien, si. Et ça répond parfaitement à la nécessité de prendre un faux nom pour ce genre de soirées.

Je sursaute légèrement. Merde, est-ce qu'il a deviné ? J'examine son visage, mais il ne me regarde pas d'un air d'expectative, comme s'il s'attendait à une confession. Je vais continuer comme ça, alors.

— Tu as raison. Personne ne croirait qu'elle s'appelle vraiment comme ça, n'est-ce pas ?

— Non, c'est exactement ça. Bien que j'aie du mal à comprendre pourquoi certains éprouvent le besoin de cacher leur nom, de toute façon. Je veux dire, c'est une grosse part de ton identité ; comment peux-tu espérer faire des rencontres sincères si tu mens sur ton état civil ?

— Oh, je suis cent pour cent d'accord. Jamais je n'utiliserais de pseudo. C'est méprisable.

— Ah, Paula, te voilà, s'exclame Éric qui débarque soudain, toujours aussi rougeaud, avec deux énormes boissons verdâtres et un grand sourire.

Je lance un regard à Brad, qui articule silencieusement :
« Paula ? »

— Tu ne m'as pas dit ce que tu voulais, continue Éric, alors je t'ai pris un cocktail à la menthe. Ça plaît toujours. Tiens.

Il me met d'autorité le verre dans la main puis reste debout là, à attendre que je le boive. Du coin de l'œil, je vois Brad qui me dévisage sans sourire, bien que je sois certaine que les commissures de ses lèvres frémissent, et je sens planer sur nous la menace d'une crise de fou rire. Ou peut-être juste sur moi.

— Allez, Paula, dit finalement Brad d'une voix qui tremble légèrement, goûte.

— Oh oui, vas-y, Paula, insiste Éric. C'est sacrément bon. (Il prend une lampée de son propre verre.) Humm, miam miam.

— Oh, Éric, écoute, merci beaucoup, mais je crois que malheureusement mon père est venu me chercher, dis-je en désignant Brad d'un geste, donc je vais devoir partir.

En récompense, je vois Brad reculer dans son siège, et son sourire vaciller. Je tends la boisson à Éric, qui s'en saisit et la serre contre sa poitrine presque avant que je l'aie lâchée.

— Ton père ? balbutie-t-il, le regard allant de l'un à l'autre. Tu as quel âge ?

— Quinze ans. C'est trop injuste. Comment tu as su où j'étais, papa ?

Brad se débat toujours avec l'idée qu'Éric ait accepté ce scénario sans broncher :

— Euh, euh, bah, je, euh…

— Ah merde, ne me dis pas que tu as encore lu mon journal ? Bordel de merde, pourquoi est-ce que je continue à écrire soigneusement tout ce que je fais avec plein de détails, et que j'oublie ce fichu machin n'importe où ?

—Surveille un peu ton langage, jeune fille, réagit Brad en se penchant vers moi. Je t'enlève 50 pence sur ton argent de poche.

—À plus, alors, dis-je à Éric qui se détourne le plus vite possible et traverse la pièce.

Alors qu'il s'enfuit dans la foule, nous l'entendons s'exclamer :

—Ça va, beauté ? Moi c'est Éric. Tu as l'air du genre de personne qui apprécie les arômes subtils du cocktail à la menthe…

Deux heures plus tard, nous sommes sur le parking, à côté de ma voiture. Brad a mes numéros de portable et de fixe, ainsi que mon adresse Hotmail. La seule chose que je ne lui ai pas donnée, c'est mon vrai nom.

—Je suis tellement content que tu aies été là, ce soir, dit-il d'une voix douce.

Il me regarde droit dans les yeux, mais cette fois encore je vois dans son regard comme une trace de… regret ? Oui, je crois que c'est ça.

—Quelque chose ne va pas ?

Les mots sont sortis avant que j'aie réfléchi. Merde, ma bouche fait une fois de plus des siennes. Pour l'amour du ciel, elle ne connaît même pas la bonne question. Tout le monde sait que personne ne répond à « Quelque chose ne va pas ? » avec franchise.

—Eh bien, oui, en quelque sorte, rétorque Brad après une courte hésitation. Ce n'est pas exactement que ça ne va pas. C'est plutôt que ça va. Trop bien. C'est difficile à expliquer.

Je pose ma main sur son bras pour le rassurer, mais aussi parce que j'ai tellement envie de le toucher. Je presse un peu, afin d'en profiter pour sentir ses muscles. C'est délicieux. De le rassurer, je veux dire.

— Non, écoute, désolée, je ne voulais pas être indiscrète. Tu n'es pas obligé de me raconter.

Il est à présent tout près de moi, et son regard parcourt mon visage, puis mes cheveux, mes yeux, mes lèvres, à nouveau mes cheveux, pendant que je contemple ses lèvres avec une intensité féroce. Je ne peux pas m'en empêcher : elles sont à hauteur de mes yeux. Et j'essaie de les attirer vers moi par la force de mon esprit, mais la télékinésie est une forme de communication qui n'a jamais fonctionné pour moi.

— Non, je sais bien, dit-il, et, de toute façon, je sais que je n'y arriverais pas. C'est juste que… (Il ferme les yeux et se masse la nuque.) Depuis que je t'ai rencontrée la semaine dernière, j'ai en quelque sorte… je veux dire, il y a eu… (Il regarde de nouveau mes lèvres, et il prend une expression douloureuse.) J'ai vraiment envie de…, dit-il lentement, avant de baisser encore une fois les paupières et de se voûter légèrement. Non, je ne peux pas. Pas avant… laisse tomber. C'est mon problème, je vais le régler. Ça n'a pas d'importance.

Je ne suis pas convaincue. Il est clair que depuis mardi dernier, soit il s'est marié, soit il a tué quelqu'un, et maintenant il le regrette parce qu'il m'a revue. J'enlève ma main de son bras :

— Oh non, tu n'es pas marié, j'espère ? dis-je, parce que de toute évidence je ne peux pas lui faire savoir que je suis au courant, pour le meurtre, ce qui me mettrait en deuxième place sur sa liste.

— Non, pour l'amour du ciel, bien sûr que non ! Pourquoi est-ce que je ferais du speed dating, si j'avais déjà quelqu'un ?

Je le regarde comme s'il était la personne la plus naïve qui se soit jamais trouvée sur un parking sombre :

— Ça s'est déjà vu.

— Eh bien, ce n'est pas le cas. Je te le promets. Et même si j'avais une femme, elle ne me comprendrait pas.

Je laisse échapper un petit rire :

— Bien sûr, qu'elle ne comprendrait pas.

Il me rend mon sourire :

— Mais toi, si. C'est pour ça que je la quitte. Notre mariage est rompu depuis des mois, de toute façon.

En réalité, je commence maintenant à me demander s'il n'est pas réellement marié et en train de faire comme si c'était une blague pour que je prenne la question à la rigolade et n'y pense plus. Et comme ça, quand je découvrirai réellement dans six mois qu'il est marié, il pourra me dire, sans mentir : « Mais, ma puce, je te l'ai dit, que j'étais marié ; tu ne t'en souviens pas ? Sur le parking de l'hôtel *Oast House*. Je croyais que ça ne te dérangeait pas, puisque tu n'as plus jamais parlé d'elle et que tu as couché avec moi plein de fois. »

Peut-être que c'est justement ce que je devrais faire. Mais au lieu de ça, je réponds :

— Faut que j'y aille. (Il acquiesce. Crotte.) On se voit bientôt.

— Tu peux y compter, dit-il.

Tout à coup il se penche et ses lèvres effleurent ma joue. À ce contact, j'ai à nouveau les genoux qui flageolent, et mes paupières se ferment sur mes yeux révulsés de plaisir. Je suis contente qu'il ne puisse pas voir mon visage, dans cet état. En fait, je suis contente que personne ne me voie.

— Bonne nuit, Libby, murmure-t-il dans mes cheveux.

Je monte dans la voiture et mets le contact, puis descends la vitre.

— Bonne nuit.

Et tandis que je sors de ma place en marche arrière et rejoins la route, je peux voir dans mon rétroviseur qu'il ne me quitte pas des yeux un instant.

Chapitre 19

Écoute active

Objectif à court terme : me décider entre Brad et Rupert. Ou peut-être, tout simplement, coucher avec les deux.

Obstacles : j'ai des valeurs. Non, je vous assure, c'est vrai.

Objectif à long terme : tout ce qui me restera à faire, ce sera de choisir ma robe.

Obstacles : il y a tellement de modèles, et il ne reste que six mois avant juin.

Rupert est en voiture, et il roule sans doute trop vite. Il a le sourire jusqu'aux oreilles et il chante sur le rythme de la radio, qui fait apparemment une journée spéciale années 1980.

— Tous les tubes des années 1980, toute la journée ! répète l'animateur.

Rupert tapote le volant et secoue la tête énergiquement en mesure. On est vendredi matin, et il sait bien qu'il devrait être au bureau, mais il a besoin de parler à une certaine personne. Quelqu'un qui l'a aidé à voir clair dans ses problèmes par le passé. Rupert espère que cette personne l'aidera à nouveau.

Il est tellement pris par Roxy Music qu'il manque de rater l'embranchement. Il écrase la pédale de frein et fait crisser les pneus en prenant le virage à la dernière minute. Il continue sur la route pendant trois ou quatre kilomètres avant de tourner derrière une haute haie et de remonter une large allée de gravier jusqu'à une imposante bâtisse de trois étages. Il se gare devant la maison, bondit hors de la voiture et franchit le seuil à la volée.

— Hou hou! Maman? Papa? Matt? Où êtes-vous, tous? Je suis là! Hou hou!

— Dans le salon, répond une voix qui semble venir de très loin.

Rupert emprunte un couloir sur la droite et le suit jusqu'au fond, où il débouche sur une grande pièce lumineuse dont l'immense baie vitrée donne sur un champ brumeux. Au fond de la pièce, un homme et une femme, tous deux âgés d'une soixantaine d'années, regardent la télévision; à genoux sur le sol, un jeune homme de vingt-cinq ans environ est absorbé par la carte de Suède d'un atlas, qu'il recopie sur une grande feuille de papier. Le dessin est plus grand que l'original, mais l'échelle est parfaitement respectée.

— Salut tout le monde! s'écrie Rupert qui entre dans le salon en trottinant.

— Rupert! Bonjour, mon chéri. (Caroline de Witter se lève pour le serrer dans ses bras.) Quelle bonne surprise!

Elle contemple son fils qui donne une accolade à son père et salue son frère:

— Salut, Matt.

— Salut, répond doucement le jeune homme sans lever les yeux. J'agrandis cette carte de Suède, ajoute-t-il, le nez pratiquement collé au papier. Je la reproduis plus grande que dans ce livre de un huitième. Celle-ci est trop petite, alors je l'agrandis. Il y a beaucoup de passages difficiles sur le bord, c'est très délicat, mais je m'en sors bien.

Il prend son temps et semble très minutieux. En fait, il est plongé dans son travail : il pose l'index sur la carte, étudie ce point pendant quelques secondes, puis le recopie avec exactitude sur sa feuille.

— C'est incroyable, dit Rupert, autant pour son frère que pour ses parents et lui-même. Comment ça va, aujourd'hui ?

— Il est calme. Il va bien, répond Caroline. Nous n'avons pas de projet, pas besoin d'aller quelque part, donc il est heureux.

— Tant mieux. Je peux l'emmener, alors ?

Elle opine :

— Bien sûr. Mais pas plus d'une demi-heure. Et pense bien à le lui dire.

— Je sais, maman. Je n'oublierai pas. Est-ce que c'est déjà arrivé ?

Elle sourit :

— Eh bien, juste une fois, mais ça a suffi…

— Oui, je sais, je m'en souviens. Et je n'ai plus jamais oublié depuis ce jour-là, n'est-ce pas ?

— Non, je ne crois pas. Mais je te le rappellerai quand même chaque fois. Au cas où. (Elle se tourne vers son deuxième fils.) Matthew, ton frère est là et il voudrait t'emmener faire une promenade d'une demi-heure. Est-ce que tu veux bien fermer l'atlas et le poser avec ta carte sur la table, maintenant, s'il te plaît ?

Matt lève les yeux, sans toutefois regarder sa mère, puis prend les objets et les pose docilement sur la table.

Il laisse les crayons de couleur étalés en désordre sur le tapis.

—Et à présent range les crayons, ajoute Caroline. J'ai oublié de le lui demander, explique-t-elle à Rupert. Maintenant, va prendre une veste dans le placard de l'entrée et enfile-la, s'il te plaît. Puis reste avec Rupert.

—Promenade d'une demi-heure, dit Matt doucement. Une demi-heure.

—Oui, mon vieux, juste une demi-heure, répond Rupert en suivant son frère dans le couloir.

—Oh, tu restes tout le week-end, n'est-ce pas, Rupe? demande Caroline alors que les deux frères se dirigent vers la porte.

—Bien sûr. Je ne vais pas rater l'anniversaire de mon petit frère, n'est-ce pas? J'arrive demain très tôt et je ne repars que dimanche soir.

Elle lui sourit tendrement:

—Merci, Rupe. Ça nous rendra vraiment service.

Une fois dehors, Rupert décide de faire le tour de la propriété mais, avant de se mettre en route, il consacre cinq minutes à Matt pour lui expliquer dans le détail quel chemin ils vont suivre. Matt ne le regarde pas, mais Rupert sait qu'il trace une carte dans sa tête. Rupert consulte sa montre et dit doucement:

—Nous rentrons à midi moins le quart.

Matt vérifie sur sa montre sans rien dire. Rupert engage la conversation alors qu'ils se promènent:

—Alors, comment ça va, petit frère? Tout va bien? Toujours occupé avec tes cartes, donc? C'est génial, ce que tu as fait pour la Suède. Tu es brillant! Je suis vraiment désolé de ne pas être venu te voir ces dernières semaines. Je voulais le faire, mais j'ai été pris par cette histoire de crèche d'entreprise, et ensuite quelque chose de merveilleux est arrivé.

Il se tourne vers Matt, espérant une réaction, un regard de son frère, un sourire, une question : « Qu'est-ce qui s'est passé, Rupe ? Qu'est-ce qui est si merveilleux ? » Mais rien ne vient. Comme toujours. Matt continue à marcher avec obstination, les yeux rivés droit devant lui, suivant le chemin tracé dans sa tête.

— J'ai besoin de te demander conseil, Matt. Ça ne t'embête pas ? (Rupert se détourne pour regarder devant lui également.) Le truc, c'est que j'ai rencontré quelqu'un. Une fille adorable, drôle et magnifique, qui s'appelle Libby. Je pense à elle tout le temps, je ne peux pas m'en empêcher. Je lui plais aussi, et cette fois-ci c'est différent parce qu'elle ne sait pas qui je suis. Elle pense que je m'appelle Brad.

— Tu t'appelles Rupert.

— Oui, mon vieux, c'est vrai, je m'appelle Rupert. Bien sûr. Mais elle ne le sait pas. Tu ne peux pas comprendre, Matt, mais si elle savait qui je suis, ça changerait tout. Elle serait différente, et moi aussi. En général, les filles ne s'intéressent à moi que pour l'argent – ou, en tout cas, c'est ce que je crois –, et ça me met mal à l'aise, alors je n'arrive pas à être naturel. Et elles ont des idées toutes faites sur ce que ce serait, de sortir avec moi. Mais, en étant Brad, je me sens différent. (Il s'anime soudain et se tourne pour regarder son frère, les yeux brillants.) Je veux dire, je suis moi, sauf que je suis décontracté parce que je sais qu'elle n'a pas d'attentes particulières à mon sujet. Je peux être vraiment moi-même. Et je lui plais, Matt. Pour ce que je suis. On ne m'avait pas transmis son numéro de téléphone, alors je suis retourné à ces soirées pour célibataires, dans l'espoir de la revoir. Et hier soir elle était là.

—Onze heures et demie, dit Matt sans le regarder.

Rupert vérifie sur sa montre.

—Je sais, mon vieux. Il nous reste un quart d'heure. Passons par le potager, maintenant. (Ils tournent à l'angle de la pelouse et passent à travers une ouverture dans la haute haie.) Alors, tu ne trouves pas que ça a l'air fantastique? Surtout maintenant, parce que depuis hier soir j'ai ses coordonnées. Et elle était tellement… (Il se tait et reste un moment à sourire à ses pieds). Elle est pleine d'humour. Et je me sens tellement à l'aise avec elle. Je voudrais passer tout mon temps en sa compagnie. (Il secoue doucement la tête et se passe la main sur la figure.) Que ce soit simple et merveilleux. Et ça l'est. Mais… Bon Dieu, j'aimerais tellement que tu puisses comprendre tout ça, Matt. Ironie du sort: après tout ce temps passé à chercher l'âme sœur sans la trouver, je rencontre deux filles en même temps. Tu imagines? (Il regarde son frère, toujours tourné vers l'avant, impassible.) Non, bien sûr que non. C'est trop ridicule. Deux d'un coup! Personne n'y croirait. Mais c'est bien ce qui s'est passé. En fait, je n'ai pas vraiment rencontré la deuxième – Beth – mais je suis complètement accro. Elle est tellement marrante, et intelligente, et pleine d'imagination, et vivante. Et quelqu'un que je connais l'a vue et m'a dit qu'en plus elle était jolie, ça t'en bouche un coin, non? Je meurs d'impatience de faire sa connaissance, pas seulement parce qu'elle est fantastique, mais aussi parce que j'ai l'impression que je n'arriverai pas vraiment à me décider tant que je ne l'aurai pas vue en chair et en os. Que je ne lui aurai pas parlé, les yeux dans les yeux. (Il se tait et marche d'un air rêveur, les mains dans les poches, pendant quelques minutes.) La différence, c'est qu'elle sait que je suis Rupert de Witter…

—Tu t'appelles Rupert.

—Oui, mon vieux, c'est vrai. Et Beth le sait, mais ce n'est peut-être pas une mauvaise chose. Sauf qu'elle imagine que j'ai… une autre tête. Elle croit que j'ai de magnifiques cheveux blonds et des dents parfaites… Bon sang, je suis trop bête! Je ne sais pas comment résoudre ce problème. J'ai l'esprit complètement vide. Laquelle choisir? Beth sait qui je suis, mais elle croit que je ressemble à un mannequin. Et Libby connaît mon apparence physique, mais elle croit que je suis quelqu'un d'autre. Je pense que je plais à chacune, et elles me charment toutes les deux. Beaucoup. Il faut que je prenne une décision, ce qui signifie que je devrai renoncer à l'une des deux, et je n'en ai pas envie. Et si je continue à les fréquenter toutes les deux quelque temps, j'aurai l'impression de les trahir. Bon sang, c'est trop compliqué! Alors, qu'est-ce que tu en penses? Libby, ou Beth? Beth, ou Libby? À ton avis?

Il regarde à nouveau son frère, mais Matt a toujours les yeux rivés droit devant. Il n'apporte ni conseil ni réconfort à Rupert, qui se passe les mains dans les cheveux.

—Eh bien, tu as peut-être raison. Je n'ai sans doute pas besoin de prendre une décision maintenant. Je veux dire, je n'en suis pas à demander leur main, n'est-ce pas? Il s'agit seulement de faire plus ample connaissance. Les gens fréquentent plus d'une personne à la fois, de nos jours, pas vrai? Ça ne pose pas de problème, tant qu'il ne s'agit que d'amitié, n'est-ce pas? (Il hoche la tête, mais fronce les sourcils en même temps.) Et puis, quand j'aurai rencontré Beth la semaine prochaine, qu'on aura bavardé, et peut-être pris un verre ensemble une fois ou deux, alors je déciderai.

— Midi moins vingt. Cinq minutes.

— Oui, je sais. Écoute, dans quelques instants on sera de retour au jardin d'hiver. Est-ce que ma solution te semble bien, alors ? Je continue à les fréquenter toutes les deux, ces jours-ci en tout cas, juste le temps de voir comment les choses évoluent ? Je veux dire, il n'y a pas de mal à avoir plus d'une amie, n'est-ce pas ? Je dois juste faire en sorte que ça n'aille pas plus loin avant que j'aie pris une décision. Je pense que j'y arriverai. J'espère. (Il s'arrête et se masse le crâne.) Je m'inquiète vraiment de la réaction de Libby quand elle saura qui je suis vraiment, cela dit. Je l'ai trompée sur mon identité quand même. Mais c'est une femme sensible et intelligente, elle comprendra pourquoi.

Il se tourne pour regarder Matt une nouvelle fois et sourit tendrement devant les cheveux emmêlés de son frère, et son visage impassible.

— Ça m'aide vraiment de discuter avec toi, tu sais, Matty, même si tu n'écoutes pas réellement. Je t'aime, vieux. Je peux te faire un câlin ?

— Midi moins le quart. On rentre maintenant.

Rupert soupire :

— Oui, mon vieux. On rentre maintenant.

Vendredi matin, je suis au boulot, assise devant mon ordinateur, le regard posé sur une rainure en forme d'éclair, comme la cicatrice d'Harry Potter, sur le bureau. Je travaille d'arrache-pied à ma préparation pour l'atelier « Motivation » de lundi, mais je suis étrangement peu concentrée. Je n'arrête pas de voir des images, tantôt de Brad, tantôt de Rupert, à cheval sur un balai, passant et repassant devant mes yeux. C'est très bizarre. D'abord Rupert, avec son abondante chevelure blonde et son sourire étincelant ; puis Brad, plus grand, plus large, les cheveux plus foncés. Chaque fois que l'un d'eux arrive, il s'approche tout près de moi, puis s'immobilise en l'air, souriant, pour me donner le temps de le mater de près. Le menton ciselé de Rupert, ses yeux de star de cinéma, sa crinière magnifique ; puis le regard chaleureux de Brad, sa barbe de trois jours, son air de gendre idéal. Chaque fois que Rupert prend la place de Brad, je suis heureuse de le voir. Et chaque fois qu'à son tour Brad remplace Rupert, ça me fait également plaisir.

Le dilemme que je rencontre est terriblement banal, basique, et ancestral. Le triangle classique : deux hommes, une femme. C'est un problème qui a poursuivi l'espèce humaine depuis la naissance de la civilisation. D'un côté, l'homme d'affaires richissime, incroyablement beau et sexy, qui n'a peut-être pas toujours été sincère, n'a communiqué que par mail et téléphone, et, autant le reconnaître, est probablement hors de ma portée. De l'autre, un garçon bien sous tous rapports, sympa, drôle, follement séduisant, avec une beauté juvénile et un air un peu dépenaillé, qui m'a rencontrée en chair et en os, m'a embrassée sur la joue avec une douceur infinie, et à qui je plais sans l'ombre d'un doute. Les manuels d'histoire et la grande littérature regorgent de situations exactement semblables à celle-là.

Bien. *Allons, Beth, reprends-toi*. Je dois absolument, absolument, absolument, avancer dans ce truc sur la « Motivation ». Je n'ai plus qu'aujourd'hui et ce week-end pour le mettre au point, et j'ai à peine commencé. La motivation repose sur le fait de se donner un objectif accessible, de s'y investir et ensuite de poser des jalons destinés à célébrer…

Oh, regardez-moi ça, la robe de Quidditch de Rupert s'est ouverte sous l'effet du vent et découvre ses pectoraux qui jouent sous sa peau douce et bronzée. Je vois ses muscles s'étirer alors qu'il reste parfaitement en place, en équilibre sur le balai lancé à pleine vitesse. Il est tellement près que je pourrais presque tendre le bras pour passer mes doigts sur sa chair et repousser le tissu de…

—Tu sais où est fourré Sean? demande Chas, qui apparaît soudain juste derrière moi.

Je tourne précipitamment les yeux vers lui et essuie en même temps la gouttelette qui perle sur ma lèvre inférieure.

—Non, Chas, je ne sais pas.

Et pourquoi il me demande, de toute façon?

—Tu as de grands projets, Beth? questionne-t-il en se frottant les mains. Plusieurs fers au feu? Plusieurs lièvres à la fois?

—Hum, oui, absolument.

—Très bien, très bien. Plus qu'une semaine, tu sais, avant qu'on ferme pour Noël. Tu n'as pas intérêt à perdre ton temps à réserver tes vacances. (Il hausse les sourcils en regardant la brochure d'Horizon, qui est mystérieusement apparue sur mon bureau.) Le monde appartient à qui, tu te souviens? Il faut savoir saisir sa chance, hein? Il n'y a pas de temps à perdre, Beth. *Carpe diem*, tu sais. Et que ça saute!

Va mourir, pauvre branleur. Je ne le dis pas à haute voix – je ne suis pas folle. Je lui envoie cette pensée par télépathie, sans cesser de sourire et d'acquiescer. Il me gratifie d'un hochement de tête et s'en va zoner plus loin.

Je jette un coup d'œil vers le bureau de Sean. Il ne figurait pas dans mon petit scénario bizarre avec les balais ; c'est intéressant. Tant mieux s'il n'est pas là aujourd'hui : sa présence pourrait commencer à compliquer les choses.

Je me tourne à nouveau vers mon ordinateur et tape sans entrain pendant quelques minutes : « La motivation première est de trouver de la nourriture et un abri. Une fois que l'on s'est procuré ces deux éléments essentiels, le besoin le plus essentiel est le sexe. De préférence en plein air, sur une couverture, quelque part. Le soleil tiède doit caresser la peau, les ombres vacillantes danser sur les corps emmêlés. Ou pourquoi pas sur un yacht, le balancement rythmique des vagues et le grincement des cordes ajoutant une note sensuelle à la passion du moment… »

Merde. Je vais me faire une tasse de thé pour me vider la tête. Je me lève, mais juste à ce moment Chas revient et frappe dans ses mains.

—Écoutez-moi tous, déclare-t-il tout haut, interrompant chacun d'entre nous dans sa tâche. J'espère que vous n'avez pas besoin que je vous rappelle l'énergie que vous devez tous déployer dans votre travail ?

Il balaie la pièce d'un regard féroce, comme s'il nous mettait au défi d'oser ne pas travailler à l'instant où il nous dévisage. Bien entendu, personne n'est plongé dans son boulot : nous avons tous levé le nez pour le regarder.

—Aujourd'hui, on est vendredi, ce qui signifie qu'il ne vous reste plus qu'une semaine, OK? Une semaine. Seulement sept petits jours. Vendredi prochain, on sera le 22, et à cette date on ferme pour Noël. Cette date est importante, OK? C'est le jour où de grandes décisions seront prises. Où notre destin sera scellé. Enfin, surtout le vôtre. Où j'attends de chacun d'entre vous un nouveau contrat, avec une signature, et un acompte à la banque. C'est d'une importance vitale. Love Learning ne survivra pas sans rentrée financière, alors il incombe à chacun d'entre vous de faire en sorte que nous recevions cet argent. Sans cela, vos emplois n'existeront plus. Je ne souhaite pas que cela se produise, mais j'ai les mains liées.

Il lève ses mains, croisées au niveau du poignet, au cas où nous ne connaîtrions pas l'expression. Il promène à nouveau sur la pièce un regard courroucé, puis s'adoucit et sourit.

—J'aurais préféré ne pas devoir vous dire ça. Par nature, je suis gentil et attentionné, et j'ai essayé de vous cacher la gravité de la situation. Mais maintenant vous êtes au courant.

Il tourne brusquement les talons et disparaît dans son bureau.

—Quel con! dit aussitôt Mike.

Fatima glousse de rire.

—Quel connard, plutôt! dit Grace dans mon dos. Bordel, ce type est un vrai trou du cul.

Je me retourne vers elle. Je la contemple alors qu'elle balaie ses cheveux vers l'arrière de ses doigts écartés, avant de les ramener aussitôt vers l'avant. Cette vision me fait grincer des dents.

— Bon, dis-je en me tripotant également une mèche de cheveux, il a raison. Et il faut reconnaître que c'était correct de sa part de ne pas laisser filtrer la gravité de la situation.

Défendre Chas me laisse un goût amer dans la bouche, d'autant plus que je suis consciente de dire n'importe quoi.

— Oh, Beth, répond Grace avec un regard apitoyé, tu es d'une telle naïveté. Il prétend qu'il a gardé cette information pour lui, et tu l'approuves aveuglément, malgré les démentis que ton cerveau ne peut manquer d'apporter. Tu ne te souviens pas, ma petite Bethy, qu'il nous a déjà dit ça la semaine dernière ? Hein ? (Elle incline la tête en me parlant, sans doute de la même façon que si elle contemplait un écureuil mort sur la route.) Peut-être que tu n'as pas compris de quoi il parlait, la dernière fois ?

Je serre et desserre les poings, et je sens tous mes muscles se tendre et mon corps prêt à bondir. Je suis en mode Je-vais-lui-arracher-les-cheveux-et-les-lui-faire-bouffer ou je-me-fais-la-malle-sur-le-champ.

— Doux Jésus, bien sûr que j'avais compris, Grace, réponds-je, surprise. Peut-être que tu n'as juste pas vu la différence entre son propos de la semaine dernière et celui d'aujourd'hui.

— Eh bien, je suis certaine que je l'aurais remarqué, s'il y en avait eu une.

— Oh oui, bien sûr, suis-je bête ! C'est un peu flippant, n'est-ce pas, qu'il ait dit la semaine dernière que quatre postes seraient supprimés et qu'il annonce aujourd'hui qu'aucun emploi ne sera conservé ? On dirait bien qu'on sera tous au chômage pour la nouvelle année.

Je penche la tête très légèrement et la regarde avec un sourire discret, les lèvres serrées, comme je pourrais contempler un enfant qui vient de faire pipi dans sa culotte. Puis, alors que je tourne tristement mon siège vers mon écran d'ordinateur, je suis récompensée par le bref spectacle de son air suffisant qui laisse place à une soudaine et violente panique. Et elle disparaît de mon champ de vision.

Mais cette nouvelle m'a secouée. J'ai toujours pensé que mon poste, au minimum, serait sauvé, étant donné que c'est moi qui ai ramené à peu près quatre-vingts pour cent de tous nos contrats. Tout à coup, il semble que nous soyons tous sur un siège éjectable. Oh là là, c'est un désastre : pour moi, pour Fatima, et pour Sean. Je jette un regard circulaire à mes collègues, tous un peu pâles et choqués. Ils ont sans nul doute également de bonnes raisons de vouloir garder leur travail, même si je ne les connais pas. Aucun d'entre nous n'a été très ouvert avec les autres, je m'en rends compte à présent, bien que nous nous soyons côtoyés pendant des années. Je ne sais même pas si Derek est gay.

Je considère la porte du bureau de Chas avec une haine voilée – je ne me laisse pas complètement aller –, et une idée me traverse l'esprit. Peut-être que l'un d'entre nous va décrocher le plus gros contrat que Love Learning ait jamais eu et prendra la place de Chas. Peut-être que l'un d'entre nous va décrocher deux énormes contrats. Sans doute que cette personne serait assurée d'obtenir le poste de Chas. Ah là là, je venais juste d'abandonner l'idée d'avoir un jour un poste de cadre dans cette boîte, puisque j'avais toujours pensé que le seul moyen pour moi d'y parvenir était ma relation avec Richard.

Mais maintenant je pourrai peut-être y arriver quand même, malgré son absence. Je jette un regard vers le bureau de Sean. Bah, il a sans doute renoncé au contrat avec *Whytelys*, de toute façon, et il doit être en ce moment même en train de monter un autre projet, presque aussi bon. Ce qui signifie que ça ne lui causera aucun tort si je me rends effectivement à ce rendez-vous, la semaine prochaine. S'ils se demandent pourquoi je suis venue alors qu'ils avaient jeté Sean à la porte de leurs locaux, je leur dirai que c'est une simple visite de suivi, cadeau de la maison. Ou bien que je vérifie s'ils n'ont pas changé de point de vue, maintenant que les esprits se sont calmés. Et ensuite je les amènerai à signer avec moi, et je rendrai à Sean ce qui est à Sean, quand il s'en apercevra. Ça ne le dérangera pas, j'en suis certaine. De toute façon, ce sera peut-être moi le patron, à ce moment-là.

Je passe le reste de la journée à travailler sur la « Motivation », enfin galvanisée par le désir d'éviscérer Chas. Ce qui montre bien qu'un objectif clair aide réellement à se concentrer sur ses tâches. J'inscris cette réflexion dans mes notes.

Alors que je suis en voiture, me dirigeant vers chez moi, mon téléphone sonne. Je me gare pour me lancer dans une recherche frénétique de l'appareil dans mon sac. J'ai en tête le visage magnifique de Rupert, attendant avec impatience et espoir que je décroche, bien que je ne pense pas qu'il ait mon numéro. Ah, voilà le téléphone. Il affiche un numéro que je ne connais pas.

—Allô ?

Oh, et si c'était lui et qu'il voulait qu'on se retrouve tout de suite pour un petit cocktail à la bonne franquette ?

—Salut, Libby, c'est Brad.

Je sens mon cœur se décrocher et je sautille un peu dans mon siège. Je m'arrête avant d'émettre un son, et fais de mon mieux pour prendre ma voix la plus sexy, ce qui est très difficile à faire tant qu'on n'a pas commencé à parler :

— Salut, comment ça va ?

Oui, c'est parfait.

— Tu sais quoi ? C'est peut-être un cliché, mais ça va beaucoup mieux, maintenant. Et c'est la pure vérité.

— Oh, vraiment ? Pourquoi, tu es assis au bord de ta piscine couverte, une bière fraîche à la main ?

Assis au bord de sa piscine couverte avec une bouteille de Carlsberg à la main, Rupert en attrape la chair de poule et tressaille légèrement :

— Bon sang, tu es forte.

— Merci. Tu as passé une bonne journée ?

— Une journée étonnamment banale. Et toi ?

Je me démonte un peu. Sa phrase me dit vraiment quelque chose, mais je n'arrive pas à savoir quoi, ni à comprendre d'où me vient cette impression.

— Je… euh…

— Libby ? Tu es toujours là ?

— Ah oui, je suis là, désolée. Je viens juste de passer sous un pont.

Petite pause.

— Tu n'es pas au volant, j'espère ?

— Non, voyons, bien sûr que non. Ce n'est vraiment pas mon genre. C'est Maurice qui conduit.

— Maurice ? dit-il d'une voix amusée. Qui est-ce ? Un vieil oncle ? Un voisin cacochyme ? Un cousin germain obèse ?

—Non, rien de tout ça. Maurice est mon chauffeur. C'est un français de vingt-quatre ans, qui s'entraîne pour l'épreuve de décathlon des Jeux olympiques. Dis bonjour, Maurice. Ah non, désolée, Brad, tu ne peux pas l'entendre, la vitre de séparation est montée.

Il rit :

—Quel dommage ! J'espère vraiment que Maurice n'aura pas de hernie étranglée ni de douleur à l'aine.

Je souris. Qui a dit que la jalousie était un péché ? Je pense au contraire que c'est terriblement agréable.

—Oh non, ne t'en fais pas, il est très costaud de ce côté-là, donc je n'ai aucune crainte à cet égard.

—Super. Je suis content pour lui. Mais tu ne m'as toujours pas dit si tu avais passé une bonne journée.

—Ah, c'est vrai ? Eh bien, ma journée a commencé de façon bizarre, a continué d'une manière embrouillée, ensuite c'était déroutant puis déconcertant avec des passages étranges.

—Et quelles sont les prévisions pour demain ?

Je réfléchis quelques instants. En réalité, je ne réfléchis pas, je me tais juste un moment pour qu'il ne pense pas que j'avais prévu cette réponse :

—Plus dégagé.

J'ai parlé d'une voix très douce, les lèvres toutes proches du téléphone.

Nous restons tous deux silencieux quelques secondes. Puis il pousse un profond soupir, interminable. Je ne suis pas sûre d'aimer ça.

—Quoi ? dis-je, en essayant de masquer mon anxiété.

—Quoi, quoi ?

—Tu as soupiré. Qu'est-ce qui se passe ?

Cette fois, j'ai vraiment l'air anxieuse.

—Non, rien. Je n'ai pas soupiré.

—Ah bon? Ah, merde, ça veut dire que tu as bâillé, alors, et c'est encore pire.

—Mais non. Ça veut juste dire que je ne suis pas triste mais fatigué. C'est mieux, non?

—Bordel, non! Ça sous-entend un manque total d'investissement de ta part. Un soupir pourrait montrer que tu es heureux, triste, déprimé, résigné, contrarié, satisfait, des tas de choses. Mais tout ça, c'est des émotions. Un bâillement n'exprime que deux possibilités: la fatigue ou l'ennui. Dans les deux cas, c'est une réaction purement physique, un réflexe qui se produit de façon automatique au niveau du corps, sans passer par le cerveau. C'est de toute évidence pire qu'un soupir, à mon avis.

—Bon sang, tu as l'air d'avoir beaucoup étudié la question!

—Eh oui. Bien obligée. Si on clarifie ce genre de choses dès le début, on a moins de risque de malentendus par la suite.

À l'autre bout du fil, Rupert sursaute, l'air surpris. Quelque chose dans ce qu'il vient d'entendre lui semble familier, mais il ne sait pas quoi exactement, ni ce que ça lui rappelle.

—OK, je ne peux rien te cacher, Libby. C'était un soupir, mais ça ne veut pas dire que je vais mal. C'est juste… que je crois que j'ai enfin les idées claires, pour la première fois depuis… oh, je ne sais pas combien de temps.

—Vraiment?

—Vraiment. Tu sais, par le passé, il y a eu tellement de fois où les choses ne se sont pas passées comme je l'espérais. À cause de… mon travail, les gens ont certaines attentes…

Il se tait, me laissant suspendue au bout du fil, sur une aire sombre au bord de la rocade, le téléphone douloureusement pressé contre mon oreille.

— Ton travail ?

Il se tait. Puis il reprend :

— Ça t'embêterait que je ne t'en dise pas plus pour le moment ? Je t'en parlerai, évidemment, tu sais. Mais pas tout de suite, si tu veux bien. Peut-être quand on se connaîtra un peu mieux.

Oh, merde, merde, merde. C'est un tueur. Je sors avec un tueur à gages international. Les conséquences pour moi seront désastreuses, et de toute évidence ça ne se terminera pas avec une belle robe de mariée blanche, une maison semi-bourgeoise de cinq pièces, et un chat. Je vois plutôt une fenêtre de chambre d'hôtel fracturée, des meubles renversés et fracassés, et mon corps nu, à plat ventre sur le lit, criblé de balles.

— Ce n'est rien d'illégal, déclare-t-il brusquement, ce qui me fait baisser la main que j'avais plaquée sur ma bouche. Libby ? Tu es toujours là ? Je t'ai fait peur, n'est-ce pas ?

Maintenant, je ne sais plus quoi penser.

— Non.

— Si, ça s'entend dans ta voix. Écoute, je t'en prie, crois-moi, il n'y a rien de dangereux ni d'illégal. Merde ! Libby ? Tu es là ?

— Oui.

— Bon. Écoute, mon boulot est juste un peu exposé, c'est tout. Promis.

Pour être honnête, s'il était tueur à gages international, il n'aurait probablement pas mis ce sujet sur le tapis. Il aurait simplement prétendu être plombier ou quelque chose dans ce goût-là.

— Tu me crois, Libby?

Je me tais un moment avant de répondre :

— Exposé, tu disais?

— Oui, oui, rien d'autre.

— Alors, tu es, je ne sais pas, le successeur de l'entraîneur de l'équipe de football d'Angleterre?

Silence surpris à l'autre bout de la ligne. Puis il reprend :

— Bon Dieu, tu m'as percé à jour. OK, bon, il va falloir me promettre de ne rien dire à personne. Gary Lineker n'est même pas encore au courant.

— Qui ça?

Il étouffe un reniflement de rire.

— Aucune importance. Le truc, c'est que si ça se sait dans les journaux, je vais devoir te tuer.

Voilà qui me réduit au silence. Par association d'idées, je pense à un silencieux. Sur un fusil avec lequel on tire à travers un oreiller. Une explosion de plumes qui s'élèvent en nuages.

— Je plaisante, dit-il en riant. Je ne vais pas vraiment te tuer.

— Dieu merci.

— Mais je te promets que bientôt tu sauras tout.

— Je meurs d'impatience. *(Et de peur, aussi, un peu.)* Et je vais devoir attendre longtemps, avant la grande révélation?

— Je ne sais pas. Il y a tellement de variables, c'est impossible à dire. Tu vas devoir faire preuve de patience.

—Bon. OK, alors.

—Merci. Mais j'avais une bonne raison pour t'appeler : j'aimerais qu'on se donne un rendez-vous. De plus de trois minutes. Le plus vite possible. Demain. (Il se tait et se racle un peu la gorge.) C'est l'anniversaire de mon frère, demain. On fait une petite fête : juste quelques proches… hum. Bref, j'aimerais vraiment que tu… je veux dire… ça me ferait vraiment plaisir… Tu veux bien venir ?

Je sautille dans mon siège quelques instants, avant de m'arrêter de peur qu'un automobiliste qui passerait par là ne pense que nous sommes deux à faire rebondir la voiture dans le noir.

—Brad, ça me fait super plaisir que tu m'invites. J'ai hâte d'y être !

Je suis libre aussi ce soir. Je ne le lui dis pas, je me contente de lui envoyer le message par télépathie. Il ne le reçoit pas, malheureusement. Ou alors il est trop poli pour répondre.

—Je viendrai te chercher à 11 h 30, dit-il. Tu habites où ?

Chapitre 20

Mauvaise performance

Objectif à court terme : traverser les seize heures et quatorze minutes qui me séparent du moment où Brad passera me chercher.

Obstacles : seize heures et quatorze minutes. Évidemment.

Objectif à long terme : Oh, c'est trop dur ! Il faut que je choisisse entre Brad et Rupert. Et ils sont tous les deux tellement parfaits, comment pourrais-je les départager ?

Obstacles : Brad et Rupert. Évidemment.

— Putain, tu ne lui as quand même pas donné notre adresse ?! s'écrie Vini, horrifiée, dix minutes plus tard.

Elle porte un justaucorps en Lycra blanc, une cape assortie, une ceinture dorée et des bottes, et ses cheveux sont relevés en deux chignons sur les côtés.

— Tu fais Carrie Fisher ?

— Natalie Portman, voyons ! Sors de ta grotte. En plus, tu ne l'as vu qu'une seule fois…

— Deux fois. Non, trois, en fait.

— D'accord, si on compte la première. Ça pourrait être un serial killer, tu ne peux pas savoir.

—C'est tout à fait possible. Je veux dire, je l'ai en effet rencontré à un speed dating, donc il a beaucoup plus de chance d'être dangereux que les types que tu ramasses dans des pubs et que tu ramènes ici.

Elle fait la moue.

—Je suis douée pour juger les gens. De toute façon, je ne le fais plus, je te l'ai dit.

—Oui, oui, je sais. En tout cas, tu ne devrais pas t'en faire, je lui ai donné rendez-vous à la Curée.

—Quoi, cette fontaine horrible ? Ce n'est pas un peu tue-l'amour ? Une meute de chiens grotesques qui déchiquettent un renard, les babines dégoulinantes de bave ou de sang frais. Ce n'est pas vraiment la Seine au clair de lune, pas vrai ?

Sa description de la statue est plutôt exacte. En fait, c'est une attraction touristique très populaire dans notre zone d'activité – des visiteurs par dizaines de milliers, au dire du conseil municipal – mais pas pour sa beauté. Les gens ont plutôt envie de se remonter le moral en constatant que leur ville n'est pas la plus mal lotie.

—On ne va pas passer la journée au pied de la statue, Vini. C'est juste un point de rencontre. C'est quoi, ça ?

Elle brandit une housse de costume et me sourit d'un air plein de sous-entendus :

—Tu m'as bien dit que tu sortais avec lui demain, n'est-ce pas ?

—Je ne sais pas. Dis-moi d'abord ce que c'est.

—Donc tu es libre ce soir. C'est une panoplie. Surprise ! Enfile-la, et je m'occuperai de ta coiffure.

Je découvre la tenue en vinyle noir zippée de *Charlie et ses drôles de dames*, un push-up, et des bottes de-la-mort-qui-tue. Elle me frise les cheveux pour qu'ils tombent sur mes épaules en fines ondulations, puis les relève de façon négligée sur les côtés et termine par un maquillage qu'elle refuse de me laisser voir avant la dernière touche.

— Ta da! s'exclame-t-elle enfin en me montrant le miroir. Barrymore en personne!

Je sursaute avec effroi, avant de regarder dans la glace et de comprendre qu'elle veut dire Drew, pas Michael. Putain, elle a raison. Je contemple mon visage, de face et de profil. La pensée me vient qu'elle avait cette idée derrière la tête quand elle a choisi ma coloration, mais je la chasse. Ça ne fait rien : la teinture magique m'a valu Brad.

— Donc, la surprise que tu m'as préparée, c'est de faire une apparition en Drew Barrymore lors de l'inauguration d'un nouveau supermarché? Et dire que je pensais que tu m'avais acheté deux tickets pour le concert de Kylie.

— Ne le prends pas comme ça. Ton rôle sort vraiment de l'ordinaire, en fait. On a une Cameron Diaz et une Lucy Liu, donc vous pouvez faire les drôles de dames. Tu vas passer toute la nuit à repousser des hommes fous de désir, tu verras.

Dans l'esprit de Vini, c'est la définition d'une bonne soirée.

— Rupert sera certainement là, ajoute-t-elle en se dirigeant vers la porte.

C'est inutile : j'avais déjà décidé de m'y rendre, en fait.

La réception a lieu dans un hôtel dont le nom de *Wickham Lodge* évoque un charmant cottage envahi par le lierre, avec des poules et des chiens dans la cour, ainsi qu'une nichée d'enfants couverts de boue en anorak et en bottes de caoutchouc, où l'on ferait bed and breakfast

– avec un vrai petit déjeuner anglais – pendant la haute saison. Mais ce n'est pas ça. C'est une énorme structure en verre et en béton de huit étages, avec environ trois cents chambres, un distributeur de billets et autant de personnalité que Britney Spears. D'ailleurs, je crois bien qu'elle y a séjourné une fois. Pas par choix. Je veux dire, de toute évidence, elle était en route vers un lieu plus attirant.

Vini me guide à travers une forêt de sapins décorés, par-delà un feston de banderoles «Joyeux Noël», et le long d'un couloir dont le calme semble inquiétant quand on pense qu'une soirée bat son plein non loin. Cet endroit est vraiment gigantesque.

—Vini, tu es certaine que les gens ont vraiment envie d'avoir Drew Barrymore et Carrie Fischer…

—C'est Natalie Portman.

—OK, Natalie Portman, alors. Est-ce que tu es bien sûre qu'ils veulent nous voir ? À une fête de Noël ? Ce n'est pas vraiment la tradition, n'est-ce pas ?

Au fur et à mesure de notre progression dans le couloir, la musique se rapproche et s'amplifie.

—Relax. On est bien attendues. Promis, dit-elle en s'arrêtant devant une double porte marquée «Salon Bingley».

Je me sens de plus en plus mal à l'aise alors que j'entends le son nous parvenir à travers les battants. Vini entre, et la première chose que je remarque dans la cohue, c'est Elvis, avec une combinaison blanche à strass, ouverte jusqu'à la taille. Mon mauvais pressentiment concernant la musique est confirmé, parce qu'Elvis chante avec plus d'enthousiasme que de talent *Can't Get You Out of My Head* dans un micro relié à un énorme équipement high-tech flanqué de deux baffles. Je cligne des yeux. Non loin, j'aperçois Sylvester Stallone, en tenue complète incluant le bandeau, les taches de sang, la veste crasseuse et la mitraillette, qui bavarde avec Audrey Hepburn, parée de l'inévitable fume-cigarette. Alors que nous les dépassons, j'entends Rambo expliquer :

— ... garder les pousses à l'intérieur jusqu'à ce moment-là, parce que s'il y a ne serait-ce qu'une seule grosse gelée...

— Par ici, me dit Vini en m'entraînant à travers la pièce. Je croise Clark Gable, Keira Knightley, Robbie Williams et Trevor McDonald, mais je vois aussi parmi eux des gens que je ne reconnais pas : des invités ordinaires. Nous nous arrêtons finalement au fond de la salle, près du bar. Il est pris d'assaut principalement par des anonymes, et je remarque que la plupart d'entre eux achètent deux boissons avant de se diriger prestement vers l'endroit où les attend Lady Di, Will Smith ou Bob Geldof. Je demande :

— On est où, là, Vini ? Est-ce que c'est vraiment une soirée organisée par quelqu'un, ou plutôt un genre de congrès de sosies ?

Elle secoue la tête :

— Non, c'est une fête. Le gars qui m'a embauchée voulait le maximum de sosies. Toute l'équipe. Et voilà.

Elle fait un grand geste du bras pour me montrer la pièce.

— Quoi, ce sont tous tes clients ? Tout ton carnet d'adresses est là ?

— Non, il en manque. Shirley Bassey est à Fuengirola, et le chien de John Travolta vient de se faire opérer. C'est trop dommage !

D'un coup de menton, elle me désigne Olivia Newton-John qui se balance en rythme, toute seule, la tête penchée de côté, un cardigan sur les épaules.

—Combien de sosies, alors?

—Trente et un, en nous comptant, répond-elle avec un sourire jusqu'aux oreilles. Il a promis de me donner un bonus de 300 livres si j'amenais plus de trente personnes, et ça a marché! Et avant que tu dises quoi que ce soit, je tiens à ajouter que j'y serais arrivée sans toi et que tu peux avoir ta part du bénéfice.

Je me tourne vers elle, les yeux brillants de colère:

—Vini, tu sais très bien que je ne vais pas… C'est combien, au fait?

—Cent cinquante.

J'en ai la mâchoire qui se décroche:

—Cent cinquante livres? Par personne? Et il y en a trente et une? Ce qui fait…

—Quatre mille six cent cinquante livres, exulte Vini en balayant la pièce du regard. L'un de ces paquets de 150 est pour moi, un autre pour toi, et je touche quinze pour cent du reste, ce qui fait 652 livres. Si on ajoute mon bonus et mes 150, ça me fait un total de 1 102 livres. Pour une soirée de travail. Bordel de merde, c'est fabuleux!

J'acquiesce, les yeux écarquillés:

—Oui, c'est clair!

—Et tu peux garder la tenue – c'est ton cadeau de Noël. J'essaie de le pousser à nous réembaucher tous pour l'année prochaine. Peut-être même tous les ans.

J'explore la pièce, les paupières plissées:

—Mais c'est qui, alors? C'est qui, notre Rockefeller?

—Bon, tu as entendu parler des projets de démolition de certains des vieux bâtiments de la zone industrielle pour construire une nouvelle salle de sport ou quelque chose comme ça ? Eh bien, ce M. Finn est le…

Elle disserte toujours, mais soudain mes oreilles ne captent plus sa voix. Le brouhaha autour de moi, chanson comprise, s'éteint, et toutes les personnes présentes s'enfoncent dans l'obscurité du pourtour de la pièce. Toutes sauf une. À moins de cinq mètres de moi, en grande conversation avec Madonna qui porte sans complexe son soutien-gorge par-dessus son tee-shirt, se trouve Rupert de Witter.

Oh, mon Dieu ! Je suis clouée au sol, les yeux rivés sur son visage sculptural, si séduisant ; ses cheveux magnifiques ; ses dents si blanches. J'enregistre tout ce que je vois : le costume bien coupé, les épaules larges et puissantes, la mâchoire carrée à la peau douce, le bronzage soutenu et doré. Subitement, Madonna s'éloigne d'un air fâché – *celle-là, elle aime trop se faire remarquer* –, et Rupert se retrouve seul. Je le vrille d'un regard si intense que je ne suis qu'à peine surprise qu'il finisse par le sentir et qu'il se tourne lentement dans ma direction. Ses yeux rencontrent les miens, et ils sont si limpides, si bleus, si perçants, que je ressens comme une décharge électrique. J'ai le ventre qui se liquéfie, et il n'est pas impossible que de la salive me coule sur le menton. Je me passe aussitôt la langue sur les lèvres. Il m'adresse un large sourire, l'air accueillant, et je sens mes genoux sur le point de se dérober. Subitement, j'éprouve une vive bouffée de reconnaissance pour Vini, qui m'a affublée de cette tenue aguicheuse. Des pensées contradictoires se bousculent dans ma tête : *Qu'est-ce que je fais dans cet accoutrement ? Quelle chance que je le porte !* Il se dirige vers moi, et comme s'il émanait un champ magnétique de sa personne plus la distance qui nous sépare diminue, plus je chancelle. Il n'est plus qu'à deux mètres quand j'entends :

— … trente-huit livres par an pour être membre. Bordel, Beth, qu'est-ce que tu regardes comme ça ? Oh !

Vini remarque la divinité qui s'approche, s'aperçoit que nous avons les yeux rivés l'un sur l'autre, et disparaît.

Il arrive près de moi, puis fait encore quelques pas, dans mon espace personnel. Je sens sa chaleur animale irradier l'air qui nous sépare, et je me demande s'il perçoit aussi la mienne. Il sourit toujours, mais d'un sourire moins large ; plus doux et séducteur, et son regard parcourt mon visage et mon cou. Je pense qu'il apprécie ce qu'il voit, car il a les sourcils qui frémissent, et ne s'éloigne pas.

— Hello, dit-il.

Essayant de ne pas trahir dans mon élocution l'émotion de me faire aborder par le millionnaire le plus incroyablement beau de tous les temps, je croasse :

— Salut. (Je lui tends la main.) Je suis…

— Je sais très bien qui tu es, dit-il en gardant ma main dans la sienne.

De vive voix, son timbre est différent, plus aigu. Je ne m'étais jamais aperçue que la voix était tellement déformée par le téléphone.

— Vraiment ?

Mon cœur bat si fort dans mes oreilles que je ne suis pas sûre d'avoir réussi à proférer un son.

— Oh oui, Miss Barrymore. Restons-en là pour le moment, d'accord ?

— Oh ! (Pour le coup, je suis un peu déçue : je croyais qu'il avait compris que j'étais Beth, la fille des mails, mais tant pis.) OK, alors. Mais moi, je sais vraiment qui vous êtes.

Cela semble lui faire plaisir, mais il essaie de faire passer ça pour de la surprise. C'est trop mignon.

— Vraiment ? Ça m'étonne. Je n'ai pas l'habitude qu'on me reconnaisse.

— C'est vrai ? J'aurais pensé…

— Surtout depuis que j'ai ces nouveaux reflets. La plupart des gens m'ont connu avec mon ancienne couleur. Avant, c'était « Lever de Soleil Doré » et « Torrent de Montagne », mais maintenant je porte « Orge d'Or » et « Fontaine d'Argent ». La plupart de mes amis prétendent que ça me va bien, mais je n'en suis pas sûr. Et toi, qu'en dis-tu ?

— Hum.

Je ne réponds pas tout de suite et commence par observer ses cheveux d'un air critique. En réalité, je ne suis pas en train d'examiner ses reflets, mais j'ai besoin de temps pour lui donner une réponse aussi spirituelle et ironique que la sienne. En plus, j'essaie de ne pas rire. Je connais Rupert, mais je ne veux pas le lui laisser deviner. J'ai juste envie de profiter du moment sans que le contrat vienne tout gâcher.

Oh, je sais ce que vous pensez : que le contrat devrait être en haut de ma liste de raisons de vouloir parler à Rupert de Witter, pas en deuxième. Ou encore moins, avouons-le, en troisième. Mais ce soir je ne suis pas Beth Sheridan, je suis Drew Barrymore, dans le rôle d'une drôle de dame. Si je révèle que je suis en réalité Beth Sheridan, la fille des mails de Love Learning, je vais perdre un peu de mon mystère. Et lui le sien.

Je veux l'observer, voir comment il est vraiment quand il abandonne sa prudence professionnelle.

— Eh bien, dis-je finalement, en prenant mon air le plus sérieux, comme dans une intense réflexion, à mon avis, votre coloration actuelle vous donne une allure formidable, l'allure de quelqu'un avec qui il faut compter, qui a une voiture fabuleuse, s'habille avec classe, traîne dans les endroits les plus sélects et fréquente régulièrement la jet-set.

Il me dévisage pendant quelques secondes, les lèvres entrouvertes.

— Impressionnant. Tu vois tout ça simplement dans ces deux couleurs ?

— Mais oui.

— C'est incroyable. (Il secoue la tête et regarde, pensif, par-dessus mon épaule gauche.) Je me demande ce que tu aurais tiré d'« Ambre Brûlé », si j'avais choisi cette teinte en plus.

Je fronce les sourcils.

— Oh, par pitié, non, pas « Ambre Brûlé ». Il n'y a que ceux qui n'y connaissent rien à la mode et n'ont leurs entrées nulle part qui portent cette nuance. Tout le monde le sait.

— C'est dingue. Vraiment ? C'est fou. Je l'ignorais. Putain. Heureusement que je ne l'ai pas choisie, alors. Merci, Drew.

Je souris de toutes mes dents. Il joue trop bien !

— C'est un plaisir.

— Super !

Il me sourit à nouveau, et même d'aussi près ses dents sont magnifiques. Pourtant, alors que je le bois des yeux, un détail qui cloche attire mon attention. Je me penche pour le regarder de plus près. Est-ce que c'est… ?

— Tes cheveux sont éblouissants, me dit-il à voix basse. J'adore les blondes.

C'est un peu direct, non ? Ça ne me plaît pas du tout. Je veux dire, et Beth, abruti ? Pour autant qu'il le sache, elle pourrait être devant son ordinateur en ce moment même, attendant un autre mail, une blague, un peu de badinage, une proposition en mariage.

— Ah, vraiment ? C'est… bien.

— Oh oui, je suis accro. Elles sont bien plus attirantes que les brunes. Teeellement plus sexy, poupée.

Et il hoche la tête d'un air approbateur, mais pas en direction de mes cheveux.

— Euh, merci.

Soudain, la fermeture Éclair de ma combinaison me semble beaucoup trop ouverte. Qu'est-ce qui a pris à Vini de descendre le zip comme ça ?

Il parvient finalement à remonter son regard jusqu'à mon visage :

— Est-ce que je peux t'offrir un verre, Miss B. ?

— Sans alcool, s'il vous plaît. Boire à jeun, ça ne me réussit pas.

— Vraiment ? (Il hausse à nouveau les sourcils.) C'est bizarre.

Et il se dirige vers le bar. Tandis que je le regarde s'éloigner, je fronce un peu les sourcils. Il est sans aucun doute très sexy, de dos également, mais jusqu'ici la conversation ne s'est pas déroulée comme je l'avais imaginé. Je sais, d'après ses mails, qu'il est charmant, drôle et charismatique, mais ce n'est pas l'image qu'il me donne ce soir. Alors que j'ai les yeux posés sur lui, il rejette ses cheveux en arrière d'un geste de la main, puis les tripote un peu, le regard au loin, et je m'aperçois qu'il a repéré son reflet dans un miroir derrière le bar. Il s'admire pendant une bonne quinzaine de secondes, tournant la tête à droite et à gauche, se touchant les cheveux, rectifiant son col. Je pourrais être flattée qu'il consacre autant de temps à son apparence, mais quelque chose dans sa façon de faire la moue tout là-bas me dit que ce n'est pas pour moi. Je ne peux m'empêcher d'afficher un air déçu alors que je l'observe. Oh zut, je suis trop bête. J'avais oublié le Facteur Glamour.

Pour être honnête, je n'ai pas tellement d'expérience du Facteur Glamour. La plupart des gens qui vivent dans une petite ville banale comme la mienne et se rendent à leur travail banal comme le mien, dans une berline cinq portes banale et une veste H&M comme les miennes n'en ont pas l'occasion. On le rencontre la plupart du temps dans l'univers fabuleux et éthéré des stars – top models beaux à se pâmer, acteurs terriblement sublimes, pop-stars éblouissantes – où la beauté va de soi, et où chacun flâne en souriant dans une brume de perfection scintillante, vénéré comme une divinité, adoré dans le monde entier.

Le Facteur Glamour, c'est une affaire de corps. Plus sculptural est le vôtre, plus vous avez de Facteur Glamour. Ces gens sont tellement sexy, magnifiques à en avoir le cœur qui s'affole, et ce depuis toujours, qu'ils ont bien compris que c'était leur meilleure arme, ce que les autres remarquaient en eux, et ils en deviennent dépendants. Plus ils sont séduisants, moins ils ont l'impression de devoir faire d'efforts dans leurs relations avec les autres. Ils plaisent à tout le monde, même en étant vaniteux, superficiels et odieux, et, du coup, ils ne cherchent pas à améliorer leur intelligence humaine. C'est la raison pour laquelle les couples de stars ne tiennent jamais, alors que les personnes que l'on voit dans le journal pour leur soixantième anniversaire de mariage ont l'air de descendre d'une union entre Skeletor et Travestor.

À moins que, tout simplement, les gens laids préfèrent rester entre eux pour se consoler.

Non, non, c'est sans nul doute le Facteur Glamour. Il y a des tas de preuves. Imaginons un homme qui réussirait, par un moyen ou un autre, à épouser Jennifer Aniston, il se contenterait probablement de se détendre et de penser qu'il est le type le plus chanceux du monde, non ? Il n'irait pas se dire : « Hum, Jen est mignonne, mais je crois que je pourrais me faire Angelina Jolie. »

Ou peut-être que si. Le salaud !

Quoi qu'il en soit, Rupert a de toute évidence du Facteur Glamour en quantité industrielle, et je n'arrive pas à croire que je n'y aie pas pensé plus tôt. À cet instant, alors que je le regarde, accoudé au bar, qui adresse des clins d'œil à Uma Thurman, je me décide définitivement : c'est Brad. Il n'y a pas moyen que j'entretienne une relation avec un crétin comme Rupert.

Oh, mais…

Non. *Allons, Beth, reprends-toi.* Il est beau, riche, drôle et charmant par mail, mais tout cela est superficiel. Il manque de tout ce qui compte, et le reste ne suffit pas à combler les trous. Je contemple ce physique à se pâmer alors qu'il revient vers moi, et je suis submergée par une vague de mélancolie ; je me sens soudain plus lourde, comme rivée au sol. Je laisse retomber mes épaules et baisse la tête. C'est la fin de cette rêverie romantique idiote.

Mais je tiens toujours à décrocher un contrat avec Horizon, alors je vais me forcer à lui parler, et peut-être faire une petite enquête improvisée en vue de notre déjeuner de la semaine prochaine, qui a maintenant perdu beaucoup de son attrait. Il pourrait manger en compagnie d'une silhouette en carton qu'il ne s'en apercevrait pas.

—Fraise-kiwi, me dit-il en arrivant près de moi. (Il me tend un grand verre de jus rose foncé.) J'espère que ça te plaît.

—Humm, ça a l'air délicieux. Alors, comment ça va, au travail, ces jours-ci?

Pour lui il a pris une boisson dorée dans un verre à liqueur, et il boit de bon cœur avant de répondre:

—Le travail? Tu sais que je suis…?

J'acquiesce:

—Oui, je connais votre boulot. Je sais qui vous êtes, je vous l'ai dit.

Il sourit, l'air presque timide. Quel hypocrite!

—Ah oui, c'est vrai, tu m'as dit ça.

Une nouvelle fois, il regarde avec mélancolie par-dessus mon épaule gauche, les yeux rivés sur quelque chose au loin, et porte sa main droite à sa tête pour passer ses doigts dans sa somptueuse chevelure. Dans cette posture, il me fait irrésistiblement penser à la photo de la brochure d'Horizon. Il reprend:

—Eh bien, ça pourrait aller mieux, pour être franc.

—Oh?

—Ouais. Bon, les choses n'ont jamais été particulièrement faciles, dans ce pays. Les gens d'ici, ils veulent juste te voir échouer, tu vois ce que je veux dire ? Et tout le monde est tellement exigeant, tout le temps. Je pense qu'on peut me pardonner de ne pas me plier à tous les caprices des autres. J'ai mes propres standards, tu vois ? C'est toujours «fais ci, mets-toi là, dépêche-toi, fais tout comme il faut». Ils passent leur temps à me bousculer et à essayer de faire les choses comme ils veulent, alors que moi, je pense que je sais mieux qu'eux ce qui est bon pour moi, tu vois ce que je veux dire ?

— Hum.

— Je sais que j'ai un truc en plus, je le sens. Un jour, je serai un grand. Tu vois, bien plus grand qu'aujourd'hui. Mais tout ce à quoi j'ai droit, c'est des petites gens qui viennent me voir avec leurs petits problèmes. Pourquoi devrais-je me soucier de leurs ennuis ? Ils ont leur boulot, moi le mien, tu vois ? Je suis bon dans mon métier, mais comment est-ce que je peux les aider, si tous les autres passent leur temps à faire n'importe quoi ?

Je hoche la tête avec sympathie :

— Vous avez complètement raison.

— De toute façon, j'ai de grands projets. Je ne vais pas rester à moisir dans ce désert artistique très longtemps. J'ai besoin de place pour grandir, pour respirer, et je ne peux pas trouver ça ici. L'Angleterre, c'est tellement provincial, tu vois ?

— Oh, euh, bon…

— Alors je pars aux States. Ces bons vieux États-Unis d'Amérique, dès que possible. Je sais qu'ils vont m'adorer, là-bas. C'est leur culture. Je vais vraiment m'intégrer dans la culture, tu vois. Mon image, ce que je représente, c'est parfait pour leur marché. Tout ce que j'ai fait ici, c'est de la gnognotte par rapport à ce que je vais réussir là-bas.

Oh, mon Dieu!... Est-ce qu'il vend Horizon?

— Alors, vous... ?

Il baisse brusquement les yeux vers moi, comme s'il venait seulement de se rappeler que j'étais là.

— Je déménage, chérie. Dans six mois, un an maximum. J'ai juste quelques affaires à régler, et ensuite je mets les bouts. Tu veux venir? (Il pose sa main sur mon cou.) Tu seras une vraie star, là-bas. Ils vont t'adorer. Qu'est-ce que tu en dis, beauté?

Quelques affaires à régler? Donc, il vend Horizon. Ce qui me donne une bouffée de panique. Est-ce qu'un contrat que je signerais avec lui tiendrait toujours après la cession? Oui, certainement. Et même si ce n'est pas le cas, je peux sans doute passer un accord pour six mois avant son départ. Ce serait déjà ça. Je lève les yeux vers son visage, pour le trouver à nouveau en train de lorgner mon décolleté. Quelle mauvaise performance... J'attrape sa main sur mon cou et l'enlève d'un air froid, avant de la laisser tomber comme une vieille chaussette. Il prend un air peiné, comme s'il se demandait quel est mon problème. Quel connard!

— Non merci. Je préfère quelque chose de plus concret.

Et ça m'est complètement égal qu'il ait une dent contre moi quand nous nous rencontrerons officiellement, mardi prochain.

Il hausse les sourcils et penche la tête vers moi.

— Les États-Unis, c'est immense, tu sais. Bien plus grand que l'Angleterre. Ça, c'est concret.

Il hoche la tête d'un air docte, comme s'il venait juste de me transmettre une précieuse pépite de savoir. De toute évidence, il ne se rend même pas compte que je viens de lui manquer de respect.

—OK.

Je souris et fais mine de m'éloigner.

—Eh, où tu vas comme ça ? Tu ne vas pas partir maintenant ? On commence à peine à se connaître.

—Justement.

Je m'échappe et rentre à la maison en taxi. Vini étant plongée dans une conversation avec Richard Gere en grande tenue d'officier, je ne vais pas la déranger. Elle a obtenu son bonus, je suis donc libre de quitter les lieux.

De retour à l'appartement, j'erre à travers les pièces pendant quelques minutes, occupée à ouvrir et à fermer les portes, à jeter un œil dans les placards avant d'en claquer les battants, à allumer et à éteindre les lumières. Je m'affale sur le canapé et attrape le programme télé, mais rien ne retient mon attention, et je me relève pour aller dans la cuisine. Il n'y a rien qui me tente dans le frigo, alors je me traîne à nouveau jusqu'au salon, puis dans ma chambre. Je me débarrasse de ma tenue de Drew et me mets au lit, espérant sans trop y croire trouver le sommeil.

Comment ai-je pu être aussi stupide à propos de Rupert ? Maintenant que je l'ai rencontré en chair et en os et que je sais exactement comment il est, tous les mails qu'il m'a envoyés, les blagues et la séduction me semblent faux. Il n'a fait ça que pour se flatter lui-même et m'a allumée juste pour se prouver qu'il pouvait le faire. Ou simplement parce qu'il s'est tout de suite rendu compte qu'il me plaisait. Bien sûr qu'il m'a plu : comme à tout le monde. C'est ça, le Facteur Glamour.

Je ferme les yeux de toutes mes forces et me retourne. Je ne vais pas penser à lui une minute de plus. Demain, je passe la journée avec Brad, et tout en lui est merveilleux.

Chapitre 21

Nouveau rebondissement

Objectif à court terme : ça au moins, c'est simple. Décrocher le contrat avec Horizon et sauver Love Learning toute seule, comme une grande.
Obstacles : Sean est peut-être aussi en train de sauver Love Learning tout seul. Bien qu'en fait ce ne soit pas un obstacle. Bien sûr que non.
Objectif à long terme : ce n'est pas compliqué non plus. Garder Brad. Pour toujours.
Obstacles : maintenant que mes sentiments pour Rupert se sont complètement évaporés, il n'y a plus d'obstacles.

À 10 heures le lendemain matin, Rupert gare sa voiture devant la maison de ses parents. Alors qu'il se dirige vers la porte d'entrée, il lève les yeux vers la bâtisse avec un frisson d'appréhension. *S'il vous plaît, faites que tout aille pour le mieux*, se dit-il, en contemplant cette vue apparemment paisible, *que ce soit un bon jour.*

Il ouvre avec sa clef, mais ne s'annonce pas en entrant, cette fois-ci. Il reste immobile quelques instants dans le hall, la tête en arrière, le regard rivé sur le balcon du premier étage, les oreilles aux aguets. Aucun son ne parvient jusqu'au rez-de-chaussée : il décide de monter.

En haut, tout semble calme. Il entrevoit un rayon d'espoir, mais en marchant silencieusement sur le palier vers la chambre du fond il commence à percevoir un gémissement étouffé, qui lui fait dresser les cheveux sur la tête et lui donne la chair de poule.

—Oh non…, soupire-t-il doucement en arrivant à la porte.

Le son est plus net ici, mais il reste faible, et c'est celui qu'il a redouté d'entendre depuis qu'il s'est levé ce matin.

Il toque une fois, puis entre. La pièce est vaste et lumineuse, et chacun de ses murs est blanc, tout comme le sol et le plafond. Seuls quelques rares éléments décoratifs viennent rompre la monotonie de l'espace : des cartes d'Europe sur les cloisons ; un lit, un bureau, une chaise, un placard. Le son ténu, qui part dans les aigus, provient du lit où une silhouette est pelotonnée en position fœtale et se balance d'avant en arrière.

Caroline de Witter se tient debout au milieu de la chambre, son corps tendu vers le lit. On pourrait presque sentir son désir d'avancer, d'enlacer et de réconforter son fils. Elle a serré ses bras autour d'elle à défaut de pouvoir enlacer son fils, et des larmes silencieuses roulent sur ses joues. Quand la porte s'ouvre, elle se tourne vers Rupert, et son visage se froisse alors qu'elle vient enlacer son aîné.

—Oh, Rupe, je suis tellement contente que tu sois là. Je ne sais plus quoi faire. On a passé presque deux heures à essayer de le convaincre de descendre, mais il ne veut pas bouger. Papa est parti faire une pause dans la remise, et je ne m'en sors pas toute seule.

Elle reste un moment à sangloter tandis que Rupert la tient contre lui et lui caresse le dos d'un geste rassurant.

—Ce n'est pas grave, maman. Ça ne fait rien, n'est-ce pas? S'il ne veut pas de fête d'anniversaire, il n'est pas obligé, pas vrai?

—Non, je sais, mais je… j'ai juste pensé… que peut-être…

—Maman, tu sais bien qu'il n'en profitera pas. Tu le sais.

Elle renifle et se dégage de son étreinte.

—Mais… je pensais juste que cette fois-ci, peut-être…

Rupert secoue la tête :

—Il ne va pas changer, maman. Il ne changera jamais. Il n'aura jamais envie de fêter son anniversaire. (Caroline a les lèvres qui tremblent en entendant ces mots, alors Rupert la prend par les épaules.) Oh, maman, ne te mets pas dans tous tes états. Ça ne fait rien. C'est vrai. Ce n'est rien qu'un bout de gâteau et des cadeaux… Ça n'a pas d'importance.

Elle prend une grande inspiration, un peu tremblante, et fait un pas pour s'éloigner de Rupert avant de se tourner à nouveau vers la silhouette qui se balance.

—Ce n'est pas la fête qui me chagrine, dit-elle si doucement que Rupert l'entend à peine. Ça m'est égal qu'il ne mange pas de gâteau et qu'il ne déballe pas ses cadeaux. Qu'on ne puisse pas chanter «Joyeux anniversaire» et le regarder souffler les bougies. (Elle garde un moment les yeux figés sur le lit, puis se tourne vers Rupert, le visage baigné de larmes.) C'est juste… je ne peux pas… je ne supporte pas de le voir dans cet état. C'est trop pour moi. Il souffre, et je suis sa maman, je veux l'aider, mais il n'y a rien que je puisse faire. Je voudrais le prendre dans mes bras, le serrer fort et lui dire que tout va bien, que je suis là, que je vais m'occuper de lui et que je l'aime. Je l'aime tellement fort…

Sa voix se brise, et elle couvre son visage de ses mains pendant un moment, les épaules secouées de sanglots. Rupert ne la quitte pas du regard, les yeux pleins de larmes lui aussi, et il sent sa gorge se serrer une fois de plus. Il a les mêmes désirs qu'elle.

— Je voudrais pouvoir lui dire que je l'aime, Rupert. Et je voudrais qu'il me le dise aussi. Je voudrais tellement qu'il me le dise aussi !

Rupert s'avance, prend sa mère dans ses bras, et la berce comme elle voudrait le faire pour son plus jeune fils, lui chuchote que tout va bien, la réconforte. Après quelques minutes, ils se dirigent ensemble vers la porte, sortent sur le palier et referment doucement derrière eux.

En bas, dans la cuisine, Rupert prépare une théière tandis que Caroline reste à sangloter près du feu dans le salon. Pendant que la bouilloire chauffe, il courbe la tête, les yeux clos, les mains plaquées sur ses joues. Maintenant qu'il est seul, qu'il échappe au regard des autres, il s'autorise une larme qui roule entre ses cils serrés et coule lentement, sans obstacle, sur son visage.

Comme l'eau se met à bouillir, il s'essuie la figure et prépare le thé, qu'il apporte ensuite à sa mère. Celle-ci lui adresse un sourire mouillé.

— Je suis désolée, Rupe, dit-elle en prenant sa tasse.

— Désolée ? Mais pourquoi ? Tu n'as pas de raison de t'excuser.

Elle secoue la tête :

— Au contraire. J'ai été lamentable, je le sais. Tu n'as pas à devoir supporter ça quand tu viens. Comme si tu n'avais pas déjà assez de soucis.

—Maman, ne dis pas de bêtises. Je ne «supporte» rien. Je suis venu rendre visite à mon frère pour son anniversaire, et à mes parents. Ce n'est pas une corvée.

Elle sourit avec reconnaissance.

—C'est vraiment idiot, cela dit, n'est-ce pas? Je veux dire, je le connais, je sais que ce sera toujours comme ça, mais je ne peux pas m'empêcher… d'espérer. Tu sais? Je continue de me dire «peut-être qu'aujourd'hui, peut-être que cette fois-ci…» Je voudrais seulement…

Il lui touche doucement la main.

—Je sais. Moi aussi. C'est parce que c'est son anniversaire… La déception se fait toujours plus forte à son anniversaire.

—Eh bien, c'est sans doute parce que ça le met toujours dans cet état.

—Ouais, bon, montre-moi quelqu'un qui ne se sente pas comme ça pour son anniversaire!

Elle rit tristement.

—Ah, Rupert. Que ferais-je sans toi? Tu es un si bon garçon!

—Maman, par pitié, j'ai trente-quatre ans…

—Je sais, j'étais là quand tu es né.

Il sourit.

—Écoute, je vais aller à la remise chercher papa, et ensuite je préparerai à manger pour vous deux. D'accord?

Elle acquiesce, et il lui frotte affectueusement la main:

—À tout de suite.

Dans le jardin, l'herbe est blanche et craquante de givre. Les empreintes de son père en direction de l'appentis sont bien visibles, mais Rupert ne les suit pas. Il remonte le col de sa veste et se dirige, à travers l'ouverture de la haie, vers le potager. Il reste à côté des rangées de terre nues, et sort son téléphone.

—Salut, c'est Brad, dit-il doucement.

À l'appartement, j'ai déjà commencé à me préparer pour mon rendez-vous avec Brad, bien que je parte seulement dans deux heures. Je ne veux pas risquer d'être en retard, cela dit. On ne sait jamais ce qu'il y aura comme circulation à 11 heures le samedi matin. J'ai fini de me coiffer, et je choisis à présent les vêtements que je vais porter. Le téléphone m'interrompt dans mes réflexions alors que j'hésite entre un style chic décontracté et décontracté chic. Ou carrément aguicheur.

—Salut, comment ça va?

Je m'assieds sur le lit, un sourire jusqu'aux oreilles. Il m'appelle alors que nous nous voyons dans deux heures; il faut qu'il soit drôlement impatient! Puis mon sourire s'évanouit. On se voit dans deux heures; pourquoi me téléphone-t-il? La seule raison que je voie pour qu'il me contacte deux heures avant notre rendez-vous est qu'il veut annuler.

—Ça va, dit-il d'une voix douce. Et toi?

Je n'aime pas ça. Pourquoi ne va-t-il pas droit au but?

—Pareil.

—Tant mieux. Écoute, Libby, c'est à propos de tout à l'heure.

Je le savais. Je ne réponds rien, pourtant, parce qu'un silence glacial en dit plus qu'une longue jérémiade.

—Je voulais que tu viennes à la fête aujourd'hui parce que j'avais vraiment envie de te présenter… je veux dire, ce n'était pas grand-chose, juste mes parents, et mon frère bien sûr, et un ou deux autres membres de la famille. Et à part ça, aussi, il y a quelque chose que je voulais te dire. Que je dois te dire. (Il se tait, et je l'entends respirer en marchant.) J'avais tout préparé, le moment où je te le dirais, les mots exacts que j'emploierais. Et je pensais que si tu voyais le vrai… moi… ma famille, tu sais, alors la raison pour laquelle… alors peut-être que tu ne serais pas… que tu ne penserais pas… du mal de moi. Ça n'a pas de sens, ce que je raconte. Désolé.

Je me tais toujours, mais cette fois, j'essaie de donner un caractère chaud et réconfortant au silence. Les choses ont l'air d'aller très mal, et je m'en veux vraiment de m'être montrée distante auparavant. Je réussis enfin à demander :

—Qu'est-ce qui se passe, Brad ?

—Je suis désolé, Libby. Il n'y aura pas de fête, finalement. Il y avait un risque que ça arrive. Écoute, je ne préfère pas en parler au téléphone. Est-ce qu'on peut quand même se voir ? Je peux venir te chercher dans une demi-heure… Tu seras prête ?

Trois informations extrêmement importantes me tombent dessus dans un court laps de temps. Bing ! Il n'annule pas. Bing ! Et il avance notre rendez-vous de deux heures. Bing ! C'est tellement fantastique que j'ai commencé à me préparer il y a une heure. J'essaie de me retenir de sauter partout avec un grand sourire, parce que de toute évidence quelque chose de négatif vient de lui arriver et il n'a pas le moral, du coup après avoir sautillé en silence pendant quelques secondes je m'assieds et me calme avant de lui répondre de ma voix la plus douce et compatissante.

—Bien sûr, ne t'inquiète pas, c'est parfait. On se retrouve toujours à la Curée ?

Une demi-heure plus tard, je me gare sur le parking de la zone d'activité. De ma place, je vois que Brad est déjà là, assis sur le banc près de la statue, occupé à regarder sa montre et à scruter les alentours, d'un côté puis de l'autre, avant un nouveau regard à son poignet. C'est cruel, mais je choisis de rester dans la voiture deux minutes, à le contempler en train de compter les minutes jusqu'à ce que j'arrive. Il est absolument superbe. La tension visible sur son visage et dans sa posture est incroyablement séduisante. Je ne le quitte pas des yeux. Cet homme grand, sexy et inquiet, et le fait qu'il soit là et que ce soit moi qu'il attende, me coupe le souffle. Moi, la petite Beth Sheridan. Euh, je veux dire Libby. Faut que je règle ça.

Finalement, n'y tenant plus, je sors de la voiture et me dirige vers lui. Il se lève dès qu'il me voit, et un large sourire se dessine sur son visage. De même que sur le mien. C'est un vrai combat de continuer à marcher, alors que mes genoux ont décidé que je devais m'allonger. Et que d'autres parties de moi sont d'accord.

— Salut, toi, dit-il quand j'arrive à ses côtés.

— Hello.

Il fait aussitôt un pas en avant, tout près de moi, et je sais qu'il va m'embrasser, il est suffisamment près pour le faire, et c'est la révolution dans mon ventre. Il lève la main à hauteur de mon visage, et je ferme à demi les yeux, dans l'attente du contact sur mon cou et de ses lèvres sur les miennes. Finalement il hésite, et laisse retomber son bras. Il baisse les yeux vers le sol, détourne un peu le regard et vacille d'un pied sur l'autre. Je frémis toujours, et j'ai l'impression que je vais exploser s'il ne

m'attrape pas sur-le-champ pour... *faire quelque chose.*
Mais il ne bouge pas.

— Si on allait se balader ? demande-t-il. Il y a certains détails que j'aimerais t'expliquer.

J'acquiesce – je lui dois moi aussi des explications –, et nous nous mettons en route.

Lors de notre promenade, il ne me prend pas la main, ne passe pas son bras autour de mes épaules, bien que je lui envoie des signaux de détresse évidents. Nous laissons nos mains pendre à nos côtés et nous frôlons une ou deux fois, déclenchant une explosion d'étincelles chez moi, mais il ne semble pas s'en apercevoir. Rapidement, il est plongé dans son récit à propos de son frère, Matt, un jeune autiste, dont c'est l'anniversaire aujourd'hui. Sa maman, me raconte-t-il, a eu beaucoup de mal à accepter l'incapacité de Matt à exprimer, ou même à ressentir, des émotions. Il parle sans me regarder, les yeux rivés droit devant lui, mais je sens dans sa voix que ce n'est pas seulement sa mère qui souffre de ne pas être aimée ou reconnue par Matt.

— Le truc, c'est qu'il est incroyablement intelligent, me dit-il alors que nous sortons de la ville. Tu vois, il sait qui je suis. Je suis allé le voir hier, pour discuter d'un sujet. (Il me lance un regard en biais.) Je sais qu'il ne comprend pas, mais ça m'aide, d'une certaine façon, de parler des choses avec lui, même s'il ne dit rien. Et il me reconnaît, c'est ce qui compte. Bien que je ne vive plus avec lui, et que je n'appartienne pas à son quotidien, il m'a quand même appelé par mon prénom, lorsque je lui ai parlé. Il a dit : « Tu t'appelles R... »

Il se tait subitement, et je me tourne pour le regarder. Il me dévisage mais détourne les yeux dès que je pose les miens sur lui :

— Il a dit : « Tu t'appelles Brad. » Donc je sais qu'il me connaît.

Je ne sais pas quoi répondre. Je ne peux pas lui donner de conseil : c'est un domaine inconnu pour moi. Ce qui ne m'empêche pas de deviner que des platitudes du genre : « Je suis sûre qu'il t'aime à sa façon » ne sont pas d'une grande utilité. Finalement je me décide pour : « Ça doit être terriblement dur pour vous tous », et il hoche la tête.

— En effet. Enfin, surtout pour maman. Papa a tendance à se couper de tout ça quand ça devient trop dur, ce qui peut sembler égoïste, mais nous avons accepté cette manière de gérer la situation. Je pense que papa comprend bien mieux que maman. Quand Matt est dans un mauvais jour, elle essaie toujours de le réconforter, et ça ne fait qu'empirer les choses. Papa sait que la meilleure chose à faire, c'est de s'éloigner et de laisser Matt se calmer tout seul.

Nous marchons quelque temps en silence. Je meurs de faim, mais je ne peux pas le dire : notre relation n'en est pas encore au stade où l'on avoue avoir des fonctions biologiques.

— Tu as faim ? demande-t-il en s'arrêtant tout d'un coup pour me faire face. (Je hoche la tête avec douceur, et il sourit.) Bien. Moi aussi. Allons déjeuner. (Et, juste à ce moment-là, je m'aperçois que nous sommes arrivés devant le *Perroquet du Pirate*.) Tu es déjà venue ici ?

—Hum, une ou deux fois. C'est plutôt rigolo. Mais je n'y ai jamais mangé, cela dit. Je me demande ce qu'ils servent.

La carte propose des Croquettes de poisson du Flibustier, une Poitrine de poulet du Corsaire ou une Soupe de la Vigie. Nous nous sourions en lisant le menu, et je commande le potage. Je ne veux surtout pas bâfrer comme un cachalot – bouche ouverte comme un four, absorbant tout élément comestible à ma portée. Brad choisit le Burger de Barbe-Bleue, avec des galettes de pomme de terre.

—Et toi ? Est-ce que tu as des frères et sœurs ? me demande-t-il tandis que nous mangeons.

Je secoue la tête :

—Ce qui s'en rapproche le plus, c'est Vini ; tu l'as rencontrée.

—Ah oui, l'incomparable Miss Jones. Qu'est-ce qu'elle devient ?

—Franchement énervante, dis-je en pensant à la soirée à laquelle elle m'a traînée hier. Elle dirige une agence de sosies, Fake Face.

—Le nom est super.

—Oui, c'est vrai. Quoi qu'il en soit, elle devait amener autant de clones que possible à une soirée hier soir, alors elle m'a obligée à y aller, déguisée en…

Soudain, mon image dans cette combinaison sexy et ces bottes, avec la coiffure, le maquillage et le décolleté, me semble complètement ridicule. Je ne peux pas le dire.

—Déguisée en qui ? Allez, Libby ! Tu en as trop dit ou pas assez. J'ai besoin de savoir, pour pouvoir imaginer.

Je secoue la tête en riant.

— Non, c'est trop gênant. Il suffit que tu saches que ce crétin de Rupert de Witter s'est mis à baver en me voyant.

Il tressaille en entendant ce nom, et je me souviens soudain qu'ils se connaissent et que je les ai vus se serrer la main à la fête de Noël d'Horizon. Merde, ils sont sans doute amis.

— Qu'est-ce que tu veux dire ? me demande-t-il d'une voix pressante.

— Oh, écoute, Brad, je suis désolée. Tu le connais ?

Il me dévisage pendant quelques secondes, comme si je venais de le mettre au défi de me donner la racine carrée de six cent quatre-vingt-treize. Puis il répond :

— Hum, bon, oui, il se trouve que je le fréquente. Un peu. Pourquoi, tu le connais, toi ?

— Non, pas vraiment. Pas au sens propre du terme. J'ai travaillé chez Horizon, il y a quelques années, et récemment j'ai…

Oups, je ne peux pas lui parler de l'histoire avec Love Learning : il pourrait essayer de me joindre au boulot et découvrir que je ne m'appelle pas réellement Libby. Ce qui ne serait pas une mauvaise chose en soi, mais je veux le lui dire moi-même. C'est un vrai tue-l'amour d'apprendre d'une tierce personne que la femme à laquelle vous vous êtes confié à propos de votre frère autiste vous a donné un faux nom.

— Bref, il ne correspond pas à l'image que je m'étais faite de lui, on va dire ça comme ça.

— Pourquoi ? Qu'est-ce qu'il a fait ?

Sa voix est toujours pressante, anxieuse. Ils doivent être proches.

—Oh non, rien. Franchement. C'est juste… bah, il ne pouvait pas détacher ses yeux de mon… tu sais, dis-je en louchant vers le bas, et nous avons bavardé et il se révèle être incroyablement superficiel, égocentrique et vaniteux. Ce dont j'aurais dû me douter, n'est-ce pas ? Je veux dire, vu sa fortune, comment pourrait-il en être autrement ? Il doit sans aucun doute s'entourer à chaque instant de flatteurs débiles dont l'unique désir est de faire tout ce qu'il demande. Beurk. Je n'ai que du mépris pour ça. Pourquoi est-ce que les gens comme lui, qui ont beaucoup d'argent, sont toujours persuadés que le monde entier n'est là que pour leur amusement ?

Il reste silencieux un moment, et je suis là, plongée dans un abîme d'angoisse, à me répéter que j'ai insulté gravement son meilleur ami. Mais il ajoute, doucement, presque distraitement :

—Je ne m'étais pas aperçu que c'était à ce point.

Ce qui me fait me sentir encore plus mal, maintenant que je suis convaincue que je viens de détruire une amitié vieille de vingt-cinq ans.

—Oh non, ne dis pas ça, je suis sûre qu'il n'en est rien. Il était peut-être simplement dans un mauvais jour, tu sais. Peut-être qu'il venait de se faire plaquer et voulait se venger sur l'ensemble de la population féminine. Peut-être qu'il était bourré. Ou qu'il s'était cogné l'orteil. Ou qu'il couvait un rhume et se sentait vraiment ronchon à cause de…

—Non. Non, Libby, on n'a aucune excuse quand on se tient mal. Les autres aussi attrapent des rhumes, se font larguer ou se cognent l'orteil, mais ils ne se comportent pas comme ça. (Il secoue la tête.) Il va falloir que je règle ça. J'y pensais, de toute façon, et cela fait déjà trop longtemps que ça dure. Tout cela est ridicule.

Il prononce ces derniers mots plus pour lui-même que pour moi, et cela me donne l'impression qu'une pieuvre promène ses tentacules glacés le long de ma colonne vertébrale. Il en parle comme s'il existait une relation illicite entre Rupert et lui, et c'est vraiment flippant. Est-ce possible qu'ils partagent un horrible secret qu'ils aimeraient enterrer depuis des années mais sans le pouvoir, car chacun menace de dénoncer l'autre et que tous deux ont trop à perdre pour prendre ce risque ? Oh, et s'ils avaient tous les deux trempé dans une affaire… de crime ? On entend des histoires comme ça tout le temps – deux hommes qui ont bien réussi, heureux, respectés, aisés, et qui ont fait tomber un parpaing sur la tête du gardien du campus il y a quinze ans.

À moins qu'ils ne soient secrètement amants.

—Tu… tu n'es pas… ? Rupert et toi, vous êtes… ? Vous n'êtes… pas… ?

—Quoi ? Qu'est-ce qui t'inquiète comme ça ?

À nouveau, il lève la main, mais cette fois-ci il n'arrête pas son geste, ne se dégonfle pas à la dernière minute, mais tend le bras et touche ma joue du bout des doigts. C'est à peine un frôlement, mais cela suffit à me donner un frisson comme une décharge électrique.

—Qu'est-ce qui se passe, là-dedans ?

J'en perds la parole. L'endroit que ses doigts ont effleuré vient juste de s'embraser.

—Écoute, quelle que soit ton hypothèse sur ma relation avec Rupert, je peux t'assurer qu'elle est fausse. Je t'expliquerai tout ça, très bientôt, mais…

— Mais quoi ? Pourquoi tu ne me le dis pas maintenant ?

Il baisse les yeux vers mon visage, son regard rivé sur le mien. Puis secoue la tête presque imperceptiblement.

— Je ne peux pas. Pas alors que je sais ce que tu ressens pour… lui. J'ai besoin de le faire quand… une autre fois. Quand je pourrai tout t'expliquer comme il faut, sans risquer de gâcher… ce qu'il y a entre nous.

Ça ne va pas. De toute évidence, il s'agit de quelque chose de grave.

— De tout gâcher ? Tu crois que me révéler cette… chose…, quelle qu'elle soit, peut détruire notre relation ?

Il secoue à nouveau la tête.

— Je ne sais pas. J'espère que non. (Il soupire encore une fois et regarde mes mains.) Je sais que ça semble de mauvais augure, mais je te jure que tu n'as pas de raison de t'en faire.

— Vraiment ? Mais si j'avais raison de m'inquiéter, est-ce que tu me le dirais, de toute façon ? Par exemple, si tu avais tué ton gardien avec un parpaing quand tu avais vingt ans, tu te confierais à moi ?

En entendant cette question, il éclate de rire, mais je ne pense pas que ce soit matière à plaisanter.

— Oh non, non, non, Libby, ce n'est rien de ce genre. Je te jure. Je n'ai pas de squelette dans le placard, même pas des petits. Pas l'ombre d'un cadavre de souris.

Je le dévisage, brûlant d'envie de le croire. *Est-ce qu'un serial killer aurait d'aussi jolis yeux ?*

— Aucun ?

— Aucun. Je te le promets. Je n'ai jamais été en prison, je n'ai jamais fait de mal à personne, n'ai jamais – à ma connaissance – enfreint la loi.

—Et tu n'as pas de frère jumeau?

Il fait «non» de la tête avec un sourire:

—Non, non, absolument pas.

—Donc tu es bien Brad… Brad quoi? Quel est ton nom de famille?

—Witt.

—Witt? Brad Witt? Tu te fous de moi! Vraiment?

—Parfaitement.

—Waouh. D'accord. Bon, alors, tu es réellement Brad Witt?

Il hésite un court instant puis détourne le regard.

—Euh, en fait, non. Je ne m'appelle pas vraiment Brad. J'ai pris un faux nom parce que sous ma vraie identité je suis incroyablement connu et puissant, et que je ne voulais pas que tu le saches avant de m'apprécier pour ce que je suis vraiment.

Je souris.

—Ouais, bien sûr, d'accord. J'ai aussi pris un faux nom.

Et j'attire sa tête vers moi pour lui déposer un baiser sur la joue.

Chapitre 22

Retours favorables

Objectif à court terme : donner à huit personnes un intense sentiment de motivation et d'engagement, par le simple pouvoir de ma parole et de mes graphiques.
Obstacles : je n'en ai pas grand-chose à foutre.
Objectif à long terme : que Brad s'engage auprès de moi pour toute la vie. Ou au moins qu'il m'invite à nouveau à déjeuner. (Oh, et aussi le contrat avec Horizon.)
Obstacles : j'attends toujours de ses nouvelles. (Et je m'occupe de R. de W. – Connard !)

Le lundi matin, je suis à mon poste dès 7 heures, occupée à revoir mon truc sur la « Motivation ». J'ai posé mon téléphone portable sur mon bureau, à portée de main, au cas où Brad m'appellerait. Il m'a dit samedi qu'il me contacterait aujourd'hui, donc j'attends son coup de fil plus ou moins depuis qu'on est aujourd'hui : ça fait donc sept heures.

Quand je l'ai embrassé, samedi, il a été un peu étonné, mais content, et ensuite il n'arrêtait pas de sourire. Je l'ai surpris une ou deux fois avec un air un peu anxieux, mais dès qu'il s'est aperçu que je le regardais, il s'est remis à sourire. Il ne m'a pas rendu mon baiser, cela dit, et on n'a pas eu d'autre contact physique, malgré mon rayon tracteur fixé sur lui dans une tentative pour attirer son corps vers le mien. Ça n'a pas marché – une fois de plus. Mes signaux de détresse non plus. Bon, c'est reposant, après un Rupert plutôt lubrique, de rencontrer un homme qui prend son temps. Brad en vaut vraiment la peine – je peux faire preuve de patience. Je crois.

Tout est prêt pour l'atelier «Motivation», et il me reste encore plus d'une heure avant de devoir démarrer, alors je consulte ma messagerie professionnelle. J'ai reçu trois nouveaux messages : un de Fatima, un de Sean et un de Rupert. J'ouvre celui de Fatima en premier. Il s'intitule : «Ma voiture!»

Coucou Beth, devine quoi? J'ai vendu ma voiture ce week-end! Un type qui m'avait appelée est venu la voir hier soir, et il m'a donné 10000 livres en liquide, juste comme ça! Il viendra la chercher dans quelques jours. Merde, quel soulagement! Je n'ai plus de souci à me faire. Je vais aller liquider mon emprunt ce midi, et il ne me restera plus que 3896,47 livres à payer. Je mets d'autres trucs en vente également, alors bientôt je ne devrai plus que 2000 ou 3000 livres, que je pourrai rembourser facilement, surtout que je ne vais sans doute pas perdre mon boulot vu que j'ai signé ce contrat avec l'animalerie. Et tout ça, c'est grâce à toi. Tu es une super copine. À tout à l'heure pour une pause-thé.

Bisous, Fati.

Je sais ce que vous pensez : dépêche-toi d'ouvrir le message de Rupert. Oui, moi aussi j'ai envie de le lire. Mais je prends mon temps. Je veux savourer le moment où il se remettra à me faire de la lèche et où je pourrais lui dire : « Tu as loupé le coche, branleur ! » Il n'est pas au courant que j'ai une dent contre lui, souvenez-vous, donc les mails que je recevrai de lui aujourd'hui ont de grandes chances d'être tout guillerets et faussement amicaux. Une moue de dégoût se forme sur mon visage à cette pensée, du coup je me concentre sur la bonne nouvelle de Fatima, et ça ne rate pas : un sourire se dessine. Je me tourne vers elle, à son bureau près du mien, et elle lève les yeux vers moi. Elle a les joues rosies et les yeux qui pétillent. Elle m'adresse un sourire ravi, et je lui réponds. Puis je m'aperçois que Mike est assis près d'elle, de l'autre côté, et qu'ils sont en grande conversation ; elle se retourne vers lui, leurs têtes si proches l'une de l'autre qu'elles se touchent presque. Il est manifestement en train de l'aider avec le contrat de l'animalerie. Quel raseur… Il ne peut pas la laisser profiter tranquillement de son bonheur quelques instants ?

Bref. Le message suivant est de Sean. Il est juste là, à son bureau, alors la raison pour laquelle il n'est pas venu me parler m'échappe. Bien que je préfère ça. Je ne me réjouis pas à l'idée de lui annoncer que je sors avec Brad. Pauvre homme, si inquiet à propos de son petit garçon, avec tous les soucis d'argent qu'ont les jeunes parents, et maintenant en plus la fille de ses rêves a rencontré quelqu'un d'autre. Quand est-ce qu'il aura enfin de la chance ? J'ouvre le message.

Salut, beauté. Ça fait un moment qu'on s'est pas parlé. Tout va bien de ton côté ? Désolé de t'avoir un peu négligée, j'ai été très occupé. J'ai à peu près fini de régler ce truc, alors je peux me rattraper quand tu veux.

Biz, Sean.

Ça ne correspond pas vraiment à l'idée que je me fais d'une proposition romantique : Il peut se rattraper ? Quand je veux ? Il n'a pas compris, pas vrai ? J'ai encore plus de peine pour lui, maintenant. Non seulement il m'a perdue ainsi que son fils, ne peut pas rivaliser avec le beau-père, mais en plus il n'a aucun talent en matière de séduction. Quelle chance aurait-il de démarrer une autre histoire d'amour ?

Bon, la pitié c'est très bien, mais on ne peut pas fonder une relation là-dessus, quoi que Vini ait pu en dire quand elle sortait avec le sosie de Dean Gaffney, l'année dernière. Je clique sur « Répondre » et tape à toute vitesse.

Sean,
Merci pour cette charmante proposition, mais depuis la dernière fois qu'on s'est vus j'ai rencontré quelqu'un. C'est assez sérieux. Je suis navrée de te laisser tomber.

Beth.

J'ajoute « Bisous », avant de changer d'avis et de l'effacer. Ce n'est pas bien de le torturer avec de faux espoirs. Il faut qu'il sache qu'il n'y a aucune chance que quelque chose se produise entre nous. J'hésite pendant presque une minute avant de cliquer sur «Envoyer», sachant que le jour va s'assombrir pour lui quand il le lira, que tout lui semblera juste un petit peu plus… difficile. Mais je dois le faire. Il faut qu'il commence à faire son deuil pour pouvoir avancer. Je lui dois bien ça. Je laisse traîner mon curseur au-dessus du bouton d'envoi, puis, lui jetant un dernier regard par-dessus mon épaule, je clique.

À peine l'ai-je expédié que je presse mes doigts sur ma bouche en regrettant mon geste. Comment ai-je pu être insensible à ce point? Il ne devrait pas apprendre cette mauvaise nouvelle par mail, c'est trop froid. La moindre des choses aurait été que je le lui dise en face. Peut-être en lui tapotant le bras et avec un petit laïus sur le mode: «Ce n'est pas toi, c'est moi.» Oh non, je suis une vraie salope. J'aimerais pouvoir plonger la main dans les tuyaux et rattraper le message, ou remonter le temps. Malheureusement, ce n'est pas possible, alors je me contente de m'affaisser légèrement et de tendre l'oreille dans l'attente de la réaction de Sean dans mon dos, le souffle étouffé, le sanglot réprimé, le visage enfoui dans les mains.

J'entends l'alerte de sa messagerie, la souris qui clique pour ouvrir le mail, une courte pause pendant qu'il lit, et… et plus rien. J'ose un regard rapide par-dessus mon épaule pour voir ce qu'il fait et l'observe alors que, d'un seul clic brutal, il l'efface! Je tressaille comme s'il m'avait giflée et me retourne vers mon propre bureau, bouche bée et les yeux toujours écarquillés. Comment a-t-il pu faire ça? Pourquoi n'est-il pas écrasé de chagrin? Je hasarde un deuxième coup d'œil, mais à présent il est sur Internet, occupé à surfer sur des sites de vacances! On dirait presque que ça lui est égal que j'aie rompu avec lui.

Et maintenant le mail de Rupert. Il a écrit comme objet « Lisez-moi s'il vous plaît », mais je l'ignore un moment. Je prends le temps de m'armer de volonté contre la déferlante d'images de ce beau visage qui va s'abattre sur moi. La brochure d'Horizon est posée sur mon bureau, ouverte comme d'habitude à la dernière page, et j'examine la photo en y superposant mes souvenirs de lui tel que je l'ai vu à la soirée. Il me semblait avoir repéré quelque chose qui n'allait pas, ce soir-là, et alors que je contemple le cliché avec attention, j'arrive à me convaincre que ce détail s'y retrouve : une ligne de démarcation orange le long de sa mâchoire, là où finit le hâle artificiel. Bref, ce que j'ai vu est soit du bronzage en institut, soit du fond de teint, mais dans l'un et l'autre cas ce n'est pas très attirant. Je me penche sur la brochure, concentrée. Oui, elle est bien là, cette marque sur le contour de son visage. À moins que ce ne soit seulement la virilité parfaite de ce menton carré ?

Non, allons, Beth, reprends-toi. Je sais comment il était, vendredi – vaniteux et superficiel. Il m'a sans doute oubliée dès l'instant où je me suis éloignée, et rien de ce qui me concerne ne restera dans sa mémoire. Ou bien, non, peut-être une chose. Deux choses. « Des jolis nénés », aurait-il probablement dit, si on lui avait demandé de me décrire un peu plus tard.

OK. Je suis prête. J'ouvre le message et commence à le lire.

Ma très chère Beth,
Est-ce que tout va bien pour vous ? Je sais que nous avons convenu de nous retrouver pour déjeuner demain, mais j'espérais échanger un mail

ou deux avec vous d'ici là. J'apprécie vraiment nos conversations. L'absence de nouvelles de votre part me préoccupe. J'ai l'impression qu'il s'est produit un événement qui vous fait hésiter à poursuivre notre amitié. Me trompé-je ? Beth, je trouverais très difficile d'accepter la fin de notre amitié et de notre correspondance, si telle était votre décision. Je voulais vous dire que je vous apprécie beaucoup et que je commençais à espérer que nous pourrions devenir plus que des partenaires professionnels. Je n'ai pas honte de l'admettre ; le médium froid et impersonnel de l'informatique me donne le courage dont j'ai besoin pour ces propos intimes. Mais j'imagine que vous avez vraisemblablement deviné mes sentiments dans nos échanges, de toute façon ? Bref, je pense que quelque chose s'est produit, qui vous a fait changer d'opinion à mon égard, et que vous êtes en train de mettre un terme à notre relation. Ai-je raison ?

Oh, il est tellement sensible et perspicace. En apparence. Je secoue la tête, comme pour en chasser la poussière. S'il n'était pas un tel branleur inculte, je trouverais ce mail incroyablement touchant. Mais il est bel et bien tel que je viens de le décrire, et donc la lecture de ce message ne me séduit guère. Pas le moins du monde. Je clique sur « Répondre ».

Ce que vous ignorez, c'est que c'est à moi que vous avez parlé, à la soirée, vendredi. Vous avez été très clair sur la nature de vos intentions.

Je me retiens d'en écrire plus. Je ne veux pas qu'il sache à quel point je suis déçue, et combien j'espérais que nous serions plus que des amis. Ça paraît tellement pathétique, maintenant que je sais comment il est vraiment. La réponse ne se fait pas attendre.

On s'est rencontrés ? Vraiment ? À une soirée ? Oh, non, Beth, que vous ai-je dit ? Ça a l'air affreux, je sais, mais malheureusement je ne m'en souviens pas. Les gens que je croise ne me disent pas toujours comment ils s'appellent, et je dois avouer à ma grande honte que, même quand ils le font, je rencontre tellement de gens chaque jour qu'il m'arrive d'oublier aussitôt leur nom.

Vous ai-je offensée d'une manière ou d'une autre ? Dans ce cas, j'aimerais que vous sachiez que rien de ce que je vous ai dit, en personne, à cette soirée ou quelque part ailleurs, n'était vrai. Ce n'était pas moi. Je veux dire, pas ma vraie personnalité. Le vrai moi, c'est celui qui vous écrit, qui vous admire, vous respecte, et éprouve de l'affection pour vous. Beaucoup d'affection. Je vous expliquerai tout le moment venu, mais pour l'instant je veux seulement m'assurer que vous ne me détestez pas. Je n'en dors plus, ça me rend grincheux et ça me perturbe dans mon travail, alors, s'il vous plaît, laissez ma vie reprendre son cours, Beth. Dites-moi que vous ne me haïssez pas à cause d'une parole que j'ai proférée à cette soirée.

Bises affectueuses,
Rupert.

Oh, merde. Il m'attire toujours autant. Mon cerveau a beau souligner le fait qu'il soit juste un connard hypocrite qui veut seulement rentrer dans mes bonnes grâces par pure vanité, toutes les autres parties de mon corps clament à l'unisson que le cerveau ferait mieux de la fermer. Et n'est-ce pas le mail le plus merveilleux et romantique que j'aie jamais reçu? Ça ressemble si peu à ce qu'il était à la soirée – on dirait quelqu'un d'autre. Le Rupert qui m'a parlé ce soir-là n'aurait jamais été capable d'élaborer un tel discours. Le Facteur Glamour avait anéanti toute faculté à converser qu'il aurait pu un jour détenir. Ce Rupert-ci est l'exact opposé de tout cela. Je sens de l'activité tout en bas de mon ventre, comme si cette partie de mon corps commençait quelques préparatifs au cas où elle aurait de la visite. Pour l'amour du ciel, qu'est-ce qui m'arrive? Je suis amoureuse de Brad, alors les seules visites dans cette région seront les siennes, et les siennes uniquement. Quand je serai prête.

Attendez une minute. Et si ce n'était pas Rupert qui écrivait ses mails, mais quelqu'un d'autre, comme Steve Martin qui joue le secrétaire pour Daryl Hannah dans *Roxanne*? Je suis très attirée par cette personne qui se fait appeler Rupert et m'envoie des mails, mais j'ai toutes les raisons de croire que le vrai Rupert de Witter n'est qu'un crétin superficiel. Il est beau et désirable, mais aussi égocentrique et inculte. Et je ne pourrais pas craquer pour quelqu'un qui est si passionnément amoureux de quelqu'un d'autre que moi – en l'occurrence, de lui-même.

Je clique sur « Répondre ».

Qui êtes-vous, en vrai?

C'est court, mais efficace. C'est une façon de lui dire que je suis prête à lui parler, mais avec prudence, et aussi que je me méfie de lui et que je sais qu'il n'est pas Rupert de Witter.

Je suis Rupert de Witter. Vous le savez très bien. L'homme que vous avez rencontré la semaine dernière était...

À ce moment-là, mon téléphone fait entendre la musique de *Superman* à plein volume pour me signaler l'arrivée d'un texto. Je détourne à regret mes yeux de l'écran, sachant que c'est forcément Brad, mais en ouvrant le message je découvre que ce n'est pas du tout lui, mais un dénommé Nigel.

Salut s'est Nigel. T été ou la semaine derniaire? Je t'es attendut 2 heures au P&roqu& du Pirrate, mes t'ai pas venue. Sa va? On se voye bientot? Gros bizous, ton chevallier servent, Nigel.

Quoi? Mais c'est qui, Nigel? Je ne connais personne de ce nom. J'y mets le temps, mais subitement je me rappelle le texto mystérieux que j'ai reçu la semaine dernière de la part d'un Nigel qui prétendait que j'avais coché sa case au speed dating. Sur le coup, j'ai pensé que c'était Vini qui me faisait une blague, puisque je n'avais coché qu'une seule personne, Brad en l'occurrence, et j'ai répondu... Oh, merde. Putain de bordel. J'ai proposé un rendez-vous au *Perroquet du Pirate*, et j'ai oublié. Or maintenant je sais que j'ai coché la mauvaise case par erreur, et ce malheureux Nigel doit avoir coché la mienne en espérant recevoir mes coordonnées, ce qui signifie qu'il a vraiment imaginé que je l'avais choisi, qu'il m'a réellement envoyé ce texto et qu'il a sincèrement cru que je serais au *Perroquet du Pirate* la semaine dernière. Aïe, qu'est-ce que je vais faire de lui ?

Eh bien, Nigel va devoir attendre, car c'est l'heure pour moi d'aller animer l'atelier « Motivation ».

J'ai la tête à l'envers, avec des images de Brad et de Rupert qui n'arrêtent pas de surgir dans mon esprit, l'apparition de chacun d'entre eux provoquant des séismes à certains endroits de mon corps, et du coup j'ai l'impression de passer ma journée entre fièvre voluptueuse et frissons d'anxiété. Je ne sais pas comment je fais pour m'en sortir, mais à la fin de la séance les huit stagiaires me gratifient d'une salve d'applaudissements spontanés, et l'un d'entre eux pousse même des acclamations. En partant, ils me serrent tous la main en me remerciant avec effusion et en me racontant combien ils sont désormais déterminés à mener à bien telle candidature, à décrocher telle promotion, à courir tel marathon. Ils ont le visage radieux et enthousiaste, ils vibrent de nombreuses opportunités, plus rien n'est impossible, ils peuvent le faire, ils ont la motivation de s'y tenir, d'aller au bout de leurs projets. Je n'en ai vraiment rien à foutre.

Et ça ne me ressemble pas du tout. En temps normal, j'ai beaucoup de fierté professionnelle. Mais durant ces deux dernières semaines, j'ai été tellement déconcentrée par Rupert que je ne me suis pas du tout investie dans le reste. Même mes gestes inconscients n'ont pas réussi à retenir mon attention, sans parler des gestes conscients. Je suis décidée à revenir à la normale dès que j'aurai assuré le contrat avec Horizon, mais pour le moment je me dirige vers mon bureau avec une seule chose en tête. Je m'assieds rapidement et ouvre ma messagerie professionnelle.

Il est 16 h 30, et je n'ai pas écrit à Rupert depuis ce matin. Il est sans aucun doute en train de penser que rien de ce qu'il peut dire ne réparera ce qui s'est passé quand nous nous sommes rencontrés la semaine dernière, et que je veux mettre un terme à notre relation. Il faut que je finisse de lire son message et que je lui réponde.

Mon cerveau exige de savoir pourquoi je prends cette peine alors que je suis déjà folle amoureuse de Brad, ce qui n'est juste ni vis-à-vis de lui, ni de Rupert, ni de moi-même; mais les autres parties de ma personne, qui sont majoritaires, me conseillent vivement de ne pas mettre tous mes œufs dans le même panier. En tout cas, pas avant d'avoir la certitude que l'un des paniers est supérieur, et sans doute mieux équipé pour offrir le plus grand confort pour tous les œufs, jusqu'à ce que la mort les sépare.

Allant droit à ma boîte de réception, je rouvre le deuxième message de Rupert. Le temps que la page s'affiche, je vois qu'aucun autre mail de lui n'est arrivé, et j'éprouve un pincement au cœur. Il doit avoir abandonné.

Je suis Rupert de Witter. Vous le savez très bien. L'homme que vous avez rencontré la semaine dernière était juste un idiot, qui essayait de se

393

faire passer pour autre chose que ce qu'il est, par plaisanterie. Si j'avais su que c'était vous, cela ne se serait jamais produit. La soirée se serait achevée bien autrement, croyez-moi.

C'est la stricte vérité. Si vous êtes toujours en colère contre moi, je vous en prie, écrivez-moi pour me le dire. Cela m'évitera de rester encore de longues heures à attendre pour rien devant l'ordinateur. En l'absence de réponse de votre part, je considérerai que vous êtes plongée dans une profonde méditation. Ou inconsciente, sur un brancard aux urgences.

Bises, Rupert.

Eh bien, je n'ai pas donné signe de vie, alors est-ce qu'il en a déduit que tout allait de nouveau bien entre nous ? J'espère. Je réponds aussitôt.

Étiez-vous sous l'emprise d'une substance illicite, dans ce cas ? Ou de l'alcool ? Ou étiez-vous simplement en train de vous divertir ? Parce qu'une autre fille que moi aurait pu s'y laisser prendre. Cela semble un peu cruel, c'est tout.

Au siège d'Horizon, Rupert a la tête entre les mains, les coudes posés sur son bureau. Il se passe les doigts dans les cheveux. Avec un froncement de sourcils, il regarde l'écran puis se lève, se dirige vers la fenêtre pour la quinzième fois, se frotte à nouveau le front, puis revient vers son fauteuil. Il s'assied, puis saisit son téléphone portable, et parcourt le répertoire jusqu'à « Libby ». Au moment où il choisit «Appeler» dans le menu, l'alerte de sa boîte de réception retentit, le faisant sursauter. Sans un regard, il laisse tomber à grand bruit l'appareil sur le bureau et s'empare de la souris, la pointe vers le nouveau mail pour voir de qui il vient. Un sourire de soulagement lui monte aux lèvres alors qu'il le survole, puis il tape une réponse.

De: Rupert de Witter
À: Beth Sheridan
Objet: Vraiment soulagé que vous ne soyez pas sur un brancard

Je sais. Vous avez raison. C'était égoïste et puéril, et cela aurait pu être blessant. De fait, cela vous a blessée, donc c'était blessant, sans aucun doute. Mais je n'étais pas sous l'emprise d'une drogue, Beth. Ce n'est pas mon genre. La possibilité que j'aie été très légèrement éméché existe, mais cela n'excuse pas ce qui s'est passé. Tout ce que je peux faire, c'est vous supplier de tourner la page. Ce n'était pas ma vraie personnalité. Ma vraie personnalité, la voici. C'est moi, Rupert de Witter, d'Horizon Holidays, qui vous parle, Beth Sheridan de Love Learning, brûlant d'espoir que vous me répondiez.

Bises, R.

Oh, mon Dieu! C'est la panique dans mon ventre. Manifestement, les parties concernées accélèrent leurs préparatifs, sous l'impulsion de mes sentiments à la lecture de ce mail, mais le fait que Rupert ne soit pas présent matériellement à côté de moi, et qu'il se trouve même dans un autre bâtiment, dans un autre quartier, rendant impossible tout contact physique, leur a, de toute évidence, échappé. Elles ne se calment pas quand je leur murmure :

— Vous perdez votre temps, mes petites.

À vrai dire, je ne suis pas sûre d'avoir envie qu'elles se calment. Je tape :

> Êtes-vous réellement en train de me dire la vérité,
> à présent ? Je veux dire, toute la vérité ? Ou bien
> y a-t-il autre chose qu'il faudrait que je sache ?

Je ne sais pas ce que j'espère au juste, mais je reprendrais bien une dose de cette passion. La réponse ne se fait pas attendre. En la lisant, je sens un sourire s'épanouir spontanément sur mon visage.

> Je suis absolument sûr qu'il y a beaucoup d'autres
> choses que vous devriez savoir, Beth. Il est certain
> que j'aimerais vous en dire plus, et aussi mieux
> vous connaître. J'espère de tout cœur que vous
> ressentez la même chose. Mais en ce qui concerne
> la soirée le type que vous avez rencontré ne
> vaut vraiment pas la peine d'être connu. Serait-il
> possible de tourner la page ?
>
> Bises, R.

La presque totalité de ma personne est parfaitement convaincue qu'il parle de faire plus ample connaissance, peut-être lors d'un événement mondain, afin de voir si quelque chose peut éclore. Ce qui est fantastique. Le reste de moi-même, minoritaire mais très localisé, a réussi à se mettre à croire qu'il espère me «connaître» au sens biblique. Je glisse un peu dans mon siège en tapant ma réponse.

Je tournerais certainement la page si je le pouvais. Malheureusement, j'ai un petit problème. Vous voyez, j'ai un peu le béguin pour lui. Ça fait un moment que ça dure. Alors même s'il s'est comporté de façon vraiment bizarre vendredi, ce que je peux oublier, je doute beaucoup de pouvoir l'oublier, lui.

Je contemple le message pendant une éternité avant de cliquer sur «Envoyer». J'ai l'impression de trahir Brad, avec qui je me sens liée, en réalité. Mais je parviens facilement à me rappeler que nous ne nous sommes engagés à rien, que nous sommes libres tous les deux de voir qui nous voulons et d'envoyer des mails à tout millionnaire sexy qui croiserait notre chemin.

Et aussi, bien sûr, c'est très direct. Il n'y a ni sous-entendu ni double sens dans ce mail. C'est franc, on ne peut pas s'y tromper. Je clique. C'est tout.

Je passe environ quatre-vingt-quinze secondes les yeux rivés sur l'ordinateur, cherchant à provoquer l'arrivée d'un message de Rupert par la seule force de ma volonté, et, pour la première fois de ma vie, cette méthode fonctionne. Je m'approche de l'écran, le cœur battant à se rompre, et ouvre le mail.

Je ne saurais vous dire ce que j'éprouve en lisant cela, Beth. Je suis sûr que vous avez conscience de la folle attirance que j'ai pour vous, parce que je suis incapable de jouer les types distants pour me faire désirer. Oh, c'est merveilleux de voir que vous ressentez la même chose. Mais cela m'inquiète un peu que vous ayez le béguin pour celui que vous avez rencontré à la soirée, ce bel homme qui s'est conduit comme un bouffon et vous a blessée. Est-ce lui et son image qui vous attirent, Beth ?

Ces fameuses parties de moi-même ont fini leurs préparatifs et me crient en chœur : « Vas-y, vas-y ! » Pendant un bref instant, je ferme les yeux et me laisse aller, puis je les rouvre et relis le message. C'est tellement bizarre, cette façon qu'il a de parler de lui à la troisième personne comme ça. Il s'est manifestement complètement détaché de son comportement de l'autre soir, ce qui me donne à penser qu'il n'était vraiment pas lui-même. C'était peut-être une blague, un pari, ou quelque chose comme ça. Quoi qu'il en soit, la distance qu'il prend à présent vis-à-vis de ces actes montre bien qu'il les regrette. Je réponds.

Je ne comprends pas. Vous êtes bien cette personne-là, celui qui a réagi à ma boutade, écrit tous ces mails pleins d'humour qui m'ont fait rire. Vous êtes celui qui a commandé toutes ces bougies au *Madeleine's* et plaisanté au sujet d'une montgolfière au téléphone. (C'était bien une plaisanterie, n'est-ce pas ?) C'est tout cela qui m'attire, Rupert. Pas le type de la soirée. Désolée, mais je préfère que vous le sachiez. Je ne pourrais pas prétendre être votre amie si j'étais incapable de vous signaler quand vous vous comportez comme un abruti.

Dans son bureau, Rupert lit ce mail, prend une inspiration profonde, puis expire lentement, calmement. Un sourire au coin des lèvres creuse ses fossettes, pendant qu'il rédige un nouveau message.

Est-ce que nous sommes amis, alors?

À l'autre bout du réseau, je déchiffre ces mots et me surprends à froncer légèrement les sourcils. Je ne sais pas vraiment si c'est bon signe ou pas. Veut-il que nous soyons amis? Se réjouit-il de cette amitié? Ou regrette-t-il un peu que nous soyons amis, parce qu'il souhaiterait bien plus? Il n'y a qu'une seule façon de le découvrir.

J'espère bien. Cela serait délicat, une fois votre contrat avec Love Learning signé, si nous n'étions pas en bonne intelligence.

Oui, oui, je sais, c'est un prétexte. Mais je n'ai écrit cela que dans l'espoir de provoquer une réaction, peut-être une sorte de déclaration disant que ce qu'il recherche n'a rien à voir avec Love Learning.

La sonnerie de la boîte mail retentit.

Vous avez de nouveau ça en tête, alors, petite chipie? Toujours professionnelle! Je suis impressionné. Et assez excité, pour être franc. La vérité, c'est que je n'ai pas arrêté de penser à vous de tout le week-end. Dès que je pense à notre rendez-vous de demain, je perds toute concentration. Que faites-vous en ce moment?

Tout à coup, je prends conscience du reste de l'équipe, tout autour de moi. Sean est toujours assis à son bureau, dans mon dos, et Fatima est près de Mike, en diagonale. À côté de Mike, la place de Derek est vide – il passe trois jours à Brighton pour une formation « Être un Bon Manager », heureusement. Il ne pourrait pas lire les messages sur mon écran, mais il me verrait sans nul doute rougir, et mes pupilles dilatées ne lui échapperaient pas, non plus que mon souffle rauque. Ni le fait que je glisse un peu plus dans mon siège. Il faut que j'essaie d'avoir l'air moins excitée, par respect des convenances. Mon mail suivant est un signe de mon état, plus que toute autre chose.

Eh bien, vous savez très bien ce que je suis en train de faire, Rupert. Je suis collée à mon écran d'ordi, le souffle court, et je caresse le clavier pour vous envoyer un nouveau message provocant.

C'est une description assez exacte. Un peu gênée, je m'écarte du moniteur et me force à m'asseoir correctement. Puis je bondis à nouveau vers l'ordinateur quand le texte suivant s'affiche.

Vous n'avez pas de travail, alors, Miss Professionnelle? Vous avez du temps à perdre? L'oisiveté
est mère de tous les vices...

Oh non, me critiquerait-il? Me suis-je ridiculisée
dans mon dernier message? Est-il en train de se défaire
de tout respect pour moi? J'écris:

Non, j'ai fini tout ce que j'avais à faire. Je suis très
efficace. Et je ne considère pas que converser avec
vous soit une perte de temps.

Je clique sur « Envoyer », puis tambourine des doigts
sur le bureau avec impatience, en attendant sa réponse.
Quand elle arrive, mon cœur s'arrête de battre pendant
une seconde avant de se décrocher.

Je peux être à la Curée dans dix minutes. Et vous?

Oh, mon Dieu! Dans mon ventre, c'est la fête, et
je ressens encore plus fort les encouragements que me
prodiguaient déjà certaines parties de mon corps. Je
crois qu'elles commencent à se rendre compte, et moi
avec, que leurs préparatifs frénétiques n'ont peut-être
pas été vains. J'envoie un rapide « OK » et avant d'avoir
pu y penser à deux fois j'ai enfilé mon manteau et éteint
mon ordinateur. Je vais vraiment rencontrer Rupert de
Witter officiellement, en sachant qui il est, et surtout,
en étant reconnue de lui. Ce n'est certainement pas un
rendez-vous d'affaires, et j'ai l'impression que nous
venons d'effectuer les préliminaires. À moins que ce
ne soit seulement une impression. Oh, et si ce n'était

qu'une impression ? Bon, je verrai bien ce qui se passera quand on y sera. S'il m'attrape brusquement et se met à m'embrasser avec passion, je saurai que ce n'est pas le cas.

Allons, mes genoux, reprenez-vous, le reste de moi compte sur vous pour m'amener là-bas.

— À plus, dis-je d'un air désinvolte en me hâtant vers la sortie, sans accorder un regard aux autres ni me soucier qu'ils m'aient ou non entendue ou vue partir.

J'ouvre la porte à la volée d'une main, ajuste mon manteau en m'aidant de l'autre, me jette dans le couloir et lève les yeux juste à temps pour m'apercevoir que je viens de rentrer dans Richard.

Chapitre 23

Retours défavorables

Objectif à court terme : euh…
Obstacles : …
Objectif à long terme : …
Obstacles : …

— Houla, ne tombe pas, poulette, dit-il en me passant le bras autour de la taille. (Je lève les yeux vers lui, et il s'arrête dans son élan.) Bordel de merde ! C'est toi, Beth ? Ben ça alors, tu es magnifique ! Viens ici.

J'ai le souffle coupé, les jambes en coton, le corps entier incapable de mouvement alors que je contemple, bouche bée, cette apparition devant moi. En moins d'une seconde, j'ai balayé du regard sa silhouette tout entière et remarqué son nouveau bronzage ; ses cheveux, un peu plus longs et plus clairs, qui lui tombent maintenant sur les yeux ; sa chemise au col ouvert et aux manches roulées ; ses yeux qui me détaillent avec admiration ; ses bras tendus vers moi pour m'étreindre. Tout à coup, le sang qui s'était récemment activé ailleurs me remonte à la tête, je reprends ma respiration péniblement, le monde se met à tourner, je chancelle un peu, heurte le mur, me tords la cheville et balance les mains en hurlant lorsque je perds complètement l'équilibre. Alors que je m'écroule dans les bras de Richard, je l'entends s'écrier :

— Oh, merde ! Venez m'aider !

Cela ne figure pas sur la liste de choses que j'aurais aimé être en train de faire quand Richard reviendrait. Même pas dans le top 100. Je suis censée être adorable, plongée dans une activité valorisante, les cheveux à peine ébouriffés, un doux sourire aux lèvres, vivant ma vie avec plaisir, sans souffrir de son absence des trois derniers mois, et sans me rendre compte qu'il est rentré et m'observe avec passion, tapi dans l'ombre. Tomber la tête la première dans ses bras ne colle vraiment pas dans le tableau.

Je ne suis par terre que quinze secondes, ce qui est plutôt embarrassant en fait. Je veux dire, si l'on doit se blesser devant l'élu de son cœur, il faut au moins lui donner une chance d'être malade d'angoisse, de composer le numéro du SAMU avec frénésie, de bercer notre tête avec tendresse et de courir dans le sillage de notre brancard à l'hôpital. Je suis prête à me relever avant que Richard ait seulement eu le temps de se mordre la lèvre.

Quand je lève les yeux, je perçois un peu d'agitation, les gens se précipitent, la panique commence tout juste, des visages inquiets apparaissent. J'entends Richard expliquer :

— … juste tombée, je ne sais pas pourquoi…

Et Fatima demander :

— Qui est-ce ? Que s'est-il passé ? Oh, Richard !

Puis tout semble se figer, deux paires d'yeux rencontrent les miens, et Richard conclut :

— Oh non, tout va bien, elle a repris connaissance. Remettez-vous au travail.

Fatima repart dans le bureau, et ses mots me parviennent :

— Eh, les gens, devinez quoi ? Richard est de retour ! Beth s'est pris une gamelle !

Puis d'autres voix lui répondent :

— Richard est rentré ? Quand ça ?

Puis je perçois, déçue, le bruit de mes collègues qui retournent à leurs places. J'ai envie de crier : « Je pourrais très bien être vraiment malade, vous savez ! » Mais Richard se tient toujours accroupi à mes côtés. Et il a tout de même l'air un peu anxieux.

— Coucou, toi, dit-il doucement, les mains posées sur les genoux.

— Tu es revenu.

— Ouais, bon, le Portugal, c'est très surfait, tu sais.

— Vraiment ?

— Ouais. Un vrai cauchemar, du début à la fin. Je te raconterai plus tard. (Il me prend la main et la caresse du pouce. Ma main meurt et s'envole au paradis.) Tu crois que tu peux te lever, maintenant ?

Je hoche la tête. Je suis incapable de parler pour le moment. Ma voix doit être partie se faire belle. Je lui laisse ma main pour qu'il me tire tendrement dans ses bras.

— Super. (Il lâche ma main, repose les siennes sur ses genoux et se lève.) Tu peux venir dans le bureau, s'il te plaît ? Je vais faire une déclaration.

Et il franchit la porte, me laissant étalée par terre comme une guirlande qui se serait détachée du sapin.

Mon premier geste est de me précipiter aux toilettes pour retoucher mon rouge à lèvres. Je sais bien que Richard m'a demandé de venir écouter son discours, mais ça ne le dérangera pas que je ne sois pas là. Il pourra me mettre au jus plus tard. Oh, mon Dieu ! J'ai les yeux qui se révulsent et les genoux qui flageolent à la pensée que Richard me mette au jus. *Allons, Beth, reprends-toi.*

Mon reflet semble en forme, en fait. Un peu pâle, peut-être, mais j'espère que ça me donne une allure fragile et intéressante. J'applique un peu de gloss et donne du volume à mes cheveux. Puis je les lisse à nouveau. Une occasion comme celle-ci s'accommode plutôt d'un look chic et décontracté, pas d'un air de savant fou.

Quand je reviens dans le bureau, Richard est en train de finir. Je boitille jusqu'au premier rang de la petite foule qui s'est réunie devant lui.

—J'espère que je me fais bien comprendre, déclare-t-il en regardant tout le monde avec un grand sourire.

Je joins les mains comme Keira Knightley en train de contempler des chiots, et je refrène mon envie de sautiller de plaisir, mais personne ne semble partager mon enthousiasme. Fatima se mordille la lèvre, les sourcils froncés ; Mike secoue légèrement la tête ; même Cath a l'air un peu perturbée. De l'index elle se gratte le nez.

—Alors sortez d'ici, passez des coups de fil, introduisez-vous dans des réunions, mentez, trichez, furetez, racontez-leur n'importe quoi, ça m'est égal, du moment que vous vous débrouillez pour les faire signer dans la case. OK ? *Capiche ?* Poussez-les à s'engager pour tout ce que vous pourrez, peu importe quoi. C'est sérieux. Tous les moyens sont bons, vous avez carte blanche. Il nous faut un paiement complet à l'avance, ou au minimum un dépôt de cinquante pour cent, d'accord ? Ce vendredi, je veux des dossiers et des sous de la part de chacun d'entre vous. Ça vous laisse encore quatre jours. Encore. Quatre. Jours. Bien, parfait. Foncez, maintenant.

Et il tourne les talons et disparaît dans son bureau.

— Oh, mon Dieu, tu as entendu ça, Beth ? s'exclame Fatima. Tu te rends compte ?

Mais je ne lui réponds pas, trop occupée à me diriger à toutes jambes vers la porte de Richard, à l'ouvrir à la volée, et à entrer.

Je le surprends au moment où il s'installe dans l'énorme fauteuil pivotant en cuir noir que Chas a acheté il y a environ un mois. Il saisit les accoudoirs, les parcourt des doigts et opine d'un air satisfait.

— C'est plutôt pas mal, non ? (Il s'appuie contre le dossier, et le siège s'incline suffisamment pour qu'il puisse s'étendre, les pieds sur le bureau.) Ah, oui, fantastique. (Il croise les mains derrière la tête.) C'est bon d'être de retour.

— Ce fauteuil a coûté plus de 1 500 livres.

Il tourne les yeux vers moi, sourcils levés.

— Vraiment ? Putain. Il est en peau de quoi ? D'être humain ? Ah ! Ah ! Ah !

— Il y a un lecteur de CD et des enceintes intégrés, une fonction massage, une machine à glaçons…

— Cool, le massage ! C'est quel bouton ? D'habitude c'est sous l'accoudoir… Ah oui, j'ai trouvé. (Le fauteuil se met à bourdonner et à vibrer.) Humm, c'est incroyable, Beth. Il faut absolument que tu l'essaies. Allons, viens par ici.

Je fais un pas dans sa direction, puis m'arrête.

— Richard, il faut que je te dise que Chas s'est comporté de façon complètement irresponsable pendant

407

ton absence. L'argent qu'il a claqué dans ce siège aurait pu payer le salaire de l'un d'entre nous pendant un mois de plus. Il nous annonce à grand bruit que nous nous trouvons dans une situation désespérée, mais, à côté de ça, il dépense une somme folle pour des futilités comme celle-ci.

— Faire beaucoup de bruit pour rien, comme c'est shakespearien ! Ah ! Ah ! Ah ! Ah !

J'esquisse un sourire, puis me force à reprendre un air sérieux.

— Richard, je ne plaisante pas.

Apparemment, je viens de le doucher, et il se redresse.

— Non, désolé, Beth, tu as raison. C'était irresponsable de sa part, et je vais renvoyer ce fauteuil au magasin. C'est ce que j'ai décidé de faire dès que je l'ai vu, en fait. Je veux dire, LL ne peut pas se permettre ce genre de dépenses, particulièrement en ce moment. (Il se penche vers moi et fait une petite moue, avec un air d'enfant tout penaud.) Ze voulais zuste zouer un peu avec, avant que le vilain monsieur vienne le prendre.

Je ris. Je craque toujours pour son tempérament farceur.

— Je n'aime pas jouer les rabat-joie, mais je voulais que tu saches ce qui se passe.

— Je sais ce qui se passe, Beth, dit-il en reprenant son sérieux. Viens t'asseoir, tu veux bien ? Merci. Bon. Maintenant, d'après ce que j'ai pu comprendre, la seule personne qui a fait rentrer des sommes correctes ces derniers mois, c'est toi. Est-ce exact ?

— Eh bien…

—Tu n'as pas besoin d'avoir de scrupules à l'égard de tes collègues, Beth. Les scrupules et les affaires ne font pas bon ménage.

—Ce n'est pas ça, c'est juste que je ne sais pas si…

—OK, bon, c'est comme tu veux. Ça ne fait rien, de toute façon. La vérité, c'est que j'ai besoin de toi, plus que jamais, et de ton talent pour dénicher des gros contrats. Qu'en dis-tu? Est-ce que tu peux le faire?

—Quoi, tu veux que j'aille fureter, mentir et tricher?

Il sourit et fronce les sourcils en même temps.

—Oui, s'il le faut. Mais je doute que ce soit nécessaire. Telle que je te connais ma Bethy, tu vas emballer cet accord sans même recourir à des pratiques douteuses, n'est-ce pas?

Je ne peux m'empêcher de sourire en entendant cela. C'est bon de sentir ses talents reconnus, particulièrement par la personne dont on rêve qu'elle nous remarque. Je veux dire, qu'elle les remarque.

—J'espère que je serai à la hauteur.

—Ne t'en fais pas, dit-il, désinvolte.

Il donne une grande impulsion par terre avec son pied pour faire un tour complet avec son fauteuil. Puis recommence. Je le regarde quelque temps et commence à avoir moi-même la tête qui tourne. C'est sûrement l'amour. J'entends ma voix demander:

—Alors, tu es rentré pour de bon?

Cette question semble pathétique, même à mes propres oreilles. Je me retiens juste à temps d'ajouter: «As-tu quitté Sabrina?»

—Ouais, répond-il avec un large sourire en s'arrêtant dans un grand frottement de pieds. Tu sais quoi,

409

cet endroit m'a vraiment manqué. Tout le monde ici m'a manqué. Toi aussi, Beth.

: Il me dévisage, toute son attention concentrée sur moi, et me dit que je lui ai manqué. Mon cœur fait un petit bond de joie.

—C'est vrai?

—Ouais. Je veux dire, c'était super, n'est-ce pas, de travailler ensemble pendant toutes ces années? L'excitation de signer de nouveaux contrats, le boulot énorme pour les écrire, le plaisir de mener le travail à terme. Ça m'a manqué.

—À moi aussi.

—Ouais, mais ce n'était pas pareil pour toi, n'est-ce pas? Toi, tu as pu continuer comme avant, les accords, les recherches, la préparation, la réussite. Toutes ces choses où tu excelles. Moi, là-bas, je ne pouvais rien faire de tout ça. Bon sang, ce don que tu as pour repérer quelqu'un qui pourrait avoir besoin de formation, avant même qu'il le sache lui-même. Tu es une sorte de légende vivante, ici, tu sais.

—Vraiment?

Je rougis de plaisir. C'est exactement comme ça que j'imaginais le retour de Richard. Bon, à part le fait de me tordre la cheville et de pousser un hurlement dans ses oreilles. Et qu'il n'ait pas déboulé en demandant où j'étais. Ni ne m'ait observée en secret, tapi dans l'ombre. Mais quelle importance, de toute façon? Il me parle, nous sommes seuls, il m'a dit que je lui avais manqué, et maintenant il ajoute que je suis une légende vivante.

—Ah, ouais. Tu sais, tous ces contrats!

Il me sourit, et ses yeux, tachetés d'or, sont pour moi si familiers, si bien-aimés, que je me sens en sécurité rien qu'à les voir.

—La formation en management, les cours en ligne, la compagnie d'assurances. C'était fantastique. Tout le monde l'a dit.

—Comment ça, tout le monde? Je pensais que tu étais le seul à le savoir. Les autres croyaient tous qu'on avait monté ces projets ensemble, non? On s'était mis d'accord pour prétendre être tous deux responsables de ces succès, afin que personne ne se mette à dépendre de l'un d'entre nous.

Il regarde par terre, puis sur le côté, ensuite de l'autre côté, mes genoux, mes mains, par terre à nouveau.

—Hum. Ben, j'étais tellement enthousiaste chaque fois, que je n'ai pas pu m'empêcher de me confier à une ou deux personnes.

—Mais qui ça?

Il sourit et saisit mes deux mains, se lève et me fait quitter ma chaise également.

—N'en parlons plus. Pas tout de suite. Tu veux bien que je t'invite à dîner? Tu dois mourir de faim. En tous cas, je suis affamé. Viens.

Il m'emmène à *Pizza Hut*. Je savais que ce serait là: c'est son restaurant préféré. On y est allés si souvent ensemble que c'est un peu «chez nous». On a même «notre table», celle dans le coin près de la fenêtre, où on s'est assis souvent. En réalité, Richard ne sait pas que c'est notre table, et du coup il ne pense pas à la demander.

Une fois que nous avons passé la commande, il se rend au buffet d'entrées, et je le regarde depuis ma

411

place. Il optimise la capacité de son bol en le bordant de grandes feuilles de laitue choisies avec stratégie, et mets les tomates dans ses poches, afin de pouvoir se servir davantage. Lorsqu'il revient vers notre table, il étend ses doigts au-dessus de la montagne de salade pour éviter une avalanche de maïs et de lardons.

—Pourquoi tu fais ça? dis-je alors que le sommet vacille.

—Quoi?

—Tout ce tralala avec les entrées. Ce n'est pas la peine.

Il me regarde comme si des feuilles de laitue s'étaient mises à pousser sur le haut de mon crâne.

—Je suis un homme d'affaires, Bethy. Je n'arriverais à rien si je ne prenais pas systématiquement tout ce que je peux avoir, n'est-ce pas?

—Mais ce n'est pas… je veux dire, ça te donne l'air… (Il me dévisage toujours d'un air incrédule, alors je laisse tomber.) Ça ne fait rien.

—Ouais, rien de rien, poupée. Faut pas avoir froid aux yeux en affaires, tu sais. Pas de place pour les faibles. Excusez-moi, crie-t-il quand une jeune fille passe en courant presque, l'air stressée, à côté de notre table. On a une chance d'avoir nos boissons aujourd'hui? Je veux dire, j'ai plein de choses prévues demain, donc je ne pourrai pas revenir les chercher.

—Oh, désolée, je vais vous les apporter, répond-elle avec un sourire nerveux avant de se précipiter vers les cuisines.

—Bon sang, quel service, ici! dit Richard, la bouche pleine de pâtes à la tomate. Ils feraient mieux d'embaucher des chimpanzés! (Il hausse la voix sur ce dernier mot, et les clients de la table d'à côté lui jettent un coup d'œil.) Alors, quand est-ce que tu as fait… ça ? (Il agite sa fourchette de haut en bas, en la pointant vaguement dans ma direction.) C'est fantastique. Tu aurais dû le faire depuis des années, tu sais.

—Hum, merci. J'avais juste besoin de changement.

—Ouais, tu en avais carrément besoin, ma poulette. Je veux dire, ça te va vraiment bien. Tu vois ce que je veux dire ?

Il me considère, par-dessus son plat, et son expression est différente. Il ne m'a jamais regardée comme ça avant.

—Merci. Et où est Sabrina, alors ? Ici avec toi ?

Finalement, j'ai réussi à glisser la question. J'espère juste que ce n'était pas trop maladroit.

Il fait entendre une exclamation maussade avant d'enfourner une autre pleine fourchette. J'attends patiemment pendant qu'il mâche et qu'il avale.

—Je ne sais pas où elle est, et putain, ça m'est bien égal !

—C'est vrai ?

—Ouais. Quelle conne ! Elle s'est mise à me les briser dès qu'on est arrivés là-bas. Elle ne s'arrêtait jamais. « Il y a trop de désordre, pas assez de nourriture, pas assez d'argent, pourquoi tu ne t'es pas encore mis au travail ? » Des plaintes, toute la sainte journée. J'ai commencé à me sentir en prison, alors j'ai creusé un tunnel pour m'évader, et je me suis cassé. Maintenant, je suis de nouveau un agent libre. Pas d'attaches, pas de responsabilités. Il n'y a que mes désirs qui comptent.

—Oh.

Depuis toutes ces années que nous nous connaissons, il ne m'a jamais envoyé ce genre de signal. Il ne m'a jamais dit que j'étais belle. Jamais essayé de regarder dans mon décolleté, comme il est manifestement en train de le faire en ce moment même. On croirait qu'il vient seulement de se rendre compte que j'ai des seins.

—Alors, raconte-moi à qui tu as parlé de ces contrats, dis-je, dans une tentative de revenir à une conversation plus neutre.

Ce qui est plutôt raté, je ne vais pas tarder à m'en apercevoir.

—Oh, euh, pas à tout le monde, bien sûr. Chas est au courant.

—Bon. (Je m'en doutais.) Mais pourquoi, au juste, lui as-tu proposé de s'occuper de Love Learning en ton absence ? Il est affreux.

Richard renifle.

—Tu as sans doute raison. Mais c'est le mari de ma sœur, et elle me l'a demandé. Il a de l'expérience en matière de direction, apparemment.

—Ouais, mais ça veut probablement dire qu'il arrive à venir en vélo jusqu'au bureau le matin sans se tromper de direction.

Il éclate de rire et postillonne une miette par-dessus la table.

—Excellent, Bethy ! Il faut que je m'en souvienne. Trop drôle !

—Alors, tu en as parlé à quelqu'un d'autre ?

—Euh, laisse-moi réfléchir. Hum. Ah oui, je crois que je l'ai dit à Grace. Et à Skye.

Grace. Oh non. Il l'a dit à Grace. Pourquoi diable ? C'est surtout à cause d'elle qu'on a décidé de ne pas révéler que j'étais la seule personne derrière ces contrats.

« Waouh, Bethy, tu es trop forte ! » avait dit Richard, surexcité, lorsque j'avais rapporté un énième accord juteux. «Tu pourrais te charger de la prospection à toi toute seule, et personne n'aurait à s'en faire!»

Mais je lui avais fait remarquer que si l'on annonçait aux autres que j'étais capable de dénicher suffisamment de clients pour faire tourner l'entreprise, ils allaient en effet totalement cesser de s'en faire.

«Surtout Grace», avais-je dit, d'un air sage. «Tu crois vraiment que quelqu'un comme elle va continuer à travailler dur, une fois qu'elle saura que je me charge de tout? Tu plaisantes! Elle va se contenter de rester à son bureau à balancer ses cheveux, et être payée à rien faire.»

Et maintenant, le souvenir de ce jour, il y a trois semaines, où Chas nous a annoncé pour la première fois que nous avions besoin de nouveaux contrats me revient à l'esprit. Elle m'a demandé si j'allais décrocher une grosse prestation et sauver la compagnie, puis elle a prétendu que c'était une plaisanterie. Mais elle n'est pas partie à la chasse aux clients, ce soir-là, n'est-ce pas? Elle avait des choses plus importantes à faire. Par exemple, s'amuser, prendre du bon temps et ne pas s'en faire, pendant que je revenais avec un contrat de-la-mort-qui-tue.

— Merde, Beth, on dirait que tu vas tomber dans les pommes. Tu ne serais pas en cloque, par hasard?

— Mais pourquoi Grace?

Il détourne les yeux et regarde son verre.

— Eh bien, tu sais, dans la situation dans laquelle nous nous trouvions à l'époque, nous étions en train de discuter, de bavarder, à propos de LL et des gens qui y travaillaient, et j'étais en quelque sorte en train de chanter tes louanges, tu vois. Si Bethy n'était pas là, et blablabla. Ce genre de choses.

Je secoue la tête. Ça ne fait pas sens.

— Mais ça se passait où ? Je ne comprends pas. Dans quelles circonstances est-ce que vous avez pu vous retrouver à avoir une conversation dans ce goût-là ? C'était à la pause-déjeuner, ou quelque chose comme ça ?

— Euh, non, ce n'était pas au bureau, en fait.

— Mais où, alors ? Sur le parking ? Mais même comme ça, pourquoi est-ce que tu aurais…

— Non, Beth, pas sur le parking. On était… on était au lit. OK ?

— Au… ?

Je me le prends en pleine figure, et bien. J'en ai le souffle coupé comme si j'avais reçu un coup de poing, et je suis incapable de parler. Grace et Richard, ensemble, dans un lit. L'image s'affiche dans mon cerveau en Technicolor : lui, penché vers elle qui se soulève à sa rencontre. J'ai envisagé, imaginé, rêvé ce scénario de si nombreuses fois, au fil des années – une chambre, des amants enlacés, la peau moite, des murmures haletants –, mais chaque fois que je l'ai vu, c'était moi, dans ce lit. Mes mains sur le dos de Richard. Mes cheveux sur l'oreiller. Mon nom sur ses lèvres. Oh non. J'ai envie de vomir.

Et là, alors que je suis assise chez *Pizza Hut* avec un tourbillon d'images et d'informations déferlant à grand bruit dans ma tête, une autre de ses paroles fait son chemin dans mon cerveau :

— Skye ?

Il hoche la tête avec bonne humeur et enfourne un gros morceau de pizza.

— Oui, elle est au courant. Même si je regrette plutôt ce coup-là. En fait, elle est carrément tordue, si tu vois

416

ce que je veux dire. Son genre de délire, ce n'est pas trop pour moi.

Il oublie de mentionner qu'elle doit avoir dans les dix-huit ans, et lui trente-sept. Et qu'il est son patron.

J'ai cessé de manger. J'ai l'estomac en feu, et continuer de m'alimenter à cet instant ne pourrait que déclencher un désastre. Mais ce n'est pas fini pour autant.

—Richard, est-ce que tu peux me dire un truc ? Il faut que je sache… Est-ce que tu as aussi couché avec Fatima ?

—Ah ! Eh bien, il se trouve que non. On s'est embrassés quelques fois – ou du moins j'ai essayé –, mais je suis presque certain qu'elle est lesbienne. Une goudou enragée. Je ne vois pas d'autre explication. Elle m'a toujours repoussé, alors…

Il hausse les épaules et continue à bâfrer sa pizza, qui lui laisse les lèvres luisantes de graisse. Je les regarde. J'ai rêvé de cette bouche pendant huit ans, et je n'ai jamais rien eu, même pas l'ombre d'un petit bisou. Je voulais sentir ces lèvres frôler les miennes, les serrer, les presser, les écraser de désir. Je me racontais qu'il y avait quelque chose entre nous ; nous étions si proches, inséparables, partenaires au travail comme dans la vie, mais nous ne sommes jamais allés plus loin en raison de sa fidélité envers sa copine. Elle était le seul obstacle entre nous, et ça suscitait mon respect. Mon amour, même. Maintenant, je découvre qu'il a essayé de coucher avec toutes les filles du boulot, sauf moi. J'ai les yeux qui picotent, mais je ne vais pas pleurer ici. Il continue de se goinfrer joyeusement. Il n'a même pas remarqué que je ne touche pas mon assiette.

—Super gâterie, hein, Beth ? marmonne-t-il, la bouche pleine. Ah ! Ah ! Ah ! Peut-être plus tard, alors ? Ah ! Ah ! Ah !

Je vois ma vie défiler : Richard chez Horizon, en train d'insulter Rupert de Witter, de le traiter d'abruti, de lancer des objets à travers la pièce, de faire des colères, de hurler. La porte du bureau fermée quand il avait des « réunions » avec d'autres assistantes et d'autres membres du personnel qui venaient de tous les services de l'entreprise. Pourquoi est-ce que la fille des Croisières venait lui rendre visite, alors qu'elle ne s'occupait pas de formation ? Tout fait sens, à présent.

Et soudain un souvenir que je croyais oublié me revient : une conversation téléphonique entre Richard et Rupert de Witter. Encore des jurons, des cris, Richard rouge de colère, hurlant que Rupert ne pourrait pas le faire parce que lui, Richard, partirait avant que ça arrive. Je pensais que Richard avait démissionné par principe. Maintenant, je vois clairement que Rupert était sur le point de le virer.

D'autres images défilent dans ma tête, des débuts de Love Learning jusqu'au départ de Richard, il y a trois mois. « Beth va le faire », dit-il à Grace, à Derek ou à Sean. « Elle est vraiment douée pour ça. Ça ne t'embête pas, Beth, n'est-ce pas ? » Et ça ne m'embêtait pas, j'étais contente de le faire, quoi que ce soit, parce que ça renforçait le lien entre nous, et nous rapprochait. C'était la preuve qu'il avait besoin de moi, qu'il voulait de moi.

Je lève les yeux vers son visage, si familier, si chéri, et je me sens rompre les amarres et dériver. Il se transforme, se ratatine, se métamorphose en quelque chose de nouveau, juste là, à côté du buffet de desserts. Il n'y a pas de changement visible dans ses traits ; son visage est le même. Mais à présent, à la place de ses yeux brillants, pétillants, pleins d'humour, je vois deux cavités sombres, débordant de cynisme. À la place du sourire juvénile, je reconnais un rictus lubrique. Au lieu d'un homme plein de fierté, d'intégrité et d'honneur, je discerne un manipulateur bas de gamme, pas très net. J'étais prête à lui tomber dans les bras quand je l'ai vu, cet après-midi – d'ailleurs, je n'en suis pas passée loin –, mais maintenant j'ai l'impression d'être séparée de lui par une bonne couche de dégoût, semblable au film graisseux qui lui enduit les lèvres.

Il sourit toujours, probablement enchanté par sa blague sur la « gâterie », et je ressens plus que jamais le besoin de m'éloigner de lui. À nouveau. J'attrape mon manteau sur le dossier de ma chaise, et il hausse les sourcils d'un air connaisseur :

— Pressée de retourner au travail, Bethy ? dit-il d'un air suggestif, en essuyant la sauce tomate de ses lèvres toujours souriantes.

J'acquiesce :

— Oui, et maintenant.

Chapitre 24

Promouvoir l'égalité des chances

Objectif à court terme : on s'en fiche ! Ma vie est déjà fantastique.
Obstacles : …
Objectif à long terme : …
Obstacles : …

De retour à l'appartement, je m'aperçois avec surprise que je suis seule. Le scénario du retour de Richard que je me suis raconté depuis trois mois a toujours culminé avec la scène où il m'accompagnait chez moi, plongeait son regard sérieux dans le mien par-dessus sa flûte de champagne tandis que nous discutions littérature, écoutions nos airs préférés et dansions des slows dans le salon sur des chansons particulièrement émouvantes, avant de nous jeter l'un sur l'autre dans une frénésie lubrique. Mais je suis là, debout dans l'entrée glaciale, éclairée seulement par le clignotement erratique des guirlandes du sapin, toujours avec mon manteau, mon sac sur l'épaule, la porte fermée sur Richard, resté dehors. Enfin, il est sans doute parti, maintenant. Je suis sûre qu'il est capable de saisir un sous-entendu. Mais juste au cas où ce serait au-dessus de ses capacités, je lui ai déclaré qu'il n'entrerait pas, même si tous les autres hommes de la planète avaient succombé à un étrange virus basé sur la testostérone et qu'il était l'unique survivant.

Vini est également sortie, et ça me soulage. Je ne peux vraiment pas supporter l'idée qu'elle ait eu raison, encore une fois. Elle a laissé un mot sur la table de la cuisine pour dire qu'elle dîne dehors avec Kylie Minogue et Jason Donovan, donc j'ai l'appartement pour moi toute seule.

Je suis debout. Dans l'entrée. Apparemment incapable de remuer. Je pense, pense, pense, et mon cerveau est tellement pris par cette activité qu'il ne peut rien produire d'autre. Même pas cette impulsion électrique qui permet de bouger les membres.

Pourtant, je finis par sentir certains muscles se mettre spontanément en mouvement. Mon cerveau est un projecteur pointé directement vers Richard – qui revient, a couché avec Grace et Skye, est un connard – et maintenant, enfin, mon visage réagit à ces révélations. Je m'attends à des pleurs : des hoquets, des sanglots, des vagissements hystériques, bouche grande ouverte ; la figure silencieuse, ruisselante de larmes sur l'oreiller, douloureusement, une boule dans le ventre. Mais rien de tout cela ne se produit. En fait, c'est carrément le contraire. Quand je me mets enfin en route vers ma chambre, j'aperçois mon image dans le miroir au-dessus de la cheminée, et je découvre avec délices qu'elle est souriante.

Je m'endors aussitôt et rêve que je cours le long d'un quai en noir et blanc alors que mon train s'en va avec force cris, sifflements et nuages de vapeur ; puis me réveille en sursaut à deux heures du matin avec l'horrible prise de conscience que j'ai laissé Rupert m'attendre à la Curée. Jésus Marie Joseph dans un wagon-lit.

Bondissant hors du lit, je décide bêtement de m'habiller et d'accourir là-bas, mais le ridicule de la situation m'apparaît, alors que j'enfile mon jean. Je veux dire, c'est vraiment stupide de me préparer à prendre le volant pour me rendre dans la zone industrielle par cette température glaciale à 2 heures du matin, alors que c'est de toute évidence une perte de temps. Il aurait bien trop froid, après avoir attendu dix heures dans ces conditions arctiques, pour être capable d'entreprendre quoi que ce soit.

Je plaisante. Évidemment que je n'ai pas pensé qu'il serait encore là. Même pas pendant, disons, huit secondes.

Il ne me reste plus qu'à retourner me coucher et à me tortiller pendant cinq heures avant qu'il soit enfin l'heure de me lever, d'aller au travail et de lui envoyer un mail. Je passe la plus grande partie de cette fin de nuit allongée sur le dos, les bras le long du corps, les yeux fermés de toutes mes forces, désespérément concentrée sur un message télépathique que j'essaie de lui transmettre ; et, à un moment, j'arrive même à me persuader que je reçois une réponse de lui. Les yeux à présent ouverts, je porte ma main à ma bouche quand la silhouette indistincte d'un homme se forme progressivement dans l'ombre au pied de mon lit, et c'est une vision douloureuse : il est déprimé, voûté, avachi ; toute animation semble l'avoir quitté. En le regardant, je prends conscience avec une angoisse grandissante que je suis responsable de la tristesse de cet homme, que c'est ma faute s'il est dévasté, que je suis la cause de sa souffrance. C'est tellement évident qu'il nourrissait des espoirs pour notre rendez-vous, qu'il pensait que quelque chose était en train de naître entre nous, et qu'en l'abandonnant là-bas pendant des heures j'ai anéanti tous ses rêves et qu'il est maintenant bien plus malheureux que s'il n'avait jamais entendu parler de Beth Sheridan.

Oh, c'est vraiment fantastique!

Non, je ne veux pas dire que je me réjouis de sa tristesse. Bien sûr que non. Je l'aime, pourquoi serais-je contente qu'il souffre?

Mais est-ce possible pour une fille de ne pas être secrètement un peu euphorique en constatant que le millionnaire sexy avec lequel elle a passé deux semaines à flirter par mail, arrangé un rendez-vous qui n'a pas eu lieu, puis qu'elle a rencontré sans qu'il connaisse son identité, avant de badiner à nouveau, et à qui elle a fini par poser un lapin involontaire quand son ancien patron est revenu, est triste et brisé parce qu'elle ne s'est pas montrée? C'est impossible, voilà la vérité. S'il ne tenait pas à moi, s'il ne brûlait pas de désir de me rencontrer, de me serrer dans ses bras, de m'aimer, de consacrer cinquante ans à m'adorer, alors il n'aurait pas été aussi écrasé de chagrin en ne me voyant pas venir, n'est-ce pas? Je regarde, ravie, la silhouette sombre se détourner et s'éloigner tristement, d'un pas lourd; j'ai le cœur qui bat à se rompre, les pupilles dilatées, les lèvres entrouvertes. C'est peut-être méprisable, mais ce désespoir m'excite.

Mes pupilles se dilatent, si bien que je finis par m'apercevoir qu'il s'agit seulement de ma robe de chambre suspendue à une patère sur la porte.

Après une nuit qui a duré environ vingt-cinq ans, c'est enfin le matin, et je me traîne hors du lit, groggy, enfile des vêtements et me rend au bureau, les yeux vitreux. En réalité, on est mardi 19 décembre, ce qui signifie que j'ai un rendez-vous avec Rupert de Witter à 13 heures et un autre avec le directeur régional de *Whytelys* à 15 heures, donc juste avant de partir je prends une longue douche avec le luxueux gel douche Lauren Oliver que Vini m'a offert pour Noël. Je me tartine de la lotion parfumée qui va avec, retourne mes tiroirs pour retrouver mon ensemble de lingerie le plus sexy, consacre une heure à mes cheveux et à mon maquillage, et emprunte à Vini une panoplie de Susan Sarandon. C'est seulement après avoir fait tout cela que je conduis, les yeux vitreux, jusqu'au travail.

En vérité, je ne suis pas groggy, malgré mon insomnie. Je sais que Richard est dans son bureau, derrière la porte à panneaux, et j'y jette un regard en passant, mais pour la première fois depuis des années cela ne me procure ni tension ni anxiété. Je suis revigorée, énergisée par mon détachement à son égard, et c'est avec enthousiasme que je m'assieds à ma place, sans même me soucier de ma posture. Maintenant que Richard est de retour, je n'ai plus besoin de m'en préoccuper. Quand bien même il ne serait pas rentré, passer tout mon temps à prendre ces poses inconfortables et peu naturelles me semble un peu ridicule, à présent. Enfin, pas qu'un peu.

J'ouvre aussitôt ma messagerie professionnelle pour voir ce que Rupert m'a envoyé, le cas échéant. Tout au fond de ma tête, j'entends une minuscule voix me rappeler que je suis amoureuse de Brad – en fait, elle n'est pas minuscule, pas même petite, et ce n'est pas non plus tout au fond –, mais j'essaie de ne pas l'écouter pour le moment, malgré ses hurlements de cochon qu'on égorge, ses sautillements furieux et son doigt pointé sur moi d'un air accusateur. Aujourd'hui, je dois me consacrer à Rupert, et j'explique au goret hurlant ainsi qu'à moi-même que c'est à cause du contrat avec Horizon. Si je ne règle pas la situation avec lui avant notre rendez-vous à 13 heures, il n'apposera jamais sa signature dans la case. Pas s'il pense que l'une des employées de Love Learning manque suffisamment de considération, d'organisation et de la plus élémentaire politesse, pour le laisser poireauter en vain pendant quinze heures près d'une fontaine hideuse, en plein hiver.

Je me demande combien de temps il a attendu avant de renoncer ? Il doit bien exister des enregistrements des systèmes de vidéosurveillance. Comment faire pour mettre la main dessus ? Peut-être que je pourrais aller au commissariat et raconter que je m'inquiète pour mon…

Non, cette information n'est pas pertinente. Du moins en ce qui concerne le contrat. Je pourrai lui poser la question quand nous serons mariés.

Oh, putain, reprends-toi ! Je ne vais pas épouser Rupert mais Brad. Dans l'immédiat, je dois présenter des excuses à Rupert, pour le bien de Love Learning, du contrat et de mon emploi.

OK. Bon, un rapide survol de ma boîte de réception m'apprend qu'il ne m'a pas écrit, ce qui signifie que je vais devoir prendre l'initiative de le faire. Ce qui est normal, évidemment. C'est moi qui suis en faute, c'est donc à moi de faire le premier pas. Au fond de moi, j'espérais des récriminations ou de la colère – quelque chose de perfide et de sarcastique aurait été parfait, cela m'aurait servi de point d'appui pour essayer d'arrondir les angles, mais il n'y a rien, pas même une bonne vieille vacherie. D'accord, bon, OK. Je me lance.

Cher Rupert,

Merde. Et s'il ne m'a pas écrit parce qu'il ne veut plus rien avoir à faire avec moi, après la façon dont je l'ai traité hier ?

Ça ne fait rien. Je dois faire le premier pas afin d'établir un état des lieux. Je n'ai rien à perdre.

Cher Rupert,

Oh non. Et si tout ce qui s'est passé hier n'était qu'une blague ? S'il n'avait jamais imaginé que je le prenne au sérieux et ne s'était même pas rendu à la Curée, après avoir lancé cette proposition par boutade ? Nos mails étaient plutôt farfelus, et nous étions justement en train de plaisanter à ce moment-là, alors il a pu penser que ce serait drôle. En lui écrivant maintenant pour arranger les choses, j'aurais l'air d'une idiote tristement pathétique.

Non, c'est faux, parce qu'il supposera que j'avais bien compris que c'était une plaisanterie et que mon message d'excuse pour le lapin que je lui ai posé est aussi une blague. OK.

Cher Rupert,

Le pire, c'est d'imaginer sa tête quand il lira ce mail idiot où je m'excuse pour mon absence. Je veux dire, je rêve qu'une expression ravie anime subitement son visage, qu'il se penche vers son écran, impatient, et clique aussitôt sur « Répondre », puis compose une magnifique e-lettre d'amour, dans laquelle il me dit combien ces deux heures d'attente dans l'obscurité glaciale, hier, ont mis en lumière ses sentiments pour moi (ainsi que ses sourcils étincelants de givre) parce qu'il n'aurait affronté cela pour personne d'autre que moi et qu'il a acquis la certitude que ce qu'il veut, c'est bien plus qu'une relation de travail. Mais il est possible également qu'il fronce les sourcils d'un air surpris en se demandant de quoi je peux bien vouloir parler, qu'il supprime aussitôt le mail et poursuive sa journée comme si de rien n'était. Le troisième scénario – probablement le pire – est celui dans lequel il appelle ses amis et ses collègues pour lire le message et que tous rient ensemble à mes dépens.

Mais cela ne fait rien, car après le déjeuner d'aujourd'hui je n'aurai plus besoin d'avoir à faire à lui. À moins qu'il ne le désire. Et je ne saurais pas s'il le désire ou non tant que je ne lui aurai pas envoyé de mail. Alors pourquoi ne pas le faire tout de suite ?

Cher Rupert,

Maintenant que j'ai décidé de m'y mettre, je m'aper-çois que je n'y arrive pas. Je ne sais pas quoi dire. Un simple « désolée de vous avoir fait faux bond hier » ne saurait suffire. En outre, il faut que ça puisse passer pour une plaisanterie, au cas où ça en aurait été une pour lui. Crotte.

À ce moment-là, mon téléphone sonne dans mon sac, ce qui me donne une excuse idéale pour penser à autre chose qu'à ce maudit message pendant quelque temps.

427

Merci, Seigneur. Je farfouille dans ma besace et parviens de justesse à décrocher avant que la sonnerie s'arrête.

— Allô ?

— Hum, bredouille une voix féminine, est-ce que c'est bien Beth Sheridan ?

Je cligne des yeux. Je ne reconnais pas du tout ces intonations. Je jette un coup d'œil au numéro affiché, mais il ne me dit rien non plus. Cela me met tout de suite mal à l'aise, et je commence à froncer les sourcils.

— Oui, c'est moi-même. Qui est à l'appareil ?

— Ici Maggie Farrell, des urgences du Edward Hospital. Nous avons reçu ce matin quelqu'un qui a vos coordonnées dans son agenda…

J'ai le souffle coupé, et je reprends juste suffisamment d'air pour croasser :

— Vini ?

— Hum, c'est mademoiselle Lavinia Jones. Elle est entrée à la suite d'un choc à…

— J'arrive.

Douze minutes plus tard, je franchis en courant les portes coulissantes de l'hôpital et hurle pratiquement à pleins poumons le nom de Vini à l'adolescente qui tient la réception, derrière une vitre pare-balles. Il s'avère que Vini a reçu un coup à la tête ce matin. On l'a trouvée assise sur le trottoir en ville, et celui qui l'a découverte était si inquiet à son sujet qu'il a appelé une ambulance.

— Nous ne savons pas très bien comment c'est arrivé, me dit l'infirmière en me conduisant vers un box fermé.

— Que voulez-vous dire ? Qu'en dit Vini ?

— Eh bien, elle n'en sait rien.

— Comment est-ce possible ?

L'infirmière s'arrête, la main sur le rideau, et baisse la voix :

— Le choc sur la boîte crânienne a provoqué une commotion assez sévère, qui a affecté ses souvenirs, murmure-t-elle. Elle a perdu la mémoire à court terme.

— Ah. D'accord. (L'amnésie. J'en ai déjà entendu parler.) Alors elle ne se souvient pas de ce qui s'est passé ce matin… c'est plutôt courant, non, après une blessure à la tête ?

— Pas tant que ça. Et je ne suis pas certaine que vous ayez bien compris. Elle ne se souvient pas de ce qui s'est passé ce matin, ni de rien de ce qui est arrivé ensuite.

— Oui…

— Je veux dire, vraiment rien. Elle ne se souvient même pas qu'elle a eu un accident. Elle ne se rappelle pas ce qu'elle m'a dit trois ou quatre minutes avant. Elle est incapable de créer de nouveaux souvenirs, du moins pour le moment.

Et, sur cette déclaration fracassante, elle tire le rideau.

Vini est allongée sur le lit, tout habillée, et lance autour d'elle des regards anxieux. Elle vient manifestement de pleurer, et elle a une énorme bosse rouge et bleue au milieu du front. Elle semble tellement petite, étendue là. On lui a enlevé ses chaussures, et son collant rayé rose et violet est filé au genou. On voit sa peau rougie à travers. Sa veste en vinyle orange est accrochée au dossier d'une chaise.

— Coucou, dis-je en m'asseyant au bord du lit.

Elle tourne la tête pour me regarder, mais ses yeux sont absents. Ça me met mal à l'aise, et je détourne rapidement le regard.

—Je croyais que je rêvais que je faisais des courses avec Adam, explique-t-elle. Je ne sais pas ce qui s'est passé.

Elle renifle, et une larme roule sur sa joue.

—Ce n'est rien, réponds-je en lui prenant la main. Tu t'es fait une bosse sur la tête.

—C'est vrai ?

—Oui. Mais tu vas bien. Tu es à l'hôpital, maintenant, et on s'occupe de toi. Ne t'en fais pas.

—Oh. À l'hôpital ? Qu'est-ce qui s'est passé ?

—Tu ne t'en souviens pas. Mais ça ne fait rien, ce qui compte c'est que tu ailles bien, maintenant.

—Vraiment ? demande-t-elle comme si elle avait du mal à le croire. Où suis-je ?

—Aux urgences, au Edward Hospital. On t'a déjà fait une radio, et maintenant ils attendent les résultats.

—Vraiment ? Je ne m'en souviens pas du tout.

—Ah bon ? Eh bien c'est sans doute à cause de ta bosse.

Elle tourne à nouveau les yeux vers moi :

—Quoi ?

—J'ai dit, c'est sans doute à cause de ta bosse.

—De quoi tu parles ? Quelle bosse ? Je rêvais que je faisais des courses de Noël avec Adam. Je ne sais même pas ce qui s'est passé.

—Tu t'es fait une bosse sur la tête…

—C'est vrai ?

Notre conversation se poursuit de la sorte pendant la demi-heure suivante tandis que nous attendons les résultats de la radio. Ils arrivent finalement, et ils sont bons, mais le docteur veut que Vini passe maintenant un scanner, et l'attente reprend. Du moins pour moi. Vini croit qu'elle vient de se réveiller. Pendant que je discute avec le médecin, elle nous regarde d'un air perplexe, comme un enfant qui écoute ses parents parler des traites de la maison. Quand il s'en va, elle dit :

— Je ne sais même pas ce qui se passe. Je rêvais que je faisais des courses avec Adam.

— Non, tu t'es fait une bosse sur la tête.

— C'est vrai ?

Après trente autres minutes à ce régime, je commence à éprouver un désir irrésistible d'écouter des mots différents, comme le besoin de chips qu'on ressent lorsqu'on vient de se gaver de chocolat. J'en suis au point où j'envisage d'engager la conversation avec une vieille dame que j'entends gémir quelque part, quand soudain une main tire le rideau et un homme brun, de grande taille, avec une barbichette, fait irruption. Il me lance un regard et un « ça va ? » presque inaudible avant de se diriger vers le lit et de se pencher vers Vini. Elle le regarde et dit :

— Je croyais que je rêvais que nous faisions des courses. Ah, ah ! Voici donc Adam.

— Oui, Livvy, nous faisions effectivement des courses, dit-il en s'asseyant. Tu es tombée dans un escalier...

Je ne peux m'empêcher de l'interrompre :

— Un escalier ? Quel escalier ? Où ça ?

Il se tourne brièvement vers moi et répond :

— Près de la bibliothèque.

Il reporte son attention sur Vini, à qui je demande :

— Tu ne t'en souviens pas ?

Mais je m'aperçois aussitôt que je n'ai pas posé la bonne question, alors je recommence :

— Qu'est-ce qui s'est passé ?

Il me regarde à nouveau :

— Elle a trébuché et dévalé une volée de marches.

Sans blague, ai-je envie de répondre, mais je me retiens.

—D'accord, mais comment s'est-elle cogné la tête ? Vous étiez avec elle ? Est-ce vous qui avez appelé l'ambulance ? *(Et qui êtes-vous, bordel ?)*

Je ne prononce pas cette dernière phrase non plus.

—Où suis-je ? dit alors Vini.

—À l'hôpital, commence Adam.

Mais je n'ai pas la patience d'attendre :

—Racontez-moi ce qui s'est passé ce matin. S'il vous plaît.

—À l'hôpital ? Pourquoi ?

—Tu t'es fait une bosse sur la tête, Liv.

—C'est vrai ?

—Oui, mais maintenant tu vas bien.

Il se tourne vers moi :

—On marchait vers un grand magasin, Liv me parlait de ce qu'elle comptait acheter, et elle a dû se prendre les pieds dans quelque chose. Je ne sais pas quoi, ajoute-t-il aussitôt en me voyant ouvrir la bouche. Je tenais tranquillement sa main dans la mienne, quand d'un coup elle m'a échappé et est partie en vol plané.

—Oh non, elle a complètement quitté le sol ?

—Je croyais que je rêvais que je faisais des courses.

—Tu faisais vraiment des courses. Tu es à l'hôpital, maintenant. Non, elle ne s'est pas vraiment envolée. C'est juste une expression.

—Ah, OK.

Merde, évidemment que c'est une expression. Ce que je peux être bête !

—Je ne sais même pas ce qui s'est passé.

—Si, tu le sais, Liv, c'est juste que tu oublies tout le temps. Bref, elle a roulé sur ces trois marches comme un mauvais cascadeur, alors j'ai rigolé, parce que je pensais qu'elle allait se sentir vraiment idiote dans une minute, dès qu'elle s'arrêterait de dégringoler.

— Est-ce que j'ai une bosse sur la tête ?

— Oui ! C'est bien, tu commences à te souvenir !

— Et ensuite ?

J'aimerais qu'il cesse de lui répondre : ça ne sert vraiment à rien.

— Et alors, arrivée en bas de l'escalier, elle est tombée sur les genoux, mais comme elle avait de l'élan elle a continué et elle s'est cogné la tête sur le mur d'en face. (Il regarde la figure ruisselante de larmes de Vini, plein de tendresse.) Boum !

— Oh là là !

— Putain, dit Vini, avant d'éclater en sanglots.

— Oh, ne pleure pas, ma Livvy, lui dit Adam en écartant doucement ses cheveux de son visage. Pourquoi tu pleures ?

— J'sais pas.

— Tu as mal quelque part ? (Elle hoche la tête.) C'est où, que ça fait mal ?

— J'sais pas.

Eh bien, il y a là beaucoup d'autres questions sans réponses, si vous voulez mon avis. Par exemple, sur quoi a-t-elle trébuché ? Que s'est-il passé ensuite ? Pourquoi lui tenait-elle la main, et qui peut bien être ce type ?

— Écoutez, dis-je. (Ils obéissent tous les deux.) Ce que j'aimerais savoir, c'est comment vous êtes au courant de tout ça. Comment connaissez-vous Vini ? Pourquoi faisiez-vous des courses ensemble ? Êtes-vous l'un de ses clients ?

Il sourit.

—Non, pas du tout. Bon sang, je ferais qui, Groucho Marx?

Je secoue la tête.

—Non, elle ne l'a pas dans ses registres. S'ils n'étaient pas morts, on pourrait avoir les Marx Brothers au complet pour le prix d'un sosie.

—C'est vrai? Bref, non, je ne suis pas un sosie, je suis Adam… le petit ami de Livvy.

—Son « petit ami »?

—Oui, c'est comme un mari, mais en moins définitif.

—Ah, ah! Vous vous êtes rencontrés comment, alors?

—Au speed dating, il y a trois semaines.

Je le dévisage :

—Impossible!

—Mais si, c'est possible. Demandez à Livvy.

Je reste quelques instants à le foudroyer du regard, mais nous savons tous deux qu'il m'a eue. Sans parler du fait qu'elle est probablement incapable actuellement de se rappeler quelle est la partie du corps sur laquelle on passe habituellement une brosse à cheveux, il se trouve qu'elle ne m'a même pas encore annoncé qu'elle avait un petit ami. C'est inimaginable qu'elle me raconte comment ils se sont rencontrés.

—Dans ce cas, comment expliquez-vous que je sois allée à ce speed dating et que je ne vous aie pas vu?

—Je sais que vous y étiez. Je vous ai croisée. Souvenez-vous, Beth, je me suis cogné dans Livvy devant la porte. J'étais entré par erreur, je devais en fait couvrir le congrès de marionnettistes. Quand je l'ai aperçue, je ne pouvais en croire mes yeux. Je veux dire, ça faisait des années que j'essayais de la contacter…

— Oh là, attendez une minute. Comment connaissez-vous mon nom ? Qu'entendez-vous par « des années que j'essayais de la contacter »… ?

Mais à cet instant, par une illumination subite, je prends conscience que je connais cet homme, depuis des années, et je le remets soudain si facilement que je ne comprends pas comment j'ai fait pour ne pas tilter plus tôt.

— Oooh ! Adam Beresford ! Merde alors ! Adam, de Saint-Leo ?

— Pfff, il était temps ! C'est sympa de te souvenir de moi si vite, Beth, sachant que j'ai été assis juste derrière toi en cours de français pendant deux ans. J'aime bien ta nouvelle couleur de cheveux, au passage.

— Oh là là, je n'arrive pas à y croire ! C'est hallucinant ! Comment tu vas ? Qu'est-ce que tu deviens ? Tu habites toujours par ici ? Tu as gardé contact avec les autres ? Malcolm Riley ? Tessa Harris, qu'on surnommait « T'as vu mes cheveux » ? Rob le bricoleur ? Je n'y crois pas !

Il opine, enthousiaste, et arbore un sourire aussi large que le mien. Ça me fait vraiment bizarre de voir un corps d'adulte sous un visage qui aura toujours seize ans dans mes souvenirs.

— Ouais, Rob est marié, deux enfants ; il travaille dans une banque.

— Je ne te crois pas !

Il rit :

— Non, c'est vrai. Malc vit avec un certain Ian. Ils ont des chiens.

— Ouais, je ne suis pas surprise.

— Sans blague ? Bon sang, je suis resté comme deux ronds de flan quand je l'ai su ! Je n'en revenais pas.

—Arrête! Malc le Talc, avec sa serviette de piscine abricot?

—Ah oui, j'avais oublié ce détail. Oui, d'accord, maintenant que j'y repense…

—Je rêvais que je faisais du shopping… C'était un joli rêve, dit une petite voix en provenance du lit.

Adam Beresford avait un gros béguin pour Vini au lycée, mais elle était trop branchée eye-liner noir et rangers pour remarquer un garçon en pantalon noir bien repassé et en pull-over gris. Mais il ne l'a pas oubliée. Il est maintenant photographe pour le journal local, et c'est lui qui a pris des photos de Vini quand il l'a aperçue avec le capitaine Jack Sparrow, cette fois-là. Et pas parce qu'il a cru que la réputation de cette petite ville insignifiante était parvenue jusqu'aux oreilles de Johnny Depp à Hollywood et qu'il venait faire un saut. Adam a aussitôt reconnu Vini, et comme il avait son appareil sur lui il l'a photographiée. Et dire que pendant tout ce temps elle a cru qu'elle avait été repérée par un paparazzi!

—Tu imagines comme j'étais furieux quand j'ai été désigné pour suivre le congrès de marionnettistes? me confie-t-il. (Assis de part et d'autre du lit de Vini qui s'est assoupie, nous chuchotons pour ne pas la réveiller.) Je veux dire, des marionnettes?! Qui se rencontrent? Bordel, ce n'est pas de l'info, ça!

—Non, en effet.

—Mais finalement c'était pour le mieux, conclut-il en se tournant pour contempler avec amour le visage de Vini endormie. (Elle a la bouche ouverte et produit un petit grognement à chaque expiration.) Si je ne m'étais pas rendu dans cet hôtel ce soir-là, je ne serais pas ici en ce moment.

De toute évidence, Vini ne peut pas me donner sa version des événements pour le moment, mais il semble bien qu'Adam soit l'homme dans lequel elle s'est cognée devant la pièce du speed dating. Cela faisait des années qu'il essayait de la contacter – par le site d'anciens amis par lequel j'ai retrouvé Vini pour notre colocation –, et après l'avoir vu ce jour-là, et l'avoir aussitôt reconnu (contrairement à moi), elle lui a enfin répondu. Elle a dû le trouver à son goût en le rencontrant en chair et en os. Ils se sont vus clandestinement quelques fois, ce qui explique le gloss rose, et ensuite ils se sont donné rendez-vous au *mix n' match*.

— Elle n'est allée à ce truc que pour t'offrir une chance de rencontrer quelqu'un, ajoute-t-il à mon grand embarras.

Bordel, comme si j'avais besoin d'aide sur le chapitre de l'amour ! *En fait, j'ai un millionnaire très sexy en vue, merci beaucoup*, ai-je envie de rétorquer, mais je me retiens. Je regarde Vini, qui ronfle doucement, allongée là, et j'essaie très fort de lui en vouloir, mais malgré mes efforts je n'arrive pas à m'empêcher de sourire en la voyant. Oh, elle a tellement de chance ! Je veux dire, le binoclard dégingandé dont les yeux ne semblaient pas avoir de cils, qui l'a adorée de loin pendant plus de dix ans s'est transformé en un type sexy et baraqué, avec de longs cils fournis. Ah, les merveilles de la testostérone ! Je parie qu'elle regrette de ne pas avoir répondu à ses mails pendant ces dix années. Si seulement elle avait compris tout de suite qu'il n'aurait pas seize ans et une stature de crevette toute sa vie !

Chapitre 25

Établir des relations positives

Objectif à court terme : arriver au *Madeleine's* à 13 heures.
Obstacles : il est déjà 13 h 45.
Objectif à long terme : amener Rupert à me pardonner de lui avoir fait faux bond deux fois de suite. Et, plus tard, changer le plomb en or.
Obstacles : je n'ai pas de plomb.

Le médecin décide de garder Vini en observation, et ils parviennent même à lui trouver une chambre. Adam doit aller travailler quelques heures, du coup je reste avec elle alors qu'on la conduit en fauteuil dans les couloirs blancs aseptisés. Elle lance des regards éperdus autour d'elle, anxieuse et confuse à la fois. Elle continue à prétendre qu'elle vient de rêver, mais elle commence à former quelques souvenirs, maintenant.

— Je crois que j'ai eu un genre d'accident, dit-elle à un moment, d'une petite voix effrayée.

Une heure plus tard, on l'emmène pour son scanner, et encore quelques heures après les résultats arrivent : rien à signaler. Je suis tellement soulagée que je manque de me mettre à pleurer, mais je parviens à me retenir, parce que Vini elle-même est en larmes et que ça me semble incroyablement pathétique de sangloter alors que c'est elle qui souffre.

— Je vais juste aux toilettes, dis-je précipitamment en me ruant dans le couloir.

Je ne m'étais même pas aperçue que j'étais si inquiète à son sujet.

Adam finit par revenir, et je les laisse ensemble, avec sa grosse bosse bleue pour leur tenir compagnie. Et finalement, maintenant que je sais qu'elle va s'en sortir, maintenant qu'on n'a plus besoin de moi et que je commence à penser à ce que j'étais censée faire aujourd'hui, je m'autorise enfin à songer à Rupert. Je me suis interdit de regarder ma montre, ou aucune des huit cents millions d'horloges qui semblent se battre pour occuper chaque centimètre carré des murs de cet endroit maudit, mais, malgré cela, j'ai une mauvaise impression à propos de notre rendez-vous à déjeuner. Je suis certaine d'être en retard, et quand je finis par regarder l'heure, ma montre – et mon estomac – m'annoncent qu'il est 13 h 50. Crotte de bique de crotte de bique.

Dans la voiture, je sors mon téléphone portable et cherche le numéro du *Madeleine's*, puis je les appelle pour leur demander de dire à Rupert que je ne peux pas venir. Je ne vais pas le faire poireauter une nouvelle fois.

— Bien sûr, je vais l'informer, répond le maître d'hôtel. Souhaitez-vous que je lui transmette un message?

Oui, pouvez-vous lui dire que je suis folle amoureuse de lui et que je veux qu'il prenne immédiatement le volant pour venir me rejoindre sur le parking de l'hôpital où il me fera l'amour avec passion sous le panneau « Radiologie », s'il vous plaît?

Je ne prononce pas cette phrase. À la place, je dis simplement :

— Est-ce que vous pouvez juste lui dire que je suis vraiment désolée, s'il vous plaît ?

— Bien sûr.

Au moins, il ne fera pas le pied de grue une deuxième fois. Enfin, si, mais en tout cas il ne restera pas deux heures sans nouvelles de moi. Et je ne peux même pas y aller maintenant – ça me permettrait d'y être en retard, mais d'y être quand même – parce que j'ai un autre rendez-vous cet après-midi, à *Whytelys*.

Je songe un instant à laisser tomber le directeur de *Whytelys* pour rejoindre Rupert, mais je sais au fond de moi que c'est une mauvaise idée. Des deux contrats, celui avec *Whytelys* serait le plus lucratif, et je dois garder mon objectif à l'esprit. Je sais qu'on n'obtient rien sans travail et sans sacrifices, mais ça me donne un sentiment de tristesse, de lourdeur, de faire ce choix.

Je retourne au travail, la tête pleine d'images de Rupert désespéré, comme dans ma vision de la nuit dernière. OK, je sais que c'était seulement ma robe de chambre, mais je pense quand même à lui comme ça. Cela me fait du bien, et du mal, d'imaginer son désespoir.

De retour à mon bureau, j'ouvre ma messagerie professionnelle et vérifie mes mails. Rien de Rupert – sans surprise, puisqu'il est toujours en train de manger (avec tristesse) ces délicieuses croquettes de saumon –, mais j'ai reçu un mail de Richard et un autre d'un certain Anthony Davies. Il se présente comme le secrétaire particulier du directeur régional de *Whytelys*, confirme simplement le rendez-vous de cet après-midi et me donne des indications pour me rendre dans leurs locaux. Je reste quelques instants les yeux rivés sur le message, à me demander pourquoi je n'ai pas annulé cette réunion grotesque ou, au moins, mis Sean au courant pour qu'il puisse s'y rendre. Je jette un coup d'œil vers son bureau, mais il est à nouveau absent. De toute façon, après sa rencontre catastrophique l'autre jour, il ne voudrait sans doute pas s'exposer à l'humiliation de se présenter une deuxième fois. Alors pourquoi est-ce que j'y vais? On l'a déjà envoyé promener, qu'est-ce qui m'a pris de me mettre dans la situation de subir le même traitement?

La vérité, c'est que je pense que j'ai de meilleures chances que Sean de leur faire bonne impression et de m'assurer la signature du contrat. C'est ce que j'ai soigneusement évité de me dire à moi-même jusqu'à cet instant, mais à présent je peux être honnête. Cela m'arrive de plus en plus souvent.

Bon, et alors? Sean a échoué avec *Whytelys*, mais ça ne m'interdit pas d'essayer. Si je réussis, tout le monde en tirera des bénéfices, y compris Sean et son petit garçon. Je regarde l'itinéraire, et estime que je dois partir aux environs de deux heures et demie – dans une demi-heure. Très bien. Ça me laisse plein de temps pour écrire à Rupert.

Avant de commencer à rédiger ce message important et difficile, je jette un rapide coup d'œil à celui de Richard. Il dit qu'il a passé un merveilleux moment hier soir, espère que moi aussi et m'invite chez lui aujourd'hui après le travail pour « dîner et tout ce qui s'ensuit ». Je sais qu'il ne parle pas d'un café et de profiteroles. Je clique sur « Répondre ».

Richard,
Merci pour cette charmante proposition, mais tu peux te la mettre là où je pense, et l'enfoncer avec une lampe torche.

Beth.

Puis j'efface et je tape :

Tu as loupé le coche, chéri.

Je contemple longuement ces mots avant de finir par annuler l'envoi du message. Puis je supprime le sien.

C'est le moment d'écrire à Rupert. Je ne peux plus remettre à plus tard. J'ouvre un nouveau mail et commence à rédiger.

Cher Rupert,
Je sais qu'à moins de m'être fait renverser par un taxi au pied de l'Empire State Building et de me retrouver paraplégique, je ne peux pas avoir d'excuse pour ne pas vous avoir rejoint hier, mais j'ai une raison, même si elle n'est pas excellente. Juste au moment où je quittais précipitamment le bureau pour me rendre à la Curée, une ombre immense s'est étendue sur l'immeuble et le parking, et, quand j'ai levé les yeux, j'ai vu un énorme disque argenté qui flottait à trente mètres du sol. Après un rapide coup d'œil, j'ai continué à me hâter vers ma voiture. Par malchance, les créatures qui pilotaient cet étrange disque m'ont repérée, parce que j'étais la seule à être sortie du

bâtiment, alors ils m'ont enlevée avec leur rayon tracteur et m'ont gardée pendant vingt-quatre ans. Finalement, ils en ont eu assez de moi et m'ont ramenée sur la Terre, et par un phénomène inexplicable c'étaient le moment et le lieu exacts où ils m'avaient kidnappée. Imaginez ma joie quand j'ai découvert que j'étais à nouveau dans cette bonne vieille année 2006, à la même date et à la même minute où je me précipitais vers vous.

Je me suis mise à courir vers mon auto, espérant que vous seriez toujours en train de m'attendre, mais à ce moment-là j'ai glissé sur une plaque de verglas et je me suis tordu la cheville. Heureusement, c'était la gauche et en plus je ne m'étais pas fait trop mal, alors j'ai continué à me diriger vers la voiture. Mais soudain la lanière de ma chaussure s'est cassée, et la chaussure a volé. Je l'ai ramassée et j'ai repris mon chemin vers mon véhicule. Lorsque je suis montée dedans, je me suis aperçue que j'avais laissé mes veilleuses allumées et que la batterie était complètement à plat. Heureusement, il y avait justement un type qui s'installait dans sa voiture, garée à côté de la mienne, alors je lui ai demandé s'il avait des câbles. Il en avait, et j'ai pu faire démarrer le moteur. Juste quand je quittais ma place en marche arrière, une femme est passée derrière moi, et je l'ai renversée. Elle s'est relevée aussitôt, s'est excusée et est repartie. À cet instant, mon téléphone portable a sonné. Je me suis mise au point mort pour répondre; c'était ma mère qui appelait pour me dire qu'elle avait fait piquer le chien. Ensuite elle m'a annoncé qu'elle partait quelques jours à Lisbonne en dernière minute et qu'elle allait embarquer d'un instant à l'autre. Je lui ai dit au revoir et j'ai raccroché. J'ai passé la première et j'ai commencé à rouler, quand j'ai remarqué tout à coup que la voiture ne répondait pas correctement. De toute évidence, j'avais un pneu crevé. Je suis ressortie, ai rapidement changé la roue, suis remontée. J'étais enfin prête à prendre la route vers la Curée et à vous retrouver, mais, à ce moment-là, un de mes collègues est sorti en courant sur le parking pour me dire que notre directeur, Richard Love, venait de revenir d'un séjour de quatre mois au Portugal et qu'on m'attendait à l'intérieur pour une réunion. J'ai coupé le moteur et je suis rentrée en boitillant, lentement. Puis je suis retournée en boitillant, toujours lentement, à la voiture pour éteindre les veilleuses, et suis repartie en boitillant encore vers le bâtiment.

Donc, comme vous le voyez, j'ai fait tout ce que j'ai pu pour être à notre rendez-vous, mais malgré les nombreux coups de pouce du destin je n'y suis pas arrivée.

La raison de mon absence à notre déjeuner d'aujourd'hui est beaucoup plus terre à terre. Ma colocataire a eu un genre d'accident et souffre d'une commotion qui lui fait perdre la mémoire à court terme. J'ai dû rester la plus grande partie de la journée à l'hôpital à ses côtés pendant qu'elle passait une série d'examens, dont elle ne se souvient pas du tout. Je suis vraiment désolée de vous avoir fait faux bond deux fois de suite. On pourrait croire que j'essaie de vous éviter, mais je veux que vous sachiez que ce n'est absolument pas le cas. J'ai vraiment envie de vous rencontrer, si vous êtes toujours d'accord. Quand vous voulez, sauf cet après-midi car je dois faire réparer ma roue.

Faites-moi savoir si vous souhaitez toujours me voir, en dehors du travail. Je reste devant mon ordinateur pour attendre votre réponse.

Amitiés,

Beth.

PS: Au fait, j'ai cinquante-deux ans, maintenant.

Je le relis avant de l'envoyer. Puis je le relis une deuxième fois. Ensuite, je me lève, me rends à la cuisine, prépare une tasse de thé, fais pipi, reviens à mon bureau et le relis une troisième fois. Je pense que c'est bon. C'est suffisamment humoristique pour passer si jamais le rendez-vous à la Curée était une plaisanterie ; c'est assez long pour lui montrer, s'il était sérieux, que je suis sincèrement désolée de ne pas être venue et que je suis prête à me traîner à ses genoux pour me faire pardonner ; et c'est assez drôle pour le faire sourire et le pousser à me donner une autre chance. Oh, pourvu que ça marche ! Je clique sur « Envoyer », éteins l'ordinateur, et me mets en route vers *Whytelys*.

Les bureaux de leur équipe de direction sont en réalité très faciles à trouver. Ils sont situés dans un centre commercial de la ville la plus proche, au-dessus d'un magasin de déstockage de leur chaîne. Je suis un peu en avance, alors je jette un rapide coup d'œil aux pantalons brodés en élasthanne. Même à moins vingt-cinq pour cent, ça ne fait pas envie. À 15 heures pile, on me fait entrer dans une petite pièce étouffante où un homme assis derrière un bureau se présente comme Gregory Matheson, directeur pour notre région.

— Vous dites que vous êtes de Love Learning ? me demande-t-il tandis que nous nous installons.

J'ouvre la bouche, prête à expliquer en toute hâte pourquoi je suis là, étant donné qu'ils ont déjà rencontré et éconduit un autre membre de notre équipe, mais il continue à parler :

— J'ai déjà entendu ce nom, mais je n'en sais guère plus, je dois l'avouer. Nous n'avons encore jamais fait appel à un prestataire extérieur pour la formation, alors si vous arrivez à me convaincre, et je suis tout disposé à l'être, cela sera un grand saut pour *Whytelys*. (Il me tend la main avec un sourire.) Alors, allez-y. Persuadez-moi.

Je cale. Ce n'est pas le discours de quelqu'un qui aurait rencontré un représentant de Love Learning récemment et l'aurait jeté hors des locaux au milieu des rires. J'ai la gorge serrée par la confusion, et je ne peux plus parler. Je m'éclaircis la voix et déglutis plusieurs fois tout en faisant semblant de consulter des papiers que je tiens à la main. Il ne s'agit en réalité que des indications de trajet qu'ils m'ont envoyées, mais il ne peut pas le savoir. Je pointe le texte avec mon index et fronce les sourcils.

— Hum, je suis désolée, M. Matheson…

— Appelez-moi Greg.

— Oh, d'accord. Bref, je suis désolée, Greg, mais on m'a dit que vous aviez déjà rencontré un représentant de Love Learning ? Est-ce que c'est une erreur ?

Il acquiesce :

— Il me semble que oui, Miss Sheridan.

— Appelez-moi Beth.

— D'accord, Beth. Oui, comme je vous le disais, *Whytelys* n'a jamais envisagé de recourir à des prestataires de formation extérieurs jusqu'ici.

— Ah. (Je contemple à nouveau ma feuille.) Oh, non, attendez, désolée. C'est moi qui me trompe. J'ai mal lu. Quelle idiote ! D'après mes informations, vous avez eu un appel de Love Learning il y a à peu près deux semaines pour préparer cet entretien. Est-ce que c'est exact ?

Je sais que je prends des risques, mais je me sens soudain glacée, et j'ai besoin de savoir.

Il secoue la tête avec un petit rire.

— Je ne sais pas où vous allez chercher vos renseignements, Beth, mais je crains qu'ils ne soient à nouveau erronés. La seule personne de chez Love Learning à qui j'aie jamais parlé, c'est vous.

J'acquiesce, souriante, et regarde une fois de plus mon papier, mais j'ai à nouveau le souffle coupé. J'ai la tête qui bourdonne, la gorge serrée ; je toussote. Sean n'est jamais venu ici. Il ne les a même jamais contactés. Ce qui m'amène à me demander pourquoi il m'a dit qu'il l'avait fait ? Est-ce qu'il n'a raconté tout ça que pour m'impressionner ? Pour me donner envie de sortir avec lui ? Ça semble à peine croyable.

— Quelque chose ne va pas ? interroge Greg, penché vers moi, l'air inquiet.

Je secoue la tête et me tapote la poitrine en me raclant la gorge. Je croasse :

—J'ai un peu mal à la gorge. Désolée. Est-ce que je pourrais vous demander un verre d'eau, si ça ne vous embête pas ?

—Bien sûr. Rien d'embêtant à cela. (Il appuie sur un bouton dans son bureau et parle dans un interphone.) Anthony, pourriez-vous apporter un verre d'eau à Miss Sheridan, s'il vous plaît ?

Il a raison : ce n'était en effet pas très embêtant.

Anthony est incroyablement efficace, il arrive moins d'une minute plus tard avec un gobelet d'eau glacée. J'en bois la moitié, puis le pose par terre. J'ai le cerveau en ébullition, des impulsions électriques qui parcourent mes synapses, des millions de connexions qui créent de nouveaux chemins neuronaux. Toute cette activité fait apparaître une possibilité, mais vais-je oser la tenter ? En ai-je envie ?

—Je suis vraiment désolée, dis-je.

Il agite la main comme pour chasser mes excuses, un grand sourire aux lèvres, mais je le vois jeter un coup d'œil à sa montre. Je dois faire vite :

—Eh bien, comme je vous le disais, j'ai apparemment été mal informée au sujet de vos intentions vis-à-vis de Love Learning. Ce qui est plutôt une bonne nouvelle, je dois dire. Car ça aurait compliqué les choses.

—Ah ? Alors, vous n'êtes pas de chez eux ?

L'image de Richard surgit devant mes yeux, et je pense à toute la loyauté dont j'ai fait preuve à son égard, en vain, pendant toutes ces années. À Grace qui couchait avec lui pendant que j'abattais son travail. À Derek, toujours hautain ; à Skye, l'écervelée ; à Cath, tellement léthargique. Et à Sean qui m'a menti à propos de ce contrat, pour une raison qui m'échappe. Qu'est-ce que je leur dois, à présent ? Est-ce que c'est chez Love Learning que se trouve mon avenir, ou est-ce que je n'aurais pas plutôt besoin d'un gros changement ? Je pose mon bloc sur mes genoux et adresse un grand sourire à Greg, en le regardant droit dans les yeux :

— Non. Je suis une ancienne de Love Learning, donc je les connais bien, mais aujourd'hui je suis ici pour représenter une nouvelle société qui vient juste de se monter. Elle s'appelle Gagnez au Change.

— Ah, je vois. Eh bien, quelle sorte de formation propose Gagnez au Change pour une chaîne de grands magasins comme la nôtre, dans ce cas ?

Je n'arrive pas à croire que j'aie fait ça. Je suis dans ma voiture, sur le chemin du retour, et je pousse un petit cri de temps en temps. Ce n'est pas un hurlement de peur. C'est un gloussement d'excitation irrépressible. Il semblerait que je sois en train de me lancer dans les affaires, et Greg Matheson en a été informé presque avant moi. Je sautille dans mon siège en couinant de plus belle. J'ai l'impression que quelqu'un est en train de me gonfler un ballon dans la poitrine.

Bon. Ça ne rigole plus, maintenant. Je me suis débrouillée pour présenter l'offre de formation de Gagnez au Change de façon plutôt cohérente, je pense, et j'ai promis d'envoyer quelques brochures à Greg dans les cinq jours. Si j'arrive à décrocher un contrat avec *Whytelys* et un avec Horizon, je serai lancée, même si ça représente tellement de travail que je vais devoir embaucher quelqu'un tout de suite. Oh non, ça veut dire des entretiens d'embauche. Pour ça, il me faut des locaux. Je me demande où il y en a en ce moment.

Mais avant de trouver des locaux il va falloir que j'aie des commandes. Ce qui signifie que je dois faire des brochures immédiatement. Ce qui implique de passer la nuit sur l'ordinateur. Par chance, la politique de formation ridicule et tragiquement dépassée d'Horizon m'a obligée à suivre un stage sur PowerPoint quand je travaillais là-bas.

À 6 h 50 le lendemain matin, je suis devant la photo-copieuse couleur, en train d'imprimer discrètement la mini-brochure que j'ai passé la nuit à préparer. Ce n'est pas facile d'être discret quand on trimballe plus de deux cents feuilles de papier, mais personne ne me regarde, donc je pense que je n'ai rien à craindre. Ou du moins je ne vois personne me regarder. Et vous savez quoi ? S'il y a quelqu'un, quelque part, qui me regarde en secret, je m'en fous. Soudain, monter Gagnez au Change est devenu la chose la plus importante dans ma vie. Plus importante que le visage que je présenterais à quelqu'un qui m'observerait en secret, que de m'assurer que mes cheveux tombent bien, que je ne souris pas trop, que je ne fronce pas les sourcils Et c'est seulement maintenant que je m'aperçois que j'en avais envie depuis des mois. Sans doute depuis que Richard est parti.

Merde, non. J'en ai rêvé depuis des années, même quand Richard était là ; je pensais juste que je voulais Richard plus que ma propre boîte. C'est la raison pour laquelle l'un de mes objectifs à long terme était de devenir chef. Seulement, pas de Love Learning.

Finalement, maintenant que j'y pense, je ferais mieux de ne pas trop sourire quand même. Je ne voudrais pas que quelqu'un vienne voir ce que je fais, après avoir remarqué mon énorme sourire surexcité et s'être dit : « Il n'y a rien de très amusant à photocopier des brochures, alors qu'est-ce qui peut bien faire sourire Beth comme ça, près de la photocopieuse ? »

Je paierai pour l'encre et le papier, de toute façon, donc ce n'est pas un problème. Mais je ne suis pas certaine que Chas ou Richard souriraient en disant : « Oh, OK, Beth, fonce, utilise nos équipements pour monter une boîte rivale, c'est très bien », même si je leur disais que je vais leur envoyer un chèque dans quelques jours pour les rembourser.

De toute façon, pour l'instant, seul Derek est arrivé, et il est caché derrière un journal invraisemblablement encombrant, donc je suis presque certaine que personne ne m'observe. Ce qui, pour une fois, est une bonne chose. J'ai passé la majeure partie de la nuit à établir ces brochures puis à faire des recherches Internet sur les démarches pour monter une petite entreprise, alors je serais vraiment contrariée si quelqu'un déboulait maintenant en disant : « Qu'est-ce que tu t'imagines que tu vas faire, espèce de chienne ? »

En fait, avec de bons conseils, c'est étonnamment facile de monter une entreprise. J'ai déjà ma propre conseillère, qui m'aide à faire mon plan de développement. Au besoin, je peux travailler dans ma salle de séjour. Et, après Noël, j'ai un rendez-vous à la banque pour un prêt. C'est fou tout ce qu'on peut faire à 3 heures du matin avec Internet.

OK, les quarante photocopies ont fini de s'imprimer, je n'ai plus qu'à les rassembler et à les traîner jusqu'à mon bureau pour les agrafer.

Je pensais trouver le bureau désert en arrivant si tôt ce matin. À ma grande surprise, Richard était déjà là.

—Ah, merde ! a-t-il hurlé en me voyant. Putain, Beth, tu m'as fait peur !

Il avait des papiers à la main et les a lâchés brusquement.

—Désolée.

—Non, non, pas de problème. Alors. Tu es là, donc. En avance. Pour travailler, sans aucun doute. Très bien. J'ai toujours pu compter sur ma petite Bethy pour faire le travail, n'est-ce pas ? Eh bien, tu as l'air d'avoir du pain sur la planche, alors je vais… (Il s'éloignait de moi à reculons, en direction de la porte à panneaux.) … te laisser finir. Bon. OK. À plus, alors.

Oui, je sais, c'était vraiment bizarre, mais j'avais tellement peur qu'il ne se rende compte de ce que j'étais en train de faire, et puis je me suis sentie tellement rassurée quand ça ne s'est pas produit, que je me suis contentée de pousser un gros soupir de soulagement et de continuer à faire mes photocopies. L'original de la brochure était dans un sac de courses, alors il ne pouvait pas l'avoir vu, mais je me sentais tellement coupable que je n'aurais pas été étonnée que le mot « traîtresse » apparaisse brusquement sur mon front en lettres de sang.

Au moment où tout le monde arrive et où Derek émerge enfin de son journal, les brochures sont prêtes et bien en sécurité dans le sac de courses, qui est rangé dans le coffre de ma voiture (oui, je suis même arrivée à sortir sur le parking avec une grosse pile de papiers sans que Derek s'en aperçoive). On est le 20 décembre, il ne reste plus que deux jours avant qu'on ferme pour Noël, du coup on n'a pas de stage en cours pour la fin de la semaine. Pour la plupart, nous avons des tâches administratives et des recherches à faire, mais je n'arrive pas à me concentrer. Toute tâche que j'entreprendrais pour Love Learning maintenant serait en compétition directe avec, disons, moi, alors je serais vraiment bête de me mettre au travail.

C'est mon excuse pour ne rien faire aujourd'hui. Dieu seul sait ce que les autres ont inventé. Grace regarde des hôtels clubs en Turquie sur Internet, Derek fait des mots croisés, Ali et Skye ont disparu – sans doute dans la salle de formation, pour consommer leur relation. Peut-être que tout le monde est occupé en secret à monter sa propre boîte rivale et se justifie de ne pas travailler de la même manière que moi.

De toute façon, ça m'est égal. J'ai les doigts qui me démangent de vérifier si Rupert m'a répondu. J'ouvre ma messagerie, l'estomac tournant comme le tambour d'une machine à laver.

Je n'ai qu'un nouveau message, et il a été envoyé il y a environ dix minutes. Il vient de Rupert. J'ai le cœur qui bondit, et je me mets à sourire. Tout va bien. Il a eu mon mail, et ça lui a plu, il me pardonne de ne pas être venue hier ni lundi, et il écrit à présent pour arranger un autre rendez-vous, ce qui signifie que je peux encore décrocher le contrat avec Horizon et démarrer ma propre boîte, qu'on est toujours bons amis, et peut-être même plus. J'ouvre le mail.

Très chère Beth,
Comme vous le savez, j'ai reçu un message hier m'informant que vous n'étiez plus mon interlocuteur chez Love Learning et que toutes mes relations avec votre compagnie se feraient désormais par

le biais d'un autre représentant. J'en ai été très surpris, pour ne pas dire attristé, mais je suppose que vous avez de bonnes raisons. J'ai beaucoup apprécié votre mail d'hier qui m'expliquait pourquoi vous n'aviez pas pu venir me retrouver près de la fontaine lundi, mais j'en ai déduit, ainsi que de l'autre mail, que le retour de Richard Love avait entraîné des changements majeurs dans votre existence, qui vous empêchent désormais d'avoir des relations avec moi.

Ce fut un vrai plaisir de vous écrire, Beth. Vous avez, à vous seule, suffisamment recommandé Love Learning à mon attention pour me donner envie de réserver des prestations. Je ne peux qu'espérer que vous serez la formatrice qui viendra chez Horizon pour chaque stage, car je crois seulement en vous, pas en Love Learning.

Je vous souhaite le meilleur pour l'avenir, chère Beth, et beaucoup de chance dans tout ce que vous entreprendrez.

Votre ami,
Rupert de Witter.

Chapitre 26

Objectifs secrets

Objectif à court terme : décrocher le contrat avec *Whytelys*, trouver des locaux, recruter du personnel, définir un programme, décrocher le...
Obstacles : pas assez de temps.
Objectif à long terme : oublier Rupert. Épouser Brad.
Obstacles : oublier Rupert.

Je détaille les mots, essayant de comprendre la blague, de déceler le sens caché, mais je n'y arrive pas. J'ai à nouveau la gorge serrée par la confusion, sauf que, cette fois, c'est douloureux. Ça me fait si mal que la douleur gagne mes yeux, les fait larmoyer. Il ne veut rien avoir à faire avec moi. Si l'on avait fini par se rencontrer, cela aurait été pour qu'il me largue. C'est l'équivalent électronique d'un bouquet de fleurs : « Tu es plutôt mignonne, mais je ne veux pas de toi. »

Je me mords la lèvre et m'accroche de toutes mes forces à mon self-control. Non, tout va bien, je ne suis pas abandonnée. Brad continue à bien m'aimer. Et c'est réciproque. Je ne suis pas complètement indigne d'être désirée.

Cette idée me console pendant trois secondes, puis j'aperçois la brochure d'Horizon sur mon bureau, ouverte comme toujours à la dernière page, et Brad sort de mes pensées.

Je verrouille mon clavier et me lève, sans savoir réellement où aller ni que faire. Pour finir, je me rends là où vont toutes les filles quand elles se sont fait jeter par le millionnaire sexy dont elles sont tombées amoureuses au fil de trois semaines de marivaudage par courrier électronique et qu'elles ont désespérément besoin de réconfort et de consolation : dans les toilettes des femmes.

Il n'y a personne, heureusement, alors je m'approche du miroir et me regarde pleurer. En réalité, ça ne m'aide pas du tout. J'ai le nez rouge, les yeux qui larmoient, le visage fripé, l'air blessée et abandonnée, alors je reste à sangloter sur mon sort pendant quelque temps.

Après un moment, je décèle quelque chose d'autre, enfoui, à peine visible. Qu'est-ce que c'est que ça ? Je me penche vers le miroir pour regarder derrière les rêves brisés et l'amour à sens unique. J'arrête de pleurer, et mon reflet change : il devient concentré, sérieux, et, à ce moment-là, je vois clairement ce que j'avais seulement aperçu, et je me demande comment j'ai fait pour ne pas le distinguer dès le début. C'est de la détermination. Et de la frustration. De l'indignation. Du cynisme. De la fureur. C'est surtout de la fureur, une rage incandescente, bouillante, qui me brûle de l'intérieur alors qu'elle se répand dans mes veines comme de la lave en fusion. Dans ce message, Rupert ne me plaquait pas. Il réagissait au fait qu'il croyait que je l'avais plaqué, ce que je ne ferais jamais. Soyons honnêtes, personne ne le ferait. Je regarde avec horreur dans le miroir tandis que mon reflet se déforme devant mes yeux, comme le portrait de Dorian Gray, passant d'un seul coup de l'image d'une fille douce et blessée à celle d'une harpie vengeresse, méchante et aigrie. J'en suis presque à grogner comme un animal furieux quand je prends clairement conscience d'avoir été poignardée dans le dos. Par un de mes collègues. L'une des personnes avec lesquelles je travaille a menti à Rupert, m'a évincée, et s'est présentée comme son nouvel interlocuteur. Quelqu'un est en train d'essayer de me voler le contrat avec Horizon.

Toujours plantée devant le miroir, je plisse les yeux, plutôt impressionnée par ma propre rage farouche. Je ne vais pas rester les bras croisés. Je vais sortir d'ici pour récupérer Rupert et trouver qui est derrière tout cela. Parce qu'il est hors de question que je me rende sans me battre.

Je fonce vers la porte en tapant des pieds, tête baissée, poings fermés, crachant presque du feu par les naseaux. Puis je m'arrête, fais demi-tour, retourne vers le miroir et m'applique à lisser ces rides de colère et à retrouver mon doux sourire. Cela n'a rien à voir avec le fait de vouloir être jolie au cas où Richard, ou quelqu'un d'autre, jetterait justement un coup d'œil dans ma direction. Il s'agit de cacher ma fureur et de paraître béatement inconsciente de l'énorme machette qui dépasse de mon dos, afin que, si la personne qui m'a fait ça pose par hasard les yeux sur moi, elle ne s'aperçoive pas que je suis sur sa piste. De cette façon, elle ne ressentira pas le besoin de couvrir ses traces, ce qui me donnera de bien meilleures chances de découvrir qui cache des intentions, disons, euh, cachées.

Je suis de retour dans la pièce principale, et soudain tout me semble suspect. Ce qui, il y a seulement quelques instants, avait l'air d'un groupe de gens calmes et détendus – et certes pas très productif aujourd'hui – innocemment assis à leur bureau, ou occupés à se tourner les pouces, s'est transformé en une salle de travail chargée de murmures sinistres et de menaces à peine voilées. Y a-t-il des intentions cachées dans les coins ? Des micros dans les téléphones ? Ou dans le chapeau géant de Fatima ? À présent, plus rien n'est sûr, on n'est en sûreté nulle part. Comme un prédateur, je suis en alerte, les yeux allant et venant vivement, les oreilles dressées, le nez frémissant. Je donne quelques petits coups de langue pour goûter l'air et plisse les yeux. Mes papilles ne m'apprennent rien, mais ça me donne un sentiment de puissance. J'ai l'impression que mon dos se cambre et que les plumes de mon cou gonflent pour me faire paraître plus grande, et je ne suis pas loin de traverser les dalles de moquette sur la pointe des pieds, les bras ballants.

— Tu as une sciatique ? dit Cath derrière moi.

Je me retourne d'un coup :

— Quoi ?

Elle hausse les sourcils d'un millimètre :

— Ça m'arrive souvent, répond-elle avec un hochement de tête. J'ai reconnu les symptômes. Il faut que tu prennes des anti-inflammatoires : c'est la seule chose qui marche.

Je la dévisage :

— Bon, d'accord, merci, Cath.

Je me redresse un peu et continue mon chemin vers mon bureau, en observant mes collègues d'un œil nouveau. Je croise Ali, qui tient quelque chose dans son dos. Qu'essaie-t-il de me cacher? Je m'arrête près de l'armoire à dossiers et fais semblant de chercher une chemise pour le regarder s'approcher de la place de Skye. Et voilà que Skye lève les yeux vers lui, sourit, tend la main pour prendre quelque chose. C'est un petit objet rectangulaire et brillant – on dirait un mini-magnétophone! Est-ce possible? Oh non, ils ont fait ça ensemble, ils m'ont espionnée, ont installé un micro sur mon bureau et écouté tout ce que j'ai... Ah non, c'est une bouteille de parfum. Qui aurait cru que ça se ressemblait à ce point?

Pfff, c'est sans espoir. Je suis vraiment nulle pour repérer les gens qui semblent se comporter normalement alors que dans le même temps ils s'affairent derrière mon dos pour me voler mes idées et amener ma chute. Ce dont j'ai besoin, c'est d'une attitude de traître vraiment flagrante, mais celui qui m'a poignardée par-derrière ne va de toute évidence pas se mettre à me dévisager froidement en se frottant les mains et en ricanant.

Je lance un regard furtif tout autour de la pièce.

Non, j'avais raison, personne n'est en train de se comporter comme ça. Alors, comment faire? Il faut que j'utilise la puissance de mon intellect. Que je réfléchisse. Que je voie si mes synapses sont encore capables de faire ces connexions surprenantes. Je m'assieds, coudes sur la table, la tête dans les mains, concentrée. Allez, cerveau, c'est à toi.

Premièrement, c'est dans les jours qui ont suivi le retour de Richard que Rupert a reçu le message qui l'informait que je n'étais plus son contact.

Je ne dis pas qu'il y a un lien. Vous savez bien, tant que sa culpabilité n'a pas été démontrée, il est présumé innocent, pas vrai ? J'ai besoin de preuves avant d'aller montrer un coupable du doigt, que je le veuille ou non ; il mérite au moins cela. D'un autre côté, tout le monde sait que les coïncidences, ça n'existe pas, et que Richard est un sale connard dépourvu de morale. Je garde l'esprit ouvert, mais je n'ai aucun doute sur le fait que Richard soit le responsable. La question, c'est comment a-t-il eu vent de ce qui se passait avec Horizon ? Comment était-il au courant de mes contacts avec Rupert ? Je n'ai découvert la possibilité qu'Horizon veuille changer sa politique de formation qu'à travers ce minuscule article dans ce magazine nautique. Je suis absolument certaine que personne d'autre ne l'a lu. Ou si quelqu'un l'a lu, il n'a pas fait, comme moi, le lien avec nos prestations. À l'époque, Horizon n'avait pas fait état de ses intentions, ni lancé d'appel d'offres, donc leur situation n'était pas connue du public. Ce qui signifie que Richard a dû se faufiler partout pour m'espionner, comme un crotale vicieux.

Attendez. Je viens d'avoir une idée. J'ai peut-être tort de condamner Richard comme ça, finalement. Peut-être qu'Horizon a annoncé entre-temps qu'ils recherchaient un prestataire de formation, que Richard leur a envoyé un mail pour se présenter et leur a dit qu'il serait leur contact pour Love Learning. Ça fait un moment que je ne suis pas allée sur leur site Web, l'information s'y trouve peut-être. Oh, peut-être que j'ai mal jugé Richard – encore une fois – et que maintenant qu'il est revenu il travaille dur, tout simplement, pour faire rentrer de l'argent dans les caisses, qui en ont bien besoin. Bordel, il est là, à s'échiner comme un esclave pour essayer de sauver la boîte et nos emplois à nous tous, et je l'accuse sans raison d'espionnage industriel.

Aussitôt, je me connecte à Internet et fais une recherche sur Horizon Holidays. Je parcours l'ensemble de leur site, d'Aberystwyth à Zanzibar, mais je ne trouve aucune mention de nouveaux projets de formation. OK, bon, peut-être que ça ne veut rien dire. Peut-être que c'est dans les pages d'actualité économique... Non. Et si c'était sur les plus gros sites d'enseignement et de développement ? Non, ici non plus.

Donc Richard est bien un connard vicieux et rampant, qui a un porte-monnaie à la place du cœur. Si l'on excepte le fait que je me sois trompée sur lui pendant huit ans, on peut dire que je l'ai bien jugé.

Je me retrouve, sourcils froncés, à tapoter mon bureau du bout de mon crayon. Je suis sûre que si je parvenais à comprendre comment il m'a trahie j'aurais la certitude que c'est bien lui. Et si j'avais la preuve que c'est lui je comprendrais comment il a fait.

— Arrête avec ce bruit ! hurle quelqu'un à travers la pièce.

Je sursaute, et le stylo m'échappe, s'envole et atterrit par terre derrière mon bureau. Putain, maintenant je dois reculer ma chaise, me pencher, le ramasser...

Alors que je relève la tête, le crayon dans la main, mes yeux se posent par hasard sur un dos vêtu d'une chemise de lin. Je me fige sur ma chaise, toujours penchée à la recherche de mon crayon. J'ai à nouveau le cerveau qui crépite et je pourrais presque l'entendre alors qu'il passe tout seul d'une idée à une autre et tire des conclusions, avec autant de précision et de froideur qu'un ordinateur. L'idée découle de l'information qui découle de la prise

461

de conscience ; toutes les pensées et tous les sentiments se mélangent, s'étendent et se construisent pour produire, à la fin, un constat clair et lumineux que je sais, avec autant de certitude que j'ai jamais pu en avoir, qu'il est la vérité.

Il n'y a qu'une autre personne dans ce bureau qui connaissait les projets d'Horizon, et cette personne était au courant parce que je les lui avais racontés moi-même. Et si je l'ai fait c'est parce qu'il m'avait parlé des siens.

Sean.

Chapitre 27

Réflexion

MEEEEEERDE!

Chapitre 28

Recherche

Objectif à court terme : ne poignarder personne.
Obstacles : j'ai vraiment, vraiment, vraiment envie
de poignarder quelqu'un.
Objectif à long terme : décrocher le contrat avec
Horizon, et me venger par la même occasion.
Obstacles : j'ai vraiment, vraiment, vraiment
envie de poignarder quelqu'un.

Je suis toujours penchée en avant, le crayon à la main,
pétrifiée dans mon siège. Mes yeux sont rivés sur cette
chemise bleue en lin. Les secondes s'égrènent au ralenti,
mais je ne peux pas bouger. Mon sang, qui s'était figé,
finit par se remettre à circuler, d'abord lentement comme
un train à vapeur, puis de plus en plus vite.

—Des anti-inflammatoires, me dit Cath en passant
quelque part derrière moi, au loin.

Je commence à me redresser, sans détacher le regard
du dos de Sean, le cerveau toujours en effervescence,
des souvenirs, lointains ou récents, défilant dans ma
tête comme une bobine de pellicule. Sean qui, après
des années à travailler ensemble, me prête soudain
attention, le lendemain de mon changement de couleur
de cheveux – mais c'était aussi deux jours après l'annonce

par Chas de la menace de suppression d'emplois. Sa façon de sourire en plissant les yeux, son naturel évasif, le mystère planant sur ses loisirs.

Oh, euh, non, ça, c'est éclairci, en réalité. De toute évidence, il passait simplement du temps avec son petit garçon et ne voulait pas que tout le monde…

Merde. Je m'arrête à nouveau et reste immobile dans mon fauteuil. Son petit garçon. Mon cerveau assemble les pièces sans relâche, et le petit Alfie n'a jamais vraiment collé dans le décor. Les yeux toujours rivés sur le dos de Sean, je me lève et me dirige vers lui. En m'approchant, je vois qu'il consulte une page Web sur Horizon. Je fais semblant de ne pas m'apercevoir qu'il la réduit, faisant apparaître un site sur les quads. De mon air le plus innocent, je lui demande en passant :

— Un cadeau de Noël pour le petit Albie ?

— Pfff, punaise, j'aimerais bien, rétorque-t-il l'air de rien. Il adorerait en avoir un, mais je ne pourrai jamais me le permettre. Sauf si je gagne au loto.

— Oh, bon, on ne sait jamais, parviens-je à répondre, malgré le fait que je manque de m'étrangler lorsqu'il néglige de me corriger alors que j'ai appelé son fils « Albie ».

Je continue mon chemin, réussissant par miracle à mettre un pied devant l'autre sans trébucher ni me cogner comme quelqu'un qui ne regarde pas où il va. Je suis entièrement tournée vers l'intérieur, vers ce que Sean m'a raconté à propos de son enfant, au pub, l'autre soir. Je suis certaine qu'il m'a dit qu'il se prénommait Alfie – je m'en souviens parce que c'était le nom de mon chat quand j'avais douze ans. Mais, lorsque j'ai prononcé le prénom Albie, il n'a pas bronché. Ce qui signifie…

Je me dirige vers la porte du fond, parce que mon crâne est sur le point d'exploser et que je ne veux pas que quelqu'un le voie.

De retour dans les toilettes, je m'enferme dans une cabine et m'assieds. Je reste les yeux écarquillés et rivés sur la porte un moment, puis me prends la tête dans les mains. Je me suis fait avoir. Waouh, il m'a bien eue. Ce qui s'est passé m'apparaît à présent avec une telle clarté que je n'arrive pas à croire que je me sois laissé faire. J'ai toujours pensé que Sean n'était pas digne de confiance, un peu sournois et superficiel, le genre de personne qui vendrait la maison de sa grand-mère alors qu'elle habite encore dedans, mais j'ai changé d'avis sur lui. Il est parvenu à ce résultat simplement en évoquant Alfie.

Les images déferlent dans mon cerveau, l'une après l'autre : Sean qui me parle de son idée au sujet de *Whytelys*. Sean au pub, bouleversé, désespéré par la perspective de perdre son emploi. Sean mystérieusement devenu papa d'un garçon de neuf ans du jour au lendemain. Puis Richard qui me dit que tout le monde est au courant que j'ai décroché tous ces contrats à moi toute seule. Maintenant je vois, car à présent c'est évident que dans « tout le monde » il incluait Sean. Sean savait dès le début que s'il voulait signer un accord présentable, le premier endroit où commencer ses recherches n'était pas dans la grand-rue ou la zone industrielle, mais sur le bureau en diagonale derrière le sien.

Comment ai-je pu avoir raison à ce point à son sujet ?

Quelques instants plus tard, je me lève et rejoins ma place, où je m'assieds et me mets à contempler son dos avec une telle fixité que je ne suis pas surprise qu'il finisse par sentir deux marques de brûlure sur sa chemise et se retourner. Nos regards se rencontrent, et je sais, par la façon dont il écarquille les yeux, dont il entrouvre la bouche et dont il recule sans le vouloir dans son siège, que je ne lui présente pas un doux sourire. Nous nous regardons quelques secondes en chiens de faïence, puis il dit :

— Putain, Beth, tu ne pourrais pas arrêter de faire ce bruit avec ton crayon ? Ça me rend dingue !

Je m'immobilise, crayon levé, sans le quitter des yeux. Il soutient mon regard une seconde de plus, puis baisse les yeux.

— Eh bien, merci, marmonne-t-il avant de se remettre à poignarder un collègue dans le dos.

Je serre la pointe du crayon entre mes doigts. Eh bien, au moins je n'ai pas de raison de me sentir coupable de lui voler le contrat *Whytelys*. Je veux dire, techniquement, je ne lui ai même pas volé…

Oh non ! Le contrat *Whytelys*. Encore une fois, je comprends combien j'ai été bête. Brusquement, la raison pour laquelle ils n'avaient aucune idée de ce dont je parlais quand j'ai mentionné l'appel d'un autre représentant de Love Learning devient claire. Sean ne les a même pas appelés, et y a encore moins mis les pieds. Il a tout inventé. Il était trop flemmard pour faire des recherches ou préparer quoi que ce soit, ou même passer des coups de fil ou se déplacer pour des rendez-vous, alors il s'est inventé un faux contrat, un fils imaginaire, et il a pleuré en faisant semblant de se confier à moi pour gagner ma confiance et me faire révéler l'accord sur lequel je travaillais. Comme ça il pourrait avoir mon contrat, son emploi serait sauvé, et tout ça sans remuer le petit doigt. Je glisse hors de mon siège et me dirige vers lui à pas de loup, serrant dans mon poing le crayon bien affûté. J'ai lu qu'en plantant un crayon bien taillé dans l'oreille ou l'œil de quelqu'un on pouvait le tuer, presque à tous les coups. Alors, si je le lui enfonce, mais pas assez fort pour le tuer, je vais sans aucun doute lui causer d'atroces souffrances, et je ne prendrai que dix-huit mois ferme, ou quelque chose comme ça.

Bien entendu, je n'ai pas l'intention de le faire. Ce serait totalement stupide ; me faire arrêter pour des violences physiques me ferait sans aucun doute rater le contrat *Whytelys*. Ce que je dois faire, c'est le défier pour l'accord avec Horizon, découvrir ce qu'il a arrangé exactement et le lui voler à mon tour. L'air détaché, je passe à côté de sa place avec nonchalance pour me rendre à la cuisine, dans l'intention évidente de préparer une boisson.

— Qui veut boire quelque chose ? dis-je à la cantonade en m'arrêtant près du bureau de Sean.

J'essaie de laisser accidentellement mes yeux se poser sur ce qui s'y trouve, mais assez vite je dois renoncer à cette idée pour noter toutes les commandes de boissons chaudes. Crotte.

Je consacre le reste de la journée à trouver des excuses pour passer à côté de la place de Sean et traîner à proximité, comme Chevy Chase quand il tente d'arnaquer Dan Aykroyd dans le brillant *Drôles d'espions*. Malheureusement, tout ce que je réussis à faire, c'est à le rendre fou, et à lui faire clairement deviner que je m'ingénie à le surveiller discrètement.

— Encore un café ? demande-t-il d'un air ironique à 14 h 30, quand je me lève pour la troisième fois.

— Je vais aux toilettes, réponds-je avec nonchalance, en regardant exprès de l'autre côté pour bien lui faire comprendre que je ne cherche pas à voir ce qu'il fait.

— Tu as la courante ? me glisse-t-il aimablement à 14 h 50 quand je le frôle à nouveau.

— J'ai envie de chips, expliqué-je, ce qui bien sûr m'interdit de retourner à mon bureau sans le paquet en question.

Ce qui m'oblige à me rendre au bout du couloir pour en acheter au distributeur. Après avoir fait un petit détour par ma place pour prendre de la monnaie.

— Tu te dégourdis les jambes ? est le commentaire de 15 h 25, alors que je m'étire et bâille à proximité de sa table.

— Je cherche une agrafeuse, réponds-je en me penchant pour l'attraper.

Finalement, il ferme sa session, rassemble ses papiers et quitte le bureau. Par la fenêtre, je le vois rejoindre sa voiture, jeter un coup d'œil à sa montre, s'engouffrer dans son véhicule et s'éloigner.

J'aurais pu le suivre, mais je doute qu'il travaille encore ce soir. Il va plus vraisemblablement assister à un combat de coqs illégal, ou jouer d'importantes sommes au poker dans un bar enfumé. Au lieu de le filer, j'ai décidé de concentrer toute mon énergie à des recherches de-la-mort-qui-tue au sujet d'Horizon. Je veux tout connaître sur cette entreprise : leurs perspectives de bénéfices, performances boursières, plan de retraite, taux de renouvellement du personnel, avantages annexes, risques, pourcentage de satisfaction des employés. Je dois savoir quel type de voitures conduisent les hauts dirigeants, combien d'enfants ils ont, et où leurs épouses aiment partir en vacances. C'est la meilleure façon de me venger de Sean.

Je suis tellement absorbée par cette histoire d'Horizon que, quand je lève le nez de mon ordinateur, tout le monde est rentré chez soi, et je me retrouve toute seule. Je consulte l'horloge : 18 h 10. Waouh ! Ça fait deux heures que je travaille là-dessus. Je m'étire. J'ai faim. Je quitte ma chaise et regarde tout autour de moi, dans le bureau désert. C'est un peu sinistre, sans aucune autre présence que la mienne ; tout est immobile, silencieux comme la chambre d'un enfant endormi. Je cligne des yeux, et il me semble voir la photocopieuse bouger légèrement, avec un bruit sourd, comme les jouets qui prennent vie dans *Toy Story*. Mais ce n'est pas le cas. Alors que je commence à me détourner, secouant la tête avec un sourire, j'entends à nouveau quelque chose. Un coup sourd, étouffé, qui ne vient pas de la machine inanimée et parfaitement immobile, mais de derrière la porte à panneaux.

De toute évidence, Richard est là, travaillant tard également, même si ce qu'il peut bien faire est un mystère. Je suis aussi certaine qu'on peut l'être qu'il n'est pas en train de se débattre pour mener à bien des recherches intensives dans une tentative de dernière minute de décrocher le contrat et le cœur de Rupert de Witter.

Peu importe ce qu'il fabrique. Ça ne me regarde pas. Si j'arrive à obtenir un accord avec Horizon et *Whytelys* pour Gagnez au Change, je quitterai cette boîte, et plus rien de ce que Richard pourra faire ne m'intéressera jamais. Enfin, si l'on excepte le fait que je vais surveiller tous ses faits et gestes compulsivement à partir d'aujourd'hui. Je ne peux pas laisser mon principal rival prendre de l'avance sur moi.

Quand je détourne les yeux de la porte à panneaux, l'idée me traverse l'esprit que mon vrai rival, en ce moment, c'est Sean, et que c'est maintenant, avec personne dans les parages, que se présente la meilleure occasion pour moi de mener une petite enquête discrète : c'est-à-dire de passer son bureau au peigne fin pour voir ce qu'il mijote.

Un œil toujours sur la porte en bois, je me lève et m'approche de sa place. Cela ne me procure presque aucun plaisir de fouiller dans ses affaires, croyez-moi, mais c'est la guerre, et c'est lui qui a ouvert les hostilités. Aucun son ne me parvient du bureau de Richard, alors je m'empare prestement des quatre dossiers qui traînent sur la table de Sean et les parcours.

La sensation capiteuse de me trouver sur le point de faire une importante découverte se dissipe aussitôt, et je laisse retomber mes épaules. Tous ces dossiers contiennent d'authentiques préparations de formation et des notes de recherche. Merde. Je les remets soigneusement en place, espérant ne pas me tromper d'ordre, et m'attaque aux tiroirs. C'était évident qu'il n'aurait rien oublié de suspect sur le dessus de sa table, c'était idiot de ma part de chercher là. Les gens qui ont des choses à cacher les rangent toujours dans les tiroirs de leur bureau. Et les ferment à clef, apparemment. Putain, ça va de soi ! Celui du bas aussi. J'essaie encore celui du haut, juste au cas où je n'aurais pas tiré assez fort, puis à nouveau celui du bas, secouant si fort que le meuble lui-même se met à bouger. Aucun des deux ne cède.

Je retourne à ma place en traînant les pieds et m'assieds. Eh bien, c'est à peu près tout ce que j'avais comme idées. Je repense soudain à un encadré que j'ai vu dans le journal quand j'avais dix-sept ans, qui annonçait que les services secrets recrutaient. Je l'avais déchiré et étais en train de remplir le formulaire, enthousiaste, la tête pleine de voyages, de destinations exotiques et de missions dangereuses, lorsque Maman était entrée et m'avait dit :

— Agent secret, ma chérie ? Ça ne te correspond pas vraiment, si ?

Sauf que… mes yeux tombent sur la corbeille à papier, sous le bureau de Sean. Il y a une chance infime… Obéissant à une impulsion subite, je me lève et vais la chercher, puis la pose par terre, à côté de mon fauteuil. À ce moment-là, la porte à panneaux s'ouvre à la volée, et Richard apparaît, une liasse de papiers à la main.

— Merde ! s'écrie-t-il.

En même temps, je hurle :

— Putain !

Nous restons à nous dévisager, les yeux écarquillés, tous deux apparemment horrifiés d'avoir été pris la main dans le sac. Sauf que je suis innocemment assise à mon poste, une corbeille à mes pieds, et qu'il émerge de son propre bureau, portant des documents. Toutes les apparences suggèrent que nous sommes tous deux parfaitement innocents, mais nous agissons comme si nous étions coupables. J'ai le cœur qui bat si fort que ça fait trembler tout mon corps, et cela n'a rien à voir avec les épaules viriles de Richard.

— Ah, tu es encore là, finit-il par dire, sa main libre toujours sur la poignée de la porte et sans faire aucun mouvement pour pénétrer plus avant dans la pièce.

— Ouais.

—Hum. Moi aussi. J'étais juste… euh…

Il regarde derrière lui et fait un geste vague en direction de sa table.

—OK.

J'ai du mal à le regarder dans les yeux avec la corbeille suspecte posée à mes pieds et la conscience de la traîtrise que je suis en ce moment même en train de fomenter, mais il éprouve également des difficultés à maintenir le contact visuel. En réalité, il a vraiment l'air mal à l'aise – il gigote, se dandine d'un pied sur l'autre, se racle la gorge, tripote sa cravate.

—Bon, finit-il par déclarer, en soulevant les papiers qu'il tient à la main, je ferais mieux de descendre ça à…

Je n'ai pas la moindre idée de ce qu'il veut dire, mais je hoche la tête d'un air encourageant.

—Oh ouais, tu as raison.

Plus vite il s'en va et me laisse le champ libre, mieux c'est.

Il ferme le battant derrière lui, hésite un moment, finit par lancer « à plus » et s'en va.

Hum. Il mijote manifestement quelque chose. C'est la deuxième fois aujourd'hui que je le fais sursauter et que je le vois sur ses gardes. Je contemple sa porte quelque temps. Je devrais sans doute aller y mettre le nez, au cas où. Mais au cas où quoi ? Au cas où il aurait déposé une bombe ? À moins qu'il n'ait été en train de faire des photocopies, tard le soir, aux frais de la princesse ? Quel crime horrible ! Nan, laissons tomber. On s'en fiche. Il faut que je découvre ce que Sean trafique.

Je m'agenouille par terre à côté de la corbeille et regarde son contenu. Par chance, Chas a insisté pour que tous les déchets organiques soient jetés dans la poubelle de la cuisine. Cath a réagi à cette exigence par « Et merde, je vais continuer à jeter mes ordures dans la corbeille à papier, et c'est tout », parce que la cuisine est tellement loin de sa place. Mais ce n'est pas le cas de Sean. Sa corbeille est presque vide, je n'y trouve que quelques feuilles de papier roulées en boule. Je les repêche toutes et les étale sur le sol. Il y a quelques pages A4 de vieilles formations sur « Le Service Après-Vente », avec quelques corrections gribouillées à la main dans les marges, ce qui signifie qu'en fait il s'est consacré à du bon travail honnête aujourd'hui. Mais ces feuilles pourraient être là depuis un moment : les poubelles ne sont pas vidées tous les jours.

OK. Rien d'intéressant jusqu'ici. Je les roule à nouveau en boule en essayant de rétablir le plus exactement possible leur forme initiale et les replace dans la corbeille. Les trois pages restantes semblent provenir d'un carnet.

Cela paraît prometteur. Enthousiaste, je les lisse sur le sol, mais je m'aperçois très vite qu'elles sont toutes vierges. Pour l'amour du ciel, ce type n'a jamais entendu parler d'écologie ?

Sur une intuition subite, je saisis un crayon gras et en frotte doucement la première feuille. J'ai vu faire ce geste si souvent dans des films que ça doit forcément marcher. Tous ces scénaristes différents ne peuvent quand même pas se tromper, si ?

Malheureusement, on dirait bien. Tout ce que j'obtiens, c'est une tache grisâtre avec quelques lignes blanches timides au milieu, complètement illisibles. Je froisse à nouveau le papier et le jette dans la corbeille dont il vient. Ce genre de trucs a le don de me mettre en colère. Je veux dire, c'est incroyable le nombre de bobards qu'on nous raconte tous les jours dans les films, simplement parce que ce sont des moyens faciles de faire avancer l'intrigue. Il faut que le héros arrive à trouver où le méchant a emmené l'otage, et, bien sûr, tous les méchants éprouvent un besoin irrépressible de noter le nom de l'hôtel et le numéro de chambre, de même que des indications claires et précises pour s'y rendre, sur le bloc à côté du téléphone, au stylo-bille, en appuyant bien fort, puis d'arracher la feuille et de l'emporter, laissant une empreinte bien nette derrière eux.

Pas Sean, cependant. Quoi qu'il ait écrit sur ce carnet, il n'a pas pressé assez fort. Ce connard sournois.

Je me rassieds sur ma chaise. Encore une fois, j'ai épuisé toutes les solutions qui s'offraient à mon esprit, et je dois admettre qu'elles n'étaient pas si nombreuses. Bordel de merde ! Je contemple les deux dernières pages, me demandant ce que je vais bien pouvoir faire, à présent. Hum. C'est vraiment étrange qu'il ait jeté trois feuilles blanches. Ça n'a pas de sens. Je me l'imagine, assis à son bureau, le calepin ouvert, arrachant une page, la roulant en boule et la laissant tomber dans la corbeille. Puis il recommence, deux fois. Alors il ferme le bloc, le range dans le tiroir, donne un tour de clef. Pourquoi ferait-il une chose pareille ?

Parce que, Beth, espèce de demeurée, il ne voulait pas que quelqu'un vienne colorier la première page de son carnet avec un crayon gras et découvrir ce qu'il mijote, voilà pourquoi. Oooh ! Mon cerveau s'est remis à fonctionner. Je me rue sur les deux feuilles restées sur le sol et passe ma mine sur la première. Je vois apparaître quelques lignes verticales et horizontales de plus, mais je n'arrive toujours pas à lire. Je la jette rapidement à la poubelle et attrape la troisième, pour la frotter comme on gratte une carte de jeu. Cette fois, je touche le gros lot :

**LANGHORNE HOTEL, VENDREDI, 14 H
SALON WILLOUGHBY
MISE EN PLACE JEUDI À PARTIR DE 18 H**

Bingo ! Je me redresse, toujours accroupie, tandis qu'une délicieuse onde de plaisir me parcourt. Ah ! Je t'ai eu, espèce de faux-cul vicieux ! Toutes ces semaines à regarder des rediffusions de *Clair de lune* et de *Jonathan Creek* quand John Wilson, de l'agence immobilière, m'a plaquée avec un bouquet de fleurs, ont fini par payer. Qui aurait besoin des services secrets, alors qu'il suffit de s'affaler devant la télé ? Va te faire foutre, maman.

Je ne le pensais pas. Pardon, maman.

OK. C'est le moment de passer à l'action. Je remets rapidement les feuilles en boule et les repose dans la corbeille, mais, en la rapportant à sa place, l'idée me vient que Sean est probablement le genre de branleur méfiant et rusé qui dispose le vieux papier d'une certaine façon dans sa poubelle, ou pose quelque chose d'invisible en équilibre sur le dessus, afin de savoir si quelqu'un a essayé de l'espionner et de fouiller dans ses ordures. Pfff, il faut être un sacré connard pour soupçonner ses propres collègues de fouiner dans sa corbeille en son absence. Pauvre type ! Je contemple la poubelle. Il est hors de question que j'aille racler le fond avec mes ongles pour retrouver et ramasser un cheveu. Même pas la peine d'y penser.

Une demi-heure plus tard, je roule joyeusement vers la maison dans ma voiture remplie de détritus, laissant toutes les corbeilles du bureau mystérieusement vides. Enfin, j'espère que ce n'est pas trop mystérieux. Je préférerais que chacun suppose, en arrivant demain matin, que la femme de ménage les a vidées au début de son service, avant notre venue, et que, de cette façon, tout papier incriminant qui s'y serait trouvé est passé inaperçu. Sean n'aura aucun moyen de savoir que je suis restée tard ce soir et que j'ai découvert son petit arrangement avant qu'on ait vidé les corbeilles.

Ce qui ne me laisse plus qu'une chose à faire : appeler le *Langhorne Hotel* pour vérifier que les notes de Sean dans son carnet correspondent bien à ce que je crois, c'est-à-dire à une présentation par lui-même des prestations de Love Learning à Horizon Holidays. Puis il faudra que je rassemble toutes mes informations sur Horizon afin d'offrir un exposé encore meilleur, plus détaillé et plus convaincant. Il faudra que j'arrive bien en avance au *Langhorne Hotel* vendredi pour disposer mes affaires sans que Sean m'aperçoive et voie clair dans mon jeu. Puis il faudra que je réfléchisse à une façon de saboter sa présentation et de me glisser habilement pour faire la mienne à la place, gagnant ainsi le contrat et du même coup suffisamment de travail pour lancer ma propre société de formation et assurer un emploi pour moi et deux employés.

OK, techniquement, ça fait quatre choses, mais elles se résument toutes à une seule : conquérir Horizon.

Et peut-être Rupert avec.

Chapitre 29

Action décisive

Objectif à court terme : poignarder Sean dans le dos sans pitié, retourner le couteau dans la plaie et casser le manche, lui arracher tout ce qu'il aurait en main, le pousser de côté et l'abandonner par terre, impuissant, dans une mare de bave, anéanti et sanguinolent.

Obstacles : euh… non, rien.

Objectif à long terme : j'ai du mal à voir plus loin que le court terme pour le moment.

Obstacles : voir ci-dessus.

Le salon Willoughby est silencieux et immense. Des festons de verdure artificielle piquetée de baies rouges et de petites lumières blanches ont été arrangés avec goût au plafond. La moquette, épaisse, étouffe les sons, et n'importe qui pourrait se promener ici, ramassant les sachets pour les ouvrir et les fouiller, les remplacer par d'autres, sans que personne s'en aperçoive. Quelqu'un a disposé quatre rangées de six chaises. Sur chaque siège, on a posé une brochure Love Learning en papier glacé, bleu marine et blanc, et un sachet de cadeaux d'entreprise avec des bons de spa, du papier à lettres, des échantillons d'eau de Cologne et un beau stylo. Devant les chaises, quelqu'un a installé un rétroprojecteur sur un guéridon et une boîte de onze diapositives. Dans le fond de la salle, deux grandes tables mises bout à bout sont chargées d'une vingtaine de tasses et de soucoupes, d'un assortiment de boissons – une Thermos de thé, une autre de vin chaud, de l'eau, du jus d'orange et du café. Il y a aussi plusieurs plateaux d'argent – qui annoncent des pains d'épice et des biscuits à venir –, et je les contemple, stupéfaite. Où Sean peut-il avoir la tête ? Il sait très bien que Love Learning ne peut pas se permettre de telles largesses pour le moment. Heureusement que j'ai décidé de régler la facture moi-même.

Derrière ces tables, une paire de rideaux rouges, très épais, barre l'accès au reste de la pièce, qui serait beaucoup trop grande sans cela. C'est derrière ces tentures que je suis cachée.

Par chance, cette deuxième partie de la pièce est déserte ce matin. Je ne sais pas ce que j'aurais fait si une réunion ou une formation s'étaient tenues là. Enfin, si, je sais. Je serais quand même debout au même endroit, à lancer des coups d'œil répétés entre les pans de velours, priant pour que ma présence inexplicable autant que silencieuse au fond de la salle ne distraie pas trop les participants.

Nous sommes vendredi matin, il est à peu près 8 h 30. J'ai passé les deux derniers jours à faire désespérément semblant de rien, tout en restant tard, en arrivant tôt, et en évitant studieusement tout contact avec les autres. Je crois que personne ne s'est aperçu de rien.

Brad m'a appelée, et nous avons bavardé au téléphone, mais je n'ai pas pu trouver le temps de le voir. Nous passons toute la journée de demain ensemble, cela dit.

479

Je crois qu'il a de grands projets, peut-être au bord de l'eau. J'aimerais bien une longue excursion en bateau, avec un déjeuner un peu chic. Ou bien une promenade en barque sur le canal, avec un pique-nique au champagne, et du saumon fumé. Il a téléphoné mercredi, pendant que j'étais au travail, et a laissé plusieurs messages adorables. Le premier disait :

« Salut, Libby, ce n'est que moi, Brad, ton amant de trois minutes ; je me demandais si techniquement on était un couple ou si j'étais sans m'en apercevoir devenu un harceleur ? Si c'est le cas, je suis vraiment désolé. Je vais aller me rendre de ce pas. »

J'ai souri en écoutant ces mots et j'allais prendre le téléphone pour l'appeler, quand il a émis un nouveau bip pour m'indiquer qu'il y avait un autre message, laissé quatre minutes après le premier :

« C'est encore moi. Bon, la police n'a rien voulu savoir. Ils disent que si la personne que je suis "censé" – ce sont leurs termes exacts – harceler n'a pas porté plainte, alors, techniquement, je ne suis même pas un harceleur ! C'est une faille intéressante, non ? En tout cas, puisque tu n'as pas déposé de plainte, j'en déduis que nous sommes toujours un couple, et je vais donc continuer à te téléphoner et à te poursuivre jusqu'à ce que tu n'en puisses plus et que tu finisses par me parler. »

Après un autre bip, le troisième message, laissé quatorze minutes plus tard, a commencé :

« Je me disais que je m'étais peut-être mal exprimé tout à l'heure, ce qui expliquerait que tu ne m'aies pas rappelé. Bon, au cas où tu aurais le moindre doute, j'aimerais vraiment te voir. Tout de suite, si possible. Bon, bien sûr, je te vois en ce moment même, mais ce n'est pas pareil, à travers des jumelles. S'il te plaît, appelle-moi dès que tu peux. Il y a un point sur lequel je voudrais vraiment… me jeter à l'eau. Salut. »

Le temps que j'aie sorti de ma voiture le contenu de toutes les corbeilles du bureau, trié les canettes de Coca et autres reliefs de repas dégoûtants (apparemment Cath n'est pas la seule qui ne s'embête pas à respecter la règle du tri des ordures), mis tout le papier dans des sacs spéciaux prêts à être collectés lundi pour le recyclage, puis passé la soirée à écrire ma présentation de-la-mort-qui-tue pour Horizon, il était plus de onze heures et demie du soir lorsque j'ai entendu ses messages, alors je ne l'ai pas rappelé. Ce serait indélicat et grossier de le déranger aussi tard, et je ne sais même pas s'il partage son appartement avec quelqu'un, alors je pourrais me retrouver à réveiller plusieurs personnes. En supposant qu'il soit chez lui quand j'appelle. Et, si ce n'est pas le cas, je ne voudrais certainement pas interrompre… ce qu'il pourrait être en train de faire à 23 h 40.

D'un autre côté, avec qui un célibataire indépendant d'une trentaine d'années pourrait bien cohabiter, je me le demande. S'il s'agit de ses parents, je ferais mieux de prendre de la distance. J'ai déjà vu comment ce genre de situation se terminait. Il y aura des remarques narquoises, des commentaires perfides sur ma coiffure ou mes habits, de la nourriture que je ne peux pas manger, des sorties auxquelles je ne peux pas participer. Finalement, les efforts entrepris pour me faire paraître stupide ou dépourvue d'éducation provoqueront une terrible dispute entre Brad et moi, qui débouchera sur une confrontation entre sa mère et moi, où elle niera tout en bloc, tout sucre tout miel, puis le prendra dans ses bras et m'adressera un sourire triomphant par-dessus l'épaule de Brad. Je préfère éviter.

Je suis vraiment allée me coucher, mais en moins de dix minutes je m'étais relevée pour l'appeler. Où avais-je la tête ? Bien sûr que non, il n'habite pas avec ses parents. Et si c'est le cas téléphoner à minuit est une bonne façon de m'en rendre compte.

Bon, ce n'est pas le cas. Ou, en tout cas, c'est ce qu'il affirme, et c'est déjà bien. S'il vit en réalité avec eux, et ment à ce sujet, ça veut dire que j'ai déjà gagné la bataille. Bref, nous avons eu une conversation charmante, qui a duré plus de deux heures et s'est achevée quand il m'a demandé de passer la journée avec lui samedi. Il a quelque chose d'important à me dire, apparemment.

— Pourquoi tu ne me le dis pas maintenant ?

Le silence s'est éternisé avant qu'il réponde :

— Non, ce n'est pas possible. Je veux voir ton visage. J'ai besoin de connaître ta réaction.

— Écoute, si tu habites avec tes parents, dis-le-moi. Ce n'est pas la peine de me raconter des salades.

Il a ri.

— Mais je ne mens pas ! Je te l'ai dit, mes parents vivent avec mon frère, à la sortie de la ville.

— OK.

— Pourquoi tu prends ce ton suspicieux ? C'est vrai !

— Oui, d'accord. Pas de problème. Je te crois.

— Parfait, alors.

Après une courte pause, il a pris une grande inspiration, et, quand il s'est remis à parler, c'était comme si quelqu'un avait augmenté les basses dans sa voix. Elle était devenue grave et sérieuse, un peu rocailleuse

– manifestement chargée de l'émotion profonde de me dire la vérité.

— Ce n'est pas dans ma nature de mentir, Libby. Je veux que tu le saches.

J'ai senti un frisson me parcourir, et mon ventre s'animer de chaudes vibrations. Il m'avait déjà parlé avec ce timbre-là. J'ai laissé un petit silence avant de répondre, pour qu'il comprenne que je partageais son sérieux et son émotion.

— Moi non plus. J'ai horreur de ça. Les gens qui mentent pensent juste que tout le monde est stupide à part eux. Sans oublier qu'une fée meurt à chaque mensonge prononcé.

— Ah, Libby, tu as bien raison.

OK, bon, techniquement, c'est mon nom, donc ce n'est pas un bobard. J'ai décidé de lui en parler, mais je ne peux pas le faire au téléphone, et je ne l'ai pas vu depuis quelques jours, du coup je n'ai pas eu l'occasion. Mais si je survis à la journée d'aujourd'hui, quand je saurai si je vais ou non quitter Love Learning ce soir, alors je le lui dirai. On a toute la journée de demain pour se révéler nos secrets.

Il n'y a que deux possibilités pour la journée qui s'annonce : soit elle sera fantastique, et ce sera le plus beau jour de ma vie, je vais assurer le contrat avec Horizon et quitter Love Learning, exactement comme Richard Cœur de Pierre est parti d'Horizon il y a toutes ces années, sauf que cette fois-ci je m'écarte de lui, et de Grace, ainsi que de tous les autres, la tête haute, réprimant à grand-peine un rire hystérique et ravi ; ou… pas. Je n'ose même pas mettre de mots sur ce que l'autre scénario pourrait impliquer. Je fonctionne par tranches de dix minutes, pour le moment. Si j'arrive simplement à me sortir de la présentation de cet après-midi, il sera toujours temps de penser aux résultats.

Soudain, mon téléphone sonne dans mon sac. Je vois que c'est Richard qui tente de me mettre la main dessus. Je lâche le rideau et me retourne instinctivement, comme s'il était là, avançant vers moi à grands pas, grognant de rage et se demandant ce qui me prend d'essayer de saboter les efforts de Sean pour décrocher un gros contrat, mais la pièce est toujours vide. Je reporte mon regard sur le téléphone que je tiens à la main, le doigt posé sur la touche « Décrocher », mais je n'appuie pas. Je ne veux pas lui parler maintenant. Ni plus tard. Jamais, en fait. Il faudra pourtant que je regagne le bureau. Je ne peux pas me permettre que Sean s'interroge sur les raisons de mon absence. Il n'a pas l'air d'être sur le point d'arriver, de toute façon, donc c'est maintenant que je dois mener une action décisive.

Aussitôt, je me glisse entre les rideaux pour pénétrer dans la moitié de la pièce que Sean a réservée et passe quelques instants à remplacer toutes les brochures Love Learning par des prospectus Gagnez au Change, puis la boîte de diapositives par un petit sac contenant les miennes, et je cache celles de Sean par terre, à l'autre bout de la partie fermée de la pièce. Seigneur, s'il vous plaît, faites qu'il ne revienne pas ici et ne découvre pas ce que j'ai fait. J'ai astucieusement donné à mes documents une couverture semblable par son dessin et ses couleurs à celles de Love Learning, et quelqu'un qui se contenterait de passer la tête pour vérifier que tout est toujours en place ne remarquerait pas la différence. Sans doute. J'espère. S'il vous plaît, Seigneur.

Il n'y a rien de plus que je puisse faire. Si je ne suis pas de retour à ma table dans dix minutes, tout le monde va commencer à se poser des questions.

Quand j'arrive au bureau, une activité frénétique et une impression de panique règnent. On dirait que chacun a quitté son poste pour courir dans tous les sens, transportant des papiers, fouillant partout, retournant les tiroirs. Même Cath est debout. Fatima m'attrape le bras dès que j'entre et s'exclame, avant de s'enfuir :

— Oh, Beth, heureusement que tu es là, c'est tellement affreux !

Mike est à genoux par terre, occupé à passer en revue une quantité de documents étalés autour de lui, et il lève les yeux vers moi, avec un hochement de tête attristé. Il est sur le point de me dire quelque chose, mais je me détourne pour regarder le bureau de Sean. S'il vous plaît, faites qu'il y soit, s'il vous plaît…

Il n'y est pas. Oh non, oh merde, ça pourrait signifier qu'il est en route pour le *Langhorne* où il va faire les cent pas en se rongeant les ongles pendant quelques heures en attendant l'arrivée des participants. Et, s'il entre, il va nécessairement vérifier ses diapositives et s'apercevoir qu'elles ont disparu. Ce qui implique qu'il va remarquer que les brochures ont un drôle d'air, et se rendre compte que ce ne sont pas celles de LL, mais les miennes. Alors il va commencer à froncer les sourcils en se demandant ce qui peut bien se passer et va découvrir que je suis derrière tout ça dès qu'il les aura regardées plus attentivement et vu mon nom et le logo de ma société sur la première page. Il s'emparera de mes documents et les jettera à travers la pièce, déchiquettera mes diapositives, grognera et hurlera, le visage levé vers le néon, de la bave s'échappant de ses lèvres et éclaboussant le velours des sièges. Et, quand il aura fini, il contactera Rupert, avancera l'heure de la réunion et fera sa présentation plutôt sans que j'en sois informée et que je sois en mesure de l'en empêcher.

Ah non, le voilà. Jésus Marie Joseph en costard-cravate, j'ai besoin de m'asseoir.

Peut-être qu'il a déjà appelé pour changer l'heure quand même, pour se débarrasser de moi, juste au cas où, à la suite d'une erreur improbable, j'en aurais effectivement après lui. Oh non, je parie qu'il l'a fait. Il me connaît, donc il sait qu'il y a une chance que j'aie envie d'utiliser mon impressionnante intelligence pour comprendre ce qui est en train de se produire. Il faudrait qu'il soit bête pour s'en tenir au plan de départ.

Eh bien, il n'y a qu'une seule façon d'en avoir le cœur net. Je sors mon répertoire et trouve le numéro du secrétaire de Rupert. Je n'ai pas le courage de lui parler en personne, avec tout ce qui arrive par ailleurs. Sa voix magnifique me démotiverait complètement, alors que je dois faire la présentation de ma vie cet après-midi. Je ne peux pas la faire après – et encore moins pendant – une bouffée de désir. Je n'aurais pas la bonne tête.

Quand l'assistant décroche et que je me présente, il me répond que Rupert lui a demandé de lui passer directement tout appel de Love Learning. Paniquée, je me mets à bredouiller que ce n'est pas la peine, que j'appelle seulement pour confirmer l'heure de la réunion :

— Je vais le voir tout à l'heure, de toute façon, donc s'il veut me parler, il pourra le faire à ce moment-là. Ce n'est vraiment pas nécessaire de le déranger.

— Bon…

Il hésite. Je me mords la lèvre pour m'empêcher d'en dire plus. Je ne veux pas avoir l'air d'être prête à tout pour ne surtout pas avoir de conversation avec lui. Même si c'est le cas. Parce que j'ai vraiment, vraiment envie d'entendre à nouveau sa voix. L'assistant reprend enfin la parole :

— OK, mais je vous serais reconnaissant si vous évitiez de lui dire que vous avez appelé.

— Absolument, du moment que vous n'en faites rien non plus. Je ne voudrais pas qu'il pense que je ne suis pas capable de retenir l'heure d'une réunion.

— Ah oui, bien sûr. Parfait. (Il laisse échapper un soupir de soulagement, et sa voix s'adoucit, plus détendue.) Eh bien, d'après son agenda, il se rend au *Langhorne Hotel* aujourd'hui à 14 heures.

Je ferme les yeux et sens tous mes muscles se décontracter sous l'effet de cette bonne nouvelle. Sean est tellement arrogant – ou me sous-estime à tel point – qu'il a pensé que je ne m'apercevrais de rien.

— Merci mon Dieu !

— Pardon ?

— Je disais : comme c'est curieux !

Une idée est en train de germer dans mon esprit.

— Ah ? Pourquoi ?

— Eh bien, j'ai inscrit 13 h 30 dans mon agenda, et je sais que le formateur, M. Cousins, a également retenu cet horaire. Mais vous avez 14 heures. Je me demande pourquoi.

Je l'entends pianoter sur son clavier d'ordinateur, tourner des pages à toute vitesse et remuer des feuilles volantes.

—Eh bien, je… c'est écrit là… je l'ai noté… je ne peux pas…

—Écoutez, ça n'a pas… Comment vous appelez-vous ?

—Jason.

—Bon, Jason, ça n'a pas vraiment d'importance, ce n'est qu'une demi-heure. Je suis sûre que nous pouvons tous patienter.

—Oh non, surtout pas ! Non, non, non ! M. de Witter déteste être en retard. Il serait vraiment mal à l'aise s'il découvrait en arrivant qu'il a fait attendre tout le monde. Il dit toujours que ce n'est pas professionnel. Et que c'est grossier envers la personne qui reçoit. Il serait furieux contre moi.

—Oh ! C'est compliqué, dans ce cas-là. Vous voyez, je n'ai pas moyen de contacter le formateur et de lui annoncer le changement d'horaire. Il n'est pas ici pour le moment, et je ne le verrai vraisemblablement qu'au début de la réunion.

Il se fait un long silence pendant lequel j'entends encore des papiers qu'on déplace et des pages qu'on tourne. Je ferme les yeux et croise les doigts des deux mains, tout en me mordant la lèvre de plus belle. Finalement, il m'annonce, hésitant, comme si l'idée lui venait en même temps qu'il parle :

—Euh, bon, je suppose que je pourrais lui dire que c'est à 13 h 30… je veux dire, la plupart du temps, il ne se souvient pas des horaires, alors… et pour les autres, ce sera facile de les informer du changement. Après tout, je suis là pour ça, non ?

—Eh bien, oui, sans doute. Ça me semble une bonne idée. De cette façon, tout le monde sera là en même temps, et c'est le principal. Je vous laisse vous en charger, alors, Jason ?

— Oui, oui, pas de problème, je suis sûr que ça va aller. Oh, mais n'oubliez pas, ne lui dites pas que vous avez appelé, d'accord ?

— Je ne dirai rien si vous ne dites rien.

Waouh. Je suis devenue une traîtresse. Non seulement je vole le rendez-vous de mon collègue, mais en plus je viens de changer l'heure pour qu'il ne soit même pas là ! Comme c'est sournois et méprisable. Et en plus ça me plaît.

Non, non, je ne suis pas une traîtresse. Je me suis juste débrouillée pour récupérer ma réunion volée par ce pervers. Je suis toujours droite et honorable, mais maintenant je suis prête à tout pour voir le bien triompher. Oui, je suis toujours l'héroïne courageuse qui a la justice de son côté.

— Crotte de bique, ronchonne Fatima qui passe près de moi en courant.

Une idée me traverse soudain l'esprit :

— Fati !

Elle s'arrête d'un coup, se retourne à toute vitesse pour me regarder, l'air terriblement anxieuse :

— Oui, Beth ?

— Je me demandais si tu pourrais me rendre un petit service. Peut-être avec Mike. Mais tu ne dois en parler à personne, d'accord ?

Son visage se détend de manière infinitésimale.

— Bien sûr, Beth. Tout ce que tu voudras.

— C'est super, Fati, merci. Est-ce que tu es libre à partir de 13 heures, aujourd'hui ?

Cinq minutes plus tard, j'entre dans la cuisine où je trouve Sean debout à côté de la bouilloire, tournant le dos à la porte. Je recule aussitôt et retourne dans le bureau. J'ai peut-être le bien de mon côté, mais, si je lui parle maintenant, je vais sans doute tout lui avouer et causer ainsi ma propre perte.

Alors que je passe devant la porte à panneaux, elle s'ouvre et laisse apparaître Chas, l'air agité. Il me voit et me prend par le bras :

—Seigneur ! Je t'ai cherchée partout.

—Non, non, moi c'est Beth. Je sais que c'est bientôt Noël, mais je ne crois pas que le Seigneur fasse une apparition cette année.

—Ferme-la et viens par ici.

Il me tire dans le bureau et ferme la porte.

—Que se passe-t-il, Chas ?

Il fourre ses mains dans ses poches et s'approche de la fenêtre à grands pas.

—On est dans la merde jusqu'au cou, Beth. Voilà ce qui se passe. C'est gentil de te joindre à nous, au fait.

Je jette un coup d'œil à l'horloge murale. Il n'est que 8 h 50, donc, techniquement, je ne suis pas en retard. J'aimerais protester contre cette attaque injuste, mais je m'élève au-dessus de ça. J'ai le bien de mon côté :

—Et pourquoi sommes-nous dans la merde ?

—Parce que ton mec arrogant, miteux, sournois et voleur nous a tous eus, voilà pourquoi. (Il se tourne pour me faire face, le visage déformé par la rage.) Et n'essaie pas de me dire que tu n'étais pas au courant.

—Qu... quoi ? (Est-ce qu'il parle de Sean ? C'est de notoriété publique que je suis sortie deux fois avec lui.) Bon, oui, je sais pour le...

—Bien sûr que tu es au courant, espèce de garce! Vous avez tout manigancé ensemble, n'est-ce pas?

—Quoi?

Je fais un pas vers lui en même temps que lui vers moi, et nous ne sommes plus qu'à cinquante centimètres l'un de l'autre. Je me dresse plus haut que lui alors que nous nous regardons en chiens de faïence, et il finit par baisser les yeux et se détourner.

—Ce n'est pas la peine de nier, Beth, dit-il à voix basse. Tout le monde est au courant. On vous a vus ensemble, il te cherchait ce matin, il n'y a pas moyen que tu aies été en dehors de tout ça. Alors même si tu n'es pas directement impliquée, si tu savais ce qu'il tramait et que tu n'as rien fait pour l'en empêcher, tu es complice. Ou comme on appelle ça. J'ai appelé la police. Je préfère te prévenir.

Je lève les mains.

—Quoi? Attends. Attends une minute. Chas, de quoi tu parles, bordel de merde? Je veux dire, je ne pense pas que ça intéresse la police que Sean m'ait volé ma réunion. Même si techniquement je suppose que c'est un genre d'espionnage industriel…

—Mais qu'est-ce que tu racontes, bordel? Ça n'a rien à voir avec Sean, ni avec ta petite réunion de merde.

—Bon, alors, de quoi…? Tu sais, ce n'est pas une réunion de merde, c'est au contraire très bien, et ça pourrait déboucher…

—Ton homme bien-aimé, ce salaud de Richard Love, est encore une fois parti avec la caisse, et il est retourné au Portugal. Autrement dit, on est complètement baisés.

Je le regarde, bouche bée:

—Il…? Au…?

Soudain, la pièce se met à tourner, et je n'ai pas d'autre solution que de m'écrouler sur la moquette, d'où je contemple Chas, la bouche toujours ouverte.

Chas me regarde sans rien dire. Finalement, il demande :

— Tu n'étais pas au courant, alors ?

Je n'arrive ni à parler ni à bouger.

— J'aurais juré…

Il se tait et me laisse tranquille, ce qui me permet de mettre de l'ordre dans mes idées. Richard a monté Love Learning, qui a rencontré le succès et rapporté beaucoup d'argent, et c'est ce moment qu'il a choisi pour partir. Chas a dirigé la boîte pendant trois mois, et pendant tout ce temps-là nous avons galéré, au point qu'il nous menace de suppression de postes si nous ne ramenions pas de nouveaux contrats. Je lève la tête :

— Tu as dit « encore une fois » ?

Il me regarde pendant quelques secondes, puis opine du chef.

— Pourquoi crois-tu que nous soyons déjà dans de tels ennuis financiers ?

Je ferme les yeux. Je ne peux pas les garder ouverts, la pièce tangue trop.

— Comment a-t-il… ?

— Oh, il était très malin. Il prenait des petites sommes, trafiquait les comptes, effaçait ses traces. Tu sais. Personne ne pouvait le prendre.

— Et maintenant ?

— Eh bien, c'est ça, le truc. Cette fois-ci, c'est différent. C'est plutôt du genre cambriolage, il n'a pas essayé de se cacher. C'est tellement évident que c'est lui.

Il y a quelque chose qui ne va pas dans sa voix. Ce n'est pas le ton de quelqu'un qui est sur le point de faire arrêter le coupable.

—Alors, Chas, si c'est évident que c'est lui, la police va le prendre, n'est-ce pas? Je veux dire, ce n'est qu'une question de temps, pas vrai?

Il secoue la tête avec tristesse et retourne vers la fenêtre.

—Malheureusement, ce connard a eu de la chance. Il était tellement pressé, pour une raison ou une autre, qu'il n'a même pas pris la peine de passer les papiers à la déchiqueteuse, semble-t-il. On a trouvé un morceau de papier sous le bureau, qui laisse à penser qu'il a tout bonnement jeté toutes les preuves dans sa corbeille à papier. Je veux dire, c'est ridicule, ce serait tellement facile de l'arrêter et de récupérer tout l'argent, si ces papiers étaient là, intacts, à nous attendre. Mais…

—Mais?

Il pousse un profond soupir et hausse les épaules.

—La femme de ménage est venue tôt ce matin et a vidé toutes les corbeilles. Toutes les preuves ont été depuis longtemps déposées à la décharge, ou déchiquetées, ou transformées en pâte à papier, ou les trois à la fois. Il n'y a plus d'espoir.

À nouveau, j'écarquille les yeux, et mon cerveau se remet à produire ce crépitement électrique. Je me lève. En fait, je saute presque. Chas se retourne d'un coup et arrondit les yeux en me voyant. J'ai l'impression de léviter au-dessus du sol, les cheveux dressés sur la tête. Ce n'est pourtant pas le cas.

—Chas, tu ne vas pas le croire, mais j'ai d'excellentes nouvelles à t'annoncer.

Chapitre 30

Résultats

Objectif à court terme : faire une présentation de-la-mort-qui-tue aux cadres d'Horizon sans trébucher, baver, m'évanouir, tomber, pouffer de rire ou sauter sur quelqu'un dans un accès de frénésie sexuelle.
Obstacles : le visage de Rupert. Oh là là !
Objectif à long terme : rester droite pour Horizon. Puis passer toute la journée de demain allongée…
Obstacles : à peu près vingt-quatre heures.

13 h 15. Il fait un froid de canard, mais le temps est sec et ensoleillé, heureusement. Je marche d'un pas vif vers la porte d'entrée du *Langhorne*, la tête haute, un attaché-case à la main. Je suis habillée en femme d'affaires avec un long manteau de laine noir, la jupe noire de Nicole Kidman et un chemisier blanc, les cheveux relevés, le maquillage irréprochable. J'arbore un discret sourire supérieur, j'irradie de confiance et de maîtrise de moi, et je suis consciente d'être une entrepreneuse pleine d'avenir, sur le point de réussir mon exposé et d'assurer un contrat lucratif pour ma propre société. Je ressemble sans doute à Richard Branson, le fondateur de *Virgin*. Sans la barbe.

Je crois que je vais vomir.

La petite Mini rouge de Fatima est garée devant l'hôtel – on ne peut pas se tromper, avec la plaque d'immatriculation FAT 5 – donc elle et Mike doivent déjà être là. Merci, Seigneur.

J'entre dans le salon Willoughby par les portes du fond, ce qui me permet de regarder entre les rideaux comme un enfant qui attend que son premier spectacle de Noël commence. Je peux voir tous les parents – je veux dire, les cadres – qui s'installent sur les chaises et feuillettent mes brochures Gagnez au Change. Certains les dévorent littéralement et les commentent avec leurs voisins. Oh, s'il vous plaît, faites que ça leur plaise !

Je parcours la foule des yeux sans répit, guettant l'arrivée d'une tête aux reflets blonds, mais je ne l'aperçois pas encore. J'ai l'estomac qui fait des nœuds et je suis plus nerveuse que jamais auparavant. C'est l'heure d'un dernier passage aux toilettes.

Devant le miroir, je lisse mes cheveux et retouche mon maquillage. J'ai les mains qui tremblent pendant que je tamponne du gloss sur mes lèvres. Je ne sais pas si ce qui m'angoisse le plus, c'est de réussir à décrocher ce contrat ; de monter ma boîte ; de poignarder Sean, de tourner la lame et de casser le manche pour qu'il ne puisse pas sortir le couteau et essayer de survivre ; ou de rencontrer Rupert. Je me penche pour examiner mon reflet, mais je tremble tellement que tout ce que je vois, c'est une image floue, vacillante. En fait, je pense que c'est lié à la saleté de la glace, mais il n'en est pas moins vrai que je tremble. J'ai le cœur qui bat deux fois plus vite que la normale, je suis aussi essoufflée que si j'avais monté les escaliers en courant, et j'ai l'impression que je suis proche de la crise de panique. C'est ridicule – je ne me souviens pas de la dernière fois que j'ai été dans cet état. Je sais que certains de mes collègues sont encore très nerveux avant d'animer une formation, mais ce n'est pas mon cas, du coup je n'ai pas de stratégie pour me calmer. Que font-ils pour faire passer le trac ? Fatima est toujours dans tous ses états, au moins une heure avant ses séances. Mais rien de ce qu'elle peut faire n'a d'efficacité sur son anxiété, alors elle n'essaie même plus, et y va toute tremblante. Certains pensent que l'inquiétude leur donne une certaine pugnacité. Je crois que Fatima trouve que ça confère simplement à sa voix une qualité exotique, vibrante.

Sean arrive toujours le plus tard possible, se débarrasse de son manteau et file directement dans la salle de formation, pour ne pas avoir le temps de s'inquiéter, j'imagine. Bon, ça ne marcherait pas pour moi : je me fais un sang d'encre depuis que j'ai organisé cette réunion, mercredi dernier.

Derek se contente de se racler abondamment la gorge et de se tapoter le cou, comme s'il était sur le point d'aller chanter *Nessun Dorma* quelque part. Mike passe vingt minutes à compter et à classer ses diapositives. Et Cath sort toujours pour avaler une grande quantité de toxines et de substances cancérogènes afin de se sentir mieux.

Bon, rien de tout cela ne peut marcher pour moi. J'ai déjà vérifié les diapos, et je ne vais pas commencer à fumer : j'ai entendu que ça prenait au moins un mois d'acquérir la technique, avant ça ne vous apporte rien, à part vous faire vomir. À la place, je retourne dans la partie déserte du salon Willoughby et reprends un verre d'eau.

Après notre conversation, Chas est ressorti dans la pièce commune et a mis un terme aux recherches frénétiques. Ensuite, il a relu tous les contrats que chacun avait réussi à signer depuis le début de la crise et a calculé si Love Learning pouvait continuer à fonctionner. Mike était arrivé à décrocher une prestation de trois mois avec le restaurant italien de la zone piétonne ; et Cath avait, à un moment durant ces trois dernières semaines, soulevé son combiné téléphonique pour joindre le grand magasin de fournitures de bureau de la zone industrielle, puis réussi à les convaincre de souscrire à des formations en accueil, en après-vente, en management et en comptabilité. Avec ces deux gros accords et les quatre plus modestes que les autres avaient obtenus, il semble que la boîte puisse continuer à tourner pour le moment. Avec un ou deux ajustements mineurs.

—Apparemment, Richard devrait aller en prison, a déclaré Chas à une assistance pétrifiée. Cela signifie que tous ses avoirs vont être gelés pendant un certain temps. Donc, je vais prendre définitivement les rênes de Love Learning, nous allons redémarrer de zéro, et il va falloir se séparer au minimum de deux membres du personnel. Vraiment désolé.

Ça m'arrange. Dans le salon Willoughby, les sièges sont en train de se remplir. Fatima circule dans la pièce, en chemisier blanc et jupe noire, et propose du thé, du café ou du jus d'orange aux cadres ; et Mike, en chemise blanche et pantalon noir, passe une dernière fois mes diapositives en revue et s'assure qu'elles sont dans l'ordre, qu'il n'en manque aucune. Je m'approche de Fatima.

—Oh là là, Beth, heureusement que tu es là, je commençais à paniquer. Je pensais que j'allais devoir faire moi-même l'exposé, n'est-ce pas, Mike ? J'y ai vraiment cru. Ça m'a mise dans un état…

Je remarque qu'elle porte des petits rennes en guise de boucles d'oreilles.

—Bon, ne t'en fais pas, ça ne sera pas nécessaire. Je suis là.

—Ah oui, ouf. J'allais le faire, tu sais. Je l'aurais fait, même si c'était sûr que j'allais tout rater, j'en suis certaine. Mais j'aurais essayé, dans tous les cas.

—Je sais, Fatima. Merci. Écoute, Fati, je ne crois pas que tu puisses laisser ta voiture là où elle est : il y a une ligne jaune.

Elle fronce les sourcils :

—De quoi tu parles, Beth ? Tu as le trac, toi aussi ? Ça te fait perdre la boule ? J'ai vendu ma Mini. C'est même toi qui m'as dit de le faire. Tu t'en souviens, n'est-ce pas ?

—Tiens, c'est bizarre. Je viens de voir une Mini rouge avec ton numéro – FAT 5 – garée devant l'hôtel. C'est bien la tienne ?

—Non, Beth, espèce de nouille ! Je te l'ai dit, je l'ai vendue.

—OK. Bien sûr. Aucune importance. Tu ne te rappelles pas à qui tu l'as vendue, par hasard ?

—Nan.

—Bon, à quoi il ressemblait ? Tu t'en souviens ?

—Pas vraiment.

—Bon, ses cheveux. Tu te rappelles la couleur ? Par exemple, est-ce qu'ils étaient, tu sais, euh, je ne sais pas, disons blonds ? Très épais et brillants ? Dans le genre qui donne envie d'y passer la main ?

Elle me regarde sans comprendre.

—Non. Il n'était certainement pas blond. Brun, je crois. Très élégant.

—Ah, OK.

Évidemment. Il y a une grosse quinzaine de cadres d'Horizon ici, ça pourrait être n'importe lequel d'entre eux. Pourquoi est-ce que j'ai tout de suite pensé…? Ça ne fait rien. Il faut que je me concentre. Fatima a l'air un peu perdue, alors je lui adresse un grand sourire, et elle se décontracte à vue d'œil. Elle n'est sans doute pas la personne la plus futée que je connaisse, mais elle a un sens du contact fantastique. Je la suis des yeux alors qu'elle évolue dans l'assistance qui attend, bavardant avec les cadres, attirant des sourires, les aidant à se détendre et à se sentir bien. Et Mike manque peut-être un peu de fantaisie, mais il n'a pas son pareil pour planifier, vérifier et revérifier que tout est prêt. Ils forment les deux tiers de l'équipe de Gagnez au Change, et ils me seront précieux quand il s'agira de m'organiser et de m'occuper de mes clients.

Mon téléphone portable sonne à nouveau, et je ressors en courant dans le couloir.

—Beth Sheridan, Love… Je veux dire, Gagnez au Change, à votre écoute.

—Ah, bonjour, Miss Sheridan, ici Anthony Davies, l'assistant de Greg Matheson.

Merde! Ça y est. C'est l'appel que j'attendais. C'est le contrat *Whytelys*. Bordel! Ce n'est vraiment pas le moment. Comme si je n'étais pas déjà réduite en un tas de *jelly* bafouillante, bégayante et incapable d'aligner deux mots.

—Oh, bonjour Anthony, je suis contente d'avoir de vos nouvelles. Que puis-je faire pour vous?

Pas trop mal pour un tas de jelly.

—Eh bien, M. Matheson m'a demandé de vous contacter pour convenir d'une entrevue avec son service juridique, dans l'optique de discuter les termes d'un éventuel contrat avec Gagnez au Change. Quand est-ce que vous êtes libre?

Il me faut quelques secondes pour retrouver l'usage de la parole.

— C'est une excellente nouvelle, Anthony. Puis-je vous passer mon assistante, Fatima, qui prendra le rendez-vous ? Merci beaucoup.

Je mets le téléphone en mode muet, agite les bras en sautant, la bouche ouverte dans un grand cri silencieux pendant au moins quinze secondes, puis je rajuste mon chemisier et retourne dans la pièce, où je fais signe à Fatima de s'approcher. Je lui tends l'appareil :

— Sors et réponds à Anthony, lui dis-je, essoufflée.

— C'est qui ?

— Il est de chez *Whytelys*. Ils veulent qu'on se rencontre. Pour discuter d'un contrat.

Fatima écarquille les yeux, sourit d'une oreille à l'autre et commence à serrer les poings dans l'intention évidente de sautiller pendant quinze secondes.

— Pas maintenant, dis-je.

Elle hoche la tête et respire profondément pour se calmer.

— OK. Alors, je suis libre… bon, tous les jours. Mais il ne faut pas qu'il le sache. Tu n'as qu'à fixer le rendez-vous, par exemple, le 28 ou quelque chose comme ça. Mettons l'après-midi. Fais semblant de vérifier mon agenda. Fais-le attendre pendant que tu agites des papiers, tu vois ce que je veux dire ?

Elle acquiesce d'un air sérieux, me prend le téléphone des mains et s'éloigne en le portant devant elle comme un objet précieux. Je la regarde partir, puis me glisse à nouveau entre les rideaux afin de me faufiler vers la sortie sans être vue. J'ai besoin d'un peu d'air frais.

Bon. Je suis dehors, sur le trottoir, à me geler les miches. Il est 13 h 22, et toujours pas de trace de Rupert. Encore huit minutes. Il a tout le temps d'arriver. Il sera sans doute là dans une ou deux minutes. Je n'ai pas besoin de m'en faire, je vais me contenter de rentrer et de l'attendre dans le salon. Mais qu'est-ce que je vais faire s'il ne vient pas ? Je ferais mieux de l'attendre ici. Ça ne dérangera pas les cadres d'Horizon d'attendre leur patron. Mais Jason, son assistant, a dit qu'il détestait être en retard. Et si je fais patienter tout le monde et que du coup il se sent bête en arrivant ? Sauf que je ne peux pas commencer sans lui, c'est encore pire. Ou pas ? Peut-être que ce serait plus facile pour moi s'il n'était pas là, assis au premier rang, beau et séduisant, pour me déconcentrer et me faire baver ? Peut-être que je pourrais simplement appeler Jason, pour m'assurer qu'il a bien transmis le changement d'horaire. Si je ne démarre pas à temps, Sean va arriver ; il va me prendre la main dans le sac, et tout sera fichu.

Reprends-toi, Beth, voyons ! C'est ridicule. Je suis professionnelle, et c'est pour ça que je vais commencer exactement à l'heure que j'ai…

Oh, bordel de merde. Voilà Sean.

C'est sa voiture qui entre dans l'allée. Je cours vers l'intérieur et me précipite à l'avant de la pièce, où je prends position : pointeur laser dans la main droite, rétroprojecteur à ma gauche, première diapositive prête à être insérée. Je regarde Mike, assis à côté du projecteur, essayant de se faire tout petit, et il hoche la tête avec solennité, les deuxième et troisième diapositives prêtes à être présentées quand j'en aurai besoin. À ma montre, il est 13 h 27. Est-ce que je peux déjà commencer ? Je jette un coup d'œil à l'horloge murale, puis à la porte. Sean est là, en train de garer sa voiture. 13 h 28. Les cadres m'apparaissent comme un flou rose et gris, terrifiant. Ils se sont tournés vers moi, pleins d'attente, et le silence se fait dans la pièce. Toujours 13 h 28. Merde! Sur le côté de la salle, Fatima me dévisage, horrifiée, et je prends soudain conscience que je suis restée voûtée, l'air revêche, pendant au moins une minute, devant tout le monde. Le fait que je ne cesse de regarder par-dessus mon épaule ajoute à l'image de psychotique échappée de prison dont j'ai lu qu'elle n'était pas la plus adaptée pour présenter un argumentaire de vente.

Je me force à arborer un sourire détendu et fais un signe de tête en direction de l'interrupteur. Fatima fronce les sourcils et articule silencieusement: «Quoi?» Sean doit être arrivé à la réception à l'heure qu'il est, en train de dire à l'hôtesse qui se tient debout dans l'entrée: «Ça vous va si j'entre directement?» Elle lui sourit, il poursuit son chemin, par-delà la double porte en verre, sur l'horrible moquette beige à motifs. J'écarquille les yeux en direction de Fatima, regarde l'interrupteur, puis les lampes, et à nouveau l'interrupteur. Elle acquiesce et fait silencieusement: «Oh!» 13 h 29. Sean arrive à la porte principale du salon, fait un mouvement vers la poignée. Fatima s'approche de l'interrupteur, tend la main, appuie sur le bouton, et l'obscurité engloutit la pièce à l'instant même où les portes s'ouvrent à la volée et où Sean apparaît, pétrifié sur le pas de la porte, les yeux rivés sur moi, puis contemple bouche bée l'ensemble de la salle, la compréhension et l'horreur s'affichant en même temps sur son visage alors que je souris et dis à l'assistance:

— Bonjour à tous. Je m'appelle Beth Sheridan et je vais vous expliquer ce que ma société de formation, Gagnez au Change, peut apporter à Horizon.

Chapitre 31

Conclusion

Objectif à court terme : atteindre le distributeur d'alcool le plus proche et boire pour être calme (c'est-à-dire dans le coma).

Obstacles : les cadres d'Horizon, qui sont tellement séduits qu'ils veulent tous me parler de contrat. Crotte.

Objectif à long terme : épouser Brad, de préférence demain.

Obstacles : il n'a sans doute pas déposé sa queue-de-pie au pressing. (Bordel, il faut vraiment que je me reprenne.)

Quarante-cinq minutes plus tard. J'ai fini mon exposé et je me sens illuminée de l'intérieur par une chaude lueur qui se propage à mon visage en un sourire serein, alors que je parcours la pièce avec grâce, légère. Les cadres ont adoré mon topo, surtout le passage où j'ai pu mentionner mon emploi chez Horizon et parler de la consternante organisation de la formation chez eux, en étant crédible.

— Attendez, m'a demandé l'un d'eux vers le début, est-ce qu'on n'était pas censés rencontrer Love Learning ?

— Si. (Je hoche la tête et souris, comme si je l'admirais d'avoir remarqué quelque chose qui n'aurait pas sauté aux yeux.) Je travaillais pour Love Learning jusqu'à aujourd'hui, mais ils n'ont pas pu vous présenter cet exposé en raison d'un imprévu.

Je n'en révèle pas plus, car je sais qu'ils apprendront la méprisable désertion de Richard demain à la première heure par les radios locales. Le fait que le petit ami de ma colocataire travaille pour le journal du coin est déjà en train de se révéler utile. Il écrit également un article sur Gagnez au Change ; c'est Vini qui a eu l'idée, quand elle a retrouvé la mémoire. Je poursuis :

— Alors je me suis dit que, plutôt que de repartir les mains vides, vous pourriez découvrir que Gagnez au Change vous rendrait autant de services, sinon plus, que Love Learning.

Et le patron n'est pas du genre à filer avec la caisse. Je ne le dis pas, cependant. Laissons-les arriver d'eux-mêmes à cette conclusion, demain matin.

Un ou deux m'ont serré la main et m'ont déclaré qu'il était grand temps de revoir leur politique de formation, et qu'ils souhaitaient prendre un rendez-vous. Ce sont Fatima et Mike qui gèrent mon planning à présent, alors je les leur envoie tous. Une queue de trois personnes s'est formée à côté de Fatima, pendant que les autres se servent du vin chaud et du pain d'épice de Noël de l'autre côté de la salle. L'atmosphère est saturée de la senteur revigorante de la cannelle et du murmure bas des conversations détendues. Soudain, une haleine brûlante me remplit l'oreille en même temps que quatre mots cinglants :

— Espèce de petite garce !

Je pivote, mon sourire toujours bien arrimé à ma figure, et trouve Sean debout là, les lèvres retroussées de rage. Je lui adresse un signe de tête :

—Oh, salut, Sean. Ça va ?

—Ne me fais pas le coup de me demander comment je vais, connasse. Putain, qu'est-ce que tu fabriques ?

Je fronce les sourcils d'un air interrogateur :

—Mais, Sean, tu n'es pas au courant ? Je viens juste de présenter un exposé brillamment construit (si je puis me permettre) et qui a rencontré un franc succès auprès de ces charmants cadres de chez Horizon. Je les ai convaincus que leur stratégie de formation ne va pas du tout et que ce qu'ils doivent faire s'ils veulent qu'Horizon continue à prospérer et à avancer dans le XXIe siècle avec des équipes qui se sentent valorisées, et qui soient dotées de ce qui se fait de plus à la page en matière de savoir, de savoir-faire et de savoir-être, dont elles ont besoin non seulement pour faire leur travail comme il faut mais pour exceller dans leur domaine, est de se débarrasser de toutes leurs pratiques, de tout leur matériel de formation, et de charger Gagnez au Change de tous leurs projets présents et futurs de remise à niveau. Est-ce que ça répond à ta question ?

Il approche brutalement son visage du mien, si près que nos nez se frôlent. C'est curieux de se dire que la dernière fois que nous nous sommes tenus ainsi, nous nous sommes presque embrassés. Il ne me montrait pas autant de dents à ce moment-là, bien sûr.

—Putain, ce que tu es drôle… Sauf que c'est mon exposé, dans ma salle, avec mes participants, pour signer mon contrat. Ce qui fait de toi une sale petite voleuse, d'après mes critères.

— Tes critères ? Ceux qui te disent que tu peux dérober le travail de tes collègues sans que ça pose problème ?

Il fait mine de répondre, puis se ravise, sourcils froncés.

— Mais de quoi tu parles, bordel de merde ?

— Le contrat avec Horizon m'appartient, comme tu le sais pertinemment. Tu m'as volé l'idée, profitant de ce que j'étais trop… je ne sais quoi pour remarquer ton petit manège. (Je croise les bras.) Je n'ai fait que le récupérer. C'est tout.

Il agite l'index vers moi.

— Non, ce n'est pas tout. C'est Love Learning qui a payé tout ça. Ce qui fait de toi une belle arnaqueuse, aussi.

— Une « belle-arnaqueuse » ? C'est-à-dire intrusive comme une belle-mère ? Ou fatigante comme une belle-sœur ?

— Oh, bordel de…

— Mijaurée comme une belle-fille ?

— … merde. Tu peux rigoler autant que tu veux, mais ça m'a coûté presque 2 000 livres, et je suis sûr que la police trouvera ça très intéressant quand je leur annoncerai que tu…

— Oh oui, Sean, tu as bien raison, ils seront très intéressés.

J'ai baissé le ton pour que les participants ne m'entendent pas, et ça me donne une voix rauque, menaçante. Cela nous prend tous les deux un peu par surprise.

— Parce que j'ai réglé intégralement la facture moi-même, et elle s'élevait à 975 livres, TVA comprise. Alors, si tu dois aller réclamer 2 000 livres à une société qui croule déjà sous les dettes à cause de détournements de fonds, et dont les comptes vont donc être passés au peigne fin, peut-être que tu devrais y penser à deux fois. Tu ne crois pas ?

Il arrondit les lèvres, apparemment sur le point de prononcer un mot commençant par « P », puis s'arrête, plisse les yeux, referme la bouche et s'éloigne vers la porte à grands pas. Je le vois pivoter, me menacer d'un autre « P » rageur et s'en aller.

Putain !

Je me retourne vers la pièce, un peu tremblante, mais portée par le sentiment que je pourrais pourfendre des dragons. Je fais un petit tour, en souriant aux cadres, en bavardant à propos de l'exposé, en hochant la tête aux souvenirs de mon passage chez Horizon et des gens qui s'y trouvaient alors.

— Tu te souviens de Cruella, du service d'impression ? Elle avait les cheveux blancs, avec une horrible tache jaune sur le devant, à cause des clopes qu'elle fumait à la chaîne. Elle s'est mariée !

Mais mon but caché est de dénicher Rupert. La présentation s'est mieux déroulée, et de loin, que tout ce que je pouvais espérer, et ma boîte est officiellement lancée, donc je devrais simplement flotter dans une bulle de bonheur, comme si j'étais la reine de la formation, mais ce n'est pas le cas. Je suis vraiment très contente, évidemment, mais une petite partie de moi – enfin, une assez grande partie en fait, voire toutes les parties, pour être honnête, et pas seulement celles auxquelles vous pensez – est très déçue qu'il ne soit pas là. Je veux dire, c'était inscrit dans son agenda, il était impatient de venir, donc je sais qu'il n'avait rien à cette heure-là.

Brève image mentale de Rupert avec « rien ». Je chancelle un peu et me rattrape au bord de la table près des pains d'épice. Fatima se tourne dans ma direction, inquiète, alors je lui adresse mon sourire rassurant. Je pense que ce vin chaud m'est monté à la tête.

De toute façon, ce n'est pas comme si Rupert avait délibérément décidé de m'éviter : il ne savait même pas que ce serait moi qui ferais la présentation d'aujourd'hui. De son point de vue, il n'a fait qu'éviter son nouveau contact, M. S. Cousins. Ce ver de terre. Si seulement j'avais ravalé ma fierté et répondu à ce mail de Rupert, ou que je l'avais appelé pour lui demander qui prétendait être son nouveau contact…

Bref, ça n'a plus d'importance, maintenant. J'ai repris ma réunion des griffes de Sean, de toute façon, sans l'aide de personne, et si j'en crois l'allure légèrement épuisée de Fatima et de Mike, les réservations pleuvent. C'est sans doute tant mieux que Rupert n'ait pas été dans l'assistance, avec ses yeux magnifiques posés sur moi. Je me serais peut-être évanouie, et cela aurait été difficile de retomber sur mes pieds après ça.

En plus, j'avais un choix épineux à faire, et avec l'absence de Rupert la question s'est en quelque sorte résolue d'elle-même. Toute relation que j'ai pu imaginer avoir avec Rupert est caduque puisque je suis complètement amoureuse de…

— Brad !

Je laisse échapper cette exclamation en le voyant, avant d'avoir le temps de prendre un air détendu et professionnel. Quelques-uns des cadres se retournent, mais je suis ravie, le regard rivé sur Brad qui est apparu par magie devant moi, tout en yeux marron rieurs et en cheveux ébouriffés. Je lui adresse un large sourire sans le quitter des yeux, vibrante du désir de l'attraper pour m'enrouler autour de ce buste sexy. Mon corps s'approche de lui contre mon gré, comme si j'étais sur un tapis roulant. Je reprends :

— Oh, c'est vraiment super de te voir. Mais qu'est-ce que tu fais là ? Oh, mince, tu bosses aussi chez Horizon, n'est-ce pas ? J'avais complètement oublié. Heureusement que je ne t'ai pas aperçu plus tôt, ça m'aurait complètement déconcentrée... (Il penche la tête de côté et fronce un peu les sourcils en me regardant.) Quoi ? Qu'est-ce qu'il y a ?

Il hausse les épaules :

— Je ne sais pas trop. Ça dépend de toi, en fait.

— De moi ?

Je commence à m'inquiéter.

— Eh bien, oui. Parce que je suis un peu perdu, Beth. Ou devrais-je dire Libby ? Je suis désolé, à qui ai-je l'honneur, exactement ? Est-ce cette merveilleuse jeune femme si sincère, qui déteste les menteurs de tout poil ? Ou... pas ?

Je porte la main à ma bouche. Oh, merde. Oh, merde, merde, merde de merde. Comment ai-je pu ne pas y penser ? Comment ai-je pu passer à côté ?

— Oh, Brad, zut, écoute, ce n'est pas vraiment un mensonge, je veux dire, mon prénom c'est Elizabeth, alors techniquement je suis aussi bien Libby que Beth. En fait, bien sûr que je suis Libby et Beth, ça tu le sais maintenant, ce que je veux dire c'est que mon diminutif, euh mes diminutifs sont, ou du moins pourraient être l'un comme l'autre, ce qui signifie que ça ne compte pas comme un mensonge que je...

— Miss Sheridan, je vais devoir vous demander de vous taire un moment, s'il vous plaît, dit-il. Merci. Alors. Passons les faits en revue, voulez-vous ? Bon. (Il lève une main, un doigt tendu.) Premièrement : tu t'es sans vergogne présentée à moi comme t'appelant Libby, alors que tu savais très bien que ton diminutif le plus habituel était Beth ; deuxièmement, tu ne m'as jamais expliqué les règles des différents diminutifs…

— Excusez-moi, monsieur, je suis désolé de…

L'un des cadres vient d'apparaître. Brad se tourne vers lui, impatient.

— Euh, est-ce que ça peut attendre, s'il vous plaît ? Je suis occupé.

— Oui, monsieur, mais il y a un problème.

— Eh bien, nous le réglerons au bureau. J'y serai dans quelques minutes, d'accord ?

J'ai un pincement au cœur. Je n'ai que quelques minutes avant qu'il s'en aille. Oh, mais nous avons la journée de demain devant nous. La déception s'efface aussitôt au profit d'une impatience surexcitée qui me fait sourire. Je sens les muscles de mon visage qui commencent à se fatiguer de toute cette gymnastique. J'imagine mes émotions, épuisées, essayant de prendre le temps de s'asseoir quelques minutes avant de devoir recommencer à courir partout et à changer de place.

— Non, monsieur, malheureusement ça ne peut pas attendre. C'est votre voiture.

— Quoi ?

Une femme en tailleur, les cheveux tirés en arrière, se faufile jusqu'à nous :

— Rupert, tu bloques l'entrée de l'hôtel, espèce d'idiot !

Rupert ? Est-ce qu'elle a dit « Rupert » ? Je relève la tête d'un coup pour parcourir la pièce des yeux, tentant de voir à qui elle s'adresse. Oh, où est-il ?

— OK, écoute, est-ce que ça peut attendre juste une minute ?

— Désolée, mais non, Rupe. Ça bouche le passage.

C'est toujours la même bonne femme. En me retournant, je la trouve juste à côté de Brad. En train de le regarder. De lui parler. De l'appeler Rupert. Et il lui répond. Mes yeux font l'aller et retour entre elle et lui tandis que mon cerveau est à nouveau incapable de fonctionner et que mes émotions ont sauté sur leurs pieds et se sont mises à courir partout en hurlant et en agitant les bras en l'air. Que diable… ?

Brad – ou Rupert – me regarde de près, visiblement inquiet.

— Voilà les clefs, dit-il précipitamment en les lançant au type. (Il ne me quitte pas des yeux.) Ramenez ma voiture au bureau, s'il vous plaît. Je vous y rejoins dans une heure.

— D… désolé, monsieur, c'est laquelle… ?

— Une Mini rouge, avec un toit en damier, garée juste devant. (Son regard est toujours rivé sur le mien.) Vous voulez bien vous en occuper maintenant, Jason ?

Jason et la bonne femme disparaissent de mon champ de vision. Bien qu'ils n'y soient jamais entrés. Tout ce que je vois, c'est… Rupert.

— Maaiiis… ?

— Je savais que tu allais me poser cette question. Viens avec moi.

Il me prend par la main et m'entraîne vers les rideaux du fond de la salle. Nous nous glissons dans la partie déserte, puis il s'arrête et s'approche de moi, les mains sur mes bras.

— Tuuu…, dis-je.

—Tu as parfaitement raison, répond-il en repoussant doucement mes cheveux de ma figure. C'était vraiment idiot. Mais j'avais une très bonne excuse, je te le promets, Beth.

—Qu…?

—Bon, d'accord. La voici : être Rupert de Witter en permanence, ça a beaucoup d'avantages. C'est tellement facile d'obtenir un service de qualité, des réservations de dernière minute dans les restaurants huppés, des bougies partout…

Je porte à nouveau la main à ma bouche. Les bougies, au *Madeleine's*. Tout cela organisé pour moi par Rupert – qui n'est autre que Brad. Brad a fait tout ça pour moi. Mais Brad est Rupert. Il y a encore trente secondes, je n'étais même pas consciente que Brad savait que j'étais allée au *Madeleine's* ce jour-là, encore moins qu'il était derrière tout ça. Je crois que je suis bel et bien sur le point de m'évanouir. Non, non, tout va bien. Je ne vais pas tomber dans les pommes. Rupert fronce les sourcils.

—Oh non, tu vas bien ? Tu es pâle comme un linge.

Il pose sa main sur mon visage et me conduit, de l'autre, vers la fenêtre, sans jamais détourner ses yeux des miens.

Je hoche la tête :

—Hun hun…

—Bon, je ne vais pas prendre de risque. Ne bouge pas.

Et après un dernier regard prolongé sur ma figure il disparaît entre les rideaux.

Bordel de merde ! Rupert et Brad ne font qu'un !

—Allez, viens vite t'asseoir. (Il est revenu aussitôt, portant l'une des chaises utilisées de l'autre côté.) S'il te plaît. Tu m'inquiètes.

Obéissante, je m'approche et m'installe sur le siège proposé. Rupert me dévisage de près pendant quelques instants, comme un parent qui borde un enfant.

—Tout va bien? (J'acquiesce.) Tu es sûre? Tu veux que j'aille te chercher à boire? De l'eau? Du brandy? Du thé? Que dirais-tu d'un verre de…?

Je secoue la tête. Il se tait. Me regarde avec franchise. Puis se frotte le visage de la main et s'approche de la fenêtre.

—OK, Mademoiselle Qui-Que-Vous-Soyez. Je vais tout vous expliquer. Mais promettez-moi de ne pas vous évanouir, d'accord? Bon. Je vais être parfaitement honnête avec toi sur les raisons qui m'ont poussé à agir comme ça. C'était impardonnable et je n'ai aucune excuse, mais tout est la faute de mon ami Hector. Non, c'est vrai. C'était son idée d'utiliser un faux nom.

—Il le fait aussi? Bordel, mais qu'est-ce que vous…?

—Non, non. (Il revient vers moi en toute hâte, secouant la tête.) Bon sang, non, ce n'est pas ce que je voulais dire. Je voulais juste dire que… l'idée m'est venue en parlant avec lui. Ce n'était pas exactement son idée en soi. Il ne me l'a pas vraiment suggérée.

J'acquiesce:

—Donc ce n'était ni son idée ni une suggestion de sa part, mais c'est sa faute.

Il se détourne:

—Tu as raison, c'est vrai que c'est affreux de dire ça. Mais, en toute honnêteté, je n'essaie pas de lui faire porter le chapeau. C'est juste que… Il a rencontré une fille, tu vois, et, à ce moment-là, elle ne savait pas qui il était…

—Et c'est qui?

—Hector McCarthy, le propriétaire de MacCarthy Systems. En tout cas…

—Ooh!

McCarthy Systems, c'est cette énorme société de maintenance informatique dans la zone industrielle. C'est encore plus grand qu'Horizon. J'écarquille les yeux.

—J'ignorais que les millionnaires avaient un comportement grégaire. Est-ce que c'est par un sixième sens inné que vous vous rassemblez en groupes sans même vous en rendre compte?

Il secoue la tête en riant.

—Non, non, bien sûr que non.

—Alors, quand vous vous êtes rencontrés, vous vous êtes aperçus que vous aviez beaucoup de points communs? Du genre, vous aviez la même voiture, habitiez dans la même rue, ce type de choses?

Il me sourit:

—Nous conduisons tous deux une Bentley.

Je fais un grand geste des mains:

—Tu vois bien: c'est une preuve matérielle. Vous n'êtes qu'une bande de phénomènes de foire.

Il sourit toujours, mais ses yeux sont devenus tristes.

—En réalité, nous sommes absolument normaux, mais les gens croient forcément… (Il se tait et secoue la tête.) Je m'égare. Où en étais-je? Ah oui, Hector et Rachel. Il me parlait d'elle, et elle paraissait tellement adorable – mignonne, charmante, drôle – que je me suis senti horriblement jaloux. Je voulais la même chose. (Il se tourne pour me faire face, puis fronce les sourcils.) Bon sang, tu es sûre que ça va? Tu es carrément verdâtre, maintenant!

Eh bien, évidemment. Vous connaissez des filles qui ne verdissent pas quand le millionnaire sexy dont elles sont folles amoureuses leur dit avec une telle éloquence qu'une autre fille est fantastique? Je devine que c'est une traînée. Une telle perfection n'existe pas. Je lui adresse un doux sourire:

— Tout va bien. Continue.

Il se penche un peu:

— Tu es sûre? OK. Donc Hector est tout amouraché de cette fille incroyable, superbe…

— Ouais, ça va, j'ai compris. Ensuite?

Il fronce les sourcils, surpris, en me regardant, puis son visage s'éclaire d'un grand sourire.

— OK, la suite. Cette fille ne savait pas qui il était quand ils se sont rencontrés. Ce qui signifie qu'elle a d'abord dû faire sa connaissance, être séduite, simplement par lui-même, et pas par son statut. (Il se tait et contemple le sol pendant quelques instants.) Depuis que j'ai Horizon, c'est-à-dire quasiment depuis que je suis en âge de travailler, ça a toujours été clair que les gens n'étaient pas tout le temps très… vrais. Ça m'a ouvert les yeux, Lib, je t'assure. Des gens que je connaissais vaguement à l'école il y a quinze ans, ou que j'ai rencontrés une fois à une soirée, de simples connaissances, m'appellent constamment pour qu'on se voie. Il y a un repas de promo, un dîner, un barbecue. C'est un assaut constant, et je ne me fais aucune illusion: ce n'est pas parce qu'ils pensent que je serai un invité charmant et que j'amuserai la galerie. (Il prend une voix nasale un peu ridicule.) «Mes compagnons de table préférés? Oh, eh bien, c'est facile. Jésus-Christ,

Oscar Wilde, Stephen Fry et le type qui possède Horizon Holidays. » Je n'y crois pas trop !

Il se tait pendant un moment, les yeux à présent rivés sur les lourds rideaux qui nous séparent toujours de ses employés. Puis il se tourne, et son regard rencontre à nouveau le mien.

— J'ai été amoureux, autrefois, me dit-il avec franchise, ou du moins je l'ai cru. Je me suis même marié. J'avais vingt-sept ans, et elle en avait onze de plus. Elle aimait le train de vie que je lui offrais, mais c'était la seule chose qui lui plaisait en moi.

— Ooh…

Il hoche la tête.

— Voilà. Tu sais tout. C'est pour ça que j'ai prétendu être un certain Brad, lors de ce truc de speed dating. Et, en plus, il y avait évidemment le risque que tu sois une « serial killeuse » munie d'une hache.

Je ris.

— Oh, pour l'amour du ciel, Br… Rupert, c'est tout simplement ridicule. Les serial killers ne vont pas au speed dating.

— Vraiment ?

— Bien sûr. Ce n'est pas parce que ce sont des tueurs psychotiques assoiffés de sang qu'ils sont des rebuts de la société.

Il cligne des yeux :

— Des rebuts de la société ? C'est comme ça que tu vois le client moyen du speed dating ?

— Oh oui, absolument.

Il lève les sourcils et se détourne un peu :

— Moi aussi ?

Il me considère d'un air si sérieux, si intense, et sa voix est si douce et si timide, que je perçois une réelle anxiété, malgré son sourire qui pourrait faire penser qu'il plaisante. En le regardant, je repense à la silhouette écrasée de chagrin de ma robe de chambre dans la nuit de lundi, et un frisson de désir me parcourt.

— Non, non, bien sûr que non, pas toi. Pas le moins du monde. Tu es juste un tricheur.

Il me contemple toujours, ses yeux ne quittant pas les miens. Puis il baisse les paupières :

— Je n'aurais pas dû te mentir, Li… Beth. Dès que je t'ai connue, je l'ai regretté. Comme tu l'as dit l'autre fois, prendre un faux nom, c'est comme si on ne rencontrait pas vraiment la personne, parce qu'on cache son identité.

— En fait, je crois que c'est toi qui l'as dit.

— Oui, tu as raison, mais tu étais d'accord.

— C'est vrai.

— Ce que je veux dire, c'est qu'une fois que c'était fait, c'était très difficile de revenir en arrière. Tu vois, j'en avais envie, je voulais le faire, mais…

— Mais tu t'amusais trop à échanger des mails aguicheurs avec quelqu'un d'autre, sous ta vraie identité.

— Ah ! Oui. C'est vrai.

Je croise les bras, mimant la colère.

— C'est vraiment méprisable. Je veux dire, comment as-tu pu flirter ainsi avec moi, pendant que tu avais une relation avec, disons, moi ? Je sais qu'il s'est avéré par la suite que nous étions une seule et même personne, mais ça aurait pu ne pas être le cas. Et alors tu nous aurais menées toutes les deux en bateau.

— Je sais. Mais j'étais attiré par vous deux, alors ça m'était impossible de… (Il arrête de faire les cent pas et se tourne pour me faire complètement face.) Hé, écoute, attends un peu. N'oublions pas, Mademoiselle Incognita, que tu faisais exactement la même chose : tu flirtais avec moi pendant que tu sortais avec…, tu sais bien, moi.

— D'accord, mais au moins j'avais l'intention de rompre avec toi dès que j'ai compris que c'était sérieux avec toi. Ce qui est plus que ce que tu ne peux en dire.

— Mais j'étais déchiré, chaque fois qu'on se rencontrait. Bon sang, Libby, j'avais tellement envie de te prendre dans mes bras et de t'embrasser, mais je ne m'en sentais pas le droit à cause de mes sentiments pour Beth. Pour toi. (Il se tait.) De toute façon, tu n'as pas cassé avec moi, n'est-ce pas ? C'est moi qui t'ai larguée.

— C'est faux !

— C'est vrai.

— Non. Tu ne m'as pas larguée. Tu as juste écrit un message qui disait que ton contact avait changé et que je ne correspondrai plus avec toi.

— Oui, je sais, et ça voulait dire que tu devais cesser de flirter avec moi parce que Richard Love était de retour et que tu avais une liaison avec lui.

— Jamais de la vie !

— Vraiment ?

— Oui ! Je n'ai jamais eu de relation avec lui. Ce type est un connard.

— Ah ! D'accord. Alors pourquoi as-tu quitté Horizon en même temps que lui, il y a six ans ?

Je le regarde, les yeux écarquillés :

— Tu t'en souviens ?

— Absolument. Richard qui s'en va, et son assistante qui le suit ! Comment aurais-je pu oublier ça ?

518

—Je veux dire, tu te souvenais que c'était moi?

Un long silence s'établit. Il répond finalement:

—En vérité, non. Je ne me rappelais pas ton nom. Mais je me souvenais de toi. Je ne parle pas de ton visage ni rien – je ne crois pas que nous nous soyons rencontrés, n'est-ce pas?

Je secoue la tête:

—Bien sûr que non – sinon je me serais rendu compte que tu étais Rupert.

—Ah oui, bien sûr. Donc je ne connaissais pas ton visage et je ne me rappelais pas ton nom, mais je me souvenais que l'assistante de Ricky était partie avec lui et que je m'étais dit sur le moment que c'était une drôle d'idée. Je veux dire, elle – enfin, toi – a pris un énorme risque ce jour-là en envoyant tout balader pour le suivre. J'ai juste supposé que tu étais folle amoureuse de lui. C'était la seule explication possible.

Nos regards se croisent et restent rivés l'un à l'autre pendant quelques instants. Les fameuses parties de ma personne recommencent à se préparer, et, cette fois-ci, non seulement il est dans le même quartier que moi, mais il est dans la même pièce du même bâtiment. Et nous sommes dans un hôtel. Je leur donne le feu vert. Je croasse:

—Oh là là... alors pendant des années j'ai fantasmé sur une photo qui s'est révélée ne pas être la tienne...

—Fantasmé?

—... alors que dans le même temps tu pensais que j'étais amoureuse de Richard.

Cela ne servirait à rien de lui révéler à quel point il était proche de la vérité.

— Oui. Et quand nous avons commencé à correspondre, et que Rhonda m'a déclaré que ton nom lui disait quelque chose…

— Attends un peu. Comment est-ce que Rhonda a su qu'on s'écrivait?

Il hausse les sourcils :

— J'ai dû en parler à une ou deux personnes.

— Oh non. Tu plaisantes?

Il sourit de toutes ses dents :

— Non, je l'ai vraiment fait. Ils ont trouvé tes mails absolument hilarants. Toutes ces histoires de chaussures et de yétis. C'était extra.

— Hum.

— Oh, écoute, ne t'en fais pas. Dès que ça a commencé à devenir plus… intime, j'ai cessé de les leur montrer.

— Bon, d'accord. Donc, Rhonda a reconnu mon nom…?

— Oui. Elle pensait que ça lui disait quelque chose, alors j'ai fait une recherche dans la base de données et j'ai découvert que tu avais démissionné sans préavis, en même temps jour pour jour que Ricky. Et que tu étais son assistante de formation. J'ai, avec ma grande intelligence, déduit de ces quelques détails que tu étais la fille qui l'avait suivi.

— Ah, bien joué. Tu n'avais pas tellement d'indices.

— Merci. Donc, après ça, une fois que j'ai su qui tu étais, j'avais le sentiment très fort d'être en rivalité avec Ricky pour gagner ton cœur. Tu aurais très bien pu l'avoir épousé dans l'intervalle. J'aurais dû être plus prudent, mais j'étais encouragé par le fait que tu ne signes pas tes mails « Beth Love ». Et j'étais tout simplement entraîné. Presque aussitôt après, j'étais amoureux.

Je me sens de nouveau chancelante. Sans doute le manque d'oxygène.

—Vraiment?

C'est tout ce que j'arrive à dire, dans un soupir. Il va bientôt falloir que je me remette à respirer.

Il se tait, sourit et reprend d'une voix plus douce:

—Complètement. (Il parle lentement.) Je pensais à toi tout le temps. Chaque instant se passait à attendre ton prochain message. J'avais tellement envie de faire quelque chose pour toi, quelque chose qui changerait ta vie. Alors j'ai acheté la voiture de ton amie.

—Alors c'était toi! Oh! Pourquoi?

—Eh bien, mon ami Harris, le comptable, m'a tout raconté après votre déjeuner au *Madeleine's*. Bon sang, j'aurais tellement voulu être là. Ça avait l'air tellement parfait, juste comme je l'imaginais.

—Pourquoi tu n'es pas venu, alors? Tu as vraiment été appelé?

Il me jette un coup d'œil, puis baisse les yeux.

—Non. Je n'ai pas eu le courage de te rencontrer, finalement, à cause de cette fichue photo. Tu t'attendais forcément à découvrir un Adonis aux cheveux d'or, et je serais arrivé, et ça aurait été la fin.

—Mais c'est rid…

—Non, pas du tout. Je te l'ai dit, je ne suis pas doué pour… ce genre de choses.

—Quel genre de choses?

—Parler. Et j'avais le handicap supplémentaire d'être incroyablement attiré par toi. J'avais déjà le trac, alors, quand je me suis souvenu que tu pensais voir ce demi-dieu tout bronzé, je n'ai pas eu la force de venir.

—Et tu as envoyé ton comptable.

—Exactement. En fait, ce n'est pas vraiment mon comptable, plutôt un ami qui fait ma comptabilité. Et il m'a tout raconté. Il est tombé lui-même sous ton charme, je dois dire. Il n'arrêtait pas de me répéter comme tu étais jolie, mignonne, comme tu t'inquiétais pour ton amie qui avait des ennuis d'argent. Alors j'ai téléphoné à Love Learning, j'ai demandé à parler à la personne qui vendait une Mini, fixé un rendez-vous, et je l'ai achetée en liquide sur-le-champ.

Je suis stupéfaite. C'est comme Darcy, dans *Orgueil et Préjugés*, qui court après Wickham et Lydia pour les pousser à se marier, tout ça par amour pour Elizabeth. Sauf que Lydia, c'est Fatima, et que Wickham, c'est… euh, la Mini rouge avec son toit en damier, mais qu'importent les détails. Je contemple cet homme magnifique, en pensant que Fatima se trouve de l'autre côté du rideau, et je sens mon cœur qui gonfle un peu.

—Je n'arrive pas à croire que tu aies fait ça, dis-je dans un souffle, en le buvant des yeux.

Il se tient à présent tout près de ma chaise.

—Je l'ai fait pour toi, dit-il, exactement comme Darcy. À cause de mes sentiments pour toi. Parce que je voulais faire quelque chose pour toi, et que le problème de voiture de ton amie était à peu près tout ce que je savais sur toi à ce moment-là.

J'ai la respiration coupée. Je contemple son visage, si près du mien, qui me dévore des yeux, attendant ma réaction avec anxiété. Mais je ne peux lui répondre, parce que je n'ai plus le moindre souffle. Je parviens finalement à croasser :

—Elle était tellement ravie…

— Tant mieux. Je suis content d'avoir pu faire plaisir à quelqu'un.

— Tu m'as fait plaisir à moi aussi.

— C'est pour ça que je l'ai fait.

— Merci.

Nous restons un moment, gênés, à nous demander tous deux frénétiquement, pleins d'espoir – moi, du moins – si nous allons nous embrasser. Il se penche plus près, je retiens mon souffle, puis il s'écarte à nouveau, toussote et détourne les yeux. Il se redresse et s'écarte de quelques pas.

— Beth, dit-il en me tournant le dos, sa voix subitement plus grave d'une octave, je sais que je ne suis pas ce à quoi tu t'attendais, ou espérais. Je ne suis pas l'homme de la brochure d'Horizon. Loin de là. Mais cet homme, celui de la photo, ne te mérite pas, de toute façon. Il est peut-être beau, séduisant, mais il n'a rien d'autre.

Il ne me regarde toujours pas, alors je me lève pour le rejoindre.

— Mais c'est qui, en fait ?

Il se retourne, l'anxiété bien lisible sur son visage. J'ai l'estomac qui fait des nœuds.

— Saul Ruggiero. C'est son nom de scène, en tout cas.

— Son nom de scène ?

— Tout à fait. En réalité, il s'appelle Jeff Staines. C'est un cousin éloigné qui essaie de percer dans le mannequinat. Il a obtenu quelques petits contrats en Angleterre, mais rien qui vaille la peine d'être noté. Pour je ne sais quelles raisons, il pense à…

— … partir en Amérique.

Il acquiesce.

— Oui, c'est ça. Je ne vais pas pleurer son départ, pour être honnête. Chaque fois qu'il sort, il se débrouille pour vexer quelqu'un, et c'est moi qui dois réparer les dégâts. (Il baisse les yeux vers moi.) Ça ne m'avait jamais dérangé jusqu'à maintenant.

— Alors ce n'est pas toi que j'ai rencontré au supermarché, à la recherche d'anchois ?

— Ça devait être Jeff.

— Et c'est aussi à Jeff que j'ai parlé à la soirée, la semaine dernière.

Il opine du chef.

— Mais que fait sa photo dans la brochure, à la place de la tienne ? Je ne comprends pas.

Il soupire :

— Quand les brochures ont été imprimées pour la première fois, il y a douze ans, les gens de mon équipe de marketing pensaient que… eh bien, ils pensaient que ma propre photo n'était pas… assez sexy.

Je le regarde, les yeux écarquillés, avec ses larges épaules, ses magnifiques yeux marron, ses cheveux ébouriffés.

— Ils n'ont quand même pas dit ça ?!

Il hoche la tête, l'air résigné.

— Malheureusement, si. J'étais très jeune à l'époque, je voulais à tout prix que l'entreprise marche, alors j'ai accepté tout ce qu'ils m'ont suggéré.

— Je n'arrive pas à croire qu'ils aient dit ça.

Il me fait cette petite mimique à la Richard Gere, mélange de petit rire soulagé et de sourire en coin :

— Tu n'es pas d'accord ?

Il lève à nouveau les yeux vers moi, et je me débrouille pour hocher la tête. Il s'approche, me prend le visage dans ses mains. Nous sommes serrés l'un contre l'autre.

— Tu penses qu'ils avaient tort ?

— Huumm humm.

Je lui envoie une déferlante de messages télépathiques très explicites, et soudain, enfin, ils semblent faire de l'effet. Il s'approche encore plus près, ses lèvres à quelques millimètres des miennes, parcourant ma nuque du bout des doigts.

— Alors, si je voulais t'embrasser maintenant, tu n'y verrais pas d'objection ?

— Non, non.

— C'est la meilleure nouvelle de la journée.

Et alors qu'il penche son visage vers le mien et pose sa bouche sur la mienne, je ferme les yeux et je me sens fondre, mes oreilles s'emplissent de musique, une mélodie romantique et belle qui nous enveloppe, résonne dans la pièce, envahit l'espace, joyeuse, triomphante, comme…

— C'est ton téléphone ? demande-t-il soudain en s'écartant.

Je prends conscience que l'air que je croyais imaginer est en réalité le thème de *Superman* et qu'il sort de mon sac pour m'informer que j'ai reçu un texto.

— Oh oui. Désolée.

Nous nous séparons, et je farfouille dans ma besace, dont je parviens finalement à extraire mon portable pour consulter le message. Il dit :

Jeu te largue, cherry. T'en pire pour toa. Ton admir-
rateur Nigel n° 15 bisoux.

CENTRAL PARK

DÉCOUVREZ AUSSI CHEZ MILADY ROMANCE :

En librairie ce mois-ci

The Fell Types are digitally reproduced by Igino Marini.
www.iginomarini.com

Achevé d'imprimer en mars 2013
Par CPI Brodard & Taupin - La Flèche (France)
N° d'impression : 72089
Dépôt légal : avril 2013
Imprimé en France
81121000-1